THE SPACE OPERA RENAISSANCE

THE SPACE OPERA RENAISSANCE

EDITED BY DAVID G. HARTWELL

& KATHRYN CRAMER

TOR®

A TOM DOHERTY ASSOCIATES BOOK
NEW YORK

This is a work of fiction. All the characters and events portrayed in these stories are either fictitious or are used fictitiously.

THE SPACE OPERA RENAISSANCE

Copyright © 2006 by David G. Hartwell and Kathryn Cramer

This book is printed on acid-free paper.

A Tor Book
Published by Tom Doherty Associates, LLC
175 Fifth Avenue
New York, NY 10010

www.tor.com

Tor® is a registered trademark of Tom Doherty Associates, LLC.

Library of Congress Cataloging-in-Publication Data

The space opera renaissance / [edited by] David G. Hartwell and Kathryn Cramer.—1st ed.
    p. cm.
  "A Tom Doherty Associates book."
  ISBN-13: 978-0-765-30617-3
  ISBN-10: 0-765-30617-4
  1. Science fiction, American. 2. Science fiction, English. I. Hartwell, David G. II. Cramer, Kathryn, 1962–
  PS648.S3S55 2006
  813'.0876208—dc22   2005034503

First Edition: July 2006

Printed in the United States of America

0 9 8 7 6 5 4 3 2 1

COPYRIGHT
ACKNOWLEDGMENTS

CONTENTS

V. MIXED SIGNALS/MIXED CATEGORIES (TO THE LATE 1990s)

VI. NEXT WAVE (TWENTY-FIRST CENTURY)

INTRODUCTION

HOW SHIT BECAME SHINOLA: DEFINITION AND REDEFINITION OF SPACE OPERA

PROLOGUE

When we introduced our anthology *The Ascent of Wonder*, nearly fifteen years ago, we reported that we had decided to unsolve the problem of what hard SF means. We had discovered in our researches during the preparation of the book that nearly everyone thought they knew what hard SF was, but that when we pressed them for a definition and examples, quite a variety of contradictory statements and dissimilar examples were the result. So we decided to represent all claims to hard SF, and to try to reproduce them in our story notes and story selections. We did this to locate the center by considering all the edges, as well as the main areas of agreement. And then we wrote our introductory essays, attempting to generalize.

In the case of space opera, we immediately found a similar set of problems. Nearly all reviewers and commentators, and many writers and readers we have spoken to, agree that good new space opera is one of the most notable features of the current SF literature. *Locus* even devoted a special issue to space opera in 2003, with essays by prominent writers. But there is no general agreement as to what it is, which writers are the best examples, or even which works are space opera—especially among the writers.

So we are in this book attempting to pursue clarification by representing perhaps conflicting examples, and attempting to set contemporary space opera in its historical context. In the case of space opera, however, as opposed to hard SF, we had the ironic advantage of starting with a clear definition and showing how literary politics and other factors worked over the decades to deconstruct and alter it into something significantly different.

What used to be science fantasy (along with some hard SF) is now space opera, and what used to be space opera is entirely forgotten. Let us explain:

I. SPACE OPERA IS TRIPE

For the past twenty years (1982–2002), the Hugo Award for best novel has generally been given to space opera—from David Brin, C. J. Cherryh, and Orson Scott Card to Lois McMaster Bujold, Dan Simmons, and Vernor Vinge. (The shorter-fiction awards have been distributed much more widely over the range of SF and fantasy styles and possibilities.) One might go so far as to say that the Hugo Award for best novel has always gone primarily to space opera, as currently defined and understood, though many of the earlier winners, up to the end of the 1970s, would have been mortally offended to have their books so labeled. Space opera used to be a pejorative locution designating not a subgenre or mode at all, but the worst form of formulaic hackwork: really bad SF.

A lot of people don't remember this, and that distorts our understanding of both our present and our past in SF. Perfectly intelligent but ignorant people are writing revisionist history, especially in the last decade, inventing an elaborate age of space opera based on wholesale redefinitions of the term made up in the fifties, sixties, and seventies to justify literary political agendas. To say it flatly, before the mid-1970s, no one in the history of science fiction ever consciously and intentionally set out to write something called space opera. (Except Jack Vance and Samuel R. Delany: Vance accepted an assignment from Berkley Books in the late 1960s to write a novel to fit the title *Space Opera*—at the same time Philip K. Dick got an assignment to write a book called *The Zap Gun*. These were editorial jokes to be shared with the fans. And Delany, as usual ahead of the literary curve, wrote several intentionally literary space operas, most significantly his novel *Nova*, which he described to me, greatly to my surprise at the time in 1968, as grand space opera.) Nevertheless, some of the surviving writers from the early days of adventure SF now call their work, and the work of others, space opera, as a kind of ironic badge of honor, perhaps following the lead of Leigh Brackett in the 1970s (see below, and also the Jack Williamson story note).

On the other hand, there are a number of examples of works from the late 1940s on, published as intentional parodies of space opera, that apply the term to works either fairly or unfairly for humorous effect, often poking fun at the big names of the past. A once-famous example is "The Swordsmen of Varnis" (1950). This, too, is literary politics and redefinition (which we will discuss more in the story notes). Nevertheless, there is now a real body of work, that gets nominated for awards and often wins them, that is authentically and consciously written as space opera. Much of it is on one cutting edge or another of SF in the last two decades—and there are a number of cutting edges.

Here is the origin and description of the term from the early dictionary of SF, the *Fancyclopedia II* (1959):

> **Space Opera** ([coined by Wilson] Tucker) A hack science-fiction story, a dressed-up Western; so called by analogy with "horse opera" for Western bangbangshootemup movies and "soap opera" for radio and video yellowdrama. [To here, the entire entry from *Fancyclopedia*, 1944.] Of course, some space operas are more crass about their nature than others; early Captain Video TVcasts were a hybrid of original space scenes and footage from old Western movies (purporting to represent a Spy Ray checking up on the Captain's Earthly agents). Terry Carr once unearthed a publication *genommen Space Western Comics,* in which a character named Spurs Jackson adventured in a futuristic Western setting with his "space vigilantes," and the old prewar *Planet Comics* intermittently ran a strip about the Fifth Martian Lancers and their struggles with rebel tribesmen.

But this is a watered-down version of the original definition, lacking some of the precision and clarity with which Tucker wrote. What Bob Tucker actually said in his fanzine in 1941 was:

> In these hectic days of phrase-coining, we offer one. Westerns are called "horse operas," the morning housewife tear-jerkers are called "soap operas." For the hacky, grinding, stinking, outworn space-ship yarn, or world-saving for that matter, we offer "space opera."

We emphasize that this original definition applied to all bad SF hackwork. It did not refer to good space stories in *Astounding,* or to E. E. "Doc" Smith and Edmond

Hamilton, leading lights of the field, but to the subliterate hackwork appearing in, say, *Amazing* in those days and never reprinted or praised today. It did not confine itself to the future, or off-Earth settings, or refer to any "good old days." Those twists of the term were introduced later, mostly after the 1950s.

Space opera was still a negative term in the 1950s. An ad on the back cover of the early issues (1950) of *Galaxy* (then an ambitious new magazine) that bore the headline "You'll never see it in *Galaxy*" gave a stereotypical example of space opera for the time.

YOU'LL NEVER SEE IT IN GALAXY

Jets blasting, Bat Durston came screeching down through the atmosphere of Bbllizznaj, a tiny planet seven billion light years from Sol. He cut out his super-hyper-drive for the landing . . . and at that point, a tall, lean spaceman stepped out of the tail assembly, proton gun-blaster in a space-tanned hand.

"Get back from those controls, Bat Durston," the tall stranger lipped thinly. "You don't know it, but this is your last space trip."

Hoofs drumming, Bat Durston came galloping down through the narrow pass at Eagle Gulch, a tiny gold colony 400 miles north of Tombstone. He spurred hard for a low overhang of rim-rock . . . and at that point a tall, lean wrangler stepped out from behind a high boulder, six-shooter in a sun-tanned hand.

"Rear back and dismount, Bat Durston," the tall stranger lipped thinly. "You don't know it, but this is your last saddle-jaunt through these here parts."

Sound alike? They should—one is merely a western transplanted to some alien and impossible planet. If this is your idea of science fiction, you're welcome to it! YOU'LL NEVER FIND IT IN GALAXY!

What you will find in GALAXY is the finest science fiction . . . authentic, plausible, thoughtful . . . written by authors who do not automatically switch over from crime waves to Earth invasions; by people who know and love science fiction . . . for people who also know and love it.

It seems likely that the *Galaxy* ad helped to introduce some confusion into the pejorative meaning and to spark a popular redefinition of space opera as any hackneyed SF filled with stereotypes borrowed from Westerns. See the story note for "The Swordsmen of Varnis" for more detail on this usage, and for the conflation of different types of SF stories under the broadening term "space opera," especially including the *Planet Stories* tales of Leigh Brackett.

When the term appeared in review columns in the fifties, we recall some critic, perhaps even James Blish, referring in passing to Edmond Hamilton's hackwork series, *Captain Future*, as an example of space opera, while distinguishing it from his better work. And we recall Damon Knight praising Leigh Brackett (reprinted in *In Search of Wonder*, 2nd ed., p. 262):

Leigh Brackett's *The Long Tomorrow* is a startling performance from the gifted author of so much, but so entirely different, science-fantasy. Miss Brackett is celebrated among fans for her intense, moody, super-masculine epics of doomed heroes on far planets, all extremely poetic and fantastical, and all very much alike.

But there was little sense, in criticism and reviewing of the fifties, of "space opera" meaning anything other than "hacky, grinding, stinking, outworn" SF stories of any kind. Here is Knight again, on Edmund Cooper's collection *Tomorrow's Gift* (1958). He dismisses five of the ten stories in the collection by saying

> . . . the rest are mostly space-opera, with many evidences of careless and indifferent writing: but even these are partly redeemed by their endings. After a frantic comic-book brouhaha, Cooper will abruptly turn to a paragraph of calm description, e.g., of a lunar landscape: and the hidden meaning of the story blooms.
>
> All the same, this is to say that seven-eighths of a given story may be tripe; the proportion is too high.

Thus he establishes a parallel between space opera and tripe. And some of the stories do not take place in what are now called space opera settings.

Note also that Knight used the term "science-fantasy" as a neutral term describing Brackett's work. That term was generally applied to writers or works from the time of Edgar Rice Burroughs on, including Brackett, C. L. Moore, Ray Bradbury (his Mars stories), who wrote a variety of SF that in some essential way violated known contemporary science. It was later applied with equal justice to Marion Zimmer Bradley's Darkover novels. "Science fantasy" (usually without the hyphen) as a term did not fall out of currency until the 1980s, and I would submit that it is still a useful locution.

On the other hand, the process of folding the Edgar Rice Burroughs tradition of science fantasy set on another planet (now often called planetary romance) into space opera was accomplished by the early 1950s in some popular circles if not in Knight's. Fredric Brown characterizes space opera loosely in a story note in the anthology *Science Fiction Carnival*—"the type of science fiction known as space opera (the all-action type which is analogous to the type of Western known as horse opera)"—but the story introduced is an obvious parody of Burroughs's Martian tales, and Leigh Brackett's science fantasies in *Planet Stories* and elsewhere.

Still, after the fifties ended, the term "space opera"'s meaning began to be regularly confused with fondness for outworn, clunky, old-fashioned SF, guilty pleasures. An interesting example of shifted usage beginning is once again from Damon Knight, in a story note in *A Century of Science Fiction* (1962) on Edmond Hamilton's realistic tale "What's It Like Out There?": "Space travel stories in American SF magazines began somewhat soberly, but quickly turned into wild and wooly space opera in which larger and larger fleets of rocket ships went faster and farther, with less and less regard for fuel and acceleration. The king of this kind of space-adventure writing was Edmond Hamilton." While Knight is not characterizing space opera as good SF, he is narrowing the definition and focusing the term on space fiction of a particular sort, instead of using it as a general synonym for crud. Nor is he including planetary romances. Knight's position on this did not, as we will see, prevail.

We don't know the first time anyone used the term in reference to Doc Smith, or the early work of John W. Campbell, Jr., but by sometime before the middle of the 1960s, but sometimes as early as 1950, it was so used, though not universally.

The example we find in 1950, from the great fanzine *Slant*, is complicated by context. Clive Jackson comments on space opera (Slant 4: fanac.org/fanzines/Slant/Slant4-16.html):

> Personally, I like it. I think it's a very good form for s-f, if only because one can make one's puppets live without going too deeply into their emotions and mental struggles, which must tend to give them a present-day characterisation. It seems to me that to give persons engaged in interstellar travel the same character-structure as mid-twentieth century people is all wrong, yet it's constantly being done. Many of Dr.

Smith's All-American half-backs would be more at home fighting Indians with Winchester repeaters than they are chasing Boskonians with Lenses.

[These views on the great Smith are not those of the typesetter, J. White.]

By the time of the March 1970 issue of the fanzine *Yandro*, Buck Coulson reviewed reissues of Doc Smith's Lensman series, saying, "I don't care all that much for the books . . . the story is a science fiction classic . . . and I suppose they can be considered the ultimate in space opera." That use of "space opera" confirmed a shift in meaning to give space opera an air of nostalgic approval. Defenders of American SF in the fanzines from the attacks of the New Wave did this often in the later sixties, we recall. In 1968, in *Yandro* #179, Buck Coulson used the term three times. James Schmitz's *The Witches of Karres* "suffers a diminution in quality after the first section. The remainder of the book is space opera. Very well-handled space opera, but not quite in tune with the original idea. Despite this flaw, it's an excellent book." He dismisses Poul Anderson's Flandry novel, *We Claim These Stars*, as "a space opera potboiler." (In *Yandro* #174 he concludes that Murray Leinster's *SOS from Three Worlds* is "good space opera.") And he comments on Edmond Hamilton's *Starwolf #2: The Closed Worlds*: "This is space opera crossed with the poetic imagery evident in most of Leigh Brackett's work, and some of Hamilton's previous stories. It's not high-quality literature, but it's highly entertaining. . . ."

And in 1968, classic SF writer George O. Smith, in the *Analog* letters column Brass Tacks, refers to *Star Trek* as "our favorite space opera." Surely a harbinger of things to come.

II. SPACE OPERA IS DEAD

The next signpost was the New Wave project in England. Pushing for a revolution, Michael Moorcock and J. G. Ballard in the early 1960s used their prestige and polemical gifts to condemn most SF of prior decades.

In the 1960s the myriad proud star-fleets dispatched in fiction since the 1930s started heading home. J. G. Ballard was one of those pressing the recall button ("Which Way to Inner Space?" NW 118, May 1962): "I think science fiction should turn its back on space, on interstellar travel, extra-terrestrial life forms, galactic wars and the overlap of these ideas that spreads across the margins of nine-tenths of magazine s-f. . . ." (Colin Greenland, *The Entropy Exhibition*, p. 44, quoting Ballard)

They declared space fiction over with, and the fiction of the near future, inner space, and the human mind the only true contemporary SF. In the process, they conflated all SF adventure in distant futures or distant in space with space opera and said it was all bad, all literary history, and no longer a living part of SF.

The success of the New Wave in communicating its new vision was hampered by its assumption that everybody knew what it was on about, or that if they didn't it didn't matter. More damaging was its aim not just to improve or enlarge traditional sf, but to replace it altogether. This would have been ambitious if the new writers were talking only in terms of the genre, a small section of the publishing industry whose limits were pre-set, but their determination to abolish genre sf and subsume its functions within a larger and more exacting kind of fiction made the ambition a vain one. (Greenland, p. 189)

New Wave associates in the later sixties and early seventies, including Harry Harrison (in the parodies *Bill, The Galactic Hero,* and *Star Smashers of the Galaxy Rangers*), M. John Harrison (in the Besterian deconstruction *The Centauri Device*), and Brian Aldiss (in his two-volume anthology *Space Opera* and *Galactic Empires*), enforced these ideas by parody or example.

When Aldiss edited *Space Opera* in 1974, he was approaching the height of his reputation both as a writer and as a literary critic (and was also editing with Harry Harrison a prestigious *SF: The Year's Best* anthology series). In his introduction, he substituted the term "space opera" for that body of work generally known and praised as science fantasy, as well as for space adventures of any sort, and in line with the New Wave project pronounced space opera dead, except as a hothouse cultivation:

> Essentially space opera was born in the pulp magazines, flourished there, and died there. It is still being written, but in the main by authors who owe their inspiration and impetus to the pulps.

But in an important departure from the New Wave, he presented space opera as a guilty pleasure for readers of good, serious SF:

> This is not a serious anthology. Both volumes burst with voluptuous vacuum. They have been put together to amuse.

Aldiss also gave a lengthy description that amounts to a redefinition:

> The term is both vague and inspired, and must have been coined [here Aldiss is being especially coy—the origins of the term were well known and clear] with both affection and some scorn. . . . Its parameters are marked by a few mighty concepts standing like watch-towers along a lonely frontier. What goes on between them is essentially simple—a tale of love or hate, triumph or defeat—because it is the watch-towers that matter. We are already familiar with some of them: the question of reality, the limitations of knowledge, exile, the sheer immensity of the universe, the endlessness of time.

In effect, this elaborate description is a wholesale redefinition of science fantasy as space opera as the good old stuff. And it drops the horse opera analogy entirely. Westerns are no longer cited as the comparison or the influence on story structure.

It used to be possible before about 1973 for SF critics to distinguish space opera (from the 1920s to the 1970s) from popular SF adventure (as written by, for instance, Poul Anderson or Henry Kuttner, and sometimes called science fantasy, sometimes later called planetary romance). The SF adventures of Edgar Rice Burroughs and, later, Leigh Brackett were fast-paced, colorful, heroic, and (at least in Brackett's case) well written, for all their pulp clichés and borrowing from Western story structures and stereotypes. They were never considered mere hackwork—all the leading SF writers wrote for, and needed, the money—although a taste for Burroughs, say, was often considered a guilty pleasure by the 1950s. But that distinction has collapsed, and with the advent and acceptance of Aldiss's redefinition the usage began to disappear. Aldiss's is still the original working definition for some SF people today, and especially some academics.

Aldiss's redefinition of space opera collapsed all adventure forms into merely varieties of space opera and they are since then usually indistinguishable in SF discussions—as are the aforementioned works of Edward E. Smith, once an early model of good, hard SF adventure. Doc Smith got published in *Astounding,* even in the Campbell Golden Age years, and Robert A. Heinlein respected, and praised,

Smith's works. But Smith is now redefined as the poster child of early space opera, replacing Edmond Hamilton.

And the days of SF before the 1950s are often referred to as the days of Space Opera, and that's at least a partial triumph for the literary politicians of the British New Wave. Here's how Jack Williamson now remembers Edmond Hamilton, his close friend:

> Hamilton's skills were perfectly tuned for the pulps. He lived his stories, hammering the typewriter keys so hard as he approached the climax that the letter "o" cut holes in the paper. Depending more on plot action than on subtleties of style or character, his stories moved fast. He wrote them fast, commonly sending them out in first draft. He was prolific, his space operas earning him a reputation as "World-Wrecker" or "World-Saver" Hamilton. (Jack Williamson, from "Edmond Hamilton: As I Knew Him," 1999)

And here's how those days were perceived by some rude young writers given to parody, insulting their elders in the early 1970s (to the tune of the *Bat Masterson* TV series theme song): "Oh when the field was very young/There was a man named Williamson/He wrote a lot, he was a hack/They called him Jack/Jack Williamson." I hasten to add that these same parodists respected and do respect Williamson as a writer who improved to the point where his best work attained classic status by the late 1940s and who grew and changed as a writer every decade thereafter. But they had no fondness for his early hackwork.

III. EVERYTHING YOU KNOW IS WRONG

And now for the next signpost. Leigh Brackett (the wife of Edmond Hamilton), by the mid-1970s, was one of the respected elder writers of SF: In the middle and late 1970s, Del Rey Books reissued nearly all her early tales, calling them space opera as a contemporary term of praise!

Brackett herself contributed a provocative and surprisingly defensive introductory essay—but perhaps she was in part identifying with critical attitudes more often expressed about Edmond Hamilton's work than hers. Still, it is unquestionably true that some of the opprobrium loosely flung at space opera in the 1940s and 1950s struck and wounded her. Now she could strike back, clearly in opposition to Brian Aldiss's anthology:

> *Planet*, unashamedly, published "space opera." Space opera, as every reader doubtless knows, is a pejorative term often applied to a story that has an element of adventure. Over the decades, brilliant and talented new writers appear, receiving great acclaim, and each and every one of them can be expected to write at least one article stating flatly that the day of space opera is over and done, thank goodness, and that henceforward these crude tales of interplanetary nonsense will be replaced by whatever type of story that writer happens to favor—closet dramas, psychological dramas, sex dramas, etc., but by God *important* dramas, containing nothing but Big Thinks.

Brackett's piece is an interesting piece of historical literary insecurity and defensive power politics:

> It was fashionable for a while, among certain elements of science-fiction fandom, to hate *Planet Stories*. They hated the magazine, apparently, because it was not *Astounding Stories*. . . . Of course *Planet* wasn't *Astounding*; it never pretended to be *Astounding*, and that was a mercy for a lot of us who would have starved to death if John W.

Campbell, Jr., had been the sole and only market for our wares . . . we who wrote for *Planet* tended to be more interested in wonders than we were in differential calculus or the theory and practice of the hydraulic ram, even if we knew all about such things. (I didn't.) *Astounding* went for the cerebrum, *Planet* for the gut, and it always seemed to me that one target was as valid as the other. *Chacun à son gout. (Best of Planet Stories #1, 1976)*

Here is the blurb copy written for the back cover of the paperback by Lester or Judy-Lynn del Rey:

PLANET STORIES
1939–1955

During the golden age of the pulps—those fabulous magazines featuring larger-than-life heroes battling monstrous aliens on hostile planets or pursuing the luscious god-desses of golden worlds—some 70 issues of *Planet Stories* were published. When the magazine folded, along with most of the other pulps, the space opera all but disap-peared. Gone were those marvelous stories that drew us out beyond our narrow skies into the vastness of interstellar space where a billion nameless planets might harbor life forms infinitely numerous and strange.

Here's how that shift happened: Lester del Rey had set out to bring SF back to its roots as non-literary, or even anti-literary, entertainment, to specifically reject the in-cursions of Modernism into SF after what he declared the pretension and excesses and failed experiments of the New Wave. Lester and his new wife, Judy-Lynn, accepted the New Wave conflation of "SF adventure" and "space opera" (and dropped the term "sci-ence fantasy") and used the terms synonymously—both in Judy's marketing for Del Rey Books and in Lester's review columns in *Analog*—as terms of approbation.

I (David) often heard them speak about space opera in public without realizing, until years later, the effect it was having: to finally and entirely reverse the polarity of space opera. Back then I thought they were just crass marketers. At the time, in the late 1970s, while Gardner Dozois and Terry Carr and Charlie Brown and I and a bunch of others sat around at Worldcon dead-dog parties joking about the del Reys' passionate, lowest-common-denominator, anti-literary SF populism, "space opera" was becoming a term of approbation, denoting a subgenre: the *best* kind of contem-porary and past SF—just the type of SF Aldiss had described as dead.

In his 1978 book on the history of SF, *The World of Science Fiction, 1926–1976*, (p. 325), Lester del Rey offered his own new definition of space opera: "Almost any story involving space, though it properly deals with those in which action takes pre-cedence over other writing details. Analogous to horse opera for westerns." He even in that book went to the extreme of denying that any writer could set out to write SF as art. This, of course, flew in the face of both the Knight/Merril/Sturgeon axis in the USA, and of the New Worlds crew in the UK. Moorcock, Ballard, Aldiss, and the rest all believed that SF could be good art and that good writers could aspire to art through the new SF of inner space—if they discarded the traditions of hackwork (space opera).

It took nearly ten years to confirm the further redefinition, but by the early years of the 1980s, the del Reys' efforts succeeded in altering the perceived meaning of "space opera" entirely. Their model by the end of the 1970s at Del Rey became *Star Wars* (the book and the film) and its sequels. Lester del Rey says of *Star Wars* in his book (p. 370): "It is obviously an example of what has been called 'space opera,' long one of the favorite forms of adventure science fiction."

And in the end Del Rey Books happily attached Brackett's considerable prestige and authority to the *Star Wars* project when Brackett, also an accomplished screenwriter, did the script for *The Empire Strikes Back*. The Del Rey novelization of the film has her name on it as well as the novelizer's. And so in the popular mind, within a few years, *Star Wars* was conflated with *Star Trek* fiction to contour the new image of space opera: By the early 1980s, "space opera" was a code term in U.S. marketing circles for bestselling popular SF entertainment.

IV. THE NEW SPACE OPERA WAVES

Here's the big irony: The del Reys were conservative, and were shooting for a restoration of past virtues, and instead hit the future and opened new possibilities for literary ambition. What they did was to allow and encourage the postmodern conflation of marketing and art, the inclusion of media in the artistic project of SF, and the mixing of all levels and kinds of art in individual works. They established the artistic environment for works they would never have considered publishing or supporting. They set the stage for a variety of kinds of new work, including postmodern space opera.

Many readers and writers and nearly all academics and media fans who entered SF after 1975 have never understood the origin of "space opera" as a pejorative and some may be surprised to learn of it. Thus the term "space opera" reentered the serious discourse on contemporary SF in the 1980s with a completely altered meaning: Henceforth, "space opera" meant, and still generally means, colorful, dramatic, large-scale science fiction adventure, competently and sometimes beautifully written, usually focused on a sympathetic, heroic central character and plot action (this bit is what separates it from other literary postmodernisms) and usually set in the relatively distant future and in space or on other worlds, characteristically optimistic in tone. It often deals with war, piracy, military virtues, and very large-scale action, large stakes.

What is centrally important is that this permits a writer to embark on a science fiction project that is ambitious in both commercial and literary terms. Easy usage of the term as approbation did not regularly occur until the end of the 1990s, and I repeat the point stated in the opening of this essay that most works now called space opera were not written with that term in mind, even in the early 1990s. Usually the writers saw themselves as writing SF adventure or even hard SF.

The new traditions of contemporary space opera come only partly from the Del Rey marketing and philosophical changes, though they start there. Good writers immediately began in the 1980s to trace their own roots back to space opera classics of the past, and thereby recategorize and implicitly reevaluate those past works in many cases. The most ambitious parts of contemporary space opera now derive from such models as Brackett's *The Sword of Rhiannon*, Charles Harness's "The Rose," Jack Vance's *The Dying Earth*, the Norstrilia stories of Cordwainer Smith, Samuel R. Delany's *Nova*, Larry Niven and Jerry Pournelle's *The Mote in God's Eye*, Michael Moorcock's Dancers at the End of Time series, Norman Spinrad's *Riding the Torch* and *The Void Captain's Tale*, C.J. Cherryh's *Downbelow Station*, Gene Wolfe's four-volume Book of the New Sun (and particularly its sequel, *The Urth of the New Sun*), Orson Scott Card's *Ender's Game* et seq., David Brin's Uplift series, Melissa Scott's *Five-Twelfths of Heaven*, Mike Resnick's *Santiago*, Lois McMaster Bujold's Miles Vorkosigan series, Colin Greenland's *Take Back Plenty* et seq., and Iain M. Banks's *Consider Phlebas* and the succeeding novels in his Culture series.

Together such works formed not one cutting edge but many, a constellation of models (once the definitional barriers were removed so they might all be considered as part of a space opera tradition or subgenre) for ambitious younger writers by the end of the 1980s, an exciting decade for space opera indeed.

Because Banks's novels were bestsellers in England, spectacularly and unexpectedly successful, Banks, in spite of his relatively small impact in the US, was the foremost model in the UK as the 1990s began. Paul Kincaid, in an essay on 1990s SF, "The New Optimism," called him the most influential writer in Britain today, and said, "His huge commercial success (bigger than any genre writer except for Terry Pratchett) has spawned a host of successors, from those opportunistically likened to him in publishing blurbs to those who have genuinely been inspired by his approach, his vigorous literary style, or his view of the future."

There is no one thing that is *the* new space opera, though, no matter (given the evidence of the *Locus* special issue on the New Space Opera) how some British critics and writers would like to think so, and claim it as predominantly theirs. There are a number of dissimilar yet important and ambitious individual writers sometimes doing space opera in the SF world, all of them sometimes stretching genre boundaries, including Dan Simmons, John Varley, David Brin, Iain Banks, Catherine Asaro, Orson Scott Card, John Clute, Peter F. Hamilton, Lois McMaster Bujold, M. John Harrison, Donald Kingsbury, David Weber, Ken MacLeod, Alastair Reynolds, Mike Resnick, C. J. Cherryh, and many others. Some of them have made a valid claim to be writing ambitious space opera (some of the time), and all of them are or have been popular and influential and called "space opera" by others. Since the reversal of polarity of the term *space opera* in the 1970s was a covert literary battle, not a public argument and discussion, the nature of space opera boundaries has been fluid and imprecise, constantly updated by new examples—hey, look at *Startide Rising;* look at *Ender's Game;* look at *Santiago;* look at *Use of Weapons;* look at *Hyperion;* look at *A Fire Upon the Deep;* look at *Appleseed.* The new space opera of the past twenty years is arguably the foundation of the literary cutting edge of SF in the new millennium.

The dominant form of the renaissance of space opera is the novel. Indeed, some of the masters of contemporary space opera have written no short fiction in this form, or only occasionally and even then only novellas. Still, there are more than enough examples to fill this substantial anthology and more. We have selected from among the major writers of recent decades typical examples of the varieties of contemporary space opera that together show the richness and ambition of what has now become a major form of SF.

In closing, we note that the majority of Web sites devoted to space opera today are media fan sites, and with deadpan sincerity they generally trace the origins of film and TV space opera back to *Captain Video* and forward to its contemporary flowering in *Star Wars, Star Trek,* and *Babylon 5.* The authors of *Fancyclopedia* may be laughing. But we are not. There are more of them than of us.

David G. Hartwell & Kathryn Cramer
Pleasantville, New York

REDEFINED WRITERS

Chubby, brownette Eunice Kinnison sat in a rocker, reading the Sunday papers and listening to the radio. Her husband Ralph lay sprawled upon the davenport, smoking a cigarette and reading the current issue of EXTRAORDINARY STORIES against an unheard background of music. Mentally, he was far from Tellus, flitting in his super-dreadnaught through parsec after parsec of vacuous space.

—E. E. "Doc" Smith, Ph.D., *Triplanetary*, Chapter 5: "1941"

EDMOND HAMILTON

Edmond Hamilton [1904–1977] (tribute page: www.pulpgen.com/pulp/edmond_hamilton) was the great original writer of space opera in science fiction. Jack Williamson says: "With his tales of the Interstellar Patrol, beginning with 'Crashing Suns' (1928), he was arguably the inventor of space opera. Long on future progress, if a bit short on hard science, he imagined a vast interstellar civilization, always in danger of some cosmic catastrophe to be averted at the last instant by his little band of human and alien heroes."

Hamilton was born in Youngstown, Ohio, and lived with his parents across the state line in New Castle, Pennsylvania, until the 1940s, when he married Leigh Brackett. He said in an interview with Patrick Nielsen Hayden, in 1975 (www.pulpgen.com/pulp/edmond_hamilton/twibbet_interview.html), that he was profoundly influenced as a young man in the teens and early twenties by the pulp SF of Homer Eon Elint. "He'd write stories about moving the Earth to Jupiter and things like that. And those fired my imagination. I've always been glad to say, I owe this and that to Mr. Flint." He sold his first story to *Weird Tales* in 1925, and his next forty stories thereafter. Most of them were science fiction, which *Weird Tales* (since the term "science fiction" was not coined until 1930) called "weird-scientific" tales.

By the early 1930s he was one of the giants of science fiction. He was the first genre writer to conceive of interstellar flight ("I think so. On a wide scale, anyway. One thing I've found out, over the years, is that, anytime you think that you were the originator of some new idea, 'I was the first to do that,' you'll find some old fellow who did it back around 1895. Every darn time."—PNH interview), and also the first to write of friendly aliens ("Yes . . . I think I was, in one sense. I began that in 1932, with a story called 'Renegade.' It was published under the title of 'Conquest of Two Worlds.' They thought the title wasn't science-fictional enough. . . . But it seemed to me wrong to always make the Earthman in the right. Let's show him up to be something different."—PNH interview).

It is one of the sad ironies of literary history that his work is nearly forgotten today, while the work of his contemporary, E. E. "Doc" Smith, Ph.D., who died in the 1960s, although in some ways inferior to Hamilton's, is still popular and in print. His best friend, Jack Williamson, is still alive and writing SF and space opera in his nineties. Williamson says:

> Hamilton's skills were perfectly tuned for the pulps . . . his stories moved fast. He wrote them fast, commonly sending them out in first draft. He was prolific, his space operas earning him a reputation as "World-Wrecker" or "World-Saver" Hamilton.
>
> . . .
>
> He wrote nearly all the short novels for *Captain Future*, which was published quarterly from 1940 through 1944. They were the purest sort of pulp, tailored to fit a formula devised by Mort Weisinger, his editor at the "Thrilling" group. Besides the captain himself, the characters were a robot, an android, and a brain in a box. The pattern dictated everything, even the paragraphs in which the characters were introduced and the order of events in the opening chapter.
>
> . . .
>
> World War II changed everything. The old pulp markets disappeared. Though Ed was able to adapt when he tried, with such fine stories as "He That Hath Wings," he spent most of the next twenty years as one of the top script writers for the Superman and Batman comics.
>
> (all three quotes from "Edmond Hamilton: As I Knew Him" by Jack Williamson)

Hamilton also says in the PNH interview that he (and his wife also) declined to submit stories to John W. Campbell after he became editor at *Astounding*, because it cost too much in time to rewrite and revise to Campbell's edits. "I never sent him a story again. Reason being: I could not make a living writing for John Campbell. And he didn't like his writers . . . to write for other magazines."

Unfortunately this is the career of a good writer who developed a successful repository of techniques and a set of professional attitudes in the pulp era and never changed them entirely, even after the era ended.

It is easy to assume with historical hindsight that Wilson Tucker in his fanzine in 1941—when Hamilton was hacking out Captain Future pulp novellas for a living—did not have Hamilton's early work in mind when he defined space opera as "filthy, stinking hackwork." But on the other hand it may plausibly have seemed that the former great was going downhill at the same time that Smith and Williamson were selling to Campbell at higher rates, with more ambitious material. Gary Westphal (who assumes that "space opera" is a term of approval) makes that case in his essay on space opera in *The Cambridge Companion to Science Fiction*:

> Despite the accomplishments of Smith and contemporaries like Campbell, Williamson, Ray Cummings, and Clifford D. Simak, the most prolific and prominent writer of classic space operas was Edmond Hamilton. Particularly fond of stories involving planets being threatened or blown to pieces, Hamilton earned the epithets "World-Saver" and "World-Wrecker," and the reference to "world-saving" in Tucker's definition suggests that Hamilton might have been the principal target of his approbation [sic—ed.]. Yet Hamilton proved capable of producing more subdued, even wistful, varieties of space opera, like "The Dead Planet" (1946), where a group of explorers hear the holographic testimony of a long-dead alien civilization that sacrificed itself to save the galaxy from virulent energy-beings; finally, we learn the aliens were in fact the human race. Hamilton also crafted the first space opera franchise, *Captain Future*, a magazine said to prefigure *Star Trek* in describing the recurring exploits of a spaceship captain and his crew—a robot, an android, and a disembodied brain.

But we think it is not necessarily the case. Nor did Hamilton: "In a 1977 interview given just before his death, Edmond Hamilton, one of the founders of the subgenre, was still able to say, 'Bob Tucker invented that term when he was a fan, and I was reproaching him last spring again for having done so. I'm an old space opera fan; I don't like to see it mocked.'" (Quoted in David Pringle's essay "What Is This Thing Called Space Opera?") We think that the pejorative term was aimed at the much less capable imitators of the patterns of world-saving and warring interstellar fleets originated by Hamilton, then prevalent in the lesser pulp magazines such as *Amazing Stories* in the early 1940s. But it is also very likely that as the years passed and the term became more widely used, it became easy to assume that Hamilton and Smith and Williamson were the original targets of opprobrium.

After Hamilton married Brackett, and after he became a successful script writer for comic books—in those days considered a form lacking in any aesthetic value, lower class than the pulps (and at about the same time that Alfred Bester gave up writing for comics)—he did produce more ambitious work from time to time, since the pressure of paying the bills was less and the time to revise and rewrite available. He continued to publish new material into the 1970s, but was not regarded as having kept up with the genre. His collection *The Best of Edmond Hamilton* (1977) is a worthwhile sampling of his short fiction, most of it from before 1939. The first volumes of a new set of Hamilton story collections appeared in 1999 and 2002, and a third, collecting his early SF, has been announced, so the new fashion for space opera may be doing his posthumous reputation some good. His work deserves reassessment. He should be remembered for his best, not his average.

"The Star Stealers" is from the very beginning of his career and from near the very beginning of genre science fiction. It was first published in *Weird Tales* in February 1929. One can see how both comics and TV space opera (*Star Trek*, in particular) and later movies such as the *Star Wars* films were influenced by this strain of adventure SF. It was all there in 1929, fast-paced, large-scale, a bit clunky and absurd, and filled with images of wonder. There are many crudities, but one can easily apprehend how this fiction moved in the estimation of generations of SF readers from astonishing cutting-edge SF to trash to pulp nostalgia over the decades.

THE STAR STEALERS

EDMOND HAMILTON

As I stepped into the narrow bridgeroom the pilot at the controls there turned toward me, saluting.

"Alpha Centauri dead ahead, sir," he reported.

"Turn thirty degrees outward," I told him, "and throttle down to eighty light-speeds until we've passed the star."

Instantly the shining levers flicked back under his hands, and as I stepped over to his side I saw the arrows of the speed-dials creeping backward with the slowing of our flight. Then, gazing through the broad windows which formed the room's front side, I watched the interstellar panorama ahead shifting sidewise with the turning of our course.

The narrow bridgeroom lay across the very top of our ship's long, cigarlike hull, and through its windows all the brilliance of the heavens around us lay revealed. Ahead flamed the great double star of Alpha Centauri, two mighty blazing suns which dimmed all else in the heavens, and which crept slowly sidewise as we veered away from them. Toward our right there stretched along the inky skies the far-flung powdered fires of the galaxy's thronging suns, gemmed with the crimson splendors of Betelgeuse and the clear brilliance of Canopus and the hot white light of Rigel. And straight ahead, now, gleaming out beyond the twin suns we were passing, shone the clear yellow star that was the sun of our own system.

It was the yellow star that I was watching, now, as our ship fled on toward it at eighty times the speed of light; for more than two years had passed since our cruiser had left it, to become a part of that great navy of the Federation of Stars which maintained peace over all the Galaxy. We had gone far with the fleet, in those two years, cruising with it the length and breadth of the Milky Way, patrolling the space-lanes of the Galaxy and helping to crush the occasional pirate ships which appeared to levy toll on the interstellar commerce. And now that an order flashed from the authorities of our own solar system had recalled us home, it was with an unalloyed eagerness that we looked forward to the moment of our return. The stars we had touched at, the peoples of their worlds, these had been friendly enough toward us, as fellow-members of the great Federation, yet for all their hospitality we had been glad enough to leave them. For though we had long ago become accustomed to the alien and unhuman forms of the different stellar races, from the strange brain-men of Algol to the bird-like people of Sirius, their worlds were not human worlds, not the familiar eight little planets which swung around our own sun, and toward which we were speeding homeward now.

While I mused thus at the window the two circling suns of Alpha Centauri had dropped behind us, and now, with a swift clicking of switches, the pilot beside me turned on our full speed. Within a few minutes our ship was hurtling on at almost a thousand light-speeds, flung forward by the power of our newly invented de-transforming generators, which could produce propulsion-vibrations of almost a thousand times the frequency of the light-vibrations. At this immense velocity, matched by few other craft in the Galaxy, we were leaping through millions of miles of space each second, yet the gleaming yellow star ahead seemed quite unchanged in size.

Abruptly the door behind me clicked open to admit young Dal Nara, the ship's second-officer, descended from a long line of famous interstellar pilots, who grinned at me openly as she saluted.

"Twelve more hours, sir, and we'll be there," she said.

I smiled at her eagerness. "You'll not be sorry to get back to our little sun, will you?" I asked, and she shook her head.

"Not I! It may be just a pin-head beside Canopus and the rest, but there's no place like it in the Galaxy. I'm wondering, though, what made them call us back to the fleet so suddenly."

My own face clouded, at that. "I don't know," I said, slowly. "It's almost unprecedented for any star to call one of its ships back from the Federation fleet, but there must have been some reason—"

"Well," she said cheerfully, turning toward the door, "it doesn't matter what the reason is, so long as it means a trip home. The crew is worse than I am—they're scrapping the generators down in the engine-room to get another lightspeed out of them."

I laughed as the door clicked shut behind her, but as I turned back to the window the question she had voiced rose again in my mind, and I gazed thoughtfully toward the yellow star ahead. For as I had told Dal Nara, it was a well-nigh unheard-of thing for any star to recall one of its cruisers from the great fleet of the Federation. Including as it did every peopled star in the Galaxy, the Federation relied entirely upon the fleet to police the interstellar spaces, and to that fleet each star contributed its quota of cruisers. Only a last extremity, I knew, would ever induce any star to recall one of its ships, yet the message flashed to our ship had ordered us to return to the solar system at full speed and report at the Bureau of Astronomical Knowledge, on Neptune. Whatever was behind the order, I thought, I would learn soon enough, for we were now speeding over the last lap of our homeward journey; so I strove to put the matter from my mind for the time being.

With an odd persistence, though, the question continued to trouble my thoughts in the hours that followed, and when we finally swept in toward the solar system twelve hours later, it was with a certain abstractedness that I watched the slow largening of the yellow star that was our sun. Our velocity had slackened steadily as we approached that star, and we were moving at a bare one light-speed when we finally swept down toward its outermost, far-swinging planet, Neptune, the solar system's point of arrival and departure for all interstellar commerce. Even this speed we reduced still further as we sped past Neptune's single circling moon and down through the crowded shipping-lanes toward the surface of the planet itself.

Fifty miles above its surface all sight of the planet beneath was shut off by the thousands of great ships which hung in dense masses above it—that vast tangle of interstellar traffic which makes the great planet the terror of all inexperienced pilots. From horizon to horizon, it seemed, the ships crowded upon each other, drawn from every quarter of the Galaxy. Huge grain-boats from Betelgeuse, vast, palatial liners from Arcturus and Vega, ship-loads of radium ores from the worlds that circle giant Antares, long, swift mailboats from distant Deneb—all these and myriad others swirled and circled in one great mass above the planet, dropping down one by one as the official traffic-directors flashed from their own boats the brilliant signals which allowed a lucky one to descend. And through occasional rifts in the crowded mass of ships could be glimpsed the interplanetary traffic of the lower levels, a swarm of swift little boats which darted ceaselessly back and forth on their comparatively short journeys, ferrying crowds of passengers to Jupiter and Venus and Earth, seeming like little toy-boats beside the mighty bulks of the great interstellar ships above them.

As our own cruiser drove down toward the mass of traffic, though, it cleared away from before us instantly; for the symbol of the Federation on our bows was known from Canopus to Fomalhaut, and the cruisers of its fleet were respected by all the traffic of the Galaxy. Arrowing down through this suddenly opened lane, we sped smoothly down toward the planet's surface, hovering for a moment above its perplexing maze of white buildings and green gardens, and then slanting down toward the mighty flat-roofed building which housed the Bureau of Astronomical Knowledge. As we sped down toward its roof I could not but contrast the warm, sunny green panorama beneath with the icy desert which the planet had been until two hundred thousand years before, when the scientists of the solar system had devised the great heat-transmitters which catch the sun's heat near its blazing surface and fling it out as high-frequency vibrations to the receiving-apparatus on Neptune, to be transformed back into the heat which warms this world. In a moment, though, we were landing gently upon the broad roof, upon which rested scores of other shining cruisers whose crews stood outside them watching our arrival.

Five minutes later I was whirling downward through the building's interior in one of the automatic little cone-elevators, out of which I stepped into a long white corridor. An attendant was awaiting me there, and I followed him down the corridor's length to a high black door at its end, which he threw open for me, closing it behind me as I stepped inside.

It was an ivory-walled, high-ceilinged room in which I found myself, its whole farther side open to the sunlight and breezes of the green gardens beyond. At a desk across the room was sitting a short-set man with gray-streaked hair and keen, inquiring eyes, and as I entered he sprang up and came toward me.

"Ran Rarak!" he exclaimed. "You've come! For two days, now, we've been expecting you."

"We were delayed off Aldebaran, sir, by generator trouble," I replied, bowing, for I had recognized the speaker as Hurus Hol, chief of the Bureau of Astronomical Knowledge. Now, at a motion from him, I took a chair beside the desk while he resumed his own seat.

A moment he regarded me in silence, and then slowly spoke. "Ran Rarak," he said, "you must have wondered why your ship was ordered back here to the solar system. Well, it was ordered back for a reason which we dared not state in an open message, a reason which, if made public, would plunge the solar system instantly into a chaos of unutterable panic!"

He was silent again for a moment, his eyes on mine, and then went on. "You know, Ran Rarak, that the universe itself is composed of infinite depths of space in which float great clusters of suns, star-clusters which are separated from each other by billions of light-years of space. You know, too, that our own cluster of suns, which we call the Galaxy, is roughly disklike in shape, and that our own particular sun is situated at the very edge of this disk. Beyond lie only those inconceivable leagues of space which separate us from the neighboring star-clusters, or island-universes, depths of space never yet crossed by our own cruisers or by anything else of which we have record.

"But now, at last, something has crossed those abysses, is crossing them; since over three weeks ago our astronomers discovered that a gigantic dark star is approaching our Galaxy from the depths of infinite space—a titanic, dead sun which their instruments showed to be of a size incredible, since, dark and dead as it is, it is larger than the mightiest blazing suns in our own Galaxy, larger than Canopus or Antares or Betelgeuse—a dark, dead star millions of times larger than our own fiery sun—a gigantic wanderer out of some far realm of infinite space, racing toward our Galaxy at a velocity inconceivable!

"The calculations of our scientists showed that this speeding dark star would not race into our Galaxy but would speed past its edge, and out into infinite space again, passing no closer to our own sun, at the edge, than some fifteen billion miles. There was no possibility of collision or danger from it, therefore; and so though the approach of the dark star is known to all in the solar system, there is no idea of any peril connected with it. But there is something else which has been kept quite secret from the peoples of the solar system, something known only to a few astronomers and officials. And that is that during the last few weeks the path of this speeding dark star has changed from a straight path to a curving one, that it is curving inward toward the edge of our Galaxy and will now pass our own sun, in less than twelve weeks, at a distance of less than three billion miles, instead of fifteen! And when this titanic dead sun passes that close to our own sun there can be but one result. Inevitably our own sun will be caught by the powerful gravitational grip of the giant dark star and carried out with all its planets into the depths of infinite space, never to return!"

Hurus Hol paused, his face white and set, gazing past me with wide, unseeing eyes. My brain whirling beneath the stunning revelation, I sat rigid, silent, and in a moment he went on.

"If this thing were known to all," he said slowly, "there would be an instant, terrible panic over the solar system, and for that reason only a handful have been told. Flight is impossible, for there are not enough ships in the Galaxy to transport the trillions of the solar system's population to another star in the four weeks that are left to us. There is but one chance—one blind, slender chance—and that is to turn aside this onward-thundering dark star from its present inward-curving path, to cause it to pass our sun and the Galaxy's edge far enough away to be harmless. And it is for this reason that we ordered your return.

"For it is my plan to speed out of the Galaxy into the depths of outer space to meet this approaching dark star, taking all of the scientific apparatus and equipment which might be used to swerve it aside from this curving path it is following. During the last week I have assembled the equipment for the expedition and have gathered together a force of fifty star-cruisers which are even now resting on the roof of this building, manned and ready for the trip. These are only swift mail-cruisers, though, specially equipped for the trip, and it was advisable to have at least one battle-cruiser for flag-ship of the force, and so your own was recalled from the Federation fleet. And although I shall go with the expedition, of course, it was my plan to have you yourself as its captain.

"I know, however, that you have spent the last two years in the service of the Federation fleet; so if you desire, another will be appointed to the post. It is one of danger—greater danger, I think, than any of us can dream. Yet the command is yours, if you wish to accept it."

Hurus Hol ceased, intently scanning my face. A moment I sat silent, then rose and stepped to the great open window at the room's far side. Outside stretched the greenery of gardens, and beyond them the white roofs of buildings, gleaming beneath the faint sunlight. Instinctively my eyes went up to the source of light, the tiny sun, small and faint and far, here, but still—the sun. A long moment I gazed up toward it, and then turned back to Hurus Hol.

"I accept, sir," I said.

He came to his feet, his eyes shining. "I knew that you would," he said, simply, and then: "All has been ready for days, Ran Rarak. We start at once."

Ten minutes later we were on the broad roof, and the crews of our fifty ships were rushing to their posts in answer to the sharp alarm of a signal bell. Another five minutes and Hurus Hol, Dal Nara and I stood in the bridgeroom of my own cruiser, watching the white roof drop behind and beneath as we slanted up from it. In a moment the half-hundred cruisers on that roof had risen and were racing up behind us, arrowing with us toward the zenith, massed in a close, wedge-shaped formation.

Above, the brilliant signals of the traffic-boats flashed swiftly, clearing a wide lane for us, and then we had passed through the jam of traffic and were driving out past the incoming lines of interstellar ships at swiftly mounting speed, still holding the same formation with the massed cruisers behind us.

Behind and around us, now, flamed the great panorama of the Galaxy's blazing stars, but before us lay only darkness—darkness inconceivable, into which our ships were flashing out at greater and greater speed. Neptune had vanished, and far behind lay the single yellow spark that was all visible of our solar system as we fled out from it. Out—out—out—rocketing, racing on, out past the boundaries of the great Galaxy itself into the lightless void, out into the unplumbed depths of infinite space to save our threatened sun.

2

Twenty-four hours after our start I stood again in the bridgeroom, alone except for the silent, imperturbable figure of my ever-watchful wheelman, Nal Jak, staring out with him into the black gulf that lay before us. Many an hour we had stood side by side thus, scanning the interstellar spaces from our cruiser's bridgeroom, but never yet had my eyes been confronted by such a lightless void as lay before me now.

Our ship, indeed, seemed to be racing through a region where light was all but non-existent, a darkness inconceivable to anyone who had never experienced it. Behind lay the Galaxy we had left, a great swarm of shining points of light, contracting slowly as we sped away from it. Toward our right, too, several misty little patches of light glowed faintly in the darkness, hardly to be seen; though these, I knew, were other galaxies or star-clusters like our own—titanic conglomerations of thronging suns dimmed to those tiny flickers of light by the inconceivable depths of space which separated them from ourselves.

Except for these, though, we fled on through a cosmic gloom that was soul-shaking in its deepness and extent, an infinite darkness and stillness in which our ship seemed the only moving thing. Behind us, I knew, the formation of our fifty ships was following close on our track, each ship separated from the next by a five hundred mile interval and each flashing on at exactly the same speed as ourselves. But though we knew they followed, our fifty cruisers were naturally quite invisible to us, and as I gazed now into the tenebrous void ahead the loneliness of our position was overpowering.

Abruptly the door behind me snapped open, and I half turned toward it as Hurus Hol entered. He glanced at our speed-dials, and his brows arched in surprise.

"Good enough," he commented. "If the rest of our ships can hold this pace it will bring us to the dark star in six days."

I nodded, gazing thoughtfully ahead. "Perhaps sooner," I estimated. "The dark star is coming toward us a tremendous velocity, remember. You will notice on the telechart—"

Together we stepped over to the big telechart, a great rectangular plate of smoothly burnished silvery metal which hung at the bridgeroom's end-wall, the one indispensable aid to interstellar navigation. Upon it were accurately reproduced, by means of projected and reflected rays, the positions and progress of all heavenly bodies near the ship. Intently we contemplated it now. At the rectangle's lower edge there gleamed on the smooth metal a score or more of little circles of glowing light, of varying sizes, representing the suns of the edge of the Galaxy behind us. Outermost of these glowed the light-disk that was our own sun, and around this Hurus Hol had drawn a shining line or circle lying more than four billion miles from our sun, on the chart. He had computed that if the approaching dark star came closer than that to our sun its mighty gravitational attraction would inevitably draw the latter out with it into space; so the shining line represented, for us, the danger line: And creeping down toward that line and toward our sun, farther up on the blank metal of the great chart, there moved a single giant circle of deepest black, an ebon disk a hundred times the diameter of our glowing little sun-circle, which was sweeping down toward the Galaxy's edge in a great curve.

Hurus Hol gazed thoughtfully at the sinister dark disk, and then shook his head. "There's something very strange about that dark star," he said, slowly. "That curving path it's moving in is contrary to all the laws of celestial mechanics. I wonder if—"

Before he could finish, the words were broken off in his mouth. For at that moment there came a terrific shock, our ship dipped and reeled crazily, and then was whirling blindly about as though caught and shaken by a giant hand. Dal Nara, the pilot, Hurus Hol and I were slammed violently down toward the bridgeroom's end with the first crash, and then I clung desperately to the edge of a switch-board as we spun dizzily about. I had a flashing glimpse, through the windows, of our fifty cruisers whirling blindly about like wind-tossed straws, and in another glimpse saw two of them caught and slammed together, both ships smashing like eggshells beneath the terrific impact, their crews instantly annihilated. Then, as our own ship dipped crazily downward again, I saw Hurus Hol creeping across the floor toward the controls, and in a moment I had slid down beside him. Another instant and we had our hands on the levers, and were slowly pulling them back into position.

Caught and buffeted still by the terrific forces outside, our cruiser slowly steadied to an even keel and then leapt suddenly forward again, the forces that held us seeming to lessen swiftly as we flashed on. There came a harsh, grating sound that brought my heart to my throat as one of the cruisers was hurled past us, grazing us, and then abruptly the mighty grip that held us had suddenly disappeared and we were humming on through the same stillness and silence as before.

I slowed our flight, then, until we hung motionless, and then we gazed wildly at each other, bruised and panting. Before we could give utterance to the exclamations on our lips, though, the door snapped open and Dal Nara burst into the bridgeroom, bleeding from a cut on her forehead.

"What was that?" she cried, raising a trembling hand to her head. "It caught us there like toys—and the other ships—"

Before any of us could answer her a bell beside me rang sharply and from the diaphragm beneath it came the voice of our message-operator.

"Ships 37, 12, 19 and 44 reported destroyed by collisions, sir," he announced, his own voice tremulous. "The others report that they are again taking up formation behind us."

"Very well," I replied. "Order them to start again in three minutes, on Number One speed-scale."

As I turned back from the instrument I drew a deep breath. "Four ships destroyed in less than a minute," I said. "And by *what?*"

"By a whirlpool of ether-currents, undoubtedly," said Hurus Hol. We stared at him blankly, and he threw out a hand in quick explanation. "You know that there are currents in the ether—that was discovered ages ago—and that those currents in the Galaxy have always been found to be comparatively slow and sluggish, but out here in empty space there must be currents of gigantic size and speed, and apparently we stumbled directly into a great whirlpool or maelstrom of them. We were fortunate to lose but four ships," he added soberly.

I shook my head. "I've sailed from Sirius to Rigel," I said, "and I never met anything like that. If we meet another—" The strangeness of our experience, in fact, had unnerved me, for even after we had tended to our bruises and were again racing on through the void, it was with a new fearfulness that I gazed ahead. At any moment, I knew, we might plunge directly into some similar or even larger maelstrom of ether-currents, yet there was no way by which we could avoid the danger. We must drive blindly ahead at full speed and trust to luck to bring us through, and now I began to understand what perils lay between us and our destination.

As hour followed hour, though, my fearfulness gradually lessened, for we encountered no more of the dread maelstroms in our onward flight. Yet as we hummed on and on and on, a new anxiety came to trouble me, for with the passing of each day we were putting behind us billions of miles of space, and were flashing nearer and nearer toward the mighty dark star that was our goal. And even as we fled on we could see, on the great telechart, the dark disk creeping down to meet us, thundering on toward the Galaxy from which, unless we succeeded, it would steal a star.

Unless we succeeded! But could we succeed? Was there any force in the universe that could turn aside this oncoming dark giant in time to prevent the theft of our sun? More and more, as we sped on, there grew in my mind doubt as to our chance of success. We had gone forth on a blind, desperate venture, on a last slender chance, and now at last I began to see how slender indeed was that chance. Dal Nara felt it, too, and even Hurus Hol, I think, but we spoke no word to each other of our thoughts, standing for hours on end in the bridgeroom together, and gazing silently and broodingly out into the darkness where lay our goal.

On the sixth day of our flight we computed, by means of our telechart and flight-log, that we were within less than a billion miles of the great dark star ahead, and had slackened our speed until we were barely creeping forward, attempting to locate our goal in the dense, unchanged darkness ahead.

Straining against the windows, we three gazed eagerly forward, while beside me Nal Jak, the wheelman, silently regulated the ship's speed to my orders. Minutes passed while we sped on, and still there lay before us only the deep darkness. Could it be that we had missed our way, that our calculations had been wrong? Could it be—and then the wild speculations that had begun to rise in my mind were cut short by a low exclamation from Dal Nara, beside me. Mutely she pointed ahead.

At first I could see nothing, and then slowly became aware of a feeble glow of light in the heavens ahead, an area of strange, subdued light which stretched across the whole sky, it seemed, yet which was so dim as to be hardly visible to our straining eyes. But swiftly, as we watched it, it intensified, strengthened, taking shape as a mighty circle of pale luminescence which filled almost all the heavens ahead. I gave a low-voiced order to the pilot which reduced our speed still further, but even so the light grew visibly stronger as we sped on.

"Light!" whispered Hurus Hol. "Light on a dark star! It's impossible—and yet—"

And now, in obedience to another order, our ship began to slant sharply up toward the mighty circle's upper limb, followed by the half-hundred ships behind us.

And as we lifted higher and higher the circle changed before our eyes into a sphere—a tremendous, faintly glowing sphere of size inconceivable, filling the heavens with its vast bulk, feebly luminous like the ghost of some mighty sun, rushing through space to meet us as we sped up and over it. And now at last we were over it, sweeping above it with our little fleet at a height of a half-million miles, contemplating in awed silence the titanic dimensions of the faint-glowing sphere beneath us.

For in spite of our great height above it, the vast globe stretched from horizon to horizon beneath us, a single smooth, vastly curving surface, shining with the dim, unfamiliar light whose source we could not guess. It was not the light of fire, or glowing gases, for the sun below was truly a dead one, vast in size as it was. It was a *cold* light, a faint but steady phosphorescence like no other light I had ever seen, a feeble white glow which stretched from horizon to horizon of the mighty world beneath. Dumfoundedly we stared down toward it, and then, at a signal to the pilot, our ship began to drop smoothly downward, trailed by our forty-odd followers behind. Down, down, we sped, slower and slower, until we suddenly started as there came from outside the ship a high-pitched hissing shriek.

"Air!" I cried. "This dark star has an atmosphere! And that light upon it—see!" And I flung a pointing hand toward the surface of the giant world below. For as we dropped swiftly down toward that world we saw at last that the faint light which illuminated it was not artificial light, or reflected light, but light inherent in itself, since all the surface of the mighty sphere glowed with the same phosphorescent light, its plains and bills and valleys alike feebly luminous, with the soft, dim luminosity of radio-active minerals. A shining world, a world glowing eternally with cold white light, a luminous, titanic sphere that rushed through the darkness of infinite space like some pale gigantic moon. And upon the surface of the glowing plains beneath us rose dense and twisted masses of dark leafless vegetation, distorted tree-growths and tangles of low shrubs that were all of deepest black in color, springing out of that glowing soil and twisting blackly and grotesquely above its feeble light, stretching away over plain and hill and valley like the monstrous landscape of some undreamed-of hell!

And now, as our ship slanted down across the surface of the glowing sphere, there gleamed ahead a deepening of that glow, a concentration of that feeble light which grew stronger as we raced on toward it. And it was a city! A city whose mighty buildings were each a truncated pyramid in shape, towering into the air for thousands upon thousands of feet, a city whose every building and street and square glowed with the same faint white light as the ground upon which they stood, a metropolis out of nightmare, the darkness of which was dispelled only by the light of its own great glowing structures and streets. Far away stretched the mass of these structures, a luminous mass which covered square mile upon square mile of the surface of this glowing world, and far beyond them there lifted into the dusky air the shining towers and pyramids of still other cities.

We straightened, trembling, turning toward each other with white faces. And then, before any could speak, Dal Nara had whirled to the window and uttered a hoarse shout. "Look!" she cried, and pointed down and outward toward the titanic, glowing buildings of the city ahead; for from their truncated summits were rising suddenly a swarm of long black shapes, a horde of long black cones which were racing straight up toward us.

I shouted an order to the pilot, and instantly our ship was turning and slanting sharply upward, while around us our cruisers sped up with us. Then, from beneath, there sped up toward us a shining little cylinder of metal which struck a cruiser racing beside our own. It exploded instantly into a great flare of blinding light, enveloping the cruiser it had struck, and then the light had vanished, while with it had vanished the ship it had enveloped. And from the cones beneath and beyond there leapt toward us other of the metal cylinders, striking our ships now by the dozens, flaring and vanishing with them in great, silent explosions of light.

"Etheric bombs!" I cried. "And our ship is the only battlecruiser—the rest have no weapons!"

I turned, cried another order, and in obedience to it our own cruiser halted suddenly and then dipped downward, racing straight into the ascending swarm of attacking cones. Down we flashed, down, down, and toward us sprang a score of the metal cylinders, grazing along our sides. And then, from the sides of our own downward-swooping ship there sprang out brilliant shafts of green light, the deadly de-cohesion ray of the ships of the Federation Fleet. It struck a score of the cones beneath and they flamed with green light for an instant and then flew into pieces, spilling downward in a great shower of tiny fragments as the cohesion of their particles was destroyed by the deadly ray. And now our cruiser had crashed down through the swarm of them and was driving down toward the luminous plain below, then turning and racing sharply upward again while from all the air around us the black cones swarmed to the attack.

Up, up, we sped, and now I saw that our blow had been struck in vain, for the last of our ships above were vanishing beneath the flares of the etheric bombs. One only of our cruisers remained, racing up toward the zenith in headlong flight with a score of the great cones in hot pursuit. A moment only I glimpsed this, and then we had turned once more and were again diving down upon the attacking cones, while all around us the etheric bombs filled the air with the silent, exploding flares. Again as we swooped downward our green rays cut paths of annihilation across the swarming cones beneath; and then I heard a cry from Hurus Hol, whirled to the window and glimpsed above us a single great cone that was diving headlong down toward us in a resistless, ramming swoop. I shouted to the pilot, sprang to the controls, but was too late to ward off that deadly blow. There was a great crash at the rear of our cruiser; it spun dizzily for a moment in midair, and then was tumbling crazily downward like a falling stone toward the glowing plain a score of miles below.

3

I think now that our cruiser's mad downward plunge must have lasted for minutes, at least, yet at the time it seemed over in a single instant. I have a confused memory of the bridgeroom spinning about us as we whirled down, of myself throwing back the controls with a last, instinctive action, and then there came a ripping, rending crash, a violent shock, and I was flung into a corner of the room with terrible force.

Dazed by the swift action of the last few minutes I lay there motionless for a space of seconds, then scrambled to my feet. Hurus Hol and Dal Nara were staggering up likewise, the latter hastening at once down into the cruiser's hull, but Nal Jak, the wheelman, lay motionless against the wall, stunned by the shock. Our first act was to bring him back to consciousness by a few rough first-aid measures, and then we straightened and gazed about us.

Apparently our cruiser's keel was resting upon the ground, but was tilted over at a sharp angle, as the slant of the room's floor attested. Through the broad windows we could see that around our prostrate ship lay a thick, screening grove of black tree-growths which we had glimpsed from above, and into which we had crashed in our mad plunge downward. As I was later to learn, it was only the shock-absorbing qualities of the vegetation into which we had fallen, and my own last-minute rush to the controls, which had slowed our fall enough to save us from annihilation.

There was a buzz of excited voices from the crew in the hull beneath us, and then I turned at a sudden exclamation from Hurus Hol, to find him pointing up through the observation windows in the bridgeroom's ceiling. I glanced up, then shrank back. For high above were circling a score or more of the long black cones which had attacked us, and which were apparently surveying the landscape for some clue to our fate. I gave a sharp catch of indrawn breath as they dropped lower toward us, and we crouched with pounding hearts while they dropped lower toward us, and while they dropped nearer. Then we uttered simultaneous sighs of relief as the long shapes above suddenly drove back up toward the zenith, apparently certain of our annihilation, massing and wheeling and then speeding back toward the glowing city from which they had risen to attack us.

We rose to our feet again, and as we did so the door clicked open to admit Dal Nara. She was a bruised, disheveled figure, like the rest of us, but there was something like a grin on her face.

"That cone that rammed us shattered two of our rear vibration-projectors," she announced, "but that was all the damage. And outside of one man with a broken shoulder the crew is all right."

"Good!" I exclaimed. "It won't take long to replace the broken projectors."

She nodded. "I ordered them to put in two of the spares," she explained. "But what then?"

I considered for a moment. "None of our other cruisers escaped, did they?" I asked.

Dal Nara slowly shook her head. "I don't think so," she said. "Nearly all of them were destroyed in the first few minutes. I saw Ship 16 racing up in an effort to escape, heading back toward the Galaxy, but there were cones hot after it and it couldn't have got away."

The quiet voice of Hurus Hol broke in upon us. "Then we alone can take back word to the Federation of what is happening here," he said. His eyes suddenly flamed. "Two things we know," he exclaimed. "We know that this dark star's curving path through space, which will bring it so fatally near to our own sun in passing, is a path contrary to all the laws of astronomical science. And we know now, too, that upon this dark star world, in those glowing cities yonder, live beings of some sort who possess, apparently, immense intelligence and power."

My eyes met his. "You mean—" I began, but he interrupted swiftly.

"I mean that in my belief the answer to this riddle lies in that glowing city yonder, and that it is there we must go to find that answer."

"But how?" I asked. "If we take the cruiser near it they'll sight us and annihilate us."

"There is another way," said Hurus Hol. "We can leave the cruiser and its crew hidden here, and approach the city on foot—get as near to it as possible—learn what we can about it."

I think that we all gasped at that suggestion, but as I quickly revolved it in my mind I saw that it was, in reality, our only chance to secure any information of value to take back to the Federation. So we adopted the idea without further discussion and swiftly laid our plans for the venture. At first it was our plan for only us three to go, but at Dal Nara's insistence we included the pilot in our party, the more quickly because I knew her to be resourceful and quick-witted.

Two hours we spent in sleep, at the suggestions of Hurus Hol, then ate a hasty meal and looked to our weapons, small projectors of the de-cohesion ray similar to the great ray-tubes of the cruiser. Already the ship's two shattered vibration-projectors had been replaced by new spares, and our last order was for the crew and under-officers to await our return without moving beyond the ship in any event. Then the cruiser's hull-door snapped open and we four stepped outside, ready for our venture.

The sandy ground upon which we stood glowed with the feeble white light which seemed to emanate from all rock and soil on this strange world, a weird light which beat upward upon us instead of down. And in this light the twisted, alien forms of the leafless trees around us writhed upward into the dusky air, their smooth black branches tangling and intertwining far above our heads. As we paused there Hurus Hol reached down for a glowing pebble, which he examined intently for a moment.

"Radio-active," he commented. "All this glowing rock and soil." Then he straightened, glanced around, and led the way unhesitatingly through the thicket of black forest into which our ship had fallen.

Silently we followed him, in single file, across the shining soil and beneath the distorted arches of the twisted trees, until at last we emerged from the thicket and found ourselves upon the open expanse of the glowing plain. It was a weird landscape which met our eyes, a landscape of glowing plains and shallow valleys patched here and there with the sprawling thickets of black forest, a pale, luminous world whose faint light beat feebly upward into the dusky, twilight skies above. In the distance, perhaps two miles ahead, a glow of deeper light flung up against the hovering dusk from the massed buildings of the luminous city, and toward this we tramped steadily onward, over the shining plains and gullies and once over a swift little brook whose waters glowed as they raced like torrents of rushing light. Within an hour we had drawn to within a distance of five hundred feet from the outermost of the city's pyramidal buildings, and crouched in a little clump of dark tree-growths, gazing fascinatedly toward it.

The scene before us was one of unequaled interest and activity. Over the masses of huge, shining buildings were flitting great swarms of the long black cones, moving from roof to roof, while in the shining streets below them moved other hordes of active figures, the people of the city. And as our eyes took in these latter I think that we all felt something of horror, in spite of all the alien forms which we were familiar with in the thronging worlds of the Galaxy.

For in these creatures was no single point of resemblance to anything human, nothing which the appalled intelligence could seize upon as familiar. Imagine an upright cone of black flesh, several feet in diameter and three or more in height, supported by a dozen or more smooth long tentacles which branched from its lower end—supple, boneless octopus-arms which held the cone-body upright and which served both as arms and legs. And near the top of that cone trunk were the only features, the twin tiny orifices which were the ears and a single round and red-rimmed white eye, set between them. Thus were these beings in appearance, black tentacle-creatures, moving in unending swirling throngs through streets and squares and buildings of their glowing city.

Helplessly we stared upon them, from our place of concealment. To venture into sight, I knew, would be to court swift death. I turned to Hurus Hol, then started as there came from the city ahead a low, waxing sound-note, a deep, powerful tone of immense volume which sounded out over the city like the blast of a deep-pitched horn. Another note joined it, and another, until it seemed that a score of mighty horns were calling across the city, and then they died away. But as we looked now we saw that the shining streets were emptying, suddenly, that the moving swarms of black tentacle-creatures were passing into the pyramidal buildings, that the cones above were slanting down toward the roofs and coming to rest. Within a space of minutes the streets seemed entirely empty and deserted, and the only sign of activity over all the city was the hovering of a few cones that still moved restlessly above it. Astounded, we watched, and then the explanation came suddenly to me.

"It's their sleep-period!" I cried. "Their night! These things must rest, must sleep, like any living thing, and as there's no night on this glowing world those horn-notes must signal the beginning of their sleep-period."

Hurus Hol was on his feet, his eyes suddenly kindling. "It's a chance in a thousand to get inside the city!" he exclaimed.

The next moment we were out of the shelter of our concealing trees and were racing across the stretch of ground which separated us from the city. And five minutes later we were standing in the empty, glowing streets, hugging closely the mighty sloping walls of the huge buildings along it.

At once Hurus Hol led the way directly down the street toward the heart of the city, and as we hastened on beside him be answered to my question, "We must get to the city's center. There's something there which I glimpsed from our ship, and if it's what I think—"

He had broken into a run, now, and as we raced together down the bare length of the great, shining avenue, I, for one, had an unreassuring presentiment of what would happen should the huge buildings around us disgorge their occupants before we could get out of the city. Then Hurus Hol had suddenly stopped short, and at a motion from him we shrank swiftly behind the corner of a pyramid's slanting walls. Across the street ahead of us were passing a half-dozen of the tentacle-creatures, gliding smoothly toward the open door of one of the great pyramids. A moment we crouched, holding our breath, and then the things had passed inside the building and the door had slid shut behind them. At once we leapt out and hastened on.

We were approaching the heart of the city, I judged, and ahead the broad, shining street we followed seemed to end in a great open space of some sort. As we sped toward it, between the towering luminous lines of buildings, a faint droning sound came to our ears from ahead, waxing louder as we hastened on. The clear space ahead was looming larger, nearer, now, and then as we raced past the last great building on the street's length we burst suddenly into view of the opening ahead and stopped, staring dumfoundedly toward it.

It was no open plaza or square, but a pit—a shallow, circular pit not more than a hundred feet in depth but all of a mile in diameter, and we stood at the rim or edge of it. The floor was smooth and flat, and upon that floor there lay a grouped mass of hundreds of half-globes or hemispheres, each fifty feet in diameter, which were resting upon their flat bases with their curving sides uppermost. Each of these hemispheres was shining with light, but it was very different light from the feeble glow of the buildings and streets around us, an intensely brilliant blue radiance which was all but blinding to our eyes. From these massed, radiant hemispheres came the loud droning we had heard, and now we saw, at the pit's farther edge, a cylindrical little room or structure of metal which was supported several hundred feet above the pit's floor by a single slender shaft of smooth round metal, like a great bird-cage. And toward this cage-structure Hurus Hol was pointing now, his eyes flashing.

"It's the switch-board of the thing!" he cried. "And these brilliant hemispheres—the unheard-of space-path of this dark star—it's all clear now! All—"

He broke off, suddenly, as Nal Jak sprang back, uttering a cry and pointing upward. For the moment we had forgotten the hovering cones above the city, and now one of them was slanting swiftly downward, straight toward us.

We turned, ran back, and the next moment an etheric bomb crashed down upon the spot where we had stood, exploding silently in a great flare of light. Another bomb fell and flared, nearer, and then I turned with sudden fierce anger and aimed the little ray-projector in my hand at the hovering cone above. The brilliant little beam cut across the dark shape; the black cone hovered still for a moment, then crashed down into the street to destruction. But now, from above and beyond, other cones were slanting swiftly down toward us, while from the pyramidal buildings beside us hordes of the black tentacle-creatures were pouring out in answer to the alarm.

In a solid, resistless swarm they rushed upon us. I heard a yell of defiance from Dal Nara, beside me, the hiss of our rays as they clove through the black masses in terrible destruction, and then they were upon us. A single moment we whirled about in a wild mêlée of men and cone-creatures, of striking human arms and coiling tentacles; then there was a shout of warning from one of my friends, something hard descended upon my head with crushing force, and all went black before me.

4

Faint light was filtering through my eyelids when I came back to consciousness. As I opened them I sat weakly up, then fell back. Dazedly I gazed about me. I was lying in a small, square room lit only by its own glowing walls and floor and ceiling, a room whose one side slanted steeply upward and inward, pierced by a small barred window that was the only opening. Opposite me I discerned a low door of metal bars, or grating, beyond which lay a long, glowing-walled corridor. Then all these things were suddenly blotted out by the anxious face of Hurus Hol, bending down toward me.

"You're awake!" he exclaimed, his face alight. "You know me, Ran Rarak?"

For answer I struggled again to a sitting position, aided by the arm of Dal Nara, who had appeared beside me. I felt strangely weak, exhausted, my head throbbing with racing fires.

"Where are we?" I asked, at last. "The fight in the city—I remember that—but where are we now? And where's Nal Jak?"

The eyes of my two friends met and glanced away, while I looked anxiously toward them. Then Hurus Hol spoke slowly.

"We are imprisoned in this little room in one of the great pyramids of the glowing city," he said. "And in this room you have lain for weeks, Ran Rarak."

"Weeks?" I gasped, and he nodded. "It's been almost ten weeks since we were captured there in the city outside," he said, "and for all that time you've lain here out of your head from that blow you received, sometimes delirious and raving, sometimes completely unconscious. And in all that time this dark star, this world, has been plunging on through space toward our Galaxy, and our sun, and the theft and doom of that sun. Ten more days and it passes our sun, stealing it from the Galaxy. And I, who have learned at last what forces are behind it all, lie prisoned here.

"It was after we four were brought to this cell, after our capture, that I was summoned before our captors, before a council of those strange tentacle-creatures which was made up, I think, of their own scientists. They examined me, my clothing, all about me, then sought to communicate with me. They did not speak— communicating with each other by telepathy—but they strove to enter into communication with me by a projection of pictures on a smooth wall, pictures of their dark star world, pictures of our own Galaxy, our own sun—picture after picture, until at last I began to understand the drift of them, the history and the purpose of these strange beings and their stranger world.

"For ages, I learned, for countless eons, their mighty sun had flashed through the infinities of space, alone except for its numerous planets upon which had risen these races of tentacle-creatures. Their sun was flaming with life, then, and on their circling planets they had attained to immense science, immense power, as their system rolled on, a single wandering star, through the depths of uncharted space. But as the slow eons passed, the mighty sun began to cool, and their planets to grow colder and colder. At last it had cooled so far that to revive its dying fires they dislodged one of their own planets from its orbit and sent it crashing into their sun, feeding its waning flames. And when more centuries had passed and it was again cooling they followed the same course, sending another planet into it, and so on through the ages, staving off the death of their sun by sacrificing their worlds, until at last but one planet was left to them. And still their sun was cooling, darkening, dying.

"For further ages, though, they managed to preserve a precarious existence on their single planet by means of artificial heat-production, until at last their great sun had cooled and solidified to such a point that life was possible upon its dark, dead surface. That surface, because of the solidified radio-active elements in it, shone always with pale light, and to it the races of the tentacle-creatures now moved. By means of great air-current projectors they transferred the atmosphere of their planet to the dark star itself and then cast loose their planet to wander off into space by itself, for its orbit had become erratic and they feared that it would crash into their own great dark star world, about which it had revolved. But on the warm, shining surface of the great dark star they now spread out and multiplied, raising their cities from its glowing rock and clinging to its surface as it hurtled on and on and on through the dark infinities of trackless space.

"But at last, after further ages of such existence, the tentacle-races saw that again they were menaced with extinction, since in obedience to the inexorable laws of nature their dark star was cooling still further, the molten fires at its center which warmed its surface gradually dying down, while that surface became colder and colder. In a little while, they knew, the fires at its center would be completely dead, and their great world would be a bitter, frozen waste, unless they devised some plan by which to keep warm its surface.

"At this moment their astronomers came forward with the announcement that their dark-star world, plunging on through empty space, would soon pass a great starcluster or Galaxy of suns at a distance of some fifteen billion miles. They could not invade the worlds of this Galaxy, they knew, for they had discovered that upon those worlds lived countless trillions of intelligent inhabitants who would be able to repel their own invasion, if they attempted it. There was but one expedient left, therefore, and that was to attempt to jerk a sun out of this Galaxy as they passed by it, to steal a star from it to take out with them into space, which would revolve around their own mighty dark world and supply it with the heat they needed.

"The sun which they fixed on to steal was one at the Galaxy's very edge, our own sun. If they passed this at fifteen billion miles, as their course then would cause them to do, they could do nothing. But if they could change their dark star's course, could curve inward to pass this sun at some three billion miles instead of fifteen, then the powerful gravitational grip of their own gigantic world would grasp this sun and carry it out with it into space. The sun's planets, too, would be carried out, but these they planned to crash into the fires of the sun itself, to increase its size and splendor. All that was needed, therefore, was some method of curving their world's course inward, and for this they had recourse to the great gravity-condensers which they had already used to shift their own planets.

"You know that it is gravitational force alone which keeps the suns and planets to their courses, and you know that the gravitational force of any body, sun or planet, is radiated out from it in all directions, tending to pull all things toward that body. In the same way there is radiated outward perpetually from the Galaxy that combined attractive gravitational force of all its swarming suns, and a tiny fraction of this outward-radiating force, of course, struck the dark star, pulling it weakly toward the

Galaxy. If more of that outward-radiating force could strike the dark star, it would be pulled toward the Galaxy with more power, would be pulled nearer toward the Galaxy's edge, as it passed.

"It was just that which their gravity-condenser accomplished. In a low pit at the heart of one of their cities—this city, in fact—they placed the condenser, a mass of brilliant hemispherical ray-attracters which caused more of the Galaxy's outward-shooting attractive force to fall upon the dark star, thereby pulling the dark star inward toward the Galaxy's edge in a great curve. When they reached a distance of three billion miles from the Galaxy's edge they planned to turn off the great condenser, and their dark star would then shoot past the Galaxy's edge, jerking out our sun with it, from that edge, by its own terrific gravitational grip. If the condenser were turned off before they came that close, however, they would pass the sun at a distance too far to pull it out with them, and would then speed on out into space alone, toward the freezing of their world and their own extinction. For that reason the condenser, and the great cage-switch of the condenser, were guarded always by hovering cones, to prevent its being turned off before the right moment.

"Since then they have kept the great gravity-condenser in unceasing operation, and their dark star has swept in toward the Galaxy's edge in a great curve. Back in our own solar system I saw and understood what would be the result of that inward curve, and so we came here—and were captured. And in those weeks since we were captured, while you have lain here unconscious and raving, this dark star has been plunging nearer and nearer toward our Galaxy and toward our sun. Ten more days and it passes that sun, carrying it out with it into the darkness of boundless space, unless the great condenser is turned off before then. Ten more days, and we lie here, powerless to warn any of what forces work toward the doom of our sun!"

There was a long silence when Hurus Hol's voice had ceased—a whispering, brain-crushing silence which I broke at last with a single question.

"But Nal Jak—?" I asked, and the faces of my two companions became suddenly strange, while Dal Nara turned away. At last Hurus Hol spoke.

"It was after the tentacle-scientists had examined me," he said gently, "that they brought Nal Jak down to examine. I think that they spared me for the time being because of my apparently greater knowledge, but Nal Jak they—vivisected."

There was a longer hush than before, one in which the brave, quiet figure of the wheelman, a companion in all my service with the fleet, seemed to rise before my suddenly blurring eyes. Then abruptly I swung down from the narrow bunk on which I lay, clutched dizzily at my companions for support, and walked unsteadily to the square, barred little window. Outside and beneath me lay the city of the dark-star people, a mighty mass of pyramidal, glowing buildings, streets thronged with their dark, gliding figures, above them the swarms of the racing cones. From our little window the glowing wall of the great pyramid which held us slanted steeply down for fully five hundred feet, and upward above us for twice that distance. And as I raised my eyes upward I saw, clear and bright above, a great, far-flung field of stars—the stars of our own Galaxy toward which this world was plunging. And burning out clearest among these the star that was nearest of all, the shining yellow star that was our own sun.

I think now that it was the sight of that yellow star, largening steadily as our dark star swept on toward it, which filled us with such utter despair in the hours, the days, that followed. Out beyond the city our cruiser lay hidden in the black forest, we knew, and could we escape we might yet carry word back to the Federation of what was at hand, but escape was impossible. And so, through the long days, days measurable only by our own time-dials, we waxed deeper into an apathy of dull despair.

Rapidly my strength came back to me though the strange food supplied us once a day by our captors was almost uneatable. But as the days fled by, my spirits sank lower and lower, and less and less we spoke to each other as the doom of our sun approached, the only change in any thing around us being the moment each twenty-four hours when the signal-horns called across the city, summoning the hordes in its streets to their four-hour sleep-period. At last, though, we woke suddenly to realization of the fact that nine days had passed since my awakening, and that upon the next day the dark star would be plunging past the burning yellow star above us and jerking it into its grip. Then, at last, all our apathy dropped from us, and we raged against the walls of our cells with insensate fury. And then, with startling abruptness, came the means of our deliverance.

For hours there had been a busy clanging of tools and machines somewhere in the great building above us, and numbers of the tentacle-creatures had been passing our barred door carrying tools and instruments toward some work being carried out overhead. We had come to pay but little attention to them, in time, but as one passed there came a sudden rattle and clang from outside, and turning to the door we saw that one of the passing creatures had dropped a thick coil of slender metal chain upon the floor and had passed on without noticing his loss.

In an instant we were at the door and reaching through its bars toward the coil, but though we each strained our arms in turn toward it the thing lay a few tantalizing inches beyond our grasp. A moment we surveyed it, baffled, fearing the return at any moment of the creature who had dropped it, and then Dal Nara, with a sudden inspiration, lay flat upon the floor, thrusting her leg out through the grating. In a moment she had caught the coil with her foot, and in another moment we had it inside examining it.

We found that though it was as slender as my smallest finger the chain was of incredible strength, and when we roughly estimated the extent of its thick-coiled length we discovered that it would be more than long enough to reach from our window to the street below. At once, therefore, we secreted the thing in a corner of the room and impatiently awaited the sleep-period, when we could work without fear of interruption.

At last, after what seemed measureless hours of waiting, the great horns blared forth across the city outside, and swiftly its streets emptied, the sounds in our building quieting until all was silence, except for the humming of a few watchful cones above the great condenser, and the deep droning of the condenser itself in the distance. At once we set to work at the bars of our window.

Frantically we chipped at the rock at the base of one of the metal bars, using the few odd bits of metal at our command, but at the end of two hours had done no more than scratch away a bare inch of the glowing stone. Another hour and we had laid bare from the rock the lower end of the bar, but now we knew that within minutes the sleep-period of the city outside would be ending, and into the streets would be swarming its gliding throngs, making impossible all attempts at escape. Furiously we worked, dripping now with sweat, until at last when our timedials showed that less than half an hour remained to us I gave over the chipping at the rock and wrapped our chain firmly around the lower end of the bar we had loosened. Then stepping back into the cell and bracing ourselves against the wall below the window, we pulled backward with all our strength.

A tense moment we strained thus, the thick bar holding fast, and then abruptly it gave and fell from its socket in the wall to the floor, with a loud, ringing clang. We lay in a heap on the floor, panting and listening for any sound of alarm, then rose and swiftly fastened the chain's end to one of the remaining bars. The chain itself we dropped out of the window, watching it uncoil its length down the mighty building's glowing side until its end trailed on the empty glowing street far below. At once I motioned Hurus Hol to the window, and in a moment he had squeezed through its bars and was sliding slowly down the chain, hand under hand. Before he was ten feet down Dal Nara was out and creeping downward likewise, and then I too squeezed through the window and followed them, downward, the three of us crawling down the chain along the huge building's steeply sloping side like three flies.

I was ten feet down from the window, now, twenty feet, and glanced down toward the glowing, empty street, five hundred feet below, and seeming five thousand. Then, at a sudden sound from above me, I looked sharply up, and as I did so the most sickening sensation of fear I had ever experienced swept over me. For at the window we had just left, twenty feet above me, one of the tentacle-creatures was leaning out, brought to our cell, I doubted not, by the metal bar's ringing fall, his white, red-rimmed eye turned full upon me.

I heard sighs of horror from my two companions beneath me, and for a single moment we hung motionless along the chain's length, swinging along the huge pyramid's glowing side at a height of hundreds of feet above the shining streets below. Then the creature raised one of its tentacles, a metal tool in its grasp, which he brought down in a sharp blow on the chain at the window's edge. Again he repeated the blow, and again.

He was cutting the chain!

5

For a space of seconds I hung motionless there, and then as the tool in the grasp of the creature above came down on the chain in another sharp blow the sound galvanized me into sudden action.

"Slide on down!" I cried. They didn't, however, but followed me up the chain, though Dal Nara and I alone came to grips with the horrible dead-star creature. I gripped the links with frantic hands, pulling myself upward toward the window and the creature at the window, twenty feet above me.

Three times the tool in his hand came down upon the chain while I struggled up toward him, and each time I expected the strand to sever and send us down to death, but the hard metal withstood the blows for the moment, and before he could strike at it again I was up to the level of the window and reaching up toward him.

As I did so, swift black tentacles thrust out and gripped Dal Nara and me, while another of the snaky arms swept up with the tool in its grasp for a blow on my head. Before it could fall, though, I had reached out with my right hand, holding to the chain with my left, and had grasped the body of the thing inside the window, pulling him outside before he had time to resist. As I did so my own hold slipped a little, so that we hung a few feet below the window, both clinging to the slender chain and both striking futilely at each other, he with the metal tool and I with my clenched fist.

A moment we hung there, swaying hundreds of feet above the luminous stone street, and then the creature's tentacle coiled swiftly around my neck, tightening, choking me. Hanging precariously to our slender strand with one hand I struck out blindly with the other, but felt consciousness leaving me as that remorseless grip tightened. Then with a last effort I gripped the chain firmly with both hands, doubled my feet under me, and kicked out with all my strength. The kick caught the cone-body of my opponent squarely, tearing him loose from his own hold on the chain, and then there was a sudden wrench at my neck and I was free of him, while beneath Dal Nara and I glimpsed his dark body whirling down toward the street below, twisting and turning in its fall along the building's slanting side and then crashing finally down upon the smooth, shining street below, where it lay a black little huddled mass.

Hanging there I looked down, panting, and saw that Hurus Hol had reached the chain's bottom and was standing in the empty street, awaiting us. Glancing up I saw that the blows of the creature I had fought had half severed one of the links above me, but there was no time to readjust it; so with a prayer that it might hold a few moments longer Dal Nara and I began our slipping, sliding progress downward.

The sharp links tore our hands cruelly as we slid downward, and once it seemed to me that the chain gave a little beneath our weight. Apprehensively I looked upward, then down to where Hurus Hol was waving encouragement. Down, down we slid, not daring to look beneath again, not knowing how near we might be to the bottom. Then there was another slight give in the chain, a sudden grating catch, and abruptly the weakened link above snapped and we dropped headlong downward—ten feet into the arms of Hurus Hol.

A moment we sprawled in a little heap there on the glowing street and then staggered to our feet. "Out of the city!" cried Hurus Hol. "We could never get to the condenser-switch on foot—but in the cruiser there's a chance. And we have but a few minutes now before the sleep-period ends!"

Down the broad street we ran, now, through squares and avenues of glowing, mighty pyramids, crouching down once as the ever-hovering cones swept by above, and then racing on. At any moment, I knew, the great horns might blare across the city, bringing its swarming thousands into its streets, and our only chance was to win free of it before that happened. At last we were speeding down the street by which we had entered the city, and before us lay that street's end, with beyond it the vista of black forest and glowing plain over which we had come. And now we were racing over that glowing plain, a quarter-mile, a half, a mile. . . .

Abruptly from far behind came the calling, crescendo notes of the mighty horns, marking the sleep-period's end, bringing back into the streets the city's tentacle-people. It could be but moments now, we knew, before our escape was discovered, and as we panted on at our highest speed we listened for the sounding of the alarm behind us.

It came! When we had drawn to within a half-mile of the black forest where our cruiser lay hidden, another great tumult of horn-notes burst out over the glowing city behind, high and shrill, and raging. And glancing back we saw swarms of the black cones rising from the pyramidal buildings' summits, circling, searching, speeding out over the glowing plains around the city, a compact mass of them racing straight toward us.

"On!" cried Hurus Hol. "It's our last chance—to get to the cruiser!"

Staggering, stumbling, with the last of our strength we sped on, over the glowing soil and rocks, toward the rim of the black forest which lay now a scant quarter-mile ahead. Then suddenly Hurus Hol stumbled, tripped and fell. I halted, turned toward him, then turned again as Dal Nara shouted thickly and pointed upward. We had been sighted by the speeding cones above and two of them were driving straight down toward us.

A moment we stood there, rigid, while the great cones dipped toward us, waiting for the death that would crash down upon us from them. Then suddenly a great dark shape loomed in the air above and behind us, from which sprang out swift shafts of brilliant green light, the dazzling de-cohesion ray, striking the two swooping cones and sending them down in twin torrents of shattered wreckage. And now the mighty bulk behind us swept swiftly down upon us, and we saw that it was our cruiser.

Smoothly it shot down to the ground, and we stumbled to its side, through the waiting open door. As I staggered up to the bridgeroom the third officer was shouting in my ear. "We sighted you from the forest," he was crying. "Came out in the cruiser to get you—"

But now I was in the bridgeroom, brushing the wheelman from the controls, sending our ship slanting sharply up toward the zenith. Hurus Hol was at my side, now, pointing toward the great telechart and shouting something in my ear. I glanced over, and my heart stood still. For the great dark disk on the chart had swept down to within an inch of the shining line around our sun-circle, the danger-line.

"The condenser!" I shouted. "We must get to that switch—turn it off! It's our only chance!"

We were racing through the air toward the luminous city, now, and ahead a mighty swarm of the cones was gathering and forming to meet us, while from behind and from each side came other swarms, driving on toward us. Then the door clicked open and Dal Nara burst into the bridgeroom.

"The ship's ray-tubes are useless!" she cried. "They've used the last charge in the ray-tanks!"

At the cry the controls quivered under my hands, the ship slowed, stopped. Silence filled the bridgeroom, filled all the cruiser, the last silence of despair. We had failed. Weaponless our ship hung there, motionless, while toward it from all directions leaped the swift and swarming cones, in dozens, in scores, in hundreds, leaping toward us, long black messengers of death, while on the great telechart the mighty dark star leapt closer toward the shining circle that was our sun, toward the fateful line around it. We had failed, and death was upon us.

And now the black swarms of the cones were very near us, and were slowing a little, as though fearing some ruse on our part, were slowing but moving closer, closer, while we awaited them in a last utter stupor of despair. Closer they came, closer, closer . . .

A ringing, exultant cry suddenly sounded from somewhere in the cruiser beneath me, taken up by a sudden babel of voices, and then Dal Nara cried out hoarsely, beside me, and pointed up through our upper observation-windows toward a long, shining, slender shape that was driving down toward us out of the upper air, while behind it drove a vast swarm of other and larger shapes, long and black and mighty.

"It's our own ship!" Dal Nara was shouting, insanely. "It's Ship 16! They escaped, got back to the Galaxy—and look there—behind them—it's the fleet, the Federation fleet!"

There was a wild singing of blood in my ears as I looked up, saw the mighty swarm of black shapes that were speeding down upon us behind the shining cruiser, the five thousand mighty battle-cruisers of the Federation fleet.

The fleet! The massed fighting-ships of the Galaxy, cruisers from Antares and Sirius and Regulus and Spica, the keepers of the Milky Way patrol, the picked fighters of a universe! Ships with which I had cruised from Arcturus to Deneb, beside which I had battled in many an interstellar fight. The fleet! They were straightening, wheeling, hovering, high above us, and then they were driving down upon the massed swarms of cones around us in one titanic, simultaneous swoop.

Then around us the air flashed brilliant with green rays and bursting flares, as decohesion rays and etheric bombs crashed and burst from ship to ship. Weaponless our cruiser hung there, at the center of that gigantic battle, while around us the mighty cruisers of the Galaxy and the long black cones of the tentacle-people crashed and whirled and flared, swooping and dipping and racing upon each other, whirling down to the glowing world below in scores of shattered wrecks, vanishing in silent flares of blinding light. From far away across the surface of the luminous world beneath, the great swarms of cones drove on toward the battle, from the shining towers of cities far away, racing fearlessly to the attack, sinking and falling and crumbling beneath the terrible rays of the leaping ships above, ramming and crashing with them to the ground in sacrificial plunges. But swiftly, now, the cones were vanishing beneath the brilliant rays.

Then Hurus Hol was at my side, shouting and pointing down toward the glowing city below. "The condenser!" he cried, pointing to where its blue radiance still flared on. "The dark star—look!" He flung a hand toward the telechart, where the dark star disk was but a scant half-inch from the shining line around our sun-circle, a tiny gap that was swiftly closing. I glanced toward the battle that raged around us, where the Federation cruisers were sending the cones down to destruction by swarms, now, but unheeding of the condenser below. A bare half-mile beneath us lay that condenser, and its cage-pillar switch, which a single shaft of the green ray would have destroyed instantly. And our ray-tubes were useless!

The wild resolve flared up in my brain and I slammed down the levers in my hands, sent our ship racing down toward the condenser and its upheld cage like a released thunderbolt of hurtling metal. "Hold tight!" I screamed as we thundered down. "I'm going to ram the switch!"

And now up toward us were rushing the brilliant blue hemispheres of the pit, the great pillar and upheld cage beside them, toward which we flashed with the speed of lightning. Crash!—and a tremendous shock shook the cruiser from stem to stern as its prow tore through the upheld metal cage, ripping it from its supporting pillar and sending it crashing to the ground. Our cruiser spun, hovered for a moment as though to whirl down to destruction, then steadied, while we at the window gazed downward, shouting.

For beneath us the blinding radiance of the massed hemispheres had suddenly snapped out! Around and above us the great battle had died, the last of the cones tumbling to the ground beneath the rays of the mighty fleet, and now we turned swiftly to the telechart. Tensely we scanned it. Upon it the great dark-star disk was creeping still toward the line around our sun-circle, creeping slower and slower toward it but still moving on, on, on. . . . Had we lost, at the last moment? Now the black disk, hardly moving, was all but touching the shining line, separated from it by only a hair's-breadth gap. A single moment we watched while it hovered thus, a moment in which was settled the destiny of a sun. And then a babel of incoherent cries came from our lips. For the tiny gap was *widening!*

The black disk was moving back, was curving outward again from our sun and from the Galaxy's edge, curving out once more into the blank depths of space whence it had come, without the star it had planned to steal. Out, out, out—and we knew, at last, that we had won.

And the mighty fleet of ships around us knew, from their own charts. They were massing around us and hanging motionless while beneath us the palely glowing gigantic dark star swept on, out into the darkness of trackless space until it hung like a titanic feeble moon in the heavens before us, retreating farther and farther from the shining stars of our Galaxy, carrying with it the glowing cities and the hordes of the tentacle-peoples, never to return. There in the bridgeroom, with our massed ships around us, we three watched it go, then turned back toward our own yellow star, serene and far and benignant, that yellow star around which swung our own eight little worlds. And then Dal Nara flung out a hand toward it, half weeping now.

"The sun!" she cried. "The sun! The good old sun, that we fought for and saved! Our sun, till the end of time!"

It was on a night a week later that Dal Nara and I said farewell to Hurus Hol, standing on the roof of that same great building on Neptune from which we had started
with our fifty cruisers weeks before. We had learned, in that week, how the only survivor of those cruisers, Ship 16, had managed to shake off the pursuing cones in that
first fierce attack and had sped back to the Galaxy to give the alarm, of how the
mighty Federation fleet had raced through the Galaxy from beyond Antares in answer to that alarm, speeding out toward the approaching dark star and reaching it just
in time to save our own ship, and our sun.

The other events of that week, the honors which had been loaded upon us, I shall
not attempt to describe. There was little in the solar system which we three could not
have had for the asking, but Hurus Hol was content to follow the science that was his
life-work, while Dal Nara, after the manner of her sex through all the ages, sought a
beauty parlor, and I asked only to continue with our cruiser in the service of the Federation fleet. The solar system was home to us, would always be home to us, but never,
I knew, would either of us be able to break away from the fascination of the great
fleet's interstellar patrol, the flashing from sun to sun, the long silent hours in cosmic
night and stellar glare. We would be star-rovers, she and I, until the end.

So now, ready to rejoin the fleet, I stood on the great building's roof, the mighty
black bulk of our cruiser behind us and the stupendous canopy of the Galaxy's glittering suns over our heads. In the streets below, too, were other lights, brilliant flares,
where thronging crowds still celebrated the escape of their worlds. And now Hurus
Hol was speaking, more moved than ever I had seen him.

"If Nal Jak were here—" he said, and we were all silent for a moment. Then his
hand came out toward us and silently we wrung it, turning toward the cruiser's door.

As it slammed shut behind us we were ascending to the bridgeroom, and from
there we glimpsed now the great roof dropping away beneath us as we slanted up from
it once more, the dark figure of Hurus Hol outlined for a moment at its edge against
the lights below, then vanishing. And the world beneath us was shrinking, vanishing
once more, until at last of all the solar system behind us there was visible only the single yellow spark that was our sun.

Then about our outward-racing cruiser was darkness, the infinite void's eternal
night—night and the unchanging, glittering hosts of wheeling, flaming stars.

JACK WILLIAMSON

Jack Williamson [1908–] was one of the first and is still one of the best science fiction writers. He lives in Portales, New Mexico, where there is now a Williamson SF library at the University of Eastern New Mexico, where he taught English for twenty years. Critic John Clute remarks (www.infinitematrix.net/columns/clute1.html):

> The personal miracle of Jack Williamson's career is that he wrote himself out of the belatedness that governed the genre when he began; and that for several decades after 1940 his creative mind paced the train. He rode a long ways up the line, which is a very high score for a man. Until he got to here.

What Clute is driving at is that Williamson, who was born in Bisbee, Arizona Territory, in 1908, lived in Mexico and Texas, moved with the family to New Mexico by covered wagon the year he was seven, and grew up on an isolated ranch, living in his imagination.

> I was just out of a country high school, with no money or job, nowhere to go, when Hugo Gernsback launched *Amazing Stories* in 1926. Immediately fascinated, I started writing "scientifiction." He bought my first story in 1928, the year before he invented the term "science fiction."

And he won the Hugo Award and a Nebula Award for his novella "The Ultimate Earth" at age 94. His most recent novel is *The Stonehenge Gate* (2005).

The OED gives him credit for inventing the word "terraforming." "I used to claim," he says in an interview (www.scifi.com/sfw/issue284/interview.html), "I'd been first to use the the term *genetic engineering*, in my novel *Dragon's Island*, published in 1951, but now I understand that some scientist beat me by a couple of years. Claiming firsts can be risky, but in vitro insemination is described in "The Girl from Mars," published in 1929. The space habitat, rotated to simulate gravity, is invented in "The Prince of Space," 1931. There are organ banks and organ transplants in *The Reefs of Space*, a novel I wrote with Fred Pohl several years before the first heart transplant. My Seetee stories, revised for *Seetee Ship*, were the first fiction about antimatter."

Williamson says, in his introduction to *Skylark Three* by Edward E. Smith, Ph.D. (2003), that Smith is the pioneer creator of space opera, and recounts how Smith and young John W. Campbell, Jr., as writers in the early 1930s, competed to increase the scale of space battles and mighty conflicts with superweapons. This is certainly in line with the narrative of the age of space opera that is commonly and confidently mentioned as the way it was, even by scholars who should know better. Williamson, of course, has his own definition, or avoidance of one:

> What is space opera? Definitions differ. Marion Zimmer Bradley was offended when I once implied that she was writing it. I hadn't meant to be derogatory. I like to use "space opera" as a label for the whole literature of man in space, a great epic tale of discovery and expansion across the galaxy. The term is drawn from "horse opera," a name often used in disdain for the western films that were a Hollywood staple for half a century. Most of those story lines, of course, were cheap and trite; I suppose Sturgeon's Law prevails. Nevertheless, I think both horse opera and space opera owe their popularity to their universal appeal. Both embody the tradition of the classic epic.

> The hero in a true epic is larger than life. He has a great cause. He breaks frontiers. He battles great enemies. He creates a new society.

Williamson himself is and has been a commercial writer devoted to science fiction, and consistently interested in the relationship of science to fiction. In his own variety of space opera, ideas from science always play a part, and so he has often been regarded as part of the hard SF core of the genre. It is no surprise to us that Marion Zimmer Bradley, who devoted much of her writing life to science fantasy in the Brackett tradition, would feel upset about being called a space opera writer by someone whom others ranked generally above that hackwork level during the years of her professional career. She had also been a fan in the 1940s and knew the social signals. One has to know that Williamson just got better as a writer through each decade of the eight (thus far) that he has published, but that he remains an unassuming craftsman who remembers his own times writing whatever he could get paid for. He wrote for comics. He wrote for TV, for *Captain Video*, the very definition of hack space opera (see the *Fancyclopedia* definition in our introductory essay). He was never too proud to write SF in any medium, and never anticipated much in the way of literary respect for his work, though he was certainly pleased when it came. So, of course, he has a benign interpretation, even of words coined to insult.

"The Prince of Space" fits comfortably within the contemporary boundaries of space opera, but was in the era of its publication simply a respectable science fiction story about a space pirate and aliens, with one original hard SF idea that became part of the common hoard of the genre, at least through and beyond the imagery of Kubrick and Clarke's *2001: A Space Odyssey*—the space station, spinning in space to create artificial gravity.

THE PRINCE OF SPACE

JACK WILLIAMSON

CHAPTER I

TEN MILLION EAGLES REWARD!

"Space Flier Found Drifting with Two Hundred Dead!
Notorious Interplanetary Pirate—Prince of Space—Believed
to Have Committed Ghastly Outrage!"

Mr. William Windsor, a hard-headed, grim-visaged newspaperman of forty, stood nonchalantly on the moving walk that swept him briskly down Fifth Avenue. He smiled with pardonable pride as he listened to the raucous magnetic speakers shouting out the phrases that drew excited mobs to the robot vending machines which sold the yet damp news strips of printed shorthand. Bill had written the account of the outrage; he had risked his life in a mad flight upon a hurtling sunship to get his concise story to New York in time to beat his competitors. Discovering the inmost details of whatever was puzzling or important or exciting in this day of 2131, regardless of risk to life or limb, and elucidating those details to the ten million avid readers of the great daily newspaper, *The Herald-Sun*, was the prime passion of Bill's life.

Incidentally, the reader might be warned at this point that Bill is not, properly speaking, a character in this narrative; he is only an observer. The real hero is that amazing person who has chosen to call himself "The Prince of Space." This history is drawn from Bill's diary, which he kept conscientiously, expecting to write a book of the great adventure.

Bill stepped off the moving sidewalk by the corner vending machine, dropped a coin in the slot, and received a copy of the damp shorthand strip delivered fresh from the presses by magnetic tube. He read his story, standing in a busy street that rustled quietly with the whir of moving walks and the barely audible drone of the thousands of electrically driven heliocars which spun smoothly along on rubber-tired wheels, or easily lifted themselves to skimming flight upon whirling helicopters.

Heliographic advices from the Moon Patrol flier *Avenger* state that the sunship *Helicon* was found today, at 16:19, Universal Time, drifting two thousand miles off the lunar lane. The locks were open, air had escaped, all on board were frozen and dead. Casualties include Captain Stormburg, the crew of 71 officers and men, and 132 passengers, of whom 41 were women. The *Helicon* was bound to Los Angeles from the lunarium health resorts at Tycho on the Moon. It is stated that the bodies were barbarously torn and mutilated, as if the most frightful excesses had been perpetrated upon them. The cargo of the sunship had been looted. The most serious loss is some thousands of tubes of the new radioactive metal, vitalium, said to have been worth nearly a million eagles.

A crew was put aboard the *Helicon* from the *Avenger*, her valves were closed, and she will be brought under her own motor tubes to the interplanetary base at Miami, Florida, where a more complete official examination will be made. No attempt has been made to identify the bodies of the dead. The passenger list is printed below.

Military officials are inclined to place blame for the outrage upon the notorious interplanetary outlaw, who calls himself "The Prince of Space." On several occasions the "Prince" has robbed sunships of cargoes of vitalium, though he has never before committed so atrocious a deed as the murder of scores of innocent passengers. It is stated that the engraved calling card, which the "Prince" is said always to present to the captain of a captured sunship, was not found on the wreck.

Further details will be given the public as soon as it is possible to obtain them.

The rewards offered for the "Prince of Space," taken dead or alive, have been materially increased since the outrage. The total offered by the International Confederation, Interplanetary Transport Lunar Mining Corporation, Sunship Corporation, Vitalium Power Company, and various other societies, corporations, newspapers, and individuals, is now ten million eagles.

"Ten million eagles!" Bill exclaimed. "That would mean a private heliocar, and a long, long vacation in the South Seas!"

He snorted, folded up the little sheet and thrust it into his green silk tunic, as he sprang nimbly upon the moving sidewalk.

"What chance have I to see the Prince of Space?"

About him, the slender spires of widely spaced buildings rose two hundred stories into a blue sky free from dust or smoke. The white sun glinted upon thousands of darting heliocars, driven by silent electricity. He threw back his head, gazed longingly up at an amazing structure that rose beside him—at a building that was the architectural wonder of the twenty-second century.

Begun in 2125, Trainor's Tower had been finished hardly a year. A slender white finger of aluminum and steel alloy, it rose twelve thousand feet above the canyons of the metropolis. Architects had laughed, six years ago, when Dr. Trainor, who had been an obscure western college professor, had returned from a vacation trip to the moon and announced his plans for a tower high enough to carry an astronomical observatory giving mountain conditions. A building five times as high as any in existence! It was folly, they said. And certain skeptics inquired how an impecunious professor would get funds to put it up. The world had been mildly astonished when the work began. It was astounded when it was known that the slender tower had safely reached its full height of nearly two and a half miles. A beautiful thing it was, in its slim strength—girder-work of glistening white metal near the ground, and but a slender white cylinder for the upper thousands of feet of its amazing height.

The world developed a hungry curiosity about the persons who had the privilege of ascending in a swift elevator to the queer, many-storied cylindrical building atop the astounding tower. Bill had spent many hours in the little waiting room before the locked door of the elevator shaft—bribes to the guard had been a heavy drain upon a generous expense account. But not even bribery had won him into the sacred elevator.

He had given his paper something, however, of the persons who passed sometimes through the waiting room. There was Dr. Trainor, of course, a mild, bald man, with kindly blue eyes and a slow, patient smile. And Paula, his vivaciously beautiful daughter, a slim, small girl, with amazingly expressive eyes. She had been with her father on the voyage to the moon. Scores of others had passed through; they ranged from janitors and caretakers to some of the world's most distinguished astronomers and solar engineers—but they were uniformly reticent about what went on in Trainor's Tower.

And there was Mr. Cain—"The mysterious Mr. Cain," as Bill had termed him. He had seen him twice, a slender man, tall and wiry, lean of face, with dark, quizzical eyes. The reporter had been able to learn nothing about him—and what Bill could not unearth was a very deep secret. It seemed that sometimes Cain was about Trainor's Tower and that more often he was not. It was rumored that he had advanced funds for building it and for carrying on the astronomical research for which it was evidently intended.

Impelled by habit, Bill sprang off the moving walk as he glided past Trainor's Tower. He was standing, watching the impassive guard, when a man came past into the street. The man was Mr. Cain, with a slight smile upon the thin, dark face that was handsome in a stern, masculine sort of way. Bill started, pricked up his ears, so to speak, and resolved not to let this mysterious young man out of sight until he knew something about him.

To Bill's vast astonishment, Mr. Cain advanced toward him, with a quick, decisive step, and a speculative gleam lurking humorously in his dark eyes. He spoke without preamble.

"I believe you are Mr. William Windsor, a leading representative of the *Herald-Sun*."

"True. And you are Mr. Cain—the mysterious Mr. Cain!"

The tall young man smiled pleasantly.

"Yes. In fact, I think the 'mysterious' is due to you. But Mr. Windsor—"

"Just call me Bill."

"—I believe that you are desirous of admission to the Tower."

"I've done my best to get in."

"I am going to offer you the facts you want about it, provided you will publish them only with my permission."

"Thanks!" Bill agreed. "You can trust me."

"I have a reason. Trainor's Tower was built for a purpose. That purpose is going to require some publicity very shortly. You are better able to supply that publicity than any other man in the world."

"I can do it—provided—"

"I am sure that our cause is one that will enlist your enthusiastic support. You will be asked to do nothing dishonorable."

Mr. Cain took a thin white card from his pocket, scrawled rapidly upon it, and handed it to Bill, who read the words, "Admit bearer. Cain."

"Present that at the elevator, at eight tonight. Ask to be taken to Dr. Trainor."

Mr. Cain walked rapidly away, with his lithe, springy step, leaving Bill standing, looking at the card, rather astounded.

At eight that night, a surprised guard let Bill into the waiting room. The elevator attendant looked at the card.

"Yes. Dr. Trainor is up in the observatory."

The car shot up, carrying Bill on the longest vertical trip on earth. It was minutes before the lights on the many floors of the cylindrical building atop the tower were flashing past them. The elevator stopped. The door swung open, and Bill stepped out beneath the crystal dome of an astronomical observatory.

He was on the very top of Trainor's Tower.

The hot stars shone, hard and clear, through a metal-ribbed dome of polished vitrolite. Through the lower panels of the transparent wall, Bill could see the city spread below him—a mosaic of fine points of light, scattered with the colored winking eyes of electric signs; it was so far below that it seemed a city in miniature.

Slanting through the crystal dome was the huge black barrel of a telescope, with ponderous equatorial mounting. Electric motors whirred silently in its mechanism, and little lights winked about it. A man was seated at the eyepiece—he was Dr. Trainor, Bill saw—he was dwarfed by the huge size of the instrument.

There was no other person in the room, no other instrument of importance. The massive bulk of the telescope dominated it.

Trainor rose and came to meet Bill. A friendly smile spread over his placid face. Blue eyes twinkled with mild kindliness. The subdued light in the room glistened on the bald dome of his head.

"Mr. Windsor, of the *Herald-Sun*, I suppose?" Bill nodded, and produced a notebook. "I am very glad you came. I have something interesting to show you. Something on the planet Mars."

"What—"

"No. No questions, please. They can wait until you see Mr. Cain again."

Reluctantly, Bill closed his notebook. Trainor seated himself at the telescope, and Bill waited while he peered into the tube, and pressed buttons and moved bright levers. Motors whirred, and the great barrel swung about.

"Now look," Trainor commanded.

Bill took the seat, and peered into the eyepiece. He saw a little circle of a curious luminous blue-blackness, with a smaller disk of light hanging in it, slightly swaying. The disk was an ocherous red, with darker splotches and brilliantly white polar markings.

"That is Mars—as the ordinary astronomer sees it," Trainor said. "Now I will change eyepieces, and you will see it as no man has ever seen it except through this telescope."

Rapidly he adjusted the great instrument, and Bill looked again.

The red disk had expanded enormously, with great increase of detail. It had become a huge red globe, with low mountains and irregularities of surface plainly visible. The prismatic polar caps stood out with glaring whiteness. Dark, green-gray patches, splotched burned orange deserts, and thin, green-black lines—the controversal "canals" of Mars—ran straight across the planet, from white caps toward the darker equatorial zone, intersecting at little round greenish dots.

"Look carefully," Trainor said. "What do you see in the edge of the upper right quadrant, near the center of the disk and just above the equator?"

Bill peered, saw a tiny round dot of blue—it was very small, but sharply edged, perfectly round, bright against the dull red of the planet.

"I see a little blue spot."

"I'm afraid you see the death-sentence of humanity!"

Ordinarily Bill might have snorted—newspapermen are apt to become exceedingly skeptical. But there was something in the gravity of Trainor's words, and in the strangeness of what he had seen through the giant telescope in the tower observatory, that made him pause.

"There's been a lot of fiction," Bill finally remarked, "in the last couple of hundred years. Wells' old book, 'The War of the Worlds,' for example. General theory seems to be that the Martians are drying up and want to steal water. But I never really—"

"I don't know what the motive may be," Trainor said. "But we know that Mars has intelligent life—the canals are proof of that. And we have excellent reason to believe that that life knows of us, and intends us no good. You remember the Enbers Expedition?"

"Yes. In 2099. Enbers was a fool who thought that if a sunship could go to the moon, it might go to Mars just as well. He must have been struck by meteorites."

"There is no reason why Enbers might not have reached Mars in 2100," said Trainor. "The heliographic dispatches continued until he was well over half way. There was no trouble then. We have very good reason to think that he landed, that his return was prevented by intelligent beings on Mars. We know that they are using what they learned from his captured sunship to launch an interplanetary expedition of their own!"

"And that blue spot has something to do with it?"

"We think so. But I have authority to tell you nothing more. As the situation advances, we will have need for newspaper publicity. We want you to take charge of that. Mr. Cain, of course, is in supreme charge. You will remember your word to await his permission to publish anything."

Trainor turned again to the telescope.

With a little clatter, the elevator stopped again at the entrance door of the observatory. A slender girl ran from it across to the man at the telescope.

"My daughter Paula, Mr. Windsor," said Trainor.

Paula Trainor was an exquisite being. Her large eyes glowed with a peculiar shade of changing brown. Black hair was shingled close to her shapely head. Her face was small, elfinly beautiful, the skin almost transparent. But it was the eyes that were remarkable. In their lustrous depths sparkled mingled essence of childish innocence, intuitive, age-old wisdom, and quick intelligence—intellect that was not coldly reasonable, but effervescent, flashing to instinctively correct conclusions. It was an oddly baffling face, revealing only the mood of the moment. One could not look at it and say that its owner was good or bad, indulgent or stern, gentle or hard. It could be, if she willed, the perfect mirror of the moment's thought—but the deep stream of her character flowed unrevealed behind it.

Bill looked at her keenly, noted all that, engraved the girl in the notebook of his memory. But in her he saw only an interesting feature story.

"Dad's been telling you about the threatened invasion from Mars, eh?" she inquired in a low, husky voice, liquid and delicious. "The most thrilling thing, isn't it? Aren't we lucky to know about it, and to be in the fight against it!—instead of going on like all the rest of the world, not dreaming there is danger?"

Bill agreed with her.

"Think of it! We may even go to Mars, to fight 'em on their own ground!"

"Remember, Paula," Trainor cautioned. "Don't tell Mr. Windsor too much."

"All right, Dad."

Again the little clatter of the elevator. Mr. Cain had come into the observatory, a tall, slender young man, with a quizzical smile, and eyes dark and almost as enigmatic as Paula's.

Bill, watching the vivacious girl, saw her smile at Cain. He saw her quick flush, her unconscious tremor. He guessed that she had some deep feeling for the man. But he seemed unaware of it. He merely nodded to the girl, glanced at Dr. Trainor, and spoke briskly to Bill.

"Excuse me, Mr. Win—er, Bill, but I wish to see Dr. Trainor alone. We will communicate with you when it seems necessary. In the meanwhile, I trust you to forget what you have seen here tonight, and what the Doctor has told you. Good evening."

Bill, of necessity, stepped upon the elevator. Five minutes later he left Trainor's

Tower. Glancing up from the vividly bright, bustling street, with its moving ways and darting heliocars, he instinctively expected to see the starry heavens that had been in view from the observatory.

But a heavy cloud, like a canopy of yellow silk in the light that shone upon it from the city, hung a mile above. The upper thousands of feet of the slender tower were out of sight above the clouds.

After breakfast next morning Bill bought a shorthand news strip from a robot purveyor. In amazement and some consternation he read:

Prince of Space Raids Trainor's Tower

Last night, hidden by the clouds that hung above the city, the daring interplanetary outlaw, the self-styled Prince of Space, suspected of the *Helicon* outrage, raided Trainor's Tower. Dr. Trainor, his daughter Paula, and a certain Mr. Cain are thought to have been abducted, since they are reported to be missing this morning.

It is thought that the raiding ship drew herself against the Tower, and used her repulsion rays to cut through the walls. Openings sufficiently large to admit the body of a man were found this morning in the metal outer wall, it is said.

There can be no doubt that the raider was the "Prince of Space" since a card engraved with that title was left upon a table. This is the first time the pirate has been known to make a raid on the surface of the earth—or so near it as the top of Trainor's Tower.

Considerable alarm is being felt as a result of this and the *Helicon* outrage of yesterday. Stimulated by the reward of ten million eagles, energetic efforts will be made on the part of the Moon Patrol to run down this notorious character.

CHAPTER II

BLOODHOUNDS OF SPACE

Two days later Bill jumped from a landing heliocar, presented his credentials as special correspondent, and was admitted to the Lakehurst base of the Moon Patrol. Nine slender sunships lay at the side of the wide, high-fenced field, just in front of their sheds. In the brilliant morning sunlight they scintillated like nine huge octagonal ingots of polished silver.

These war-fliers of the Moon Patrol were eight-sided, about twenty feet in diameter and a hundred long. Built of steel and the new aluminum bronzes, with broad vision panels of heavy vitrolite, each carried sixteen huge positive ray tubes. These mammoth vacuum tubes, operated at enormous voltages from vitalium batteries, were little different in principle from the "canal ray" apparatus of some centuries before. Their "positive rays," or streams of atoms which had lost one or more electrons, served to drive the sunship by reaction—by the well-known principle of the rocket motor.

And the sixteen tubes mounted in twin rings about each vessel served equally well as weapons. When focused on a point, the impact-pressure of their rays equaled that of the projectile from an ancient cannon. Metal in the positive ray is heated to fusion, living matter carbonized and burned away. And the positive charge carried by the ray is sufficient to electrocute any living being in contact with it.

This Moon Patrol fleet of nine sunships was setting out in pursuit of the Prince of Space, the interplanetary buccaneer who had abducted Paula Trainor and her father, and the enigmatic Mr. Cain. Bill was going aboard as special correspondent for the *Herald-Sun*.

On the night before the *Helicon*, the sunship which had been attacked in space, had been docked at Miami by the rescue crew put aboard from the *Avenger*. The world had been thrown into a frenzy by the report of the men who had examined the two hundred dead on board.

"Blood sucked from *Helicon* victims!" the loud speakers were croaking. "Mystery of lost sunship upsets world! Medical examination of the two hundred corpses found on the wrecked space flier show that the blood had been drawn from the bodies, apparently through curious circular wounds about the throat and trunk. Every victim bore scores of these inexplicable scars. Medical men will not attempt to explain how the wounds might have been made.

"In a more superstitious age, it might be feared that the Prince of Space is not man at all, but a weird vampire out of the void. And, in fact, it has been seriously suggested that, since the wounds observed could have been made by no animal known on earth, the fiend may be a different form of life, from another planet."

Bill found Captain Brand, leader of the expedition, just going on board the slender, silver *Fury*, flagship of the fleet of nine war-fliers. He had sailed before with this bluff, hard-fighting guardsman of the space lanes; he was given a hearty welcome.

"Hunting down the Prince is a good-sized undertaking, from all appearances," Bill observed.

"Rather," big, red-faced Captain Brand agreed. "We have been after him seven or eight times in the past few years—but I think his ship has never been seen. He must have captured a dozen commercial sunships."

"You know, I rather admire the Prince—" Bill said, "or did until that *Helicon* affair. But the way those passengers were treated is simply unspeakable. Blood sucked out!"

"It is hard to believe that the Prince is responsible for that. He has never needlessly murdered anyone before—for all the supplies and money and millions worth of vitalium he has taken. And he has always left his engraved card—except on the *Helicon*.

"But anyhow, we blow him to eternity on sight!"

The air-lock was open before them, and they walked through, and made their way along the ladder (now horizontal, since the ship lay on her side) to the bridge in the bow. Bill looked alertly around the odd little room, with its vitrolite dome and glistening instruments, while Captain Brand flashed signals to the rest of the fleet for sealing the locks and tuning the motor ray generators.

A red rocket flared from the *Fury*. White lances of flame darted from the downturned vacuum tubes. As one, the nine ships lifted themselves from the level field. Deliberately they upturned from horizontal to vertical positions. Upward they flashed through the air, with slender white rays of light shooting back from the eight rear tubes of each.

Bill, standing beneath the crystal dome, felt the turning of the ship. He felt the pressure of his feet against the floor, caused by acceleration, and sat down in a convenient padded chair. He watched the earth become a great bowl, with sapphire sea on the one hand and green-brown land and diminishing, smokeless city on the other. He watched the hazy blue sky become deepest azure, then black, with a million still stars bursting out in pure colors of yellow and red and blue. He looked down again, and saw the earth become convex, an enormous bright globe, mistily visible through haze or air and cloud.

Swiftly the globe drew away. And a tiny ball of silver, half black, half rimmed with blinding flame, sharply marked with innumerable round craters, swam into view beyond the misty edge of the globe—it was the moon.

Beyond them flamed the sun—a ball of blinding light, winged with a crimson sheet of fire—hurling quivering lances of white heat through the vitrolite panels. Blinding it was to look upon it, unless one wore heavily tinted goggles.

Before them hung the abysmal blackness of space, with the canopy of cold hard stars blazing as tiny scintillant points of light, at an infinite distance away. The Galaxy was a broad belt of silvery radiance about them, set with ten thousand many-colored jewels of fire. Somewhere in the vastness of that void they sought a daring man, who laughed at society, and called himself the Prince of Space.

The nine ships spread out, a thousand miles apart. Flickering heliographs—swinging mirrors that reflected the light of the sun—kept them in communication with bluff Captain Brand, while many men at telescopes scanned the black, star-studded sweep of space for the pirate of the void.

Days went by, measured only by chronometer, for the winged, white sun burned ceaselessly. The earth had shrunk to a little ball of luminous green, bright on the sun-ward side, splotched with the dazzling white of cloud patches and polar caps.

Sometimes the black vitalium wings were spread, to catch the energy of the sun. The sunship draws its name from the fact that it is driven by solar power. It utilizes the remarkable properties of the rare radioactive metal, vitalium, which is believed to be the very basis of life, since it was first discovered to exist in minute traces in those complex substances so necessary to all life, the vitamins. Large deposits were discovered at Kepler and elsewhere on the moon during the twenty-first century. Under the sun's rays vitalium undergoes a change to triatomic form, storing up the vast energy of sunlight. The vitalium plates from the sunshine are built into batteries with alternate sheets of copper, from which the solar energy may be drawn in the form of electric current. As the battery discharges, the vitalium reverts to its stabler allotropic form, and may be used again and again. The Vitalium Power Company's plants in Arizona, Chili, Australia, the Sahara, and the Gobi now furnish most of the earth's power. The sunship, recharging its vitalium batteries in space, can cruise indefinitely.

It was on the fifth day out from Lakehurst. The *Fury*, with her sister ships spread out some thousands of miles to right and left, was cruising at five thousand miles per hour, at heliocentric elevation 93.243546, ecliptic declination 7° 18' 46" north, right ascension XIX hours, 20 min., 31 sec. The earth was a little green globe beside her, and the moon a thin silver crescent beyond.

"Object ahead!" called a lookout in the domed pilot-house of the *Fury*, turning from his telescope to where Captain Brand and Bill stood smoking, comfortably held to the floor by the ship's acceleration. "In Scorpio, about five degrees above Antares. Distance fifteen thousand miles. It seems to be round and blue."

"The Prince, at last!" Brand chuckled, an eager grin on his square chinned face, light of battle flashing in his blue eyes.

He gave orders that set the heliographic mirrors flickering signals for all nine of the Moon Patrol fliers to converge about the strange object, in a great crescent. The black fins that carried the charging vitalium plates were drawn in, and the full power of the motor ray tubes thrown on, to drive ahead each slender silver flier at the limit of her acceleration.

Four telescopes from the *Fury* were turned upon the strange object. Captain Brand and Bill took turns peering through one of them. When Bill looked, he saw the infinite black gulf of space, silvered with star-dust of distant nebulae. Hanging in the blackness was an azure sphere, gleaming bright as a great globe cut from turquoise. Bill was reminded of a similar blue globe he had seen—when he had stood at the enormous telescope on Trainor's Tower, and watched a little blue circle against the red deserts of Mars.

Brand took two or three observations, figured swiftly.

"It's moving," he said. "About fourteen thousand miles per hour. Funny! It is moving directly toward the earth, almost from the direction of the planet Mars. I wonder—" He seized the pencil, figured again. "Queer. That thing seems headed for the earth, from a point on the orbit of Mars, where that planet was about forty days ago. Do you suppose the Martians are paying us a visit?"

"Then it's not the Prince of Space?"

"I don't know. Its direction might be just a coincidence. And the Prince might be a Martian, for all I know. Anyhow, we're going to find what that blue globe is!"

Two hours later the nine sunships were drawn up in the form of a great half circle, closing swiftly on the blue globe, which had been calculated to be about one hundred feet in diameter. The sunships were nearly a thousand miles from the globe, and scattered along a curved line two thousand miles in length. Captain Brand gave orders for eight forward tubes on each flier to be made ready for use as weapons. From his own ship he flashed a heliographic signal.

"The *Fury*, of the Moon Patrol, demands that you show ship's papers, identification tags for all passengers, and submit to search for contraband."

The message was three times repeated, but no reply came from the azure globe. It continued on its course. The slender white sunships came plunging swiftly toward it, until the crescent they formed was not two hundred miles between the points, the blue globe not a hundred miles from the war-fliers.

Then Bill, with his eye at a telescope, saw a little spark of purple light appear beside the blue globe. A tiny, bright point of violet-red fire, with a white line running from it, back to the center of the sphere. The purple spark grew, the white line lengthened. Abruptly, the newspaperman realized that the purple was an object hurtling toward him with incredible speed.

Even as the realization burst upon him, the spark became visible as a little red-blue sphere, brightly luminous. A white beam shone behind it, seemed to push it with ever-increasing velocity. The purple globe shot past, vanished, The white ray snapped out.

"A weapon!" he exclaimed.

"A weapon and a warning!" said Brand, still peering through another eyepiece. "And we reply!"

"Heliograph!" he shouted into a speaking tube. "Each ship will open with one forward tube, operating one second twelve times per minute. Increase power of rear tubes to compensate repulsion."

White shields flickered. Blindingly brilliant rays, straight bars of dazzling opalescence, burst intermittently from each of the nine ships, striking across a hundred miles of space to batter the blue globe with a hail of charged atoms.

Again a purple spark appeared from the sapphire globe, with a beam of white fire behind it. A tiny purple globe, hurtling at an inconceivable velocity before a lance of white flame. It reached out, with a certain deliberation, yet too quickly for a man to do more than see it.

It struck a sunship, at one tip of the crescent formation.

A dazzling flash of violet flame burst out. The tiny globe seemed to explode into a huge flare of red-blue light. And where the slim, eight-sided ship had been was a crushed and twisted mass of metal.

"A solid projectile!" Brand cried. "And driven on the positive ray! Our experts have tried it, but the ray always exploded the shell. And that was some explosion! I don't know what—unless atomic energy!"

The eight sunships that remained were closing swiftly upon the blue globe. The dazzling white rays flashed intermittently from them. They struck the blue globe squarely—the fighting crews of the Moon Patrol are trained until their rays are directed with deadly accuracy. The azure sphere, unharmed, shone with bright radiance—it seemed that a thin mist of glittering blue particles was gathering about it, like a dust of powdered sapphires.

Another purple spark leapt from the turquoise globe.

In the time that it took a man's eyes to move from globe to slim, glistening sunship, the white ray had driven the purple spark across the distance. Another vivid flash of violet light. And another sunship became a hurtling mass of twisted wreckage.

"We are seven!" Brand quoted grimly.

"Heliograph!" he shouted into the mouthpiece. "Fire all forward tubes one second twenty times a minute. Increase rear power to maximum."

White rays burst from the seven darting sunships, flashing off and on. That sapphire globe grew bright, with a strange luminosity. The thin mist of sparkling blue particles seemed to grow more dense about it.

"Our rays don't seem to be doing any good," Brand muttered, puzzled. "The blue about that globe must be some sort of vibratory screen."

Another purple spark, with the narrow white line of fire behind it, swept across to the flier from the opposite horn of the crescent, burst into a sheet of blinding red-violet light. Another ship was a twisted mass of metal.

"Seven no longer!" Brand called grimly to Bill.

"Looks as if the Prince has got us beaten!" the reporter cried.

"Not while a ship can fight!" exclaimed the Captain. "This is the Moon Patrol!"

Another tiny purple globe traced its line of light across the black, star-misted sky. Another sunship crumpled in a violet flash.

"They're picking 'em off the ends," Bill observed. "We're in the middle, so I guess we're last."

"Then," said Captain Brand, "we've got time to ram 'em."

"Control!" he shouted into the speaking tube. "Cut off forward tubes and make all speed for the enemy. Heliograph! Fight to the end! I am going to ram them!"

Another red-blue spark moved with its quick deliberation. A purple flash left another ship in twisted ruin.

Bill took his eye from the telescope. The blue globe, bright under the rays, with the sapphire mist sparkling about it, was only twenty miles away. He could see it with his naked eye, drifting swiftly among the familiar stars of Scorpio.

It grew larger very swiftly.

With the quickness of thought, the purple sparks moved out alternately to right and to left. They never missed. Each one exploded in purple flame, crushed a sunship.

"Three fliers left," Bill counted, eyes on the growing blue globe before them. "Two left. Good-by, Brand." He grasped the bluff Captain's hand. "One left. Will we have time?"

He looked forward. The blue globe, with the dancing, sparkling haze of sapphire swirling about it, was swiftly expanding.

"The last one! Our turn now!"

He saw a tiny fleck of purple light dart out of the expanding azure sphere that they had hoped to ram. Then red-violet flame seemed to envelope him. He felt the floor of the bridge tremble beneath his feet: He heard the beginning of a shivering crash like that of shattering glass. Then the world was mercifully dark and still.

CHAPTER III

THE CITY OF SPACE

Bill lay on an Alpine glacier, a painful broken leg inextricably wedged in a crevasse. It was dark, frightfully cold. In vain he struggled to move, to seek light and warmth, while the grim grip of the ice held him, while bitter wind howled about him and the piercing cold of the blizzard crept numbingly up his limbs.

He came to with a start, realized that it was a dream. But he was none the less freezing, gasping for thin frigid air, that somehow would not come into his lungs. All about was darkness. He lay on cold metal.

"In the wreck of the *Fury!*" he thought. "The air is leaking out. And the cold of space! A frozen tomb!"

He must have made a sound, for a groan came from beside him. He fought to draw breath, tried to speak. He choked, and his voice was oddly high and thin.

"Who are—"

He ended in a fit of coughing, felt warm blood spraying from his mouth. Faintly he heard a whisper beside him.

"I'm Brand. The Moon Patrol—fought to the last!"

Bill could speak no more, and evidently the redoubtable captain could not. For a long time they lay in freezing silence. Bill had no hope of life, he felt only very grim satisfaction in the fact that he and Brand had not been killed outright.

But suddenly he was thrilled with hope. He heard a crash of hammer blows upon metal, sharp as the sound of snapping glass in the thin air. Then he heard the thin hiss of an oxygen lance.

Someone was cutting a way to them through the wreckage. Only a moment later, it seemed, a vivid bar of light cleft the darkness, searched the wrecked bridge, settled upon the two limp figures. Bill saw grotesque figures in clumbrous metal space suits clambering through a hole they had cut. He felt an oxygen helmet being fastened about his head, heard the thin hiss of the escaping gas, and was once more able to breathe.

Again he slipped into oblivion.

He awoke with the sensation that infinite time had passed. He sat up quickly, feeling strong, alert, fully recovered in every faculty, a clear memory of every detail of the disastrous encounter with the strange blue globe-ship springing instantly to his mind.

He was in a clean bed in a little white-walled room. Captain Brand, a surprised grin on his bluff, rough-hewn features, was sitting upon another bed beside him. Two attendants in white uniform stood just inside the door; and a nervous little man in black suit, evidently a doctor, was hastily replacing gleaming instruments in a leather bag.

A tall man appeared suddenly in the door, clad in a striking uniform of black, scarlet, and gold—black trousers, scarlet military coat and cap, gold buttons and decorations. He carried in his hand a glittering positive ray pistol.

"Gentlemen," he said in a crisp, gruff voice, "you may consider yourselves prisoners of the Prince of Space."

"How come?" Brand demanded.

"The Prince was kind enough to have you removed from the wreck of your ship, and brought aboard the *Red Rover*, his own sunship. You have been kept unconscious until your recovery was complete."

"And what do you want with us now?" Brand was rather aggressive.

The man with the pistol smiled. "That, gentlemen, I am happy to say, rests largely with yourselves."

"I am an officer in the Moon Patrol," said Brand. "I prefer death to anything—"

"Wait, Captain. You need have none but the kindest feelings for my master, the Prince of Space. I now ask you nothing but your word as an officer and a gentleman that you will act as becomes a guest of the Prince. Your promise will lose you nothing and win you much."

"Very good, I promise," Brand agreed after a moment. "—for twenty-four hours."

He pulled out his watch, looked at it. The man in the door lowered his pistol, smiling, and walked across to shake hands with Brand.

"Call me Smith," he introduced himself. "Captain of the Prince's cruiser, *Red Rover*."

Still smiling, he beckoned toward the door.

"And if you like, gentlemen, you may come with me to the bridge. The *Red Rover* is to land in an hour."

Brand sprang nimbly to the floor, and Bill followed. The flier was maintaining a moderate acceleration—they felt light, but were able to walk without difficulty. Beyond the door was a round shaft, with a ladder through its length. Captain Smith clambered up the ladder. Brand and Bill swung up behind him.

After an easy climb of fifty feet or so, they entered a domed pilot-house, with vitrolite observation panels, telescopes, maps and charts, and speaking tube—an arrangement similar to that of the *Fury*.

Black, star-strewn heavens lay before them. Bill looked for the earth, found it visible in the periscopic screens, almost behind them. It was a little green disk, the moon but a white dot beside it.

"We land in an hour!" he exclaimed.

"I didn't say where," said Captain Smith, smiling. "Our landing place is a million miles from the earth."

"Not on earth! Then where—"

"At the City of Space."

"The City of Space!"

"The capital of the Prince of Space. It is not a thousand miles before us."

Bill peered ahead, through the vitrolite dome, distinguished the bright constellation of Sagittarius with the luminous clouds of the Galaxy behind it.

"I don't see anything—"

"The Prince does not care to advertise his city. The outside of the City of Space is covered with black vitalium—which furnishes us with power. Reflecting none of the sun's rays, it cannot be seen by reflected light. Against the black background of space it is invisible, except when it occults a star."

Captain Smith busied himself with giving orders for the landing. Bill and Brand stood for many minutes looking forward through the vitrolite dome, while the motor ray tubes retarded the flier. Presently a little black point came against the silver haze of the Milky Way. It grew, stars vanishing behind its rim, until a huge section of the heavens was utterly black before them.

"The City of Space is in a cylinder," Captain Smith said. "Roughly five thousand feet in diameter, and about that high. It is built largely of meteoric iron which we captured from a meteorite swarm—making navigation safe and getting useful metal at the same time. The cylinder whirls constantly, with such speed that the centrifugal force against the sides equals the force of gravity on the earth. The city is built around the inside of the cylinder—so that one can look up and see his neighbor's house apparently upside down, a mile above his head. We enter through a lock in one end of the cylinder."

A vast disk of dull black metal was now visible a few yards outside the vitrolite panels. A huge metal valve swung open in it, revealing a bright space beyond. The *Red Rover* moved into the chamber, the mighty valve closed behind her, air hissed in about her, an inner valve was opened, and she slipped into the City of Space.

They were, Bill saw, at the center of an enormous cylinder. The sides, half a mile away, above and below them, were covered with buildings along neat, tree-bordered streets, scattered with green lawns, tiny gardens, and bits of wooded park. It seemed very strange to Bill, to see these endless streets about the inside of a tube, so that one by walking a little over three miles in one direction would arrive again at the starting point, in the same way that one gets back to the starting point after going around the earth in one direction.

At the ends of the cylinder, fastened to the huge metal disks, which closed the ends, were elaborate and complex mechanisms, machines strange and massive. "They must be for heating the city," Bill thought, "and for purifying the air, for furnishing light and power, perhaps even for moving it about." The lock through which they had entered was part of this mechanism.

In the center of each end of the cylinder hung a huge light, seeming large and round as the sun, flooding the place with brilliant mellow rays.

"There are five thousand people here," said Captain Smith. "The Prince has always kept the best specimens among his captives, and others have been recruited besides. We are self-sustaining as the earth is. We use the power of the sun—through our vitalium batteries. We grow our own food. We utilize our waste products—matter here goes through a regular cycle of life and death as on the earth. Men eat food containing carbon, breathe in oxygen, and breathe out carbon dioxide; our plants break up the carbon dioxide, make more foods containing the same carbon, and give off the oxygen for men to breathe again. Our nitrogen, or oxygen and hydrogen, go through similar cycles. The power of the sun is all we need from outside."

Captain Smith guided his "guests" down the ladder, and out through the ship's airlock. They entered an elevator. Three minutes later they stepped off upon the side of the great cylinder that housed the City, and entered a low building with a broad concrete road curving up before it. As they stepped out, it gave Bill a curious dizzy feeling to look up and see busy streets, inverted, a mile above his head. The road before them curved smoothly up on either hand, bordered with beautiful trees, until its ends met again above his head.

The centrifugal force that held objects against the sides of the cylinder acted in precisely the same way as gravity on the earth—except that it pulled *away* from the center of the cylinder, instead of *toward* it.

A glistening heliocar came skimming down upon whirling heliocopters, dropped to rubber tires, and rolled up beside them. A young man of military bearing, clad in a striking uniform of red, black, and gold, stepped out, saluted stiffly.

"Captain Smith," he said, "the Prince desires your attendance at his private office immediately with your guests."

Smith motioned Bill and Captain Brand into the richly upholstered body of the heliocar. Bill, gazing up at the end of the huge cylinder with a city inside it, caught sight, for the first time, of the exterior of the *Red Rover*, the ship that had brought them to the City of Space. It lay just beside the massive machinery of the air-lock, supported in a heavy metal cradle, with the elevator tube running straight from it to the building behind them.

"Look, Brand!" Bill gasped. "That isn't the blue globe. It isn't the ship we fought at all!"

Brand looked. The *Red Rover* was much the same sort of ship that the *Fury* had been. She was slender and tapering, cigar-shaped, some two hundred feet in length and twenty-five in diameter—nearly twice as large as the *Fury*. She was cylindrical, instead of octagonal, and she mounted twenty-four motor tubes, in two rings fore and aft, of twelve each, instead of eight.

Brand turned to Smith. "How's this?" he demanded. "Where is the blue globe? Did you have two ships?"

A smile flickered over Smith's stern face. "You have a revelation waiting for you. But it is better not to keep the Prince waiting."

They stepped into the heliocar. The pilot sprang to his place, set the electric motors whirring. The machine rolled easily forward, took the air on spinning helicopters. The road, lined with green gardens and bright cottages, dropped away "below" them, and other houses drew nearer "above." In the center of the cylinder the young man dextrously inverted the flier; and they continued on a straight line toward an imposing concrete building which now seemed "below."

The heliocar landed; they sprang out and approached the imposing building of several stories. Guards uniformed in scarlet, black and gold standing just outside the door held ray pistols in readiness. Smith hurried his "guests" past; they entered a long, high-ceilinged room. It gave a first impression of stately luxury. The walls were paneled with rich dark wood, hung with a few striking paintings. It was almost empty of furniture; a heavy desk stood alone toward the farther end. A tall young man rose from behind this desk, advanced rapidly to meet them.

"My guests, sir," said Smith. "Captain Brand of the *Fury*, and a reporter."

"The mysterious Mr. Cain!" Bill gasped.

Indeed, Mr. Cain stood before him, a tall man, slender and wiry, with a certain not unhandsome sternness in his dark face. A smile twinkled in his black, enigmatic eyes—which none the less looked as if they might easily flash with fierce authority.

"And Mr. Win—or, I believe you asked me to call you Bill. You seem a very hard man to evade!"

Still smiling enigmatically, Mr. Cain took Bill's hand, and then shook hands with Captain Brand.

"But—are you the Prince of Space?" Bill demanded.

"I am. Cain was only a *nom de guerre*, so to speak. Gentlemen, I welcome you to the City of Space!"

"And you kidnapped yourself?"

"My men brought the *Red Rover* for me."

"Dr. Trainor and his daughter—" Bill ejaculated.

"They are friends of mine. They are here."

"And that blue globe!" said Captain Brand. "What was that?"

"You saw the course it was following?"

"It was headed to intersect the orbit of the earth—and its direction was on a line that cuts the orbit of Mars where that planet was forty days ago."

The Prince turned to Bill. "And you have seen something like that blue globe before?"

"Why, yes. The little blue circle on Mars—that I saw through the great telescope on Trainor's Tower."

A sober smile flickered across the dark lean face of the Prince.

"Then, gentlemen, you should believe me. The earth is threatened with a dreadful danger from Mars. The blue globe that wrecked your fleet was a ship from Mars. It was another Martian flier that took the *Helicon*. I believe I have credit for that ghastly exploit of sucking out the passengers' blood." His smile became grimly humorous. "One of the consequences of my position."

"Martian fliers?" echoed Captain Brand. "Then how did we come to be on your ship?"

"I haven't any weapon that will meet those purple atomic bombs on equal terms—though we are now working out a new device. I had Smith cruising around the blue globe in our *Red Rover* to see what he could learn. He was investigating the wrecks, and found you alive."

"You really mean that men from Mars have come this near the earth?" Captain Brand was frankly incredulous.

"Not men," the Prince corrected, smiling. "But *things* from Mars have done it. They have already landed on earth, in fact."

He turned to the desk, picked up a broad sheet of cardboard.

"I have a color photograph here."

Bill studied it, saw that it looked like an aerial photograph of a vast stretch of mountain and desert, a monotonous expanse of gray, tinged with green and red.

"A photograph, taken from space, of part of the state of Chihuahua, Mexico. And see!"

He pointed to a little blue disk in the green-gray expanse of a plain, just below a narrow mountain ridge, with the fine green line that marked a river just beside it.

"That blue circle is the first ship that came. It was the things aboard it that sucked the blood out of the people on the *Helicon*."

Captain Brand was staring at the tall, smiling man, with a curious expression on his red, square-chinned face. Suddenly he spoke.

"Your Highness, or whatever we must call you—"

"Just call me Prince. Cain is not my name. Once I had a name—but now I am nameless!"

The thin dark face suddenly lined with pain, the lips closed in a narrow line. The Prince swept a hand across his high forehead, as if to sweep something unpleasant away.

"Well, Prince, I'm with you. That is, if you want an officer from the Moon Patrol." A sheepish smile overspread his bluff features. "I would have killed a man for suggesting that I would ever do such a thing. But I'll fight for you as well as I ever did for the honor of the Patrol."

"Thanks, Brand!" The Prince took his hand, smiling again.

"Count me in too, of course," said Bill.

"Both of you will be valuable men," said the Prince.

He picked up a sheaf of papers, scanned them quickly, seemed to mark off one item from a sheet and add another.

"The *Red Rover* sets out for the earth in one hour, gentlemen. We're going to try a surprise attack on that blue globe in the desert. You will both go aboard."

"And I'm going too!" A woman's voice, soft and a little husky, spoke beside them. Recognizing it, Bill turned to see Paula Trainor standing behind them, an eager smile on her elfinly beautiful face. Her amazing eyes were fixed upon the Prince, their brown depths filled, for the moment, with passionate wistful yearning.

"Why, no, Paula," the Prince said. "It's dangerous!"

Tears swam mistily in the golden orbs. "I will go! I must! I must!" The girl cried out the words, a sobbing catch in her voice.

"Very well, then," the Prince agreed, smiling absently. "Your father will be along of course. But anything will be likely to happen."

"But you will be there in danger, too!" cried the girl.

"We start in an hour," said the Prince. "Smith, you may take Brand and Windsor back aboard the *Red Rover*."

"Curse his fatherly indifference!" Bill muttered under his breath as they walked out through the guarded door. "Can't he see that she loves him?"

Smith must have heard him, for he turned to him, spoke confidentially. "The Prince is a determined misogynist. I think an unfortunate love affair was what ruined his life—back on the earth. He left his history, even his name, behind him. I think a woman was the trouble. He won't look at a woman now."

They were outside again, startled anew by the amazing scene of a street of houses and gardens, that curved evenly up on either side of them and met above, so that men were moving about, head downward directly above them.

The heliocar was waiting. The three got aboard, were lifted and swiftly carried to the slender silver cylinder of the *Red Rover*, where it hung among the ponderous machinery of the air-lock, on the end of the huge cylinder that housed the amazing City of Space.

"I will show you your rooms," said Captain Smith. "And in an hour we are off to attack the Martians in Mexico."

CHAPTER IV

VAMPIRES IN THE DESERT

Forty hours later the *Red Rover* entered the atmosphere of the earth, above northern Mexico. It was night, the desert was shrouded in blackness. The telescopes revealed only the lights at ranches scattered as thinly as they had been two centuries before.

Bill was in the bridge-room, with Captain Smith.

"The blue globe that destroyed your fleet has already landed here," Smith said. "We saw both of them before they slipped into the shadow of night. They were right together, and it seems that a white metal building has been set up between them."

"The Prince means to attack? In spite of those purple atomic bombs?" Bill seemed surprised.

"Yes. They are below a low mountain ridge. We land on the other side of the hill, a dozen miles off, and give 'em a surprise at dawn."

"We'd better be careful," Bill said doubtfully. "They're more likely to surprise us. If you had been in front of one of those little purple bombs, flying on the white ray!"

"We have a sort of rocket torpedo that Doc Trainor invented. The Prince means to try that on 'em."

The *Red Rover* dropped swiftly, with Smith's skilled hands on the controls. It seemed but a few minutes until the dark shadow of the earth beneath abruptly resolved itself into a level plain scattered with looming shapes that were clumps of mesquite and sagebrush. The slim silver cylinder came silently to rest upon the desert, beneath stars that shone clearly, though to Bill they seemed dim in comparison with the splendid wonders of space.

Three hours before dawn, five men slipped out through the air-lock. The Prince himself was the leader, with Captains Brand and Smith, Bill, and a young officer named Walker. Each man carried a searchlight and a positive ray pistol. And strapped upon the back of each was a rocket torpedo—a smooth, white metal tube, four feet long and as many inches thick, weighing some eighty pounds.

Dr. Trainor, kindly, bald-headed old scientist, was left in charge of the ship. He and his daughter came out of the air-lock into the darkness, to bid the five adventurers farewell.

"We should be back by night," said the Prince, his even white teeth flashing in the darkness. "Wait for us until then. If we don't come, return at once to the City of Space. I want no one to follow us, and no attempt made to rescue us if we don't come back. If we aren't back by tomorrow night we shall be dead."

"Very good, sir," Trainor nodded.

"I'm coming with you, then," Paula declared suddenly.

"Absolutely you are not!" cried the Prince. "Dr. Trainor, I command you not to let your daughter off the ship until we return."

Paula turned quickly away, a slim pillar of misty white in the darkness. Bill heard a little choking sound; he knew that she had burst into tears.

"I can't let you go off into such danger, without me!" she cried, almost hysterical. "I can't!"

The Prince swung a heavy torpedo higher on his shoulders, and strode off over bare gravel toward the low rocky slope of the mountain that lay to northward, faintly revealed in the light of the stars. The other four followed silently. The slender sunship, with the old scientist and his sobbing daughter outside the air-lock, quickly vanished behind them.

With only an occasional cautious flicker of the flashlights the five men picked their way over bare hard ground, among scattered clumps of mesquite. Presently they crossed a barren lava bed, clambering over huge blocks of twisted black volcanic rock. Up the slope of the mountain they struggled, sweating under heavy burdens, blundering into spiky cactus, stumbling over boulders and sagebrush.

When the silver and rose of dawn came in the purple eastern sky, the five lay on bare rock at the top of the low ridge, overlooking the flat, mesquite-covered valley beyond. The valley floor was a brownish green in the light of morning, the hills that rose far across it a hazy blue-gray, faintly tinged with green on age-worn slopes.

Like a string of emeralds dropped down the valley lay an endless wandering line of cottonwoods, of a light and vivid green that stood out from the somber plain. These trees traced the winding course of a stream, the Rio Casas Grandes.

Lying against the cottonwoods, and rising above their tops, were two great spheres of blue, gleaming like twin globes of lapis lazuli in the morning light. They were not far apart, and between them rose a curious domed structure of white, silvery metal.

Each of the five men lifted his heavy metal tube, leveled it across a boulder before him. The Prince, alert and smiling despite the dust and stain of the march through the desert, spoke to the others.

"This little tube along the top of the torpedo is a telescope sight. You will peer through, get the cross hairs squarely upon your target, and hold them there. Then press this nickeled lever. That starts the projectile inside the case to spinning so that inertia will hold it true. Then, being certain that the aim is correct, press the red button. The torpedo is thrown from the case by compressed air, and a positive ray mechanism drives it true to the target. When it strikes, about fifty pounds of Dr. Trainor's new explosive, *trainite*, will be set off.

"Walker, you and Windsor take the right globe. Smith and Brand, the left. I'll have a shot at that peculiar edifice between them."

Bill balanced his torpedo, peered through the telescope, and pressed the lever. The hum of a motor came from the heavy tube.

"All ready?" the Prince inquired.

"Ready," each man returned.

"Fire!"

Bill pressed the red button. The tube drove heavily backward in his hands, and then was but a light, sheet-metal shell. He saw a little gleam of white light before him, against the right blue globe, a diminishing point. It was the motor ray that drove the torpedo speeding toward its mark.

Great flares of orange light hid the two azure spheres and the white dome between them. The spheres and the dome crumpled and vanished, and a thin haze of bluish smoke swirled about them.

"Good shooting!" the Prince commented. "This motor torpedo of Trainor's ought to put a lot of the old fighting equipment in the museum—if we were disposed to bestow such a dangerous toy upon humanity.

"But let's get over and see what happened."

Grasping ray pistols, they sprang to their feet and plunged down the rocky slope. It was five miles to the river. Nearly two hours later it was, when the five men slipped out of the mesquites, to look two hundred yards across an open, grassy flat to the wall of green trees along the river.

Three great heaps of wreckage lay upon the flat. At the right and the left were crumpled masses of bright silver metal—evidently the remains of the globes. In the center was another pile of bent and twisted metal, which had been the domed building.

"Funny that those blue globes look like ordinary white metal now," said Smith.

"I wonder if the blue is not some sort of etheric screen?" Brand commented. "When we were fighting, our rays seemed to take no effect. It occurred to me that some vibratory wall might have stopped them."

"It's possible," the Prince agreed. "I'll take up the possibilities with Trainor. If they have such a screen, it might even be opaque to gravity. Quite a convenience in maneuvering a ship."

As they spoke, they were advancing cautiously, stopping to pick up bits of white metal that had been scattered about by the explosion.

Suddenly Bill's eyes caught movement from the pile of crumpled metal that had been the white dome. It seemed that a green plant was growing quickly from among the ruins. Green tendrils shot up amazingly. Then he saw on the end of a twisted stalk a glowing purple thing that looked somehow like an eye.

At first sight of the thing he had stopped in amazement, leveling his deadly ray pistol and shouting, "Look out!"

Before the shout had died in his throat, before the others had time to turn their heads, they caught the flash of metal among the twining green tentacles. The thing was lifting a metal object.

Then Bill saw a tiny purple spark dart from a bright little mechanism that the green tendrils held. He saw a blinding flash of violet light. His consciousness was cut off abruptly.

The next he knew he was lying on his back on rocky soil. He felt considerably bruised and battered, and his right eye was swollen so that he could not open it. Struggling to a sitting position, he found his hands and feet bound by bloody manacles of unfamiliar design. Captain Brand was lying on his elbow beside him, half under the thin shade of a mesquite bush. Brand looked much torn and disheveled; blood was streaming across his face from a gash in his scalp. His hands and feet also were bound with fetters of white metal.

"What happened?" Bill called dazedly.

"Not so loud," Brand whispered. "The thing—a Martian left alive, I guess it is.

Must have been somewhere out in the brush when we shot. It blew us up with an atomic bomb. Smith and Walker dead—blown to pieces."

"And the Prince?"

"I can speak for myself."

Hearing the familiar low voice, Bill turned. He saw the Prince squatted down, in the blazing sunshine, hands and feet manacled, hat off and face covered with blood and grime.

"Was it that—that green thing?" Bill asked.

"Looks like a sort of animated plant," said the Prince. "A bunch of green tentacles, that it uses for hands. Three purple eyes on green stalks. Just enough of a body to join it all together. Not like anything I ever saw. But the Martians, originating under different conditions, ought to be different."

"What is going to happen now?" Bill inquired.

"Probably it will suck our blood—as it did to the passengers of the *Helicon*," Brand suggested grimly.

Windsor fell silent. It was almost noon. The desert sun was very hot. The motionless air was oppressive with a dry, parching heat; and flies buzzed annoyingly about his bleeding cuts. Wrists and ankles ached under the cruel pressure of the manacles.

"Wish the thing would come back, and end the suspense," Brand muttered.

Bill reflected with satisfaction that he had no relatives to be saddened by his demise. He had no great fear of death. Newspaper work in the twenty-second century is not all commonplace monotony; your veteran reporter is pretty well inured to danger.

"Glad I haven't anyone to worry about me," he observed.

"So am I," the Prince said bitterly. "I left them all, years ago."

"But you have someone!" Bill cried. "It isn't my business to say it, but that makes no difference now. And you're a fool not to know. Paula Trainor loves you! This will kill her!"

The Prince looked up, a bitter smile visible behind the bloody grime on his thin dark face.

"Paula—in love with me! We're friends, of course. But love! I used to believe in love. I have not been always a nameless outcast of space. Once I had name, family—even wealth and position. I trusted my name and my honor to a beautiful woman. I loved her! She said she loved me—I thought she meant it. She used me for a tool. I was trustful; she was clever."

The dark eyes of the Prince burned in fierce anger.

"When she was through with me she left me to die in disgrace. I barely escaped with my life. She had robbed me of my name, wealth, position. She named me the outlaw. She made me appear a traitor to those who trusted me—then laughed at me. She laughed at me and called me a fool. I was—but I won't be again!

"At first I was filled with anger at the whole world, at the unjust laws and the silly conventions and the cruel intolerance of men. I became the pirate of space. A pariah. Fighting against my own kind. Struggling desperately for power."

For a few moments he was moodily silent, slapping at the flies that buzzed around his bloody wounds.

"I gained power. And I learned of the dangers from Mars. First I was glad. Glad to see the race of man swept out. Parasites men seemed. Insects. Life—what is it but a kind of decay on a mote in space? Then I got a saner view, and built the City of Space, to save a few men. Then because the few seemed to have noble qualities, I resolved to try to save the world.

"But it is too late. We have lost. And I have had enough of love, enough of women, with their soft, alluring bodies, and the sweet lying voices, and the heartless scheming."

The Prince fell into black silence, motionless, heedless of the flies that swarmed about him. Presently Brand contrived, despite his manacles, to fish a packet of cigarettes from his pocket, extract one, and tossed the others to Bill, who managed to light one for the Prince. The three battered men sat in dazzling sun and blistering heat, smoking and trying to forget heat and flies and torturing manacles—and the death that loomed so near.

It was early noon when Bill heard a little rustling beyond the mesquites. In a moment the Martian appeared. A grotesque and terrifying being it was. Scores of green tentacles, slender and writhing, grew from an insignificant body. Three lidless, purple eyes, staring, alien, and malevolent, watched them alertly from foot-long green stalks that rose above the body. The creature half walked on tentacles extended below it, half dragged itself along by green appendages that reached out to grasp mesquite limbs above it. One inch-thick coil carried a curious instrument of glittering crystal and white metal—it was a strange, gleaming thing, remotely like a ray pistol. And fastened about another tentacle was a little metal ring, from which an odd-looking little bar dangled.

The thing came straight for the Prince. Bill screamed a warning. The Prince saw it, twisted himself over on the ground, tried desperately to crawl away. The thing reached out a slender tentacle, many yards long. It grasped him about the neck, drew him back.

In a moment the dreadful being was crouching in a writhing green mass above the body of the manacled man. Once he screamed piteously, then there was no sound save loud, gasping breaths. His muscles knotted as he struggled in agony against the fetters and the coils of the monster.

Bill and Captain Brand lay there, unable either to escape or to give assistance. In silent horror they watched the scene. They saw that each slender green tentacle ended in a sharp-edged suction disk. They watched the disks forcing themselves against the throat of the agonized man, tearing a way through his clothing to his body. They saw constrictions move down the rubber-like green tentacles as if they were sucking, while red drops oozed out about the edge of the disks.

"Our turn next," muttered Captain Brand.

"And after us, the world!" Bill breathed, tense with horror.

A narrow, white beam, blindingly brilliant, flashed from beyond the dull green foliage of the mesquite. It struck the crouching monster waveringly. Without a sound, it leapt, flinging itself aside from the body of the Prince. It raised its curious weapon. A tiny purple spark darted from it.

A shattering crash rang out at a little distance. There was a thin scream—a woman's scream.

Then the white ray stabbed at the monster again, and it collapsed in a twitching heap of thin green coils, upon the still body of the Prince.

A slender girl rushed out of the brush, tossed aside a ray pistol, and flung herself upon the monster, trying to drag it from the Prince. It was Paula Trainor. Her clothing was torn. Her skin was scratched and bleeding from miles of running through the desert of rocks and cactus and thorny mesquite. She was evidently exhausted. But she flung herself with desperate energy to the rescue of the injured man.

The body of the dead thing was light enough. But the sucking disks still clung to the flesh. They pulled and tore it when she tugged at them. She struggled desperately to drag them loose, by turns sobbing and laughing hysterically.

"If you can help us get loose, we might help," Bill suggested.

The girl raised a piteous face. "Oh, Mr. Bill—Captain Brand! Is he dead?"

"I think not, Miss Paula. The thing had just jumped on him. Buck up!"

"See the little bar—it looks like a sliver of aluminum—fastened to the metal ring about that coil?" Brand said. "It might be the key for these chains. End of it seems to be shaped about right. Suppose you try it?"

In nervous haste, the girl tore the little bar from its ring. With Brand's aid, she was able to unlock his fetters. The Captain lost no time in freeing Bill and removing the manacles from the unconscious Prince.

The thin, rubber-like tentacles could not be torn loose. Brand cut them with his knife. He found them tough and fibrous. Red blood flowed from them when they were severed.

Bill carried the injured man down to the shade of the cottonwoods, brought water to him in a hat from the muddy little stream below. In a few minutes he was conscious, though weak from loss of blood.

Captain Brand, after satisfying himself that Paula had killed the Martian, and that it was the only one that had survived in the wreckage of the blue globes and the metal dome, set off to cross the mountain and bring back the sunship.

When the *Red Rover* came into view late that evening, a beautiful slender bar of silver against the pyrotechnic gold and scarlet splendor of the desert sunset, the Prince of Space was hobbling about, supported on Bill's arm, examining the wreckage of the Martian fliers.

Paula was hovering eagerly about him, anxious to aid him. Bill noticed the pain and despair that clouded her brown eyes. She had been holding the Prince's head in her arms when he regained consciousness. Her lips had been very close to his, and bright tears were brimming in her golden eyes.

Bill had seen the Prince push her away, then thank her gruffly when he had found what she had done.

"Paula, you have done a great thing for the world," Bill had heard him say.

"It wasn't the world at all! It was for you!" the girl had cried, tearfully.

She had turned away, to hide her tears. And the Prince had said nothing more.

The *Red Rover* landed beside the wreckage of the Martian fliers. After a few hours spent in examining and photographing the wrecks, in taking specimens of the white alloy of which they were built, and of other substances used in the construction, they all went back on the sunship, taking the dead Martian and other objects for further study. Brand took off for the upper atmosphere.

"Captain Brand," the Prince said as they stood in the bridge room, "since the death of poor Captain Smith this morning, I believe you are the most skillful sunship officer in my organization. Hereafter you are in command of the *Red Rover*, with Harris and Vincent as your officers.

"We have a huge task before us. The victory we have won is but the first hand in the game that decides the fate of Earth."

CHAPTER V

THE TRITON'S TREASURE

"I must have at least two tons of vitalium," the Prince of Space told Bill, when the newspaperman came to the bridge of the *Red Rover* after twenty hours in the bunk. The Prince was pale and weak from loss of blood, but seemed to suffer no other ill effects from his encounter with the Martian.

"Two tons of vitalium!" Bill exclaimed. "A small demand! I doubt if there is that much on the market, if you had all the Confederation's treasury to buy it with."

"I must have it, and at once! I am going to fit out the *Red Rover* for a voyage to Mars. It will take that much vitalium for the batteries."

"We are going to Mars!"

"The only hope for humanity is for us to strike first and to strike hard!"

"If the world knew of the danger, we could get help."

"That's where you come in. I told you that I should need publicity. It is your business to tell the public about things. I want you to tell humanity about the danger from Mars. Make it convincing and make it strong! Say anything you like so long as you leave the Prince of Space out of it. I have the body of the Martian that attacked me preserved in alcohol. You have that and the wreckage in the desert to substantiate your story. I will land you at Trainor's Tower in New York tonight. You will have twenty-four hours to convince the world, and raise two tons of vitalium. It has to be done!"

"A big order," Bill said doubtfully. "But I'll do my best."

The city was a bright carpet of twinkling lights when the *Red Rover* darted down out of a black sky, hovering for a moment over. Trainor's Tower. When it flashed away, Bill was standing alone on top of the loftiest building on earth, in his pocket a sheaf of manuscript on which he had been at work for many hours, beside him a bulky package that contained the preserved body of the weird monster from Mars.

He opened the trapdoor—which was conveniently unlocked—took up the package, and clambered down a ladder into the observatory. An intent man was busy at the great telescope—which pointed toward the red planet Mars. The man looked understandingly at Bill, and nodded toward the elevator.

In half an hour Bill was exhibiting his package and his manuscript to the night editor of the *Herald-Sun*.

"The greatest news in the century!" he cried. "The Earth attacked by Mars! It was a Martian ship that took the *Helicon*. I have one of the dead creatures from Mars in this box."

The astounded editor formed a quick opinion that his star reporter had met with some terrifying experience that had unsettled his brain. He listened skeptically while Bill related a true enough account of the cruise of the Moon Patrol ships, and of the battle with the blue globe. Bill omitted any mention of the City of Space and its enigmatic ruler; but let it be assumed that the *Fury* had rammed the globe and that it had fallen in the desert. He ended with a wholly fictitious account of how a mysterious scientist had picked him up in a sunship, had told him of the invaders from Mars, and had sent him to collect two tons of vitalium to equip his ship for a raid on Mars. Bill had spent many hours in planning his story; he was sure that it sounded as plausible as the amazing reality of the Prince of Space and his wonderful city.

The skeptical editor was finally convinced, as much by his faith in Bill's probity as by the body of the green monster, the scraps of a strange white metal, and the photographs, which he presented as material evidence. The editor radioed to have a plane sent from El Paso, Texas, to investigate the wrecks. When it was reported that they were just as Bill had said, the *Herald-Sun* issued an extra, which carried Bill's full account, with photographs of the dead monster, and scientific accounts of the other evidence. There was an appeal for two tons of vitalium, to enable the unknown scientist to save the world by making a raid on Mars.

The story created an enormous sensation all over the world. A good many people believed it. The *Herald-Sun* actually received half a million eagles in subscriptions to buy the vitalium—a sum sufficient to purchase about eleven ounces of that precious metal.

Most of the world laughed. It was charged that Bill was insane. It was charged that the *Herald-Sun* was attempting to expand its circulation by a baseless canard. Worse, it was charged that Bill, perhaps in complicity with the management of the great newspaper, was making the discovery of a new sort of creature in some far corner of the world the basis for a gigantic fraud, to secure that vast amount of vitalium.

Examination proved that the wrecks in the desert had been demolished by explosion instead of by falling. A court injunction was filed against the *Herald-Sun* to prevent collection of the subscriptions, and Bill might have been arrested, if he had not wisely retired to Trainor's Tower.

Finally, it was charged that the pirate, the Prince of Space, was at the bottom of it—possibly the charge was suggested by the fact that the chief object of the Prince's raids had always been vitalium. A rival paper asserted that the pirate must have captured Bill and sent him back to Earth with this fraud.

Public excitement became so great that the reward for the capture of Prince of Space, dead or alive, was raised from ten to fifteen million eagles.

Twenty-four hours later after he had been landed on Trainor's Tower, Bill was waiting there again, with bright stars above him, and the carpet of fire that was New York spread in great squares beneath him. The slim silver ship came gliding down, and hung just beside the vitrolite dome while eager hands helped him through the air-lock. Beyond, he found the Prince waiting, with a question in his eyes.

"No luck," Bill grunted hopelessly. "Nobody believed it. And the town was getting too hot for me. Lucky I had a getaway."

The Prince smiled bitterly as the newspaperman told of his attempt to enlist the aid of humanity.

"About what I expected," he said. "Men will act like men. It might be better, in the history of the cosmos, to let the Martians have this old world. They might make something better of it. But I am going to give humanity a chance—if I can. Perhaps man will develop into something better, in a million years."

"Then there is still a chance—without the vitalium?" Bill asked eagerly.

"Not without vitalium. We have to go to Mars. We must have the metal to fit our flier for the trip. But I have needed vitalium before; when I could not buy it. I took it."

"You mean—piracy!" Bill gasped.

"Am I not the Prince of Space—'notorious interplanetary outlaw' as you have termed me in your paper? And is not the good of the many more than the good of the few? May I not take a few pounds of metal from a rich corporation, to save the earth for humanity?"

"I told you to count me in," said Bill. "The idea was just a little revolutionary."

"We haven't wasted any time while you were in New York. I have means of keeping posted on the shipments of vitalium from the moon. We have found that the sun-ship *Triton* leaves the moon in about twenty hours, with three months production of the vitalium mines in the Kepler crater. It should be well over two tons."

Thirty hours later the *Red Rover* was drifting at rest in the lunar lane, with ray tubes dead and no light showing. Men at her telescopes scanned the heavens moonward for sight of the white repulsion rays of the *Triton* and her convoy.

Bill was with Captain Brand in the bridge-room. Eager light flashed in Brand's eyes as he peered through the telescopes, watched his instruments, and spoke brisk orders into the tube.

"How does it feel to be a pirate?" Bill asked, "after so many years spent hunting them down?"

Captain Brand grinned. "You know," he said, "I've wanted to be a buccaneer ever since I was about four years old. I couldn't, of course, so I took the next best thing, and hunted them. I'm not exactly grieving my heart out over what has happened. But I feel sorry for my old pals of the Moon Patrol. Somebody is going to get hurt!"

"And it may be we," said Bill. "The *Triton* will be convoyed by several war-fliers, and she can fight with her own rays. It looks to me like a hard nut to crack."

"I used to dream about how I would take a ship if I were the Prince of Space," said Captain Brand. "I've just been talking our course of action over with him. We've agreed on a plan."

In an hour the Prince and Dr. Trainor entered the bridge. Paula appeared in a few moments. Her face was drawn and pale; unhappiness cast a shadow in her brown eyes. Eagerly, she asked the Prince how he was feeling.

"Oh, about as well as ever, thanks," the lean young man replied in a careless voice. His dark, enigmatic eyes fell upon her face. He must have noticed her pallor and evident unhappiness. He met her eyes for a moment, then took a quick step toward her. Bill saw a great tenderness almost breaking past the bitter cynicism in those dark eyes. Then the Prince checked himself, spoke shortly:

"We are preparing for action, Paula. Perhaps you should go back to your stateroom until it is over."

The girl turned silently and moved out of the room. Bill thought she would have tottered and fallen if there had been enough gravity or acceleration to make one fall.

In a few minutes a little group of flickering lights appeared among the stars ahead, just beside the huge, crater-scarred, golden disk of the moon.

"The *Triton* and her convoy!" shouted the men at the telescopes.

"All men to their stations, and clear the ship for action!" Captain Brand gave the order.

"Two Moon Patrol sunships are ahead, cruising fifty miles apart," came the word from the telescope. "A hundred miles behind them is the *Triton*, with two more Patrol fliers twenty-five miles behind her and fifty miles apart."

Brand spoke to the Prince, who nodded. And Brand gave the order.

"Show no lights. Work the ship around with the gyroscopes until our rear battery of tubes will cover the right Patrol ship of the leading pair, and our bow tubes the other."

The whir of the electric motors came from below. The fliers swung about, hanging still in the path of the approaching *Triton*.

"All ready, sir," came a voice from the tube.

A few anxious minutes went by. Then the *Red Rover*, dark and silent, was hanging squarely between the two forward Patrol ships, about twenty-five miles from each of them.

"Fire constantly with all tubes, fore and aft, until the enemy appears to be disabled," Brand gave the order. The Prince spoke to him, and he added, "Inflict no unnecessary damage."

Dazzling white rays flashed from the tubes. Swiftly, they found the two forward sunships. The slender octagons of silver shone white under the rays. They reeled, whirled about, end over end, under the terrific pressure of atomic bombardment. In a moment they glowed with dull red incandescence, swiftly became white. A bluish haze spread about them—the discharge of the electric energy carried by the atoms, which would electrocute any man not insulated against it.

From the three other ships flaming white rays darted, searching for the *Red Rover*. But they had hardly found the mark when Brand ordered his rays snapped out. The two vessels he had struck were but whirling masses of incandescent wreckage—completely out of the battle, though most of the men aboard them still survived in their insulated cells.

The Prince himself spoke into the tube. "Maneuver number forty-one. Drive for the *Triton*."

Driven by alternate burst from front and rear motor tubes, the *Red Rover* started a curiously irregular course toward the treasure ship. Spinning end over end, describing irregular curves, she must have been an almost impossible target.

And twice during each spin, when her axis was in line with the *Triton*, all tubes were fired for an instant, striking the treasure ship with a force that reeled and staggered her, leaving her plates half-fused, twisted and broken.

Three times a ray caught the *Red Rover* for an instant, but her amazing maneuvers, which had evidently been long practised by her crew, carried her on a course so erratic and puzzling that the few rays that found her were soon shaken off.

Before the pirate flier reached the *Triton*, the treasure vessel was drifting helpless, with all rays out. The *Red Rover* passed by her, continuing on her dizzily whirling course until she was directly between the two remaining fliers.

"Hold her still," the Prince then shouted into the tube. "And fire all rays, fore and aft."

Blinding opalescent rays jetted viciously from the two rings of tubes. Since the *Red Rover* lay between the two vessels, they could not avoid firing upon each other. Her own rays, being fired in opposite directions, served to balance each other and hold her at rest, while the rays of the enemy, as well as those of the pirate that impinged upon them, tended to send them into spinning flight through space.

Blinding fluorescence obscured the vitrolite panels, and the stout walls of the *Red Rover* groaned beneath the pressure of the hail of atoms upon them. Swiftly they would heat, soften, collapse. Or the insulation would burn away and the electric charge electrocute her passengers.

The enemy was in a state as bad. The white beams of the pirate flier had found them earlier, and could be held upon them more efficiently. It was a contest of endurance.

Suddenly the jets of opalescence snapped off the pirate. Bill gazing out into stardusted space, saw the two Patrol vessels spinning in mad flight before the pressure of the rays, glowing white in incandescent twisted ruin.

A few minutes later the *Red Rover* was drifting beside the *Triton* holding the wrecked treasure-flier with electromagnetic plates. The air-lock of the pirate vessel opened to release a dozen men in metal vacuum suits, armed with ray pistols and equipped with wrecking tools and oxygen lances. The Prince was their leader.

They forced the air-lock of the *Triton*, and entered the wreck. In a few minutes grotesque metal-suited figures appeared again, carrying heavy leaden tubes filled with the precious vitalium.

The *Red Rover* was speeding into space, an hour later, under full power. The Prince of Space was in the bridge room, with Bill, Captain Brand, Dr. Trainor, and Paula. Bill noticed that the girl seemed pathetically joyous at the Prince's safety, though he gave her scant attention.

"We have the two tons of vitalium," said the Prince. "Nearly forty-six hundred pounds, in fact. Easily enough to furnish power for the voyage to Mars. We have the metal—provided we can get away with it."

"Is there still danger?" Paula inquired nervously.

"Yes. Most of the passengers of the *Triton* were still alive. When I gave her captain my card, he told me that they sent a heliographic S.O.S. as soon as we attacked. Some forty or fifty fliers of the Moon Patrol will be hot on our trail."

The *Red Rover* flew on into space, under all her power. Presently the lookouts picked up a score of tiny flickering points of light behind them. The Moon Patrol was in hot pursuit.

"Old friends of mine," said Captain Brand. "Every one of them would give his life to see us caught. And I suppose every one of them feels now that he has a slice of that fifteen million eagles reward! The Moon Patrol never gives up and never admits defeat."

Tense, anxious hours went by while every battery was delivering its maximum current, and every motor tube was operating at its absolutely highest potential.

Paula waited on the bridge, anxiously solicitous for the Prince's health—he was still pale and weak from the adventure in the desert. Presently, evidently noticing how tired and worried she looked, he sent her to her stateroom to rest. She went, in tears.

"No chance to fight, if they run us down," said Captain Brand. "We can handle four, but not forty."

Time dragged heavily. The *Red Rover* flew out into space, past the moon, on such a course as would not draw pursuit toward the City of Space. Her maximum acceleration was slightly greater than that of the Moon Patrol fliers, because of the greater number and power of her motor tubes. Steadily she forged away from her pursuers.

At last the flickering lights behind could be seen no longer.

But the *Red Rover* continued in a straight line, at the top of her speed, for many hours, before she turned and slipped cautiously toward the secret City of Space. She reached it in safety, was let through the air-lock. Once more Bill looked out upon the amazing city upon the inner wall of a spinning cylinder. He enjoyed the remarkable experience of a walk along a street three miles in length, which brought him up in an unbroken curve, and back to where he had started.

It took a week to refit the *Red Rover*, in preparation for the voyage to Mars. Her motor ray tubes were rebuilt, and additional vitalium generators installed. The precious metal taken from the *Triton* was built into new batteries to supply power for the long voyage. Good stocks of food, water, and compressed oxygen were taken aboard, as well as weapons and scientific equipment of all variety.

"We start for Mars in thirty minutes," Captain Brand told Bill when the warning gong had called him and the others aboard.

CHAPTER VI

THE RED STAR OF WAR

The *Red Rover* slipped out through the great airlock of the City of Space, and put her bow toward Mars. The star of the war-god hung before her in the silver-dusted darkness of the faint constellation of Capricornus, a tiny brilliant disk of ocherous red. The Prince of Space, outlawed by the world of his birth, was hurtling out through space in a mad attempt to save that world from the horrors of Martian invasion.

The red point that was Mars hung almost above them, it seemed, almost in the center of the vitrolite dome of the bridge. "We are not heading directly for the planet," Captain Brand told Bill. "Its orbital velocity must be considered. We are moving toward the point that it will occupy in twenty days."

"We can make it in twenty days? Three million miles a day?"

"Easily, if the vitalium holds out, and if we don't collide with a meteorite. There is no limit to speed in space, certainly no practical limit. Acceleration is the important question."

"We may collide with a meteorite you say? Is there much danger?"

"A good deal. The meteorites travel in swarms which follow regular orbits about the sun. We have accurate charts of the swarms whose orbits cross those of the earth and moon. Now we are entering unexplored territory. And most of them are so small, of course, that no telescope would reveal them in time. Merely little pebbles, moving with a speed about a dozen times that of a bullet from an old-fashioned rifle."

"And what are we going to do if we live to get to Mars?"

"A big question!" Brand grinned. "We could hardly mop up a whole planet with the motor rays. Trainor has a few of his rocket torpedoes, but not enough to make much impression upon a belligerent planet. The Prince and Trainor have a laboratory rigged up down below. They are doing a lot of work. A new weapon, I understand. I don't know what will come of it."

Presently Bill found his way down the ladder to the laboratory. He found the Prince of Space and Dr. Trainor hard at work. He learned little by watching them, save that they were experimenting upon small animals, green plants, and samples of the rare vitalium. High tension electricity, electron tubes, and various rays seemed to be in use.

Noticing his interest, the Prince said, "You know that vitalium was first discovered in vitamins, in infinitesimal quantities. The metal seems to be at the basis of all life. It is the trace of vitalium in chlorophyl which enables the green leaves of plants to utilize the energy of sunlight. We are trying to determine the nature of the essential force of life—we know that the question is bound up with the radioactivity of vitalium. We have made a good deal of progress, and complete success would give us a powerful instrumentality."

Paula was working with them in the laboratory, making a capable and eager assistant—she had been her father's helper since her girlhood. Bill noticed that she seemed happy only when near the Prince, that the weight of unhappiness and trouble left her brown eyes only when she was able to help him with some task, or when her skill brought a word or glance of approval from him.

The Prince himself seemed entirely absorbed in his work; he treated the girl courteously enough, but seemed altogether impersonal toward her. To him, she seemed only to be a fellow-scientist. Yet Bill knew that the Prince was aware of the girl's feelings—and he suspected that the Prince was trying to stifle a growing reciprocal emotion of his own.

Bill spent long hours on the bridge with Captain Brand, staring out at the star-scattered midnight of space. The earth shrank quickly, until it was a tiny green disk, with the moon an almost invisible white speck beside it. Day by day, Mars grew larger. It swelled from an ocher point to a little red disk.

Often Bill scanned the spinning scarlet globe through a telescope. He could see the white polar caps, the dark equatorial regions, the black lines of the canals. And after many days, he could see the little blue circle that had been visible in the giant telescope on Trainor's Tower.

"It must be something enormous, to stand out so plainly," he said when he showed it to Captain Brand.

"I suppose so. Even now, we could see nothing with a diameter of less than a mile or so."

"If it's a ship, it must be darned big—big enough for the whole race of 'em to get aboard."

Bill was standing, a few hours later, gazing out through the vitrolite panels at the red-winged splendor of the sun, when suddenly he heard a series of terrific crashes. The ship rocked and trembled beneath him; he heard the reverberation of hammered metal, and the hiss of escaping air.

"Meteorite!" screamed Brand.

Wildly, he pointed to the vitrolite dome above. In three places the heavy crystal was shattered, a little hole drilled through it, surrounded with radiating cracks. In two other sections the heavy metal wall was dented. Through the holes, the air was hissing out. It formed a white cloud outside, and glistening frost gathered quickly on the crystal panels.

Bill felt the air suddenly drawn from his lungs. He gasped for breath. The bridge was abruptly cold. Little particles of snow danced across it.

"The air is going!" Brand gasped. "We'll suffocate!"

He touched a lever and a heavy cover fell across the ladder shaft, locked itself, making the floor an airtight bulkhead.

"That's right," Bill tried to say. "Give others—chance."

His voice had failed. A soaring came in his ears. He felt as if a malignant giant were sucking out his breath. The room grew dark, swam about him. He reeled; he was blind. A sudden chill came over his limbs—the infinite cold of space. He felt hot blood spurting from his nose, freezing on his face. Faintly he heard Brand moving, as he staggered and fell into unconsciousness.

When he looked about again, air and warmth were coming back. He saw that the shaft was still sealed, but air was hissing into the room through a valve. Captain Brand lay inert beside him on the floor. He looked up at the dome, saw that soft rubber patches had been placed over the holes, where air-pressure held them fast. The Captain had saved the ship before he fell.

In a moment the door opened. Dr. Trainor rushed in, with Prince and others behind him. They picked up the unconscious Brand and rushed him down to the infirmary. The plucky captain had been almost asphyxiated, but administration of pure oxygen restored him to consciousness. On the following day he was back on the bridge.

The *Red Rover* had been eighteen days out from the City of Space. The loss of air due to collision with the meteorites had brought inconveniences, but good progress had been made. It was only two more days to Mars. The forward tubes had been going many hours, to retard the ship.

"Object dead ahead!" called a lookout from his telescope.

"A small blue globe, coming directly toward us," he added, a moment later.

"Another of their ships, setting out for the earth," Brand muttered. "It will about cook our goose!"

In a few moments the Prince and Dr. Trainor had rushed up the ladder from the laboratory. The blue globe was rushing swiftly toward them; and the *Red Rover* was plunging forward at many thousand miles per hour.

"We can't run from it," said Brand. "It is still fifty thousand miles away, but we are going far too fast to stop in that distance. We will pass it in about five minutes."

"If we can't stop, we go ahead," the Prince said, smiling grimly.

"We might try a torpedo on 'em," suggested Dr. Trainor. He had mounted a tube to fire his rocket torpedoes from the bridge. "It will have all the speed its own motor rays can develop, *plus* what the ship has at present, *plus* the relative velocity of the globe. That might carry it through."

The Prince nodded assent.

Trainor slipped a slender, gleaming rocket into his tube, sighted it, moved the lever that set the projectile to spinning, and fired. The little white flame of the motor rays dwindled and vanished ahead of them. Quickly, Trainor fired again, and then a third time.

"Switch off the rays and darken the lights," the Prince ordered. "With combined speeds of ten thousand miles a minute, we might pass them without being seen—if they haven't sighted us already."

For long seconds they hurtled onward in tense silence. Bill was at a telescope. Against the silver and black background of space, the little blue disk of the Martian ship was growing swiftly.

Suddenly a bright purple spark appeared against the blue, grew swiftly brighter.

"An atomic bomb!" he cried. "They saw us. We are lost!"

He tensed himself, waiting for the purple flash that would mean the end. But the words were hardly out of his mouth when he saw a tiny sheet of violet flame far ahead of them. It flared up suddenly, and vanished as abruptly. The blue disk of the ship still hung before them, but the purple spark was gone. For a moment he was puzzled. Then he understood.

"The atomic bomb struck a torpedo!" he shouted. "It's exploded. And if they think it was we—"

"Perhaps they can't see us, with the rays out," Brand said.

"It is unlikely," Trainor observed, "that the bomb actually struck one of our torpedoes. More likely it was set to be detonated by the gravitational attraction of any object that passed near it."

Still watching the azure globe, Bill saw a sudden flare of orange light against it. A great burst of yellow flame. The blue ball crumpled behind the flame. The orange went out, and the blue vanished with it. Only twisted scraps of white metal were left.

"The second torpedo struck the Martian!" Bill cried.

"And you notice that the blue went out," said Dr. Trainor. "It must be merely a vibratory screen."

The *Red Rover* hurtled on through space, toward the crimson planet that hour by hour and minute by minute expanded before her. The blue disk was now plainly visible against the red. It was apparently a huge globe of azure, similar to the ships they had met, but at least a mile in diameter. She lay just off the red desert, near an important junction of "canals."

"Some huge machine, screened by the blue wall of vibration," Dr. Trainor suggested.

During the last two days the Prince and Dr. Trainor, and their eager assistant, Paula, had worked steadily in the laboratory, without pause for rest. Bill was with them when the Prince threw down his pencil and announced the result of his last calculation.

"The problem is solved," he said. "And its answer means both success and failure. We have mastered the secret of life. We have unlocked the mystery of the ages! A terrific force is at our command—a force great enough to sweep man to the millennium, or to wipe out a planet! But that force is useless without the apparatus to release it."

"We have the laboratory—" Trainor began.

"But we lack one essential thing. We must have a small amount of cerium, one of the rare earth metals. For the electrode, you know, inside the vitalium grid in our new vacuum tube. And there is not a gram of cerium in all our supplies."

"We can go back to the Earth—" said Trainor.

"That will mean forty days gone, before we could come back—more than forty, because we would have to stop at the City of Space to refit. And all the perils of the meteorites again. I am sure that in less than forty days the Martians will be putting the machine in that enormous blue globe to its dreadful use."

"Then we must land on Mars and find the metal!" said Captain Brand, who had been listening by the door.

"Exactly," said the Prince. "You will pick out a spot that looks deserted, at a great distance from the blue globe. Somewhere in the mountains, as far back as possible from the canals. Land there just after midnight. We will have mining and prospecting equipment ready to go to work when day comes. Almost any sort of ore ought to yield the small quantity of cerium we need."

"Very good, sir," said Brand.

A few hours later the *Red Rover* was sweeping around Mars, on a long curve, many thousands of miles from the surface of the red planet.

"We'll pick out the spot to land while the sun is shinning on it," Captain Brand told Bill. "Then we can keep over it, as it sweeps around into the shadow, timing ourselves to land just after midnight."

"Isn't there danger that we may be seen?"

"Of course. We can only minimize it by keeping a few thousand miles above the surface as long as it is day, and landing at night, and in a deserted section."

As they drew nearer, the telescope revealed the surface of the hostile planet more distinctly. Bill peered intently into an eyepiece, scanning the red globe for signs of its malignant inhabitants.

"The canals seem to be strips of greenish vegetation, irrigated from some sort of irrigation system that brings water from the melting ice-caps," he said.

"Lowell, the old American astronomer, knew that two hundred years ago," said Captain Brand, "though some of his contemporaries claimed that they could not see the 'canals.'"

"I can make out low green trees, and metal structures. I think there are long pipes, as well as open channels, to spread the water. And I see a great dome of white metal—it must be five hundred feet across. . . . There are several of them in sight, mostly located where the canals intersect."

"They might be great community buildings—cities," suggested Brand. "On account of the dust-storms that so often hide the surface of the planet, it would probably be necessary to cover a city up in some way."

"And I see something moving. A little blue dot, it seems. Probably a little flier on the same order as those we have seen; but only a few feet in diameter. It seemed to be sailing from one of the white domes to another."

Brand moved to another telescope.

"Yes, I see them. Two in one place. They seem to be floating along, high and fast. And just to the right is a whole line of them, flying one behind the other. Crossing a patch of red desert."

"What's this?" Bill cried in some excitement. "Looks like animals of some kind in a pen. They look like people, almost."

"What! Let me see!"

Brand rushed over from his telescope. Bill relinquished him the instrument. "See. Just above the center of the field. Right in the edge of that cultivated strip, by what looks like a big aluminum water-pipe."

"Yes. Yes, I see something. A big stockade. And it has things in it. But not men, I think. They are gray and hairy. But they seem to walk on two legs."

"Something like apes, maybe."

"I've got it," cried Brand. "They're domestic animals! The ruling Martians are parasites. They must have something to suck blood out of. They live on these creatures!"

"Probably so," Bill admitted. "Do you suppose they will keep people penned up that way, if they conquer the world?"

"Likely." He shuddered. "No good in thinking of it. We must be selecting the place to land."

He returned to his instrument.

"I've got it," he said presently. "A low mountain, in a big sweep of red desert. About sixty degrees north of the equator. Not a canal or a white dome in a hundred miles."

Long hours went by, while the *Red Rover* hung above the chosen landing place, waiting for it to sweep into the shadow of night. Bill peered intently through his telescope, watching the narrow strips of vegetation across the bare stretches of orange desert. He studied the bright metal and gray masonry of irrigation works, the widely scattered, white metal domes that seemed to cover cities, the hurtling blue globes that flashed in swift flight between them. Two or three times he caught sight of a tiny, creeping green thing that he thought was one of the hideous, blood-sucking Martians. And he saw half a dozen broad metal pens, or pastures, in which the hairy gray bipeds were confined.

Shining machines were moving across the green strips of fertile land, evidently cultivating them.

The Prince, Dr. Trainor, and Paula were asleep in their staterooms. Bill retired for a short rest, came back to find the planet beneath them in darkness. The *Red Rover* was dropping swiftly, with Captain Brand still at the bridge.

Rapidly, the stars vanished in an expanding circle below them. Phobos and Deimos, the small moons of Mars, hurtling across the sky with different velocities shed scant light upon the barren desert below. Captain Brand eased the ship down, using the rays as little as possible, to cut down the danger of detection.

The *Red Rover* dropped silently to the center of a low, cliff-rimmed plateau that rose from the red, sandy desert. In the faint light of stars and hurtling moons, the ocherous waste lay flat in all directions—there are no high mountains on Mars. The air was clear, and so thin that the stars shone with hot brilliance, almost, Bill thought, as if the ship were still out in space.

Silent hours went by, as they waited for dawn. The thin white disk of the nearer moon slid down beneath the black eastern horizon, and rose again to make another hurtling flight.

Just before dawn the Prince appeared, an eager smile on his alert lean face, evidently well recovered from the long struggling in the laboratory.

"I've all the mining machinery ready," Captain Brand told him. "We can get out as soon as it's warm enough—it's a hundred and fifty below zero out there now."

"It ought to warm up right soon after sunrise—thin as this air is. You seem to have picked about the loneliest spot on the planet, all right. There's a lot of danger, though, that we may be discovered before we get the cerium."

"Funny feeling to be the first men on a new world," said Bill.

"But we're not the first," the Prince said. "I am sure that Envers landed on Mars—I think the Martian ships are based on a study of his machinery."

"Envers may have waited here in the desert for the sun to rise, just as we are doing," murmured Brand. "In fact, if he wanted to look around without being seen, he may have landed right near here. This is probably the best place on the planet to land without being detected."

CHAPTER VII

A MINE ON MARS

The sun came up small and white and hot, shining from a black sky upon an endless level orange waste of rocks and sand, broken with a black swamp in the distant north.

Even from the eminence of the time-worn plateau, the straight horizon seemed far nearer than on earth, due to the greater curvature of the planet's surface.

Men were gathering about the air-lock, under the direction of the Prince, assembling mining equipment.

"Shall we be able to go out without vacuum suits?" Bill asked Captain Brand.

"I think so, when it gets warm enough. The air is light—the amount of oxygen at the surface is about equal to that in the air nine miles above sea level on earth. But the pull of gravity here is only about one-third as much as it is on the earth, and less oxygen will be required to furnish energy. I think we can stand it, if we don't take too much exertion."

The rays of the oddly small sun beat fiercely through the thin air. Soon the Prince went into the air-lock, closed the inner door behind him and started the pumps. When the dial showed the pressures equalized he opened the outer door, and stepped out upon the red rocks.

All were watching him intently, through the vitrolite panels. Paula clasped her hands in nervous anxiety. Bill saw the Prince step confidently out, sniff the air as though testing it, and take a few deep breaths. Then he drew his legs beneath him and made an astounding leap, that carried him twenty feet high. He fell in a long arc, struck on his shoulder in a pile of loose red sand. He got up, gasping for air as if the effort had exhausted him, and staggered back to the air-lock. Quickly he sealed the outer door behind him, opened the valve, and raised the pressure.

"Feels funny," he said when he opened the inner door. "Like trying to breathe on top of a mountain—only more so. The jump was great fun, but rather exhausting. I imagine it would be dangerous for a fellow with a weak heart. All right to come out now. Air is still cool, but the rocks are getting hot under the sun."

He held open the door. "The guards will come first."

Six of the thirty-odd members of the crew had been detailed to act as guards, to prevent surprise, Each was to carry two rocket torpedoes—such a burden was not too much upon this planet, with its lesser gravity. They would watch from the cliffs at the edge of the little plateau upon which the sunship had landed.

Bill and four other men entered the air-lock—and Paula. The girl had insisted upon having some duty assigned to her, and this had seemed easier than the mining.

The door was closed behind them, the air pumped out until Bill gasped for breath and heard a drumming in his ears. Then the outer door was opened and they looked out upon Mars. Motion was easy, yet the slightest effort was tiring. Bill found himself panting merely from the exertion of lifting the two heavy torpedoes to his shoulders.

With Paula behind him, he stepped through the outer door. The air felt chill and thin. Loose red sand crumbled yieldingly under their feet.

They separated at the door, Bill starting toward the south end of the pleateau, Paula toward the north point, and the men going to stations along the sides.

"Just lie at the top of the cliffs and watch," the Prince had ordered. "When you have anything to report, flash with your ray pistols, in code. Signal every thirty minutes, anyhow. We will have a man watching from the bridge. Report to him anything moving. We will fire off a red signal rocket when you are to come back."

He had tried to keep Paula from going out, but the girl had insisted. At last he had agreed.

"Better to have you keeping watch than handling a pick and shovel, or pushing a barrow," he had told her. "But I hate to see you go so far off. Something might happen. If they find us, though, they will probably get us all. Don't get hurt."

Bill had seen the Prince looking anxiously at the slender, brown-eyed girl as they entered the air-lock. He had seen him move forward quickly, as though to ask her to come back—move forward, and then turn aside with a flush that became a bitterly cynical smile.

As Bill walked across the top of the barren red plateau, he looked back at the girl moving slowly in the opposite direction. He had glanced at her eyes as they left the ship. They were shadowed, heavy-lidded. In their brown depths lurked despair and tragic determination. Bill, watching her now, thought that all life had gone out of her. She seemed a dull automaton, driven only by the energy of a determined will. All hope and life and vivacity had gone from her manner. Yet she walked as if she had a stern task to do.

"I wonder—" Bill muttered. "Can she mean—suicide?"

He turned uncertainly, as if to go after her. Then, deciding that his thought was mere fancy, he trudged on across the red plateau to his station.

Behind him, he saw other parties emerging from the air-lock. The Prince and Dr. Trainor were setting up apparatus of some kind, probably, Bill thought, to take magnetic and meteorological observations. Men with prospecting hammers were scattering over all the plateau.

"Almost any sort of ferruginous rock is sure to contain the tiny amount of cerium we need," Dr. Trainor had said.

Bill reached the end of the plateau. The age-worn cliffs of red granite and burned lava fell sheer for a hundred feet, to a long slope of talus. Below the rubble of sand and boulders the flat desert stretched away, almost visibly curving to vanish beneath the near red horizon.

It was a desolate and depressing scene, this view of a dead and sun-baked planet. There was no sign of living thing, no moving object, no green of life—the canals, with their verdure, were far out of sight.

"Hard to realize there's a race of vampires across there, living in great metal domes," Bill muttered, as he threw himself flat on the rocks at the lip of the precipice, and leveled one of the heavy torpedoes before him. "But I don't blame 'em for wanting to go to a more cheerful world."

Looking behind him, he soon saw men busy with electric drills not a hundred yards from the slender silver cylinder that was the *Red Rover*. The earth quivered beneath him as a shot was set off, and he saw a great fountain of crushed rock thrown into the air.

Men with barrows, an hour later, were wheeling the crushed rock to gleaming electrical reducing apparatus that Dr. Trainor and the Prince were setting up beside the sunship. Evidently there had been no difficulty in finding ore that carried a satisfactory amount of cerium.

Bill continued to scan the orange-red desert below him through the powerful telescope along the rocket tube. He kept his watch before him, and at half-hour intervals sent the three short flashes with his ray pistol, which meant "All is well."

Two hours must have gone by before he saw the blue globe. It came into view low over the red rim of the desert below him, crept closer on a wavering path.

"Martian ship in view," he signalled. "A blue globe, about ten feet in diameter. Follows curious winding course, as if following something."

"Keep rocket trained upon it," came the cautiously flashed reply. "Fire if it observes us."

"Globe following animals," he flashed back. "Two grayish bipeds leaping before it. Running with marvelous agility."

He was peering through the telescope sight of the rocket tube. Keeping the cross hairs upon the little blue globe, he could still see the creatures that fled before it. They were almost like men—or erect, hairy apes. Bipeds, they were, with human-like arms, and erect heads. Covered with short gray hair or fur, they carried no weapons.

They fled from the globe at a curious leaping run, which carried them over the flat red desert with remarkable speed. They came straight for the foot of the cliff from which Bill watched, the blue globe close behind them. When one of them stumbled over a block of lava and fell sprawling headlong on the sand, the other gray creature stopped to help it. The blue globe stopped, too, hanging still twenty feet above the red sand, waited for them to rise and run desperately on again.

Bill felt a quick flood of sympathy for the gray creatures. One had stopped to help the other. That meant that they felt affection. And the globe had waited for them to run again. It seemed to be baiting them maliciously. Almost he fired the rocket. But his orders had been not to fire unless the ship were discovered.

Now they were not a mile away. Suddenly Bill perceived a tiny, light-gray object grasped close to the breast of one of the gray bipeds. Evidently it was a young one, in the arms of its mother. The other creature seemed a male. It was the mother that had fallen.

They came on toward the cliff.

They were very clearly in view, and not five hundred yards below, when the female fell again. The male stopped to aid her, and the globe poised itself above them, waited. The mother seemed unable to rise. The other creature lifted her, and she fell limply back.

As if in rage, the gray male sprang toward the blue globe, crouching.

A tiny purple spark leapt from it. A flash of violet fire enveloped him. He was flung twisted and sprawling to the ground. Burned and torn and bleeding, he drew himself to all fours, and crept on toward the blue globe.

Suddenly the sphere dropped to the ground. A round panel swung open in its side—it was turned from Bill, so that he could not see within. Green things crept out. They were creatures like the one he had seen in the Mexican desert—a cluster of slender, flexible green tentacles, with suction disks, an insignificant green body, and three malevolent purple eyes, at the ends of foot-long stalks.

There were three of the things.

The creeping male flung himself madly upon one of them. It coiled itself about him; suction disks fastened themselves against his skin. For a time he writhed and struggled, fighting in agony against the squeezing green coils. Then he was still.

One of the things grasped the little gray object in the mother's arms. She fought to shield it, to cover it with her own body. It was torn away from her, hidden in the hideously writhing green coils.

The third of the monsters flung itself upon the mother, wrapping snake-like tentacles about her, dragging her struggling body down shuddering and writhing in agony while the blood of life was sucked from it.

Bill watched, silent and trembling with horror.

"The things chased them—for fun!" he muttered fiercely. "Just a sample of what it will be on the earth—if we don't stop 'em."

Presently the green monsters left their victims—which were now mere shriveled husks. They dragged themselves back into the blue globe, which rose swiftly into the air. The round panel had closed.

From his station on the cliff, Bill watched the thing through the telescope sight of the rocket, keeping the cross hairs upon it. It came up to his own level—above it. Suddenly it paused. He was sure that the things in it had seen the *Red Rover*.

Quickly, he pressed a little nickeled lever. A soft whir came from the rocket tube.

He pressed the red button. The torpedo leapt forward, with the white rays driving back. The empty shell was flung back in Bill's hand.

A great burst of vivid orange flame enveloped the cobalt globe. It disintegrated into a rain of white metal fragments.

"Take that, damn you!" he muttered in fierce satisfaction.

"Globe brought down successfully," he flashed. "Evidently it had sighted us. Green Martians from it had killed gray bipeds. May I inspect remains?"

"You may," permission was flashed back from the Prince. "But be absent not over half an hour."

In a moment another message came. "All lookouts be doubly alert. Globe may be searched for. Miners making good progress. We can leave by sunset. Courage! —The Prince."

Strapping the remaining rocket torpedo to his shoulders, and thrusting his ray pistol ready in his belt, Bill walked back along the brink of the precipice until he saw a comparatively easy way to the red plain below, and scrambled over the rim. Erosion of untold ages had left cracks and irregularities in the rock. Because of the slighter gravity of Mars, it was a simple feat to support his weight with the grip of his fingers on a ledge. In five minutes he had clambered down to the bank of talus. Hurriedly he scrambled down over great fallen boulders, panting and gasping for breath in the thin air.

He reached the red sand of the plain—it was worn by winds of ages into an impalpable scarlet dust, that rose in a thin, murky cloud about him, and settled in a blood-colored stain upon his perspiring limbs. The dry dust yielded beneath his feet as he made his way toward the silent gray bodies, making his progress most difficult.

Almost exhausted, he reached the gray creatures, examined them. They were far different from human beings, despite obvious similarities. Each of their "hands" had but three clawed digits; a curious, disk-like appendage took the place of the nose. In skeletal structure they were far different from *homo sapiens*.

Wearily Bill trudged back to the towering red cliff, red dust swirling up about him. He was oddly exhausted by his exertions, trifling as they had been. The murky red dust he inhaled was irritating to his nostrils; he choked and sneezed. Sweat ran in muddy red streams from his body, and he was suddenly very thirsty.

All the top of the red granite plateau—it was evidently the stone heart of an ancient mountain—was hidden from him. He could see nothing of the *Red Rover* or any of her crew. He could see no living thing.

The flat plain of red dust lay about him, curving below a near horizon. Loose dust sucked at his feet, rose about him in a suffocating saffron cloud. The sun, a little crimson globe in a blue-black sky, shone blisteringly. The sky was soberly dark, cold and hostile. In alarmed haste, he struggled toward the grim line of high, red cliffs.

Then he saw a round white object in the red sand.

Pausing to gasp for breath and to rub the sweat and red mud from his forehead, he kicked at it curiously. A sun-bleached human skull rolled out of the scarlet dust. He knew at once that it was human, not a skull of a creature like the gray things behind him on the sand.

With the unpleasant feeling that he was opening the forbidden book of some forgotten tragedy, he fell to his knees in the dust, and scooped about with his fingers. His right had closed upon a man's thigh bone. His left caught in a rotten leather belt, that pulled a human vertebra out of the dust. The belt had a tarnished silver buckle, and he looked at it with a gasp.

It bore an elaborate initial "E."

"E!" he muttered. "Envers! He got to Mars. And died here. Trying to get to the mountain, I guess. Lord! what a death! A man all alone, in the dust and the sun. A strange world. Strange monsters."

The loneliness of the red desert, the mystery of it, and its alien spirit, wrapped itself about him like a mantle of fear. He staggered to his feet, and set off at a stumbling run through the sand toward the cliff. But in a moment he paused,

"He might have left something!" he muttered.

He turned, and plodded back to where he had left the skull and the rotted belt, and dug again with his fingers. He found the rest of the skeleton, even bits of hair, clothing and human skin, preserved in the dry dust. He found an empty canteen, a rusty pocketknife, buttons, coins, and a ray pistol that was burned out.

Then his plowing fingers brought up a little black book from the dust.

It was Envers' diary.

Most of it was still legible. It is available in printed form today, and gives a detailed account of the tragic venture. The hopeful starting from earth. The dangers and discouragements of the voyage. A mutiny; half the crew killed. The thrill of landing on a new planet. The attack of the blue globes. How they took the ship, carried their prisoners to the pens, where they tried to use them to breed a new variety of domestic animals. Envers' escape, his desperate attempt to find the ship where they had landed in the desert.

Bill did not read it all then. He took time to read only that last tragic entry.

"Water all gone. See now I will never reach mountain where I landed. Probably they have moved sunship anyhow. Might have been better to have stayed in the pen. Food and water there. . . . But how could God create such things? So hideous, so malignant! I pray they will not use my ship to go to earth. I hoped to find and destroy it. But it is too late."

Thick red dust swirled up in Bill's face. He tried to breathe, choked and sneezed and strangled. Looking up from the yellowed pages of the dead explorer's notebook, he saw great clouds of red dust hiding the darkly blue sky in the east. It seemed almost that a colossal red-yellowed cylinder was being rolled swiftly upon him from eastward:

A dust-storm was upon him! One of the terrific dust-storms of Mars, so fierce that they are visible to astronomers across forty million miles of space.

Clutching the faded note-book, he ran across the sand again, toward the red cliffs. The wind howled behind him, overtook him and came screaming about his ears. Red dust fogged chokingly about his head. The line of cliffs before him vanished in a murky red haze. The wind blew swiftly, yet it was thin, exerting little force. The dusty air became an acrid fluid, choking, unbreathable.

Blindly, he staggered on, toward the rocks. He reached them, fought his way up the bank of talus, scrambling over gigantic blocks of lava. The base of the cliff was before him, a massive, perpendicular wall, rising out of sight in red haze. He skirted it, saw a climbable chimney, scrambled up.

At last he drew himself over the top, and lay flat. Scarlet dust-clouds swirled about him: he could not see twenty yards. He made no attempt to find the *Red Rover*; he knew he could not locate it in the dust.

Hours passed as he lay there, blinded, suffocating, feeling the hot misery of acrid dust and perspiration caked in a drying mud upon his skin. Thin winds screamed about the rocks, hot as a furnace-blast. He leveled his torpedo, tried to watch. But he could see only a murky wall of red, with the sun biting through it like a tiny, round blood-ruby.

The red sun had been near the zenith. Slowly it crept down, toward an unseen horizon. It alone gave him an idea of direction, and of the passage of time. Then it, too, vanished in the dust.

Suddenly the wind was still. The dust settled slowly. In half an hour the red sun came into view again, just above the red western horizon. Objects about the mile-long plateau began to take shape. The *Red Rover* still lay where she had been, in the center. Men were still busily at work at the mining machinery—they had struggled on through the storm.

"All lookouts signal reports," the Prince flashed from the ship.

"Found Envers' body and brought his diary," Bill flashed when it came his turn.

"Now preparing to depart," came from the Prince. "Getting apparatus aboard. Have the required cerium. Return signal will be fired soon."

Bill watched the dusty sky, over whose formerly dark-blue face the storm had drawn a yellowish haze. In a few minutes he saw a blue globe. Then another, and a third. They were far toward the southeast, drifting high and fast through the saffron haze. It seemed that they were searching out the route over which the globe that he had brought down must have come.

"Three globe-ships in sight," he signalled. "Approaching us."

Some of the other lookouts had evidently seen them, for he saw the flicker of other ray pistols across the plateau.

Without preamble, the red signal rocket was fired. Bill heard the report of it—sharp and thin in the rare atmosphere. He saw the livid scarlet flare.

He got to his feet, shouldered the heavy rocket tube, and ran stumbling back to the *Red Rover*. He saw other men running; saw men struggling to get the mining machinery back on the ship.

Looking back, he saw the three blue globes swimming swiftly nearer. Then he saw others, a full score of them. They were far off, tiny circles of blue in the saffron sky. They seemed to be rapidly flying toward the *Red Rover*.

He looked expectantly northward, toward the end of the plateau to which Paula had gone. He saw nothing of her. She was not returning in answer to the signal rocket.

He was utterly exhausted when he reached the sunship, panting, gasping for the thin air. The others were all like himself, caked with dried red mud, gasping asthmatically from exertion and excitement. Men were struggling to get pieces of heavy machinery aboard the flier—vitalium power generators that had been used to heat the furnaces, and even a motor ray tube that had been borrowed from the ship's power plant for emergency use in the improvised smelter.

The Prince and Dr. Trainor were laboring furiously over an odd piece of apparatus. On the red sand beside the silver sunship, they had set up a tripod on which was mounted a curious glistening device. There were lenses, prisms, condensers, mirrors. The core of it seemed to be a strange vacuum tube—which had an electrode of cerium, surrounded with a queer vitalium grid. A tiny filament was glowing in it; and the induction coil which powered the tube, fed by vitalium batteries, was buzzing incessantly.

"Better get aboard, and off!" Bill cried. "No use to lose our lives, our chance to save the world—just for a little mining machinery."

The Prince looked up in a moment, leaving the queer little device to Dr. Trainor. "Look at the Martian ships!" he cried, sweeping out an arm. "Must be thirty in sight, swarming up like flies. We couldn't get away. And against those purple atomic bombs, the torpedoes wouldn't have a chance. Besides, we have some of the ship's machinery out here. Some generators, and a ray tube."

Bill looked up, saw the swarming blue globes, circling above them in the saffron sky, some of them not a mile above. He shrugged hopelessly, then looked anxiously off to the north again, scanning the red plateau.

"Paula! What's become of her?" he demanded.

"Paula? Is she gone?" The Prince turned from the tripod, looked around suddenly. "Paula! What could have happened to her?"

"A broken heart has happened to her," Bill told him.

"You think—you think—" stammered the Prince. There was sudden alarm in his dark eyes, and a great tender longing. His bitterly cynical smile was gone.

"Bill, she can't be gone!" he cried, almost in agony.

"You know she was on lookout duty at the north end of the plateau. She hasn't come back."

"I've got to find her!"

"What is it to you? I thought you didn't care!" Bill was stern.

"I thought I didn't, except as a friend. But I was wrong. If she's gone, Bill—it will kill me!"

The Prince spun about with abrupt decision.

"Get everything aboard, and fit the ship to take off, as soon as possible," he ordered. "Dr. Trainor is in command. Give him any help he needs. Brand, test everything when the tube is replaced; keep the ship ready to fly." He turned swiftly to Trainor, who still worked deftly over the glittering little machine on the tripod. "Doc, you can operate that by yourself, as well as if I were here. Do your best—for mankind! I'm going to find your daughter."

Trainor nodded in silent assent, his fingers busy.

The Prince, sticking a ray pistol in his belt, set off at a desperate run toward the north end of the plateau. After a moment's hesitation, Bill staggered along behind him, still carrying the rocket torpedo strapped to his back.

It was only half a mile to the end of the plateau. In a few minutes the Prince was there. Bill staggered up just as he was reading a few scrawled words on a scrap of paper that he had found fastened to a boulder where Paula had been stationed.

"To the Prince of Space" it ran. "I can't go on. You must know that I love you—desperately. It was maddening to be with you, to know that you don't care. I know the story of your life, know that you can never care for me. The red dust is blowing now, and I am going down in the desert to die. Please don't look for me—it will do no good. Pardon me for writing this, but I wanted you to know—why I am going. Because I love you. Paula."

CHAPTER VIII

THE VITOMATON

"I love Paula!" cried the Prince. "It happened all at once—when you said she was gone. Like a burst of light. Yet it must have been growing for weeks. It was getting so I couldn't work in the lab, unless she was there. God! It must have been hard for her. I was fighting it; I tried to hide what I was beginning to feel, tried to treat her as if she were a man. Now—she's gone!"

Bill looked back to the *Red Rover*, half a mile behind them. She lay still, burnished silver cylinder on the red sand. He could see Trainor beside her, still working over the curious little device on the tripod. All the others had gone aboard. And a score of blue globe-ships, like little sapphire moons, were circling a few thousand feet above, drifting around and around, with a slow gliding motion, like buzzards circling over their carrion-prey.

The Prince had buried his face in his hands, standing in an attitude of utter dejection.

Bill turned, looked over the red flat sand of the Martian desert. Far below, leading toward the near horizon, he saw a winding line of foot-prints, half obliterated by the recent dust-storm. Far away they vanished below the blue-black sky.

"Her tracks," he said, pointing.

"Tracks!" the Prince looked up, eager, hopeful determination flashing in his dark eyes. "Then we can follow! It may not be too late!"

He ran toward the edge of the cliff.

Bill clutched his sleeve. "Wait! Think what you're doing, man! We're fighting to save the world. You can't run off that way! Anyhow, the sun is low. It is getting cool already. In two minutes after the sun goes down it will be cold as the devil! You'll die in the desert!"

The Prince tugged away. "Hang the world! If you knew the way I feel about Paula—Lord, what a fool I've been! To drive her to this!"

Agony was written on his dark face; he bit his thin lip until blood oozed out and mingled indistinguishably with the red grime on his face. "Anyhow, the *vitomaton* is finished. Trainor can use it as well as I. I've got to find Paula—or die trying."

He started toward the brink of the precipice again. After the hesitation of a moment, Bill started after him. The Prince turned suddenly.

"What the devil are you doing here?"

"Well," said Bill, "the *Red Rover* is not a very attractive haven of refuge, with all those Martian ships flying around it. And I have come to think a good deal of Miss Paula. I'd like to help you find her."

"Don't come," said the Prince. "Probably it is death—"

"I'm not exactly an infant. I've been in tight places before. I've even an idea of what it would be like to die at night in this desert—I found the bones of a man in the dust today. But I want to go."

The Prince grasped Bill's hand. For a moment a tender smile of friendship came over the drawn mask of mingled despair and determination upon his lean face.

Presently the two of them found an inclining ledge that ran down the face of the red granite cliff, and scrambled along to the flat plain of acrid dust below. In desperate haste they plodded gasping along, following the scant traces of Paula's footprints that the storm had left. A hazy red cloud of dust rose about them, stinging their nostrils. They strangled and gasped for breath in the thin, dusty air. Sweaty grime covered them with a red crust.

For a mile they followed the trail. Then Paula had left the sand for a bare ledge of age-worn volcanic rock. The wind had erased what traces she might have left here. They skirted the edge of the ledge, but no prints were visible in the sand. The small red eye of the sun was just above the ocherous western rim of the planet. Their perspiring bodies shivered under the first chill of the frozen Martian night.

"It's no use," Bill muttered, sitting down on a block of timeworn granite, and wiping the red mud from his face. "She's probably been gone for hours. No chance."

"I've got to find her!" the Prince cried, his lean, red-stained face tense with determination. "I'll circle about a little, and see if I can't pick up the trail."

Bill sat on the rock. He looked back at the low dark rim of cliffs, a mile behind, grim and forbidding against the somber, indigo sky. The crimson, melancholy splendor of the Martian sunset was fading in the west.

The silver sunship was out of sight behind the cliffs. But he could see the little blue globes, like spinning moons of sapphire, circling watchfully above it. They were lower now, some of them not a thousand feet above the hidden sunship.

Abruptly, one of them was enveloped in a vivid flare of orange light. Its blue gleam flickering out, and it fell in fragments of twisted white metal. Bill knew that it had been struck with a rocket torpedo.

The reply was quick and terrible. Slender, dazzling shafts of incandescent white-ness stabbed down toward the ship, each of them driving before it a tiny bright spark of purple fire, coruscating, iridescent.

They were the atomic bombs, Bill knew. A dozen of them must have been fired, from as many ships. In a few seconds he heard the reports of their explosions—in the thin, still air, they were mere sharp cracks, like pistol reports. They exploded below the line of his vision. No more torpedoes were fired from the unseen sunship. Bill could see nothing of it; but he was sure that it had been destroyed.

He heard the Prince's shout, thin and high in the rare atmosphere. It came from a hundred yards beyond him.

"I've found the trail."

Bill got up, trudged across to follow him. The Prince waited, impatiently, but gasping for breath. Just half of the red disk of the sun was visible in the indigo sky above the straight horizon, and a chill breeze blew upon them.

"I guess that ends the chance for the world!" Bill gasped.

"I suppose so. Some fool must have shot that torpedo off, contrary to orders. The *vitomaton* might have saved us, if Trainor had had a chance to use it."

They plodded on through the dust, straining their eyes to follow the half-obliterated trail in the fading light. It grew colder very swiftly, for Mars has no such thick blanket atmosphere to hold the heat of day as has the earth.

Twilight was short. Splendid wings of somber crimson flame hung for a moment in the west. A brief golden glow shone where it had been. Then the sky was dark, and the million stars were standing out in cold, motionless majesty—scintillantly bright, unfeeling watchers of the drama in the desert.

Bill felt tingling cold envelope his limbs. The sweat and mud upon him seemed freezing. He saw the white glitter of frost appear suddenly upon his garments, even upon the red dust. The thin air he breathed seemed to freeze his lungs. He trembled. His skin became a stiff, numb, painful garment, hindering his movements. The Prince staggered on ahead of him, a vague dark shadow in the night, crying out at in-tervals in a queer, strained voice.

Bill stopped, looked back, shivering and miserable.

"No use to go on," he muttered. "No use." He stood still, vainly flapping his numb arms against his sides. A vivid picture came to him—a naked, staring, sun-bleached skull, lying in the red dust. "Bones in the dust," he muttered. "Bones in the dust. En-vers' bones. And Paula's, The Prince's. Mine."

He saw something that made him stare, oblivious of the cold.

The red cliff had become a low dark line, below the star-studded sky. The score of little cobalt moons were still drifting around and around, in endless circles, watching, waiting. They were bright among the stars.

A little green cloud came up into view, above the dark rim of the cliff. A little spinning wisp of greenish vapor. A tiny sphere of swirling radiance. It shone with the clear lucent green of spring, of all verdure, of life itself. It spun, and it shone with live green light.

With inconceivable speed, it darted upward. It struck one of the blue globes. A sparkling mist of dancing emerald atoms flowed over the azure sphere, dissolved it, melted it away.

Bill rubbed his eyes. Where the sapphire ship had been was now only a swirling mass of green mist, a cloud of twinkling emerald particles, shining with a supernal viridescent radiance that somehow suggested *life*.

Abruptly as the first tiny wisp of green luminescence had appeared, this whirling cloud exploded. It burst into scores of tiny globes of sparkling, vibrant atoms. The green cloud had eaten and grown. Now it was reproducing itself like a living thing that feeds and grows and sends off spores.

And each of the little blobs of viridity flew to an azure sphere. It seemed to Bill as if the blue ships drew them—or as if the green globules of swirling mist were *alive*, seeking food.

In an instant, each swirling spiral of emerald mist had struck a blue globe. Vibrant green haze spread over every sphere. And the spheres melted, faded, vanished in clouds of swirling viridescent vapor.

It all happened very suddenly. It was hardly a second, Bill thought, after the first of the swirling green blobs had appeared, before the last of the Martian fliers had become a mass of incandescent mist. Then, suddenly as they had come, the green spirals vanished. They were blotted out.

The stars shone cold and brilliant, in many-colored splendor, above the dark line of the cliffs. The Martian ships were gone.

"The *vitomaton!*" Bill muttered. "The Prince said something about the *vitomaton*. A new weapon, using the force of life. And the green was like a living thing, consuming the spheres!"

Suddenly he felt the bitter cold again. He moved, and his garments were stiff with frost. The cold had numbed his limbs—most of the pain had gone. He felt a curious lightness, an odd sense of relief, of freedom—and a delicious, alarming desire for sleep. But leaden pain of cold still lurked underneath, dull, throbbing.

"Move! Move!" he muttered through cold-stiffened lips. "Move! Keep warm!"

He stumbled across the dust in the direction the Prince had taken. The cold tugged at him. His breath froze in swirls of ice. With all his will he fought the deadly desire for sleep.

He had not gone far when he came upon a dark shape in the night. It was the Prince, carrying Paula in his arms.

"I found her lying on the sand," he gasped to Bill. "She was awake. She was glad—forgave me—happy now."

The Prince was exhausted, struggling through the sand, burdened with the girl in his arms.

"Why go on?" Bill forced the words through his freezing face. "Never make it. They shot atomic bombs at *Red Rover*. Then something happened to them. Green light."

"The *vitomaton!*" gasped the Prince. "Vortex of spinning, disintegrated atoms. Controlled by wireless power. Alive! Consumes all matter! Disintegrates it into atomic nothingness!"

He staggered on toward the dark line of cliffs, clasping the inert form of the girl to his body.

"But Paula! I love her. I must carry her to the ship. It is my fault. We must get to the ship."

Bill struggled along beside him. "Too far!" he muttered.

"Miles, in the night. In the cold. We'll never—"

He stopped, with a thin, rasping cry.

Before him, above the narrow black line of the cliffs, a slender bar of luminescent silver had shot up into view. It was the slim, tapering cylinder of the *Red Rover*, with her twelve rear motor rays driving white and dazzling against the mountain she was leaving. The sunship, unharmed, driving upward into space!

"My God!" Bill screamed. "Leaving us!" He staggered forward, a pitiful, trembling figure, encased in stiff, frost-covered garments. He waved his arms, shouted. It was vain, almost ludicrous.

The Prince had stopped, still holding Paula in his arms.

"They think—Martians got us!" he called in a queer voice. "Stop them! Fire torpedo—at boulder. They will see!"

Bill heard the gasping voice. He unfastened the heavy tube that he still carried on his shoulder, leveled it before him. With numb, trembling fingers, he tried to move the levers. His fingers seemed frozen; they would not move. Tears burst from his eyes, freezing on his cheeks. He stood holding the heavy tube in his arms, sobbing like a baby.

Above them, the slender white cylinder of the *Red Rover* was driving out into star-gemmed space, dazzling opalescent rays shooting back at the dark mountain behind her.

"They go," Bill babbled. "They think we are dead. Have not time to wait. Go to fight for world."

He collapsed in a trembling heap upon the loose, frosty sand.

The Prince had suddenly laid Paula on the ground, was beside him.

"Lift the rocket," he gasped. "Aim. I will fire."

Bill raised the heavy tube mechanically, sighted through the telescope. His trembling was so violent that he could hardly hold it upon the rock. The Prince tried with his fingers to move the lever, in vain. Then he bent, pressed his chin against it. It slipped, cut a red gash in his skin. Again he tried, and the whir of the motor responded. He got his chin upon the little red button, pressed it. The empty shell drove back, fell from Bill's numbed hands and clattered on the sand.

The torpedo struck with a burst of orange light.

The Prince picked up Paula again, clasped her chilled body to him. Bill watched the *Red Rover*. Suddenly he voiced a glad, incoherent cry. The white rays that drove her upward were snapped out. The slim silver ship swung about, came down on a long swift glide.

In a moment, it seemed, she swept over them, with a searchlight sweeping the red sand. The white beam found the three. Quickly the ship dropped beside them. Grotesque figures in vacuum suits leapt from the airlock.

In a few seconds they were aboard, in warmth and light. Hot, moist air hissed into the lock about them, and they could breathe easily again. The sizzling of the air through the valves was the last impression of which Bill was conscious, until he found himself waking up in a comfortable bed, feeling warm and very hungry. Captain Brand was standing with his blue eyes peering through the door.

"Just looked in to see you as I was going on duty, Bill," he said. "Doctor Trainor says you're all right now. The Prince and Paula are too. You were all rather chilled, but nothing was seriously frozen. Lucky you shot off the rocket. We had given up hope for you didn't dare stay.

"Funny change has come over the Prince. He's been up a good while, sitting by Paula's bed. How's that for the misogynist—the hermit outlaw of space? Well, come on up to the bridge when you've had some breakfast. The battle with Mars is going to be fought out in the next few hours. Ought to be something interesting to see."

Having delivered his broadside of information so fast that the sleepy Bill could hardly absorb it, the bluff old space-captain withdrew his head, and went on.

An hour later Bill entered the bridge-room.

Gazing through the vitrolite panels, he saw the familiar aspect of interplanetary space—hard, brilliant points of many-colored light scintillating in a silver-dusted void of utter blackness. The flaming, red-winged sun was small and far distant. Earth was a huge green star, glowing with indescribably beautiful liquid emerald brilliance; the moon a silver speck beside it.

The grim red disk of Mars filled a great space in the heavens. Bill looked for a little blue dot that had been visible upon the red planet for so long—the tiny azure circle that he had first seen from the telescope in Trainor's Tower. He found the spot where it should be, on the upper limb of the planet. But it was gone.

"The thing has left Mars," Captain Brand told him. "It has set out on its mission of doom to Earth!"

"What is it?"

"It is armored with one of their blue vibratory screens. What hellish contrivances of war it has in it, and what demoniac millions of Martians, no one knows. It is enormous, more than a mile in diameter."

"Can we do anything?"

"I hardly see how we can do anything. But we can try. Trainor and the Prince are coming with their *vitomaton*."

"Say, didn't they shoot their atomic bombs at the ship last night?" Bill asked. "It was out of sight, but I imagined they had wrecked it."

"One of the lookouts who was late getting back brought down one of their globes with a rocket. They fired a lot of the purple bombs to scare us. But I think they meant to take us alive. In the interest of their science, I suppose. And Dr. Trainor got the *vitomaton* ready before they had done anything."

Bill was peering out into the star-strewn ebon gulf. Captain Brand pointed. He saw a tiny blue globe, swimming among the stars.

"There's the infernal thing! Carrying its cargo of horror to our earth!"

In a few moments Dr. Trainor, the Prince, and Paula came one by one up the ladder to the bridge. Trainor carried the tripod; the Prince brought a little black case which contained the strange vacuum tube with the cerium electrode, and its various accessories; Paula had a little calculating machine and a book of mathematical tables.

Trainor and the Prince set up the tripod in the center of the room, and mounted the little black case upon it. The apparatus looked not very different from a small camera. Working with cool, brisk efficiency, Paula began operating the calculating machine, taking numbers from the book, and calling out the results to the Prince, who was setting numerous small dials on the apparatus.

Dr. Trainor peered through a compact little telescope which was evidently an auxiliary part of the apparatus, training the machine on the tiny blue disk that was the messenger of doom from Mars. From time to time he called out numbers which seemed to go into Paula's calculations.

Looking curiously at Paula and the Prince, Bill could see no sign of an understanding between them. Both seemed absorbed in the problem before them. They were impersonal as any two collaborating scientists.

At last Dr. Trainor raised his eyes from the little telescope, and the Prince paused, with his fingers on a tiny switch. The induction coil, in the circuit of a powerful vitalium generator, was buzzing monotonously, while purple fire leapt between its terminals. Paula was still efficiently busy over the little calculating machine, pressing its keys while the motors whirred inside it.

"We're all ready," Trainor announced, "as soon as Paula finishes the integration." He turned to Bill and Captain Brand, who were eying the apparatus with intense interest. "If you will look inside this electron tube, when the Prince closes the switch, you will see a tiny green spark come into being. Just at the focus of the rays from the cerium electrode, inside the vitalium helix grid.

"That green spark is a living thing!

"It has in it the vital essence. It can consume matter—feed itself. It can grow. It can divide, reproduce itself. It responds to stimuli—it obeys the signals we send from this directional beam transmitter." He tapped an insignificant little drum.

"And it ceases to be, when we cut off the power.

"It is a living thing, that eats. And it is more destructive than anything else that eats, for it destroys the atoms that it takes into itself. It resolves them into pure vibratory energy, into free protons and electrons."

Paula called out another number, in her soft, husky voice. The Prince swiftly set a last dial, pressed a tiny lever. Bill, peering through the thin walls of a little electron tube, saw a filament light, saw the thin cerium disk grow incandescent, apparently under cathode bombardment. Then he saw a tiny green spark come into being, in a fine helix of gleaming vitalium wire. For a little time it hung there, swinging back and forth a little, growing slowly.

Deliberately, one by one, the Prince depressed keys on a black panel behind the tube. The little green spark wavered. Suddenly it shot forward, out through the wall of the tube. It swam uncertainly through the air in the room, growing until it was large as a marble. The Prince flicked down another key, and it darted out through a vitrolite panel, towards the blue globe from Mars.

It had cut a little round hole in the transparent crystal, a hole the size of a man's finger. The matter in it had vanished utterly. And the little viridescent cloud of curdled light that hung outside had grown again. It was as large as a man's fist—a tiny, whirling spiral of vibrant emerald particles.

Air hissed through the little hole, forming a frozen, misty cloud outside. Captain Brand promptly produced a little disk of soft rubber, placed it against the opening. Air-pressure held it tight, sealing the orifice.

The Prince pressed another key, the little swirling green sphere was whisked away—it vanished. The Prince stood intent, fingers on the banks of keys, eyes on red pointers that spun dizzily on tiny dials. Another key clicked down suddenly. He moved a dial, and looked expectantly out through the vitrolite panel.

Bill saw the green film run suddenly over the tiny blue globe floating among the stars. The azure sphere seemed to melt away, to dissolve into sparkling green radiance. In a moment, where the great blue ship had been, was only a spinning spiral of glistening viridescence.

"Look at Mars!" cried the Prince. "This is a challenge. If they want peace, they shall have it. If they want war, they shall feel the power of the *vitomaton!*"

Bill turned dazedly to look at the broad disk of the red planet. It was not relatively very far away. He could see the glistening white spot that was the north polar cap, the vast ocherous deserts, the dark equatorial markings, the green-black lines of the canals. For all the grimness of its somber, crimson color, it was very brilliant against the darkness of the spangled void.

An amazing change came swiftly over Mars.

A bluish tinge flowed over orange-red deserts. A thin blue mist seemed to have come suddenly into the atmosphere of the planet. It darkened, became abruptly solid. A wall of blue hid the red world. Mars became a colossal globe. Her surface was as real, as smooth and unbroken, as that of the ship they had just destroyed.

Mars had become a sphere of polished sapphire.

"A wall of vibration, I suppose," said the Prince. "What a science to condemn to destruction!"

Huge globes of purple fire—violet spheres large as the ship they had just destroyed—driven on mighty rays, leapt out from a score of points on the smooth azure armor that covered a world. With incredible speed, they converged toward the *Red Rover.*

"Atomic bombs with a vengeance!" cried the Prince. "One of those would throw the earth out of its orbit, into the sun." He turned briskly to Paula. "Quick now! Integrations for the planet!"

She sprang to the calculating machine; slim fingers flew over the keys. Trainor swung his apparatus toward the smooth azure ball that Mars had become, peered through his telescope, called out a series of numbers to Paula. Quickly she finished, gave her results to the Prince.

He bent over the banks of keys again.

Bill watched the enormous blue globe of Mars in fascinated horror, followed the huge, luminescent red-purple atomic bombs, that were hurtling out toward them, driven on broad white rays.

"An amazing amount of power in those atomic bombs," Dr. Trainor commented, his mild eyes bright with scientific enthusiasm. "I doubt that space itself is strong enough to hold up under their explosion. If they hit us, I imagine it will break down the continuum, blow us out of the universe altogether, out of space and time!"

Bill was looking at the whirling green spiral that hung where the Martian flier had been. He saw it move suddenly, dart across the star-dusted darkness of space. It plunged straight for the blue ball of Mars, struck it. A viridescent fog ran quickly over the enormous azure globe.

Mars melted away.

The planet dissolved in a huge, madly spinning cloud of brilliant green mist that shone with an odd light—with a light of *life!* A world faded into a nebulous spiral of green. Mars became a spinning cloud of dust as if of malachite.

A tiny lever flicked over, under the Prince's fingers. And the green light went out.

Where Mars had been was nothing! The stars shone through, hot and clear. A machine no larger than a camera had destroyed a world. Bill was dazed, staggered.

Solemnly, almost sadly, the Prince moved a slender, tanned hand across his brow. "A terrible thing," he said slowly. "It is a terrible thing to destroy a world. A world that had been eons in the making, and that might have changed the history of the cosmos. . . . But they voted for war. We had no choice."

He shook his head suddenly, and smiled. "It's all over. The great mission of my life—completed. Doctor I want you to pack the *vitomaton* very carefully, and lock it up in our best safe, and try to forget the combination. A great invention. But I hope we never need to use it again."

Then the Prince of Space did a thing that was amazing to most of his associates as the destruction of Mars had been. He walked quickly to Paula Trainor, and put his arms around her. He slowly tilted up her elfin face, where the golden eyes were laughing now, with a great, tender light of gladness shining in them. He bent, and kissed her warm red lips, with a hungry eagerness that was almost boyish.

A happy smile was dancing in his eyes when he looked up at the astounded Captain Brand and the others.

"Allow me," he said, "to present the Princess of Space!"

Some months later, when Bill was landed on Trainor's Tower, on a visit from his new home in the City of Space, he found that the destruction of Mars had created an enormous sensation. Astronomers were manfully inventing fantastic hypotheses to explain why the red planet had first turned blue, then green, and finally vanished utterly. The sunships of the Moon Patrol were still hunting merrily for the Prince of Space. Since the loss of the *Triton's* treasure, the reward for his capture had been increased to twenty-five million eagles.

LEIGH BRACKETT

Leigh Brackett [1915–1978] was born in Los Angeles, and raised near Santa Monica. She spent her youth as an athletic tomboy—and reading stories by Edgar Rice Burroughs and H. Rider Haggard—and she began writing fantastic adventures of her own. A recent biographical note (in her collected early stories, *The Martian Quest*) tells us that several of these early efforts were read by Henry Kuttner, who critiqued her stories and introduced her to the SF personalities then living in California, including Cleve Cartmill, Robert A. Heinlein, Julius Schwartz, Jack Williamson, Edmond Hamilton—and another as yet unpublished writer, Ray Bradbury. She sold her first story to John W. Campbell at *Astounding* in 1939, but immediately moved to the science fantasy pulps, becoming a stalwart of *Planet Stories*. She also wrote hardboiled mystery fiction (her first novel was *No Good from a Corpse*, 1943).

Brackett married Edmond Hamilton on New Year's Eve in 1946, and the couple maintained homes in the high desert of California and the rural farmland of Kinsman, Ohio. Jack Williamson, in his essay "Edmond Hamilton: As I Knew Him," says, "She had met him in 1940, the year her first story was published, when we were in Los Angeles with Julius Schwartz, Ed's literary agent. She had begun as a writer of literate and colorful fantasy and science fiction, and mysteries of the 'hardboiled' sort. During the war she had become a successful screenwriter, writing scripts for *The Big Sleep* . . . for Howard Hawks, in collaboration with William Faulkner. When I asked about Faulkner, she called him a courteous Southern gentleman, concerned chiefly with getting back to Mississippi with his half grand a week."

Her friend and admirer Michael Moorcock said in an essay, "Like so many of her heroes, Leigh preferred the outlaw life. She always said her first love was science fantasy. She said it defiantly, when it generally paid less than other pulp fiction. When it paid less, indeed, than other kinds of science fiction. If she had chosen, in her fiction, to hang out more with the scum of the LA streets rather than the dregs of the spacelanes, she could have made a lot more money. . . . Her keen sense of freedom made her, like many other fine writers of her generation, choose the more precarious living of writing science fantasy." And further, "There was a time when the kind of science fantasy Brackett made her own was looked down upon as a kind of bastard progeny of science fiction (which was about scientific speculation) and fantasy (which was about magic)."

A few weeks before her death, in 1978, she turned in the first-draft screenplay for *The Empire Strikes Back*, and the film was posthumously dedicated to her. The connection between Brackett, the queen of space opera, and *Star Wars*, the biggest SF film of its day, was very potent in establishing a link between space opera and commercial success.

Since a literary genre is a form of conversation among writers, one useful approach is to find writers who say they're writing space opera and see what they do and say about it. This means including writers who seem out of place, have a bad attitude, or choose unorthodox tactics for yoking the science to the fiction. If one scours interviews and essays for what these writers think they're doing, it quickly becomes apparent that they do not agree on what SF is or ought to be, nor on how to do it. This disagreement is very fertile ground for a growing literature. Leigh Brackett said, in the introduction to her only anthology, *The Best of Planet Stories #1*, that she was writing space opera:

> For fifteen years, from 1940 to 1955, when the magazine ceased publication, I had the
> happiest relationship possible for a writer with the editors of *Planet Stories*. They gave

me, in the beginning, a proving-ground where I could gain strength and confidence in the exercise of my fledgling skills a thing of incalculable value for a young writer. They sent me checks, which enabled me to keep on eating. In later years, they provided a steady market for the kind of stories I liked best to write. In short, I owe them much. . . . *Planet*, unashamedly, published "space opera."

And from the same essay, her panegyric to space opera:

The so-called space opera is the folk-tale, the hero-tale, of our particular niche in history. No more than a few years back, Ziolkovsky was a visionary theoretician. Goddard, a genius before his time, had to pretend that his rockets were for high-altitude research only because he was afraid to use the word "space." The important men, who were carrying their brains in their hip-pockets, continued to sit upon them, sneering, until Sputnik went up and frightened the daylights out of them. But the space opera has been telling us tales of spaceflight, of journeys to other worlds in this solar system, of journeys to the world of other stars, even to other galaxies; the space opera has been telling them of decades, with greater or less skill but with enormous love and enthusiasm. These stories served to stretch our little minds, to draw us out beyond our narrow skies into the vast glooms of interstellar space, where the great suns ride in splendor and the bright nebulae fling their veils of fire parsecs-long across the universe; where the Coal-sack and the Horsehead make patterns of black mystery; where the Cepheid variables blink their evil eyes and a billion nameless planets may harbor life-forms infinitely numerous and strange. Escape fiction? Yes, indeed! But in its own ironic way, as we see now, it was an escape into a reality which even now some people are still trying to fight off as the Devil fights holy water, afraid to look up and Out.

By the mid-1970s, at least one European literary critic maintained (in "Le Space Opera et l'Heroic Fantasy") that space opera has two poles, Edgar Rice Burroughs and Edmond Hamilton. In the latter, "the combat spreads over at least a galaxy, mankind confronts a hostile, alien race and the destiny of the universe is in the balance." The Burroughs type is more pictorial, "the anachronistic, baroque world of the first adventures of Flash Gordon." If any living writer then occupied the senior position as polar opposite of Hamilton, it was Brackett.

David Pringle, in his 1990s essay on the history and development of space opera, expands on this point:

. . . There was another, less serious, more crowd-pleasing form of space travel fiction in existence before space opera. If the latter emerged around 1928, with "Doc" Smith's *The Skylark of Space* and Hamilton's "Interstellar Patrol" stories as its best-known early examples, then the former had already produced its paradigm text more than a decade and a half earlier . . . Edgar Rice Burroughs's "Under the Moons of Mars," serialized in *All-Story* magazine in 1912 and later republished as *A Princess of Mars*. The form this tale exemplified is what has come to be known as the "planetary romance." I find this a tremendously useful label for another distinct subgenre of popular sf, one that contrasts with space opera in several ways, though it has some things in common. Many casual commentators have confused the two forms. . . .

Moorcock says, in the same essay quoted earlier:

It's commonly known, because Ray has said so, that Ray Bradbury's Mars, like Ballard's Vermillion Sands, is not a million miles from Brackett's Mars. And before the whole world realised how good he was, Bradbury regularly appeared in the same pulps. Leigh would have credited Edgar Rice Burroughs for everything, but Burroughs lacked her poetic vision, her specific, characteristic talent, and in my view her finest Martian adventure stories remain superior to all others.

The central character of "Enchantress of Venus," Erik John Stark, is also the hero of many of Brackett's Martian stories, and of three novels written in the 1970s. Born on Mercury and raised by subhuman savages, he is a Tarzan figure who wanders the solar system and is here on the strange watery Venus of early SF. This story is one of the archetypes or models of space opera as it came to be understood by the 1970s, and as it has been understood since.

ENCHANTRESS OF VENUS

LEIGH BRACKETT

The ship moved slowly across the Red Sea, through the shrouding veils of mist, her sail barely filled by the languid thrust of the wind. Her hull, of a thin light metal, floated without sound, the surface of the strange ocean parting before her prow in silent rippling streamers of flame.

Night deepened toward the ship, a river of indigo flowing out of the west. The man known as Stark stood alone by the after rail and watched its coming. He was full of impatience and a gathering sense of danger, so that it seemed to him that even the hot wind smelled of it.

The steersman lay drowsily over his sweep. He was a big man, with skin and hair the color of milk. He did not speak, but Stark felt that now and again the man's eyes turned toward him, pale and calculating under half-closed lids, with a secret avarice.

The captain and the two other members of the little coasting vessel's crew were forward, at their evening meal. Once or twice Stark heard a burst of laughter, half-whispered and furtive. It was as though all four shared in some private joke, from which he was rigidly excluded.

The heat was oppressive. Sweat gathered on Stark's dark face. His shirt stuck to his back. The air was heavy with moisture, tainted with the muddy fecundity of the land that brooded westward behind the eternal fog.

There was something ominous about the sea itself. Even on its own world, the Red Sea is hardly more than legend. It lies behind the Mountains of White Cloud, the great barrier wall that hides away half a planet. Few men have gone beyond that barrier, into the vast mystery of Inner Venus. Fewer still have come back.

Stark was one of that handful. Three times before he had crossed the mountains, and once he had stayed for nearly a year. But he had never quite grown used to the Red Sea.

It was not water. It was gaseous, dense enough to float the buoyant hulls of the metal ships, and it burned perpetually with its deep inner fires. The mists that clouded it were stained with the bloody glow. Beneath the surface Stark could see the drifts of flame where the lazy currents ran, and the little coiling bursts of sparks that came upward and spread and melted into other bursts, so that the face of the sea was like a cosmos of crimson stars.

It was very beautiful, glowing against the blue, luminous darkness of the night. Beautiful, and strange.

There was a padding of bare feet, and the captain, Malthor, came up to Stark, his outline dim and ghostly in the gloom.

"We will reach Shuruun," he said, "before the second glass is run."

Stark nodded. "Good."

The voyage had seemed endless, and the close confinement of the narrow deck had got badly on his nerves.

"You will like Shuruun," said the captain jovially. "Our wine, our food, our women—all superb. We don't have many visitors. We keep to ourselves, as you will see. But those who do come . . ."

He laughed, and clapped Stark on the shoulder. "Ah, yes. You will be happy in Shuruun!"

It seemed to Stark that he caught an echo of laughter from the unseen crew, as though they listened and found a hidden jest in Malthor's words.

Stark said, "That's fine."

"Perhaps," said Malthor, "you would like to lodge with me. I could make you a good price."

He had made a good price for Stark's passage from up the coast. An exorbitantly good one.

Stark said, "No."

"You don't have to be afraid," said the Venusian, in a confidential tone. "The strangers who come to Shuruun all have the same reason. It's a good place to hide. We're out of everybody's reach."

He paused, but Stark did not rise to his bait. Presently he chuckled and went on, "In fact, it's such a safe place that most of the strangers decide to stay on. Now, at my house, I could give you . . ."

Stark said again, flatly, "No."

The captain shrugged. "Very well. Think it over, anyway." He peered ahead into the red, coiling mists. "Ah! See there?" He pointed, and Stark made out the shadowy loom of cliffs. "We are coming into the strait now."

Malthor turned and took the steering sweep himself, the helmsman going forward to join the others. The ship began to pick up speed. Stark saw that she had come into the grip of a current that swept toward the cliffs, a river of fire racing ever more swiftly in the depths of the sea.

The dark wall seemed to plunge toward them. At first Stark could see no passage. Then, suddenly, a narrow crimson streak appeared, widened, and became a gut of boiling flame, rushing silently around broken rocks. Red fog rose like smoke. The ship quivered, sprang ahead, and tore like a mad thing into the heart of the inferno.

In spite of himself, Stark's hands tightened on the rail. Tattered veils of mist swirled past them. The sea, the air, the ship itself, seemed drenched in blood. There was no sound, in all that wild sweep of current through the strait. Only the sullen fires burst and flowed.

The reflected glare showed Stark that the Straits of Shuruun were defended. Squat fortresses brooded on the cliffs. There were ballistas, and great windlasses for the drawing of nets across the narrow throat. The men of Shuruun could enforce their law, that barred all foreign shipping from their gulf.

They had reason for such a law, and such a defense. The legitimate trade of Shuruun, such as it was, was in wine and the delicate laces woven from spider-silk. Actually, however, the city lived and throve on piracy, the arts of wrecking, and a contraband trade in the distilled juice of the *vela* poppy.

Looking at the rocks and the fortresses, Stark could understand how it was that Shuruun had been able for more centuries than anyone could tell to victimize the shipping of the Red Sea, and offer a refuge to the outlaw, the wolf's-head, the breaker of taboo.

With startling abruptness, they were through the gut and drifting on the still surface of this all but landlocked arm of the Red Sea.

Because of the shrouding fog, Stark could see nothing of the land. But the smell of it was stronger, warm damp soil and the heavy, faintly rotten perfume of vegetation half jungle, half swamp. Once, through a rift in the wreathing vapor, he thought he glimpsed the shadowy bulk of an island, but it was gone at once.

After the terrifying rush of the strait, it seemed to Stark that the ship barely moved. His impatience and the subtle sense of danger deepened. He began to pace the deck, with the nervous, velvet motion of a prowling cat. The moist, steamy air seemed all but unbreathable after the clean dryness of Mars, from whence he had come so recently. It was oppressively still.

Suddenly he stopped, his head thrown back, listening.

The sound was borne faintly on the slow wind. It came from everywhere and nowhere, a vague dim thing without source or direction. It almost seemed that the night itself had spoken—the hot blue night of Venus, crying out of the mists with a tongue of infinite woe.

It faded and died away, only half heard, leaving behind it a sense of aching sadness, as though all the misery and longing of a world had found voice in that desolate wail.

Stark shivered. For a time there was silence, and then he heard the sound again, now on a deeper note. Still faint and far away, it was sustained longer by the vagaries of the heavy air, and it became a chant, rising and falling. There were no words. It was not the sort of thing that would have need of words. Then it was gone again.

Stark turned to Malthor. "What was that?"

The man looked at him curiously. He seemed not to have heard.

"That wailing sound," said Stark impatiently.

"Oh, that." The Venusian shrugged. "A trick of the wind. It sighs in the hollow rocks around the strait."

He yawned, giving place again to the steersman, and came to stand beside Stark. The Earthman ignored him. For some reason, that sound half heard through the mists had brought his uneasiness to a sharp pitch.

Civilization had brushed over Stark with a light hand. Raised from infancy by half-human aboriginals, his perceptions were still those of a savage. His ear was good.

Malthor lied. That cry of pain was not made by any wind.

"I have known several Earthmen," said Malthor, changing the subject, but not too swiftly. "None of them were like you."

Intuition warned Stark to play along. "I don't come from Earth," he said. "I come from Mercury."

Malthor puzzled over that. Venus is a cloudy world, where no man has ever seen the Sun, let alone a star. The captain had heard vaguely of these things. Earth and Mars he knew of. But Mercury was an unknown word.

Stark explained. "The planet nearest the Sun. It's very hot there. The Sun blazes like a huge fire, and there are no clouds to shield it."

"Ah. That is why your skin is so dark." He held his own pale forearm close to Stark's and shook his head. "I have never seen such skin," he said admiringly. "Nor such great muscles."

Looking up, he went on in a tone of complete friendliness, "I wish you would stay with me. You'll find no better lodgings in Shuruun. And I warn you, there are people in the town who will take advantage of strangers—rob them, even slay them. Now, I am known by all as a man of honor. You could sleep soundly under my roof."

He paused, then added with a smile, "Also, I have a daughter. An excellent cook—and very beautiful."

The woeful chanting came again, dim and distant on the wind, an echo of warning against some unimagined fate.

Stark said for the third time, "No."

He needed no intuition to tell him to walk wide of the captain. The man was a rogue, and not a very subtle one.

A flint-hard, angry look came briefly into Malthor's eyes. "You're a stubborn man. You'll find that Shuruun is no place for stubbornness."

He turned and went away. Stark remained where he was. The ship drifted on through a slow eternity of time. And all down that long still gulf of the Red Sea, through the heat and the wreathing fog, the ghostly chanting haunted him, like the keening of lost souls in some forgotten hell.

Presently the course of the ship was altered. Malthor came again to the afterdeck, giving a few quiet commands. Stark saw land ahead, a darker blur on the night, and then the shrouded outlines of a city.

Torches blazed on the quays and in the streets, and the low buildings caught a ruddy glow from the burning sea itself. A squat and ugly town, Shuruun, crouching witch-like on the rocky shore, her ragged skirts dipped in blood.

The ship drifted in toward the quays.

Stark heard a whisper of movement behind him, the hushed and purposeful padding of naked feet. He turned, with the astonishing swiftness of an animal that feels itself threatened, his hand dropping to his gun.

A belaying pin, thrown by the steersman, struck the side of his head with stunning force. Reeling, half blinded, he saw the distorted shapes of men closing in upon him. Malthor's voice sounded, low and hard. A second belaying pin whizzed through the air and cracked against Stark's shoulder.

Hands were laid upon him. Bodies, heavy and strong, bore his down. Malthor laughed.

Stark's teeth glinted bare and white. Someone's cheek brushed past, and he sank them into the flesh. He began to growl, a sound that should never have come from a human throat. It seemed to the startled Venusians that the man they had attacked had by some wizardry become a beast, at the first touch of violence.

The man with the torn cheek screamed. There was a voiceless scuffling on the deck, a terrible intensity of motion, and then the great dark body rose and shook itself free of the tangle, and was gone, over the rail, leaving Malthor with nothing but the silken rags of a shirt in his hands.

The surface of the Red Sea closed without a ripple over Stark. There was a burst of crimson sparks, a momentary trail of flame going down like a drowned comet, and then—nothing.

2

Stark dropped slowly downward through a strange world. There was no difficulty about breathing, as in a sea of water. The gases of the Red Sea support life quite well, and the creatures that dwell in it have almost normal lungs.

Stark did not pay much attention at first, except to keep his balance automatically. He was still dazed from the blow, and he was raging with anger and pain.

The primitive in him, whose name was not Stark but N'Chaka, and who had fought and starved and hunted in the blazing valleys of Mercury's Twilight Belt, learning lessons he never forgot, wished to return and slay Malthor and his men. He regretted that he had not torn out their throats, for now his trail would never be safe from them.

But the man Stark, who had learned some more bitter lessons in the name of civilization, knew the unwisdom of that. He snarled over his aching head, and cursed the Venusians in the harsh, crude dialect that was his mother tongue, but he did not turn back. There would be time enough for Malthor.

It struck him that the gulf was very deep.

Fighting down his rage, he began to swim in the direction of the shore. There was no sign of pursuit, and he judged that Malthor had decided to let him go. He puzzled over the reason for the attack. It could hardly be robbery, since he carried nothing but the clothes he stood in, and very little money.

No. There was some deeper reason. A reason connected with Malthor's insistence that he lodge with him. Stark smiled. It was not a pleasant smile. He was thinking of Shuruun, and the things men said about it, around the shores of the Red Sea.

Then his face hardened. The dim coiling fires through which he swam brought him memories of other times he had gone adventuring in the depths of the Red Sea.

He had not been alone then. Helvi had gone with him—the tall son of a barbarian kinglet up-coast by Yarell. They had hunted strange beasts through the crystal forests of the sea-bottom and bathed in the welling flames that pulse from the very heart of Venus to feed the ocean. They had been brothers.

Now Helvi was gone, into Shuruun. He had never returned.

Stark swam on. And presently he saw below him in the red gloom something that made him drop lower, frowning with surprise.

There were trees beneath him. Great forest giants towering up into an eerie sky, their branches swaying gently to the slow wash of the currents.

Stark was puzzled. The forests where he and Helvi had hunted were truly crystalline, without even the memory of life. The "trees" were no more trees in actuality than the branching corals of Terra's southern oceans.

But these were real, or had been. He thought at first that they still lived, for their leaves were green, and here and there creepers had starred them with great nodding blossoms of gold and purple and waxy white. But when he floated down close enough to touch them, he realized that they were dead—trees, creepers, blossoms, all.

They had not mummified, nor turned to stone. They were pliable, and their colors were very bright. Simply, they had ceased to live, and the gases of the sea had preserved them by some chemical magic, so perfectly that barely a leaf had fallen.

Stark did not venture into the shadowy denseness below the topmost branches. A strange fear came over him, at the sight of that vast forest dreaming in the depths of the gulf, drowned and forgotten, as though wondering why the birds had gone, taking with them the warm rains and the light of day.

He thrust his way upward, himself like a huge dark bird above the branches. An overwhelming impulse to get away from that unearthly place drove him on, his half-wild sense shuddering with an impression of evil so great that it took all his acquired common-sense to assure him that he was not pursued by demons.

He broke the surface at last, to find that he had lost his direction in the red deep and made a long circle around, so that he was far below Shuruun. He made his way back, not hurrying now, and presently clambered out over the black rocks.

He stood at the end of a muddy lane that wandered in toward the town. He followed it, moving neither fast nor slow, but with a wary alertness.

Huts of wattle-and-daub took shape out of the fog, increased in numbers, became a street of dwellings. Here and there rush-lights glimmered through the slitted windows. A man and a woman clung together in a low doorway. They saw him and sprang apart, and the woman gave a little cry. Stark went on. He did not look back, but he knew that they were following him quietly, at a little distance.

The lane twisted snakelike upon itself, crawling now through a crowded jumble of houses. There were more lights, and more people, tall white-skinned folk of the swamp-edges, with pale eyes and long hair the color of new flax, and the faces of wolves.

Stark passed among them, alien and strange with his black hair and sun-darkened skin. They did not speak, nor try to stop him. Only they looked at him out of the red fog, with a curious blend of amusement and fear, and some of them followed him, keeping well behind. A gang of small naked children came from somewhere among the houses and ran shouting beside him, out of reach, until one boy threw a stone and screamed something unintelligible except for one word—*Lhari*. Then they all stopped, horrified, and fled.

Stark went on, through the quarter of the lacemakers, heading by instinct toward the wharves. The glow of the Red Sea pervaded all the air, so that it seemed as though the mist was full of tiny drops of blood. There was a smell about the place he did not like, a damp miasma of mud and crowding bodies and wine, and the breath of the *vela* poppy. Shuruun was an unclean town, and it stank of evil.

There was something else about it, a subtle thing that touched Stark's nerves with a chill finger. Fear. He could see the shadow of it in the eyes of the people, hear its undertone in their voices. The wolves of Shuruun did not feel safe in their own kennel. Unconsciously, as this feeling grew upon him, Stark's step grew more and more wary, his eyes more cold and hard.

He came out into a broad square by the harbor front. He could see the ghostly ships moored along the quays, the piled casks of wine, the tangle of masts and cordage dim against the background of the burning gulf. There were many torches here. Large low buildings stood around the square. There was laughter and the sound of voices from the dark verandas, and somewhere a woman sang to the melancholy lilting of a reed pipe.

A suffused glow of light in the distance ahead caught Stark's eye. That way the streets sloped to a higher ground, and straining his vision against the fog, he made out very dimly the tall bulk of a castle crouched on the low cliffs, looking with bright eyes upon the night, and the streets of Shuruun.

Stark hesitated briefly. Then he started across the square toward the largest of the taverns.

There were a number of people in the open space, mostly sailors and their women. They were loose and foolish with wine, but even so they stopped where they were and stared at the dark stranger, and then drew back from him, still staring.

Those who had followed Stark came into the square after him and then paused, spreading out in an aimless sort of way to join with other groups, whispering among themselves.

The woman stopped singing in the middle of a phrase.

A curious silence fell on the square. A nervous sibilance ran round and round under the silence, and men came slowly out from the verandas and the doors of the wine shops. Suddenly a woman with disheveled hair pointed her arm at Stark and laughed, the shrieking laugh of a harpy.

Stark found his way barred by three tall young men with hard mouths and crafty eyes, who smiled at him as hounds smile before the kill.

"Stranger," they said. "Earthman."

"Outlaw," answered Stark, and it was only half a lie.

One of the young men took a step forward. "Did you fly like a dragon over the Mountains of White Cloud? Did you drop from the sky?"

"I came on Malthor's ship."

A kind of sigh went round the square, and with it the name of Malthor. The eager faces of the young men grew heavy with disappointment. But the leader said sharply, "I was on the quay when Malthor docked. You were not on board."

It was Stark's turn to smile. In the light of the torches, his eyes blazed cold and bright as ice against the sun.

"Ask Malthor the reason for that," he said. "Ask the man with the torn cheek. Or perhaps," he added softly, "you would like to learn for yourselves."

The young men looked at him, scowling, in an odd mood of indecision. Stark settled himself, every muscle loose and ready. And the woman who had laughed crept closer and peered at Stark through her tangled hair, breathing heavily of the poppy wine.

All at once she said loudly, "He came out of the sea. That's where he came from. He's . . ."

One of the young men struck her across the mouth and she fell down in the mud. A burly seaman ran out and caught her by the hair, dragging her to her feet again. His face was frightened and very angry. He hauled the woman away, cursing her for a fool and beating her as he went. She spat out blood, and said no more.

"Well," said Stark to the young men. "Have you made up your minds?"

"Minds!" said a voice behind them—a harsh-timbred, rasping voice that handled the liquid vocables of the Venusian speech very clumsily indeed. "They have no minds, these whelps! If they had, they'd be off about their business, instead of standing here badgering a stranger."

The young men turned, and now between them Stark could see the man who had spoken. He stood on the steps of the tavern. He was an Earthman, and at first Stark thought he was old, because his hair was white and his face deeply lined. His body was wasted with fever, the muscles all gone to knotty strings twisted over bone. He leaned heavily on a stick, and one leg was crooked and terribly scarred.

He grinned at Stark and said, in colloquial English, "Watch me get rid of 'em!"

He began to tongue-lash the young men, telling them that they were idiots, the misbegotten offspring of swamp-toads, utterly without manners, and that if they did not believe the stranger's story they should go and ask Malthor, as he suggested. Finally he shook his stick at them, fairly screeching.

"Go on, now. Go away! Leave us alone—my brother of Earth and I!"

The young men gave one hesitant glance at Stark's feral eyes. Then they looked at each other and shrugged, and went away across the square half sheepishly, like great loutish boys caught in some misdemeanor.

The white-haired Earthman beckoned to Stark. And, as Stark came up to him on the steps he said under his breath, almost angrily, "You're in a trap."

Stark glanced back over his shoulder. At the edge of the square the three young men had met a fourth, who had his face bound up in a rag. They vanished almost at once into a side street, but not before Stark had recognized the fourth man as Malthor.

It was the captain he had branded.

With loud cheerfulness, the lame man said in Venusian, "Come in and drink with me, brother, and we will talk of Earth."

3

The tavern was of the standard low-class Venusian pattern—a single huge room under bare thatch, the wall half open with the reed shutters rolled up, the floor of split logs propped up on piling out of the mud. A long low bar, little tables, mangy skins and heaps of dubious cushions on the floor around them, and at one end the entertainers—two old men with a drum and a reed pipe, and a couple of sulky, tired-looking girls.

The lame man led Stark to a table in the corner and sank down, calling for wine. His eyes, which were dark and haunted by long pain, burned with excitement. His hands shook. Before Stark had sat down he had begun to talk, his words stumbling over themselves as though he could not get them out fast enough.

"How is it there now? Has it changed any? Tell me how it is—the cities, the lights, the paved streets, the women, the Sun. Oh Lord, what I wouldn't give to see the Sun again, and women with dark hair and their clothes on!" He leaned forward, staring hungrily into Stark's face, as though he could see those things mirrored there. "For God's sake, talk to me—talk to me in English, and tell me about Earth!"

"How long have you been here?" asked Stark.

"I don't know. How do you reckon time on a world without a Sun, without one damned little star to look at? Ten years, a hundred years, how should I know? Forever. Tell me about Earth."

Stark smiled wryly. "I haven't been there for a long time. The police were too ready with a welcoming committee. But the last time I saw it, it was just the same."

The lame man shivered. He was not looking at Stark now, but at some place far beyond him.

"Autumn woods," he said. "Red and gold on the brown hills. Snow. I can remember how it felt to be cold. The air bit you when you breathed it. And the women wore high-heeled slippers. No big bare feet tromping in the mud, but little sharp heels tapping on clean pavement."

Suddenly he glared at Stark, his eyes furious and bright with tears.

"Why the hell did you have to come here and start me remembering? I'm Larrabee. I live in Shuruun. I've been here forever, and I'll be here till I die. There isn't any Earth. It's gone. Just look up into the sky, and you'll know it's gone. There's nothing anywhere but clouds, and Venus, and mud."

He sat still, shaking, turning his head from side to side. A man came with wine, put it down, and went away again. The tavern was very quiet. There was a wide space empty around the two Earthmen. Beyond that people lay on the cushions, sipping the poppy wine and watching with a sort of furtive expectancy.

Abruptly, Larrabee laughed, a harsh sound that held a certain honest mirth.

"I don't know why I should get sentimental about Earth at this late date. Never thought much about it when I was there."

Nevertheless, he kept his gaze averted, and when he picked up his cup his hand trembled so that he spilled some of the wine.

Stark was staring at him in unbelief. "Larrabee," he said. "You're Mike Larrabee. You're the man who got half a million credits out of the strong room of the *Royal Venus*."

Larrabee nodded. "And got away with it, right over the Mountains of White Cloud, that they said couldn't be flown. And do you know where that half a million is now? At the bottom of the Red Sea, along with my ship and my crew, out there in the gulf. Lord knows why I lived." He shrugged. "Well, anyway, I was heading for Shuruun when I crashed, and I got here. So why complain?"

He drank again, deeply, and Stark shook his head.

"You've been here nine years, then, by Earth time," he said. He had never met Larrabee, but he remembered the pictures of him that had flashed across space on police bands. Larrabee had been a young man then, dark and proud and handsome.

Larrabee guessed his thought. "I've changed, haven't I?"

Stark said lamely, "Everyone thought you were dead."

Larrabee laughed. After that, for a moment, there was silence. Stark's ears were straining for any sound outside. There was none.

He said abruptly, "What about this trap I'm in?"

"I'll tell you one thing about it," said Larrabee. "There's no way out. I can't help you. I wouldn't if I could, get that straight. But I can't, anyway."

"Thanks," Stark said sourly. "You can at least tell me what goes on."

"Listen," said Larrabee. "I'm a cripple, and an old man, and Shuruun isn't the sweetest place in the solar system to live. But I do live. I have a wife, a slatternly wench I'll admit, but good enough in her way. You'll notice some little dark-haired brats rolling in the mud. They're mine, too. I have some skill at setting bones and such, and so I can get drunk for nothing as often as I will—which is often. Also, because of this bum leg, I'm perfectly safe. So don't ask me what goes on. I take great pains not to know."

Stark said, "Who are the Lhari?"

"Would you like to meet them?" Larrabee seemed to find something very amusing in that thought. "Just go on up to the castle. They live there. They're the Lords of Shuruun, and they're always glad to meet strangers."

He leaned forward suddenly. "Who are you anyway? What's your name, and why the devil did you come here?"

"My name is Stark. And I came here for the same reason you did."

"Stark," repeated Larrabee slowly, his eyes intent. "That rings a faint bell. Seems to me I saw a *Wanted* flash once, some idiot that had led a native revolt somewhere in the Jovian Colonies—a big cold-eyed brute they referred to colorfully as the wild man from Mercury."

He nodded, pleased with himself. "Wild man, eh? Well, Shuruun will tame you down!"

"Perhaps," said Stark. His eyes shifted constantly, watching Larrabee, watching the doorway and the dark veranda and the people who drank but did not talk among themselves. "Speaking of strangers, one came here at the time of the last rains. He was Venusian, from up-coast. A big young man. I used to know him. Perhaps he could help me."

Larrabee snorted. By now, he had drunk his own wine and Stark's too. "Nobody can help you. As for your friend, I never saw him. I'm beginning to think I should never have seen you." Quite suddenly he caught up his stick and got with some difficulty to his feet. He did not look at Stark, but said harshly, "You better get out of here." Then he turned and limped unsteadily to the bar.

Stark rose. He glanced after Larrabee, and again his nostrils twitched to the smell of fear. Then he went out of the tavern the way he had come in, through the front door. No one moved to stop him. Outside, the square was empty. It had begun to rain.

Stark stood for a moment on the steps. He was angry, and filled with a dangerous unease, the hair-trigger nervousness of a tiger that senses the beaters creeping toward him up the wind. He would almost have welcomed the sight of Malthor and the three young men. But there was nothing to fight but the silence and the rain.

He stepped out into the mud, wet and warm around his ankles. An idea came to him, and he smiled, beginning now to move with a definite purpose, along the side of the square.

The sharp downpour strengthened. Rain smoked from Stark's naked shoulders, beat against thatch and mud with a hissing rattle. The harbor had disappeared behind boiling clouds of fog, where water struck the surface of the Red Sea and was turned again instantly by chemical action into vapor. The quays and the neighboring streets were being swallowed up in the impenetrable mist. Lightning came with an eerie bluish flare, and thunder came rolling after it.

Stark turned up the narrow way that led toward the castle.

Its lights were winking out now, one by one, blotted by the creeping fog. Lightning etched its shadowy bulk against the night, and then was gone. And through the noise of the thunder that followed, Stark thought he heard a voice calling.

He stopped, half crouching, his hand on his gun. The cry came again, a girl's voice, thin as the wail of a seabird through the driving rain. Then he saw her, a small white blur in the street behind him, running, and even in that dim glimpse of her every line of her body was instinct with fright.

Stark set his back against a wall and waited. There did not seem to be anyone with her, though it was hard to tell in the darkness and the storm.

She came up to him, and stopped, just out of his reach, looking at him and away again with a painful irresoluteness. A bright flash showed her to him clearly. She was young, not long out of her childhood, and pretty in a stupid sort of way. Just now her mouth trembled on the edge of weeping, and her eyes were very large and scared. Her skirt clung to her long thighs, and above it her naked body, hardly fleshed into womanhood, glistened like snow in the wet. Her pale hair hung dripping over her shoulders.

Stark said gently, "What do you want with me?"

She looked at him, so miserably like a wet puppy that he smiled. And as though that smile had taken what little resolution she had out of her, she dropped to her knees, sobbing.

"I can't do it," she wailed. "He'll kill me, but I just can't do it!"

"Do what?" asked Stark.

She stared up at him. "Run away," she urged him. "Run away *now!* You'll die in the swamps, but that's better than being one of the Lost Ones!" She shook her thin arms at him. *"Run away!"*

4

The street was empty. Nothing showed, nothing stirred anywhere. Stark leaned over and pulled the girl to her feet, drawing her in under the shelter of the thatched eaves.

"Now then," he said. "Suppose you stop crying and tell me what this is all about."

Presently, between gulps and hiccoughs, he got the story out of her.

"I am Zareth," she said. "Malthor's daughter. He's afraid of you, because of what you did to him on the ship, so he ordered me to watch for you in the square, when you would come out of the tavern. Then I was to follow you, and . . ."

She broke off, and Stark patted her shoulder. "Go on."

But a new thought had occurred to her. "If I do, will you promise not to beat me, or . . ." She looked at his gun and shivered.

"I promise."

She studied his face, what she could see of it in the darkness, and then seemed to lose some of her fear.

"I was to stop you. I was to say what I've already said, about being Malthor's daughter and the rest of it, and then I was to say that he wanted me to lead you into an ambush while pretending to help you escape, but that I couldn't do it, and would help you to escape anyhow because I hated Malthor and the whole business about the Lost Ones. So you would believe me, and follow me, and I would lead you into the ambush."

She shook her head and began to cry again, quietly this time, and there was nothing of the woman about her at all now. She was just a child, very miserable and afraid. Stark was glad he had branded Malthor.

"But I can't lead you into the ambush. I do hate Malthor, even if he is my father, because he beats me. And the Lost Ones . . ." She paused. "Sometimes I hear them at night, chanting way out there beyond the mist. It is a very terrible sound."

"It is," said Stark. "I've heard it. Who are the Lost Ones, Zareth?"

"I can't tell you that," said Zareth. "It's forbidden even to speak of them. And anyway," she finished honestly, "I don't even know. People disappear, that's all. Not our own people of Shuruun, at least not very often. But strangers like you—and I'm sure my father goes off into the swamps to hunt among the tribes there, and I'm sure he comes back from some of his voyages with nothing in his hold but men from some captured ship. Why, or what for, I don't know. Except I've heard the chanting."

"They live out there in the gulf, do they, the Lost Ones?"

"They must. There are many islands there."

"And what of the Lhari, the Lords of Shuruun? Don't they know what's going on? Or are they part of it?"

She shuddered, and said, "It's not for us to question the Lhari, nor even to wonder what they do. Those who have are gone from Shuruun, nobody knows where."

Stark nodded. He was silent for a moment, thinking. Then Zareth's little hand touched his shoulder.

"Go," she said. "Lose yourself in the swamps. You're strong, and there's something about you different from other men. You may live to find your way through."

"No. I have something to do before I leave Shuruun." He took Zareth's damp fair head between his hands and kissed her on the forehead. "You're a sweet child, Zareth, and a brave one. Tell Malthor that you did exactly as he told you, and it was not your fault I wouldn't follow you."

"He will beat me anyway," said Zareth philosophically, "but perhaps not quite so hard."

"He'll have no reason to beat you at all, if you tell him the truth—that I would not go with you because my mind was set on going to the castle of the Lhari."

There was a long, long silence, while Zareth's eyes widened slowly in horror, and the rain beat on the thatch, and fog and thunder rolled together across Shuruun.

"To the castle," she whispered. "Oh, no! Go into the swamps, or let Malthor take you—but don't go to the castle!" She took hold of his arm, her fingers biting into his flesh with the urgency of her plea. "You're a stranger, you don't know. . . . Please, don't go up there!"

"Why not?" asked Stark. "Are the Lhari demons? Do they devour men?" He loosened her hands gently. "You'd better go now. Tell your father where I am, if he wishes to come after me."

Zareth backed away slowly, out into the rain, staring at him as though she looked at someone standing on the brink of hell, not dead, but worse than dead. Wonder showed in her face, and through it a great yearning pity. She tried once to speak, and then shook her head and turned away, breaking into a run as though she could not endure to look upon Stark any longer. In a second she was gone.

Stark looked after her for a moment, strangely touched. Then he stepped out into the rain again, heading upward along the steep path that led to the castle of the Lords of Shuruun.

The mist was blinding. Stark had to feel his way, and as he climbed higher, above the level of the town, he was lost in the sullen redness. A hot wind blew, and each flare of lightning turned the crimson fog to a hellish purple. The night was full of a vast hissing where the rain poured into the gulf. He stopped once to hide his gun in a cleft between the rocks.

At length he stumbled against a carven pillar of black stone and found the gate that hung from it, a massive thing sheathed in metal. It was barred, and the pounding of his fists upon it made little sound.

Then he saw the gong, a huge disc of beaten gold beside the gate. Stark picked up the hammer that lay there, and set the deep voice of the gong rolling out between the thunderbolts.

A barred slit opened and a man's eyes looked out at him. Stark dropped the hammer.

"Open up!" he shouted. "I would speak with the Lhari!"

From within he heard an echo of laughter. Scraps of voices came to him on the wind, and then more laughter, and then, slowly, the great valves of the gate creaked open, wide enough only to admit him.

He stepped through, and the gateway shut behind him with a ringing clash.

He stood in a huge open court. Enclosed within its walls was a village of thatched huts, with open sheds for cooking, and behind them were pens for the stabling of beasts, the wingless dragons of the swamps that can be caught and broken to the goad.

He saw this only in vague glimpses, because of the fog. The men who had let him in clustered around him, thrusting him forward into the light that streamed from the huts.

"He would speak with the Lhari!" one of them shouted, to the women and children who stood in the doorways watching. The words were picked up and tossed around the court, and a great burst of laughter went up.

Stark eyed them, saying nothing. They were a puzzling breed. The men, obviously, were soldiers and guards to the Lhari, for they wore the harness of fighting men. As obviously, these were their wives and children, all living behind the castle walls and having little to do with Shuruun.

But it was their racial characteristics that surprised him. They had interbred with the pale tribes of the Swamp-Edges that had peopled Shuruun, and there were many with milk-white hair and broad faces. Yet even these bore an alien stamp. Stark was puzzled, for the race he would have named was unknown here behind the Mountains of White Cloud, and almost unknown anywhere on Venus at Sea-level, among the sweltering marshes and the eternal fogs.

They stared at him even more curiously, remarking on his skin and his black hair and the unfamiliar modeling of his face. The women nudged each other and whispered, giggling, and one of them said aloud, "They'll need a barrel-hoop to collar that neck!"

The guards closed in around him. "Well, if you wish to see the Lhari, you shall," said the leader, "but first we must make sure of you."

Spear-points ringed him round. Stark made no resistance while they stripped him of all he had, except for his shorts and sandals. He had expected that, and it amused him, for there was little enough for them to take.

"All right," said the leader. "Come on."

The whole village turned out in the rain to escort Stark to the castle door. There was about them the same ominous interest that the people of Shuruun had had, with one difference. They knew what was supposed to happen to him, knew all about it, and were therefore doubly appreciative of the game.

The great doorway was square and plain, and yet neither crude nor ungraceful. The castle itself was built of the black stone, each block perfectly cut and fitted, and the door itself was sheathed in the same metal as the gate, darkened but not corroded.

The leader of the guard cried out to the warder, "Here is one who would speak with the Lhari!"

The warder laughed. "And so he shall! Their night is long, and dull."

He flung open the heavy door and cried the word down the hallway. Stark could hear it echoing hollowly within, and presently from the shadows came servants clad in silks and wearing jeweled collars, and from the guttural sound of their laughter Stark knew that they had no tongues.

Stark faltered, then. The doorway loomed hollowly before him, and it came to him suddenly that evil lay behind it and that perhaps Zareth was wiser than he when she warned him from the Lhari.

Then he thought of Helvi, and of other things, and lost his fear in anger. Lightning burned the sky. The last cry of the dying storm shook the ground under his feet. He thrust the grinning warder aside and strode into the castle, bringing a veil of the red fog with him, and did not listen to the closing of the door, which was stealthy and quiet as the footfall of approaching Death.

Torches burned here and there along the walls, and by their smoky glare he could see that the hallway was like the entrance—square and unadorned, faced with the black rock. It was high, and wide, and there was about the architecture a calm reflective dignity that had its own beauty, in some ways more impressive than the sensuous loveliness of the ruined palaces he had seen on Mars.

There were no carvings here, no paintings nor frescoes. It seemed that the builders had felt that the hall itself was enough, in its massive perfection of line and the somber gleam of polished stone. The only decoration was in the window embrasures. These were empty now, open to the sky with the red fog wreathing through them, but there were still scraps of jewel-toned panes clinging to the fretwork, to show what they had once been.

A strange feeling swept over Stark. Because of his wild upbringing, he was abnormally sensitive to the sort of impressions that most men receive either dully or not at all.

Walking down the hall, preceded by the tongueless creatures in their bright silks and blazing collars, he was struck by a subtle *difference* in the place. The castle itself was only an extension of the minds of its builders, a dream shaped into reality. Stark felt that that dark, cool, curiously timeless dream had not originated in a mind like his own, nor like that of any man he had ever seen.

Then the end of the hall was reached, the way barred by low broad doors of gold fashioned in the same chaste simplicity.

A soft scurrying of feet, a shapeless tittering from the servants, a glancing of malicious, mocking eyes. The golden doors swung open, and Stark was in the presence of the Lhari.

5

They had the appearance in that first glance, of creatures glimpsed in a fever-dream, very bright and distant, robed in a misty glow that gave them an allusion of unearthly beauty.

The place in which the Earthman now stood was like a cathedral for breadth and loftiness. Most of it was in darkness, so that it seemed to reach without limit above and on all sides, as though the walls were only shadowy phantasms of the night itself. The polished black stone under his feet held a dim translucent gleam, depthless as water in a black tarn. There was no substance anywhere.

Far away in this shadowy vastness burned a cluster of lamps, a galaxy of little stars to shed a silvery light upon the Lords of Shuruun.

There had been no sound in the place when Stark entered, for the opening of the golden doors had caught the attention of the Lhari and held it in contemplation of the stranger. Stark began to walk toward them in this utter stillness.

Quite suddenly, in the impenetrable gloom somewhere to his right, there came a sharp scuffling and a scratching of reptilian claws, a hissing and a sort of low angry muttering, all magnified and distorted by the echoing vault into a huge demoniac whispering that swept all around him.

Stark whirled around, crouched and ready, his eyes blazing and his body bathed in cold sweat. The noise increased, rushing toward him. From the distant glow of the lamps came a woman's tinkling laughter, thin crystal broken against the vault. The hissing and snarling rose to hollow crescendo, and Stark saw a blurred shape bounding at him.

His hands reached out to receive the rush, but it never came. The strange shape resolved itself into a boy of about ten, who dragged after him on a bit of rope a young dragon, new and toothless from the egg, and protesting with all its strength.

Stark straightened up, feeling let down and furious—and relieved. The boy scowled at him through a forelock of silver curls. Then he called him a very dirty word and rushed away, kicking and hauling at the little beast until it raged like the father of all dragons and sounded like it, too, in that vast echo chamber.

A voice spoke. Slow, harsh, sexless, it rang thinly through the vault. Thin—but a steel blade is thin, too. It speaks inexorably, and its word is final.

The voice said, "Come here, into the light."

Stark obeyed the voice. As he approached the lamps, the aspect of the Lhari changed and steadied. Their beauty remained, but it was not the same. They had looked like angels. Now that he could see them clearly, Stark thought that they might have been the children of Lucifer himself.

There were six of them, counting the boy. Two men, about the same age as Stark, with some complicated gambling game forgotten between them. A woman, beautiful, gowned in white silk, sitting with her hands in her lap, doing nothing. A woman, younger, not so beautiful perhaps, but with a look of stormy and bitter vitality. She wore a short tunic of crimson, and a stout leather glove on her left hand, where perched a flying thing of prey with its fierce eyes hooded.

The boy stood beside the two men, his head poised arrogantly. From time to time he cuffed the little dragon, and it snapped at him with its impotent jaws. He was proud of himself for doing that Stark wondered how he would behave with the beast when it had grown its fangs.

Opposite him, crouched on a heap of cushions, was a third man. He was deformed, with an ungainly body and long spidery arms, and in his lap a sharp knife lay on a block of wood, half formed into the shape of an obese creature half woman, half pure evil. Stark saw with a flash of surprise that the face of the deformed young man, of all the faces there, was truly human, truly beautiful. His eyes were old in his boyish face, wise, and very sad in their wisdom. He smiled upon the stranger, and his smile was more compassionate than tears.

They looked at Stark, all of them, with restless, hungry eyes. They were the pure breed, that had left its stamp of alienage on the pale-haired folk of the swamps, the serfs who dwelt in the huts outside.

They were of the Cloud People, the folk of the High Plateaus, kings of the land on the farther slopes of the Mountains of White Cloud. It was strange to see them here, on the dark side of the barrier wall, but here they were. How they had come, and why, leaving their rich cool plains for the fetor of these foreign swamps, he could not guess. But there was no mistaking them—the proud fine shaping of their bodies, their alabaster skin, their eyes that were all colors and none, like the dawn sky, their hair that was pure warm silver.

They did not speak. They seemed to be waiting for permission to speak, and Stark wondered which one of them had voiced that steely summons.

Then it came again. "Come here—come closer." And he looked beyond them, beyond the circle of lamps into the shadows again, and saw the speaker.

She lay upon a low bed, her head propped on silken pillows, her vast, her incredibly gigantic body covered with a silken pall. Only her arms were bare, two shapeless masses of white flesh ending in tiny hands. From time to time she stretched one out and took a morsel of food from the supply laid ready beside her, snuffling and wheezing with the effort, and then gulped the tidbit down with a horrible voracity.

Her features had long ago dissolved into a shaking formlessness, with the exception of her nose, which rose out of the fat curved and cruel and thin, like the bony beak of the creature that sat on the girl's wrist and dreamed its hooded dreams of blood. And her eyes . . .

Stark looked into her eyes and shuddered. Then he glanced at the carving half formed in the cripple's lap, and knew what thought had guided the knife.

Half woman, half pure evil. And strong. Very strong. Her strength lay naked in her eyes for all to see, and it was an ugly strength. It could tear down mountains, but it could never build.

He saw her looking at him. Her eyes bored into his as though they would search out his very guts and study them, and he knew that she expected him to turn away, unable to bear her gaze. He did not. Presently he smiled and said, "I have outstared a rock-lizard, to determine which of us should eat the other. And I've outstared the very rock while waiting for him."

She knew that he spoke the truth. Stark expected her to be angry, but she was not. A vague mountainous rippling shook her and emerged at length as a voiceless laughter.

"You see that?" she demanded, addressing the others. "You whelps of the Lhari—not one of you dares to face me down, yet here is a great dark creature from the gods know where who can stand and shame you."

She glanced again at Stark. "What demon's blood brought you forth, that you have learned neither prudence nor fear?"

Stark answered somberly, "I learned them both before I could walk. But I learned another thing also—a thing called anger."

"And you are angry?"

"Ask Malthor if I am, and why!"

He saw the two men start a little, and a slow smile crossed the girls face.

"Malthor," said the hulk upon the bed, and ate a mouthful of roast meat dripping with fat. "That is interesting. But rage against Malthor did not bring you here. I am curious, Stranger. Speak."

"I will."

Stark glanced around. The place was a tomb, a trap. The very air smelled of danger. The younger folk watched him in silence. Not one of them had spoken since he came in, except the boy who had cursed him, and that was unnatural in itself. The girl leaned forward, idly stroking the creature on her wrist so that it stirred and ran its knife-like talons in and out of their bony sheathes with sensuous pleasure. Her gaze on Stark was bold and cool, oddly challenging. Of them all, she alone saw him as a man. To the others he was a problem, a diversion—something less than human.

Stark said, "A man came to Shuruun at the time of the last rains. His name was Helvi, and he was son of a little king by Yarell. He came seeking his brother, who had broken taboo and fled for his life. Helvi came to tell him that the ban was lifted, and he might return. Neither one came back."

The small evil eyes were amused, blinking in their tallowy creases. "And so?"

"And so I have come after Helvi, who is my friend."

Again there was the heaving of that bulk of flesh, the explosion of laughter that hissed and wheezed in snake-like echoes through the vault.

"Friendship must run deep with you, Stranger. Ah, well. The Lhari are kind of heart. You shall find your friend."

And as though that were the signal to end their deferential silence, the younger folk burst into laughter also, until the vast hall rang with it, giving back a sound like demons laughing on the edge of Hell.

The cripple only did not laugh, but bent his bright head over his carving, and sighed.

The girl sprang up. "Not yet, Grandmother! Keep him awhile."

The cold, cruel eyes shifted to her. "And what will you do with him, Varra? Haul him about on a string, like Bor with his wretched beast?"

"Perhaps—though I think it would need a stout chain to hold him." Varra turned and looked at Stark, bold and bright, taking in the breadth and the height of him, the shaping of the great smooth muscles, the iron line of the jaw. She smiled. Her mouth was very lovely, like the red fruit of the swamp tree that bears death in its pungent sweetness.

"Here is a man," she said. "The first man I have seen since my father died."

The two men at the gaming table rose, their faces flushed and angry. One of them strode forward and gripped the girl's arm roughly.

"So I am not a man," he said, with surprising gentleness. "A sad thing for one who is to be your husband. It's best that we settle that now, before we wed."

Varra nodded. Stark saw that the man's fingers were cutting savagely into the firm muscle of her arm, but she did not wince.

"High time to settle it all, Egil. You have borne enough from me. The day is long overdue for my taming. I must learn now to bend my neck, and acknowledge my lord."

For a moment Stark thought she meant it, the note of mockery in her voice was so subtle. Then the woman in white, who all this time had not moved nor changed expression, voiced again the thin, tinkling laugh he had heard once before. From that, and the dark suffusion of blood in Egil's face, Stark knew that Varra was only casting the man's own phrases back at him. The boy let out one derisive bark, and was cuffed into silence.

Varra looked straight at Stark. "Will you fight for me?" she demanded.

Quite suddenly, it was Stark's turn to laugh. "No!" he said.

Varra shrugged. "Very well, then. I must fight for myself."

"Man," snarled Egil. "I'll show you who's a man, you scapegrace little vixen!"

He wrenched off his girdle with his free hand, at the same time bending the girl around so he could get a fair shot at her. The creature of prey, a Terran falcon, clung to her wrist, beating its wings and screaming, its hooded head jerking.

With a motion so quick that it was hardly visible, Varra slipped the hood and flew the creature straight for Egil's face.

He let go, flinging up his arms to ward off the talons and the tearing beak. The wide wings beat and hammered. Egil yelled. The boy Bor got out of range and danced up and down shrieking with delight.

Varra stood quietly. The bruises were blackening on her arm, but she did not deign to touch them. Egil blundered against the gaming table and sent the ivory pieces flying. Then he tripped over a cushion and fell flat, and the hungry talons ripped his tunic to ribbons down the back.

Varra whistled, a clear peremptory call. The creature gave a last peck at the back of Egil's head and flopped sullenly back to its perch on her wrist. She held it, turning toward Stark. He knew from the poise of her that she was on the verge of launching her pet at him. But she studied him and then shook her head.

"No," she said, and slipped the hood back on. "You would kill it."

Egil had scrambled up and gone off into the darkness, sucking a cut on his arm. His face was black with rage. The other man looked at Varra.

"If you were pledged to me," he said, "I'd have that temper out of you!"

"Come and try it," answered Varra.

The man shrugged and sat down. "It's not my place. I keep the peace in my own house." He glanced at the woman in white, and Stark saw that her face, hitherto blank of any expression, had taken on a look of abject fear.

"You do," said Varra, "and, if I were Arel, I would stab you while you slept. But you're safe. She had no spirit to begin with."

Arel shivered and looked steadfastly at her hands. The man began to gather up the scattered pieces. He said casually, "Egil will wring your neck some day, Varra, and I shan't weep to see it."

All this time the old woman had eaten and watched, watched and eaten, her eyes glittering with interest.

"A pretty brood, are they not?" she demanded of Stark. "Full of spirit, quarreling like young hawks in the nest. That's why I keep them around me, so—they are such sport to watch. All except Treon there." She indicated the crippled youth. "He does nothing. Dull and soft-mouthed, worse than Arel. What a grandson to be cursed with! But his sister has fire enough for two." She munched a sweet, grunting with pride.

Treon raised his head and spoke, and his voice was like music, echoing with an eerie liveliness in that dark place.

"Dull I may be, Grandmother, and weak in body, and without hope. Yet I shall be the last of the Lhari. Death sits waiting on the towers, and he shall gather you all before me. I know, for the winds have told me."

He turned his suffering eyes upon Stark and smiled, a smile of such woe and resignation that the Earthman's heart ached with it. Yet there was a thankfulness in it too, as though some long waiting was over at last.

"You," he said softly, "Stranger with the fierce eyes, I saw you come, out of the darkness, and where you set foot there was a bloody print. Your arms were red to the elbows, and your breast was splashed with the redness, and on your brow was the symbol of death. Then I knew, and the wind whispered into my ear, 'It is so. This man shall, pull the castle down, and its stones shall crush Shuruun and set the Lost Ones free'."

He laughed, very quietly. "Look at him, all of you. For he will be your doom!"

There was a moment's silence, and Stark, with all the superstitions of a wild race thick within him, turned cold to the roots of his hair. Then the old woman said disgustedly, "Have the winds warned you of this, my idiot?"

And with astonishing force and accuracy she picked up a ripe fruit and flung it at Treon.

"Stop your mouth with that," she told him. "I am weary to death of your prophecies."

Treon looked at the crimson juice trickling slowly down the breast of his tunic, to drip upon the carving in his lap. The half formed head was covered with it. Treon was shaken with silent mirth.

"Well," said Varra, coming up to Stark, "what do you think of the Lhari? The proud Lhari, who would not stoop to mingle their blood with the cattle of the swamps. My half-witted brother, my worthless cousins, that little monster Bor who is the last twig of the tree—do you wonder I flew my falcon at Egil?"

She waited for an answer, her head thrown back, the silver curls framing her face like wisps of storm-cloud. There was a swagger about her that at once irritated and delighted Stark. A hellcat, he thought, but a mighty fetching one, and bold as brass. Bold—and honest. Her lips were parted, midway between anger and a smile.

He caught her to him suddenly and kissed her, holding her slim strong body as though she were a doll. He was in no hurry to set her down. When at last he did, he grinned and said, "Was that what you wanted?"

"Yes," answered Varra. "That was what I wanted." She spun about, her jaw set dangerously. "Grandmother . . ."

She got no farther. Stark saw that the old woman was attempting to sit upright, her face purpling with effort and the most terrible wrath he had ever seen.

"You," she gasped at the girl. She choked on her fury and her shortness of breath, and then Egil came soft-footed into the light, bearing in his hand a thing made of black metal and oddly shaped, with a blunt, thick muzzle.

"Lie back, Grandmother," he said. "I had a mind to use this on Varra—"

Even as he spoke he pressed a stud, and Stark in the act of leaping for the sheltering darkness, crashed down and lay like a dead man. There had been no sound, no flash, nothing, but a vast hand that smote him suddenly into oblivion.

Egil finished,—"but I see a better target."

6

Red. Red. Red. The color of blood. Blood in his eyes. He was remembering now. The quarry had turned on him, and they had fought on the bare, blistering rocks.

Nor had N'Chaka killed. The Lord of the Rocks was very big, a giant among lizards, and N'Chaka was small. The Lord of the Rocks had laid open N'Chaka's head before the wooden spear had more than scratched his flank.

It was strange that N'Chaka still lived. The Lord of the Rocks must have been full fed. Only that had saved him.

N'Chaka groaned, not with pain, but with shame. He had failed. Hoping for a great triumph, he had disobeyed the tribal law that forbids a boy to hunt the quarry of a man, and he had failed. Old One would not reward him with the girdle and the flint spear of manhood. Old One would give him to the women for the punishment of little whips. Tika would laugh at him, and it would be many seasons before Old One would grant him permission to try the Man's Hunt.

Blood in his eyes.

He blinked to clear them. The instinct of survival was prodding him. He must arouse himself and creep away, before the Lord of the Rocks returned to eat him.

The redness would not go away. It swam and flowed, strangely sparkling. He blinked again, and tried to lift his head, and could not, and fear struck down upon him like the iron frost of night upon the rocks of the valley.

It was all wrong. He could see himself clearly, a naked boy dizzy with pain, rising and clambering over the ledges and the shale to the safety of the cave. He could see that, and yet he could not move.

All wrong. Time, space, the universe, darkened and turned.

A voice spoke to him. A girl's voice. Not Tika's and the speech was strange.

Tika was dead. Memories rushed through his mind, the bitter things, the cruel things. Old One was dead, and all the others . . .

The voice spoke again, calling him by a name that was not his own.

Stark.

Memory shattered into a kaleidoscope of broken pictures, fragments, rushing, spinning. He was adrift among them. He was lost, and the terror of it brought a scream into his throat.

Soft hands touching his face, gentle words, swift and soothing. The redness cleared and steadied, though it did not go away, and quite suddenly he was himself again, with all his memories where they belonged.

He was lying on his back, and Zareth, Malthor's daughter, was looking down at him. He knew now what the redness was. He had seen it too often before not to know. He was somewhere at the bottom of the Red Sea—that weird ocean in which a man can breathe.

And he could not move. That had not changed, nor gone away. His body was dead.

The terror he had felt before was nothing to the agony that filled him now. He lay entombed in his own flesh, staring up at Zareth, wanting an answer to a question he dared not ask.

She understood, from the look in his eyes.

"It's all right," she said, and smiled. "It will wear off. You'll be all right. It's only the weapon of the Lhari. Somehow it puts the body to sleep, but it will wake again."

Stark remembered the black object that Egil had held in his hands. A projector of some sort, then, beaming a current of high-frequency vibration that paralyzed the nerve centers. He was amazed. The Cloud People were barbarians themselves, though on a higher scale than the swamp-edge tribes, and certainly had no such scientific proficiency. He wondered where the Lhari had got hold of such a weapon.

It didn't really matter. Not just now. Relief swept over him, bringing him dangerously close to tears. The effect would wear off. At the moment, that was all he cared about.

He looked up at Zareth again. Her pale hair floated with the slow breathing of the sea, a milky cloud against the spark-shot crimson. He saw now that her face was drawn and shadowed, and there was a terrible hopelessness in her eyes. She had been alive when he first saw her—frightened, not too bright, but full of emotion and a certain dogged courage. Now the spark was gone, crushed out.

She wore a collar around her white neck, a ring of dark metal with the ends fused together for all time.

"Where are we?" he asked.

And she answered, her voice carrying deep and hollow in the dense substance of the sea, "We are in the place of the Lost Ones."

Stark looked beyond her, as far as he could see, since he was unable to turn his head. And wonder came to him.

Black walls, black vault above him, a vast hall filled with the wash of the sea that slipped in streaks of whispering flame through the high embrasures. A hall that was twin to the vault of shadows where he had met the Lhari.

"There is a city," said Zareth dully. "You will see it soon. You will see nothing else until you die."

Stark said, very gently, "How do you come here, little one?"

"Because of my father. I will tell you all I know, which is little enough. Malthor has been slaver to the Lhari for a long time. There are a number of them among the captains of Shuruun, but that is a thing that is never spoken of—so I, his daughter, could only guess. I was sure of it when he sent me after you."

She laughed, a bitter sound. "Now I'm here, with the collar of the Lost Ones on my neck. But Malthor is here, too." She laughed again, ugly laughter to come from a young mouth. Then she looked at Stark, and her hand reached out timidly to touch his hair in what was almost a caress. Her eyes were wide, and soft, and full of tears.

"Why didn't you go into the swamps when I warned you?"

Stark answered stolidly, "Too late to worry about that now." Then, "You say Malthor is here, a slave?"

"Yes." Again, that look of wonder and admiration in her eyes. "I don't know what you said or did to the Lhari, but the Lord Egil came down in a black rage and cursed my father for a bungling fool because he could not hold you. My father whined and made excuses, and all would have been well—only his curiosity got the better of him and he asked the Lord Egil what had happened. You were like a wild beast, Malthor said, and he hoped you had not harmed the Lady Varra, as he could see from Egil's wounds that there had been trouble.

"The Lord Egil turned quite purple. I thought he was going to fall in a fit."

"Yes," said Stark. "That was the wrong thing to say." The ludicrous side of it struck him, and he was suddenly roaring with laughter. "Malthor should have kept his mouth shut!"

"Egil called his guard and ordered them to take Malthor. And when he realized what had happened, Malthor turned on me, trying to say that it was all my fault, that I let you escape."

Stark stopped laughing.

Her voice went on slowly, "Egil seemed quite mad with fury. I have heard that the Lhari are all mad, and I think it is so. At any rate, he ordered me taken too, for he wanted to stamp Malthor's seed into the mud forever. So we are here."

There was a long silence. Stark could think of no word of comfort, and as for hope, he had better wait until he was sure he could at least raise his head. Egil might have damaged him permanently, out of spite. In fact, he was surprised he wasn't dead.

He glanced again at the collar on Zareth's neck. Slave. Slave to the Lhari, in the City of the Lost Ones.

What the devil did they do with slaves, at the bottom of the sea?

The heavy gases conducted sound remarkably well, except for an odd property of diffusion which made it seem that a voice came from everywhere at once. Now, all at once, Stark became aware of a dull clamor of voices drifting towards him.

He tried to see, and Zareth turned his head carefully so that he might.

The Lost Ones were returning from whatever work it was they did.

Out of the dim red murk beyond the open door they swam, into the long, long vastness of the hall that was filled with the same red murk, moving slowly, their white bodies trailing wakes of sullen flame. The host of the damned drifting through a strange red-lit hell, weary and without hope.

One by one they sank onto pallets laid in rows on the black stone floor, and lay there, utterly exhausted, their pale hair lifting and floating with the slow eddies of the sea. And each one wore a collar.

One man did not lie down. He came toward Stark, a tall barbarian who drew himself with great strokes of his arms so that he was wrapped in wheeling sparks. Stark knew his face.

"Helvi," he said, and smiled in welcome.

"Brother!"

Helvi crouched down—a great handsome boy he had been the time Stark saw him, but he was a man now, with all the laughter turned to grim deep lines around his mouth and the bones of his face standing out like granite ridges.

"Brother," he said again, looking at Stark through a glitter of unashamed tears. "Fool." And he cursed Stark savagely because he had come to Shuruun to look for an idiot who had gone the same way, and was already as good as dead.

"Would you have followed me?" asked Stark.

"But I am only an ignorant child of the swamps," said Helvi. "You come from space, you know the other worlds, you can read and write—you should have better sense!"

Stark grinned. "And I'm still an ignorant child of the rocks. So we're two fools together. Where is Tobal?"

Tobal was Helvi's brother, who had broken taboo and looked for refuge in Shuruun. Apparently he had found peace at last, for Helvi shook his head.

"A man cannot live too long under the sea. It is not enough merely to breathe and eat. Tobal overran his time, and I am close to the end of mine." He held up his hand and then swept it down sharply, watching the broken fires dance along his arms.

"The mind breaks before the body," said Helvi casually, as though it were a matter of no importance.

Zareth spoke. "Helvi has guarded you each period while the others slept."

"And not I alone," said Helvi. "The little one stood with me."

"Guarded me!" said Stark. "Why?"

For answer, Helvi gestured toward a pallet not far away. Malthor lay there, his eyes half open and full of malice, the fresh scar livid on his cheek.

"He feels," said Helvi, "that you should not have fought upon his ship."

Stark felt an inward chill of horror. To lie here helpless, watching Malthor come toward him with open fingers reaching for his helpless throat . . .

He made a passionate effort to move, and gave up, gasping. Helvi grinned.

"Now is the time I should wrestle you, Stark, for I never could throw you before." He gave Stark's head a shake, very gentle for all its apparent roughness. "You'll be throwing me again. Sleep now, and don't worry."

He settled himself to watch, and presently in spite of himself Stark slept, with Zareth curled at his feet like a little dog.

There was no time down there in the heart of the Red Sea. No daylight, no dawn, no space of darkness. No winds blew, no rain nor storm broke the endless silence.

Only the lazy currents whispered by on their way to nowhere, and the red sparks danced, and the great hall waited, remembering the past.

Stark waited, too. How long he never knew, but he was used to waiting. He had learned his patience on the knees of the great mountains whose heads lift proudly into open space to look at the Sun, and he had absorbed their own contempt for time.

Little by little, life returned to his body. A mongrel guard came now and again to examine him, pricking Stark's flesh with his knife to test the reaction, so that Stark should not malinger.

He reckoned without Stark's control. The Earthman bore his prodding without so much as a twitch until his limbs were completely his own again. Then he sprang up and pitched the man half the length of the hall, turning over and over, yelling with startled anger.

At the next period of labor, Stark was driven with the rest out into the City of the Lost Ones.

7

Stark had been in places before that oppressed him with a sense of their strangeness or their wickedness—Sinharat, the lovely ruin of coral and gold lost in the Martian wastes; Jekkara, Valkis—the Low-Canal towns that smell of blood and wine; the cliff-caves of Arianrhod on the edge of Darkside, the buried tomb-cities of Callisto. But this—this was nightmare to haunt a man's dreams.

He stared about him as he went in the long line of slaves, and felt such a cold shuddering contraction of his belly as he had never known before.

Wide avenues paved with polished blocks of stone, perfect as ebon mirrors. Buildings, tall and stately, pure and plain, with a calm strength that could outlast the ages. Black, all black, with no fripperies of paint or carving to soften them, only here and there a window like a drowned jewel glinting through the red.

Vines like drifts of snow cascading down the stones. Gardens with close-clipped turf and flowers lifting bright on their green stalks, their petals open to a daylight that was gone, their heads bending as though to some forgotten breeze. All neat, all tended, the branches pruned, the fresh soil turned this morning—by whose hand?

Stark remembered the great forest dreaming at the bottom of the gulf, and shivered. He did not like to think how long ago these flowers must have opened their young bloom to the last light they were ever going to see. For they were dead—dead as the forest, dead as the city. Forever bright—and dead.

Stark thought that it must always have been a silent city. It was impossible to imagine noisy throngs flocking to a market square down those immense avenues. The black walls were not made to echo song or laughter. Even the children must have moved quietly along the garden paths, small wise creatures born to an ancient dignity.

He was beginning to understand now the meaning of that weird forest. The Gulf of Shuruun had not always been a gulf. It had been a valley, rich, fertile, with this great city in its arms, and here and there on the upper slopes the retreat of some noble or philosopher—of which the castle of the Lhari was a survivor.

A wall or rock had held back the Red Sea from this valley. And then, somehow, the wall had cracked, and the sullen crimson tide had flowed slowly, slowly into the fertile bottoms, rising higher, lapping the towers and the treetops in swirling flame, drowning the land forever. Stark wondered if the people had known the disaster was coming, if they had gone forth to tend their gardens for the last time so that they might remain perfect in the embalming gases of the sea.

The columns of slaves, herded by overseers armed with small black weapons similar to the one Egil had used, came out into a broad square whose farther edges were veiled in the red murk. And Stark looked on ruin.

A great building had fallen in the center of the square. The gods only knew what force had burst its walls and tossed the giant blocks like pebbles into a heap. But there it was, the one untidy thing in the city, a mountain of debris.

Nothing else was damaged. It seemed that this had been the place of temples, and they stood unharmed, ranked around the sides of the square, the dim fires rippling through their open porticoes. Deep in their inner shadows Stark thought he could make out images, gigantic things brooding in the spark-shot gloom.

He had no chance to study them. The overseers cursed them on, and now he saw what use the slaves were put to. They were clearing away the wreckage of the fallen building.

Helvi whispered, "For sixteen years men have slaved and died down here, and the work is not half done. And why do the Lhari want it done at all? I'll tell you why. Because they are mad, mad as swamp-dragons gone *musth* in the spring!"

It seemed madness indeed, to labor at this pile of rocks in a dead city at the bottom of the sea. It was madness. And yet the Lhari, though they might be insane, were not fools. There was a reason for it, and Stark was sure it was a good reason—good for the Lhari, at any rate.

An overseer came up to Stark, thrusting him roughly toward a sledge already partly loaded with broken rocks. Stark hesitated, his eyes turning ugly, and Helvi said,

"Come on, you fool! Do you want to be down flat on your back again?"

Stark glanced at the little weapon, blunt and ready, and turned reluctantly to obey. And there began his servitude.

It was a weird sort of life he led. For a while he tried to reckon time by the periods of work and sleep, but he lost count, and it did not greatly matter anyway.

He labored with the others, hauling the huge blocks away, clearing out the cellars that were partly bared, shoring up weak walls underground. The slaves clung to their old habit of thought, calling the work-periods "days" and the sleep-periods "nights."

Each "day" Egil, or his brother Cond, came to see what had been done, and went away black-browed and disappointed, ordering the work speeded up.

Treon was there also much of the time. He would come slowly in his awkward crabwise way and perch like a pale gargoyle on the stones, never speaking, watching with his sad beautiful eyes. He woke a vague foreboding in Stark. There was something awesome in Treon's silent patience, as though he waited the coming of some black doom, long delayed but inevitable. Stark would remember the prophecy, and shiver.

It was obvious to Stark after a while that the Lhari were clearing the building to get at the cellars underneath. The great dark caverns already bared had yielded nothing, but the brothers still hoped. Over and over Cond and Egil sounded the walls and the floors, prying here and there, and chafing at the delay in opening up the underground labyrinth. What they hoped to find, no one knew.

Varra came, too. Alone, and often, she would drift down through the dim mist-fires and watch, smiling a secret smile, her hair like blown silver where the currents played with it. She had nothing but curt words for Egil, but she kept her eyes on the great dark Earthman, and there was a look in them that stirred his blood. Egil was not blind, and it stirred his too, but in a different way.

Zareth saw that look. She kept as close to Stark as possible, asking no favors, but following him around with a sort of quiet devotion, seeming contented only when she was near him. One "night" in the slave barracks she crouched beside his pallet, her hand on his bare knee. She did not speak, and her face was hidden by the floating masses of her hair.

Stark turned her head so that he could see her, pushing the pale cloud gently away.

"What troubles you, little sister?"

Her eyes were wide and shadowed with some vague fear. But she only said, "It's not my place to speak."

"Why not?"

"Because . . ." Her mouth trembled, and then suddenly she said, "Oh, it's foolish, I know. But the woman of the Lhari . . ."

"What about her?"

"She watches you. Always she watches you! And the Lord Egil is angry. There is something in her mind, and it will bring you only evil. I know it!"

"It seems to me," said Stark wryly, "that the Lhari have already done as much evil as possible to all of us."

"No," answered Zareth, with an odd wisdom. "Our hearts are still clean."

Stark smiled. He leaned over and kissed her. "I'll be careful, little sister."

Quite suddenly she flung her arms around his neck and clung to him tightly, and Stark's face sobered. He patted her, rather awkwardly, and then she had gone, to curl up on her own pallet with her head buried in her arms.

Stark lay down. His heart was sad, and there was a stinging moisture in his eyes.

The red eternities dragged on. Stark learned what Helvi had meant when he said that the mind broke before the body. The sea bottom was no place for creatures of the upper air. He learned also the meaning of the metal collars, and the manner of Tobal's death.

Helvi explained.

"There are boundaries laid down. Within them we may range, if we have the strength and the desire after work. Beyond them we may not go. And there is no chance of escape by breaking through the barrier. How this is done I do not understand, but it is so, and the collars are the key to it.

"When a slave approaches the barrier the collar brightens as though with fire, and the slave falls. I have tried this myself, and I know. Half paralyzed, you may still crawl back to safety. But if you are mad, as Tobal was, and charge the barrier strongly . . ."

He made a cutting motion with his hands.

Stark nodded. He did not attempt to explain electricity or electronic vibrations to Helvi, but it seemed plain enough that the force with which the Lhari kept their slaves in check was something of the sort. The collars acted as conductors, perhaps for the same type of beam that was generated in the hand-weapons. When the metal broke the invisible boundary line it triggered off a force-beam from the central power station, in the manner of the obedient electric eye that opens doors and rings alarm bells. First a warning—then death.

The boundaries were wide enough, extending around the city and enclosing a good bit of forest beyond it. There was no possibility of a slave hiding among the trees, because the collar could be traced by the same type of beam, turned to low power, and the punishment meted out to a retaken man was such that few were foolish enough to try that game.

The surface, of course, was utterly forbidden. The one unguarded spot was the island where the central power station was, and here the slaves were allowed to come sometimes at night. The Lhari had discovered that they lived longer and worked better if they had an occasional breath of air and a look at the sky.

Many times Stark made that pilgrimage with the others. Up from the red depths they would come, through the reeling bands of fire where the currents ran, through the clouds of crimson sparks and the sullen patches of stillness that were like pools of blood, a company of white ghosts shrouded in flame, rising from their tomb for a little taste of the world they had lost.

It didn't matter that they were so weary they had barely the strength to get back to the barracks and sleep. They found the strength. To walk again on the open ground, to be rid of the eternal crimson dusk and the oppressive weight on the chest—to look up into the hot blue night of Venus and smell the fragrance of the *liha*-trees borne on the land wind . . . They found the strength.

They sang here, sitting on the island rocks and staring through the mists toward the shore they would never see again. It was their chanting that Stark had heard when he came down the gulf with Malthor, that wordless cry of grief and loss. Now he was here himself, holding Zareth close to comfort her and joining his own deep voice into that primitive reproach to the gods.

While he sat, howling like the savage he was, he studied the power plant, a squat blockhouse of a place. On the nights the slaves came guards were stationed outside to warn them away. The blockhouse was doubly guarded with the shock-beam. To attempt to take it by force would only mean death for all concerned.

Stark gave that idea up for the time being. There was never a second when escape was not in his thoughts, but he was too old in the game to break his neck against a stone wall. Like Malthor, he would wait.

Zareth and Helvi both changed after Stark's coming. Though they never talked of breaking free, both of them lost their air of hopelessness. Stark made neither plans nor promises. But Helvi knew him from of old, and the girl had her own subtle understanding, and they held up their heads again.

Then, one "day" as the work was ending, Varra came smiling out of the red murk and beckoned to him, and Stark's heart gave a great leap. Without a backward look he left Helvi and Zareth, and went with her, down the wide still avenue that led outward to the forest.

8

They left the stately buildings and the wide spaces behind them, and went in among the trees. Stark hated the forest. The city was bad enough, but it was dead, honestly dead, except for those neat nightmare gardens. There was something terrifying about these great trees, full-leafed and green, rioting with flowering vines and all the rich undergrowth of the jungle, standing like massed corpses made lovely by mortuary art. They swayed and rustled as the coiling fires swept them, branches bending to that silent horrible parody of wind. Stark always felt trapped there, and stifled by the stiff leaves and the vines.

But he went, and Varra slipped like a silver bird between the great trunks, apparently happy.

"I have come here often, ever since I was old enough. It's wonderful. Here I can stoop and fly like one of my own hawks." She laughed and plucked a golden flower to set in her hair, and then darted away again, her white legs flashing.

Stark followed. He could see what she meant. Here in this strange sea one's motion was as much flying as swimming, since the pressure equalized the weight of the body. There was a queer sort of thrill in plunging headlong from the treetops, to arrow down through a tangle of vines and branches and then sweep upward again.

She was playing with him, and he knew it. The challenge got his blood up. He could have caught her easily but he did not, only now and again he circled her to show his strength. They sped on and on, trailing wakes of flame, a black hawk chasing a silver dove through the forests of a dream.

But the dove had been fledged in an eagle's nest. Stark wearied of the game at last. He caught her and they clung together, drifting still among the trees with the momentum of that wonderful weightless flight.

Her kiss at first was lazy, teasing and curious. Then it changed. All Stark's smoldering anger leaped into a different kind of flame. His handling of her was rough and cruel, and she laughed, a little fierce voiceless laugh, and gave it back to him, and remembered how he had thought her mouth was like a bitter fruit that would give a man pain when he kissed it.

She broke away at last and came to rest on a broad branch, leaning back against the trunk and laughing, her eyes brilliant and cruel as Stark's own. And Stark sat down at her feet.

"What do you want?" he demanded. "What do you want with me?"

She smiled. There was nothing sidelong or shy about her. She was bold as a new blade.

"I'll tell you, wild man."

He started. "Where did you pick up that name?"

"I have been asking the Earthman Larrabee about you. It suits you well." She leaned forward. "This is what I want of you. Slay me Egil and his brother Cond. Also Bor, who will grow up worse than either—although that I can do myself, if you're averse to killing children, though Bor is more monster than child. Grandmother can't live forever, and with my cousins out of the way she's no threat. Treon doesn't count."

"And if I do—what then?"

"Freedom. And me. You'll rule Shuruun at my side."

Stark's eyes were mocking. "For how long, Varra?"

"Who knows? And what does it matter? The years take care of themselves." She shrugged. "The Lhari blood has run out, and it's time there was a fresh strain. Our children will rule after us, and they'll be men."

Stark laughed. He roared with it.

"It's not enough that I'm a slave to the Lhari. Now I must be executioner and herd bull as well!" He looked at her keenly. "Why me, Varra? Why pick on me?"

"Because, as I have said, you are the first man I have seen since my father died. Also, there is something about you . . ."

She pushed herself upward to hover lazily, her lips just brushing his.

"Do you think it would be so bad a thing to live with me, wild man?"

She was lovely and maddening, a silver witch shining among the dim fires of the sea, full of wickedness and laughter. Stark reached out and drew her to him.

"Not bad," he murmured. "Dangerous."

He kissed her, and she whispered, "I think you're not afraid of danger."

"On the contrary, I'm a cautious man." He held her off, where he could look straight into her eyes. "I owe Egil something on my own, but I will not murder. The fight must be fair, and Cond will have to take care of himself."

"Fair! Was Egil fair with you—or me?"

He shrugged. "My way, or not at all."

She thought it over a while, then nodded. "All right. As for Cond, you will give him a blood debt, and pride will make him fight. The Lhari are all proud," she added bitterly. "That's our curse. But it's bred in the bone, as you'll find out."

"One more thing. Zareth and Helvi are to go free, and there must be an end to this slavery."

She stared at him. "You drive a hard bargain, wild man!"

"Yes or no?"

"Yes and no. Zareth and Helvi you may have, if you insist, though the gods know what you see in that pallid child. As to the other . . ." She smiled very mockingly. "I'm no fool, Stark. You're evading me, and two can play that game."

He laughed. "Fair enough. And now tell me this, witch with the silver curls— how am I to get at Egil that I may kill him?"

"I'll arrange that."

She said it with such vicious assurance that he was pretty sure she would arrange it. He was silent for a moment, and then he asked,

"Varra—what are the Lhari searching for at the bottom of the sea?"

She answered slowly, "I told you that we are a proud clan. We were driven out of the High Plateaus centuries ago because of our pride. Now it's all we have left, but it's a driving thing."

She paused, and then went on. "I think we had known about the city for a long time, but it had never meant anything until my father became fascinated by it. He would stay down here days at a time, exploring, and it was he who found the weapons and the machine of power which is on the island. Then he found the chart and the metal book, hidden away in a secret place. The book was written in pictographs—as though it was meant to be deciphered—and the chart showed the square with the ruined building and the temples, with a separate diagram of catacombs underneath the ground.

"The book told of a secret—a thing of wonder and of fear. And my father believed that the building had been wrecked to close the entrance to the catacombs where the secret was kept. He determined to find it."

Sixteen years of other men's lives. Stark shivered. "What was the secret, Varra?"

"The manner of controlling life. How it was done I do not know, but with it one might build a race of giants, of monsters, or of gods. You can see what that would mean to us, a proud and dying clan."

"Yes," Stark answered slowly. "I can see."

The magnitude of the idea shook him. The builders of the city must have been wise indeed in their scientific research to evolve such a terrible power. To mold the living cells of the body to one's will—to create, not life itself but its form and fashion . . .

A race of giants, or of gods. The Lhari would like that. To transform their own degenerate flesh into something beyond the race of men, to develop their followers into a corps of fighting men that no one could stand against, to see that their children were given an unholy advantage over all the children of men . . . Stark was appalled at the realization of the evil they could do if they ever found that secret.

Varra said, "There was a warning in the book. The meaning of it was not quite clear, but it seemed that the ancient ones felt that they had sinned against the gods and been punished, perhaps by some plague. They were a strange race, and not human. At any rate, they destroyed the great building there as a barrier against anyone who should come after them, and then let the Red Sea in to cover their city forever. They must have been superstitious children, for all their knowledge."

"Then you all ignored the warning, and never worried that a whole city had died to prove it."

She shrugged. "Oh, Treon has been muttering prophecies about it for years. Nobody listens to him. As for myself, I don't care whether we find the secret or not. My belief is it was destroyed along with the building, and besides, I have no faith in such things."

"Besides," mocked Stark shrewdly, "you wouldn't care to see Egil and Cond striding across the heavens of Venus, and you're doubtful just what your own place would be in the new pantheon."

She showed her teeth at him. "You're too wise for your own good. And now goodbye." She gave him a quick, hard kiss and was gone, flashing upward, high above the treetops where he dared not follow.

Stark made his way slowly back to the city, upset and very thoughtful.

As he came back into the great square, heading toward the barracks, he stopped, every nerve taut.

Somewhere, in one of the shadowy temples, the clapper of a votive bell was swinging, sending its deep pulsing note across the silence. Slowly, slowly, like the beating of a dying heart it came, and mingled with it was the faint sound of Zareth's voice, calling his name.

9

He crossed the square, moving very carefully through the red murk, and presently he saw her.

It was not hard to find her. There was one temple larger than all the rest. Stark judged that it must once have faced the entrance of the fallen building, as though the great figure within was set to watch over the scientists and the philosophers who came there to dream their vast and sometimes terrible dreams.

The philosophers were gone, and the scientists had destroyed themselves. But the image still watched over the drowned city, its hand raised both in warning, and in benediction.

Now, across its reptilian knees, Zareth lay. The temple was open on all sides, and Stark could see her clearly, a little white scrap of humanity against the black unhuman figure.

Malthor stood beside her. It was he who had been tolling the votive bell. He had stopped now, and Zareth's words came clearly to Stark.

"Go away, go away! They're waiting for you. Don't come in here!"

"I'm waiting for you, Stark," Malthor called out, smiling. "Are you afraid to come?" And he took Zareth by the hair and struck her, slowly and deliberately, twice across the face.

All expression left Stark's face, leaving it perfectly blank except for his eyes, which took on a sudden lambent gleam. He began to move toward the temple, not hurrying even then, but moving in such a way that it seemed an army could not have stopped him.

Zareth broke free from her father. Perhaps she was intended to break free.

"Egil!" she screamed. "It's a trap . . ."

Again Malthor caught her and this time he struck her harder, so that she crumpled down again across the image that watched with its jeweled, gentle eyes and saw nothing.

"She's afraid for you," said Malthor. "She knows I mean to kill you if I can. Well, perhaps Egil is here also. Perhaps he is not. But certainly Zareth is here. I have beaten her well, and I shall beat her again, as long as she lives to be beaten, for her treachery to me. And if you want to save her from that, you outland dog, you'll have to kill me. Are you afraid?"

Stark was afraid. Malthor and Zareth were alone in the temple. The pillared colonnades were empty except for the dim fires of the sea. Yet Stark was afraid, for an instinct older than speech warned him to be.

It did not matter. Zareth's white skin was mottled with dark bruises, and Malthor was smiling at him, and it did not matter.

Under the shadow of the roof and down the colonnade he went, swiftly now, leaving a streak of fire behind him. Malthor looked into his eyes, and his smile trembled and was gone.

He crouched. And at the last moment, when the dark body plunged down at him as a shark plunges, he drew a hidden knife from his girdle and struck.

Stark had not counted on that. The slaves were searched for possible weapons every day, and even a sliver of stone was forbidden. Somebody must have given it to him, someone . . .

The thought flashed through his mind while he was in the very act of trying to avoid that death blow. *Too late, too late, because his own momentum carried him onto the point . . .*

Reflexes quicker than any man's, the hair-trigger reactions of a wild thing. Muscles straining, the center of balance shifted with an awful wrenching effort, hands grasping at the fire-shot redness as though to force it to defy its own laws. The blade ripped a long shallow gash across his breast. But it did not go home. By a fraction of an inch, it did not go home.

While Stark was still off balance, Malthor sprang.

They grappled. The knife blade glittered redly, a hungry tongue eager to taste Stark's life. The two men rolled over and over, drifting and tumbling erratically, churning the sea to a froth of sparks, and still the image watched, its calm reptilian features unchangingly benign and wise. Threads of a darker red laced heavily across the dancing fires.

Stark got Malthor's arm under his own and held it there with both hands. His back was to the man now. Malthor kicked and clawed with his feet against the backs of Stark's thighs, and his left arm came up and tried to clamp around Stark's throat. Stark buried his chin so that it could not, and then Malthor's hand began to tear at Stark's face, searching for his eyes.

Stark voiced a deep bestial sound in his throat. He moved his head suddenly, catching Malthor's hand between his jaws. He did not let go. Presently his teeth were locked against the thumb-joint, and Malthor was screaming, but Stark could give all his attention to what he was doing with the arm that held the knife. His eyes had changed. They were all beast now, the eyes of a killer blazing cold and beautiful in his dark face.

There was a dull crack, and the arm ceased to strain or fight. It bent back upon itself, and the knife fell, drifting quietly down. Malthor was beyond screaming now. He made one effort to get away as Stark released him, but it was a futile gesture, and he made no sound as Stark broke his neck.

He thrust the body from him. It drifted away, moving lazily with the suck of the currents through the colonnade, now and again touching a black pillar as though in casual wonder, wandering out at last into the square. Malthor was in no hurry. He had all eternity before him.

Stark moved carefully away from the girl, who was trying feebly now to sit up on the knees of the image. He called out, to some unseen presence hidden in the shadows under the roof,

"Malthor screamed your name, Egil. Why didn't you come?"

There was a flicker of movement in the intense darkness of the ledge at the top of the pillars.

"Why should I?" asked the Lord Egil of the Lhari. "I offered him his freedom if he could kill you, but it seems he could not—even though I gave him a knife, and drugs to keep your friend Helvi out of the way."

He came out where Stark could see him, very handsome in a tunic of yellow silk, the blunt black weapon in his hands.

"The important thing was to bait a trap. You would not face me because of this—" He raised the weapon. "I might have killed you as you worked, of course, but my family would have had hard things to say about that. You're a phenomenally good slave."

"They'd have said hard words like 'coward,' Egil," Stark said softly. "And Varra would have set her bird at you in earnest."

Egil nodded. His lip curved cruelly. "Exactly. That amused you, didn't it? And now my little cousin is training another falcon to swoop at me. She hooded you today, didn't she, Outlander?"

He laughed. "Ah well. I didn't kill you openly because there's a better way. Do you think I want it gossiped all over the Red Sea that my cousin jilted me for a foreign slave? Do you think I wish it known that I hated you, and why? No. I would have killed Malthor anyway, if you hadn't done it, because he knew. And when I have killed you and the girl I shall take your bodies to the barrier and leave them there together, and it will be obvious to everyone, even Varra, that you were killed trying to escape."

The weapon's muzzle pointed straight at Stark, and Egil's finger quivered on the trigger stud. Full power, this time. Instead of paralysis, death. Stark measured the distance between himself and Egil. He would be dead before he struck, but the impetus of his leap might carry him on, and give Zareth a chance to escape. The muscles of his thighs stirred and tensed.

A voice said, "And it will be obvious how and why *I* died, Egil? For if you kill them, you must kill me too."

Where Treon had come from, or when, Stark did not know. But he was there by the image, and his voice was full of a strong music, and his eyes shone with a fey light.

Egil had started, and now he swore in fury. "You idiot! You twisted freak! How did you come here?"

"How does the wind come, and the rain? I am not as other men." He laughed, a somber sound with no mirth in it. "I am here, Egil, and that's all that matters. And you will not slay this stranger who is more beast than man, and more man than any of us. The gods have a use for him."

He had moved as he spoke, until now he stood between Stark and Egil.

"Get out of the way," said Egil.

Treon shook his head.

"Very well," said Egil. "If you wish to die, you may."

The fey gleam brightened in Treon's eyes. "This is a day of death," he said softly, "but not of his, or mine."

Egil said a short, ugly word, and raised the weapon up.

Things happened very quickly after that. Stark sprang, arching up and over Treon's head, cleaving the red gases like a burning arrow. Egil started back, and shifted his aim upward, and his finger snapped down on the trigger stud.

Something white came between Stark and Egil, and took the force of the bolt.

Something white. A girl's body, crowned with streaming hair, and a collar of metal glowing bright around the slender neck.

Zareth.

They had forgotten her, the beaten child crouched on the knees of the image. Stark had moved to keep her out of danger, and she was no threat to the mighty Egil, and Treon's thoughts were known only to himself and the winds that taught him. Unnoticed, she had crept to a place where one last plunge would place her between Stark and death.

The rush of Stark's going took him on over her, except that her hair brushed softly against his skin. Then he was on top of Egil, and it had all been done so swiftly that the Lord of the Lhari had not had time to loose another bolt.

Stark tore the weapon from Egil's hand. He was cold, icy cold, and there was a strange blindness on him, so that he could see nothing clearly but Egil's face. And it was Stark who screamed this time, a dreadful sound like the cry of a great cat gone beyond reason or fear.

Treon stood watching. He watched the blood stream darkly into the sea, and he listened to the silence come, and he saw the thing that had been his cousin drift away on the slow tide, and it was as though he had seen it all before and was not surprised.

Stark went to Zareth's body. The girl was still breathing, very faintly, and her eyes turned to Stark, and she smiled.

Stark was blind now with tears. All his rage had run out of him with Egil's blood, leaving nothing but an aching pity and a sadness, and a wondering awe. He took Zareth very tenderly into his arms and held her, dumbly, watching the tears fall on her upturned face. And presently he knew that she was dead.

Sometime later Treon came to him and said softly, "To this end she was born, and she knew it, and was happy. Even now she smiles. And she should, for she had a better death than most of us." He laid his hand on Stark's shoulder. "Come, I'll show you where to put her. She will be safe there, and tomorrow you can bury her where she would wish to be."

Stark rose and followed him, bearing Zareth in his arms.

Treon went to the pedestal on which the image sat. He pressed in a certain way upon a series of hidden springs, and a section of the paving slid noiselessly back, revealing stone steps leading down.

10

Treon led the way down, into darkness that was lightened only by the dim fires they themselves woke in passing. No currents ran here. The red gas lay dull and stagnant, closed within the walls of a square passage built of the same black stone.

"These are the crypts," he said. "The labyrinth that is shown on the chart my father found." And he told about the chart, as Varra had.

He led the way surely, his misshapen body moving without hesitation past the mouths of branching corridors and the doors of chambers whose interiors were lost in shadow.

"The history of the city is here. All the books and the learning, that they had not the heart to destroy. There are no weapons. They were not a warlike people, and I think that the force we of the Lhari have used differently was defensive only, protection against the beasts and the raiding primitives of the swamps."

With a great effort, Stark wrenched his thoughts away from the light burden he carried.

"I thought," he said dully, "that the crypts were under the wrecked building."

"So we all thought. We were intended to think so. That is why the building was wrecked. And for sixteen years we of the Lhari have killed men and women with dragging the stones of it away. But the temple was shown also in the chart. We thought it was there merely as a landmark, an identification for the great building. But I began to wonder . . ."

"How long have you known?"

"Not long. Perhaps two rains. It took many seasons to find the secret of this passage. I came here at night when the others slept."

"And you didn't tell?"

"No!" said Treon. "You are thinking that if I had told, there would have been an end to the slavery and the death. But what then? My family, turned loose with the power to destroy a world, as this city was destroyed? No! It was better for the slaves to die."

He motioned Stark aside, then, between doors of gold that stood ajar, into a vault so great that there was no guessing its size in the red and shrouding gloom.

"This was the burial place of their kings," said Treon softly. "Leave the little one here."

Stark looked around him, still too numb to feel awe, but impressed even so.

They were set in straight lines, the beds of black marble—lines so long that there was no end to them except the limit of vision. And on them slept the old kings, their bodies, marvelously embalmed, covered with silken palls, their hands crossed upon their breasts, their wise unhuman faces stamped with the mark of peace.

Very gently, Stark laid Zareth down on a marble couch, and covered her also with silk, and closed her eyes and folded her hands. And it seemed to him that her face, too, had that look of peace.

He went out with Treon, thinking that none of them had earned a better place in the hall of kings than Zareth.

"Treon," he said.

"Yes?"

"That prophecy you spoke when I came to the castle—I will bear it out."

Treon nodded. "That is the way of prophecies."

He did not return toward the temple, but led the way deeper into the heart of the catacombs. A great excitement burned within him, a bright and terrible thing that communicated itself to Stark. Treon had suddenly taken on the stature of a figure of destiny, and the Earthman had the feeling that he was in the grip of some current that would plunge on irresistibly until everything in its path was swept away. Stark's flesh quivered.

They reached the end of the corridor at last. And there, in the red gloom, a shape sat waiting before a black, barred door. A shape grotesque and incredibly misshapen, so horribly malformed that by it Treon's crippled body appeared almost beautiful. Yet its face was as the faces of the images and the old kings, and its sunken eyes had once held wisdom, and one of its seven-fingered hands was still slim and sensitive.

Stark recoiled. The thing made him physically sick, and he would have turned away, but Treon urged him on.

"Go closer. It is dead, embalmed, but it has a message for you. It has waited all this time to give that message."

Reluctantly, Stark went forward.

Quite suddenly, it seemed that the thing spoke.

Behold me. Look upon me, and take counsel before you grasp that power which lies beyond the door!

Stark leaped back, crying out, and Treon smiled.

"It was so with me. But I have listened to it many times since then. It speaks not with a voice, but within the mind, and only when one has passed a certain spot."

Stark's reasoning mind pondered over that. A thought-record, obviously, triggered off by an electronic beam. The ancients had taken good care that their warning would be heard and understood by anyone who should solve the riddle of the catacombs. Thought-images, speaking directly to the brain, know no barrier of time or language.

He stepped forward again, and once more the telepathic voice spoke to him.

"We tampered with the secrets of the gods. We intended no evil. It was only that we love perfection, and wished to shape all living things as flawless as our buildings and our gardens. We did not know that it was against the Law . . .

"I was one of those who found the way to change the living cell. We used the unseen force that comes from the Land of the Gods beyond the sky, and we so harnessed it that we could build from the living flesh as the potter builds from the clay. We healed the halt and the maimed, and made those stand tall and straight who came crooked from the egg, and for a time we were as brothers to the gods themselves. I myself, even I, knew the glory of perfection. And then came the reckoning.

"The cell, once made to change, would not stop changing. The growth was slow, and for a while we did not notice it, but when we did it was too late. We were becoming a city of monsters. And the force we had used was worse than useless, for the more we tried to mold the monstrous flesh to its normal shape, the more the stimulated cells grew and grew, until the bodies we labored over were like things of wet mud that flow and change even as you look at them.

"One by one the people of the city destroyed themselves. And those of us who were left realized the judgment of the gods, and our duty. We made all things ready, and let the Red Sea hide us forever from our own kind, and those who should come after.

"Yet we did not destroy our knowledge. Perhaps it was our pride only that forbade us, but we could not bring ourselves to do it. Perhaps other gods, other races wiser than we, can take away the evil and keep only the good. For it is good for all creatures to be, if not perfect, at least strong and sound.

"But heed this warning, whoever you may be that listen. If your gods are jealous, if your people have not the wisdom or the knowledge to succeed where we failed in controlling this force, then touch it not! Or you, and all your people, will become as I."

The voice stopped. Stark moved back again, and said to Treon incredulously, "And your family would ignore that warning?"

Treon laughed. "They are fools. They are cruel and greedy and very proud. They would say that this was a lie to frighten away intruders, or that human flesh would not be subject to the laws that govern the flesh of reptiles. They would say anything, because they have dreamed this dream too long to be denied."

Stark shuddered and looked at the black door. "The thing ought to be destroyed."

"Yes," said Treon softly.

His eyes were shining, looking into some private dream of his own. He started forward, and when Stark would have gone with him he thrust him back, saying, "No. You have no part in this." He shook his head.

"I have waited," he whispered, almost to himself. "The winds bade me wait, until the day was ripe to fall from the tree of death. I have waited, and at dawn I knew, for the wind said, *Now is the gathering of the fruit at hand.*"

He looked suddenly at Stark, and his eyes had in them a clear sanity, for all their feyness.

"You heard, Stark. 'We made those stand tall and straight who came crooked from the egg'. I will have my hour. I will stand as a man for the little time that is left."

He turned, and Stark made no move to follow. He watched Treon's twisted body recede, white against the red dusk, until it passed the monstrous watcher and came to the black door. The long thin arms reached up and pushed the bar away.

The door swung slowly back. Through the opening Stark glimpsed a chamber that held a structure of crystal rods and discs mounted on a frame of metal, the whole thing glowing and glittering with a restless bluish light that dimmed and brightened as though it echoed some vast pulse-beat. There was other apparatus, intricate banks of tubes and condensers, but this was the heart of it, and the heart was still alive.

Treon passed within and closed the door behind him.

Stark drew back some distance from the door and its guardian, crouched down, and set his back against the wall. He thought about the apparatus. Cosmic rays, perhaps—the unseen force that came from beyond the sky. Even yet, all their potentialities were not known. But a few luckless spacemen had found that under certain conditions they could do amazing things to human tissue.

It was a line of thought Stark did not like at all. He tried to keep his mind away from Treon entirely. He tried not to think at all. It was dark there in the corridor, and very still, and the shapeless horror sat quiet in the doorway and waited with him. Stark began to shiver, a shallow animal-twitching of the flesh.

He waited. After a while he thought Treon must be dead, but he did not move. He did not wish to go into that room to see.

He waited.

Suddenly he leaped up, cold sweat bursting out all over him. A crash had echoed down the corridor, a clashing of shattered crystal and a high singing note that trailed off into nothing.

The door opened.

A man came out. A man tall and straight and beautiful as an angel, a strong-limbed man with Treon's face, Treon's tragic eyes. And behind him the chamber was dark. The pulsing heart of power had stopped.

The door was shut and barred again. Treon's voice was saying, "There are records left, and much of the apparatus, so that the secret is not lost entirely. Only it is out of reach."

He came to Stark and held out his hand. "Let us fight together, as men. And do not fear. I shall die, long before this body changes." He smiled, the remembered smile that was full of pity for all living things. "I know, for the winds have told me."

Stark took his hand and held it.

"Good," said Treon. "And now lead on, stranger with the fierce eyes. For the prophecy is yours, and the day is yours, and I who have crept about like a snail all my life know little of battles. Lead, and I will follow."

Stark fingered the collar around his neck. "Can you rid me of this?"

Treon nodded. "There are tools and acid in one of the chambers."

He found them, and worked swiftly, and while he worked Stark thought, smiling—and there was no pity in that smile at all.

They came back at last into the temple, and Treon closed the entrance to the catacombs. It was still night, for the square was empty of slaves. Stark found Egil's weapon where it had fallen, on the ledge where Egil died.

"We must hurry," said Stark. "Come on."

11

The island was shrouded heavily in mist and the blue darkness of the night. Stark and Treon crept silently among the rocks until they could see the glimmer of torchlight through the window-slits of the power station.

There were seven guards, five inside the blockhouse, two outside to patrol.

When they were close enough, Stark slipped away, going like a shadow, and never a pebble turned under his bare foot. Presently he found a spot to his liking and crouched down. A sentry went by not three feet away, yawning and looking hopefully at the sky for the first signs of dawn.

Treon's voice rang out, the sweet unmistakable voice. "Ho, there, guards!"

The sentry stopped and whirled around. Off around the curve of the stone wall someone began to run, his sandals thud-thudding on the soft ground, and the second guard came up.

"Who speaks?" one demanded. "The Lord Treon?"

They peered into the darkness, and Treon answered, "Yes." He had come forward far enough so that they could make out the pale blur of his face, keeping his body out of sight among the rocks and the shrubs that sprang up between them.

"Make haste," he ordered. "Bid them open the door, there." He spoke in breathless jerks, as though spent. "A tragedy—a disaster! Bid them open!"

One of the men leaped to obey, hammering on the massive door that was kept barred from the inside. The other stood goggle-eyed, watching. Then the door opened, spilling a flood of yellow torchlight into the red fog.

"What is it?" cried the men inside. "What has happened?"

"Come out!" gasped Treon. "My cousin is dead, the Lord Egil is dead, murdered by a slave."

He let that sink in. Three or more men came outside into the circle of light, and their faces were frightened, as though somehow they feared they might be held responsible for this thing.

"You know him," said Treon. "The great black-haired one from Earth. He has slain the Lord Egil and got away into the forest, and we need all extra guards to go after him, since many must be left to guard the other slaves, who are mutinous. You, and you—" He picked out the four biggest ones. "Go at once and join the search. I will stay here with the others."

It nearly worked. The four took a hesitant step or two, and then one paused and said doubtfully.

"But, my lord, it is forbidden that we leave our posts, for any reason. Any reason at all, my lord! The Lord Cond would slay us if we left this place."

"And you fear the Lord Cond more than you do me," said Treon philosophically. "Ah, well, I understand."

He stepped out, full into the light.

A gasp went up, and then a startled yell. The three men from me inside had come out armed only with swords, but the two sentries had their shock-weapons. One of them shrieked,

"It is a demon, who speaks with Treon's voice!"

And the two black weapons started up.

Behind them, Stark fired two silent bolts in quick succession, and the men fell, safely out of the way for hours. Then he leaped for the door.

He collided with two men who were doing the same thing. The third had turned to hold Treon off with his sword until they were safely inside.

Seeing that Treon, who was unarmed, was in danger of being spitted on the man's point, Stark fired between the two lunging bodies as he fell, and brought the guard down. Then he was involved in a thrashing tangle of arms and legs, and a lucky blow jarred the shock-weapon out of his hand.

Treon added himself to the fray. Pleasuring in his new strength, he caught one man by the neck and pulled him off. The guards were big men, and powerful, and they fought desperately. Stark was bruised and bleeding from a cut mouth before he could get in a finishing blow.

Someone rushed past him into the doorway. Treon yelled. Out of the tail of his eyes Stark saw the Lhari sitting dazed on the ground. The door was closing.

Stark hunched up his shoulders and sprang.

He hit the heavy panel with a jar that nearly knocked him breathless. It slammed open, and there was a cry of pain and the sound of someone falling. Stark burst through, to find the last of the guards rolling every which way over the floor. But one rolled over onto his feet again, drawing his sword as he rose. He had not had time before.

Stark continued his rush without stopping. He plunged headlong into the man before the point was clear of the scabbard, bore him over and down, and finished the man off with savage efficiency.

He leaped to his feet, breathing hard, spitting blood out of his mouth, and looked around the control room. But the others had fled, obviously to raise the warning.

The mechanism was simple. It was contained in a large black metal oblong about the size and shape of a coffin, equipped with grids and lenses and dials. It hummed softly to itself, but what its source of power was Stark did not know. Perhaps those same cosmic rays, harnessed to a different use.

He closed what seemed to be a master switch, and the humming stopped, and the flickering light died out of the lenses. He picked up the slain guard's sword and carefully wrecked everything that was breakable. Then he went outside again.

Treon was standing up, shaking his head. He smiled ruefully.

"It seems that strength alone is not enough," he said. "One must have skill as well."

"The barriers are down," said Stark. "The way is clear."

Treon nodded, and went with him back into the sea. This time both carried shock-weapons taken from the guards—six in all, with Egil's. Total armament for war.

As they forged swiftly through the red depths, Stark asked, "What of the people of Shuruun? How will they fight?"

Treon answered, "Those of Malthor's breed will stand for the Lhari. They must, for all their hope is there. The others will wait, until they see which side is safest. They would rise against the Lhari if they dared, for we have brought them only fear in their lifetimes. But they will wait, and see."

Stark nodded. He did not speak again.

They passed over the brooding city, and Stark thought of Egil and of Malthor who were part of that silence now, drifting slowly through the empty streets where the little currents took them, wrapped in their shrouds of dim fire.

He thought of Zareth sleeping in the hall of kings, and his eyes held a cold, cruel light.

They swooped down over the slave barracks. Treon remained on watch outside. Stark went in, taking with him the extra weapons.

The slaves still slept. Some of them dreamed, and moaned in their dreaming, and others might have been dead, with their hollow faces white as skulls.

Slaves. One hundred and four, counting the women.

Stark shouted out to them, and they woke, starting up on their pallets, their eyes full of terror. Then they saw who it was that called them, standing collarless and armed, and there was a great surging and a clamor that stilled as Stark shouted again, demanding silence. This time Helvi's voice echoed his. The tall barbarian had wakened from his drugged sleep.

Stark told them, very briefly, all that happened.

"You are freed from the collar," he said. "This day you can survive or die as men, and not slaves." He paused, then asked, "Who will go with me into Shuruun?"

They answered with one voice, the voice of the Lost Ones, who saw the red pall of death begin to lift from over them. The Lost Ones, who had found hope again.

Stark laughed. He was happy. He gave the extra weapons to Helvi and three others that he chose, and Helvi looked into his eyes and laughed too.

Treon spoke from the open door. "They are coming!"

Stark gave Helvi quick instructions and darted out, taking with him one of the other men. With Treon, they hid among the shrubbery of the garden that was outside the hall, patterned and beautiful, swaying its lifeless brilliance in the lazy drifts of fire.

The guards came. Twenty of them, tall armed men, to turn out the slaves for another period of labor, dragging the useless stones.

And the hidden weapons spoke with their silent tongues.

Eight of the guards fell inside the hall. Nine of them went down outside. Ten of the slaves died before the remaining three were overcome.

Now there were twenty swords among ninety-four slaves, counting the women.

They left the city and rose up over the dreaming forest, a flight of white ghosts with flames in their hair, coming back from the red dusk and the silence to find the light again.

Light, and vengeance.

The first pale glimmer of dawn was sifting through the clouds as they came up among the rocks below the castle of the Lhari. Stark left them and went like a shadow up the tumbled cliffs to where he had hidden his gun on the night he had first come to Shuruun. Nothing stirred. The fog lifted up from the sea like a vapor of blood, and the face of Venus was still dark. Only the high clouds were touched with pearl.

Stark returned to the others. He gave one of his shock-weapons to a swamp-lander with a cold madness in his eyes. Then he spoke a few final words to Helvi and went back with Treon under the surface of the sea.

Treon led the way. He went along the face of the submerged cliff, and presently he touched Stark's arm and pointed to where a round mouth opened in the rock.

"It was made long ago," said Treon, "so that the Lhari and their slavers might come and go and not be seen. Come—and be very quiet."

They swam into the tunnel mouth, and down the dark way that lay beyond, until the lift of the floor brought them out of the sea. Then they felt their way silently along, stopping now and again to listen.

Surprise was their only hope. Treon had said that with the two of them they might succeed. More men would surely be discovered, and meet a swift end at the hands of the guards.

Stark hoped Treon was right.

They came to a blank wall of dressed stone. Treon leaned his weight against one side, and a great block swung slowly around on a central pivot. Guttering torchlight came through the crack. By it Stark could see that the room beyond was empty.

They stepped through, and as they did so a servant in bright silks came yawning into the room with a fresh torch to replace the one that was dying.

He stopped in mid-step, his eyes widening. He dropped the torch. His mouth opened to shape a scream, but no sound came, and Stark remembered that these servants were tongueless—to prevent them from telling what they saw or heard in the castle, Treon said.

The man spun about and fled, down a long dim-lit hall. Stark ran him down without effort. He struck once with the barrel of his gun, and the man fell and was still.

Treon came up. His face had a look almost of exaltation, a queer shining of the eyes that made Stark shiver. He led on, through a series of empty rooms, all somber black, and they met no one else for a while.

He stopped at last before a small door of burnished gold. He looked at Stark once, and nodded, and thrust the panels open and stepped through.

12

They stood inside the vast echoing hall that stretched away into darkness until it seemed there was no end to it. The cluster of silver lamps burned as before, and within their circle of radiance the Lhari started up from their places and stared at the strangers who had come in through their private door.

Cond, and Arel with her hands idle in her lap. Bor, pummeling the little dragon to make it hiss and snap, laughing at its impotence. Varra, stroking the winged creature on her wrist, testing with her white finger the sharpness of its beak. And the old woman, with a scrap of fat meat halfway to her mouth.

They had stopped, frozen, in the midst of these actions. And Treon walked slowly into the light.

"Do you know me?" he said.

A strange shivering ran through them. Now, as before, the old woman spoke first, her eyes glittering with a look as rapacious as her appetite.

"You are Treon," she said, and her whole vast body shook.

The name went crying and whispering off around the dark walls, *Treon! Treon!*

Treon! Cond leaped forward, touching his cousin's straight strong body with hands that trembled.

"You have found it," he said. "The secret."

"Yes." Treon lifted his silver head and laughed, a beautiful ringing bell-note that sang from the echoing corners. "I found it, and it's gone, smashed, beyond your reach forever. Egil is dead, and the day of the Lhari is done."

There was a long, long silence, and then the old woman whispered, *"You lie!"*

Treon turned to Stark.

"Ask him, the stranger who came bearing doom upon his forehead. Ask him if I lie."

Cond's face became something less than human. He made a queer crazed sound and flung himself at Treon's throat.

Bor screamed suddenly. He alone was not much concerned with the finding or the losing of the secret, and he alone seemed to realize the significance of Stark's presence. He screamed, looking at the big dark man, and went rushing off down the hall, crying for the guard as he went, and the echoes roared and racketed. He fought open the great doors and ran out, and as he did so the sound of fighting came through from the compound.

The slaves, with their swords and clubs, with their stones and shards of rock, had come over the wall from the cliffs.

Stark had moved forward, but Treon did not need his help. He had got his hands around Cond's throat, and he was smiling. Stark did not disturb him.

The old woman was talking, cursing, commanding, choking on her own apoplectic breath. Arel began to laugh. She did not move, and her hands remained limp and open in her lap. She laughed and laughed, and Varra looked at Stark and hated him.

"You're a fool, wild man," she said. "You would not take what I offered you, so you shall have nothing—only death."

She slipped the hood from her creature and set it straight at Stark. Then she drew a knife from her girdle and plunged it into Treon's side.

Treon reeled back. His grip loosened and Cond tore away, half throttled, raging, his mouth flecked with foam. He drew his short sword and staggered in upon Treon.

Furious wings beat and thundered around Stark's head, and talons were clawing for his eyes. He reached up with his left hand and caught the brute by one leg and held it. Not long, but long enough to get one clear shot at Cond that dropped him in his tracks. Then he snapped the falcon's neck.

He flung the creature at Varra's feet, and picked up the gun again. The guards were rushing into the hall now at the lower end, and he began to fire at them.

Treon was sitting on the floor. Blood was coming in a steady trickle from his side, but he had the shock-weapon in his hands, and he was still smiling.

There was a great boiling roar of noise from outside. Men were fighting there, killing, dying, screaming their triumph or their pain. The echoes raged within the hall, and the noise of Stark's gun was like a hissing thunder. The guards, armed only with swords, went down like ripe wheat before the sickle, but there were many of them, too many for Stark and Treon to hold for long.

The old woman shrieked and shrieked, and was suddenly still.

Helvi burst in through the press, with a knot of collared slaves. The fight dissolved into a whirling chaos. Stark threw his gun away. He was afraid now of hitting his own men. He caught up a sword from a fallen guard and began to hew his way to the barbarian.

Suddenly Treon cried his name. He leaped aside, away from the man he was fighting, and saw Varra fall with the dagger still in her hand. She had come up behind him to stab, and Treon had seen and pressed the trigger stud just in time.

For the first time, there were tears in Treon's eyes.

A sort of sickness came over Stark. There was something horrible in this specta-cle of a family destroying itself. He was too much the savage to be sentimental over Varra, but all the same he could not bear to look at Treon for a while.

Presently he found himself back to back with Helvi, and as they swung their swords—the shock-weapons had been discarded for the same reason as Stark's gun—Helvi panted, "It has been a good fight, my brother! We cannot win, but we can have a good death, which is better than slavery!"

It looked as though Helvi was right. The slaves, unfortunately, weakened by their long confinement, worn out by overwork, were being beaten back. The tide turned, and Stark was swept with it out into the compound, fighting stubbornly.

The great gate stood open. Beyond it stood the people of Shuruun, watching, hanging back—as Treon had said, they would wait and see.

In the forefront, leaning on his stick, stood Larrabee the Earthman.

Stark cut his way free of the press. He leaped up onto the wall and stood there, breathing hard, sweating, bloody, with a dripping sword in his hand. He waved it, shouting down to the men of Shuruun.

"What are you waiting for, you scuts, you women? The Lhari are dead, the Lost Ones are freed—must we of Earth do all your work for you?"

And he looked straight at Larrabee.

Larrabee stared back, his dark suffering eyes full of a bitter mirth. "Oh, well," he said in English. "Why not?"

He threw back his head and laughed, and the bitterness was gone. He voiced a high, shrill rebel yell and lifted his stick like a cudgel, limping toward the gate, and the men of Shuruun gave tongue and followed him.

After that, it was soon over.

They found Bor's body in the stable pens, where he had fled to hide when the fighting started. The dragons, maddened by the smell of the blood, had slain him very quickly.

Helvi had come through alive, and Larrabee, who had kept himself carefully out of harm's way after he had started the men of Shuruun on their attack. Nearly half the slaves were dead, and the rest wounded. Of those who had served the Lhari, few were left.

Stark went back into the great hall. He walked slowly, for he was very weary, and where he set his foot there was a bloody print, and his arms were red to the elbows, and his breast was splashed with the redness. Treon watched him come, and smiled, nodding.

"It is as I said. And I have outlived them all."

Arel had stopped laughing at last. She had made no move to run away, and the tide of battle had rolled over her and drowned her unaware. The old woman lay still, a mountain of inert flesh upon her bed. Her hand still clutched a ripe fruit, clutched convulsively in the moment of death, the red juice dripping through her fingers.

"Now I am going, too," said Treon, "and I am well content. With me goes the last of our rotten blood, and Venus will be the cleaner for it. Bury my body deep, stranger with the fierce eyes. I would not have it looked on after this."

He sighed and fell forward.

Bor's little dragon crept whimpering out from its hiding place under the old woman's bed and scurried away down the hall, trailing its dragging rope.

Stark leaned on the taffrail, watching the dark mass of Shuruun recede into the red mists.

The decks were crowded with the outland slaves, going home. The Lhari were gone, the Lost Ones freed forever, and Shuruun was now only another port on the Red Sea. Its people would still be wolfs-heads and pirates, but that was natural and as it should be. The black evil was gone.

Stark was glad to see the last of it. He would be glad also to see the last of the Red Sea.

The off-shore wind set the ship briskly down the gulf. Stark thought of Larrabee, left behind with his dreams of winter snows and city streets and women with dainty feet. It seemed that he had lived too long in Shuruun, and had lost the courage to leave it.

"Poor Larrabee," he said to Helvi, who was standing near him. "He'll die in the mud, still cursing it."

Someone laughed behind him. He heard a limping step on the deck and turned to see Larrabee coming toward him.

"Changed my mind at the last minute," Larrabee said. "I've been below, lest I should see my muddy brats and be tempted to change it again." He leaned beside Stark, shaking his head. "Ah, well, they'll do nicely without me. I'm an old man, and I've a right to choose my own place to die in. I'm going back to Earth, with you."

Stark glanced at him. "I'm not going to Earth."

Larrabee sighed. "No. No, I suppose you're not. After all, you're no Earthman, really, except for an accident of blood. Where are you going?"

"I don't know. Away from Venus, but I don't know yet where."

Larrabee's dark eyes surveyed him shrewdly. "'A restless, cold-eyed tiger of a man', that's what Varra said. He's lost something, she said. He'll look for it all his life, and never find it."

After that there was silence. The red fog wrapped them, and the wind rose and sent them scudding before it.

Then, faint and far off, there came a moaning wail, a sound like broken chanting that turned Stark's flesh cold.

"All on board heard it. They listened, utterly silent, their eyes wide, and somewhere a woman began to weep.

Stark shook himself. "It's only the wind," he said roughly, "in the rocks by the strait."

The sound rose and fell, weary, infinitely mournful, and the part of Stark that was N'Chaka said that he lied. It was not the wind that keened so sadly through the mists. It was the voices of the Lost Ones who were forever lost—Zareth, sleeping in the hall of kings, and all the others who would never leave the dreaming city and the forest, never find the light again.

Stark shivered, and turned away, watching the leaping fires of the strait sweep toward them.

CLIVE JACKSON

Clive Jackson is the name of a science fiction fan who in 1950 and 1951 seemed to be destined for a professional career in the field but has since disappeared. He was an articulate and knowledgeable fan critic and a talented writer. But nothing is known of what became of him. In *Slant* #4, Jackson commented on space opera in the course of a commentary on the film *Destination Moon* (fanac.org/fanzines/Slant/Slant4-16.html):

> Personally, I like it. I think it's a very good form for s-f, if only because one can make one's puppets live without going too deeply into their emotions and mental struggles, which must tend to give them a present-day characterisation. . . .

Then Jackson continues:

> I suppose it was inevitable that s-f films should come to be classified by the public as trash, just as the prozines are, because the worthwhile productions will be lost from view under the usual pile of rubbish. But if DM had had a fair chance we might have seen some more of such honest work. I should have loved to see just one of Dr. Smith's space operas on celluloid, if only to find out how they conveyed to the average audience that the Lensmen were about to sling a contra-terrene planet at the enemy through a hyperspacial tube!

Jackson's story was first published in Walt Willis's distinguished fanzine, *Slant*, as by "Geoffrey Cobbe" in 1950, and reprinted in the American magazine *Other Worlds*. When it was reprinted in 1953 in *Science Fiction Carnival*, edited by Fredric Brown and Mack Reynolds, they called it a parody of space opera. It seems to us that this is a very strong indication that the pejorative term is broadening in colloquial usage and by the early 1950s includes much of what (then and still) is called science fantasy (and sometimes now called planetary romance), the tradition of Edgar Rice Burroughs's novels of the planet Mars, and of Leigh Brackett (one thinks of her classic science fantasy *The Sword of Rhiannon*). Yet Brown's thumb-rule definition (which is in fact a redefinition) is even broader.

The kernel of the story survives as a visual gag in the first Indiana Jones film.

THE SWORDSMEN OF VARNIS

CLIVE JACKSON

The twin moons brooded over the red deserts of Mars and the ruined city of Khua-Loanis. The night wind sighed around the fragile spires and whispered at the fretted lattice windows of the empty temples, and the red dust made it like a city of copper.

It was close to midnight when the distant rumble of racing hooves reached the city, and soon the riders thundered in under the ancient gateway. Tharn, Warrior Lord of Loanis, leading his pursuers by a scant twenty yards, realized wearily that his lead was shortening, and raked the scaly flanks of his six-legged vorkl with cruel spurs. The faithful beast gave a low cry of despair as it tried to obey and failed.

In front of Tharn in the big double saddle sat Lehni-tal-Loanis, Royal Lady of Mars, riding the ungainly animal with easy grace, leaning forward along its arching neck to murmur swift words of encouragement into its flattened ears. Then she lay back against Tharn's mailed chest and turned her lovely face up to his, flushed and vivid with the excitement of the chase, amber eyes aflame with love for her strange hero from beyond time and space.

"We shall win this race yet, my Tharn," she cried. "Yonder through that archway lies the Temple of the Living Vapor, and once there we can defy all the Hordes of Varnis!" Looking down at the unearthly beauty of her, at the subtle curve of throat and breast and thigh, revealed as the wind tore at her scanty garments, Tharn knew that even if the Swordsmen of Varnis struck him down his strange odyssey would not have been in vain.

But the girl had judged the distance correctly and Tharn brought their snorting vorkl to a sliding, rearing halt at the great doors of the Temple, just as the Swordsmen reached the outer archway and jammed there in a struggling, cursing mass. In seconds they had sorted themselves out and came streaming across the courtyard, but the delay had given Tharn time to dismount and take his stand in one of the great doorways. He knew that if he could hold it for a few moments while Lehni-tal-Loanis got the door open, then the secret of the Living Vapor would be theirs, and with it mastery of all the lands of Loanis.

The Swordsmen tried first to ride him down, but the doorway was so narrow and deep that Tharn had only to drive his sword-point upward into the first vorkl's throat and leap backward as the dying beast fell. Its rider was stunned by the fall, and Tharn bounded up onto the dead animal and beheaded the unfortunate Swordsman without compunction. There were ten of his enemies left and they came at him now on foot, but the confining doorway prevented them from attacking more than four abreast, and Tharn's elevated position upon the huge carcass gave him the advantage he needed. The fire of battle was in his veins now, and he bared his teeth and laughed in their faces, and his reddened sword wove a pattern of cold death which none could pass.

Lehni-tal-Loanis, running quick cool fingers over the pitted bronze of the door, found the radiation lock and pressed her glowing opalescent thumb-ring into the socket, gave a little sob of relief as she heard hidden tumblers falling. With agonizing slowness the ancient mechanism began to open the door; soon Tharn heard the girl's clear voice call above the clashing steel, "Inside, my Tharn, the secret of the Living Vapor is ours!"

But Tharn, with four of his foes dead now, and seven to go, could not retreat from his position on top of the dead vorkl without grave risk of being cut down, and Lehni-tal-Loanis, quickly realizing this, sprang up beside him, drawing her own slim blade and crying, "Aie, my love! I will be your left arm!"

Now the cold hand of defeat gripped the hearts of the Swordsmen of Varnis: two, three, four more of them mingled their blood with the red dust of the courtyard as Tharn and his fighting princess swung their merciless blades in perfect unison. It seemed that nothing could prevent them now from winning the mysterious secret of the Living Vapor, but they reckoned without the treachery of one of the remaining Swordsmen. Leaping backward out of the conflict he flung his sword on the ground in disgust. "Aw, the Hell with it!" he grunted, and unclipping a proton gun from his belt he blasted Lehni-tal-Loanis and her Warrior Lord out of existence with a searing energy-beam.

II.

DRAFTEES (1960S)

New space opera is twenty-eight years old. It began, and almost ended, in 1975, when M. John Harrison's *The Centauri Device* took a British New Wave sensibility to the stars. Its cover claimed it as a galaxy-spanning space adventure in the great tradition, that stood comparison with the classic works of E.E. "Doc" Smith and A.E. Van Vogt. Anyone who bought it under that misapprehension was likely to hurl it across the room. Its hero would have been, to Smith and Van Vogt, at best a villain: "He had sung revolutionary songs and pushed meta-amphetamines to the all-night workers on Morpheus—not because he was in any way committed to the insurrection that finally blew the planet apart, but because he was stuck there and broke." For its author, it was intended to terminate space opera, not to expand it. Mike Harrison wanted to knot its legs behind its neck and to walk away, brushing his palms.

—Ken MacLeod in *Locus*

CORDWAINER SMITH

Cordwainer Smith (pseudonym for Dr. Paul Myron Anthony Linebarger) [1913–1966] (www.cordwainer-smith.com) was a professor of Asiatic studies at Johns Hopkins University, School of Advanced International Studies. He was closely linked with the U.S. intelligence community with a special interest in propaganda techniques and psychological warfare. According to a biography at the Arlington National Cemetery Web site, Linebarger taught at Duke University from 1937 to 1946. He also wrote as Felix C. Forrest, a pun in reference to his Chinese name Lin Bah Loh (Forest of Incandescent Bliss), and as Carmichael Smith. He published three contemporary novels under those pseudonyms in the 1940s. He was a spy, a trickster, a secret agent, an impressive theoretician who wrote the first and standard text *Psychological Warfare*.

When he was six, he lost the sight of one eye in an accident. This added to his sense of being different, according to his daughter, Rosana Hart (www.cordwainer-smith.com), and must have been the beginning of the theme of pain and suffering that ran through his life. Linebarger's own psychological problems, as well as his keen interest in psychological warfare, caused him to explore modern psychiatry and psychoanalysis. These themes, as well as Christian philosophy and allegory, and also psychological warfare, run all through the science fiction he published as Cordwainer Smith. A psychobiography of Linebarger by scholar Alan Elms has been in preparation for more than twenty-five years and is forthcoming.

The first science fiction story published under the pseudonym Cordwainer Smith was "Scanners Live in Vain," in 1949. It had been written in 1945. The Arlington biographer says:

> This story is a full-blown allegory of the coming of the New Covenant, and reveals a very sophisticated understanding both of the Biblical narrative and typology (e.g., the smell of roast lamb reminds the central character of the smell of burning people), and of the theological and philosophical tenets of the Christian religion.

Robert Silverberg calls it "one of the classic stories of science fiction. For me it was a revelation. I read it over and over, astonished by its power."

Yet it was not widely anthologized in the early 1950s, and his second story, "The Game of Rat and Dragon," although it was another milestone in SF, widely read and praised, simply made him a two-story wonder. He did not begin to sell fiction regularly until 1959. He flourished in the magazines and the low end of the paperback market in the early 1960s, and shortly after his death, in 1966, all his fiction was more or less out of print. He died, like Leigh Brackett, at age fifty-three.

But as is evident from Silverberg's comment, his work was vividly remembered by the fans and writers. If there is one fan who did the most to keep his work alive between 1966 and 1975, it is J. J. Pierce, who wrote extensively on Smith. His literary renaissance was in the 1970s, when Del Rey Books collected his work in paperback, introduced by Pierce, and published his only novel, *Norstrilia* (1975), complete for the first time (it had been done in two edited paperback volumes as two separate books in the 1960s). They trumpeted the return of a classic writer. To finish Smith's apotheosis, the distinguished fan small press NESFA did *The Rediscovery of Man: The Complete Short Science Fiction of Cordwainer Smith* (1993), which remains in print. And an award was created by Linebarger's estate, now given each year at the World

Science Fiction Convention to a deceased writer of distinction whose works have fallen out of currency.

It was clear by the time of his death that all but five stories were set in a future called the Instrumentality of Mankind, a future history that has been obsessively studied by many fans since. Until the 1990s, most of the Smith scholarship was done by fans. And although his stories (like those of Brackett) frequently had all the earmarks of what is now called space opera, they were not called that during his lifetime. Smith is quoted in Karen Hellekson's *The Science Fiction of Cordwainer Smith*: "In my stories I use exotic settings, but the settings are like the function of a Chinese stage. They are intended to lay bare the human mind, to throw torches over the underground lakes of the human soul, to show the chambers wherein the ageless dramas of self-respect, God, courage, sex, love, hope, envy, decency and power go on forever." The body of work is now often referred to as one of the historic models of space opera, and Smith's influence continues.

"The Game of Rat and Dragon" appeared in 1955. It is an unusual tale of the horrors of interstellar travel: Interstellar space, the dark between the stars, is the realm of nightmares. The telling involves two of Smith's obsessions, cats and telepathy. The monsters of nightmare are inconceivable. Human telepaths intuit these entities as dragons; their feline "partners," the great cat warriors Captain Wow and the Lady May, apprehend them as enormous rats. Light is their nemesis. If humans leave the protection of suns, they die or are driven mad. So interstellar travel is an eternal war.

THE GAME OF RAT AND DRAGON

CORDWAINER SMITH

I. THE TABLE

Pinlighting is a hell of a way to earn a living. Underhill was furious as he closed the door behind himself. It didn't make much sense to wear a uniform and look like a soldier if people didn't appreciate what you did.

He sat down in his chair, laid his head back in the headrest, and pulled the helmet down over his forehead.

As he waited for the pin-set to warm up, he remembered the girl in the outer corridor. She had looked at it, then looked at him scornfully.

"Meow." That was all she had said. Yet it had cut him like a knife.

What did she think he was—a fool, a loafer, a uniformed nonentity? Didn't she know that for every half-hour of pinlighting, he got a minimum of two months' recuperation in the hospital?

By now the set was warm. He felt the squares of space around him, sensed himself at the middle of an immense grid, a cubic grid, full of nothing. Out in that nothingness, he could sense the hollow aching horror of space itself and could feel the terrible anxiety which his mind encountered whenever it met the faintest trace of inert dust.

As he relaxed, the comforting solidity of the Sun, the clockwork of the familiar planets and the Moon rang in on him. Our own solar system was as charming and as simple as an ancient cuckoo clock filled with familiar ticking and with reassuring noises. The odd little moons of Mars swung around their planet like frantic mice, yet their regularity was itself an assurance that all was well. Far above the plane of the ecliptic, he could feel half a ton of dust more or less drifting outside the lanes of human travel.

Here there was nothing to fight, nothing to challenge the mind, to tear the living soul out of a body with its roots dripping in effluvium as tangible as blood.

Nothing ever moved in on the solar system. He could wear the pin-set forever and be nothing more than a sort of telepathic astronomer, a man who could feel the hot, warm protection of the Sun throbbing and burning against his living mind.

Woodley came in.

"Same old ticking world," said Underhill. "Nothing to report. No wonder they didn't develop the pin-set until they began to planoform. Down here with the hot Sun around us, it feels so good and so quiet. You can feel everything spinning and turning. It's nice and sharp and compact. It's sort of like sitting around home."

Woodley grunted. He was not much given to flights of fantasy.

Undeterred, Underhill went on, "It must have been pretty good to have been an ancient man. I wonder why they burned up their world with war. They didn't have to planoform. They didn't have to go out to earn their livings among the stars. They didn't have to dodge the Rats or play the Game. They couldn't have invented pin-lighting because they didn't have any need of it, did they, Woodley?"

Woodley grunted, "Uh-huh." Woodley was twenty-six years old and due to retire in one more year. He already had a farm picked out. He had gotten through ten years of hard work pinlighting with the best of them. He had kept his sanity by not think-ing very much about his job, meeting the strains of the task whenever he had to meet them, and thinking nothing more about his duties until the next emergency arose.

Woodley never made a point of getting popular among the Partners. None of the Partners liked him very much. Some of them even resented him. He was suspected of thinking ugly thoughts of the Partners on occasion, but since none of the Partners ever thought a complaint in articulate form, the other pinlighters and the Chiefs of the Instrumentality left him alone.

Underhill was still full of the wonder of their job. Happily he babbled on, "What does happen to us when we planoform? Do you think it's sort of like dying? Did you ever see anybody who had his soul pulled out?"

"Pulling souls is just a way of talking about it," said Woodley. "After all these years, nobody knows whether we have souls or not."

"But I saw one once. I saw what Dogwood looked like when he came apart. There was something funny. It looked wet and sort of sticky as if it were bleeding and it went out of him—and you know what they did to Dogwood? They took him away, up in that part of the hospital where you and I never go—way up at the top part where the others are, where the others always have to go if they are alive after the Rats of the Up-and-Out have gotten them."

Woodley sat down and lit an ancient pipe. He was burning something called tobacco in it. It was a dirty sort of habit, but it made him look very dashing and adventurous.

"Look here, youngster. You don't have to worry about that stuff. Pinlighting is getting better all the time. The Partners are getting better. I've seen them pinlight two Rats forty-six million miles apart in one and a half milliseconds. As long as peo-ple had to try to work the pin-sets themselves, there was always the chance that with a minimum of four-hundred milliseconds for the human mind to set a pinlight, we wouldn't light the Rats up fast enough to protect our planoforming ships. The Part-ners have changed all that. Once they get going, they're faster than Rats. And they always will be. I know it's not easy, letting a Partner share your mind—"

"It's not easy for them, either," said Underhill.

"Don't worry about them. They're not human. Let them take care of themselves. I've seen more pinlighters go crazy from monkeying around with Partners than I have ever seen caught by the Rats. How many of them do you actually know of that got grabbed by Rats?"

Underhill looked down at his fingers, which shone green and purple in the vivid light thrown by the tuned-in pin-set, and counted ships. The thumb for the *Androm-eda*, lost with crew and passengers, the index finger and the middle finger for *Release Ships* 43 and 56, found with their pin-sets burned out and every man, woman, and child on board dead or insane. The ring finger, the little finger, and the thumb of the other hand were the first three battleships to be lost to the Rats—lost as people real-ized that there was something out there *underneath space itself* which was alive, capri-cious, and malevolent.

Planoforming was sort of funny. It felt like—

Like nothing much.

Like the twinge of a mild electric shock.

Like the ache of a sore tooth bitten on for the first time.

Like a slightly painful flash of light against the eyes.

Yet in that time, a forty-thousand-ton ship lifting free above Earth disappeared somehow or other into two dimensions and appeared half a light-year or fifty light-years off.

At one moment, he would be sitting in the Fighting Room, the pin-set ready and the familiar solar system ticking around inside his head. For a second or a year (he could never tell how long it really was, subjectively), the funny little flash went through him and then he was loose in the Up-and-Out, the terrible open spaces between the stars, where the stars themselves felt like pimples on his telepathic mind and the planets were too far away to be sensed or read.

Somewhere in this outer space, a gruesome death awaited, death and horror of a kind which Man had never encountered until he reached out for interstellar space itself. Apparently the light of the suns kept the Dragons away.

Dragons. That was what people called them. To ordinary people, there was nothing, nothing except the shiver of planoforming and the hammer blow of sudden death or the dark spastic note of lunacy descending into their minds.

But to the telepaths, they were Dragons.

In the fraction of a second between the telepaths' awareness of a hostile something out in the black, hollow nothingness of space and the impact of a ferocious, ruinous psychic blow against all living things within the ship, the telepaths had sensed entities something like the Dragons of ancient human lore, beasts more clever than beasts, demons more tangible than demons, hungry vortices of aliveness and hate compounded by unknown means out of the thin, tenuous matter between the stars.

It took a surviving ship to bring back the news—a ship in which, by sheer chance, a telepath had a light-beam ready, turning it out at the innocent dust so that, within the panorama of his mind, the Dragon dissolved into nothing at all and the other passengers, themselves non-telepathic, went about their way not realizing that their own immediate deaths had been averted.

From then on, it was easy—almost.

Planoforming ships always carried telepaths. Telepaths had their sensitiveness enlarged to an immense range by the pin-sets, which were telepathic amplifiers adapted to the mammal mind. The pin-sets in turn were electronically geared into small dirigible light bombs. Light did it.

Light broke up the Dragons, allowed the ships to reform three-dimensionally, skip, skip, skip, as they moved from star to star.

The odds suddenly moved down from a hundred to one against mankind to sixty to forty in mankind's favor.

This was not enough. The telepaths were trained to become ultrasensitive, trained to become aware of the Dragons in less than a millisecond.

But it was found that the Dragons could move a million miles in just under two milliseconds and that this was not enough for the human mind to activate the light beams.

Attempts had been made to sheathe the ships in light at all times.

This defense wore out.

As mankind learned about the Dragons, so too, apparently, the Dragons learned about mankind. Somehow they flattened their own bulk and came in on extremely flat trajectories very quickly.

Intense light was needed, light of sunlike intensity. This could be provided only by light bombs. Pinlighting came into existence.

Pinlighting consisted of the detonation of ultra-vivid miniature photonuclear bombs, which converted a few ounces of a magnesium isotope into pure visible radiance.

The odds kept coming down in mankind's favor, yet ships were being lost.

It became so bad that people didn't even want to find the ships because the rescuers knew what they would see. It was sad to bring back to Earth three hundred bodies ready for burial and two hundred or three hundred lunatics, damaged beyond repair, to be wakened, and fed, and cleaned, and put to sleep, wakened and fed again until their lives were ended.

Telepaths tried to reach into the minds of the psychotics who had been damaged by the Dragons, but they found nothing there beyond vivid spouting columns of fiery terror bursting from the primordial id itself, the volcanic source of life.

Then came the Partners.

Man and Partner could do together what man could not do alone. Men had the intellect. Partners had the speed.

The Partners rode their tiny craft, no larger than footballs, outside the spaceships. They planoformed with the ships. They rode beside them in their six-pound craft ready to attack.

The tiny ships of the Partners were swift. Each carried a dozen pinlights, bombs no bigger than thimbles.

The pinlighters threw the Partners—quite literally threw—by means of mind-to-firing relays directly at the Dragons.

What seemed to be Dragons to the human mind appeared in the form of gigantic Rats in the minds of the Partners.

Out in the pitiless nothingness of space, the Partners' minds responded to an instinct as old as life. The Partners attacked, striking with a speed faster than man's, going from attack to attack until the Rats or themselves were destroyed. Almost all the time it was the Partners who won.

With the safety of the interstellar skip, skip, skip of the ships, commerce increased immensely, the population of all the colonies went up, and the demand for trained Partners increased.

Underhill and Woodley were a part of the third generation of pinlighters and yet, to them, it seemed as though their craft had endured forever.

Gearing space into minds by means of the pin-set, adding the Partners to those minds, keying up the minds for the tension of a fight on which all depended—this was more than human synapses could stand for long. Underhill needed his two months' rest after half an hour of fighting. Woodley needed his retirement after ten years of service. They were young. They were good. But they had limitations.

So much depended on the choice of Partners, so much on the sheer luck of who drew whom.

II. THE SHUFFLE

Father Moontree and the little girl named West entered the room. They were the other two pinlighters. The human complement of the Fighting Room was now complete.

Father Moontree was a red-faced man of forty-five who had lived the peaceful life of a farmer until he reached his fortieth year. Only then, belatedly, did the authorities find he was telepathic and agree to let him late in life enter upon the career of pinlighter. He did well at it, but he was fantastically old for this kind of business.

Father Moontree looked at the glum Woodley and the musing Underhill. "How're the youngsters today? Ready for a good fight?"

"Father always wants a fight," giggled the little girl named West. She was such a little little girl. Her giggle was high and childish. She looked like the last person in the world one would expect to find in the rough, sharp dueling of pinlighting.

Underhill had been amused one time when he found one of the most sluggish of the Partners coming away happy from contact with the mind of the girl named West.

Usually the Partners didn't care much about the human minds with which they were paired for the journey. The Partners seemed to take the attitude that human minds were complex and fouled up beyond belief, anyhow. No Partner ever questioned the superiority of the human mind, though very few of the Partners were much impressed by that superiority.

The Partners liked people. They were willing to fight with them. They were even willing to die for them. But when a Partner liked an individual the way, for example, that Captain Wow or the Lady May liked Underhill, the liking had nothing to do with intellect. It was a matter of temperment, of feel.

Underhill knew perfectly well that Captain Wow regarded his, Underhill's, brains as silly. What Captain Wow liked was Underhill's friendly emotional structure, the cheerfulness and glint of wicked amusement that shot through Underhill's unconscious thought patterns, and the gaiety with which Underhill faced danger. The words, the history books, the ideas, the science—Underhill could sense all that in his own mind, reflected back from Captain Wow's mind, as so much rubbish.

Miss West looked at Underhill. "I bet you've put stickum on the stones."

"I did not!"

Underhill felt his ears grow red with embarrassment. During his novitiate, he had tried to cheat in the lottery because he got particularly fond of a special Partner, a lovely young mother named Murr. It was so much easier to operate with Murr and she was so affectionate toward him that he forgot pinlighting was hard work and that he was not instructed to have a good time with his Partner. They were both designed and prepared to go into deadly battle together.

One cheating had been enough. They had found him out and he had been laughed at for years.

Father Moontree picked up the imitation-leather cup and shook the stone dice which assigned them their Partners for the trip. By senior rights he took first draw.

He grimaced. He had drawn a greedy old character, a tough old male whose mind was full of slobbering thoughts of food, veritable oceans full of half-spoiled fish. Father Moontree had once said that he burped cod liver oil for weeks after drawing that particular glutton, so strongly had the telepathic image of fish impressed itself upon his mind. Yet the glutton was a glutton for danger as well as for fish. He had killed sixty-three Dragons, more than any other Partner in the service, and was quite literally worth his weight in gold.

The little girl West came next. She drew Captain Wow. When she saw who it was, she smiled.

"I *like* him," she said. "He's such fun to fight with. He feels so nice and cuddly in my mind."

"Cuddly, hell," said Woodley. "I've been in his mind, too. It's the most leering mind in this ship, bar none."

"Nasty man," said the little girl. She said it declaratively, without reproach.

Underhill, looking at her, shivered.

He didn't see how she could take Captain Wow so calmly. Captain Wow's mind *did* leer. When Captain Wow got excited in the middle of a battle, confused images of Dragons, deadly Rats, luscious beds, the smell of fish, and the shock of space all scrambled together in his mind as he and Captain Wow, their consciousnesses linked together through the pin-set, became a fantastic composite of human being and Persian cat.

That's the trouble with working with cats, thought Underhill. It's a pity that nothing else anywhere will serve as Partner. Cats were all right once you got in touch with them telepathically. They were smart enough to meet the needs of the flight, but their motives and desires were certainly different from those of humans.

They were companionable enough as long as you thought tangible images at them, but their minds just closed up and went to sleep when you recited Shakespeare or Colegrove, or if you tried to tell them what space was.

It was sort of funny realizing that the Partners who were so grim and mature out here in space were the same cute little animals that people had used as pets for thousands of years back on Earth. He had embarrassed himself more than once while on the ground saluting perfectly ordinary non-telepathic cats because he had forgotten for the moment that they were not Partners.

He picked up the cup and shook out his stone dice.

He was lucky—he drew the Lady May.

The Lady May was the most thoughtful Partner he had ever met. In her, the finely bred pedigree mind of a Persian cat had reached one of its highest peaks of development. She was more complex than any human woman, but the complexity was all one of emotions, memory, hope, and discriminated experience—experience sorted through without benefit of words.

When he had first come into contact with her mind, he was astonished at its clarity. With her he remembered her kittenhood. He remembered every mating experience she had ever had. He saw in a half-recognizable gallery all the other pinlighters with whom she had been paired for the fight. And he saw himself radiant, cheerful, and desirable.

He even thought he caught the edge of a longing—

A very flattering and yearning thought: *What a pity he is not a cat.*

Woodley picked up the last stone. He drew what he deserved—a sullen, scarred old tomcat with none of the verve of Captain Wow. Woodley's Partner was the most animal of all the cats on the ship, a low, brutish type with a dull mind. Even telepathy had not refined his character. His ears were half chewed off from the first fights in which he had engaged. He was a serviceable fighter, nothing more.

Woodley grunted.

Underhill glanced at him oddly. Didn't Woodley ever do anything but grunt?

Father Moontree looked at the other three. "You might as well get your Partners now. I'll let the Go-Captain know we're ready to go into the Up-and-Out."

III. THE DEAL

Underhill spun the combination lock on the Lady May's cage. He woke her gently and took her into his arms. She humped her back luxuriously, stretched her claws, started to purr, thought better of it, and licked him on the wrist instead. He did not have the pin-set on, so their minds were closed to each other, but in the angle of her mustache and in the movement of her ears, he caught some sense of the gratification she experienced in finding him as her Partner.

He talked to her in human speech, even though speech meant nothing to a cat when the pin-set was not on.

"It's a damn shame, sending a sweet little thing like you whirling around in the coldness of nothing to hunt for Rats that are bigger and deadlier than all of us put together. You didn't ask for this kind of fight, did you?"

For answer, she licked his hand, purred, tickled his cheek with her long fluffy tail, turned around and faced him, golden eyes shining.

For a moment, they stared at each other, man squatting, cat standing erect on her hind legs, front claws digging into his knee. Human eyes and cat eyes looked across an immensity which no words could meet, but which affection spanned in a single glance.

"Time to get in," he said.

She walked docilely to her spheroid carrier. She climbed in. He saw to it that her miniature pin-set rested firmly and comfortably against the base of her brain. He made sure that her claws were padded so that she could not tear herself in the excitement of battle.

Softly he said to her, "Ready?"

For answer, she preened her back as much as her harness would permit and purred softly within the confines of the frame that held her.

He slapped down the lid and watched the sealant ooze around the seam. For a few hours, she was welded into her projectile until a workman with a short cutting arc would remove her after she had done her duty.

He picked up the entire projectile and slipped it into the ejection tube. He closed the door of the tube, spun the lock, seated himself in his chair, and put his own pin-set on.

Once again he flung the switch.

He sat in a small room, *small, small, warm, warm,* the bodies of the other three people moving close around him, the tangible lights in the ceiling bright and heavy against his closed eyelids.

As the pin-set warmed, the room fell away. The other people ceased to be people and became small glowing heaps of fire, embers, dark red fire, with the consciousness of life burning like old red coals in a country fireplace.

As the pin-set warmed a little more, he felt Earth just below him, felt the ship slipping away, felt the turning Moon as it swung on the far side of the world, felt the planets and the hot, clear goodness of the sun which kept the Dragons so far from mankind's native ground.

Finally, he reached complete awareness.

He was telepathically alive to a range of millions of miles. He felt the dust which he had noticed earlier high above the ecliptic. With a thrill of warmth and tenderness, he felt the consciousness of the Lady May pouring over into his own. Her consciousness was as gentle and clear and yet sharp to the taste of his mind as if it were scented oil. It felt relaxing and reassuring. He could sense her welcome of him. It was scarcely a thought, just a raw emotion of greeting.

At last they were one again.

In a tiny remote corner of his mind, as tiny as the smallest toy he had ever seen in his childhood, he was still aware of the room and the ship, and of Father Moontree picking up a telephone and speaking to a Go-Captain in charge of the ship.

His telepathic mind caught the idea long before his ears could frame the words. The actual sound followed the idea the way that thunder on an ocean beach follows the lightning inward from far out over the seas.

"The Fighting Room is ready. Clear to planoform, sir."

IV. THE PLAY

Underhill was always a little exasperated the way that Lady May experienced things before he did.

He was braced for the quick vinegar thrill of planoforming, but he caught her report of it before his own nerves could register what happened.

Earth had fallen so far away that he groped for several milliseconds before he found the Sun in the upper rear right-hand corner of his telepathic mind.

That was a good jump, he thought. *This way we'll get there in four or five skips.*

A few hundred miles outside the ship, the Lady May thought back at him, "O warm, O generous, O gigantic man! O brave, O friendly, O tender and huge Partner! O wonderful with you, with you so good, good, good, warm, warm, now to fight, now to go, good with you . . ."

He knew that she was not thinking words, that his mind took the clear amiable babble of her cat intellect and translated it into images which his own thinking could record and understand.

Neither one of them was absorbed in the game of mutual greetings. He reached out far beyond her range of perception to see if there was anything near the ship. It was funny how it was possible to do two things at once. He could scan space with his pin-set mind and yet at the same time catch a vagrant thought of hers, a lovely, affectionate thought about a son who had had a golden face and a chest covered with soft, incredibly downy white fur.

While he was still searching, he caught the warning from her.

We jump again!

And so they had. The ship had moved to a second planoform. The stars were different. The sun was immeasurably far behind. Even the nearest stars were barely in contact. This was good Dragon country, this open, nasty, hollow kind of space. He reached farther, faster, sensing and looking for danger, ready to fling the Lady May at danger wherever he found it.

Terror blazed up in his mind, so sharp, so clear, that it came through as a physical wrench.

The little girl named West had found something—something immense, long, black, sharp, greedy, horrific. She flung Captain Wow at it.

Underhill tried to keep his own mind clear. "Watch out!" he shouted telepathically at the others, trying to move the Lady May around.

At one corner of the battle, he felt the lustful rage of Captain Wow as the big Persian tomcat detonated lights while he approached the streak of dust which threatened the ship and the people within.

The lights scored near misses.

The dust flattened itself, changing from the shape of a sting ray into the shape of a spear.

Not three milliseconds had elapsed.

Father Moontree was talking human words and was saying in a voice that moved like cold molasses out of a heavy jar, "C-a-p-t-a-i-n." Underhill knew that the sentence was going to be "Captain, move fast!"

The battle would be fought and finished before Father Moontree got through talking.

Now, fractions of a millisecond later, the Lady May was directly in line.

Here was where the skill and speed of the Partners came in. She could react faster than he. She could see the threat as an immense Rat coming directly at her.

She could fire the light-bombs with a discrimination which he might miss.

He was connected with her mind, but he could not follow it.

His consciousness absorbed the tearing wound inflicted by the alien enemy. It was like no wound on Earth—raw, crazy pain which started like a burn at his navel. He began to writhe in his chair.

Actually he had not yet had time to move a muscle when the Lady May struck back at their enemy.

Five evenly spaced photonuclear bombs blazed out across a hundred-thousand miles.

The pain in his mind and body vanished.

He felt a moment of fierce, terrible, feral elation running through the mind of the Lady May as she finished her kill. It was always disappointing to the cats to find out that their enemies disappeared at the moment of destruction.

Then he felt her hurt, the pain and the fear that swept over both of them as the battle, quicker than the movement of an eyelid, had come and gone. In the same instant there came the sharp and acid twinge of planoform.

Once more the ship went skip.

He could hear Woodley thinking at him. "You don't have to bother much. This old son-of-a-gun and I will take over for a while."

Twice again the twinge, the skip.

He had no idea where he was until the lights of the Caledonia space port shone below.

With a weariness that lay almost beyond the limits of thought, he threw his mind back into rapport with the pin-set, fixing the Lady May's projectile gently and neatly in its launching tube.

She was half dead with fatigue, but he could feel the beat of her heart, could listen to her panting, and he grasped the grateful edge of a "Thanks" reaching from her mind to his.

V. THE SCORE

They put him in the hospital at Caledonia.

The doctor was friendly but firm. "You actually got touched by that Dragon. That's as close a shave as I've ever seen. It's all so quick that it'll be a long time before we know what happened scientifically, but I suppose you'd be ready for the insane asylum now if the contact had lasted several tenths of a millisecond longer. What kind of cat did you have out in front of you?"

Underhill felt the words coming out of him slowly. Words were such a lot of trouble compared with the speed and the joy of thinking, fast and sharp and clear, mind to mind! But words were all that could reach ordinary people like this doctor.

His mouth moved heavily as he articulated words. "Don't call our Partners cats. The right thing to call them is Partners. They fight for us in a team. You ought to know we call them Partners, not cats. How is mine?"

"I don't know," said the doctor contritely. "We'll find out for you. Meanwhile, old man, you take it easy. There's nothing but rest that can help you. Can you make yourself sleep, or would you like us to give you some kind of sedative?"

"I can sleep," said Underhill. "I just want to know about the Lady May."

The nurse joined in. She was a little antagonistic. "Don't you want to know about the other people?"

"They're okay," said Underhill. "I knew that before I came in here."

He stretched his arms and sighed and grinned at them. He could see they were relaxing and were beginning to treat him as a person instead of a patient.

"I'm all right," he said. "Just let me know when I can go see my Partner."

A new thought struck him. He looked wildly at the doctor. "They didn't send her off with the ship, did they?"

"I'll find out right away," said the doctor. He gave Underhill a reassuring squeeze of the shoulder and left the room.

The nurse took a napkin off a goblet of chilled fruit juice.

Underhill tried to smile at her. There seemed to be something wrong with the girl. He wished she would go away. First she had started to be friendly and now she was distant again. *It's a nuisance being telepathic*, he thought. *You keep trying to reach even when you are not making contact.*

Suddenly she swung around on him.

"You pinlighters! You and your damn cats!"

Just as she stamped out, he burst into her mind. He saw himself a radiant hero, clad in his smooth suede uniform, the pin-set crown shining like ancient royal jewels around his head. He saw his own face, handsome and masculine, shining out of her mind. He saw himself very far away and he saw himself as she hated him.

She hated him in the secrecy of her own mind. She hated him because he was— she thought—proud and strange and rich, better and more beautiful than people like her.

He cut off the sight of her mind and, as he buried his face in the pillow, he caught an image of the Lady May.

"She *is* a cat," he thought. "That's all she is—a *cat!*"

But that was not how his mind saw her—quick beyond all dreams of speed, sharp, clever, unbelievably graceful, beautiful, wordless, and undemanding.

Where would he ever find a woman who could compare with her?

SAMUEL R. DELANY

Samuel R. Delany [1942–] (tribute site: www.pcc.com/~jay/delany) lives in New York City, and is currently a professor at Temple University in Philadelphia. One of the dazzling young talents of the 1960s in SF, he published nine SF novels between 1962 and 1968, culminating in the grand space opera *Nova* (1968). All of those early novels can usefully be approached as space opera. He published ten short stories in the 1960s as well, collected in *Driftglass* (1971).

Delany then spent five years writing the massive and influential novel *Dhalgren* (1975), which is not quite SF but never mind, and followed it with two masterly SF novels, *Triton* (1976) and *Stars in My Pocket Like Grains of Sand* (1984), and a brilliant collection of linked fantasy stories, *Tales of Nevèrÿon* (1979), which launched a fantasy series that included three more books in the 1980s. He also began to publish literary criticism and theory in the 1970s, and is perhaps now the most important living critic of SF. He has not written another SF novel to date. His autobiography, *The Motion of Light in Water: Sex and Science Fiction Writing in the East Village 1957–1965* (1988), won awards and illuminates the rich environment out of which the fiction emerged in the 1960s. It's a stunner, telling more than you ever thought you might want to know about being a young gay/bisexual black SF writer in the 1960s. To say that Delany has led an interesting life is to understate. *Empire Star* was published as the short half of an Ace Double in mass-market paperback.

In 1978, Delany wrote an introduction to the graphic-novel version of *Empire Star, Empire* (illustrated by Howard V. Chaykin—from the 1960s to the 1990s, Delany has occasionally written for comics), titled "Some Notes on Space Opera." In it, he said, "We all know science fiction provides action and adventure, as well as a look at the visions of different worlds, different cultures, different values. But it is just the multiplicity of worlds, each careening in its particular orbit about the vast sweep of interstellar night, that may be the subtlest, most pervasive, and finally the most valuable thing in science fiction. It's a basic image that, if you let it, can almost totally revise that gravity-bound, upper/lower organization, which holds down (or holds up) so much of our thinking."

This is a fascinating parallel to Le Guin's position, elucidated in the note to "The Shobies' Story," elsewhere in this anthology. About *Empire Star*, Delany says:

> The whole concept of an endless, linear vertical measure, ever mounting and with no ceiling, has given way to the concept of relative unfixed centers, different worlds, different points of view, related only by direction, distance, and trajectory. . . . In the most recent star maps and computer simulation models of the million-plus galaxies so far discovered, though they indeed show many, many clusters (the Virgo Cluster, the Local Supercluster, the Coma Cluster, and M81, among those that have been named) there is nothing to suggest a center. Rather, they spread in nets throughout the greater multiverse—the concept beginning to replace that of the "universe," in place since the presocratic Greeks and ready for an update.
>
> . . .
>
> Does this mean that linear, *high/low, up/down* thinking is impossible in space opera? Not at all. It's as prevalent here as it is in any other product of our single world. You'll even find some in *Empire Star*. But what keeps the whole thing interesting is the way in which the basic space-opera construct, the worlds to come and the flights between them, suggest, by their de-centerings, ways to *under*-cut that up/down thinking,

to *over*-come it, ways to surprise it and to subvert it: the space-opera construct is always suggesting something more—and more exciting.

Delany is here providing one of the earliest statements of a rationale for the writing of space opera as a respectable enterprise for ambitious contemporary writers with intellectual aspirations.

Critic Russell Letson, writing in the *Locus* special issue on New Space Opera in 2003, tried to reason his way into a definition, or at least a characterization, of space opera along similar lines:

> If we take the term as more than a joke (or an arbitrary noise made when pointing to something), then "space" has to do with the physical setting and "opera" with the scale and emotional pitch of the action. Like its musical counterpart, it pushes everything up the intensity scale, and like the cartoon vision of grand opera, it's over the top, all horned helmets and marching animals and high priests and grand gestures and outsized emotions—gods and monsters, with aliens and starships thrown in for good measure.
>
> The enduring traits of space opera seem to be those of scale: interplanetary or interstellar space, preferably at least partly settled and governed, so it can be a "world" for human action. But it also needs to be big and mysterious, a place of extremes, and full of hidden treasures and dangers. Then you add action suited to this kind of world, preferably (again) with huge stakes—saving planets (or the empire or civilization), averting (or committing) genocide, discovering the Meaning of Life or the Center of the Galaxy. Space opera isn't just any old narrative-containing vessel; it's a vessel for supersized stories that celebrate the sense that the universe is a supersized kind of place. It cuts Creation down to size at the same time that it celebrates how big and scary it is. I think at its best it's about the sublime.

Delany's ambitious novels of the 1960s were not called space opera by the critics and reviewers of the day, though, except when someone was attacking them. Rather they were most often praised as cutting-edge speculative fiction, and Delany was one of the primary figures of the avant garde in SF of the time. But it is precisely Delany's willingness to wallow in the lowest form while writing at the highest levels of stylistic sophistication that gave his fiction both popularity and the odor of radical change in the 1960s.

"Basically, during the sixties, Moorcock and the writers associated with the New Wave did not particularly enjoy my work," says Delany, in response to our queries about the situation when *Empire Star* was published. "Though we all got along well socially, Moorcock told me that the only book of mine he liked enough to publish himself was *Empire Star*—no doubt because the political allegory of North American slavery and the Lll was so clear. But when *Nova* was reviewed in *New Worlds* by M. John Harrison, the basic thrust of his review was: What a shame someone so talented is wasting his time with this far future space opera nonsense. And in his history of *New Worlds*, published in *Foundation* during the 70s, Moorcock dismisses the one story of mine his magazine published, 'Time Considered as a Helix of Semi-Precious Stones,' as 'derivative' and 'space opera.'

"The New Wave did not condemn all space opera outright. They were, after all, the great proponents of Bester's *Tiger, Tiger!* (*The Stars My Destination*). Nevertheless, for them the term was still generally pejorative. For them to like a space opera, a strong anti-authoritarian current had to run through the work—or a clear liberal political allegory needed to be woven into it. The truth was, both were rare in the space operas generally produced in those days.

"It's interesting that today the anti-authoritarian message that the New Wave writers craved has become a standard convention, if not a cliché, of the more space operatic SF films of the last thirty years—from the *Alien* films through the *Matrix* trilogy. You can see it growing stronger and stronger through the *Star Wars* hexology—not to mention in fantasies such as *The Lord of the Rings*."

EMPIRE STAR

SAMUEL R. DELANY

Being set on the idea
  Of getting to Atlantis,
You have discovered of course
  Only the Ship of Fools is
Making the voyage this year,
As gales of abnormal force.
    Are predicted, and that you
    Must, therefore, be ready to
Behave absurdly enough
    To pass for one of The Boys,
At least appearing to love
  Hard liquor, horseplay and noise.
                —W. H. Auden

. . . truth is a point of view about things.
                —Marcel Proust

ONE

He had:
    a waist-length braid of blond hair;
    a body that was brown and slim and looked like a cat's, they said, when he curled
up, half-asleep, in the flicker of the Field Keeper's fire at New Cycle;
    an ocarina;
    a pair of black boots and a pair of black gloves with which he could climb walls
and across ceilings;
    gray eyes too large for his small, feral face;
    brass claws on his left hand with which he had killed, to date, three wild kepards
that had crept through a break in the power fence during his watch at New Cycle
(and in a fight once with Billy James—a friendly scuffle where a blow had suddenly
come too fast and too hard and turned it into for real—he had killed the other boy;
but that had been two years ago when he had been sixteen, and he didn't like to think
about it);
    eighteen years of rough life in the caves of the satellite Rhys attending the un-
derground fields while Rhys cycloided about the red giant Tau Ceti;

a propensity for wandering away from the Home Caves to look at the stars, which had gotten him in trouble at least four times in the past month, and in the past fourteen years had earned him the sobriquet, Comet Jo;

an uncle named Clemence whom he disliked.

Later, when he had lost all but, miraculously, the ocarina, he thought about these things and what they had meant to him, and how much they defined his youth, and how poorly they had prepared him for maturity.

Before he began to lose, however, he gained: two things, which, along with the ocarina, he kept until the end. One was a devil kitten named Di'k. The other was me. I'm Jewel.

I have a multiplex consciousness, which means I see things from different points of view. It's a function of the overtone series in the harmonic pattern of my internal structuring. So I'll tell a good deal of the story from the point of view called, in literary circles, the omniscient observer.

Crimson Ceti bruised the western crags. Tyre, giant as solar Jupiter, was a black curve across a quarter of the sky, and the white dwarf Eye silvered the eastern rocks. Comet Jo, with hair the hue of wheat, walked behind his two shadows, one long and gray, one squat and rusty. His head was back, and in the rush of wine-colored evening he stared at the first stars. In his long-fingered right hand, with the nails gnawed like any boy might, he held his ocarina. He should go back, he knew; he should crawl from under the night and into the luminous cocoon of the Home Cave. He should be respectful to his Uncle Clemence; he should not get into fights with the other boys on Field Watch. There were so many things he should do—

A sound:

Rock and non-rock in conflict.

He crouched, and his clawed left hand, deadly on the lean arm, jumped to protect his face. Kepards struck for the eyes. But it was not a kepard. He lowered his claw.

The devil-kitten came scrambling from the crevice, balancing on five of its eight legs, and hissed. It was a foot long, had three horns, and large gray eyes the color of Jo's own. It giggled, which devil-kittens do when upset, usually because they have lost their devil-cat parents—which are fifty feet long and perfectly harmless, unless they step on you accidentally.

"Wha' madda?" Comet Jo asked. "Ya ma and pa run off?"

The devil-kitten giggled again.

"Sum' wrong?" Jo persisted.

The kitten looked over its left shoulder and hissed.

"Le' ta' look." Comet Jo nodded. "Com'n, kitty." Frowning, he started forward, the motion of his naked body over the rocks as graceful as his speech was rude. He dropped from a ledge to crumbling red earth, yellow hair clouding his shoulders in mid-leap, then falling in his eyes. He shook it back. The kitten rubbed his ankle, giggled again, and darted around the boulder.

Jo followed—then threw himself back against the rock. The claws of his left hand and the nubs of his right ground on the granite. He sweated. The large vein along the side of his throat pulsed furiously, while his scrotum tightened like a prune.

Green slop frothed and flamed in a geyser two feet taller than Jo was. There were things in that fuming mess he couldn't see, but he could sense them—writhing, shrieking silently, dying in great pain. One of the things was trying hard to struggle free.

Oblivious to the agony within, the devil-kitten pranced to the base, spat haughtily, and pranced back.

As Jo chanced a breath, the thing inside broke out. It staggered forward, smoking. It raised gray eyes. Long wheat-colored hair caught on a breeze and blew back from its shoulders, as, for a moment, it moved with a certain catlike grace. Then it fell forward.

Something under fear made Comet Jo reach out and catch its extended arms. Hand caught claw. Claw caught hand. It was only when Comet Jo was kneeling and the figure was panting in his arms that he realized it was his double.

Surprise exploded in his head, and his tongue was one of the things jarred loose. "Who you?"

"You've got to take . . ." the figure began, coughed, and for a moment its features lost clarity: ". . . to take . . ." it repeated.

"Wha'? *Wha'*?" Jo was baffled and scared.

". . . take a message to Empire Star." The accent was the clean, precise tone of off-worlders' Interling. "You have to take a message to Empire Star!"

"Wha' I say?"

"Just get there and tell them . . ." It coughed again. "Just get there . . . no matter how long it . . ."

"Wha' hell I say when I ge' there?" Jo demanded. Then he thought of all the things he should have already asked. "Whe' ya fum? Whe' ya go? Wha' happen?"

Struck by a spasm, the figure arched its back and flipped from Jo's arms. Comet Jo reached out to pry the mouth open and keep it from swallowing its tongue, but before he touched it, it . . . melted.

It bubbled and steamed, frothed and smoked.

The larger phenomenon had quieted down, was only a puddle now, sloshing the weeds. The devil-kitten went to the edge, sniffed, then pawed something out. The puddle stilled, then began to evaporate—fast. The kitten picked the thing up in its mouth and, blinking rapidly, came and laid it between Jo's knees, then sat back to wash its fluffy pink chest.

Jo looked down.

The thing was multicolored, multifaceted, multiplexed, and me.

I'm jewel.

TWO

Oh, we had traveled so long, Norn, Ki, Marbika, and myself, to have it end so suddenly and disastrously. I had warned them, of course, when our original ship had broken down and we had taken the organiform cruiser from S. Doradus. Things went beautifully as long as we stayed in the comparatively dusty region of the Magellanic Cloud, but when we reached the emptier space of the Home Spiral, there was nothing for the encysting mechanism to catalyze against.

We were going to swing around Ceti and head for Empire Star with our burden of good news and bad, our chronicle of success and defeat. But we lost our crust, and the organiform, like a wild amoeba, plopped onto the satellite Rhys. The strain was fatal. Ki was dead when we landed. Marbika had broken up into a hundred idiot components, which were struggling and dying in the nutrient jelly, where we were suspended.

Norn and I had a quick consultation. We put a rather faulty perceptor scan over a hundred-mile radius from the crash. The organiform had already started to destroy itself. Its primitive intelligence blamed us for the accident, and it wanted to kill. The perceptor scan showed a small colony of Terrans, who worked producing plyasil, which grew in the vast underground caves. There was a small Transport Station about twenty miles south where the plyasil was shipped to Galactic-Center to be distributed among the stars. But the satellite itself was incredibly backward. "This is about as simplex a community as I've ever run into that you could still call intelligent," Norn commented. "I can't detect more than ten minds in the whole place that have ever been to another star-system; and *they* all work at the Transport Station."

"Where they have nonorganic, reliable ships that won't get hostile and crack up," I said. "Because of this one we've both got to die, and we'll never get to Empire Star now. That's the sort of ship we should have been on. This thing—bah!" The temperature of the proto-photoplasm was getting uncomfortable.

"There's a child somewhere around here," Norn said. "And a . . . what the hell is that, anyway?"

"The Terrans call it a devil-kitten," I said, picking up the information.

"That certainly isn't a simplex mind."

"It's not exactly multiplex either," I said. "But it's something. Maybe it could get the message through."

"But its intelligence is sub-moronic," Norn said. "The Terrans at least have a fair amount of gray matter. If we could only get the both of them cooperating. That child is rather bright—but so simplex! The kitten is complex, at least—so at least it could carry the message. Well, let's try. See if you can get them over here. If you crystallize, you can put off dying for a while, can't you?"

"Yes," I said, uncomfortably, "but I don't know if I want to. I don't think I can take being that passive, being just a point of view."

"Even passive," Norn said, "you can be very useful, especially to that simplex boy. He's going to have a hard time, if he agrees."

"Oh, all right," I said. "I'll crystallize. But I won't like it. You go on out and see what you can do."

"Damn," Norn said, "I don't like dying. I don't want to die. I want to live, and go to Empire Star and tell them."

"Hurry up," I said. "You're wasting time."

"All right, all right. What form do you think I should take?"

"Remember, you're dealing with a simplex mind. There's only one form you can take that he's likely to pay much attention to and not chalk up to a bad dream tomorrow morning."

"All right," Norn repeated. "Here goes. Good-bye, Jewel."

"Good-bye," I said and began to crystallize.

Norn struggled forward, and the boiling jelly sagged as he broke through onto the rocks where the child was waiting. *Here, kitty, kitty, kitty,* I projected toward the devil-kitten. It was very cooperative.

THREE

Comet Jo walked back to the caves, playing slow tunes on the ocarina, and thinking. The gem (which was Jewel, which was me) hung in the pouch at his waist. The devil-kitten was snapping at fireflies, then stopping to pick bristles out of its foot cups. Once it rolled on its back and hissed at a star; then it scurried after Comet. It was not a simplex mind at all.

Comet reached the ledge of Toothsome. Glancing over the rock, he saw Uncle Clemence at the door of the cave, looking very annoyed. Comet stuck his tongue in his cheek and hunted for leftover lunch, because he knew he wasn't going to get any dinner.

Above him someone said, "Hey, stupid! Unca' Clem is mad on y', an' how!"

He looked up. His fourth cousin Lilly was hanging onto the edge of a higher precipice, staring down.

He motioned, and she came down to stand beside him. Her hair was cut in a short brush, which he always envied girls. "Tha' ya' devil-kitty? Wha's's name?"

"It ain't none o' mine," he said. "Hey, who says ya can use my boots and gloves, huh?"

She was wearing the knee-high black boots and the elbow-length gloves that Charona had given him for his twelfth birthday.

"I wanted to wait for ya an' tell ya how mad Unca' Clem is. An' I had to hang up there whe' I could see ya comin' in."

"Jhup, ya did! Gimme. Ya jus' wan'ed to use 'em. Now gimme. I di'n' say ya could use 'em."

Reluctantly Lilly shucked the gloves. "Jhup ya," she said. "Ya won' lemme use 'em?" She stepped out of the boots.

"No," Comet said.

"All right," Lilly said. She turned around and called, "*Unca' Clem!*"

"Hey . . . !" Jo said.

"Unca' Clem, Comet's back!"

"Shedup!" Comet hissed, then turned and ran back across the ledge.

"Unca' Clem, he's runnin' away again—" Just then the devil-kitty stuck two of its horns into Lilly's ankles, picked up the gloves and boots in his mouth, and ran after Comet—which was a very multiplex thing to do, considering no one had said anything to him at all.

Fifteen minutes later Comet was crouching in the starlit rocks, scared and mad. Which was when the devil-kitty walked up and dropped the boots and gloves in front of him.

"Huh?" said Comet, as he recognized them in the maroon half-dark. "Hey, thanks!" And he picked them up and put them on. "Charona," he said, standing up. "I'm gonna go see Charona." Because Charona had given him the boots, and because Charona was never mad at him, and because Charona would be likely to know what Empire Star was.

He started off, then turned back and frowned at the devil-kitten. Devil-kittens are notoriously independent, and do not fetch and carry for human beings like dogs. "Devil-kitty," he said. "D'kitty. Di'k; that's a name. Di'k, you wanna come wi' me?" which was a surprisingly un-simplex thing to do—anyway, it surprised me.

Comet Jo started off. Di'k followed.

It rained toward dawn. The spray drooled his face and jeweled his eyelashes as he hung from the underside of the cliff, looking down at the gate of the Transport Area. He hung like a sloth. Di'k sat in the cradle of his belly.

Between the rocks in the reddening light, two plyasil trucks crept forward. In a minute Charona would come to let them in. Leaning his head back until the world was upside down, he could see across the rocky valley, spanned by the double cusp of Brooklyn Bridge, to the loading platforms where the star ships balanced in the dawn's red rain.

As the trucks came out of the thicket of chupper vines that at one point arbored the road, he saw Charona marching toward the gate. 3-Dog ran ahead of her, barking through the mesh at the vehicles as they halted. The devil-kitten shifted nervously from one foot to another. One way in which it resembled its namesake was its dislike for dogs.

Charona pulled the gate lever, and the bars rolled back. As the truck trundled through, Jo hollered down from the cliff, "Hey, Charona, hol' 'em up f'me!"

She lifted her bald head and twisted her wrinkled face. "Who art thou aloft?" 3-Dog barked.

"Watch it," Jo called, then let go of the rocks and twisted in the air. He and Di'k both took the fall rolling. He sprang open before her, light on his booted feet.

"Well!" she laughed, putting her fists in the pouch of her silver skin suit that glistened with rain. "Thou art an agile elf. Where has thou been a-hiding for the best part of the month?"

"The New Cycle watch," he said, grinning. "See, I'm wearin' ya' present."

"And it's good to see thee with them. Come in, come in, so I can close the gate."

Comet ducked under the half-lowered bars. "Hey, Charona," he said as they started down the wet road together, "wh' Empire Star? An' whe' it? An' how I ge' 'ere?" By unspoken consent they turned off the road to make their way over the rougher earth of the valley beneath the tongue of metal called Brooklyn Bridge.

"'Tis a great, great star, lad, that thy great-great-great-grandfathers on Earth called Aurigae. It is seventy-two degrees around the hub of the galaxy from here at a hyperstatic distance of fifty-five point nine, and—to quote the ancient maxim—thou canst not get there from here."

"Why?"

Charona laughed. 3-Dog ran ahead and barked at Di'k, who arched, started to say something back in kittenish, thought better of it, and pranced away. "One could hitch a ride on a transport and get started; but *thou* couldst not. Which is the important part."

Comet Jo frowned.

"Why cou'nt I?" He swiped at a weed and tore off the head. "I gonna ge' off this planet—now!"

Charona raised the bare flesh where her eyebrows would have been. "Thou seemst a mite determined. Thou art the first person born here to tell me that in four hundred years. Return thou, Comet Jo, to thine uncle and make peace in the Home Cave."

"Jhup," said Comet Jo and kicked a small stone. "I wanna go. Why can' I go?"

"Simplex, complex, and multiplex," Charona said. And I woke up in the pouch. Perhaps there was hope, after all. If there was someone to explain it to him, the journey would be easier. "This is a simplex society here, Comet. Space travel is not a part of it. Save for trucking the plyasil here, and a few curious children like thyself, nobody ever comes inside the gates. And in a year, thou wilt cease to come, and all thy visits will eventually mean to thee is that thou wilt be a bit more lenient with thine own when they will wander to the gates or come back to the Home Caves with magic trinkets from the stars. To travel between worlds, one must deal with at least complex beings, and often multiplex. Thou wouldst be lost as how to conduct thyself. After half an hour in a spaceship, thou wouldst turn around and decide to go back, dismissing the whole idea as foolish. The fact that thou hast a simplex mind is good, in a way, because thou remainest safe at Rhys. And even though thou comest through the gates, thou art not likely to be 'corrupted,' as it were, even by visits to the Transport Area, nor by an occasional exposure to something from the stars, like those boots and gloves I gave thee."

She seemed to have finished, and I felt sad, for that certainly was no explanation. And by now I knew that Jo would journey.

But Comet reached for his pouch, pushed aside the ocarina, and lifted me out into the palm of his hand. "Charona, ya ever see wonna these?"

Together they loomed above me. Beyond the tines of Comet's claws, beyond their shadowed faces, the black ribbon of Brooklyn Bridge scribed the mauve sky. His palm was warm beneath my dorsal facet. A cool droplet splashed my frontal faces, distorting theirs.

"Why . . . I think . . . No, it cannot be. Where didst thou retrieve it?"

He shrugged. "Jus' foun' it. Wha'cha think it is?"

"It looks for all the light of the seven suns to be a crystallized Tritovian."

She was right, of course, and I knew immediately that here was a well-traveled spacewoman. Crystallized, we Tritovians are not that common.

"Gotta take him to Empire Star."

Charona thought quietly behind the wrinkled mask of her face, and I could tell from the overtones that they were multiplex thoughts, with images of space and the stars seen in the blackness of galactic night, weird landscapes that were unfamiliar even to me. The four hundred years as gate guardian to the Transport Area of Rhys had leveled her mind to something nearly simplex. But multiplexity had awakened.

"I shall try and explain something to thee, Comet. Tell me, what's the most important thing there is?"

"Jhup," he answered promptly, then saw her frowning. He got embarrassed. "I mean plyasil. I din' mean to use no dirty words." And I was dropped back in his pouch.

"Words don't bother me, Comet. In fact, I always found it a little funny that thy people had such a thing as a 'dirty word' for plyasil. Though I suppose 'tis not so funny when I recall the 'dirty words' on the world I came from. Water was the taboo term where I grew up—there was very little of it, and thou dared not refer to it by other than its chemical formula in a technological discussion, and never in front of your teacher. And on Earth, in our great-great-grandfather's time, food once eaten and passed from the body could not be spoken of by its common name in polite company."

"But wha' dirty about food an' water?"

"What's dirty about jhup?"

He was surprised at her use of the common slang. But she was always dealing with truckers and loaders who had notoriously filthy mouths and lacked respect for everything—said Uncle Clemence.

"I dunno."

"It's an organic plastic that grows in the flower of a mutant strain of grain that only blooms with the radiation that comes from the heart of Rhys in the darkness of the caves. It's of no use to anyone on this planet, except as an alloy strengthener for other plastics, and yet it is Rhys' only purpose in the Universal plan—to supply the rest of the galaxy. For there are places where it is needed. All men and women on Rhys work to produce or process or transport it. That is all it is. Nowhere in my definition have I mentioned anything about dirt."

"Well, if a bag of it breaks open and spills, it's sort of . . . well not dirty, but messy."

"Spilled water or spilled food is messy too. But none of them by nature so."

"You just don' talk about certain things in front o' nice people. That's what Unca' Clem says." Jo finally took refuge in his training. "An' like ya say, jhup is the most important thing there is, so that's why you have to . . . well, be a little respectful."

"I didn't say it. You did. And that is why thou hast a simplex mind. If thou passeth through the second gate and asketh a ride of a Transport captain—and thou wilt probably get it, for they are a good lot—thou wilt be in a different world, where plyasil means only forty credits a ton and is a good deal less important than derny, kibblepobs, clapper boxes, or boysh, all of which bring above fifty. And thou might shout the name of any of them, and be thought nothing more than noisy."

"I ain't gonna go shoutin' nothing aroun'," Comet Jo assured her. "An' all I can get from ya' jabber about 'simplex' is that I know how to be polite, even if a lotta other people don'—I know I'm not as polite as I should be, but I do know how."

Charona laughed. 3-Dog ran back and rubbed her hip with his head.

"Perhaps I can explain it in purely metaphorical terms, though painfully I know that thou wilt not understand until thou hast seen for thyself. Stop and look above."

They paused in the broken stone and looked up.

"See the holes?" she asked.

In the plating that floored the bridge, here and there were pinpricks of light.

"They just look like random dots, do they not?"

He nodded.

"That's the simplex view. Now start walking and keep looking."

Comet started to walk, steadily, staring upward. The dots of light winked out, and here and there others appeared, then winked out again, and more, or perhaps the original ones, returned.

"There's a superstructure of girders above the bridge that gets in the way of some of the holes and keeps thee from perceiving all at once. But thou art now receiving the complex view, for thou art aware that there is more than what is seen from any one spot. Now, start to run, and keep thy head up."

Jo began to run along the rocks. The rate of flickering increased, and suddenly he realized that the holes were in a pattern, six-pointed stars crossed by diagonals of seven holes each. It was only with the flickering coming so fast that the entire pattern could be perceived—

He stumbled, and skidded onto his hands and knees.

"Didst thou see the pattern?"

"Eh . . . yeah." Jo shook his head. His palms stung through the gloves, and one knee was raw.

"That was the multiplex view."

3-Dog bent down and licked his face.

Di'k watched a little scornfully from the fork of a trident bush.

"Thou hast also encountered one of the major difficulties of the simplex mind attempting to encompass the multiplex view. Thou art very likely to fall flat on thy face. I really do not know if thou wilt make the transition, though thou art young, and older people than thou have had to harken. Certainly I wish thee luck. Though for the first few legs of thy journey, thou canst always turn around and come back, and even with a short hop to Ratshole thou wilt have seen a good deal more of the universe than most of the people of Rhys. But the farther thou goest, the harder it will be to return."

Comet Jo pushed 3-Dog aside and stood up. His next question came both from fear of his endeavor and the pain in his hands. "Brooklyn Bridge," he said, still looking up. "Why they call it Brooklyn Bridge?" He asked it as one asks a question without an answer, and had his mind been precise enough to articulate its true meaning, he would have asked, "Why is that structure there to trip me up at all?"

But Charona was saying, "On Earth, there is a structure similar to this that spans between two islands—though it is a little smaller than this one here. 'Bridge' is the name for this sort of structure, and Brooklyn is the name of the place it leads to, so it was called Brooklyn Bridge. The first colonists brought the name with them and gave it to what thou seest here."

"Ya mean there's a reason?"

Charona nodded.

Suddenly an idea caught in his head, swerved around a corner, and came up banging and clanging behind his ears. "Will I get to see Earth?"

"'Twill not take thee too far afield," Charona said.

"And c'n I see Brooklyn Bridge?" His feet had started to move in the boots.

"I saw it four hundred years ago, and 'twas still standing then."

Comet Jo suddenly jumped up and tried to beat his fists against the sky, which was a beautifully complex action that gave me more hope; then he ran forward, leaped against one of the stanchions of the bridge and, from sheer exuberance, scurried up a hundred feet of thermoplast.

Stopping at two girders' groin, he looked down. "Hey, Charona! I'm gonna go Earth! Me, Comet Jo, I'm gonna go Earth an' see Brooklyn Bridge!"

Below us the gatekeeper smiled and stroked 3-Dog's head.

FOUR

They came up from beneath the balustrade as the rain ceased. Climbing over the railing, they strolled across the water-blackened tarmac toward the second gate. "Thou art sure?" Charona asked him once more.

A little warily, he nodded.

"And what should I say to thy Uncle when he comes inquiring, which he will."

At the thought of Uncle Clemence, the wariness increased. "Jus' say I gone away."

Charona nodded, pulled the second lever, and the gate rose.

"And wilt thou be taking that?" Charona pointed to Di'k.

"Sure. Why not?" And at that he strode bravely forward. Di'k looked right, left, then ran after him. Charona would have gone through herself to accompany the boy, but suddenly there was a signal light flashing, which said her presence was required at the first gate again. So only her gaze went with him, as the gate lowered. Then she turned back, this time across the bridge.

He had never done more than look through the second gate at the bulbous forms of the ships, at the loading buildings, at the mechanical loaders and sledges that plied the pathways of the Transport Area. When he stepped through, he looked around, waiting for the world to be very different, as Charona had warned. But his conception of *different* was rather simplex, so that twenty feet along he was disappointed.

Another twenty feet and disappointment was replaced by ordinary curiosity. A saucer-sled was sliding toward him, and a tall figure guided it austerely down the slip. There was a small explosion of fear and surprise when he realized the saucer was coming directly at him. A moment later it stopped.

The woman standing there—and it took him a minute to figure it out, for her hair was long like a man's and elaborately coiffed like no one's he'd ever seen—wore a glittering red dress, where panels of different textures (though the color was all the same) wrapped her or swung away in the damp dawn breeze. Her hair and lips and nails were red, he realized. That *was* odd. She looked down at him, and said, "You are a beautiful boy."

"Wha'?" asked Comet.

"I said you are a beautiful boy."

"Well, jhup, I mean . . . well . . . ." Then he stopped looking at his feet and stared back up at her.

"But your hair is a mess."

He frowned. "Whaddya mean it's a mess?"

"I mean exactly what I say. And *where* did you learn to speak Interling? Or am I just getting a foggy telepathic equivalent of your oral utterance?"

"Wha'?"

"Never mind. You are still a beautiful boy. I will give you a comb, and I will give you diction lessons. Come to me on the ship—you *will* be taking my ship, since there is no other one leaving soon. Ask for San Severina."

The saucer-disk turned to slide away.

"Hey, whe'ya goin'?" Comet Jo called.

"Comb your hair first, and we shall discuss it at lessons." She removed something from a panel of her dress and tossed it to him.

He caught it, looked at it. It was a red comb.

He pulled his mass of hair across his shoulder for inspection. It was snarled from the night's journey to the Transport Area. He struck at it a few times, hoping that perhaps the comb was some special type that would make unsnarling easier. It wasn't. So it took him about ten minutes, and then, to avoid repeating the ordeal as long as possible, he braided it deftly down one shoulder. Then he put the comb to his pouch and took out the ocarina.

He was passing a pile of cargo when he saw a young man a few years his senior perched on top of the boxes, hugging his knees and staring down at him. He was barefooted, shirtless, and his frayed pants were held on by rope. His hair was of some indiscriminately sexless length and a good deal more snarled than Jo's had been. He was very dirty, but he was grinning.

"Hey!" Jo said. "Know where I can getta ride outta here?"

"T'chapubna," the boy said, pointing across the field, "f'd jhup n' Lll."

Jo felt a little lost that the only thing he understood in the sentence was a swear word.

"I wanna get a ride," Jo repeated.

"T'chapubna," the boy said, and pointed again. Then he put his hands to his mouth as though he too were playing an ocarina.

"You wanna try?" Jo asked and then wished he hadn't, because the boy was so dirty.

But the boy shook his head, smiling. "Jus' a shuttle-bum. Can' make no music." Which half made sense, maybe. "Where ya from?" Jo asked.

"Jus' a shuttle-bum," the boy repeated. Now he pointed to the pink moon-moon above the horizon. "Dere n' back, dere n' back, 'sall I ever been." He smiled again.

"Oh," Jo said, and smiled because he couldn't think of anything else to do. He wasn't sure if he'd gotten any information from the conversation or not. He started playing the ocarina again and kept walking.

He headed directly for a ship this time; the one being loaded.

Jo crossed what seemed acres of tarmac.

A beefy man was supervising the robo-loaders, checking things off against a list. His greasy shirt was still damp from the rain, and he had tied it across his hairy stomach, which bulged below and above the knot.

Another boy, this one closer to Jo's age, was leaning against a guy cable that ran from the ship. Like the first, he was dirty, shoeless, and shirtless. One pant leg was torn off at the knee, and two belt loops were held together with a twist of wire. The weatherburned face even lacked the readiness to smile that the other's held. The boy leaned out from the guy and swung his body slowly around, to watch Jo as he came past.

Jo started to approach the big man checking the loading, but the man had gotten very busy reorganizing the pile that one of the loaders had done incorrectly, so Jo stepped back. He looked at the boy again, gave a half-smile and nodded. Comet didn't feel much like getting into a conversation, but the boy nodded shortly back, and the man looked like he was going to be busy for a while.

"Ya a shuttle-bum?" Jo asked.

The boy nodded.

"Ya go from there n' back?" he asked, pointing toward the disk of the moon-moon.

The boy nodded again.

"Any chance my hoppin' a ride out toward . . . well, anywhere?"

"There is if you want to take a job," the boy said.

The accent surprised Jo.

"Sure," Jo said. "If I gotta work, I don't mind."

The boy pulled himself upright on the wire. "Hey, Elmer," he called. The man looked back, then flipped a switch on his wrist-console, and the robo-loaders all halted. *That was simple,* Jo thought.

"What dost thou wish?" Elmer asked, turning around and wiping his forehead.

"We have that second shuttle-bum. The kid wants a job."

"Well and good," Elmer said. "Thou wilt take care of him, then. He looks a likely lad, but feed him well and he'll work, I warrant." He grinned and turned back to the robo-loaders.

"You're hired," the boy said. "My name's Ron."

"I'm Jo," Jo said. "They call me Comet Jo."

Ron laughed out loud and shook Jo's hand. "I'll never figure it. I've been running the stasiscurrents for six months now, and every tried and true spaceman you meet is Bob or Hank or Elmer. Then, the minute you hit some darkside planet or one-product simplex culture, everybody's Starman, or Cosmic Smith, or Comet Jo." He clapped Jo on the shoulder. "Don't take offense, but thou wilt lose thy 'comet' soon enough."

Jo took no offense, mainly because he wasn't sure what Ron was talking about, but he smiled. "Whe' ya from?"

"I'm taking a year off from Centauri University to bounce around the stars, work a little when I have to. I've been shuttle-bumming across this quarter of the spiral for a couple of months. You notice Elmer here's got me talking like a real spaceman?"

"That guy sittin' back there? He from the . . . University too?"

"Hank? That darkside, noplex kid who was sitting on the cargo?" Ron laughed.

"Noplex?" Jo asked. He connected the word to the others he had learned that morning. "Like simplex, complex, and that stuff?"

Ron apparently realized that the query was serious. "There's no such thing as no-plex, really. But sometimes you wonder. Hank just bums between Rhys and moon-moon. His folks are h-poor, and I don't even think he can read and write his name. Most shuttle-bums come from similar situations, thou wilt discover. They just have their one run, usually between two planets, and that's all they'll ever see. But I star hop too. I want to make mate's position before the Half Spin is over, so I can go back to school with some money, but thou must begin somewhere. How far are you going?"

"Empire Star," Jo said. "Do ya . . . I mean doest thou know whe' it is?"

"Trying to pick up a spaceman's accent already?" Ron asked. "Don't worry, it'll rub off on you before you know. Empire Star? I guess it's about seventy, seventy-five degrees around galactic center."

"Seventy-two degrees, at a distance of 55.9," Jo said.

"Then why did you ask me?" Ron said.

" 'Cause that don' tell me nothin'."

Ron laughed again. "Oh. I see. Thou hast never been in space before?"

Jo shook his head.

"I see," repeated Ron, and the laugh got louder. "Well, it will mean something shortly. Believe thou me, it will!" Then Ron saw Di'k. "Is that yours?"

Jo nodded. "I can take him wi' me, can' I?"

"Elmer's the Captain. Ask him."

Jo looked at the Captain, who was furiously rearranging a cargo pile to balance on the loader. "All right," he said, and started toward him. "Elm—"

Ron grabbed his shoulder. Jo swung around. "Wha'? Jhup—"

"Not *now*, noplex! Wait till he's finished."

"But *you* just—"

"You're not me," Ron explained, "and he wasn't trying to balance the load when I stopped him. If you call him by his name, he has to stop, and you might have killed him if that load fell over."

"Oh. Wha' should I call him?"

"Try 'Captain,'" Ron said. "That's what he is, and when you call him that, he doesn't have to stop what he's doing unless it's convenient. Only call him Elmer if it's an emergency." He looked sideways at Jo. "On second thought, let somebody else decide if it's an emergency or not. To you he's 'Captain' until he tells you otherwise."

"Was it an emergency when you called him?"

"He wanted another shuttle-bum for this trip, but I also saw that he wasn't doing anything he couldn't stop, and . . . well, you've just got a lot to learn."

Jo looked crestfallen.

"Cheer up," Ron said. "You do nice things on the sweet potato there. I have a guitar inside—I'll get it out, and we can play together, hey?" He grabbed hold of the guy line and started to climb hand over hand. He disappeared into the overhanging hatch. Jo watched, wide-eyed. Ron wasn't even wearing gloves.

Just then Captain Elmer said, "Hey, thou canst take thy kitten, but thou must leave those gloves and boots."

"Huh? Why?"

"Because I say so. Ron?"

The shuttle-bum looked out of the hatch. "What?" He was holding a guitar.

"Explain to him about culture-banned artifacts."

"Okay," Ron said, and slid down the guy wire again with his feet and one hand. "You better chuck those now."

Reluctantly Jo began to peel them from his hands and feet.

"You see, we're going to be running to some complex cultures, with a technology a lot below the technology that made those boots. If they got out, it might disrupt their whole culture."

"We couldn't make them boots," Jo said, "and Charona gave . . .'em to me."

"That's because you're simplex here. Nothing could disrupt *your* culture, short of moving it to another environment. And even then, you'd probably come up with the same one. But complex cultures are touchy. We're taking a load of jhup to Genesis. Then the Lll will go on to Ratshole. You can probably pick up a ride there to Earth if you want. I guess you want to see Earth. Everybody does."

Jo nodded.

"From Earth you can go anywhere. Maybe you'll even get a ride straight on to Empire Star. What do you have to go there for?"

"Gotta take a message."

"Yeah?" Ron began to tune the guitar.

Jo opened his pouch and took me out—I rather wished he wouldn't go showing me around to everyone. There were some people who would get rather upset if I showed up, crystallized or not.

"This," Jo said. "I gotta take this there."

Ron peered at me. "Oh, I see." He put the guitar down. "I guess it's good you're going with the shipment of Lll then."

I smiled to myself. Ron was a multiplexually educated young man. I shuddered to think what would have happened had Jo shown me to Hank; the other shuttle-bum would just as likely have tried to make Jo trade me for something or other, and that would have been disastrous.

"What's Lll?" Jo asked. "Is that one of the things more important than jhup?"

"Good lord, yes," Ron said. "You've never seen any, have you?"

Jo shook his head.

"Come on, then," said Ron. "We can play later. Up into the hatch with you, and throw your boots and gloves away."

Jo left them on the tarmac and began to climb the cable. It was easier than he'd anticipated, but he was sweating at the top. Di'k simply climbed up the ship's hull with his cupped feet and was waiting for him in the hatch.

Jo followed Ron down a hallway, down through another hatchway, down a short ladder. "The Lll are in here," Ron said before a circular door. He was still holding the guitar by the neck. He pushed open the door, and something grabbed Jo by the stomach and twisted. Tears mounted in his eyes, and his mouth opened. His breath began to come very slowly.

"Really hit you, didn't it?" Ron said, his voice soft. "Let's go inside."

Jo was scared, and when he stepped into the half-darkness, his gut fell twenty feet with each step. He blinked to clear his vision, but the tears came again.

"Those are the Lll," Ron said.

Jo saw tears on Ron's weathered face. He looked forward again.

They were chained by the wrists and ankles to the floor; seven of them, Jo counted. Their great green eyes blinked in the blue cargo light. Their backs were humped, their heads shaggy. Their bodies seemed immensely strong.

"What am I . . ." Jo tried to say, but something caught in his throat, and the sound rasped. "What am I feelin'?" he whispered, for it was as loud as he could speak.

"Sadness," Ron said.

Once named, the emotion grew recognizable—a vast, overpowering sadness that drained all movement from his muscles, all joy from his eyes.

"They make me feel . . . sad?" Jo asked. "Why?"

"They're slaves," Ron said. "They build—build beautifully, wonderfully. They're extremely valuable. They built over half the Empire. And the Empire protects them, this way."

"Protects . . . ?" Jo asked.

"You can't get near them without feeling like this."

"Then who would buy them?"

"Not many people. But enough so that they are incredibly valuable slaves."

"Why don't they turn 'em *loose?*" Jo asked, and the sentence became a cry halfway through.

"Economics," Ron said.

"How can ya think 'bout economics feelin' like . . . this?"

"Not many people can," Ron said. "That's the Lll's protection."

Jo knuckled his eyes. "Let's get outta here."

"Let's stay awhile," Ron countered. "We'll play for them now." He sat down on a crate, put his guitar on his lap, and pulled from it a modal chord. "Play," Ron said. "I'll follow you."

Jo began to blow, but his breath was so weak that the note quavered and died half-sung. "I . . . I don' wanna," Jo protested.

"It's your job, shuttle-bum," Ron said, simply. "You have to take care of the cargo once it's aboard. They like music, and it will make them happy."

"Will it . . . make me happier too?" Jo asked.

Ron shook his head. "No."

Jo raised the ocarina to his mouth, filled his lungs, and blew. The long notes filled the hold of the ship, and as Jo closed his eyes, the tears melted the darkness behind his lids. Ron's obligato wove around the melody Jo coaxed from his ocarina. Each note took on a pungency like perfume and called up before Jo, as he played with eyes shut and streaming, the New Cycle when the plyasil had failed, the funeral of Billy James, the day that Lilly laughed at him when he had tried to kiss her behind the generator of the power fence, the time when the slaughtered kepards had been weighed and he had learned that his weighed ten pounds less than Yl Odic's—and Yl was three years his junior and everybody was always saying how wonderful she was—in short, every unhappy and painful memory of his simplex existence.

When they left the hold half an hour later and, as Ron secured the hatch, the feeling rolled from him like a receding wave, Jo felt exhausted; and he was quivering.

"Hard work, huh?" Ron said, smiling. Tears had streaked the dust on his face.

Jo didn't say anything, only tried to keep from sobbing in earnest with homesickness that still constricted his throat. *You can always turn around and go home*, Charona had said. He almost started to. But a voice over the loudspeaker said, "Will the Beautiful Boy please come for his Interling lesson."

"That's San Severina," Ron said. "She's our only passenger. The Lll belong to her."

An entire matrix of emotions broke open in Jo's head at once, among them outrage, fear, and curiosity. Curiosity won out.

"Her cabin's just up that way and around the corner," Ron said.

Jo started forward. How, he wondered, could she possibly bring herself to own those incredible creatures?

FIVE

"A vast improvement," San Severina said when he opened her door. "I'm sure you're wondering how I could possibly bring myself to own those incredible creatures."

She sat in an opulent bubble chair, sheathed in blue from neck to ankles. Her hair, her lips, her nails were blue.

"It isn't easy."

Jo stepped inside. One wall was covered with crowded bookshelves.

"You, at least," San Severina went on, "only have to feel it when you are in their presence. I, as owner, am subjected to that feeling throughout the entire duration of my ownership. It is part of the contract."

"You feel that way . . . now?"

"Rather more intensely than you did just then. My sensitivity band is a good deal wider than yours."

"But . . . why?"

"It cannot be helped. I have eight worlds, fifty-two civilizations, and thirty-two thousand three hundred and fifty-seven complete and distinct ethical systems to rebuild. I cannot do it without Lll. Three of those worlds are charred black, without a drop of water on their surfaces. One is half-volcanic and must be completely recrusted. Another has lost a good deal of its atmosphere. The other three are at least habitable."

"Wha' happened?" Jo asked incredulously.

"War," said San Severina. "And it is so much more disastrous today than it was a thousand years back. Sixty-eight billion, five hundred thousand, two hundred and five people, reduced to twenty-seven. There was nothing to do but pool our remaining wealth and agree to purchase the Lll. I am bringing them back now, by way of Earth."

"Lll," Jo repeated. "Wha' *are* they?"

"Didn't you ask that other young man?"

"Yeah, but—"

San Severina's smile stopped him. "Ah, the seeds of complexity. When you receive one answer, you ask for a second. Very good. I will give you a second. They are the shame and tragedy of the multiplex universe. No man can be free until they are free. While they are bought and sold, any man may be bought and sold—if the price is high enough. Now come, it's time for your Interling lesson. Would you get me that book?"

Obedient but bewildered, Jo fetched the book from the desk.

"Why I gotta learn speakin'?" he asked as he handed it to her.

"So people can understand you. You have a long journey, at the end of which you must deliver a message, quite precisely, quite accurately. It would be disastrous if you were misheard."

"I don' even know wha' is it!" Jo said.

"You will by the time you deliver it," San Severina said. "But you'd best get to work now."

Jo looked at the book apprehensively. "You got somethin' I can maybe learn it real quick wi', in my sleep or sompin'—like hypnotizin'?" He recalled his disappointment with her comb.

"I have nothing like that with me now," San Severina said sadly. "I thought the other young man explained. We're passing through some rather primitive complex societies. No culture-banned artifacts allowed. I'm afraid you'll have to do it the hard way."

"Jhup," Jo said. "I wanna go home."

"Very well. But you'll have to hitch a ride back from Ratshole. We're a hundred and fifty-three thousand miles away from Rhys already."

"Huh?"

San Severina rose and raised a set of Venetian blinds that covered one wall. Beyond the glass: darkness, the stars, and the red rim of Ceti.

Comet Jo stood with his mouth open.

"While you're waiting, we might get some studying done."

The rim of Ceti grew smaller.

SIX

The actual work on the ship was certainly as easy as tending the underground fields of plyasil. Save for the Lll, it was comparatively pleasant, once it became routine. San Severina's wit and charm made the language lessons a peak of pleasure in an otherwise enjoyable day. Once she rather surprised both Jo and me by saying during one lesson when he seemed particularly recalcitrant and demanded another reason for why he had to improve his Interling: "Besides, think how tiring your clumsy speech will be to your readers."

"My what?" He had already, with difficulty, mastered his final consonants.

"You have undertaken an enterprise of great pith and moment, and I am sure someday somebody will set it down. If you don't improve your diction, you will lose your entire audience before page forty. I suggest you seriously apply yourself, because you are in for quite an exciting time, and it would be rather sad if everyone abandoned you halfway through because of your atrocious grammar and pronunciation."

Her Multiplexedness San Severina certainly had *my* number down.

Four days out, Jo was watching Elmer carefully while he sat whistling at the

T-ward viewport. When he had (definitely) decided that the Captain was not engaged in anything it would be fatal to interrupt, he put his hands behind his back and said, "Elmer?"

Elmer looked around. "Yeah. What is it?"

"Elmer, how come everybody knows more about what I'm doing on this boat than I do?"

"Because they've been doing it longer than thou hast."

"I don't mean about my work. I mean about my trip and the message and everything."

"Oh." Elmer shrugged. "Simplex, complex, and multiplex."

Jo was used to having the three words shoved at him in answer to just about anything he didn't comprehend, but this time he said, "I want another answer."

The Captain leaned forward on his knees, thumbed the side of his nose, and frowned. "Look, thou hast come on board, telling us that thou must take a message to Empire Star about the Lll, so we—"

"Elmer, wait a minute. How do you know the message concerns the Lll?"

Elmer looked surprised. "Doesn't it?"

"I don't know," Jo said.

"Oh," Elmer said. "Well, I do. It does concern the Lll. How it concerns the Lll thou wilt have to find out later, but I can assure thee that it does. That's why Ron showed them to thee first off, and why San Severina is so interested in thee."

"But how does everybody know when I don't?" He felt exasperation growing again in the back of his throat.

"Thou art going to Empire Star," Elmer began again, patiently, "and it is the Empire that protects the Lll."

Comet Jo nodded.

"They are extremely concerned about them, as they should be, as we all are. Thou hast with thee a crystallized Tritovian, and the Tritovians have spearheaded the movement for the emancipation of the Lll. They have worked for it for nearly a thousand years. Therefore, the probability is very high that thy message concerns the Lll."

"Oh . . . that makes sense. But San Severina seems to know things she couldn't even see or figure out."

Elmer gestured for Jo to come closer. "For a person to survive a war that reduces sixty-eight billion people to twenty-seven individuals, that person must know a great deal. And it's a little silly to be surprised that such a person knows a trifle more than thou or I. It's not only silly, it is *unbelievably* simplex. Now get back to work, shuttle-bum."

Having to admit that it was pretty simplex after all, Jo went down in the hole to turn over the boysh and rennedox the kibblepobs. He would not have to play for the Lll again until after supper.

Two days after that, they landed in Ratshole. San Severina took him shopping in the open market and bought him a black velvet contour-cloak with silver embroidery whose patterns changed with the pressure of the light under which it was viewed. Next she took him to a body salon. During the trip he had gotten as grimy as any other shuttle-bum. Holding him gently by the ear, she extended him to the white-smocked proprietor. "Groom this," she said.

"For what?" the proprietor asked.

"First for Earth, then for a long journey."

When they were finished, his braid was gone, his claws had been clipped, and he had been cleaned from teeth to toenails. "How do you like yourself?" she asked, placing the cloak over his shoulders.

Jo ran his hand over his short, yellow hair. "I look like a girl." He frowned. Then he looked at his fingernails. "I just hope I don't run into any kepards on the way." Now he looked at the mirror again. "The cloak's great, though."

When they went outside again, Di'k looked once at Jo, blinked, and got so upset that he giggled himself into the hiccups and had to be carried back to the Transport Area while his belly was scratched and he pulled himself together.

"It's a shame I'm going to have to get dirty again," he told San Severina. "But it's dirty work."

San Severina laughed. "Most delightfully simplex child! You will travel the rest of the way to Earth as my protégé."

"But what about Ron and Elmer?"

"They have already taken off. The Lll have been transferred to another ship."

Jo was surprised, sad, then curious.

"San Severina?"

"Yes?"

"Why have you been doing all this for me?"

She kissed his cheek, then danced back from a halfhearted swipe Di'k made with his horns. Jo was still scratching his tummy. "Because you are a very beautiful boy, and very important."

"Oh," he said.

"Do you understand?"

"No." They continued to the ship.

A week later they stood together on a rocky rise, watching the comparatively tiny disk of the sun set behind the Brooklyn Bridge. A thin worm of water crawled along the dried, black mud ditch still referred to in their guidebook as the East River. The jungle whispered behind them. Across the "river" the webbed cables lowered the bridge itself to the white sands of Brooklyn. "It's smaller than the one at home," Jo said. "But it's very nice."

"You sound disappointed."

"Oh, not with the bridge," Jo said.

"Is it because I have to leave you here?"

"Well . . ." He stopped. "I'd like to say yes. Because I think it would make you feel better. But I don't want to lie."

"The truth is always multiplex," San Severina said, "and you must get in the habit of dealing with multiplexity. What's on your mind?"

"Remember I was saying how nice everybody has been up till now? And you said I could stop expecting people to be nice once I got to Earth? That scares me."

"I also said there would be things other than people that would be nice."

"But people means any sapient being from any life-system. You taught me that. What else, if it's not people?" Suddenly he caught her hand. "You're going to leave me all alone, and I may never see you again!"

"That's right," she said. "But I wouldn't just throw you out into the universe with nothing. So I will give you a piece of advice: find the Lump."

"Eh . . . where do you suggest I find it?" He was bewildered again.

"It's too big to come to Earth. I last saw it on the Moon. It was waiting to have an adventure. You might be just what it's waiting for. I'm sure it will be nice to you; it was always very nice to me."

"It's not a people?"

"No. There, I've given you your advice. I'm going now. I have a lot to do, and you have some idea of the pain I am in till it's accomplished."

"San Severina!"

She stopped.

"That day on Ratshole, when we went shopping, and you laughed and called me a delightfully simplex child—when you laughed, were you happy?"

Smiling, she shook her head. "The Lll are always with me. I must go now."

She backed away, till the leaves brushed across her silver lips, dress, and fingertips. Then she turned, carrying with her the incredible sadness of Lll ownership. Jo watched her, then turned back to see the last points of sunlight melt from the sand.

It was night when he got back to the Transport Terminal. Earth was a large enough tourist area so that there were always people beneath the glittering ceiling. He had not even begun to think about how he was going to get to the Moon, and was walking around expending his curiosity, when a portly, well-dressed gentleman began a conversation. "I say there, young fellow, but you've been here for some time, haven't you? Waiting for a ship?"

"No," Jo said.

"I saw you here this afternoon with that charming young lady, and I couldn't help seeing you this evening. My name's Oscar." He extended his hand.

"Comet Jo," Jo said, and shook it.

"Where you off to?"

"I'd like to get to the Moon. I hitchhiked in from Rhys."

"My, my! That's a long way. What ship are you taking?"

"I don't know. I guess you can't hitch from the terminal very well, can you? I suppose I'd do better to try a commercial stop."

"Certainly, if you wanted to hitch. Of course, if Alfred doesn't show up, maybe you can use his ticket. He's missed two ships already; I don't know why I stick around here waiting for him. Except that we *did* make plans to go together."

"To the Moon?"

"That's right."

"Oh, great," Jo said, brightening. "I hope he doesn't get here—" He caught himself. "That came out all simplex, didn't it?"

"The truth is always multiplex," intoned Oscar.

"Yeah. That's what *she* said."

"The young lady you were with this afternoon?"

Jo nodded.

"Who was she, anyway?"

"San Severina."

"I've heard the name. What was she doing in this arm of the galaxy?"

"She just bought some Lll. She had some work to do."

"Bought *some* Lll, eh? And she didn't leave you with any money for a ticket? You'd think she could spare you the hundred and five credits for Moon fare."

"Oh, she's a very generous person," Jo said. "And you mustn't think badly of her because she bought the Lll. It's awfully sad to own them."

"If I had enough money to buy Lll," said Oscar, "nothing, but *nothing* could make me sad. *Some* Lll? How many did she buy?"

"Seven."

Oscar put his hand on his forehead and whistled. "And the price goes up geometrically! It costs four times as much to buy two as it does to buy one, you know. She didn't give you *any* fare?"

Jo shook his head.

"That's incredible. I never heard of such a thing. Have you any idea how fabulously wealthy that woman must be?"

Jo shook his head again.

"You're not very bright, are you?"

"I never asked how much they cost, and she never told me. I was just a shuttle-bum on her ship."

"Shuttle-bum? That sounds exciting. I always wanted to do something like that when I was your age. Never had the nerve, though." The portly man suddenly looked around the terminal with a perturbed expression. "Look, Alfred isn't going to show up. Use his ticket. Just go up to the desk and ask for it."

"But I don't have any of Alfred's identification," Jo said.

"Alfred never has his identification with him. Always losing his wallet and things like that. Whenever I make reservations for him, I always stipulate that he will probably not have any identification with him. Just tell them you're Alfred A. Douglas. They'll give it to you. Hurry up now."

"Well, okay." He made his way through the people to one of the desk clerks.

"Excuse me," he said. "You've got a ticket for A. Douglas?"

The desk clerk looked through his clipboard. "Yeah. It's right here." He grinned at Jo. "You must have had a pretty good time while you were on Earth."

"Huh?"

"This ticket's been waiting for you for three days."

"Oh," Jo said. "Well, I was sort of in bad shape, and I didn't want my parents to see me till I got myself together."

The desk clerk nodded and winked. "Here's your ticket."

"Thanks," Jo said, and went back to Oscar.

"The next ship's boarding right now," Oscar said. "Come along, come along. He'll just have to figure out some other way to get there."

On the ship, Jo asked, "Do you know if the Lump is still on the Moon?"

"I would expect so. He never goes anywhere, that I've heard of."

"Do you think I'll have trouble finding him?"

"I doubt it. Isn't that a beautiful view out the window?"

Oscar was recounting still another off-color story when they walked from the terminal on Luna. A bright crescent of sunlight lined the plastidome that arched a mile above their heads. The lunar mountains curved away on their right, and Earth hung like a greenish poker chip behind them.

Suddenly someone cried, "*There* they are!"

A woman screamed and moved backward.

"Get them!" someone else called.

"What in the . . . ?" Oscar began to splutter.

Jo looked around. Habit made him raise his left hand. But the claws were gone. Four men—one behind, one in front, one on either side . . . He ducked and bumped into Oscar, who . . . fell apart! Pieces went whirling and skittering about and under his feet.

He looked around, as the four men also exploded. The buzzing, humming fragments whirled through the air, circling him, drawing closer, blurring the bewildered faces of the other debarkees. Then suddenly all the pieces coalesced, and Jo was in shaking darkness. A light came on, just as he collapsed.

"Bosie!" someone shrieked. "Bosie . . . !"

Jo landed in a bubble chair in a very small room which seemed to be moving, but he couldn't be sure. A voice that was Oscar's said, "April fool. Surprise."

"Jhup!" Jo exclaimed, and stood up. "Wha' the jhup is goin'—what's going on?"

"April fool," the voice repeated. "It's my birthday. You look a mess; you haven't let all this upset you?"

"I'm scared to death. What is this? Who are you?"

"I'm the Lump," the Lump said. "I thought you knew."

"Knew what?"

"All that business with Oscar and Alfred and Bosie. I thought you were just playing along."

"Playing along with what? Where am I?"

"On the Moon, of course. I just thought it would be a clever way of getting you here. San Severina *didn't* pay your fare, you know. I suppose she just assumed I would. Well, since I'm footing the bill, you have to allow me a little fun. You didn't get it?"

"Get what?"

"It was a literary allusion. I make them all the time."

"Well, watch it, next time. What are you, anyway?"

"A linguistic ubiquitous multiplex. Lump to you."

"Some sort of computer?"

"*Um-hum.* More or less."

"Well, what's supposed to happen now?"

"You're supposed to tell *me*," the Lump said. "I just help."

"Oh," Jo said.

There was a giggle from behind the bubble chair, and Di'k marched out, sat down in front of Jo, and looked at him reproachfully.

"Where are you taking me?"

"To my home console. You can rest up and make plans there. Sit back and relax. We'll be there in three or four minutes."

Jo sat back. He didn't relax, but he took out his ocarina and played on it until a door opened in the front wall.

"Home again, home again, back the same day," said the Lump. "Won't you come in?"

SEVEN

"I"—he flung his cape at the console—"have got"—he hurled the pouch against the glass wall—"to get outta here!" His final gesture was a flying kick at Di'k. Di'k dodged; Jo stumbled, and regained his balance shaking.

"Who's stopping you?" the Lump asked.

"Jhup ya," Jo grunted. "Look, I've been here for three weeks, and every time I get ready to go, we end up in one of those ridiculous conversations that last for nine hours, and then I'm too tired." He walked down the hall and picked up his cloak. "All right, so I'm stupid. But why do you take such delight in rubbing it in? I can't help it if I'm a dark-sided noplex—"

"You're not noplex," the Lump said. "Your view of things is quite complex by now—though there is a good deal of understandable nostalgia for your old simplex perceptions. Sometimes you try to support them just for the sake of argument. Like the time we were discussing the limiting psychological factors in the apprehension of the specious present, and you insisted on maintaining that—"

"Oh, no you don't!" Jo said. "I'm not getting into another one." By now he'd reached his pouch at the other end of the hall. "I'm leaving. Di'k, let's go."

"You," said the Lump, a lot more authoritatively than it usually spoke, "are being silly."

"So I'm simplex. I'm still going."

"Intelligence and plexity have nothing to do with each other."

"There's the spaceship you just spent four days teaching me how to use," Jo said, pointing off through the glass wall. "You put a hypno implant of the route in my head the first night I was here. What under the light of seven suns is stopping me?"

"Nothing is *stopping* you," replied the Lump. "And if you would get it out of your head that something was, you could relax and do this thing sensibly."

Exasperated, Jo turned to face the sixty-foot wall of microlinks and logic-blocks, with their glitter of check lights and reprogram keyboards. "Lump, I *like* it here. You're great to have for a friend, you really are. But I get all my food, all my exercise, everything; and I'm going crazy. Do you think it's easy just to walk out and leave you like this?"

"Don't be so emotional," the Lump said. "I'm not set up to deal with that sort of thing."

"Do you know that since I've stopped being a shuttle-bum, I've done less work than I ever have in my life during any comparable period?"

"You have also changed more than you have during any comparable period."

"Look, Lump, try and understand." Jo dropped his cloak and walked back over to the console. It was a large mahogany desk. He pulled out the chair, crawled in under it, and hugged his knees. "Lump, I don't think you *do* understand. So listen. Here you are, in touch with all the libraries and museums of this arm of the galaxy. You've got lots of friends, people like San Severina and the other people who're always stopping by to see you. You write books, make music, paint pictures. Do you think you could be happy in a little one-product culture where there was nothing to do on Saturday night except get drunk, with just one teletheater, and no library, where maybe four people had been to the University, and you never saw them anyway because they were making too much money, and everybody knew everybody else's business?"

"No."

"Well, I could, Lump."

"Why did you leave, then?"

"Well . . . because of the message. And because there were a lot of things I don't think I really appreciated. I don't think I was ready to leave. *You* couldn't be happy there. *I* could. It's as simple as that, and I don't really think you fully comprehend that."

"I do," Lump said. "I hope you can be happy in someplace like that. Because that's what most of the universe is composed of. You're slated to spend a great deal of time in places like that, and if you *couldn't* appreciate them, it would be rather sad."

Di'k looked under the desk and then jumped into Jo's lap. It was always ten degrees warmer under the desk, and the two warmblooded creatures, Di'k and Jo, independently or together, sought the spot out again and again.

"Now *you* listen," Lump said.

Jo leaned his head against the side of the desk. Di'k jumped down from his lap, went out, and came back a moment later dragging the plastic pouch. Jo opened it and took out the ocarina.

"There are things I can tell you, most of which I have already told you. There are things you have to ask me. Very few of them have you asked. I know much more about you than you know about me. And if we are to be friends—which is very important for you and for me—that situation must be changed."

Jo put his ocarina down. "That's right—I don't know that much about you, Lump. Where do you come from?"

"I was built by a dying Lll to house its disassociating consciousness."

"Lll?" Jo asked.

"You'd almost forgotten about them, hadn't you?"

"No I didn't."

"You see, my mind is a Lll mind."

"But you don't make me sad."

"I'm half Lll and half machine. So I forfeit the protection."

"You're a Lll?" Jo asked again, incredulously. "It never occurred to me. Now that you've told me, do you think it will make any difference?"

"I doubt it," the Lump said. "But if you say anything about some of your best friends, I will lose a great deal of respect for you."

"What about my best friends?" Jo asked.

"Another allusion. It's all just as well you didn't get it."

"Lump, why don't we go on together?" Jo said suddenly. "I am leaving—that I've made up my mind to. Why don't you come with me?"

"Delightful idea. I thought you'd never ask. That's the only way you could get out of here anyway. Of course, the area in which we're going is very hostile to free Lll. It's right into Empire territory. They protect Lll, and they get rather upset if one shrugs off their protection and decides to stay free on her or his own. Some of the things they have been known to do are atrocious."

"Well, if anybody asks, just say you're a computer. Like I said, I wouldn't have known if you hadn't said anything."

"I do *not* intend to pass," the Lump said sternly.

"Then *I'll* say you're a computer. But let's get going. We'll be here for hours if this keeps up. I can feel another one of those discussions starting." He stood up from under the desk and started for the door.

"Comet?"

Jo stopped and looked back over his shoulder. "What? Don't change your mind on me now."

"Oh, no. I'm definitely going. But . . . well, if I were—now be honest—just lumping along the street, do you really think people would just say, 'Oh, there goes a linguistic ubiquitous multiplex,' and not think about Lll?"

"That's what I'd say if I said anything at all."

"All right. Take the tube to Journal Square, and I'll meet you in forty minutes."

Di'k octopeded after Jo as he ran across the cracked, dusty plain of the Moon toward the egg-shaped spaceship.

The tube was an artificial stasis current that took ships quickly beyond Pluto, where they could leave the system without fear of heavy solar-dust damage.

The great slab of plastic, some ten miles on either side—Journal Square—supported buildings, its own atmosphere, and several amusement areas. Jo parked his ship on a side street and stepped into the chill air.

Soldiers were practicing drill formation in the square.

"What are they doing that for?" he asked one uniformed man resting on the side.

"It's the field brigade of the Empire Army. They'll be heading out of there in a few days; they won't be here long."

"I wasn't objecting," Jo said. "Just curious."

"Oh," the soldier said, and offered no further explanation.

"Where are they going?" Jo asked after a moment.

"Look," the soldier said, turning to Jo as he would to a persistent child, "everything about the Empire Army that you can't see immediately is secret. If where they're going doesn't concern you, forget it. If it does, go see if you can get clearance from Prince Nactor."

"Nactor?" Jo asked.

"That one." The soldier pointed to a dark man with a goatee who was leading one platoon.

"I don't think it does," Jo said.

The soldier gave him a disgusted look, got up, and moved away. Together black capes swung out as the men snapped briskly around a turn.

Then there was a commotion among the spectators. People looked up and began to point and talk excitedly.

It caught the sun, spinning toward the square, getting larger and larger. It was roughly cubical and—huge! As one face turned toward the light, another disappeared, till Jo suddenly regained his sense of proportion: it was nearly a quarter of a mile long on each side.

It struck the square, and Jo and all the soldiers—and one of the taller buildings—fell down. There was mass confusion, sirens sounded, and people ran to and from the object.

Jo started running toward it. Low gravity got him there fairly quickly. There were a couple of large cracks in the square that jagged out across the area. He leaped across one and saw stars below him.

Catching his breath, he landed on the other side and proceeded a little more slowly. The object, he realized, was covered with some sort of boiling jelly; the jelly looked surprisingly familiar, but he could not place it. The face of the object that was turned toward him, he could make out through the mildly smoking slop, was glass. And beyond the glass, dim in the interior transplutonian night: microlinks, logic-blocks, and the faint glitter of check-lights.

"Lump!" Jo cried, running forward.

"*Shhhh,*" a familiar voice said, muffled by jelly. "I'm trying not to attract attention."

Soldiers were marching by now. "What the hell *is* that thing, anyway?" said one.

"It's a linguistic ubiquitous multiplex," said the other.

The first scratched his head and looked up and down the length of the wall. "Ubiquitous as hell, isn't it?"

A third was examining the edge of a crack in the square. "Think they're gonna have to get a damned Lll in here to rebuild this?"

Lump whispered, "Just let one of them say anything to my face. Just one—"

"Oh, shut up," Jo said, "or I won't let you marry my daughter."

"What's that supposed to mean?"

"It's an allusion," Jo explained. "I did some reading while you were taking a nap last week."

"Very funny, very funny," the Lump said.

The soldiers started to walk away. "They won't get no Lll in," one of the soldiers said, scratching his ear. "This is soldier work. We do all the real building around here anyway. Wish there *was* a damned Lll around, though."

Several of Lump's check-lights changed color behind the jelly.

"What's that jhup all over you?" Jo asked, stepping back now.

"My spaceship," the Lump said. "I'm using an organiform. They're much more comfortable for inanimate objects like me. Haven't you ever seen one before?"

"No—yes! Back on Rhys. That's what the Tritovian and those other things came in."

"Odd," said Lump. "They don't usually use organiforms. They're not particularly inanimate."

More people were gathering around the computer. The sirens were getting close.
"Let's just get out of here," Jo said. "Are you all right?"

"I'm fine," Lump said. "I just wonder about the square."

"Bloody but unbowed," Jo said. "That's another allusion. Get going and we'll reconnoiter at Tantamount."

"Fine," Lump said. "Step back. I'm taking off."

There was a bubbling, a tremendous *suck,* and Jo staggered in the wind. People started screaming again.

Back at Jo's ship, Di'k was hiding under the dashboard with forepaws over his head. Jo pushed the takeoff button, and the robo-crew took over. The confusion of the square dropped beneath them. He ran over his hyperstasis checkout, then signaled for the jump.

The stasis generators surged, and the ship began to slip into hyperstasis. He hadn't finished slipping when the ship lurched and he smashed forward into the dashboard. His wrists took the shock, and he bounced away with both of them aching. Di'k screeched.

EIGHT

Jo pried his canines out of his lower lip.

"You're not playing chess," the voice went on. "If you occupy my square, I will not be removed from the board. Look out, next time."

"Gnnnnnnng," Jo said, rubbing his mouth.

"Same to you and many more."

Jo shook his head and put on his sensory helmet. It smelled like old jhup. It sounded like scrap metal being crushed under a hydraulic press. But it looked beautiful.

Ramps curved away into structures that blossomed like flowers. Thin spires erupted at their tips in shapes of metal, and fragile observation domes were supported on slender pylons.

"You might come out of there and see if you've done any damage to us."

"Oh," Jo said. "Yeah. Sure."

He started to the lock and was about to release it when he realized the warning light was still on. "Hey," he called back toward the intercom, "there's no air out there."

"I thought you were going to take care of that," the voice answered. "Just a second." The light went off.

"Thanks," Jo said. He pulled the release. "What are you, anyway?"

Outside the lock a balding man in a white smock was coming down one of the ramps. "This is the Geodesic Survey Station that you almost ran down, youngster." His voice was much diminished, in person. "You better get on inside the force-field, before this atmosphere escapes. I don't know what you thought you were doing anyway."

"I was finishing up a stasis jump, on my way to Tantamount. Simplex of me, wasn't it?" Jo started back up the ramp with the man, who shrugged.

"I never pass judgments like that," the man said. "Now tell me your specialty."

"I don't have one, I don't think."

The man frowned. "I don't think we need a synthesizer right now. They tend to be extremely long-lived."

"I know just about everything there is to know about raising and storing plyasil," Jo said.

The man smiled. "I'm afraid that wouldn't do much good. We're only up to volume one hundred and sixty-seven: *Bba* to *Bbaab*."

"It's common term is jhup," Jo said.

The man smiled benignly at him. "*Jh* is still a long way away. But if you're alive in five or six hundred years, we'll take your application."

"Thanks," Jo said. "But I'll just forget it."

"Very well," the man said, turning to him. "Good-bye."

"Well, what about the damage to *my* ship? Aren't you going to check me over? You're not supposed to be here, in the first place. I've got through clearance on this path."

"Young man," the gentleman said, "first of all, we have priority. Second of all, if you don't want a job, you are abusing our hospitality by using up our air. Third of all, there is advance work being done in *biology, human*—and if you bother me anymore, I'll ship you off for a specimen and have you cut up in little pieces. And don't think I won't."

"What about my message?" Jo demanded. "I've got to get a message through concerning the Lll, to Empire Star. And it's important. That's why I rammed into you in the first place."

The man's face had become hostile.

"Eventually," he said, evenly, "we will finish our project, and there will be enough knowledge so that Lll will be economically unfeasible, because building will be able to proceed without them. If you want to benefit the Lll, I'll order you sliced up immediately. Father is working on the adenoids now. There is a raft of work to be done on the bicuspids. We've just started the colon, and the duodenum is a complete mystery. If you want to deliver your message, deliver it here."

"But I don't know what it is!" Jo said, backing out toward the edge of the force-field. "I think I'll be going."

"We have a computer for just such problems as yours," the man said. "Not with a lungful of *our* air, you're not," he added, and lunged toward Jo.

Jo saw where he was lunging and simply wasn't there.

The force-field was permeable, and he ducked through, sprang to the lock of his ship, and slammed it behind him. The warning light blinked on less than a second afterward.

He threw her into reverse and prayed that the automatic pilot could still negotiate the currents and move to a deeper stasis level. It did, if a little jerkily. The Geodesic Survey Station faded from the viewplates of the sensory helmet that was lying face-up on the dashboard.

He reconnoitered easily with Lump in an orbit around Tantamount. It was a planet of iced methane with so much volcanic activity that the surface was constantly being broken and exploded. It was the single daughter of an intensely hot white dwarf, so that from here they looked like two eyes, one jeweled and glittering, one of silver-gray, spying on the night.

"Lump, I want to go home. Back to Rhys. Give up the whole thing."

"What in the world for?" came the computer's incredulous voice over the intercom.

Jo leaned on his elbows, looking morosely at his ocarina. "The multiplex universe doesn't appeal to me. I don't like it. I want to get away from it. If I'm complex now, it's too bad, it's a mistake, and if I ever get back to Rhys, I'll try as hard as I can to be simplex. I really will."

"What's got into you?"

"I just don't like the people. I think it's that simple. You ever heard of the Geodesic Survey Station?"

"Certainly have. You run into them?"

"Yeah."

"That *is* unfortunate. Well, there are certain sad things in the multiplex universe that must be dealt with. And one of the things is simplexity."

"Simplexity?" Jo asked. "What do you mean?"

"And you better be thankful that you have acquired as much multiplexity of vision as you have, or you never would have gotten away from them alive. I've heard tell of other simplex creatures encountering them. They don't come back."

"They're simplex?"

"Good God, yes. Couldn't you tell?"

"But they're compiling all that information. And the place they live—it's beautiful. They couldn't be stupid and have built that."

"First of all, most of the Geodesic Survey Station was built by Lll. Second of all, as I have said many times before, intelligence and plexity do not necessarily go together."

"But how was I supposed to know?"

"I suppose it won't hurt to outline the symptoms. Did they ask you a single question?"

"No."

"That's the first sign, though not conclusive. Did they judge you correctly, as you could tell from their statements about you?"

"No. They thought I was looking for a job."

"Which implies that they should have asked questions. A multiplex consciousness always asks questions when it has to."

"I remember," Jo said, putting down the ocarina, "when Charona was trying to explain it to me, she asked me what was the most important thing there was. If I asked them that, I know what they would have said: their blasted dictionary, or encyclopedia, or whatever it is."

"Very good. Anyone who can give a nonrelative answer to that question is simplex."

"I said jhup," Jo recalled wistfully.

"They're in the process of cataloging all the knowledge in the Universe."

"That's more important than jhup, I suppose," Jo said.

"From a complex point of view, perhaps. But from a multiplex view, they're about the same. First of all, it's a rather difficult task. When last I heard, they were already up to the B's, but I'm sure they don't have a thing on Aaaaaaaaaaaaaaaaaaavdqx."

"What's . . . well, what you just said?"

"It's the name for a rather involved set of deterministic moral evaluations taken through a relativistic view of the dynamic moment. I was studying it some years back."

"I wasn't familiar with the term."

"I just made it up. But what it stands for is quite real, and well worth an article. I don't think they could even comprehend it. But from now on, I shall refer to it as Aaaaaaaaaaaaaaaaaaavdqx, and there are two of us who know the word now—so it's valid."

"I guess I get the point."

"Besides, cataloging all knowledge, even all available knowledge, while admirable, is . . . well, the only word is simplex."

"Why?"

"One can learn all one needs to know; or one can learn what one wants to know.

But to need to learn all one wants to know, which is what the Geodesic Survey Station is doing, even falls apart semantically. What's the matter with your ship?"

"The Geodesic Survey Station again. We collided."

"I don't like the looks of it."

"My takeoff was sort of jerky."

"Don't like the looks of it at all. Especially considering how far we have to go. Why don't you hop on over here and travel with me? This organiform is a beauty, and I think I've got my landings and takeoffs a little more under control."

"If you promise not to break my back when we land."

"Promise," the Lump said. "I'll open up. Swing around to your left and you can leave that jalopy right where it is."

They made contact.

"Jo," Lump said, as the flexible tube attached to his air lock, "if you really want to, you can go back. But there comes a point where going back is harder than going on. You've received a great deal of very specialized education. Not only what San Severina and I have tried to teach you, but even back on Rhys you were learning."

Jo started through the tube. "I still wanna go home." He slowed his pace as he moved toward the console room. "Lump, sometimes, even if you're simplex, you ask yourself, who am I? All right, you say the Geodesic Survey Station was simplex. That makes me feel a little better. But I'm still a very ordinary kid who would like to get back to a jhup field, and maybe fight off some wild kepards. That's who I am. That's what I know."

"If you went back, you would find the people around you very much like you found the Geodesic Survey. You left your home, Jo, because you weren't happy. Remember why?"

Jo reached the console room but stopped, his hands on either jamb. "Jhup, yeah. Sure I remember. Because I thought I was different. Then the message came along, and I thought that was proof I was special. Else they wouldn't have given it to me. Don't you see, Lump"—he leaned forward on his hands—"if I really knew I was something special—I mean if I was sure—then I wouldn't get so upset by things like the Survey Station. But most of the time I just feel lost and unhappy and ordinary."

"You're you, Jo. You're you and everything that went into you, from the way you sit for hours and watch Di'k when you want to think, to the way you turn a tenth of a second faster in response to something blue than to something red. You're all you ever thought, all you ever hoped, and all you ever hated, too. And all you've learned. You've been learning a lot, Jo."

"But if I knew that it was mine, Lump. That's what I want to be sure of: that the message was really important and that I was the only one who could deliver it. If I really knew that this education I'd gotten had made me—well, like I say, something special—then I wouldn't mind going on. Jhup, I'd be happy to do it."

"Jo, you're you. And that's as important as you want to make it."

"Maybe that's the most important thing there is, Lump. If there is an answer to that question, Lump, that's what it is, to know you're yourself and nobody else."

Just as Jo stepped inside the console room, the speakers from the communications unit began to whisper. As Jo looked around, the whisper increased. "What's that, Lump?"

"I'm not sure."

The door closed, the tube fell away, and the wrecked cruiser drifted back. Jo watched it through the glass wall covered with vaguely distorting organiform.

The speaker was laughing now.

Di'k scratched his ear with one foot.

"It's coming from over there," Lump said. "It's coming awfully fast, too."

Laughter got louder, reached hysteria, filled the high chamber. Something hurtled by the Lump's glass wall, then suddenly swung around and came up short, twenty feet away.

The laughing stopped and was replaced by exhausted gasps.

The thing outside looked like a huge chunk of rock, only the front face had been polished. As they drifted slightly in the glare of Tantamount, the white light slipped from the surface; Jo saw it was a transparent plate. Behind it a figure leaned forward, hands over his head, feet wide apart. Even from here Jo could see the chest heave in time to the panting that stormed through the console room. "Lump, turn down the volume, will you?"

"Oh, I'm sorry." The panting ceased to be something happening inside his ear and settled to a reasonable sound a respectable number of feet away. "Do you want to speak to him, or shall I?"

"You go ahead."

"Who are you?" Lump asked.

"Ni Ty Lee. Who are you, blast it, to be so interesting?"

"I'm the Lump. I've heard of you, Ni Ty Lee."

"I've never heard of you, Lump. But I should have, I know. Why are you so interesting?"

Jo whispered, "Who is he?"

"Shhh," the Lump said. "Tell you later. What were you doing, Ni Ty Lee?"

"I was running toward that sun there, and staring at it, and thinking how beautiful it was, and laughing because it was so beautiful, and laughing because it was going to destroy me, and still be beautiful, and I was writing a poem about how beautiful that sun was and how beautiful the planet that circled it was: and I was doing all that until I saw something more interesting to do, and that was find out who *you* were."

"Then come aboard and find out some more."

"I already know you're a linguistic ubiquitous multiplex with a Lll-based consciousness," Ni Ty Lee answered. "Is there any more I should find out before I sail into the fires?"

"I have a boy on board your own age that you know nothing about at all."

"Then I'm coming over. Get your tube out." He started forward.

"How did he know you were Lll?" Jo asked as the chunk of rock approached.

"I don't know," Lump said. "Some people can tell right off. That's better than the ones who sit around and talk to you for an hour before they get around to asking. Only I bet he doesn't know *which* Lll I am."

The tube connected up with Ni's vessel. A moment later the door opened, and Ni Ty Lee stepped leisurely inside, his thumbs in his pants pockets, and looked around.

Jo was still wearing the black cape San Severina had bought him on Ratshole. Ni Ty Lee, however, looked like a shuttle-bum. He was barefooted. He wore no shirt. His faded work pants had one frayed knee. His too-long hair was silver-blond and clutched at his ears and forehead; his face was high-cheeked, with sloping Oriental eyes the color of slate chips.

The face fixed on Jo and grinned. "Hello," he said, and came forward.

He extended his hand, and Jo started to shake it. There were claws on the fingers of his right hand.

Ni's head leaned to the side. "I'm going to write a poem about the expressions that just went over your face. You're from Rhys, and you used to work in the jhup fields, and curl up by the fires at New Cycle, and kill kepards when they broke through." He made a small, sad, amused sound without opening his mouth. "Hey, Lump. I know all about him now, and I'll be on my way." He began to turn.

"Were you on Rhys? You were really on Rhys?" Jo said.

Ni turned back. "Yes. I was. Three years ago. Hitched there as a shuttle-bum and worked for a while down in field seven. That's where I got these." He held up his claws.

A pulsing ache had begun in the back of Jo's throat that he had not felt since first he had played for the Lll. "I worked field seven just before New Cycle."

"Did Keeper James ever knock some sense into that brat son of his? I get along with most people, but I got into a fight four times with that pesky know-it-all. And once I nearly killed him."

"I . . . I did," Jo whispered.

"Oh," Ni said. He blinked. "Well, I guess I can't really say I'm surprised." But he looked taken aback nevertheless.

"You really were there?" Jo asked. "You're not just . . . reading my mind?"

"I was there. In the flesh. For three and a half weeks."

"That's not very long," Jo said.

"I didn't say I was there a *long* time."

"But you *were* really there," Jo repeated.

"It's not that big a universe, friend. It's too bad your culture was so simplex, or there'd be more to know about you and I'd stay longer." He turned once more to leave.

"Wait a minute!" Jo called. "I want . . . I *need* to talk to you."

"You do?"

Jo nodded.

Ni Ty put his hands back in his pockets. "Nobody's needed me for a long time. That should be interesting enough to write a poem about." He swaggered over to the console and sat down on top of the desk. "I'll hang around awhile, then. What do you need to talk about?"

Jo was silent, while his mind darted. "Well, what's your spaceship made of?" he asked at last.

Ni Ty looked up at the ceiling. "Hey, Lump," he called, "is this guy putting me on? He doesn't really need to know what my ship is made of, does he? If he's putting me on, I'm going to go. People put me on all the time, and I know all about that, and it doesn't interest me a bit."

"He needs to warm up to what's important," Lump said. "And you need to be patient."

Ni Ty looked back at Jo. "You know, he's right. I'm always leaving words and paragraphs out of my poems because I write too fast. Then nobody understands them. I don't know too much about being patient, either. This might be very interesting after all. This your ocarina?"

Jo nodded.

"I used to play one of these things." He put it to his lips and ran through a bright melody that slowed suddenly at the end.

The knot in Jo's throat tightened further. The tune was the first song he had ever learned on the instrument.

"That's the only tune I ever learned. I should have stuck with it longer. Here, you play. Maybe that'll warm you up."

Jo just shook his head.

Ni Ty shrugged, turned the ocarina over in his hands, then said, "Does it hurt?"

"Yeah," Jo said, after a while.

"I can't help it," Ni Ty said. "I've just done a lot of things."

"May I interject?" the Lump said.

Ni shrugged again. "Sure."

Jo nodded.

"You will find, during your reading, Jo, that certain authors seem to have discovered all the things you have discovered, done all you've done. There was one ancient science fiction writer, Theodore Sturgeon, who would break me up every time I read him. He seemed to have seen every flash of light on a window, every leaf shadow on a screen door, that I have ever seen; done everything I had ever done from playing the guitar to laying over for a couple of weeks on a boat in Arransas Pass, Texas. And he was supposedly writing fiction, and that four thousand years ago. Then you learn that lots of other people find the same things in the same writer, who have done none of the things you've done and seen none of the things you've seen. That's a rare sort of writer. But Ni Ty Lee is that sort. I have read many of your poems, Ni Ty. My appreciation, were I to express it, I'm sure would only prove embarrassing."

"Gee," Ni Ty said. "Thanks." And he got a grin on his face that was too big to hide even by looking at his lap. "I lose most of the best ones. Or don't write them down. I wish I could show you some of them. They're really nice."

"I wish you could too," said the Lump.

"Hey." Ni Ty looked up. "But you need me. I can't even remember what you asked."

"About your ship," Jo said.

"I just hollowed out a chunk of nonporous meteor and bolted in a Kayzon Drive in the back, and ran my controls for igneous permeability."

"Yes, yes!" cried the Lump. "That's exactly how it's done! Bolted the Kayzon in with a left-handed ratchet. The threads run backwards, don't they? It was years ago, but it was such a beautiful little ship!"

"You're right about the threads," Ni Ty said. "Only I used a pliers."

"It doesn't matter. Just that you really did it. I told you, Jo, with some writers, it's just uncanny."

"There's a problem, though," Ni Ty said. "I never do anything long enough to really get to know it—just long enough to identify it in a line or a sentence, then I'm on to something else. I think I'm afraid. And I write to make up for all the things I really can't do."

At which point I began to twinge a little. I had said the same thing to Norn an hour before we'd cracked up on Rhys, when we had been discussing my last book. Remember me? I'm Jewel.

"But you're only my age," Jo said at last. "How could you do all this and write all this so early?"

"Well, I . . . I mean, it's . . . I guess I don't really know. I just do. I suppose there's a lot I never will do because I'm too busy writing."

"Another interjection," the Lump said. "Would it embarrass you if I told him the story?"

Ni Ty shook his head.

"It's like Oscar and Alfred," Lump said.

Ni Ty looked surprisingly relieved. "Or Paul V. and Arthur R.," he added.

"Like Jean C. and Raymond R.," said Lump, in rhythm.

"Or Willy and Colette."

"It's a recurrent literary pattern," the Lump explained. "An older writer, a younger writer—often a mere child—and something tragic. And something wonderful is given to the world. It's been happening every twenty-five or fifty years since Romanticism."

"Who was the older writer?" Jo asked.

Ni Ty looked down. "Muels Aranlyde."

"I've never heard of him," Jo said.

Ni Ty blinked. "Oh. I thought everybody knew about the whole, unpleasant mess."

"I'd like to meet him," Jo offered.

"I doubt you ever will," said the Lump. "What happened was very, very tragic."

"Aranlyde was Lll." Ni Ty took a breath and began to explain. "We made a long trip together, and . . ."

"You made a long trip with a Lll?"

"Well, he was really only part—" Then he stopped. "I can't help it," he said. "It's what I've done. I swear I can't help it."

"You know about the sadness of the Lll, then," Jo said.

Ni Ty nodded. "Yes. You see, I sold him. I was desperate, I needed the money, and he told me to go ahead."

"You sold him? But why—"

"Economics."

"Oh."

"And with it I bought a less expensive Lll to rebuild the world we had destroyed; so I know about the sadness of Lll, and the sadness of Lll ownership—though it was a small world, and only took a little while. I was explaining that to San Severina only days ago, and she got very upset—she too has bought and sold Lll and used them to rebuild a—"

"You know San Severina?"

"Yes. She gave me Interling lessons when I was a shuttle-bum—"

"No!" Jo cried.

Ni Ty shook his head and whispered, "I swear I can't help it! I swear!"

"No!" He turned and put his hands over his ears, crouched down and staggered.

Behind him, Ni Ty cried out, "Lump, you said he needed me?"

"You are fulfilling his need very well."

Jo whirled. "Get out of here!"

Ni Ty looked frightened and stood up from the desktop.

"It's my life, damn it, not yours. It's mine!" He grabbed Ni's clawed hand. "Mine. I gave it up—but that doesn't mean you can have it."

Ni sucked a quick breath. "It's not interesting now," he said quickly, edging from the desk. "I've been through this too many times before."

"But I haven't!" Jo cried. He felt as if something in him had been raped and outraged. "You can't steal my life!"

Suddenly Ni pushed him. Jo slipped to the deck, and the poet stood over him, shaking now. "What the hell makes you think it's yours? Maybe you stole it from me. How come I never get to finish anything out? How come any time I get a job, fall in love, have a child, suddenly I'm jerked away and flung into another dung heap where I have to start the same mess all over again? Are you doing that to me? Are you jerking me away from what's mine, picking up for yourself the thousand beautiful lives I've started?" Suddenly he closed his eyes and flung his left hand against his right shoulder. With his head back he hissed to the ceiling, "God, I've said this so many times before! And it bores me, damn it! It bores me!" He'd raked the claws across his shoulder, and five lines of blood trickled to his chest—and for one horrid instant the scene came flashing into Jo's mind when he'd run from Lilly's laughter and stood with his eyes clenched and his head back, and pulled his talons across his shoulder. He shook the memory from his head and blinked his eyes. There was a lot of old scar tissue banding Ni Ty's shoulder under the path the fresh welts cut.

"Always returning, always coming back, always the same things over and over and over!" Ni Ty cried.

He lurched toward the door.

"Wait!"

Jo flipped to his belly and scrabbled to his knees after him.

"What are you going to do?" He threw himself around Ni Ty and put his arm across the door.

Ni Ty put his clawed hand around Jo's forearm. Jo shook his head—Billy James had blocked his way from the corral, and he had put his claws on the boy's arm so, and that's how it all started . . .

"I'm going to get in my ship," Ni Ty said evenly, "and I'm going to face that sun and jam the throttle all the way. I've done it once laughing. This time I'll probably cry. And that damn well better be interesting."

"But *why?*"

"Because someday—" and Ni Ty's face twisted with the strain of words— "somebody else is going to come plunging toward a silver sun, first laughing, then crying, and they'll have read about this, and they'll remember, and suddenly they'll know, don't you see? They'll know that they're not the only ones—"

"But nobody will ever read what you have to say about—"

Ni Ty slapped his arm away and ran down the tube, just missing Di'k, who was stepping down with a sheaf of paper in his mouth.

The tube popped free, and the organifoam swarmed together as the door closed in the console room. Jo saw Ni Ty bending at the controls; then he stood and pressed his face and hands against the viewport as the automatic pilot took the hollow meteor into the glare of the sun. Jo squinted after it till his lids ached. The sobbing that came over the intercom lasted for perhaps a minute after the ship was out of sight.

Jo rubbed his hand across his forehead and turned from the wall.

Di'k was sitting on the sheaf of papers, chewing on a dog-eared corner. "What are those?"

"Ni Ty's poems," the Lump said. "The last batch he was working on."

"Di'k, did you steal them out of his ship?" Jo demanded.

"With somebody like that, the only thing you can do is get their work away from them before they destroy it. That's how everything of his we have has been obtained. This has all happened before," Lump said wearily.

"But Di'k didn't know that," Jo said. "You were just stealing, weren't you?" He tried to sound reproving.

"You underestimate your devil-kitten," the Lump said. "He does not have a simplex mind."

Jo bent over and tugged the papers from under Di'k, who finally rolled over and slapped at his hands a couple of times. Then he took them to the desk and crawled underneath.

Three hours later, when he emerged, Jo walked slowly over to the glass wall and squinted once more at the white dwarf. He turned, blew three notes on his ocarina, then dropped his hand. "I think that's the most multiplex consciousness I've encountered so far."

"He may be," Lump said. "But then, so are you, now."

"I hope he doesn't plunge into the sun," Jo said.

"He won't if he finds something more interesting between here and there."

"There's not much out there."

"It doesn't take much to interest a mind like Lee's."

"The thing you were saying about multiplexity and understanding points of view. He completely took over my point of view, and you were right; it was uncanny."

"It takes a multiplex consciousness to perceive the multiplexity of another consciousness, you know."

"I can see why," Jo said. "He was using all his experiences to understand mine. It made me feel funny."

"You know he wrote those poems before he even knew you existed."

"That's right. But that just makes it stranger."

"I'm afraid," Lump said, "you've set up your syllogism backwards. You were using your experiences to understand his."

"I was?"

"You've had a lot of experiences recently. Order them multiplexually and they will be much clearer. And when they are clear enough, enough confusion will remain so that you ask the proper questions."

Jo was silent for a moment, ordering. Then he said, "What was the name of the Lll your mind is based on?"

"Muels Aranlyde," the Lump said.

Jo turned back to the window. "Then this has all happened before."

After another minute of silence, the Lump said, "You know you will have to make the last leg of the trip without me."

"I'd just begun to order that out," Joe said. "Multiplexually."

"Good."

"I'll be scared as hell."

"You needn't be," Lump said.

"Why not?"

"You've got a crystallized Tritovian in your pouch."

He was referring to me, of course. I hope you haven't forgotten me, because the rest of the story is going to be incomprehensible if you have.

NINE

"What am I supposed to do with it?" Jo asked.

He laid me on a velvet cloth on the desk. The lights in the high ceiling of the console room were dim and had haloes in the faint fog from the humidifiers.

"What's the most multiplex thing you can do when you are not sure what to do?"

"Ask questions."

"Then ask."

"Will it answer?"

"There's an easier way to find that out than by asking me," Lump said.

"Just a second," Jo said. "I have to order my perceptions multiplexually, and it may take a little time. I'm not used to it." After a moment he said, "Why will I have to join the Empire Army and serve Prince Nactor?"

"Excellent," Lump said. "I've been wondering about that one myself."

Because, I broadcast, *the army is going your way.* It was a relief to be able to speak. But that's one of the hardships of crystallization: you can only answer when asked directly.

Incidentally, between the time that Jo said, "I'm not used to it," and the time he asked his question, the radio had come blaring on, and Prince Nactor's voice had announced that all humans in the area were up for immediate conscription, to which Lump had said, "I guess that takes care of your problem." So there's nothing mysterious about Jo's question at all. I want to stress, for those who have followed the argument to this point, that multiplexity is perfectly within the laws of logic. I left the incident out because I thought it was distracting and assumed it was perfectly deducible from Jo's question what had happened, sure that the multiplex reader would supply it for himself. I have done this several times throughout the story.

"Why can't I just deliver my message and go on about my business?" Jo asked.

In crystallization one has the seeming activity of being able to ask rhetorical questions. *Are you ready to deliver the message?* I broadcast.

Jo pounded both fists on the desk. The room seemed to shake as I rocked back and forth.

"Jhup! What *is* the message? That's what I have to find out now. What *is* it?"

Someone has come to free the Lll.

Jo stood up, and concern deepened the young lines of his face. "That's a very important message." The concern turned to a frown. "When will I be ready to deliver it?"

Whenever someone has come to free them.

"But I've come all this way . . ." Jo stopped. "Me? Me free them? But . . . I may be ready to deliver the message, but how will I know when I'm ready to free them?"

If you don't know, I broadcast, *obviously that's not the message.*

Jo felt confused and ashamed. "But it ought to be."

He'd asked no questions, so I could broadcast nothing. But Lump said it for me: "That's the message, but you have misunderstood it. Try and think of another interpretation that contains no contradictions."

Jo turned from the table. "I don't see enough," he said, discouraged.

"Sometimes one must see through someone else's eyes," Lump said. "At this point, I would say if you could use Jewel's, you would be doing yourself a great service."

"Why?"

"You are becoming more and more intimately concerned with the Lll, and our struggle for release. The Tritovians are the most active of the non-Lll species in this struggle. It's that simple. Besides, it would greatly facilitate your military career."

"Can it be done?" Jo asked.

"A very simple operation," Lump said. "You can perform it yourself. Go get the Tritovian."

Jo went back to the desk and lifted me from the velvet.

"Now pull up your right eyelid."

Jo did. And did other things at Lump's instruction. A minute later he screamed in pain, whirled from the desk, and fell to his knees, with his hands over his face.

"The pain will go away in a little while," the Lump said calmly. "I can give you some eyewash if the stinging is too bad."

Jo shook his head. "It's not the pain, Lump," he whispered. "I see. I see you and me and Di'k and Jewel, only all at the same time. And I see the military ship waiting for me, and even Prince Nactor. But the ship is a hundred and seventy miles away, and Di'k is behind me, and you're all around me, and Jewel's inside me, and I'm . . . not me anymore."

"You better practice walking for a little while," Lump said. "Spiral staircases are particularly difficult at first. On second thought, you'd better get used just to sitting still and thinking. Then we'll go on to more complicated things."

"I'm not me anymore," Jo repeated softly.

"Play your ocarina," Lump suggested.

Jo watched himself remove the instrument from his pouch and place it on his own lips, saw his lids close, one over his left eye, one over the glittering presence that had replaced his right. He heard himself begin a long, slow tune, and with his eyes shut he watched Di'k come tentatively over, then nuzzle his lap.

.   .   .

A little later Jo said, "You know, Lump, I don't think talking to Jewel got me anything."

"Certainly not as much as looking through him."

"I'm still awfully foggy about that message."

"You've got to make allowances. When people become as militant as he is, the most multiplex minds get downright linear. But his heart's in the right place. Actually, he said a great deal to you if you can view it multiplexually."

Jo watched his own face become concentrated. It was rather runny, he thought in passing—like an overanxious, towheaded squirrel wearing a diamond monocle. "The message must be the words: *Someone has come to free the Lll*. And I have to be ready to free the Lll. Only it's not me that's going to free them." He waited for Lump to approve his reasoning. There was only silence, however. So he went on: "I wish it were me. But I guess there're reasons why it can't be. I have to be ready to deliver the message, too. The only way I can really be ready is if I make sure whoever is going to free the Lll is ready."

"Very good," the Lump said.

"Where am I going to find this person, and how can I make sure he's ready to free the Lll?"

"You may have to get him ready yourself."

"Me?"

"You've received quite an education in the past few months. You are going to have to impart a good deal of that education to somebody as simplex as you were when you began this journey."

"And lose whatever uniqueness Ni Ty left me with?"

"Yes."

"Then I won't do it," Jo said.

"Oh, come on."

"Look, my old life was stolen from me. Now you want me to give my new life to somebody else. I won't do it."

"That's a very selfish way of—"

"Besides, I know enough about simplex cultures to know that the only thing you could do to them with an army that might shake loose one or two people is destroy it. And I won't."

"Oh," said the Lump. "You've figured that out."

"Yes, I did. And it would be very painful."

"The destruction will happen whether you go or not. The only difference will be that you won't be able to deliver your message."

"Won't he be ready without me?"

"The point is you will have no way to know."

"I'll take the chance," Jo said. "I'm going someplace else. I'll take the gamble that everything will work out for the best, whether I'm there or not."

"You have no idea how risky that is. Look, we have some time. Let's take a little side trip. I want to show you something that will change your mind."

"Lump, I don't think I could take any exposure to slave-driven, exploited, long-suffering Lll right now. That's where you want to take me, isn't it?"

"Lll suffering is something that happens to you, not to Lll," the Lump said. "It is impossible to understand the suffering of the Lll from the point of view of the Lll itself unless you are one. Understanding is one of the things the Empire protects them from. Even the Lll can't agree on what's so awful about their situation. But there is enough concurrence so you must take our word. There are certain walls that multiplexity cannot scale. Occasionally it can blow them up, but it is very difficult and leaves scars in the earth. And admitting their impermeability is the first step in their destruction. I am going to show you something that you can appreciate in any plex you like. We are going to talk to San Severina."

TEN

"Is this one of the worlds she rebuilt with the Lll?" Jo asked, looking through the silver streets of the empty city, then back to the rolling woody hills that crept to the edge of the breeze-brushed lake behind them.

"This is one of them," said Oscar. "It's the first one finished and will be the last to be repopulated."

"Why?" Jo asked, stepping over the new cast-iron gutter grating on the curb. The bluish sun flamed in the spiral window that circled the great tower to their left. A magnificent fountain sat empty on their right. Jo ran his fingers over the dry, granite rim of the forty-foot pool as they turned past.

"Because she is here."

"How much work remains to be done?"

"All the worlds have been rebuilt. Forty-six of the civilizations have been reestablished. But it's those ethical systems that take time. They'll be in the works for another six months or more." Oscar gestured toward a black metal door, studded with brass. "Right through there."

Jo looked around at the tremendous spires. "It's beautiful," he said. "It really is. I think I understand a little more why she wanted to rebuild it."

"In here," Oscar said.

Jo stepped inside.

"Down these steps."

Their feet echoed in the dim, wide stairwell.

"Right through here." Oscar pushed open a smaller door in the gray stone wall.

As Jo stepped through, he wrinkled his nose. "Smells funn—"

She was naked.

Here wrists and ankles were chained to the floor.

When the gray blade of light fell across her humped back, she reared against the shackles and howled. Her lips pulled back from teeth he hadn't realized were so long. The howl stopped in a grinding rasp.

He watched her.

He watched himself watching her and watched himself back into the door and the door swing to and clank closed behind him.

Strain had caused the muscles of her shoulders to grow hard and defined. Her neck was corded, her shaggy, matted hair hung half across her face. *A comb!* he thought nonsensically. *Oh lord, a red comb!* And watched tears start in his real eye. The other grew crusty dry.

"They keep her here, now," Oscar said. "The chains are just short enough so she can't kill herself."

"Who—"

"There were twenty-six others, remember. Oh, she passed the point a long time ago where if she could release them, she would. But the others keep her here now, like this. And her Lll go on working."

"That's not fair!" Jo cried. "Why doesn't somebody turn her loose!"

"She knew what she was getting into. She told them before that they would have to do this. She knew her limitations." Oscar made a pained face. "Seven of them. That's more than any one person's ever owned at one time. It really *is* too much. And the sadness increases the more the Lll build. Geometrically. Like the price."

Jo stared at her, appalled, fascinated, torn.

"You came here to talk to her," Oscar said. "Go ahead."

Jo walked forward gingerly and watched himself do so. There were scabs on her wrists and ankles.

"San Severina?"

She pulled back, a constrained choking in her throat.

"San Severina, I've got to talk to you."

A thin trickle of blood wormed across the ligaments on the back of her left hand.

"Can't you talk to me? San Severina—"

With rattling links, she lunged for him, her teeth snapping on what would have been his leg had he not dodged back. She bit into her tongue and collapsed shrieking on the stone, her mouth awash with blood.

Jo only saw that he was beating on the door and Oscar was holding him. Oscar got the handle opened, and they stumbled into the bottom of the stairwell. Oscar was breathing hard too as they started up the steps. "I almost felt sorry for her," he said, halfway up.

Shocked, Jo turned to him on the stairway. "You don't . . ."

"I feel sorry for the Lll," Oscar said. "I am one, remember."

Jo watched himself begin to climb the steps again, carrying his own confusion. "I feel sorry for her," Jo said.

"Enough to join the army?" Oscar said.

"Jhup," Jo said. "Yes."

"I had hoped so."

As they stepped out of the upper door and onto the street again, Jo squinted in the light. "Ni Ty," he said after a moment. "He said he'd come to speak to San Severina a few days ago."

Oscar nodded.

"Here? He saw her like this?"

Oscar nodded again.

"Then he's done this too," Jo said. He started down the street. "I hope he made the sun."

"They couldn't put her to sleep with something or maybe hypnotize her?" Jo mused, staring through the glass wall back in the console room.

"When she goes to sleep, the Lll cease building," the Lump explained. "It's part of the contract. Ownership must be conscious ownership at all times, for the Lll to function."

"That's what I'd more or less figured. How can you even be sure she's conscious inside that . . . beast? Can anybody get through to her?"

"That beast is *her* protection," Lump explained. "Are you ready to leave?"

"As much as I'll ever be."

"Then I want you to take a complex statement with you that is further in need of multiplex evaluation: The only important elements in any society are the artistic and the criminal, because they alone, by questioning the society's values, can force it to change."

"Is that true?"

"I don't know. I haven't evaluated it multiplexually. But let me say, further, that you are going to change a society. You haven't got the training that, say, Ni Ty has to do it artistically."

"I'm already with you, Lump," Jo said. "Lump, where's the army going, anyway?"

"Empire Star," Lump told him. "Have you any idea what your first criminal action is going to be?"

Jo paused a moment. "Well, up until you told me what our destination was, it was going to be going AWOL. Now I'm not so sure."

"Good," Lump said. "Good-bye, Jo."

"Good-bye."

ELEVEN

Almost immediately Jo decided he did not like the army. He had been on the ten-mile spaceship for three minutes, milling around with the other recruits, when Prince Nactor strode by. As the recruits stepped back, Prince Nactor saw Di'k. The devil-kitten was kicking his legs in the air and chirping. As Jo went to pick him up, Prince Nactor said, "Is that yours?"

"Yes, sir," Jo said.

"Well, you can't bring that aboard."

"Of course, sir," Jo said. "I'll take care of it right away."

With his expanded vision, there was no problem locating someplace on that battleship where he could hide Di'k. It had been reconverted a few years back, and a lot of the old equipment had been removed, to be replaced by more compact components. The old view-chamber which had housed the direct-contact photo-regenerator had been done away with, and the compartment on the glass-walled hull had been first used as storage for things that would never be needed, then sealed up.

Jo slipped away, swiped a croten-wrench from the maintenance cabinet, and found the sealed hatchway. He wrenched off the stripping, shooed Di'k through into the darkness, started to close the door, but got an idea. He went back up to maintenance, took an alphabetic stencil, a can of yellow paint, and a brush. Back at the hatch he lettered onto the door:

AUTHORIZED ENTRANCE
FOR J-O PERSONS
ONLY

He got back upstairs in time to be issued uniform and equipment. The quartermaster demanded his allowance card. Jo explained that he didn't have one. The quartermaster went to chew out the control computer. Jo went back down to the hatch and walked in. There was a small hallway, and the top of his yellow head brushed the ceiling and got dusty. Then he heard music.

He'd heard an instrument like that, a long time ago, back when he'd been a shuttle-bum. Ron's guitar. Only this was a guitar played differently, much faster. And the voice—he'd never heard a voice like that. It was slow, and rich as his ocarina.

He waited, tempted to look and see, but resisted. He heard the song through once, and the melody repeated, so he took his instrument and began to play with the singing. The singing stopped; the guitar stopped. Jo played to the end of the melody, then stepped out.

She was sitting on the floor in front of a pile of crystal blocks. The glass wall of the spaceship let in the white light of Tantamount. She looked up from her guitar, and the face—it was a beautiful face, fine-featured, dark, with heavy brown hair that fell to one shoulder—twisted in silent terror.

"What are you doing?" Jo asked.

She backed against the wall of crystal blocks, her hand flat on the blond face of the guitar, fingers sliding across the wood and leaving paths of glimmer on the varnish.

"Have you seen Di'k?" Jo asked. "A devil-kitten about so big, eight legs, horns? Came in about fifteen minutes ago?"

She shook her head hard, a violence in the motion that told him the negation was general and not connected with his particular question.

"Who are you?" he asked.

Just then Di'k stepped out from behind the crystal blocks, pranced in front of the girl, lay on his back, kicked his legs in the air, meowed, stuck his tongue out, and was, in short, perfectly engaging. Jo reached out and scratched Di'k's belly with his bare toe. He was still naked from the induction physical, and his uniform was over his arm.

The girl was wearing a white blouse that came up around her neck, and a dark skirt that came just below her knees. Whatever frightened her about him seemed to be behind his uniform, because she stared at it as though she were trying to see through it. He could see in the shifting muscles of her face the thoughts becoming more confused.

"I like your singing," Jo said. "You shouldn't be afraid. My name's Jo. What are you doing here?"

Suddenly she clamped her eyes, let the guitar fall face down in her lap, and clapped her hands on her ears. "Singing," she said quickly. "I'm just singing. Singing's the most important thing there is, you know. I'm not hurting anybody. No, don't say anything more to me. I refuse to answer any questions."

"You look pretty confused," Jo said. "Do you want to ask any?"

She shook her head, then hunched it down between her shoulders as if to avoid a blow.

Jo frowned, moved his mouth to one side of his face, then the other. He chewed the inside of his lip and said at last, "I don't believe you're really that simplex." She just crouched farther back against the crystal blocks. "You know, I'm not really a soldier."

She looked up. "Then why do you have the uniform?"

"See! You just asked one."

"Oh!" She sat up and put her hand over her mouth.

"I have the uniform because I came very close to being a soldier. I only have to wear it when I go outside. If it frightens you, I'll put it away." He tossed it over the crystal pile. The girl lowered her shoulders and visibly relaxed. "You're hiding from the soldiers," Jo said slowly. "If they find you, you'd prefer they thought you were simplex. Are you going to Empire Star too?"

She nodded.

"Who are you?"

She picked up the guitar. "I'd rather not say. It's not that I don't trust you. But the fewer people on this battleship who know, the better."

"All right. But would you answer another one, then?"

"Yes. All these soldiers under Prince Nactor are going to Empire Star to kill me, unless I get there first."

"That's not the answer to the question I was going to ask."

She looked dreadfully embarrassed.

"But I guess it's a pretty good one." Jo smiled.

She reached out to scratch Di'k's belly. "Someday I'll learn how to do that answer-before-you're-asked bit. It's so impressive when it comes off. I thought you were going to ask what this was all about."

Jo looked puzzled. Then he laughed. "You're hiding from the soldiers by . . .

staying under their noses! Very multiplex! Very multiplex!" He lowered himself cross-legged to the floor on the other side of Di'k.

"Also, if I go with them, it's fairly certain I won't get there *after* they do. At worst we'll arrive at the same time." She pursed her mouth. "But I've got to contrive some way to get there first."

Jo scratched Di'k too, and their fingers touched knuckles. He grinned. "Only I was going to ask you where you were coming from. I know where you're going and where you are now."

"Oh," she said. "Do you know Miss Perrypicker's?"

"Who?"

"Where. Miss Perrypicker's Finishing Academy for Young Ladies."

"What's that?"

"That's where I come from. It's a perfectly dreadful place where basically nice girls are taken from the best families and taught how to appear so simplex you wouldn't believe it."

"I didn't believe *you*," Jo said.

She laughed. "I'm one of Miss Perrypicker's failures. I suppose there's a lot there to enjoy—tennis, antigrav volleyball, water polo, four-walled handball—which is my favorite—and three-D chess. A few teachers did slip in who actually knew something. But singing and playing the guitar, which is what I really like to do, I picked up on my own."

"You do it very well."

"Thanks." She pulled from the strings a descending run of chords, opened her lips, and ejected a melody that rose on slow, surprising intervals that plucked sympathetic strings of pleasure, nostalgia, and joy that Jo had not felt since he had sung for the Lll.

She stopped. "That's a song the Lll made. It's one of my favorites."

"It's beautiful," Jo said blinking. "Go on, please. Sing the rest."

"That's all there is," she said. "Very short. Just those six notes. It does what it has to do, then stops. Everything that Lll make is very economical."

"Oh," Jo said. The melody was like a rainbow slick over his mind, calming, spreading.

"I'll sing anoth—"

"No," Jo said. "Let me just think about that one awhile."

She smiled and dropped her hand, silent, over the strings.

Jo's hand meandered over Di'k's stomach. The devil-kitten was snoring softly. "Tell me," Jo said, "why does Prince Nactor want to kill you at Empire Star?"

"My father is very ill," she explained. "I was called home suddenly from Miss Perrypicker's because it looks like he's going to die any day. When he does, I shall inherit the reins of the Empire—if I'm there. If not, Prince Nactor will seize them. We've been racing each other all the way."

"You're a princess of the Empire?"

She nodded.

"You must be pretty important," Jo said wonderingly.

"I won't be anything if I don't beat Nactor. He's been waiting for this for years."

"Why should you have them and not Nactor?"

"For one thing, I'm going to free the Lll. Prince Nactor wants to keep them under his protection."

"I see." He nodded and hugged his knees. "How are you going to do this, and why won't Nactor?"

"Economics," the girl said. "I have the support of the twenty-six richest men in the Empire. They trust me to deal with the matter multiplexually. They are waiting at

Empire Star to hear what the outcome between myself and Nactor will be. They refuse to support Nactor, and all he's left with is the army. Although he is quite a multiplex man, he only has the one tool of force to pry with. If you only have one direction in which you can push, you might as well be simplex, whether you want to be or not. So they await me, assembled in the brass-columned council chamber, while the tessellations of the stained-glass windows cast their many shadows on the blue tiles, and somewhere in a crystal bed, my father lies dying . . ."

"Jhup," said Jo, impressed.

"I've never been there. I read about it in a novel by Muels Aranlyde. We all read his political trilogy at Miss Perrypicker's. Do you know his work?"

Jo shook his head. "Only . . ."

"Yes?"

"I think I have a message for them, there in the council chamber."

"You do?"

"That's why I'm going to Empire Star. I have a message to deliver, and I think I must be fairly close to delivering it."

"What is it?"

Jo let go of his knees now. "You're not anxious to tell me who you are; I think I'd best keep my message to myself until I get to the council chamber."

"Oh." She tried to look content, but curiosity kept struggling to the surface of her face.

"I'll tell you this," Jo said, half-smiling. "It concerns the Lll."

"Oh," she repeated, more slowly. Suddenly she rose up on her knees, leaning over her guitar. "Look, I'll make a deal with you! You can't get into the council chamber without my help—"

"Why not?"

"Nobody can. The great iris of energy that guards the chamber only opens to twenty-eight mind patterns—you better read up on it in your Aranlyde. Twenty-six of them are inside already. My father's dying, and I doubt if his is still recognizable. So there's just me left. I'll help you get into the council chamber if you help me beat Prince Nactor."

"All right," Jo said. "All right. That's fair. What sort of help do you need?"

"Well," she said, sitting back down. "You've got that uniform, so you can sneak in and out of here."

Jo nodded and waited for her to go on.

But she shrugged. Then looked questioningly. "That's something, isn't it?"

"You mean I have to figure out the rest," Jo said. "I'll try. What sort of help have you had already?"

"I've got a small computer running interference for me."

"I may be small," a voice said from beneath Jo's uniform where it lay over the piled blocks, "but I haven't reached my full growth yet."

"Huh?" Jo said.

"That's a Lump," the girl said. "He's a linguistic—"

"—ubiquitous multiplex," Jo finished. "Yeah. I've met one before." For the first time he realized that the haphazard crystals were logic-blocks. But there were surprisingly few. He'd been used to seeing them organized over the sixty-foot wall in the console room.

"It was his idea to hide out in the battleship."

Jo nodded, then stood. "Maybe," Jo said, "if everybody works together, we can muddle through this thing. Though I have a feeling it's going to be a little confusing. Say, one thing I've been meaning to ask. What planet around Empire Star are we going to?"

The girl looked very surprised.

"Well, we're not going inside the star itself, are we?"

Lump said, "I don't think he knows. You really should read Aranlyde."

"I guess he doesn't know," she said, and bit at a knuckle. "Should I tell him?"

"Let me."

"You mean people *do* live in the star?"

"People could," Lump said. "The surface temperature of Aurigae is less than two thousand degrees Fahrenheit. It's a very dim star, and it shouldn't be difficult to devise a refrigeration plant to bring that down to a reasonable—"

"They don't live inside," the girl said. "But there are no planets around Aurigae."

"Then where—"

"Let me. Please," the Lump repeated. "Aurigae is not only the largest star in the galaxy—hundreds of times the mass of Sol, thousands of times as big. But it is not just simply a star—"

"It's more complicated—" the girl began.

"Multiplicated," Lump said. "Aurigae has been known to be an eclipsing binary for ages. But there are at least seven giant stars—giant compared to Sol—doing a rather difficult, but beautiful, dance around one another out there."

"All around one point," the girl said. "That point is the center of Empire."

"The still point," said Lump, "in the turning world. That's an allusion. It's the gravitational center of that vast multiplex of matter. It's also the center of the Empire's power."

"It's the origin of the reins of Empire," the girl said.

"Can you imagine the incredible strain both space and time are subjected to at that point? The fibers of reality are parted there. The temporal present joins the spatial past there with the possible future, and they get totally mixed up. Only the most multiplex of minds can go there and find their way out again the same way they went in. One is always arriving on Wednesday and coming out again on Thursday a hundred years ago and a thousand light years away."

"It's a temporal and spatial gap," the girl explained. "The council controls it, and that's how it keeps its power. I mean, if you can go into the future to see what's going to happen, then go into the past to make sure it happens like you want it, then you've just about got the universe in your pocket, more or less."

"More or less," Jo said. "How old are you?"

"Sixteen," the girl said.

"Two years younger than I am," said Jo. "And how many times have you been through the gap at Empire Star?"

"Never," she said, surprised. "This is the first time I've ever been away from Miss Perrypicker's. I've only read about it."

Jo nodded. "Tell me—" he pointed toward the pile of logic-blocks—"is Lump there based on a Lll consciousness?"

"I say—" began the Lump.

"You know, you're really very gauche," the girl announced, straightening. "What possible difference could that make to you—"

"It doesn't," Jo said. He sighed. "Only I think this has all happened before. I also think I have a lot of things to tell you."

"What things?"

"What's he talking about?" Lump asked.

"Listen," Jo said. "It's going to take a bit longer to free the Lll than you think right now. You're going to have to undergo the unbearable sadness of Lll ownership yourself—"

"Oh, I would never own a—"

"You will," Jo said sadly. "You'll own more than anyone else has ever owned. That's probably the only way you will be able to free them." Jo shook his head. "There will be a war, and a lot of what you hold most beautiful and important will be destroyed."

"Oh, a war! With who?"

Jo shrugged. "Perhaps Prince Nactor."

"Oh, but even with war, I wouldn't—Oh, Lump, you know I wouldn't ever—"

"Many people will be killed. The economics will be such, I imagine, that the council and you will decide that purchasing the Lll is the only way to rebuild. And you will. You will have a great deal of sadness and worse to carry, both of you. But a long time from now, while what I am telling you about now is happening, you will run into a boy." Jo glanced at his reflection on the glass. "I was going to say that he looks like me. But he doesn't, not that much. His eyes—well, he doesn't have this glass thing in place of his right eye. His hands—he'll have claws on his left. He'll be a lot browner than I am because he's spent more time outside than I have recently. His speech will be almost unintelligible. Though his hair will be about the color of mine, it will be much longer and a mess—" Suddenly Jo reached for his pouch and dug inside. "Here. Keep this, until you meet him. Then give it to him." He handed her the red comb.

"I'll keep it," she said, puzzled. She turned it around to look at it. "If he speaks all that poorly, I can give him diction lessons in Interling. Miss Perrypicker was a real fanatic about diction."

"I know you can," Jo said. "Both of you, remember me, and when he comes to you, try and make him as much like me as you can. Here, you'll recognize him this way." He pointed to Di'k. "He'll have one of these for a pet. He'll be going to Empire Star like we are now, only by then you'll be going someplace else. He'll have a message to deliver, but he won't know what it is. He's very unsure of himself, and he won't understand how you can bring yourself to own such incredible creatures as the Lll."

"But *I* don't understand how—"

"By then you will," Jo said. "Reassure him. Tell him he'll learn what his message is by the time he has to deliver it. He's a very insecure little boy."

"You don't make him sound very attractive."

Jo shrugged. "Perhaps by then your band of sensitivity will be broader. There'll be something about him—"

"You know," she said suddenly, looking up from the comb, "I think *you're* a very beautiful boy!" Then self-surprise and modesty contended for possession of her smile.

Jo broke out laughing.

"I didn't mean to . . . Oh, I'm sorry if I said any—"

"No!" Jo rolled back on the floor. "No, that's all right!" He kicked his feet in the air. "No, everything's perfectly all right." He rolled back to a sitting position. Then his laughter stopped.

She had twined her hands together, catching a fold of her skirt.

"I didn't mean to laugh at you," Jo said.

"It's not that."

He leaned forward. "Then tell me what it is."

"It's just that—well, since I left Miss Perrypicker's the weirdest things have been happening to me. And everybody I run into seems to know a bleb of a lot more about what's going on than I do."

". . . bleb?"

"Oh, dear. I didn't mean to say that either. Miss Perrypicker would have a fit."

"Eh . . . what exactly is *bleb?*"

She giggled and involuntarily hushed her voice as she leaned toward him. "It's what all the girls at Miss Perrypicker's *pick*!"

Jo nodded. "I get the general idea. You haven't been multiplex very long, have you?"

"I haven't. And up until a few weeks ago"—she pointed to Lump—"he was called Lusp."

"Really," Lump said, "you don't have to tell him *everything*."

"That's all right," Jo said. "I understand."

"I've been having so many adventures since I got started. And they all come out so weird."

"What sort of adventures?" Jo asked. "Tell me about them."

"The last thing was on the ship I was on before that one—I didn't have to hide there—there was a shuttle-bum who I was giving Interling lessons to. It turned out he had written the most marvelous poems. They completely changed my life, I think— sounds rather melodramatic, I know, and I suppose you wouldn't understand how. But anyway, he introduced me to Lump. Lump was a friend of his before he was a Lump. Lump says he got the idea of hiding in the battleship from him. Apparently an army had been after *this* boy, too, once, and—"

"Ni Ty had done it before?"

"How did you know his name?"

"I'm familiar with his poems," Jo said. "I understand how they changed your life. He lets you know how much of your life is yours and how much belongs to history."

"Yes. Yes, that's exactly how it struck me!" She looked into her lap. "And if you're a princess of the Empire, so much belongs to history there's hardly any left for you."

"Sometimes—" he reached into his pouch and took out his ocarina—"even if you're not. Play with me."

"All right," she said, and picked up her guitar.

They made a soft, climbing melody. Beyond the glass wall night sped by. It might as well have been still and listening, as the youngsters made their music and their ship hove forward.

"You look at me," she said at last, "as though you know so much about me. Are you reading my mind?"

Jo shook his head. "Just simplex, complex, and multiplex."

"You speak as though you know, too."

"I know that Lump there was based on Muels Aranlyde's consciousness."

She turned. "Lump . . . you didn't tell me!"

"I didn't know. Ni Ty didn't tell me. He just told me I was Lll-based. He didn't say *which* Lll."

"And you're San Severina."

She whirled back. "But you said before that you didn't know—"

"And now I say I do."

"As time progresses," Lump stated, "people learn. That's the only hope."

Through the battleship wall the dark and flaming masses of the multiplex system of Empire Star were just visible.

San Severina went to the wall and leaned her cheek against the glass. "Jo, have you ever been through the time gap at Empire Star? Maybe that's why you know so much about the future."

"No. But you're going to."

She raised her head, and her eyes widened. "Oh, you'll come with me, won't you? I'd be scared to go alone!"

She touched his shoulder.

"Jo, do you know whether we'll win or not?"

"I only know that, win or lose, it will take longer than we think."

Her hand slipped down his arm and seized his. "But you will help me! You *will* help!"

He raised his hands and placed both of them on her shoulders. Her hand came up with his. "I'll help you," he said. Empire Star drew nearer. "Of course I'll help you, San Severina. How could I refuse after what you've done for me?"

"What have I done?" she asked, puzzled again.

"*Shhh*," he said and touched her lips with a finger. "If you ask questions that nobody can answer, you just have to wait and see."

Di'k hiccuped in his sleep, and Lump coughed discreetly. They turned to look at Empire Star again, and, from the protective socket of bone and flesh, I too looked, and saw much further.

I'm Jewel.

TWELVE

The multiplex reader has by now discovered that the story is much longer than she thinks, cyclic and self-illuminating. I must leave out a great deal; only order your perceptions multiplexually, and you will not miss the lacunae.

No end at all! I hear from one complex voice.

Unfair. Look at the second page. There I told you that there was an end and that Di'k, myself, and the ocarina were with him till then.

A tile for the mosaic?

Here's a piece. The end came sometime after San Severina (after many trips through the gap), bald, wrinkled, injured, healed, and aged a hundred years, was allowed to give up her sovereignty and with it her name and a good many of her more painful memories. She took a great 3-Dog for her companion and the name Charona and retired to a satellite called Rhys, where for five hundred years she had nothing more taxing to do than guard the gate of the Transport Area and be kind to children, which suited her old age.

Another tile? *Bleb* is water, picked drop by drop from the leaves of lile-ferns at dawn by the girls of Miss Perrypicker's Finishing Academy for Young Ladies.

Oh, I could tell you good news and bad, of successes and defeats. Prince Nactor waged a war that charred eight worlds, destroyed fifty-two civilizations and thirty-two thousand three hundred and fifty-seven complete and distinct ethical systems, a small defeat. A great victory, now: Prince Nactor, through a chain of circumstances I leave you to deduce, fear-crazed, clammy with sweat, fled at midnight through the jungles of Central Park on Earth when Di'k yawned, emerged from behind a clump of trees, and stepped on him, quite by accident—Di'k having gained by then his adult size of fifty feet.

I have told you how San Severina, aged and bald and called Charona, first taught the child, Comet Jo, about simplex, complex, and multiplex under a place called Brooklyn Bridge on a satellite called Rhys. As well I could tell you how Jo, as old and as wrinkled and then called Norn, first taught the child San Severina the song they played together in the abandoned chamber of a battleship, on a world unnamed in this story so far—under a place called Brooklyn Bridge.

I could tell you how, at the final emancipation of the Lll, when the crowds silenced before the glorious music, a man named Ron, who as a boy had himself sung for the Lll while a shuttle-bum, tears quivering in the corners of his eyes, his throat half-blocked with emotion, both then and now, turned to the Lll standing next to him in the tremendous crush of people and whispered (indicating not only the straining attentions around him, and the incredible effect of the brief song, but as well the shattering culmination the emancipation represented), "Have you ever seen anything like it before?"

The Lll was silent, but the Oriental youngster standing by him shot back with shocking, subdued rage, "Yeah. *I* have!" and then to the Lll, "Come *on*, Muels, let's get *out* of here, huh?" and the Lll and the boy began to push their way toward the edge of the crowd, to begin a journey as incredible as the one I have recounted, while Ron stayed there, open-mouthed, incredulous at the sacrilege.

A joyous defeat: When Prince Nactor burned Jo's body on the ice-blasted plains of the planet that circled Tantamount—joyous, because it freed Jo to be able to use many other bodies, many other names.

A tragic victory: When the Lump destroyed Prince Nactor's mind, only a few hours before the incident with Di'k in Central Park, by crashing his full growth—several times as big as we have seen him to date—into the Geodesic Survey Station, where Nactor had secreted his brain in an ivory egg flushed with nutrient fluid deep within the station—tragic, because the Lump too was finally destroyed in the collision.

Or I can tell you the very end, happening at the same time as the very beginning, when at last someone *had* come to free the Lll, and Comet Jo—still called Norn, then—Ki, Marbika, and myself were bringing the message from S. Doradus to Empire Star in an organiform, when suddenly the encycsting mechanism broke down and we went out of control. As the rest of us fought to save the ship, I turned for a moment and saw Norn standing at the front, staring out at the glittering sun at which we hurtled. He had begun to laugh.

Struggling to pull us back on course, I demanded, "And just what's so funny?"

He shook his head slowly, without looking away. "Did you eyer read any of the poems of Ni Ty Lee, Jewel?"

As I said, this was at the beginning, and I hadn't yet. I wasn't crystallized then, either. "This is no time to discuss literature!" I shouted—even though a moment before the breakdown, he'd been patiently listening for hours as I had detailed a book I was intending to write.

Ki came swimming through the proto-photoplasm. "I don't think there's anything we can do." The light through the greenish jelly gleamed on his fear-stained face.

I looked back at Norn, who still hadn't moved, as the blot of illumination spread over the darkness. The laughter had stopped, and tears glistened on his face.

"There's a satellite," Marbika cried from the interior darkness. "Maybe we can crash-land—"

We did.

On a place called Rhys where there was nothing but a one-product simplex society with a Transport Area.

They died. I was the only one able to go on, though Norn gave the message over to someone else to carry, and I went with them to see that it was delivered—

Or have I told you this part of the story before?

I doubt it.

In this vast multiplex universe there are almost as many satellites called Rhys as there are places called Brooklyn Bridge. It's a beginning. It's an end. I leave to you the problem of ordering your perceptions and making the journey from one to the other.

—*New York City,*
Sept 1965

ROBERT SHECKLEY

Robert Sheckley [1928–2005] (www.sheckley.com) was one of the great SF writers, whose reputation was based primarily on the quality of his quirky, subversive, satirical short fiction, a body of work admired by everyone from Kingsley Amis, J. G. Ballard, and Harlan Ellison to Roger Zelazny, with whom he collaborated. As an ironic investigator of questions of identity and of the nature of reality, he was a peer of Philip K. Dick and Kurt Vonnegut. Sheckley first came to prominence in the 1950s as one of the leading writers in *Galaxy*, became a novelist in the 1960s, and produced fiction that was thought-provoking, memorable, and stylish.

Sheckley never wrote a space opera (though he did write TV scripts for *Captain Video* very early in his career), nor was he so constituted that he could ever take one seriously. But he sure could parody it. This story is from 1972, when nearly all the hip, ambitious writers were trying to get beyond the space opera roots of SF into a more mature literary territory. Some (including Ballard and Aldiss) called it the literature of inner space, others speculative fiction or speculative literature, which meant many things to many individual writers but amounted to more sophisticated and adult fiction, whether it be actual SF or not. Between the middle 1960s and the end of the 1970s, there were a number of parodies of space opera, written with the intent of killing it off. This is one of them.

Brian Aldiss, in *Space Operas*, says of this story, "There is a noble tradition of great and epical adventure in science fiction. Beginning, perhaps, with Edgar Rice Burroughs, it continues through the wide screen space opera epics of E. E. Smith, Ph.D., on through Jack Williamson, and even the very young John W. Campbell, Jr. . . . Robert Sheckley has finished off the up until now endless saga, written *finis* to those mighty tomes, killed the entire literature dead."

As we noted in the general introduction to this anthology, Brian Aldiss was engaging in a complex bit of literary politics in creating and describing space opera in new ways in that anthology. And as we also noted, his comments ironically helped to inspire a resurgence of space opera in the 1970s.

ZIRN LEFT UNGUARDED, THE JENGHIK PALACE IN FLAMES, JON WESTERLEY DEAD

ROBERT SHECKLEY

The bulletin came through blurred with fear. "Somebody is dancing on our graves," said Charleroi. His gaze lifted to include the entire Earth. "This will make a fine mausoleum."

"Your words are strange," she said. "Yet there is that in your manner which I find pleasing . . . Come closer, stranger, and explain yourself."

I stepped back and withdrew my sword from its scabbard. Beside me, I heard a metallic hiss; Ocpetis Marn had drawn his sword, too, and now he stood with me, back to back, as the Megenth horde approached.

"Now shall we sell our lives dearly, Jon Westerley," said Ocpetis Marn in the peculiar guttural hiss of the Mnerian race.

"Indeed we shall," I replied. "And there will be some more than one widow to dance the Passagekeen before this day is through."

He nodded. "And some disconsolate fathers will make the lonely sacrifice to the God of Deteriorations."

We smiled at each other's staunch words. Yet it was no laughing matter. The Megenth bucks advanced slowly, implacably, across the green and purple moss-sward. They had drawn their *raftii*—those long, curved, double-pointed dirks that had struck terror in the innermost recesses of the civilized galaxy. We waited.

The first blade crossed mine. I parried and thrust, catching the big fellow full in the throat. He reeled back, and I set myself for my next antagonist.

Two of them came at me this time. I could hear the sharp intake of Ocpetis's breath as he hacked and hewed with his sword. The situation was utterly hopeless.

I thought of the unprecedented combination of circumstances that had brought me to this situation. I thought of the Cities of the Terran Plurality, whose very existence depended upon the foredoomed outcome of this present impasse. I thought of autumn in Carcassone, hazy mornings in Saskatoon, steel-colored rain falling on the Black Hills. Was all this to pass? Surely not. And yet—why not?

. . . .

We said to the computer: "These are the factors, this is our predicament. Do us the favor of solving our problem and saving our lives and the lives of all Earth."

The computer computed. It said: "The problem cannot be solved."

"Then how are we to go about saving Earth from destruction?"

"You don't," the computer told us.

We left sadly. But then Jenkins said, "What the hell—that was only one computer's opinion."

That cheered us up. We held our heads high. We decided to take further consultations.

The gypsy turned the card. It came up Final Judgement. We left sadly. Then Myers said, "What the hell—that's only one gypsy's opinion."

That cheered us up. We held our heads high. We decided to take further consultations.

You said it yourself: "'A bright blossom of blood on his forehead.' You looked at me with strange eyes. Must I love you?"

It all began so suddenly. The reptilian forces of Megenth, long quiescent, suddenly began to expand due to the serum given them by Charles Engstrom, the power-crazed telepath. Jon Westerley was hastily recalled from his secret mission to Angos II. Westerley had the supreme misfortune of materializing within a ring of Black Force, due to the inadvertent treachery of Ocpetis Marn, his faithful Mnerian companion, who had, unknown to Westerley, been trapped in the Hall of Floating Mirrors, and his mind taken over by the renegade Santhis, leader of the Entropy Guild. That was the end for Westerley, and the beginning of the end for us.

The old man was in a stupor. I unstrapped him from the smouldering control chair and caught the characteristic sweet-salty-sour odor of manginee—that insidious narcotic grown only in the caverns of Ingidor—whose insidious influence had subverted our guard posts along the Wall Star Belt.

I shook him roughly. "Preston!" I cried. "For the sake of Earth, for Magda, for everything you hold dear—tell me what happened."

His eyes rolled. His mouth twitched. With vast effort he said, "Zirn! Zirn is lost, is lost, is lost!"

His head lolled forward. Death rearranged his face.

Zirn lost! My brain worked furiously. That meant that the High Star Pass was open, the negative accumulators no longer functioning, the drone soldiers overwhelmed. Zirn was a wound through which our lifeblood would pour. But surely there was a way out?

President Edgars looked at the cerulean telephone. He had been warned never to use it except in the direst emergency, and perhaps not even then. But surely the present situation justified? . . . He lifted the telephone.

"Paradise Reception, Miss Ophelia speaking."

"This is President Edgars of Earth. I must speak to God immediately."

"God is out of his office just now and cannot be reached. May I be of service?"

"Well, you see," Edgars said, "I have this really bad emergency on my hands. I mean, it looks like the end of everything."

"Everything?" Miss Ophelia asked.

"Well, not *literally* everything. But it does mean the destruction of us. Of Earth and all that. If you could just bring this to God's attention—"

"Since God is omniscient, I'm sure he knows all about it."

"I'm sure he does. But I thought that if I could just speak to him personally—"

"I'm afraid that is not possible at this time. But you could leave a message. God is very good and very fair, and I'm sure he will consider your problem and do what is right and godly. He's wonderful, you know. I love God."

"We all do," Edgars said sadly.

"Is there anything else?"

"No. Yes! May I speak with Mr. Joseph J. Edgars, please?"

"Who is that?"

"My father. He died ten years ago."

"I'm sorry, sir. That is not permitted."

"Can you at least tell me if he's up there with you people?"

"Sorry, we are not allowed to give out that information."

"Well, can you tell me if *anybody* is up there? I mean, is there really an afterlife? Or is it maybe only you and God up there? Or maybe only you?"

"For information concerning the afterlife," Miss Ophelia said, "kindly contact your nearest priest, minister, rabbi, mullah, or anyone else on the accredited list of God representatives. Thank you for calling."

There was a sweet tinkle of chimes. Then the line went dead.

"What did the Big Fellow say?" asked General Muller.

"All I got was double-talk from his secretary."

"Personally, I don't believe in superstitions like God," General Muller said. "Even if they happen to be true, I find it healthier not to believe. Shall we get on with it?"

They got on with it.

Testimony of the robot who might have been Dr. Zach:

"My true identity is a mystery to me, and one which, under the circumstances, I do not expect to be resolved. But I was at the Jenghik Palace. I saw the Megenth warriors swarm over the crimson balustrades, overturn the candelabra, smash, kill, destroy. The governor died with a sword in his hand. The Terran Guard made their last stand in the Dolorous Keep, and perished to a man after mighty blows given and received. The ladies of the court defended themselves with daggers so small as to appear symbolic. They were granted quick passage. I saw the great fire consume the bronze eagles of Earth. The subject peoples had long fled. I watched the Jenghik Palace— that great pile, marking the furthest extent of Earth's suzerainty, topple soundlessly into the dust from which it sprung. And I knew then that all was lost, and that the fate of Terra—of which planet I consider myself a loyal son, despite the fact that I was (presumably) crafted rather than created, produced rather than born—the fate of divine Terra, I say, was to be annihilated utterly, until not even the ghost of a memory remained.

"You said it yourself: 'A star exploded in his eye.' This last day I must love you. The rumors are heavy tonight, and the sky is red. I love it when you turn your head just so. Perhaps it is true that we are chaff between the iron jaws of life and death. Still, I prefer to keep time by my own watch. So I fly in the face of the evidence. I fly with you.

"It is the end, I love you, it is the end."

III.

TRANSITIONS / REDEFINERS
(LATE 1970S TO LATE 1980S)

I'm tempted to overstate and say that space opera *is* science fiction. But it is certainly close to the center of the SF tradition, along with a handful of other ur-forms such as the planetary romance, the scientific romance, the cosmology epic, the superman story, and so on. It's probably no accident that most of these deal with extremes of space or time or human condition—they're about the ability of the world to be amazing and astounding and a source of fantastic adventures. I suspect that as long as SF is around, somebody will keep reinventing the space opera.

—Russell Letson in *Locus*

DAVID BRIN

David Brin [1950–] (www.davidbrin.com) lives in Encinitas, California. He is a physicist whose first novel, *Sundiver,* was published in 1980, the year before he finished his Ph.D. thesis. His novel *Startide Rising* (1983) won both the Hugo and Nebula Awards for best novel, and his novel *Uplift War* (1987) was also a Hugo Award winner. His stories are collected in *The River of Time* (1986), *Otherness* (1994), and *Tomorrow Happens* (2003). He is characteristically interested in futures in which the human condition is improved, and in which heroic action is a possibility. His most recent book is a graphic novel, *The Life Eaters* (2004), based on his novella "Thor Meets Captain America."

Although Brin is known as a hard SF writer (one of the famous "three Bs"), he doesn't let that get in the way of a good story. As John Clute put it, "he writes tales in which the physical constraints governing the knowable Universe are flouted with high-handed panache." His optimism, showmanship, and unornamented prose place him in the literary tradition of John W. Campbell and Robert A. Heinlein.

Earlier in his career, it might have been insulting to group Brin with the writers of space opera. It is only in the late 1990s that his major series, the Uplift novels, has been redefined as space opera (as opposed to the heretofore more respectable terms "hard SF" or "adventure SF"). He said, "My Uplift series of far future space tales proved popular enough to draw me into a recent trilogy—*Brightness Reef, Infinity's Shore,* and *Heaven's Reach.* Added to three earlier novels—*Sundiver, Startide Rising,* and *The Uplift War*—they form a cluster of adventures in the unabashedly proud space-opera tradition . . . though I hope with some ideas mixed in with all the dash and sci-fi élan." Brin is one of the first of a new generation of writers (preceded by C. J. Cherryh and followed by Lois McMaster Bujold) who entered SF and often choose to write ambitious space opera.

An interviewer asked New Space Opera writer M. John Harrison, still a leading polemicist for UK SF <www.zone-sf.com/mjharrison.html>, "Do you think there is a clear difference between American and British SF and fantasy? Do you think there's much communication between the two, or are [Ken] MacLeod, [Iain] Banks and [China] Mieville writing something fundamentally different from, say, David Brin, Dan Simmons, and George R. R. Martin?" Harrison replied, "I couldn't suggest much in the way of common ground between Brin and MacLeod, or Brin and Mieville. If a book is the bill of goods it is trying to sell, then there are primary ideological differences between most British fiction and most US fiction, whether it's SF or chick-lit. I incline to think that we're doing something completely different to the Americans—although, thankfully, none of us is exactly certain what it is."

There is currently a disagreement as to whether New Space Opera is a broad SF phenomenon, as we maintain in this book, or whether all the really good stuff is politically engaged from the left and characteristically British. Thankfully, so that the controversy may continue, no one is exactly certain what space opera, let alone New Space Opera, is.

In contrast to what is generally done in space opera, Brin tends to choose ordinary people as his characters. In a 1997 *Locus* interview, he remarked:

> One of the rules I try to follow is that normal people are going to be involved even in heroic events. Even if you have superior protagonists, I hate to make them *slans.* I hate the whole *Ubermensch,* superman temptation that pervades science fiction. I believe no protagonist should be so competent, so awe-inspiring, that a committee of twenty really hard-working, intelligent people couldn't do the same thing. . . .

In "Temptation," a part of his Uplift saga, sentient dolphins are dropped off by humans to colonize a planet because the dolphins are reverting under the stress of space travel. The planet has genetically engineered leviathan creatures living in its oceans that serve as habitats for many sentient races who have visited the planet previously. It was first published in the anthology *Far Horizons*, and in the story note there Brin says:

> Some people say you can't have everything. For instance, if a story offers action, it must lack philosophy. If it involves science, character must suffer. This has especially been said about one of the core types of science fiction, the genre sometimes called *space opera*. Is it possible to depict grand adventures and heroic struggles cascading across lavish future settings—complete with exploding planets and vivid special effects—while still coming up with something worth calling a novel?
>
> I'm one of those who believe it's worth a try—and have attempted it in the *Uplift* novels, which are set several hundred years into a dangerous future, in a cosmos that poor humans barely comprehend.

And in an interview, he said: "Each story in the Uplift Universe deals with some issue of good and evil—or the murky realm between. One that I've been confronting lately is the insidious and arrogant, but all too commonplace, assumption that words are more important than actions."

His comment on this story is:

> In my story "Temptation"—an offshoot adventure from events depicted in *Infinity's Shore*—we confronted that old malignant notion—the ever-lurking temptation of wishful thinking. As the dolphin characters conclude, it is possible to mix science and art. We can combine honesty with extravagant self-expression. We are not limited beings.

TEMPTATION

DAVID BRIN

MAKANEE

Jijo's ocean stroked her flank like a mother's nuzzling touch, or a lover's caress. Though it seemed a bit disloyal, Makanee felt this alien ocean had a silkier texture and finer taste than the waters of Earth, the homeworld she had not seen in years.

With gentle beats of their powerful flukes, she and her companion kept easy pace beside a tremendous throng of fishlike creatures—red-finned, with violet gills and long translucent tails that glittered in the slanted sunlight like plasma sparks behind a starship. The school seemed to stretch forever, grazing on drifting clouds of plankton, moving in unison through coastal shallows like the undulating body of a vast complacent serpent.

The creatures were beautiful . . . and delicious. Makanee performed an agile twist of her sleek gray body, lunging to snatch one from the teeming mass, provoking only a slight ripple from its nearest neighbors her casual style of predation must be new to Jijo, for the beasts seemed quite oblivious to the dolphins. The rubbery flesh tasted like exotic mackerel.

"I can't help feeling guilty," she commented in Underwater Anglic, a language of clicks and squeals that was well suited to a liquid realm where sound ruled over light.

Her companion rolled alongside the school, belly up, with ventral fins waving languidly as he grabbed one of the local fish for himself.

"Why guilty?" Brookida asked, while the victim writhed between his narrow jaws. Its soft struggle did not interfere with his train of word-glyphs, since a dolphin's mouth plays no role in generating sound. Instead a rapid series of ratcheting sonar impulses emanated from his brow. "Are you ashamed because you live? Because it feels good to be outside again, with a warm sea rubbing your skin and the crash of waves singing in your dreams? Do you miss the stale water and moldy air aboard ship? Or the dead echoes of your cramped stateroom?"

"Don't be absurd," she snapped back. After three years confined aboard the Terran survey vessel, *Streaker*, Makanee had felt as cramped as an overdue fetus, straining at the womb. Release from that purgatory was like being born anew.

"It's just that we're enjoying a tropical paradise while our crewmates—"

"—must continue tearing across the cosmos in foul discomfort, chased by vile enemies, facing death at every turn. Yes, I know."

Brookida let out an expressive sigh. The elderly geophysicist switched languages, to one more suited for poignant irony.

> * Winter's tempest spends
> * All is force against the reef
> * Sparing the lagoon. *

The Trinary haiku was expressive and wry. At the same time though, Makanee could not help making a physician's diagnosis. She found her old friend's sonic patterns rife with undertones of *Primal*—the natural cetacean demi-language used by wild *Tursiops truncatus* dolphins back on Earth—a dialect that members of the modern *amicus* breed were supposed to avoid, lest their minds succumb to tempting ancient ways. Mental styles that lured with rhythms of animal-like purity.

She found it worrisome to hear Primal from Brookida, one of her few companions with an intact psyche. Most of the other dolphins on Jijo suffered to some degree from stress-atavism. Having lost the cognitive focus needed by engineers and starfarers, they could no longer help Streaker in its desperate flight across five galaxies. Planting this small colony on Jijo had seemed a logical solution, leaving the regressed ones for Makanee to care for in this gentle place, while their shipmates sped on to new crises elsewhere.

She could hear them now, browsing along the same fishy swarm just a hundred meters off. Thirty neo-dolphins who had once graduated from prestigious universities. Specialists chosen for an elite expedition—now reduced to splashing and squalling, with little on their minds but food, sex, and music. Their primitive calls no longer embarrassed Makanee. After everything her colleagues had gone through since departing Terra—on a routine one-year survey voyage that instead stretched into a hellish three—it was surprising they had any sanity left at all.

Such suffering would wear down a human, or even a tymbrimi. But our race is just a few centuries old. Neo-dolphins have barely started the long Road of Uplift. Our grip on sapience is still slippery.

And now another trail beckons us.

After debarking with her patients, Makanee had learned about the local religion of the Six Races who already secretly settled this isolated world, a creed centered on *the Path of Redemption*—a belief that salvation could be found in blissful ignorance and nonsapience.

It was harder than it sounded. Among the "sooner" races who had come to this world illegally, seeking refuge in simplicity, only one had succeeded so far, and Makanee doubted that the *human* settlers would ever reclaim true animal innocence, no matter how hard they tried. Unlike species who were uplifted, humans had earned their intelligence the hard way on Old Earth, seizing each new talent or insight at frightful cost over the course of a thousand harsh millennia. They might become ignorant and primitive—but never simple. Never innocent.

We neo-dolphins will find it easy, however. We've only been tool-users for such a short time—a boon from our human patrons that we never sought. It's simple to give up something you received without struggle. Especially when the alternative—the Whale Dream—calls seductively, each time you sleep.

An alluring sanctuary. The sweet trap of timelessness.

From clackety sonar emanations, she sensed her assistants—a pair of fully conscious volunteers—keeping herd on the reverted ones, making sure the group stayed together. Things seemed pleasant here, but no one knew for sure what dangers lurked in Jijo's wide sea.

We already have three wanderers out there somewhere. Poor little Peepoe and her two wretched kidnappers. I promised Kaa we'd send out search parties to rescue her. But how? Zhaki and Mopol have a huge head start, and half a planet to hide in.

Tkett's out there looking for her right now, and we'll start expanding the search as soon as the patients are settled and safe. But they could be on the other side of Jijo by now. Our only real hope is for Peepoe to escape that pair of dolts somehow and get close enough to call for help.

It was time for Makanee and Brookida to head back and take their own turn shepherding the happy-innocent patients. Yet, she felt reluctant. Nervous.

Something in the water rolled through her mouth with a faint metallic tang, tasting like *expectancy*.

Makanee swung her sound-sensitive jaw around, seeking clues. At last she found a distant tremor. A faintly familiar resonance, coming from the west.

Brookida hadn't noticed yet.

"Well," he commented, "it won't be long till we are truly part of this world, I suppose. A few generations from now, none of our descendants will be using Anglic, or any Galactic language. We'll be guileless innocents once more, ripe for readoption and a second chance at uplift. I wonder what our new patrons will be like."

Makanee's friend was goading her gently with the bittersweet destiny anticipated for this colony, on a world that seemed made for cetaceans. A world whose comfort was the surest way to clinch a rapid devolution of their disciplined minds. Without constant challenges, the Whale Dream would surely reclaim them. Brookida seemed to accept the notion with an ease that disturbed Makanee.

"We still *have* patrons," she pointed out. "There are humans living right here on Jijo."

"Humans, yes. But uneducated, lacking the scientific skills to continue guiding us. So our only remaining option must be—"

He stopped, having at last picked up that rising sound from the west. Makanee recognized the unique hum of a speed sled.

"It is Tkett," she said. "Returning from his scouting trip. Let's go hear what he found out."

Thrashing her flukes, Makanee jetted to the surface, spuming the moist, stale air from her lungs and drawing in a deep breath of sweet oxygen. Then she spun about and kicked off toward the engine noise, with Brookida following close behind.

In their wake, the school of grazing fishoids barely rippled in its endless, sinuous dance, darting in and out of luminous shoals, feeding on whatever the good sea pressed toward them.

The archaeologist had his own form of mental illness—wishful thinking.

Tkett had been ordered to stay behind and help Makanee with the reverted ones, partly because his skills weren't needed in Streaker's continuing desperate flight across the known universe. In compensation for that bitter exile, he had grown obsessed with studying the Great Midden, that deep underwater trash heap where Jijo's ancient occupants had dumped nearly eve sapient-made object when this planet was abandoned by starfaring culture, half a million years ago.

"I'll have a wonderful report to submit when we get back to Earth," he rationalized, in apparent confidence that all their troubles would pass, and eventually he would make it home to publish his results. It was a special kind of derangement, without featuring any sign of stress-atavism or reversion. Tkett still spoke Anglic perfectly. His work was flawless and his demeanor cheerful. He was pleasant, functional, and mad as a hatter.

Makanee met the sled a kilometer west of the pod, where Tkett pulled up short in order not to disturb the patients. "Did you find any traces of Peepoe?" she asked when he cut the engine.

Tkett was a wonderfully handsome specimen of *Tursiops amicus*, with speckled mottling along his sleek gray flanks. The permanent dolphin-smile presented twin rows of perfectly white, conical teeth. While still nestled on the sled's control platform, Tkett shook his sleek gray head left and right.

"Alas, no. I went about two hundred klicks, following those faint traces we picked up on deep-range sonar. But it grew clear that the source wasn't Zhaki's sled."

Makanee grunted disappointment. "Then what was it?" Unlike the clamorous sea of Earth, this fallow planet wasn't supposed to have motor noises permeating its thermal-acoustic layers.

"At first I started imagining all sorts of unlikely things, like sea monsters, or Jophur submarines," Tkett answered. "Then the truth hit me."

Brookida nodded nervously, venting bubbles from his blowhole. "Yessssss?"

"It must be a *starship*. And ancient, piece-of-trash wreck, barely puttering along—"

"Of course!" Makanee thrashed her tail. "Some of the decoys didn't make it into space."

Tkett murmured ruefully over how obvious it now seemed. When *Streaker* made its getaway attempt, abandoning Makanee and her charges on this world, the earthship fled concealed in a swarm of ancient relics that dolphin engineers had resurrected from trash heaps on the ocean floor. Though Jijo's surface now was a fallow realm of savage tribes, the deep underwater canyons still held thousands of battered, abandoned spacecraft and other debris from when this section of Galaxy Four had been a center of civilization and commerce. Several dozen of those derelicts had been reactivated in order to confuse *Streaker's* foe—a fearsome Jophur battleship—but some of the hulks must have failed to haul their bulk out of the sea when the time came. Those failures were doomed to drift aimlessly underwater until their engines gave our and they tumbled once more to the murky depths.

As for the rest, there had been no word whether *Streaker's* ploy succeeded beyond luring the awful dreadnought away toward deep space. At least Jijo seemed a friendlier place without it. For now.

"We should have expected this," the archaeologist continued. "When I got away from the shoreline surf noise, I thought I could detect at least three of the hulks, bumping around out here almost randomly. It seems kind of sad, when you think about it. Ancient ships, not worth salvaging when the Buyur abandoned Jijo, waiting in an icy, watery tomb for just one last chance to climb back out to space. Only these couldn't make it. They're stranded here."

"Like us," Makanee murmured.

Tkett seemed not to hear.

"In fact, I'd like to go back out there and try to catch up with one of the derelicts."

"Whatever for?"

Tkett's smile was still charming and infectious . . . which made it seem even crazier, under these circumstances.

"I'd like to use it as a scientific instrument," the big neo-dolphin said.

Makanee felt utterly confirmed in her diagnosis.

PEEPOE

Captivity wasn't as bad as she had feared.

It was worse.

Among natural, presapient dolphins on Earth, small groups of young males would sometimes conspire to isolate a fertile female from the rest of the pod, herding her away for private copulation—especially if she was about to enter heat. By working together, they might monopolize her matings and guarantee their own reproductive success, even if she clearly preferred a local alpha-ranked male instead. That ancient behavior pattern persisted in the wild because, while native *Tursiops* had both traditions and a kind of feral honor, they could not quite grasp or carry out the concept of *law*—a code that all must live by, because the entire community has a memory transcending any individual.

But modern, uplifted *amicus* dolphins did have law! And when young hoodlums occasionally let instinct prevail and tried that sort of thing back home, the word for it was *rape*. Punishment was harsh. As with human sexual predators, just one of the likely outcomes was permanent sterilization.

Such penalties worked. After three centuries, some of the less desirable primal behaviors were becoming rare. Yet, uplifted neo-dolphins were still a young race. Great stress could yank old ways back to the fore, from time to time.

And we Streakers have sure been under stress.

Unlike some devolved crewmates, whose grip on modernity and rational thought had snapped under relentless pressure, Zhaki and Mopol suffered only partial atavism. They could still talk and run complex equipment, but they were no longer the polite, almost shy junior ratings she had met when *Streaker* first set out from Earth under Captain Creideiki, before the whole cosmos seemed to implode all around the dolphin crew.

In abstract, she understood the terrible strain that had put them in this state. Perhaps, if she were offered a chance to kill Zhaki and Mopol, Peepoe might call that punishment a bit too severe.

On the other fin, sterilization was much too good for them.

Despite sharing the same culture, and a common ancestry as Earth mammals, dolphins and humans looked at many things differently. Peepoe felt more annoyed at being kidnapped than violated. More pissed off than traumatized. She wasn't able to stymie their lust completely, but with various tricks—playing on their mutual jealousy and feigning illness as often as she could—Peepoe staved off unwelcome attentions for long stretches.

But if I find out they murdered Kaa, I'll have their entrails for lunch.

Days passed and her impatience grew. Peepoe's real time limit was fast approaching. *My contraception implant will expire. Zhaki and his pal have fantasies about populating Jijo with their descendants, but I like this planet far too much to curse it that way.*

She vowed to make a break for it. But how?

Sometimes she would swim to a channel between the two remote islands where her kidnappers had brought her, and drift languidly, listening. Once, Peepoe thought she made out something faintly familiar—a clicking murmur, like a distant crowd of dolphins. But it passed, and she dismissed it as wishful thinking. Zhaki and Mopol had driven the sled at top speed for days on end with her strapped to the back, before they halted by this strange archipelago and removed her sonar-proof blindfold. She had no idea how to find her way back to the old coastline where Makanee's group had settled.

When I do escape these two idiots. I may be consigning myself to a solitary existence for the rest of my days.

Oh well, you wanted the life of an explorer. There could be worse fates than swimming all the way around this beautiful world, eating exotic fish when you're hungry, riding strange tides and listening to rhythms no dolphin ever heard before.

The fantasy had a poignant beauty—though ultimately, it made her lonely and sad.

The ocean echoed with anger, engines, and strange noise.

Of course it was all a matter of perspective. On noisy Earth, this would have seemed eerily quiet. Terran seas buzzed with a cacophony of traffic, much of it caused by her own kind as neo-dolphins gradually took over managing seventy percent of the home planet's surface. In mining the depths, or tending fisheries, or caring for those sacredly complex simpletons called whales, more and more responsibilities fell to up-lifted 'fins using boats, subs, and other equipment. Despite continuing efforts to re-duce the racket, home was still a raucous place.

In comparison, Jijo appeared as silent as a nursery. Natural sound-carrying ther-mal layers reported waves crashing on distant shorelines and intermittent groaning as minor quakes rattled the ocean floor. A myriad buzzes, clicks, and whistles came from Jijo's own subsurface fauna—fishy creatures that evolved here, or were introduced by colonizing leaseholders like the Buyur, long ago. Some distant rumbles even hinted at *large* entities, moving slowly, languidly across the deep . . . perhaps pondering long, slow thoughts.

As days stretched to weeks, Peepoe learned to distinguish Jijo's organic rhythms . . . punctuated by a grating din whenever one of the boys took the sled for a joy ride, stampeding schools of fish, or careening along with the load indicator show-ing red. At this rate the machine wouldn't stand up much longer, though Peepoe kept hoping one of them would break his fool neck first.

With or without the sled, Zhaki and Mopol could rack her down if she just swam away. Even when they left piles of dead fish to ferment atop some floating reeds, and got drunk on the foul carcasses, the two never let their guard down long enough to let her steal the sled. It seemed that one or the other was always sprawled across the sad-dle. Since dolphins only sleep one brain hemisphere at a time, it was impossible to take them completely by surprise.

Then, after two months of captivity, she detected signs of something drawing near.

Peepoe had been diving in deeper water for a tasty kind of local soft-shell crab when she first heard it. Her two captors were having fun a kilometer away, driving their speedster in tightening circles around a panicked school of bright silvery fishoids. But when she dived through a thermal boundary layer, separating warm wa-ter above from cool saltier liquid below—the sled's racket abruptly diminished.

Blessed silence was one added benefit of this culinary exploit. Peepoe had been doing a lot of diving lately.

This time, however, the transition did more than spare her the sled's noise for a brief time. it also brought forth a *new* sound. A distant rumble, channeled by the shilly stratum. With growing excitement, Peepoe recognized the murmur of an en-gine! Yet the rhythms struck her as unlike any she had heard on Earth or elsewhere.

Puzzled, she kicked swiftly to the surface, filled her lungs with fresh air, and dived back down to listen again.

This deep current offers an excellent sonic grove, she realized, *focusing sound rather than diffusing it. Keeping the vibrations well confined. Even the sled's sensors may not pick it up for quite a while.*

Unfortunately, that also meant she couldn't tell how far away the source was.

If I had a breathier unit . . . if it weren't necessary to keep surfacing for air . . . I could swim a great distance masked by this thermal barrier. Otherwise, it seems hopeless. They can use the sled's monitors on long-range scan to detect me when I broach and exhale.

Peepoe listened for a while longer, and decided.

I think it's getting closer . . . but slowly. The source must still be far away. If I made a dash now, I won't get far before they catch me.

And yet, she daren't risk Mopol and Zhaki picking up the new sound. If she must wait, it meant keeping them distracted till the time was right.

There was just one way to accomplish that.

Peepoe grimaced. Rising toward the surface, she expressed disgust with a vulgar Trinary demi-haiku.

* May sun roast your backs,
　　* And hard sand scrape your bottoms,
　　　* Til you itch madly. . . .
* . . . as if with a good case of the clap! *

MAKANEE

She sent a command over her neural link, ordering the tools of her harness to fold away into streamlined recesses, signaling that the inspection visit was over.

The chief of the kiqui, a little male with purple gill-fringes surrounding a squat head, let himself drift a meter or so under the water's surface, spreading all four webbed hands in a gesture of benediction and thanks. Then he thrashed around to lead his folk away, back toward the nearby island where they made their home. Makanee felt satisfaction as she watched the small formation of kicking amphibians, clutching their stone-tipped spears.

Who would have thought that we dolphins, youngest registered sapient race in the Civilization of Five Galaxies, would become patrons ourselves, just a few centuries after humans started uplifting us.

The kiqui were doing pretty well on Jijo, all considered. Soon after being released onto a coral atoll, not far offshore, they started having babies.

Under normal conditions, some elder race would find an excuse to take the kiqui away from dolphins, fostering such a promising presapient species into one of the rich, ancient family lines that ruled oxygen-breathing civilization in the Five Galaxies. But here on Jijo things were different. They were cut off from starfaring culture, a vast bewildering society of complex rituals and obligations that made the ancient Chinese Imperial court seem like a toddler's sandbox, by comparison. There were advantages and disadvantages to being a castaway from all that.

On the one hand, Makanee would no longer have to endure the constant tension of running away from huge oppressive battlefleets or aliens whose grudges went beyond earthling comprehension.

On the other hand, there would be no more performances of symphony, or opera, or bubble-dance for her to attend.

Never again must she endure disparaging sneers from exalted patron-level beings, who considered dolphins little more than bright beasts.

Nor would she spend another lazy Sunday in her snug apartment in cosmopolitan Melbourne-Under, with multicolored fish cruising the coral garden just outside her window while she munched salmon patties and watched an all-dolphin cast perform *Twelfth Night* on the telly.

Makanee was marooned, and would likely remain so for the rest of her life, caring for two small groups of sea-based colonists, hoping they could remain hidden from trouble until a new era came. An age when both might resume the path of uplift.

Assuming some metal nutrient supplements could be arranged, the kiqui had apparently transplanted well. Of course, they must be taught tribal taboos against overhunting any one species of local fauna, so their presence would not become a curse on this world. But the clever little amphibians already showed some understanding, expressing the concept in their own, emphatic demi-speech.

Rare is precious!
Not eat-or-hurt rare/precious things/fishes/beasts!
Only eat/hunt many-of-a-kind!

She felt a personal stake in this. Two years ago, when *Streaker* was about to depart poisonous Kithrup, masked inside the hulk of a crashed Thennanin warship, Makanee had taken it upon herself to beckon a passing tribe of kiqui with some of their own recorded calls, attracting the curious group into *Streaker's* main airlock just before the surrounding water boiled with exhaust from revving engines. What then seemed an act of simple pity turned into a kind of love affair, as the friendly little amphibians became favorites of the crew. Perhaps now their race might flourish in a kinder place than unhappy Kithrup. It felt good to know *Streaker* had accomplished at least one good thing out of its poignant, tragic mission.

As for dolphins, how could anyone doubt their welcome in Jijo's warm sea? Once you learned which fishoids were edible and which to avoid, life became a matter of snatching whatever you wanted to eat, then splashing and lolling about. True, she missed her *holoson* unit, with its booming renditions of whale chants and baroque chorales. But here she could take pleasure in listening to an ocean whose sonic purity was almost as fine as its vibrant texture.

Almost . . .

Reacting to a faint sensation, Makanee swung her sound-sensitive jaw around, casting right and left.

There! She heard it again. A distant rumbling that might have escaped notice amid the underwater cacophony on Earth. But here it seemed to stand out from the normal swish of current and tide.

Her patients—the several dozen dolphins whose stress-atavism had reduced them to infantile innocence—called such infrequent noises *boojums.* Or else they used a worried upward trill in Primal Delphin—one that stood for strange monsters of the deep. Sometimes the far-off grumbles did seem to hint at some huge, living entity, rumbling with basso-profundo pride, complacently assured that it owned the entire vast sea. Or else it might be just frustrated engine noise from some remnant derelict machine, wandering aimlessly in the ocean's immensity.

Leaving the kiqui atoll behind, Makanee swam back toward the underwater dome where she and Brookida, plus a few still-sapient nurses, maintained a small base to keep watch over their charges. It would be good to get out of the weather for a while. Last night she had roughed it, keeping an eye on her patients during a rain squall. An unpleasant, wearying experience.

We modern neo-fins are spoiled. It will take us years to get used to living in the elements, accepting whatever nature sends our way, without complaining or making ambitious plans to change the way things are.

That human side of us must be allowed to fade away.

PEEPOE

She made her break around midmorning the next day.

Zhaki was sleeping off a hangover near a big mat of driftweed, and Mopol was using the sled to harass some unlucky penguinlike seabirds, who were trying to feed their young by fishing near the island's lee shore. It seemed a good chance to slip away, but Peepoe's biggest reason for choosing this moment was simple. Diving deep below the thermal layer, she found that the distant rumble had peaked, and appeared to have turned away, diminishing with each passing hour.

It was now, or never.

Peepoe had hoped to steal something from the sled first. A utensil harness per-haps, or a breather tube, and not just for practical reasons. In normal life, few neo-dolphins spent a single day without using cyborg tools, controlled by cable links to the brain's temporal lobes. But for months now her two would-be "husbands" hadn't let her connect to anything at all! The neural tap behind her left eye ached from disuse.

Unfortunately, Mopol nearly always slept on the sled's saddle, barely ever leaving except to eat and defecate.

He'll be desolated when the speeder finally breaks down, she thought, taking some solace from that.

So the decision was made, and Ifni's dice were cast. She set out with all the gifts and equipment nature provided—completely naked—into an uncharted sea.

For Peepoe, escaping captivity began unlike any human novel or fantasholo. In such stories, the heroine's hardest task was normally the first part, sneaking away. But here Peepoe faced no walls, locked rooms, dogs, or barbed wire. Her "guards" let her come and go as she pleased. In this case, the problem wasn't getting started, but win-ning a big enough head start before Zhaki and Mopol realized she was gone.

Swimming under the thermocline helped mask her movements at first. it left her vulnerable to detection only when she went up for air. But she could not keep it up for long. The *Tursiops* genus of dolphins weren't deep divers by nature, and her speed at depth was only a third what it would be by skimming near the surface.

So, while the island was still above the horizon behind her, Peepoe stopped slink-ing along silently below and instead began her dash for freedom in earnest—racing toward the sun with an endless series of powerful back archings and fluke-strokes, go-ing deep only occasionally to check her bearings against the far-off droning sound.

It felt exhilarating to slice through the wavetops, flexing her body for all it was worth. Peepoe remembered the last time she had raced along this way—with Kaa by her side—when Jijo's waters had seemed warm, sweet, and filled with possibilities.

Although she kept low-frequency sonar clickings to a minimum, she did allow herself some short-range bursts, checking ahead for obstacles and toying with the sur-rounding water, bouncing reflections off patches of sun-driven convection, letting echoes wrap themselves around her like rippling memories. Peepoe's sonic transmis-sions remained soft and close—no louder than the vibrations given off by her kicking tail—but the patterns grew more complex as her mind settled into the rhythms of movement. Before long, returning wavelets of her own sound meshed with those of current and tide, overlapping to make phantom sonar images.

Most of these were vague shapes, like the sort that one felt swarming at the edges of a dream. But in time several fell together, merging into something larger. The com-posite echo seemed to bend and thrust when she did—as if a spectral companion now swam nearby, where her squinting eye saw only sunbeams in an empty sea.

Kaa, she thought, recognizing a certain unique zest whenever the wraith's bottle nose flicked through the waves.

Among dolphins, you did not have to die in order to come back as a ghost . . . though it helped. Sometimes the only thing required was vividness of spirit—and Kaa surely was, or had been, vivid.

Or perhaps the nearby sound-effigy fruited solely from Peepoe's eager imagina-tion.

In fact, dolphin logic perceived no contradiction between those two explana-tions. Kaa's essence might really be there—and not be—at the same time. Whether real or mirage, she was glad to have her lover back where he belonged—by her side.

I've missed you, she thought.

Anglic wasn't a good language for phantoms. No human grammar was. Perhaps that explained why the poor bipeds so seldom communed with their beloved lost.

Peepoe's visitor answered in a more ambiguous, innately delphin style.

> * Till the seaweed's flower
>   * Shoots forth petals made of moonbeams
>   * I will swim with you *

Peepoe was content with that. For some unmeasured time, it seemed as if a real companion, her mate, swam alongside, encouraging her efforts, sharing the grueling pace. The water divided before her, caressing her flanks like a real lover.

Then, abruptly, a new sound intruded. A distant grating whine that threatened to shatter all illusions.

Reluctantly, she made herself clamp down, silencing the resonant chambers surrounding her blowhole. As her own sonar vibrations ceased, so did the complex echoes, and her phantom comrade vanished. The waters ahead seemed to go black as Peepoe concentrated, listening intently.

There it was.

Coming from behind her. Another engine vibration, this one all too familiar, approaching swiftly as if skimmed across the surface of the sea.

They know, she realized. *Zhaki and Mopol know I'm gone, and they're coming after me.*

Peepoe wasted no more time. She bore down with her flukes, racing through the waves faster than ever. Stealth no longer mattered. Now it was a contest of speed, endurance, and luck.

TKETT

It took him most of a day and the next night to get near the source of the mysterious disturbance, pushing his power sled as fast as he dared. Makanee had ordered Tkett not to overstrain the engine, since there would be no replacements when it wore out.

"Just be careful out there," the elderly dolphin physician had urged, when giving permission for this expedition. *"Find out what it is . . . whether it's one of the derelict spacecraft that Suessi and the engineers brought back to life as decoys. If so, don't mess with it! Just come back and report. We'll discuss where to go from there."*

Tkett did not have disobedience in mind. At last not explicitly. But if it really was a starship making the low, uneven grumbling noise, a host of possibilities presented themselves. What if it proved possible to board the machine and take over the makeshift controls that *Streaker's* crew had put in place?

Even if it can't fly, it's cruising around the ocean. I could use it as a submersible and visit the Great Midden.

That vast undersea trench was where the Buyur had dumped most of the dross of their mighty civilization, when it came time for them to abandon Jijo and return its surface to fallow status. After packing up to leave, the last authorized residents of this planet used titanic machines to scrape away their cities, then sent all their buildings and other works tumbling into an abyss where the slow grinding of tectonic plates would draw the rubble inward, melting and reshaping new ores to be used by others in some future era; when Jijo was opened for legal settlement once again.

To an archaeologist, the Midden seemed the opportunity of a lifetime.

I'd learn so much about the Buyur! We might examine whole classes of tools that no Earthling has ever seen. The Buyur were rich and powerful. They could afford the very best in the Civilization of Five Galaxies, while we Terran newcomers can only buy the dregs. Even stuff the Buyur threw away—their toys and broken trinkets—could provide valuable data for the Terragens Council.

Tkett wasn't a complete fool. He knew what Makanee and Brookida thought of him.

They consider me crazy to be optimistic about going home. To believe any of us will see Earth again, or let the industrial tang of its waters roll through our open jaws, or once more surf the riptides of Ranga Roa.

Or give a university lecture. Or dive through the richness of a worldwide data network, sharing ideas with a fecund civilization at light-speed. Or hold challenging conversations with others who share your intellectual passions.

He had signed aboard *Streaker* to accompany Captain Creideiki and a neo-dolphin intellectual elite in the greatest mental and physical adventure any group of cetaceans ever faced—the ultimate test of their new sapient race. Only now Creideiki was gone, presumed dead, and Tkett had been ejected by *Streaker's* new commander, exiled from the ship at its worst moment of crisis. Makanee might feel complacent over being put ashore as "nonessential" personnel, but it churned Tkett's guts to be spilled into a warm, disgustingly placid sea while his crewmates were still out there, facing untold dangers among the bleeding stars.

A voice broke in from the outside, before his thoughts could spiral any further toward self-pity.

> \# *give me give me* GIVE ME
> \# *snout-smacking pleasure*
> \# *of a good fight!*\#

That shrill chatter came from the sled's rear compartment, causing Tkett's flukes to thrash in brief startlement. It was easy to forget about his quiet passenger for long stretches of time. Chissis spoke seldom, and then only in the throwback protolanguage, Primal Delphin.

Tkett quashed his initial irritation. After all, Chissis was unwell. Like several dozen other members of the crew, her modern mind had crumpled under the pressure of *Streaker's* long ordeal, taking refuge in older ways of thought. One had to make allowances, even though Tkett could not imagine how it was possible for anyone to abandon the pleasures of rationality, no matter how insistently one heard the call of the Whale Dream.

After a moment, Tkett realized that her comment had been more than just useless chatter. Chissis must have sensed some meaning from his sonar clicks. Apparently she understood and shared his resentment over Gillian Baskin's decision to leave them behind on Jijo.

"You'd rather be back in space right now, wouldn't you?" he asked. "Even though you can't read an instrument panel anymore? Even with Jophur battleships and other nasties snorting down *Streaker's* neck, closing in for the kill?"

His words were in Underwater Anglic. Most of the reverted could barely comprehend it anymore. But Chissis squawled from the platform behind Tkett, throwing a sound burst that sang like the sled's engine, thrusting ever forward, obstinately defiant.

> \# *smack the Jophur! smack the sharks!*
> \# SMACK THEM! \#

Accompanying her eager-repetitive message squeal, there came a sonar crafted by the fatty layers of her brow, casting a brief veil of illusion around Tkett. He briefly visualized Chissis, joyfully ensconced in the bubble nose of a *lamprey*-class torpedo, personally piloting it on course toward a huge alien cruiser, penetrating all of the cyberdisruptive fields that Galactic spacecraft used to stave off digital guidance systems, zeroing in on her target with all the instinct and native agility that dolphins inherited from their ancestors.

Loss of speech apparently had not robbed some "reverted" ones of either spunk or ingenuity. Tkett sputtered laughter. Gillian Baskin had made a real mistake leaving this one behind! Apparently you did not need an engineer's mind in order to have the heart of a warrior.

"No wonder Makanee let you come along on this trip," he answered. "You're a bad influence on the others, aren't you?"

It was her turn to emit a laugh—sounding almost exactly like his own. A ratcheting raspberry-call that the masters of uplift had left alone. A deeply cetacean shout that defied the sober universe for taking so many things too seriously.

> # *Faster faster FASTER!*
> > # *Engines call us . . .*
> > > # *offering a ride . . . #*

Tkett's tail thrashed involuntarily as her cry yanked something deep within. Without hesitating, he cranked up the sled's motor, sending it splashing through the foamy white-tops, streaking toward a mysterious object whose song filled the sea.

PEEPOE

She could sense Zhaki and Mopol closing in from behind. They might be idiots, but they knew what they wanted and how to pilot their sled at maximum possible speed without frying the bearings. Once alerted to her escape attempt, they cast ahead using the machine's deep-range sonar. She felt each loud *ping* like a small bite along her backside. By now they knew exactly where she was. The noise was meant to intimidate her.

It worked. *I don't know how much longer I can keep on.* Peepoe thought while her body burned with fatigue. Each body-arching plunge through the waves seemed to take more out of her. No longer a joyful sensation, the ocean's silky embrace became a clinging drag, taxing and stealing her hard-won momentum, making Peepoe earn each dram of speed over and over again.

In comparison, the hard vacuum of space seemed to offer a better bargain. What you bought, you got to keep. Even the dead stayed on trajectory, tumbling ever onward. Space travel tended to promote belief in "progress," a notion that old-style dolphins used to find ridiculous, and still had some trouble getting used to.

I should be fairly close to the sound I was chasing . . . whatever's making it. I'd be able to tell, if only those vermin behind me would turn off the damned sonar and let me listen in peace!

Of course the pinging racket was meant to disorient her. Peepoe only caught occasional sonic-glimpses of her goal, and then only by diving below the salt-boundary layer, something she did as seldom as possible, since it always slowed her down.

The noise of the sled's engine sounded close. Too damned close. At any moment Zhaki and Mopol might swerve past to cut her off, then start spiraling inward, herding her like some helpless sea animal while they chortled, enjoying their macho sense of power.

I'll have to submit . . . bear their punishment . . . put up with bites and whackings till they're convinced I've become a good cow.

None of that galled Peepoe as much as the final implication of her recapture.

I guess this means I'll have to kill the two of them.

It was the one thing she'd been hoping to avoid. Murder among dolphins had been rare in olden times, and the genetic engineers worked to enhance this innate distaste. Anyway, Peepoe had wished to avoid making the choice. A clean getaway would have sufficed.

She didn't know how she'd do it. Not yet.

But I'm still a Terragens officer, while they relish considering themselves wild beasts. How hard can it be?

Part of her knew that she was drifting, fantasizing. This might even be the way her subconscious was trying to rationalize surrendering the chase. She might as well give up now, before exhaustion claimed all her strength.

No! I've got to keep going.

Peepoe let out a groan as she redoubled her efforts, bearing down with intense drives of her powerful tail flukes. Each moment that she held them off meant just a little more freedom. A little more dignity.

It couldn't last, of course. Though it felt exultant and defiant to give it one more hard push, the burst of speed eventually faded as her body used up its last reserves. Quivering, she fell at last into a languid glide, gasping for air to fill her shuddering lungs.

Too bad. I can hear it . . . the underwater thing I was seeking . . . not far away now.

But Zhaki and Mopol are closer still . . .

What took Peepoe some moments to recall was that the salt-thermal barrier deadened sound from whatever entity was cruising the depths below. For her to hear it now, however faintly, meant that it had to be—

A tremor rocked Peepoe. She felt the waters *bulge* around her, as if pushed aside by some massive creature, far under the ocean's surface. Realization dawned, even as she heard Zhaki's voice, shouting gleefully only a short distance away.

It's right below me. The thing! It's passing by, down there in the blackness.

She had only moments to make a decision. Judging from cues in the water, it was both very large and very far beneath her. Yet Peepoe felt nowhere near ready to attempt a deep dive while each breath still sighed with ragged pain.

She heard and felt the sled zoom past, spotting her two tormentors sprawled on the machine's back, grinning as they swept by dangerously close. Instinct made her want to turn away and flee, or else go below for as long as her lungs could hold out. But neither move would help, so she stayed put.

They'll savor their victory for a little while, she thought, hoping they were confident enough not to use the sled's stunner on her. Anyway, at this short range, what could she do?

It was hard to believe they hadn't picked up any signs of the behemoth by now. Stupid, single-minded males, they had concentrated all of their attention on the hunt for her.

Zhaki and Mopol circled around her twice, spiraling slowly closer, leering and chattering.

Peepoe felt exhausted, still sucking air for her laboring lungs. But she could afford to wait no longer. As they approached for the final time, she took one last, body-stretching gasp through her blowhole, arched her back, and flipped over to dive nose first into the deep.

At the final instant, her tail flukes waved at the boys. A gesture that she hoped they would remember with galling regret.

Blackness consumed the light and she plunged, kicking hard to gain depth while her meager air supply lasted. Soon, darkness welcomed Peepoe. But on passing the boundary layer, she did not need illumination any more. Sound guided her, the throaty rumble of something huge, moving gracefully and complacently through a world where sunshine never fell.

TKETT

He had several reasons to desire a starship, even one that was unable to fly. It could offer a way to visit the Great Midden, for instance, and explore its wonders. A partly operational craft might also prove useful to the Six Races of Jijo, whose bloody war against Jophur aggressors was said to be going badly ashore.

Tkett also imagined using such a machine to find and rescue Peepoe.

The beautiful dolphin medic—one of Makanee's assistants—had been kidnapped shortly before *Streaker* departed. No one held out much hope of finding her, since the ocean was so vast and the two dolphin felons—Mopol and Zhaki—had an immensity to conceal her in. But that gloomy calculation assumed that searchers must travel by sled! A *ship* on the other hand—even a wreck that had lain on an ocean-floor garbage dump for half a million years—could cover a lot more territory and listen with big underwater sonaphones, combing for telltale sounds from Peepoe and her abductors. It might even be possible to sift the waters for Earthling DNA traces. Tkett had heard of such techniques available for a high price on Galactic markets. Who knew what wonders the fabled Buyur took for granted on their elegant starcraft?

Unfortunately, the trail kept going hot and cold. Sometimes he picked up murmurs that seemed incredibly close—channeled by watery layers that focused sound. Other times they vanished altogether.

Frustrated, Tkett was willing to try anything. So when Chissis started getting agitated, squealing in Primal that a *great beast* prowled to the southwest, he willingly turned the sled in the direction she indicated.

And soon he was rewarded. Indicators began flashing on the control panel, an down his neural-link cable, connecting the sled to an implanted socket behind his left eye. In addition to a surge of noise, mass displacement anomalies suggested something of immense size was moving ponderously just ahead, and perhaps a hundred meters down.

"I guess we better go find out what it is," he told his passenger, who clicked her agreement.

go chase go chase go chase ORCAS!

She let out squawls of laughter at her own cleverness. But minutes later, as they plunged deeper into the sea—both listening and peering down the shaft of the sled's probing headlights—Chissis ceased chuckling and became silent as a tomb.

Great Dreamers! Tkett stared in awe and surprise at the object before them. It was unlike any starship he had ever seen before. Sleek metallic sides seemed to go on and on forever as the titanic machine trudged onward across the sea floor, churning up mud with thousands of shimmering, crystalline legs!

As if sensing their arrival, a mammoth hatch began rising open—in benign welcome, he hoped.

No resurrected starship. Tkett began to suspect he had come upon something entirely different.

PEEPOE

Her rib cage heaved.

Peepoe's lungs filled with a throbbing ache as she forced herself to dive ever deeper, much lower than would have been wise, even if she weren't fatigued to the very edge of consciousness.

The sea at this depth was black. Her eyes made out nothing. But that was not the important sense, underwater. Sonar clicks, emitted from her brow, grew more rapid as she scanned ahead, using her sensitive jaw as an antenna to sift the reflections.

It's big. . . . she thought when the first signs returned.

Echo outlines began coalescing, and she shivered.

It doesn't sound like metal. The shape . . . seems less artificial than something—

A thrill of terror coursed her spine as she realized that the thing ahead had outlines resembling a gigantic living creature! A huge mass of fins and trailing tentacles, resembling some monster from the stories dolphin children would tell each other at night, secure in their rookeries near one of Earth's great port cities. What lay ahead of Peepoe, swimming along well above the canyon floor, seemed bigger and more intimidating than the giant squid who fought *Physeter* sperm whales, mightiest of all the cetaceans.

And yet, Peepoe kept arching her back, pushing hard with her flukes, straining ever downward. Curiosity compelled her. Anyway, she was closer to the creature than the sea surface, where Zhaki and Mopol waited.

I might as well find out what it is.

Curiosity was just about all she had left to live for.

When several tentacles began reaching for her, the only remaining question in her mind was about death.

I wonder who I'll meet on the other side.

MAKANEE

The dolphins in the pod—her patients—all woke about the same time from their afternoon siesta, screaming.

Makanee and her nurses joined Brookida, who had been on watch, swimming rapid circles around the frightened reverts, preventing any of them from charging in panic across the wide sea. Slowly, they all calmed down from a shared nightmare.

It was a common enough experience back on Earth, when unconscious sonar clicks from two or more sleeping dolphins would sometimes overlap and interfere, creating false echoes. The ghost of something terrifying. That most cetaceans sleep just one brain hemisphere at a time did not help. In a way, that seemed only to make the dissonance more eerie, and the fallacious sound-images more credibly scary.

Most of the patients were inarticulate, emitting only a jabber of terrified Primal squeals. But there were a dozen or so borderline cases who might even recover their faculties someday. One of these moaned nervously about *Tkett* and a *city of spells.*

Another one chittered nervously, repeating over and over, the name of Peepoe.

TKETT

Well, at least the machine has air inside, he thought. *We can survive here, and learn more.*

In fact, the huge underwater edifice—bigger than all but the largest starships—

seemed rather accommodating, pulling back metal walls as the little sled entered a spacious airlock. The floor sank in order to provide a pool for Tkett and Chissis to debark from their tight cockpits and swim around. It felt good to get out of the cramped confines, even though Tkett knew that coming inside might be a mistake.

Makanee's orders had been to do an inspection from the outside, then hurry home. But that was when they expected to find one of the rusty little spacecraft that *Streaker's* engineers had resurrected from some sea floor dross-pile. As soon as Tkett saw *this* huge cylindrical thing, churning along the sea bottom on a myriad caterpillar legs that gleamed like crystal stalks, he knew that nothing on Jijo could stand in the way of his going aboard.

Another wall folded aside, revealing a smooth channel that stretched ahead—water below and air above—beckoning the two dolphins down a hallway that shimmered as it continued transforming before their eyes. Each panel changed color with the glimmering luminescence of octopus skin, seeming to convey *meaning* in each transient, flickering shade. Chissis thrashed her tail nervously as objects kept slipping through seams in the walls. Sometimes these featured a camera lens at the end of an articulated arm, peering at them as they swam past.

Not even the Buyur could afford to throw away something as wonderful as this, Tkett thought, relishing a fantasy of taking this technology home to Earth. At the same time, the mechanical implements of his tool harness quivered, responding to nervous twitches that his brain sent down the neural tap. He had no weapons that would avail in the slightest if the owners of this place proved to be hostile.

The corridor spilled at last into a wide chamber with walls and ceiling that were so corrugated that he could not estimate its true volume. Countless bulges and spires protruded inward, half of them submerged, and the rest hanging in midair. All were bridged by cables and webbing that glistened like spiderwebs lined with dew. Many of the branches carried shining spheres or cubes or dodecahedrons that dangled like geometric fruit, ranging from half a meter across to twice the length of a bottlenose dolphin.

Chissis let out a squawl, colored with fear and awe.

> # *coral that bites! coral bites bites!*
> > # *See the critters, stabbed by coral!* #

When he saw what she meant, Tkett gasped. The hanging "fruits" were mostly transparent. They contained things that *moved* . . . creatures who writhed or hopped or ran in place, churning their arms and legs within the confines of their narrow compartments.

Adaptive optics in his right eye whirred, magnifying and zooming toward one of the crystal-walled containers. Meanwhile, his brow cast forth a stream of nervous sonar clicks—useless in the air—as if trying to penetrate this mystery with yet another sense.

I don't believe it!

He recognized the shaggy creature within a transparent cage.

Ifni! It's a hoon. A miniature hoon!

Scanning quickly, he found individuals of other species . . . four-legged urs with their long necks whipping nervously, like muscular snakes . . . minuscule traeki that resembled their Jophur cousins, looking like tapered stacks of doughnuts, piled high . . . and tiny versions of wheeled g'Keks, spinning their hubs madly, as if they were actually going somewhere. In fact, every member of the Commons of Six Races of Jijo—fugitive clans that had settled this world illegally during the last two thousand years—could be seen here, represented in lilliputian form.

Tkett's spine shuddered when he made out several cells containing slim bipedal forms. Bantamweight human beings, whose race had struggled against lonely ignorance on old Terra for so many centuries, nearly destroying the world before they finally matured enough to lead the way toward the true sapiency for the rest of Earthclan. Before Tkett's astonished eye, these members of the patron race were now reduced to leaping and cavorting within the confines of dangling crystal spheres.

PEEPOE

Death would not be so mundane . . . nor hurt in such familiar ways. when she began regaining consciousness, there was never any doubt which world this was. The old cosmos of life and pain.

Peepoe remembered the sea monster, an undulating behemoth of fins, tendrils, and phosphorescent scales, more than a kilometer long and nearly as wide, flapping wings like a manta ray as it glided well above the seafloor. When it reached up for her, she never thought of fleeing toward the surface, where mere enslavement waited. Peepoe was too exhausted y that point, and too transfixed by the images—both sonic and luminous—of a true leviathan.

The tentacle was gentler than expected, in grabbing her unresisting body and drawing it toward a widening beaklike maw. As she was pulled between a pair of jagged-edged jaws, Peepoe had let blackness finally claim her, moments before the end. The last thought to pass through her head was a Trinary haiku.

*Arrogance is answered
    *When each of us is reclaimed.
        *Rejoin the food chain!

Only there turned out to be more to her life, after all. Expecting to become pulped food for huge intestines, she wakened instead, surprised to find herself in another world.

A blurry world, at first. She lay in a small, pool, that much was evident. But it took moments to restore focus, meanwhile, out of the pattern of her bemused sonar clickings, a reflection seemed to mold itself, unbidden, surrounding Peepoe with Trinary philosophy.

*In the turning of life's cycloid,
    *Pulled by sun and moon insistence,
*Once a springtime storm may toss you,
    *Over reefs that have no channel,
*Into some lagoon untraveled,
    *Where strange fishes, spiny-poisoned,
*Taunt you, forlorn, isolated . . .

It wasn't an auspicious thought-poem, and Peepoe cut it off sharply, lest such stark sonic imagery trigger panic. The Trinary fog clung hard, though. It dissipated only with fierce effort, leaving a sense of dire warning in its wake.

Rising to the surface, Peepoe lifted her head and inspected the pool, lined by a riot of dense vegetation. Dense jungle stretched on all sides, brushing the rough-textured ceiling and cutting off small inhabitants, from flying insectoids to clambering things that peered at her shyly from behind sheltering leaves and shadows.

A habitat, she realized. Things lived here, competed, preyed on each other, died, and were recycled in a familiar ongoing synergy. The largest starships often contained ecological life-support systems, replenishing both food and oxygen supplies in the natural way.

But this is no starship. It can't be. The huge shape I saw could never fly. It was a sea beast, meant for the underwater world. It must have been alive!

Well, was there any reason why a gigantic animal could not keep an ecology going inside itself, like the bacterial cultures that helped Peepoe digest her own food?

So now what? Am I supposed to take part in all of this somehow? Or have I just begun a strange process of being digested?

She set off with a decisive push of her flukes. A dolphin without tools wasn't very agile in an environment like this. Her monkey-boy cousins—humans and chimps—would do better. But Peepoe was determined to explore while her strength lasted.

A channel led out of the little pool. Maybe something more interesting lay around the next bend.

TKETT

One of the spiky branches started moving, bending and articulating as it bent lower toward the watery surface where he and Chissis waited. At its tip, one of the crystal "fruits" contained a quadrupedal being—an urs whose long neck twisted as she peered about with glittering black eyes.

Tkett knew just a few things about this species. For example, they hated water in its open liquid form. Also the females were normally as massive as a full-grown human, yet this one appeared to be as small as a diminutive urrish male, less than twenty centimeters from nose to tail. Back in the Civilization of Five Galaxies, urs were known as great engineers. Humans didn't care for their smell (the feeling was mutual), but interactions between the two starfaring clans had been cordial. Urs weren't among the persecutors of Earthclan.

Tkett had no idea why an offshoot group of urs came to this world, centuries ago, establishing a secret and illegal colony on a world that had been declared off-limits by the Migration Institute. As one of the Six Races, they now galloped across Jijo's prairies, tending herds and working metals at forges that used heat from fresh volcanic lava pools. To find one here, under the sea, left him boggled and perplexed.

The creature seemed unaware of the dolphins who watched from nearby. From certain internal reflections, Tkett guessed that the glassy confines of the enclosure were transparent only in one direction. Flickering scenes could be made out, playing across the opposite internal walls. He glimpsed hilly countryside covered with swaying grass. The little urs galloped along, as if unencumbered and unenclosed.

The sphere dropped closer, and Tkett saw that it was choked with innumerable microscopic *threads* that crisscrossed the little chamber. Many of these terminated at the body of the urs, especially the bottoms of her flashing hooves.

Resistance simulators! Tkett recognized the principle, though he had never seen such a magnificent implementation. Back on Earth, humans and chimps would sometimes put on full bodysuits and VR helmets before entering chambers where a million needles made up the floor, each one computer controlled. As the user walked along a fictitious landscape, depicted visually in goggles he wore, the needles would rise and fall, simulating the same rough terrain underfoot. Each of these small crystal containers apparently operated in the same way, but with vastly greater texture and sophistication. So many tendrils pushing, stroking or stimulating each patch of skin, could feign wind blowing through urrish fur, or simulate the rough sensation of holding a tool . . . perhaps even the delightful rub and tickle of mating.

Other stalks descended toward Tkett and Chissis, holding many more virtual-reality fruits, each one containing a single individual. All of Jijo's sapient races were present, though much reduced in stature. Chissis seemed especially agitated to see small humans that ran about, or rested, or bent in apparent concentration over indiscernible tasks. None seemed aware of being observed.

It all felt horribly creepy, yet the subjects did not give an impression of lethargy or unhappiness. They seemed vigorous, active, interested in whatever engaged them. Perhaps they did not even know the truth about their peculiar existence.

Chissis snorted her uneasiness, and Tkett agreed. Something felt weird about the way these microenvironments were being paraded before the two of them, as if the mind—or minds—controlling the whole vast apparatus had some point it was trying to make, or some desire to communicate.

Is the aim to impress us?

He wondered about that, then abruptly realized what it must be about.

. . . all of Jijo's sapient races were present . . .

In fact, that was no longer true. Another species of thinking beings now dwelled on this world, the newest one officially sanctioned by the Civilization of Five Galaxies.

Neo-dolphins.

Oh, certainly the reverts like poor Chissis were only partly sapient anymore. And Tkett had no illusions about what Dr. Makanee thought of his own mental state. Nevertheless, as stalk after stalk bent to present its fruit before the two dolphins, showing off the miniature beings within—all of them busy and apparently happy with their existence—he began to feel as if he was being *wooed*.

"Ifni's boss . . ." he murmured aloud, amazed at what the great machine appeared to be offering. "It wants us to become part of all this!"

PEEPOE

A village of small grass huts surrounded the next pool she entered.

Small didn't half describe it. The creatures who emerged to swarm around the shore stared at her with wide eyes, set in skulls less than a third of normal size.

They were humans and hoons, mostly . . . along with a few traeki and a couple of glavers . . . all races whose full-sized cousins lived just a few hundred kilometers away, on a stretch of Jijo's western continent called The Slope.

As astonishing as she found these lilliputians, they stared in even greater awe at her. *I'm like a whale to them,* she realized, noting with some worry that many of them brandished spears or other weapons.

She heard a chatter of worried conversation as they pointed at her long gray bulk. That meant their brains were large enough for speech. Peepoe noted that the creatures' heads were out of proportion to their bodies, making the humans appear rather childlike . . . until you saw the men's hairy, scarred torsos, or the women's breasts, pendulous with milk for hungry babies. Their rapid jabber grew more agitated by the moment.

I'd better reassure them, or risk getting harpooned.

Peepoe spoke, starting with Anglic, the wolfling tongue most used on Earth. She articulated the words carefully with her gene-modified blowhole.

"Hello, f-f-folks! How are you doing today?"

That got a response, but not the one she hoped for. The crowd onshore backed away hurriedly, emitting upset cries. This time she thought she made out a few words in a time-shifted dialect of Galactic Seven, so she tried again in that language.

"Greetings! I bring you news of peaceful arrival and friendly intentions!"

This time the crowd went nearly crazy, leaping and cavorting in excitement, though whether it was pleasure or indignation seemed hard to tell at first.

Suddenly, the mob parted and went silent as a figure approached from the line of huts. It was a hoon, taller than average among these midgets. He wore an elaborate headdress and cape, while the dyed throat-sac under his chin flapped and vibrated to a sonorous beat. Two human assistants followed, one of them beating a drum. The rest of the villagers then did an amazing thing. They all dropped to their knees and covered their ears. Soon Peepoe heard a rising murmur.

They're humming. I do believe they're trying not to hear what the big guy is saying!

At the edge of the pool, the hoon lifted his arms and began chanting in a strange version of Galactic Six.

"Spirits of the sky, I summon thee by name . . . Kataranga!

"Spirits of the water, I beseech thy aid . . . Dupussien!

"By my knowledge of your secret names, I command thee to gather and surround this monster. Protect the people of the True Way!"

This went on for a while. At first Peepoe felt bemused, as if she were watching a documentary about some ancient human tribe, or the Prob'shers of planet Horse. Then she began noticing something strange. Out of the jungle, approaching on buzzing wings, there began appearing a variety of insectlike creatures. At first just a few, then more. Flying zigzag patterns toward the chanting shaman, they started gathering in a spiral-shaped swarm.

Meanwhile, ripples in the pool tickled Peepoe's flanks, revealing another convergence of ingathering beasts—this time swimmers—heading for the point of shore nearest the summoning hoon.

I don't believe this, she thought. It was one thing for a primitive priest to invoke the forces of nature. It was quite another to sense those forces *responding* quickly, unambiguously, and with ominous threatening behavior.

Members of both swarms, the fliers and the swimmers, began making darting forays toward Peepoe. She felt several sharp stings on her dorsal fin, and some more from below, on her ventral side.

They're attacking me!

Realization snapped her out of a bemused state.

Time to get out of here, she thought, as more of the tiny native creatures could be seen arriving from all directions.

Peepoe whirled about, sending toward shore a wavelet that interrupted the yammering shaman, sending him scurrying backward with a yelp. Then, in a surge of eager strength, she sped away from there.

TKETT

Just when he thought he had seen enough, one of the crystal fruits descended close to the pool where he and Chissis waited, stopping only when it brushed the water, almost even with their eyes. The walls vibrated for a moment . . . then spilt open!

The occupant, a tiny g'Kek with spindly wheels on both sides of a tapered torso, rolled toward the gap, regarding the pair of dolphins with four eyestalks that waved as they peered at Tkett. Then the creature spoke in a voice that sounded high-pitched but firm, using thickly accented Galactic Seven.

"We were aware that new settlers had come to this world. But imagine our surprise to find that this time they are swimmers, who found us before we found them! No summoning call had to be sent through the Great Egg. No special collector robots dispatched to pick up

volunteers from shore. How clever of you to arrive just in time, only days and weeks before the expected moment when this universe splits asunder!"

Chissis panted nervously, filling the sterile chamber with rapid clicks while Tkett bit the water hard with his narrow jaw.

"I . . . have no idea what y-y-you're talking about," he stammered in reply.

The miniature g'Kek twisted several eyestalks around each other. Tkett had an impression that it was consulting or communing with some entity elsewhere. Then it rolled forward, unwinding the stalks to wave at Tkett again.

"If an explanation is what you seek, then that is what you shall have."

PEEPOE

The interior of the great leviathan seemed to consist of one leaf-shrouded pool after another, in a complex maze of little waterways. Soon quite lost, Peepoe doubted she would ever be able to find her way back to the thing's mouth.

Most of the surrounding areas consisted of dense jungle, though there were also rocky escarpments and patches of what looked like rolling grassland. Peepoe had also passed quite a few villages of little folk. In one place an endless series of ramps and flowing bridges had been erected through the foliage, comprising what looked like a fantastic scale-model roller coaster, interspersed amid the dwarf trees. Little g'Keks could be seen zooming along this apparatus of wooden planks and vegetable fibers, swerving and teetering on flashing wheels.

Peepoe tried to glide past the shoreline villages innocuously, but seldom managed it without attracting some attention. Once, a war party set forth in chase after her, riding upon the backs of turtlelike creatures, shooting tiny arrows and hurling curses in quaint-sounding jargon she could barely understand. Another time, a garishly attired urrish warrior swooped toward her from above, straddling a flying lizard whose wings flapped gorgeously and whose mouth belched small but frightening bolts of flame! Peepoe retreated, overhearing the little urs continue to shout behind her, challenging the "sea monster" to single combat.

It seemed she had entered a world full of beings who were as suspicious as they were diminished in size. Several more times, shamans and priests of varied races stood at the shore, gesturing and shouting rhythmically, commanding hordes of beelike insects to sting and pursue her until she fled beyond sight. Peepoe's spirits steadily sank . . . until at last she arrived at a broad basin where many small boats could be seen, cruising under brightly painted sails.

To her surprise, this time the people aboard shouted with amazed pleasure upon spotting her, not fear or wrath! With tentative but rising hope, she followed their beckonings to shore where, under the battlements of a magnificently ornate little castle, a delegation descended to meet her beside a wooden pier.

Their apparent leader, a human wearing gray robes and a peaked hat, grinned as he gestured welcome, enunciating in an odd but lilting version of Anglic.

"Many have forgotten the tales told by the First. But we know you, oh noble dolphin! You are remembered from tales passed down since the beginning! How wonderful to have you come among us now, as the Time of Change approaches. In the name of the Spirit Guides, we offer you our hospitality and many words of power!"

Peepoe mused on everything she had seen and heard.

Words, eh? Words can be a good start.

She had to blow air several times before her nervous energy dispelled enough to speak.

"All right then. Can you start by telling me what in Ifni's name is going on here?"

GIVERS OF WONDER

A Time of Changes comes. Worlds are about to divide.

Galaxies that formerly were linked by shortcuts of space and time will soon be sundered. The old civilization—including all the planets you came from—will no longer be accessible. Their ways won't dominate this part of the cosmos any more.

Isolated, this island realm of one hundred billion stars (formerly known as Galaxy Four) will soon develop its own destiny, fostering a bright new age. It has been foreseen that Jijo will provide the starting seed for a glorious culture, unlike any other. The six . . . and now seven! . . . sapient species who came sneaking secretly to this world as refugees—skulking in order to hide like criminals on a forbidden shore—will prosper beyond all their wildest imagings. They will be cofounders of something great and wonderful. Forerunners of all the starfaring races who may follow in this fecund stellar whirlpool.

But what *kind* of society should it be? One that is a mere copy of the noisy, bickering, violent conglomeration that exists back in "civilized" space? One based on crude so-called sciences? Physics, cybernetics, and biology? We have learned that such obsessions lead to soullessness. A humorless culture, operated by reductionists who measure the cost/benefit ratios of everything and know the value of nothing!

There must be something better.

Indeed, consider how the *newest* sapient races—fresh from uplift—look upon their world with a childlike sense of wonder! What if that feeling could be made to last?

To those who have just discovered it, the *power of speech itself* is glorious. A skill with words seems to hold all the potency anyone should ever need! Still heedful of their former animal ways, these infant species often use their new faculty of self-expression to perceive patterns that are invisible to older "wiser" minds.

Humans were especially good at this, during the long ages of their lonely abandonment, on isolated Earth. They had many names for their systems of wondrous cause and effect, traditions that arose in a myriad land bound tribes. But nearly all of these systems shared certain traits in common:

—a sense that the world is made of spirits, living in each stone or brook or tree.

—an eager willingness to perceive all events, even great storms and the movements of planets, as having a *personal* relationship with the observer.

—a conviction that nature can be swayed by those favored with special powers of sight, voice, or mind, raising those elite ones above other mere mortals.

—a profound belief in the power of words to persuade and control the world.

"Magic" was one word that humans used for this way of looking at the universe. We believe it is a better way, offering drama, adventure, vividness, and romance. Yet, magic can take many forms. And there is still some dispute over the details. . . .

ALTERNATING VIEWS OF TEMPTATION

Tkett found the explanation bizarre and perplexing at first. How did it relate to this strange submersible machine whose gut was filled with crystal fruit, each containing an intelligent being who leaped about and seemed to focus fierce passion on things only he or she could see?

Still, as an archaeologist he had some background studying the tribal human past, so eventually a connection clicked in his mind.

"You . . . you are using technology to give each individual a private world! B-but there's more to it than that, isn't there? Are you saying that every hoon, or human, or traeki inside these crystal c-containers gets to cast *magic spells?* They don't just manipulate false objects by hand, and see tailored illusions . . . they also shout incantations and have the satisfaction of watching them come *true?*"

Tkett blinked several times, trying to grasp it all.

"Take that woman over there." He aimed his rostrum at a nearby cube wherein a female human grinned and pointed amid a veritable cloud of resistance threads.

"If she has an enemy, can she mold a clay figure and stick pins in it to cast a spell of pain?"

The little g'Kek spun its wheels before answering emphatically.

"True enough, oh perceptive dolphin! Of course she has to be creative. Talent and a strong will are helpful. And she must adhere to the accepted lore of her simulated tribe."

"Arbitrary rules, you mean."

The eye stalks shrugged gracefully. "Arbitrary, but elegant and consistent. And there is another requirement.

"Above all, our user of magic must intensely believe."

Peepoe blinked at the diminutive wizard standing on the nearby dock, in the shadow of a fairy-tale castle.

"You mean people in this place can command the birds and insects and other beasts using words alone?"

She had witnessed it happen dozen of times, but to hear it explained openly like this felt strange.

The gray-cloaked human nodded, speaking rapidly, eagerly. "Special words! The power of secret *names*. Terms that each user must keep closely guarded."

"But—"

"Above all, most creatures will only obey those with inborn talent. Individuals who possess great force of will. Otherwise, if they heeded everybody, where would be the awe and envy that lie at the very heart of sorcery? If *anyone* can do a thing, it soon loses all worth. A miracle palls when it becomes routine.

"It is said that technology used to be like that, back in the Old Civilization. Take what happened soon after Earth-humans discovered how to fly. Soon *everybody* could soar through the sky, and people took the marvel for granted. How tragic! That sort of thing does not happen here. We preserve wonder like a precious resource."

Peepoe sputtered.

"But all this—" She flicked her jaws, spraying water toward the jungle and the steep, fleshy cliffs beyond. "All of this smacks of technology! That absurd fire-breathing dragon, for instance. Clearly bioengineered! Somebody set up this whole thing as . . . as an . . ."

"As an experiment?" the gray-clad mage conceded with a nod. His beard shook as he continued with eager fire in his piping voice.

"That has never been secret! Every since our ancestors were selected, from among Jijo's landbound Six Races, to come dwell below the sea in smaller but mightier bodies, we knew that one purpose would be to help the Buyur fine-tune their master plan."

Tkett reared back in shock, churning water with his flukes. He stared at the many-eyed creature who had been explaining this weird chamber-of-miniatures.

"The B-Buyur! They left Jijo half a million years ago. How could they even know about human culture, let alone set up this elaborate—"

"Of course the answer to that question is simple," replied the little g'Kek, peering with several eyestalks from its cracked crystal shell. "Our Buyur lords never left! They have quietly observed and guided this process ever since the first ship of refugees slunk down to Jijo, preparing for the predicted day when natural forces would sever all links between Galaxy Four—half an eon ago—made sure that no other techno-sapients remained in this soon-to-be isolated starry realm. So it will belong to *our* descendants, living in a culture far different than the dreary one our ancestors belonged to."

Tkett had heard of the Buyur, of course—among the most powerful members of the Civilization of Five Galaxies, and one of the few elder races known for a sense of humor . . . albeit a strange one. It was said that they believed in *long* jokes, that took ages to plan and execute.

Was that because the Buyur found Galactic culture stodgy and stifling? (Most Earthlings would agree.) Apparently they foresaw all of the changes and convulsions that were today wracking the linked starlanes, and began preparing millennia ago for an unparalleled opportunity to put their own stamp on an entirely new branch of destiny.

Peepoe nodded, understanding part of it at last.

"This leviathan . . . this huge organic beast . . . isn't the only experimental container cruising below the waves. There are others! Many?"

"Many," confirmed the little gray-bearded human wizard. "The floating chambers take a variety of forms, each accommodating its own colony of sapient beings. Each habitat engages its passengers in a life that is rich with magic, though in uniquely different ways.

"Here, for instance, we sapient beings experience physically active lives, in a totally real environment. It is the wild creatures around us who were altered! Surely you have heard that the Buyur was master gene-crafters? In this experimental realm, each insect, fish, and flower knows its own unique and secret *name*. By learning and properly uttering such names, a mage like me can wield great power."

Tkett listened as the cheerful g'Kek explained the complex experiment taking place in the chamber of crystalline fruits.

"In *our* habitat, each of us gets to live in his or her own world—one that is rich, varied, and physically demanding, even if it is mostly a computer-driven simulation. Within such an ersatz reality every one of us can be the lead magician in a society or tribe of lesser peers. Or the crystal fruits can be linked, allowing shared encounters between equals. Either way, it is a vivid life, filled with more excitement than the old way of so-called engineering.

"A life in which the mere act of believing can have power, and wishing sometimes makes things come true!"

Peepoe watched the gray magician stroke his beard while describing the range of Buyur experiments.

"There are many other styles, modes, and implementations being tried out, in scores of other habitats. Some emphasize gritty 'reality,' while others go so far as to eliminate physical form entirely, encoding their subjects as digital personae in wholly computerized worlds."

Downloading personalities, Peepoe recognized the concept. *It was tried back home and never caught on, even though boosters said it ought to, logically.*

"There is an ultimate purpose to all of these experiments," the human standing on the nearby pier explained, like a proselyte eager for a special convert. "We aim to find exactly the right way to implement a new society that will thrive across the star-lanes of Galaxy Four, once separation is complete and all the old hyperspatial transit paths are gone. When this island whirlpool of a hundred billion stars is safe at last from interference by the Old Civilization, it will be time to start our own. One that is based on a glorious new principle.

"By analyzing the results of each experimental habitat, the noble Buyur will know exactly how to implement a new realm of magic and wonders. Then the age of the true miracles can begin."

Listening to this, Peepoe shook her head.

"You don't sound much like a rustic feudal magician. I just bet you're something else, in disguise.

"Are *you* a Buyur?"

The g'Kek bowed within its crystal shell. "That's a very good guess, my dolphin friend. Though of course the real truth is complicated. A real Buyur would weigh more than a metric ton and somewhat resemble an Earthling frog!"

"Nevertheless you—" Tkett prompted.

"I have the honor of serving as a spokesman-intermediary. . . ."

". . . to help persuade you dolphins—the newest promising colonists on Jijo—that joining us will be your greatest opportunity for vividness, adventure, and a destiny filled with marvels!"

The little human wizard grinned, and Peepoe realized that the others nearby must not have heard or understood a bit of it. Perhaps they wore earplugs to protect themselves against the power of the mage's words. Or else Anglic was rarely spoken, here. Perhaps it was a "language of power."

Peepoe also realized—she was both being tested and offered a choice.

Out there in the world, we few dolphin settlers face an uncertain existence. Makanee has no surety that our little pod of reverts will survive the next winter, even with help from the other colonists ashore. Anyway, the Six Races have troubles of their own, fighting Jophur invaders.

She had to admit that this offer had tempting aspects. After experiencing several recent Jijo storms, Peepoe could see the attraction of bringing all the other *Streaker* exiles aboard some cozy undersea habitat—presumably one with bigger stretches of open water—and letting the Buyur perform whatever technomagic it took a reduce dolphins in size so they would fit their new lives. How could that be any worse than the three years of cramped hell they had all endured aboard poor *Streaker*?

Presumably someday, when the experiments were over, her descendants would be given back their true size, after they had spent generations learning to weave spells and cast incantations with the best of them.

Oh, we could manage that, she thought. *We dolphins are good at certain artistic types of verbal expression. After all, what is Trinary but our own special method of using sound to persuade the world? Talking it into assuming vivid sonic echoes and dreamlike shapes? Coaxing it to make sense in our own cetacean way?*

The delicious temptation of it all reached out to Peepoe.

What is the alternative? Assuming we ever find a way back to civilization, what would we go home to? A gritty fate that at best offers lots of hard work, where it can take half a lifetime just to learn the skills you need to function usefully in a technological society.

Real life isn't half as nice as the tales we first hear in storybooks. Everybody learns at some point that it's a disappointing world out there—a universe where good is seldom purely handsome and evil doesn't obligingly identify itself with red glowing eyes. A complex society filled with trade-offs and compromises, as well as committees and political opponents who always have much more power than you think they deserve.

Who wouldn't prefer a place where the cosmos might be talked into giving you what you want? Or where wishing sometimes makes things true?

"We already have two volunteers from your esteemed race," the g'Kek spokesman explained, causing Tkett to quiver in surprise. With a flailing of eyestalks, the wheeled figure commanded that a hologram appear, just above the water's surface.

Tkett at once saw two large male dolphins lying calmly on mesh hammocks while tiny machines scurried all over them, spinning webs of some luminescent material. Chissis, long-silent and brooding, abruptly recognized the pair, and shouted Primal recognition.

> # Caught! Caught in nets as they deserved!
> # Foolish Zhaki—Nasty Mopol! #

"Ifni!" Tkett commented. "I think you're right. But what's being done to them?"

"They have already accepted our offer," said the little wheeled intermediary.

"Soon those two will dwell in realms of holographic and sensual delights, aboard a different experimental station than this one. Their destiny is assured, and let me promise you—they will be happy."

"You're sure those two aren't *here* aboard this vessel, near me?" Peepoe asked nervously, watching Zhaki and Mopol undergo their transformation via a small image that the magician had conjured with a magic phrase and a wave of one hand.

"No. Your associates followed a lure to one of our neighboring experimental cells—to their senses it appeared to be a 'leviathan' resembling one of your Earthling blue whales. Once they had come aboard, preliminary appraisal showed that their personalities will probably thrive best in a world of pure fantasy.

"They eagerly accepted this proposal."

Peepoe nodded, shocked only at her own lack of emotion—either positive or negative—toward this final disposal of her tormentors. They were gone from her life, and that was all she really cared about. Let Ifni decide whether their destination qualified as permanent imprisonment, or a strange kind of heaven.

Well, now they can have harems of willing cows, to their hearts' content, she thought. *Good riddance.*

Anyway, she had other quandaries to focus on, closer at hand.

"What've you got p-planned for me?"

The gray wizard spread his arms in eager consolation.

"Nothing frightening or worrisome, oh esteemed dolphin-friend! At this point we are simply asking that you choose!

"Will you join us? No one is coerced. But how could anybody refuse? If one lifestyle does not suit you, pick another! Select from a wide range of enchanted worlds, and further be assured that your posterity will someday be among the magic-welders who establish a new order across a million suns."

Tkett saw implications that went beyond the offer itself. The plan of the Buyur—its scope and the staggering range of their ambition—left him momentarily dumbfounded.

They want to set up a whole, galaxy-spanning civilization, based on what they consider to be an ideal way of life. Someday soon, after this "Time of Changes" has ruptured the old intergalaxy links, the Buyur will be free from any of the old constraints of law and custom that dominated oxygen-breathing civilization for the last billion years.

Then, out of this planet there will spill a new wave of starships, crewed by the Seven Races of Jijo, commanded by bold captains, wizards, and kings . . . a mixture of themes from old-time science fiction and fantasy . . . pouring forth toward adventure! Over the course of several ages, they will fight dangers, overcome grave perils, discover and uplift new species. Eventually, the humans and urs and traekis and others will become revered leaders of a galaxy that is forever filled with high drama.

In this realm, boredom will be the ultimate horror. Placidity the ultimate crime. The true masters—the Buyur—will see to that.

Like the Great Oz, manipulating levers behind a curtain, the Buyur will use their high technology to provide every wonder. As for dragons? They will gene-craft or manufacture them. Secret factories will build sea monsters and acid-mouthed aliens, ready for battle.

It will be a galaxy run by special-effects wizards! A perpetual theme park, whose inhabitants use magic spells instead of engineering to get what they want. Conjurers and monarchs will replace tedious legislatures, impulse will supplant deliberation, and lists of secret names will substitute for physics.

Nor will our descendants ask too many questions, or dare to pull back the curtain and expose Oz. Those who try won't have descendants!

Cushioned by hidden artifice, in time people will forget nature's laws.

They will flourish in vivid kingdoms, forever setting forth heroically, returning triumphally, or dying bravely . . . but never asking why.

Tkett mused on this while filling the surrounding water with intense sprays of sonar clicks. Chissis, who had clearly not understood much of the g'Kek's convoluted explanation, settled close by, rolling her body through the complex rhythms of Tkett's worried thoughts.

Finally, he felt that he grasped the true significance of it all.

Tkett swam close to the crystal cube, raising one eye until it was level with the small representative of the mighty Buyur.

"I think I get what's going on here," he said.

"Yes?" the little g'Kek answered cheerfully. "And what is your sage opinion, oh dolphin-friend. What do you think of this great plan?"

Tkett lifted his head high out of the water, rising up on churning flukes, emitting chittering laughter from his blowhole. At the same time, a sardonic Trinary haiku floated from his clicking brow.

> *Sometimes sick egos
>   *foster in their narrow brains
>   *Really stupid jokes!

Some aspects of the offer were galling, such as the smug permanence of Buyur superiority in the world to come. Yet, Peepoe felt tempted.

After all, what else awaits us here on Jijo? Enslavement by the Jophur? Or the refuge of blessed dimness that the sages promise, if we follow the so-called Path of Redemption? Doesn't this offer a miraculous way out of choosing between those two unpalatable destinies?

She concentrated hard to sequester her misgivings, focusing instead on the advantages of the Buyur plan. And there were plenty, such as living in a cosmos where hidden technology made up for nature's mistakes. After all, wasn't it cruel of the Creator to make a universe where so many fervent wishes were ignored? A universe where prayers were mostly answered—if at all—within the confines of the heart? Might the Buyur plan rectify this oversight for billions and trillions? For all the inhabitants of a galaxy-spanning civilization! Generosity on such a scale was hard to fathom.

She compared this ambitious goal with the culture waiting for the *Streaker* survivors, should they ever make it back home to the other four galaxies, where myriad competitive, fractious races bickered endlessly. Overreliant on an ancient Library of unloving technologies, they seldom sought innovation or novelty. Above all, the desires of individual beings were nearly always subordinated to the driving needs of nation, race, clan, and philosophy.

Again, the Buyur vision looked favorable compared to the status quo.

A small part of her demanded: *Are these our only choices? What if we could come up with alternatives that go beyond simpleminded—*

She quashed the question fiercely, packing it off to far recesses of her mind.

"I would love to learn more," she told the gray wizard. "But what about my comrades? The other dolphins who now live on Jijo? Won't you need them, too?"

"In order to have a genetically viable colony, yes." The spokesman agreed. "If you agree to join us, we will ask you first to go and persuade others to come."

"Just out of curiosity, what would happen if I refused?"

The sorcerer shrugged. "Your life will resume much as it would have, if you had never found us. We will erase all conscious memory of this visit, and you will be sent home. later, when we have had a chance to refine our message, emissaries will come visit your pod of dolphins. But as far as you know, you will hear the proposal as if for the first time."

"I see. And again, those who refuse will be memory-wiped . . . and again each time you return. Kind of gives you an advantage in proselytizing, doesn't it?"

"Perhaps. Still, no one is compelled to join against their will." The little human smiled. "So, what is your answer? Will you help convey our message to your peers? We sense that you understand and sympathize with the better world we aim toward. Will you help enrich the Great Stew of Races with wondrous dolphin flavors?"

Peepoe nodded. "I will carry your vision to the others."

"Excellent! In fact, you can start without even leaving this pool! For I can now inform you that a pair of your compatriots already reside aboard one of our nearby vessels . . . and those two seem to be having trouble appreciating the wondrous life we offer."

"Not Zhaki and Mopol!" Peepoe pushed back with her ventral fins, clicking nervously. She wanted nothing further to do with them.

"No, no." The magician assured. "Please, wait calmly while we open a channel between ships and all will become clear."

TKETT

"Hello, Peepoe," he said to the wavering image in front of him. "I'm glad you look well. We were all worried sick about you. But I figured when we saw Zhaki and Mopol you must be nearby."

The holo showed a sleek female dolphin, looking exquisite but tired in a jungle-shrouded pool, beside a miniature castle. Tkett could tell a lot about the style of "experiment" aboard her particular vessel, just by observing the crowd of natives gathered by the shore. Some of them were dressed as armored knights, riding upon rearing steeds, while gaily attired peasants doffed their caps to passing lords and ladies. It was a far different approach than the crystal fruits that hung throughout *this* vessel—semitransparent receptacles where individuals lived permanently immersed in virtual realities.

And yet, the basic principle was similar.

"*Hi, Tkett,*" Peepoe answered. "*Is that Chissis with you? You both doing all right?*"

"Well enough, I guess. Though I feel like the victim of some stupid fraternity practical—"

"*Isn't it exciting?*" Peepoe interrupted, cutting off what Tkett had been about to say. "*Across all the ages, visionaries have come up with countless utopian schemes. But this one could actually w-w-work!*"

Tkett stared back at her, unable to believe he was hearing this.

"Oh yeah?" he demanded. "What about free will?"

"*The Buyur will provide whatever your will desires.*"

"Then how about truth!"

"*There are many truths, Tkett. Countless vivid subjective interpretations will thrive in a future filled with staggering diversity.*"

"Subjective, exactly! That's an ancient and d-despicable perversion of the word *truth*, and you know it. Diversity is wonderful, all right. There may indeed be many cultures, many art forms, even many styles of wisdom. But *truth* should be about finding out what's really real, what's repeatable and verifiable, whether it suits your fancy or not!"

Peepoe sputtered a derisive raspberry.

"*Where's the fun in that?*"

"Life isn't just about having fun, or getting whatever you want!" Tkett felt his guts roil, forcing sour bile up his esophagus. "Peepoe, there's such a thing as growing up! Finding out how the world actually works, despite the way you think things *ought* to be. Objectivity means I accept that the universe doesn't revolve around me."

"*In other words, a life of limitations.*"

"That we overcome with knowledge! With new tools and skills."

"*Tools made of dead matter, designed by committees, mass-produced and sold on shop counters.*"

"Yes! Committees, teams, organizations, and enterprises, all of them made up of individuals who have to struggle every day with their egos in order to cooperate with others, making countless compromises along the way. It ain't how things happen in a child's fantasy. It's not what we yearn for in our secret hearts, Peepoe. I know that! But it's how adults get things done.

"Anyway, what's wrong with buying miracles off a shop counter? So we take for granted wonders that our ancestors would've given their tail fins for. Isn't that what they'd have wanted for us? You'd prefer a world where the best of everything is kept reserved for wizards and kings?"

Tkett felt a sharp jab in his side. The pain made him whirl, still bitterly angry, still flummoxed with indignation.

"What is it!" He demanded sharply of Chissis, even though the little female could not answer.

She backed away from his bulk and rancor, taking a snout-down submissive posture. But from her brow came a brief burst of caustic Primal.

> # idiot idiot idiot idiot
> > # idiots keep talking human talk-talk
> # while the sea tries to teach #

Tkett blinked. Her phrasings were sophisticated, almost lucid. In fact, it was a lot like a simple Trinary chiding-poem, that a dolphin mother might use with her infant.

Through an act of hard self-control, he forced himself to consider.

While the sea tries to teach . . .

It was a common dolphin turn of phrase, implying that one should listen *below* the surface, to meanings that lay hidden.

He whirled back to examine the hologram, wishing it had not been designed by beings who relied so much on sight, and ignored the subtleties of sound transmission.

"*Think about it, Tkett,*" Peepoe went on, as if their conversation had been interrupted. "*Back home, we dolphins are the youngest client race of an impoverished, despised clan, in danger of being conquered or rendered extinct at any moment. Yet now we're being offered a position at the top of a new pantheon, just below the Buyur themselves.*

"*What's more, we'd be good at this! Think about how dolphin senses might extend the range of possible magics. Our sound-based dreams and imagery. Our curiosity and reckless sense of adventure! And that just begins to hint at the possibilities when we finally come into our own. . . .*"

Tkett concentrated on sifting the background. The varied pulses, whines and clicks that melted into the ambiance whenever any neo-dolphin spoke. At first it seemed Peepoe was emitting just the usual mix of nervous sonar and blowhole flutters.

Then he picked out a single, floating phrase . . . in ancient Primal . . . that interleaved itself amid the earnest logic of sapient speech.

> # sleep on it sleep on it sleep on it sleep on it #

At first the hidden message confused him. It seemed to support the rest of her argument. So then why make it secret?

Then another meaning occurred to him.

Something that even the puissant Buyur might not have thought of.

PEEPOE

Her departure from the habitat was more gay and colorful than her arrival.

Dragons flew by over head, belching gusts of heat that were much friendlier than before. Crowds of boats, ranging from canoes to bejeweled galleys pulled by sweating oarsmen, accompanied Peepoe from one pool to the next. Ashore, local wizards performed magnificent spectacles in her honor, to the awed wonder of gazing onlookers, while Peepoe swam gently past amid formations of fish whose scales glittered unnaturally bright.

With six races mixing in a wild variety of cultural styles, each village seemed to celebrate its own uniqueness in a profusion of architectural styles. The general attitude seemed both proud and fiercely competitive. But today all feuds, quests, and noble campaigns had been put aside in order to see her off.

"See how eagerly we anticipate the success of your mission," the gray magician commented as they reached the final chamber. In a starship, this space would be set aside for an airlock, chilly and metallic. But here, the breath of a living organism sighed all around them as the great maw opened, letting both wind and sunshine come suddenly pouring through.

Nice of them to surface like this, sparing me the discomfort of a long climb out the abyss.

"Tell the other dolphins what joy awaits them!" the little mage shouted after Peepoe as she drifted past the open jaws, into the light.

"Tell them about the vividness and adventure! Soon days of experimentation will be over, and all of this will be full-sized, with a universe lying before us!"

She pumped her flukes in order to rear up, looking back at the small gray figure in a star-spangled gown, who smiled as his arms spread wide, causing swarms of obedient bright creatures to hover above his head, converging to form a living halo.

"I will tell them," she assured.

Then Peepoe whirled and plunged into the cool sea, setting off toward a morning rendezvous.

TKETT

He came fully conscious again, only to discover with mild surprise that he was already swimming fast, leaping and diving through the ocean's choppy swells, propelled by powerful, rhythmic fluke-strokes.

Under other circumstances it might have been disorienting to wake up in full motion. Except that a pair of dolphins flanked Tkett, one on each side, keeping perfect synchrony with his every arch and leap and thrust. That made it instinctively easy to literally swim in his sleep.

How long has this been going on?

He wasn't entirely sure. It felt like perhaps an hour or two. Perhaps longer.

Behind him, Tkett heard the low thrum of a sea sled's engine, cruising on low power as it followed the three of them on autopilot.

Why aren't we using the sled? he wondered. Three could fit, in a pinch. And that way they could get back to Makanee quicker, to report that . . .

Stale air exchanged quickly for fresh as he breached, performing each move with flawless precision, even as his mind roiled with unpleasant confusion.

. . . to report that Mopol and Zhaki are dead.

We found Peepoe, safe and well, wandering the open ocean.

As for the "machine" noises we were sent to investigate . . .

Tkett felt strangely certain there was a story behind all that. A story that Peepoe would explain later, when she felt the time was right.

Something wonderful, he recited, without quite knowing why. A flux of eagerness seemed to surge out of nowhere, priming Tkett to be receptive when she finally told everyone in the pod about the good news.

He could not tell why, but Tkett felt certain that more than just the sled was following behind them.

·   ·   ·

"Welcome back to the living," Peepoe greeted in crisp Underwater Anglic, after their next breaching.

"Thanks I . . . seem to be a bit muddled right now."

"Well, that's not too surprising. You've been half-asleep for a long time. In fact, one might say you *half slept* through something really important."

Something about her words flared like a glowing spark within him—a triggered release that jarred Tkett's smooth pace through the water. He reentered the water at a wrong angle, smacking his snout painfully. It took a brief struggle to get back in place between the two females, sharing the group's laminar rhythm.

I . . . slept. I slept on it.

Or rather, half of him had done so.

It slowly dawned on him why that was significant.

There aren't many water-dwellers in the Civilization of Five Galaxies, he mused, reaching for threads that had lain covered under blankets of repose. *I guess the Buyur never figured . . .*

A shiver of brief pain lanced from right to left inside his skull, as if a part of him that had been numb just came to life.

The Buyur!

Memories flowed back unevenly, at their own pace.

They never figured on a race of swimmers discovering their experiments, hidden for so long under Jijo's ocean waves. They had no time to study us. To prepare before the encounter. And they especially never took into account the way a cetacean's brain works.

An air-breathing creature who lives in the sea has special problems. Even after millions of years evolving for a wet realm, dolphins still faced a never-ending danger of drowning. Hence, sleep was no simple matter.

One way they solved the problem was to sleep one brain hemisphere at a time.

Like human beings, dolphins had complex internal lives, made up of many temporary or persistent subselves that must somehow reconcile under an overall persona. but this union was made even more problematic when human genetic meddlers helped turn fallow dolphins into a new information stored in one side was frustratingly hard to get at from the other.

And sometimes that proved advantageous.

The side that knew about the Buyur—the one that had slept while amnesia was imposed on the rest—had much less language ability than the other half of Tkett's brain. Because of this, only a few concepts could be expressed in words at first. Instead, Tkett had to replay visual and sonic images, reinterpreting and extrapolating them, holding a complex conversation of inquiry between two sides of his whole self.

It gave him a deeper appreciation for the problems—and potential—of people like Chissis.

I've been an unsympathetic bastard, he realized.

Some of this thought emerged in his sonar echoes as an unspoken apology. Chissis brushed against him the next time their bodies flew through the air, and her touch carried easy forgiveness.

"So," Peepoe commented when he had taken some more time to settle his thoughts, "is it agreed what we'll tell Makanee?"

Tkett summed up his determination.

"We'll tell everything . . . and then some!"

Chissis concurred.

\# *Tell them tell them*
   \# *Orca-tricksters*
\# *Promise fancy treats*
   \# *But take away freedom!* \#

Tkett chortled. There was a lot of Trinary elegance in the little female's Primal burst—a transition from animal-like emotive squawks toward the kind of expressiveness she used to be so good at, back when she was an eager researcher and poet, before three years of hell aboard *Streaker* hammered her down. Now a corner seemed to be turned. Perhaps it was only a matter of time till this crewmate returned to full sapiency . . . and all the troubles that would accompany that joy.

"Well," Peepoe demurred, "by one way of looking at things, the Buyur seem to be offering us more freedom. Our descendants would experience a wider range of personal choices. More power to achieve their wishes. More dreams would come true."

"As fantasies and escapism," Tkett dismissed. "The Buyur would turn everybody into egotists . . . solipsists! In the real world, you have to grow up eventually, and learn to negotiate with others. Be part of a culture. Form teams and partnerships. Ifni, what does it take to have a good *marriage*? Lots of hard work and compromises, leading to something better and more complicated than either person could've imagined!"

Peepoe let out a short whistle of surprise.

"Why, Tkett! In your own prudish, tight-vented way, I do believe you're a romantic."

Chissis shared Peepoe's gentle, teasing laughter, so that it penetrated him in stereo, from both sides. A human might have blushed. But dolphins can barely conceal their emotions from each other, and seldom try.

"Seriously," he went on. "I'll fight the Buyur because they would keep us in a playpen for eons to come, denying us the right to mature and learn for ourselves how the universe ticks. Magic may be more romantic than science. But science is *honest* . . . and it works.

"What about you, Peepoe? What's your reason?"

The was a long pause. Then she answered with astonishing vehemence.

"I can't stand all that *kings and wizards* dreck! Should somebody rule because his father was a pompous royal? Should all the birds and beasts and fish obey you just because you know some secret words that you won't share with others? Or on account of the fact that you've got a loud voice and your egotistic *will* is bigger than others'?

"I seem to recall we fought free of such idiotic notions ages ago, on Earth . . . or at least humans did. They never would've helped us dolphins get to the stars if they hadn't broken out of those sick thought patterns first.

"You want to know why I'll fight them, Tkett? Because Mopol and Zhaki will be right at home down there—one of them dreaming he's Superman, and the other one getting to be King of the Sea."

The three dolphins swam on, keeping pace in silence while Tkett pondered what their decision meant. In all likelihood, resistance was going to be futile. After all, the Buyur were overwhelmingly powerful and had been preparing for half a million years. Also, the incentive they were offering would make all prior temptations pale in comparison. Among the Six Races ashore—and the small colony of dolphins—many would leap to accept, and help make the new world of *magical wonder* compulsory.

We've never had an enemy like this before, he realized. *One that takes advantage of our greatest weakness, by offering to make all our dreams come true.*

    ·   ·   ·

Of course there was one possibility they hadn't discussed. That they were only seeing the surface layers of a much more complicated scheme . . . perhaps some long and desperately unfunny practical joke.

It doesn't matter, Tkett thought. We have to fight this anyway, or we'll never grow strong and wise enough to "get" the joke. And we'll certainly never be able to pay the Buyur back, in kind. Not if they control all the hidden levers in Oz.

For a while their journey fell into a grim mood of hopelessness. No one spoke, but sonar clicks from all three of them combined and diffused ahead. Returning echoes seemed to convey the sea's verdict on their predicament.

No chance. But good luck anyway.

Finally, little Chissis broke their brooding silence, after arduously spending the last hour composing her own Trinary philosophy glyph.

In one way, it was an announcement—that she felt ready to return to the struggles of sapiency.

At the same time, the glyph also expressed her manifesto. For it turned out that she had a different reason for choosing to fight the Buyur. One that Tkett and Peepoe had not expressed, though it resonated deep within.

> * *Both the hazy mists of dreaming,*
> >   * *And the stark-clear shine of daylight,*
> * *Offer treasures to the seeker,*
> >   * *And a trove of valued insights.*

> * *One gives open, honest knowledge.*
> >   * *And the skill to achieve wonders.*
> * *But the other (just as needed!)*
> >   * *Fills the soul and sets hearts a' stir.*

> * *What need then for ersatz magic?*
> >   * *Or for contrived Disney marvels?*
> * *God and Ifni made a cosmos.*
> >   * *Filled with wonders . . . let's go live it!*

Peepoe sighed appreciatively.

"I couldn't have said it better. Screw the big old frogs! We'll make magic of our own."

They were tired and the sun was dropping well behind them by the time they caught sight of shore, and heard other dolphins chattering in the distance. Still, all three of them picked up the pace, pushing ahead through Jijo's silky waters.

Despite all the evidence of logic and their senses, the day still felt like morning.

DAVID DRAKE

David Drake [1945–] (www.david-drake.com) lives near Chapel Hill, North Carolina. He was born in Iowa and graduated from the University of Iowa with a BA in history (with honors) and Latin; he was drafted out of law school and served in the army from 1969 to 1971, spending most of 1970 as an interrogator with the Eleventh Armored Cavalry Regiment, the Blackhorse, in Vietnam and Cambodia. He sold his first story to August Derleth of Arkham House in 1966 while an undergraduate, and continued to sell stories in law school at Duke, in the army, and while working as an attorney. In 1979 his first book, the military SF collection *Hammer's Slammers*, and his first novel, *The Dragon Lord* (a swords-and-sorcery piece), were published. He's written or cowritten forty-nine books; edited or coedited about thirty; done plot outlines for another twenty-odd, the books themselves being written by another author. His most recent books include *Master of the Cauldron* (2004) and *The Way to Glory* (2005).

He says on his Web site, "I'm probably best known for my military SF, but that's never been more than about a quarter of my output. While all my work has been in the fantasy/SF genre, within these bounds I've written about everything except for romance—humor, thriller, epic fantasy, S&S, military SF, space opera, historical (both fantasy and SF)." And later, "Frequently I write about soldiers or veterans: military SF. Because of that I'm accused of writing militaristic SF by those who either don't know the difference between description and advocacy or who deny there is a difference." He also includes on his Web site an essay on his feeling about his military experiences and military SF (originally published as an afterword to *The Tank Lords*), and comments on what he sees as his literary influences: "One strand is pulp fiction— literally, stories from the '30s and '40s collected into anthologies in the '50s, when I started reading SF and fantasy. Robert E. Howard, in particular, then when I got to college the Tolkien trilogy in the SUI Library before the books came out in paperback. The other strand is Latin authors and the classics more generally (though the Greek mostly in translation). I've got a separate section on this site on the classics, but the short version is that Tacitus and Caesar in their different ways are models for prose in any language, and the ability of some of the poets (Ovid and Juvenal spring first to mind) to handle tricky problems like continuous action and capsule description can teach any writer. They certainly taught me."

Drake is generally regarded, by those few critics who pay attention to the category, as the leading writer of military SF today, and for the past two decades. Often his SF novels are military space opera, and his career has been tied closely to the commercial success of Baen Books. When the cyberpunk revolution of the 1980s was launched, Drake was named in Bruce Sterling's agitprop fanzine, *Cheap Truth* (along with Vernor Vinge, Dean Ing, Janet Morris, and several others), as one of the examples of what was politically wrong with SF.

Since its unlikely birth, SF has been a trash medium, its appeal restricted to a subcultural faithful. But that appeal is widening and is being culturally legitimized. With the advent of the Strategic Defense Initiative, the elements, themes, and modes of thought native to science fiction have become central to worldwide political debate.

One SF splinter group has shown a laudable quickness in grasping SF's new political potential. Unlike traditional SF "movements," this group of writers is not marked by literary innovation but by its radical ideology. For purposes of discussion we will refer to them as the "Pournelle Disciples."

This group has a number of strengths. The first is their solid publishing base . . . Baen Books. A second is their claim to tradition, especially the gung-ho technolatry that has marked genre SF since the days of Gernsback. Another crucial advantage is their ideological solidarity, which gives them the sort of shock-troop discipline that Lenin installed in the Bolsheviks. In this case, their Lenin is the redoubtable ex-Marxist Jerry Pournelle, who wears multiple hats as writer, editor, theorist, and political organizer. (Bruce Sterling in *Cheap Truth # 13*)

In the course of his scathing attack on this group, Sterling calls David Drake "a Disciple stalwart who specializes in military tales of a purported 'gut-wrenching hyperrealism.'" Sterling's attitude mapped closely to the political attitudes in the UK and European SF communities of the 1980s, and basically all American military SF writers were marginalized, and conflated with militarists in the popular critical discourse outside the US (and in some circles in the US as well), used as a symbol of what was wrong (militarism) with American SF both in the US and abroad. Note Iain M. Banks's comment (see the story note for Banks, later in this book) on saving space opera for the left. Drake meanwhile continued his commercially successful career throughout, with frequent forays into space opera in the most traditional sense, of large-scale battles among the stars. His work is not widely known outside the US.

One of Drake's most individual contributions to space opera was the novel *Ranks of Bronze* (1986). Based on a 1976 short story of the same name, it imagines military campaigns among the stars in the distant future for Crassus's lost Roman legions.

A Roman legion is snatched from Earth into space to be used as mercenaries owned and operated by superior aliens out for profit, to fight relatively low-cost, low-technology wars on alien planets against alien races with whom they have no personal quarrel, and perhaps only dimly comprehend. No one in the legion has any choice in this. The soldiers behave in a convincingly plausible way, the way Roman soldiers would. They are a very effective fighting force and can most often win. They are moved without notice from one planet to another, fight (sometimes die). They are wretched.

This is military SF with the contemporary politics stripped off, and removed from the level of policy decisions. The soldiers go to a place. They are told whom to fight. They win or die. They go to the next place. This is, it seems to me, the true experience of the ordinary fighting man or woman in a military organization throughout history, who has very limited choice. Various individuals manifest good or bad behavior, sanity or craziness, cleverness or stupidity. And luck matters. No one has the big picture, which may be known when the fighting is over and may not. The ones who do the job best tend to survive and perhaps rise in the ranks. Some of them are bad and/or crazy, but they are not stupid, which leads to death. There is very little moral choice possible, but the characters we tend to admire are those who are sane, careful, and make moral choices as they can. And try to live with them afterward. There is no access to those who make policy in Drake's military fiction. All in all it is a fairly dark vision of human life.

By using SF as a distancing device, and by further using classical mercenaries as soldier characters, Drake constructs a fictional space in which he can investigate and portray certain kinds of human behavior, heroism, loyalty, cowardice, the strategic working out of detailed military actions and the impact on them of individuals behaving well or not, of high and low technology for killing functioning properly or not. And he can do this with something analogous to clinical detachment as the killing commences, without advocating policy. No one who reads Drake properly can imagine him advocating war.

RANKS OF BRONZE

DAVID DRAKE

The rising sun is a dagger point casting long shadows toward Vibulenus and his cohort from the native breastworks. The legion had formed ranks an hour before; the enemy is not yet stirring. A playful breeze with a bitter edge skitters out of the south, and the tribune swings his shield to his right side against it.

"When do we advance, sir?" his first centurion asks. Gnaeus Clodius Calvus, promoted to his present position after a boulder had pulped his predecessor during the assault on a granite fortress far away. Vibulenus only vaguely recalls his first days with the cohort, a boy of eighteen in titular command of four hundred and eighty men whose names he had despaired of learning. Well, he knows them now. Of course, there are only two hundred and ninety-odd left to remember.

Calvus's bearded, silent patience snaps Vibulenus back to the present. "When the cavalry comes up, they told me. Some kinglet or other is supposed to bring up a couple of thousand men to close our flanks. Otherwise, we're hanging. . . ."

The tribune's voice trails off. He stares across the flat expanse of gravel toward the other camp, remembering another battle plain of long ago.

"Damn Parthians," Calvus mutters, his thought the same.

Vibulenus nods. "Damn Crassus, you mean. He put us *there*, and that put us *here*. The stupid bastard. But he got his, too."

The legionaries squat in their ranks, talking and chewing bits of bread or dried fruit. They display no bravado, very little concern. They have been here too often before. Sunlight turns their shield-facings green: not the crumbly fungus of verdigris but the shimmering sea-color of the harbor of Brundisium on a foggy morning.

Oh, Mother Vesta, Vibulenus breathes to himself. He is five foot two, about average for the legion. His hair is black where it curls under the rim of his helmet and he has no trace of a beard. Only his eyes make him appear more than a teenager; they would suit a tired man of fifty.

A trumpet from the command group in the rear sings three quick bars. "Fall in!" the tribune orders, but his centurions are already barking their own commands. These too are lost in the clash of hobnails on gravel. The Tenth Cohort could form ranks in its sleep.

Halfway down the front, a legionary's cloak hooks on a notch in his shield rim. He tugs at it, curses in Oscan as Calvus snarls down the line at him. Vibulenus makes a mental note to check with the centurion after the battle. That fellow should have been issued a replacement shield before disembarking. He glances at his own. How many shields has he carried? Not that it matters. Armor is replaceable. He is wearing his fourth cuirass, now, though none of them have fit like the one his father had bought him the day Crassus granted him a tribune's slot. Vesta . . .

A galloper from the command group skids his beast to a halt with a needlessly brutal jerk on its reins. Vibulenus recognizes him—Pompilius Falco. A little swine when he joined the legion, an accomplished swine now. Not bad with animals, though. "We'll be advancing without the cavalry," he shouts, leaning over in his saddle. "Get your line dressed."

"Osiris's bloody dick we will!" the tribune snaps. "Where's our support?"

"Have to support yourself, I guess," shrugs Falco. He wheels his mount. Vibulenus steps forward and catches the reins.

"Falco," he says with no attempt to lower his voice, "you tell our deified Commander to get somebody on our left flank if he expects the Tenth to advance. There's too many natives—they'll hit us from three sides at once."

"You afraid to die?" the galloper sneers. He tugs at the reins.

Vibulenus holds them. A gust of wind whips at his cloak. "Afraid to get my skull split?" he asks. "I don't know. Are you, Falco?" Falco glances at where the tribune's right hand rests. He says nothing. "Tell him we'll fight for him," Vibulenus goes on. "We won't let him throw us away. We've gone that route once." He looses the reins and watches the galloper scatter gravel on his way back.

The replacement gear is solid enough, shields that do not split when dropped and helmets forged without thin spots. But there is no craftsmanship in them. They are heavy, lifeless. Vibulenus still carries a bone-hilted sword from Toledo that required frequent sharpening but was tempered and balanced—poised to slash a life out, as it has a hundred times already. His hand continues to caress the palm-smoothed bone, and it calms him somewhat.

"Thanks, sir."

The thin-featured tribune glances back at his men. Several of the nearer ranks give him a spontaneous salute. Calvus is the one who spoke. He is blank-faced now, a statue of mahogany and strap-bronze. His stocky form radiates pride in his leader. Leader—no one in the group around the standards can lead a line soldier, though they may give commands that will be obeyed. Vibulenus grins and slaps Calvus's burly shoulder. "Maybe this is the last one and we'll be going home," he says.

Movement throws a haze over the enemy camp. At this distance it is impossible to distinguish forms, but metal flashes in the virid sunlight. The shadow of bodies spreads slowly to right and left of the breastworks as the natives order themselves. There are thousands of them, many thousands.

"Hey-*yip!*" Twenty riders of the general's bodyguard pass behind the cohort at an earthshaking trot. They rein up on the left flank, shrouding the exposed depth of the infantry. Pennons hang from the lances socketed behind their right thighs, gay yellows and greens to keep the lance heads from being driven too deep to be jerked out. The riders' faces are sullen under their mesh face guards. Vibulenus knows how angry they must be at being shifted under pressure—under his pressure—and he grins again. The bodyguards are insulted at being required to fight instead of remaining nobly aloof from the battle. The experience may do them some good.

At least it may get a few of the snotty bastards killed.

"Not exactly a regiment of cavalry," Calvus grumbles.

"He gave us half of what was available," Vibulenus replies with a shrug. "They'll do to keep the natives off our back. Likely nobody'll come near, they look so mean."

The centurion taps his thigh with his knobby swagger stick. "Mean? We'll give 'em mean."

All the horns in the command group sound together, a cacophonous bray. The jokes and scufflings freeze, and only the south wind whispers. Vibulenus takes a last look down his ranks—each of them fifty men abreast and no more sway to it than a tight-stretched cord would leave. Five feet from shield boss to shield boss, room to swing a sword. Five feet from nose guard to the nose guards of the next rank, men ready to step forward individually to replace the fallen or by ranks to lock shields with the front line in an impenetrable wall of bronze. The legion is a restive dragon, and its teeth glitter in its spears; one vertical behind each legionary's shield, one slanted from each right hand to stab or throw.

The horns blare again, the eagle standard slants forward, and Vibulenus's throat joins three thousand others in a death-rich bellow as the legion steps off on its left foot. The centurions are counting cadence and the ranks blast it back to them in the crash-jingle of boots and gear.

Striding quickly between the legionaries, Vibulenus checks the dress of his cohort. He should have a horse, but there are no horses in the legion now. The command group rides rough equivalents which are . . . very rough. Vibulenus is not sure he could accept one if his parsimonious employers offered it.

His men are a smooth bronze chain that advances in lock step. Very nice. The nine cohorts to the right are in equally good order, but Hercules! there are so few of them compared to the horde swarming from the native camp. Somebody has gotten overconfident. The enemy raises its own cheer, scattered and thin at first. But it goes on and on, building, ordering itself to a blood-pulse rhythm that moans across the intervening distance, the gap the legion is closing at two steps a second. Hercules! there is a crush of them.

The natives are close enough to be individuals now: lanky, long-armed in relation to a height that averages greater than that of the legionaries. Ill-equipped, though. Their heads are covered either by leather helmets or beehives of their own hair. Their shields appear to be hide and wicker affairs. What could live on this gravel waste and provide that much leather? But of course Vibulenus has been told none of the background, not even the immediate geography. There is some place around that raises swarms of warriors, that much is certain.

And they have iron. The black glitter of their spearheads tightens the tribune's wounded chest as he remembers.

"Smile, boys," one of the centurions calls cheerfully, "here's company." With his words a javelin hums down at a steep angle to spark on the ground. From a spear-thrower, must have been. The distance is too long for any arm Vibulenus has seen, and he has seen his share.

"Ware!" he calls as another score of missiles arc from the native ranks. Legionaries judge them, raise their shields or ignore the plunging weapons as they choose. One strikes in front of Vibulenus and shatters into a dozen iron splinters and a knobby shaft that looks like rattan. One or two of the men have spears clinging to their shield faces. Their clatter syncopates the thud of boot heels. No one is down.

Vibulenus runs two paces ahead of his cohort, his sword raised at an angle. It makes him an obvious target: a dozen javelins spit toward him. The skin over his ribs crawls, the lumpy breadth of scar tissue scratching like a rope over the bones. But he can be seen by every man in his cohort, and somebody has to give the signal. . . .

"Now!" he shouts vainly in the mingling cries. His arm and sword cut down abruptly. Three hundred throats give a collective grunt as the cohort heaves its own massive spears with the full weight of its rush behind them. Another light javelin glances from the shoulder of Vibulenus's cuirass, staggering him. Calvus's broad right palm catches the tribune, holds him upright for the instant he needs to get his balance.

The front of the native line explodes as the Roman spears crash into it.

Fifty feet ahead there are orange warriors shrieking as they stumble over the bodies of comrades whose armor has shredded under the impact of the heavy spears. "At 'em!" a front-rank file-closer cries, ignoring his remaining spear as he drags out his short sword. The trumpets are calling something but it no longer matters what: tactics go hang, the Tenth is cutting its way into another native army.

In a brief spate of fury, Vibulenus holds his forward position between a pair of legionaries. A native, orange-skinned with bright carmine eyes, tries to drag himself out of the tribune's path. A Roman spear has gouged through his shield and arm, locking all three together. Vibulenus's sword takes the warrior alongside the jaw. The blood is paler than a man's.

The backward shock of meeting has bunched the natives. The press of undisciplined reserves from behind adds to their confusion. Vibulenus jumps a still-writhing body and throws himself into the wall of shields and terrified orange faces. An iron-headed spear thrusts at him, misses as another warrior jostles the wielder. Vibulenus slashes downward at his assailant. The warrior throws his shield up to catch the sword, then collapses when a second-rank legionary darts his spear through the orange abdomen.

Breathing hard with his sword still dripping in his hand, Vibulenus lets the pressing ranks flow around him. Slaughter is not a tribune's work, but increasingly Vibulenus finds that he needs the swift violence of the battle line to release the fury building within him. The cohort is advancing with the jerky sureness of an ox-drawn plow in dry soil.

A windrow of native bodies lies among the line of first contact, now well within the Roman formation. Vibulenus wipes his blade on a fallen warrior, leaving two sluggish runnels filling on the flesh. He sheathes the sword. Three bodies are sprawled together to form a hillock. Without hesitation the tribune steps onto it to survey the battle.

The legion is a broad awl punching through a belt of orange leather. The cavalry on the left stand free in a scatter of bodies, neither threatened by the natives nor making any active attempt to drive them back. One of the mounts, a hairless brute combining the shape of a wolfhound with the bulk of an ox, is feeding on a corpse his rider has lanced. Vibulenus was correct in expecting the natives to give them a wide berth; thousands of flanking warriors tremble in indecision rather than sweep forward to surround the legion. It would take more discipline than this orange rabble has shown to attack the toad-like riders on their terrible beasts.

Behind the lines, a hundred paces distant from the legionaries whose armor stands in hammering contrast to the naked autochthones, is the Commander and his remaining score of guards. He alone of the three thousand who have landed from the starship knows why the battle is being fought, but he seems to stand above it. And if the silly bastard still has half his bodyguard with him—Mars and all the gods, what must be happening on the right flank?

The inhuman shout of triumph that rises half a mile away gives Vibulenus an immediate answer.

"Prepare to disengage!" he orders the nearest centurion. The swarthy noncom, son of a North African colonist, speaks briefly into the ears of two legionaries before sending them to the ranks forward and back of his. The legion is tight for men, always has been. Tribunes have no runners, but the cohort makes do.

Trumpets blat in terror. The native warriors boil whooping around the Roman right flank. Legionaries in the rear are facing about with ragged suddenness, obeying instinct rather than the orders bawled by their startled officers. The command group suddenly realizes the situation. Three of the bodyguard charge toward the oncoming orange mob. The rest of the guards and staff scatter into the infantry.

The iron-bronze clatter has ceased on the left flank. When the cohort halts its advance, the natives gain enough room to break and flee for their encampment. Even the warriors who have not engaged are cowed by the panic of those who have; by the panic, and the sprawls of bodies left behind them.

"About face!" Vibulenus calls through the indecisive hush, "and pivot on your left flank. There's some more barbs want to fight the Tenth!"

The murderous cheer from his legionaries overlies the noise of the cohort executing his order.

As it swings, Vibulenus runs across the new front of his troops, what had been the rear rank. The cavalry, squat-bodied and grim in their full armor, shows sense enough to guide their mounts toward the flank of the Ninth Cohort as Vibulenus rotates his men away from it. Only a random javelin from the native lines appears to hinder them. Their comrades who remained with the Commander have been less fortunate.

A storm of javelins has disintegrated the half-hearted charge. Two of the mounts have gone down despite their heavy armor. Behind them, the Commander lies flat on the hard soil while his beast screams horribly above him. The shaft of a stray missile projects from its withers. Stabbing up from below, the orange warriors fell the remaining lancer and gut his companions as they try to rise. Half a dozen of the bodyguards canter nervously back from their safe bolthole among the infantry to try to rescue their employer. The wounded mount leaps at one of the lancers. The two beasts tangle with the guard between them. A clawed hind leg flicks his head. Helmet and head rip skyward in a spout of green ichor.

"Charge!" Vibulenus roars. The legionaries who can not hear him follow his running form. The knot of cavalry and natives is a quarter mile away. The cohorts of the right flank are too heavily engaged to do more than defend themselves against the new thrust. Half the legion has become a bronze worm, bristling front and back with spear-points against the surging orange flood. Without immediate support, the whole right flank will be squeezed until it collapses into a tangle of blood and scrap metal. The Tenth Cohort is their support, all the support there is.

"Rome!" the fresh veterans leading the charge shout as their shields rise against the new flight of javelins. There are gaps in the back ranks, those just disengaged. Behind the charge, men hold palms clamped over torn calves or lie crumpled around a shaft of alien wood. There will be time enough for them if the recovery teams land— which they will not do in event of a total disaster on the ground.

The warriors snap and howl at the sudden threat. Their own success has fragmented them. What had been a flail slashing into massed bronze kernels is now a thousand leaderless handfuls in sparkling contact with the Roman line. Only the leaders bunched around the command group have held their unity.

One mount is still on its feet and snarling. Four massively-equipped guards try to ring the Commander with their maces. The Commander, his suit a splash of blue against the gravel, tries to rise. There is a flurry of mace strokes and quickly-riposting spears, ending in a clash of falling armor and an agile orange body with a knife leaping the crumpled guard. Vibulenus's sword, flung over-arm, takes the native in the throat. The inertia of its spin cracks the hilt against the warrior's forehead.

The Tenth Cohort is on the startled natives. A moment before the warriors were bounding forward in the flush of victory. Now they face the cohort's meat-axe suddenness—and turn. At sword-point and shield edge, as inexorable as the rising sun, the Tenth grinds the native retreat into panic while the cohorts of the right flank open order and advance. The ground behind them is slimy with blood.

Vibulenus rests on one knee, panting. He has retrieved his sword. Its stickiness bonds it to his hand. Already the air keens with landing motors. In minutes the recovery teams will be at work on the fallen legionaries, building life back into all but the brain-hacked or spine-severed. Vibulenus rubs his own scarred ribs in aching memory.

A hand falls on the tribune's shoulder. It is gloved in a skin-tight blue material; not armor, at least not armor against weapons. The Commander's voice comes from the small plate beneath his clear, round helmet. Speaking in Latin, his accents precisely flawed, he says, "You are splendid, you warriors."

Vibulenus sneers though he does not correct the alien. Warriors are capering heroes, good only for dying when they meet trained troops, when they meet the Tenth Cohort.

"I thought the Federation Council had gone mad," the flat voice continues, "when it ruled that we must not land weapons beyond the native level in exploiting inhabited worlds. All very well to talk of the dangers of introducing barbarians to modern weaponry, but how else could my business crush local armies and not be bled white by transportation costs?"

The Commander shakes his head in wonder at the carnage about him. Vibulenus silently wipes his blade. In front of him, Falco gapes toward the green sun. A javelin points from his right eyesocket. "When we purchased you from your Parthian captors it was only an experiment. Some of us even doubted it was worth the cost of the longevity treatments. In a way you are more effective than a Guard Regiment with lasers; out-numbered, you beat them with their own weapons. They can't even claim 'magic' as a salve to their pride. And at a score of other job sites you have done as well. And so cheaply!"

"Since we have been satisfactory," the tribune says, trying to keep the hope out of his face, "will we be returned home now?"

"Oh, goodness, no," the alien laughs, "you're far too valuable for that. But I have a surprise for you, one just as pleasant I'm sure—females."

"You found us real women?" Vibulenus whispers.

"You really won't be able to tell the difference," the Commander says with paternal confidence.

A million suns away on a farm in the Sabine hills, a poet takes the stylus from the fingers of a nude slave girl and writes, very quickly, *And Crassus's wretched soldier takes a barbarian wife from his captors and grows old waging war for them.*

The poet looks at the line with a pleased expression. "It needs polish, of course," he mutters. Then, more directly to the slave, he says, "You know, Leuconoe, there's more than inspiration to poetry, a thousand times more; but this came to me out of the air."

Horace gestures with his stylus toward the glittering night sky. The girl smiles back at him.

LOIS MCMASTER BUJOLD

Lois McMaster Bujold [1949–] (www.dendarri.com) is among the most popular and respected SF writers today. She is the only writer in SF to have won the Hugo Award for best novel four times, as many as Robert A. Heinlein, the previous record holder: for *The Vor Game* (1990), *Barrayar* (1991), *Mirror Dance* (1994), *Paladin of Souls* (2003). She burst into prominence in 1986 when her first three novels came out all in one year. She has written a few shorter pieces, but most of her work is novels of science fiction (and in recent years fantasy) that have won her many awards and since the late 1990s have often appeared on bestseller lists.

If there is such a thing as the new old space opera, it is what Bujold began to write in the eighties and early nineties, the years in which all critical attention was focused on cyberpunk. C. J. Cherryh had already written this way for a decade, during which Orson Scott Card, Mike Resnick, David Brin, and others began. It looks back to the traditions of SF in prior decades, carrying them forward, reinterpreting them for the times, but not blowing them into the air and leaving them in pieces on the ground, as M. John Harrison had attempted earlier in *The Centauri Device,* or reducing them to absurdity, as Harry Harrison had in *Star Smashers of the Galaxy Rangers.*

Gwyneth Jones, in an essay in *Locus,* said, "SF evolution is not straightforward. What cyberpunk bequeathed to the twenty-first century was not science, nor politics, but a plot. In the largely masculine phenomenon of New Space Opera, futuristic noir replaces the baroque political intrigue of former doyennes like Carolyn Cherryh and Lois McMaster Bujold." And it is obvious in retrospect that Cherryh and Bujold were in fact the queens of space opera, at least in the US.

Her trademark series of novels and stories is built around a central character, Miles Vorkosigan, an unusual SF figure, a crippled and somewhat Byronic antihero aristocrat, sometime space pirate and sometime soldier. Critic Sylvia Kelso, in an essay on Bujold, says:

> Early books are epitomized by *The Warrior's Apprentice:* unabashed space opera, clearly military space opera . . . shards of untoward reality, so to speak, puncture the light-hearted adventure envelope, just as Miles's character repeatedly contradicts what we expect of the classic young male sf protagonist.
>
> In these books Miles appears what Joan Baez once called Bob Dylan: a "genius brat," a manic loose cannon who triumphs where superiors and enemies fail, an outlaw, a white Coyote prevailing not by gun or fist but wits. Considering his position as a democratic aristocrat, his rebellions against his rank and future status, and his stance on the outside of authority, he also looks a perfect anti-hero.
>
> In this subversion of the sf heroic model, the comedy is critical, and although some is drawn by the cultures and other characters, much centers on Miles.

Her space opera is usually military and often romantic. Bujold said in a speech on wars of the future reprinted on her Web site, "The psychology of war and war-making, armies and the military, does fascinate me. I've looked at film clips of ranks of guys marching in goose step, and thought, 'Y'know . . . I don't think they could ever get a bunch of women to do something so incredibly goofy-looking and take it seriously.' The military and its psychological techniques for group cohesion is an intensely, inherently weird way for people to organize themselves. It's also remarkably powerful." And also:

As speculative fiction writers, to create convincing wars on our pages, ones that will ring true to people of real experience, we're compelled to look at what changes in both geography and technology might wring. My own Miles Vorkosigan adventure series begins with a not very original bit of science fictional astro-geography—the vision or scenario of defined and limited wormhole jumps between star systems. In strategic and tactical terms, a wormhole is the equivalent of straits, mountain passes, and especially bridges and tunnels, writ large and in odd dimensions. So I can raid real history for tales of battles turning around these sorts of choke points, and extrapolate (and, not incidentally, simplify—this is a novel, you know).

In such moments one is reminded of what made Robert A. Heinlein famous and popular in SF in his day and beyond. Bujold is still in the middle of her career, with more decades to go as an active figure and writer. She has not yet achieved the heights of success of Heinlein, but that appears within her reach.

"Weatherman" is one of her few short stories. It is of the planetary romance variety of space opera, a long episode within a larger space opera framework of interstellar war, with a hard SF attitude. It chronicles a period of time in the very early career of young military officer Miles Vorkosigan, told with all the irony and wit that have made Bujold famous.

WEATHERMAN

LOIS MCMASTER BUJOLD

"Ship duty!" chortled the ensign three ahead of Miles in line. Glee lit his face as his eyes sped down his orders, the plastic flimsy rattling just slightly in his hands. "I'm to be junior weaponry officer on the Imperial Cruiser *Commodore Vorhalas*. Reporting at once to Tanery Base Shuttleport for orbital transfer." At a pointed prod he removed himself with an unmilitary skip from the way of the next man in line, still muttering delight under his breath.

"Ensign Plause." The aging sergeant manning the desk managed to look bored and superior at the same time, holding the next packet up with deliberation between thumb and forefinger. How long had he been holding down this post at the Imperial Military Academy? Miles wondered. How many hundreds—thousands—of young officers had passed under his bland eye at this first supreme moment of their careers? Did they all start to look alike after a few years? The same fresh green uniforms. The same shiny blue plastic rectangles of shiny new-won rank armoring the high collars. The same hungry eyes, the go-to-hell graduates of the Imperial Services's most elite school with visions of military destiny dancing in their heads. *We don't just march on the future, we charge it.*

Plause stepped aside, touched his thumbprint to the lock-pad, and unzipped his envelope in turn.

"Well?" said Ivan Vorpatril, just ahead of Miles in line. "Don't keep us in suspense."

"Language school," said Plause, still reading.

Plause spoke all four of Barrayar's native languages perfectly already. "As student or instructor?" Miles inquired.

"Student."

"Ah, ha. It'll be galactic languages, then. Intelligence will be wanting you, after. You're bound off-planet for sure," said Miles.

"Not necessarily," said Plause. "They could just sit me in a concrete box somewhere, programming translating computers till I go blind." But hope gleamed in his eyes.

Miles charitably did not point out the major drawback of intelligence, the fact that you ended up working for Chief of ImpSec Simon Illyan, the man who remembered *everything*. But perhaps on Plause's level, he would not encounter the acerb Illyan.

"Ensign Vorpatril," intoned the sergeant. "Ensign Vorkosigan."

Tall Ivan collected his packet and Miles his, and they moved out of the way with their two comrades.

Ivan unzipped his envelope. "Ha. Imperial HQ in Vorbarr Sultana for me. I am to be, I'll have you know, aide-de-camp to Commodore Jollif, Operations." He bowed and turned the flimsy over. "Starting tomorrow, in fact."

"Ooh," said the ensign who'd drawn ship duty, still bouncing slightly. "Ivan gets to be a *secretary*. Just watch out if General Lamitz asks you to sit on his lap, I hear he—"

Ivan flipped him an amiable rude gesture. "Envy, sheer envy. I'll get to live like a civilian. Work seven to five, have my own apartment in town—no girls on that ship of yours up there, I might point out." Ivan's voice was even and cheerful, only his eyes failing to totally conceal his disappointment. Ivan had wanted ship duty, too. They all did.

Miles did. *Ship duty. Eventually, command, like my father, his father, his, his . . .* A wish, a prayer, a dream . . . he hesitated for self-discipline, for fear, for a last lingering moment of high hope. He thumbed the lock pad and unzipped the envelope with deliberate precision. A single plastic flimsy, a handful of travel passes. . . . His deliberation lasted only for the brief moment it took him to absorb the short paragraph before his eyes. He stood frozen in disbelief, began reading again from the top.

"So what's up, coz?" Ivan glanced down over Miles's shoulder.

"Ivan," said Miles in a choked voice, "Have I got a touch of amnesia, or did we indeed never have a meteorology course on our sciences track?"

"Five-space math, yes. Xenobotany, yes." Ivan absently scratched a remembered itch. "Geology and terrain evaluation, yes. Well, there was aviation weather, back in our first year."

"Yes, but . . ."

"So what have they done to you this time?" asked Plause, clearly prepared to offer congratulations or sympathy as indicated.

"I'm assigned as Chief Meteorology Officer, Lazkowski Base. Where the hell is Lazkowski Base? I've never even heard of it!"

The sergeant at the desk looked up with a sudden evil grin. "I have, sir," he offered. "It's on a place called Kyril Island, up near the arctic circle. Winter training base for infantry. The grubs call it Camp Permafrost."

"*Infantry?*" said Miles.

Ivan's brows rose, and he frowned down at Miles. "Infantry? You? That doesn't seem right."

"No, it doesn't," said Miles faintly. Cold consciousness of his physical handicaps washed over him.

Years of arcane medical tortures had almost managed to correct the severe deformities from which Miles had nearly died at birth. Almost. Curled like a frog in infancy, he now stood almost straight. Chalk-stick bones, friable as talc, now were almost strong. Wizened as an infant homunculus, he now stood almost four-foot-nine. It had been a trade-off, toward the end, between the length of his bones and their strength, and his doctor still opined that the last six inches of height had been a mistake. Miles had finally broken his legs enough times to agree with him, but by then it was too late. But not a mutant, not . . . it scarcely mattered any more. If only they would let him place his strengths in the Emperor's service, he would make them forget his weaknesses. The deal was understood.

There had to be a thousand jobs in the Service to which his strange appearance and hidden fragility would make not one whit of difference. Like aide-de-camp, or Intelligence translator. Or even a ship's weaponry officer, monitoring his computers. It had been understood, surely it had been understood. But infantry? Someone was not playing fair. Or a mistake had been made. That wouldn't be a first. He hesitated a long moment, his fist tightening on the flimsy, then headed toward the door.

"Where are you going?" asked Ivan.

"To see Major Cecil."

Ivan exhaled through pursed lips. "Oh? Good luck."

Did the desk sergeant hide a small smile, bending his head to sort through the next stack of packets? "Ensign Draut," he called. The line moved up one more.

·   ·   ·

Major Cecil was leaning with one hip on his clerk's desk, consulting about something on the vid, as Miles entered his office and saluted.

Major Cecil glanced up at Miles and then at his chrono. "Ah, less than ten minutes. I win the bet." The major returned Miles's salute as the clerk, smiling sourly, pulled a small wad of currency from his pocket, peeled off a one-mark note, and handed it across wordlessly to his superior. The major's face was only amused on the surface; he nodded toward the door, and the clerk tore off the plastic flimsy his machine had just produced and exited the room.

Major Cecil was a man of about fifty, lean, even-tempered, watchful. Very watchful. Though he was not the titular head of Personnel, that administrative job belonging to a higher-ranking officer, Miles had spotted Cecil long ago as the final-decision man. Through Cecil's hands passed at the last every assignment for every Academy graduate. Miles had always found him an accessible man, the teacher and scholar in him ascendant over the officer. His wit was dry and rare, his dedication to his duty intense. Miles had always trusted him. Till now.

"Sir," he began. He held out his orders in a frustrated gesture. "What *is* this?"

"Cecil's eyes were still bright with his private amusement as he pocketed the mark-note. "Are you asking me to read them to you, Vorkosigan?"

"Sir, I question—" Miles stopped, bit his tongue, began again. "I have a few questions about my assignment."

"Meteorology Officer, Lazkowski Base," Major Cecil recited.

"It's . . . not a mistake, then? I got the right packet?"

"If that's what that says, you did."

"Are . . . you aware the only meteorology course I had was aviation weather?"

"I am." The major wasn't giving away a thing.

Miles paused. Cecil's sending his clerk out was a clear signal that this discussion was to be frank. "Is this some kind of punishment?" *What have I ever done to you?*

"Why, Ensign," Cecil's voice was smooth, "it's a perfectly normal assignment. My job is to match personnel requests with available candidates. Every request must be filled by someone."

"Any tech school grad could have filled this one." With an effort, Miles kept the snarl out of his voice, uncurled his fingers. "Better. It doesn't require an Academy cadet."

"That's right," agreed the major.

"*Why*, then?" Miles burst out. His voice came out louder than he'd meant it to.

Cecil sighed, straightened. "Because I have noticed, Vorkosigan, watching you— and you know very well you were the most closely-watched cadet ever to pass through these halls barring Emperor Gregor himself—"

Miles nodded shortly.

"That despite your demonstrated brilliance in some areas, you have also demonstrated some chronic weaknesses. And I'm not referring to your physical problems, which everybody but me thought were going to take you out before your first year was up—you've been surprisingly sensible about those—"

Miles shrugged. "Pain hurts, sir. I don't court it."

"Very good. But your most insidious chronic problem is in the area of . . . how shall I put this precisely . . . subordination. You argue too much."

"No, I don't," Miles began indignantly, then shut his mouth.

Cecil flashed a grin. "Quite. Plus your rather irritating habit of treating your superior officers as your, ah . . . ." Cecil paused, apparently groping again for just the right word.

"Equals?" Miles hazarded.

"Cattle," Cecil corrected judiciously. "To be driven to your will. You're a manipulator *par excellence*, Vorkosigan. I've been studying you for three years now, and your group dynamics are fascinating. Whether you were in charge or not, somehow it was always your ideas that ended up getting carried out."

"Have I been . . . that disrespectful, sir?" Miles's stomach felt cold.

"On the contrary. Given your background, the marvel is that you conceal that, ah, little arrogant streak so well. But Vorkosigan," Cecil dropped at last into perfect seriousness, "the Imperial Academy is not the whole of the Imperial Service. You've made your comrades appreciate you because here, brains are held at a premium. You were picked first for any strategic team for the same reason you were picked last for any purely physical contest—these young hot-shots wanted to win. All the time. Whatever it took."

"I can't be ordinary and survive, sir!"

Cecil tilted his head. "I agree. And yet, sometime, you must also learn how to command ordinary men. And be commanded by them!

"This isn't a punishment, Vorkosigan, and it isn't my idea of a joke. Upon my choices may depend not only our fledgling officers' lives, but also those of the innocents I inflict 'em on. If I seriously miscalculate, overmatch or mismatch a man with a job, I not only risk him, but also those around him. Now, in six months (plus unscheduled overruns), the Imperial Orbital Shipyard is going to finish commissioning the *Prince Serg*."

Miles's breath caught.

"You've got it," Cecil nodded. "The newest, fastest, deadliest thing His Imperial Majesty has ever put into space. And with the longest range. It will go out, and stay out, for longer periods than anything we've ever had before. It follows that everyone on board will be in each other's hair for longer unbroken periods than ever before. High Command is actually paying some attention to the psych profiles on this one. For a change.

"Listen, now," Cecil leaned forward. So did Miles, reflexively. "If you can keep your nose clean for just six months on an isolated downside post—bluntly, if you prove you can handle Camp Permafrost, I'll allow as how you can handle anything the Service might throw at you. And I'll support your request for a transfer to the *Prince*. But if you screw up, there will be nothing I or anybody else can do for you. Sink or swim, Ensign."

Fly, thought Miles. *I want to fly.* "Sir . . . just how much of a pit is this place?"

"I wouldn't want to prejudice you, Ensign Vorkosigan," said Cecil piously.

And I love you too, sir. "But . . . infantry? My physical limits . . . won't prevent my serving if they're taken into account, but I can't pretend they're not there. Or I might as well jump off a wall, destroy myself immediately, and save everybody time." *Dammit, why did they let me occupy some of Barrayar's most expensive classroom space for three years if they meant to kill me outright?* "I'd always assumed they were going to be taken into account."

"Meteorology Officer is a technical speciality, Ensign," the major reassured him. "Nobody's going to try and drop a full field pack on you and smash you flat. I doubt there's an officer in the Service who would choose to explain your dead body to the Admiral." His voice cooled slightly. "Your saving grace. Mutant."

Cecil was without prejudice, merely testing. Always testing. Miles ducked his head. "As I may be, for the mutants who come after me."

"You've figured that out, have you?" Cecil's eye was suddenly speculative, faintly approving.

"Years ago, sir."

"Hm." Cecil smiled slightly, pushed himself off the desk, came forward and extended his hand. "Good luck, then, Lord Vorkosigan."

Miles shook it. "Thank you, sir." He shuffled through the stack of travel passes, ordering them.

"What's your first stop?" asked Cecil.

Testing again. Must be a bloody reflex. Miles answered unexpectedly, "The Academy archives."

"Ah!"

"For a downloading of the Service meteorology manual. And supplementary material."

"Very good. By the way, your predecessor in the post will be staying on a few weeks to complete your orientation."

"I'm extremely glad to hear that, sir," said Miles sincerely.

"We're not trying to make it impossible, Ensign."

Merely very difficult. "I'm glad to know that, too. Sir." Miles's parting salute was almost subordinate.

Miles rode the last leg to Kyril Island in a big automated air-freight shuttle with a bored back-up pilot and eighty tons of supplies. He spent most of the solitary journey frantically swotting up on weather. Since the flight schedule went rapidly awry due to hours-long delays at the last two loading stops, he found himself reassuringly further along in his studies than he'd expected by the time the air-shuttle rumbled to a halt at Lazkowski Base.

The cargo bay doors opened to let in watery light from a sun skulking along near the horizon. The high-summer breeze was about five degrees above freezing. The first soldiers Miles saw were a crew of black-coveralled men with loaders under the direction of a tired-looking corporal, who met the shuttle. No one appeared to be specially detailed to meet a new weather officer. Miles shrugged on his parka and approached them.

A couple of the black-clad men, watching him as he hopped down from the ramp, made remarks to each other in Barrayaran Greek, a minority dialect of Earth origin, thoroughly debased in the centuries of the Time of Isolation. Miles, weary from his journey and cued by the all-too-familiar expressions on their faces, made a snap decision to ignore whatever they had to say by simply pretending not to understand their language. Plause had told him often enough that his accent in Greek was execrable anyway.

—Look at that, will you? Is it a kid?

—I knew they were sending us baby officers, but this is a new low.

—Hey, that's no kid. It's a damn dwarf of some sort. The midwife sure missed her stroke on that one. Look at it, it's a mutant!

With an effort, Miles kept his eyes from turning toward the commentators. Increasingly confident of their privacy, their voices rose from whispers to ordinary tones.

—So what's it doing in uniform, ha?

—Maybe it's our new mascot.

The old genetic fears were so subtly ingrained, so pervasive even now, you could get beaten to death by people who didn't even know quite why they hated you but simply got carried away in the excitement of a group feedback loop. Miles knew quite well he had always been protected by his father's rank, but ugly things could happen to less socially fortunate odd ones. There had been a ghastly incident in the Old Town section of Vorbarr Sultana just two years ago, a destitute crippled man found castrated with a broken wine bottle by a gang of drunks. It was considered Progress that it was a scandal, and not simply taken for granted. A recent infanticide in the

Vorkosigan's own district had cut even closer to the bone. Yes, rank, social or military, had its uses. Miles meant to acquire all he could before he was done.

Miles twitched his parka back so that his officer's collar tabs showed clearly. "Hello, Corporal. I have orders to report in to a Lieutenant Ahn, the base Meteorology Officer. Where can I find him?"

Miles waited a beat for his proper salute. It was slow in coming, the corporal was still goggling down at him. It dawned on him at last that Miles might really be an officer.

Belatedly, he saluted. "Excuse me, uh, what did you say, sir?"

Miles returned the salute blandly and repeated himself in level tones.

"Uh, Lieutenant Ahn, right. He usually hides out—that is, he's usually in his office. In the main administration building." The corporal swung his arm around to point toward a two-story prefab sticking up beyond a rank of half-buried warehouses at the edge of the tarmac, maybe a kilometer off. "You can't miss it, it's the tallest building on the base."

Also, Miles noted, well-marked by the assortment of comm equipment sticking out of the roof. Very good.

Now, should he turn his pack over to these goons and pray that it would follow him to his eventual destination, whatever it was? Or interrupt their work and commandeer a loader for transport? He had a brief vision of himself stuck up on the prow of the thing like a sailing ship's figurehead, being trundled toward his meeting with destiny along with half a ton of Underwear, Thermal, Long, 2 doz per unit crate, Style #6774932. He decided to shoulder his duffel and walk.

"Thank you, Corporal." He marched off in the indicated direction, too conscious of his limp and his leg-braces concealed beneath his trouser legs taking up their share of the extra weight. The distance turned out to be farther than it looked, but he was careful not to pause or falter till he'd turned out of sight beyond the first warehouse-unit.

The base seemed nearly deserted. Of course. The bulk of its population was the infantry trainees who came and went in two batches per winter. Only the permanent crew was here now, and Miles bet most of them took their long leaves during this brief summer breathing space. Miles wheezed to a halt inside the Admin building without having passed another man.

The Directory and Map Display, according to a hand-lettered sign taped across its vid plate, was down. Miles wandered up the first and only hallway to his right, searching for an occupied office, any occupied office. Most doors were closed, but not locked, lights out. An office labeled *Gen. Accounting* held a man in black fatigues with red lieutenant's tabs on the collar, totally absorbed in his holovid which was displaying long columns of data. He was swearing under his breath.

"Meteorology Office. Where?" Miles called in the door.

"Two." The lieutenant pointed upward without turning around, crouched more tightly, and resumed swearing. Miles tiptoed away without disturbing him further.

He found it at last on the second floor, a closed door labeled in faded letters. He paused outside, set down his duffel, and folded his parka atop it. He checked himself over. Fourteen hours' travel had rumpled his initial crispness. Still, he'd managed to keep his green undress uniform and half-boots free of foodstains, mud, and other unbecoming accretions. He flattened his cap and positioned it precisely in his belt. He'd crossed half a planet, half a lifetime, to achieve this moment. Three years training to a fever pitch of readiness lay behind him. Yet the Academy years had always had a faint air of pretense, We-are-only-practicing; now, at last, he was face to face with the real thing, his first real commanding officer. First impressions could be vital, especially in his case. He took a breath and knocked.

A gravelly muffled voice came through the door, words unrecognizable. Invitation? Miles opened it and strode in.

He had a glimpse of computer interfaces and vid displays gleaming and glowing along one wall. He rocked back at the heat that hit his face. The air within was blood-temperature. Except for the vid displays, the room was dim. At a movement to his left, Miles turned and saluted. "Ensign Miles Vorkosigan, reporting for duty as ordered, sir," he snapped out, looked up, and saw no one.

The movement had come from lower down. An unshaven man of about forty dressed only in his skivvies sat on the floor, his back against the comconsole desk. He smiled up at Miles, raised a bottle half-full of amber liquid, mumbled, "Salu', boy. Love ya," and fell slowly over.

Miles gazed down on him for a long, long, thoughtful moment.

The man began to snore.

After turning down the heat, shedding his tunic, and tossing a blanket over Lieutenant Ahn (for such he was), Miles took a contemplative half-hour and thoroughly examined his new domain. There was no doubt, he was going to require instruction in the office's operations. Besides the satellite real-time images, automated data seemed to be coming in from a dozen micro-climate survey rigs spotted around the island. If procedural manuals had ever existed, they weren't around now, not even on the computers. After an honorable hesitation, bemusedly studying the snoring, twitching form on the floor, Miles also took the opportunity to go through Ahn's desk and comconsole files.

Discovery of a few pertinent facts helped put the human spectacle before. Miles into a more understandable perspective. Lieutenant Ahn, it seemed, was a twenty-year man within weeks of retirement. It had been a very, very long time since his last promotion. It had been an even longer time since his last transfer; he'd been Kyril Island's only weather officer for the last fifteen years.

This poor sod has been stuck on this iceberg since I was six years old, Miles calculated, and shuddered inwardly. Hard to tell, at this late date, if Ahn's drinking problem were cause or effect. Well, if he sobered up enough within the next day to show Miles how to go on, well and good. If he didn't, Miles could think of half a dozen ways, ranging from the cruel to the unusual, to bring him around whether he wanted to be conscious or not. If Ahn could just be made to disgorge a technical orientation, he could return to his coma till they came to roll him onto outgoing transport, for all Miles cared.

Ahn's fate decided, Miles donned his tunic, stowed his gear behind the desk, and went exploring. Somewhere in the chain of command there must be a conscious, sober, and sane human being who was actually doing his job, or the place couldn't even function on this level. Or maybe it was run by corporals, who knew? In that case, Miles supposed, his next task must be to find and take control of the most effective corporal available.

In the downstairs foyer a human form approached Miles, silhouetted at first against the light from the front doors. Jogging in precise double-time, the shape resolved into a tall, hard-bodied man in sweat pants, T-shirt, and running shoes. He had clearly just come in off some condition-maintaining five-kilometer run, with maybe a few hundred push-ups thrown in for dessert. Iron-grey hair, iron-hard eyes; he might have been a particularly dyspeptic drill sergeant. He stopped short to stare down at Miles, startlement compressing to a thin-lipped frown.

Miles stood with his legs slightly apart, threw back his head, and stared up with equal force. The man seemed totally oblivious to Miles's collar tabs. Exasperated, Miles snapped, "Are all the keepers on vacation, or is anybody actually running this bloody zoo?"

The man's eyes sparked, as if their iron had struck flint; they ignited a little warning light in Miles's brain, one mouthy moment too late. *Hi, there, sir!* cried the hysterical commenter in the back of Miles's mind, with a skip, bow, and flourish. *I'm your newest exhibit!* Miles suppressed the voice ruthlessly. There wasn't a trace of humor in any line of that seamed countenance looming over him.

With a cold flare of his carved nostril, the Base Commander glared down at Miles and growled, "*I* run it, Ensign."

Dense fog was rolling in off the distant, muttering sea by the time Miles finally found his way to his new quarters. The officers' barracks and all around it were plunged into a grey, frost-scummed obscurity. Miles decided it was an omen.

Oh, God, it was going to be a long winter.

Rather to Miles's surprise, when he arrived at Ahn's office next morning at an hour he guessed might represent beginning-of-shift, he found the lieutenant awake, sober, and in uniform. Not that the man looked precisely *well*; pasty-faced, breathing stertorously, he sat huddled staring slit-eyed at a computer-colorized weather vid. The holo zoomed and shifted dizzyingly at signals from the remote controller he clutched in one damp and trembling palm.

"Good morning, sir." Miles softened his voice out of mercy, and closed the door behind himself without slamming it.

"Ha?" Ahn looked up, and returned his salute automatically. "What the devil are you, ah . . . Ensign?"

"I'm your replacement, sir. Didn't anyone tell you I was coming?"

"Oh, yes!" Ahn brightened right up. "Very good, come in." Miles, already in, smiled briefly instead. "I meant to meet you on the shuttlepad," Ahn went on. "You're early. But you seem to have found your way all right."

"I came in yesterday, sir."

"Oh. You should have reported in."

"I did, sir."

"Oh." Ahn squinted at Miles in worry. "You did?"

"You promised you'd give me a complete technical orientation to the office this morning, sir," Miles added, seizing the opportunity.

"Oh," Ahn blinked. "Good." The worried look faded slightly. "Well, ah . . ." Ahn rubbed his face, looking around. He confined his reaction to Miles's physical appearance to one covert glance, and, perhaps deciding they must have gotten the social duties of introduction out of the way yesterday, plunged at once into a description of the equipment lining the wall, in order from left to right.

Literally an introduction; all the computers had women's names. Except for a tendency to talk about his machines as though they were human, Ahn seemed coherent enough as he detailed his job, only drifting into randomness, then hung-over silence, when he accidently strayed from the topic. Miles steered him gently back to weather with pertinent questions, and took notes. After a bewildered brownian trip around the room Ahn rediscovered his office procedural disks at last, stuck to the undersides of their respective pieces of equipment. He made fresh coffee on a non-regulation brewer—named "Georgette"—parked discreetly in a corner cupboard, then took Miles up to the roof of the building to show him the data-collection center there.

Ahn went over the assorted meters, collectors, and samplers rather perfunctorily. His headache seemed to be growing worse with the morning's exertions. He leaned heavily on the corrosion-proof railing surrounding the automated station and squinted out at the distant horizon. Miles followed him around dutifully as he appeared to meditate deeply for a few minutes on each of the cardinal compass points. Or maybe that introspective look just meant he was getting ready to throw up.

It was pale and clear this morning, the sun up—the sun had been up since two hours after midnight, Miles reminded himself. They were just past the shortest nights of the year for this latitude. From this rare high vantage point, Miles gazed out with interest at Lazkowski Base and the flat landscape beyond.

Kyril Island was an egg-shaped lump about seventy kilometers wide and a hundred and sixty kilometers long, and over five hundred kilometers from the next land of any description. *Lumpy and brown* described most of it, both base and island. The majority of the nearby buildings, including Miles's officers' barracks, were dug in, topped with native turf. Nobody had bothered with agricultural terraforming here. The island retained its original Barrayaran ecology, scarred by use and abuse. Long fat rolls of turf covered the barracks for the winter infantry trainees, now empty and silent. Muddy water-filled ruts fanned out to deserted marksmanship ranges, obstacle courses, and pocked live-ammo practice areas.

To the near south, the leaden sea heaved, muting the sun's best efforts at sparkle. To the far north a grey line marked the border of the tundra at a chain of dead volcanic mountains.

Miles had taken his own officers' short course in winter maneuvers in the Black Escarpment, mountain country deep in Barrayar's second continent; plenty of snow, to be sure, and murderous terrain, but the air had been dry and crisp and stimulating. Even today, at high summer, the sea dampness seemed to creep up under his loose parka and gnaw his bones at every old break. Miles shrugged against it, without effect.

Ahn, still draped over the railing, glanced sideways at Miles at this movement. "So tell me, ah, Ensign, are you any relation to *the* Vorkosigan? I wondered, when I saw the name on the orders the other day."

"My father," said Miles shortly.

"Good God." Ahn blinked and straightened, then sagged self-consciously back onto his elbows as before. "Good God," he repeated. He chewed his lip in fascination, dulled eyes briefly alight with honest curiosity. "What's he really like?"

What an impossible question, Miles thought in exasperation. Admiral Count Aral Vorkosigan. The colossus of Barrayaran history in this half-century. Conqueror of Komarr, hero of the ghastly retreat from Escobar. For six teen years Lord Regent of Barrayar during Emperor Gregor's troubled minority; the Emperor's trusted Prime Minister in the four years since. Destroyer of Vordarian's Pretendership, engineer of the peculiar victory of the third Cetagandan war, unshaken tiger-rider of Barrayar's murderous internecine politics for the past two decades. *The* Vorkosigan.

I have seen him laugh in pure delight, standing on the dock at Vorkosigan Surleau and yelling instructions over the water, the morning I first sailed, dumped, and righted the skimmer by myself. I have seen him weep till his nose ran, more dead drunk than you were yesterday, Ahn, the night we got the word Major Duvallier was executed for espionage. I have seen him rage, so brick-red we feared for his heart, when the reports came in fully detailing the stupidities that led to the last riots in Solstice. I have seen him wandering around Vorkosigan House at dawn in his underwear, yawning and prodding my sleepy mother into helping him find two matching socks. He's not like anything, Ahn. He's the original.

"He cares about Barrayar," Miles said aloud at last, as the silence grew awkward. "He's . . . a hard act to follow." *And, oh yes, his only child is a deformed mutant. That, too.*

"I should think so." Ahn blew out his breath in sympathy, or maybe it was nausea.

Miles decided he could tolerate Ahn's sympathy. There seemed no hint in it of the damned patronizing pity, nor, interestingly, of the more common repugnance. *It's because I'm his replacement here,* Miles decided. *I could have two heads and he'd still be overjoyed to meet me.*

"That what you're doing, following in the old man's footsteps?" said Ahn equably. And more dubiously, looking around, "Here?"

"I'm Vor," said Miles impatiently. "I serve. Or at any rate, I try to. Wherever I'm put. That was the deal."

Ahn shrugged bafflement, whether at Miles or at the vagaries of the Service that had sent him to Kyril Island Miles could not tell. "Well." He pushed himself up off the rail with a grunt. "No wah-wah warnings today.'

"No what warnings?"

Ahn yawned, and tapped an array of figures—pulled out of thin air, as far as Miles could tell—into his report panel representing hour-by-hour predictions for today's weather. "Wah-wah. Didn't anybody tell you about the wah-wah?"

"No . . ."

"They should have, first thing. Bloody dangerous, the wah-wah."

Miles began to wonder if Ahn was trying to diddle his head. Practical jokes could be a subtle enough form of victimization to penetrate even the defenses of rank, Miles had found. The honest hatred of a beating inflicted only physical pain.

Ahn leaned across the railing again to point. "You notice all those ropes, strung from door to door between buildings? That's for when the wah-wah comes up. You hang onto 'em to keep from being blown away. If you lose your grip, don't fling out your arms to try and stop yourself. I've seen more guys break their wrists that way. Go into a ball and roll."

"What the hell's a wah-wah? Sir."

"Big wind. Sudden. I've seen it go from dead calm to a hundred and sixty kilometers, with a temperature drop from sixteen degrees cee above freezing to thirty below, in seven minutes. It can last from ten minutes to two days. They almost always blow up from the northwest, here, when conditions are right. The remote station on the coast gives us about a twenty-minute warning. We blow a siren. That means you must never let yourself get caught without your cold gear, or less than fifteen minutes away from a bunker. There's bunkers all around the grubs' practice fields out there." Ahn waved his arm in that direction. He seemed quite serious, even earnest. "You hear that siren, you run like hell for cover. The size you are, if you ever got picked up and blown into the sea, they'd never find you again."

"All right," said Miles, silently resolving to check out these alleged facts in the base's weather records at the first opportunity. He craned his neck for a look at Ahn's report panel. "Where did you read off those numbers from, that you just entered on there?"

Ahn stared at his report panel in surprise. "Well—they're the right figures."

"I wasn't questioning their accuracy," said Miles patiently. "I want to know how you came up with them. So I can do it tomorrow, while you're still here to correct me."

Ahn waved his free hand in an abortive, frustrated gesture. "Well . . ."

"You're not just making them up, are you?" said Miles in suspicion.

"No!" said Ahn. "I hadn't thought about it, but . . . it's the way the day smells, I guess." He inhaled deeply, by way of demonstration.

Miles wrinkled his nose and sniffed experimentally. Cold, sea salt, shore slime, damp and mildew. Hot circuits in some of the blinking, twirling array of instruments beside him. The mean temperature, barometric pressure, and humidity of the present moment, let alone that of eighteen hours into the future, was not to be found in the olfactory information pressing on *his* nostrils. He jerked his thumb at the meteorological array. "Does that thing have any sort of a smell-o-meter to duplicate whatever it is you're doing?"

Ahn looked genuinely nonplussed, as if his internal system, whatever it was, had been dislocated by his sudden self-consciousness of it. "Sorry, Ensign Vorkosigan. We have the standard computerized projections, of course, but to tell you the truth I haven't used 'em in years. They're not accurate enough."

Miles stared at Ahn, and came to a horrid realization. Ahn wasn't lying, joking, or making this up. It was the fifteen years' experience, gone subliminal, that was carrying out these subtle functions. A backlog of experience Miles could not duplicate. *Nor would I wish to,* he admitted to himself.

Later in the day, while explaining with perfect truth that he was orienting himself to the systems, Miles covertly checked out all of Ahn's startling assertions in the base meteorological archives. Ahn hadn't been kidding about the wah-wah. Worse, he hadn't been kidding about the computerized projections. The automated system produced local predictions of 86% accuracy, dropping to 73% at a week's long-range forecast. Ahn and his magical nose ran an accuracy of 96%, dropping to 94% at a week's range. *When Ahn leaves, this island is going to experience a 10 to 21% drop in forecast accuracy. They're going to notice.*

Weather Officer, Lazkowski Base, was clearly a more responsible position than Miles had at first realized. The weather here could be deadly.

And this guy is going to leave me alone on this island with six thousand armed men, and tell me to go sniff for wah-wahs?

On the fifth day, when Miles had just about decided that his first impression had been too harsh, Ahn relapsed. Miles waited an hour for Ahn and his nose to show up at the weather office to begin the day's duties. At last he pulled the routine readings from the substandard computerized system, entered them anyway, and went hunting.

He ran Ahn down at last still in his bunk, in his quarters in the officers' barracks, sodden and snoring, stinking of stale . . . fruit brandy? Miles shuddered. Shaking, prodding, and yelling in Ahn's ear failed to rouse him. He only burrowed deeper into his bedclothes and noxious miasma, moaning. Miles regretfully set aside visions of violence, and prepared to carry on by himself. He'd be on his own soon enough anyway.

He limp-marched off to the motor pool. Yesterday Ahn had taken him on a scheduled maintenance patrol of the five remote-sensor weather stations nearest the base. The outlying six had been planned for today. Routine travel around Kyril Island was accomplished in an all-terrain vehicle called a scat-cat, which had turned out to be almost as much fun to drive as an anti-grav sled. Scat-cats were ground-hugging iridescent teardrops that tore up the tundra, but were guaranteed not to blow away in the wah-wah winds. Base personnel, Miles had been given to understand, had grown extremely tired of picking lost anti-grav sleds out of the frigid sea.

The motor pool was another half-buried bunker like most of the rest of Lazkowski Base, only bigger. Miles routed out the corporal, what's his name, Olney, who'd signed Ahn and himself out the previous day. The tech who assisted him, driving the scat-cat up from the underground storage to the entrance, also looked faintly familiar. Tall, black fatigues, dark hair—that described eighty percent of the men on the base—it wasn't until he spoke that his heavy accent cued Miles. He was one of the sotto voice commenters Miles had overheard on the shuttlepad. Miles schooled himself not to react.

Miles went over the vehicle's supply check-list carefully before signing for it, as Ahn had taught him: All scat-cats were required to carry a complete cold-survival kit at all times. Corporal Olney watched with faint contempt as Miles fumbled around finding everything. *All right, so I'm slow,* Miles thought irritably. *New and green. This is the only way I'm gonna get less new and green. Step by step.* He controlled his self-consciousness with an effort. Previous painful experience had taught him it was a most dangerous frame of mind. *Concentrate on the task, not the bloody audience. You've always had an audience. Probably always will.*

Miles spread out the map flimsy across the scat-cat's shell, and pointed out his projected itinerary to the corporal. Such a briefing was also safety SOP, according to Ahn. Olney grunted acknowledgment with a finely-tuned look of long-suffering boredom, palpable but just short of something Miles would be forced to notice.

The black-clad tech, Pattas, watching over Miles's uneven shoulder, pursed his lips and spoke. "Oh, Ensign *sir.*" Again, the emphasis fell just short of irony. "You going up to Station Nine?"

"Yes?"

"You might want to be sure and park your scat-cat, uh, out of the wind, in that hollow just below the station." A thick finger touched the map flimsy on an area marked in blue. "You'll see it. That way your scat-cat'll be sure of restarting."

"The power pack in these engines is rated for space," said Miles. "How could it not restart?"

Olney's eye lit, then went suddenly very neutral. "Yes, but in case of a sudden wah-wah, you wouldn't want it to blow away."

I'd blow away before it would. "I thought these scat-cats were heavy enough not to."

"Well, not *away,* but they have been known to blow *over,*" murmured Pattas.

"Oh. Well, thank you."

Corporal Olney coughed. Pattas waved cheerfully as Miles drove out.

Miles's chin jerked up in the old nervous tic. He took a deep breath and let his hackles settle, as he turned the scat-cat away from the base and headed cross-country. He powered up to a more satisfying speed, lashing through the brown bracken-like growth. He had been what, a year and a half? two years? at the Imperial Academy proving and re-proving his competence to every bloody man he crossed every time he did anything. The third year had perhaps spoiled him, he was out of practice. Was it going to be like this every time he took up a new post? Probably, he reflected bitterly, and powered up a bit more. But he'd known that would be part of the game when he'd demanded to play.

The weather was almost warm today, the pale sun almost bright, and Miles almost cheerful by the time he reached Station Six, on the eastern shore of the island. It was a pleasure to be alone for a change, just him and his job. No audience. Time to take his time and get it all right. He worked carefully, checking power packs, emptying samplers, looking for signs of corrosion, damage, or loose connections in the equipment. And if he dropped a tool, there was no one about to make comments about spastic mutants. With the fading tension, he made fewer fumbles, and the tic vanished. He finished, stretched, and inhaled the damp air benignly, reveling in the unaccustomed luxury of solitude. He even took a few minutes to walk along the shore-line, and notice the intricacies of the small sea-life washed up there.

One of the samplers in Station Eight was damaged, a humidity-meter shattered. By the time he'd replaced it he realized his itinerary timetable had been overly optimistic. The sun was slanting down toward green twilight as he left Station Eight. By the time he reached Station Nine, in an area of mixed tundra and rocky outcrops near the northern shore, it was almost dark.

Station Ten, Miles reconfirmed by checking his map flimsy by pen-light, was up in the volcanic mountains among the glaciers. Best not try to go hunting it in the dark. He would wait out the brief four hours till dawn. He reported his change-of-plan via comm-link to the base, 160 kilometers to the south. The man on duty did not sound terribly interested. Good.

With no watchers, Miles happily seized the opportunity to try out all that fascinating gear packed in the back of the scat-cat. Far better to practice now, when conditions were good, than in the middle of some later blizzard. The little two-man bubble-shelter, when set up, seemed almost palatial for Miles's short and lonely splendor. In winter it was meant to be insulated with packed snow. He positioned it downwind of the scat-cat, parked in the recommended low spot a few hundred meters from the weather station, which was perched on a rocky outcrop.

Miles reflected on the relative weight of the shelter versus the scat-cat. A vid that Ahn had shown him of a typical wah-wah remained vivid in his mind. The portable latrine traveling sideways in the air at a hundred kilometers an hour had been particularly impressive. Ahn hadn't been able to tell him if there'd been anyone in it at the time the vid was shot. Miles took the added precaution of attaching the shelter to the scat-cat with a short chain. Satisfied, he crawled inside.

The equipment was first-rate. He hung a heat-tube from the roof and touched it on, and basked in its glow, sitting cross-legged. Rations were of the better grade. A pull tab heated a compartmentalized tray of stew with vegetables and rice. He mixed an acceptable fruit drink from the powder supplied. After eating and stowing the remains, he settled on a comfortable pad, shoved a book-disk into his viewer, and prepared to read away the short night.

He had been rather tense these last few weeks. These last few years. The book-disk, a Betan novel of manners which the Countess had recommended to him, had nothing whatsoever to do with Barrayar, military maneuvers, mutation, politics, or the weather. He didn't even notice what time he dozed off.

He woke with a start, blinking in the thick darkness gilded only with the faint copper light from the heat-tube. He felt he had slept long, yet the transparent sectors of the bubble-shelter were pitchy black. An unreasoning panic clogged his throat. Dammit, it didn't matter if he overslept, it wasn't like he would be late for an exam, here. He glanced at the glowing readout on his wrist chrono.

It ought to be broad daylight.

The flexible walls of the shelter were pressing inward. Not one-third of the original volume remained, and the floor was wrinkled. Miles shoved one finger against the thin cold plastic. It yielded slowly, like soft butter, and retained the dented impression. What the *hell* . . . ?

His head was pounding, his throat constricted, the air was stuffy and wet. It felt just like . . . like oxygen depletion and CO_2 excess in a space emergency. *Here?* The vertigo of his disorientation seemed to tilt the floor.

The floor *was* tilted, he realized indignantly, pulled deeply downward on one side, pinching one of his legs. He convulsed from its grip. Fighting the CO_2-induced panic, he lay back, trying to breathe slower and think faster.

I'm underground. Sunk in some kind of quicksand. Quick-mud. Had those two bloody bastards at the motor-pool set him up for this? He'd fallen for it, fallen right in it.

Slow-mud, maybe. The scat-cat hadn't settled noticably in the time it had taken him to set up this shelter. Or he would have twigged to the trap. Of course, it had been dark. But if he'd been settling for hours, asleep. . . .

Relax, he told himself frantically. The tundra surface, the free air, might be a mere ten centimeters overhead. Or ten meters . . . *relax!* He felt about the shelter for something to use as a probe. There'd been a long, telescoping, knife-bitted tube for sampling glacier ice. Packed in the scat-cat. Along with the comm link. Now located, Miles gauged by the angle of the floor, about two-and-a-half meters down and to the west of his present location. It was the scat-cat that was dragging him down. The bubble-shelter alone might well have floated in the tundra-camouflaged mud-pond. If he could detach the chain, might it rise? Not fast enough. His chest felt stuffed with cotton. He had to break through to air soon, or asphyxiate. Womb, tomb. Would his parents be there to watch, when he was found at last, when this grave was opened, scat-cat and shelter winched out of the bog by heavy hovercab. . . . his body frozen rictus-mouthed in this hideous parody of an amniotic sac . . . *relax.*

He stood, and shoved upward against the heavy roof. His feet sank in the pulpy floor, but he was able to jerk loose one of the bubble's interior ribs, now bent in an overstrained curve. He almost passed out from the effort, in the thick air. He found the top edge of the shelter's opening, and slid his finger down the burr-catch just a few centimeters. Just enough for the pole to pass through. He'd feared the black mud would pour in, drowning him at once, but it only crept in extrusive blobs, to fall with oozing plops. The comparison was obvious and repulsive. *God, and I thought I'd been in deep shit before.*

He shoved the rib upward. It resisted, slipping in his sweating palms. Not ten centimeters. Not twenty. A meter, a meter and a third, and he was running short on probe. He paused, took a new grip, shoved again. Was the resistance lessening? Had he broken through to the surface? He heaved it back and forth, but the sucking slime sealed it still.

Maybe, maybe a little less than his own height between the top of the shelter and breath. Breath, death. How long to claw through it? How fast did a hole in this stuff close? His vision was darkening, and it wasn't because the light was going dim. He turned the heat tube off and stuck it in the front pocket of his jacket. The uncanny dark shook him with horror. Or perhaps it was the CO_2. Now or never.

On an impulse, he bent and loosened his boot-catches and belt buckle, then zipped open the burr by feel. He began to dig like a dog, heaving big globs of mud down into the little space left in the bubble. He squeezed through the opening, braced himself, took his last breath, and pressed upward.

His chest was pulsing, his vision a red blur, when his head broke the surface. Air! He spat black muck and bracken bits, and blinked, trying with little success to clear his eyes and nose. He fought one hand up, then the other, and tried to pull himself up horizontal, flat like a frog. The cold confounded him. He could feel the muck closing around his legs, numbing like a witch's embrace. His toes pressed at full extension on the shelter's roof. It sank and he rose a centimeter. The last of the leverage he could get by pushing. Now he must pull. His hands closed over bracken. It gave. More. More. He was making a little progress, the cold air raking his grateful throat. The witch's grip tightened. He wriggled his legs, futilely, one last time. All right, now. Heave!

His legs slid out of his boots and pants, his hips sucked free, and he rolled away. He lay spread-eagled for maximum support on the treacherous surface, face up to the grey swirling sky. His uniform jacket and long underwear were soaked with slime, and he'd lost one thermal sock, as well as both boots and his trousers.

It was sleeting.

They found him hours later, curled around the dimming heat-tube, crammed into an eviscerated equipment bay in the automated weather station. His eyesockets were hollow in his black-streaked face, his toes and ears white. His numb purple fingers jerked two wires across each other in a steady, hypnotic tattoo, the Service emergency code. To be read out in bursts of static in the barometric pressure meter in base's weather room. If and when anybody bothered to look at the suddenly-defective reading from this station, or noticed the pattern in the white noise.

His fingers kept twitching in this rhythm for minutes after they pulled him free of his little box. Ice cracked off the back of his uniform jacket as they tried to straighten his body. For a long time they could get no words from him at all, only a shivering hiss. Only his eyes burned.

Floating in the heat tank in the base infirmary, Miles considered crucifixion for the two saboteurs from the motor pool from several angles. Such as upside-down. Dangling over the sea at low altitude from an anti-grav sled. Better still, staked out face-up in a bog in a blizzard. . . . But by the time his body had warmed up, and the corpsman had pulled him out of the tank to dry, be reexamined, and eat a supervised meal, his head had cooled.

It hadn't been an assassination attempt. And therefore, not a matter he was compelled to turn over to Simon Illyan, dread Chief of Imperial Security and Miles's father's left-hand man. The vision of the sinister officers from Imperial Security coming to take those two jokers away, far away, was lovely, but impractical, like shooting mice with a maser cannon. Anyway, where could Imperial Security possibly send them that was worse than here?

They'd meant his scat-cat to bog, to be sure, while he serviced the weather station, and for Miles to have the embarrassment of calling the base for heavy equipment to pull it out. Embarrassing, not lethal. They could not have—no one could have—foreseen Miles's inspired safety-conscious precaution with the chain, which was in the final analysis what had almost killed him. At most it was a matter for Service Security, bad enough, or for normal discipline.

He dangled his toes over the side of his bed, one of a row in the empty infirmary, and pushed the last of his food around on his tray. The corpsman wandered in, and glanced at the remains.

"You feeling all right now, sir?"

"Fine," said Miles morosely.

"You, uh, didn't finish your tray."

"I often don't. They always give me too much."

"Yeah, I guess you are pretty, um . . ." The corpsman made a note on his report panel, leaned over to examine Miles's ears, and bent to inspect his toes, rolling them between practiced fingers. "It doesn't look like you're going to lose any pieces, here. Lucky."

"Do you treat a lot of frostbite?" *Or am I the only idiot?* Present evidence would suggest it.

"Oh, once the grubs arrive, this place'll be crammed. Frostbite, pneumonia, broken bones, contusions, concussions . . . gets real lively, come winter. Wall-to-wall moro—unlucky trainees. And a few unlucky instructors, that they take down with 'em." The corpsman stood, and tapped a few more entries on his panel. "I'm afraid I have to mark you as recovered now, sir."

"Afraid?" Miles raised his brows inquiringly.

The corpsman straightened, in the unconscious posture of a man transmitting official bad news. That old they-told-me-to-say-this-it's-not-my-fault look. "You are ordered to report to the base commander's office as soon as I release you, sir."

Miles considered an immediate relapse. No. Better to get the messy parts over with. "Tell me, corpsman, has anyone else ever sunk a scat-cat?"

"Oh, sure. The grubs lose about five or six a season. Plus minor bog-downs. The engineers get real pissed about it. The commandant promised them next time he'd . . . ahem!" The corpsman lost his voice, suddenly.

Wonderful, thought Miles. Just great. He could see it coming. It wasn't like he couldn't see it coming.

.   .   .

Miles dashed back to his quarters for a quick change of clothing, guessing a hospital robe might be inappropriate for the coming interview. He immediately found he had a minor quandry. His black fatigues seemed too relaxed, his dress greens too formal for office wear anywhere outside Imperial HQ at Vorbarr Sultana. His undress greens' trousers and half-boots were still at the bottom of the bog. He had only brought one of each uniform style with him; his spares, supposedly in transit, had not yet arrived.

He was hardly in a position to borrow from a neighbor. His uniforms were privately made to his own fit, at approximately four times the cost of Imperial issue. Part of that cost was for the effort of making them indistinguishable on the surface from the machine cut, while at the same time partially masking the oddities of his body through subtleties of hand-tailoring. He cursed under his breath, and shucked on his dress greens, complete with mirror-polished boots to the knees. At least the boots obviated the leg braces.

General Stanis Metzov, read the sign on the door, *Base Commander.* Miles had been assiduously avoiding the base commander ever since their first unfortunate encounter. This had not been hard to do in Ahn's company, despite the pared population of Kyril Island this month; Ahn avoided everybody. Miles now wished he'd tried harder to strike up conversations with brother officers in mess. Permitting himself to stay isolated, even to concentrate on his new tasks, had been a mistake. In five days of even the most random conversation, someone must surely have mentioned Kyril Island's voracious killer mud.

A corporal manning the comconsole in an antechamber ushered Miles through to the inner office. He must now try to work himself back round to Metzov's good side, assuming the general had one. Miles needed allies. General Metzov looked across his desk unsmiling as Miles saluted and stood waiting.

Today, the general was aggressively dressed in black fatigues. At Metzov's altitude in the hierarchy, this stylistic choice usually indicated a deliberate identification with The Fighting Man. The only concession to his rank was their pressed neatness. His decorations were stripped down to a mere modest three, all high combat commendations. Pseudo-modest, pruned of the surrounding foliage, they leapt to the eye. Mentally, Miles applauded, even envied, the effect. Metzov looked his part, the combat commander, absolutely, unconsciously natural.

A fifty-fifty chance with the uniform, and I had to guess wrong, Miles fumed as Metzov's eye traveled sarcastically down, and back up, the subdued glitter of his dress greens. All right, so Metzov's eyebrows signalled, Miles now looked like some kind of Vorish headquarters twit. Not that that wasn't another familiar type. Miles decided to decline the roasting and cut Metzov's inspection short by forcing the opening.

"Yes, sir?"

Metzov leaned back in his chair, lips twisting. "I see you found some pants, Ensign Vorkosigan. And, ah . . . riding boots, too. You know, there are no horses on this island."

None at Imperial Headquarters, either, Miles thought irritably. *I didn't design the damn boots.* His father had once suggested his staff officers must need them for riding hobbyhorses, high horses, and nightmares. Unable to think of a useful reply to the general's sally, Miles stood in dignified silence, chin lifted, parade rest. "Sir."

Metzov leaned forward, clasping his hands, abandoning his heavy humor, eyes gone hard again. "You lost a valuable, fully-equipped scat-cat as a result of leaving it parked in an area clearly marked as a Permafrost Inversion Zone. Don't they teach map-reading at the Imperial Academy any more, or is it to be all diplomacy in the New Service—how to drink tea with the ladies?"

Miles called up the map in his mind. He could see it clearly. "The blue areas were labelled P.I.Z. Those initials were not defined. Not in the key or anywhere."

"Then I take it you also failed to read your manual."

He'd been buried in manuals ever since he'd arrived. Weather office procedural's equipment tech-specs . . . "Which one, sir?"

"Lazkowski Base Regulations."

Miles tried frantically to remember if he'd ever seen such a disk. "I . . . think Lieutenant Ahn may have given me a copy . . . night before last." Ahn had in fact dumped an entire carton of disks out on Miles's bed in officers' quarters. He was doing some preliminary packing, he'd said, and was willing Miles his library. Miles had read two weather disks before going to sleep that night. Ahn, clearly, had returned to his own cubicle to do a little preliminary celebrating. The next morning Miles had taken the scat-cat out. . . .

"And you haven't read it yet?"

"No, sir."

"Why not?"

I was set up, Miles's thought wailed. He could feel the highly-interested presence of Metzov's clerk, undismissed, standing witness by the door behind him. Making this a public, not a private, dressing-down. And if only he'd read the damn manual, would those two bastards from the motor pool have even been *able* to set him up? Will or nill, he was going to get down-checked for this one. "No excuse, sir."

"Well, Ensign, in Chapter Three of Lazkowski Base Regulations you will find a complete description of all the permafrost zones, together with the rules for avoiding them. You might look into it, when you can spare a little leisure from . . . drinking tea."

"Yes, sir." Miles's face was set like glass. The general had a right to skin him with a vibra-knife, if he chose—in *private*. The authority lent Miles by his uniform barely balanced the deformities that made him a target of Barrayar's historically-grounded, intense genetic prejudices. A public humiliation that sapped that authority before men he must also command came very close to an act of sabotage. Deliberate, or unconscious?

The general was only warming up. "The Service may still provide warehousing for excess Vor lordlings at Imperial Headquarters, but out here in the real world, where there's fighting to be done, we have no use for drones. Now, I fought my way up through the ranks. I saw casualties in Vordarian's Pretendership before you were born—"

I WAS a casualty in Vordarian's Pretendership before I was born, thought Miles, his irritation growing wilder. The soltoxin gas that had almost killed his pregnant mother and made Miles what he was, had been a purely military poison.

"—and I fought the Komarr Revolt. You infants who've come up in the past decade and more have no concept of combat. These long periods of unbroken peace weaken the Service. If they go on much longer, when a crisis comes there'll be no one left who's had any real practice in a crunch."

Miles's eyes crossed slightly, from internal pressure. *Then should His Imperial Majesty provide a war every five years, as a convenience for the advancement of his officers' careers?* His mind boggled slightly over the concept of "real practice." Had Miles maybe acquired his first clue why this superb-looking officer had washed up on Kyril Island?

Metzov was still expanding, self-stimulated. "In a real combat situation, a soldier's equipment is vital. It can be the difference between victory and defeat. A man who loses his equipment loses his effectiveness as a soldier. A man disarmed in a technological war might as well be a woman, useless! And you disarmed *yourself!*"

Miles wondered sourly if the general would then agree that a woman armed in a technological war might as well be a man. . . . no, probably not. Not a Barrayaran of his generation.

Metzov's voice descended again, dropping from military philosophy to the immediately practical. Miles was relieved. "The usual punishment for a man bogging a scat-cat is to dig it out himself. By hand. I understand that won't be feasible, since the depth to which you sank yours is a new camp record. Nevertheless, you will report at 1400 to Lieutenant Bonn of Engineering, to assist him as he sees fit."

Well, that was certainly fair. And would probably be educational, too. Miles prayed this interview was winding down. *Dismissed, now?* But the general fell silent, squinty-eyed and thoughtful.

"For the damage you did to the weather station," Metzov began slowly, then sat up more decisively—his eyes, Miles could almost swear, lighting with a faint red glow, the corner of that seamed mouth twitching upward, "you will supervise basic-labor detail for one week. Four hours a day. That's in addition to your other duties. Report to Sergeant Neuve, in Maintenance, at 0500 daily."

A slight choked inhalation sounded from the corporal still standing behind Miles, which Miles could not interpret. Laughter? Horror?

But . . . *unjust!* And he would lose a significant fraction of the precious time remaining to decant technical expertise from Ahn. . . . "The damage I did to the weather station was not a stupid accident like the scat-cat, sir! It was necessary, to my survival."

General Metzov fixed him with a very cold eye. "Make that six hours a day, Ensign Vorkosigan."

Miles spoke through his teeth, words jerked out as though by pliers. "Would you have preferred the interview you'd be having right now if I'd permitted myself to freeze, sir?"

Silence fell, very dead. Swelling, like a road-killed animal in the summer sun.

"You are dismissed, Ensign," General Metzov hissed at last. His eyes were glittering slits.

Miles saluted, about-faced, and marched, stiff as any ancient ramrod. Or board. Or corpse. His blood beat in his ears; his chin jerked upward. Past the corporal, who was standing at attention doing a fair imitation of a waxwork. Out the door, out the outer door. Alone at last in the Administration Building's lower corridor.

Miles cursed himself silently, then out loud. He really had to try to cultivate a more normal attitude toward senior officers. It was his bloody upbringing that lay at the root of the problem, he was sure. Too many years of tripping over herds of generals, admirals, and senior staff at Vorkosigan House, at lunch, dinner, all hours. Too much time sitting quiet as a mouse, cultivating invisibility, permitted to listen to their extremely blunt arguments and debate on a hundred topics. He saw them as they saw each other, maybe. When a normal ensign looked at his commander, he ought to see a god-like being, not a, a . . . future subordinate. New ensigns were supposed to be a subhuman species anyway.

And yet . . . *What is it about this guy Metzov?* He'd met others of the type before, of assorted political stripes. Many of them were cheerful and effective soldiers, as long as they stayed out of politics. As a party, the military conservatives had been eclipsed ever since the bloody fall of the cabal of officers responsible for the disastrous Escobar invasion, over two decades ago. But the danger of revolution from the far right, some would-be junta assembling to save the Emperor from his own government, remained quite real in Miles's father's mind, he knew.

So, was it some subtle political odor emanating from Metzov that had raised the hairs on the back of Miles's neck? Surely not. A man of real political subtlety would seek to use Miles, not abuse him. *Or are you just pissed because he stuck you on some humiliating garbage detail?* A man didn't have to be politically extreme to take a certain sadistic joy in sticking it to a representative of the Vor class. Could be Metzov had been diddled in the past himself by some arrogant Vor lord. Political, social, genetic . . . the possibilities were endless.

Miles shook the static from his head, and limped off to change to his black fatigues and locate Base Engineering. No help for it now, he was sunk deeper than his scat-cat. He'd simply have to avoid Metzov as much as possible for the next six months. Anything Ahn could do so well, Miles could surely do too.

Lieutenant Bonn prepared to probe for the scat-cat. The engineering lieutenant was a slight man, maybe twenty-eight or thirty years old, with a craggy face surfaced with pocked sallow skin, reddened by the climate. Calculating brown eyes, competent-looking hands, and a sardonic air which, Miles sensed, might be permanent and not merely directed at himself. Bonn and Miles squished about atop the bog, while two engineering techs in black insulated coveralls sat perched on their heavy hovercab, safely parked on a nearby rocky outcrop. The sun was pale, the endless wind cold and damp.

"Try about there, sir," Miles suggested, pointing, trying to estimate angles and distances in a place he had only seen at dusk. "I think you'll have to go down at least two meters."

Lieutenant Bonn gave him a joyless look, raised his long metal probe to the vertical, and shoved it into the bog. It jammed almost immediately. Miles frowned puzzlement. Surely the scat-cat couldn't have floated upward. . . .

Bonn, looking unexcited, leaned his weight into the rod and twisted. It began to grind downward.

"What did you run into?" Miles asked.

"Ice," Bonn grunted. " 'Bout three centimeters thick right now. We're standing on a layer of ice, underneath this surface crud, just like a frozen lake except it's frozen mud."

Miles stamped experimentally. Wet, but solid. Much as it had felt when he had camped on it.

Bonn, watching him, added, "The ice thickness varies with the weather. From a few centimeters to solid-to-the-bottom. Midwinter, you could park a freight shuttle on this bog. Come summer, it thins out. It can thaw from seeming-solid to liquid in a few hours, when the temperature is just right, and back again."

"I . . . think I found that out."

"Lean," ordered Bonn laconically, and Miles wrapped his hands around the rod and helped shove. He could feel the scrunch as it scraped past the ice layer. And if the temperature had dropped a little more, the night he'd sunk himself, and the mud refroze, would he have been able to punch up through the icy seal? He shuddered inwardly, and zipped his parka half-up, over his black fatigues.

"Cold?" said Bonn.

"Thinking."

"Good. Make it a habit." Bonn touched a control, and the rod's sonic probe beeped at a teeth-aching frequency. The readout displayed a bright teardrop shape a few meters over. "There it is." Bonn eyed the numbers on the readout. "It's really down there, isn't it? I'd let you dig it out with a teaspoon, ensign, but I suppose winter would set in before you were done." He sighed and stared down at Miles as though picturing the scene.

Miles could picture it, too. "Yes, sir," he said carefully.

They pulled the probe back out. Cold mud slicked the surface under their gloved hands. Bonn marked the spot and waved to his techs. "Here, boys!" They waved back, hopped down off the hovercab, and swung within. Bonn and Miles scrambled well out of the way, on to the rocks toward the weather station.

The hovercab whined into the air and positioned itself over the bog. Its heavy-duty space-rated tractor beam punched downward. Mud, plant matter, and ice geysered out in all directions with a roar. In a couple of minutes, the beam had created an oozing crater, with a glimmering pearl at the bottom. The crater's sides began to slump inward at once, but the hovercab operator narrowed and reversed his beam, and the scat-cat rose, noisily sucking free from its matrix. The limp bubble shelter dangled repellently from its chain. The hovercab set its load down delicately in the rocky area, and landed beside it.

Bonn and Miles trooped over to view the sodden remains. "You weren't *in* that bubble-shelter, were you, Ensign?" said Bonn, prodding it with his toe.

"Yes, sir. I was. Waiting for daylight. I . . . fell asleep."

"But you got out before it sank."

"Well, no. When I woke up, it was all the way under."

Bonn's crooked eyebrows rose. "How far?"

Miles's flat hand found the level of his chin.

Bonn looked startled. "How'd you get out of the suction?"

"With difficulty. And adrenaline, I think. I slipped out of my boots and pants. Which reminds me, may I take a minute and look for my boots, sir?"

Bonn waved a hand, and Miles trudged back out onto the bog, circling the ring of muck spewed from the tractor beam, keeping a safe distance from the now water-filling crater. He found one mud-coated boot, but not the other. Should he save it, on the off-chance he might have one leg amputated someday? It would probably be the wrong leg. He sighed, and climbed back up to Bonn.

Bonn frowned down at the ruined boot dangling from Miles's hand. "You could have been killed," he said in a tone of realization.

"Three times over. Smothered in the bubble shelter, trapped in the bog, or frozen waiting for rescue."

Bonn gave him a penetrating stare. "Really." He walked away from the deflated shelter, idly, as if seeking a wider view, Miles followed. When they were out of earshot of the techs, Bonn stopped and scanned the bog. Conversationally, he remarked, "I heard—unofficially—that a certain motor-pool tech named Pattas was bragging to one of his mates that he'd set you up for this. And you were too stupid to even realize you'd been had. That bragging could have been . . . not too bright, if you'd been killed."

"If I'd been killed, it wouldn't have mattered if he'd bragged or not." Miles shrugged. "What a Service investigation missed, I flat guarantee the Imperial Security investigation would have found."

"You knew you'd been set up?" Bonn studied the horizon.

"Yes."

"I'm surprised you didn't call Imperial Security in, then."

"Oh? Think about it, sir."

Bonn's gaze returned to Miles, as if taking inventory of his distasteful deformities. "You don't add up for me, Vorkosigan. Why did they let you in the Service?"

"Why d'you think?"

"Vor privilege."

"Got it in one."

"Then why are you here? Vor privilege gets sent to HQ."

"Vorbarr Sultana is lovely this time of year," said Miles agreeably. And how was his cousin Ivan enjoying it right now? "But I want ship duty."

"And you couldn't arrange it?" said Bonn skeptically.

"I was told to earn it. That's why I'm here. To prove I can handle the Service. Or . . . not. Calling in a wolf pack from ImpSec within a week of my arrival to turn the base and everyone on it inside-out looking for assassination conspiracies—where, I judge, none exist—would not advance me toward my goal. No matter how entertaining it might be." Messy charges, his word against their two words—even if Miles had pushed it to a formal investigation, with fast-penta to prove him right, the ruckus could hurt him far more in the long run than his two tormentors. No. No revenge was worth the *Prince Serg*.

"The motor pool is in Engineering's chain of command. If Imperial Security fell on it, they'd also fall on me." Bonn's brown eyes glinted.

"You're welcome to fall on anyone you please, sir. But if you have unofficial ways of receiving information, it follows you must have unofficial ways of sending it, too. And after all, you've only my word for what happened." Miles hefted his useless single boot, and heaved it back into the bog.

Thoughtfully, Bonn watched it arc and splash down in a pool of brown meltwater. "A Vor lord's word?"

"Means nothing in these degenerate days." Miles bared his teeth in a smile of sorts. "Ask anyone."

"Huh." Bonn shook his head, and started back toward the hovercab.

Next morning Miles reported to the maintenance shed for the second half of the scat-cat retrieval job, cleaning all the mud-caked equipment. The sun was bright today, and had been up for hours but Miles's body knew it was only 0500. An hour into his task he'd begun to warm up, feel better, and get into the rhythm of the thing.

At 0630, the deadpan Lieutenant Bonn arrived, and delivered two helpers unto Miles.

"Why, Corporal Olney. Tech Pattas. We meet again." Miles smiled with acid cheer. The pair exchanged an uneasy look. Miles kept his demeanor absolutely even.

He then kept everyone, starting with himself, moving briskly. The conversation seemed to automatically limit itself to brief, wary technicalities. By the time Miles had to knock off and go report to Lieutenant Ahn, the scat-cat and most of the gear had been restored to better condition than when Miles had received it.

He wished his two helpers, now driven to near-twitchiness by uncertainty, an earnest good day. Well, if they hadn't figured it out by now, they were hopeless. Miles wondered bitterly why he seemed to have so much better luck establishing rapport with bright men like Bonn. Cecil had been right, if Miles couldn't figure out how to command the dull as well, he'd never make it as a Service officer. Not at Camp Permafrost, anyway.

The following morning, the third of his official punishment seven, Miles presented himself to Sergeant Neuve. The sergeant in turn presented Miles with a scat-cat full of equipment, a disk of the related equipment manuals, and the schedule for drain and culvert maintenance for Lazkowski Base. Clearly, it was to be another learning experience. Miles wondered if General Metzov had selected this task personally. He rather thought so.

On the bright side, he had his two helpers back again. This particular civil engineering task had apparently never fallen on Olney or Pattas before either, so they had no edge of superior knowledge with which to trip Miles. They had to stop and read the manuals first, too. Miles swotted procedures and directed operations with a good cheer that edged toward manic as his helpers became glummer.

There was, after all, a certain fascination to the clever drain-cleaning devices. And excitement. Flushing pipes with high pressure could produce some surprising effects. There were chemical compounds that had some quite military properties, such as the ability to dissolve anything instantly, including human flesh. In the following three days Miles learned more about the infrastructure of Lazkowski Base than he'd ever imagined wanting to know. He'd even calculated the point where one well-placed charge could bring the entire system down, if he ever decided he wanted to destroy the place.

On the sixth day, Miles and his team were sent to clear a blocked culvert out by the grubs' practice fields. It was easy to spot. A silver sheet of water lapped the raised roadway on one side; on the other only a feeble trickle emerged to creep away down the bottom of a deep ditch.

Miles took a long telescoping pole from the back of their scat-cat, and probed down into the water's opaque surface. Nothing seemed to be blocking the flooded end of the culvert. Whatever it was must be jammed farther in. Joy. He handed the pole back to Pattas and wandered over to the other side of the road, and stared down into the ditch. The culvert, he noted, was something over half a meter in diameter. "Give me a light," he said to Olney.

He shucked his parka and tossed it into the scat-cat, and scrambled down into the ditch. He aimed his light into the aperture. The culvert evidently curved slightly; he couldn't see a damned thing. He sighed, considering the relative width of Olney's shoulders, Pattas's, and his own.

Could there be anything further from ship duty than this? The closest he'd come to anything of a sort was spelunking in the Dendarii Mountains. Earth and water, versus fire and air. He seemed to be building up a helluva supply of yin, the balancing yang to come had better be stupendous.

He gripped the light tighter, dropped to hands and knees, and shinnied into the drain.

The icy water soaked the trouser knees of his black fatigues. The effect was numbing. Water leaked around the top of one of his gloves. It felt like a knife blade on his wrist.

Miles meditated briefly on Olney and Pattas. They had developed a cool, reasonably efficient working relationship over the last few days, based, Miles had no illusions, on a fear of God instilled in the two men by Miles's good angel Lieutenant Bonn. How did Bonn accomplish that quiet authority, anyway? He had to figure that one out. Bonn was good at his job, for starters, but what else?

Miles scraped round the curve, shone his light on the clot, and recoiled, swearing. He paused a moment to regain control of his breath, examined the blockage more closely, and backed out.

He stood up in the bottom of the ditch, straightening his spine vertebra by creaking vertebra. Corporal Olney stuck his head over the road's railing, above. "What's in there, ensign?"

Miles grinned up at him, still catching his breath. "Pair of boots."

"That's all?" said Olney.

"Their owner is still wearing 'em."

Miles called the base surgeon on the scat-cat's comm link, urgently requesting his presence with forensic kit, body bag, and medical transport. Miles and his crew then blocked the upper end of the drain with a plastic signboard forcibly borrowed from the empty practice field beyond. Now so thoroughly wet and cold that it made no difference, Miles crawled back into the culvert to attach a rope to the anonymous booted ankles. When he emerged, the surgeon and his corpsman had arrived.

The surgeon, a big, balding man, peered dubiously into the drainpipe. "What could you see in there, Ensign? What happened?"

"I can't see anything from this end but legs, sir," Miles reported. "He's got himself wedged in there but good. Drain crud up above him, I'd guess. We'll have to see what spills out with him."

"What the hell was he doing in there?" The surgeon scratched his freckled scalp.

Miles spread his hands. "Seems a peculiar way to commit suicide. Slow and chancy, as far as drowning yourself goes."

The surgeon raised his eyebrows in agreement. Miles and the surgeon had to lend their weight on the rope to Olney, Pattas, and the corpsman before the stiff form wedged in the culvert began to scrape free.

"He's *stuck*," observed the corpsman, grunting. The body jerked out at last with a gush of dirty water. Pattas and Olney stared from a distance; Miles glued himself to the surgeon's shoulder. The corpse, dressed in sodden black fatigues, was waxy and blue. His collar tabs and the contents of his pockets identified him as a private from Supply. His body bore no obvious wounds, but for bruised shoulders and scraped hands.

The surgeon spoke clipped, negative preliminaries into his recorder. No broken bones, no nerve disruptor blisters. Preliminary hypothesis, death from drowning or hypothermia or both, within the last twelve hours. He flipped off his recorder and added over his shoulder, "I'll be able to tell for sure when we get him laid out back at the infirmary."

"Does this sort of thing happen often around here?" Miles inquired mildly.

The surgeon shot him a sour look. "I slab a few idiots every year. What d'you expect, when you put five thousand kids between the ages of eighteen and twenty together on an island and tell 'em to go play war? I admit, this one seems to have discovered a completely new method of slabbing himself. I guess you never see it all."

"You think he did it to himself, then?" True, it would be real tricky to kill a man and *then* stuff him in there.

The surgeon wandered over to the culvert and squatted, and stared into it. "So it would seem. Ah, would you take one more look in there, ensign, just in case?"

"Very well, sir." Miles hoped it was the last trip. He'd never have guessed drain cleaning would turn out to be so . . . thrilling. He slithered all the way under the road to the leaky board, checking every centimeter, but found only the dead man's dropped hand light. So. The private had evidently entered the pipe on purpose. With intent. What intent? Why go culvert-crawling in the middle of the night in the middle of a heavy rainstorm? Miles skinned back out and turned the light over to the surgeon.

Miles helped the corpsman and surgeon bag and load the body, then had Olney and Pattas raise the blocking board and return it to its original location. Brown water gushed, roaring, from the bottom end of the culvert and roiled away down the ditch. The surgeon paused with Miles, leaning on the road railing and watching the water level drop in the little lake.

"Think there might be another one at the bottom?" Miles inquired morbidly.

"This guy was the only one listed as missing on the morning report," the surgeon replied, "so probably not." He didn't look like he was willing to bet on it, though.

The only thing that did turn up, as the water level fell, was the private's soggy parka. He'd clearly tossed it over the railing before entering the culvert, from which it had fallen or blown into the water. The surgeon took it away with him.

"You're pretty cool about that," Pattas noted, as Miles turned away from the back of the medical transport and the surgeon and corpsman drove off.

Pattas was not that much older than Miles himself. "Haven't you ever had to handle a corpse?"

"No. You?"

"Yes."

"Where?"

Miles hesitated. Events of three years ago flickered through his memory. The brief months he'd been accidentally caught in desperate combat, far from home, was not a secret to be mentioned, or even hinted at, here. But it had surely taught him the difference between "practice" and "real," between war and war games, and that death had subtler vectors than direct touch. "Before," Miles said dampingly. "Couple of times."

Pattas shrugged, veering off. "Well," he allowed grudgingly over his shoulder, "at least you're not afraid to get your hands dirty. Sir."

Miles's brows crooked, bemused. *No. That's not what I'm afraid of.*

Miles marked the drain "cleared" on his report panel, turned the scat-cat, their equipment, and a very subdued Olney and Pattas back in to Sergeant Neuve in Maintenance, and headed for the officers' barracks. He'd never wanted a hot shower more in his entire life.

He was squelching down the corridor toward his quarters, shivering, when another officer stuck his head out a door. "Ah, Ensign Vorkosigan?"

"Yes?"

"You got a vid call a while ago. I encoded the return for you."

"Call?" Miles stopped. "Where from?"

"Vorbarr Sultana."

Miles felt a chill in his belly. Some emergency at home? "Thanks." He reversed direction, and beelined for the end of the corridor and the vidconsole booth that the officers on this level shared.

He slid damply into the seat and punched up the message. The number was not one he recognized. He entered it, and his charge code, and waited. It chimed several times, then the vidplate hissed to life. His cousin Ivan's handsome face materialized over it, and grinned at him.

"Ah, Miles. There you are."

"Ivan! Where the devil are you? What is this?"

"Oh, I'm at home. And that doesn't mean my mother's. I thought you might like to see my new flat."

Miles had the vague, disoriented sensation that he'd somehow tapped a line into some parallel universe, or alternate astral plane. Vorbarr Sultana, yes. He'd lived in the capital himself, in a previous incarnation. Eons ago.

Ivan lifted his vid pick-up, and aimed it around, dizzyingly. "It's fully furnished. I took over the lease from an Ops captain who was being transferred to Komarr. A real bargain. I just got moved in yesterday. Can you see the balcony?"

Miles could see the balcony, drenched in late afternoon sunlight the color of warm honey. The Vorbarr Sultana skyline rose like a fairytale city, swimming in the summer haze beyond. Scarlet flowers swarmed over the railing, so red in the level light they almost hurt his eyes. Miles felt like drooling into his shirt pocket, or bursting into tears. "Nice flowers," he choked.

"Yeah, m'girlfriend brought 'em."

"Girlfriend?" Ah yes, human beings had come in two sexes, once upon a time. One smelled much better than the other. Much. "Which one?"

"Tatya."

"Have I met her?" Miles struggled to remember.

"Naw, she's new."

Ivan stopped waving the vid pick-up around, and reappeared over the vidplate. Miles's exacerbated senses settled slightly. "So how's the weather up there?" Ivan peered at him more closely. "Are you wet? What have you been doing?"

"Forensic . . . plumbing," Miles offered after a pause.

"What?" Ivan's brow wrinkled.

"Never mind." Miles sneezed. "Look, I'm glad to see a familiar face and all that," he was, actually, a painful, strange gladness, "but I'm in the middle of my duty day, here."

"I got off-shift a couple of hours ago," Ivan remarked. "I'm taking Tatya out for dinner in a bit. You just caught me. So just tell me quick, how's life in the infantry?"

"Oh, great. Lazkowski Base is the real thing, y'know." Miles did not define what real thing. "Not a . . . warehouse for excess Vor lordlings like Imperial Headquarters."

"I do my job!" said Ivan, sounding slightly stung. "Actually, you'd like my job. We process information. It's amazing, all the stuff Ops accesses in a day's time. It's like being on top of the world. It would be just your speed."

"Funny. I've thought that Lazkowski Base would be just yours, Ivan. Suppose they could have got our orders reversed?"

Ivan tapped the side of his nose and sniggered. "I wouldn't tell." His humor sobered in a glint of real concern. "You, ah, take care of yourself up there, eh? You really don't look so good."

"I've had an unusual morning. If you'd sod off, I could go get a shower."

"Oh, right. Well, take care."

"Enjoy your dinner."

"Right-oh. 'Bye."

Voices from another universe. At that, Vorbarr Sultana was only a couple of hours away by sub-orbital flight. In theory. Miles was obscurely comforted, to be reminded that the whole planet hadn't shrunk to the lead-grey horizons of Kyril Island, even if his part of it seemed to have.

Miles found it difficult to concentrate on the weather, the rest of that day. Fortunately his superior didn't much notice. Since the scat-cat sinking Ahn had tended to maintain a guilty, nervous silence around Miles except when directly prodded for specific information. When his duty-day ended Miles headed straight for the infirmary.

The surgeon was still working, or at least sitting, at his desk console when Miles poked his head around the doorframe. "Good evening, sir."

The surgeon glanced up. "Yes, Ensign? What is it?"

Miles took this as sufficient invitation despite the unencouraging tone of voice, and slipped within. "I was wondering what you'd found out about that fellow we pulled from the culvert this morning."

The surgeon spread his hand, palm up. "Not that much to find out. His ID checked. He died of drowning. All the physical and metabolic evidence—stress, hypothermia, the hematomas—are consistent with his being stuck in there for a bit less than half an hour before death. I've ruled it death by misadventure."

"Yes, but why?"

"Why?" The surgeon's eyebrows rose. "He slabbed himself, you'll have to ask him, eh?"

"Don't you want to find out?"

"To what purpose?"

"Well . . . to know, I guess. To be sure you're right."

The surgeon gave him a dry stare. "I'm not questioning your medical findings, sir," Miles added hastily. "But it was just so damn weird. Aren't you curious?"

"Not any more," said the surgeon. "I'm satisfied it wasn't suicide or foul play, so whatever the details, it comes down to death from stupidity in the end, doesn't it?"

Miles wondered if that would have been the surgeon's final epitaph on him, if he'd sunk himself with the scat-cat. "I suppose so, sir."

Standing outside the infirmary afterward in the damp wind, Miles hesitated. The corpse, after all, was not Miles's personal property. Not a case of finders-keepers. He'd turned the situation over to the proper authority. It was out of his hands now. And yet . . .

There were still several hours of daylight left. Miles was having trouble sleeping anyway, in these almost-endless days. He returned to his quarters, pulled on sweat pants and shirt and running shoes, and went jogging.

The road was lonely, out by the empty practice fields. The sun crawled crabwise toward the horizon. Miles broke from a jog back to a walk, then to a slower walk. His leg-braces chafed, beneath his pants. One of these days very soon he would take the time to get the brittle long bones in his legs replaced with synthetics. At that, elective surgery might be a quasi-legitimate way to lever himself off Kyril Island, if things got too desperate before his six months were up. It seemed like cheating, though.

He looked around, trying to imagine his present surroundings in the dark and heavy rain. If he had been the private, slogging along this road about midnight, what would he have seen? What could possibly have attracted the man's attention to the ditch? Why the hell had he come out here in the middle of the night in the first place? This road wasn't on the way to anything but an obstacle course and a firing range.

There was the ditch . . . no, his ditch was the next one, a little farther on. Four culverts pierced the raised roadway along this half-kilometer straight stretch. Miles found the correct ditch and leaned on the railing, staring down at the now-sluggish trickle of drain water. There was nothing attractive about it now, that was certain. Why, why, why . . . ?

Miles sloped along up the high side of the road, examining the road surface, the railing, the sodden brown bracken beyond. He came to the curve and turned back, studying the opposite side. He arrived back at the first ditch, on the base-ward end of the straight stretch, without discovering any view of charm or interest.

Miles perched on the railing and meditated. All right, time to try a little logic. What overwhelming emotion had led the private to wedge himself in the drain, despite the obvious danger? Rage? What had he been pursuing? Fear? What could have been pursuing him? Error? Miles knew all about error. What if the man had picked the wrong culvert . . . ?

Impulsively, Miles slithered down into the first ditch. Either the man had been methodically working his way through all the culverts—if so, had he been working from the base out, or from the practice fields back?—or else he had missed his intended target in the dark and rain and got into the wrong one. Miles would give them all a crawl-through if he had to, but he preferred to be right the first time. Even if there wasn't anybody watching. This culvert was slightly wider in diameter than the second, lethal one. Miles pulled his hand light from his belt, ducked within, and began examining it centimeter by centimeter.

"Ah," he breathed in satisfaction, midway beneath the road. There was his prize, stuck to the upper side of the culvert's arc with sagging tape. A package, wrapped in waterproof plastic. How *interesting*. He slithered out and sat in the mouth of the culvert, careless of the damp but carefully out of view from the road above.

He placed the packet on his lap and studied it with pleasurable anticipation, as if it had been a birthday present. Could it be drugs, contraband, classified documents, criminal cash? Personally, Miles hoped for classified documents, though it was hard to imagine anyone classifying anything on Kyril Island except maybe the efficiency reports. Drugs would be all right, but a spy ring would be just *wonderful*. He'd be a Security hero—his mind raced ahead, already plotting the next move in his covert investigation. Following the dead man's trail through subtle clues to some ringleader, who knew how high up? The dramatic arrests, maybe a commendation from Simon Illyan himself. . . . The package was lumpy, but crackled slightly—plastic flimsies?

Heart hammering, he eased it open—and slumped in stunned disappointment. A pained breath, half laugh, half moan, puffed from his lips.

Pastries. A couple of dozen lisettes, a kind of miniature popover glazed and stuffed with candied fruit, made, traditionally, for the midsummer day celebration. Month-and-a-half-old stale pastries. What a cause to die for. . . .

Miles's imagination, fueled by knowledge of barracks life, sketched in the rest readily enough. The private had received this package from some sweetheart, mother, sister, and sought to pro tect it from ravenous mates, who would have wolfed it all down in seconds. Perhaps the man, starved for home, had been rationing them out to himself morsel by morsel in a lingering masochistic ritual, pleasure and pain mixed with each bite. Or maybe he'd just been saving them for some special occasion.

Then came the two days of unusually heavy rain, and the man had begun to fear for his secret treasure's, ah, liquidity margin. He'd come out to rescue his cache, missed the first ditch in the dark, gone at the second in desperate determination as the waters rose, realized his mistake too late. . . .

Sad. A little sickening. But not *useful.* Miles sighed, bundled the lisettes back up, and trotted off with the package under his arm, back to the base to turn it over to the surgeon.

The surgeon's only comment, when Miles caught up with him and explained his findings, was "Yep. Death from stupidity, all right." Absently, he bit into a lisette and sniffed.

Miles's time on maintenance detail ended the next day without his finding anything in the sewers of greater interest than the drowned man. It was probably just as well. The following day Ahn's office corporal arrived back from his long leave. Miles discovered that the corporal, who'd been working the weather office for some two years, was a ready reservoir of the greater part of the information Miles had spent the last two weeks busting his brains to learn. He didn't have Ahn's nose, though.

Ahn actually left Camp Permafrost sober, walking up the transport's ramp under his own power. Miles went to the shuttle pad to see him off, not certain if he was glad or sorry to see the weatherman go. Ahn looked happy, though, his lugubrious face almost illuminated.

"So where are you headed, once you turn in your uniforms?" Miles asked him.

"The equator."

"Ah? Where on the equator?"

"*Anywhere* on the equator," Ahn replied with fervor.

Miles trusted he'd at least pick a spot with a suitable land mass under it.

Ahn hesitated on the ramp, looking down at Miles. "Watch out for Metzov," he advised at last.

This warning seemed remarkably late, not to mention maddeningly vague. Miles gave Ahn an exasperated look, up from under his raised eyebrows. "I doubt I'll be much featured on his social calendar."

Ahn shifted uncomfortably. "That's not what I meant."

"What do you mean?"

"Well . . . I don't know. I once saw . . ."

"What?"

Ahn shook his head. "Nothing. It was a long time ago. A lot of crazy things were happening, at the height of the Komarr revolt. But it's better that you should stay out of his way."

"I've had to deal with old martinets before."

"Oh, he's not exactly a martinet. But he's got a streak of . . . he can be a funny kind of dangerous. Don't ever really threaten him, huh?"

"Me, threaten Metzov?" Miles's face screwed up in bafflement. Maybe Ahn wasn't as sober as he smelled after all. "Come on, he can't be that bad, or they'd never put him in charge of trainees."

"He doesn't command the grubs. They have their own hierarchy—comes in with 'em—the instructors report to their own commander. Metzov's just in charge of the base's permanent physical plant." Ahn paused. "You're a pushy little sod, Vorkosigan. Just don't . . . ever push him to the edge, or you'll be sorry. And that's all I'm going to say." Ahn shut his mouth determinedly, and headed up the ramp.

I'm already sorry, Miles thought of calling after him. Well, his punishment week was over now. Perhaps Metzov had meant the labor detail to humiliate Miles, but actually it had been quite interesting. Sinking his scat-cat, now, *that* had been humiliating. That he had done to *himself.* Miles waved one last time to Ahn as he disappeared into the transport shuttle, shrugged, and headed back across the tarmac toward the now-familiar admin building.

It took fully a couple of minutes, after Miles's corporal had left the weather office for lunch, for Miles to yield to the temptation to scratch the itch Ahn had planted in his mind, and punch up Metzov's public record on the comconsole. The mere listing of the base commander's dates, assignments, and promotions was not terribly informative, though a little knowledge of history filled in between the lines.

Metzov had entered the Service some thirty-five years ago. His most rapid promotions had occurred, not surprisingly, during the conqest of Komarr about twenty-five years ago. He had somehow managed to end up on the correct side during Vordarian's Pretendership two decades past—picking the wrong side in that civil affray would have been Miles's first guess why such an apparently competent officer had ended up marking out his later years on ice on Kyril Island. But the dead halt to Metzov's career seemed to come during the Komarr Revolt, some sixteen years back now. No hint in this file as to why, but for a cross-reference to another file. An Imperial Security code, Miles recognized. Dead end there.

Or maybe not. Lips compressed thoughtfully, Miles punched through another code on his comconsole.

"Operations, Commodore Jollif's office," Ivan began formally as his face materialized over the comconsole vid plate, then, "Oh, hello, Miles. What's up?"

"I'm doing a little research. Thought you might help me out."

"I should have known you wouldn't call me at HQ just to be sociable. So what d'you want?"

"Ah . . . do you have the office to yourself, just at present?"

"Yeah, the old man's stuck in committee." Ivan's eyes narrowed in suspicion. "Why do you ask?"

Miles relaxed slightly. "I want you to pull a file for me." He reeled off the code-string.

Ivan's hand started to tap it out, then stopped. "Are you crazy? That's an Imperial Security file. No can do!"

"Of course you can, you're right there, aren't you?"

Ivan shook his head smugly. "Not any more. The whole ImpSec file system's been made super-secure. You can't transfer data out of it except through a coded filter-cable, which you must physically attach. Which I would have to sign for. Which I would have to explain why I wanted it and produce authorization. You got an authorization for this? Ha. I thought not."

Miles frowned frustration. "Surely you can call it up on the internal system."

"On the internal system, yes. What I can't do is connect the internal system to any external system for a data dump. So you're out of luck."

"You got an internal system comconsole in that office?"

"Sure."

"So," said Miles impatiently, "call up the file, turn your desk around, and let the two vids talk to each other. You can do that, can't you?"

Ivan scratched his head. "Would that work?"

"Try it!" Miles drummed his fingers while Ivan dragged his desk around and fiddled with focus. The signal was degraded but readable. "There, I thought so. Scroll it up for me, would you?"

Fascinating, utterly fascinating. The file was a collection of secret reports from an ImpSec investigation into the mysterious death of a prisoner in Metzov's charge, a Komarran rebel who had killed his guard and had himself been killed while attempting to escape. When ImpSec had demanded the Komarran's body for an autopsy, Metzov had turned over cremated ashes and an apology; if only he had been told a few hours earlier the body was wanted, etc. The investigating officer hinted at charges of illegal torture—perhaps in revenge for the death of the guard?—but was unable to amass enough evidence to obtain authorization to fast-penta the Barrayaran witnesses, including a certain Tech-ensign Ahn. The investigating officer had lodged a formal protest of his superior officer's decision to close the case, and there it ended. Apparently. If there was any more to the story it existed only in Simon Illyan's remarkable head, a secret file Miles was not about to attempt to access. Or in his father's—Admiral Vorkosigan was obsessed with Komarr, his "perfect conquest" that had gone so wrong. And Metzov's career had stopped, literally, cold.

"Miles," Ivan interrupted for the fourth time, "I really don't think we should be doing this. This is slit-your-throat-before-reading stuff, here."

"If we shouldn't do it, we shouldn't be able to do it. You'd still have to have the cable for flash-downloading. No real spy would be dumb enough to sit there inside Imperial HQ by the hour and scroll stuff through by hand, waiting to be caught and shot."

"That does it." Ivan killed the Security file with a swat of his hand. The vid image wavered wildly as Ivan dragged his desk back around, followed by scrubbing noises as he frantically rubbed out the tracks in his carpet with his boot. "I didn't do this, you hear?"

"I didn't mean you. We're not spies." Miles subsided glumly. "Still . . . I suppose somebody ought to tell Illyan about the little hole they overlooked in his Security arrangements."

"Not me!"

"Why not you? Put it in as a brilliant theoretical suggestion. Maybe you'll earn a commendation. Don't tell 'em we actually did it, of course. Or maybe we were just testing your theory, eh?"

"You," said Ivan severely, "are career-poison. Never darken my vidplate again. Except at home, of course."

Miles grinned, and permitted his cousin to escape. He sat a while in the office, watching the colorful weather holos flicker and change, and thinking about his base commander, and the kinds of accidents that could happen to defiant prisoners.

Well, it had all been very long ago. Metzov himself would probably be retiring in another five years, with his status as a double-twenty-years-man and a pension, to merge into the population of unpleasant old men. Not so much a problem to be solved as to be outlived, at least by Miles. His ultimate purpose at Lazkowski Base, Miles reminded himself, was to escape Lazkowski Base, silently as smoke. Metzov would be left behind in time.

In the next weeks Miles settled into a tolerable routine. For one thing, the grubs arrived. All five thousand of them. Miles's status rose on their shoulders, to that of almost-human. Lazkowski Base suffered its first real snow of the season as the days shortened, plus a mild wah-wah lasting half a day, both of which Miles managed to predict accurately in advance.

Even more happily, Miles was completely displaced as the most famous idiot on the island (an unwelcome notoriety earned by the scat-cat sinking) by a group of grubs who managed one night to set their barracks on fire while lighting fart-flares. Miles's strategic suggestion at the officers' fire-safety meeting next day that they tackle the problem with a logistical assault on the enemy's fuel supply, i.e., eliminate red bean stew from the menu, was shot down with one icy glower from General Metzov, though in the hallway later, an earnest captain from Ordnance stopped Miles to thank him for trying.

So much for the glamour of the Imperial Service. Miles took to spending long hours alone in the weather office, studying chaos theory, his readouts, and the walls. Three months down, three to go. It was getting darker.

Miles was out of bed and half dressed before it penetrated his sleep-stunned brain that the galvanizing klaxon was not the wah-wah warning. He paused with a boot in his hand. Not fire or enemy attack, either. Not his department, then, whatever it was. The rhythmic blatting stopped. They were right, silence was golden.

He checked the glowing digital clock. It claimed mid-evening. He'd only been asleep about two hours, having fallen into bed exhausted after a long trip up-island in a snowstorm to repair wind damage to Weather Station Eleven. The comm link by his bed was not blinking its red call light to inform him of any surprise duties he must carry out. He could go back to bed.

Silence was *baffling*.

He pulled on the second boot and stuck his head out his door. A couple of other officers had done the same, and were speculating to each other on the cause of the alarm. Lieutenant Bonn emerged from his quarters and strode down the hall, jerking on his parka. His face looked strained, half worry, half annoyance.

Miles grabbed his own parka and galloped after him. "You need a hand, Lieutenant?"

Bonn glanced down at him, and pursed his lips. "I might," he allowed.

Miles fell in beside him, secretly pleased by Bonn's implicit judgment that he might in fact be useful. "So what's up?"

"Some sort of accident in a toxic stores bunker. If it's the one I think, we could have a real problem."

They exited the double-doored heat-retaining vestibule from the officers' quarters into a night gone crystal cold. Fine snow squeaked under Miles's boots and swept along the ground in a faint east wind. The brightest stars overhead held their own against the base's lights. The two men slid into Bonn's scat-cat, their breath smoking until the canopy-defrost cut in. Bonn headed west out of the base at high acceleration.

A few kilometers past the last practice fields, a row of turf-topped barrows hunched in the snow. A cluster of vehicles were parked at the end of one bunker—a couple of scat-cats, including the one belonging to the base fire marshal, and medical transport. Handlights moved among them. Bonn slewed in and pulled up, and popped his door. Miles followed him, crunching rapidly across the packed ice.

The surgeon was directing a pair of corpsmen, who were loading a foil-blanketed shape and a second coverall-clad soldier who shivered and coughed onto the med transport. "All of you, put everything you're wearing into the destruct bin when you hit the door," he called after them. "Blankets, bedding, splints, everything. Full decontamination showers for you all before you even start to worry about that broken leg of his. The pain-killer will hold him through it, and if it doesn't, ignore the screams and keep scrubbing. I'll be right behind you." The surgeon shuddered, turning away, whistling dismay through his teeth.

Bonn headed for the bunker door. "Don't open that!" the surgeon and the fire marshal called together. "There's nobody left inside," the surgeon added. "All evacuated now."

"What exactly happened?" Bonn scrubbed with a gloved hand at the frosted window set in the door, in an effort to see inside.

"Couple of guys were moving stores, to make room for a new shipment coming in tomorrow," the fire marshal, a lieutenant named Yaski, filled him in rapidly. "They dumped their loader over, one got pinned underneath with a broken leg."

"That . . . took ingenuity," said Bonn, obviously picturing the mechanics of the loader in his mind.

"They had to have been horsing around," said the surgeon impatiently. "But that's not the worst of it. They took several barrels of fetaine over with them. And at least two broke open. The stuff's all over the place in there. We've sealed the bunker as best we could. Clean-up," the surgeon exhaled, "is your problem. I'm gone." He looked like he wanted to crawl out of his own skin, as well as his clothes. He waved, making quickly for his scat-cat to follow his corpsmen and their patients through medical decontamination.

"Fetaine!" Miles exclaimed in startlement. Bonn had retreated hastily from the door. Fetaine was a mutagenic poison invented as a terror weapon but never, so far as Miles knew, used in combat. "I thought that stuff was obsolete. Off the menu." His academy course in Chemicals and Biologicals had barely mentioned it.

"It is obsolete," said Bonn grimly. "They haven't made any in twenty years. For all I know this is the last stockpile on Barrayar. Dammit, those storage barrels shouldn't have broken open even if you'd dropped 'em out a shuttle."

"Those storage barrels are at least twenty years old, then," the marshal pointed out. "Corrosion?"

"In that case," Bonn craned his neck, "what about the rest of them?"

"Exactly," nodded Yaski.

"Isn't fetaine destroyed by heat?" Miles asked nervously, checking to make sure they were standing around discussing this *up*wind of the bunker. "Chemically dissociated into harmless components, I heard."

"Well, not exactly harmless," said Lieutenant Yaski. "But at least they don't unravel all the DNA in your balls."

"Are there any explosives stored in there, Lieutenant Bonn?" Miles asked.

"No, only the fetaine."

"If you tossed a couple of plasma mines through the door, would the fetaine all be chemically cracked before the roof melted in?"

"You wouldn't want the roof to melt in. Or the floor. If that stuff ever got loose in the permafrost . . . But if you set the mines on slow heat release, and threw a few kilos of neutral plas-seal pellets in with 'em, the bunker might be self-sealing." Bonn's lips moved in silent calculation. ". . . Yeah, that'd work. In fact, that could be the safest way to deal with that crap. Particularly if the rest of the barrels are starting to lose integrity too."

"Depending on which way the wind is blowing," put in Lieutenant Yaski, looking back toward the base and then at Miles.

"We're expecting a light east wind with dropping temperatures till about 0700 tomorrow morning," Miles answered his look. "Then it'll shift around to the north and blow harder. Potential wah-wah conditions starting around 1800 tomorrow night."

"If we're going to do it that way, we'd better do it tonight, then," said Yaski.

"All right," said Bonn decisively. "I'll round up my crew, you round up yours. I'll pull the plans for the bunker, calculate the charges' release-rate, and meet you and the ordnance chief in Admin in an hour."

Bonn posted the fire marshal's sergeant as guard to keep everyone well away from the bunker. An unenviable duty, but not unbearable in present conditions, and the guard could retreat inside his scat-cat when the temperature dropped, toward midnight. Miles rode back with Bonn to the base Administration building to double-check his promises about wind direction at the weather office.

Miles ran the latest data through the weather computers, that he might present Bonn with the most refined possible update on predicted wind vectors over the next 26.7 hour Barrayaran day. But before he had the printout in his hand, he saw Bonn and Yaski out the window, down below, hurrying away from the Admin building into the dark. Perhaps they were meeting with the ordnance chief elsewhere? Miles considered chasing after them, but the new prediction was not significantly different from the older one. Did he really need to go watch them cauterize the poison dump? It could be interesting—educational. On the other hand, he had no real function there now. As his parents' only child—as the father, perhaps, of some future Count Vorkosigan it was arguable if he even had the right to expose himself to such a vile mutagenic hazard for mere curiosity. There seemed no immediate danger to the base—till the wind shifted, anyway. Or was cowardice masquerading as logic? Prudence was a virtue, he had heard.

Now thoroughly awake, and too rattled to even imagine re-capturing sleep, he pottered around the weather office, and caught up on all the routine files he had set aside that morning in favor of the repairs junket. An hour of steady plugging finished off everything that even remotely looked like work. When he found himself compulsively dusting equipment and shelves, he decided it was time to go back to bed, sleep or no sleep. But a shifting light from the window caught his eye, a scat-cat pulling up out front.

Ah, Bonn and Yaski, back. Already? That had been fast, or hadn't they started yet? Miles tore off the plastic flimsy with the new wind readout and headed downstairs to the Base Engineering office at the end of the corridor.

Bonn's office was dark. But light spilled into the corridor from the Base Commander's office. Light, and angry voices rising and falling. Clutching the flimsy; Miles approached.

The door was open to the inner office. Metzov sat at his desk console, one clenched fist resting on the flickering colored surface. Bonn and Yaski stood tensely before him. Miles rattled the flimsy cautiously to announce his presence.

Yaski's head swiveled around, and his gaze caught Miles. "Send Vorkosigan, he's a mutant already, isn't he?"

Miles gave a vaguely directed salute and said immediately, "Pardon me, sir, but no, I'm not. My last encounter with a military poison did teratogenic damage, not genetic. My future children should be as healthy as the next man's. Ah, send me where, sir?"

Metzov glowered across at Miles, but did not pursue Yaski's unsettling suggestion. Miles handed the flimsy wordlessly to Bonn, who glanced at it, grimaced, and stuffed it savagely into his trouser pocket.

"Of *course* I intended them to wear protective gear," continued Metzov to Bonn in irritation. "I'm not mad."

"I understood that, sir. But the men refuse to enter the bunker even with contamination gear," Bonn reported in a flat, steady voice. "I can't blame them. The standard precautions are inadequate for fetaine, in my estimation. The stuff has an incredibly high penetration value, for its molecular weight. Goes right through permeables."

"You can't *blame* them?" repeated Metzov in astonishment. "Lieutenant, you gave an order. Or you were supposed to."

"I did, sir, but—"

"But—you let them sense your own indecision. Your weakness. Dammit, when you give an order you have to give it, not dance around it."

"Why do we have to save this stuff?" said Yaski plaintively.

"We've been over that. It's our charge," Metzov grunted at him. "Our orders. You can't ask a man to give an obedience you don't give yourself."

What, blind? "Surely Research still has the recipe," Miles put in, feeling he was at last getting the alarming drift of this argument. "They can mix up more if they really want it. Fresh."

"Shut up, Vorkosigan," Bonn growled desperately out of the corner of his mouth, as General Metzov snapped, "Open your lip tonight with one more sample of your humor, Ensign, and I'll put you on charges."

Miles's lips closed over his teeth in a tight glassy smile. Subordination. The *Prince Serg*, he reminded himself. Metzov could go drink the fetaine, for all Miles cared, and it would be no skin off his nose. His clean nose, remember?

"Have you never heard of the fine old battlefield practice of shooting the man who disobeys your order, Lieutenant?" Metzov went on to Bonn.

"I . . . don't think I can make that threat, sir," said Bonn stiffly.

And besides, thought Miles, *we're not on a battlefield. Are we?*

"Techs!" said Metzov in a tone of disgust. "I didn't say threaten, I said shoot. Make one example, the rest will fall in line."

Miles decided he didn't much care for Metzov's brand of humor, either. Or was the general speaking literally?

"Sir, fetaine is a violent mutagen," said Bonn doggedly. "I'm not at all sure the rest *would* fall into line, no matter what the threat. It's a pretty unreasonable topic. I'm . . . a little unreasonable about it myself."

"So I see." Metzov stared at him coldly. His glare passed on to Yaski, who swallowed and stood straighter, his spine offering no concession. Miles tried to cultivate invisibility.

"If you're going to go on pretending to be military officers, you techs need a lesson in how to extract obedience from your men," Metzov decided. "Both of you go and assemble your crews in front of Admin in twenty minutes. We're going to have a little old-fashioned discipline parade."

"You're not—seriously thinking of shooting anyone, are you?" said Lieutenant Yaski in alarm.

Metzov smiled sourly. "I doubt I'll have to." He regarded Miles. "What's the outside temperature right now, Weather Officer?"

"Five degrees of frost, sir," replied Miles, careful now to speak only when spoken to. "And the wind?"

"Winds from the east at nine kilometers per hour, sir."

"Very good." Metzov's eye gleamed wolfishly. "Dismissed, gentlemen. See if you can carry out your orders, this time."

General Metzov stood, heavily gloved and parka-bundled, beside the empty metal banner pole in front of Admin, and stared down the half-lit road. Looking for what?

Miles wondered. It was pushing midnight now. Yaski and Bonn were lining up their tech crews in parade array, some fifteen thermal-coveralled and parka-clad men.

Miles shivered, and not just from the cold. Metzov's seamed face looked angry. And tired. And old. And scary. He reminded Miles a bit of his grandfather on a bad day. Though Metzov was in fact younger than Miles's father; Miles had been a child of his father's middle-age, some generational skew there. His grandfather, the old General Count Piotr himself, had sometimes seemed a refugee from another century. Now, the really old-fashioned discipline parades had involved lead-lined rubber hoses. How far back in Barrayaran history was Metzov's mind rooted?

Metzov smiled, a gloss over rage, and turned his head at a movement down the road. In a horribly cordial voice he confided to Miles, "You know, Ensign, there was a secret behind that carefully-cultivated inter-service rivalry they had back on Old Earth. In the event of a mutiny you could always persuade the army to shoot the navy, or vice versa, when they could no longer discipline themselves. A hidden disadvantage to a combined Service like ours."

"Mutiny!" said Miles, startled out of his resolve to speak only when spoken to. "I thought the issue was poison exposure."

"It *was*. Unfortunately, due to Bonn's mishandling, it's now a matter of principle." A muscle jumped in Metzov's jaw. "It had to happen sometime, in the New Service. The Soft Service."

Typical Old Service talk, that, old men bullshitting each other about how tough they'd had it in the old days. "Principle, sir, what principle? It's *waste disposal*," Miles choked.

"It's a mass refusal to obey a direct order, Ensign. Mutiny by any barracks-lawyer's definition. Fortunately, this sort of thing is easy to dislocate, if you move quickly, while it's still small and confused."

The motion down the road resolved itself into a platoon of grubs in their winter-white camouflage gear, marching under the direction of a Base sergeant. Miles recognized the sergeant as part of Metzov's personal power-net, an old veteran who'd served under Metzov as far back as the Komarr Revolt, and who had moved on with his master.

The grubs, Miles saw, had been armed with lethal nerve-disruptors, which were purely anti-personnel hand weapons. For all the time they spent learning about such things, the opportunity for even advanced trainees such as these to lay hands on fully powered deadly weapons was rare, and Miles could sense their nervous excitement from here.

The sergeant lined the grubs up in a cross-fire array around the stiff-standing techs, and barked an order. They presented their weapons, and aimed them, the silver bell-muzzles gleaming in the scattered light from the Admin building. A twitchy ripple ran through Bonn's men. Bonn's face was ghastly white, his eyes glittering like jet.

"Strip," Metzov ordered through set teeth.

Disbelief, confusion; only one or two of the techs grasped what was being demanded, and began to undress. The others, with many uncertain glances around, belatedly followed suit.

"When you are again ready to obey your orders." Metzov continued in a parade-pitched voice that carried to every man, "you may dress and go to work. It's up to you." He stepped back, nodded to his sergeant, and took up a pose of parade rest. "That'll cool 'em off," he muttered to himself, barely loud enough for Miles to catch. Metzov looked like he fully expected to be out here no more than five minutes; he looked like he was already thinking of warm quarters and a hot drink.

Olney and Pattas were among the techs, Miles noted, along with most of the rest of the Greek-speaking cadre who had plagued Miles early on. Others Miles had seen around, or talked to during his private investigation into the background of the drowned man, or barely knew. Fifteen naked men starting to shiver violently as the dry snow whispered around their ankles. Fifteen bewildered faces beginning to look terrified. Eyes shifted toward the nerve-disruptors trained on them. *Give in*, Miles urged silently. *It's not worth it.* But more than one pair of eyes flickered at him, and squeezed shut in resolution.

Miles silently cursed the anonymous clever boffin who'd invented fetaine as a terror weapon, not for his chemistry, but for his insight into the Barrayaran psyche. Fetaine could surely never have been used, could never be used. Any faction trying to do so must rise, up against itself and tear apart in moral convulsions.

Yaski, standing back from his men, looked thoroughly horrified. Bonn, his expression black and brittle as obsidian, began to strip off his gloves and parka.

No, no, no! Miles screamed inside his head. *If you join them they'll never back down. They'll know they're right.* Bad mistake, bad . . . Bonn dropped the rest of his clothes in a pile, marched forward, joined the line, wheeled, and locked eyes with Metzov. Metzov's eyes narrowed with new fury. "So," he hissed, "you convict yourself. Freeze, then."

How had things gone so bad, so fast? Now would be a good time to remember a duty in the weather office, and get the hell out of here. If only those shivering bastards would back down, Miles could get through this night without a ripple in his record. He had no duty, no function here. . . .

Metzov's eye fell on Miles. "Vorkosigan, you can either take up a weapon and be useful, or consider yourself dismissed."

He could leave. Could he leave? When he made no move, the sergeant walked over and thrust a nerve disruptor into Miles's hand. Miles took it up, still struggling to think with brains gone suddenly porridge. He did retain the wit to make sure the safety was "on" before pointing the disruptor vaguely in the direction of the freezing men.

This isn't going to be a mutiny. It's going to be a massacre.

One of the armed grubs giggled nervously. What had they been told they were doing? What did they *believe* they were doing? Eighteen, nineteen-year-olds—could they even recognize a criminal order? Or know what to do about it if they did?

Could Miles?

The situation was ambiguous, that was the problem. It didn't quite fit. Miles knew about criminal orders, every academy man did. His father came down personally and gave a one-day seminar on the topic to the seniors at mid-year. He'd made it a requirement to graduate, by Imperial fiat back when he'd been Regent. What exactly constituted a criminal order, when and how to disobey it. With vid evidence from various historical test cases and bad examples, including the politically disastrous Solstice Massacre that had taken place under the Admiral's own command. Invariably one or more cadets had to leave the room to throw up during that part.

The other instructors hated Vorkosigan's Day. Their classes were subtly disrupted for weeks afterward. One reason Admiral Vorkosigan didn't wait till any later in the year. He almost always had to make a return trip a few weeks after, to talk some disturbed cadet out of dropping out at almost the finale of his schooling. Only the academy cadets got this live lecture, as far as Miles knew, though his father talked of canning it on holovid and making it a part of basic training Service-wide. Parts of the seminar had been a revelation even to Miles.

But this . . . If the techs had been civilians, Metzov would clearly be in the wrong. If this had been in wartime, while being harried by some enemy, Metzov might be within his rights, even duty. This was somewhere between Soldiers disobeying, but passively. Not an enemy in sight. Not even a physical situation threatening, necessarily, lives on the base (except theirs), though when the wind shifted that could change. *I'm not ready for this, not yet, not so soon. My career . . .*

Claustrophobic panic rose in Miles's chest, like a man with his head caught in a drain. The nerve disruptor wavered just slightly in his hand. Over the parabolic reflector he could see Bonn standing dumbly, too congealed now even to argue any more. Ears were turning white out there, and fingers and feet. One man crumpled into a shuddering ball, but made no move to surrender. Was there any softening of doubt yet, in Metzov's rigid neck?

For a lunatic moment Miles envisioned thumbing off the safety and shooting Metzov. And then what, shoot the grubs? He couldn't possibly get them all before they got him.

I could be the only soldier here under thirty who's ever killed an enemy before, in battle or out of it. The grubs might fire out of ignorance, or sheer curiosity. They didn't know enough *not* to. *What we do in the next half-hour will replay in our heads as long as we breathe.*

He could try doing nothing. Only follow orders. How much trouble could he get into, only following orders? Every commander he'd ever had agreed, he needed to follow orders better. *Think you'll enjoy your ship duty, then, Ensign Vorkosigan, you and your pack of frozen ghosts? At least you'd never be lonely. . . .*

Miles, still holding up the nerve disruptor, faded backward, out of the grubs' line-of-sight, out of the corner of Metzov's eye. Tears stung and blurred his vision. From the cold, no doubt.

He sat on the ground. Pulled off his gloves and boots. Let his parka fall, and his shirts. Trousers and thermal underwear atop the pile, and the nerve-disruptor nested carefully on them. He stepped forward. His leg braces felt like icicles against his calves.

I hate passive resistance. I really, really hate it.

"What the hell do you think *you're* doing, Ensign?" Metzov snarled as Miles limped past him.

"Breaking this up, sir," Miles replied steadily. Even now some of the shivering techs flinched away from him, as if his deformities might be contagious. Pattas didn't draw away, though. Nor Bonn.

"Bonn tried that bluff. He's now regretting it. It won't work for you either, Vorkosigan." Metzov's voice shook too, though not from the cold.

You should have said "Ensign." What's in a name? Miles could see the ripple of dismay run through the grubs, that time. No, this hadn't worked for Bonn. Miles might be the only man here for whom this sort of individual intervention could work. Depending on how far gone Mad Metzov was by now.

Miles spoke now for both Metzov's benefit and the grubs'. "It's possible—barely—that Service Security wouldn't investigate the deaths of Lieutenant Bonn and his men, if you diddled the record, claimed some accident. I guarantee Imperial Security will investigate mine."

Metzov grinned strangely. "Suppose no witnesses survive to complain?"

Metzov's sergeant looked as rigid as his master. Miles thought of Ahn, drunken Ahn, silent Ahn. What had Ahn seen, once long ago, when crazy things were happening on Komarr? What kind of surviving witness had he been? A guilty one, perhaps? "S-s-sorry, sir, but I see at least ten witnesses, behind those nerve disruptors." Silver parabolas—they looked enormous, like serving dishes, from this new angle. The change in point of view was amazingly clarifying. No ambiguities now.

Miles continued, "Or do you propose to execute your firing squad and then shoot yourself? Imperial Security will fast-penta everyone in sight. You can't silence me. Living or dead, through my mouth or yours—or theirs—I will testify." Shivers racked Miles's body. Astonishing, the effect of just that little bit of east wind, at this temperature. He fought to keep the shakes out of his voice, lest cold be mistaken for fear.

"Small consolation, if you—ah—permit yourself to freeze, I'd say, Ensign." Metzov's heavy sarcasm grated on Miles's nerves. The man still thought he was winning. Insane.

Miles's bare feet felt strangely warm, now. His eyelashes were crunchy with ice. He was catching up fast to the others, in terms of freezing to death, no doubt because of his smaller mass. His body was turning a blotchy purple-blue.

The snow-blanketed base was so silent. He could almost hear the individual snow grains skitter across the sheet ice. He could hear the vibrating bones of each man around him, pick out the hollow frightened breathing of the grubs. Time stretched.

He could threaten Metzov, break up his complacency with dark hints about Komarr, *the truth will out.* . . . He could call on his father's rank and position. He could . . . dammit, Metzov must realize he was overextended, no matter how mad he was. His discipline parade bluff hadn't worked and now he was stuck with it, stonily defending his authority unto death. *He can be a funny kind of dangerous, if you really threaten him.* . . . It was hard to see through the sadism to the underlying fear. But it had to be there, underneath. . . . Pushing wasn't working. Metzov was practically petrified with resistance. What about pulling . . . ?

"But consider, sir," Miles's words stuttered out persuasively, "the advantages to yourself of stopping now. You now have clear evidence of a mutinous, er, conspiracy. You can arrest us all, throw us in the stockade. It's a better revenge, 'cause you get it all and lose nothing. I lose my career, get a dishonorable discharge or maybe prison— do you think I wouldn't rather die? Service Security punishes the rest of us for you. You get it all."

Miles's words had hooked him; Miles could see it, in the red glow fading from the narrowed eyes, in the slight bending of that stiff, stiff neck. Miles had only to let the line out, refrain from jerking on it and renewing Metzov's fighting frenzy, *wait.* . . .

Metzov stepped nearer, bulking in the half-light, haloed by his freezing breath. His voice dropped, pitched to Miles's ear alone. "A typical soft Vorkosigan answer. Your father was soft on Komarran scum. Cost us lives. A court-martial for the Admiral's little boy—that might bring down that holier-than-thou buggerer, eh?"

Miles swallowed icy spit. *Those who do not know their history,* his thought careened, *are doomed to keep stepping in it.* Alas, so were those who did, it seemed. "Thermo the damned fetaine spill," he whispered hoarsely, "and see."

Lieutenant Yaski had taken the opportunity afforded by Miles's attention-arresting nude arrival on center stage to quietly disappear into the Admin building and make several frantic calls. But by the time the trainee's commander, the base surgeon, and Metzov's second-in-command arrived, primed to persuade or perhaps sedate and confine Metzov, the decision had been made. Miles, Bonn, and the techs were already dressed and being marched, stumbling, toward the stockade bunker under the argus-eyes of the nerve disruptors.

"Am I s-supposed to th-thank you for this?" Bonn asked Miles through chattering teeth. Their hands and feet swung like paralyzed lumps; he leaned on Miles, Miles hung on him, hobbling down the road together.

"We got what we wanted, eh? He's going to plasma the fetaine on-site before the wind shifts in the morning. Nobody dies. Nobody gets their nuts curdled. We win. I think." Miles emitted a deathly cackle through numb lips.

"I never thought," wheezed Bonn, "that I'd ever meet anybody crazier than Metzov."

"I didn't do anything you didn't," protested Miles. "Except I made it work. Sort of. It'll all look different in the morning, anyway."

"Yeah. Worse," Bonn predicted glumly.

.   .   .

Miles jerked up out of an uneasy doze on his cell cot when the door hissed open. They were bringing Bonn back.

Miles rubbed his unshaven face. "What time is it out there, lieutenant?"

"Dawn." Bonn looked as pale, stubbled, and criminally low as Miles felt. He eased himself down on his cot with a pained grunt.

"What's happening?"

"Service Security's all over the place. They flew in a captain from the mainland, just arrived, who seems to be in charge. Metzov's been filling his ear, I think. They're just taking depositions, so far."

"They get the fetaine taken care of?"

"Yep." Bonn vented a grim snicker. "They just had me out to check it, and sign the job off. The bunker made a neat little oven, all right."

"Ensign Vorkosigan, you're wanted," said the security guard who'd delivered Bonn. "Come with me now."

Miles creaked to his feet and limped toward the cell door. "See you later, lieutenant."

"Right. If you spot anybody out there with breakfast, why don't you use your political influence to send 'em my way, eh?"

Miles grinned bleakly. "I'll try."

Miles followed the guard up the stockade's short corridor. Lazkowski Base's stockade was not exactly what one would call a high-security facility, being scarcely more than a living quarters bunker with doors that only locked from the outside and no windows. The weather usually made a better guard than any force screen, not to mention the 500-kilometer-wide ice water moat surrounding the island.

The base security office was busy this morning. Two grim strangers stood waiting by the door, a lieutenant and a big sergeant with the Horus-eye insignia of Imperial Security on their sleek uniforms. *Imperial* Security, not Service Security. Miles's very own Security, who had guarded his family all his father's political life. Miles regarded them with possessive delight.

The base security clerk looked harried, his desk console lit up and blinking. "Ensign Vorkosigan, sir, I need your palm print on this."

"All right. What am I signing?"

"Just the travel orders, sir."

"What? Ah . . ." Miles paused, holding up his plastic-mitted hands. "Which one?"

"The right, I guess would do, sir."

With difficulty, Miles peeled off the right mitten with his awkward left. His hand glistened with the medical gel that was supposed to be healing the frostbite. His hand was swollen, red-blotched and mangled-looking, but the stuff must be working. All his fingers now wriggled. It took three tries, pressing down on the ID pad, before the computer recognized him.

"Now yours, sir," the clerk nodded to the Imperial Security lieutenant. The ImpSec man laid his hand on the pad and the computer bleeped approval. He lifted it and glanced dubiously at the sticky sheen, looked around futilely for some towel, and wiped it surreptitiously on his trouser seam just behind his stunner holster. The clerk dabbed nervously at the pad with his uniform sleeve, and touched his intercom.

"Am I glad to see you fellows," Miles told the ImpSec officer. "Wish you'd been here last night."

The lieutenant did not smile in return. "I'm just a courier, Ensign. I'm not supposed to discuss your case."

General Metzov ducked through the door from the inner office, a sheaf of plastic flimsies in one hand and a Service Security captain at his elbow, who nodded warily to his counterpart on the Imperial side.

The general was almost smiling. "Good morning, Ensign Vorkosigan." His glance took in Imperial Security without dismay. Dammit, ImpSec should be making that near-murderer shake in his combat boots. "It seems there's a wrinkle in this case even I hadn't realized. When a Vor lord involves himself in a military mutiny, a charge of high treason follows automatically."

"What?" Miles swallowed, to bring his voice back down. "Lieutenant, I'm not under arrest by *Imperial* Security, am I?"

The lieutenant produced a set of handcuffs and proceeded to attach Miles to the big sergeant. *Overholt*, read the name on the man's badge, which Miles mentally redubbed Overkill. He had only to lift his arm to dangle Miles like a kitten.

"You are being detained, pending further investigation," said the lieutenant formally.

"How long?"

"Indefinitely."

The lieutenant headed for the door, the sergeant and perforce Miles following. "Where?" Miles asked frantically.

"Imperial Security Headquarters."

Vorbarr Sultana! "I need to get my things—"

"Your quarters have already been cleared."

"Will I be coming back here?"

"I don't know, Ensign."

Late dawn was streaking Camp Permafrost with grey and yellow when the scatcat deposited them at the shuttlepad. The Imperial Security sub-orbital courier shuttle sat on the icy concrete like a bird of prey accidently placed in a pigeon cote. Slick and black and deadly, it seemed to break the sound barrier just resting there. Its pilot was at the ready, engines primed for takeoff.

Miles shuffled awkwardly up the ramp after Sergeant Overkill, the handcuff jerking coldly on his wrist. Tiny ice crystals danced in the northeasterly wind. The temperature would be stabilizing this morning, he could tell by the particular dry bite of the relative humidity in his sinuses. Dear God, it was past time to get off this island.

Miles took one last sharp breath, then the shuttle door sealed behind them with a snaky hiss. Within was a thick, upholstered silence that even the howl of the engines scarcely penetrated.

At least it was warm.

Autumn in the city of Vorbarr Sultana was a beautiful time of year, and today was exemplary. The air was high and blue, the temperature cool and perfect, and even the tang of industrial haze smelled good. The autumn flowers were not yet frosted off, but the Earth-import trees had turned their colors. Miles glimpsed one such tree as he was hustled out of the Security lift van and into a back entrance to the big blocky building that was Imperial Security Headquarters. An Earth maple, with carnelian leaves and a silver-grey trunk, across the street. Then the door closed. Miles held that tree before his mind's eye, trying to memorize it, just in case he never saw another.

The Security lieutenant produced passes that sped Miles and Overholt through the door guards, and led them into a maze of corridors to a pair of lift tubes. They entered the up tube, not the down one. So, Miles was not being taken directly to the ultra-secure cell block beneath the building. Miles woke to what this meant, and wished wistfully for the down tube.

They were ushered into an office on an upper level, past a Security captain, then into an inner office. A man, slight, bland, civilian-clothed, with brown hair greying at the temples, sat at his very large comconsole desk, studying a vid. He glanced up at Miles's escort. "Thank you, lieutenant, sergeant. You may go."

Overholt detached Miles from his wrist as the lieutenant asked, "Uh, will you be safe, sir?"

"I expect so," said the man dryly.

Yeah, but what about me? Miles wailed inwardly. The two soldiers exited, and left Miles alone, standing literally on the carpet. Unwashed, unshaven, still wearing the faintly reeking black fatigues he'd flung on—only last night? Face weather-raked, with his swollen hands and feet still encased in their plastic medical mittens—his toes now wriggled in their squishy matrix. No boots. He had dozed, in a jerky inter-mittent exhaustion, on the two-hour shuttle flight, without being noticeably re-freshed. His throat was raw, his sinuses felt stuffed with packing fiber, and his chest hurt when he breathed.

Simon Illyan, Chief of Barrayaran Imperial Security, crossed his arms and looked Miles over slowly, from head to toe and back again. It gave Miles a skewed sense of *deja vu.*

Practically everyone on Barrayar feared this man's name, though few knew his face. This effect was carefully cultivated by Illyan, building in part—but only in part—on the legacy of his formidable predecessor, the legendary Security Chief Ne-gri, Illyan and his department in turn had provided security for Miles's father for the twenty years of his political career, and had slipped up only once, during the night of the infamous soltoxin attack. Offhand, Miles knew of no one Illyan feared except Miles's mother. He'd once asked his father if this was guilt about the soltoxin, but Count Vorkosigan had replied, No, it was only the lasting effect of vivid first impres-sions. Miles had called Illyan "Uncle Simon" all his life until he'd entered the Ser-vice, "Sir" after that.

Looking at Illyan's face now, Miles thought he finally grasped the distinction be-tween exasperation, and utter exasperation.

Illyan finished his inspection, shook his head, and groaned, "Wonderful. Just wonderful."

Miles cleared his throat. "Am I . . . really under arrest, sir?"

"That is what this interview will determine," Illyan sighed, leaning back in his chair. "I have been up since two hours after midnight over this escapade. Rumors are flying all over the Service, as fast as the vid net can carry them. The facts appear to be mutating every forty minutes, like bacteria. I don't suppose you could have picked some more public way to self-destruct? Attempted to assassinate the Emperor with your pocket-knife during the Birthday Review, say, or raped a sheep in the Great Square during rush hour?" The sarcasm melted to genuine pain. "He had so much hope of you. How could you betray him so?"

No need to ask who "he" was. *The* Vorkosigan. "I . . . don't think I did, sir. I don't know."

A light blinked on Illyan's comconsole. He exhaled, with a sharp glance at Miles, and touched a control. The second door to his office, in the wall to the right of his desk, slid open, and two men in dress greens ducked through.

Prime Minister Admiral Count Aral Vorkosigan wore the uniform as naturally as an animal wears its fur. He was a man of no more than middle height, stocky, grey-haired, heavy-jawed, scarred, almost a thug's body and yet with the most penetrating grey eyes Miles had ever encountered. He was flanked by his aide, a tall blond lieu-tenant named Jole. Miles had met Jole on his last home leave. Now, there was a per-fect officer, brave and brilliant—he'd served in space, been decorated for some courage and quick thinking during a horrendous on-board accident, been rotated through HQ while recovering from his injuries, and promptly been snapped up as his military liaison by the Prime Minister, who had a sharp eye for hot new talent. Jaw-dropping gorgeous, to boot, he ought to be making recruiting vids. Miles sighed in hopeless jealousy every time he ran across him; Jole was even worse than Ivan, who while darkly handsome had never been accused of brilliance.

"Thanks, Jole," Count Vorkosigan murmured to his aide, as his eye found Miles. "I'll see you back at the office."

"Yes, sir." So dismissed, Jole ducked back out, glancing back at Miles and his superior with worried eyes, and the door hissed closed again.

Illyan still had his hand pressed to a control on his desk. "Are you officially here?" he asked Count Vorkosigan.

"No."

Illyan keyed something off—recording equipment, Miles realized. "Very well," he said, editorial doubt injected into his tone.

Miles saluted his father. His father ignored the salute and embraced him gravely, wordlessly, sat in the room's only other chair, crossed his arms and booted ankles, and said, "Continue, Simon."

Illyan, who had been cut off in the middle of what had been shaping up, in Miles's estimation, to a really classic reaming, chewed his lip in frustration. "Rumors aside," Illyan said to Miles, "what really happened last night out on that damned island?"

In the most neutral and succinct terms he could muster, Miles described the previous night's events, starting with the fetaine spill and ending with his arrest/detainment/to-be-determined by Imperial Security. His father said nothing during the whole recitation, but he had a light pen in his hand which he kept turning absently around and over, *tap* against his knee, around and over.

Silence fell when Miles finished. The light pen was driving Miles to distraction. He wished his father would put the damned thing away, or drop it, or anything.

His father slipped the light pen back into his breast pocket, thank God, leaned back, and steepled his fingers, frowning. "Let me get this straight. You say Metzov hopscotched the command chain and dragooned *trainees* for his firing squad?"

"Ten of them. I don't know if they were volunteers or not, I wasn't there for that part."

"Trainees." Count Vorkosigan's face was dark. "Boys."

"He was babbling something about it being like the army versus the navy, back on Old Earth."

"Huh?" said Illyan.

"I don't think Metzov was any too stable when he was exiled to Kyril Island after his troubles in the Komarr Revolt, and fifteen years of brooding about it didn't improve his grip." Miles hesitated. "Will . . . General Metzov be questioned about his actions at all, sir?"

"General Metzov, by your account," said Admiral Vorkosigan, "dragged a platoon of eighteen-year-olds into what came within a hair of being a mass torture-murder."

Miles nodded in memory. His body still twinged with assorted agony.

"For that sin, there is no hole deep enough to hide him from my wrath. Metzov will be taken care of, all right." Count Vorkosigan was terrifyingly grim.

"What about Miles and the mutineers?" asked Illyan.

"Necessarily, I fear we will have to treat that as a separate matter."

"Or two separate matters," said Illyan suggestively.

"Mm. So, Miles, tell me about the men on the other end of the guns."

"Techs, sir, mostly. A lot of greekies."

Illyan winced. "Good God, had the man no political sense at all?"

"None that I ever saw. I thought it would be a problem." Well, later he'd thought of it, lying awake on his cell cot after the med squad left. The other political ramifications had spun through his mind. Over half the slowly freezing techs had been of the Greek-speaking minority. The language separatists would have been rioting in the streets, had it become a massacre, sure to claim the general had ordered the greekies into the clean-up as racial sabotage. More deaths, chaos reverberating down the timeline like the consequences of the Solstice Massacre? "It . . . occurred to me, that if I died with them, at least it would be crystal clear that it hadn't been some plot of your government or the Vor oligarchy. So that if I lived, I won, and if I died, I won too. Or at least served. Strategy, of sorts."

Barrayar's greatest strategist of this century rubbed his temples, as if they ached. "Well . . . of sorts, yes."

"So," Miles swallowed, "what happens now, sirs? Will I be charged with high treason?"

"For the second time in four years?" said Illyan. "Hell, no. I'm not going through that again. I will simply disappear you, until this blows over. Where to, I haven't figured yet. Kyril Island is out."

"Glad to hear it." Miles's eyes narrowed. "What about the others?"

"The trainees?" said Illyan.

"The techs. My . . . fellow mutineers."

Illyan twitched at the term.

"It would be seriously unjust if I were to slither up some Vor-privileged line and leave them standing charges alone," Miles added.

"The public scandal of your trial would damage your father's Centrist coalition. Your moral scruples may be admirable, Miles, but I'm not sure I can afford them."

Miles stared steadily at the Prime Minister. "Sir?"

Count Vorkosigan sucked thoughtfully on his lower lip. "Yes, I could have the charges against them quashed, by Imperial flat. That would involve another price, though." He leaned forward intently, eyes peeling Miles. "You could never serve again. Rumors will travel even without a trial. No commander would have you, after. None could trust you, trust you to be a real officer, not an artifact protected by special privilege. I can't ask anyone to command you with his head cranked over his shoulder all the time."

Miles exhaled, a long breath. "In a weird sense, they were my men. Do it, Kill the charges."

"Will you resign your commission, then?" demanded Illyan. He looked sick.

Miles felt sick, nauseous and cold. "I will." His voice was thin.

Illyan looked up suddenly from a blank brooding stare at his comconsole. "Miles, how did you know about General Metzov's questionable actions during the Komarr Revolt? That case was Security-classified."

"Ah . . . didn't Ivan tell you about the little leak in the ImpSec files, sir?"

"What?"

Damn Ivan. "May I sit down, sir?" said Miles faintly. The room was wavering, his head thumping. Without waiting for permission, he sat cross-legged on the carpet, blinking. His father made a worried movement toward him, then restrained himself. "I'd been checking up on Metzov's background because of something Lieutenant Ahn said. By the way, when you go after Metzov, I strongly suggest you fast-penta Ahn first. He knows more than he's told. You'll find him somewhere on the equator, I expect."

"My *files*, Miles."

"Uh, yes, well, it turns out that if you face a secured console to an outgoing console, you can read off Security files from anywhere in the vid net. Of course, you have to have somebody inside HQ who can and will aim the consoles and call up the files for you. And you can't flash-download. But I, uh, thought you should know, sir."

"Perfect security," said Count Vorkosigan in a choked voice. Chortling, Miles realized in startlement.

Illyan looked like a man sucking on a lemon. "How did you," Illyan began, stopped to glare at the Count, started again, "how did you figure this out?"

"It was obvious."

"Air-tight security, you said," murmured Count Vorkosigan, suppressing a wheezing laugh. "The most expensive yet devised. Proof against the cleverest viruses, the most sophisticated eavesdropping equipment, you said. And two ensigns waft right through it?"

Goaded, Illyan snapped, "I didn't promise it was idiot-proof!"

Count Vorkosigan wiped his eyes and sighed. "Ah, the human factor. We will correct the defect, Miles. Thank you."

"You're a bloody loose cannon, boy, firing in all directions," Illyan growled to Miles, craning his neck to see over his desk to where Miles sat in a slumping heap. "This, on top of your earlier escapade, on top of it all—house arrest isn't enough. You ought to be locked in a cell with your hands tied behind your back. Just so I can get a decent night's sleep."

Miles, who thought he might kill for a decent hour's sleep right now, could only shrug. Maybe Illyan could be persuaded to let him go to that nice quiet cell soon.

Count Vorkosigan had fallen silent, a strange thoughtful glow starting in his eye. Illyan noticed the expression, too, and paused.

"Simon," said Count Vorkosigan, "there's no doubt Imperial Security will have to go on watching Miles. For his sake, as well as mine."

"And the Emperor's," put in Illyan dourly. "And Barrayar's. And the innocent bystanders'."

"But what better, more direct and efficient way for you to watch him than if he is assigned *to* Imperial Security?"

"What?" said Illyan and Miles together, in the same sharp horrified tone. "You're not serious," Illyan went on, as Miles added, "Security was never on my top-ten list of assignment choices."

"Not choice. Aptitude. Major Cecil discussed it with me at one time, as I recall. But as Miles says, he didn't put it on his list."

He hadn't put Arctic Weatherman on his list either, Miles recalled.

"You had it right the first time," said Illyan. "No commander in the Service will want him now. Not excepting myself."

"None that I could, in honor, lean on to take him. Excepting yourself. I have always," Count Vorkosigan flashed a peculiar grin, "leaned on you, Simon."

Illyan looked faintly stunned, as a top tactician beginning to see himself outmaneuvered.

"Besides," Count Vorkosigan went on in that same mild persuasive voice, "it would allow us to send him off-planet till this blows over."

Illyan brightened slightly. "How far off-planet?"

A strange shadow of—pain?—passed over Count Vorkosigan's face and vanished, as swiftly as a cloud across the sun. "As far as he's needed," he replied steadily. "It works on several levels. We can put it about that it's an unofficial exile, departure in disgrace. It will buy off my political enemies, who would otherwise try to stir profit from this mess. It will tone down the appearance of our condoning a mutiny, which no military service can afford."

"True exile," said Miles. "Even if unofficial."

"Oh yes," Count Vorkosigan agreed softly. "But, ah—not true disgrace."

Not? But . . . *off-planet?* Ship duty? Some kind of ship duty, it had to be, he couldn't *get* off-planet except aboard a ship. Miles's heart rose in his aching chest for the first time since he'd left Kyril Island.

"Can he be trusted on detached duties, without supervision?" said Illyan doubtfully.

"Apparently." The Count's smile was like the gleam off a knife blade. "Security can use his talents. Security more than any other department needs his talents."

"To see the obvious?"

"And the less obvious. Many officers may be trusted with the Emperor's life. Rather fewer with his honor."

Illyan, reluctantly, made a vague acquiescent gesture. Count Vorkosigan, perhaps prudently, did not troll for greater enthusiasm from his Security chief at this time, but turned to Miles and said, "You look like you need an infirmary."

"I need a bed."

"How about a bed in an infirmary?"

Miles coughed, and blinked blearily. "Yeah, that'd do."

"Come on, we'll find one."

He stood, and staggered out on his father's arm, his feet squishing in their plastic bags.

"Other than that, how was Kyril Island, Ensign Vorkosigan?" inquired the Count. "You didn't vid home much, your mother noticed."

"I was busy, Lessee. The climate was ferocious, the terrain was lethal, a third of the population including my immediate superior was dead drunk most of the time. The average IQ equalled the mean temperature in degrees cee, there wasn't a woman for five hundred kilometers in any direction, and the base commander was a homicidal psychotic. Other than that, it was lovely."

"Doesn't sound like it's changed in the smallest detail in twenty-five years."

"You've been there?" Miles squinted. "And yet you let *me* get sent there?"

"I commanded Lazkowski Base for five months, once, while waiting for my captaincy of the cruiser *General Vorkraft*. During the period my career was, so to speak, in political eclipse."

So to speak. "How'd you like it?"

"I can't remember much. I was drunk most of the time. Everybody finds their own way of dealing with Camp Permafrost. I might say, you did rather better than I."

"I find your subsequent survival . . . encouraging, sir."

"I thought you might. That's why I mentioned it. It's not otherwise an experience I'd hold up as an example."

Miles looked up at his father. "Did . . . I do the right thing, sir? Last night?"

"Yes," said the Count simply. "A right thing. Perhaps not the best of all possible right things. Three days from now you may think of a cleverer tactic, but you were the man on the ground at the time. I try not to second-guess my field commanders."

Miles nodded, satisfied.

IAIN M. BANKS

Iain M. Banks [1954–] (www.iainbanks.net) lives in Fife, Scotland. His first published novel, *The Wasp Factory* (1984), was a powerful contemporary horror novel. His second, *Walking on Glass* (1985), and third, *The Bridge* (1986)—both of which had elements of the fantastic—confirmed him as a significant contemporary writer. Then he successfully published his first SF novel, *Consider Phlebas* (1987), set in the complex and unusual and very distant future of the Culture (which Banks illuminates in his essay "A Few Notes on the Culture"). According to his friend Ken MacLeod, "Iain M. Banks wrote four full-scale works of new space opera and collected numerous rejections on all of them before slipping under the radar as a mainstream writer and then exploding onto the SF scene with *Consider Phlebas*, the fourth to be written. It found and made a market for the other three. They were new then, and they will endure as SF."

It is difficult to underestimate the importance of Banks to UK SF: Critic Rob Latham summarized his early fame in 1994 in a review essay in *The New York Review of Science Fiction*: "I generally agree with John Clute's assessment, in his entry on the author for the new Clute-Nicholls encyclopedia, that Banks might well be 'the greatest UK SF writer' to have emerged during the 1980s—if not with mainstream novelist Fay Weldon's more ambiguously laconic judgment . . . that he is 'the great white hope of contemporary British literature.'" He has published eleven literary novels, all bestsellers in the UK, to date—they sell even better than his science fiction. Though his reputation is very high, he still awaits comparable success in the US market. As noted in the general introduction to this book, Banks's massive success in the UK provided a primary model to British SF writers for commercial and artistic success specifically through space opera at the start of the 1990s.

Banks's SF novels of the Culture include *The Player of Games* (1988), *Use of Weapons* (1990), *Excession* (1996), *Inversions* (1998), and *Look to Windward* (2000). His story collection, *The State of the Art* (1989), contains a few Culture stories. Jeff VanderMeer said, in an NYRSF review of the last novel, "Nowhere has Banks demonstrated more ingenuity than in his far-future Culture novels. These 'space operas,' set against the backdrop of a universe-wide (somewhat suspect) utopia, succeed because Banks simultaneously delights in science fiction tropes and seeks to subvert them. At least two Culture novels, *Consider Phlebas* and *Use of Weapons*, qualify as masterpieces." Perhaps equally significant, they were all bestsellers in the UK. His recent SF includes *The Algebraist* (2005), a space opera in a new setting.

Furthermore, Banks took as his mission to "reclaim the moral high ground of space opera for the Left." In doing so, he jettisons a lot of space opera's traditional furniture. As John Clute notes, "the Culture has very carefully been conceived in genuine post-scarcity terms. In other words, it boasts no hierarchies bent on maintaining power through control of limited resources. There are no Empires in the Culture, no tentacled Corporations, no Enclave whose hidden knowledge gives its inhabitants a vital edge in their attempts to maintain independence against the military hardware of the far-off Czar at the apex of the pyramid of power."

Gwyneth Jones provides further context, in the course of reviewing Ken MacLeod: "Space opera writers and readers like high-concept ideas, and have limited regard for human details. It may seem ironic, but it's not really surprising that the two UK male writers who can match the rather brutal optimism of the US classics, Iain Banks and his brother-in-arms Ken MacLeod, both take a Marxist line: Banks with his Communist-bloc 'Culture' novels, and MacLeod with his 'hard-left libertarian' factions. There's no distance between the hard left and the hard right when it comes to brutal optimism."

"A Gift from the Culture" is one of Banks's few short stories, and of them, one of the even fewer that give glimpses of the Culture. In this story, written more than a decade before the real-world War on Terror, Banks's protagonist is coerced into committing mass murder, seeming now a bit uncomfortably like Luke Skywalker as Mohamed Atta.

A GIFT FROM THE CULTURE

IAIN M. BANKS

Money is a sign of poverty. This is an old Culture saying I remember every now and again, especially when I'm being tempted to do something I know I shouldn't, and there's money involved (when is there not?).

I looked at the gun, lying small and precise in Cruizell's broad, scarred hand, and the first thing I thought—after: Where the hell did they get one of *those?*—was: Money is a sign of poverty. However appropriate the thought might have been, it wasn't much help.

I was standing outside a no-credit gambling club in Vreccis Low City in the small hours of a wet weeknight, looking at a pretty, toy-like handgun while two large people I owed a lot of money to asked me to do something extremely dangerous and worse than illegal. I was weighing up the relative attractions of trying to run away (they'd shoot me), refusing (they'd beat me up; probably I'd spend the next few weeks developing a serious medical bill), and doing what Kaddus and Cruizell asked me to do, knowing that while there was a chance I'd get away with it—uninjured, and solvent again—the most likely outcome was a messy and probably slow death while assisting the security services with their enquiries.

Kaddus and Cruizell were offering me all my markers back, plus—once the thing was done—a tidy sum on top, just to show there were no hard feelings.

I suspected they didn't anticipate having to pay the final instalment of the deal.

So, I knew that logically what I ought to do was tell them where to shove their fancy designer pistol, and accept a theoretically painful but probably not terminal beating. Hell, I could switch the pain off (having a Culture background does have some advantages), but what about that hospital bill?

I was up to my scalp in debt already.

"What's the matter, Wrobik?" Cruizell drawled, taking a step nearer, under the shelter of the club's dripping eaves. Me with my back against the warm wall, the smell of wet pavements in my nose and a taste like metal in my mouth. Kaddus and Cruizell's limousine idled at the kerb; I could see the driver inside, watching us through an open window. Nobody passed on the street outside the narrow alley. A police cruiser flew over, high up, lights flashing through the rain and illuminating the underside of the rain clouds over the city. Kaddus looked up briefly, then ignored the passing craft. Cruizell shoved the gun towards me. I tried to shrink back.

"Take the gun, Wrobik," Kaddus said tiredly. I licked my lips, stared down at the pistol.

"I can't," I said. I stuck my hands in my coat pockets.

"Sure you can," Cruizell said. Kaddus shook his head.

"Wrobik, don't make things difficult for yourself; take the gun. Just touch it first, see if our information is correct. Go on; take it." I stared, transfixed, at the small pistol. "Take the gun, Wrobik. Just remember to point it at the ground, not at us; the driver's got a laser on you and he might think you meant to use the gun on us . . . come on; take it, touch it."

I couldn't move, I couldn't think. I just stood, hypnotized. Kaddus took hold of my right wrist and pulled my hand from my pocket. Cruizell held the gun up near my nose; Kaddus forced my hand onto the pistol. My hand closed round the grip like something lifeless.

The gun came to life; a couple of lights blinked dully, and the small screen above the grip glowed, flickering round the edges. Cruizell dropped his hand, leaving me holding the pistol; Kaddus smiled thinly.

"There, that wasn't difficult, now was it?" Kaddus said. I held the gun and tried to imagine using it on the two men, but I knew I couldn't, whether the driver had me covered or not.

"Kaddus," I said, "I can't do this. Something else; I'll do anything else, but I'm not a hit-man; I can't—"

"You don't have to be an expert, Wrobik," Kaddus said quietly. "All you have to be is . . . whatever the hell you are. After that, you just point and squirt: like you do with your boyfriend." He grinned and winked at Cruizell, who bared some teeth. I shook my head.

"This is crazy, Kaddus. Just because the thing switches on for me—"

"Yeah; isn't that funny." Kaddus turned to Cruizell, looking up to the taller man's face and smiling. "Isn't that funny, Wrobik here being an alien? And him looking just like us."

"An alien *and* queer," Cruizell rumbled, scowling. "Shit."

"Look," I said, staring at the pistol, "it . . . this thing, it . . . it might not work," I finished lamely. Kaddus smiled.

"It'll work. A ship's a big target. You won't miss." He smiled again.

"But I thought they had protection against—"

"Lasers and kinetics they can deal with, Wrobik; this is something different. I don't know the technical details; I just know our radical friends paid a lot of money for this thing. That's enough for me."

Our radical friends. This was funny, coming from Kaddus. Probably he meant the Bright Path. People he'd always considered bad for business, just terrorists. I'd have imagined he'd sell them to the police on general principles, even if they did offer him lots of money. Was he starting to hedge his bets, or just being greedy? They have a saying here: Crime whispers; money talks.

"But there'll be people on the ship, not just—"

"You won't be able to see them. Anyway; they'll be some of the Guard, Naval brass, some Administration flunkeys, Secret Service agents . . . What do you care about them?" Kaddus patted my damp shoulder. "You can do it."

I looked away from his tired grey eyes, down at the gun, quiet in my fist, small screen glowing faintly. Betrayed by my own skin, my own touch. I thought about that hospital bill again. I felt like crying, but that wasn't the done thing amongst the men here, and what could I say? I *was a woman. I was Culture.* But I had renounced these things, and now I am a man, and now I am here in the Free City of Vreccis, where nothing is free.

"All right," I said, a bitterness in my mouth, "I'll do it."

Cruizell looked disappointed. Kaddus nodded. "Good. The ship arrives Ninthday;

you know what it looks like?" I nodded. "So you won't have any problems," Kaddus smiled thinly. "You'll be able to see it from almost anywhere in the City." He pulled out some cash and stuffed it into my coat pocket. "Get yourself a taxi. The underground's risky these days." He patted me lightly on the cheek; his hand smelt of expensive scents. "Hey, Wrobik; cheer up, yeah? You're going to shoot down a fucking starship. It'll be an experience." Kaddus laughed, looking at me and then at Cruizell, who laughed too, dutifully.

They went back to the car; it hummed into the night, tyres ripping at the rain-filled streets. I was left to watch the puddles grow, the gun hanging in my hand like guilt.

"I am a Light Plasma Projector, model LPP 91, series two, constructed in A/4882.4 at Manufactury Six in the Spanshacht-Trouferre Orbital, Ørvolöus Cluster. Serial number 3685706. Brain value point one. AM battery powered, rating: indefinite. Maximum power on single-bolt: 3.1×8^{10} joules, recycle time 14 seconds. Maximum rate of fire: 260 RPS. Use limited to Culture genofixed individuals only through epidermal gene analysis. To use with gloves or light armour, access 'modes' store via command buttons. Unauthorized use is both prohibited and punishable. Skill requirement 12-75%C. Full instructions follow; use command buttons and screen to replay, search, pause or stop . . .

"Instructions, part one: Introduction. The LPP 91 is an operationally-intricate general-purpose 'peace'-rated weapon not suitable for full battle use; its design and performance parameters are based on the recommendations of—"

The gun sat on the table, telling me all about itself in a high, tinny voice while I lay slumped in a lounger, staring out over a busy street in Vreccis Low City. Underground freight trains shook the rickety apartment block every few minutes, traffic buzzed at street level, rich people and police moved through the skies in fliers and cruisers, and above them all the starships sailed.

I felt trapped between these strata of purposeful movements.

Far in the distance over the city, I could just see the slender, shining tower of the city's Lev tube, rising straight towards and through the clouds, on its way to space. Why couldn't the Admiral use the Lev instead of making a big show of returning from the stars in his own ship? Maybe he thought a glorified elevator was too undignified. Vainglorious bastards, all of them. They deserved to die (if you wanted to take that attitude), but why did I have to be the one to kill them? Goddamned phallic starships.

Not that the Lev was any less prick-like, and anyway, no doubt if the Admiral had been coming down by the tube Kaddus and Cruizell would have told me to shoot *it* down; holy shit. I shook my head.

I was holding a long glass of jahl—Vreccis City's cheapest strong booze. It was my second glass, but I wasn't enjoying it. The gun chattered on, speaking to the sparsely furnished main room of our apartment. I was waiting for Maust, missing him even more than usual. I looked at the terminal on my wrist; according to the time display he should be back any moment now. I looked out into the weak, watery light of dawn. I hadn't slept yet.

The gun talked on. It used Marain, of course; the Culture's language. I hadn't heard that spoken for nearly eight standard years, and hearing it now I felt sad and foolish. My birthright; my people, my language. Eight years away, eight years in the wilderness. My great adventure, my renunciation of what seemed to me sterile and lifeless to plunge into a more vital society, my grand gesture . . . well, now it seemed like an empty gesture, now it looked like a stupid, petulant thing to have done.

I drank some more of the sharp-tasting spirit. The gun gibbered on, talking about beam-spread diameters, gyroscopic weave patterns, gravity-contour mode, line-of-sight mode, curve shots, spatter and pierce settings . . . I thought about glanding something soothing and cool, but I didn't; I had vowed not to use those cunningly altered glands eight years ago, and I'd broken that vow only twice, both times when I was in severe pain. Had I been courageous I'd have had the whole damn lot taken out, returned to their human-normal state, our original animal inheritance . . . but I am not courageous. I dread pain, and cannot face it naked, as these people do. I admire them, fear them, still cannot understand them. Not even Maust. In fact, least of all Maust. Perhaps you cannot ever love what you completely understand.

Eight years in exile, lost to the Culture, never hearing that silky, subtle, complexly simple language, and now when I do hear Marain, it's from a gun, telling me how to fire it so I can kill . . . what? Hundreds of people? Maybe thousands; it will depend on where the ship falls, whether it explodes (could primitive starships explode? I had no idea; that was never my field). I took another drink, shook my head. I couldn't do it.

I am Wrobik Sennkil, Vreccile citizen number . . . (I always forget; it's on my papers), male, prime race, aged thirty; part-time freelance journalist (between jobs at the moment), and full-time gambler (I tend to lose but I enjoy myself, or at least I did until last night). But I am, also, still Bahlln-Euchersa Wrobich Vress Schennil dam Flaysse, citizen of the Culture, born female, species mix too complicated to remember, aged sixty-eight, standard, and one-time member of the Contact section.

And a renegade; I chose to exercise the freedom the Culture is so proud of bestowing upon its inhabitants by leaving it altogether. It let me go, even helped me, reluctant though I was (but could I have forged my own papers, made all the arrangements by myself? No, but at least, after my education into the ways of the Vreccile Economic Community, and after the module rose, dark and silent, back into the night sky and the waiting ship, I have turned only twice to the Culture's legacy of altered biology, and not once to its artefacts. Until now; the gun rambles on). I abandoned a paradise I considered dull for a cruel and greedy system bubbling with life and incident; a place I thought I might find . . . what? I don't know. I didn't know when I left and I don't know yet, though at least here I found Maust, and when I am with him my searching no longer seems so lonely.

Until last night that search still seemed worthwhile. Now utopia sends a tiny package of destruction, a casual, accidental message.

Where *did* Kaddus and Cruizell get the thing? The Culture guards its weaponry jealously, even embarrassedly. You can't buy Culture weapons, at least not from the Culture. I suppose things go missing though; there is so much of everything in the Culture that objects must be mislaid occasionally. I took another drink, listening to the gun, and watching that watery, rainy-season sky over the rooftops, towers, aerials, dishes and domes of the Great City. Maybe guns slip out of the Culture's manicured grasp more often than other products do; they betoken danger, they signify threat, and they will only be needed where there must be a fair chance of losing them, so they must disappear now and again, be taken as prizes.

That, of course, is why they're built with inhibiting circuits which only let the weapons work for Culture people (sensible, non-violent, non-acquisitive Culture people, who *of course* would only use a gun in self-defence, for example, if threatened by some comparative barbarian . . . oh the self-satisfied Culture: its imperialism of smugness). And even this gun is antique; not obsolescent (for that is not a concept the Culture really approves of—it builds to last), but outdated; hardly more intelligent than a household pet, whereas modern Culture weaponry is sentient.

The Culture probably doesn't even make handguns any more. I've seen what it calls Personal Armed Escort Drones, and if, somehow, one of those fell into the hands of people like Kaddus and Cruizell, it would immediately signal for help, use its motive power to try and escape, shoot to injure or even kill anybody trying to use or trap it, attempt to bargain its way out, and destruct if it thought it was going to be taken apart or otherwise interfered with.

I drank some more jahl. I looked at the time again; Maust was late. The club always closed promptly, because of the police. They weren't allowed to talk to the customers after work: he always came straight back . . . I felt the start of fear, but pushed it away. Of course he'd be all right. I had other things to think about. I had to think this thing through. More jahl.

No, I couldn't do it. I left the Culture because it bored me, but also because the evangelical, interventionist morality of Contact sometimes meant doing just the sort of thing we were supposed to prevent others doing; starting wars, assassinating . . . all of it, all the bad things . . . I was never involved with Special Circumstances directly, but I knew what went on (Special Circumstances; Dirty Tricks, in other words. The Culture's tellingly unique euphemism). I refused to live with such hypocrisy and chose instead this honestly selfish and avaricious society, which doesn't pretend to be good, just ambitious.

But I have lived here as I lived there, trying not to hurt others, trying just to be myself; and I cannot be myself by destroying a ship full of people, even if they are some of the rulers of this cruel and callous society. I can't use the gun; I can't let Kaddus and Cruizell find me. And I will not go back, head bowed, to the Culture.

I finished the glass of jahl.

I had to get out. There were other cities, other planets, besides Vreccis; I'd just had to run; run and hide. Would Maust come with me though? I looked at the time again; he was half an hour late. Not like him. Why was he late? I went to the window, looking down to the street, searching for him.

A police APC rumbled through the traffic. Just a routine cruise; siren off, guns stowed. It was heading for the Outworlder's Quarter, where the police had been making shows of strength recently. No sign of Maust's svelte shape swinging through the crowds.

Always the worry. That he might be run over, that the police might arrest him at the club (indecency, corrupting public morals, and homosexuality; that great crime, even worse than not making your pay-off!), and, of course, the worry that he might meet somebody else.

Maust. Come home safely, come home to me.

I remember feeling cheated when I discovered, towards the end of my regendering, that I still felt drawn to men. That was long ago, when I was happy in the Culture, and like many people I had wondered what it would be like to love those of my own original sex; it seemed terribly unfair that my desires did not alter with my physiology. It took Maust to make me feel I had not been cheated. Maust made everything better. Maust was my breath of life.

Anyway, I would not be a woman in this society.

I decided I needed a refill. I walked past the table.

". . . will not affect the line-stability of the weapon, though recoil will be increased on power-priority, or power decreased—"

"Shut up!" I shouted at the gun, and made a clumsy attempt to hit its Off button; my hand hit the pistol's stubby barrel. The gun skidded across the table and fell to the floor.

"Warning!" The gun shouted. "There are no user-serviceable parts inside! Irreversible deactivation will result if any attempt is made to dismantle or—"

"Quiet, you little bastard," I said (and it did go quiet). I picked it up and put it in the pocket of a jacket hanging over a chair. Damn the Culture; damn all guns. I went to get more drink, a heaviness inside me as I looked at the time again. Come home, please come home . . . and then come away, come away with me . . .

I fell asleep in front of the screen, a knot of dull panic in my belly competing with the spinning sensation in my head as I watched the news and worried about Maust, trying not to think of too many things. The news was full of executed terrorists and famous victories in small, distant wars against aliens, outworlders, subhumans. The last report I remember was about a riot in a city on another planet; there was no mention of civilian deaths, but I remember a shot of a broad street littered with crumpled shoes. The item closed with an injured policeman being interviewed in hospital.

I had my recurring nightmare, reliving the demonstration I was caught up in three years ago; looking, horrified, at a wall of drifting, sun-struck stun gas and seeing a line of police mounts come charging out of it, somehow more appalling than armoured cars or even tanks, not because of the visored riders with their long shock-batons, but because the tall animals were also armoured and gas-masked; monsters from a ready-made, mass-produced dream; terrorizing.

Maust found me there hours later, when he got back. The club had been raided and he hadn't been allowed to contact me. He held me as I cried, shushing me back to sleep.

"Wrobik, I can't. Risåret's putting on a new show next season and he's looking for new faces; it'll be big-time, straight stuff. A High City deal. I can't leave now; I've got my foot in the door. Please understand." He reached over the table to take my hand. I pulled it away.

"I can't do what they're asking me to do. I can't stay. So I have to go; there's nothing else I can do." My voice was dull. Maust started to clear away the plates and containers, shaking his long, graceful head. I hadn't eaten much; partly hangover, partly nerves. It was a muggy, enervating mid-morning; the tenement's conditioning plant had broken down again.

"Is what they're asking really so terrible?" Maust pulled his robe tighter, balancing plates expertly. I watched his slim back as he moved to the kitchen. "I mean, you won't even tell me. Don't you trust me?" His voice echoed.

What could I say? That I didn't know if I did trust him? That I loved him but: only he had known I was an outworlder. That had been my secret, and I'd told only him. So how did Kaddus and Cruizell know? How did Bright Path know? My sinuous, erotic, faithless dancer. Did you think because I always remained silent that I didn't know of all the times you deceived me?

"Maust, please; it's better that you don't know."

"Oh," Maust laughed distantly; that aching, beautiful sound, tearing at me. "How terribly dramatic. You're protecting me. How awfully gallant."

"Maust, this is serious. These people want me to do something I just can't do. If I don't do it they'll . . . they'll at least hurt me, badly. I don't know what they'll do. They . . . they might even try to hurt me through you. That was why I was so worried when you were late; I thought maybe they'd taken you."

"My dear, poor Wrobbie," Maust said, looking out from the kitchen, "it has been a long day; I think I pulled a muscle during my last number, we may not get paid after the raid—Stelmer's sure to use that as an excuse even if the filth didn't swipe the takings—and my ass is still sore from having one of those queer-bashing pigs poking his finger around inside me. Not as romantic as your dealings with gangsters and baddies, but important to me. I've enough to worry about. You're overreacting. Take a pill or something; go back to sleep; it'll look better later." He winked at me, disappeared. I listened to him moving about in the kitchen. A police siren moaned overhead. Music filtered through from the apartment below.

I went to the door of the kitchen. Maust was drying his hands. "They want me to shoot down the starship bringing the Admiral of the Fleet back on Ninthday," I told him. Maust looked blank for a second, then sniggered. He came up to me, held me by the shoulders.

"Really? And then what? Climb the outside of the Lev and fly to the sun on your magic bicycle?" He smiled tolerantly, amused. I put my hands on his and removed them slowly from my shoulders.

"No. I just have to shoot down the ship, that's all. I have . . . they gave me a gun that can do it." I took the gun from the jacket. He frowned, shaking his head, looked puzzled for a second, then laughed again.

"With that, my love? I doubt you could stop a motorized pogo-stick with that little—"

"Maust, please; believe me. This can do it. My people made it and the ship . . . the state has no defence against something like this."

Maust snorted, then took the gun from me. Its lights flicked off. "How do you switch it on?" He turned it over in his hand.

"By touching it; but only I can do it. It reads the genetic make-up of my skin, knows I am Culture. Don't look at me like that; it's true. Look." I showed him. I had the gun recite the first part of its monologue and switched the tiny screen to holo. Maust inspected the gun while I held it.

"You know," he said after a while, "this might be rather valuable."

"No, it's worthless to anyone else. It'll only work for me, and you can't get round its fidelities; it'll deactivate."

"How . . . faithful," Maust said, sitting down and looking steadily at me. "How neatly everything must be arranged in your 'Culture.' I didn't really believe you when you told me that tale, did you know that, my love? I thought you were just trying to impress me. Now I think I believe you."

I crouched down in front of him, put the gun on the table and my hands on his lap. "Then believe me that I can't do what they're asking, and that I am in danger; perhaps we both are. We have to leave. Now. Today or tomorrow. Before they think of another way to make me do this."

Maust smiled, ruffled my hair. "So fearful, eh? So desperately anxious." He bent, kissed my forehead. "Wrobbie, Wrobbie; I can't come with you. Go if you feel you must, but I can't come with you. Don't you know what this chance means to me? All my life I've wanted this; I may not get another opportunity. I have to stay, whatever. You go; go for as long as you must and don't tell me where you've gone. That way they can't use me, can they? Get in touch through a friend, once the dust has settled. Then we'll see. Perhaps you can come back; perhaps I'll have missed my big chance anyway and I'll come to join you. It'll be all right. We'll work something out."

I let my head fall to his lap, wanting to cry. "I can't leave you."

He hugged me, rocking me. "Oh, you'll probably find you're glad of the change. You'll be a hit wherever you go, my beauty; I'll probably have to kill some knife-fighter to win you back."

"Please, please come with me," I sobbed into his gown.

"I can't, my love, I just can't. I'll come to wave you goodbye, but I can't come with you."

He held me while I cried; the gun lay silent and dull on the table at his side, surrounded by the debris of our meal.

·   ·   ·

I was leaving. Fire escape from the flat just before dawn, over two walls clutching my travelling bag, a taxi from General Thetropsis Avenue to Intercontinental Station . . . then I'd catch a Railtube train to Bryme and take the Lev there, hoping for a standby on almost anything heading Out, either trans or inter. Maust had lent me some of his savings, and I still had a little high-rate credit left; I could make it. I left my terminal in the apartment. It would have been useful, but the rumours are true; the police can trace them, and I wouldn't put it past Kaddus and Cruizell to have a tame cop in the relevant department.

The station was crowded. I felt fairly safe in the high, echoing halls, surrounded by people and business. Maust was coming from the club to see me off; he'd promised to make sure he wasn't followed. I had just enough time to leave the gun at Left Luggage. I'd post the key to Kaddus, try to leave him a little less murderous.

There was a long queue at Left Luggage; I stood, exasperated, behind some naval cadets. They told me the delay was caused by the porters searching all bags and cases for bombs; a new security measure. I left the queue to go and meet Maust; I'd have to get rid of the gun somewhere else. Post the damn thing, or even just drop it in a waste bin.

I waited in the bar, sipping at something innocuous. I kept looking at my wrist, then feeling foolish. The terminal was back at the apartment; use a public phone, look for a clock. Maust was late.

There was a screen in the bar, showing a news bulletin. I shook off the absurd feeling that somehow I was already a wanted man, my face liable to appear on the news broadcast, and watched today's lies to take my mind off the time.

They mentioned the return of the Admiral of the Fleet, due in two days. I looked at the screen, smiling nervously. *Yeah, and you'll never know how close the bastard came to getting blown out of the skies.* For a moment or two I felt important, almost heroic.

Then the bombshell; just a mention—an aside, tacked on, the sort of thing they'd have cut had the programme been a few seconds over—that the Admiral would be bringing a guest with him; an ambassador from the Culture. I choked on my drink.

Was *that* who I'd really have been aiming at if I'd gone ahead?

What was the Culture doing anyway? An ambassador? The Culture knew everything about the Vreccile Economic Community, and was watching, analyzing; content to leave ill enough alone for now. The Vreccile people had little idea how advanced or widely spread the Culture was, though the court and Navy had a fairly good idea. Enough to make them slightly (though had they known it, still not remotely sufficiently) paranoid. What was an ambassador for?

And who was really behind the attempt on the ship? Bright Path would be indifferent to the fate of a single outworlder compared to the propaganda coup of pulling down a starship, but what if the gun hadn't come from them, but from a grouping in the court itself, or from the Navy? The VEC had problems; social problems, political problems. Maybe the President and his cronies were thinking about asking the Culture for aid. The price might involve the sort of changes some of the more corrupt officials would find terminally threatening to their luxurious lifestyles.

Shit, I didn't know; maybe the whole attempt to take out the ship was some loony in Security or the Navy trying to settle an old score, or just skip the next few rungs on the promotion ladder. I was still thinking about this when they paged me.

I sat still. The station PA called for me, three times. A phonecall. I told myself it was just Maust, calling to say he had been delayed; he knew I was leaving the terminal at the apartment so he couldn't call me direct. But would he announce my name all over a crowded station when he knew I was trying to leave quietly and unseen? Did he still take it all so lightly? I didn't want to answer that call. I didn't even want to think about it.

My train was leaving in ten minutes; I picked up my bag. The PA asked for me again, this time mentioning Maust's name. So I had no choice.

I went to Information. It was a viewcall.

"Wrobik," Kaddus sighed, shaking his head. He was in some office; anonymous, bland. Maust was standing, pale and frightened, just behind Kaddus' seat. Cruizell stood right behind Maust, grinning over his slim shoulder. Cruizell moved slightly, and Maust flinched. I saw him bite his lip. "Wrobik," Kaddus said again. "Were you going to leave so soon? I thought we had a date, yes?"

"Yes," I said quietly, looking at Maust's eyes. "Silly of me. I'll . . . stick around for . . . a couple of days. Maust, I—" The screen went grey.

I turned round slowly in the booth and looked at my bag, where the gun was. I picked the bag up. I hadn't realized how heavy it was.

I stood in the park, surrounded by dripping trees and worn rocks. Paths carved into the tired top-soil led in various directions. The earth smelled warm and damp. I looked down from the top of the gently sloped escarpment to where pleasure boats sailed in the dusk, lights reflecting on the still waters of the boating lake. The duskward quarter of the city was a hazy platform of light in the distance. I heard birds calling from the trees around me.

The aircraft lights of the Lev rose like a rope of flashing red beads into the blue evening sky; the port at the Lev's summit shone, still uneclipsed, in sunlight a hundred kilometres overhead. Lasers, ordinary searchlights and chemical fireworks began to make the sky bright above the Parliament buildings and the Great Square of the Inner City; a display to greet the returning, victorious Admiral, and maybe the ambassador from the Culture, too. I couldn't see the ship yet.

I sat down on a tree stump, drawing my coat about me. The gun was in my hand; on, ready, ranged, set. I had tried to be thorough and professional, as though I knew what I was doing; I'd even left a hired motorbike in some bushes on the far side of the escarpment, down near the busy parkway. I might actually get away with this. So I told myself, anyway. I looked at the gun.

I'd considered using it to try and rescue Maust, or maybe using it to kill myself; I'd even considered taking it to the police (another, slower form of suicide). I'd also considered calling Kaddus and telling him I'd lost it, it wasn't working, I couldn't kill a fellow Culture citizen . . . anything. But in the end; nothing.

If I wanted Maust back I had to do what I'd agreed to do.

Something glinted in the skies above the city; a pattern of falling, golden lights. The central light was brighter and larger than the others.

I had thought I could feel no more, but there was a sharp taste in my mouth, and my hands were shaking. Perhaps I would go berserk, once the ship was down, and attack the Lev too; bring the whole thing smashing down (or would part of it go spinning off into space? Maybe I ought to do it just to see). I could bombard half the city from here (hell, don't forget the curve shots; I could bombard the *whole* damn city from here); I could bring down the escort vessels and attacking planes and police cruisers; I could give the Vreccile the biggest shock they've ever had, before they got me . . .

The ships were over the city. Out of the sunlight, their laserproof mirror hulls were duller now. They were still falling; maybe five kilometres up. I checked the gun again.

Maybe it wouldn't work, I thought.

Lasers shone in the dust and grime above the city, producing tight spots on high and wispy clouds. Searchlight beams faded and spread in the same haze, while fire-works burst and slowly fell, twinkling and sparkling. The sleek ships dropped majesti-cally to meet the welcoming lights. I looked about the tree-lined ridge; alone. A warm breeze brought the grumbling sound of the parkway traffic to me.

I raised the gun and sighted. The formation of ships appeared on the holo display, the scene noon-bright. I adjusted the magnification, fingered a command stud; the gun locked onto the flagship, became rock-steady in my hand. A flashing white point in the display marked the centre of the vessel.

I looked round again, my heart hammering, my hand held by the field-anchored gun. Still nobody came to stop me. My eyes stung. The ships hung a few hundred me-tres above the state buildings of the Inner City. The outer vessels remained there; the centre craft, the flagship, stately and massive, a mirror held up to the glittering city, descended towards the Great Square. The gun dipped in my hand, tracking it.

Maybe the Culture ambassador wasn't aboard the damn ship anyway. This whole thing might be a Special Circumstances set-up; perhaps the Culture was ready to in-terfere now and it amused the planning Minds to have me, a heretic, push things over the edge. The Culture ambassador might have been a ruse, just in case I started to suspect . . . I didn't know. I didn't know anything. I was floating on a sea of possibili-ties, but parched of choices.

I squeezed the trigger.

The gun leapt backwards, light flared all around me. A blinding line of brilliance flicked, seemingly instantaneously, from me to the starship ten kilometres away. There was a sharp detonation of sound somewhere inside my head. I was thrown off the tree stump.

When I sat up again the ship had fallen. The Great Square blazed with flames and smoke and strange, bristling tongues of some terrible lightning; the remaining lasers and fireworks were made dull. I stood, shaking, ears ringing, and stared at what I'd done. Late-reacting sprinterceptiles from the escorts criss-crossed the air above the wreck and slammed into the ground, automatics fooled by the sheer velocity of the plasma bolt. Their warheads burst brightly amongst the boulevards and buildings of the Inner City, a bruise upon a bruise.

The noise of the first explosion smacked and rumbled over the park.

The police and the escort ships themselves were starting to react. I saw the lights of police cruisers rise strobing from the Inner City; the escort craft began to turn slowly above the fierce, flickering radiations of the wreck.

I pocketed the gun and ran down the damp path towards the bike, away from the escarpment's lip. Behind my eyes, burnt there, I could still see the line of light that had briefly joined me to the starship; bright path indeed, I thought, and nearly laughed. A bright path in the soft darkness of the mind.

I raced down to join all the other poor folk on the run.

IV.

VOLUNTEERS: REVISIONARIES (EARLY 1990S)

I like the idea of Space Opera more as furniture than as genre, since this explains how leftist writers in England can embrace it at the same time that it's being appropriated for almost opposite purposes by writers such as Orson Scott Card, who is essentially another galaxy—(or at least species)—destroyer, but with the caveat that we probably ought to feel bad about committing genocide, and it was all a trick anyway. In other words, maybe there is no inherent meaning in the form. Maybe it's all furniture and props, and not a form at all.

—Gary K. Wolfe in *Locus*

DAN SIMMONS

Dan Simmons [1948–] (www.dansimmons.com) lives outside of Denver in Colorado. He was for many years a schoolteacher, and has been a full-time writer since 1987. His early fiction was horror. He based his first, World Fantasy Award–winning novel, *Song of Kali* (1985), on a year he spent in India traveling on a group Fulbright Fellowship for educators.

For reasons of length, his first SF novel was published in two parts: *Hyperion* (1989), winner of the Hugo Award for Best Novel, and *The Fall of Hyperion* (1990). He returned to the Hyperion universe with *Endymion* (1996) and *The Rise of Endymion* (1997), another novel in two volumes, the four comprising The Hyperion Cantos.

Space operas by Card, Brin, Cherryh, Simmons, Bujold, and Vernor Vinge won best novel every year between 1986 and 1993, and this suggests the central importance of space opera to ambitious US writers (and to the reading audience) in those years. It also shows that, in the heydey of cyberpunk, space opera was the dominant mode in popular SF. And Simmons was a central figure.

Only one space opera won between 1996 and 2005. One wonders if this reflects changing audience tastes, or a shift in the focus of ambition among the leading writers. In all but one of the years in that decade, there was in fact only one space opera nominated. This certainly suggests that post-1995 space opera did not achieve the popular impact of the earlier wave.

In the 1990s and beyond, Simmons wrote many varieties of fiction in and out of genre. His most recent books are *A Winter's Haunting* (2002), winner of the 2003 Colorado Book Award for Best Genre Novel; *Ilium* (2003), Simmons's return to space opera; *Hard as Nails* (2003), a hard-boiled mystery featuring his continuing character Joe Kurtz; and *Olympos* (2005), the sequel to *Ilium*. He said in a *Locus* interview, "Why write across genre lines then? For me, it's . . . the appeal of trying to master the different styles, learn the necessary tropes and protocols, and to honor the best writing in these various genres. It's pure celebration, in the same way my first SF novel, *Hyperion*, was a celebration of the various forms of SF, from Jack Vance to cyberpunk." The broad canvas of space opera obviously appeals to him, as all his SF novels to date are space opera.

In a headnote to this story, which is set in the universe of The Hyperion Cantos, Simmons said, "The four Hyperion books cover more than thirteen centuries in time, tens of thousands of light-years in space, more than three thousand pages of the reader's time, the rise and fall of at least two major interstellar civilizations, and more ideas than the author could shake an epistemological stick at. They are, in other words, space opera."

As the reviewer in *The New York Times* said of the last book in the series, "Yet *The Rise of Endymion*, like its three predecessors, is also a full-blooded action novel, replete with personal combats and battles in space that are distinguished from the formulaic space opera by the magnitude of what is at stake—which is nothing less than the salvation of the human soul." It is an amusing footnote to the space opera renaming game that critic John Clute, according to David Pringle, "coined the unholy phrase 'entelechy opera' in a review of Dan Simmons's novels."

ORPHANS OF THE HELIX

DAN SIMMONS

The great spinship translated down from Hawking space into the red-and-white double light of a close binary. While the 684,300 people of the Amoiete Spectrum Helix dreamt on in deep cryogenic sleep, the five AIs in charge of the ship conferred. They had encountered an unusual phenomenon and while four of the five had agreed it important enough to bring the huge spinship out of C-plus Hawking space, there was a lively debate—continuing for several microseconds—about what to do next.

The spinship itself looked beautiful in the distant light of the two stars, white and red light bathing its kilometer-long skin, the starlight flashing on the three thousand environmental deep-sleep pods, the groups of thirty pods on each of the one hundred spin hubs spinning past so quickly that the swing arms were like the blur of great, overlapping fan blades, while the three thousand pods themselves appeared to be a single, flashing gem blazing with red and white light. The Aeneans had adapted the ship so that the hubs of the spinwheels along the long, central shaft of the ship were slanted—the first thirty spin arms angled back, the second hub angling its longer thirty-pod arms forward, so that the deep-sleep pods themselves passed between each other with only microseconds of separation, coalescing into a solid blur that made the ship under full spin resemble exactly what its name implied—*Helix*. An observer watching from some hundreds of kilometers away would see what looked to be a rotating human double DNA helix catching the light from the paired suns.

All five of the AIs decided that it would be best to call in the spin pods. First the great hubs changed their orientation until the gleaming helix became a series of three thousand slowing carbon-carbon spin arms, each with an ovoid pod visible at its tip through the slowing blur of speed. Then the pod arms stopped and retracted against the long ship, each deep-sleep pod fitting into a concave nesting cusp in the hull like an egg being set carefully into a container.

The *Helix*, no longer resembling its name so much now so as a long, slender arrow with command centers at the bulbous, triangular head, and the Hawking drive and larger fusion engines bulking at the stern, morphed eight layers of covering over the nested spin arms and pods. All of the AIs voted to decelerate toward the G8 white star under a conservative four hundred gravities and to extend the containment field to class twenty. There was no visible threat in either system of the binary, but the red giant in the more distant system was—as it should be—expelling vast amounts of dust and stellar debris. The AI who took the greatest pride in its navigational skills and caution warned that the entry trajectory toward the G8 star should steer very clear of the L_1 Roche lobe point because of the massive heliosphere shock waves there, and all five AIs began charting a deceleration course into the G8 system that would avoid the worst of the heliosphere turmoil. The radiation shock waves there could be dealt with easily using even a class-three containment field, but with 684,300 human souls aboard and under their care, none of the AIs would take the slightest chance.

Their next decision was unanimous and inevitable. Given the reason for the deviation and deceleration into the G8 system, they would have to awaken humans. Saigyō, AI in charge of personnel lists, duty rosters, psychology profiles, and who had made it its business to meet and know each of the 684,300 men, women, and children, took several seconds to review the list before deciding on the nine people to awaken.

Dem Lia awoke with none of the dull hangover feel of the old-fashioned cryogenic fugue units. She felt rested and fit as she sat up in her deep-sleep crèche, the unit arm offering her the traditional glass of orange juice.

"Emergency?" she said, her voice no more thick or dull than it would have been after a good night's sleep.

"Nothing threatening the ship or the mission," said Saigyō, the AI. "An anomaly of interest. An old radio transmission from a system which may be a possible source of resupply. There are no problems whatsoever with ship function or life support. Everyone is well. The ship is in no danger."

"How far are we from the last system we checked?" said Dem Lia, finishing her orange juice and donning her shipsuit with its emerald green stripe on the left arm and turban. Her people had traditionally worn desert robes, each robe the color of the Amoiete Spectrum that the different families had chosen to honor, but robes were impractical for spinship travel where zero g was a frequent environment.

"Six thousand three hundred light-years," said Saigyō.

Dem Lia stopped herself from blinking. "How many years since last awakening?" she said softly. "How many years' total voyage ship time? How many years' total voyage time-debt?"

"Nine ship years and one hundred two time-debt years since last awakening," said Saigyō. "Total voyage ship time, thirty-six years. Total voyage time-debt relative to human space, four hundred and one years, three months, one week, five days."

Dem Lia rubbed her neck. "How many of us are you awakening?"

"Nine."

Dem Lia nodded, quit wasting time chatting with the AI, glanced around only once at the two-hundred-some sealed sarcophagi where her family and friends continued sleeping, and took the main shipline people mover to the command deck, where the other eight would be gathering.

The Aeneans had followed the Amoiete Spectrum Helix people's request to construct the command deck like the bridge of an ancient torchship or some Old Earth, pre-Hegira seagoing vessel. The deck was oriented one direction to down and Dem Lia was pleased to notice on the ride to the command deck that the ship's containment field held at a steady one gee. The bridge itself was about twenty-five meters across and held command-nexus stations for the various specialists, as well as a central table—round, of course—where the awakened were gathering, sipping coffee and making the usual soft jokes about cryogenic deep-sleep dreams. All around the great hemisphere of the command deck, broad windows opened onto space: Dem Lia stood a minute looking at the strange arrangement of the stars, the view back along the seemingly infinite length of the *Helix* itself where heavy filters dimmed the brilliance of the fusion-flame tail that now reached back eight kilometers toward their destination—and the binary system itself, one small white star and one red giant, both clearly visible. The windows were not actual windows, of course; their holo pickups could be changed and zoomed or opaqued in an instant, but for now the illusion was perfect.

Dem Lia turned her attention to the eight people at the table. She had met all of them during the two years of ship training with the Aeneans, but knew none of these individuals well. All had been in the select group of fewer than a thousand chosen for possible awakening during transit. She checked their color-band stripes as they made introductions over coffee.

Four men, five women. One of the other women was also an emerald green, which meant that Dem Lia did not know if command would fall to her or the younger woman. Of course, consensus would determine that at any rate, but since the emerald green band of the Amoiete Spectrum Helix poem and society stood for resonance with nature, ability to command, comfort with technology, and the preservation of endangered life-forms—and all 684,300 of the Amoiete refugees could be considered endangered life-forms this far from human space—it was assumed that in unusual awakenings the greens would be voted into overall command.

In addition to the other green—a young, redheaded woman named Res Sandre—there was: a red-band male, Patek Georg Dem Mio; a young, white-band female named Den Soa whom Dem Lia knew from the diplomacy simulations; an ebony-band male named Jon Mikail Dem Alem; an older yellow-band woman named Oam Rai whom Dem Lia remembered as having excelled at ship system's operations; a white-haired blue-band male named Peter Delen Dem Tae whose primary training would be in psychology; an attractive female violet-band—almost surely chosen for astronomy—named Kem Loi; and an orange male—their medic, whom Dem Lia had spoken to on several occasions—Samuel Ria Kem Ali, known to everyone as Dr. Sam.

After introductions there was a silence. The group looked out the windows at the binary system, the G8 white star almost lost in the glare of the *Helix*'s formidable fusion tail.

Finally the red, Patek Georg, said, "All right, ship. Explain."

Saigyō's calm voice came over the omnipresent speakers. "We were nearing time to begin a search for earthlike worlds when sensors and astronomy became interested in this system."

"A *binary* system?" said Kem Loi, the violet. "Certainly not in the red giant system?" The Amoiete Spectrum Helix people had been very specific about the world they wanted their ship to find for them—G2 sun, earthlike world at least a 9 on the old Solmev Scale, blue oceans, pleasant temperatures—paradise, in other words. They had tens of thousands of light-years and thousands of years to hunt. They fully expected to find it.

"There are no worlds left in the red-giant system," agreed Saigyō the AI affably enough. "We estimate that the system was a G2 yellow-white dwarf star . . ."

"Sol," muttered Peter Delen, the blue, sitting at Dem Lia's right.

"Yes," said Saigyō. "Much like the Old Earth's sun. We estimate that it became unstable on the main sequence hydrogen-burning stage about three and one half million standard years ago and then expanded to its red giant phase and swallowed any planets that had been in system."

"How many AUs out does the giant extend?" asked Res Sandre, the other green.

"Approximately one-point-three," said the AI.

"And no outer planets?" asked Kem Loi. Violets in the *Helix* were dedicated to complex structures, chess, the love of the more complex aspects of human relationships, and astronomy. "It would seem that there would be some gas giants or rocky worlds left if it only expanded a bit beyond what would have been Old Earth's or Hyperion's orbit."

"Maybe the outer worlds were very small planetoids driven away by the constant outgassing of heavy particles," said Patek Georg, the red-band pragmatist.

"Perhaps no worlds formed here," said Den Soa, the white-band diplomat. Her voice was sad. "At least in that case no life was destroyed when the sun went red giant."

"Saigyō," said Dem Lia, "why are we decelerating in toward this white star? May we see the specs on it, please?"

Images, trajectories, and data columns appeared over the table.

"What is that?" said the older yellow-band woman, Oam Rai.

"An Ouster forest ring," said Jon Mikail Dem Alem. "All this way. All these years. And some ancient Ouster Hegira seedship beat us to it."

"Beat us to what?" asked Res Sandre, the other green. "There are no planets in this system are there, Saigyō?"

"No, ma'am," said the AI.

"Were you thinking of restocking on their forest ring?" said Dem Lia. The plan had been to avoid any Aenean, Pax, or Ouster worlds or strongholds found along their long voyage away from human space.

"This orbital forest ring is exceptionally bountiful," said Saigyō the AI, "but our real reason for awakening you and beginning the in-system deceleration is that someone living on or near the ring is transmitting a distress signal on an early Hegemony code band. It is very weak, but we have been picking it up for two hundred and twenty-eight light-years."

This gave them all pause. The *Helix* had been launched some eighty years after the Aenean Shared Moment, that pivotal event in human history which had marked the beginning of a new era for most of the human race. Previous to the Shared Moment, the Church-manipulated Pax society had ruled human space for three hundred years. These Ousters would have missed all of Pax history and probably most of the thousand years of Hegemony history that preceded the Pax. Added to that, the *Helix*'s time-debt added more than four hundred years of travel. If these Ousters had been part of the original Hegira from Old Earth or from the Old Neighborhood Systems in the earliest days of the Hegemony, they may well have been out of touch with the rest of the human race for fifteen hundred standard years or more.

"Interesting," said Peter Delen Dem Tae, whose blue-band training included profound immersion in psychology and anthropology.

"Saigyō, play the distress signal, please," said Dem Lia.

There came a series of static hisses, pops, and whistles with what might have been two words electronically filtered out. The accent was early Hegemony Web English.

"What does it say?" said Dem Lia. "I can't quite make it out."

"Help us," said Saigyō. The AI's voice was tinted with an Asian accent and usually sounded slightly amused, but his tone was flat and serious now.

The nine around the table looked at one another again in silence. Their goal had been to leave human and posthuman Aenean space far behind them, allowing their people, the Amoiete Spectrum Helix culture, to pursue their own goals, to find their own destiny free of Aenean intervention. But Ousters were just another branch of human stock, attempting to determine their own evolutionary path by adapting to space, their Templar allies traveling with them, using their genetic secrets to grow orbital forest rings and even spherical startrees completely surrounding their suns.

"How many Ousters do you estimate live on the orbital forest ring?" asked Den Soa, who with her white training would probably be their diplomat if and when they made contact.

"Seven hundred million on the thirty-degree arc we can resolve on this side of the sun," said the AI. "If they have migrated to all or most of the ring, obviously we can estimate a population of several billion."

"Any sign of Akerataeli or the zeplens?" asked Patek Georg. All of the great forest rings and startree spheres had been collaborative efforts with these two alien races, which had joined forces with the Ousters and Templars during the Fall of the Hegemony.

"None," said Saigyō. "But you might notice this remote view of the ring itself in the center window. We are still sixty-three AUs out from the ring . . . this is amplified ten thousand times."

They all turned to look at the front window where the forest ring seemed only thousands of kilometers away, its green leaves and yellow and brown branches and braided main trunk curving away out of sight, the G8 star blazing beyond.

"It looks wrong," said Dem Lia.

"This is the anomaly that added to the urgency of the distress signal and decided us to bring you out of deep sleep," said Saigyō, his voice sounding slightly bemused again. "This orbital forest ring is not of Ouster or Templar bioconstruction."

Doctor Samuel Ria Kem Ali whistled softly. "An alien-built forest ring. But with human-descended Ousters living on it."

"And there is something else we have found since entering the system," said Saigyō. Suddenly the left window was filled with a view of a machine—a spacecraft—so huge and ungainly that it almost defied description. An image of the *Helix* was superimposed at the bottom of the screen to give scale. The *Helix* was a kilometer long. The base of this other spacecraft was at least a thousand times as long. The monster was huge and broad, bulbous and ugly, carbon black and insectoidal, bearing the worst features of both organic evolution and industrial manufacture. Centered in the front of it was what appeared to be a steel-toothed maw, a rough opening lined with a seemingly endless series of mandibles and shredding blades and razor-sharp rotors.

"It looks like God's razor," said Patek Georg Dem Mio, the cool irony undercut slightly by a just-perceptible quaver in his voice.

"God's razor my ass," said Jon Mikail Dem Alem softly. As an ebony, life support was one of his specialties, and he had grown up tending the huge farms on Vitus-Gray-Balianus B. "That's a threshing machine from hell."

"Where is it?" Dem Lia started to ask, but already Saigyō had thrown the plot on the holo showing their deceleration trajectory in toward the forest ring. The obscene machine-ship was coming in from above the ecliptic, was some twenty-eight AUs ahead of them, was decelerating rapidly but not nearly as aggressively as the *Helix*, and was headed directly for the Ouster forest ring. The trajectory plot was clear—at its current rate of deceleration, the machine would directly intercept the ring in nine standard days.

"This may be the cause of their distress signal," the other green, Res Sandre, said dryly.

"If it were coming at me or my world, I'd scream so loudly that you'd hear me two hundred and twenty-eight light-years away without a radio," said the young white-band, Den Soa.

"If we started picking up this weak signal some two hundred twenty-eight light-years ago," said Patek Georg, "it means that either that thing has been decelerating in-system *very* slowly, or . . ."

"It's been here before," said Dem Lia. She ordered the AI to opaque the windows and to dismiss itself from their company. "Shall we assign roles, duties, priorities, and make initial decisions?" she said softly.

The other eight around the table nodded soberly.

To a stranger, to someone outside the Spectrum Helix culture, the next five minutes would have been very hard to follow. Total consensus was reached within the first two minutes, but only a small part of the discussion was through talk. The combination of hand gestures, body language, shorthand phrases, and silent nods that had evolved through four centuries of a culture determined to make decisions through consensus worked well here. These people's parents and grandparents knew the necessity of command structure and discipline—half a million of their people had died in the short but nasty war with the Pax remnant on Vitus-Gray-Balianus B, and then another hundred thousand when the fleeing Pax vandals came looting through their system some thirty years later. But they were determined to elect command through consensus and thereafter make as many decisions as possible through the same means.

In the first two minutes, assignments were settled and the subtleties around the duties dealt with.

Dem Lia was to be in command. Her single vote could override consensus when necessary. The other green, Res Sandre, preferred to monitor propulsion and engineering, working with the reticent AI named Basho to use this time out of Hawking space to good advantage in taking stock.

The red-band male, Patek Georg, to no one's surprise, accepted the position of chief security officer—both for the ship's formidable defenses and during any contact with the Ousters. Only Dem Lia could override his decisions on use of ship weaponry.

The young white-band woman, Den Soa, was to be in charge of communications and diplomacy, but she requested and Peter Delen Dem Tae agreed to share the responsibility with her. Peter's training in psychology had included theoretical exobiopsychology.

Dr. Sam would monitor the health of everyone aboard and study the evolutionary biology of the Ousters and Templars if it came to contact.

Their ebony-band male, Jon Mikail Dem Alem, assumed command of life support—both in reviewing and controlling systems in the *Helix* along with the appropriate AI, but also arranging for necessary environments if they met with the Ousters aboard ship.

Oam Rai, the oldest of the nine and the ship's chess master, agreed to coordinate general ship systems and to be Dem Lia's principal advisor as events unfolded.

Kem Loi, the astronomer, accepted responsibility for all long-range sensing, but was obviously eager to use her spare time to study the binary system. "Did anyone notice what old friend our white star ahead resembles?" she asked.

"Tau Ceti," said Res Sandre without hesitation.

Kem Loi nodded. "And we saw the anomaly in the placing of the forest ring."

Everyone had. The Ousters preferred G2-type stars, where they could grow their orbital forests at about one AU from the sun. This ring circled its star at only 0.36 AUs.

"Almost the same distance as Tau Ceti Center from its sun," mused Patek Georg. TC^2, as it had been known for more than a thousand years, had once been the central world and capital of the Hegemony. Then it had become a backwater world under the Pax until a Church cardinal on that world attempted a coup against the beleaguered pope during the final days of the Pax. Most of the rebuilt cities had been leveled then. When the *Helix* had left human space eighty years after that war, the Aeneans were repopulating and repopularizing the ancient capital, rebuilding beautiful, classical structures on broad estates and essentially turning the lance-lashed ruins into an Arcadia. For Aeneans.

Assignments given and accepted, the group discussed the option of awakening their immediate family members from cryogenic sleep. Since Spectrum Helix families consisted of triune marriages—either one male and two females or vice versa—and since most had children aboard, this was a complicated subject. Jon Mikail discussed the life-support considerations—which were minor—but everyone agreed that it would complicate decision-making with family awake only as passengers. It was agreed to leave them in deep sleep, with the one exception of Den Soa's husband and wife. The young white-band diplomat admitted that she would feel insecure without her two loved ones with her, and the group allowed this exception to their decision with the gentle suggestion that the reawakened mates would stay off the command deck unless there was compelling reason for them to be there. Den Soa agreed at once. Saigyō was summoned and immediately began awakening of Den Soa's bond pair. They had no children.

Then the most central issue was discussed.

"Are we actually going to decelerate to this ring and involve ourselves in these Ousters' problems?" asked Patek Georg. "Assuming that their distress signal is still relevant."

"They're still broadcasting on the old bandwidths," said Den Soa, who had jack-sensed into the ship's communications system. The young woman with blond hair looked at something in her virtual vision. "And that monster machine is still headed their way."

"But we have to remember," said the red-band male, "that our goal was to avoid contact with possibly troublesome human outposts on our way out of known space."

Res Sandre, the green now in charge of engineering, smiled. "I believe that we made that general plan about avoiding Pax or Ouster or Aenean elements without considering that we would meet up with humans—or former humans—some eight thousand light-years outside the known sphere of human space."

"It could still mean trouble for everyone," said Patek Georg.

They all understood the real meaning of the red-band security chief's statement. Reds in the Spectrum Helix devoted themselves to physical courage, political convictions, and passion for art, but they also were deeply trained in compassion for other living things. The other eight understood that when he said the contact might mean trouble for "everyone," he meant not only the 684,291 sleeping souls aboard the ship, but also the Ousters and Templars themselves. These orphans of Old Earth, this band of self-evolving human stock, had been beyond history and the human pall for at least a millennium, perhaps much longer. Even the briefest contact could cause problems for the Ouster culture as well.

"We're going to go in and see if we can help . . . and replenish fresh provisions at the same time, if that's possible," said Dem Lia, her tone friendly but final. "Saigyō, at our greatest deceleration figure consistent with not stressing the internal containment fields, how long will it take us to a rendezvous point about five thousand klicks from the forest ring?"

"Thirty-seven hours," said the AI.

"Which gets us there seven days and a bit before that ugly machine," said Oam Rai.

"Hell," said Dr. Sam, "that machine could be something the Ousters built to ferry themselves through the heliosphere shock fields to the red-giant system. A sort of ugly trolley."

"I don't think so," said young Den Soa, missing the older man's irony.

"Well, the Ousters have noticed us," said Patek Georg, who was jacksensed into his system's nexus. "Saigyō, bring up the windows again, please. Same magnification as before."

Suddenly the room was filled with starlight and sunlight and the reflected light from the braided orbital forest ring that looked like nothing so much as Jack and the Giant's beanstalk, curving out of sight around the bright, white star. Only now something else had been added to the picture.

"This is real time?" whispered Dem Lia.

"Yes," said Saigyō. "The Ousters have obviously been watching our fusion tail as we've entered the system. Now they're coming out to greet us."

Thousands—tens of thousands—of fluttering bands of light had left the forest ring and were moving like brilliant fireflies or radiant gossamers away from the braid of huge leaves, bark, and atmosphere. The thousands of motes of light were headed out-system, toward the *Helix*.

"Could you please amplify that image a bit more?" said Dem Lia.

She had been speaking to Saigyō, but it was Kem Loi, who was already wired into the ship's optic net, who acted.

Butterflies of light. Wings a hundred, two hundred, five hundred kilometers across catching the solar wind and riding the magnetic-field lines pouring out of the small, bright star. But not just tens of thousands of winged angels or demons of light, hundreds of thousands. At the very minimum, hundreds of thousands.

"Let's hope they're friendly," said Patek Georg.

"Let's hope we can still communicate with them," whispered young Den Soa. "I mean . . . they could have forced their own evolution any direction in the last fifteen hundred years."

Dem Lia set her hand softly on the table, but hard enough to be heard. "I suggest that we quit speculating and hoping for the moment and get ready for this rendezvous in . . ." She paused.

"Twenty-seven hours eight minutes if the Ousters continue sailing out-system to meet us," said Saigyō on cue.

"Ros Sandre," Dem Lia said softly, "why don't you and your propulsion AI begin work now on making sure that our last bit of deceleration is mild enough that it isn't going to fry a few tens of thousands of these Ousters coming to greet us. That would be a bad overture to diplomatic contact."

"If they *are* coming out with hostile intent," said Patek Georg, "the fusion drive would be one of our most potent weapons against . . ."

Dem Lia interrupted. Her voice was soft but brooked no argument. "No discussion of war with this Ouster civilization until their motives become clear. Patek, you can review all ship defensive systems, but let us have no further group discussion of offensive action until you and I talk about it privately."

Patek Georg bowed his head.

"Are there any other questions or comments?" asked Dem Lia. There were none.

The nine people rose from the table and went about their business.

A largely sleepless twenty-four-plus hours later, Dem Lia stood alone and god-sized in the white star's system, the G8 blazing away only a few yards from her shoulder. The braided worldtree was so close that she could have reached out and touched it, wrapped her god-sized hand around it, while at the level of her chest the hundreds of thousands of shimmering wings of light converged on the *Helix*, whose deceleration fusion tail had dwindled to nothing. Dem Lia stood on nothing, her feet planted steadily on black space, the alien forest ring roughly at her belt line, the stars a huge sphere of constellations and foggy galactic scatterings far above, around, and beyond her.

Suddenly Saigyō joined her. The tenth-century monk assumed his usual virreal pose: cross-legged, floating easily just above the plane of the ecliptic a few respectful yards from Dem Lia. He was shirtless and barefoot, and his round belly added to the sense of good feeling that emanated from the round face, squinted eyes, and ruddy cheeks.

"The Ousters fly the solar winds so beautifully," muttered Dem Lia.

Saigyō nodded. "You notice, though, that they're really surfing the shock waves riding out along the magnetic-field lines. That gives them those astounding bursts of speed."

"I've been told that, but not seen it," said Dem Lia. "Could you . . ."

Instantly the solar system in which they stood became a maze of magnetic-field lines pouring from the G8 white star, curving at first and then becoming as straight and evenly spaced as a barrage of laser lances. The display showed this elaborate pattern of magnetic-field lines in red. Blue lines showed the uncountable paths of cosmic rays flowing into the system from all over the galaxy, aligning themselves with the magnetic-field lines and trying to corkscrew their way up the field lines like swirling salmon fighting their way upstream to spawn in the belly of the star. Dem Lia noticed that magnetic-field lines pouring from both the north and south poles of the sun were kinked and folded around themselves, thus deflecting even more cosmic waves that should otherwise have had an easy trip up smooth polar-field lines. Dem Lia changed metaphors, thinking of sperm fighting their way toward a blazing egg, and being cast aside by vicious solar winds and surges of magnetic waves, blasted away by shock waves that whipped out along the field lines as if someone had forcefully shaken a wire or snapped a bullwhip.

"It's stormy," said Dem Lia, seeing the flight path of so many of the Ousters now rolling and sliding and surging along these shock fronts of ions, magnetic fields, and cosmic rays, holding their positions with wings of glowing forcefield energy as the solar wind propagated first forward and then backward along the magnetic-field lines, and finally surfing the shock waves forward again as speedier bursts of solar winds crashed into more sluggish waves ahead of them, creating temporary tsunami that rolled out-system and then flowed backward like a heavy surf rolling back in toward the blazing beach of the G8 sun.

The Ousters handled this confusion of geometries, red lines of magnetic-field lines, yellow lines of ions, blue lines of cosmic rays, and rolling spectra of crashing shock fronts with seeming ease. Dem Lia glanced once out to where the surging heliosphere of the red giant met the seething heliosphere of this bright G8 star and the storm of light and colors there reminded her of a multihued, phosphorescent ocean crashing against the cliffs of an equally colorful and powerful continent of broiling energy. A rough place.

"Let's return to the regular display," said Dem Lia, and instantly the stars and forest ring and fluttering Ousters and slowing *Helix* were back—the last two items quite out of scale to show them clearly.

"Saigyō," said Dem Lia, "please invite all of the other AIs here now."

The smiling monk raised thin eyebrows. "All of them here at once?"

"Yes."

They appeared soon, but not instantly, one figure solidifying into virtual presence a second or two before the next.

First came Lady Murasaki, shorter even than the diminutive Dem Lia, the style of her three-thousand-year-old robe and kimono taking the acting commander's breath away. *What beauty Old Earth had taken for granted*, thought Dem Lia. Lady Murasaki bowed politely and slid her small hands in the sleeves of her robe. Her face was painted almost white, her lips and eyes were heavily outlined, and her long, black hair was done up so elaborately that Dem Lia—who had worn short hair most of her life—could not even imagine the work of pinning, clasping, combing, braiding, shaping and washing such a mass.

Ikkyū stepped confidently across the empty space on the other side of the virtual *Helix* a second later. This AI had chosen the older persona of the long-dead Zen Poet: Ikkyū looked to be about seventy, taller than most Japanese, quite bald, with wrinkles of concern on his forehead and lines of laughter around his bright eyes. Before the flight had begun, Dem Ria had used the ship's history banks to read about the fifteenth-century monk, poet, musician, and calligrapher: it seemed that when the historical, living Ikkyū had turned seventy, he had fallen in love with a blind singer just forty years his junior and scandalized the younger monks when he moved his love into the temple to live with him. Dem Lia liked Ikkyū.

Basho appeared next. The great *haiku* expert chose to appear as a gangly seventeenth-century Japanese farmer, wearing the coned hat and clog shoes of his profession. His fingernails always had some soil under them.

Ryōkan stepped gracefully into the circle. He was wearing beautiful robes of an astounding blue with gold trim. His hair was long and tied in a queue.

"I've asked you all here at once because of the complicated nature of this rendezvous with the Ousters," Dem Lia said firmly. "I understand from the log that one of you was opposed to translating down from Hawking space to respond to this distress call."

"I was," said Basho, his speech in modern post-Pax English but his voice gravel-rough and as guttural as a Samurai's grunt.

"Why?" said Dem Lia.

Basho made a gesture with his gangly hand. "The programming priorities to which we agreed did not cover this specific event. I felt it offered too great a potential for danger and too little benefit in our true goal of finding a colony world."

Dem Lia gestured toward the swarms of Ousters closing on the ship. They were only a few thousand kilometers away now. They had been broadcasting their peaceful intentions across the old radio bandwidths for more than a standard day. "Do you still feel that it's too risky?" she asked the tall AI.

"Yes," said Basho.

Dem Lia nodded, frowning slightly. It was always disturbing when the AIs disagreed on an important issue, but that was why the Aeneans had left them Autonomous after the breakup of the TechnoCore. And that was why there were five to vote.

"The rest of you obviously saw the risk as acceptable?"

Lady Murasaki answered in her low, demure voice, almost a whisper. "We saw it as an excellent possibility to restock new foodstuffs and water, while the cultural implications were more for you to ponder and act on than for us to decide. Of course, we had not detected the huge spacecraft in the system before we translated out of Hawking space. It might have affected our decision."

"This is a human-Ouster culture, almost certainly with a sizable Templar population, that may not have had contact with the outside human universe since the earliest Hegemony days, if then," said Ikkyū with great enthusiasm. "They may well be the farthest-flung outpost of the ancient Hegira. Of all humankind. A wonderful learning opportunity."

Dem Lia nodded impatiently. "We close to rendezvous within a few hours. You've heard their radio contact—they say they wish to greet us and talk, and we've been polite in return. Our dialects are not so diverse that the translator beads can't handle them in face-to-face conversations. But how can we know if they actually come in peace?"

Ryōkan cleared his throat. "It should be remembered that for more than a thousand years, the so-called Wars with the Ousters were provoked—first by the Hegemony and then by the Pax. The original Ouster deep-space settlements were peaceful places and this most-distant colony would have experienced none of the conflict."

Saigyō chucked from his comfortable perch on nothing. "It should also be remembered that during the actual Pax wars with the Ousters, to defend themselves, these peaceful, space-adapted humans learned to build and use torchships, modified Hawking drive warships, plasma weapons, and even some captured Pax Gideon drive weapons." He waved his bare arm. "We've scanned every one of these advancing Ousters, and none carry a weapon—not so much as a wooden spear."

Dem Lia nodded. "Kem Loi has shown me astronomical evidence which suggests that their moored seedship was torn away from the ring at an early date—possibly only years or months after they arrived. This system is devoid of asteroids, and the Oort cloud has been scattered far beyond their reach. It is conceivable that they have neither metal nor an industrial capacity."

"Ma'am," said Basho, his countenance concerned, "how can we know that? Ousters have modified their bodies sufficiently to generate forcefield wings that can extend for hundreds of kilometers. If they approach the ship closely enough, they could theoretically use the combined plasma effect of those wings to attempt to breach the containment fields and attack the ship."

"Beaten to death by angels' wings," Dem Lia mused softly. "An ironic way to die."

The AIs said nothing.

"Who is working most directly with Patek Georg Dem Mio on defense strategies?" Dem Lia asked into the silence.

"I am," said Ryōkan.

Dem Lia had known that, but she still thought, *Thank God it's not Basho.* Patek Georg was paranoid enough for the AI-human interface team on this specialty.

"What are Patek's recommendations going to be when we humans meet in a few minutes?" Dem Lia bluntly demanded from Ryōkan.

The AI hesitated only the slightest of perceptible instants. AIs understood both discretion and loyalty to the human working with them in their specialty, but they also understood the imperatives of the elected commander's role on the ship.

"Patek Georg is going to recommend a hundred-kilometer extension of the class-twenty external containment field," said Ryōkan softly. "With all energy weapons on standby and pre-targeted on the three hundred nine thousand, two hundred and five approaching Ousters."

Dem Lia's eyebrows rose a trifle. "And how long would it take our systems to lance more than three hundred thousand such targets?" she asked softly.

"Two-point-six seconds," said Ryōkan.

Dem Lia shook her head. "Ryōkan, please tell Patek Georg that you and I have spoken and that I want the containment field not at a hundred-klick distance, but maintained at a steady one kilometer from the ship. It may remain a class-twenty field—the Ousters can actually see the strength of it, and that's good. But the ship's weapons systems will not target the Ousters at this time. Presumably, they can see our targeting scans as well. Ryōkan, you and Patek Georg can run as many simulations of the combat encounter as you need to feel secure, but divert no power to the energy weapons and allow no targeting until I give the command."

Ryōkan bowed. Basho shuffled his virtual clogs but said nothing.

Lady Murasaki fluttered a fan half in front of her face. "You trust," she said softly.

Dem Lia did not smile. "Not totally. Never totally. Ryōkan, I want you and Patek Georg to work out the containment-field system so that if even one Ouster attempts to breach the containment field with focused plasma from his or her solar wings, the containment field should go to emergency class thirty-five and instantly expand to five hundred klicks."

Ryōkan nodded. Ikkyū smiled slightly and said, "That will be one very quick ride for a great mass of Ousters, Ma'am. Their personal energy systems might not be up to containing their own life support under that much of a shock, and it's certain that they wouldn't decelerate for half an AU or more."

Dem Lia nodded. "That's their problem. I don't think it will come to that. Thank you all for talking to me."

All six human figures winked out of existence.

Rendezvous was peaceful and efficient.

The first question the Ousters had radioed the *Helix* twenty hours earlier was, "Are you Pax?"

This had startled Dem Lia and the others at first. Their assumption was that these people had been out of touch with human space since long before the rise of the Pax. Then the ebony, Jon Mikail Dem Alem, said, "The Shared Moment. It has to have been the Shared Moment."

The nine looked at each other in silence at this. Everyone understood that Aenea's "Shared Moment" during her torture and murder by the Pax and TechnoCore had been shared by every human being in human space—a gestalt resonance along the Void Which Binds that had transmitted the dying young woman's thoughts and memories and knowledge along those threads in the quantum fabric of the universe which existed to resonate empathy, briefly uniting everyone originating from Old Earth human stock. But out here? So many thousands of light-years away?

Dem Lia suddenly realized how silly that thought was. Aenea's Shared Moment of almost five centuries ago must have propagated everywhere in the universe along the quantum fabric of the Void Which Binds, touching alien races and cultures so distant as to be unreachable by any technology of human travel or communication while adding the first self-aware human voice to the empathic conversation that had been going on between sentient and sensitive species for almost twelve billion years. Most of those species had long since become extinct or evolved beyond their original form, the Aeneans had told Dem Lia, but their empathic memories still resonated in the Void Which Binds.

Of course the Ousters had experienced the Shared Moment five hundred years ago.

"No, we are not Pax," the *Helix* had radioed back to the three-hundred-some thousand approaching Ousters. "The Pax was essentially destroyed four hundred standard years ago."

"Do you have followers of Aenea aboard?" came the next Ouster message.

Dem Lia and the others had sighed. Perhaps these Ousters had been desperately waiting for an Aenean messenger, a prophet, someone to bring the sacrament of Aenea's DNA to them so that they could also become Aeneans.

"No," the *Helix* had radioed back. "No followers of Aenea." They then tried to explain the Amoiete Spectrum Helix and how the Aeneans had helped them build and adapt this ship for their long voyage.

After some silence, the Ousters had radioed, "Is there anyone aboard who has met Aenea or her beloved, Raul Endymion?"

Again the nine had looked blankly at each other. Saigyō, who had been sitting cross-legged on the floor some distance from the conference table, spoke up. "No one on board met Aenea," he said softly. "Of the Spectrum family who hid and helped Raul Endymion when he was ill on Vitus-Gray-Balianus B, two of the marriage partners were killed in the war with the Pax there—one of the mothers, Dem Ria, and the biological father, Alem Mikail Dem Alem. Their son by that triune—a boy named Bin Ria Dem Loa Alem—was also killed in the Pax bombing. Alem Mikail's daughter by a previous triune marriage was missing and presumed dead. The surviving female of the triune, Dem Loa, took the sacrament and became an Aenean not many weeks after the Shared Moment. She farcast away from Vitus-Gray-Balianus B and never returned."

Dem Lia and the others waited, knowing that the AI wouldn't have gone on at such length if there were not more to the story.

Saigyō nodded. "It turns out that the teenage daughter, Ces Ambre, presumed killed in the Pax Base Bombasino massacre of Spectrum Helix civilians, had actually been shipped offworld with more than a thousand other children and young adults. They were to be raised on the final Pax stronghold world of St. Theresa as born-again Pax Christians. Ces Ambre received the cruciform and was overseen by a cadre of religious guards there for nine years before that world was liberated by the Aeneans and Dem Loa learned that her daughter was still alive."

"Did they reunite?" asked young Den Soa, the attractive diplomat. There were tears in her eyes. "Did Ces Ambre free herself of the cruciform?"

"There was a reunion," said Saigyō. "Dem Loa freecast there as soon as she learned that her daughter was alive. Ces Ambre chose to have the Aeneans remove the cruciform, but she reported that she did not accept Aenea's DNA sacrament from her triune stepmother to become Aenean herself. Her dossier says that she wanted to return to Vitus-Gray-Balianus B to see the remnants of the culture from which she had been kidnapped. She continued living and working there as a teacher for almost sixty standard years. She adopted her former family's band of blue."

"She suffered the cruciform but chose not to become Aenean," muttered Kem Loi, the astronomer, as if it were impossible to believe.

Dem Lia said, "She's aboard in deep sleep."

"Yes," said Saigyō.

"How old was she when we embarked?" asked Patek Georg.

"Ninety-five standard years," said the AI. He smiled. "But as with all of us, she had the benefit of Aenean medicine in the years before departure. Her physical appearance and mental capabilities are of a woman in her early sixties."

Dem Lia rubbed her cheek. "Saigyō, please awaken Citizen Ces Ambre. Den Soa, could you be there when she awakens and explain the situation to her before the Ousters join us? They seem more interested in someone who knew Aenea's husband than in learning about the Spectrum Helix."

"Future husband at that point in time," corrected the ebony, Jon Mikail, who was a bit of a pedant. "Raul Endymion was not yet married to Aenea at the time of his short stay on Vitus-Gray-Balianus B."

"I'd feel privileged to stay with Ces Ambre until we meet the Ousters," said Den Soa with a bright smile.

While the great mass of Ousters kept their distance—five hundred klicks—the three ambassadors were brought aboard. It had been worked out by radio that the three could take one-tenth normal gravity without discomfort, so the lovely solarium bubble just aft and above the command deck had its containment field set at that level and the proper chairs and lighting adapted. All of the *Helix* people thought it would be easier conversing with at least some sense of up and down. Den Soa added that the Ousters might feel at home amongst all the greenery there. The ship easily morphed an airlock onto the top of the great solarium bubble, and those waiting watched the slow approach of two winged Ousters and one smaller form being towed in a transparent spacesuit. The Ousters who breathed air on the ring, breathed 100 percent oxygen so the ship had taken care to accommodate them in the solarium. Dem Lia realized that she felt slightly euphoric as the Ouster guests entered and were shown to their specially tailored chairs, and she wondered if it was the pure O, or just the novelty of the circumstances.

Once settled in their chairs, the Ousters seemed to be studying their five

Spectrum Helix counterparts—Dem Lia, Den Soa, Patek Georg, the psychologist Peter Delen Dem Tae, and Ces Ambre, an attractive woman with short, white hair, her hands now folded neatly on her lap. The former teacher had insisted in dressing in her full robe and cowl of blue, but a few tabs of stiktite sewn at strategic places kept the garment from billowing at each movement or ballooning up off the floor.

The Ouster delegation was an interesting assortment of types. On the left, in the most elaborately constructed low-g chair, was a true space-adapted Ouster. Introduced as Far Rider, he was almost four meters tall—making Dem Lia feel even shorter than she was. The Spectrum Helix people always having been generally short and stocky, not through centuries on high-g planets, just because of the genetics of their founders—and the space-adapted Ouster looked far from human in many other ways. Arms and legs were mere long, spidery attachments to the thin torso. The man's fingers must have been twenty centimeters long. Every square centimeter of his body—appearing almost naked under the skintight sweat-coolant, compression layer—was covered with a self-generated forcefield, actually an enhancement of the usual human body aura, which kept him alive in hard vacuum. The ridges above and beneath his shoulders were permanent arrays for extending his forcefield wings to catch the solar wind and magnetic fields. Far Rider's face had been genetically altered far from basic human stock: the eyes were black slits behind bulbous, nictitating membranes; he had no ears but a gridwork on the side of his head that suggested the radio receiver; his mouth was the narrowest of slits, lipless—he communicated through radio-transmitting glands in his neck.

The Spectrum Helix delegation had been aware of this Ouster adaptation and each was wearing a subtle hearplug, which, in addition to picking up Far Rider's radio transmissions, allowed them to communicate with their AIs on a secure tightband.

The second Ouster was partially adapted to space, but clearly more human. Three meters tall, he was thin and spidery, but the permanent field of forcefield ectoplasmic skin was missing, his eyes and face were thin and boldly structured, he had no hair—and he spoke early Web English with very little accent. He was introduced as Chief Branchman and historian Keel Redt, and it was obvious that he was the chosen speaker for the group, if not its actual leader.

To the Chief Branchman's left was a Templar—a young woman with the hairless skull, fine bone structure, vaguely Asian features, and large eyes common to Templars everywhere—wearing the traditional brown robe and hood. She introduced herself as the True Voice of the Tree Reta Kasteen, and her voice was soft and strangely musical.

When the Helix Spectrum contingent had introduced themselves, Dem Lia noticed the two Ousters and the Templar staring at Ces Ambre, who smiled back pleasantly.

"How is that you have come so far in such a ship?" asked Chief Branchman Keel Redt.

Dem Lia explained their decision to start a new colony of the Amoiete Spectrum Helix far from Aenean and human space. There was the inevitable question about the origins of the Amoiete Spectrum Helix culture, and Dem Lia told the story as succinctly as possible.

"So if I understand you correctly," said True Voice of the Tree Reta Kesteen, the Templar, "your entire social structure is based upon an opera—a work of entertainment—that was performed only once, more than six hundred standard years ago."

"Not the *entire* social structure," Den Soa responded to her Templar counterpart. "Cultures grow and adapt themselves to changing conditions and imperatives, of course. But the basic philosophical bedrock and structure of our culture was contained in that one performance by the philosopher-composer-poet-holistic artist, Halpul Amoiete."

"And what did this . . . poet . . . think of a society being built around his single multimedia opera?" asked the Chief Branchman.

It was a delicate question, but Dem Lia just smiled and said, "We'll never know. Citizen Amoiete died in a mountain-climbing accident just a month after the opera was performed. The first Spectrum Helix communities did not appear for another twenty standard years."

"Do you worship this man?" asked Chief Branchman Keel Redt.

Ces Ambre answered. "No. None of the Spectrum Helix people have ever deified Halpul Amoiete, even though we have taken his name as part of our society's. We do, however, respect and try to live up to the values and goals for human potential which he communicated in his art through that single, extraordinary Spectrum Helix performance."

The Chief Branchman nodded as if satisfied.

Saigyō's soft voice whispered in Dem Lia's ear. "They are broadcasting both visual and audio on a very tight coherent band which is being picked up by the Ousters outside and being rebroadcast to the forest ring."

Dem Lia looked at the three sitting across from her, finally resting her gaze on Far Rider, the completely space-adapted Ouster. His human eyes were essentially invisible behind the gogglelike, polarized, and nictitating membranes that made him look almost insectoid. Saigyō had tracked Dem Lia's gaze, and his voice whispered in her ear again. "Yes. He is the one broadcasting."

Dem Lia steepled her fingers and touched her lips, better to conceal the subvocalizing. "You've tapped into their tightbeam?"

"Yes, of course," said Saigyō. "Very primitive. They're broadcasting just the video and audio of this meeting, no data subchannels or return broadcasts from either the Ousters near us or from the forest ring."

Dem Lia nodded ever so slightly. Since the *Helix* was also carrying out complete holocoverage of this meeting, including infrared study, magnetic-resonance analysis of brain function, and a dozen other hidden but intrusive observations, she could hardly blame the Ousters for recording the meeting. Suddenly her cheeks reddened. Infrared. Tightbeam physical scans. Remote neuro-MRI. Certainly the fully space-adapted Ouster could *see* these probes—the man, if man he still was, lived in an environment where he could see the solar wind, sense the magnetic-field lines, and follow individual ions and even cosmic rays as they flowed over and under and through him in hard vacuum. Dem Lia subvocalized, "Shut down all of our solarium sensors except the holocameras."

Saigyō's silence was his assent.

Dem Lia noticed Far Rider suddenly blinking as if someone had shut off blazing lights that had been shining in his eyes. The Ouster then looked at Dem Lia and nodded slightly. The strange gap of a mouth, sealed away from the world by the layer of forcefield and clear ectodermal skin plasma, twitched in what the Spectrum woman thought might be a smile.

It was the young Templar, Rita Kasteen who had been speaking. ". . . so you see we passed through what was becoming the Worldweb and left human space about the time the Hegemony was establishing itself. We had departed the Centauri system some time after the original Hegira had ended. Periodically, our seedship would drop into real space—the Templars joined us from God's Grove on our way out—so we had fatline news and occasional firsthand information of what the interstellar Worldweb society was becoming. We continued outbound."

"Why so far?" asked Patek Georg.

The Chief Branchman answered, "Quite simply, the ship malfunctioned. It kept us in deep cryogenic fugue for centuries while its programming ignored potential systems for an orbital worldtree. Eventually, as the ship realized its mistake—twelve hundred of us had already died in fugue crèches never designed for such a lengthy voyage—the ship panicked and began dropping out of Hawking space at every system, finding the usual assortment of stars that could not support our Templar-grown tree ring or that would have been deadly to Ousters. We know from the ship's records that it almost settled us in a binary system consisting of a black hole that was gorging on its close red-giant neighbor."

"The accretion disk would have been pretty to watch," said Den Soa with a weak smile.

The Chief Branchman showed his own thin-lipped smile. "Yes, in the weeks or months we would have had before it killed us. Instead, working on the last of its reasoning power, the ship made one more jump and found the perfect solution—this double system, with the white-star heliosphere we Ousters could thrive in, and a tree ring already constructed."

"How long ago was that?" asked Dem Lia.

"Twelve-hundred-and-thirty-some standard years," broadcast Far Rider.

The Templar woman leaned forward and continued the story. "The first thing we discovered was that this forest ring had nothing to do with the biogenetics we had developed on God's Grove to build our own beautiful, secret startrees. This DNA was so alien in its alignment and function that to tamper with it might have killed the entire forest ring."

"You could have started your own forest ring growing in and around the alien one," said Ces Ambre. "Or attempted a startree sphere as other Ousters have done."

The True Voice of the Tree Reta Kasteen nodded. "We had just begun attempting that—and diversifying the protogene growth centers just a few hundred kilometers from where we had parked the seedship in the leaves and branches of the alien ring, when . . ." She paused as if searching for the right words.

"The Destroyer came," broadcast Far Rider.

"The Destroyer being the ship we observe approaching your ring now?" asked Patek Georg.

"Same ship," broadcast Far Rider. The two syllables seemed to have been spat out.

"Same monster from hell," added the Chief Branchman.

"It destroyed your seedship," said Dem Lia. So that was why the Ousters seemed to have no metal and why there was no Templar-grown forest ring braiding this alien one.

Far Rider should his head. "It *devoured* the seedship, along with more than twenty-eight thousand kilometers of the tree ring itself—every leaf, fruit, oxygen pod, water tendril—even our protogene growth centers."

"There were far fewer purely space-adapted Ousters in those days," said Reta Kasteen. "The adapted ones attempted to save the others, but many thousands died on that first visit of the Destroyer . . . the Devourer . . . the Machine. We obviously have many names for it."

"Ship from hell," said the Chief Branchman, and Dem Lia realized that he was almost certainly speaking literally, as if a religion had grown up based upon hating this machine.

"How often does it come?" asked Den Soa.

"Every fifty-seven years," said the Templar. "Exactly."

"From the red giant system?" asked Den Soa.

"Yes," broadcast Far Rider. "From the hell star."

"If you know its trajectory," said Dem Lia, "can't you know far ahead of time the sections of your forest ring it will . . . devastate, devour? Couldn't you just not colonize, or at the very least evacuate, those areas? After all, most of the tree ring has to be unpopulated . . . the ring's surface area has to be equal to more than half a million Old Earths or Hyperions."

Chief Branchman Keel Redt showed his thin smile again. "About now—some seven or eight standard days out—the Destroyer, for all its mass, not only completes its deceleration cycle, but carries out complicated maneuvers that will take it to some populated part of the ring. Always a populated area. A hundred and four years ago, its final trajectory took it to a massing of O_2 pods where more than twenty million of our non–fully space-adapted Ousters had made their homes, complete with travel tubes, bridges, towers, city-sized platforms and artificially grown life-support pods that had been under slow construction for more than six hundred standard years."

"All destroyed," said True Voice of the Tree Reta Kasteen with sorrow in her voice. "Devoured. Harvested."

"Was there much loss of life?" asked Dem Lia, her voice quiet.

Far Rider shook his head and broadcast, "Millions of fully space-adapted Ousters rallied to evacuate the oxygen breathers. Fewer than a hundred died."

"Have you tried to communicate with the . . . machine?" asked Peter Delem Dem Tae.

"For centuries," said Reta Kasteen, her voice shaking with emotion. "We've used radio, tightbeam, maser, the few holo transmitters we still have, Far Rider's people have even used their wingfields—by the thousands—to flash messages in simple, mathematical code."

The five Amoiete Spectrum Helix people waited.

"Nothing," said the Chief Branchman in a flat voice. "It comes, it chooses its populated section of the ring, and it devours. We have never had a reply."

"We believe that it is completely automated and very ancient," said Reta Kasteen. "Perhaps millions of years old. Still operating on programming developed when the alien ring was built. It harvests these huge sections of the ring, limbs, branches, tubules with millions of gallons of tree-ring manufactured water . . . then returns to the red-star system and, after a pause, returns our way again."

"We used to believe that there was a world left in that red-giant system," broadcast Far Rider. "A planet which remains permanently hidden from us on the far side of that evil sun. A world which built this ring as its food source, probably before their G2 sun went giant, and which continues to harvest in spite of the misery it causes us. No longer. There is no such planet. We now believe that the Destroyer acts alone, out of ancient, blind programming, harvesting sections of the ring and destroying our settlements for no reason. Whatever or whoever lived in that red giant system has long since fled."

Dem Lia wished that Kem Loi, their astronomer was there. She knew that she was on the command deck watching. "We saw no planets during our approach to this binary system," said the green-banded commander. "It seems highly unlikely that any world that could support life would have survived the transition of the G2 star to the red giant."

"Nonetheless, the Destroyer passes very close to that terrible red star on each of its voyages," said the Ouster Chief Branchman. "Perhaps some sort of artificial environment remains—a space habitat—hollowed-out asteroids. An environment which requires this plant ring for its inhabitants to survive. But it does not excuse the carnage."

"If they had the ability to build this machine, they could have simply fled their system when the G2 sun went critical," mused Patek Georg. The red-band looked at Far Rider. "Have you tried to destroy the machine?"

The lipless smile beneath the ectofield twitched lizard-wide on Far Rider's strange face. "Many times. Scores of thousands of true Ousters have died. The machine has an energy defense that lances us to ash at approximately one hundred thousand klicks."

"That could be a simple meteor defense," said Dem Lia.

Far Rider's smile broadened so that it was very terrible. "If so, it suffices as a very efficient killing device. My father died in the last attack attempt."

"Have you tried traveling to the red giant system?" asked Peter Delem.

"We have no spacecraft left," answered the Templar.

"On your own solar wings then?" asked Peter, obviously doing the math in his head on the time such a round trip would take. Years—decades at solar sailing velocities—but well within an Ouster's life span.

Far Rider moved his hand with its elongated fingers in a horizontal chop. "The heliosphere turbulence is too great. Yet we have tried hundreds of times—expeditions upon which scores depart and none or only a few return. My brother died on such an attempt six of your standard years ago."

"And Far Rider himself was terribly hurt," said Reta Kasteen softly. "Sixty-eight of the best deep spacers left—two returned. It took all of what remains of our medical science to save Far Rider's life, and that meant two years in recovery pod nutrient for him."

Dem Lia cleared her throat. "What do you want us to do?"

The two Ousters and the Templar leaned forward. Chief Branchman Keel Redt spoke for all of them. "If, as you believe, as we have become convinced, that there is no inhabited world left in the red giant system, kill the Destroyer now. Annihilate the harvesting machine. Save us from this mindless, obsolete, and endless scourge. We will reward you as handsomely as we can—foods, fruits, as much water as you need for your voyage, advanced genetic techniques, our knowledge of nearby systems, anything."

The Spectrum Helix people glanced at one another. Finally Dem Lia said, "If you are comfortable here, four of us would like to excuse ourselves for a short time to discuss this. Ces Ambre would be delighted to stay with you and talk if you so wish."

The Chief Branchman made a gesture with both long arms and huge hands. "We are completely comfortable. And we are more than delighted to have this chance to talk to the venerable M. Ambre—the woman who saw the husband of Aenea."

Dem Lia noticed that the young Templar, Reta Kesteen, looked visibly thrilled at the prospect.

"And then you will bring us your decision, yes?" radioed Far Rider, his waxy body, huge eyeshields, and alien physiology giving Dem Lia a slight chill. This was a creature that fed on light, tapped enough energy to deploy electromagnetic solar wings hundreds of kilometers wide, recycled his own air, waste, and water, and lived in an environment of absolute cold, heat, radiation, and hard vacuum. Humankind had come a long way from the early hominids in Africa on Old Earth.

And if we say no, thought Dem Lia, *three-hundred-thousand-some angry space-adapted Ousters just like him might descend on our spinship like the angry Hawaiians venting their wrath on Captain James Cook when he caught them pulling the nails from the hull of his ship. The good captain ended up not only being killed horribly, but having his body eviscerated, burned, and boiled into small chunks.* As soon as she thought this, Dem Lia knew better. These Ousters would not attack the *Helix.* All of her intuition told her that. *And if they do,* she thought, *our weaponry will vaporize the lot of them in two-point-six seconds.* She felt guilty and slightly nauseated at her own thoughts as she made her farewells and took the lift down to the command deck with the other three.

.   .   .

"You saw him," said True Voice of the Tree Reta Kasteen a little breathlessly. "Aenea's husband?"

Ces Ambre smiled. "I was fourteen standard years old. It was a long time ago. He was traveling from world to world via farcaster and stayed a few days in my second triune parents' home because he was ill—a kidney stone—and then the Pax troopers kept him under arrest until they could send someone to interrogate him. My parents helped him escape. It was a very few days a very many years ago." She smiled again. "And he was not Aenea's husband at that time, remember. He had not taken the sacrament of her DNA, nor even grown aware of what her blood and teachings could do for the human race."

"But you *saw* him," pressed Chief Branchman Keel Redt.

"Yes. He was in delirium and pain much of the time and handcuffed to my parents' bed by the Pax troopers."

Reta Kesteen leaned closer. "Did he have any sort of . . . *aura* . . . about him?"

"Oh, yes," said Ces Ambre with a chuckle. "Until my parents gave him a sponge bath. He had been traveling hard for many days."

The two Ousters and the Templar seemed to sit back in disappointment.

Ces Ambre leaned forward and touched the Templar woman's knee. "I apologize for being flippant—I know the important role that Raul Endymion played in all of our history—but it was long ago, there was much confusion, and at that time on Vitus-Gray-Balianus B I was a rebellious teenager who wanted to leave my community of the Spectrum and accept the cruciform in some nearby Pax city."

The other three visibly leaned back now. The two faces that were readable registered shock. "You *wanted* to accept that . . . that . . . *parasite* into your body?"

As part of Aenea's Shared Moment, every human everywhere had seen—had known—had felt the full *gestalt*—of the reality behind the "immortality cruciform"—a parasitic mass of AI nodes creating a TechnoCore in real space, using the neurons and synapses of each host body in any way it wished, often using it in more creative ways by *killing* the human host and using the linked neuronic web when it was at its most creative—during those final seconds of neural dissolution before death. Then the Church would use TechnoCore technology to resurrect the human body with the Core cruciform parasite growing stronger and more networked at each death and resurrection.

Ces Ambre shrugged. "It represented immortality at the time. And a chance to get away from our dusty little village and join the real world—the Pax."

The three Ouster diplomats could only stare.

Ces Ambre raised her hands to her robe and slipped it open enough to show them the base of her throat and the beginning of a scar where the cruciform had been removed by the Aeneans. "I was kidnapped to one of the remaining Pax worlds and put under the cruciform for nine years," she said so softly that her voice barely carried to the three diplomats. "And most of this time was *after* Aenea's shared moment—after the absolute revelation of the Core's plan to enslave us with those despicable things."

The True Voice of the Tree Reta Kesteen took Ces Ambre's older hand in hers. "Yet you refused to become Aenean when you were liberated. You joined what was left of your old culture."

Ces Ambre smiled. There were tears in her eyes, and those eyes suddenly looked much older. "Yes. I felt I owed my people that—for deserting them at the time of crisis. Someone had to carry on the Spectrum Helix culture. We had lost so many in the wars. We lost even more when the Aeneans gave us the option of joining them. It is hard to refuse to become something like a god."

Far Rider made a grunt that sounded like heavy static. "This is our greatest fear next to the Destroyer. No one is now alive on the forest ring who experienced the

Shared Moment, but the details of it—the glorious insights into empathy and the binding powers of the Void Which Binds, Aenea's knowledge that many of the Aeneans would be able to farcast—freecast—anywhere in the universe. Well, the Church of Aenea has grown here until at least a fourth of our population would give up their Ouster or Templar heritage and become Aenean in a second."

Ces Ambre rubbed her cheek and smiled again. "Then it's obvious that no Aeneans have visited this system. And you have to remember that Aenea insisted that there be no 'Church of Aenea,' no veneration or beatification or adoration. That was paramount in her thoughts during the Shared Moment."

"We know," said Reta Kasteen. "But in the absence of choice and knowledge, cultures often turn to religion. And the possibility of an Aenean being aboard with you was one reason we greeted the arrival of your great ship with such enthusiasm and trepidation."

"Aeneans do not arrive by spacecraft," Ces Ambre said softly.

The three nodded. "When and if the day ever comes," broadcast Far Rider, "it will be up to the individual conscience of each Ouster and Templar to decide. As for me, I will always ride the great waves of the solar wind."

Dem Lia and the other three returned.

"We've decided to help," she said. "But we must hurry."

There was no way in the universe that Dem Lia or any of the other eight humans or any of the five AIs would risk the *Helix* in a direct confrontation with the Destroyer or the Harvester or whatever the hell the Ousters wanted to call their nemesis. It was not just by engineering happenstance that the three thousand life-support pods carrying the 684,300 Spectrum Helix pioneers in deep cryogenic sleep were egg-shaped. This culture had all their eggs in one basket—literally—and they were not about to send that basket into battle. Already Basho and several of the other AIs were brooding about the proximity to the oncoming harvesting ship. Space battles could easily be fought across twenty-eight AUs of distance—while traditional lasers, or lances, or charged particle-beam weapons would take more than a hundred and ninety-six minutes to creep that distance—Hegemony, Pax, and Ouster ships had all developed hyperkinetic missiles able to leap into and out of Hawking space. Ships could be destroyed before radar could announce the presence of the incoming missile. Since this "harvester" crept around its appointed rounds at sublight speed, it seemed unlikely that it would carry C-plus weaponry, but "unlikely" is a word that has undone the planning and fates of warriors since time immemorial.

At the Spectrum Helix engineers' request, the Aeneans had rebuilt the *Helix* to be truly modular. When it reached its utopian planet around its perfect star, sections would free themselves to become probes and aircraft and landers and submersibles and space stations. Each of the three thousand individual life pods could land and begin a colony on its own, although the plans were to cluster the landing sites carefully after much study of the new world. By the time the *Helix* was finished deploying and landing its pods and modules and probes and shuttles and command deck and central fusion core, little would be left in orbit except the huge Hawking drive units with maintenance programs and robots to keep them in perfect conditions for centuries, if not millennia.

"We'll take the system exploratory probe to investigate this Destroyer," said Dem Lia. It was one of the smaller modules, adapted more to pure vacuum than to atmospheric entry, although it was capable of some morphing, but compared to most of the *Helix*'s peaceful subcomponents the probe was armed to the teeth.

"May we accompany you?" said Chief Branchman Keel Redt. "None of our race has come closer than a hundred thousand kilometers to the machine and lived."

"By all means," said Dem Lia. "The probe's large enough to hold thirty or forty of us, and only three are going from our ship. We will keep the internal containment field at one-tenth gee and adapt the seating accordingly."

The probe was more like one of the old combat torchships than anything else, and it accelerated out toward the advancing machine under 250 gravities, internal containment fields on infinite redundancy, external fields raised to their maximum of class twelve. Dem Lia was piloting. Den Soa was attempting to communicate with the gigantic ship via every means available, sending messages of peace on every band from primitive radio to modulated tachyon bursts. There was no response. Patek Georg Dem Mio was meshed into the defense counterattack virtual umbilicals of his couch. The passengers sat at the rear of the probe's compact command deck and watched. Saigyō had decided to accompany them, and his massive holo sat bare-chested and cross-legged on a counter near the main viewport. Dem Lia made sure to keep their trajectory aimed *not* directly at the monstrosity, in the probability that it had simple meteor defenses: if they kept traveling toward their current coordinates, they would miss the ship by tens of thousands of kilometers above the plane of the ecliptic.

"Its radar has begun tracking us," said Patek Georg when they were six hundred thousand klicks away and decelerating nicely. "Passive radar. No weapons acquisition. It doesn't seem to be probing us with anything except simple radar. It will have no idea if life-forms are aboard our probe or not."

Dem Lia nodded. "Saigyō," she said softly, "at two hundred thousand klicks, please bring our coordinates around so that we will be on intercept course with the thing." The chubby monk nodded.

Somewhat later, the probe's thrusters and main engines changed tune, the starfield rotated, and the image of the huge machine filled the main window. The view was magnified as if they were only five hundred klicks from the spacecraft. The thing was indescribably ungainly, built only for vacuum, fronted with metal teeth and rotating blades built into mandible-like housings, the rest looking like the wreckage of an old space habitat that had been mindlessly added onto for millennium after millennium and then covered with warts, wattles, bulbous sacs, tumors, and filaments.

"Distance, one hundred eighty-three thousand klicks and closing," said Patek Georg.

"Look how blackened it is," whispered Den Soa.

"And worn," radioed Far Rider. "None of our people have ever seen it from this close. Look at the layers of cratering through the heavy carbon deposits. It is like an ancient, black moon that has been struck again and again by tiny meteorites."

"Repaired, though," commented the Chief Branchman gruffly. "It operates."

"Distance one hundred twenty thousand klicks and closing," said Patek Georg. "Search radar has just been joined by acquisition radar."

"Defensive measures?" said Dem Lia, her voice quiet.

Saigyō answered. "Class-twelve field in place and infinitely redundant. CPB deflectors activated. Hyperkinetic countermissiles ready. Plasma shields on maximum. Countermissiles armed and under positive control." This meant simply that both Dem Lia and Patek Georg would have to give the command to launch them, or—if the human passengers were killed—Saigyō would do so.

"Distance one hundred five thousand klicks and closing," said Patek Georg. "Relative delta-v dropping to one hundred meters per second. Three more acquisition radars have locked on."

"Any other transmission?" asked Dem Lia, her voice tight.

"Negative," said Den Soa at her virtual console. "The machine seems blind and dumb except for the primitive radar. Absolutely no signs of life aboard. Internal communications show that it has . . . intelligence . . . but not true AI. Computers more likely. Many series of physical computers."

"*Physical* computers!" said Dem Lia, shocked. "You mean silicon . . . chips . . . stone axe-level technology?"

"Or just above," confirmed Den Soa at her console. "We're picking up magnetic bubble-memory readings, but nothing higher."

"One hundred thousand klicks . . ." began Patek Georg, and then interrupted himself. "The machine is firing on us."

The outer containment fields flashed for less than a second.

"A dozen CPBs and two crude laser lances," said Patek Georg from his virreal point of view. "Very weak. A class-one field could have countered them easily."

The containment field flickered again.

"Same combination," reported Patek. "Slightly lower energy settings."

Another flicker.

"Lower settings again," said Patek. "I think it's giving us all it's got and using up its power doing it. Almost certainly just a meteor defense."

"Let's not get overconfident," said Dem Lia. "But let's see all of its defenses."

Den Soa looked shocked. "You're going to *attack* it?"

"We're going to see if we *can* attack it," said Dem Lia. "Patek, Saigyō, please target one lance on the top corner of that protuberance there . . ." She pointed her laser stylus at a blackened, cratered, fin-shaped projection that might have been a radiator two klicks high. ". . . and one hyperkinetic missile . . ."

"*Commander!*" protested Den Soa.

Dem Lia looked at the younger woman and raised her finger to her lips. "One hyperkinetic with plasma warhead removed, targeted at the front lower leading edge of the machine, right where the lip of that aperture is."

Patek Georg repeated the command to the AI. Actual target coordinates were displayed and confirmed.

The CPB struck almost instantly, vaporizing a seventy-meter hole in the radiator fin.

"It raised a class-point-six field," reported Patek Georg. "That seems to be its top limit of defense."

The hyperkinetic missile penetrated the containment field like a bullet through butter and struck an instant later, blasting through sixty meters of blackened metal and tearing out through the front feeding-orifice of the harvesting machine. Everyone aboard watched the silent impact and the almost mesmerizing tumble of vaporized metal expanding away from the impact site and the spray of debris from the exit wound. The huge machine did not respond.

"If we had left the warhead on," murmured Dem Lia, "and aimed for its belly, we would have a thousand kilometers of exploding harvest machine right now."

Chief Branchman Keel Redt leaned forward in his couch. Despite the one-tenth g field, all of the couches had restraint systems. His was activated now.

"Please," said the Ouster, struggling slightly against the harnesses and airbags. "Kill it now. Stop it now."

Dem Lia shifted to look at the two Ousters and the Templar. "Not yet," she said. "First we have to return to the *Helix*."

"We will lose more valuable time," broadcast Far rider, his tone unreadable.

"Yes," said Dem Lia. "But we still have more than six standard days before it begins harvesting."

The probe accelerated away from the blackened, cratered, and newly scarred monster.

.   .   .

"You will not destroy it, then?" demanded the Chief Branchman as the probe hurried back to the *Helix*.

"Not now," responded Dem Lia. "It might still be serving a purpose for the race that built it."

The young Templar seemed to be close to tears. "Yet your own instruments—far more sophisticated than our telescopes—told you that there are no worlds in the red giant system."

Dem Lia nodded. "Yet you yourselves have mentioned the possibility of space habitats, can cities, hollowed-out asteroids . . . our survey was neither careful nor complete. Our ship was intent upon entering your star system with maximum safety, not carrying out a careful survey of the red giant system."

"For such a small probability," said the Chief Branchman Ouster in a flat, hard voice, "you are willing to risk so many of our people?"

Saigyō's voice whispered quietly in Dem Lia's subaudio circuit. "The AIs have been analyzing scenarios of several million Ousters using their solar wings in a concentrated attack on the *Helix*."

Dem Lia waited, still looking at the Chief Branchman.

"The ship could defeat them," finished the AI, "but there is some real probability of damage."

To the Chief Branchman, Dem Lia said, "We're going to take the *Helix* to the red giant system. The three of you are welcome to accompany us."

"How long will the round trip last?" demanded Far Rider.

Dem Lia looked to Saigyō. "Nine days under maximum fusion boost," said the AI. "And that would be a powered perihelion maneuver with no time to linger in the system to search every asteroid or debris field for life-forms."

The two Ousters were shaking their heads. Reta Kasteen drew her hood lower, covering her eyes.

"There's another possibility," said Dem Lia. To Saigyō, she pointed toward the *Helix*, now filling the main viewscreen. Thousands of energy-winged Ousters parted as the probe decelerated gently through the ship's containment field and aligned itself for docking.

They gathered in the solarium to decide. All ten of the humans—Den Soa's wife and husband had been invited to join in the vote but had decided to stay below in the crew's quarters—all five of the AIs, and the three representatives of the forest-ring people. Far Rider's tightbeam continued to carry the video and audio to the three hundred thousand nearby Ousters and the billions waiting on the great curve of tree ring beyond.

"Here is the situation," said Dem Lia. The silence in the solarium was very thick. "You know that the *Helix*, our ship, contains an Aenean-modified Hawking drive. Our faster-than-light passage does harm the fabric of the Void Which Binds, but thousands of times less than the old Hegemony or Pax ships. The Aeneans allowed us this voyage." The short woman with the green band around her turban paused and looked at both Ousters and the Templar woman before continuing. "We could reach the red giant system in . . ."

"Four hours to spin up to relativistic velocities, then the jump," said Res Sandre. "About six hours to decelerate into the red giant system. Two days to investigate for life. Same ten-hour return time."

"Which, even with some delays, would bring the *Helix* back almost two days before the Destroyer begins its harvesting. If there is no life in the red-giant system, we will use the probe to destroy the robot harvester."

"But . . ." said Chief Branchman Keel Redt with an all-too-human iron smile. His face was grim.

"*But* it is too dangerous to use the Hawking drive in such a tight binary system," said Dem Lia, voice level. "Such short-distance jumps are incredibly tricky anyway, but given the gas and debris the red giant is pouring out . . ."

"You are correct. It would be folly." It was Far Rider broadcasting on his radio band. "My clan has passed down the engineering from generation to generation. No commander of any Ouster seedship would make a jump in this binary system."

True Voice of the Tree Reta Kasteen was looking from face to face. "But you have these powerful fusion engines . . ."

Dem Lia nodded. "Basho, how long to survey the red-giant system using maximum thrust with our fusion engines?"

"Three and one-half days transit time to the other system," said the hollow-cheeked AI. "Two days to investigate. Three and one-half days back."

"There is no way we could shorten that?" said Oam Rai, the yellow. "Cut safety margins? Drive the fusion engines harder?"

Saigyō answered. "The nine-day round-trip is posited upon ignoring all safety margins and driving the fusion engines at one hundred twelve percent of their capacity." He sadly shook his bald head. "No, it cannot be done."

"But the Hawking drive . . ." said Dem Lia, and everyone in the room appeared to cease breathing except for Far Rider, who had never been breathing in the traditional sense. The appointed Spectrum Helix commander turned to the AIs. "What are the probabilities of disaster if we try this?"

Lady Murasaki stepped forward. "Both translations—into and out of Hawking space—will be far too close to the binary system's Roche lobe. We estimate probability of total destruction of the *Helix* at two percent, of damage to some aspect of ship's systems at eight percent, and specifically damage to the pod life-support network at six percent."

Dem Lia looked at the Ousters and the Templar. "A six percent chance of losing hundreds—thousands—of our sleeping relatives and friends. Those we have sworn to protect until arrival at our destination. A two percent chance that our entire culture will die in the attempt."

Far Rider nodded sadly. "I do not know what wonders your Aenean friends have added to your equipment," he broadcast, "but I would find those figures understated. It is an impossible binary system for a Hawking drive jump."

Silence stretched. Finally Dem Lia said, "Our options are to destroy the harvesting machine for you without knowing if there is life—perhaps an entire species—depending upon it in the red giant system, however improbable. And we cannot do that. Our moral code prevents it."

Reta Kasteen's voice was very small. "We understand."

Dem Lia continued, "We could travel by conventional means and survey the system. This means you will have to suffer the ravages of this Destroyer a final time, but if there is no life in the red giant system, we will destroy the machine when we return on fusion drive."

"Little comfort to the thousands or millions who will lose their homes during this final visit of the Destroyer," said Chief Branchman Keel Redt.

"No comfort at all," agreed Dem Lia.

Far Rider stood to his full four-meter height, floating slightly in the one-tenth gravity. "This is not your problem," he broadcast. "There is no reason for you to risk any of your people. We thank you for considering . . ."

Dem Lia raised a hand to stop him in mid-broadcast. "We're going to vote now. We're voting whether to jump to the red giant system via Hawking drive and get back here before your Destroyer begins destroying. If there is an alien race over there, perhaps we can communicate in the two days we will have in-system. Perhaps they can reprogram their machine. We have all agreed that the odds against it accidentally 'eating' your seedship on its first pass after you landed are infinitesimal. The fact that it constantly harvests areas on which you've colonized—on a tree ring with the surface area equal to half a million Hyperions—suggests that it is programmed to do so, as if eliminating abnormal growths or pests."

The three diplomats nodded.

"When we vote," said Dem Lia, "the decision will have to be unanimous. One 'no' vote means that we will not use the Hawking drive."

Saigyō had been sitting cross-legged on the table, but now he moved next to the other four AIs who were standing. "Just for the record," said the fat little monk, "the AIs have voted five to zero against attempting a Hawking drive maneuver."

Dem Lia nodded. "Noted," she said. "But just for the record, for this sort of decision, the AIs' vote does not count. Only the Amoiete Spectrum Helix people or their representatives can determine their own fate." She turned back to the other nine humans. "To use the Hawking drive or not? Yes or no? We ten will account to the thousands of others for the consequences. Ces Ambre?"

"Yes." The woman in the blue robe appeared as calm as her startlingly clear and gentle eyes.

"Jon Mikail Dem Alem?"

"Yes," said the ebony life-support specialist in a thick voice. "Yes."

"Oam Rai?"

The yellow-band woman hesitated. No one on board knew the risks to the ship's systems better than this person. A two percent chance of destruction must seem an obscene gamble to her. She touched her lips with her fingers. "There are two civilizations we are deciding for here," she said, obviously musing to herself. "Possibly three."

"Oam Rai?" repeated Dem Lia.

"Yes," said Oam Rai.

"Kem Loi?" said Dem Lia to the astronomer.

"Yes." The young woman's voice quavered slightly.

"Patek Georg Dem Mio?"

The red-band security specialist grinned. "Yes. As the ancient saying goes, no guts, no glory."

Dem Lia was irritated. "You're speaking for 684,288 sleeping people who might not be so devil-may-care."

Patek Georg's grin stayed in place. "My vote is yes."

"Dr. Samuel Ria Kem Ali?"

The medic looked as troubled as Patek had brazen. "I must say . . . there are so many unknowns . . ." He looked around. "Yes," he said. "We must be sure."

"Peter Delem Dem Tae?" Dem Lia asked the blue-banded psychologist.

The older man had been chewing on a pencil. He looked at it, smiled, and set it on the table. "Yes."

"Res Sandre?"

For a second the other green-band woman's eyes seemed to show defiance, almost anger. Dem Lia steeled herself for the veto and the lecture that would follow.

"Yes," said Res Sandre. "I believe it's a moral imperative."

That left the youngest in the group.

"Den Soa?" said Dem Lia.

The young woman had to clear her throat before speaking. "Yes. Let's go look."

All eyes turned to the appointed commander.

"I vote yes," said Dem Lia. "Saigyō, prepare for maximum acceleration toward the translation point to Hawking drive. Kem Loi, you and Res Sandre and Oam Rai work on the optimum inbound translation point for a systemwide search for life. Chief Branchman Redt. Far Rider, True Voice of the Tree Kasteen, if you would prefer to wait behind, we will prepare the airlock now. If you three wish to come, we must leave immediately."

The Chief Branchman spoke without consulting the others. "We wish to accompany you, Citizen Dem Lia."

She nodded. "Far Rider, tell your people to clear a wide wake. We'll angle above the plane of the ecliptic outward bound, but our fusion tail is going to be fierce as a dragon's breath."

The fully space-adapted Ouster broadcast, "I have already done so. Many are looking forward to the spectacle."

Dem Lia grunted softly. "Let's hope it's not more of a spectacle than we've all bargained for," she said.

The *Helix* made the jump safely, with only minor upset to a few of the ship's subsystems. At a distance of three AUs from the surface of the red giant, they surveyed the system. They had estimated two days, but the survey was done in less than twenty-four hours.

There were no hidden planets, no planetoids, no hollowed-out asteroids, no converted comets, no artificial space habitats—no sign of life whatsoever. When the G2 star had finished its evolution into a red giant at least three million years earlier, its helium nuclei began burning its own ash in a high-temperature second round of fusion reactions at the star's core while the original hydrogen fusion continued in a thin shell far from that core, the whole process creating carbon and oxygen atoms that added to the reaction and . . . presto . . . the short-lived rebirth of the star as a red giant. It was obvious that there had been no outer planets, no gas giants, no rocky worlds beyond the new red sun's reach. Any inner planets had been swallowed whole by the expanding star. Outgassing of dust and heavy radiation had all but cleared the solar system of anything larger than nickel-iron meteorites.

"So," said Patek Georg, "that's that."

"Shall I authorize the AIs to begin full acceleration toward the return translation point?" said Res Sandre.

The Ouster diplomats had been moved to the command deck with their specialized couches. No one minded the one-tenth gravity on the bridge because each of the Amoiete Spectrum specialists—with the exception of Ces Ambre—was enmeshed in a control couch and in touch with the ship on a variety of levels. The Ouster diplomats had been silent during most of the search, and they remained silent now as they turned to look at Dem Lia at her center console.

The elected commander tapped her lower lip with her knuckle. "Not quite yet." Their searches had brought them all around the red giant, and now they were less than one AU from its broiling surface. "Saigyō, have you looked inside the star?"

"Just enough to sample it," came the AI's affable voice. "Typical for a red giant at this stage. Solar luminosity is about two thousand times that of its G8 companion. We sampled the core—no surprises. The helium nuclei there are obviously engaged despite their mutual electrical repulsion."

"What is its surface temperature?" asked Dem Lia.

"Approximately three thousand degrees Kelvin," came Saigyō's voice. "About half of what the surface temperature had been when it was a G2 sun."

"Oh, my God," whispered the violet-band Kem Loi from her couch in the astronomy station nexus. "Are you thinking . . ."

"Deep-radar the star, please," said Dem Lia.

The graphics holos appeared less than twenty minutes later as the star turned and they orbited it. Saigyō said, "A single rocky world. Still in orbit. Approximately four-fifths Old Earth's size. Radar evidence of ocean bottoms and former riverbeds."

Dr. Samuel said, "It was probably earthlike until its expanding sun boiled away its seas and evaporated its atmosphere. God help whoever or whatever lived there."

"How deep in the sun's troposphere is it?" asked Dem Lia.

"Less than a hundred and fifty thousand kilometers," said Saigyō.

Dem Lia nodded. "Raise the containment fields to maximum," she said softly. "Let's go visit them."

It's like swimming under the surface of a red sea, Dem Lia thought as they approached the rocky world. Above them, the outer atmosphere of the star swirled and spiraled, tornadoes of magnetic fields rose from the depths and dissipated, and the containment field was already glowing despite the thirty micromonofilament cables they had trailed out a hundred and sixty thousand klicks behind them to act as radiators.

For an hour the *Helix* stood off less than twenty thousand kilometers from what was left of what could once have been Old Earth or Hyperion. Various sensors showed the rocky world through the swirling red murk.

"A cinder," said Jon Mikail Dem Alem.

"A cinder filled with life," said Kem Loi at the primary sensing nexus. She brought up the deep-radar holo. "Absolutely honeycombed. Internal oceans of water. At least three billion sentient entities. I have no idea if they're humanoid, but they have machines, transport mechanisms, and citylike hives. You can even see the docking port where their harvester puts in every fifty-seven years."

"But still no understandable contact?" asked Dem Loi. The *Helix* had been broadcasting basic mathematical overtures on every bandwidth, spectrum, and communications technology the ship had—from radio maser to modulated tachyons. There had been a return broadcast of sorts.

"Modulated gravity waves," explained Ikkyū. "But not responding to our mathematical or geometrical overtures. They are picking up our electromagnetic signals but not understanding them, and we can't decipher their gravitonic pulses."

"How long to study the modulations until we can find a common alphabet?" demanded Dem Lia.

Ikkyū's lined face looked pained. "Weeks, at least. Months more likely. Possibly years." The AI returned the disappointed gaze of the humans, Ousters and Templar. "I am sorry," he said, opening his hands. "Humankind has only contacted two sentient alien races before, and *they* both found ways to communicate with *us*. These . . . beings . . . are truly alien. There are too few common referents."

"We can't stay here much longer," said Res Sandre at her engineering nexus. "Powerful magnetic storms are coming up from the core. And we just can't dissipate the heat quickly enough. We have to leave."

Suddenly Ces Ambre, who had a couch but no station or duties, stood, floated a meter above the deck in the one-tenth g, moaned, and slowly floated to the deck in a dead faint.

Dr. Sam reached her a second before Dem Lia and Den Soa. "Everyone else stay at your stations," said Dem Lia.

Ces Ambre opened her startlingly blue eyes. "They are so *different*. Not human at all . . . oxygen breathers but not like the Seneschai empaths . . . modular . . . multiple minds . . . so fibrous . . ."

Dem Lia held the older woman. "Can you communicate with *them?*" she said urgently. "Send *them* images?"

Ces Ambre nodded weakly.

"Send them the image of their harvesting machine and the Ousters," said Dem Lia sternly. "Show them the damage their machine does to the Ouster city clusters. Show them that the Ousters are . . . human . . . sentient. Squatters, but not harming the forest ring."

Ces Ambre nodded again and closed her eyes. A moment later she began weeping. "They . . . are . . . so . . . *sorry,*" she whispered. "The machine brings back no . . . pictures . . . only the food and air and water. It is programmed . . . as you suggested, Dem Lia . . . to eliminate infestations. They are . . . so . . . so . . . *sorry* for the loss of Ouster life. They offer the suicide of . . . of their species . . . if it would atone for the destruction."

"No, no, no," said Dem Lia squeezing the crying woman's hands. "Tell them that won't be necessary." She took the older woman by the shoulders. "This will be difficult, Ces Ambre, but you have to ask them if the harvester can be reprogrammed. Taught to stay away from the Ouster settlements."

Ces Ambre closed her eyes for several minutes. At one point it looked as if she had stopped breathing. Then those lovely eyes opened wide. "It can. They are sending the reprogramming data."

"We are receiving modulated graviton pulses," said Saigyō. "Still no translation possible."

"We don't need a translation," said Dem Lia, breathing deeply. She lifted Ces Ambre and helped her back to her couch. "We just have to record it and repeat it to the Destroyer when we get back." She squeezed Ces Ambre's hand again. "Can you communicate our thanks and farewell?"

The woman smiled. "I have done so. As best I can."

"Saigyō," said Dem Lia. "Get us the hell out of here and accelerate full speed to the translation point."

The *Helix* survived the Hawking space jump back into the G8 system with no damage. The Destroyer had already altered its trajectory toward populated regions of the forest ring, but Den Soa broadcast the modulated graviton recordings while they were still decelerating, and the giant harvester responded with an indecipherable gravitonic rumble of its own and dutifully changed course toward a remote and unpopulated section of the ring. Far Rider used his tightbeam equipment to show them a holo of the rejoicing on the ring cities, platforms, pods, branches, and towers, then he shut down his broadcast equipment.

They had gathered in the solarium. None of the AIs was present or listening, but the humans, Ousters, and Templar sat in a circle. All eyes were on Ces Ambre. That woman's eyes were closed.

Den Soa said very quietly, "The beings . . . on that world . . . they had to build the tree ring before their star expanded. They built the harvesting spacecraft. Why didn't they just . . . leave?"

"The planet was . . . is . . . home," whispered Ces Ambre, her eyes still shut tight. "Like children . . . not wanting to leave home . . . because it's dark out there. Very dark . . . empty. They love . . . *home.*" The older woman opened her eyes and smiled wanly.

"Why didn't you tell us that you were Aenean?" Dem Lia said softly.

Ces Ambre's jaw set in resolve. "I am *not* Aenea. My mother, Dem Loa, gave me the sacrament of Aenea's blood—through her own, of course—after rescuing me from the hell of St. Theresa. But I decided *not* to use the Aenean abilities. I chose *not* to follow the others, but to remain with the Amoiete."

"But you communicated telepathically with . . ." began Patek Georg.

Ces Ambre shook her head and interrupted quickly. "It is *not* telepathy. It is . . . being connected . . . to the Void Which Binds. It is hearing the language of the dead and of the living across time and space through pure empathy, memories not one's own." The ninety-five-year-old woman who looked middle-aged put her hand on her brow. "It is *so* tiring. I fought for so many years not to pay attention to the voices . . . to join in the memories. That is why the cryogenic deep sleep is so . . . restful."

"And the other Aenean abilities?" Dem Lia asked, her voice still very soft. "Have you freecast?"

Ces Ambre shook her head, with her hand still shielding her eyes. "I did not want to *learn* the Aenean secrets," she said. Her voice sounded very tired.

"But you could if you wanted to," said Den Soa, her voice awestruck. "You could take one step—freecast—and be back on Vitus-Gray-Balianus B or Hyperion or Tau Ceti Center or Old Earth in a second, couldn't you?"

Ces Ambre lowered her hand and looked fiercely at the young woman. "But I *won't.*"

"Are you continuing with us in deep sleep to our destination?" asked the other green-band, Res Sandre. "To our final Spectrum Helix colony?"

"Yes," said Ces Ambre. The single word was a declaration and a challenge.

"How will we tell the others?" asked Jon Mikail Dem Alem. "Having an Aenean . . . a potential Aenean . . . in the colony will change . . . everything."

Dem Lia stood. "In my final moments are your consensus-elected commander, I could make this an order, Citizens. Instead, I ask for a vote. I feel that Ces Ambre and only Ces Ambre should make the decision as to whether or not to tell our fellow Spectrum Helix family about her . . . gift. At any time after we reach our destination." She looked directly at Ces Ambre. "Or never, if you so choose."

Dem Lia turned to look at each of the other eight. "And we shall never reveal the secret. Only Ces Ambre has the right to tell the others. Those in favor of this, say aye."

It was unanimous.

Dem Lia turned to the standing Ousters and Templar. "Saigyō assures me that none of this was broadcast on your tightbeam."

Far Rider nodded.

"And your recording of Ces Ambres's contact with the aliens through the Void Which Binds?"

"Destroyed," broadcast the four-meter Ouster.

Ces Ambre stepped closer to the Ousters. "But you still want some of my blood . . . some of Aenea's sacramental DNA. You still want the choice."

Chief Branchman Keel Redt's long hands were shaking. "It would not be for us to decide to release the information or allow the sacrament to be distributed . . . the Seven Councils would have to meet in secret . . . the Church of Aenea would be consulted . . . or . . ." Obviously the Ouster was in pain at the thought of millions or billions of his fellow Ousters leaving the forest ring forever, freecasting away to human-Aenean space or elsewhere. Their universe would never be the same. "But the three of us do not have the right to reject it for everyone."

"But we hesitate to ask . . ." began the True Voice of the Tree Reta Kasteen.

Ces Ambre shook her head and motioned to Dr. Samuel. The medic handed the Templar a small quantity of blood in a shockproof vial. "We drew it just a while ago," said the doctor.

"You must decide," said Ces Ambre. "That is always the way. That is always the curse."

Chief Branchman Keel Redt stared at the vial for a long moment before he took it in his still-shaking hands and carefully set it away in a secure pouch on his Ouster forcefield armor. "It will be interesting to see what happens," said the Ouster.

Dem Lia smiled. "That's an ancient Old Earth curse, you know. Chinese. 'May you live in interesting times.'"

Saigyō morphed the airlock and the Ouster diplomats were gone, sailing back to the forest ring with the hundreds of thousands of other beings of light, tacking against the solar wind, following magnetic lines of force like vessels of light carried by swift currents.

"If you all don't mind," said Ces Ambre, smiling, "I'm going to return to my deep-sleep crèche and turn in. It's been a long couple of days."

The originally awakened nine waited until the *Helix* had successfully translated into Hawking space before returning to deep sleep. When they were still in the G8 system, accelerating up and away from the ecliptic and the beautiful forest ring which now eclipsed the small, white sun, Oam Rai pointed to the stern window, and said, "Look at that."

The Ousters had turned out to say good-bye. Several billion wings of pure energy caught the sunlight.

A day into Hawking space while conferring with the AIs was enough to establish that the ship was in perfect form, the spin arms and deep-sleep pods functioning as they should, that they had returned to course, and that all was well. One by one, they returned to their crèches—first Den Soa and her mates, then the others. Finally only Dem Lia remained awake, sitting up in her creche in the seconds before it was to be closed.

"Saigyō," she said, and it was obvious from her voice that it was a summons.

The short, fat, Buddhist monk appeared.

"Did you know that Ces Ambre was Aenean, Saigyō?"

"No, Dem Lia."

"How could you not? The ship has complete genetic and med profiles on every one of us. You must have known."

"No, Dem Lia, I assure you that Citizen Ces Ambre's med profiles were within normal Spectrum Helix limits. There was no sign of post-humanity Aenean DNA. Nor clues in her psych profiles."

Dem Lia frowned at the hologram for a moment. Then she said, "Forged bio records then? Ces Ambre or her mother could have done that."

"Yes, Dem Lia."

Still propped on one elbow, Dem Lia said, "To your knowledge—to any of the AI's knowledge—are there other Aeneans aboard the *Helix*, Saigyō?"

"To our knowledge, no," said the plump monk, his face earnest.

Dem Lia smiled. "Aenea taught that evolution had a direction and determination," she said softly, more to herself than to the listening AI. "She spoke of a day when all the universe would be green with life. Diversity, she taught, is one of evolution's best strategies."

Saigyō nodded and said nothing.

Dem Lia lay back on her pillow. "We thought the Aeneans so generous in helping us preserve our culture—this ship—the distant colony. I bet the Aeneans have helped a thousand small cultures cast off from human space into the unknown. They want the diversity—the Ousters, the others. They want many of us to pass up their gift of godhood."

She looked at the AI, but the Buddhist monk's face showed only his usual slight smile. "Good night, Saigyō. Take good care of the ship while we sleep." She pulled the top of the crèche shut and the unit began cycling her into deep cryogenic sleep.

"Yes, Dem Lia," said the monk to the now-sleeping woman.

The *Helix* continued its great arc through Hawking space. The spin arms and life pods wove their complex double helix against the flood of false colors and four-dimensional pulsations which had replaced the stars.

Inside the ship, the AIs had turned off the containment-field gravity and the atmosphere and the lights. The ship moved on in darkness.

Then, one day, about three months after leaving the binary system, the ventilators hummed, the lights flickered on, and the containment-field gravity activated. All 684,300 of the colonists slept on.

Suddenly three figures appeared in the main walkway halfway between the command-center bridge and the access portals to the first ring of life-pod arms. The central figure was more than three meters tall, spiked and armored, bound about with chrome razorwire. Its faceted eyes gleamed red. It remained motionless where it had suddenly appeared.

The figure on the left was a man in early middle age, with curly, graying hair, dark eyes, and pleasant features. He was very tan and wore a soft blue cotton shift, green shorts, and sandals. He nodded at the woman and began walking toward the command center.

The woman was older, visibly old even despite Aenean medical techniques, and she wore a simple gown of flawless blue. She walked to the access portal, took the lift up the third spin arm, and followed the walkway down into the one-g environment of the life pod. Pausing by one of the crèches, she brushed ice and condensation from the clear faceplate of the umbilically monitored sarcophagus.

"Ces Ambre," muttered Dem Loa, her fingers on the chilled plastic centimeters above her triune stepdaughter's lined cheek. "Sleep well, my darling. Sleep well."

On the command deck, the tall man was standing among the virtual AIs.

"Welcome, Petyr, son of Aenea and Endymion," said Saigyō with a slight bow.

"Thank you, Saigyō. How are you all?"

They told him in terms beyond language or mathematics. Petyr nodded, frowned slightly, and touched Basho's shoulder. "There are too many conflicts in you, Basho? You wished them reconciled?"

The tall man in the coned hat and muddy clogs said, "Yes, please, Petyr."

The human squeezed the AI's shoulder in a friendly embrace. Both closed their eyes for an instant.

When Petyr released him, the saturnine Basho smiled broadly. "Thank you, Petyr."

The human sat on the edge of the table, and said, "Let's see where we're headed."

A holocube four meters by four meters appeared in front of them. The stars were recognizable. The *Helix*'s long voyage out from human-Aenean space was traced in red. Its projected trajectory proceeded ahead in blue dashes—blue dashes extending toward the center of the galaxy.

Petyr stood, reached into the holo cube, and touched a small star just to the right of the projected path of the *Helix*. Instantly that section magnified.

"This might be an interesting system to check out," said the man with a comfortable smile. "Nice G2 star. The fourth planet is about a seven-point-six on the old

Solmev Scale. It would be higher, but it has evolved some very nasty viruses and some very fierce animals. Very fierce."

"Six hundred eighty-five light-years," noted Saigyō. "Plus forty-three light-years course correction. Soon."

Petyr nodded.

Lady Murasaki moved her fan in front of her painted face. Her smile was provocative. "And when we arrive, Petyr-san, will the nasty viruses somehow be gone?"

The tall man shrugged. "Most of them, my Lady. Most of them." He grinned. "But the fierce animals will still be there." He shook hands with each of the AIs. "Stay safe, my friends. And keep our friends safe."

Petyr trotted back to the nine-meter chrome-and-bladed nightmare in the main walkway just as Dem Loa's soft gown swished across the carpeted deckplates to join him.

"All set?" asked Petyr.

Dem Loa nodded.

The son of Aenea and Raul Endymion set his hand against the monster standing between them, laying his palm flat next to a fifteen-centimeter curved thorn. The three disappeared without a sound.

The *Helix* shut off its containment-field gravity, stored its air, turned off its interior lights, and continued on in silence, making the tiniest of course corrections as it did so.

COLIN GREENLAND

Colin Greenland [1954–] lives in Cambridge, England. His first book was the standard work on the British New Wave, *The Entropy Exhibition: Michael Moorcock and the British "New Wave" in Science Fiction* (1983). He was a coeditor of *Interzone* in the 1980s and coauthored the famous editorial in *Interzone* #7 calling for a new "radical hard SF." With John Clute and David Pringle, he was coeditor of *Interzone: The 1st Anthology* (1985). His profile at www.infinityplus.co.uk/misc/cg.htm says he "made his name in the columns of the *New Statesman*, *The Face*, and *The Sunday Times*, where he patiently explained to a sceptical world about SF and fantasy." For two years he was Arts Council Writer in Residence at the Science Fiction Foundation. His interviews with Michael Moorcock have been collected and published under the title *Death Is No Obstacle* (1992). Most of his novels have not appeared in the US even now, and he has been known in the US primarily as a literary critic.

But his particular claim to importance in space opera is as the author of *Take Back Plenty* (1990), winner of both the British SF Association and Arthur C. Clarke Awards as best novel, one of the origins and engines of nineties UK space opera. The Plenty series, including sequels *Seasons of Plenty* (1995), *The Plenty Principle* (1997), a collection of stories featuring a previously untold adventure of the young Captain Jute, and *Mother of Plenty* (1998), was an important paradigm for British SF writers, though it had much less impact in the US.

Ken MacLeod, in an essay in *Locus*, said, "Colin Greenland eased space opera's limbs out of the contorted shape in which Harrison had left them, visibly drawing on him while lightening his tone, in *Take Back Plenty*. Its title adumbrates its cheerful, brazen reappropriation of the Golden Age Solar system: Greenland's Venus has jungles, his Mars has canals, but his characters are space truckers and musicians who could have reeled out of any of Harrison's dives into a cold Camden morning."

This assertion entirely ignores the existence and evolution of American space opera between 1970 and 1990, much of which was either not reprinted in the UK or was not recognized as space opera, a continuing problem in clarifying the tradition. But it does underscore the continuing impact of Greenland's space operas on writers in the UK, where *Take Back Plenty* was a breath of fresh air after two decades of a fashion for, in Brian Aldiss's phrase, "pure bracing gloom." It made much less impact in the US because there was so much popular space opera available in the 1980s and 1990s.

We asked Greenland for comments and he responded:

Alastair Reynolds, Adam Roberts, Ken MacLeod, Justina Robson, Charles Stross—looking around now, it's hard to believe that space opera was once off-limits to British sf writers. Worse, it was held in deep scorn. *Star Wars*, we admitted, was huge fun, but it was mindless fun. At the beginning of the eighties, struggling with the first impulses of what became the Tabitha Jute trilogy, I was assured kindly but firmly by sf fans and fellow writers alike that whether on screen or in print the form was bankrupt, "untenable" (that was Bruce Sterling), inherently simplistic, blatantly imperialistic, and quite unable to support intelligent life.

I didn't have a lot of counter-evidence. On these shores, in those days, sf was in the grip of a sort of glum Puritanism. We wanted the meaning—future shock, cognitive dissonance, alienation, all that—but the metaphors were embarrassing, tainted, politically incorrect. "British space opera" was an archaism that described the less interesting work of John Brunner, or more specifically Ted Tubb, the absolute paradigm of reliable generic British sf writers knocked flat by the tsunami of the New Wave. Though Brian Aldiss, in his short fiction especially, delighted in the subgenre he identified as "widescreen baroque," the rest of Michael Moorcock's motley crew had followed J. G. Ballard in pulling out of the Space Race.

No one was more conscious of that than I, who had just finished studying the process at doctorate level, and written it up in *The Entropy Exhibition*. At the same time, curiously enough, two of my Oxford contemporaries were busy writing novels that were thoroughly space-operatic: Michael Scott Rohan's *Run to the Stars* and David Langford's *The Space Eater* were both published in 1982. Significantly, perhaps, neither man continued in that vein. Still, something was going on, an intention tremor in the string of the pendulum.

Phillip Mann's *Master of Paxwax* and *Fall of the Families*, a pair of space operas from New Zealand, were published here in 1986 and 1987, but like two more famous books of the same period, *Consider Phlebas* and *The Player of Games*, they seemed rather tame to me. Certainly, part of that response was the entirely unreasonable conviction to which any writer must always be liable, that there was a book I very much wanted to exist, and they weren't it. If Iain Banks, especially, was going to turn his hand to sf, I was not prepared to accept anything less weird or ambitious or singular than *The Wasp Factory*, or *Walking on Glass*. Still, I was encouraged to see I wasn't the only one working to answer the meanness and fear of the Thatcher years with a vision of interplanetary plenty.

The book I held in highest esteem was one from a dozen years earlier. *Look*, I would say to anyone who showed the slightest interest. *It's weird, it's fun, it's literate, it's humane, it's even political, and it's space opera. No genre is beyond redemption. You just have to work at it.* That exemplary work was *The Centauri Device* by M. John Harrison.

I once made the mistake of telling Mr. Harrison how much I was inspired by *The Centauri Device*. He looked decidedly affronted. "Well you shouldn't be," he said truculently. "It's a very bad book." Too late The damage was done.

This story, from 1996, has nevertheless a kind of early 1980s, pre-cyberpunk, Sterling feel. It is a Ballardian space opera, about a mad artist on Umbriel, one of the moons of Neptune, and features Tabitha Jute, the cynical, working-class, hard-boiled woman space captain who was the central character of the Plenty novels. It is Leigh Brackett for the 1990s.

THE WELL WISHERS

COLIN GREENLAND

On Umbriel, where the Dream Wells are, it is always one kind of night or another. Great nights and little ones succeed each other, darkness overlapping darkness, with only the silver-fretted heavens for relief. Sol, when Uranus does not eclipse it, is too far away to be much help. Most of its light expires on the crawl out here. So daytime is a technicality, like longitude, or irrational numbers. It can be proved to exist, but troubles few sleepers.

On Umbriel you can really concentrate on your dreams.

The ship sat alone on the field beneath the beacon. The terrain was the same all over, salty white with outcrops raw and jagged black, and there didn't seem to be much in the way of occupation; but tiny, outlying settlements like this could be horribly snotty about their zoning regulations, and the agency could be brutally literal about their policy of not rehiring careless drivers; so Tabitha Jute had opted for the field.

No one appeared to give her a welcome, or even a clue. There was no traffic, no workers, no one just hanging about, as there usually was on even the most insignificant moons. The woman who had acknowledged her approach and cleared her landing had been a recording.

"NOT A VERY FRIENDLY PLACE, CAPTAIN, IS IT?" said Alice.

Captain Jute was still new enough to this ship to be surprised by her remark. She suspected somebody had fiddled with the programming of the persona, raising the sensitivity levels, amplifying the affinity circuits. One day she would have to get inside and poke around Bergen Kobold Persona 5N179476.900, given name Alice, to see what made her tick.

"No, Alice, it isn't," she said. "Never mind. I don't suppose we'll be here long."

Tabitha suited up and stepped out into a landscape like a frozen sea. She felt the salt crust crunch silently under her boots as she sprang slowly across to the office.

No one had come to meet her. There was one man on the inside of a horseshoe counter big enough for twelve. He sitting with his chair in recline, watching AV.

Captain Jute opened her helmet. "Hi," she said.

The man lifted an indifferent hand.

The air was high oxygen, and warm. It smelt of peppermint cycler freshener.

On the AV were a young man and a young woman in a jeep. They were pretending to be riding along, while film of a mountain road played behind them. They were talking to each other, and laughing.

"Is there a message for me?"

"Nope," said the field officer, his eyes not leaving the screen.

The Captain unpopped her left cuff. She tapped up the job details.

"Can you tell me where this is?"

The man gave the Captain's com set the merest glance and pointed through the wall. "Twenty minutes," he said. He didn't look where he was pointing.

"Where's the phone?"

He pointed at that in the same way.

"She won't answer," he said.

Captain Jute made a long step to the phone. She plugged in and started pressing the tabs.

She heard it ring, once. Then a muffled tape came on playing a forgotten pop song. There was a hustling, robotic beat; a woman's voice singing sluggishly, sullenly, along with it. If there were words, they didn't seem to have anything to do with making a phonecall.

Tabitha waited for a message, but the music was all there was. After a while she pulled her plug. "She never answers," said the field officer. Hands laced across his stomach, he watched his show. "Twenty minutes," he said again. "You've got a car." He stated it as a general principle.

"I'm saving up," she said.

"Forty-five minutes," he said.

Through the triple-glazing she could see the tracks of many vehicles, or maybe the same vehicle driving around in all directions. She could see the low plateau where the beacon was. Between there and here, roughly north-west, lay a low dull brown dome. In the distance were three or four lights, small, sharp and unwavering, like fallen stars.

On the screen the young people were still taking their imaginary ride. Only the man was talking now. The woman watched his face and smiled. The scarf on her head flapped like a flag in the artificial slipstream.

"Where do I get a car?" asked Captain Jute.

The man said: "You wait a couple of hours, I'll take you."

She wasn't going to get into that. "There must be a cab."

"I doubt it. This is apogee," he told her, as if she might not have noticed. "No one comes here at apogee."

"People come here?" said Captain Jute, snapping up her cuff. "That way?" she asked him.

He pointed again, east, a short stab in the scented air. "Big place with all the windows."

He keyed the door for her.

"She won't let you in," he said.

Captain Jute reached for her sealing tab. The contact name was Morton Godfrey. A man's name, she had supposed.

"I'm just making a pick-up," she said.

The field officer watched the people on the screen with unwavering attention, like a lover or a spy. Perhaps he had written the script and wanted to make sure they got it right.

"She never lets anyone in," he said.

The house occupied a rise on the far side of the plateau. It was a low irregular pile of silver aluminium saucers. There were a lot of saucers, and they did have a lot of windows, thought Tabitha, coming up the slope. All the windows were alight, as if Mr Godfrey's employer was throwing a fabulous party.

A camera scrutinized the approaching Captain. In her phones a robot voice said: *"State your business."*

"Careways Agency pick-up for Morton Godfrey," she said. She went up to the camera and showed her wrist. Artworks, the goods description field said.

"Mr Godfrey is not available."

"Whose house is this?"

"This is the house of Princess Badroulboudour," the robot said. "She is not available."

"Was it something I said?" Captain Jute asked it.

"I am not enabled to answer that question," said the robot. "No one is available to deal with you at present."

In her mind's eye she could see it, a Facto 4000, multi-capacitied and very prim. She imagined it with a feather duster in its manipulators, going down a line of grey plaster statues.

"Where can I reach them?" she asked.

"No one is available to deal with you at present," said the robot. "Your visit has been recorded and logged at 05.22.32. Please return later."

Halfway down the hill, she looked back at the house. There was no one at any of the brilliant windows, nothing moving anywhere. Behind the house, Uranus was rising with a sour and sallow face.

She called the ship.

"Where is everybody, Alice?"

"COMMUNICATIONS TRAFFIC IS LOW," Alice reported.

Captain Jute looked out towards the little bubble domes that were scattered across the corrugated plains of chemical ice. There was nothing moving down there either. She wondered who the hell would live here, and why.

"ONE CENTRE OF SOCIAL AMENITIES IS LISTED."

"A bar? Is there a bar?"

"VERY PROBABLY. THERE'S A HUNDRED-BED HOTEL."

"Someone does come here." Religious retreats, knowing her luck. The ambience was getting to her. "Who's this Princess Badroulboudour, do we know?" she asked the ship, as she called the hotel.

There was a swift pause while Alice searched. "I Can't FIND ANYTHING UNDER THAT NAME. SHALL I PUT OUT A QUERY?"

"No, Alice, doesn't matter."

The hotel answered. Tabitha could hear slow music, a couple of people talking in the background.

"Are you open?" she asked.

"Ask me nicely."

The voice was studied, coarse, good-humoured, female. She relaxed a fraction.

"I'm just in. I'm looking for fresh air and a recharge."

"You find something fresh on Umbriel, sweetheart, you let us all know about it."

The hotel was called Reveries. It was inside the brown dome she had seen from the landing field. There was no one in the cloakroom. She put her chip in the slot, and her suit in a locker.

The corridors of Reveries were silent, with thick purple carpets in case somebody accidentally made a noise. There were signs to somewhere called the Well. Captain Jute followed them.

The signs led her to a small circular chamber, with two other corridors leading off it. There were some steps going down. At the top of the steps was a tall blue glass vase holding a single flower.

The flower was large. It was ostentatious, and not very realistic. There were six broad petals of cobalt blue that curved luxuriously back from a soft grey centre. In the centre was a face.

The face was humanoid, lifesize. It had two green eyes, a broad nose, and a pair of glistening lavender lips. The eyes looked entirely vacant, but as Tabitha appeared the lips parted suddenly, as if in a little soundless sigh.

Tabitha felt the eyes of the flower follow her down the steps, and into the Well.

The Well was clean white rockfoam and vinyl, with redwood trim. There were eighteen tables, and a grand piano. The piano had a dustsheet over it, and the tables were empty.

On the jukebox at the end of the bar a saxophone was playing, while some men sang mournfully in unison in a language she didn't know. Opposite the bar was a picture window, showing a broad slice of desolation. The glass was tinted seaweed green. It didn't help.

There were six people in the room. One of them was standing behind the bar, the other five were sitting on stools in front of her. They were all older than Tabitha. They all looked at her as she came down the steps.

Tabitha hated being inspected. It made her feel she needed to hitch up her jeans and tuck her T-shirt in.

The barwoman had a head of tarnished curls and a face life had written lines on. She smiled dozily. "How do you like the air?" "It would be better with a beer," said Tabitha.

"What's your choice?"

"The cheapest," said Captain Jute. She went and sat at an empty table.

The other customers withdrew their attention. A drowsy, rumbling conversation resumed. Tabitha wasn't interested.

The Well was like any other hotel bar on any other world. The locals were leaning on the bar as if they were glued there. They were assaulting their livers with alcohol in a relaxed but businesslike way. On the little holopad of the jukebox a blond white man in a baggy suit was nursing a black saxophone that emitted floating white eggs of sound. Everything was perfectly bland and ordinary, in fact, except for the ornaments.

They didn't make good ornaments, in Captain Jute's opinion, but that was what they had to be. They were all the same size, about thirty centimetres tall, the same as the flower at the entrance; and they were all set up just above eye level, in case you wanted something to look at.

From where Tabitha sat she could see three.

One was a big transparent egg. It was full of a clear liquid, and there was some kind of creature hunched up inside it, which the egg was barely big enough to contain. The creature looked as if it might have been the offspring of a human and a fish.

The creature was partly animated, like the face in the flower. It kept making tiny squirming motions against the inside of its egg. Every time it did, strings of bubbles floated up from the corners of its mouth.

The second ornament was another creature. It was a model of a Thrant, poised as if to spring. It too seemed to be moving a little, flexing its long muscles, without ever moving its feet. It seemed to have its eye on Captain Jute.

Captain Jute hoped it wasn't actually capable of springing. She hoped that wasn't the sort of thing they found funny on Umbriel, at apogee. The third ornament was a lifesize head. It too looked human. It was bloodless white, and completely bald. There were long metal spikes sticking out of its skull. It kept smiling knowingly, and lolling out its deep red tongue.

"Hi there," said a man. He had got down off his stool at the bar and come over to her table. "Can I get you another?"

She looked at her beer. Apparently she had drunk it.

"Why not," she said.

The man was dark-skinned, with a little gold ring in each ear and a shock of shiny black hair. He was wearing a crimson blazer over a collarless shirt in blue pinstripe. He had a little beard on the point of his chin, and there was a gold ring around that too. He was dressed up a lot for someone living in a place where no one came.

Perhaps he had been expecting her.

"You're not Morton Godfrey," asked Captain Jute, "by any chance?"

They all heard that. They laughed at her, sideways.

She ignored them and concentrated on her new acquaintance. He was grinning.

"No," he said. "I'm not Morton Godfrey." He looked steadily at her, bathing her in his regard. "I'm Olister Crane," he said. He had that tone in his voice that allowed a chance she might have heard of him.

She hadn't.

He indicated the seat opposite her. "Mind if I sit down?"

"I wasn't saving it for anyone," she said.

He asked her: "So, is that your Kobold out there at the field?"

Captain Jute said it was.

"Did Mr Godfrey send for you?"

She nodded. He hadn't, but that was none of Olister Crane's business, whoever he was. She drained her tube and began the new one. Crane was not going to give up trying.

"Your name is Mo," he said. "Your name is Lucky."

She would not play. "My name is Tabitha Jute," she said.

He complimented her with his eyelashes.

"You know who Mr Godfrey works for, Captain Jute."

"A princess, apparently," she said.

Crane found her reply amusing.

"A princess," he repeated, affirmatively.

The saxophone record had stopped some minutes earlier. Now one of the customers at the bar leaned over to the panel and punched up something else.

There was a sound like steel brushes being dragged along a metal floor, and after a while, a woman crooning. She didn't sound any happier than the men with the saxophone had. On the holopad some kind of string puppet jerked and spun.

"This is where she is now," said Crane. "Princess Badroulboudour. Gracing our little colony."

He looked at Captain Jute sidelong to see how she took this disclosure. He seemed to want her to be impressed.

There was nothing more boring, thought Tabitha, drinking, than people wanting you to be impressed. Crane reminded her of her father. This was just the sort of place she could imagine he might have ended up, drinking for consolation on a dead-end moon.

"Have you seen her yet, Tabitha?" asked a white woman at the bar. Already they had adopted her, accepted her into their club. "Last year she bought some of my jewellery."

"Tell her about your jewellery, Cerise," said another man. He sounded somnolent with drink.

"You like jewellery, Tabitha?" The woman wore an iron and turquoise comb in her long blonde hair. She appraised the new member across the room. "You should wear rubies. I've got some pieces you're going to adore."

Captain Jute sat tight. She drank steadily.

"And you can read my poems," Olister Crane was saying softly to her, "and Noland's novel, and Gideam's opera." He produced a huge white handkerchief and touched it to his eyes, as if they were wet, from humour, or emotion. He was still smiling. "And maybe by then the Princess will let you see Mr Godfrey."

He lay his large hand on the table between them, an ambiguous gesture of friendship or warning.

Tabitha examined the label on her beer.

Long after everyone had stopped waiting for her to speak and gone back to talking among themselves, she asked Crane: "Where is she from, this princess?"

This stirred them all again, all her new pals sitting along the bar. They indicated the jukebox. They wanted her to look at what was on it.

The figure in the holo had changed from being a string puppet. Now it was a living human woman in an industrial grey skinsuit, only instead of hands and feet, her arms and legs ended in sprays of electrical wiring. The wires were unbraiding, multiplying while the figure tugged and struggled.

"This is her," said Cerise. "Princess B."

Tabitha watched for a moment. The trapped figure, half woman, half machine, reminded her of a woman called Devereux. Devereux lived in a private habitat off Deimos. She wasn't someone Tabitha especially wanted to be reminded of. "Do you like this stuff?" she asked Olister Crane, who was buying her another drink.

"Tabitha," said Crane chidingly. "You really don't know the Princess? She was the one who invented traipse!"

"Not my kind of thing. Put some blues on," suggested Captain Jute.

It was useless. They found her something that was more or less R&B, then talked over it.

They had a mission, to educate and inform. Either that or they were punishing her lack of interest with a lecture on their local celebrity.

"You remember that thing people used to say," said a fat woman called Georginelle, "about having to reinvent yourself thirty-two times a second. That was Princess Badroulboudour. She was the one who said that."

"Princess Badroulboudour—redesigned—the face of music—forever," claimed Gideam, the composer of operas. He was elderly, and even more overweight than Georginelle. The gravity was kind here, to people that size. Still Gideam's breathing was laboured, his voice thick with mucus. "She *became* the face of music."

The face of music was equipped with breathtakingly large eyes, and a mouth that seemed to express a personal offence at the universe, or the human condition, or something. The patrons of the Well played Tabitha some more examples of her work: restless things in different speeds, but with the same abrasive kind of rhythm. The Princess appeared in a dozen different styles: in rags; in furs; once in a weird telescopic dress whose sections slid up and down her body while she danced. Untutored, the Captain might have been unsure that they were all the same woman, though there was a uniform frenzy to the appearances, as if whatever it was she disapproved of so was on the point of devouring her whole.

Captain Jute did get the sense that the Princess's reign had been pretty temporary, like all these things. She still had no idea what traipse was, or why it mattered. She had the feeling that if she told them how pointless it all sounded to her, somebody would say: "Exactly."

Crane was still monopolizing her. "So what have you got there," he asked, "in your Kobold?"

"I'm making a pick-up," she said.

"The Captain is making a pick-up," said Crane to the rest of them, keeping his eyes on Tabitha.

"She's the lucky one," grated the barwoman.

"What are you picking up, Captain?" called the somnolent man.

"I'm picking up some artworks," said Captain Jute.

Now she had given them something. They were thrilled.

"She's working again!" Georginelle was positively exultant. She tipped back her head and clenched her fists.

The news was no surprise to Cerise. "She couldn't just retire," she said, as if that should always have been obvious to everyone. "You can't *stop*. If it's in you, you *can't* stop."

She wanted confirmation for her testimony. They gave it to her. You couldn't stop working, they all agreed. None of them at the moment seemed to be in much of a hurry to start again, nevertheless.

Everyone wanted to know what Tabitha knew. Tabitha told them again she knew nothing. She showed them her wristcom. "There, you see? Artworks. That's all it says."

"What does she want with a barge?" said Crane to the room in general. "She could just release them."

"Security, Crane," said Gideam. "There are no safeguards here. Anyone who really—wants to can—steal all your ideas."

"She doesn't want to let people know where she is," said Cerise. She said it loudly, claiming the credit for being the one to admit an unpleasing truth.

"Everyone knows where she is," stated the somnolent man, truculently. By *everyone* he seemed to mean the entire population, permanent and temporary, of Sol System.

"Princess Badroulboudour," Cerise continued in her fatalistic tone, "could put this place back on the map, if she wanted to."

"She doesn't owe Umbriel anything," Georginelle said protectively. "And she certainly doesn't owe us anything."

This had the air of a ritualistic argument. There was no way either of them was ever going to convince the other. Maybe that was traipse too.

Captain Jute said to Crane: "You're all artists."

Crane nodded slowly and rhythmically. "We are the Well Wishers," he said.

He slid his hand across the table, and made a bridge across Tabitha's wrist. He did it delicately, slowly, looking humorously into her eyes. Perhaps the idea was that she would be mesmerized. Or perhaps he was daring her to stop him.

She moved the hand. She lifted her beer to her mouth.

"You sit here and wish," she said.

Everything she said amused Olister Crane. "Yeah, then, Captain, we do. But this isn't that Well. That's just the name of the bar. That's just like a joke. The Wells of Umbriel. You know?" He sat back, searching her face. He shook his head. "You don't know anything, do you?" His voice was sympathetic, and high.

"Glory be," the barkeeper said. She was looking across the heads of her patrons, out of the green window. "If it isn't her coming."

Crane got to his feet. Georginelle and Gideam and Noland turned on their barstools. Everyone gazed out of the window.

Across the rutted white waste a big grey car was approaching.

"It's her."

They all stared. Their enthusiasm for the ex-entertainer seemed to have evaporated suddenly. They seemed oddly apprehensive, as if wondering whether she might have been listening to them talking about her.

"Do you think she's coming here?" said Georginelle, in a kind of hushed giggle.

Tabitha left the bar. In the purple corridors, she found herself running. She did not know why. Perhaps she just wanted to get on with the job. Or perhaps the songs had got to her. Perhaps the Captain feared that Princess Badroulboudour might be an unstable presence, a manifestation likely to disappear as quickly and unpredictably as it had appeared.

The grey car was an antique Rolls, a hundred years old if it was a day. It was a half-track now. It slipped silently towards her across the alien ice.

It came inside the dome and stopped, not entering the car park. Maybe proximity to other vehicles might be contaminating.

The driver's door unsealed. A human chauffeur got out. He wore a grey uniform two shades darker than the paintwork of the car. His face was completely concealed by the peak of his cap and a moulded grey plastic airmask.

He let a woman out of the back.

She wore the same model airmask, and three swathes of thick pink-speckled fur: one in a high collar around her neck; one around her hands as a muff; and one luxuriously around her ankles. On her head was a helmet of black velvet. Her costume was mulberry red, with a high-waisted jacket and a full-length skirt narrow as a stalk.

Princess Badroulboudour held her head high and her shoulders back. She gazed across the car park like a predator, suspecting enemies.

Captain Jute stepped out across the concrete. She unpopped her cuff, ready to display her credentials.

"Princess?" she said. "I'm with Careways, I'm looking for a Morton Godfrey."

With her black-gloved hand Princess Badroulboudour impatiently pulled off her airmask.

"Who is this?" she said to the chauffeur, with a dazed hauteur that made the Captain's hair prickle. "What does she want?"

The Captain recognised now the original of the holos: the head like a mannered sculpture with its taut, hollow cheeks and affronted mouth. The eyes really were as large as they looked, and made even larger with mascara.

"Careways," she said again. "You've got some artworks to go to New Malibu."

She tried to show her wristset. The woman would not focus on it. She glared.

The chauffeur stood behind his employer, too close to be properly respectful. His breast was grey and smooth and broad as a wall. His jacket bore two rows of silver buttons. The singer reached a hand back over her shoulder, as if to make sure he was there to protect her from this intruder.

"I don't suppose you're Morton Godfrey," said Tabitha to the chauffeur.

His voice was muffled by his mask, but she knew he was smiling. "At your service," he said.

His employer turned on him, as though the phrase itself was an annoyance. "Who is she?" she demanded.

Captain Jute addressed herself to Godfrey. "How much have you got?"

"Money?" asked Godfrey.

"How much of a load," said Tabitha.

The entertainer with the ludicrous pseudonym was staring at her as though to nail her to the ground where she stood. "Nothing is ready," she said.

The man in the chauffeur's uniform lifted his head a touch. His eyes were the merest glints in the shadow of his cap.

Princess Badroulboudour swept past Captain Jute. "Nothing is ready, nothing." Her voice was bored, remote.

The chauffeur followed the Princess into the hotel.

The Captain came after. "When will I be able to collect?" "How do they expect anything ever to be ready," the Princess complained, "when they won't leave you alone?" She seemed to wish to blame everyone for her deficiency: Godfrey, the agency, Tabitha—everyone except herself.

Princess Badroulboudour and Morton Godfrey flew along the purple corridors, swift as children in the easy g. Captain Jute strode after. They were leaving her behind.

"Mr Godfrey," she called.

"Not here," said the chauffeur. "Come to the house."

"I've been to the house," said the Captain.

They had gone.

When she caught up with them, the Princess had come to rest. There was another of the unpleasant ornaments, and she was standing in front of it, examining it.

The ornament was a sly-looking, dark-skinned boy with his hair shaved to a frizz. He looked about twelve. His head was too big for his body.

Princess Badroulboudour held her right elbow cupped in her left hand, her long fingers splayed against her cheek, a parody of the art connoisseur.

"It's not crap like this, you know," she said.

The boy curled his lip at them.

"Pathetic," said the Princess. She hit the thing on the side of the head with her muff. It did not react.

Tabitha wondered if Crane and his friends were hiding somewhere, watching this.

Princess Badroulboudour turned a scornful glance on the Captain. "This is the sort of stuff you're expecting, I suppose."

"I'm just the driver," said Tabitha.

The Princess's fingers lunged for her arm. "Come here, driver."

Tabitha checked an impulse to kick her. She had lost a job once before, for refusing to be treated like dirt. She let herself be pulled into a position between the singer and the statue.

"Now then. Tell me what you see."

"An ugly boy," said Captain Jute.

"It's crap," said the Princess immediately, as if that was the only acceptable answer, the answer Tabitha should have given. "But is it interesting?"

The depth of insinuation suddenly in the skinny woman's voice made Tabitha turn and stare.

The Princess was smiling now, sardonically. The discarded airmask nestling underneath her chin was the same advanced design as her chauffeur's, but finished in speckled pink to match her furs.

"I wouldn't have it in my house," Tabitha told her.

The Princess laughed throatily, seeming to read more in the reply than the Captain had intended to put there. Her chauffeur was laughing too. "Where *is* your house?" the singer asked.

Several possible replies occurred to Tabitha, all of them offensive. She hadn't got a house any more than she'd got a car. All she'd got was her superannuated barge, Bergen Kobold 009059, registered name the *Alice Liddell*.

She said nothing.

"Listen, listen, you," said the Princess, who seemed to be bound by no restraint. "What you're going to be carrying is the first collection of moondreams ever to be exhibited in a decent gallery. Do you think you can handle it?"

Tabitha held her face rigid. She spoke to Godfrey, who stood behind them. "You've got the insurance details," she said. "If you want it to go with Careways, I'll take it. If not, there's the usual cancellation fee."

"Well, perhaps you'd like to think about it," said the Princess to her, with sudden devastating charm. It was as if the Captain hadn't spoken.

"If the consignment isn't ready, there is a stopover charge," said the Captain to the chauffeur.

The Princess closed her great black-rimmed eyes. The raspberry-speckled fur seemed to bristle across her shoulders. "Sort it out," she said in an undertone, to her attendant.

Godfrey placed himself between her and the offending space pilot. His attitude to his employer was soothing, conciliatory; but he did not touch her. He pulled out a phone and flipped it open. Tabitha could hear he was speaking to the barwoman. It was a moment or two before she realised he was booking her a room.

In the bar they called the Well, the locals were at the green window, watching for the Princess to leave. More of them had gathered in the short time Captain Jute had been away. Everyone seemed to be up to date with everything. Unasked, the barkeeper pulled another tube from the fridge and held it out to Tabitha. "On the bill," she said.

Around the curve of the dome the grey car appeared, heading away across the ice.

"There she goes," said Cerise, in case anyone wasn't looking.

"Now you can take it easy, Tabitha," said Georginelle, in a congratulatory tone.

"*What* is it she's working on?" asked the novelist, Noland. He sounded like a bored parent consulting a teacher about a devious child.

"Did she tell you anything?" Cerise was avid.

"Of course she didn't tell her anything," said Olister Crane. He was moving in on her again with his dandy beard and blazer.

"She asked if I thought I could handle her moondream collection," said Tabitha, as much to get their reaction as to gratify their rampant curiosity.

They were startled. "Her *dreams?*" Cerise squeaked. Georginelle muttered something incoherent. The men smirked at each other. "Her Highness's moondream collection," drawled Crane.

"And where are you supposed to take them?" asked Noland. Mirth was evident in his voice, the imminence of ridicule.

"New Malibu," said Captain Jute.

They all laughed then.

Captain Jute shifted irritably in her chair. She felt as if they were laughing at her.

"They're for an exhibition," she said aggressively, dismissively.

"Poor *stupid* cow," declared Noland, explosively, while Georginelle made tutting, clucking noises of pity.

"They're not going anywhere," Crame assured Captain Jute.

Captain Jute put her head back. "You don't know that," she said. "She might do it. Godfrey might get her to do it."

Crane rounded his lips and shook his finger in front of his nose. "No no no no no no," he said quietly and rapidly. "The dreams don't travel."

He spoke with great gravity, acquainting her with a basic truth.

"New Malibu!" said a woman Captain Jute didn't know. They were still finding the idea pretty funny.

"Maybe hers are different," said the Captain. She wanted this job.

Cerise came over to the table. "Tabitha, look," she said. She indicated one of the ornaments, the bald head with the spikes growing out of it. "That's me. That's a dream I had."

Tabitha looked. The head winked at her. She could see now it bore a strong resemblance to Cerise.

She was completely confused now. She had no idea if this was art, or a joke, or what it was.

"I wouldn't have thought you'd get much sleep with those sticking out of your head." To her gratification, they loved that. They obviously thought it showed the right attitude.

"That's me, look," said Gideam, amid the hilarity. He pointed at the little fishman in the egg. "I'm jolly proud of that one, it's the best I've ever had. That's what—inspired me—to write—*Hatchings*."

"Those things are moondreams?" Captain Jute asked Olister Crane.

He nodded positively.

"What are they?"

"Our true selves," he said, in all seriousness.

"Which one is you?"

"Come with me and I'll show you." He stood and held out both hands.

Captain Jute got up from her chair, but she did not let him take her hands. She followed him to the stairs.

He gestured at the flower with the face. He went up the stairs to where it stood. It pursed its lips and blinked vacuously at him.

"They look solid enough," said Tabitha.

"They are," said Crane, touching one blue petal reverently, "as long as we're in the vicinity. That's why we keep them here in the bar." Like everything else, he thought that was a good joke.

Tabitha hoped Princess Badroulboudour wasn't expecting to travel to New Malibu along with her collection.

"How do you make them?"

"First, you go to a Well," said Crane, starting back down the stairs to her. "I'll show you."

She wasn't really interested. She was worn out from the journey and all the walking.

"I'm knackered," she said. "I'm going back to my ship."

"I'll drive you," said Crane, quick as a snake.

"We got you a room here, sweetheart," the barwoman called out. "It's all ready for you. Why don't you go up and get your head down for a while?"

She wondered if the woman meant to warn her against Crane. He stood there all kitted out in his crimson blazer, ready to show her his dreams.

She didn't need the warning.

The Captain rubbed her head and yawned. The ship was her cave, but it was cluttered and cramped. A hotel room would be comfortable.

She was ready for some comfort.

The room was huge. It had three enormous sofas, besides a bed big enough for four people. The extravagance of everything was almost depressing. She wouldn't possibly be here long enough to make a satisfactory dent in it.

"They really must get tourists, Alice," she said.

"THE DISCOVERY OF THE SO-CALLED DREAM WELLS QUICKLY ATTRACTED NUMBERS OF INVESTIGATORS, ENTREPRENEURS AND CURIOSITY SEEKERS TO UMBRIEL," said Alice, who had been doing some research of her own. "SINCE IT BECAME APPARENT THAT THE EFFECT IS A NATURAL PHENOMENON THAT CAN'T BE MEASURED, PREDICTED OR CONTROLLED, THE INITIAL CURIOSITY HAS ABATED SOMEWHAT."

"Somewhat," said Tabitha, sliding open a cupboard. It was full of thick soft towels in pastel colours. "I've just been seeing some of the effect, if I understand it right."

She slid open another cupboard. It was a fridge. It was stocked with shrink-wrapped snacks, shiny chocolates, tubes of the beer she had been drinking.

"Alice, will you please tell Careways the consignment isn't ready and stopover arrangements have been made," she said, reaching for a tube.

"WILL DO, CAPTAIN," replied the faithful ship. "SHALL I TELL THEM YOU AWAIT THEIR INSTRUCTIONS?"

"Yes," said Captain Jute. "Tell them that."

She launched herself lightly onto the bed and put the AV on. There were so many channels she tired of pressing the button. She put it on a fifty-second cycle and fell asleep to dream of car crashes, z-ball tournaments, overflowing carbonated drinks and glossy linkmen in blue suits. The linkmen had metal spikes growing out of their heads.

The door chimed softly, waking her. It was a squat service drone. They had sent up her suit, cleaned and recharged.

Captain Jute slept again, woke, ate, bathed at great length in real water, got drunk, watched some porn, called reception, called the ship. Careways had acknowledged, but left no message. There was no word from Godfrey. At some point, the fridge had been silently restocked.

Captain Jute did everything again, and again, in different sequences. She ate and slept and woke and stared out of the window at the rolling dance of Oberon and Titania, the night that raced away across the mountains of Uranus overhead.

Soon enough, boredom drove her back to the bar. She didn't imagine it could still be the same day by any system of measurement, but Crane was there. He was alone. He looked up and smiled, easily, as if he had been waiting for her.

"Okay," Tabitha said. "Show me these Wells, then."

They drove through a haze of salt glare. The stars were dazzling. Among them Sol was a fierce dot, as if someone outside space was trying to break in with a welding torch.

Crane looked at Tabitha sidelong. Though his ice rover was on automatic pilot, he was keeping his hands to himself.

"What, you always travel alone?" he said.

"Always," she said.

"You don't like people."

"I'm fine on my own," she said. He laughed a short silent laugh. "You're fine on your own," he said.

The dead land crept by.

"You'd do okay here," he said. "This place is made for people who are fine on their own." He sounded blithe. "The less you need, the better you'll like it."

"I'm not staying," said Tabitha.

Crane chuckled softly. "No, no," he assured her.

The car was bright yellow. She looked at its fuzzy reflection in the ice.

"What about Mr Godfrey?" she said.

"Is he bothering you?"

She was not pleased by a proprietorial assumption that seemed to underlie his reply.

"Did she bring him here?"

"The Princess brought him." The poet's voice was cool now, neutral. "He's her number one fan. A good looking man," he averred. "A big man." He smiled a wide-eyed smile.

She said nothing.

"Best not touch."

"I wasn't going to touch him," said Captain Jute, unnerved.

"No no no no no no," he said again.

She inhaled hard.

Another barren kilometre slid by.

"What about you?" she asked him, eventually. "How long have you been here?"

"Years," he said. "Years and years."

"You must like it."

"I'm a poet," he said. "I have a poet's ego. I like the idea of a corner of the universe that shows my reflection." It was obviously a line he had perfected.

"A blue flower?" she said.

"My theory is, that one was kind of a joke," he said drily. Lights flickered across the dashboard as the car turned in the direction of an oblong dome. "I like it. Don't you? I do. I think it's good."

"And it just happens?" she asked. "Naturally?"

"Well, you have to work for it," he said. "You have to concentrate."

"How many have you done?"

He shook his head, not answering.

The dome looked like a simple utilitarian construction: bluish-grey fabricate with modular units budding out of it.

"Is this it?"

"This is it," he said. "This is the main one."

It looked more like a public building on Luna than a place where people went to dream solid dreams.

"You spend a lot of time out here, do you?"

"A lot of time," he acknowledged. "It's like making babies," he said, innocently. "You have to try a lot of times before you get lucky."

"Sometimes you just don't get lucky," she told him firmly.

"That's right," said Olister Crane. He wiped the corners of his mouth with his forefinger and thumb as he drove on toward the Well.

"Not everyone can make a dream," he said.

"You write poems too," she said.

He looked at her sideways again. "I'm going to write a poem about you."

"Leave me out," she said.

"That's a good title," he said.

"I don't want you to write about me," said Captain Jute.

Crane scratched his beard. "Those are often the most interesting subjects," he said, in a playful tone. "You'd better not do it," she said. "And you'd better not have any dreams about me, either."

"I think you're too late, there," said Crane. "Everyone's dreaming about you."

Her jaw tightened.

"Oh, don't worry, Captain," he said. "Nobody's going to steal your soul."

Where they went in, at the end of one of the tube modules, the air was warm and dank as a swimming bath. It even smelled slightly of chlorine. Biofluorescents threw sickly green light around.

A dried-up old man in a grubby white orderly's jacket sat at a desk. Crane spoke to him. They chatted for a moment, about who was in. Tabitha heard no names she recognised.

The superintendent was punching something out slowly on a keyboard. "Who's your lady friend, Mr Crane?" he asked. Perhaps he thought she didn't look capable of saying her own name.

"This is Captain Jute," said Crane. "Captain Jute flies things."

Please let's not talk about Princess Bad now, thought Captain Jute to herself.

"Captain Jute is working for the Princess," said Crane.

But the old man merely cocked an eyebrow and laughed.

They went down a corridor. Someone had tried to make the place look impressive by painting huge diamonds on the walls. The diamonds were sombre red, with gold outlines. In the middle of the floor someone else had left a battered green folding chair and a couple of bundles that looked as if they might have been laundry.

Captain Jute followed Crane round the obstacles. The chair seemed to be a chair; the laundry, laundry. She wondered when the weirdness was going to start.

There were doors along the corridor. Some of them were open. Inside were empty rooms.

"People still do come?" she asked.

"In the season," Crane said.

She wondered how long ago the last season had ended.

He seemed to answer her thought. "There's no commercial potential," he said. "One thing the Wells don't make is money."

They passed a glass-walled area that seemed to hold the remains of some abandoned experiment. There was the frame of a whole body medical scanner, with all the machinery removed. On the floor were a lead-lined blanket and several empty gas cylinders.

Ahead, a woman walked slowly across the corridor, wrapped in a towel. She went through a door, which closed behind her. She did not even glance at them. Perhaps she was walking in her sleep.

"In the beginning everyone came to Umbriel," Crane was saying. "Everyone with something burning in their brain. Artists, scientists, people on campaigns. Pilgrims, crazy for mysteries. People with theories. People with too much time and money. People dying, with no time at all."

He was speaking more softly now, as they neared the end of the corridor.

"People come and make a living out of the crazy people," said Crane. "Interpreters. Dream therapists, like Georginelle there."

They entered the dome.

"Some people think everybody should see their own true self," said Crane.

In the main dome the lights were low. Around the walls stood lines of hooded, shadowy booths like prayer shrines. There was more random furniture, stray pieces of equipment. Industrial friction carpet ran around a large curved pool. "There is always some disappointment," Crane said, "inevitably. The truth is a stranger. Mostly. Not always welcome by daylight."

Around the pool at intervals were stands of long-handled tools: hooks, rakes and nets. The stands had stainless steel racks on top. Most of the racks were empty.

"So the people moved on," said Crane, going to the edge of the pool. "The seekers decided it was something else they were looking for."

"I imagine," said Captain Jute.

He ignored her.

He was looking across the pool at a small tent of milky plastic. Its occupant was just visible through the fabric, a horizontal smudge.

Crane went down on one knee.

"The people who stayed," he said. "The Well Wishers. Who knows what they're looking for."

He dipped his hand in the water.

It was not really water, obviously. It was dark as ale. It dripped greasily from his fingers.

The next steel rack along had something on it: something round. It was, once again, about the size of a human head.

Her hands clenched tight, Captain Jute went up and had a look.

The thing was a sort of fat bird with no legs, lying on its side. Its plumage was dowdy, its eye an unfinished socket. Inside it was dirty yellow, the consistency of dried-up sponge. It seemed to be disintegrating.

"We can go now," Captain Jute said. Her voice was high, tight in her throat.

Crane stood up with his back to the Well. He wiped his hands together. His face seemed illuminated with a sudden elation, or malice.

"What's the matter, Captain? It's only a dream . . ."

Across the water came a shout of complaint, muddled by the echoes into incomprehensibility. Tabitha could see a man's head sticking out of the tent. She wondered what they had woken him from.

The superintendent was sitting with his chair tipped back, his feet up on his desk. His eyes were closed.

Smiling, Crane rapped on the desk with his knuckles.

"You should be sleeping in there," he said, "not out here!"

The old man gave them a gap-toothed grin. "Not me, Mr. Crane," he croaked cheerfully. "I ain't got the talent."

There was still no word from the agency. Tabitha lay on her enormous bed. "You should have seen those things, Alice," she said.

"PERHAPS I SOON SHALL," answered the small voice from the wall, where the wristcom was in a power socket, recharging.

"Not if Crane and them are right." She rolled over and back. "Shit, this is such a waste of time."

The AV was playing a rerun of a primitive sitcom, about two Martian salt dealers and their unruly camel. Half-finished snack dishes lay on the bed, clothes and empty beer tubes around it. She had spent the rest of the day failing to get hold of anyone that might have a truck for hire.

"We're not earning anything, lying here. We ought to check in and see if we can't get a bit of local work."

"THAT WOULD PUT YOU IN TECHNICAL VIOLATION OF YOUR CAREWAYS CONTRACT, CAPTAIN. SECTION 24, PARAGRAPH 4.14: BEFORE THE TERMINATION OF THIS AGREEMENT THE OPERATOR MAY NOT ENTER INTO A SECOND OR SUBSIDIARY—"

"Don't read me that crap, Alice. They don't know what it's like out here."

"PERHAPS YOU SHOULD THINK OF THIS AS A HOLIDAY, CAPTAIN," suggested the ever-considerate ship. "HUMAN BEINGS PERFORM BETTER WITH PERIODS OF REST AND RECREATION."

"Don't let Crane hear you," said Captain Jute. She rolled herself up in the coverlet, yawning. "He has some ideas about recreation. If something doesn't happen soon, I'm going to give in, I know I—"

The phone warbled.

She threw out an arm and hit the button. "Yes?"

"Morton Godfrey's here to see you, sugar."

"Christ. At last. I'll come down."

"Uh-uh. He's on his way up." The barwoman started to cough. *"Couldn't stop him."*

"Christ. Christ."

The Captain catapulted herself off the bed and started trying to kick some of the debris out of sight under it. Misjudging the gravity, she merely succeeded in scattering it around further. There was something bright pink spilt down the front of her shirt. She scrubbed at it furiously with a complimentary tissue, without result, then grabbed her jacket with one hand and the remote with the other, attempting to put the jacket on and the AV off at the same time.

She got one arm in the jacket, and managed to kill the soundtrack. Then the door chimed.

"I'm coming!" she yelled, searching madly with her hand behind her for her second sleeve.

"CAPTAIN," said the persona, from the dangling com set, "PERHAPS—"

"Vox off," ordered the Captain, pointing the remote at the door.

Like a visitor from some more elegant age, there stood Morton Godfrey. His boots were spotless knee-length Repellex. The sourceless light of the hotel corridor turned his uniform into a suit of tailored steel.

He took off his cap and put it under his arm.

"Captain Jute."

She loped towards him, still pulling on her jacket. "You didn't have to come up," she said.

"Sorry for the intrusion," he said, walking in.

He towered over her. Without cap and mask, he looked as perfect as a royal accessory must surely have to be. A clinical fragrance radiated from him.

"The Princess is ready."

"Now? It's the middle of the night."

The chauffeur stood with his hands on hips, looking at the silently quarrelling figures on the oversized AV. "It's always the middle of the night here," he said.

"I was in bed," she said.

He looked her between the eyes. "So I imagine," he said. He circled each of his wrists briefly with the thumb and forefinger of the opposite hand. She felt her face go suddenly warm.

"I've been trying to get transport all day," she said.

"We've got transport," said Morton Godfrey, looking up at the AV again. There was something deliberate about the way he took his eyes off her. He nodded, stoically, at the screen. "Second series," he said. "They were never as good after Caligula Probert left."

Even the chauffeur was an art critic.

He glanced intently at Tabitha again, then cast an eye over the disarray of the bed, the jumble of socks and discarded meals.

"I'll come back," he said. "I'll come back at six. Can you be ready by then?"

"I've been ready," she said with asperity, "for some time."

"Well, you're not ready now," he reminded her, solemnly.

"Okay," she said. "Let's go."

"No," he said. "Get your sleep. I'll come and get you." He half winked, and held up a forefinger in confirmation. "At six." She shut the door on him. She went back and lay down on the bed, hard.

It was herself she was angry with, she realised after a moment. She had been supremely unprofessional. He could complain to the agency, get her replaced.

She rolled over.

"Vox on," she said.

The light on the wristcom blinked.

"WAS THAT MORTON GODFREY, CAPTAIN?"

"Yes. Why?"

"STRESS PATTERNS IN HIS VOICE ARE SIMILAR TO THOSE IN THE VOICE OF OLISTER CRANE," the persona reported.

Tabitha succeeded at last in turning the AV off. "Are they?" she said.

"SUGGESTING HE DESIRES YOU TOO," said the persona.

The Captain felt her face heat up again. The things this one came out with.

"I don't think so, Alice," she said. "You can delete that, please."

"YES, CAPTAIN," whispered the little voice from the wall.

"The people love her," said Morton Godfrey. "They do. Only the networks are all against her."

This place was full of men who wanted to tell her stories.

They sat at the bar, drinking coffee. The barwoman was in and out, working. No one else was around. Captain Jute once again had the sense they might be watching her, keeping out, leaving the pair of them alone.

Godfrey sat swivelled around sideways on his stool to face her. He held his coffee cup in both hands, and ran his thumbs around the bowl of it, caressing it. Captain Jute imagined those big hands caressing the neurotic designer cheekbones, the vestigial breasts.

"They don't understand her," he said. "She threatens them." He looked at her to see if she understood. When she didn't react he nodded, as if the point needed approval by somebody before he could go on.

"They're jealous of her talent."

Delay had enveloped them again. Either that or Bad was being deliberately uncooperative, which seemed entirely possible. Captain Jute had been up and dressed at six. At half seven Godfrey had phoned to say the "schedule had been changed" and he would be there at eight. It had been nearer nine when he showed up in a little metallic blue Guignuki slider, a two-seater. Now it was nearly eleven, and they were still in the bar. She did not object to his company. She was quite convinced Alice didn't know what she was talking about. Morton Godfrey was a satellite, single-minded as Umbriel or Luna. One thing only lit up his life: the reflected glamour of his primary.

"Are we going to take a look at this stuff, then?" she asked him.

"Yeah," he said. "In a minute." He put his cup down beside his cap, which lay upside down on the bar like an empty dish. He seemed to suppress a sigh. Perhaps his mistress and he had had a row.

The barwoman was unloading the glasswasher. Godfrey signalled to her.

"Doreen," he said. "Put 'Do You' on."

Doreen was feeling uncooperative too, apparently. She apologised with her eyebrows, her hands full of glassware.

Godfrey got to his feet. He walked past Tabitha to the jukebox panel and pressed the numbers.

On the holopad at the end of the bar appeared a sleek figure dressed in a black shirt and oversized powder blue man's suit.

"You've seen this," Godfrey said.

"Maybe," said Tabitha, wearily. "I don't know."

The dancing doll on the holopad swivelled her hips. The ornaments on the wall of the bar showing through her as though she were made of cellophane.

"Thirty-four takes," said Godfrey. "You wouldn't believe it." He drank his coffee.

"She was as fresh after the thirty-fourth as she was at the first. She always gave it everything she'd got."

His loyalty was touching.

Close-ups showed Princess Bad looking haughty and hermaphroditic. Her eyes had been narrower then, or they had been made to look it. She was dancing a delicate, mincing dance, while her voice on the soundtrack sang something about snow. She looked exactly like a Japanese transvestite.

"Look at that depth! Look at the resolution! They can't get work like this any-where now."

It was impossible to tell whether he was speaking about Princess Badroulboudour or the camerawork. Tabitha wondered whether the Princess would have had some-thing to say about that. Perhaps she wouldn't have minded. Perhaps it might be just the sort of thing she dreamed of in her philosophy.

The music rattled to a stop. The image melted into nothing.

"This show is really important to her," confided Godfrey, into the icebound si-lence.

Doreen wiped her hands. "Captain Jute says the Princess is working again," she said. Perhaps she had noticed the Captain's growing impatience and decided to help her out.

"Yeah. Well." The chauffeur seemed troubled by Doreen's intervention, reluctant to expand his audience to include her. He looked towards the empty holopad, as though hoping the little ghost would reappear and guide him.

"She never really stopped," he said.

"She's been doing some dreams," Doreen prompted.

"Yeah." The chauffeur rotated his coffee cup through 120° in its saucer. "This place has been really good for her," he said. "The new stuff is her best yet."

"We'd surely like to see it," said Doreen with edged good humour. She took up her crate of glasses and disappeared out the back.

Morton Godfrey's eyes flicked after her. He muttered something; and when Tabitha did not reply said softly but distinctly: "The Princess never shows work till it's finished. They know that."

He picked up his coffee and drank it off. He put the cup down precisely in its saucer. Clearly he resented the implied insult to his mistress's artistic integrity.

Captain Jute glanced at the moondreams in the bar: the spiked head, the model Thrant still flexing its muscles.

"I've been told," she said carefully, "that these things won't survive being taken away from their owners."

Godfrey looked directly at her then, for the first time since putting the disc on. In his guarded glower she was surprised by a strange vulnerability; a plea for her com-plicity. He was asking her to be good, like him, and not expose the bankruptcy of his mistress's expectations.

"We got to go," he said. "She'll be waiting." But he didn't move. He sat there looking at her unhappily.

Tabitha decided to try taking control, to see if that was what he needed. "Give her a call," she said. "Tell her we're on our way."

His eyes still on Captain Jute, Morton Godfrey pulled his phone halfway out of his pocket. Then he pushed it back in.

His hand came up and went over Tabitha's shoulder and round behind her head. She felt his broad palm cradle the back of her skull.

"I'll call her from the car," he said thickly. Then he opened his mouth and pressed it determinedly to hers.

Captain Jute had time to be shocked, and aroused, and amused, all at once. She put her hands between them, pushing at the wide wall of the chauffeur's chest, feeling the twin rows of silver buttons bite into the flesh of her palms. Eyes screwed tight shut, she twisted her head away from his, coming up for air over his shoulder. Her heart hammering, she opened her eyes then and saw at the top of the steps, where Olister Crane's dream flower leaned from its blue vase, the Princess Badroulboudour, standing watching the pair of them.

That was when she jerked backwards in fright and fell off her stool.

. . .

Captain Jute shut the forward starboard airlock and threw her helmet clumsily into the co-pilot's web.

"Prepare for departure, Alice."

"THE HOLD IS STILL EMPTY, CAPTAIN," the little ship pointed out. "THE CARGO CONSIGNMENT HASN'T YET BEEN LOADED."

"I know the fucking consignment hasn't yet been loaded!"

She was furious: with herself; with Careways; with Morton Godfrey; with Princess bloody Badroulboudour. She had come all the way out here for nothing, and wasted a week being leched over, drinking too much and watching crap AV. Now she wouldn't get paid, and no doubt Bad still had the clout to get her blacklisted with every shipping agency in the outer system.

In the low g of Umbriel her fall had been humiliating rather than painful. It had taken her a undignified minute to get her breath back into her lungs and her feet under her. By that time they had both gone.

Doreen, crouching to help her, told her she had come back just in time to see the Princess leaving, going up the steps without a word. "Godfrey stands there staring like a man that's seen the sign," said Doreen.

Tabitha rubbed her hip. "What sign?" she asked.

"The sign," said Doreen. She ran her middle finger and thumb along an invisible line in the air. "'JERUSALEM,'" she quoted. "'CLOSED FOR REDEVELOPMENT.' Then he snatches up his cap, pulls it on his head and leaps off after her. Good Lord, give me a man that'll follow me that way. You okay, hon? You want some more coffee?"

"Fucking idiot," Tabitha had said, and more in the same vein.

Doreen turned her head, lowered her chin and looked up at her from the corners of her eyes, prepared for something bad. "Did he hurt you?"

"He fucking kissed me," she said.

Doreen whipped out a cloth and started wiping the bar vigorously. "Well, at least it wasn't a total loss."

"You think it's funny?" said Tabitha hotly.

Doreen threw up her hands in surrender. "Hey, hey, sweetheart, that man's all over everyone. No offence," she purred, "but what do you expect?" She shook her curls. "If she don't know it by now, she had it coming."

"How did she look?"

"Mad as hell."

Suddenly the barkeeper had cracked up laughing, and just as suddenly the captain had joined her.

She sat at the bar and drank a refill. "Oh, Christ," she grumbled, "why can't I just get a single straightforward job for a change?"

"Hey, lover, you find something straightforward in this system, you let us all know about it," said Doreen. "Here, how about a shot of whisky in that? The real thing, Doreen's personal reserve . . ."

While the barwoman rummaged under the bar, Tabitha had reflected that when the local witticisms start to repeat, you might as well be going.

Now she sat in the cockpit of her Kobold preparing for takeoff and wondering how long it would be before she dared go back to the Careways Agency.

"At this rate I'll be calling Sanczau for another favour," she said. She hated the idea. It seemed like admitting she couldn't handle the ship their Grand Old Man had given her.

"YOU DID PROMISE BALTHAZAR PLUM YOU WOULD STAY IN TOUCH," the ship reminded her diplomatically.

"Don't talk to me now about Balthazar Plum," said Captain Jute. "He's no different from Morton Godfrey."

"I'M NOT SURE I UNDERSTAND THAT LAST REMARK, CAPTAIN," said Alice, who had not been told anything.

"Just be glad you're made of steel, Alice."

"IN FACT, STEEL PLAYS A VERY SMALL PART IN MY COMPOSITION," replied the persona. "MY PRIMARY CONSTITUENT IS A BINOMIAL POLY-SACCHARIDE OF SILICON."

"Don't try to be clever," said the Captain, ungraciously. "Status reports, please."

"EXTRAORBITAL FLIGHT APPLICATION FILED AND ACKNOWL-EDGED," said the persona. "PLASMA BALANCE 46% RISING. IMPULSE OS-CILLATIONS 120-22. PRIMARY ORIENTATION AXIS LOCK ENGAGED. VEHICLE APPROACHING."

"What?"

The external monitors flashed up a grey Rolls halftrack racing towards her across the ice.

The Captain swore again. "Come to tell me he can't let me go, has he?"

But in a moment she could see the Rolls now had a robot in the driving seat: a chunky custom-plated Facto 4000.

"Power down, Alice," said Tabitha, jockeying with the magnification, trying to see into the back seat of the car. "Christ, it's not her, is it? What does she want? If she thinks I was encouraging him, I shall laugh, I know I shall."

But the robot was alone.

Parking the Rolls neatly alongside the Kobold, it unsealed the door and let itself gently down onto the ice. It rolled the four metres to the forward port entry ladder, then reconfigured its mobilators to climb up into the airlock.

Admitted to the ship, the robot cocked its flat head up at the Captain, who stood there in the inner doorway, leaning on her arms.

"*Careways Agency operative, I have a message for you from Princess Badroulboudour,*" said the robot. "*She is ready for you to begin loading.*"

"I've already had that message, thank you," said Tabitha, reaching for the CLOSE control.

"*This message supersedes that delivered at 08.80.14 by Morton Godfrey,*" said the robot. "*This message originates at 15.06.36.*"

"You're kidding," said the Captain. "And does it come with an apology for unauthorized personal interference by a member of her royal staff?"

The robot hummed congestedly for a moment. "*That question contains more than 10% of undefined and unfamiliar terms,*" it told her. "*I am not enabled to answer that question. I am enabled only to convey you to the house and assist in the execution of your instructions, as issued by Careways Agency and detailed in Careways Agency contract 95TAF9U4.002.*"

Captain Jute whistled and shook her head as she reached for her helmet. "Can I drive?" she asked.

"*The vehicle is currently enabled to accept only my commands,*" it said, seriously.

"It is, eh?" said Captain Jute, as she tabbed Alice down to Maintain. "What happened to Mr Godfrey?"

"*I am not enabled to answer that question,*" said the Facto 4000.

.   .   .

At Princess Badroulboudour's palace all the lights were still on. The only person inside was Princess Badroulboudour; but she was all over the place. The interior décor consisted of the chromatic variations of her own identity.

A lifesize holo of a younger Princess Badroulboudour in a white dress dominated the foyer. She had been made up to look like the old movie star, Marilyn Monroe, though with black hair. She was turning away from the door and looking round at you over her shoulder; and when the wind from the grating blew her skirt up, you could see she wasn't wearing any knickers.

"There are two kinds of people who come to this house," said the owner herself, arriving on the far side of the foyer in a gold-caged lift. She indicated the replica that was wiggling and beaming and pushing its dress down with such artful ineffectuality. "The ones who immediately they see that, have to come round the front and look; and the ones who wouldn't dream of doing anything so vulgar." She sounded tired, but very much at ease. "Which kind are you?"

"I'm pretty vulgar," said Tabitha, not moving from where she stood. She had to say it loudly, to be heard over the music.

The foyer was a rounded space tiled in large rectangular sheets of something grey and opalescent. Small Princess B-style images flickered here and there like sudden puffs of orange and viridian fire, never exactly where you were looking, while the life-size holo gleamed and fluttered. Every tile, Tabitha supposed, was a possible screen. The music was not like the things they had played her in the hotel bar, but like slowed-down explosions, full of fuzz and overload. The whole effect made her feel rather sick. Presumably that was the intention.

The entertainer came across the foyer, magnificent in sleeveless lilac shimmersilk balloon pants and fishnet cape. She wore heels and lots of bulky Arabic jewellery. She seemed pretty hyper, but pleased with herself, all trace of anger and aloofness vanished.

"Vulgarity is all we've got left!" she said, or shouted. She seemed to have decided Captain Jute was her trusted colleague, her ally against the worlds. That was as confusing as anything else.

"I'm so so sorry to make you wait such an awful time," the entertainer said, leading Tabitha into the lift. "It must have been bloody dreary for you." She shut the gate with a jingling clash.

Captain Jute was trapped in a cage with Princess Badroulboudour. The planet-devouring eyes were fastened upon her.

The Captain made the position clear. "I'll be gone as soon as you can hand over the consignment," she said.

The woman looked through the bars of the cage, interested only in what she herself had to say. "I've been trying and trying and trying to make the selection," she said, as the lift rose one floor. "I just couldn't decide. And you know why I couldn't. Because all along the only thing to do was send *everything*."

They walked out of the lift into a curving corridor with glossy pink walls that met overhead. The music was just as loud up here, and the air was perfumed with a rich, dizzying musk. The whole place seemed to be a parody of the female body, as if its architecture had been extrapolated from the inner curves of its owner.

"Everything," said Princess Badroulboudour. "It's the logic of it. Exhibition."

In a dimpled niche, a miniature holo of the Princess smiled, turning sulky as they passed.

"Exhibition. That's the key, you see, the theme."

The exhibitor smiled keenly at Tabitha. She seemed to have completely forgotten the incident in the bar. Perhaps Doreen had been right, and it hadn't been that much of a shock.

The Princess ushered the Captain into a room.

The room was large, and white, with huge paintings on the walls: enormous dull things, triangles of tan and grey on dirty white. In the far corner of the room was a compact automatic cuisine. There was a glass counter where a spherical white lamp hovered. The lamp was on, like all the lights in Princess Badroulboudour's palace. On the counter were the messy preparations for a meal: crushed rectangular packets of white insulite film; an open jar of honey with a spoon in. On the floor, as if it had rolled off the counter, lay what looked like a big black watermelon with a piece torn out of it.

Princess Bad strode up to the thing as if she was going to pick it up, or give it a kick, or something. Captain Jute kept her distance. It was impossible to say what the woman might do next.

The Princess stopped beside the fallen thing and swivelled purposefully to face Tabitha with a grand, demonstrative gesture.

Tabitha went over and looked at it.

Inside the broken black shell was wet, glossy brown pulp. From the midst of it, as if modelled out of it somehow, protruded the Princess's own face. Her chin was raised, her eyes closed, her mouth open in some kind of private joke or ecstasy. There was one hand, too, the fingers sticking out. They moved, thrusting, as if the dream woman were trying to surface, to push her way out of the smothering pulp.

"Now," the Princess was saying. "Imagine." She was taking something from the counter. "You come in, just the way you've come in now, and here—"

She was putting whatever she had picked up into Tabitha's hands.

The Captain caught hold of it automatically. She looked up at the artist, bewildered; and down at what she was holding.

It was a long wire, for cutting cheese. It had a smooth wooden handle at each end, painted a cheerful buttery yellow. Princess Badroulboudour had put one handle in each of her hands.

Tabitha looked at the cheese wire. She looked at the wet black thing with the face in. What was the woman thinking of? Whatever it was, it was appalling.

Captain Jute dropped the wire hurriedly back on the counter. "I don't think so," she said. "Well, no," said the Princess in her hard, flat voice. "But you get the general idea. The settings, the appliances, it's all documented, in the background stuff they're getting. But they have to see something like that, you see, at the same time they're seeing something like this—"

While she was speaking, the artist vaulted lightly across the room, shoved open a pair of high white doors and disappeared through them.

Dazed, and more sickened than ever, Captain Jute went after her.

She found her in a room of green jungle plants. There was the noise of booming water in the music now, and birds squawking lazily.

Tabitha was almost afraid to look at what the woman wanted her to see here. But this one was a harmless, miniature, pretty version of herself, covered from head to toe in brilliant feathers. She looked comical and jolly, more like a clown than a parrot.

"These are all your dreams?" said Captain Jute. The word felt daft as she said it, inadequate.

"Don't tell me about your insurance again," said the Princess loftily, leaping ahead on some connection only she had made. "You can't insure them, I know. You can't *preserve* them. That's exactly what's interesting."

She took another head from among the greenery. It was yellowish white, like bone. Its eyes were closed, its mouth open. For its two rows of teeth, it had two metal sawblades.

"It's all about exclusivity!"

The artist's hysterical eyes shone. She turned the head in her hand. From the neck dangled a short fibrous root, like the root of an extracted tooth. There was blood on it.

Princess Bad laughed, putting the back of her wrist to her mouth. She looked as if any moment she might overbalance backwards into the foliage. "Exhibition and exclusivity," she said thickly. "Look, look, bugger this, I want some wine."

Tabitha was afraid that would mean they were going back into the room with the watermelon thing on the floor; but instead the Princess led her on along a gallery of pine and yellow metal that ran inside the outer walls of the saucer palace, past long windows that looked out onto the ice below. There was still nothing moving out there, Tabitha saw. There never would be.

As they walked the artist went on with her theme as if she had never proposed dropping it. "Exhibition and exclusivity. The Princess B no one can see. Not even—" She broke off; then spoke again, in a deliberate tone. "Where do you go when you close your eyes? That's where it started. With what happens when you walk away from yourself."

Tabitha had had more than enough of this. She spoke up.

"I thought we were all supposed to reinvent ourselves thirty-two times a second, or whatever it is."

"That's what I mean," said the Princess, ushering her into another lift, this one a more conventional steel box. "Princess Badroulboudour is the prisoner of that line. People welded me to it. The very people it was intended to liberate. They don't want to be liberated from themselves," she said slowly and scornfully, as the lift took them down into the hillside, "not for a thirty-secondth of a second. They're in love with their stupid selves. And with Princess bloody Badroulboudour!"

She looked at the toothy head, which she was still carrying. As if to underline her comment, it opened its sightless eyes and smiled up at her lovingly.

"Who I encouraged them to produce," said the Princess. "I know, I know."

Captain Jute looked at her reflection in the sliding doors.

The lift deposited them in a darkened room, too dark to see anything. The air smelled stale. To the music that had followed them all through the palace was now added a buzzing, snoring sort of noise. The water motif was still there, but bubbling now, sedately, more like a big pot than a big river. "They made me into the woman who said that line," said the Princess, walking away in the darkness. "I am never allowed to reinvent myself, not allowed to embrace the prospect of singularity."

It was Princess Bad who was in love with herself if anyone was, thought Captain Jute. She couldn't even interrupt herself to turn the light on.

"Wine," she heard her hostess say, indistinctly; then: "Lights up."

As illumination dawned all around, soft and pale amber, the Captain saw they were now in the bedroom. Hence the snoring, she presumed. The saw-toothed head lay on the bed, which was large and circular, with a censer of perforated brass hanging over it.

Below the bed a flight of wide, shallow steps led down to a small sunken pool. It seemed to be some kind of Jacuzzi. It was from there the sound of bubbling was coming, from the dark water seething in the pool.

Everywhere in the room there were clothes: clothes hanging on tiered racks, clothes discarded on the floor, clothes folded neatly or bundled together or spilling out of shelves. Here and there, images of different sizes peered out of corners. One, a skull-headed figure with several arms, lay beside the Jacuzzi, gesticulating jerkily at the ceiling.

They were all her. In Princess Bad's case, her true self was her external appearance. Apparently.

"All these are going," their maker said. She was across the room, on the far side of the bed, pouring thick red wine into two large glasses. "I wasted ages trying to work out a selection," she explained again. "Now I think the point is to show them everything. Here."

"No, thanks," said Captain Jute.

The woman seemed not to hear her. She continued to hold out the glass of wine across the bed.

"Show them what a real artist can do here," said Princess Badroulboudour smugly. It wasn't a Jacuzzi, of course. It was one of the wells. Princess Bad had her own private Dream Well. She had built her palace around it.

The water was murky, opaque in the low light. As it boiled, the Captain could see the shape of another image already forming beneath the surface.

"Are you sure these things are safe?"

The Princess laughed loudly.

She took Captain Jute back up to ground level. She spoke about the special amenities of the building, about its "homeostatic systems." She sounded more like an estate agent than an interplanetary recording star. Whatever residual awe she had still held for Captain Jute vanished completely.

"Let's see how the loading's going," said Princess Badroulboudour.

The garage was spacious. The robot was there. It was pulling racks of green plastic crates out of a goods lift and towing them up into the back of a tall spike-wheeled truck. The crates were full of dreams. Tabitha saw them blink their eyes and gesture with their tiny hands, as if to say goodbye.

The blue Guignuki slider was parked over by the wall. There was no sign of Godfrey.

Over the radio, the field officer quizzed them as they came in range. It was still the same bloke on duty. Probably he didn't have an AV of his own at home.

Tabitha leaned forward to the radio. "She let me in," she told him.

When they reached the office, the robot stopped the truck. The officer did not appear.

"Do you want to take a look?" the Captain asked him. She got half out of her seat to see if she could see him in there.

He was in the warm. He was reluctant to suit up and go out into the vacuum. *"Just give me the figures,"* he said.

She started to read him all the values, the way the regulations said you had to: weight, cubic capacity, varietal coding. "Fifty-eight human heads," she said. "No insurable value." He didn't laugh. She could just make him out now through the layers of glass: a grey blur poking at a keyboard.

The robot drove the truck onto the field. It put it beside the *Alice Liddell* in exactly the same position it had put the Rolls.

Captain Jute gave Alice the signal to open the hold. A puff of debris blew out as the pressures equalized: particles of who knew how many different worlds, a negligible addition to the mass of this one. Among the dust she spotted a lost screwdriver, an empty krilkracker bag.

Inside the hold the cargo extensors were starting to unhook themselves. "Just the drones for this one, Alice," said Tabitha, sealing her suit.

"ACTIVATING," replied the ship, pleasantly.

There was a pause, and then four squat shapes like spaceport shoe polishers waddled out onto the ice.

Beside the Captain in the truck cab, Princess Bad's 4000 extended its head, running it out along a little boom. Its selection of eyepieces swivelled rapidly until it found the right one.

"*I am enabled to transfer the consignment,*" it said in Captain Jute's earphones, as she swung herself outside.

"You can help," she told it.

The robot clambered down, looking all the time at the drones. Its manner seemed distrustful. It approached the nearest one and flashed some lights at it.

The drone turned its upper casing around and flashed some back.

The 4000 craned its head up towards the Captain, who was opening the back of the truck. "*The capacities of this model are inferior to my own,*" it informed her.

"But there are four of them," she said, "and only one of you. You'd better watch your step." While the persona plotted a course for the Asteroid Belt, Captain Jute stood up on the catwalk that ran around the hold and supervised her metal team. Together they unloaded fifty-eight masks, models and portrait busts of Princess Badroulboudour from the back of the truck, and loaded them onto the *Alice Liddell*.

It took a while. The moondreams were apt to bob about like bubbles. One left its crate entirely. The Captain slid down the ladder and intercepted it before it floated into somewhere crucial and did some damage.

The fugitive dream was a half-length figure, thirty centimetres long. It was nude, its right arm modestly covering its breasts. Its skin was the texture and colour of graphite.

The Captain held the figure under its armpits in front of her, dangling it like a baby. The moondream did not move. Inert, it hung between her hands as if stunned by the bleak light of Uranus. Belatedly the Captain wondered if she should have done something to protect them from the vacuum.

"I told you I couldn't be liable," she reminded it.

She thought she saw the grey lips twitch.

The Princess's robot rolled up and looked at her in a manner she could only call accusing. Behind it the drones were beginning to unroll the cargo retaining nets. "Wait, wait," she told them. "Last one." She tucked the cold grey torso safely back in its crate.

The ship went up into the cold black gulf under the yellow circumference of Uranus, and the cold black gulf received her. "That's better," said Captain Jute, as the last of her weight drained away and left her floating peacefully at the controls, in her web. Space suited her, she always thought to herself at about this point: the depth and the breadth and the solitude of space. Other people always wanted something from you; usually something that you hadn't got. With a good ship, you could leave their complications and entanglements behind along with their gravity. While the charting computers made the last refinements to the vectors, she thought of Morton Godfrey, the need in his eyes, the desperation in his kiss. How entangled must he have become in the endlessly bifurcating personality of Princess Badroulboudour?

"I WONDER IF YOU SHOULD CHECK THE CARGO, CAPTAIN," said Alice then.

"Oh God," sighed Captain Jute, feeding the hold cameras to the console monitors. "What's happening?"

"I BELIEVE THERE MAY BE SOME SPOILAGE," said the ship persona calmly.

Tabitha released the latches of her web and swam back through the cockpit to the door of the hold.

They were ten thousand klicks from Umbriel. Already the moondreams were suffering corrosion. Released from the supporting armature of their creator's presence, their features were melting.

The Captain reached through the retaining net and pulled the large black spheroid to her. Inside it was dry and flaking like rotting sponge, like the legless bird she had seen at the Well. The face it bore was barely recognisable.

Before she could even start to wonder what to do, and whether she felt good or bad about it, the hold com chimed.

"Callig Brabo Golp Ganshaf zero-zero-nider-zero-fiver-nider. Thif if the polee'h. Please returd ibbediately, repeat: ibbediately, to Ubbriel field."

Yes, well: it had to be the cops, in fact. No one else could simply override her receive control. And the hoarse, nonhuman accent spoke for itself. Still the Captain automatically catapulted herself back into the cockpit to check the screen.

There it was, in horrible full colour: the shaven blue dog face of an Eladeldi traffic cop.

"Captid Zhoot," she commanded. *"Returd at wuds to Ubbriel."*

The inspector was an Eladeldi too, of course. She carried some kind of anti-allergen inhaler with which she made great play, shaking it up and squirting it moodily into each nostril as she stepped in through the airlock with two squad officers behind her. "Zhoot, Tabitha, Captib," she said formally. "I ab authorived to tsurch your bessel."

Tabitha wished she had an anti-allergen inhaler of her own. It was not Umbriel she was allergic to, or even Eladeldi. It was cops. The very sight of a cop made her nervous, irascible, badly behaved. She had already shut the persona down in reflex noncooperation.

"Why?" she said, not getting up and stepping away from the controls, but rather tightening her grip on the edge of the main console. "What's happened?"

But the cop only intoned again: "I ab authorived to tsurch your bessel. Blease unfashed your web ad step away frob the codtrols."

Through the viewport Captain Jute could see the patrol ship, a Caledonian Cumulus looming over the field like a miniature fortress. Its blackened engines stuck out like gun emplacements, threatening the dirty ice.

Paws in the pockets of her uniform duster, the inspector stood in the middle of the cockpit. With a sombre jerk of her muzzle, she directed one of her subordinates into the main body of the ship. He scurried past the door of the hold, which the Captain had closed and sealed for re-entry, and on down the passage that led to the squalid and rudimentary personal quarters, astern.

"Good luck finding anything back there," Captain Jute called after him. "I never can."

She scowled mutinously at the inspector, who was now scowling suspiciously at her.

The inspector took in the rubbish in the cockpit, the empty food containers and unwashed T-shirts. She produced her inhaler again and took a couple of juicy squirts. "Steb away frob the codtrols, Captid Zhoot, blease," she said thickly. "I'b askig you dicely."

"And I'm asking you nicely what the fuck's going on," said Tabitha. But she opened her web and stepped down, reluctantly, away from the console.

At once the second squad officer took her seat, slid an unlabelled disc into the drive and started to type.

"You be careful with her," Tabitha told the interloper. "You hit one wrong tab and you'll hear about it."

The inspector stared hard at the Captain for a moment. Then came the sound of boots on the decking, and the patrolman came back along the passage with a small plastic bag of dried vegetable matter. Sternly he held it up for his chief to examine.

"Oregano," said Captain Jute.

The inspector gave the bag a tired glance, took it and stuffed it in the pocket of her coat, then waved the man back to his search.

"God knows where he found that," said the Captain.

"Obed the hold," said the inspector to the woman at the console.

"It's a mess in there, I warn you," said Captain Jute. "The cargo's a bit the worse for wear. I did tell her it wasn't recommended. Told Bad, I mean. Princess Badroulboudour. You know Princess Badroulboudour."

The inspector made a low snuffling noise in the back of her throat.

The door of the hold came open.

The mess had got worse. Some of the images had burst apart like Venusian puffballs. A sticky yellow residue was speckled all over the walls and floor like ancient kitchen fat. For a moment Captain Jute thought they might decide to pull her licence for hygiene offences.

The inspector shuffled to the lines of green crates. Between the bars she poked the flaccid remains of the parrot-princess with the end of her stylus. There was a smell like the sweet smell of corruption.

"Where were you betweed the hours of eleved ad fifteed hudred yefterday, Captid Zhoot?"

"Here," said Tabitha. "I was right here. Well, eleven: I suppose I was on the way here. From the Well."

"Which Well would thad be?"

"The bar. At the hotel."

"Yesss . . ." exhaled the inspector. She produced a zip-lock evidence bag and lugubriously packaged up the sticky glob of dead dream residue from the end of her stylus.

"Who saw you there? At the hotel?"

"Well, Doreen, obviously. Morton Godfrey. I had breakfast with him."

The inspector stared at her. Her mouth was open, her blue tongue curled. It was hard to tell what it meant, if anything.

"Then Princess Bad arrived and they left. The two of them. Together."

"Togedder," said the inspector.

"Yes," said Tabitha. "Well. She went, and he followed. Ibbediately," she said.

The inspector paid no attention to her rudeness. She started fishing with her stylus again in the crates of ruined dreams. "Where did you go betweed the bar ad here?" she asked.

"Where?" echoed Tabitha. "Nowhere. I came straight here."

"What did you do thed?"

Tabitha's head felt hot. Everyone was guilty, to the Eladeldi mind. It was just a question of identifying the particular infraction.

"I started getting ready for takeoff."

The inspector left off fishing to pull out her notebook and call up a screen of information.

"Field records," she said at length, "show takeoff at twedty-two hudred twedty-fibe. Loadig cobplete at twedty-wud sebety-sebed. Loadig cobbedsed twedty-thirty."

The inspector looked at the Captain with eyes that were black and clear; thoroughly accustomed to the human discourse of evasion and deceit; endlessly, if minimally, hopeful for a glimpse of truth.

"I was going early," said Tabitha. "I thought Princess Bad was about to cancel. Then the robot arrived and said it was still on. That must have been about fifteen hundred. A bit after, maybe. Why don't you ask it? It's a 4000, you two should get on well. Look, what the hell is all this, anyway?"

The inspector had begun prodding the contents of another crate.

"You think I nicked this lot or something?"

The inspector sniffed hard and slow. She began putting something out of the sticky, dusty ochre mess.

It was a long piece of wire. The Eladeldi pulled it out from under the net, raising it with the end of her stylus, like a wary diner encountering spaghetti for the first time.

At each end of the wire there was a yellow cylindrical wooden handle. As the wire came out of the crate, the handles caught in the slots. The inspector took a piece of cloth and gently freed them.

"Whad is this, blease?"

Tabitha rubbed her forehead. "It's like a thing for cutting cheese, I think," she said. "I don't know. I didn't know it was in there. It's not mine."

"Bud you know id."

"Yes," said Tabitha, feeling peculiar. "It belongs to the Princess. She showed it to me. At the palace. The house, I mean."

She reached out to take the implement from the inspector. The inspector gave a sudden bark, shockingly loud in the confines of the hold, and snatched it away.

"It was with one of the exhibits," said the Captain. "At the house. The robot must have packed it by mistake. Or maybe it's meant to go with it, I don't know."

Distantly, carefully, the inspector was coiling the cheese wire inside another, larger evidence bag.

The patrolman who had been searching aft appeared, saluting. With a few words in their own soft, coughing tongue, the inspector gave Captain Jute into his charge. Then she went back into the cockpit.

"Are you going to arrest me for stealing a bit of wire?" yelled the Captain.

No one answered. The patrolman pushed her face against the freezing metal wall of the hold, made her spread her arms and legs.

While she struggled as hard as she could with a big blue paw pinning the back of her neck, he frisked her unceremoniously, finding nothing. Then he led her forward, into the starboard airlock.

As the inner door started to close, Captain Jute took a last look the two silky blue figures up in the cockpit. The inspector was comparing the automatic log with something in her notebook. Her subordinate looked unhappy, as if the results were not what the inspector wanted. Her ears were drooping.

"Don't tell them anything, Alice," called the Captain, as her suit pressurized and the pumps began evacuating the lock. "Let them find out for themselves."

She knew the sequestered persona could not hear her.

In the office, the field officer was still sitting with his hands laced across his stomach, watching the AV screen. There was another cop with him, a human. When the door opened the cop straightened and turned, and saluted the Captain's escort. Captain Jute returned the salute, just for fun. Everybody stared at her sourly.

"At ease, boys," she said.

The Captain's escort pushed her hard into a chair. He signalled to the human one, who came over, scanned her fingerprints and put handcuffs on her.

The Eladeldi left the ship. Tabitha sat tight. Fear and anger and disbelief swept over her in alternating waves. They obviously had no intention of telling her what she was meant to have done. The cop and the field official were both preoccupied with the screen.

"Can I watch?" she said.

In a little while the cop hitched up his trousers and came over to her. For a moment she thought he was going to hit her. Instead, he put a hand under her armpit, hauled her to her feet, and pulled her over to the screen.

When she saw what was on it, her next clever remark died on her lips.

It was a still picture of a man, a human. He was lying out in the open, on raw ice.

The view cycled to another shot of the same man. He was naked. His face was purple, his eyeballs bursting from his head. That black growth protruding from his mouth must formerly have been his tongue. The pictures had the flat, coarse, unreal quality that told the Captain she was not looking at the special effects from some murder movie.

In any case, she recognised the man.

"Morton Godfrey," she said.

The two men studied her.

"Friend of yours?" said the cop.

"No," she said. "He worked for Princess Bad."

The chauffeur's whole neck and jaw were twisted and swollen. He looked like a mad purple moondream.

"I had a drink with him, yesterday morning," the Captain heard herself say. "I think I'm going to be sick."

The field officer kicked a wastebasket at her, just in time.

In a little while she lifted her head.

"What happened to him?" she asked, in a squeaky whisper.

The two men looked at each other, as if wondering how much pleasure there was to be derived from not telling her. "Satellite picked him up at 02.90," said the cop. "Somebody strangled him and dumped the body."

"He was a big man," said Tabitha, wonderingly.

"That the way you like them?" asked the field officer.

"Fuck off," she said. "Why's everybody so interested in me, for God's sake?"

"You were the last person seen talking to him," said the cop.

"I didn't strangle him!" she said.

On the screen, the distorted face of the dead chauffeur zoomed into pitiless close-up. The field officer was playing with the controls.

"Somebody did," he said.

The screen was full of bulging red and purple flesh.

"All they have to do now is find the cord," said the field officer.

"Wire," the cop told him. "Go back one. There. Look at that. See the depth of that, compared to the width. See? That's like a cut."

Behind her the door whisked open again. The inspector came in, followed by her team. The patrolman sprang to attention.

Captain Jute looked at her. She was numb. There was a noise in her head like a hundred engines on slow burn. "Are you going to charge me?"

The inspector barely looked at her. Her ears were stiff, the fur on the back of her neck bristling with displeasure. "You will be held for questiodig," she said roughly.

She reached in the pocket of her long coat and took out the cheese wire in its bag.

When they all saw that, the air in the room grew solid with investigative fervour.

The inspector held the bag out to her human subordinate. "Figgerprids," she ordered.

Tabitha was dreaming.

She dreamed she was swimming in a green sea, within sight of vague islands of purple-grey rock. She could taste and smell the salt of the sea. She felt uncertain about swimming in it. The sea was lively. The swell might pull her under.

In the dream, there were fountains in the sea. She could see them shooting up into the air. She felt that if she could get to one of the fountains, she would be safe from sinking.

Beneath the fountains, dark blue shapes swam indistinctly in the green sea. They were whales. The fountains were their waterspouts. In the dream, it became important that she dive beneath one of the fountains, to rescue a smaller creature which was not entirely distinct from herself.

There was a moment when she found herself taking hold of a bulky young mauve-coloured animal by its flippers and trying to pull it towards her. It was a baby whale, she thought, though it seemed more like a seal.

Then she woke, disoriented, not knowing where she was.

She got off the bunk and stood upright. The sprayfoam floor of the cell rasped the soles of her bare feet. Uranus shone in through the high, narrow slot of the window. It was just past full, and very bright.

While she stood there, thinking about nothing, the door whined open. A cop came in, one of the human ones.

"Come on, get your things," he said. His voice was dull and unsympathetic.

"What's happening?" she said. "Where are you taking me?"

"Hawaii," said the cop. He took her by the arm and led her out through the passageways of the Cumulus, that smelled of dogs, disinfectant and despair.

A small desk stood at the top of the exit ramp. Olister Crane was there, writing something on a pad with an ink pen. For a moment she wondered if it was his threatened poem.

"What am I, on bail now?"

He wore his red blazer, the gold ring around his beard. He capped the pen and slid it neatly into his breast pocket. His nails were long, but clean and well shaped.

"They know you didn't do it, Captain," he said.

In his yellow rover they rode away from the Cumulus, across the silent sea. The shock of it all reverberated in the Captain's head. She felt exhausted, filthy.

She pulled at her hair. "I need a shower," she said.

"Need a drink too, am I right?"

In the purple corridors of Reveries, they walked past the model of the ugly boy that had incensed Princess Badroulboudour. It smirked and ogled them.

"Whose is that one?" asked Captain Jute.

"He's one of mine," Crane told her, complacently. "Handsome devil, ain't I?"

It was the local equivalent of four A.M. The bar was open. Tabitha wondered when it ever closed.

Georginelle was there, drinking alone. She was horrified to hear about Tabitha's treatment. "Of course, there's no chance you'll get an apology," she said, righteously.

Tabitha said little. Of the cheese wire, she said nothing at all.

She looked around the walls. The unpleasant ornaments looked tawdry and unrealistic, as if even the temporary absence of their creators was enough to shave a degree of substance from them.

Crane was sitting close to Captain Jute. She put her hand on his forearm.

"Take me to the house," she said.

He raised his eyebrows. "My house?" he said. She could see he knew perfectly well which house she meant, but for some reason required her to say it.

·   ·   ·

On the way, they saw three flat blue spearheads go over, heading east: fliers out of the patrol ship, going to pay Princess Bad a visit.

The Captain imagined her sitting in her windowless basement room, waiting for them on the big bed. She saw her surrounded once again by all the moondreams that had disintegrated in the hold of the *Alice*: the parrot and the melon, the sawtooth and the skull—all the little versions of herself the superseded star had produced in her years of solitary musing. Captain Jute imagined her gazing into the glutinous water, striving to invoke one final, consummate portrait, in which all the faces of all the roles she had played would combine around a single centre, like the facets of a jewel.

Even before they came in sight of the palace of silver saucers, the white blaze of its lights began to pale the stars.

"They're not going to let you in," said Crane softly.

"Everyone keeps telling me that." Captain Jute was sealing up her suit. "Drop me at the next bend," she said. "You drive up to the front door, create a diversion."

"Create a diversion," repeated Crane, chuckling lazily and shaking his head. "What do you think this is, a movie?"

Soundless on the airless moon, the rover wheeled away from her, off up the hillside. He would come up with something, Tabitha was sure. Perhaps he would give the cops an impromptu poetry recital.

She went up the rest of the way quickly on all fours, trying to merge with the profile of the terrain. She could almost feel the unspeakable cold of the surface, sucking at her through her suit. She saw no one.

The robot met her at the door to the garage.

Its voice buzzed in her phones. *"No one is available to deal with you at present."*

"It's me," she said. "Captain Jute. You remember me."

The arrival of the police had unsettled it. In the circuits of the domestic 4000 there were no contingencies for the Apocalypse.

"I've come to pick up the last of the artworks," she told it.

"Your statement requires confirmation," said the robot.

"Ask the Princess," she said. She knew they would have blocked the connection by now, isolating the system from its owner with one of their handy little discs.

"Princess Badroulboudour is occupied," said the 4000. *"Your request has been recorded and logged—"*

"I can't wait," she told it. "The Princess would be very very unhappy if it got left behind."

Red lights flashed on all its displays. *"Your statement must be referred to Princess Badroulboudour,"* it said. *"Please return later."*

Captain Jute attempted to convey every impression of urgency. She swung her arms around. She hugged herself and hopped from foot to foot. "I'm leaving in fifteen minutes," she said. "I don't want to make the Princess unhappy."

The red lights flashed amber. She supposed it was reattempting the refused communication. She hoped none of the cops had been detailed to watch the other side of their com block.

"Well, it's too bad," she said. "You'll have to tell the Princess I came but you turned me away. You'll have to tell her I'm sorry I can't do what she asked."

The amber lights all went out. One light only remained.

It was red.

For a significant fraction of a second, the robot struggled.

Then the light went green.

"I shall accompany you to the Princess," said the 4000, as it opened the door.

"No, no, wait here," said the Captain. "I shall need you to drive me back to the field. You must prepare the truck!"

The 4000 spun its head. It extended another pair of eyes. It considered the truck that towered over it on its crampon tyres. By the time it reversed its mobilators, Captain Jute was on her way to the lift.

In the corridor she passed a holo of an obese Princess Badroulboudour dancing in freefall. She did not slow down to examine it. She knew everything now its frenzied presentation could possibly convey.

In the Princess's bedroom all the lights were on. There were cops everywhere. With their trace detectors they were sweeping the wardrobes, the trinket shelves, the canopy above the bed.

They would not let her out of the lift. They blocked her exit, signalling to their superiors.

The patrolman who had searched the *Alice* was there. He stood on the far side of the bed, a tracer rig around his neck. Recognising her, he alerted the inspector.

The inspector did not even glance at the intruder. She was busy. Her shoulders were hunched, her ears up. She stood with her legs bent, her front paws on her knees, her long coat hanging open.

All the inspector's attention was on Princess Badroulboudour.

The Princess stood before him in a white cowl-shirt and black leggings. She wore the chauffeur's uniform jacket draped over her shoulders. It was a nice touch, Captain Jute thought.

The Princess was as thin as a cigarette. She had no make-up on. Her face looked porous and creased, her large eyes red with emotion. She looked as if she had been up all night exercising, rehearsing the part of a woman wronged.

The Princess's Dream Well was still in ferment. People in sterile suits of white paper were shining a spotlight into it. There was a woman in scuba gear perched on the edge, directing them.

"Bad," said Tabitha over the shoulders of the cops. "All your dreams died."

The Princess shrieked. The audio tracers recoiled, whipping off their headphones.

"*There she is!* Returning to the scene of the crime," said the Princess with melodramatic relish. "Hold her tight," she ordered them. "Don't let her make a run for it."

Tabitha relaxed, folding her arms. "I'm not going anywhere," she said.

There was a flabby splosh as the frogwoman went in.

The inspector shook herself irritably. This was hard enough without distractions. She gestured her people to bring Captain Jute into the room.

"Why have you cub here?" she asked. "Is there subthig you wad to dell me?"

She panted sourly.

"No," said Captain Jute with an insolent smile. "You're getting it right now."

Meanwhile Princess Badroulboudour was launching into her aria.

Captain Jute often thought afterwards that it might have been her greatest performance. There she stood, dressed like a refugee, grandstanding in an overheated, over-lit room for a captive audience of cops. There was nothing original about the song she sang, or the simple, senseless ideas that over the years had come to comprise her character; but her projection was thunderous and her conviction total. For a minute or so she filled the scented air with the rage of grief, while her case and the last frail shell of her sanity collapsed in shreds around her like decomposing moondreams.

"She's the one, inspector! The dirty-handed slut I saw with Morton in that second-rate hotel. I warned him about her, but he was always a soft touch. No defences. Look at her! Women like her think they can take what they want. Fly in, fuck it, fly out again. Not a thought for the lives they ruin as they come and go."

Her voice broke. Her narrow bosom quivered. The tendons on her neck stood out like twine and pulled her mouth into a downturned crescent of disdain.

"She killed him. She *killed* him. God knows what she wanted him to do that he was too loyal and honest and sweet to do . . ." Her voice softened into tenderness. "She wanted him, and she couldn't have him, because he was mine, so she killed him."

She shook. Her voice began to rise again, *con tremolo*. "Because she was jealous of me. They all are, all of them. All the women who aren't lucky or talented or courageous enough to be me."

Princess Badroulboudour took hold of her arresting officer by the shoulder.

"Take her away, inspector," she commanded. "Take her away and lock her in that big black ship of yours, and carry her off into dark, cold space. And when you get to the darkest, coldest, emptiest part of space, open the door and throw her out. And let her think as the emptiness sucks her lungs out through her mouth about the man she killed and the woman whose life she destroyed."

She threw her arms out and her shoulders back, turning her head left and right, appealing to the investigators as if to a chorus line that would now link arms and echo her sentiments in deafening harmony.

But the investigators were taking no notice. They were going about their business like souvenir hunters, picking over the bedroom of this decayed celebrity.

Below the flight of steps that ran down from the bed the greasy waters of the pool were quiet now, delivered of their final burden. The Princess's last dream lay dripping on a white plastic sheet, where the frogwoman had dumped it. Captain Jute could see it, between the backs of the forensic team. It looked only half-made. Even so, it was completely recognisable.

Unlike most of the other moondreams she had seen, it had two heads. It had a large head and a smaller one. What connected the two heads could be thought of as a single snaky neck, so that the dream resembled one two-headed creature looking at itself. The larger head was bent over the smaller one, like a madonna over an infant.

The face on the upper head fluttered and writhed like an ill-tuned holo. Its eyes kept spreading wide and puckering up like unruly mouths. Perhaps, Tabitha thought, the image was enraged by its premature extraction from the mineral womb.

The lower, smaller head was turned up. It was blocky, unmoving, and bare of detail. Its brow stuck out like the peak of a cap, shading what there was of its face. All Captain Jute could see was a single gash, a curved line like a smile, the blissful smile of a fan in the front row at a concert.

Around the neck that joined the two heads a shiny, sticky string was twisted. Each end of the string was held tightly in one of the hands—spidery, inhuman little hands, with far too many fingers—that protruded from just beneath the chin of the effervescent upper head.

Over and over again, while the Captain and the cops watched, the little hands pulled the wet string tight.

PETER F. HAMILTON

Peter F. Hamilton [1960–] (www.peterfhamilton.co.uk) lives near the Rutland Water, in England. Hamilton sold his first story, "Death Day," to *Fear* magazine in 1989. He began publishing SF in the early 1990s with three SF detective novels, *Mindstar Rising* (1993), *A Quantum Murder* (1994), and *The Nano Flower* (1995). But his prominence began with a massive trilogy of thousand-page novels (in its original British form), *The Reality Dysfunction* (1996), *The Neutronium Alchemist* (1997), and a third book, *The Naked God* (2000), together the Night's Dawn Trilogy. (In the US, all three books were divided into two volumes each, so it became a six-book series.) A collection, *A Second Chance at Eden* (1998), is set in the same Confederation future as the trilogy. The whole setting is so complex that Hamilton published a nonfiction guide, *The Confederation Handbook: The Essential Guide to the Night's Dawn Series*, in 2000. Two of his three later novels to date are also space opera, *Fallen Dragon* (2001) and *Pandora's Star* (2004). After Iain M. Banks, Hamilton is the most popular British space opera writer of the last decade.

Hamilton's universe is not a hard SF construct: Dead souls come back to threaten the living, and take possession of living people. Hamilton comments in a late-1990s *Locus* interview, "Although this has a lot of military hardware and people running around shooting each other, certainly in the first volume and to some degree in the second, the military solution cannot apply. This is not militaristic SF. You have to think of a solution. . . . You can't go and shoot one of the Possessed, because you're also shooting the person whose body it is, which adds to the number of souls that want to come back."

Given the rhetoric of many of the critics of New Space Opera, it is amusing to note: "I try to make the background of my own worlds—the society, the economy, the politics—as real as I can. The plot in *Mindstar Rising* fairly much dictated what the politics would be: the right wing nationalized, the left wing denationalized. This forms a big part of the denouement at the end. I had the socialists as the bad guys, purely because of plot, but I got a lot of flak from reviewers in Britain, because they tend to be left-of-center. Three years later, I was writing about the decline of the right—I didn't get so much flak for that." Compare this to Ken MacLeod's later *Locus* essay on New Space Opera, in which he says, "British New Space Opera could be described as British SF written by people who like American SF, for people who like American SF. Or, more provocatively, left-wing SF by and for people who like right-wing SF. (This is on a spectrum where Peter F. Hamilton would have to be located towards the red end, fractionally to the right of Iain M. Banks.)" It seems to us as if Hamilton is essentially nearly apolitical, like Stephen Baxter.

But his connection to American SF is clear. Hamilton comments on E. E. Smith in the same interview: " 'Doc' Smith was a big influence. A series of reprints came out in England in the early '70s, which was when I read them. I was just mesmerized. You can project 600 years into the future, you can do a lot of things you can't do 40 years into the future, where you're trying to make things reasonably accurate. So it gives you a much broader canvas to paint on." And he adds, "I would hate to read the 'Doc' Smith books again, I've got such beautiful memories! They're exactly what a 13-year-old wanted. That is the best age to read them. . . ."

When Gardner R. Dozois used this story in his *Year's Best Science Fiction* anthology in 1998, he classified it as Modern Baroque Space Opera. And he listed other writers of the form: "*The Reality Dysfunction* has been attracting the reviews and acclaim that his prior novels did not and has suddenly put Hamilton on the map as a writer to watch, perhaps a potential rival for writers such as Dan Simmons, Iain M. Banks, Paul J. McAuley, Greg Benford, C. J. Cherryh, Stephen R. Donaldson, Colin Greenland, and other major players in the expanding subgenre of Modern Baroque Space Opera, an increasingly popular area these days." Dozois, one of the first to identify a new strain in space opera in the 1990s, happily blended the British and American writers contributing to what he saw as an international movement. We generally agree with his perception in that regard.

"Escape Route" is an engaging novella set in Hamilton's Confederation future. There's lots of action, space technology, and a big object to explore. Captain Marcus and his crew are hired to go prospecting for an asteroid of gold. They discover an alien ship thirteen thousand years old, filled with advanced technology.

ESCAPE ROUTE

PETER F. HAMILTON

Marcus Calvert had never seen an asteroid cavern quite like Sonora's before; it was disorientating even for someone who had spent 30 years captaining a starship. The centre of the gigantic rock had been hollowed out by mining machines, producing a cylindrical cavity twelve kilometers long, five in diameter. Usually, the floor would be covered in soil and planted with fruit trees and grass. In Sonora's case, the environmental engineers had simply flooded it. The result was a small freshwater sea that no matter where you were on it, you appeared to be at the bottom of a valley of water.

Floating around the grey surface were innumerable rafts, occupied by hotels, bars, and restaurants. Taxi boats whizzed between them and the wharfs at the base of the two flat cavern walls.

Marcus and two of his crew had taken a boat out to the Lomaz bar, a raft which resembled a Chinese dragon trying to mate with a Mississippi paddle steamer.

"Any idea what our charter is, Captain?" asked Katherine Maddox, the *Lady Macbeth*'s node specialist.

"The agent didn't say," Marcus admitted. "Apart from confirming it's private, not corporate."

"They don't want us for combat, do they?" Katherine asked. There was a hint of rebellion in her voice. She was in her late 40s, and like the Calverts her family had geneered their offspring to withstand both freefall and high acceleration. The dominant modifications had given her thicker skin, tougher bones, and harder internal membranes; she was never sick or giddy in freefall, nor did her face bloat up. Such changes were a formula for blunt features, and Katherine was no exception.

"If they do, we're not taking it," Marcus assured her.

Katherine exchanged an unsettled glance with Roman Zucker, the ship's fusion engineer, and slumped back in her chair.

The combat option was one Marcus had considered possible. *Lady Macbeth* was combat-capable, and Sonora asteroid belonged to a Lagrange-point cluster with a strong autonomy movement. An unfortunate combination. But having passed his 67th birthday two months ago he sincerely hoped those kinds of flights were behind him.

"This could be them," Roman said, glancing over the rail. One of Sonora's little taxi boats was approaching their big resort raft.

The trim cutter curving round towards the Lomaz had two people sitting on its red leather seats.

Marcus watched with interest as they left the taxi. He ordered his neural nanonics to open a fresh memory cell, and stored the pair of them in a visual file. The first to alight was a man in his mid-30s, dressed in expensive casual clothes; a long face and a very broad nose gave him a kind of imposing dignity.

His partner was less flamboyant. She was in her late 20s, obviously geneered;

Oriental features matched with white hair that had been drawn together in wide dreadlocks and folded back aerodynamically.

They walked straight over to Marcus's table, and introduced themselves as Antonio Ribeiro and Victoria Keef. Antonio clicked his fingers at the waitress, and told her to fetch a bottle of Norfolk Tears.

"Hopefully to celebrate the success of our business venture, my friends," he said. "And if not, it is a pleasant time of day to imbibe such a magical potion. No?"

Marcus found himself immediately distrustful. It wasn't just Antonio's phoney attitude; his intuition was scratching away at the back of his skull. Some friends called it his paranoia programme, but it was rarely wrong. A family trait, like the wanderlust which no geneering treatment had ever eradicated.

"The cargo agent said you had a charter for us," Marcus said. "He never mentioned any sort of business deal."

"If I may ask your indulgence for a moment, Captain Calvert. You arrived here without a cargo. You must be a very rich man to afford that."

"There were . . . circumstances requiring us to leave Ayachcho ahead of schedule."

"Yeah," Katherine muttered darkly. "Her husband."

Marcus was expecting it, and smiled serenely. He'd heard very little else from the crew for the whole flight.

Antonio received the tray and its precious pear-shaped bottle from the waitress, and waved away the change.

"If I may be indelicate, Captain, your financial resources are not optimal at this moment," Antonio suggested.

"They've been better."

Antonio sipped his Norfolk Tears, and grinned in appreciation. "For myself, I was born with the wrong amount of money. Enough to know I needed more."

"Mr Ribeiro, I've heard all the get-rich-quick schemes in existence. They all have one thing in common, they don't work. If they did, I wouldn't be sitting here with you."

"You are wise to be cautious, Captain. I was, too, when I first heard this proposal. However, if you would humour me a moment longer, I can assure you this requires no capital outlay on your part. At the worst you will have another mad scheme to laugh about with your fellow captains."

"No money at all?"

"None at all, simply the use of your ship. We would be equal partners sharing whatever reward we find."

"Jesus. All right, I can spare you five minutes. Your drink has bought you that much attention span."

"Thank you, Captain. My colleagues and I want to fly the Lady Macbeth on a prospecting mission."

"For planets?" Roman asked curiously.

"No. Sadly, the discovery of a terracompatible planet does not guarantee wealth. Settlement rights will not bring more than a couple of million fuseodollars, and even that is dependant on a favourable biospectrum assessment, which would take many years. We have something more immediate in mind. You have just come from the Dorados?"

"That's right," Marcus said. The system had been discovered six years earlier, comprising a red dwarf sun surrounded by a vast disc of rocky particles. Several of the larger chunks had turned out to be nearly pure metal. Dorados was an obvious name; whoever managed to develop them would gain a colossal economic resource. So much so that the governments of Omuta and Garissa had gone to war over who had that development right.

It was the Garissan survivors who had ultimately been awarded settlement by the Confederation Assembly. There weren't many of them. Omuta had deployed twelve antimatter planetbusters against their homeworld. "Is that what you're hoping to find, another flock of solid metal asteroids?"

"Not quite," Antonio said. "Companies have been searching similar disc systems ever since the Dorados were discovered, to no avail. Victoria, my dear, if you would care to explain."

She nodded curtly and put her glass down on the table. "I'm an astrophysicist by training," she said. "I used to work for Forrester-Courtney; it's a company based in the O'Neill Halo that manufactures starship sensors, although their speciality is survey probes. It's been a very healthy business recently. Consortiums have been flying survey missions through every catalogued disc system in the Confederation. As Antonio said, none of our clients found anything remotely like the Dorados. That didn't surprise me, I never expected any of Forrester-Courtney's probes to be of much use. All our sensors did was run broad spectrographic sweeps. If anyone was going to find another Dorados cluster it would be the Edenists. Their voidhawks have a big advantage; those ships generate an enormous distortion field which can literally see mass. A lump of metal 50 kilometres across would have a very distinct density signature; they'd be aware of it from at least half a million kilometres away. If we were going to compete against that, we'd need a sensor which gave us the same level of results, if not better."

"And you produced one?" Marcus enquired.

"Not quite. I proposed expanding our magnetic anomaly detector array. It's a very ancient technology; Earth's old nations pioneered it during the 20th century. Their military maritime aircraft were equipped with crude arrays to track enemy submarines. Forrester-Courtney builds its array into low-orbit resource-mapping satellites; they produce quite valuable survey data. Unfortunately, the company turned down my proposal. They said an expanded magnetic array wouldn't produce better results than a spectrographic sweep, not on the scale required. And a spectrographic scan would be quicker."

"Unfortunate for Forrester-Courtney," Antonio said wolfishly. "Not for us. Dear Victoria came to me with her suggestion, and a simple observation."

"A spectrographic sweep will only locate relatively large pieces of mass," she said. "Fly a starship 50 million kilometres above a disc, and it can spot a 50-kilometre lump of solid metal easily. But the smaller the lump, the higher the resolution you need or the closer you have to fly, a fairly obvious equation. My magnetic anomaly detector can pick out much smaller lumps of metal than a Dorado."

"So? If they're smaller, they're worth less," Katherine said. "The whole point of the Dorados is that they're huge. I've seen the operation those ex-Garissans are building up. They've got enough metal to supply their industrial stations with specialist microgee alloys for the next 2,000 years. Small is no good."

"Not necessarily," Marcus said carefully. Maybe it was his intuition again, or just plain logical extrapolation, but he could see the way Victoria Keef's thoughts were flowing. "It depends on what kind of small, doesn't it?"

Antonio applauded. "Excellent, Captain. I knew you were the right man for us."

"What makes you think they're there?" Marcus asked.

"The Dorados are the ultimate proof of concept," Victoria said. "There are two possible origins for disc material around stars. The first is accretion; matter left over from the star's formation. That's no use to us, it's mostly the light elements, carbonaceous chondritic particles with some silica aluminium thrown in if you're lucky. The second type of disc is made up out of collision debris. We believe that's what the Dorados are, fragments of planetoids that were large enough to form molten metal cores. When they broke apart the metal cooled and congealed into those hugely valuable chunks."

"But nickel iron wouldn't be the only metal," Marcus reasoned, pleased by the way he was following through. "There will be other chunks floating about in the disc."

"Exactly, Captain," Antonio said eagerly. "Theoretically, the whole periodic table will be available to us, we can fly above the disc and pick out whatever element we require. There will be no tedious and expensive refining process to extract it from ore. It's there waiting for us in its purest form; gold, silver, platinum, iridium. Whatever takes your fancy."

Lady Macbeth sat on a docking cradle in Sonora's spaceport, a simple dull-grey sphere 57 metres in diameter. All Adamist starships shared the same geometry, dictated by the operating parameters of the ZTT jump, which required perfect symmetry. At her heart were four separate life-support capsules, arranged in a pyramid formation; there was also a cylindrical hangar for her spaceplane, a smaller one for her Multiple Service Vehicle, and five main cargo holds. The rest of her bulk was a solid intestinal tangle of machinery and tanks. Her main drive system was three fusion rockets capable of accelerating her at eleven gees, clustered round an antimatter intermix tube which could multiply that figure by an unspecified amount; a sure sign of her combat-capable status. (By a legislative quirk it wasn't actually illegal to have an antimatter drive, though possession of antimatter itself was a capital crime throughout the Confederation.)

Spaceport umbilical hoses were jacked into sockets on her lower hull, supplying basic utility functions. Another expense Marcus wished he could avoid; it was inflicting further pain on his already ailing cash-flow situation. They were going to have to fly soon, and fate seemed to have decided what flight it would be. That hadn't stopped his intuition from maintaining its subliminal assault on Antonio Ribeiro's scheme. If he could just find a single practical or logical argument against it . . .

He waited patiently while the crew drifted into the main lounge in life-support capsule A. Wai Choi, the spaceplane pilot, came down through the ceiling hatch and used a stikpad to anchor her shoes to the decking. She gave Marcus a sly smile that bordered on teasing. There had been times in the last five years when she'd joined him in his cabin, nothing serious, but they'd certainly had their moments. Which, he supposed, made her more tolerant of him than the others.

At the opposite end of the spectrum was Karl Jordan, the Lady Mac's systems specialist with the shortest temper, the greatest enthusiasm, and certainly the most serious of the crew. His age was the reason, only 25; the Lady Mac was his second starship duty.

As for Schutz, who knew what emotions were at play in the cosmonik's mind; there was no visible outlet for them. Unlike Marcus, he hadn't been geneered for freefall; decades of working on ships and spaceport docks had seen his bones lose calcium, his muscles waste away, and his cardiovascular system atrophy. There were hundreds like him in every asteroid, slowly replacing their body parts with mechanical substitutes. Some even divested themselves of their human shape altogether. At 63, Schutz was still humanoid, though only 20 per cent of him was biological. His body supplements made him an excellent engineer.

"We've been offered a joint-prize flight," Marcus told them. He explained Victoria's theory about disc systems and the magnetic anomaly array. "Ribeiro will provide us with consumables and a full cryogenics load. All we have to do is take Lady Mac to a disc system and scoop up the gold."

"There has to be a catch," Wai said. "I don't believe in mountains of gold just drifting through space waiting for us to come along and find them."

"Believe it," Roman said. "You've seen the Dorados. Why can't other elements exist in the same way?"

"I don't know. I just don't think anything comes that easy."

"Always the pessimist."

"What do you think, Marcus?" she asked. "What does your intuition tell you?"

"About the mission, nothing. I'm more worried about Antonio Ribeiro."

"Definitely suspect," Katherine agreed.

"Being a total prat is socially unfortunate," Roman said. "But it's not a crime. Besides, Victoria Keef seemed levelheaded enough."

"An odd combination," Marcus mused. "A wannabe playboy and an astrophysicist. I wonder how they ever got together."

"They're both Sonora nationals," Katherine said. "I ran a check through the public data cores, they were born here. It's not that remarkable."

"Any criminal record?" Wai asked.

"None listed. Antonio has been in court three times in the last seven years; each case was over disputed taxes. He paid every time."

"So he doesn't like the tax man," Roman said. "That makes him one of the good guys."

"Run-ins with the tax office are standard for the rich," Wai said.

"Except he's not actually all that rich," Katherine said. "I also queried the local Collins Media library; they keep tabs on Sonora's principal citizens. Mr Ribeiro senior made his money out of fish breeding, he won the franchise from the asteroid development corporation to keep the biosphere sea stocked. Antonio was given a 15 per cent stake in the breeding company when he was 21, which he promptly sold for an estimated 800,000 fuseodollars. Daddy didn't approve, there are several news files on the quarrel; it became very public."

"So he is what he claims to be," Roman said. "A not-very-rich boy with expensive tastes."

"How can he pay for the magnetic detectors we have to deploy, then?" Wai asked. "Or is he going to hit us with the bill and suddenly vanish?"

"The detector arrays are already waiting to be loaded on board," Marcus said. "Antonio has several partners; people in the same leaky boat as himself, and willing to take a gamble."

Wai shook her head, still dubious. "I don't buy it. It's a free lunch."

"They're willing to invest their own money in the array hardware. What other guarantees do you want?"

"What kind of money are we talking about, exactly?" Karl asked. "I mean, if we do fill the ship up, what's it going to be worth?"

"Given its density, *Lady Mac* can carry roughly 5,000 tonnes of gold in her cargo holds," Marcus said. "That'll make manoeuvring very sluggish, but I can handle her."

Roman grinned at Karl. "And today's price for gold is three and a half thousand fuseodollars per kilogram."

Karl's eyes went blank for a second as his neural nanonics ran the conversion. "Seventeen billion fuseodollars' worth!"

He laughed. "Per trip."

"How is this Ribeiro character proposing to divide the proceeds?" Schutz asked.

"We get one third," Marcus said. "Roughly five point eight billion fuseodollars. Of which I take 30 per cent. The rest is split equally between you, as per the bounty flight clause in your contracts."

"Shit," Karl whispered. "When do we leave, Captain?"

"Does anybody have any objections?" Marcus asked. He gave Wai a quizzical look.

"Okay," she said. "But just because you can't see surface cracks, it doesn't mean there isn't any metal fatigue."

The docking cradle lifted *Lady Macbeth* cleanly out of the spaceport's crater-shaped bay. As soon as she cleared the rim her thermo-dump panels unfolded, sensor clusters rose up out of their recesses on long booms. Visual and radar information was collated by the flight computer, which datavised it directly into Marcus's neural nanonics. He lay on the acceleration couch at the centre of the bridge with his eyes closed as the external starfield blossomed in his mind. Delicate icons unfurled across the visualization, ship status schematics and navigational plots sketched in primary colours.

Chemical verniers fired, lifting Lady Mac off the cradle amid spumes of hot saffron vapour. A tube of orange circles appeared ahead of him, the course vector formatted to take them in towards the gas giant. Marcus switched to the more powerful ion thrusters, and the orange circles began to stream past the hull.

The gas giant, Zacateca, and its moon, Lazaro, had the same apparent size as Lady Mac accelerated away from the spaceport. Sonora was one of 15 asteroids captured by their Lagrange point, a zone where their respective gravity fields were in equilibrium. Behind the starship, Lazaro was a grubby grey crescent splattered with white craters. Given that Zacateca was small for a gas giant, barely 40,000 kilometres in diameter, Lazaro was an unusual companion. A moon 9,000 kilometres in diameter, with an outer crust of ice 50 kilometres deep. It was that ice which had originally attracted the interest of the banks and multistellar finance consortia. Stony iron asteroids were an ideal source of metal and minerals for industrial stations, but they were also notoriously short of the light elements essential to sustain life. To have abundant supplies of both so close together was a strong investment incentive.

Lady Mac's radar showed Marcus a serpentine line of one-tonne ice cubes flung out from Lazaro's equatorial mass-driver, gliding inertly up to the Lagrange point for collection. The same inexhaustible source which allowed Sonora to have its unique sea.

All the asteroids in the cluster had benefited from the plentiful ice, their economic growth racing ahead of equivalent settlements. Such success always bred resentment among the indigenous population, who inevitably became eager for freedom from the founding companies. In this case, having so many settlements so close together gave their population a strong sense of identity and shared anger. The cluster's demands for autonomy had become increasingly strident over the last few years. A situation agitated by numerous violent incidents and acts of sabotage against the company administration staff.

Ahead of the Lady Mac, Marcus could see the tidal hurricane Lazaro stirred up amid the wan amber and emerald stormbands of Zacateca's upper atmosphere. An ocean-sized hypervelocity maelstrom which followed the moon's orbit faithfully around the equator. Lightning crackled round its fringes, 500-kilometre-long forks stabbing out into the surrounding cyclones of ammonia cirrus and methane sleet.

The starship was accelerating at two gees now, her triple fusion drives sending out a vast streamer of arc-bright plasma as she curved around the bulk of the huge planet. Her course vector was slowly bending to align on the star which Antonio intended to prospect, 38 light years distant. There was very little information contained in the almanac file other than confirming it was a K class star with a disc.

Marcus cut the fusion drives when the Lady Mac was 7,000 kilometres past perigee and climbing steadily. The thermo-dump panels and sensor clusters sank down into their jump recesses below the fuselage, returning the ship to a perfect sphere. Fusion generators began charging the energy patterning nodes. Orange circles flashing through Marcus's mind were illustrating the slingshot parabola she'd flown, straightening up the farther the gas giant was left behind. A faint star slid into the last circle.

An event horizon swallowed the starship. Five milliseconds later it had shrunk to nothing.

.   .   .   .

"Okay, try this one," Katherine said. "Why should the gold or anything else congeal into lumps as big as the ones they say it will? Just because you've got a planetoid with a hot core doesn't mean it's producing the metallic equivalent of fractional distillation. You're not going to get an onion-layer effect with strata of different metals. It doesn't happen on planets, it won't happen here. If there is gold, and platinum and all the rest of this fantasy junk, it's going to be hidden away in ores just like it always is."

"So Antonio exaggerated when he said it would be pure," Karl retorted. "We just hunt down the highest grade ore particles in the disc. Even if it's only 50 per cent, who cares? We're never going to be able to spend it all anyway."

Marcus let the discussion grumble on. It had been virtually the only topic for the crew since they'd departed Sonora five days ago. Katherine was playing the part of chief sceptic, with occasional support from Schutz and Wai, while the others tried to shoot her down. The trouble was, he acknowledged, that none of them knew enough to comment with real authority. At least they weren't talking about the sudden departure from Ayachcho any more.

"If the planetoids did produce ore, then it would fragment badly during the collision which formed the disc," Katherine said. "There won't even be any mountain-sized chunks left, only pebbles."

"Have you taken a look outside recently?" Roman asked. "The disc doesn't exactly have a shortage of large particles."

Marcus smiled to himself at that. The disc material had worried him when they arrived at the star two days ago. *Lady Mac* had jumped deep into the system, emerging three million kilometres above the ecliptic. It was a superb vantage point. The small orange star burned at the centre of a disc 160 million kilometres in diameter. There were no distinct bands like those found in a gas giant's rings, this was a continuous grainy copper mist veiling half of the universe. Only around the star itself did it fade away; whatever particles were there to start with had long since evaporated to leave a clear band three million kilometres wide above the turbulent photosphere.

Lady Mac was accelerating away from the star at a 20th of a gee, and curving round into a retrograde orbit. It was the vector which would give the magnetic arrays the best possible coverage of the disc. Unfortunately, it increased the probability of collision by an order of magnitude. So far, the radar had only detected standard motes of interplanetary dust, but Marcus insisted there were always two crew on duty monitoring the local environment.

"Time for another launch," he announced.

Wai datavised the flight computer to run a final systems diagnostic through the array satellite. "I notice Jorge isn't here again," she said sardonically. "I wonder why that is?"

Jorge Leon was the second companion Antonio Ribeiro had brought with him on the flight. He'd been introduced to the crew as a first-class hardware technician who had supervised the construction of the magnetic array satellites. As introverted as Antonio was outgoing, he'd shown remarkably little interest in the arrays so far. It was Victoria Keef who'd familiarized the crew with the systems they were deploying.

"We should bung him in our medical scanner," Karl suggested cheerfully. "Be interesting to see what's inside him. Bet you'd find a whole load of weapon implants."

"Great idea," Roman said. "You ask him. He gives me the creeps."

"Yeah, Katherine, explain that away," Karl said. "If there's no gold in the disc, how come they brought a contract killer along to make sure we don't fly off with their share?"

"Karl!" Marcus warned. "That's enough." He gave the open floor hatch a pointed look. "Now let's get the array launched, please."

Karl's face reddened as he began establishing a tracking link between the starship's communication system and the array satellite's transponder.

"Satellite systems on line," Wai reported. "Launch when ready."

Marcus datavised the flight computer to retract the satellite's hold-down latches. An induction rail shot it clear of the ship. Ion thrusters flared, refining its trajectory as it headed down towards the squally apricot surface of the disc.

Victoria had designed the satellites to skim 5,000 kilometres above the nomadic particles. When their operational altitude was established they would spin up and start to reel out 25 gossamer-thin optical fibres. Rotation ensured the fibres remained straight, forming a spoke array parallel to the disc. Each fibre was 150 kilometres long, and coated in a reflective, magnetically sensitive film.

As the disc particles were still within the star's magnetosphere, every one of them generated a tiny wake as it traversed the flux lines. It was that wake which resonated the magnetically sensitive film, producing fluctuations in the reflectivity. By bouncing a laser pulse down the fibre and measuring the distortions inflicted by the film, it was possible to build up an image of the magnetic waves writhing chaotically through the disc. With the correct discrimination programmes, the origin of each wave could be determined.

The amount of data streaming back into the *Lady Macbeth* from the array satellites was colossal. One satellite array could cover an area of 250,000 square kilometres, and Antonio Ribeiro had persuaded the Sonora Autonomy Crusade to pay for 15. It was a huge gamble, and the responsibility was his alone. Forty hours after the first satellite was deployed, the strain of that responsibility was beginning to show. He hadn't slept since then, choosing to stay in the cabin which Marcus Calvert had assigned to them, and where they'd set up their network of analysis processors. Forty hours of his mind being flooded with near-incomprehensible neuroiconic displays. Forty hours spent fingering his silver crucifix and praying.

The medical monitor programme running in his neural nanonics was flashing up fatigue toxin cautions, and warning him of impending dehydration. So far he'd ignored them, telling himself discovery would occur any minute now. In his heart, Antonio had been hoping they would find what they wanted in the first five hours.

His neural nanonics informed him the analysis network was focusing on the mass density ratio of a three-kilometre particle exposed by satellite seven. The processors began a more detailed interrogation of the raw data.

"What is it?" Antonio demanded. His eyes fluttered open to glance at Victoria, who was resting lightly on one of the cabin's flatchairs.

"Interesting," she murmured. "It appears to be a cassiterite ore. The planetoids definitely had tin."

"Shit!" He thumped his fist into the chair's padding, only to feel the restraint straps tighten against his chest, preventing him from sailing free. "I don't care about tin. That's not what we're here for."

"I am aware of that." Her eyes were open, staring at him with a mixture of contempt and anger.

"Sure, sure," he mumbled. "Holy Mother, you'd expect us to find some by now."

"Careful," she datavised. "Remember this damn ship has internal sensors."

"I know how to follow elementary security procedures," he datavised back.

"Yes. But you're tired. That's when errors creep in."

"I'm not that tired. Shit, I expected results by now; some progress."

"We have had some very positive results, Antonio. The arrays have found three separate deposits of pitchblende."

"Yeah, in hundred-kilogram lumps. We need more than that, a lot more."

"You're missing the point. We've proved it exists here; that's a stupendous discovery. Finding it in quantity is just a matter of time."

"This isn't some astrological experiment you're running for that university which threw you out. We're on an assignment for the cause. And we cannot go back empty-handed. Got that? Cannot."

"Astrophysics."

"What?"

"You said astrological, that's fortune-telling."

"Yeah? You want I should take a guess at how much future you're going to have if we don't find what we need out here?"

"For Christ's sake, Antonio," she said out loud. "Go and get some sleep."

"Maybe." He scratched the side of his head, unhappy with how limp and oily his hair had become. A vapour shower was something else he hadn't had for a while. "I'll get Jorge in here to help you monitor the results."

"Great." Her eyes closed again.

Antonio deactivated his flatchair's restraint straps. He hadn't seen much of Jorge on the flight. Nobody had. The man kept strictly to himself in his small cabin. The Crusade's council wanted him on board to ensure the crew's continuing cooperation once they realized there was no gold. It was Antonio who had suggested the arrangement; what bothered him was the orders Jorge had received concerning himself should things go wrong.

"Hold it." Victoria raised her hand. "This is a really weird one."

Antonio tapped his feet on a stikpad to steady himself. His neural nanonics accessed the analysis network again. Satellite eleven had located a particle with an impossible mass-density ratio; it also had its own magnetic field, a very complex one. "Holy Mother, what is that? Is there another ship here?"

"No, it's too big for a ship. Some kind of station, I suppose. But what's it doing in the disc?"

"Refining ore?" he said with a strong twist of irony.

"I doubt it."

"Okay. So forget it."

"You are joking."

"No. If it doesn't affect us, it doesn't concern us."

"Jesus, Antonio; if I didn't know you were born rich I'd be frightened by how stupid you were."

"Be careful, Victoria my dear. Very careful."

"Listen, there's two options. One, it's some kind of commercial operation; which must be illegal because nobody has filed for industrial development rights." She gave him a significant look.

"You think they're mining pitchblende?" he datavised.

"What else? We thought of the concept, why not one of the black syndicates as well? They just didn't come up with my magnetic array idea, so they're having to do it the hard way."

"Secondly," she continued aloud, "it's some kind of covert military station; in which case they've tracked us from the moment we emerged. Either way, we're under observation. We have to know who they are before we proceed any further."

"A station?" Marcus asked. "Here?"

"It would appear so," Antonio said glumly.

"And you want us to find out who they are?"

"I think that would be prudent," Victoria said, "given what we're doing here."

"All right," Marcus said. "Karl, lock a communication dish on them. Give them our CAB identification code, let's see if we can get a response."

"Aye, sir," Karl said. He settled back on his acceleration couch.

"While we're waiting," Katherine said. "I have a question for you, Antonio."
She ignored the warning glare Marcus directed at her.

Antonio's bogus smile blinked on. "If it is one I can answer, then I will do so
gladly, dear lady."

"Gold is expensive because of its rarity value, right?"

"Of course."

"So here we are, about to fill *Lady Mac*'s cargo holds with 5,000 tonnes of the
stuff. On top of that you've developed a method which means people can scoop up
millions of tonnes any time they want. If we try and sell it to a dealer or a bank, how
long do you think we're going to be billionaires for, a fortnight?"

Antonio laughed. "Gold has never been that rare. Its value is completely artificial. The Edenists have the largest stockpile. We don't know exactly how much they
possess because the Jovian Bank will not declare the exact figure. But they dominate
the commodity market, and sustain the price by controlling how much is released.
We shall simply play the same game. Our gold will have to be sold discreetly, in small
batches, in different star systems, and over the course of several years. And knowledge
of the magnetic array system should be kept to ourselves."

"Nice try, Katherine," Roman chuckled. "You'll just have to settle for an income
of a hundred million a year."

She showed him a stiff finger, backed by a shark's smile.

"No response," Karl said. "Not even a transponder."

"Keep trying," Marcus told him. "Okay, Antonio, what do you want to do about it?"

"We have to know who they are," Victoria said. "As Antonio has just explained
so eloquently, we can't have other people seeing what we're doing here."

"It's what *they're* doing here that worries me," Marcus said; although, curiously,
his intuition wasn't causing him any grief on the subject.

"I see no alternative but a rendezvous," Antonio said.

"We're in a retrograde orbit, 32 million kilometres away and receding. That's going to use up an awful lot of fuel."

"Which I believe I have already paid for."

"Okay, we rendezvous."

"What if they don't want us there?" Schutz asked.

"If we detect any combat wasp launch, then we jump outsystem immediately,"
Marcus said. "The disc's gravity field isn't strong enough to affect *Lady Mac*'s patterning node symmetry. We can leave any time we want."

For the last quarter of a million kilometres of the approach, Marcus put the ship on
combat status. The nodes were fully charged, ready to jump. Thermo-dump panels
were retracted. Sensors maintained a vigilant watch for approaching combat wasps.

"They must know we're here," Wai said when they were 8,000 kilometres away.
"Why don't they acknowledge us?"

"Ask them," Marcus said sourly. *Lady Mac* was decelerating at a nominal one gee,
which he was varying at random. It made their exact approach vector impossible to
predict, which meant their course couldn't be seeded with proximity mines. The ma-
noeuvre took a lot of concentration.

"Still no electromagnetic emission in any spectrum," Karl reported. "They're certainly not scanning us with active sensors."

"Sensors are picking up their thermal signature," Schutz said. "The structure is
being maintained at 36 degrees Celsius."

"That's on the warm side," Katherine observed. "Perhaps their environmental system is malfunctioning."

"Shouldn't affect the transponder," Karl said.

"Captain, I think you'd better access the radar return," Schutz said.

Marcus boosted the fusion drives up to one and a half gees, and ordered the flight computer to datavise him the radar feed. The image which rose into his mind was of a fine scarlet mesh suspended in the darkness, its gentle ocean-swell pattern outlining the surface of the station and the disc particle it was attached to. Except Marcus had never seen any station like this before. It was a gently curved wedge-shape structure, 400 metres long, 300 wide, and 150 metres at its blunt end. The accompanying disc particle was a flattened ellipsoid of stony iron rock, measuring eight kilometres along its axis. The tip had been sheared off, leaving a flat cliff half a kilometre in diameter, to which the structure was clinging. That was the smallest of the particle's modifications. A crater four kilometres across, with perfectly smooth walls, had been cut into one side of the rock. An elaborate unicorn-horn tower rose 900 metres from its centre, ending in a clump of jagged spikes.

"Oh Jesus," Marcus whispered. Elation mingled with fear, producing a deviant adrenaline high. He smiled thinly. "How about that?"

"This was one option I didn't consider," Victoria said weakly.

Antonio looked round the bridge, a frown cheapening his handsome face. The crew seemed dazed, while Victoria was grinning with delight. "Is it some kind of radio astronomy station?" he asked.

"Yes," Marcus said. "But not one of ours. We don't build like that. It's xenoc."

Lady Mac locked attitude a kilometre above the xenoc structure. It was a position which made the disc appear uncomfortably malevolent. The smallest particle beyond the fuselage must have massed over a million tonnes; and all of them were moving, a slow, random three-dimensional cruise of lethal inertia. Amber sunlight stained those near the disc's surface a baleful ginger, while deeper in there were only phantom silhouettes drifting over total blackness, flowing in and out of visibility. No stars were evident through the dark, tightly packed nebula.

"That's not a station," Roman declared. "It's a shipwreck."

Now that *Lady Mac's* visual-spectrum sensors were providing them with excellent images of the xenoc structure, Marcus had to agree. The upper and lower surfaces of the wedge were some kind of silver-white material, a fuselage shell which was fraying away at the edges. Both of the side surfaces were dull brown, obviously interior bulkhead walls, with the black geometrical outline of decking printed across them. The whole structure was a cross-section torn out of a much larger craft. Marcus tried to fill in the missing bulk in his mind; it must have been vast, a streamlined delta fuselage like a hypersonic aircraft. Which didn't make sense for a starship. Rather, he corrected himself, for a starship built with current human technology. He wondered what it would be like to fly through interstellar space the way a plane flew through an atmosphere, swooping round stars at a hundred times the speed of light. Quite something.

"This doesn't make a lot of sense," Katherine said. "If they were visiting the telescope dish when they had the accident, why did they bother to anchor themselves to the asteroid? Surely they'd just take refuge in the operations centre."

"Only if there is one," Schutz said. "Most of our deep space science facilities are automated, and by the look of it their technology is considerably more advanced."

"If they are so advanced, why would they build a radio telescope on this scale anyway?" Victoria asked. "It's very impractical. Humans have been using linked baseline arrays for centuries. Five small dishes orbiting a million kilometres apart would provide a reception which is orders of magnitude greater than this. And why build it here? Firstly, the particles are hazardous, certainly to something that size. You can see it's been pocked by small impacts, and that horn looks broken to me. Secondly, the disc itself blocks half of the universe from observation. No, if you're going to do major radio astronomy, you don't do it from a star system like this one."

"Perhaps they were only here to build the dish," Wai said. "They intended it to be a remote research station, in this part of the galaxy. Once they had it up and running, they'd boost it into a high-inclination orbit. They had their accident before the project was finished."

"That still doesn't explain why they chose this system. Any other star would be better than this one."

"I think Wai's right about them being long-range visitors," Marcus said. "If a xenoc race like that existed close to the Confederation we would have found them by now. Or they would have contacted us."

"The Kiint," Karl said quickly.

"Possibly," Marcus conceded. The Kiint were an enigmatic xenoc race, with a technology far in advance of anything the Confederation had mastered. However, they were reclusive, and cryptic to the point of obscurity. They also claimed to have abandoned starflight a long time ago. "If it is one of their ships, then it's very old."

"And it's still functional," Roman said eagerly. "Hell, think of the technology inside. We'll wind up a lot richer than the gold could ever make us." He grinned over at Antonio, whose humour had blackened considerably.

"So what were the Kiint doing building a radio telescope here?" Victoria asked.

"Who the hell cares?" Karl said. "I volunteer to go over, Captain."

Marcus almost didn't hear him. He'd accessed the *Lady Mac*'s sensor suite again, sweeping the focus over the tip of the dish's tower, then the sheer cliff which the wreckage was attached to. Intuition was making a lot of junctions in his head. "I don't think it is a radio telescope," he said. "I think it's a distress beacon."

"It's four kilometres across!" Katherine said.

"If they came from the other side of the galaxy, it would need to be. We can't even see the galactic core from here there's so much gas and dust in the way. You'd need something this big to punch a message through."

"That's valid," Victoria said. "You believe they were signalling their homeworld for help?"

"Yes. Assume their world is a long way off, three-four thousand light years away if not more. They were flying a research or survey mission in this area and they have an accident. Three quarters of their ship is lost, including the drive section. Their technology isn't good enough to build the survivors a working stardrive out of what's left, but they can enlarge an existing crater on the disc particle. So they do that; they build the dish and a transmitter powerful enough to give God an alarm call, point it at their homeworld, and scream for help. The ship can sustain them until the rescue team arrives. Even our own zero-tau technology is up to that."

"Gets my vote," Wai said. She gave Marcus a wink.

"No way," said Katherine. "If they were in trouble they'd use a supralight communicator to call for help. Look at that ship, we're centuries away from building anything like it."

"Edenist voidhawks are pretty sophisticated," Marcus countered. "We just scale things differently. These xenocs might have a more advanced technology, but physics is still the same the universe over. Our understanding of quantum relativity is good enough to build faster than light starships, yet after 450 years of theoretical research we still haven't come up with a method of supralight communication. It doesn't exist."

"If they didn't return on time, then surely their homeworld would send out a search and recovery craft," Schutz said.

"They'd have to know the original ship's course exactly," Wai said. "And if a search ship did manage to locate them, why did they build the dish?"

Marcus didn't say anything. He knew he was right. The others would accept his scenario eventually, they always did.

"All right, let's stop arguing about what happened to them, and why they built the dish," Karl said. "When do we go over there, Captain?"

"Have you forgotten the gold?" Antonio asked. "That is why we came to this disc system. We should resume our search for it. This piece of wreckage can wait."

"Don't be crazy. This is worth a hundred times as much as any gold."

"I fail to see how. An ancient, derelict, starship with a few heating circuits operational. Come along. I've been reasonable indulging you, but we must return to the original mission."

Marcus regarded the man cautiously, a real bad feeling starting to develop. Anyone with the slightest knowledge of finance and the markets would know the value of salvaging a xenoc starship. And Antonio had been born rich. "Victoria," he said, not shifting his gaze. "Is the data from the magnetic array satellites still coming through?"

"Yes." She touched Antonio's arm. "The captain is right. We can continue to monitor the satellite results from here, and investigate the xenoc ship simultaneously."

"Double your money time," Katherine said with apparent innocence.

Antonio's face hardened. "Very well," he said curtly. "If that's your expert opinion, Victoria, my dear. Carry on by all means, Captain."

In its inert state the SII spacesuit was a broad sensor collar with a protruding respirator tube and a black football-sized globe of programmable silicon hanging from it. Marcus slipped the collar round his neck, bit on the tube nozzle, and datavised an activation code into the suit's control processor. The silicon ball began to change shape, flattening out against his chest, then flowing over his body like a tenacious oil slick. It enveloped his head completely, and the collar sensors replaced his eyes, datavising their vision directly into his neural nanonics. Three others were in the preparation compartment with him: Schutz, who didn't need a spacesuit to EVA, Antonio, and Jorge Leon. Marcus had managed to control his surprise when they'd volunteered. At the same time, with Wai flying the MSV he was glad they weren't going to be left behind in the ship.

Once his body was sealed by the silicon, he climbed into an armoured exoskeleton with an integral cold-gas manoeuvring pack. The SII silicon would never puncture, but if he was struck by a rogue particle the armour would absorb the impact.

When the airlock's outer hatch opened, the MSV was floating 15 metres away. Marcus datavised an order into his manoeuvring pack processor, and the gas jets behind his shoulder fired, pushing him towards the small egg-shaped vehicle. Wai extended two of the MSV's three waldo arms in greeting. Each of them ended in a simple metal grid, with a pair of boot clamps on both sides.

Once all four of her passengers were locked into place, Wai piloted the MSV in towards the disc. The rock particle had a slow, erratic tumble, taking 120 hours to complete its cycle. As she approached, the flattish surface with the dish was just turning into the sunlight. It was a strange kind of dawn, the rock's crumpled grey-brown crust speckled by the sharp black shadows of its own rolling prominences, while the dish was a lake of infinite black, broken only by the jagged spire of the horn rising from its centre. The xenoc ship was already exposed to the amber light, casting its bloated sundial shadow across the featureless glassy cliff. She could see the ripple of different ores and mineral strata frozen below the glazed surface, deluding her for a moment that she was flying towards a mountain of cut and polished onyx.

Then again, if Victoria's theory was right, she could well be.

"Take us in towards the top of the wedge," Marcus datavised. "There's a series of darker rectangles there."

"Will do," she responded. The MSV's chemical thrusters pulsed in compliance.

"Do you see the colour difference near the frayed edges of the shell?" Schutz asked. "The stuff's turning grey. It's as if the decay is creeping inwards."

"They must be using something like our molecular binding force generators to resist vacuum ablation," Marcus datavised. "That's why the main section is still intact."

"It could have been here for a long time, then."

"Yeah. We'll know better once Wai collects some samples from the tower."

There were five of the rectangles, arranged in parallel, one and a half metres long and one metre wide. The shell material below the shorter edge of each one had a set of ten grooves leading away down the curve.

"They look like ladders to me," Antonio datavised. "Would that mean these are airlocks?"

"It can't be that easy," Schutz replied.

"Why not?" Marcus datavised. "A ship this size is bound to have more than one airlock."

"Yeah, but five together?"

"Multiple redundancy."

"With technology this good?"

"That's human hubris. The ship still blew up, didn't it?"

Wai locked the MSV's attitude 50 metres above the shell section. "The micropulse radar is bouncing right back at me," she informed them. "I can't tell what's below the shell, it's a perfect electromagnetic reflector. We're going to have communication difficulties once you're inside."

Marcus disengaged his boots from the grid and fired his pack's gas jets. The shell was as slippery as ice, neither stikpads nor magnetic soles would hold them to it.

"Definitely enhanced valency bonds," Schutz datavised. He was floating parallel to the surface, holding a sensor block against it. "It's a much stronger field than *Lady Mac*'s. The shell composition is a real mix; the resonance scan is picking up titanium, silicon, boron, nickel, silver, and a whole load of polymers."

"Silver's weird," Marcus commented. "But if there's nickel in it our magnetic soles should've worked." He manoeuvred himself over one of the rectangles. It was recessed about five centimetres, though it blended seamlessly into the main shell. His sensor collar couldn't detect any seal lining. Halfway along one side were two circular dimples, ten centimetres across. Logically, if the rectangle was an airlock, then these should be the controls. Human back-ups were kept simple. This shouldn't be any different.

Marcus stuck his fingers in one. It turned bright blue.

"Power surge," Schutz datavised. "The block's picking up several high voltage circuits activating under the shell. What did you do, Marcus?"

"Tried to open one."

The rectangle dilated smoothly, material flowing back to the edges. Brilliant white light flooded out.

"Clever," Schutz datavised.

"No more than our programmable silicon," Antonio retorted.

"We don't use programmable silicon for external applications."

"It settles one thing," Marcus datavised. "They weren't Kiint, not with an airlock this size."

"Quite. What now?"

"We try to establish control over the cycling mechanism. I'll go in and see if I can operate the hatch from inside. If it doesn't open after ten minutes, try the dimple again. If that doesn't work, cut through it with the MSV's fission blade."

The chamber inside was thankfully bigger than the hatch: a pentagonal tube two metres wide and 15 long. Four of the walls shone brightly, while the fifth was a strip of dark-maroon composite. He drifted in, then flipped himself over so he was facing the hatch, floating in the centre of the chamber. There were four dimples just beside the hatch. "First one," he datavised. Nothing happened when he put his fingers in. "Second." It turned blue. The hatch flowed shut.

Marcus crashed down onto the strip of dark composite, landing on his left shoulder. The force of the impact was almost enough to jar the respirator tube out of his mouth. He grunted in shock. Neural nanonics blocked the burst of pain from his bruised shoulder.

Jesus! They've got artificial gravity.

He was flat on his back, the exoskeleton and manoeuvring pack weighing far too much. Whatever planet the xenocs came from, it had a gravity field about one and a half times that of Earth. He released the catches down the side of his exoskeleton, and wriggled his way out. Standing was an effort, but he was used to higher gees on Lady Mac; admittedly not for prolonged periods, though.

He stuck his fingers in the first dimple. The gravity faded fast, and the hatch flowed apart.

"We just became billionaires," he datavised.

The third dimple pressurized the airlock chamber; while the fourth depressurized it.

The xenoc atmosphere was mostly a nitrogen oxygen blend, with one per cent argon and six per cent carbon dioxide. The humidity was appalling, pressure was lower than standard, and the temperature was 42 degrees Celsius.

"We'd have to keep our SII suits on anyway, because of the heat," Marcus datavised. "But the carbon dioxide would kill us. And we'll have to go through biological decontamination when we go back to Lady Mac."

The four of them stood together at the far end of the airlock chamber, their exoskeleton armour lying on the floor behind them. Marcus had told Wai and the rest of the crew their first foray would be an hour.

"Are you proposing we go in without a weapon?" Jorge asked.

Marcus focused his collar sensors on the man who alleged he was a hardware technician. "That's carrying paranoia too far. No, we do not engage in first contact either deploying or displaying weapons of any kind. That's the law, and the Assembly regulations are very specific about it. In any case, don't you think that if there are any xenocs left after all this time they're going to be glad to see someone? Especially a space-faring species."

"That is, I'm afraid, a rather naive attitude, Captain. You keep saying how advanced this starship is, and yet it suffered catastrophic damage. Frankly, an unbelievable amount of damage for an accident. Isn't it more likely this ship was engaged in some kind of battle?"

Which was a background worry Marcus had suffered right from the start. That this starship could ever fail was unnerving. But like physical constants, Murphy's Law would be the same the universe over. He'd entered the air-lock because intuition told him the wreck was safe for him personally. Somehow he doubted a man like Jorge would be convinced by that argument.

"If it's a warship, then it will be rigged to alert any surviving crew or flight computer of our arrival. Had they wanted to annihilate us, they would have done so by now. Lady Mac is a superb ship, but hardly in this class. So if they're waiting for us on the other side of this airlock, I don't think any weapon you or I can carry is going to make the slightest difference."

"Very well, proceed."

Marcus postponed the answer which came straight to mind, and put his fingers in one of the two dimples by the inner hatchway. It turned blue.

The xenoc ship wasn't disappointing, exactly, but Marcus couldn't help a growing sense of anticlimax. The artificial gravity was a fabulous piece of equipment, the atmosphere strange, the layout exotic. Yet for all that, it was just a ship; built from the universal rules of logical engineering. Had the xenocs themselves been there, it would have been so different. A whole new species with its history and culture. But they'd gone, so he was an archaeologist rather than an explorer.

They surveyed the first deck, which was made up from large compartments and broad hallways. The interior was made out of a pale-jade composite, slightly ruffled to a snake-skin texture. Surfaces always curved together, there were no real corners. Every ceiling emitted the same intense white glare, which their collar sensors compensated for. Arching doorways were all open, though they could still dilate if you used the dimples. The only oddity were 50-centimetre hemispherical blisters on the floor and walls, scattered completely at random.

There was an ongoing argument about the shape of the xenocs. They were undoubtedly shorter than humans, and they probably had legs, because there were spiral stairwells, although the steps were very broad, difficult for bipeds. Lounges had long tables with large, rounded stool-chairs inset with four deep ridges.

After the first 15 minutes it was clear that all loose equipment had been removed. Lockers, with the standard dilating door, were empty. Every compartment had its fitted furnishings and nothing more. Some were completely bare.

On the second deck there were no large compartments, only long corridors lined with grey circles along the centre of the walls. Antonio used a dimple at the side of one, and it dilated to reveal a spherical cell three metres wide. Its walls were translucent, with short lines of colour slithering round behind them like photonic fish.

"Beds?" Schutz suggested. "There's an awful lot of them."

Marcus shrugged. "Could be." He moved on, eager to get down to the next deck. Then he slowed, switching his collar focus. Three of the hemispherical blisters were following him, two gliding along the wall, one on the floor. They stopped when he did. He walked over to the closest, and waved his sensor block over it. "There's a lot of electronic activity inside it," he reported.

The others gathered round.

"Are they extruded by the wall, or are they a separate device?" Schutz asked.

Marcus switched on the block's resonance scan. "I'm not sure, I can't find any break in the composite round its base, not even a hairline fracture; but with their materials technology that doesn't mean much."

"Five more approaching," Jorge datavised. The blisters were approaching from ahead, three of them on the walls, two on the floor. They stopped just short of the group.

"Something knows we're here," Antonio datavised.

Marcus retrieved the CAB xenoc interface communication protocol from a neural nanonics memory cell. He'd stored it decades ago, all qualified starship crew were obliged to carry it along with a million and one other bureaucratic lunacies. His communication block transmitted the protocol using a multispectrum sweep. If the blister could sense them, it had to have some kind of electromagnetic reception facility. The communication block switched to laser-light, then a magnetic pulse.

"Nothing," Marcus datavised.

"Maybe the central computer needs time to interpret the protocol," Schutz datavised.

"A desktop block should be able to work that out."

"Perhaps the computer hasn't got anything to say to us."

"Then why send the blisters after us?"

"They could be autonomous, whatever they are."

Marcus ran his sensor block over the blister again, but there was no change to its electronic pattern. He straightened up, wincing at the creak of complaint his spine made at the heavy gravity. "Okay, our hour is almost up anyway. We'll get back to *Lady Mac* and decide what stage two is going to be."

The blisters followed them all the way back to the stairwell they'd used. As soon as they started walking down the broad central hallway of the upper deck, more blisters started sliding in from compartments and other halls to stalk them.

The airlock hatch was still open when they got back, but the exoskeletons were missing.

"Shit," Antonio datavised. "They're still here, the bloody xenocs are here."

Marcus shoved his fingers into the dimple. His heartbeat calmed considerably when the hatch congealed behind them. The lock cycled obediently, and the outer rectangle opened.

"Wai," he datavised. "We need a lift. Quickly, please."

"On my way, Marcus."

"Strange way for xenocs to communicate," Schutz datavised. "What did they do that for? If they wanted to make sure we stayed, they could have disabled the airlock."

The MSV swooped over the edge of the shell, jets of twinkling flame shooting from its thrusters.

"Beats me," Marcus datavised. "But we'll find out."

Opinion on the ship was a straight split; the crew wanted to continue investigating the xenoc ship, Antonio and his colleagues wanted to leave. For once Jorge had joined them, which Marcus considered significant. He was beginning to think young Karl might have been closer to the truth than was strictly comfortable.

"The dish is just rock with a coating of aluminium sprayed on," Katherine said. "There's very little aluminium left now, most of it has boiled away in the vacuum. The tower is a pretty ordinary silicon-boron composite wrapped round a titanium load structure. The samples Wai cut off were very brittle."

"Did you carbon date them?" Victoria asked.

"Yeah." She gave her audience a laboured glance. "Give or take a decade, it's 13,000 years old."

Breath whistled out of Marcus's mouth. "Jesus."

"Then they must have been rescued, or died," Roman said. "There's nobody left over there. Not after that time."

"They're there," Antonio growled. "They stole our exoskeletons."

"I don't understand what happened to the exoskeletons. Not yet. But any entity who can build a ship like that isn't going to go creeping round stealing bits of space armour. There has to be a rational explanation."

"Yes! They wanted to keep us over there."

"What for? What possible reason would they have for that?"

"It's a warship, it's been in battle. The survivors don't know who we are, if we're their old enemies. If they kept us there, they could study us and find out."

"After 13,000 years, I imagine the war will be over. And where did you get this battleship idea from anyway?"

"It's a logical assumption," Jorge said quietly.

Roman turned to Marcus. "My guess is that some kind of mechanoid picked them up. If you look in one of the lockers you'll probably find them neatly stored away."

"Some automated systems are definitely still working," Schutz said. "We saw the blisters. There could be others."

"That seems the most remarkable part of it," Marcus said. "Especially now we know the age of the thing. The inside of that ship was brand new. There wasn't any dust, any scuff marks. The lighting worked perfectly, so did the gravity, the humidity hasn't corroded anything. It's extraordinary. As if the whole structure has been in zero-tau. And yet only the shell is protected by the molecular bonding force generators. They're not used inside, not in the decks we examined."

"However they preserve it, they'll need a lot of power for the job, and that's on top of gravity generation and environmental maintenance. Where's that been coming from uninterrupted for 13,000 years?"

"Direct mass to energy conversion," Katherine speculated. "Or they could be tapping straight into the sun's fusion. Whatever, bang goes the Edenist He3 monopoly."

"We have to go back," Marcus said.

"NO!" Antonio yelled. "We must find the gold first. When that has been achieved, you can come back by yourselves. I won't allow anything to interfere with our priorities."

"Look, I'm sorry you had a fright while you were over there. But a power supply that works for 13,000 years is a lot more valuable than a whole load of gold which we have to sell furtively," Katherine said levelly.

"I hired this ship. You do as I say. We go after the gold."

"We're partners, actually. I'm not being paid for this flight unless we strike lucky. And now we have. We've got the xenoc ship, we haven't got any gold. What does it matter to you how we get rich, as long as we do? I thought money was the whole point of this flight."

Antonio snarled at her, and flung himself at the floor hatch, kicking off hard with his legs. His elbow caught the rim a nasty crack as he flashed through it.

"Victoria?" Marcus asked as the silence became strained. "Have the satellite arrays found any heavy metal particles yet?"

"There are definitely traces of gold and platinum, but nothing to justify a rendezvous."

"In that case, I say we start to research the xenoc wreck properly." He looked straight at Jorge. "How about you?"

"I think it would be prudent. You're sure we can continue to monitor the array satellites from here?"

"Yes."

"Good. Count me in."

"Thanks. Victoria?"

She seemed troubled by Jorge's response, even a little bewildered, but she said: "Sure."

"Karl, you're the nearest thing we've got to a computer expert. I want you over there trying to make contact with whatever control network is still operating."

"You got it."

"From now on we go over in teams of four. I want sensors put up to watch the airlocks when we're not around, and start thinking about how we communicate with people inside. Wai, you and I are going to secure *Lady Mac* to the side of the shell. Okay, let's get active, people."

Unsurprisingly, none of the standard astronautics industry vacuum epoxies worked on the shell. Marcus and Wai wound up using tether cables wrapped round the whole of the xenoc ship to hold *Lady Mac* in place.

Three hours after Karl went over, he asked Marcus to join him.

Lady Mac's main airlock tube had telescoped out of the hull to rest against the shell. There was no way it could ever be mated to the xenoc airlock rectangle, but it did allow the crew to transfer over directly without having to use exoskeleton armour and the MSV. They'd also run an optical fibre through the xenoc airlock to the interior of the ship. The hatch material closed around it forming a perfect seal, rather than cutting through it.

Marcus found Karl just inside the airlock, sitting on the floor with several processor blocks in his lap. Eight blisters were slowly circling round him; two on the wall were stationary.

"Roman was almost right," he datavised as soon as Marcus stepped out of the airlock. "Your exoskeletons were cleared away. But not by any butler mechanoid. Watch." He lobbed an empty recording flek case onto the floor behind the blisters. One of them slid over to it. The green composite became soft, then liquid. The little plastic case sank through it into the blister.

"I call them cybermice," Karl datavised. "They just scurry around keeping the place clean. You won't see the exoskeletons again, they ate them, along with anything else they don't recognize as part of the ship's structure. I imagine they haven't tried digesting us yet because we're large and active; maybe they think we're friends of the xenocs. But I wouldn't want to try sleeping over here."

"Does this mean we won't be able to put sensors up?"

"Not for a while. I've managed to stop them digesting the communication block which the optical fibre is connected to."

"How?"

He pointed to the two on the wall. "I shut them down."

"Jesus, have you accessed a control network?"

"No. Schutz and I used a micro SQUID on one of the cybermice to get a more detailed scan of its electronics. Once we'd tapped the databus traffic it was just a question of running standard decryption programmes. I can't tell you how these things work, but I have found some basic command routines. There's a deactivation code which you can datavise to them. I've also got a reactivation code, and some directional codes. The good news is that the xenoc programme language is standardized." He stood and held a communication block up to the ceiling. "This is the deactivation code." A small circle of the ceiling around the block turned dark. "It's only localized, I haven't worked out how to control entire sections yet. We need to trace the circuitry to find an access port."

"Can you turn it back on again?"

"Oh yes." The dark section flared white again. "The codes work for the doors as well; just hold your block over the dimples."

"Be quicker to use the dimples."

"For now, yes."

"I wasn't complaining, Karl. This is an excellent start. What's your next step?"

"I want to access the next level of the cybermice programme architecture. That way I should be able to load recognition patterns in their memory. Once I can do that I'll enter our equipment, and they should leave it alone. But that's going to take a long time; *Lady Mac* isn't exactly heavily stocked with equipment for this kind of work. Of course, once I do get deeper into their management routines we should be able to learn a lot about their internal systems. From what I can make out the cybermice are built around a molecular synthesizer." He switched on a fission knife, its ten-centimetre blade glowing a pale yellow under the ceiling's glare. It scored a dark smouldering scar in the floor composite.

A cybermouse immediately slipped towards the blemish. This time when the composite softened the charred granules were sucked down, and the small valley closed up.

"Exactly the same thickness and molecular structure as before," Karl datavised. "That's why the ship's interior looks brand new, and everything's still working flawlessly after 13,000 years. The cybermice keep regenerating it. Just keep giving them energy and a supply of mass and there's no reason this ship won't last for eternity."

"It's almost a Von Neumann machine, isn't it?"

"Close. I expect a synthesizer this small has limits. After all, if it could reproduce anything, they would have built themselves another starship. But the principle's here, Captain. We can learn and expand on it. Think of the effect a unit like this will have on our manufacturing industry."

Marcus was glad he was in an SII suit, it blocked any give-away facial expressions. Replicator technology would be a true revolution, restructuring every aspect of human society, Adamist and Edenist alike. And revolutions never favoured the old.

I just came here for the money, not to destroy a way of life for 800 star systems.

"That's good, Karl. Where did the others go?"

"Down to the third deck. Once we solved the puzzle of the disappearing exoskeletons, they decided it was safe to start exploring again."

"Fair enough, I'll go down and join them."

"I cannot believe you agreed to help them," Antonio stormed. "You of all people. You know how much the cause is depending on us."

Jorge gave him a hollow smile. They were together in his sleeping cubicle, which made it very cramped. But it was one place on the starship he knew for certain no sensors were operational; a block he'd brought with him had made sure of that. "The cause has become dependent on your project. There's a difference."

"What are you talking about?"

"Those detector satellites cost us a million and a half fuseodollars each; and most of that money came from sources who will require repayment no matter what the outcome of our struggle."

"The satellites are a hell of a lot cheaper than antimatter."

"Indeed so. But they are worthless to us unless they find pitchblende."

"We'll find it. Victoria says there are plenty of traces. It's only a question of time before we get a big one."

"Maybe. It was a good idea, Antonio, I'm not criticising. Fusion bomb components are not easily obtainable to a novice political organization with limited resources. One mistake, and the intelligence agencies would wipe us out. No, old-fashioned fission was a viable alternative. Even if we couldn't process the uranium up to weapons-quality, we still use it as a lethal large-scale contaminant. As you say, we couldn't lose. Sonora would gain independence, and we would form the first government, with full access to the Treasury. Everyone would be reimbursed for their individual contribution to the liberation."

"So why are we mucking about in a pile of xenoc junk? Just back me up, Jorge, please. Calvert will leave it alone if we both pressure him."

"Because, Antonio, this piece of so-called xenoc junk has changed the rules of the game. In fact we're not even playing the same game any more. Gravity generation, an inexhaustible power supply, molecular synthesis, and if Karl can access the control network he might even find the blueprints to build whatever stardrive they used. Are you aware of the impact such a spectrum of radical technologies will have upon the Confederation when released all together? Entire industries will collapse from overnight obsolescence. There will be an economic depression the like of which we haven't seen since before the invention of the ZTT drive. It will take decades for the human race to return to the kind of stability we enjoy today. We will be richer and stronger because of it; but the transition years, ah . . . I would not like to be a citizen in an asteroid settlement that has just blackmailed the founding company into premature independence. Who is going to loan an asteroid such as that the funds to re-equip our industrial stations, eh?"

"I . . . I hadn't thought of that."

"Neither has the crew. Except for Calvert. Look at his face next time you talk to him, Antonio. He knows, he has reasoned it out, and he's seen the end of his captaincy and freedom. The rest of them are lost amid their dreams of exorbitant wealth."

"So what do we do?"

Jorge clamped a hand on Antonio's shoulder. "Fate has smiled on us, Antonio. This was registered as a joint venture flight. No matter we were looking for something different. By law, we are entitled to an equal share of the xenoc technology. We are already trillionaires, my friend. When we get home we can *buy* Sonora asteroid; Holy Mother, we can buy the entire Lagrange cluster."

Antonio managed a smile, which didn't quite correspond with the dew of sweat on his forehead. "Okay, Jorge. Hell, you're right. We don't have to worry about anything any more. But . . ."

"Now what?"

"I know we can pay off the loan on the satellites, but what about the Crusade council? They won't like this. They might—"

"There's no cause for alarm. The council will never trouble us again. I maintain that I am right about the disaster which destroyed the xenoc ship. It didn't have an accident. That is a warship, Antonio. And you know what that means, don't you? Somewhere on board there will be weapons just as advanced and as powerful as the rest of its technology."

It was Wai's third trip over to the xenoc ship. None of them spent more than two hours at a time inside. The gravity field made every muscle ache, walking round was like being put on a crash exercise regimen.

Schutz and Karl were still busy by the airlock, probing the circuitry of the cyber-mice, and decrypting more of their programming. It was probably the most promising line of research; once they could use the xenoc programme language they should be able to extract any answer they wanted from the ship's controlling network. Assuming there was one. Wai was convinced there would be. The number of systems operating—life-support, power, gravity—had to mean some basic management integration system was functional.

In the meantime there was the rest of the structure to explore. She had a layout file stored in her neural nanonics, updated by the others every time they came back from an excursion. At the blunt end of the wedge there could be anything up to 40 decks, if the spacing was standard. Nobody had gone down to the bottom yet. There were some areas which had no obvious entrance; presumably engineering compartments, or storage tanks. Marcus had the teams tracing the main power lines with magnetic sensors, trying to locate the generator.

Wai plodded after Roman as he followed a cable running down the centre of a corridor on the eighth deck.

"It's got so many secondary feeds it looks like a fishbone," he complained. They paused at a junction with five branches, and he swept the block round. "This way." He started off down one of the new corridors.

"We're heading towards stairwell five," she told him, as the layout file scrolled through her skull.

There were more cybermice than usual on deck eight; over 30 were currently pursuing her and Roman, creating strong ripples in the composite floor and walls. Wai had noticed that the deeper she went into the ship the more of them there seemed to be. Although after her second trip she'd completely ignored them. She wasn't paying a lot of attention to the compartments leading off from the corridors, either. It wasn't that they were all the same, rather that they were all similarly empty.

They reached the stairwell, and Roman stepped inside. "It's going down," he datavised.

"Great, that means we've got another level to climb up when we're finished."

Not that going down these stairs was easy, she acknowledged charily. If only they could find some kind of variable gravity chute. Perhaps they'd all been positioned in the part of the ship that was destroyed.

"You know, I think Marcus might have been right about the dish being an emergency beacon," she datavised. "I can't think of any other reason for it being built. Believe me, I've tried."

"He always is right. It's bloody annoying, but that's why I fly with him."

"I was against it because of the faith gap."

"Say what?"

"The amount of faith these xenocs must have had in themselves. It's awesome. So different from humans. Think about it. Even if their homeworld is only 2,000 light years away, that's how long the message is going to take to reach there. Yet they sent it believing someone would still be around to receive it, and more, act on it. Suppose that was us; suppose the *Lady Mac* had an accident a thousand light years away. Would you think there was any point in sending a lightspeed message to the Confederation, then going into zero-tau to wait for a rescue ship?"

"If their technology can last that long, then I guess their civilization can, too."

"No, our hardware can last for a long time. It's our culture that's fragile, at least compared to theirs. I don't think the Confederation will last a thousand years."

"The Edenists will be here, I expect. So will all the planets, physically if nothing else. Some of their societies will advance, possibly even to a state similar to the Kiint; some will revert to barbarism. But there will be somebody left to hear the message and help."

"You're a terrible optimist."

They arrived at the ninth deck, only to find the doorway was sealed over with composite.

"Odd," Roman datavised. "If there's no corridor or compartment beyond, why put a doorway here at all?"

"Because this was a change made after the accident."

"Could be. But why would they block off an interior section?"

"I've no idea. You want to keep going down?"

"Sure. I'm optimistic enough not to believe in ghosts lurking in the basement."

"I really wish you hadn't said that."

The tenth deck had been sealed off as well.

"My legs can take one more level," Wai datavised. "Then I'm going back."

There was a door on deck 11. It was the first one in the ship to be closed.

Wai stuck her fingers in the dimple, and the door dilated. She edged over cautiously, and swept the focus of her collar sensors round. "Holy shit. We'd better fetch Marcus."

.   .   .

Decks nine and ten had simply been removed to make the chamber. Standing on the floor and looking up, Marcus could actually see the outline of the stairwell doorways in the wall above him. By xenoc standards it was a cathedral. There was only one altar, right in the centre. A doughnut of some dull metallic substance, eight metres in diameter with a central aperture five metres across; the air around it was emitting a faint violet glow. It stood on five sableblack arching buttresses, four metres tall.

"The positioning must be significant," Wai datavised. "They built it almost at the centre of the wreck. They wanted to give it as much protection as possible."

"Agreed," Katherine replied. "They obviously considered it important. After a ship has suffered this much damage, you don't expend resources on anything other than critical survival requirements."

"Whatever it is," Schutz reported. "It's using up an awful lot of power." He was walking round it, keeping a respectful distance, wiping a sensor block over the floor as he went. "There's a power cable feeding each of those legs."

"Is it radiating in any spectrum?" Marcus asked.

"Only that light you can see, which spills over into ultraviolet, too. Apart from that, it's inert. But the energy must be going somewhere."

"Okay." Marcus walked up to a buttress, and switched his collar focus to scan the aperture. It was veiled by a grey haze, as if a sheet of fog had solidified across it. When he took another tentative step forward the fluid in his semicircular canals was suddenly affected by a very strange tidal force. His foot began to slip forwards and upwards. He threw himself backwards, and almost stumbled. Jorge and Karl just caught him in time.

"There's no artificial gravity underneath it," he datavised. "But there's some kind of gravity field wrapped around it." He paused. "No, that's not right. It pushed me."

"Pushed?" Katherine hurried to his side. "Are you sure?"

"Yes."

"My God."

"What? Do you know what it is?"

"Possibly. Schutz, hang on to my arm, please."

The cosmonik came forward and took her left arm. Katherine edged forward until she was almost under the lambent doughnut. She stretched up her right arm, holding out a sensor block, and tried to press it against the doughnut. It was as if she was trying to make two identical magnetic poles touch. The block couldn't get to within 20 centimetres of the surface, it kept slithering and sliding through the air. She held it as steady as she could, and datavised it to run an analysis of the doughnut's molecular structure.

The results made her back away.

"So?" Marcus asked.

"I'm not entirely sure it's solid in any reference frame we understand. That surface could just be a boundary effect. There's no spectroscopic data at all, the sensor couldn't even detect an atomic structure in there, let alone valency bonds."

"You mean it's a ring of energy?"

"Don't hold me to it, but I think that thing could be some kind of exotic matter."

"Exotic in what sense, exactly?" Jorge asked.

"It has a negative energy density. And before you ask, that doesn't mean antigravity. Exotic matter only has one known use, to keep a wormhole open."

"Jesus, that's a wormhole portal?" Marcus asked.

"It must be."

"Any way of telling where it leads?"

"I can't give you an exact stellar coordinate; but I know where the other end has to emerge. The xenocs never called for a rescue ship, Marcus. They threaded a wormhole with exotic matter to stop it collapsing, and escaped down it. That is the entrance to a tunnel which leads right back to their homeworld."

Schutz found Marcus in the passenger lounge in capsule C. He was floating centimetres above one of the flatchairs, with the lights down low.

The cosmonik touched his heels to a stikpad on the decking beside the lower hatch. "You really don't like being wrong, do you?"

"No, but I'm not sulking about it, either." Marcus moulded a jaded grin. "I still think I'm right about the dish, but I don't know how the hell to prove it."

"The wormhole portal is rather conclusive evidence."

"Very tactful. It doesn't solve anything, actually. If they could open a wormhole straight back home, why did they build the dish? Like Katherine said, if you have an accident of that magnitude then you devote yourself completely to survival. Either they called for help, or they went home through the wormhole. They wouldn't do both."

"Possibly it wasn't their dish, they were just here to investigate it."

"Two ancient unknown xenoc races with FTL starship technology is pushing credibility. It also takes us back to the original problem: if the dish isn't a distress beacon, then what the hell was it built for?"

"I'm sure there will be an answer at some time."

"I know, we're only a commercial trader's crew, with a very limited research capability. But we can still ask fundamental questions, like why have they kept the wormhole open for 13,000 years?"

"Because that's the way their technology works. They probably wouldn't consider it odd."

"I'm not saying it shouldn't work for that long, I'm asking why their homeworld would bother maintaining a link to a chunk of derelict wreckage?"

"That is harder for logic to explain. The answer must lie in their psychology."

"That's a cop-out; you can't simply cry alien at everything you don't understand. But it does bring us to my final query, if you can open a wormhole with such accuracy across God knows how many light years, why would you need a starship in the first place? What sort of psychology accounts for that?"

"All right, Marcus, you got me. Why?"

"I haven't got a clue. I've been reviewing all the file texts we have on wormholes, trying to find a solution which pulls all this together. And I can't do it. It's a complete paradox."

"There's only one thing left then, isn't there?"

Marcus turned to look at the hulking figure of the cosmonik. "What?"

"Go down the wormhole and ask them."

"Yeah, maybe I will. Somebody has to go eventually. What does our dear Katherine have to say on that subject? Can we go inside it in our SII suits?"

"She's rigging up some sensors that she can shove through the interface. That grey sheet isn't a physical barrier. She's already pushed a length of conduit tubing through. It's some kind of pressure membrane, apparently, stops the ship's atmosphere from flooding into the wormhole."

"Another billion fuseodollar gadget. Jesus, this is getting too big for us, we're going to have to prioritize." He datavised the flight computer, and issued a general order for everyone to assemble in capsule A's main lounge.

Karl was the last to arrive. The young systems engineer looked exhausted. He frowned when he caught sight of Marcus.

"I thought you were over in the xenoc ship."

"No."

"But you . . ." He rubbed his fingers against his temples. "Skip it."

"Any progress?" Marcus asked.

"A little. From what I can make out, the molecular synthesizer and its governing circuitry are combined within the same crystal lattice. To give you a biological analogy, it's as though a muscle is also a brain."

"Don't follow that one through too far," Roman called.

Karl didn't even smile. He took a chocolate sac from the dispenser, and sucked on the nipple.

"Katherine?" Marcus said.

"I've managed to place a visual-spectrum sensor in the wormhole. There's not much light in there, only what soaks through the pressure membrane. From what we can see it's a straight tunnel. I assume the xenocs cut off the artificial gravity under the portal so they could egress it easily. What I'd like to do next is dismount a laser radar from the MSV and use that."

"If the wormhole's threaded with exotic matter, will you get a return from it?"

"Probably not. But we should get a return from whatever is at the other end."

"What's the point?"

Three of them began to talk at once, Katherine loudest of all. Marcus held his hand up for silence. "Listen, everybody, according to Confederation law if the appointed commander or designated controlling mechanism of a spaceship or free-flying space structure discontinues that control for one year and a day then any ownership title becomes null and void. Legally, this xenoc ship is an abandoned structure which we are entitled to file a salvage claim on."

"There is a controlling network," Karl said.

"It's a sub-system," Marcus said. "The law is very clear on that point. If a starship's flight computer fails, but, say, the fusion generators keep working, their governing processors do not constitute the designated controlling mechanism. Nobody will be able to challenge our claim."

"The xenocs might," Wai said.

"Let's not make extra problems for ourselves. As the situation stands right now, we have title. We can't not claim the ship because the xenocs may return at some time."

Katherine rocked her head in understanding. "If we start examining the wormhole they might come back, sooner rather than later. Is that what you're worried about?"

"It's a consideration, yes. Personally, I'd rather like to meet them. But, Katherine, are you really going to learn how to build exotic matter and open a wormhole with the kind of sensor blocks we've got?"

"You know I'm not, Marcus."

"Right. Nor are we going to find the principle behind the artificial gravity generator, or any of the other miracles on board. What we have to do is catalogue as much as we can, and identify the areas that need researching. Once we've done that we can bring back the appropriate specialists, pay them a huge salary, and let them get on with it. Don't any of you understand yet? When we found this ship, we stopped being starship crew, and turned into the highest-flying corporate executives in the galaxy. We don't pioneer any more, we designate. So, we map out the last remaining decks. We track the power cables and note what they power. Then we leave."

"I know I can crack their programme language, Marcus," Karl said. "I can get us into the command network."

Marcus smiled at the weary pride in his voice. "Nobody is going to be more pleased about that than me, Karl. One thing I do intend to take with us is a cybermouse, preferably more than one. That molecular synthesizer is the hard evidence we need to convince the banks of what we've got."

Karl blushed. "Uh, Marcus, I don't know what'll happen if we try and cut one out of the composite. So far we've been left alone; but if the network thinks we're endangering the ship. Well . . ."

"I'd like to think we're capable of something more sophisticated than ripping a cybermouse out of the composite. Hopefully, you'll be able to access the network, and we can simply ask it to replicate a molecular synthesizer unit for us. They have to be manufactured somewhere on board."

"Yeah, I suppose they do. Unless the cybermice duplicate themselves."

"Now that'd be a sight," Roman said happily. "One of them humping away on top of the other."

His neural nanonics time function told Karl he'd slept for nine hours. After he wriggled out of his sleep pouch he air-swam into the crew lounge and helped himself to a pile of food sachets from the galley. There wasn't much activity in the ship, so he didn't even bother to access the flight computer until he'd almost finished eating.

Katherine was on watch when he dived into the bridge through the floor hatch.

"Who's here?" he asked breathlessly. "Who else is on board right now?"

"Just Roman. The rest of them are all over on the wreck. Why?"

"Shit."

"Why, what's the matter?"

"Have you accessed the flight computer?"

"I'm on watch, of course I'm accessing."

"No, not the ship's functions. The satellite analysis network Victoria set up."

Her flat features twisted into a surprised grin. "You mean they've found some gold?"

"No way. The network was reporting that satellite seven had located a target deposit three hours ago. When I accessed the network direct to follow it up I found out what the search parameters really are. They're not looking for gold, those bastards are here to get pitchblende."

"Pitchblende?" Katherine had to run a search programme through her neural nanonics encyclopedia to find out what it was. "Oh Christ, uranium. They want uranium."

"Exactly. You could never mine it from a planet without the local government knowing; that kind of operation would be easily spotted by the observation satellites. Asteroids don't have deposits of pitchblende. But planetoids do, and out here nobody is going to know that they're scooping it up."

"I knew it! I bloody knew that fable about gold mountains was a load of balls."

"They must be terrorists, or Sonora independence freaks, or black syndicate members. We have to warn the others, we can't let them back on board *Lady Mac*."

"Wait a minute, Karl. Yes, they're shits, but if we leave them over on the wreck they'll die. Even if you're prepared to do that, it's the captain's decision."

"No it isn't, not any more. If they come back then neither you, me, nor the captain is going to be in any position to make decisions about anything. They knew we'd find out about the pitchblende eventually when *Lady Mac* rendezvoused with the ore particle. They knew we wouldn't take it on board voluntarily. That means they came fully prepared to force us. They've got guns, or weapons implants. Jorge is exactly what I said he was, a mercenary killer. We can't let them back on the ship, Katherine. We can't."

"Oh Christ," she was gripping the side of her acceleration couch in reflex. Command decision. And it was all hers.

"Can we datavise the captain?" he asked.

"I don't know. We've got relay blocks in the stairwells now the cybermice have been deactivated, but they're not very reliable; the structure plays hell with our signals."

"Who's he with?"

"He was partnering Victoria. Wai and Schutz are together; Antonio and Jorge made up the last team."

"Datavise Wai and Schutz, get them out first. Then try for the captain."

"Okay. Get Roman, and go down to the airlock chamber; I'll authorize the weapons cabinet to release some maser carbines. . . . Shit!"

"What?"

"I can't. Marcus has the flight computer command codes. We can't even fire the thrusters without him."

Deck 14 appeared no different from any other as Marcus and Victoria wandered through it. The corridors were broad, and there were few doorways.

"About 60 per cent is sealed off," Marcus datavised. "This must be a major engineering level."

"Yeah. There's so many cables around here I'm having trouble cataloguing the grid." She was wiping a magnetic sensor block slowly from side to side as they walked.

His communication block reported it was receiving an encrypted signal from the *Lady Mac*. Sheer surprise made him halt. He retrieved the appropriate code file from a neural nanonics memory cell.

"Captain?"

"What's the problem, Katherine?"

"You've got to get back to the ship. Now, Captain, and make sure Victoria doesn't come with you."

"Why?"

"Captain, this is Karl. The array satellites are looking for pitchblende, not gold or platinum. Antonio's people are terrorists, they want to build fission bombs."

Marcus focused his collar sensors on Victoria, who was waiting a couple of metres down the corridor. "Where's Schutz and Wai?"

"On their way back," Katherine datavised. "They should be here in another five minutes."

"Okay, it's going to take me at least half an hour to get back." He didn't like to think about climbing 14 flights of stairs fast, not in this gravity. "Start prepping the ship."

"Captain, Karl thinks they're probably armed."

Marcus's communication block reported another signal coming on line.

"Karl is quite right," Jorge datavised. "We are indeed armed; and we also have excellent processor blocks and decryption programmes. Really, Captain, this code of yours is at least three years out of date."

Marcus saw Victoria turn towards him. "Care to comment on the pitchblende?" he asked.

"I admit, the material would have been of some considerable use to us," Jorge replied. "But of course, this wreck has changed the Confederation beyond recognition, has it not, Captain?"

"Possibly."

"Definitely. And so we no longer require the pitchblende."

"That's a very drastic switch of allegiance."

"Please, Captain, do not be facetious. The satellites were left on purely for your benefit; we didn't wish to alarm you."

"Thank you for your consideration."

"Captain," Katherine datavised. "Schutz and Wai are in the airlock."

"I do hope you're not proposing to leave without us," Jorge datavised. "That would be most unwise."

"You were going to kill us," Karl datavised.

"That is a hysterical claim. You would not have been hurt."

"As long as we obeyed, and helped you slaughter thousands of people."

Marcus wished Karl would stop being quite so blunt. He had few enough options as it was.

"Come now, Captain," Jorge said. "The *Lady Macbeth* is combat-capable; are you telling me you have never killed people in political disputes?"

"We've fought. But only against other ships."

"Don't try and claim the moral high ground, Captain. War is war, no matter how it is fought."

"Only when it's between soldiers; anything else is terrorism."

"I assure you, we have put our old allegiance behind us. I ask you to do the same. This quarrel is foolish in the extreme. We both have so much to gain."

And you're armed, Marcus filled in silently. Jorge and Antonio were supposed to be inspecting decks 12 and 13. It would be tough if not impossible getting back to the airlock before them. But I can't trust them on *Lady Mac.*

"Captain, they're moving," Katherine datavised. "The communication block in stairwell three has acquired them, strength one. They must be coming up."

"Victoria," Jorge datavised. "Restrain the captain and bring him to the airlock. I advise all of you on the ship to remain calm, we can still find a peaceful solution to this situation."

Unarmed combat programmes went primary in Marcus's neural nanonics. The black, featureless figure opposite him didn't move.

"Your call," he datavised. According to his tactical analysis programme she had few choices. Jorge's order implied she was armed, though a scan of her utility belt didn't reveal anything obvious other than a standard fission blade. If she went for a gun he would have an attack window. If she didn't, then he could probably stay ahead of her. She was a lot younger, but his geneered physique should be able to match her in this gravity field.

Victoria dropped the sensor block she was carrying, and moved her hand to her belt. She grabbed the multipurpose power tool and started to bring it up.

Marcus slammed into her, using his greater mass to throw her off balance. She was hampered by trying to keep her grip on the tool. His impact made her sway sideways, then the fierce xenoc gravity took over. She toppled helplessly, falling *fast.* The power tool was swinging round to point at him. Marcus kicked her hand, and the unit skittered away. It didn't slide far, the gravity saw to that.

Victoria landed with a terrible thud. Her neural nanonics medical monitor programme flashed up an alert that the impact had broken her collar bone. Axon blocks came on line, muting all but the briefest pulse of pain. It was her programmes again which made her twist round to avoid any follow-on blow, her conscious mind was almost unaware of the fact she was still moving. A hand scrabbled for the power tool. She snatched it and sat up. Marcus was disappearing down a side corridor. She fired at him before the targeting programme even gave her an overlay grid.

"Jorge," she datavised. "I've lost him."

"Then get after him."

Marcus's collar sensors showed him a spray of incendiary droplets fizzing out of the wall barely a metre behind him. The multipurpose tool must be some kind of laser pistol. "Katherine," he datavised. "Retract *Lady Mac*'s airlock tube. Now. Close the outer hatch and codelock it. They are not to come on board."

"Acknowledged. How do we get you back?"

"Yes, Captain," Jorge datavised. "Do tell."

Marcus dodged down a junction. "Have Wai stand by. When I need her, I'll need her fast."

"You think you can cut your way out of the shell, Captain? You have a fission blade, and that shell is held together by a molecular bonding generator."

"You touch him, shithead, and we'll fry that wreck," Karl datavised. "*Lady Mac*'s got maser cannons."

"But do you have the command codes, I wonder. Captain?"

"Communication silence," Marcus ordered. "When I want you, I'll call."

Jorge's boosted muscles allowed him to ascend stairwell three at a speed which Antonio could never match. He was soon left struggling along behind. The airlock was the tactical high ground, once he had secured that, Jorge knew he'd won. As he climbed his hands moved automatically, assembling the weapon from various innocuous-looking pieces of equipment he was carrying on his utility belt.

"Victoria?" he datavised. "Have you got him?"

"No. He broke my shoulder, the bastard. I've lost him."

"Go to the nearest stairwell, I expect that's what he's done. Antonio, go back and meet her. Then start searching for him."

"Is that a joke?" Antonio asked. "He could be anywhere."

"No he's not. He has to come up. Up is where the airlock is."

"Yes, but—"

"Don't argue. And when you find him, don't kill him. We have to have him alive. He's our ticket out. Our only ticket, understand?"

"Yes, Jorge."

When he reached the airlock, Jorge closed the inner hatch and cycled the chamber. The outer hatch dilated to show him the *Lady Macbeth*'s fuselage 15 metres away. Her airlock tube had retracted, and the fuselage shield was in place.

"This is a no-win stand-off," he datavised. "Captain, please come up to the airlock. You have to deal with me, you have no choice. The three of us will leave our weapons over here, and then we can all go back on board together. And when we return to a port none of us will mention this unfortunate incident again. That is reasonable, surely?"

Schutz had just reached the bridge when they received Jorge's datavise.

"Damn! He's disconnected our cable from the communication block," Karl said. "We can't call the captain now even if we wanted to."

Schutz rolled in midair above his acceleration couch and landed gently on the cushioning. Restraint webbing slithered over him.

"What the hell do we do now?" Roman asked. "Without the command codes we're bloody helpless."

"It wouldn't take that long for us to break open the weapons cabinet," Schutz said. "They haven't got the captain. We can go over there and hunt them down with the carbines."

"I can't sanction that," Katherine said. "God knows what sort of weapons they have."

"Sanction it? We put it to the vote."

"It's my duty watch. Nobody votes on anything. The last order the captain gave us was to wait. We wait." She datavised the flight computer for a channel to the MSV. "Wai, status please?"

"Powering up. I'll be ready for a flight in two minutes."

"Thank you."

"We have to do something!" Karl said.

"For a start you can calm down," Katherine told him. "We're not going to help Marcus by doing anything rash. He obviously had something in mind when he told Wai to get ready."

The hatchway to the captain's cabin slid open. Marcus air-swam out and grinned round at their stupefied expressions. "Actually, I didn't have any idea what to do when I said that. I was stalling."

"How the hell did you get back on board?" Roman yelped.

Marcus looked at Katherine and gave her a lopsided smile. "By being right, I'm afraid. The dish is a distress beacon."

"So what?" she whispered numbly.

He drifted over to his acceleration couch and activated the webbing. "It means the wormhole doesn't go back to the xenoc homeworld."

"You found out how to use it!" Karl exclaimed. "You opened its other end inside the *Lady Mac*."

"No. There is no other end. Yes, they built it as part of their survival operation. It was their escape route, you were right about that. But it doesn't go somewhere; it goes some*when*."

Instinct had brought Marcus to the portal chamber. It was as good as any other part of the ship. Besides, the xenocs had escaped their predicament from here. In a remote part of his mind he assumed that ending up on their homeworld was preferable to capture here by Jorge. It wasn't the kind of choice he wanted to make.

He walked slowly round the portal. The pale violet emanation in the air around it remained constant, hazing the dull surface from perfect observation. That and a faint hum were the only evidence of the massive quantity of power it consumed. Its eternal stability a mocking enigma.

Despite all the logic of argument he knew Katherine was wrong. Why build the dish if you had this ability? And why keep it operational?

That factor must have been important to them. It had been built in the centre of the ship, and built to last. They'd even reconfigured the wreck to ensure it lasted. Fine, they needed reliability, and they were masters of material science. But a one-off piece of emergency equipment lasting 13,000 years? There must be a reason, and the only logical one was that they knew they would need it to remain functional so they could come back one day.

The SII suit prevented him from smiling as realization dawned. But it did reveal a shiver ripple along his limbs as the cold wonder of the knowledge struck home.

On the *Lady Mac*'s bridge, Marcus said: "We originally assumed that the xenocs would just go into zero-tau and wait for a rescue ship; because that's what we would do. But their technology allows them to take a much different approach to engineering problems."

"The wormhole leads into the future," Roman said in astonishment.

"Almost. It doesn't lead anywhere but back to itself, so the length inside it represents time not space. As long as the portal exists you can travel through it. The xenocs went in just after they built the dish and came out again when their rescue ship arrived. That's why they built the portal to survive so long. It had to carry them through a great deal of time."

"How does that help you get here?" Katherine asked. "You're trapped over in the xenoc wreckage right now, not in the past."

"The wormhole exists as long as the portal does. It's an open tube to every second of that entire period of existence, you're not restricted which way you travel through it."

In the portal chamber Marcus approached one of the curving black buttress legs. The artificial gravity was off directly underneath the doughnut so the xenocs could rise into it. But they had been intent on travelling into the future.

He started to climb the buttress. The first section was the steepest; he had to clamp his hands behind it, and haul himself up. Not easy in that gravity field. It gradually curved over, flattening out at the top, leaving him standing above the doughnut. He balanced there precariously, very aware of the potentially lethal fall down onto the floor.

The doughnut didn't look any different from this position, a glowing ring surrounding the grey pressure membrane. Marcus put one foot over the edge of the exotic matter, and jumped.

He fell clean through the pressure membrane. There was no gravity field in the wormhole, although every movement suddenly became very sluggish. To his waving limbs it felt as if he was immersed in some kind of fluid, though his sensor block reported a perfect vacuum.

The wormhole wall was insubstantial, difficult to see in the meagre backscatter of light from the pressure membrane. Five narrow lines of yellow light materialized, spaced equidistantly around the wall. They stretched from the rim of the pressure membrane up to a vanishing point some indefinable distance away.

Nothing else happened. Marcus drifted until he reached the wall, which his hand adhered to as though the entire surface was one giant stikpad. He crawled his way back to the pressure membrane. When he stuck his hand through, there was no resistance. He pushed his head out.

There was no visible difference to the chamber outside. He datavised his communication block to search for a signal. It told him there was only the band from one of the relay blocks in the stairwells. No time had passed.

He withdrew back into the wormhole. Surely the xenocs hadn't expected to crawl along the entire length? In any case, the other end would be 13,000 years ago. Marcus retrieved the xenoc activation code from his neural nanonics, and datavised it.

The lines of light turned blue.

He quickly datavised the deactivation code, and the lines reverted to yellow. This time when he emerged out into the portal chamber there was no signal at all.

"That was ten hours ago," Marcus told his crew. "I climbed out and walked back to the ship. I passed you on the way, Karl."

"Holy shit," Roman muttered. "A time machine."

"How long was the wormhole active for?" Katherine asked.

"A couple of seconds, that's all."

"Ten hours in two seconds." She paused, loading sums into her neural nanonics. "That's a year in 30 minutes. Actually, that's not so fast. Not if they were intending to travel a couple of thousand years into the future."

"You're complaining about it?" Roman asked.

"Maybe it speeds up the further you go through it," Schutz suggested. "Or more likely we need the correct access codes to vary its speed."

"Whatever," Marcus said. He datavised the flight computer and blew the tether bolts which were holding *Lady Mac* to the wreckage. "I want flight readiness status, people, please."

"What about Jorge and the others?" Karl asked.

"They only come back on board under our terms." Marcus said. "No weapons, and they go straight into zero-tau. We can hand them over to Tranquillity's serjeants as soon as we get home." Purple course vectors were rising into his mind. He fired the manoeuvring thrusters, easing *Lady Mac* clear of the xenoc shell.

Jorge saw the sparkle of bright dust as the explosive bolts fired. He scanned his sensor collar round until he found the tethers, narrow grey serpents flexing against the speckled backdrop of drab orange particles. It didn't bother him unduly. Then the small thrusters ringing the starship's equator fired, pouring out translucent amber plumes of gas.

"Katherine, what do you think you're doing?" he datavised.

"Following my orders," Marcus replied. "She's helping to prep the ship for a jump. Is that a problem for you?"

Jorge watched the starship receding, an absurdly stately movement for an artifact that big. His respirator tube seemed to have stopped supplying fresh oxygen, paralysing every muscle. "Calvert. How?" he managed to datavise.

"I might tell you some time. Right now, there are a lot of conditions you have to agree to before I allow you back on board."

Pure fury at being so completely outmanoeuvred by Calvert made him reach automatically for his weapon. "You will come back now," he datavised.

"You're not in any position to dictate terms."

Lady Macbeth was a good 200 metres away. Jorge lined the stubby barrel up on the rear of the starship. A green targeting grid flipped up over the image, and he zeroed on the nozzle of a fusion drive tube. He datavised the X-ray laser to fire. Pale white vapour spewed out of the nozzle.

"Depressurization in fusion drive three," Roman shouted.

"The lower deflector coil casing is breached. He shot us, Marcus, Jesus Christ, he shot us with an X-ray."

"What the hell kind of weapon has he got back there?" Karl demanded.

"Whatever it is, he can't have the power capacity for many more shots," Schutz said.

"Give me fire control for the maser cannons," Roman said. "I'll blast the little shit."

"Marcus!" Katherine cried. "He just hit a patterning node. Stop him."

Neuroiconic displays zipped through Marcus's mind. Ship's systems coming on line as they shifted over to full operational status, each with its own schematic. He knew just about every performance parameter by heart. Combat sensor clusters were already sliding out of their recesses. Maser cannons powering up. It would be another seven seconds before they could be aimed and fired.

There was one system with a faster response time.

"Hang on," he yelled.

Designed for combat avoidance manoeuvres, the fusion drive tubes exploded into life two seconds after he triggered their ignition sequence. Twin spears of solar-bright plasma transfixed the xenoc shell, burning through deck after deck. They didn't even strike anywhere near the airlock which Jorge was cloistered in. They didn't have to. At that range, their infrared emission alone was enough to break down his SII suit's integrity.

Superenergized ions hammered into the wreck, smashing the internal structure apart, heating the atmosphere to an intolerable pressure. Xenoc machinery detonated in tremendous energy bursts all through the structure, the units expending themselves in spherical clouds of solid light which clashed and merged into a single wavefront of destruction. The giant rock particle lurched wildly from the explosion. Drenched in a cascade of hard radiation and subatomic particles, the unicorn tower at the centre of the dish snapped off at its base to tumble away into the darkness.

Then the process seemed to reverse. The spume of light blossoming from the cliff curved in on itself, growing in brightness as it was compressed back to its point of origin.

Lady Mac's crew were straining under the five gee acceleration of the starship's flight. The inertial guidance systems started to flash priority warnings into Marcus's neural nanonics.

"We're going back," he datavised. Five gees made talking too difficult. "Jesus, five gees and it's still pulling us in." The external sensor suite showed him the contracting fireball, its luminosity surging towards violet. Large sections of the cliff were flaking free and plummeting into the conflagration. Fissures like black lightning bolts split open right across the rock.

He ordered the flight computer to power up the nodes and retract the last sensor clusters.

"Marcus, we can't jump," Katherine datavised, her face pummelled into frantic creases by the acceleration. "It's a gravitonic emission. Don't."

"Have some faith in the old girl." He initiated the jump.

An event horizon eclipsed the *Lady Macbeth's* fuselage.

Behind her, the wormhole at the heart of the newborn micro-star gradually collapsed, pulling in its gravitational field as it went. Soon there was nothing left but an expanding cloud of dark snowdust embers.

They were three jumps away from Tranquillity when Katherine ventured into Marcus's cabin. *Lady Mac* was accelerating at a tenth of a gee towards her next jump coordinate, holding him lightly in one of the large blackfoam sculpture chairs. It was the first time she'd ever really noticed his age.

"I came to say sorry," she said. "I shouldn't have doubted."

He waved limply. "*Lady Mac* was built for combat, her nodes are powerful enough to jump us out of some gravity fields. Not that I had a lot of choice. Still, we only reduced three nodes to slag, plus the one dear old Jorge damaged."

"She's a hell of ship, and you're the perfect captain for her. I'll keep flying with you, Marcus."

"Thanks. But I'm not sure what I'm going to do after we dock. Replacing three nodes will cost a fortune. I'll be in debt to the banks again."

She pointed at the row of transparent bubbles which all held identical antique electronic circuit boards. "You can always sell some more Apollo command module guidance computers."

"I think that scam's just about run its course. Don't worry, when we get back to Tranquillity I know a captain who'll buy them from me. At least that way I'll be able to settle the flight pay I owe all of you."

"For Heaven's sake, Marcus, the whole astronautics industry is in debt to the banks. I swear I never could understand the economics behind starflight."

He closed his eyes, a wry smile quirking his lips. "We very nearly solved human economics for good, didn't we?"

"Yeah. Very nearly."

"The wormhole would have let me change the past. Their technology was going to change the future. We could have rebuilt our entire history."

"I don't think that's a very good idea. What about the grandfather paradox for a start? How come you didn't warn us about Jorge as soon as you emerged from the wormhole?"

"Scared, I guess. I don't know nearly enough about quantum temporal displacement theory to start risking paradoxes. I'm not even sure I'm the Marcus Calvert that brought this particular *Lady Macbeth* to the xenoc wreck. Suppose you really can't travel between times, only parallel realities? That would mean I didn't escape into the past, I just shifted sideways."

"You look and sound pretty familiar to me."

"So do you. But is my crew still stuck back at their version of the wreck waiting for me to deal with Jorge?"

"Stop it," she said softly. "You're Marcus Calvert, and you're back where you belong, flying *Lady Mac*."

"Yeah, sure."

"The xenocs wouldn't have built the wormhole unless they were sure it would help them get home, their true home. They were smart people."

"And no mistake."

"I wonder where they did come from?"

"We'll never know, now." Marcus lifted his head, some of the old humour emerging through his melancholia. "But I hope they got back safe."

DAVID WEBER

David Weber [1952–] (www.davidweber.net) lives in South Carolina. His short biography states: "David Mark Weber is a member of SFWA, the American Small Business Association, and the National Rifle Association. His hobbies include military history, military wargaming, RPG gaming, miniatures painting, and pistol and rifle marksmanship." So we asked him for more detailed background: "I began writing advertising copy when I was still about fifteen. . . . After high school, I supported myself as a copywriter, typesetter (I'm one of the last trained Linotype operators on the face of the planet, I feel pretty sure), proofreader, and occasional paste-up artist." He attended two colleges, got an undergraduate degree in history, and completed an MA in history before ending his academic career and going home to take over his mother's advertising agency. "I wasn't a very comfortable fit for the political and ideological landscape of the late 1970s college campuses," he says.

"I was also doing a little bit of war game design, on the side, and in the mid-1980s, Steve White and I started exchanging short stories set in the StarFire gaming universe . . . we realized that what we actually had was the makings of a novel, although neither of us had been thinking in that direction when we began. We kept going, and we wound up with a final word count of around 280,000 words." It finally sold, after much cutting, to Baen books in 1989. Shortly thereafter Baen bought seven more novels.

So starting in 1990, all of his fantasy and science fiction to date has been published by Baen Books. He is prolific, and still often collaborates with other writers. His most recent books include *The Shadow of Saganami* (2004), *We Few* (2005), and *Bolo!* (2005). Baen's promotional line is: "His novels range from epic fantasy (*Oath of Swords, The War God's Own*) to breathtaking space opera (*Path of the Fury, The Armageddon Inheritance*) to military science fiction with in-depth characterization (the celebrated and awesomely popular Honor Harrington novels)." Over the course of a bit more than a decade he has become perhaps the bestselling space opera writer in the US.

The Wikipedia entry on Weber says: "Many of his stories have militaristic, particularly naval, themes, and fit into the Military science fiction genre. He challenges current gender roles in the military by assuming that a gender-neutral military service will exist in his futures. As he often places female leading characters in what have previously been seen as traditionally male roles, he is able to explore the challenges faced by women in the military and politics. His most enduring character is Honor Harrington, whose story, together with the 'Honorverse' she populates, has been developed in thirteen novels, and four shared-universe anthologies."

Weber says, "It seems evident that if we're on the right track in terms of not simply gender equality, but human equality, then by the time we get five hundred years, or a thousand years into the future, it's going to be a done deal." And he continues, "Even Western nations have different gradations of gender equality; when you get outside Western nations, the notion of gender equality tends to become a matter of lip service, and goes downhill from there. Near-future science fiction is an extraordinarily apt tool for dealing with those issues, but far-future science fiction, I think, serves best by presenting the struggle for equality as one which has been won as it manifestly and obviously deserves to be won. That's what the Honorverse does."

Honor Harrington is a young woman who rises through the ranks in the Manticorean space navy as the series progresses. She is very reminiscent of Robert A. Heinlein's perky, bright, courageous female characters. She has an intelligent alien partner and symbiote, a six-legged treecat, who is always with her, perched on her shoulder, who can understand human speech but not speak. Nimitz, the treecat, can sense human emotions and transmit them to Honor, making it impossible for anyone to lie to her. The Harrington series is based on C. S. Forester's Horatio Hornblower series, set in the British Royal Navy in the late eighteenth and early nineteenth centuries. There is a tendency to spend pages describing ship maneuvers and tactics, sometimes to the detriment of story pacing, but many of Weber's fans apparently find it an attraction.

"From the very beginning," he says, "I had more in mind than simply a series of isolated adventures centered around my heroine. The Honor Harrington novels are, indeed, about Honor. They're also, however, an effort to tell the story of an entire war, from the perspectives of *all* of the participants in it. And it's given me an opportunity which I believe is rare in what is, after all, largely an escapist genre, in that it's let me examine some fairly serious concepts. I believe that writers of military fiction, in particular, have a responsibility to avoid sanitizing violence and trivializing the issues—and, especially, the consequences—of military conflict. One of the easiest ways to trivialize is to oversimplify. Another is to dehumanize one's opponents. I've tried to avoid doing that in the Honorverse."

One of his fans, Sheldon Brown, characterizes Weber's politics on his Web site (www.sheldonbrown.org/honorharrington.html): "Manticore is laissez-faire capitalism making everybody prosperous. Haven is a welfare state where 75 percent of the population is on the dole. The Haven state provides bread and circuses, but since the 'Dolists' are non-productive, the only way they can keep the economy afloat is by conquering, looting and absorbing more productive but less well-armed neighbors." This is, in other words, the kind of space opera that many UK readers love to hate, for its focus on the military and for its right-wing politics. As we said, though it appears to be the bestselling space opera in the US at present, it is rarely reviewed or discussed in depth. The SF critical establishment in the US at present doesn't like the military fiction or Weber's politics any better than the Brits. It is, however, extremely popular and influential in the marketplace.

Weber says, "At the moment, I'm visualizing at least another fifteen books or so in the Honorverse. Things are occurring in the latest two or three books which are going to send Honor and her friends—and many of her present enemies—up against new, and in most ways much more dangerous, adversaries. I think that the changes in direction will help me stay fresh and engaged."

MS. MIDSHIPWOMAN HARRINGTON

DAVID WEBER

"That looks like your snotty, Senior Chief."

The Marine sentry's low-pitched voice exuded an oddly gleeful sympathy. It was the sort of voice in which a Marine traditionally informed one of the Navy's "vacuum-suckers" that his trousers had just caught fire or something equally exhilarating, and Senior Chief Petty Officer Roland Shelton ignored the jarhead's tone with the lofty disdain of any superior life form for an evolutionary inferior. Yet it was a bit harder than usual this time as his eyes followed the corporal's almost invisible nod and picked the indicated target out of the crowded space dock gallery. She was certainly *someone's* snotty, he acknowledged without apparently so much as looking in her direction. Her midshipwoman's uniform was immaculate, but both it and the tethered counter-grav locker towing behind her were so new he expected to hear her squeak. There was something odd about that locker, too, as if something else half its size had been piggybacked onto it, although he paid that little attention. Midshipmen were always turning up with oddball bits and pieces of personalized gear that they hoped didn't quite violate Regs. Half the time they were wrong, but there would be time enough to straighten that out later if this particular snotty came aboard Shelton's ship. And, he conceded, she seemed to be headed for *War Maiden's* docking tube, although that might simply be a mistake on her part.

He hoped.

She was a tall young woman, taller than Shelton himself, with dark brown, fuzz-cut hair, and a severe, triangular face which seemed to have been assembled solely from a nose which might charitably be called "strong" and huge, almond-shaped eyes. At the moment the face as a whole showed no expression at all, but the light in those eyes was bright enough to make an experienced petty officer groan in resignation.

She also looked to be about thirteen years old. That probably meant she was a third-generation prolong recipient, but recognizing the cause didn't do a thing to make her look any more mature. Still, she moved well, he admitted almost grudgingly. There was an athletic grace to her carriage and an apparent assurance at odds with her youth, and she avoided collisions with ease as she made her way through the people filling the gallery, almost as if she were performing some sort of free-form dance.

Had that been all Shelton had been able to discern about her, he would probably have put her down (provisionally and a bit hopefully) as somewhat above the average of the young gentlemen and ladies senior Navy noncoms were expected to transform from pigs' ears into silk purses. Unfortunately, it was not all that he could discern, and it took most of his thirty-four T-years of experience not to let his dismay show as he observed the prick-eared, wide-whiskered, six-limbed, silky-pelted Sphinx treecat riding on her shoulder.

A treecat. A treecat in *his* ship. And in the midshipmen's compartment, at that. The thought was enough to give a man who believed in orderly procedures and Navy traditions hives, and Shelton felt a strong urge to reach out and throttle the expressionlessly smirking Marine at his shoulder.

For a few more seconds he allowed himself to hope that she might walk right past *War Maiden* to the ship she actually sought, or that she might be lost. But any possibility of dodging the pulser dart faded as she walked straight over to the heavy cruiser's tube.

Shelton and the Marine saluted, and she returned the courtesy with a crispness which managed to be both brand new and excited yet curiously mature. She gave Shelton a brief, measuring glance, almost more imagined than seen, but addressed herself solely to the sentry.

"Midshipwoman Harrington to join the ship's company, Corporal," she said in a crisp Sphinx accent, and drew a record chip in an official Navy cover slip from her tunic pocket and extended it. Her soprano was surprisingly soft and sweet for someone her height, Shelton noted as the Marine took the chip and slotted it into his memo board, although her tone was neither hesitant nor shy. Still, he had to wonder if someone who sounded as young as she looked would ever be able to generate a proper snap of command. He allowed no sign of his thoughts to cross his face, but the 'cat on her shoulder cocked its head, gazing at him with bright, grass-green eyes while its whiskers twitched.

"Yes, Ma'am," the Marine said as the chip's data matched that in his memo board and confirmed Ms. Midshipwoman Harrington's orders and legal right to come aboard *War Maiden*. He popped the chip free and handed it back to her, then nodded to Shelton. "Senior Chief Shelton's been expecting you, I believe," he said, still with that irritating edge of imperfectly concealed glee, and Harrington turned to the senior chief and arched one eyebrow.

That surprised Shelton just a bit. However composed she might appear, he'd seen thirty-plus T-years of new-penny snotties reporting for their midshipman cruises, and the light in her eyes was proof enough that she was just as excited and eager as any of the others had been. Yet that arched eyebrow held a cool authority, or perhaps assurance. It wasn't the sort of deliberately projected superiority some snotties used to hide their own anxiety or lack of confidence. It was too natural for that. But that calm, silent question, delivered with neither condescension nor defensiveness, woke a sudden glimmer of hope. There might be some solid metal in this one, the senior chief told himself, but then the 'cat wiggled its whiskers at him, and he gave himself a mental shake.

"Senior Chief Petty Officer Shelton, Ma'am," he heard himself say. "If you'll just follow me, I'll escort you to the Exec."

"Thank you, Senior Chief," she said and followed him into the tube.

With the 'cat.

Honor Harrington tried conscientiously to keep her excitement from showing as she swam the boarding tube behind Senior Chief Shelton, but it was hard. She'd known she was headed for this moment for almost half her life, and she'd sweated and worked for over three-and-a-half endless T-years at Saganami Island to reach it. Now she had, and the butterflies in her midsection propagated like particularly energetic yeast as they reached the inboard end of the tube and she caught the grab bar and swung herself through into the heavy cruiser's internal gravity behind Shelton. In her own mind, that was the symbolic moment when she left His Majesty's Space Station

Hephaestus to enter the domain of HMS *War Maiden*, and her heart beat harder and stronger as the sights and sounds and distinctive smell of a King's starship closed about her. They were subtly different somehow from those in the space station she'd left behind. No doubt that was her imagination—one artificial environment in space was very like another, after all—but the impression of differentness, of something special waiting just for her, quivered at her core.

The treecat on her shoulder made a soft scolding sound, and her mouth quirked ever so slightly. Nimitz understood her excited joy, as well as the unavoidable trepidation that went with it, but the empathic 'cats were pragmatic souls, and he recognized the signs of Honor Harrington in exhilarated mode. More to the point, he knew the importance of getting off on the right foot aboard *War Maiden*, and she felt his claws dig just a bit deeper into her uniform tunic's specially padded shoulder in a gentle reminder to keep herself focused.

She reached up and brushed his ears in acknowledgment even as her feet found the deck of *War Maiden*'s boat bay, just outside the painted line which indicated the official separation between ship and space station. At least she hadn't embarrassed herself like one of her classmates, who had landed on the wrong side of the line during one of their short, near-space training missions! A part of her wanted to giggle in memory of the absolutely scathing look the training ship's boat bay officer of the deck had bestowed upon her fellow middy, but she suppressed the temptation and came quickly to attention and saluted the OD of *this* boat bay.

"Permission to come aboard to join the ship's company, Ma'am!" she said, and the sandy-haired ensign gave her a cool, considering look, then acknowledged the salute. She brought her hand down from her beret's brim and extended it wordlessly, and Honor produced the chip of her orders once more. The BOD performed the same ritual as the Marine sentry, then nodded, popped the chip from her board, and handed it back.

"Permission granted, Ms. Harrington," she said, much less crisply than Honor but with a certain world-weary maturity. She was, after all, at least a T-year older than Honor, with her own middy cruise safely behind her. The ensign glanced at Shelton, and Honor noticed the way the other young woman's shoulders came back ever so slightly and the way her voice crisped up as she nodded to the SCPO. "Carry on, Senior Chief," she said.

"Aye, aye, Ma'am," Shelton replied, and beckoned respectfully for Honor to follow him once more as he led her towards the lifts.

Lieutenant Commander Abner Layson sat in the chair behind his desk and made an obviously careful study of his newest potential headache's orders. Midshipwoman Harrington sat very upright in her own chair, hands folded in her lap, feet positioned at precisely the right angle, and watched the bulkhead fifteen centimeters above his head with apparent composure. She'd seemed on the edge of flustered when he'd directed her to sit rather than remain at stand-easy while he perused her paperwork, but there was little sign of that in her present demeanor. Unless, of course, the steady flicking of the very tip of her treecat's tail indicated more uneasiness in the cat's adopted person than she cared to admit. Interesting that she could conceal the outward signs so readily, though, if that were the case.

He let his eyes return to his reader's display, scanning the official, tersely worded contents of her personnel jacket, while he wondered what had possessed Captain Bachfisch to specifically request such an . . . unlikely prize when the snotty cruise assignments were being handed out.

A bit young, he thought. Although her third-gen prolong made her look even younger than her calendar age, she was only twenty. The Academy was flexible about admission ages, but most midshipmen entered at around eighteen or nineteen T-years of age; Harrington had been barely seventeen when she was admitted. Which was all the more surprising given what seemed to be a total lack of aristocratic connections, patronage, or interest from on high to account for it. On the other hand, her overall grades at Saganami Island had been excellent—aside from some abysmal math scores, at least—and she'd received an unbroken string of "Excellent" and "Superior" ratings from her tactical and command simulation instructors. That was worth noting. Still, he reminded himself, many an Academy overachiever had proven a sad disappointment in actual Fleet service. Scored remarkably high on the kinesthesia tests, too, although that particular requirement was becoming less and less relevant these days. Very high marks in the flight training curriculum as well, including—his eyebrows rose ever so slightly—a new Academy sailplane record. But she might be a bit on the headstrong side, maybe even the careless one, given the official reprimand noted on her Form 107FT for ignoring her flight instruments. And that stack of black marks for lack of air discipline didn't look very promising. On the other hand, they all seemed to come from a single instance. . . .

He accessed the relevant portion of her record, and something suspiciously like a snort escaped before he could throttle it. He turned it into a reasonably convincing coughing fit, but his mouth quivered as he scanned the appended note. Buzzed the Commandant's boat during the Regatta, had she? No wonder Hartley had lowered the boom on her! Still, he must have thought well of her to stop there, although the identity of her partner in crime might also have had a bit to do with it. Couldn't exactly go tossing the King's niece out, now could they? Well, not for anything short of premeditated murder, at any rate. . . .

He sighed and tipped back his chair, pinching the bridge of his nose, and glanced at her under cover of his hand. The treecat worried him. He knew it wasn't supposed to, for regulations were uncompromising on that particular subject and had been ever since the reign of Queen Adrienne. She could not legally be separated from the creature, and she'd obviously gotten through the Academy with it without creating any major waves. But a starship was a much smaller world than Saganami Island, and she wasn't the only middy aboard.

Small jealousies and envies could get out of hand on a long deployment, and she would be the only person on board authorized to take a pet with her. Oh, Layson knew the 'cats weren't really pets. It wasn't a subject he'd ever taken much personal interest in, but the creatures' sentience was well-established, as was the fact that once they empathically bonded to a human, they literally could not be separated without serious consequences for both partners. But they *looked* like pets, and most of the Star Kingdom's citizens knew even less about them than Layson did, which offered fertile ground for misunderstandings and resentment. And the fact that the Bureau of Personnel had seen fit to assign *War Maiden* a brand new assistant tac officer, and that the ATO in any ship was traditionally assigned responsibility for the training and discipline of any midshipmen assigned to her, only deepened his worries about the possible repercussions of the 'cats presence. The exec hadn't yet had time to learn much about the ATO, but what he had learned so far did not inspire him with a lively confidence in the man's ability.

Yet even the presence of the 'cat was secondary to Layson's true concern. There had to be some reason the Captain had requested Harrington, and try though he might, the exec simply couldn't figure out what that reason might be. Such requests usually represented tokens in the patronage game the Navy's senior officers played so assiduously. They were either a way to gain the support of some well-placed potential patron by standing sponsor to a son or daughter or younger relative, or else a way to pay back a similar favor. But Harrington was a yeoman's daughter, whose only apparent aristocratic association was the highly tenuous one of having roomed with the

Earl of Gold Peak's younger offspring for a bit over two T-years. That was a fairly lofty connection, or would have been if it actually existed, but Layson couldn't see any way the Captain could have capitalized on it even if it had. So what could the reason be? Layson didn't know, and that bothered him, because it was a good executive officer's job to keep himself informed of anything which might affect the smooth functioning of the ship he ran for his captain.

"Everything seems to be in order, Ms. Harrington," he told her after a moment, lowering his hand and letting his chair come back upright. "Lieutenant Santino is our assistant tac officer, which makes him your OCT officer, as well. I'll have Senior Chief Shelton deliver you to Snotty Row when we're done here, and you can report to him once you've stowed your gear. In the meantime, however, I make it a policy to spend a few minutes with new middies when they first come aboard. It gives me a chance to get to know them and to get a feel for how they'll fit in here in *War Maiden*."

He paused, and she nodded respectfully.

"Perhaps you can start off then by telling me—briefly, of course—just why you joined the Service," he invited.

"For several reasons, Sir," she said after only the briefest of pauses. "My father was a Navy doctor before he retired and went into private practice, so I was a 'Navy brat' until I was about eleven. And I've always been interested in naval history, clear back to pre-Diaspora Earth. But I suppose the most important reason was the People's Republic, Sir."

"Indeed?" Layson couldn't quite keep the surprise out of his tone.

"Yes, Sir." Her voice was both respectful and thoughtful, but it was also very serious. "I believe war with Haven is inevitable, Sir. Not immediately, but in time."

"And you want to be along for the glory and the adventure, do you?"

"No, Sir." Her expression didn't alter, despite the bite in his question. "I want to help defend the Star Kingdom. And I *don't* want to live under the Peeps."

"I see," he said, and studied her for several more seconds. That was a viewpoint he was more accustomed to hearing from far more senior—and older—officers, not from twenty-year-old midshipwomen. It was also the reason the Royal Manticoran Navy was currently involved in the biggest buildup in its history, and the main reason Harrington's graduating class was ten percent larger than the one before it. But as Harrington had just pointed out, the looming war still lurked in the uncertain future.

And her answer *still* didn't give him a clue as to why Captain Bachfisch wanted her aboard *War Maiden*.

"Well, Ms. Harrington," he said at last, "if you want to help defend the Star Kingdom, you've certainly come to the right place. And you may have an opportunity to start doing it a bit sooner than you anticipated, as well, because we've been ordered to Silesia for antipiracy duties." The young woman sat even straighter in her chair at that, and the 'cat's tail stopped twitching and froze in the curl of a question mark. "But if you truly don't harbor dreams of glory, make it a point not to start harboring them anytime soon. As you're no doubt tired of hearing, this cruise is your true final exam."

He paused, regarding her steadily, and she nodded soberly. A midshipwoman was neither fish nor fowl in many respects. Officially, she remained an officer candidate, holding a midshipwoman's warrant but not yet an officer's commission. Her warrant gave her a temporary place in the chain of command aboard *War Maiden*; it did not guarantee that she would ever hold any authority anywhere *after* this cruise, however. Her actual graduation from the Academy was assured, given her grades and academic performance, but a muffed midshipman's cruise could very well cost her any chance at one of the career tracks which led to eventual command. The Navy always needed non-line staff officers whose duties kept them safely out of the chain of command, after all, and someone who blew his or her first opportunity to shoulder responsibility outside a classroom wasn't the person one wanted commanding a King's ship. And if she screwed up too massively on this cruise, she might receive both an Academy diploma and formal notice that the Crown did not after all require her services in *any* capacity.

"You're here to learn, and the Captain and I will evaluate your performance very carefully. If you have any hope of achieving command in your own right someday, I advise you to see to it that our evaluations are positive ones. Is that understood?"

"Yes, Sir!"

"Good." He gave her a long, steady look, then produced a small smile. "It's a tradition in the Fleet that by the time a middy has survived Saganami Island, he's like a 'cat. Fling him into the Service any way you like, and he'll land on his feet. That, at least, is the type of midshipman the Academy *tries* to turn out, and it's what will be expected of you as a member of *War Maiden*'s company. In your own case, however, there is a rather special complicating factor. One, I'm certain, of which you must be fully aware. Specifically," he pointed with his chin to the treecat stretched across the top of her chair's back, "your . . . companion."

He paused, waiting to see if she would respond. But she simply met his eyes steadily, and he made a mental note that this one had composure by the bucketful.

"No doubt you're more intimately familiar with the Regs where 'cats aboard ship are concerned than I am," he went on after a moment in a tone which said she'd damned well *better* be familiar with them. "I expect you to observe them to the letter. The fact that the two of you managed to survive Saganami Island gives me some reason to hope you'll also manage to survive *War Maiden*. But I expect you to be aware that this is a much smaller environment than the Academy, and the right to be together aboard ship carries with it the responsibility to avoid any situation which might have a negative impact on the smooth and efficient functioning of this ship's company. I trust that, also, is clearly understood. By you both."

"Yes, Sir," she said once more, and he nodded.

"I am delighted to hear it. In that case, Senior Chief Shelton will see you to your quarters, such as they are. Good luck, Ms. Harrington."

"Thank you, Sir."

"Dismissed," he said, and turned back to his data terminal as the middy braced to attention once more and then followed SCPO Shelton from the compartment.

Honor finished making up her bunk (with regulation "Saganami Island" corners on the sheets and a blanket taut enough to bounce a five-dollar coin), then detached the special piggyback unit from her locker and lifted the locker itself into the waiting bulkhead brackets. She grinned, remembering one of her classmates—from a dirt-grubber Gryphon family with no Navy connections at all—who had revealed his abysmal ignorance the day their first lockers were issued by wondering aloud why every one of them had to have exactly the same dimensions. That particular question had been answered on their first training cruise, and now Honor settled hers in place, opened the door, flipped off the counter-grav, and toggled the locking magnets once its weight had fully settled.

She gave it a precautionary shake, despite the glowing telltales which purported to show a solid seal. Others had trusted the same telltales when they shouldn't have, but this time they held, and she closed the door and attached the piggyback to the frame of her bunk. She took rather more care with it than she had with the locker, and Nimitz watched alertly from atop her pillow as she did so. Unlike the locker, which was standard Navy issue, she—or rather, her father, who had provided it as a graduation gift—had paid the better part of seventeen thousand Manticoran dollars for that unit. Which was money well spent in her opinion, since it was the life support module which would keep Nimitz alive if the compartment lost pressure. She made very certain that it was securely anchored, then hit the self-test key and nodded in satisfaction as the control panel blinked alive and the diagnostic program confirmed full functionality. Nimitz returned her nod with a satisfied bleek of his own, and she turned away to survey the rest of the berthing compartment known rather unromantically as "Snotty Row" while she awaited Senior Chief Shelton's return.

It was a largish compartment for a ship as small and as old—as *War Maiden*. In fact, it was about twice the size of her Saganami Island dorm room. Of course, that dorm room had held only two people, her and her friend Michelle Henke, while this compartment was designed to house six. At the moment, only four of the bunks had sheets and blankets on them, though, so it looked as if *War Maiden* was sailing light in the middy department.

That could be good or bad, she reflected, settling into one of the spartan, unpowered chairs at the berthing compartment's well-worn table. The good news was that it meant she and her three fellows would have a bit more space, but it would also mean there were only four of them to carry the load. Everyone knew that a lot of what any midshipwoman did on her snotty cruise always constituted little more than makework, duties concocted by the ship's officer candidate training officer and assigned only as learning exercises rather than out of any critical need on her ship's part. But a lot more of those duties were anything *but* makework. Middies were King's officers—the lowest of the low, perhaps, and only temporarily and by virtue of warrant, but still officers—and they were expected to pull their weight aboard ship.

She lifted Nimitz into her lap and ran her fingers slowly over his soft, fluffy pelt, smiling at the crackle of static electricity which followed her touch. He bleeked softly and pressed his head against her, luxuriating in her caresses, and she drew a long, slow breath. It was the first time she'd truly relaxed since packing the last of her meager shipboard belongings into her locker that morning on Saganami Island, and the respite was going to be brief.

She closed her eyes and let mental muscles unkink ever so slightly while she replayed her interview with Commander Layson. The exec of any King's ship was a being of at least demigod status, standing at the right hand of the Captain. As such, Layson's actions and attitudes were not to be questioned by a mere midshipwoman. But there'd been something, an edge she hadn't been able to pin down or define, to his questions. She tried once more to tell herself it was only first-day-aboard-ship nerves. He *was* the Exec, and it was an executive officer's job to know everything she could about the officers serving under her, even if the officers in question were mere middies. Yet that curious certainty which came to Honor seldom but was never wrong told her there was more to it than that in this case. And whether there was or not, there was no question at all that he regarded Nimitz's presence aboard *War Maiden* as an at least potential problem. For that matter, Senior Chief Shelton seemed to feel the same way, and Honor sighed.

It wasn't the first time, or the second, or even the twentieth time she'd faced that attitude. As Commander Layson had suggested, she was indeed fully conversant with what Navy regulations had to say about treecats and their adoptees in Fleet service. Most Navy personnel were not, because the situation arose so infrequently. 'Cat-human bonds were vanishingly rare even on Honor's native Sphinx. The six-limbed arboreals were almost never seen off-planet, and they were even more uncommon in the Navy than in civilian life. Honor had done a little discreet research, and as far as she could determine, no more than a dozen or so current active-duty personnel of all ranks, including herself, had been adopted. That number was minute compared to the total number of people in the Navy, so it was hardly surprising that the 'cats created a stir whenever they did turn up.

Understanding the reason for the situation didn't change it, however, and Honor had been made almost painfully well aware that Nimitz's presence was regarded as a potentially disruptive influence by the vast majority of people who were unfamiliar with his species. Even those who knew better intellectually had a tendency to regard 'cats as little more than extremely clever pets, and an unfortunate percentage of humans never bothered to learn differently even when the opportunity presented itself. The fact that 'cats were unable to form anything like the sounds of human speech only exacerbated that particular aspect of the situation, and the fact that they were so cute and cuddly helped hone the occasional case of jealous resentment over their presence.

Of course, no one who had ever seen a treecat roused to fury could possibly confuse "cute and cuddly" with "harmless." Indeed, their formidable natural armament was another reason some people worried about their presence, even though Nimitz would never harm a human being except in direct self-defense. Or in Honor's defense, which he regarded as precisely the same thing. But people who'd never seen their lethality demonstrated had a pronounced tendency to coo over the 'cats and wish that *they* could have such an adorable pet.

From there, it was a short step to resenting someone else who did have one. Honor and Nimitz had been forced to deal with that attitude more than once at the Academy, and only the fact that the Regs were on their side and that Nimitz was a natural (and unscrupulous) diplomat had gotten them past some of the worse incidents.

Well, if they'd done it on Saganami Island they could do it here, as well, she told herself, and—

The compartment hatch opened with no warning, and Honor came quickly to her feet, Nimitz in her arms as she turned to face the unexpected opening. She knew the occupied light above the hatch had been lit, and opening an occupied compartment's hatch without at least sounding the admittance chime first was a gross infraction of shipboard etiquette. It was also at least technically a privacy violation which was prohibited by Regs except in cases of emergency. The sheer unexpectedness of it created an unaccustomed confusion in Honor, and she stood frozen as a beefy senior-grade lieutenant, perhaps seven or eight T-years older than her, loomed in the doorway. He was two or three centimeters shorter than Honor, with a certain florid handsomeness, but something about his eyes woke an instinctive dislike in her. Or perhaps it was his posture, for he planted both hands on his hips and rocked forward on the balls of his feet to glower at her.

"Don't even snotties know to stand to attention in the presence of a superior officer, Snotty?" he demanded disdainfully, and a flush of anger lit Honor's high cheekbones. His eyes gleamed at the sight, and she felt the sub-audible rumble of Nimitz's snarl through her arms. She tightened her grip in warning, but the 'cat knew better than to openly display his occasional dislike for those senior to his person. He clearly thought it was one of the sillier restrictions inherent in Honor's chosen career, but he was willing to humor her in something so important to her.

She held him just a heartbeat longer, concentrating hard for the benefit of his empathic sense on how important it was for him to behave himself this time, then set him quickly on the table and came to attention.

"That's better," the lieutenant growled, and stalked into the compartment. "I'm Lieutenant Santino, the assistant tac officer," he informed her, hands still on hips while she stood rigidly at attention. "Which means that, for my sins, I'm also in charge of Snotty Row this deployment. So tell me, Ms. Harrington, just what the hell are you doing *here* instead of reporting to me?"

"Sir, I was instructed to stow my gear and get settled in here. My understanding was that Senior Chief Shelton was—"

"And what makes you think a petty officer is more important than a *commissioned* officer, Ms. Harrington?" he broke in on her.

"Sir, I didn't say he was," she replied, making her voice come out calm and even despite her mounting anger.

"You certainly implied it if you meant to say his instructions were more important than mine!"

Honor clamped her jaw tight and made no response. He was only going to twist anything she said to suit his own ends, and she refused to play his stupid game.

"*Didn't* you imply that, Ms. Harrington?" he demanded after the silence had lingered a few seconds, and she looked him squarely in the eye.

"No, Sir. I did not." The words were perfectly correct, the tone calm and unchallenging, but the expression in her dark brown eyes was unyielding. Something flickered in his own gaze, and his lips tightened, but she simply stood there.

"Then what did you mean to imply?" he asked very softly.

"Sir, I meant to imply nothing. I was merely attempting to answer your question."

"Then answer it!" he snapped.

"Sir, I was told by Commander Layson—" she delivered the Exec's name with absolutely no emphasis and watched his eyes narrow and his mouth tighten once more "—that I was to remain here until the Senior Chief returned, at which time he would take me to formally report in to you."

Santino glared at her, but the invocation of Layson's name had at least temporarily stymied him. Which was only going to make things worse in the long run, Honor decided.

"Well here I am, Ms. Harrington," he growled after a long, silent moment. "So suppose you just get started reporting in to me."

"Sir! Midshipwoman Honor Harrington reports for duty, Sir!" she barked with the sort of parade ground formality no one but an idiot or an utter newbie would use aboard ship. Anger glittered in his eyes, but she only met his gaze expressionlessly.

It's really, really stupid to antagonize him this way, girl! a voice which sounded remarkably like Michelle Henke's chided in her head. *Surely you put up with enough crap at the Academy to realize that much!*

But she couldn't help herself. And it probably wouldn't matter that much in the long term, anyway.

"Very well, Ms. Harrington," he said icily. "Now that you've condescended to join us, suppose you accompany me to the chart room. I believe I have just the thing for you to occupy yourself with until dinner."

Honor felt far more nervous than she hoped anyone could guess as she joined the party assembling outside the hatch to Captain Bachfisch's dining cabin. *War Maiden* was only three days out of Manticore orbit, and she and her fellow midshipmen had been surprised, to say the least, to discover that the Captain habitually invited his officers to dine with him. It was particularly surprising because *War Maiden* was almost thirty-five standard years old, and small for her rate. Although the captain's quarters were indisputably larger and far more splendid than Snotty Row, they were cramped and plain compared to those aboard newer, larger ships, which made his dining cabin a tight fit for even half a dozen guests. With space at such a premium, he could hardly invite all of his officers to every dinner, but he apparently rotated the guest list regularly to ensure that all of them dined with him in turn.

It was unheard of, or almost so. But Captain Courvoisier, Honor's favorite instructor at the Academy, had once suggested to her that a wise CO got to know her officers—and see to it that they knew her—as well as possible, and she wondered if this was Captain Bachfisch's way of doing just that. But whatever the Captain thought he was up to, finding herself on the guest list was enough to make any snotty nervous, especially this early in the cruise.

She looked around as unobtrusively as possible as the Captain's steward opened the hatch and she followed her seniors through it. As the most junior person present, she brought up the rear, of course, which was only marginally better than being required to lead the way. At least she didn't have to be the very first person through the hatch! But that only meant everyone else could arrive, take their seats, and turn to watch her enter the compartment last of all. She felt the weight of all those senior eyes upon her and wondered if she'd really been wise to bring Nimitz. It was entirely proper for her to do so, according to Regs, unless the invitation specifically excluded him, yet she felt suddenly uncertain and ill at ease, afraid that her seniors might find her decision presumptuous. The uncertainty made her feel physically awkward as well, as if she had somehow reverted to the gawky, oversized horse she'd always thought herself before Chief MacDougal got her seriously interested in *coup de vitesse*. Her face tried to flush, but she ordered her uneasiness sternly back into its box. This evening promised to be stressful enough without borrowing reasons to crank her adrenaline, but she could at least be grateful that Elvis Santino wasn't present. Midshipman Makira had already endured this particular ordeal, and he *had* had to put up with Santino's presence.

At least her lowly status precluded any confusion over which seat might be hers, and she scarcely needed the steward's small gesture directing her to the very foot of the table. She settled herself into the chair as unobtrusively as she could, and Nimitz, as aware as she of the need to be on his best behavior, parked himself very neatly along the top of her seat back.

The steward circled the table, moving through the dining cabin's cramped confines with the grace of long practice as he poured coffee. Honor had always despised that particular beverage, and she covered her cup with her hand as the steward approached her. The man gave her a quizzical glance, but moved on without comment.

"Don't care for coffee, huh?"

The question came from the senior-grade lieutenant seated to her left, and Honor looked at him quickly. The brown-haired, snub-nosed officer was about Santino's age, or within a year or two either way. Unlike Santino, however, his expression was friendly and his tone was pleasant, without the hectoring sneer the OCTO seemed to achieve so effortlessly.

"I'm afraid not, Sir," she admitted.

"That could be a liability in a Navy career," the lieutenant said cheerfully. He looked across the table at a round-faced, dark-complexioned lieutenant commander and grinned. "Some of us," he observed, "seem to be of the opinion that His Majesty's starships actually run on caffeine, not reactor mass. In fact, *some* of us seem to feel that it's our responsibility to rebunker regularly by taking that caffeine on internally."

The lieutenant commander looked down her nose at him and sipped from her own cup, then set it precisely back on the saucer.

"I trust, Lieutenant, that it was not your intention to cast aspersions on the quantities of coffee which certain of your hard-working seniors consume on the bridge," she remarked.

"Certainly not! I'm shocked by the very suggestion that you might think I intended anything of the sort, Ma'am!"

"Of course you are," Commander Layson agreed, then looked down the length of the table at Honor from his place to the right of the Captain's as yet unoccupied chair. "Ms. Harrington, allow me to introduce you. To your left, we have Lieutenant Saunders, our assistant astrogator. To his left, Lieutenant Commander LaVacher, our chief engineer, and to your right, Lieutenant Commander Hirake, our tac officer." LaVacher, a petite, startlingly pretty blonde, faced Layson, who sat at Hirake's right, across the table. She and the Exec completed the group of dinner guests, and Layson gave a small wave in Honor's direction. "Ladies and gentlemen, Ms. Midshipwoman Harrington."

Heads had nodded at her as the Exec named each officer in turn, and now Honor nodded respectfully back to them. Not a one of them, she noticed, seemed to exude the towering sense of superiority which was so much a part of Elvis Santino.

Saunders had just opened his mouth to say something more when the hatch leading to the captain's day cabin opened and a tall, spare man in the uniform of a senior-grade captain stepped through it. All of the other officers around the table stood, and Honor quickly followed suit. They remained standing until Captain Bachfisch had taken his own chair and made a small gesture with his right hand.

"Be seated, ladies and gentlemen," he invited.

Chairs scraped gently on the decksole as his juniors obeyed the instruction, and Honor observed Bachfisch covertly as she unfolded her snowy linen napkin and draped it across her lap. It was the first time she'd set eyes upon the man who was master after God aboard *War Maiden*, and her first impression was one of vague dissatisfaction. Captain Bachfisch had a thin, lined face and dark eyes which seemed to hold a hint of perpetual frown. In fact, he looked more like an accountant whose figures hadn't come out even than like Honor's mental image of the captain of a King's ship bound to suppress bloody piracy. Nor did his slightly nasal tenor seem the proper voice for such an exalted personage, and she felt an undeniable pang of disappointment.

But then the steward reappeared and began to serve the meal proper, which banished such mundane concerns quite handily. The quality of the food was several notches higher than anything which normally came in the way of a lowly snotty, and Honor dug in with a will. There was little conversation while they ate, and she was just as glad, for it gave her the opportunity to enjoy the food without having to worry about whether a mere midshipwoman was expected to contribute to the table talk. Not that there *was* much table talk. Captain Bachfisch, in particular, applied himself to his dinner in silence. He seemed almost unaware of his guests, and despite the gratitude Honor felt at being allowed to enjoy her meal in relative peace, she wondered why he had bothered to invite them in the first place if he only intended to ignore them. It all seemed very peculiar.

The dinner progressed from salad and an excellent potato soup through glazed chicken with sliced almonds, fluffy rice, stir-fried vegetables and sauteed mushrooms, fresh green peas, and crusty, butter-drenched rolls to a choice of three different desserts. Every time Honor glanced up, the steward seemed to be at her elbow, offering another helping, and she accepted with gusto. Captain Bachfisch might not match her mental image of a dashing and distinguished starship commander, but he set an excellent table. She hadn't tasted food this good since her last visit home.

The apple pie à la mode was even better than the glazed chicken, and Honor needed no prompting when the steward offered her a second helping. The man gave her a small, conspiratorial wink as he slid the second dessert plate in front of her, and she heard something which sounded suspiciously like a chuckle from Lieutenant Saunders' direction. She glanced at the assistant astrogator from the corner of her eye, but his expression was laudably composed. There might have been a hint of a twinkle in his own eyes, but Honor scarcely minded that. She was a direct descendant of the Meyerdahl First Wave, and she was well accustomed to the reactions her genetically modified metabolism's appetite—especially for sweets—drew from un-prepared table mates.

But in the end, she was reduced to chasing the last of the melted ice cream around the plate with her spoon, and she sat back with an unobtrusive sigh of reple-tion as the silent, efficient steward reappeared to collect the empty dishes and make them magically vanish into some private black hole. Wineglasses replaced them, and the steward presented an old-fashioned wax-sealed glass bottle for Captain Bach-fisch's inspection. Honor watched the Captain more attentively at that, for her own father was a notable wine snob in his own modest way, and she recognized another as the steward cracked the wax, drew the cork, and handed it to the Captain. Bachfisch sniffed it delicately while the steward poured a small quantity of ruby liquid into his glass, then set the cork aside and sipped the wine itself. He considered for just a mo-ment, then nodded approval, and the steward filled his glass and then circled the table to pour for each of the guests in turn.

A fresh butterfly fluttered its wings ever so gently in Honor's middle as the stew-ard filled her own glass. She was the junior officer present, and she knew what that re-quired of her. She waited until the steward had finished pouring and stepped back, then reached for her glass and stood.

"Ladies and gentlemen, the King!" She was pleased her voice came out sounding so close to normal. It certainly didn't *feel* as if it ought to have, but she appeared to be the only one aware of how nervous she felt.

"The King!" The response sounded almost too loud in the cramped dining cabin, and Honor sank back into her chair quickly, vastly relieved to have gotten through without mischance.

There was a sudden shift of atmosphere around the table, almost as if the loyalty toast were a signal the diners had awaited. It was more of a shift in attitude than any-thing else, Honor thought, trying to put a mental finger on what had changed. The Captain's guests sat back in their chairs, wineglasses in hand, and Lieutenant Com-mander Hirake actually crossed her legs.

"May I assume you got those charts properly straightened out, Joseph?" Captain Bachfisch said.

"Yes, Sir," Lieutenant Saunders replied. "You were right, Captain. They were just mislabeled, although Commander Dobrescu and I *are* still a little puzzled over why someone thought we needed updated charts on the People's Republic when we're headed in exactly the opposite direction."

"Oh, that's an easy one, Joseph," Lieutenant Commander Hirake told him. "I imagine *War Maiden's* original astrogator probably requested them for her maiden voyage. I mean, it's only been thirty-six standard years. That's about average for turn-around on LogCom requests."

Several people around the table chuckled, and Honor managed not to let her sur-prise show as Captain Bachfisch's lined, disapproving face creased in a smile of its own. The Captain waved a finger at the tac officer and shook his head.

"We can't have you talking that way about LogCom, Janice," he told her severely. "If nothing else, you'll raise future expectations which are doomed to be disappointed."

"I don't know about that, Sir," Commander Layson said. "Seems to me it took about that long to get the emitter head on Graser Four replaced, didn't it?"

"Yes, but that wasn't LogCom alone," Lieutenant Commander LaVacher put in. "The yard dogs on *Hephaestus* actually found it for us in the end, remember? I almost had to demand it at pulser point, but they *did* find it. Of course, they'd probably had it in stores for five or six years while some other poor cruiser waited for it, and we just shortstopped it."

That drew fresh chuckles, and Honor's amazement grew. The men and women in the compartment with her were suddenly very different from those who had shared the almost silent, formal dinner, and Captain Bachfisch was the most different of all. As she watched, he cocked his head at Commander Layson, and his expression was almost playful.

"And I trust that while Joseph was straightening out his charts you and Janice managed to come up with an exercise schedule which is going to make everyone onboard hate us, Abner?"

"Well, we tried, Sir." Layson sighed and shook his head. "We did our best, but I think there are probably three or four ratings in Engineering who are only going to take us in intense dislike instead."

"Hmm." Captain Bachfisch frowned. "I'm a bit disappointed to hear that. When a ship's company has as many grass-green hands as this one, a good exec shouldn't have any trouble at all coming up with a training program guaranteed to get on their bad side."

"Oh, we've managed *that*, Sir. It's just that Irma managed to hang on to most of her original watch crews, and they already know all our tricks."

"Ah? Well, I suppose that is a circumstance beyond your control," Captain Bachfisch allowed, and looked at Lieutenant Commander LaVacher. "I see it's your fault, Irma," he said.

"Guilty as charged, Sir," LaVacher admitted. "Wasn't easy, either, with BuPers hanging over my shoulder and trying to poach my most experienced people the whole time."

"I know it wasn't," the Captain said, and this time there was no teasing note in his approving voice. "I reviewed some of your correspondence with Captain Allerton. I thought right up to the last minute that we were going to lose Chief Heisman, but you finessed Allerton beautifully. I hope this isn't going to cost the Chief that extra rocker, though. We need him, but I don't want him shortchanged out of the deal."

"He won't be, Sir," Layson replied for LaVacher. "Irma and I discussed it before she ever resorted to the 'essential to efficient functioning' argument to hang onto him. We're two senior chiefs light in Engineering alone . . . and we're also going to be in Silesia more than long enough for you to exercise your own discretion in promoting Heisman to fill one of those slots."

"Good," Bachfisch said. "That's what I like to see! Intelligent ship's officers effortlessly outsmarting their natural enemies at BuPers."

It was all Honor could do not to gawk at the changeling who had replaced the dour and unsmiling man in the chair at the head of the table. Then he turned from Layson and LaVacher and looked directly down the table at her, and this time there was a definite twinkle in his deep-set eyes.

"I notice your companion has spent the entire meal on the back of your chair, Ms. Harrington," he observed. "I was under the impression that 'cats usually ate at the same time their people did."

"Uh, yes, Sir," Honor said. She felt a warmth along her cheekbones and drew a deep breath. At least his bantering with the more senior officers present had given her some opportunity to adjust before he turned his guns on her, and she took herself firmly in hand. "Yes, Sir," she said much more composedly. "Nimitz normally eats at the same time I do, but he doesn't do very well with vegetables, and we weren't sure what arrangements your steward might have made, so he ate in the berthing compartment before we came to dinner."

"I see." The Captain gazed at her for a moment, then nodded at his steward. "Chief Stennis is a capable sort, Ms. Harrington. If you'll be good enough to provide him with a list of foods suitable for your companion, I feel confident he can arrange an appropriate menu for his next dinner engagement."

"Yes, Sir," Honor said, trying unsuccessfully to hide her relief at the evidence that Nimitz's presence was welcome, and not merely something to be tolerated. "Thank you, Sir."

"You're welcome," Bachfisch replied, then smiled. "In the meantime, is there at least something we can offer him as an after dinner snack while we enjoy our wine?"

"If Chief Stennis has a little celery left over from the salad, that would be perfect, Sir. 'Cats may not do well with most vegetables, but they *all* love celery!"

"Jackson?" The Captain glanced at the steward who smiled and nodded.

"I believe I can handle that, Sir."

Chief Stennis disappeared into his pantry, and Captain Bachfisch returned his attention to Commander Layson and Lieutenant Commander Hirake. Honor settled back in her chair, and the pleased buzz of Nimitz's purr vibrated against the back of her neck. If she'd been a 'cat herself, her own purr would have been even more pleased and considerably louder. She watched *War Maiden's* captain chatting with his officers and felt a sense of ungrudging admiration. This Captain Bachfisch was a very different proposition from the formal, almost cold CO who had presided over the meal itself. She still didn't understand why he'd seemed so distant then, but she readily appreciated the skill with which he drew each of his officers in turn into the discussion now. And, she admitted, how effortlessly he had made a mere midshipwoman feel at ease in their company. His questions might be humorously phrased, and he might display an almost dangerously pointed wit, yet he had all of them involved in discussing serious issues, and he managed it as a leader, not merely as a captain. She remembered once more what Captain Courvosier had said about the need for a captain to know her officers, and realized that Bachfisch had just given her an object lesson in how a captain might go about that.

It was a lesson worth learning, and she filed it away carefully as she smiled and reached up to take the plate of celery Chief Stennis brought her.

". . . and as you can see, we have the Alpha Three upgrade to the emergency local control positions for our energy mounts," Chief MacArthur droned. The sturdy, plain-faced woman bore the hash marks of over twenty-five T-years' service on her sleeve, and the combat ribbons on her chest proved she'd paid cash to learn her weapons skills. It was unfortunate that she'd never mastered the skills of the lecture hall to go with them. Even though Honor was deeply interested in what MacArthur had to tell her, she found it difficult to keep from yawning as the dust-dry instruction continued.

She and Audrey Bradlaugh, *War Maiden's* other female middy, stood in the number four inboard wing passage, peering over MacArthur's shoulder into the small, heavily armored compartment. It didn't offer a lot of space for the men and women who would man it when the ship cleared for action, and every square centimeter of room it did have was crammed with monitors, readouts, keypads, and access panels. In between those more important bits and pieces were sandwiched the shock-mounted couches and umbilical attachment points for the mere humans of the weapon crew.

"When the buzzer goes, the crew has a maximum of fifteen minutes to don skin-suits and man stations," MacArthur informed them, and Honor and Bradlaugh nodded as if no one had ever told them so before. "Actually, of course, fifteen minutes should give time to spare, although we sometimes run a bit over on shakedown cruises. On the other hand," the petty officer glanced back at her audience, "the Captain isn't what I'd call a patient man with people who screw up his training profiles, so I wouldn't recommend dawdling."

One eyelid flickered in what might have been called a wink on a less expressionless face, and despite herself, Honor grinned at the petty officer. Not that on-mount crew duties were the most humorous subject imaginable. Honor knew that, for she'd logged scores of hours in simulators which re-created every detail of the local control command position in front of her, and her grin faded as she envisioned it in her mind. Her excellent imagination pictured every moment of the shriek of the general quarters alarm, the flashing lights of battle stations, and the sudden claustrophobic tension as the crew plugged in their skinsuit umbilicals and the hatch slammed shut behind them while powerful pumps sucked the air from the passages and compartments around them. The vacuum about their armored capsule would actually help protect it—and them—from atmosphere-transmitted shock and concussion, not to mention fires, yet she doubted anyone could ever embrace it without an atavistic shudder.

Nimitz shifted uneasily on her shoulder as he caught the sudden edge of darkness in her emotions, and she reached up to rest one hand lightly on his head. He pressed back against her palm, and she made a soft crooning sound.

"If Chief MacArthur is *boring* you, Ms. Harrington," an unpleasant voice grated unexpectedly, "I'm sure we can find some extra duty to keep you occupied."

Honor turned quickly, shoulders tightening in automatic response, and her expression was suddenly a better mask than Chief MacArthur's as she faced Elvis Santino. It was obvious the OCTO had come quietly around the bend in the passage while she and Bradlaugh were listening to MacArthur, and she castigated herself for letting him sneak up on her. Now he stood glaring at her, hands once more on hips and lip curled, and she gazed back at him in silence.

Anything she said or did would be wrong, so she said nothing. Which, of course, was *also* the wrong thing to do.

"Well, Ms. Harrington? If you're bored, just say so. I'm sure Chief MacArthur has better things to do with her time as well. *Are* you bored?"

"No, Sir." She gave the only possible answer as neutrally as possible, and Santino smiled nastily.

"Indeed? I would've thought otherwise, given the way you're humming and playing with your little pet."

Once again, there was no possible response that would not give him another opening. She felt Bradlaugh's unhappiness beside her, but Audrey said nothing, either. There wasn't anything she could say, and she'd experienced sufficient of Santino's nastiness herself. But MacArthur shifted her weight, and turned to face the lieutenant. Her non-expression was more pronounced than ever, and she cleared her throat.

"With all due respect, Sir," she said, "the young ladies have been very attentive this afternoon."

Santino turned his scowl on her.

"I don't recall asking your opinion of their attentiveness, Chief MacArthur." His voice was harsh, but MacArthur never turned a hair.

"I realize that, Sir. But again with all due respect, you just came around the corner. I've been working with Ms. Harrington and Ms. Bradlaugh for the last hour and a half. I just felt that I should make you aware of the fact that they've paid very close attention during that time."

"I see." For a moment, Honor thought the lieutenant was going to chew MacArthur out as well for having the audacity to interfere. But it seemed even Elvis Santino wasn't quite stupid enough to risk making this sort of dispute with a noncom of MacArthur's seniority and in his own shipboard department part of the official record. He rocked up and down on the balls of his feet for several seconds then returned his glare to Honor.

"No matter how much attention you've been paying, there's no excuse for slacking off," he told her. "I realize Regs permit you to carry that creature with you on duty, but I warn you not to abuse that privilege. And stop playing with it when you ought to be concentrating on what you're here to learn! I trust I've made myself sufficiently clear?"

"Yes, Sir," Honor said woodenly. "Perfectly clear."

"Good!" Santino snapped, and strode briskly away.

"Lord! What *is* his problem?" Nassios Makira groaned.

The stocky midshipman heaved himself up to sit on the edge of his upper-tier bunk, legs dangling over the side. Honor couldn't imagine why he liked perching up there so much. He was shorter than she was, true, but the deckhead was too low to let even Nassios sit fully upright on his bunk. Maybe it was *because* she was taller than he was? As a matter of fact, Nassios was one of the shortest people aboard *War Maiden*. So did he spend so much time climbing around like a 'cat or an Old Earth monkey because it was the only way he could get above eye level on everyone else?

"I don't know," Audrey Bradlaugh replied without looking up from the boot in her lap. No names had been mentioned, but she seemed in no doubt about the object of Nassios' plaint. "But I do know that complaining about him is only going to make it worse if it gets back to him," the red-haired midshipwoman added pointedly, reaching for the polish on the berthing compartment table.

"Hey, let the man talk," Basanta Lakhia put in. The dark-skinned young midshipman with the startlingly blond hair lay comfortably stretched out on his own bunk. "No one's gonna be tattling to Santino on him, and even if anyone did, it's not against Regs to discuss a senior officer."

"Not as long as the discussion isn't prejudicial to discipline," Honor corrected.

Somewhat to her surprise, she'd found herself the senior of *War Maiden*'s midshipmen on the basis of their comparative class standings. That, unfortunately, only seemed to make matters worse where Santino was concerned, since her seniority—such as it was—pushed him into somewhat closer proximity with her than with the other middies. It also gave her a greater degree of responsibility to provide a voice of reason in snotty bull sessions, and now she looked up to give Makira a rather pointed glance from where she sat beside Bradlaugh at the table, running a brush over Nimitz's pelt. It was unusual for all four of them to be off-duty at once, but middies tended to be assigned to rotating watch schedules, and this time their off-watch periods happened to overlap. In fact, they had almost two more hours before Audrey and Basanta had to report for duty.

"Honor, you know I'd never, ever want to prejudice discipline," Nassios said piously. "Or that anything *I* did could possibly prejudice it as much as *he* does," he added *sotto voce*.

"Basanta's right that no one is going to be carrying tales, Nassios," Audrey said, looking up at last. "But that's exactly the kind of crack that's going to bring him—and the Exec—down on you like a shuttle with dead counter-grav if it gets back to them."

"I know. I know," Nassios sighed. "But you've got to admit he's going awful far out of his way to make himself a royal pain, Audrey! And the way he keeps picking on Honor over Nimitz . . ."

"Maybe he thinks it's part of his job as our training officer," Honor suggested. She finished brushing Nimitz and carefully gathered up the loose fluff for disposal someplace other than in the compartment's air filters.

"Huh! Sure he does!" Basanta snorted.

"I didn't say I agreed with him if he did," Honor said serenely. "But you know as well as I do that there's still the old 'stomp on them hard enough to make them tough' school of snotty-training."

"Yeah, but it's dying out," Nassios argued. "Most of the people you run into who still think that way are old farts from the old school. You know, the ones who think starships should run on steam plants or reaction thrusters . . . or maybe oars! Santino's too young for that kind of crap. Besides, it still doesn't explain the wild hair he's got up his ass over Nimitz!"

"Maybe, and maybe not," Basanta said thoughtfully. "You may have a point, Honor—about the reason he's such a hard ass in the first place, anyway. He's not all that much older than we are, but if his OCTO worked that way, he could just be following in the same tradition."

"And the reason he keeps picking on Nimitz?" Nassios challenged.

"Maybe he's just one of those people who can't get past the image of treecats as dumb animals," Bradlaugh suggested. "Lord knows I wasn't ready for how smart the little devil is. And I wouldn't have believed Honor if she'd just told me about it either."

"That could be it," Honor agreed. "Most people can figure out the difference between a treecat and a pet once they come face-to-face with the real thing, but that's hardly universally true. I think it depends on how much imagination they have."

"And imagination isn't something he's exactly brimming over with," Basanta pointed out. "Which goes back to what Honor said in the first place. If he doesn't have much imagination—" his tone suggested that he'd had a rather more pointed noun in mind "—of his own, he probably is treating us the same way his OCTO treated him. Once he got pointed that way, he couldn't figure out another way to go."

"I don't think he needed anyone to point him in that direction," Nassios muttered, and although she was the one who'd put the suggestion forward, Honor agreed with him. For that matter, she felt morally certain that Santino's behavior was a natural product of his disposition which owed nothing to anyone else's example. Not that she doubted for a moment that his defense, if anyone senior to him called him on it, would be that he was only doing it "for their own good."

"If he ever needed a pointer, he doesn't need one anymore, that's for sure," Basanta agreed, then shook himself. "Say, has anybody seen any of the sims Commander Hirake is setting up for us?"

"No, but PO Wallace warned me they were going to be toughies," Audrey chimed in, supporting the change of subject, and Honor sat back down and gathered Nimitz into her arms while the comfortable shop talk flowed around her.

She ought, she reflected, to be happier than she'd ever been in her life, and in many ways she was. But Elvis Santino was doing his best to keep her happiness from being complete, and he was succeeding. Despite anything she might say to the others, she was morally certain the abusive, sarcastic, belittling behavior he directed at all of them, and especially at her and Nimitz, sprang from a pronounced bullying streak. Worse, she suspected that streak was aggravated by natural stupidity.

And he *was* stupid. She only had to watch him performing as *War Maiden's* assistant tac officer to know that much.

She sighed mentally and pressed her lips together, warning herself once more of the dangers inherent in allowing herself to feel contempt for anyone senior to her. Even if she never let a sign of it show outwardly, it would affect the way she responded to his orders and endless lectures on an officer's proper duties, which could only make things even worse in the end. But she couldn't help it. Her favorite subjects at the Academy had been tactics and ship handling, and she knew she had a natural gift in both areas. Santino did not. He was unimaginative and mentally lazy—at best a plodder, whose poor performance was shielded by Lieutenant Commander Hirake's sheer competence as his boss and carried by Senior Chief Del Conte's matching competence from below. She'd only had a chance to see him in the simulator once or twice, but her fingers had itched with the need to shove him aside and take over the tac console herself.

Which might be another reason he gave her so much grief, she sometimes thought. She'd done her level best not to let her contempt show, but he had access to her Academy records. That meant he knew exactly how high she'd placed in the Tactical Department, and unless he was even stupider than she thought (possible but not likely; he seemed able to zip his own shoes), he had to know she was absolutely convinced that she could have done his job at least twice as well as he could.

And that's only because I'm too naturally modest to think I could do it even better than that, she thought mordantly.

She sighed again, this time physically, pressing her face into Nimitz's coat, and admitted, if only to herself, the real reason she detested Elvis Santino. He reminded her inescapably of Mr. Midshipman Lord Pavel Young, the conceited, vicious, small-minded, oh-so-nobly born cretin who had done his level best to destroy her and her career at Saganami Island.

Her lips tightened, and Nimitz made a scolding sound and reached out to touch her cheek with one long-fingered true-hand. She closed her eyes, fighting against replaying the memory of that dreadful night in the showers yet again, then drew a deep breath, smoothed her expression, and lowered him to her lap once more.

"You okay, Honor?" Audrey asked quietly, her soft voice hidden under a strenuous argument between Nassios and Basanta over the merits of the Academy's new soccer coach.

"Hmm? Oh, sure." She smiled at the redhead. "Just thinking about something else."

"Homesickness, huh?" Audrey smiled back. "I get hit by it every so often, too, you know. Of course," her smile grew into a grin, "I don't have a treecat to keep me company when it does!"

Her infectious chuckle robbed the last sentence of any implied bitterness, and she rummaged in her belt purse for a bedraggled, rather wilted stalk of celery. All of the midshipmen who shared Snotty Row with Honor had taken to hoarding celery almost from the moment they discovered Nimitz's passion for it, and now Audrey smiled fondly as the 'cat seized it avidly and began to devour it.

"Gee, thanks a whole bunch, Audrey!" Honor growled. "You just wrecked his appetite for dinner completely!"

"Sure I did," Audrey replied. "Or I would have, if he didn't carry his own itty-bitty black hole around inside him somewhere."

"As any informed person would know, that's his stomach, not a black hole," Honor told her sternly.

"Sure. It just *works* like a black hole," Basanta put in.

"I've seen you at the mess table, too, boy-oh," Audrey told him, "and if I were you, I wouldn't be throwing any rocks around my glass foyer!"

"I'm just a growing boy," Basanta said with artful innocence, and Honor joined in the laughter.

At least if I have to be stuck with Santino, I got a pretty good bunch to share the misery with, she thought.

HMS *War Maiden* moved steadily through hyperspace. The Gregor Binary System and its terminus of the Manticore Wormhole Junction lay almost a week behind; the Silesian Confederacy lay almost a month ahead, and the heavy cruiser's company had begun to shake down. It was not a painless process. As Captain Bachfisch's after-dinner conversation with Commander Layson had suggested, much of *War Maiden*'s crew was new to the ship, for the cruiser had just emerged from an extensive overhaul period, and the Bureau of Personnel had raided her pre-overhaul crew ruthlessly while she was laid up in space dock. That always happened during a refit, of course, but the situation was worse in the RMN these days due to the Navy's expansion. Every Regular, officer and enlisted alike, knew the expansion process was actually just beginning to hit its stride . . . and that the situation was going to get nothing but worse if King Roger and his ministers stood by their obvious intention to build a fleet capable of resisting the Peeps. The Government and Admiralty faced the unenviable task of balancing the financial costs of new hardware—and especially of yard infrastructure—against the personnel-related costs of providing the manpower to crew and use that hardware, and they were determined to squeeze the last penny out of every begrudged dollar they could finagle out of Parliament. Which meant, down here at the sharp end of the stick, that *War Maiden*'s crew contained a high percentage of new recruits, with a higher percentage of newly promoted noncoms to ride herd on them than her officers would have liked, while the personnel retention problems of the Navy in general left her with several holes among her senior petty officer slots. Almost a third of her total crew were on their first long deployment, and there was a certain inevitable friction between some members of her company, without the solid core of senior noncommissioned officers who would normally have jumped on it as soon as it surfaced.

Honor was as aware of the background tension as anyone else. She and her fellow middies could scarcely have helped being aware of it under any circumstances, but she had the added advantage of Nimitz, and she only had to watch his body language to read his reaction to the crew's edginess.

The ship was scarcely a hotbed of mutiny, of course, but there was a sense of rough edges and routines just out of joint that produced a general air of unsettlement, and she occasionally wondered if that hovering feeling that things were somehow out of adjustment helped explain some of Santino's irascibility. She suspected, even as she wondered, that the notion was nonsense, nothing more than an effort to supply some sort of excuse for the way the OCTO goaded and baited the midshipmen under his nominal care. Still, she had to admit that it left *her* feeling unsettled. None of her relatively short training deployments from the Academy had produced anything quite like it. Of course, none of the ships involved in those deployments had been fresh from refit with crews composed largely of replacements, either. Could this sense of connections still waiting to be made be the norm and not the exception? She'd always known the Academy was a sheltered environment, one where corners were rounded, sharp edges were smoothed, and tables of organization were neatly adhered to, no matter how hard the instructors ran the middies. No doubt that same "classroom-perfect" organization had extended to the training ships homeported at Saganami Island, while *War Maiden* was the real Navy at last. When she thought of it that way, it was almost exciting, like a challenge to earn her adulthood by proving she could deal with the less than perfect reality of a grownup's universe.

Of course, Elvis Santino all by himself was more than enough to make any universe imperfect, she told herself as she hurried down the passage. The OCTO was in an even worse mood than usual today, and all of the middies knew it was going to be impossible to do anything well enough to satisfy him. Not that they had any choice but to try, which was how Honor came to find herself bound all the way forward to Magazine Two just so she could personally count the laser heads to confirm the computer inventory. It was pure makework, an order concocted solely to keep her occupied and let Santino once more demonstrate his petty-tyrant authority. Not that she objected all that strenuously to anything that got her out of his immediate vicinity!

She rounded a corner and turned left along Axial One, the large central passage running directly down the cruiser's long axis. *War Maiden* was old enough that her lift system left much to be desired by modern standards. Honor could have made almost the entire trip from bridge to magazine in one of the lift cars, but its circuitous routing meant the journey would actually have taken longer that way. Besides, she *liked* Axial One. *War Maiden's* internal grav field was reduced to just under .2 G in the out-sized passage, and she fell into the long, bounding, semi-swimming gait that permitted.

More modern warships had abandoned such passages in favor of better designed and laid out lift systems, although most merchantmen retained them. Convenient though they were in many ways, they represented what BuShips had decided was a dangerous weakness in a military starship which was expected to sustain and survive damage from enemy fire. Unlike the smaller shafts lift cars required, passages like Axial One posed severe challenges when it came to things like designing in blast doors and emergency air locks, and the large empty space at the very core of the ship represented at least a marginal sacrifice in structural strength. Or so BuShips had decided. Honor wasn't certain she agreed, but no flag officers or naval architects had shown any interest in seeking her opinion on the matter, so she simply chose to enjoy the opportunity when it presented itself.

Nimitz clung to her shoulder, chittering with delight of his own as the two of them sailed down the passageway with impeccable grace. It was almost as much fun as Honor's hang glider back home on Sphinx, and his fluffy tail streamed behind them. They were far from the only people making use of Axial One, and Honor knew she was technically in violation of the speed limits imposed here under nonemergency conditions, but she didn't much care. She doubted anyone was likely to take her to task for it, and if anyone did, she could always point out that Santino had ordered her to "get down there double-quick, Snotty!"

She was almost to her destination when it happened. She didn't see the events actually leading up to the collision, but the consequences were painfully obvious. A three-man work party from Engineering, towing a counter-grav pallet of crated electronic components, had collided head-on with a missile tech using a push-pull to maneuver five linked missile main drive units down the same passage. It was a near-miracle no one had suffered serious physical injury, but there'd obviously been a fair number of bruises, and it was clear that the participants' emotions were even more bruised than their hides.

"—and get your goddamn, worthless pile of frigging junk out of my fucking way!" the missile tech snarled.

"Fuck you and the horse you rode in on!" the senior rating from the Engineering party snapped back. "Nobody ever tell you forward traffic to starboard, sternward traffic to port? Or are you just naturally stupid? You were all over the goddamn place with that piece of shit! It's a damn miracle you didn't kill one of us!"

She gave the linked drive units a furious kick to emphasize her point. Unfortunately, she failed to allow for the low grav conditions, and the result was more pratfall than intimidating. She sent herself flailing through the air towards the center of the passage, where she landed flat on her posterior on the decksole, without even budging the drive units, none of which did a thing for her temper. It did, however, have the effect of infuriating the missile tech even further, and he unbuckled from his push-pull and shoved himself off the saddle with obviously homicidal intent. One of the male Engineering ratings moved to intercept him, and things were headed rapidly downhill when Honor reached out for one of the bulkhead handrails and brought herself to a semi-floating stop.

"Belay that!"

Her soprano was very little louder than normal, yet it cracked like a whip, and the disputants' heads snapped around in sheer surprise. Their surprise only grew when they saw the fuzz-haired midshipwoman who had produced the order.

"I don't know who did what to whom," she told them crisply while they gawked at her in astonishment, "and I don't really care. What matters is getting this mess sorted out and getting you people to wherever it is you're supposed to be." She glared at them for a moment, and then jabbed a finger at the senior Engineering rating. "You," she told the woman. "Chase down those loose crates, get them back on the pallet, and this time get them properly secured! You and you—" she jabbed an index finger at the other two members of the work party "—get over there and give her a hand. And *you*," she wheeled on the missile tech who had just begun to gloat at his rivals' stunned expressions, "get that push-pull back under control, tighten the grav-collars on those missile drives before they fall right out of them, and see to it that you stay in the right heavy tow lane the rest of the way to wherever you're going!"

"Uh, yes, Ma'am!" The missile tech recognized command voice when he heard it, even if it did come from a midshipwoman who looked like someone's preteen kid sister, and he knew better than to irritate the person who had produced it. He actually braced to attention before he scurried back over to the bundle of drive units and began adjusting the offending counter-grav collars, and the Engineering working party, which had already come to the same conclusion, spread out, quickly corralling their scattered crates and stacking them oh-so-neatly on their pallet. Honor stood waiting, one toe tapping gently on the decksole while Nimitz watched with interest from her shoulder and the errant ratings—the youngest of them at least six standard years older than she—gave an excellent imitation of small children under the eye of an irritated governess.

It took a remarkably short time for the confusion to be reduced to order, and all four ratings turned carefully expressionless faces back to Honor.

"That's better," she told them in more approving tones. "Now I suggest that all of you get back to doing what you're supposed to be doing just a little more carefully than you were."

"Aye, aye, Ma'am," they chorused, and she nodded. They moved off—far more sedately than before, she suspected—and she resumed her own interrupted trip.

That went fairly well, she told herself, and continued her progress along Axial One, unaware of the grinning senior chief who had arrived behind her just in time to witness the entire episode.

"So, Shellhead," Senior Master Chief Flanagan said comfortably, "what d'you think of this helpless bunch of Momma's dirtside darlings now?"

"Who, me?" Senior Chief Shelton leaned back in his own chair, heels propped on the table in the senior petty officers' mess, and grinned as he nursed a beer stein. Not many were permitted to use that nickname to his face, but Flanagan had known him for over twenty standard years. More importantly than that, perhaps, Flanagan was also *War Maid*'s Bosun, the senior noncommissioned member of her company.

"Yeah, you," Flanagan told him. "You ever see such a hapless bunch in your entire life? I swear, I think one or two of them aren't real clear on which hatch to open first on the air lock!"

"Oh, they're not as bad as all that," Shelton said. "They've got a few rough edges—hell, let's be honest, they've got a *lot* of rough edges—but we're getting them filed down. By the time we hit Silesia, they'll be ready. And some of them aren't half bad already."

"You think so?" Flanagan's eyebrows rose ever so slightly at Shelton's tone, and the senior chief nodded. "And just who, if you don't mind my asking, brought that particular bit of praise to the surface?"

"Young Harrington, as a matter of fact," Shelton said. "I came across her in Axial One this afternoon tearing a strip off a couple of work parties who'd managed to run smack into each other. 'Tronics crates all over the deck, counter-grav pallet cocked up on its side, push-pull all twisted against the bulkhead, and half a dozen missile drives ready to slip right out of their collars, not to mention a couple of ratings ready to start thumping hell out of each other over whose fault it was. And there she stood, reading them the riot act. Got their sorry asses sorted out in record time, too."

Flanagan found it a little difficult to hide his surprise at the obvious approval in Shelton's voice.

"I wouldn't've thought she had the decibels for reading riot acts," he observed, watching his friend's expression carefully. "Sweet-voiced thing like that, I'd think she'd sound sort of silly shouting at a hairy bunch of spacers."

"Nah," Shelton said with a grin. "That was the beauty of it—never cussed or even raised her voice once. Didn't have to. She may only be a snotty, but that young lady could burn the finish off a battle steel bulkhead with just her tone alone. Haven't seen anything like it in years."

"Sounds like that shithead Santino could learn a little something from his snotties, then," Flanagan observed sourly, and it was Shelton's turn to feel surprise. In all the years he'd known Flanagan, he could count the number of times he'd heard his friend use that tone of voice about a commissioned officer on the fingers of one hand. Well, maybe one and half. Not that the senior chief disagreed with the bosun.

"Actually, I think he could learn a hell of a lot from Harrington," he said after a moment. "For that matter, he could probably learn a lot from all of them. If he could keep his own mouth shut long enough to listen to them, anyway."

"And how likely is that to happen?" Flanagan snorted.

"Not very," Shelton conceded. "The man does like to hear himself talk."

"I wouldn't mind that so much, if he weren't such a bastard," Flanagan said, still with such an edge of bitter condemnation that Shelton looked across at him with the first beginnings of true alarm.

"Is there something going on that I should be hearing about, Ian?"

"Probably not anything you don't already know about," Flanagan told him moodily. "It's just that he's such a total asshole. Hell, you're in a better spot to see the way he treats the snotties like dirt than I am, and he's not a lot better with his own tac people. Even he knows better than to piss off a senior noncom, but he came down like a five-grav field on his yeoman yesterday, for a screw-up that was entirely his own fault. You know I've got no use for any officer who beats up on his people when *he's* the one who screwed the pooch. Man's the most worthless piece of crap I've seen in an officer's uniform in years, Shellhead."

"I don't know that I'd go quite that far myself," Shelton said in a considering tone. "I've seen some pretty piss-poor officers, you know. Some of them could at least give him a run for his money. On the other hand, I don't think any of them were *worse* than he is." He paused for a moment, and looked quizzically at his friend. "You know, I think it's probably against Regs for two senior petty officers to sit around and badmouth a commissioned officer over their beer this way."

"And you don't see me doing it with anyone else, do you?" Flanagan returned, then grimaced. "Ah, hell, Shellhead, you know as well as I do that Santino is the worst frigging officer in this ship. Come on, be honest. You're worried about the way he treats the snotties, aren't you?"

"Well, yeah," Shelton admitted. "I see a kid like Harrington—any of them, really, but especially Harrington—with all that promise, and there's Santino, doing his level best to crush it all out of them. I mean, it's one thing to be tough on them. It's something else entirely to ride them twenty-two hours a day out of sheer poison meanness because you know there's nothing in the world they can do to fight back."

"You can say that again," Flanagan said. "Not bad enough he's got the chain of command on his side, but they know he can flush their careers any time he damned well pleases if they don't kiss ass enough to make him happy."

"Maybe. But I've got to tell you, Ian, I don't know how much longer Harrington's going to put up with it." Shelton shook his head soberly. "I had my doubts when she turned up with that treecat of hers. First time I'd ever seen one onboard ship. I figured it was bound to make trouble in Snotty Row if nowhere else, and that Harrington might be full of herself for having it in the first place, but I was wrong on both counts. And the girl's got bottom, too. She's going to be a good one someday . . . unless Santino pushes her too hard. She's got a temper in there, however hard she tries to hide it, and Santino sticks in her craw sideways. One of these days, she's gonna lose it with him, and when she does . . ."

The two noncoms gazed at one another across the table, and neither of them any longer felt like smiling at all.

"Tell me, Ms. Harrington," Elvis Santino said, "is it possible that by some vast stretch of the imagination you actually consider this a competently done job?"

The lieutenant stood in the weapon's bay for Graser Three, the second energy mount in *War Maiden*'s port broadside. He and Honor both wore skinsuits as Regs required, since the bay was sealed only by a single hatch, not a proper air lock. When the ship cleared for action, the bay would be opened to space, the emitter assembly would train outboard, and the powered ram would move the entire weapon outward until the emitter head cleared the hull and could bring up its gravity lenses safely. Honor had always been privately amused by the fact that modern energy weapons were "run out" like some echo of the muzzleloading cannon of Old Earth's sailing navies, but at the moment all she felt was a dull, seething resentment for her training officer.

Santino was in his favorite pose, hands propped on hips and feet spread wide. All he needed to complete the handsome HD star image was a bright sun to squint into, Honor thought derisively, and wondered yet again how he could possibly be unaware of the effect that sort of posturing was bound to have on the men and women under his orders. It was more than a merely rhetorical consideration at the moment, since six of those men and women—including SCPO Shelton—stood at her back in silent witness.

"Yes, Sir, I do," she made herself say levelly, and his lips drew back to bare his teeth.

"Then I can only say your judgment is suspect, Ms. Harrington," he told her. "Even from here I can see that the access panel is still open on Ram One!"

"Yes, Sir, it is," Honor agreed. "When we got it open, we—"

"I don't recall inviting excuses, Ms. Harrington!" he snapped. "Is or is not that access panel still open?"

Honor clamped her teeth and decided it was a good thing Nimitz wasn't present. The 'cat had no vac suit. As such, he was thankfully barred from this compartment and so unable to bristle and snarl in response to Santino's attitude.

"Yes, Sir, it is," she said again after a moment, exactly as if she hadn't already agreed it was.

"And you are, perhaps, aware of the standing orders and operating procedures which require all access panels to be closed after inspection and routine maintenance?" he pressed.

"Yes, Sir, I am." Honor's voice was clearer and crisper than usual, and a small tic quivered at the corner of her mouth. Something seemed to gleam for just an instant in Santino's eyes as he observed it, and he leaned towards her.

"Then just how the hell can even *you* stand there and call this a 'competent' job?" he demanded harshly.

"Because, Sir, Ram One has a major engineering casualty," she told him. "The main actuator must have developed a short since its last routine maintenance. There are actual scorch marks inside the casing, and stages one and five both show red on the diagnostic. As per standing orders, I immediately informed Commander LaVacher in Engineering, and she instructed me to open the main breaker, red-tag the actuator, and leave the access panel open until she could get a repair crew up here to deal with it. All of which, Sir, is in my report."

Her dark eyes locked unflinchingly with his, but even as they did, she kicked herself mentally for losing her temper, for she saw the sudden rage flashing in the depths of his glare. She'd kept her voice level and even, but the entire tone of her answer—and especially that last jab about her report—had been well over the line. No one would ever be able to prove it, but she and Santino both knew she'd done it to get some of her own back, and his florid complexion darkened angrily.

"I assume you know the penalty for insubordination," he grated. She said nothing, and his color darkened further. "I asked you a question, Snotty!" he barked.

"I'm sorry, Sir. I was unaware that it was meant as a question. It sounded like a statement."

She could hardly believe it even as she heard her own voice say it, and she sensed Senior Chief Shelton and his work party behind her, watching it all. What was *wrong* with her? Why in heaven's name was she goading him back this way?

"Well it wasn't one!" Santino snapped. "So answer me!"

"Yes, Sir," she said. "I am aware of the penalty for insubordination."

"That's good, Snotty, because you just bought yourself a locker full of it! Now get out of my sight. Go directly to your quarters and remain there until I personally tell you differently!"

"Yes, Sir." She came to attention, saluted crisply, turned on her heel, and marched off with her head high while the man with the power to destroy her career before it even began glared after her.

The hatch signal chimed, and Commander Layson looked up from his display and pressed the admittance button. The hatch slid open, and Lieutenant Santino stepped through it.

"You wanted to see me, Sir?" the lieutenant said.

Layson nodded, but he said nothing, simply gazed at his assistant tactical officer with cool, thoughtful eyes. His face was expressionless, but Santino shifted slightly under that dispassionate gaze. It wasn't quite a fidget, but it was headed in that direction, and still the silence stretched out. At last, after at least three full minutes, Santino could stand it no more and cleared his throat.

"Uh, may I ask why you wanted to see me, Sir?"

"You may." Layson leaned back in his chair and folded his hands across his midsection. He sat that way for several seconds, eyes never leaving Santino's face, stretching the lieutenant's nerves a bit tighter, then went on in a neutral tone. "I understand there was some . . . difficulty with Midshipwoman Harrington this afternoon, Lieutenant," he said at last, his tone very cool. "Suppose you tell me what that was all about."

Santino blinked, then darkened. He hadn't yet gotten around to reporting

Harrington's gross insubordination, but obviously the girl had gone crying to the Exec over it already. Just a sort of thing she *would* do. He'd known even before the trouble-making, spoiled brat reported aboard what he'd have to deal with there, and he'd been grateful for the forewarning, even if it wasn't considered quite "proper" for an OCTO to have private, pre-cruise briefings on the snotties who would be in his care. She and her wretched pet and the special treatment they both got had certainly jus-tified the warnings he'd been given about her. He could see the arrogance in her eyes, of course, the way she was not so secretly convinced of her superiority to all about her. That was one of the things he'd been determined to knock out of her, in the faint hope that he might somehow salvage a worthwhile officer out of her. Yet even though today's episode had dealt a death blow to that hope, he was still vaguely surprised that even she'd had the sheer nerve to go whining to the Exec after he'd confined her to quarters, which she knew perfectly well meant no com time, either. Well, he'd just add that to the list when he wrote her fitness report.

He blinked again as he realized the Exec was still waiting, then shook himself.

"Of course, Sir," he said. "She was assigned to a routine maintenance inspection of Graser Three. When I arrived to check her progress, she'd instructed her inspec-tion party to fall out and prepared to sign off on the inspection sheet. I observed, however, that the access panel for one of the power rams was still open in violation of SOP. When I pointed this out to her, she was both insolent in attitude and insubordi-nate in her language, so I ordered her to her quarters."

"I see." Layson frowned ever so slightly. "And how, precisely, was she insolent and insubordinate, Lieutenant?"

"Well, Sir," Santino said just a bit cautiously, "I asked her if she thought she'd completed her assignment, and she said she did. Then I pointed out the open access panel and asked her if she was familiar with standard procedures and the requirement to keep such panels closed when not actually being used for inspection or repair. Her tone and manner were both insolent when she replied that she was aware of proper procedure. Only when I pressed her for a fuller explanation did she inform me that she had discovered a fault in the ram and reported it to Engineering. Obviously, I had no way to know that before she explained it to me, but once again her manner was ex-tremely insolent, and both her tone and her choice of words were, in my opinion, in-tended to express contempt for a superior officer. Under the circumstances, I saw no option but to relieve her of duty pending disciplinary action."

"I see," Layson repeated, then let his chair come upright. "Unfortunately, Lieu-tenant, I've already heard another account of the discussion which doesn't exactly tally with yours."

"Sir?" Santino drew himself up and squared his shoulders. "Sir, if Harrington has been trying to—"

"I didn't say I'd heard it from Midshipwoman Harrington," Layson said frostily, and Santino shut his mouth with a click. "Nor did I say I'd heard it from only one per-son," the Exec went on with cold dispassion. "In fact, I have six eyewitnesses, and none of them—not one, Lieutenant Santino—describes events as you just did. Would you perhaps care to comment on this minor discrepancy?"

Santino licked his lips and felt sweat prickle under the band of his beret as the ice in the Exec's voice registered.

"Sir, I can only report my own impressions," he said. "And with all due respect, Sir, I've had ample opportunity to watch Harrington's behavior and attitude over the last eight weeks. Perhaps that gives me, as her training officer, somewhat more insight into her character than a petty officer and working party who haven't had the advan-tage of that perspective."

"The *senior chief* petty officer in question," Layson said quietly, "has been in the

King's Navy for seven years longer than you've been *alive*, Lieutenant Santino. In that time, he's had the opportunity to see more midshipmen and midshipwomen than you've seen dinners. I am not prepared to entertain any suggestion that he is too inexperienced to form a reasonable and reliable opinion of Ms. Harrington's character. Do I make myself clear?"

"Yes, Sir!"

Santino was perspiring freely now, and Layson stood behind his desk.

"As a matter of fact, Mr. Santino, I asked Senior Chief Shelton to share the insight of his many years of experience with me some days ago when I began to hear a few disturbing reports about our officer candidates. As such, he was acting under my direct instructions when he gave me his version of your . . . discussion with Ms. Harrington. Frankly, I'm happy he was there, because this episode simply confirms something I'd already come to suspect. Which is, Mr. Santino, that you are clearly too stupid to pour piss out of a boot without printed instructions!"

The Exec's voice cracked like a whip on the last sentence, and Santino flinched. Then his face darkened and his lips thinned.

"Sir, I resent your implications and strongly protest your language! Nothing in the Articles of War requires me to submit to personal insults and abuse!"

"But the Articles *do* require Ms. Harrington and her fellow middies to submit to *your* personal insults and abuse?" Layson's voice was suddenly like silk wrapped around a dagger's blade. "Is that what you're saying, Mr. Santino?"

"I—" Santino began, then cut himself off and licked his lips again as he realized the Exec had set him up.

"Sir, the situations aren't parallel," he said finally. "Harrington and the other snotties are fresh out of the Academy. They're still learning that the world isn't going to stand around and wipe their noses for them. If I seemed—or if Senior Chief Shelton thought I seemed—abusive, I was simply trying to help toughen them up and turn them into proper King's officers!"

He met Layson's cold eyes defiantly, and the Exec's lip curled.

"Somehow I knew you were going to say that, Lieutenant," he observed. "And, of course, no one can prove you're lying. If I *could* prove it, I would have you up on charges so fast your head would spin. Since I can't, I will explain this to you once. I will explain it *only* once, however, and you had better by God be listening."

The Exec didn't raise his voice, but Santino swallowed hard as Layson walked around the desk, hitched a hip up to rest on it, folded his arms across his chest, and looked him straight in the eye.

"For your information, Mr. Santino, those young men and women are already King's officers. They are also in their final form at the Academy, true, and they're here for evaluation as well as training. But while they are here aboard this ship, they are just as much members of her company and King's officers as *you* are. This means they are to be treated with respect, especially by their seniors. A midshipman cruise is supposed to be stressful. It is supposed to put sufficient pressure on a midshipman—or -woman—to allow us to evaluate his ability to function under it and to teach *him* that he can hack tough assignments. It is *not* supposed to expose any of them to abuse, to bullying, or to the unearned contempt of a superior officer too stupid to know what his own duties and responsibilities are."

"Sir, I have never abused or bullied—"

"Lieutenant, you've never *stopped* bullying them!" Layson snapped. "As just one example, the term 'snotty,' while universally accepted as a slang label for a midshipman on his training cruise, is not an epithet to be hurled contemptuously at them by their own training officer! You have hectored and hounded them from the outset, and I strongly suspect that it's because you are a coward as well as stupid. After all, who expects a mere midshipwoman to stand up to a superior officer? Especially when she knows that superior officer can flush her career right out the air lock with a bad efficiency report?"

Santino stood rigid, his jaws locked, and Layson regarded him with cold contempt.

"You are relieved as officer candidate training officer for cause, effective immediately, Lieutenant Santino. I will report that fact to the Captain, and he will undoubtedly select another officer to fill that slot. In the meantime, you will prepare all records on the midshipmen formerly under your supervision for immediate transfer to that officer. Further, you will take *no* action against Midshipwoman Harrington, any other midshipman aboard this ship, Senior Chief Shelton, or any member of Ms. Harrington's work party which I or the Captain could conceivably construe as retaliation. Should you choose to do so, I assure you, you will regret it. Is that clearly understood?"

Santino nodded convulsively, and Layson gave him a thin smile.

"I'm afraid I didn't hear you, Mr. Santino. I asked if that was clearly understood."

"Yes, Sir." It came out strangled, and Layson smiled again.

"Very good, Lieutenant," he said softly. "Dismissed."

Honor never knew exactly what Commander Layson had to say to Santino that afternoon, but the vicious hatred which looked at her out of Santino's eyes told her that it had not been pleasant. She and her fellow middies did their best—by and large successfully—to restrain their rejoicing when Commander Layson announced that Lieutenant Saunders would replace him, but it was impossible to fool anyone in a world as small as a single starship.

Conditions on Snotty Row improved both drastically and immediately. There was a tough, professional-minded officer behind Saunders' cheerful face, but Santino's mocking contempt was utterly foreign to the assistant astrogator. No one but a fool— which none of *War Maiden's* middies were—would write Saunders off as an easy touch, but he obviously felt no temptation to hammer the midshipmen in his care simply because he could, and that was more than enough to endear him to them.

Unfortunately, it was impossible for the middies to completely avoid Santino even after Saunders replaced him. Tactics were one of the areas in which their training was most intense, which was why the assistant head of that department was traditionally the OCTO aboard any ship. The fact that Santino had been relieved of those duties—obviously for cause—was going to be a serious black mark on his record, which no doubt helped explain some of the hatred which so plainly burned within him. But it also made the change in assignments awkward for everyone involved. He might have been relieved as their training officer, but whatever the Exec and the Captain might have had to say to him in private, he had not been relieved of any other duties. Honor quickly noticed that Lieutenant Commander Hirake seemed to hand out a much higher percentage of their training assignments than had previously been the case, but it was impossible for any of them to report to Hirake without at least entering Santino's proximity. At least half the time, Santino was still the tac officer who actually oversaw their training sims, and none of them enjoyed it a bit when that happened. Nor did he, for that matter. He was careful to restrict himself to formalities, but the glitter in his eyes was ample proof of how difficult he found that. In some ways, it was almost hard not to sympathize with him. Given the circumstances of his relief, his contact with them as simply one more assistant department head was guaranteed to grind his nose into his disgrace. But however well Honor understood what he must be feeling, she, for one, was never tempted to feel sorry for him in the least. Besides, being Elvis Santino, it never occurred to him to blame anyone but Honor Harrington for what had happened to him, and despite anything the Exec had said to him, he was constitutionally incapable of hiding his hatred for her. Since he was going to feel that way whatever she did, she refused to strain herself trying to feel sympathy for someone who so amply merited his disgrace.

In some ways, it was almost worse now that he'd been relieved. Just as he was forced to stifle his fury at Honor on the occasions when their duties brought them into contact, she was required to act as if nothing had ever happened between them. Honor knew that there wasn't a great deal Layson could have done to decrease their contacts without far greater official provocation than Santino had given. Without stripping the man completely of his duties, there was no way to take him out of the queue. Certainly not without completing the lieutenant's public humiliation by absolutely confirming the reason he'd been relieved as OCTO in the first place. And there were times Honor wondered if perhaps Layson didn't have another reason for leaving Santino where he was. It was certainly one way to determine how she and her fellow middies would react under conditions of social strain!

For the most part though, she found herself blossoming and expanding as she was finally freed to throw herself into the learning experience a middy cruise was supposed to be. The fact that *War Maiden* arrived in Silesian space shortly after Santino's relief contributed its own weight to her happiness, although she supposed some people might have found it difficult to understand. After all, the Silesian Confederacy was a snake pit of warring factions, revolutionary governments, and corrupt system governors whose central government, such as it was, maintained its tenuous claim of rule solely on sufferance and the fact that the various unruly factions could never seem to combine effectively against it any more than they could combine effectively against one another. The casual observer, and especially the casual civilian observer, might have been excused for finding such an environment less than desirable. But Honor didn't see it that way, for the unending unrest was what had brought her ship here in the first place, and she was eager to test herself in the real world.

In a perverse sort of way, Silesia's very instability helped explain the enormous opportunities which the Confederacy offered Manticoran merchants. There was quite literally no reliable local supplier for most of the Confederacy's citizens' needs, which opened all sorts of possibilities for outside suppliers. Unfortunately, that same instability provided all manner of havens and sponsors for the privateers and pirates for whom the Star Kingdom's commerce offered what were often irresistible targets. The Royal Manticoran Navy had made its draconian policy concerning pirates (the enforcement of which was *War Maiden's* reason for being here) uncompromisingly clear over the years. The demonstration of that policy had involved quite a few pirate fatalities, but the capture of a single seven- or eight-million-ton merchantman could earn a pirate crew millions upon millions of dollars, and greed was a powerful motivator. Especially since even the stupidest pirate knew that the Star Kingdom's navy couldn't possibly cover the trade routes in depth and that no one else—with the possible exception of the Andermani—would even make the attempt.

That background explained why the Silesian Confederacy had been the RMN's main training ground for decades. It was a place to blood fledgling crews and starship commanders, gain tactical experience in small-scale engagements, and expose Navy personnel to the realities of labyrinthine political murkiness, all while doing something useful in its own right—protecting the Star Kingdom's commerce.

Still, the antipiracy effort was perpetually undersupplied with warships. That had always been true to some extent, but the steadily accelerating buildup of the battle fleet had made it worse in recent years. The increased emphasis on capital units and the Junction forts, and especially on manning such crew-intensive propositions, had reduced the availability of light units for such operational areas as Silesia.

And there was a corollary to that, one which was bound to affect HMS *War Maiden* and one Ms. Midshipwoman Harrington. For if there were fewer units available, then those which did reach Silesia could expect to be worked hard.

Honor stepped through the wardroom hatch with Nimitz on her shoulder. It had been late by *War Maiden's* onboard clock when she went off duty, and she was tired, but she wasn't yet ready for bed. The heavy cruiser had made her alpha translation into normal space in the Melchor System of the Saginaw Sector shortly before the end of Honor's watch, and she'd had an excellent vantage from which to watch the process, for she was assigned to Astrogation this month. That was a mixed blessing in her opinion. It had its exciting moments, like the ones she'd spent backing up Lieutenant Commander Dobrescu during the approach to the alpha wall. Dobrescu, *War Maiden's* astrogator, was Lieutenant Saunders' boss, and very good at his job, so there'd never been much chance that he was going to require Honor's assistance in a maneuver he'd performed hundreds of times before, but it had still been . . . not so much exciting as *satisfying* to sit in the backup chair at his side and watch the hyper log spin down to the translation locus. She still preferred Tactical to Astrogation—when Santino was absent, at least—but there *was* something about being the person who guided the ship among the stars.

Now if only she'd been any good at it . . .

Actually, she knew there was very little wrong with her astrogation in and of itself. She understood the *theory* perfectly, and as long as people would just leave her alone with the computers, she felt confident of her ability to find her way about the galaxy. Unfortunately, she was a midshipwoman. That meant she was a trainee, and to the Navy—including Dobrescu and Lieutenant Saunders (however satisfactory he might otherwise have been as an OCTO)—"trainee" meant "student," and students were expected to demonstrate their ability to do the basic calculations with no more than a hand comp and a stylus. And that was pure, sweat-popping, torment for Honor. However well she understood astrogation theory and multi-dimension math, her actual mathematical proficiency was something else altogether. She'd never been any good at math, which was all the more irritating because her aptitude scores indicated that she ought to excel at it. And, if people would just leave her alone and not stand around waiting for her to produce the right answer, she usually did come up with the correct solution in the end. For that matter, if she didn't have time to think about it and remember she was no good at math, she usually got the right answer fairly quickly. But that wasn't the way it worked during snotty-training, and she'd found herself sweating blood every time Dobrescu gave her a problem. Which was both grossly unfair—in her opinion—and stupid.

It wasn't as if Dobrescu or the astrogator of any other starship did his calculations by hand. The entire idea was ridiculous! That was what computers were for in the first place, and if a ship suffered such a massive computer failure as to take Astrogation off-line, figuring out where it was was going to be the *least* of its problems. She'd just *love* to see anyone try to manage a hyper generator, an inertial compensator, or the grav pinch of a fusion plant without computer support! But the Powers That Were weren't particularly interested in the opinions of one Ms. Midshipwoman Harrington, and so she sweated her way through the entire old-fashioned, labor-intensive, frustrating, *stupid* quill-pen-and-parchment business like the obedient little snotty she was.

At least Lieutenant Commander Dobrescu had a sense of humor.

And at least they were now safely back into normal space, with only three dinky little dimensions to worry about.

It would have been nice if Melchor had been a more exciting star to visit, given how hard Honor and her hand comp had worked to overcome the dreadful deficiencies of her ship's computers and get *War Maiden* here safely. Unfortunately, it wasn't. True, the G4 primary boasted three very large gas giants whose orbital spacing had created no less than four asteroid belts, but of its total of seven planets, only one was of any particular interest to humans. That was Arianna, the sole habitable planet of the system, which orbited Melchor at nine light-minutes, over eleven light-minutes inside the star's hyper limit. Arianna was a dry, mountainous world, with narrow, shallow seas, minimal icecaps, and a local flora which tended to the drought-hardy and low-growing. It had been settled over two hundred standard years before, but the hardscrabble colony had never moved much above the subsistence level until about fifty years ago, when an Andermani mining consortium had decided to take advantage of the resource extraction possibilities of all those asteroids. The outside investment and subsequent discovery of an unusual abundance of rare metals had brought an unexpected boom economy to the star system and attracted more immigrants in less time than the Melchor system government could ever have expected. Unfortunately for the Andermani, the local sector governor had seen that boom primarily as an opportunity to fill his own pockets. That wasn't an uncommon occurrence in Silesia, and however angry the Andermani consortium's financial backers might have been, they could not really have been very surprised when the governor began muscling in on their investment. Bribery and kickbacks were a way of life in the Confederacy, and people like the Saginaw sector governor knew how to extract them when they were not offered spontaneously. Within ten years, he and his family had owned over thirty percent of the total consortium, and the original Andermani backers had begun selling off their stock to other Silesians. Within another ten, the entire mining operation had been in Silesian hands and, like so much else in Silesian hands, running very, very poorly.

But this time around, the majority of the stockholders seemed willing to at least make an attempt to restore their fortunes, and the Star Kingdom's Dillingham Cartel had been brought onboard as a minority stockholder, with all sorts of performance incentives, to attempt to turn things back around once more. Which, in no small part, explained *War Maiden*'s presence in Melchor.

Dillingham had moved in Manticoran mining experts and begun a systematic upgrade of the extraction machinery which had been allowed to disintegrate under purely Silesian management. Honor suspected the cartel had been forced to pay high-risk bonuses to any Manticorans who had agreed to relocate here, and she knew from the general background brief Captain Bachfisch had shared with *War Maiden*'s company that Dillingham had seen fit to install some truly impressive defensive systems to protect their extraction complexes and Arianna itself. They would not have been very effective against a regular naval force, but they were more than enough to give any piratical riffraff serious pause. Unfortunately, the Confederacy's central government refused to countenance privately flagged warships in its territorial space, so Dillingham had been forced to restrict itself to orbital systems. The ban on private warships was one of the (many) stupid policies of the Confederacy, in Honor's opinion. No doubt it was an attempt to at least put a crimp in the supply of armed vessels which seemed to find a way into pirate hands with dismal regularity, but it was a singularly ineffective one. All it really did in this case was to prevent someone who might have been able to provide the entire star system with a degree of safety which was unhappily rare in Silesia from doing so. The cartel's fixed defenses created zones within the Melchor System into which no raider was likely to stray, but they couldn't possibly protect merchant ships approaching or leaving the star.

Not that the Confederacy government was likely to regard that concern as any skin off its nose. The ships coming and going to Melchor these days were almost all Manticoran—aside from the handful of Andermani who still called there—and if the foreigners couldn't take the heat, then they should get out of the kitchen. Or, as in *War Maiden's* case, call in their own governments to look after their interests. Of course, the Confederacy scarcely liked to admit that it needed foreign navies to police its own domestic space, but it had learned long ago that Manticore would send its naval units to protect its commerce whatever the Silesians wanted, so it might as well let Manticore pick up the tab for Melchor. And if the Star Kingdom lost a few merchant ships and their crews in the process, well, it served the pushy foreigners right.

Honor was scarcely so innocent as to be surprised by the situation. That didn't mean she liked it, but like anyone else who aspired to command a King's ship, she recognized the protection of the merchant trade which was the heart, blood, and sinews of the Star Kingdom's economic might as one of the Navy's most important tasks. She didn't begrudge being here to protect Manticoran lives and property, whatever she might think of the so-called local government that made her presence a necessity.

Despite all that, it was highly unlikely *War Maiden* would find anything exciting to do here. As Captain Courvosier had often warned, a warship's life was ten percent hard work, eighty-nine percent boredom, and one percent sheer, howling terror. The percentages might shift a bit in a place like Silesia, but the odds in favor of boredom remained overwhelming. Honor knew that, too, but she was still just a bit on edge and not quite ready to turn in, which explained her detour by the wardroom. Besides, she was hungry. Again.

Her eyes swept the compartment with a hint of wariness as she stepped through the hatch, but then she relaxed. A middy in the wardroom was rather like a junior probationary member of an exclusive club, only less so. He or she had a right to be there, but the tradition was that they were to be seen and not heard unless one of the more senior members of the club invited them to open their mouths. In addition, they had better be prepared to run any errands any of their seniors needed run, because none of those seniors were likely to give up any of their hard-earned rest by getting up and walking across the wardroom when there were younger and more junior legs they could send instead. In fact, the tradition of sending snotties to do the scut work was one of the Navy's longer-standing traditions, part of the semi-hazing which was part and parcel of initiating midshipmen into the tribal wisdom, and Honor didn't really mind it particularly. For the most part, at least.

But this time she was lucky. Santino was off duty, of course, or she wouldn't have been here in the first place, but Lieutenant Commander LaVacher, who, while an otherwise reasonably pleasant human being, had a pronounced talent for and took an unabashed delight in finding things for middies to do, was also absent. Lieutenant Saunders looked up from his contemplation of a book reader and nodded a casual welcome, while Commander Layson and Lieutenant Jeffers, the ship's logistics officer, concentrated on the chessboard between them and Lieutenant Livanos and Lieutenant Tergesen, LaVacher's first and second engineers, respectively, were immersed in some sort of card game with Ensign Baumann. Aside from Saunders' offhanded greeting, no one seemed to notice her at all, and she made a beeline across the compartment towards the waiting mid-rats table. The food in the wardroom was considerably inferior to that served in the officers' mess at normal mealtimes, but rated several more stars than the off-watch rations available to the denizens of Snotty Row. And perhaps even more important, from Honor's perspective, there was more of it.

Nimitz perked up on her shoulder as she spotted the cheese-stuffed celery sticks and passed one up to him, then snuck an olive out of the slightly limp looking bowl of tossed salad and popped it into her own mouth to stave off starvation while she constructed a proper sandwich for more serious attention. Mayonnaise, cold cuts, mustard, Swiss cheese, sliced onion, another layer of cold cuts, dill pickle slices, another slice of Swiss cheese, some lettuce from the salad bowl, and a tomato ring, and she was done. She added a satisfying but not overly greedy heap of potato chips to her plate to keep it company, and poured herself a large glass of cold milk and snagged two cupcakes to keep *it* company, then gathered up a few extra celery sticks for Nimitz and found a seat at one of the unoccupied wardroom tables.

"How in God's name did you put that thing together without counter-grav?"

She turned her head and smiled in response to Commander Layson's question. The Exec gazed at her sandwich for a moment longer, then shook his head in bemusement, and Lieutenant Jeffers chuckled.

"I'm beginning to understand why we seem to be running a little short on commissary supplies," he observed. "I always knew midshipmen were bottomless pits, but—"

It was his turn to shake his head, and Layson laughed out loud.

"What I don't understand," Lieutenant Tergesen said just a bit plaintively, looking up from her cards at the sound of the Exec's laughter, "is how you can stuff all that in and never gain a kilo." The dark-haired engineering officer was in her early thirties, and while she certainly wasn't obese, she *was* a shade on the plump side. "I'd be as broad across the beam as a trash hauler if I gorged on half that many calories!"

"Well, I work out a lot, Ma'am," Honor replied, which was accurate enough, if also a little evasive. People were no longer as prejudiced against "genies" as they once had been, but those like Honor who were descended from genetically engineered ancestors still tended to be cautious about admitting it to anyone they did not know well.

"I'll say she does," Ensign Baumann put in wryly. "I saw her and Sergeant Tausig sparring yesterday evening." The ensign looked around at the wardroom's occupants in general and wrinkled her nose. "She was working out full contact . . . with Tausig."

"With *Tausig?*" Layson half-turned in his own chair to look more fully at Honor. "Tell me, Ms. Harrington. How well do you know Surgeon Lieutenant Chiem?"

"Lieutenant Chiem?" Honor frowned. "I checked in with him when I joined the ship, of course, Sir. And he was present one night when the Captain was kind enough to include me in his dinner party, but I don't really *know* the doctor. Why? Should I, Sir?"

This time the laughter was general, and Honor blushed in perplexity as Nimitz bleeked his own amusement from the back of her chair. Her seniors' mirth held none of the sneering putdown or condescension she might have expected from someone like a Santino, but she was honestly at a loss to account for it. Lieutenant Saunders recognized her confusion, and smiled at her.

"From your reaction, I gather that you weren't aware that the good sergeant was the second runner-up in last year's Fleet unarmed combat competition, Ms. Harrington," he said.

"That he was—" Honor stopped, gawking at the lieutenant, then closed her mouth and shook her head.

"No, Sir, I didn't. He never—I mean, the subject never came up. Second runner-up in the *Fleet* matches? Really?"

"Really," Layson replied for the lieutenant, his tone dry. "And everyone knows Sergeant Tausig's theory of instruction normally involves thumping on his students until they either wake up in sick bay or get good enough to thump him back. So if you and Doctor Chiem haven't become close personal acquaintances, you must be pretty good yourself."

"Well, I try, Sir. And I was on the *coup de vitesse* demo team at the Academy, but—" She paused again. "But I'm not in the sergeant's league by a longshot. I only get a few pops in because he lets me."

"I beg to differ," Layson said more dryly than ever. "I hold a black belt myself, Ms. Harrington, and Sergeant Tausig has been known to spend the odd moment kicking my commissioned butt around the salle. And he has never 'let' me get a hit in. I think it's against his religion, and I very much doubt that he would decide to make an exception in your case. So if you 'get a few pops in,' you're doing better than ninety-five percent of the people who step onto the mat with him."

Honor blinked at him, still holding her sandwich for another bite. She'd known Tausig was one of the best she'd ever worked out with, and she knew he was light-years better at the *coup* than she was, but she would never have had the gall to ask to spar with him if she'd known he'd placed that high in the Fleet competition. He must have thought she was out of her mind! Why in the world had he agreed to let her? And if he was going to do that, why go so easy on her? Whatever Commander Layson might think, Honor couldn't believe that—

A high, shrill, atonal shriek cut her thought off like an ax of sound, and her sandwich thumped messily onto her plate as spinal reflex yanked her from her chair. She snatched Nimitz up and was out of the wardroom with the 'cat cradled in her arms before the plate slid off the table and the disintegrating sandwich's stuffing hit the decksole.

Lieutenant Saunders looked up from his displays and glanced at Honor over his shoulder as she arrived on the bridge, then flicked a look at the bulkhead chrono. It was only a brief glance, and then he gave her a quick, smiling nod as she crossed the command deck to him. Regs allowed her an extra five minutes to get to action stations, in order to give her time to secure Nimitz safely in his life-support module in her berthing compartment, but she'd made it in only thirteen minutes. It helped that Snotty Row was relatively close to the bridge, but it helped even more that she'd spent so many extra hours on suit drill at Saganami Island expressly because she'd known she'd have to find time to get her and Nimitz both cleared for action.

Not that even the amount of practice she'd put in could make it any less uncomfortable to make her skinsuit's plumbing connections that rapidly, she thought wryly as she settled gingerly into the assistant astrogation officer's chair. At the moment, Saunders occupied first chair in Astrogation, because Commander Dobrescu was with Commander Layson in Auxiliary Control. In fact, there was an entire backup command crew in AuxCon. Few modern heavy cruisers had auxiliary command decks, since more recent design theory regarded the provision of such a facility in so small a unit as a misuse of mass which could otherwise have been assigned to weapons or defensive systems. In newer ships of *War Maiden*'s type, an additional fire control position was provided at one end of the core hull instead, with just enough extra room for the ship's executive officer to squeeze into alongside the Tac Department personnel who manned it. But since *War Maiden* was an old enough design to provide an AuxCon, Captain Bachfisch had been able to create an entirely separate command crew to back up Commander Layson if something unpleasant should happen to the bridge.

Honor was delighted to be on the bridge itself, but because she was currently assigned to astro training duties, she'd drawn the assistant astrogator's duty here, while Basanta Lakhia filled the same duty for Dobrescu in AuxCon. The person Honor passionately envied at this moment was Audrey Bradlaugh, who sat beside Lieutenant Commander Hirake at Tactical. Honor would have given her left arm—well, a finger or two off her left hand, anyway—to sit in Audrey's chair, but at least she was luckier than Nassios. Captain Bachfisch had given Commander Layson the more experienced astrogator, but he'd kept the senior tac officer for himself, which meant Layson was stuck with Elvis Santino . . . and that Nassios had found himself stuck as Santino's assistant.

There were, Honor conceded, even worse fates than astrogation training duty.

She pushed the thought aside as she brought her own console rapidly online, and her amusement vanished and her stomach tightened when her astro plot came up and steadied. It lacked the detail of the tactical displays available to Hirake and Captain Bachfisch, but it showed enough for her to realize that this was no drill, for *War Maiden*'s arrival had interrupted a grim drama. The icon of a merchantman showed in her plot with the transponder code of a Manticoran vessel, but there was another vessel as well, the angry red bead of an unknown, presumably hostile ship less than four hundred kilometers from the merchie. The unknown vessel had her wedge up; the merchantman did not, and a jagged crimson ring strobed about its alphanumeric transponder code.

"Positive ID on the merchie, Skipper," Lieutenant Commander Hirake reported crisply. "I have her on my shipping list—RMMS *Gryphon's Pride*. She's a Dillingham Cartel ship, all right. Five-point-five million tons, a pure bulk hauler with no passenger accommodations, and she's squawking a Code Seventeen."

An invisible breeze blew across the bridge, cold on the nape of Honor's neck as the tac officer's announcement confirmed what all of them had already known. Code Seventeen was the emergency transponder code which meant "I am being boarded by pirates."

"Range to target?" Captain Bachfisch's tenor was no longer nasal. It was clipped, cool, and clear, and Honor darted a glance over her shoulder. The Captain sat in his command chair, shoulders square yet relaxed, right leg crossed over left while he gazed intently into the tactical display deployed from the chair, and the dark eyes in his thin face no longer frowned. They were the bright, fierce eyes of a predator, and Honor turned back to her own display with a tiny shiver.

"Nine-point-three-one million klicks," Hirake said, and if the Captain's voice was crisp, hers was flat. "We don't have the angle on them, either," she went on in that same disappointed tone. "The bogey's already gotten underway, and we'll never be able to pull enough vector change to run him down."

"Do you concur, Astro?"

"Aye, Sir," Saunders said with equal unhappiness. "Our base vector is away from the merchie at almost eleven thousand KPS, Captain. It'll take us forty-five minutes just to decelerate to relative rest to them, and according to my plot, the bogey is turning well over five hundred gravities."

"They're up to just over five-thirty," Hirake confirmed from Tactical.

"Even at maximum military power, we're twenty gravities slower than that, Sir," Saunders said. "At normal max, they've got over one-point-two KPS squared on us, and they're accelerating on a direct reciprocal of our heading."

"I see." Bachfisch said, and Honor understood the disappointment in his tone perfectly. The pirate ship had to be smaller than *War Maiden* to pull that sort of acceleration, which meant it was certainly more lightly armed, as well, but it didn't matter. Their relative positions and base vectors had given the pirates the opportunity to run, and their higher acceleration curve meant the heavy cruiser could never bring them into even extreme missile range.

"Very well," the Captain said after a moment. "Astro, put us on a course to intercept the merchie. And keep trying to raise them, Com."

"Aye, aye, Sir." Saunders' quiet acknowledgment sounded much too loud against the bitter background silence of the bridge.

.   .   .

There was no response to Lieutenant Sauchuk's repeated hails as *War Maiden* closed on the merchantship, and the taut silence on the heavy cruiser's bridge grew darker and more bitter with each silent minute. It took over two hours for the warship to decelerate to zero relative to the merchantman and then overtake her. *Gryphon's Pride* coasted onward at her base velocity, silent and uncaring, and the cruiser was less than a minnow as she swam toward a rendezvous with her, for the whale-like freighter outmassed *War Maiden* by a factor of almost thirty. But unlike the whale, the minnow was armed, and a platoon of her Marines climbed into their skinsuits and checked their weapons in her boat bay as Captain Bachfisch's helmsman edged his ship into position with finicky precision.

Honor was no longer on the bridge to watch. Bachfisch's eyes had passed over her with incurious impersonality while he punched up Major McKinley, the commander of *War Maiden's* embarked Marine company, on the internal com and instructed her to prepare a boarding party. But then those eyes had tracked back to his assistant astrogator's assistant.

"I'll be attaching a couple of naval officers, as well," he told McKinley, still looking at Honor.

"Yes, Sir," the Marine's reply came back, and Bachfisch released the com stud.

"Commander Hirake," he said, "please lay below to the boat bay to join the boarding party. And take Ms. Harrington with you."

"Aye, aye, Sir," the tac officer acknowledged and stood. "You have Tactical, Ms. Bradlaugh."

"Aye, aye, Ma'am," Audrey acknowledged, and darted a quick, envious glance at her cabin mate.

"Come along, Ms. Harrington," Hirake said, and Honor stood quickly.

"Sir, I request relief," she said to Saunders, and the lieutenant nodded.

"You stand relieved, Ms. Harrington," he said with equal formality.

"Thank you, Sir." Honor turned to follow Hirake through the bridge hatch, but Captain Bachfisch raised one hand in an admonishing gesture and halted them.

"Don't forget your sidearm this time," he told Hirake rather pointedly, and she nodded. "Good," he said. "In that case, people, let's be about it," he added, and waved them off his bridge.

Hirake said nothing in the lift car. Despite *War Maiden's* age and the idiosyncratic layout of her lift shafts, the trip from the bridge to the boat bay was relatively brief, but it lasted more than long enough for conflicting waves of anticipation and dread to wash through Honor. She had no idea why the Captain had picked her for this duty, but she'd heard more than enough grisly stories from instructors and noncoms at the Academy to produce a stomach-clenching apprehension. Yet hunting down pirates— and cleaning up the wreckage in their wake—was part of the duty she'd signed on to perform, and not even the queasiness in her midsection could quench her sense of excitement finally confronting its reality.

Lieutenant Blackburn's Second Platoon was waiting in the boat bay, but Honor was a bit surprised to see that Captain McKinley and Sergeant-Major Kutkin were also present. She'd assumed McKinley would send one of her junior officers, but she and Kutkin obviously intended to come along in person, for both of them were skinsuited, and the sergeant-major had a pulse rifle slung over his shoulder. Major McKinley didn't carry a rifle, but the pulser holstered at her hip looked almost like a part of her, and its grip was well worn.

The Marine officer's blue eyes examined the newcomers with clinical dispassion and just a hint of disapproval, and Hirake sighed.

"All right, Katingo," she said resignedly. "The Skipper already peeled a strip off me, so give me a damned gun."

"It's nice to know *someone* aboard the ship knows Regs," McKinley observed, and nodded to a noncom standing to one side. Honor hadn't seen him at first, but she recognized Sergeant Tausig as he stepped forward and silently passed a regulation gun belt and pulser to the tac officer. Lieutenant Commander Hirake took them a bit gingerly and buckled the belt around her waist. It was obvious to Honor that the Navy officer felt uncomfortable with the sidearm, but Hirake drew the pulser and made a brief but thorough inspection of its safety and magazine indicators before she returned it to its holster.

"Here, Ma'am," Tausig said, and Honor held out her hand for a matching belt. She felt both the major and the sergeant-major watching her, but she allowed herself to show no sign of her awareness as she buckled the belt and adjusted it comfortably. Then she turned slightly away, drew the pulser—keeping its muzzle pointed carefully away from anyone else—visually checked the safety and both magazine indicators and the power cell readout, then ejected the magazine and cleared the chamber to be certain it was unloaded. She replaced the magazine and reholstered the weapon. The military issue flapped holster was clumsy and bulky compared to the semi-custom civilian rig Honor had always carried in the Sphinx bush, but the pulser's weight felt comfortingly familiar at her hip, and Sergeant Tausig's eyes met hers with a brief flash of approval as she looked up once more.

"All right, people," Major McKinley said, raising her voice as she turned to address Blackburn's platoon. "You all know the drill. Remember, we do this by The Book, and I will personally have the ass of anyone who fucks up."

She didn't ask if her audience understood. She didn't have to, Honor thought. Not when she'd made herself clear in that tone of voice. Of course, it would have been nice if someone had told *Honor* what "the drill" was, but it was an imperfect universe. She'd just have to keep her eyes on everyone else and take her cues from them. And at least, given the Captain's parting injunction to Hirake and McKinley's response to it, she might not be the only one who needed a keeper.

The pinnace was just like dozens of other pinnaces Honor had boarded during Academy training exercises, but it didn't feel that way. Not with forty-six grim, hard-faced, armed-to-the-teeth Marines and their weapons packed into it. She sat next to Lieutenant Commander Hirake at the rear of the passenger compartment, and watched through the view port beside her as the pinnace crossed the last few hundred kilometers between *War Maiden* and *Gryphon's Pride*. The big freighter grew rapidly as they came up on it from astern, and the pinnace's pilot cut his wedge and went to reaction thrusters, then angled his flight to spiral up and around the huge hull.

Honor and Hirake were tied into the Marines' com net. There was no chatter, and Honor sensed the intensity with which the Marines fortunate enough to have view port seats, veterans all, stared out at the freighter. Then the pilot spoke over the net.

"I have debris, Major," he said in a flat, professional voice. "At your ten o'clock high position." There were a few seconds of silence, then, "Looks like bodies, Ma'am."

"I see them, Coxswain," McKinley said tonelessly. Honor was on the wrong side of the pinnace to lean closer to her port and peer forward. For a moment she felt frustrated, but then that changed into gratitude for the accident of seating that had kept her from doing just that. She would have felt ashamed and somehow unclean if

Hirake and the Marines had seen her craning her neck while she gawked at the bodies like some sort of sick disaster-watcher or a news service ghoul.

"Coming up on her main starboard midships hatch, Ma'am," the pilot reported a few minutes later. "Looks like the cargo bays are still sealed, but the forward personnel hatch is open. Want me to go for a hard docking?"

"No, we'll stick to The Book," McKinley said. "Hold position at two hundred meters."

"Aye, aye, Ma'am."

The pilot nudged the pinnace into a stationary position relative to the freighter with the pinnace's swept wing tip almost exactly two hundred meters from the hull, and Sergeant-Major Kutkin shoved all two meters of his height up out of his seat. Lieutenant Blackburn was no more than a second behind the sergeant-major, and Kutkin watched with an approving proprietary air as the lieutenant addressed his platoon.

"All right, Marines, let's do it. Carras, you've got point. Janssen, you've got the backdoor. The rest of you in standard, just like we trained for it." He waited a moment, watching as two or three of his troopers adjusted position slightly, then grunted in approval. "Helmet up and let's go," he said.

Honor unclipped her own helmet from the carry point on her chest and put it on. She gave it a little extra twist to be sure it was seated properly and raised her left arm to press the proper key on the sleeve keypad. Her helmet HUD lit immediately, and she automatically checked the telltale which confirmed a good seal and the digital readout on her oxygen supply. Both were nominal, and she took her place—as befitted her lowly status—at the very rear of the queue to the pinnace's port hatch. With so many personnel to unload, the flight crew made no effort to cycle them through the air lock. Instead, they cracked the outer hatch and vented the compartment's air to space. Honor felt the pressure tug at her for several seconds as the air bled outward, but then the sensation of unseen hands plucking at her limbs faded and her skinsuit audio pickups brought her the absolute silence of vacuum.

Corporal Carras—the same corporal, Honor realized suddenly, who had been *War Maiden's* tube sentry when she first joined the ship—pushed himself away from the pinnace. He drifted outward for four or five meters, and then engaged his skinsuit thrusters once he was sure he had cleared their safety perimeter. He accelerated smoothly towards the freighter, riding his thrusters with the practiced grace of some huge bird of prey, and the rest of his section followed.

Even with their obvious practice it took time for all of the Marines to clear the hatch for Hirake and Honor, but at last it was their turn, and despite her best effort to mirror the cool professionalism of Blackburn's Marines, Honor felt a fresh flutter of excited anxiety as she followed Hirake into the open hatch. The lieutenant commander launched herself with a gracefulness which fully matched that of the Marines, yet was somehow subtly different. She sailed away from the pinnace, and Honor pushed herself out into emptiness in the tac officer's wake.

This far out, the system primary was a feeble excuse for a star, and even that was on the far side of the freighter. The pinnace and its erstwhile passengers floated in an ink-black lee of shadow, and hull-mounted spotlights and the smaller helmet lights of skinsuits pierced the ebon dark. The pinnace's powerful spots threw unmoving circles of brilliance on the freighter's hull, picking out the sealed cargo hatch and the smaller personnel hatch which gaped open ahead of it, yet their beams were invisible, for there was no air to diffuse them. Smaller circles curtsied and danced across the illuminated area and into the darkness beyond as the helmet lights of individual Marines swept over the hull. Honor brought up her own helmet lamp as her thrusters propelled her towards the ship, and her eyes were bright. She cherished no illusion that she was a holodrama heroine about to set forth on grand adventure, yet her pulse was faster than usual, and it was all she could do not to rest her right hand on the butt of her holstered pulser.

Then something moved in the darkness. It was more sensed than seen, an uncertain shape noticed only because it briefly occluded the circle on the hull cast by someone else's light as it rotated slowly, keeping station on the ship. She rotated her own body slightly, bringing her light to bear upon it, and suddenly any temptation she might still have nursed to see this as an adventure vanished.

The crewwoman could not have been more than a very few standard years older than Honor . . . and she would never grow any older. She wore no suit. Indeed, even the standard shipboard coverall she once had worn had been half-ripped from her body and drifted with her in the blackness, tangled about her arms and shoulders like some ungainly, rucked up shroud. An expression of pure horror was visible even through the froth of frozen blood caked about her mouth and nose, and the hideousness of her death had relaxed her sphincters. It was not simply death. It was desecration, and it was ugly, and Honor Harrington swallowed hard as she came face-to-face with it. She remembered all the times she and Academy friends had teased one another, humorously threatening to "space" someone for some real or imagined misdeed, and it was no longer funny.

She didn't know how long she floated there, holding her light on the corpse which had once been a young woman until someone jettisoned her like so much garbage. It seemed later like a century, but in reality it could not have been more than a very few seconds before she tore her eyes away. She had drifted off course, she noted mechanically, and Lieutenant Commander Hirake was twenty or thirty meters ahead of her and to the right. She checked her HUD, and tapped a correction on her thruster controls. She felt a sort of surprise when her fingers moved the skinsuit gloves' finger servos with rocklike steadiness, and she accelerated smoothly to follow the tac officer through the blackness.

It was interesting, a detached corner of her brain noted almost clinically. Despite her horror, she truly was collected and almost calm—or something which counterfeited those qualities surprisingly well.

But she was very, very careful what else she let her helmet light show her.

". . . so that's about it, Sir." Commander Layson sighed, and let the memo board drop onto the corner of Captain Bachfisch's desk. "No survivors. No indications that they even tried to keep any of the poor bastards alive long enough to find out what *Gryphon's Pride* might've had in her secure cargo spaces." He leaned back in his chair and rubbed his eyes wearily. "They just came aboard, amused themselves, and butchered her entire company. Eleven men and five women. The lucky ones were killed out of hand. The others . . ." His voice trailed off, and he shook his head.

"Not exactly what our briefing told us to expect," Bachfisch said quietly. He tipped back in his own chair and gazed at the deckhead.

"No, but this is Silesia," Layson pointed out. "The only thing anyone can count on here is that the lunatics running the asylum will be even crazier than you expected," he added bitterly. "Sometimes I wish we could just go ahead and hand the damned place over to the Andies and be done with it. Let these sick bastards deal with the Andy Navy for a while with no holds barred."

"Now, Abner," Bachfisch said mildly. "You shouldn't go around suggesting things you know would give the Government mass coronaries. Not to mention the way the cartels would react to the very notion of letting someone else control one of their major market areas! Besides, would you really like encouraging someone like the Andermani to bite off that big an expansion in one chunk?"

"All joking aside, Sir, it might not be that bad a thing from our perspective. The Andies have always been into slow and steady expansion, biting off small pieces one at a time and taking time to digest between mouthfuls. If they jumped into a snake pit like Silesia, it would be like grabbing a hexapuma by the tail. They might be able to hang onto the tail, but those six feet full of claws would make it a lively exercise. Could even turn out to be a big enough headache to take them out of the expansion business permanently."

"Wishful thinking, Abner. Wishful thinking." Bachfisch pushed himself up out of his chair and paced moodily across his cramped day cabin. "I told the Admiralty we needed more ships out here," he said, then snorted. "Not that they needed to hear it from me! Unfortunately, more ships are exactly what we don't have, and with the Peeps sharpening their knives for Trevor's Star, Their Lordships aren't going to have any more to spare out this way for the foreseeable future. And the damned Silesians know it."

"I wish you were wrong, Sir. Unfortunately, you're not."

"I only wish I could decide which were worse," Bachfisch half-muttered. "The usual sick, sadistic, murdering scum like the animals that hit *Gryphon's Pride*, or the goddamn 'patriots' and their so-called privateers!"

"I think I prefer the privateers," Layson said. "There aren't as many of them, and at least some of them pretend to play by some sort of rules. And there's at least a sense of semi-accountability to the government or revolutionary committee or whoever the hell issued their letter of marque in the first place."

"I know the logic." Bachfisch chopped at the air with his right hand. "And I know we can at least sometimes lean on whoever chartered them to make them behave—or at least to turn them over to us if they *mis*behave badly enough—but that assumes we know who they are and where they came from in the first place. And anything we gain from that limited sort of accountability on their part, we lose on the capability side."

Layson nodded. It didn't take much of a warship to make a successful pirate cruiser. Aside from a few specialized designs, like the Hauptman Cartel's armed passenger liners, merchantmen were big, slow, lumbering and unarmored targets, helpless before even the lightest shipboard armament. By the same token, no sane pirate— and however sociopathic all too many of them might be, pirates as a group tended to be very sane where matters of survival were concerned—wanted to take on any warship in combat. Even here in Silesia, regular navy crews tended to be better trained and more highly motivated. Besides, a pirate's ship was his principal capital investment. He was in business to make money, not spend it patching the holes in his hull . . . assuming he was fortunate enough to escape from a regular man-of-war in the first place.

But privateers were different. Or they could be, at least. Like pirates, the financial backers who invested in a privateer expected it to be a money-making concern. But privateers also possessed a certain quasi-respectability, for interstellar law continued to recognize privateering as a legal means of making war, despite the strong opposition of nations like the Star Kingdom of Manticore, whose massive merchant marine made it the natural enemy of any legal theory which legitimized private enterprise commerce raiding. As far as Bachfisch and Layson were concerned, there was little if any practical difference between privateers and pirates, but smaller nations which could not afford to raise and maintain large and powerful navies adamantly resisted all efforts to outlaw privateering by interstellar treaty. Oh, they attended the conferences Manticore and other naval powers convened periodically to discuss the issue, but the bottom line was that they saw privateers as a cost-effective means by which even a weak nation could attack the life's blood of a major commercial power like the Star Kingdom and at least tie down major portions of its navy in defensive operations.

Bachfisch and Layson could follow the logic of that argument, however much they might detest it, but privateering as practiced in the Silesian Confederacy was a far cry from the neat theories propounded by the practice's defenders at the interstellar conferences. Breakaway system governments and an incredible variety of "people's movements" proliferated across the Confederacy like weeds in a particularly well-rotted compost heap, and at least half of them issued—sold, really—letters of marque to license privateering in the names of their revolutions. At least two-thirds of those letters went to out and out pirates, who regarded them as get-out-of-jail-free cards. Whereas piracy was a capital offense under interstellar law, privateers were legally regarded as a sort of militia, semi-civilian volunteers in the service of whatever nation had issued their letter of marque in the first place. That meant that their ships could be seized, but that they themselves were protected. The worst that could happen to them (officially, at least) was incarceration along with other prisoners of war, unless they had been so careless as to be captured in the act of murdering, torturing, raping, or otherwise treating the crews of their prizes in traditional piratical fashion.

That was bad enough, but in some ways the genuine patriots were even worse. They were far less likely to indulge themselves in atrocities, but their ships tended to be larger and better armed, and they actually did regard themselves as auxiliary naval units. That made them willing to accept risks no true for-profit pirate would consider running for a moment, up to and including an occasional willingness to engage light warships of whoever they were rebelling against that week. Which wouldn't have bothered the Royal Manticoran Navy excessively, if not for the fact that even the best privateers were still amateurs who sometimes suffered from less than perfect target identification.

The fact that some privateers invariably seemed to believe that attacks on the commerce of major powers like Manticore would somehow tempt those major powers into intervening in their own squabbles in an effort to impose an outside solution to protect their commercial interests was another factor altogether. The Star Kingdom had made it abundantly clear over the years that it would come down like the wrath of God on any revolutionary movement stupid enough to deliberately send its privateers after Manticoran merchant shipping, yet there always seemed to be a new group of lunatics who thought *they* could somehow manipulate the Star Kingdom where everyone else had failed. The Navy eventually got around to teaching them the same lesson it had taught their countless predecessors, but it was ultimately a losing proposition. That particular bunch of crazies would not offend again once the RMN crushed them, but a lot of Manticoran merchant spacers tended to get hurt first, and someone else would always be along in a year or two who would have to learn the lesson all over again.

And at the moment, the Saginaw Sector of the Confederacy (which just happened to contain the Melchor System) was in an even greater than usual state of unrest. At least two of its systems—Krieger's Star and Prism—were in open rebellion against the central government, and there were half a dozen shadow governments and liberation movements all boiling away just beneath the surface. ONI estimated that several of those insurrectionary factions had managed to open communications and establish a degree of coordination which had—yet again—taken the Confederacy's excuse for a government by surprise. Worse, The Honorable Janko Wegener, the Saginaw sector governor, was even more venal than most, and it seemed obvious to ONI that he saw the turmoil in his command area as one more opportunity to line his pockets. At the same time that Wegener fought valiantly to suppress the rebellions in his sector, he was raking off protection money in return for tacitly ignoring at least three liberation movements, and there was compelling evidence to suggest that he was actually permitting privateers to auction their prizes publicly in return for a percentage of their profits. Under the ironclad laws of cronyism which governed the Confederacy, the fact that he was a close relative of the current government's interior minister and an in-law of the premier meant Wegener could get away with it forever (or at least until the Confederacy's political parties' game of musical chairs made someone else premier), and the odds were that he would retire a very wealthy man indeed.

In the meantime, it was up to HMS *War Maiden* and her company to do what they could to keep some sort of lid on the pot he was busily stirring.

"If only we could free up a division or two of the wall and drop them in on Saginaw to pay Governor Wegener a little visit, we might actually be able to do some genuine good," Bachfisch observed after a moment. "As it is, all we're going to manage is to run around pissing on forest fires." He stared off into the distance for several seconds, then shook himself and smiled. "Which is the usual state of affairs in Silesia, after all, isn't it?"

"I'm afraid you're right there, Sir," Layson agreed ruefully. "I just wish we could have started pissing on them by getting into missile range of the bastards who killed *Gryphon's Pride*."

"You and me both," Bachfisch snorted. "But let's face it, Abner, we were luckier than we had any right to count on just to recover the ship herself. If they hadn't wasted time . . . amusing themselves with her crew and gotten her underway sooner instead—or even just killed her transponder to keep us from realizing she'd been taken—they'd have gotten away clean. The fact that we got the hull back may not be much, but it's better than nothing."

"The insurers will be pleased, anyway," Layson sighed, then made a face and shook his head quickly. "Sorry, Sir. I know that wasn't what you meant. And I know the insurers would be just as happy as we would if we'd managed to save the crew as well. It's just—"

"I know," Bachfisch said, waving away his apology. The captain took one more turn around the cabin, then parked himself in the chair behind the desk once more. He picked up Layson's memo board and punched up the display to scan the terse report himself. "At least McKinley and her people cleared the ship on the bounce," he observed. "And I notice that even Janice remembered to take a gun this time!"

"With a little prodding," Layson agreed, and they grinned at one another. "I think the problem is that she regards anything smaller than a missile or a broadside energy mount as being beneath a tac officer's dignity," the exec added.

"It's worse than that," Bachfisch said with a small headshake. "She's from downtown Landing, and I don't think she and her family spent more than a day or two all told in the bush when she was a kid." He shrugged. "She never learned to handle a gun before the Academy, and she's never actually needed one in the line of duty since. That's what Marines are for."

"Sergeant Tausig mentioned to me that Ms. Harrington seemed quite competent in that regard," Layson observed in a carefully uninflected tone.

"Good," Bachfisch said. "Of course, her family has a nice little freeholding in the Copper Wall Mountains. That's hexapuma country, and I imagine she grew up packing a gun whenever she went for a hike. Actually, I think she did quite well. At least she kept her lunch down while they recovered and bagged the bodies."

Layson managed to keep his eyebrows from rising. He'd known Harrington was from Sphinx, of course, but he hadn't known she was from the Copper Walls, so how did the Captain know? He looked at Bachfisch for a moment, then drew a deep breath.

"Excuse me, Sir. I realize it's not really any of my business, but I know you must have had a reason for specifically requesting that Ms. Harrington be assigned to us for her snotty cruise."

The sentence was a statement that was also a question, and Bachfisch leaned back in his chair and gazed steadily at his executive officer.

"You're right, I did," he said after a thoughtful pause. "Are you by any chance familiar with Captain Raoul Courvosier, Abner?"

"Captain Courvosier?" Layson's brow furrowed. "Oh, of course. He's the head of the Saganami Tactical Department, isn't he?"

"At the moment," Bachfisch said. "The grapevine says he's up for rear admiral on the current list. They're going to jump him right past commodore, and they'll probably drag him over to head the War College as soon as they do."

"I knew he had a good rep, Sir, but is he really that good?" Layson asked in considerable surprise. It was unusual, to say the least, for the RMN to jump an officer two grades in a single promotion, despite its current rate of expansion.

"He's better than that," Bachfisch said flatly. "In fact, he's probably the finest tactician and one of the three best strategists I've ever had the honor to serve under."

Abner Layson was more than simply surprised by that, particularly since that was precisely the way *he* would have described Captain Thomas Bachfisch.

"If Raoul had been born into a better family—or been even a little more willing to play the suck-up game—he would have had his commodore's star years ago," Bachfisch went on, unaware of his exec's thoughts. "On the other hand, I imagine he's done more good than a dozen commodores at the Academy. But when Raoul Courvosier tells me privately that one of his students has demonstrated in his opinion the potential to be the most outstanding officer of her generation and asks me to put her in my Snotty Row, I'm not about to turn him down. Besides, she's about due for a little offsetting career boost."

"I beg your pardon, Sir?" The question came out almost automatically, for Layson was still grappling with the completely unexpected endorsement of Honor Harrington's capabilities. Of course, he'd been very favorably impressed by her himself, but *the* outstanding officer of her generation?

"I said she's due for a career boost," Bachfisch repeated, and snorted at the confused look Layson gave him. "What? You think *I* was stupid enough to ask for Elvis Santino for my OCTO? Give me a break, Abner!"

"But—" Layson began, then stopped and looked at Bachfisch narrowly. "I'd assumed," he said very slowly, "that Santino was just a particularly obnoxious example of BuPers' ability to pound square pegs into round holes. Are you saying he wasn't, Sir?"

"I can't prove it, but I wouldn't bet against it. Oh, it could be innocent enough. That's why I didn't say anything about it to you ahead of time . . . and why I was so happy that he gave you ample grounds to bring the hammer down on him. The creep had it coming, whatever his motives may have been, but nobody who sees your report and the endorsements from Shelton and Flanagan could possibly question the fact that he was relieved for cause."

"But why would anyone want to question it in the first place?"

"Did you ever happen to encounter Dimitri Young?"

This time, despite all he could do, Layson blinked in surprise at the complete *non sequitur.*

"Uh, no, Sir. I don't believe I can place the name."

"I'm not surprised, and you didn't miss a thing," Bachfisch said dryly. "He was considerably before your time, and he resigned about the time he made commander in order to pursue a political career when he inherited the title from his father."

"Title?" Layson repeated cautiously.

"These days he's the Earl of North Hollow, and from all I hear he's just as big a loss as a human being as he ever was. What's worse, he's reproduced, and his oldest son, Pavel, was a class ahead of Harrington at Saganami."

"Why do I think I'm not going to like this, Sir?"

"Because you have good instincts. It seems that Mr. Midshipman Young and Ms. Midshipwoman Harrington had a small . . . disagreement in the showers one night."

"In the show—" Layson began sharply, then broke off. "My God," he went on a moment later in a very different tone, "she must have kicked his ass up one side and down the other!"

"As a matter of fact, she did," Bachfisch said, gazing speculatively at his exec.

"Damned straight she did," Layson said with an evil chuckle. "Ms. Harrington works out full contact with Sergeant Tausig, Sir. And she gets through his guard upon occasion."

"Does she?" Bachfisch smiled slowly. "Well, now. I suppose that *does* explain a few things, doesn't it?" He gazed sightlessly at the bulkhead, smiling at something Layson could not see, for several seconds, then shook himself back to the present.

"At any rate," he said more briskly, "Harrington sent him to the infirmary for some fairly serious repairs, and he never did manage to explain just what he was doing in the showers alone with her after hours that inspired her to kick the crap out of him. But neither did she, unfortunately, press charges against him. No," he said, shaking his head before Layson could ask the question, "I don't know why she didn't, and I don't know why Hartley couldn't get her to do it. But she didn't, and the little prick graduated with the rest of his class and went straight into the old-boy patronage system."

"And cranked the same system around to wreck Harrington's career." There was no amusement in Layson's voice this time, and Bachfisch nodded.

"That's Raoul's belief, anyway," the captain said, "and I respect his instincts. Besides, unlike you *I* did know Young's father, and I doubt very much that he's improved with age. That's one reason I have to wonder how we wound up saddled with Santino. North Hollow may not be Navy anymore, but he's got one hell of a lot of clout in the House of Lords, and he sits on the Naval Affairs Committee. So if he does want to punish her for 'humiliating' his precious son, he's in the perfect spot to do it."

"I see, Sir." Layson sat back in his chair, and his mind worked busily. There was even more going on here than he'd suspected might be the case, and he felt a brief uneasiness at the weight and caliber of the enemies his Captain appeared to be courting. But knowing Bachfisch as well as he did, he also understood perfectly. In many ways, there were actually two Royal Manticoran Navies: the one to which well-connected officers like Pavel Young and Elvis Santino belonged, where all that truly mattered was who was related to whom; and the one which produced officers like Thomas Bachfisch and—he hoped—Abner Layson, whose only claim to their rank was the fact that they put duty and responsibility before life itself. And just as the Navy of patronage and string-pullers looked after their own, so did the Navy of dedication and ability protect and nurture *its* own.

"Does Harrington know?" he asked. "I mean, know that Young and his family are out to get her?"

"I don't know. If she's as observant as I think she is—or even a quarter as good at analyzing interpersonal relationships as she is in the tactical simulator—then it's a pretty sure bet that she does. On the other hand, she didn't press charges against him in the first place, and that raises a question mark, doesn't it? In any case, I don't think a snotty cruise in the middle of Silesia is the best possible place and time for us to be explaining it to her, now is it?"

"You do have a gift for understatement, Sir."

"A modest talent, but one which has its uses," Bachfisch admitted. Then he picked up the memo board and handed it back to Layson. "But that's enough about Ms. Harrington for the moment," he said. "Right now, you and I need to give some thought to where we go from here. I've been thinking that it might be worthwhile to hang around here in Melchor for a while and use the system as a pirate lure, since this is the main magnet for our shipping at the moment. But if we do that too obviously, the local pirates—and probably Wegener—are going to get hinky. So what I was thinking was—"

Commodore Anders Dunecki replayed the brief message and clenched his jaw against the urge to swear vilely.

"Is this confirmed?" he asked the messenger without looking up from the display.

"Yes, Sir. The SN made the official announcement last week. According to their communique they picked off *Lydia* a couple of weeks before that, and Commander Presley is almost a month overdue." The nondescript man in civilian clothing shrugged unhappily. "According to the SN they took him out in Hera, and that was where he'd said he was planning to cruise with *Lydia*. We don't have absolute confirmation that it was him, of course, but all the pieces match too well for it to have been anyone else."

"But according to this—" Dunecki jabbed his chin at the holographic screen where the message footer was still displayed "—it was a heavy cruiser that nailed him." He paused, looking at the messenger expectantly, and the other man nodded. "In that case," Dunecki said, "what I want to know is how the hell the SN managed to run a ship that powerful into the area without our hearing about it. There's no way John Presley would have been careless enough to let a heavy cruiser sneak up on him if he'd known she was there to begin with. And he damned well ought to have known!"

The rage Dunecki had struggled to conceal broke through his control with the last sentence, and the messenger sat very still. Anders Dunecki was not a good man to anger, and the messenger had to remind himself that he was only the bearer of the news, and not the one responsible for its content.

"I didn't know Commander Presley as well as you did, Sir," he said carefully after a long moment of silence. "Or for as long. But I'm familiar with his record in the Council's service, and on the basis of that, I'd have to agree that he certainly would have exercised all due prudence if he'd been aware of the escalation in threat levels. Actually, as nearly as we can tell, at least two heavy cruisers, and possibly as many as three have been transferred into Saginaw in the last month and a half, and there are some indications that more will be following. Apparently—" he allowed himself a predatory smile despite the tension in Dunecki's cabin "—losses in the sector have gotten severe enough for the Navy to reinforce its presence here."

"Which is probably a good thing. Or at least an indication that we're really beginning to hurt them," Dunecki agreed, but his glass-green eyes were frosty, and the messenger's smile seemed to congeal. "At the same time," the commodore went on in the same chill tone, "if they're increasing their strength in-sector, it means the risks are going up for all of us . . . just like they did for Commander Presley. Which, in turn, makes timely intelligence on their movements more important than it ever was before. And that consideration is the reason I'm particularly concerned about Wegener's failure to warn us about this in time for *Lydia* to know she had to watch her back more carefully."

"He may not have known himself," the messenger suggested, and Dunecki snorted harshly.

"The man is Interior Minister Wegener's *nephew*, for God's sake! And he's Premier Stolar's brother-in-law, to boot—not to mention the civilian head of government and military commander-in-chief of the sector." The commodore grimaced. "Do you really think they'd send so many heavy units into his command area without even mentioning them to him?"

"Put that way, it does sound unlikely," the messenger agreed. "But if he knew about them, why didn't he warn us? Sure, we've lost *Lydia*, and a good chunk of our combat power with her, but by the same token we've also lost an equally good-sized chunk of our raiding ability. And that translates into a direct loss of income for Governor Wegener."

"If you were talking about someone placed lower in the chain of command, I'd be tempted to agree that he didn't know ahead of time," Dunecki said. "As you say, losing *Lydia* is going to cut into his revenue stream, and we've always known he was only in it for the money. But the fact is that no one in the Confed navy or government would dare send what sounds like a couple of divisions of heavy cruisers into his bailiwick without telling him they were coming. Not with his family connections to the Cabinet itself, they wouldn't! The only possible conclusion Stolar or Wegener's uncle could draw from that would be that whoever was responsible for withholding information distrusted the good governor, and that would be a fatal move career-wise for whoever made it. No, he knew about it and decided not to tell us."

"But why?" The messenger's tone was that of a man speaking almost to himself, but it was also thoughtful, as if his own mind were questing down the path it was apparent Dunecki had already explored.

"Because he's decided the time's come to pull the plug on us," Dunecki said grimly. The messenger looked up quickly in surprise, and the commodore chuckled. It was a grating sound, with absolutely no humor in it, and the expression which bared his teeth could scarcely have been called a smile.

"Think about it," he invited. "We've just agreed that we've always known Wegener was only in for the money. He certainly never shared our agenda or our ambition to achieve an independent Prism. For that matter, he has to know that we regard Prism as only the first step in liberating the entire sector, and if we manage that—or even look like we might come close to it—not even his connections to the Cabinet could save his job. Hell, they might actually go as far as throwing him to the wolves in a big, fancy inquiry or criminal trial just to prove how lily-white and innocent they themselves were! And greedy as he is, Wegener's also not stupid enough not to know that. Which means that he's always had some point in mind at which he'd cut off his relationship with us and do his damnedest to wipe out the Council and retake control of the system. From what happened to *Lydia* and what you're saying about additional reinforcements, it sounds to me as if we've been successful enough that he's finally decided the time is now."

"If you're right, this is terrible," the messenger muttered. His hands wrapped together in his lap, and he stared down at them, his eyes worried. "Losing the intelligence he's provided would be bad enough by itself, but he knows an awful lot about the Council's future plans, as well. If he acts on the basis of that knowledge . . ."

He let his voice trail off and looked back up at Dunecki.

"He doesn't know as much as he thinks he does." Dunecki's tone surprised the messenger, and his surprise grew as the commodore gave him a grim smile. "Of course he doesn't," Dunecki told him. "The Council has always known he'd turn on us the instant he decided it was no longer in his perceived interest to support us. That's why we've used him solely as an intelligence source rather than try to involve him in our strategic thinking or operational planning, and we've been very careful to use false identities or anonymous contacts whenever we dealt with him. Oh, he knows the identities of the public Council members from the independence government back in Prism, but so does everyone else in the star system. What he *doesn't* know is the identity of anyone else. And the only regular warships he knows we have are the ones he himself managed to 'lose' in our favor, like *Lydia*."

The messenger nodded slowly. The Council for an Independent Prism had been around for decades, and he'd been one of its adherents almost from its inception. But unlike Dunecki, he'd never been a member of the inner circle. He was confident that the Council trusted his loyalty, or they would never have assigned him to the duties he'd carried out for the movement, but he was also a realist. He'd known that another reason he'd been chosen for his various assignments was that the Council was willing to risk him because, in the final analysis, he was expendable. And because he was expendable—and might end up expended and in enemy hands—his superiors had always been careful to limit the information they shared with him, but he'd been active in the movement long enough to know that it was only in the last four or five years that the CIP had become a serious player even by the somewhat elastic standards of Silesia. What he didn't know were the ins and outs of how the organization had made the transition from an ineffectual fringe group to one which had managed to seize effective control of half a star system, but he knew Anders Dunecki and his brother Henryk had played a major role in that accomplishment. And although his commitment to the CIP's ultimate goal was as strong as it had ever been, he was no more a stranger to ambition than anyone else who had committed twenty years of his life to the forcible creation of a new political order.

Now he watched Commodore Dunecki with a carefully blank expression, hoping the time had come for him to learn more. Not merely out of simple curiosity (though he certainly was curious) but because the decision to share that information with him might be an indication that his longtime loyal services were finally about to earn him promotion to a higher and more sensitive level of the movement.

Dunecki gazed back at him impassively. He knew precisely what was going on in the other man's mind, and he rather wished that he could avoid taking the messenger any further into his confidence. Not that he actively distrusted the man, and certainly not because he faulted the messenger's obvious hope that he might finally be about to move beyond the thankless and dangerous role of courier. It was simply a matter of habit. After so many years of not letting the left hand know what the right hand was doing as a survival tactic it went against the grain to admit anyone any deeper into his confidence than he absolutely had to.

Unfortunately, like Anders, Henryk was out of the Prism System on operations. Dunecki knew he could have relied upon his brother to convince the Council that Governor Wegener's apparent change of attitude meant it was time to move to the next planned phase of operations. But in Henryk's absence, Dunecki was going to require another spokesman to make his case, and the messenger was all that was available.

"Wegener knows about the light cruisers and the frigates," the commodore said after a moment, "mostly because he and Commodore Nielsen were the ones who sold them to us in the first place." He watched the messenger's eyes widen slightly and chuckled. "Oh, I suspect that Nielsen thought he was simply disposing of them to regular pirates, but Wegener knew he was dealing with the CIP from the outset. After all, he was already taking a payoff from us to look the other way while we got ourselves organized in Prism, so there was no reason he shouldn't make a little more money off us by letting us buy a bunch of 'obsolescent' warships if Nielsen was willing to sign off on them for disposal. Of course, Nielsen told his Navy superiors that the ships had gone to the breakers, but I doubt any of them believed that any more than he did. Still, it's going to be at least a little embarrassing for Nielsen if any of his 'scrapped' ships wind up being taken by regular Confed naval units, although I have no doubt he has splendid paperwork to prove that he sold them to ostensibly genuine scrap dealers who have since disappeared after undoubtedly selling the hulls to us nasty rebels.

"But we're pretty sure neither Wegener nor Nielsen knows about the destroyers, and we *know* that they don't know about *Annika, Astrid,* and *Margit.* We bought the destroyers in the Tumult Sector, and *Annika, Astrid,* and *Margit* came from . . . somewhere else entirely."

He paused once more, watching the messenger's face. The odds were that the other man had already known everything Dunecki had just told him—except, perhaps, for the fact that the newly created Prism Space Navy's destroyers had come from Tumult—but his expression indicated that he was beginning to see previously unnoted implications in the information.

"The point," Dunecki went on after a moment, "is that Wegener and Nielsen have probably based their estimates of our strength on the units that they sold us. They may have made some allowance for one or two additional light units, but we've been very careful in our discussions with our 'trusted ally' the Governor to make it plain that our only ships came from them. We've even passed up two or three nice prizes that Wegener had pointed us at because we didn't have a vessel available to take them."

"Uh, excuse me, Sir," the messenger said, "but I know that you and your brother have both taken prizes. Doesn't that mean that they have to know about *Annika* and *Astrid,* at least?"

"No," Dunecki said. "Henryk and I have taken special precautions. Neither of us has disposed of any of our prizes here in the Confederacy. We have some . . . friends and associates in the People's Republic of Haven who've agreed to help out their fellow revolutionaries." The messenger's eyes narrowed, and the commodore chuckled once more. "Don't worry about it. The Legislaturalists are about as revolutionary as a hunk of nickel iron, but if it suits their purpose to pretend to support 'the People's struggle' as long as its safely outside their own borders and they can make money on it, it suits our purpose just as well to have some place legitimate privateers can dispose of their prizes and repatriate their crews without questions being asked. It's just a pity that the Peeps aren't willing to help us out with additional ships and weapons, as well."

"So Wegener, Nielsen, and the Confed Navy all think that our naval strength is less than half as great as it really is," the messenger said slowly.

"More like a third," Dunecki corrected. "The ships they know about are all ex-Confed crap, just like their own units. Of course, they don't know about the system upgrades or the . . . technical assistance we've had in improving our missile seekers and EW capability, so even the ships they expect us to have are considerably more effective than they could possibly predict."

"I can see that," the messenger replied. "But does it really matter in the long run? I mean, with all due respect, Sir, even if we're in a position to inflict serious losses on Nielsen because they underestimate our strength, he's got the entire Silesian Navy behind him. You're probably right when you call them 'crap,' but they have an awful lot more ships than we do."

"Yes, they do. But that's where the other point you weren't cleared to hear about comes in." Dunecki leaned back in his chair and regarded the messenger coolly. "Haven't you wondered just how we managed to get our hands on like-new destroyers and heavy cruisers? *Andermani* destroyers and heavy cruisers?"

"Occasionally," the messenger admitted. "I always assumed we must have found someone like Nielsen in the Empire. I mean, you and your brother both have contacts in the Andy Navy, so—"

"In the IAN? You think there's someone in the *IAN* who'd sell first-line warships on the black market?" Almost despite himself, Dunecki laughed uproariously. It took several seconds for him to get his amusement back under control, and he wiped tears of laughter from his eyes as he shook his head at the messenger. "I may have made it clear to captain in the IAN, and Henryk may have been a full commander, but trust me, the Imperial Navy isn't at all like the Confeds! Even if there were someone interested in stealing ships, there are way too many checkpoints and inspectorates. No," he shook his head. "Henryk and I did use contacts in the Empire to set it up, but they weren't with the Navy. Or not directly, anyway."

"Then who did you work with?" the messenger asked.

"Let's just say there are a few people, some of them from rather prominent Andie families, who were able to stomach having their investment stolen by Wegener and his family, but only until Wegener decided to bring in another set of foreigners to take it over and run it. That was a bit too much for them, and one or two of them spoke to their prominent relatives after Henryk and I spoke to *them*, just before he and I came home to Prism. Which brings me to the point I need you to stress to the Council when you get home."

"Yes, Sir." The messenger straightened in his chair, his expression intent, and Dunecki looked straight into his eyes.

"The Andermani money people who made our ships available in the first place have just gotten word to me that the Imperial government is finally ready to act. If we can inflict sufficient losses on the local naval forces to provide the Emperor with a pretext, the Empire will declare that the instability in this region of the Confederacy has become great enough in its opinion to threaten a general destabilization of the area. And to prevent that destabilization, the Imperial Navy will move into Saginaw and impose a cease-fire, under the terms of which the Empire will recognize the Council as the de facto legitimate government of Prism."

"Are you serious?" the messenger stared at Dunecki in disbelief. "Everyone knows the Andies have wanted to move into the Confederacy for years, but the Manties have always said no."

"True, but the Manties are focused on Haven right now. They won't have the resources or the will to take on the Empire over something as unimportant to them as Saginaw."

"But what do the Andies get out of it?"

"The Empire gets the precedent of having successfully intervened to restore order to a sector of the Confederacy, which it can use as an opening wedge for additional interventions. It won't demand any outright territorial concessions—this time. But the next time may be a slightly different story, and the time after that, and the time after that, and the time after that . . ." Dunecki let his voice trail off and smiled evilly. "As for our sponsors, the one thing the Emperor's negotiators will insist upon is that Wegener, or whoever Stolar replaces him with, revoke the trade concessions Wegener made to the Manties in Melchor and regrant them to the original Andy investors. So everybody gets what they want . . . except for the Confeds and the Manties, that is."

"My God." The messenger shook his head. "My God, it might just work."

"It damned well *will* work," Dunecki said flatly, "and it's what the Council has been working towards for the last three years. But we didn't expect such sudden confirmation that the groundwork had finally been completed in the Empire, so no one back home is ready to move. But coupling the word from my Imperial contacts with what happened to *Lydia*, I think we've just run out of time. If Wegener and Nielsen are ready to begin moving against us rather than working with us, we need to act quickly. So what I need you to do is to go back to the Council and tell them that they have to get couriers to Henryk and to Captain Traynor in the *Margit* with instructions to begin all-out operations against the Confed Navy."

"I understand, Sir, but I'm not sure they'll listen to me." The messenger smiled wryly. "I realize you're using me because you don't have anyone else available, but I'm hardly part of the inner circle, and this will be coming at them cold. So what if they refuse?"

"Oh, they won't do that," Dunecki said with cold assurance. "If it looks like they might, just tell them this." He looked levelly at the messenger across his desk, and his expression was grim. "Whatever they may want to decide, *Annika* will commence active operations against the SN one standard week from today."

"I still say there has to be a better way to do this." Midshipman Makira sounded unusually grumpy, and Honor glanced across the table and shook her head at him.

"You have got to be one of the most contrary people that I've ever met, Nassios," she told him severely.

"And just what do you mean by that?" Makira demanded.

"I mean that I don't think there's anything the Captain could do that you couldn't decide was the wrong way to go about it. Not to say that you're a nit-picker—although, now that I think about it, someone whose disposition was less naturally sunny and equable than my own probably would—but you do have an absolute gift for picking up on the potential weaknesses of an idea without paying any attention to its advantages."

"Actually," Makira said in an unusually serious tone, "I think you might have a point there. I really do have a tendency to look for problems first. Maybe that's because I've discovered that that way any of my surprises are pleasant ones. Remember, Captain Courvoisier always said that no plan survives contact with the enemy anyway. The way I see it, that makes a pessimist the ideal commander in a lot of ways."

"Maybe—as long as your pessimism doesn't prevent you from having enough confidence to take the initiative away from the bad guys and hang on to it for yourself," Honor countered. Nimitz looked up from his perch on the end of the Snotty Row table and cocked his head in truly magisterial style as he listened to his person's discussion, and Makira chuckled.

"Not fair," he protested, reaching out to stroke the 'cat's ears. "You and Nimitz are ganging up on me again!"

"Only because you're wrong," Honor informed him with a certain smugness.

"Oh, no, I'm not! Look, all I'm saying is that the way we're going about it now, this is the only star system in our entire patrol area that we're giving any cover at all to. Now," he leaned back and folded his arms, "explain to me where that statement is in error."

"It's not in error at all," she conceded. "The problem is that there isn't an ideal solution to the problem of too many star systems and not enough cruisers. We can only be in one place at a time whatever we do, and if we try to spread ourselves between too many systems, we'll just spend all of our time running around between them in hyper and never accomplish anything at all in n-space." She shrugged. "Under the circumstances, and given the fact that the Star Kingdom's presence here in Melchor is pretty much nailed down, I think it makes a lot of sense to troll for pirates right here."

"And while we're doing that," Makira pointed out, "we can be pretty sure that somewhere else in our patrol area a merchantship we ought to be protecting is about to get its ass into a world of hurt with no one there to look out for her."

"You're probably right. But without detailed advance knowledge of the schedules and orders of every merchie in the entire Saginaw Sector, it's simply impossible for anyone to predict where our shipping is going to be at any given moment, anyway. For that matter, even if we'd had detailed schedules on every civilian ship planning on moving in our area at the time we left Manticore, they'd be hopelessly out of date by now, and you know it. And there aren't any such detailed schedules in the first place, which means every single Manticoran ship in Silesia is basically its own needle inside one huge haystack. So even if we were cruising around from system to system, the odds are that we'd almost certainly be out of position to help out the merchantship you're talking about. If we *were* in position to help, it could only be a case of sheer dumb luck, and you know that as well as I do."

"But at least we'd have a chance for dumb luck to put us there!" he shot back stubbornly. "As it is, we don't even have that!"

"No, we don't—we've got something much better than that: bait. We *know* that every pirate in the sector knows about the Dillingham Cartel's installations here in Melchor. They can be pretty much certain that there are going to be Manticoran ships in and out of this system on a semi-regular basis, not to mention the possibility that they might get lucky and actually manage to pull off a successful raid on the installations themselves, despite their defenses. That's the whole point of the Captain's strategy! Instead of chasing off from star system to star system with no assurance that he'll catch up with any pirates, much less pirates in the act of raiding our shipping, he's opted to sit here and set an ambush for anybody who's tempted to hit Dillingham's people. I'd say the odds are much better that we'll actually manage to pick off a few pirates by lying in wait for them than there'd be any other way."

"But we're not even showing the flag in any other system," Makira complained. "There's no sense of presence to deter operations anywhere else in the sector."

"That's probably the single most valid criticism of our approach," Honor agreed. "Unfortunately, the Captain only has one ship and there's no way in the world to cover enough space with a single ship to actually deter anyone who can do simple math. What are the odds that *War Maiden* is going to turn up to intercept any given pirate at any given moment?" She shook her head. "No, unless the Admiralty is prepared to give the Captain at least a complete cruiser division to work with, I don't see how he can possibly be expected to create a broad enough sense of presence to actually deter anybody who's inclined to turn pirate in the first place."

"Then why bother to send us at all?" For the first time, there was a note of true bitterness in Makira's voice. "If all we're doing is trying to hold air in the lock with a screen door, then what's the damned point?"

"The same as it's always been, I suppose," Honor said. "One ship can't deter piracy throughout an entire patrol area the size of the Saginaw Sector—not in any specific sense, at least. But if we can pick off two or three of the scum, then the word will get around among the ones we don't get a shot at. At least we can make a few people who are considering the 'great adventure' as a career choice think about whether or not they really want to run the risk of being one of the unlucky ones. More to the point, the word will also get around that we're paying particular attention to Melchor, which may just remind them that the Star Kingdom takes a dim view of attacks on our nationals. I hate to say it, but in a lot of ways what we're really doing out here is encouraging the local vermin to go pick on someone else's shipping and leave ours alone."

"That's not what they told us back at the Academy," Makira said. "They told us our job was to suppress piracy, not just encourage it to go after merchies unlucky enough to belong to some poor sucker of a star nation that doesn't have a decent navy of its own!"

"Of course that's what they told us, and in an absolute sense they were right. But we live in an imperfect galaxy, Nassios, and it's been getting steadily less perfect for years now. Look," she leaned forward across the table, propping her elbows on it while her expression turned very serious, "the Navy only has so many ships and so many people, and important as Silesia is—and as important as the lives of Manticoran spacers are—we can only put so many ships in so many places. Back before the Peeps started conquering everything in sight, we could actually send a big enough chunk of the Navy off to Silesia every year to make a real hole in pirate operations here. But with so much of our available strength diverted to keeping an eye on the Peeps at places like Trevor's Star and Basilisk, we can't do that any more. We simply don't have enough hulls for that kind of deployment. So I'm sure that everyone at the Admiralty understands perfectly well that there's no way we can possibly 'suppress' piracy in our patrol areas. For that matter, I'd bet that any pirate who's not a complete imbecile knows that just as well as *we* do, and you can be absolutely sure that the Andies do!"

Nassios Makira tipped back in his chair, and his expression had gone from one that showed more than a little outrage to one of surprise. He knew that he and the other middies in *War Maiden*'s company all had exactly the same access to information, but it was suddenly apparent to him that Honor had put that information together into a far more complete and coherent picture than he ever had.

"Then why bother to send us?" he repeated, but his tone had gone from one of challenge to one that verged on the plaintive. "If we can't do any good, and everyone knows it, then why are we here?"

"I didn't say we couldn't do any good," Honor told him almost gently. "I said that we couldn't realistically expect to *suppress* piracy. The fact that we can't stamp it out or even drive a significant number of the raiders out of any given area doesn't relieve us of a moral responsibility to do whatever we *can* do. And one of the responsibilities that we have is to protect our own nationals to the greatest possible extent, however limited that extent may be compared to what we'd like to do. We can't afford for the pirates—or the Andies—to decide that we'll simply write off our commitments in Silesia, however strapped for ships we may be. And when I said that what we're really trying to do is to convince pirates to go pick on someone else's merchant shipping, I didn't mean that we had any specific victims in mind. I just meant that our objective is to convince fine locals that it's more unsafe to attack our shipping than it is to attack anyone else's. I know there are some people back home who would argue that it's in our true strategic interest to point the pirates here at anybody who competes with our own merchant marine, but they're idiots. Oh, I'm sure we could show some short-term gain if the pirate threat scared everybody looking for freight carriers in Silesia into using our merchies, but the long-term price would be stiff. Besides, once everybody was using Manticoran bottoms, the pirates would have no choice but to come after us again because there wouldn't be any other targets for them!

"Actually," she said after a moment, her tone and expression thoughtful, "there may *be* an additional advantage in pointing pirates at someone else. Everyone has relied on us to play police out here for the better part of a century and a half, but we're scarcely the only ones with an interest in what happens in Silesia. I'm sure that there have been times when the government and the Admiralty both did their very best to make sure that everyone else regarded us as the logical police force for Silesia, if only to depress Andy pretentions in the area. But now that we're having to concentrate on our own forces on the Peeps' frontiers, we need someone else to take up the slack out here. And I'm afraid the only people available are the Andies. The Confeds certainly aren't going to be able to do anything about it! So maybe there's an advantage I hadn't considered in persuading pirates to pick on Andy merchies instead of ours, if that's going to get the Andy navy involved in going after them more aggressively while we're busy somewhere else."

"Um." Makira rubbed his eyebrow while he pondered everything she'd just said. It made sense. In fact, it made a *lot* of sense, and now that she'd laid it all out, he couldn't quite understand why the same conclusions hadn't suggested themselves to him long since. But still . . .

"All right," he said. "I can see your point, and I don't guess I can really argue with it. But I still think that we could do more to convince pirates to go after someone else's shipping if we put in an appearance in more than one star system. I mean, if Melchor is the only place we ever pop a single pirate—not that we've managed to do even that much so far—then our impact is going to be very limited and localized."

"It's going to be 'limited' whatever we do. That's the inevitable consequence of only having one ship," Honor pointed out with a glimmer of amusement. "But like I said, I'm sure the word will get around. One thing that's always been true is that the 'pirate community,' for lack of a better term, has a very efficient grapevine. Captain Courvoisier says that the word always gets around when someplace turns out to be particularly hazardous to their health, so we can at least push them temporarily out of Melchor. On the other hand, what makes you think that Melchor is going to be the *only* place the Captain stakes out during our deployment? It's the place he's staking out *at the moment*, but there's no reason not to move his operations elsewhere after he feels reasonably confident that he's made an impression on the local lowlife's minds. I think the presence of the Dillingham operation here makes this the best hunting grounds we're likely to find, and it looks to me like the Captain thinks the same. But the same tactics will work just as well anyplace else there are actually pirates operating, and I'd be very surprised if we don't spend some time trolling in other systems, as well."

"Then why didn't you say so in the first place?" Makira demanded with the heat of exasperation. "You've been letting me bitch and carry on about the Captain's obsession with this system for days! Now you're going to sit there and tell me that the whole time you've actually been expecting him to eventually do what I *wanted?*"

"Well," Honor chuckled, "it's not *my* fault if what you've been letting yourself hear wasn't exactly what I've been saying, now is it? Besides, you shouldn't criticize the Captain quite so energetically unless you've really thought through what you're talking about!"

"You," Makira said darkly, "are an evil person who will undoubtedly come to an unhappy end, and if there is any justice in the universe, I'll be there to see it happen."

Honor grinned, and Nimitz bleeked a lazy laugh from the table between them.

"You may laugh . . . for now," he told them both ominously, "but There Will Come a Day when you will remember this conversation and regret it bitterly." He raised his nose with an audible sniff, and Nimitz turned his head to look up at his person. Their eyes met in complete agreement, and then Nassios Makira's arms windmilled wildly as a gray blur of treecat bounded off the table and wrapped itself firmly around his neck. The midshipman began a muffled protest that turned suddenly into a most unmilitary—and high-pitched—sound as Nimitz's long, agile fingers found his armpits and tickled unmercifully. Chair and midshipman alike went over backwards with a high, wailing laugh, and Honor leaned back in her own chair and watched with folded arms as the appropriate penalty for his ominous threat was rigorously applied.

"Well, here we are," Commander Obrad Bajkusa observed.

One might have concluded from his tone that he was less than delighted with his own pronouncement, and one would have been correct. Bajkusa had an enormous amount of respect for Commodore Dunecki as both a tactical commander and a military strategist, but he'd disliked the entire concept of this operation from the moment the commodore first briefed him on it over six T-months before. It wasn't so much that he distrusted the motives of the commodores Andermani . . . associates (although he *did* distrust them about as much as was humanly possible) as that it was Bajkusa's personal conviction that anyone who screwed around with the Royal Manticoran Navy was stupid enough that he no doubt deserved his Darwinian fate. On the surface, Dunecki's plan was straightforward and reasonable, especially given the promises of backing from the imperial Andermani court. So far as logical analysis was concerned, it was very difficult to find fault with the commodore's arguments. Unfortunately, the Manty Navy had a deplorable habit of kicking the ever-living crap out of anyone foolish enough to piss it off, and Obrad Bajkusa had no particular desire to find himself a target of such a kicking.

On the other hand, orders were orders, and it wasn't as if the Manties knew his name or address. All he had to do was keep it that way.

"All right, Hugh," he told his exec. "Let's head on in and see what we can find."

"Yes, Sir," Lieutenant Wakefield replied, and the frigate PSN *Javelin* headed in-system while the star named Melchor burned steadily ahead of her.

"Well, well. What *do* we have here?"

Senior Chief Jensen Del Conte turned his head towards the soft murmur. Sensor Tech 1/c Francine Alcott was obviously unaware that she had spoken aloud. If Del Conte had harbored any doubt about that, the expression on her dark, intense face as she leaned closer to her display would have disabused him of it quickly enough.

The senior chief watched her as her fingers flickered back and forth across her panel with the unconscious precision of a concert pianist. He had no doubt whatsoever what she was doing, and he clenched his jaw and thought very loudly in her direction.

Unfortunately, she seemed remarkably insensitive to Del Conte's telepathy, and he swallowed a silent curse. Alcott was extremely good at her job. She had both a natural aptitude for it, and the sort of energy and sense of responsibility which took her that extra kilometer from merely satisfactory to outstanding, and Del Conte knew that Lieutenant Commander Hirake had already earmarked Alcott, despite her relative youth, for promotion to petty officer before this deployment was over. But for all her undoubted technical skills, Alcott was remarkably insensitive to some of the internal dynamics of *War Maiden*'s tactical department. The fact that she had been transferred to Del Conte's watch section less than two weeks earlier made the situation worse, but the senior chief felt depressingly certain that she would have been blithely blind to certain unpleasant realities even if she'd been in the same duty section since the ship left Manticore.

Del Conte glanced over his shoulder as unobtrusively as possible, then swallowed another silent expletive. Lieutenant Santino had the watch, and he sat in the command chair at the center of the bridge looking for all the world like a competent naval officer. His forearms rested squarely upon the command chair's armrests. His squared shoulders rested firmly against the chair's upright back, his manly profile was evident as he held his head erect, and there was an almost terrifying lack of intelligence in his eyes.

Jensen Del Conte had seen more officers than he could possibly count in the course of his naval career. Some had been better than others, some had been worse; none had ever approached the abysmal depths which Elvis Santino plumbed so effortlessly. Del Conte knew Lieutenant Commander Hirake was aware of the problem, but there was very little that she could do about it, and one thing she absolutely could *not* do was to violate the ironclad etiquette and traditions of the Service by admitting to a noncommissioned officer, be he ever so senior, that his immediate superior was a complete and utter ass. The senior chief rather hoped that the lieutenant commander and the Skipper were giving Santino rope in hopes that he would manage to hang himself with it. But even if they were, that didn't offer much comfort to those unfortunate souls who found themselves serving under his immediate command—like one Senior Chief Del Conte.

Alcott continued her silent communion with her instruments, and Del Conte wished fervently that Santino's command chair were even a few meters further away from him than it was. Given its proximity, however, the lieutenant was entirely too likely to hear anything Del Conte might say to Alcott. In fact, the sensor tech was extremely fortunate that Santino hadn't already noticed her preoccupation. The lieutenant's pose of attentiveness fooled no one on the bridge, but it would have been just like him to emerge from his normal state of internal oblivion at precisely the wrong moment for Alcott. So far, he hadn't, however, and that posed a most uncomfortable dilemma for Del Conte.

The senior chief reached out and made a small adjustment on his panel, and his brow furrowed as his own display showed him a duplicate of the imagery on Alcott's. He saw immediately what had drawn her attention, although he wasn't at all certain that he would have spotted it himself without the enhancement she had already applied. Even now, the impeller signature was little more than a ghost, and the computers apparently did not share Alcott's own confidence that what she was seeing was really there. They insisted on marking the icon with the rapidly strobing amber circle which indicated a merely possible contact, and that was usually a bad sign. But Alcott possessed the trained instinct which the computers lacked, and Del Conte was privately certain that what she had was a genuine contact.

Part of the problem was the unknown's angle of approach. Whatever it was, it was overtaking from astern and very high—so high, in fact, that the upper band of War Maiden's impeller wedge was between the contact and Alcott's gravitic sensors. In theory, CIC's computers knew the exact strength of the heavy cruiser's wedge and, equipped with that knowledge, could compensate for the wedge's distorting effect. In theory. In real life, however, the wedge injected a high degree of uncertainty into any direct observation through it, which was why warships tended to rely so much more heavily on the sensor arrays mounted on their fore and aft hammerheads and on their broadsides, where their wedges did not interfere. They also carried ventral and dorsal arrays, of course, but those systems were universally regarded—with reason—as little more than precautionary afterthoughts under most circumstances. In this case, however, the dorsal arrays were the only ones that could possibly see Alcott's possible contact. The known unreliability of those arrays, coupled with the extreme faintness of the signature that had leaked through the wedge, meant that the contact (if that was what it actually was) had not yet crossed the threshold of CIC's automatic filters, so no one in CIC was so far even aware of it.

But Alcott was, and now—for his sins—Del Conte was, as well. Standing orders for such a contingency were clear, and Alcott, unfortunately, had followed them . . . mostly. She had, in fact, done precisely what she would have been expected to do if she had still been part of Lieutenant Commander Hirake's watch section, for the lieutenant commander trusted her people's abilities and expected them to routinely route their observations directly to her own plot if they picked up anything they thought she should know about. Standard operating procedure required a verbal announcement, as well, but Hirake preferred for her sensor techs to get on with refining questionable data rather than waste time reporting that they didn't yet know what it was they didn't know.

Del Conte's problem was that the lieutenant commander's attitude was that of a confident, competent officer who respected her people and their own skills. Which would have been fine, had anyone but Elvis Santino had the watch. Because what Alcott had done was exactly what Lieutenant Commander Hirake would have wanted; she had thrown her own imagery directly onto Santino's Number Two Plot . . . and the self-absorbed jackass hadn't even noticed!

Had the contact been strong enough for CIC to consider it reliable, *they* would already have reported it, and Santino would have known it was there. Had Alcott made a verbal report, he would have known. Had he bothered to spend just a little more effort on watching his own displays and a little less effort on projecting the proper HD-image of the Complete Naval Officer, he would have known. But none of those things had happened, and so he didn't have a clue. But when CIC did get around to upgrading their classification from sensor ghost to possible real contact, even Santino was likely to notice from the time chop on the imagery blinking unnoticed (at the moment) on his plot that Alcott had identified it as such several minutes earlier. More to the point, he would realize that when Captain Bachfisch and Commander Layson got around to reviewing the bridge log, *they* would realize that he ought to have been aware of the contact long before he actually got around to reporting it to *them*. Given Santino's nature, the consequences for Alcott would be totally predictable, and wasn't it a hell of a note that a senior chief in His Majesty's Navy found himself sitting here sweating bullets trying to figure out how to protect a highly talented and capable rating from the spiteful retaliation of a completely untalented and remarkably stupid officer?

None of which did anything to lessen Del Conte's dilemma. Whatever else happened, he couldn't let the delay drag out any further without making things still worse, and so he drew a deep breath.

"Sir," he announced in his most respectful voice, "we have a possible unidentified impeller contact closing from one-six-five by one-one-five."

"What?" Santino shook himself. For an instant, he looked completely blank, and then his eyes dropped to the repeater plot deployed from the base of his command chair and he stiffened.

"Why didn't CIC report this?" he snapped, and Del Conte suppressed an almost overwhelming urge to answer in terms which would leave even Santino in no doubt of the senior chief's opinion of him.

"It's still very faint, Sir," he said instead. "If not for Alcott's enhancement, we'd never have noticed it. I'm sure it's just lost in CIC's filters until it gains a little more signal strength."

He made his voice as crisp and professional as possible, praying all the while that Santino would be too preoccupied with the potential contact to notice the time chop on his plot and realize how long had passed before its existence had been drawn to his attention.

For the moment, at least, God appeared to be listening. Santino was too busy glaring at the strobing contact to worry about anything else, and Del Conte breathed a sigh of relief.

Of premature relief, as it turned out.

Elvis Santino looked down at the plot icon in something very like panic. He was only too well aware that the Captain and that asshole Layson were both out to get him. Had he been even a little less well connected within the aristocratic cliques of the Navy, Layson's no doubt scathing endorsement of his personnel file which had almost certainly accompanied the notation that he had been relieved as OCTO for cause would have been the kiss of death. As it was, he and his family were owed sufficient favors that his career would probably survive without serious damage. But there were limits even to the powers of patronage, and he dared not give the bastards any additional ammunition.

As it happened, he *had* noticed the plot time chop. Which meant that he knew that he—or at least his bridge crew, and for that matter, his own tactical personnel—had picked up the possible contact almost six full minutes before anyone had drawn it to his attention. He could already imagine the coldly formal, impeccably correct, and brutally blistering fashion in which Bachfisch (or, even worse, that ass-kisser Layson) would ream him out for not reacting sooner. The mental picture of that . . . discussion was the only thing which prevented him from ripping out Alcott's and Del Conte's lungs for having deliberately withheld the information. But Layson had already demonstrated his taste for using noncoms and ratings as spies and informants, and Santino had no doubt that the Exec would take gleeful pleasure in adding Del Conte's ass-covering version of what had happened to his own report. So instead of kicking their insolent and disloyal asses as they so richly deserved, he forced himself to remain outwardly oblivious to what they had conspired to do to him. The time would come eventually for the debt to be paid, yet for now it was one more thing he dared not attend to.

In the meantime, he had to decide how to handle the situation, and he gnawed on his lower lip while he thought hard. Del Conte—the disloyal bastard—was undoubtedly correct about the reason for CIC's silence. But if Alcott's enhancement was solid (and it looked as if it were) then the contact was bound to burn through CIC's filters in no more than another five to ten minutes, even with only the dorsal gravitics. When that happened, he would have no option but to report it to the Captain . . . at which point the fact that Alcott and Del Conte had officially fed him the data so much earlier would also become part of the official record. And the fact that they had deliberately concealed the report by failing to announce it verbally would be completely ignored while Bachfisch and Layson concentrated on the way in which he had "wasted" so much "valuable time" before reporting it to them. And Layson, in particular, was too vindictive for Santino to doubt for a moment that he would point out the fashion in which Santino had squandered the potential advantage which his own brilliantly competent Tactical Department subordinates had won him by making such an early identification of the contact.

Frustration, fury, resentment, and fear boiled back and forth behind his eyes while he tried to decide what to do, and every second that ticked away with no decision added its own weight to the chaos rippling within him. It was such a *little* thing! So what if Alcott and Del Conte had picked up the contact six minutes, or even fifteen minutes—hell, half an hour!—before CIC did? The contact was over two and a half light-minutes behind *War Maiden*. That was a good fifty million klicks, and Alcott's best guess on its acceleration was only around five hundred gravities. With an initial overtake velocity of less than a thousand kilometers per second, it would take whatever it was over five hours to overtake *War Maiden*, so how could the "lost time" possibly matter? But it would. He knew it would, because Bachfisch and Layson would never pass up the opportunity to hammer his efficiency report all over again and—

His churning thoughts suddenly paused. Of course! Why hadn't he thought of it sooner? He felt his lips twitch and managed somehow to suppress the need to grin triumphantly as he realized the solution to his dilemma. His "brilliant" subordinates had reported the contact even before CIC, had they? Well, good for them! And as the officer of the watch, wasn't it his job to confirm whether or not the contact was valid as quickly as possible—even before the computers and the highly trained plotting crews in CIC could do so? Of course it was! And *that* was the sole reason he had delayed in reporting to the Captain: to confirm that the *possible* contact was a real one.

He caught himself just before he actually rubbed his hands together in satisfaction and then turned to the helmsman.

"Prepare to roll ship seventy degrees to port and come to new heading of two-two-three," he said crisply.

Del Conte spun his chair to face the center of the bridge before he could stop himself. He knew exactly what the lieutenant intended to do, but he couldn't quite believe that even Elvis Santino could be *that* stupid. The preparatory order he'd just given was a classic maneuver. Naval officers called it "clearing the wedge," because that was exactly what it did as the simultaneous roll and turn swept the more sensitive broadside sensor arrays across the zone which had been obstructed by the wedge before the maneuver. But it was the sort of maneuver which only warships made, and *War Maiden* had gone to enormous lengths to masquerade as a fat, helpless, *unarmed* freighter expressly to lure raiders into engagement range. If this asshole—

"Sir, I'm not sure that's a good idea," the senior chief said.

"Fortunately, *I* am," Santino said sharply, unable to refrain from smacking down the disloyal noncom.

"But, Sir, we're supposed to be a merchie, and if—"

"I'm quite aware of what we're supposed to be, Senior Chief! But if in fact this is a genuine contact and not simply a figment of someone's overheated imagination, clearing the wedge should confirm it, don't you think?"

"Yes, Sir, but—"

"They're only pirates, Senior Chief," Santino said scathingly. "We can turn to clear the wedge, lock them in for CIC, and be back on our original heading before they even notice!"

Del Conte opened his mouth to continue the argument, and then shut it with a click. There was obviously no point, and it was even remotely possible that Santino was right and that the contact would never notice such a brief course change. But if the contact had them on a gravitic sensor which wasn't obstructed by a wedge, then *War Maiden* was at least nine or ten light-minutes inside its sensor range. At that range, even a brief change in heading would be glaringly obvious to any regular warship's tactical crew. Of course, if these were your typical run-of-the-mill pirates, then Santino could just possibly get away with it without anyone's noticing. It was unlikely, but it *was* possible.

And if the asshole blows it, at least my hands will be clean. I did my level best to keep him from screwing up by the numbers, and the voice logs will show it. So screw you, Lieutenant!

The senior chief gazed into the lieutenant's eyes for five more endless seconds while he fought with himself. His stubborn sense of duty pulled one way, urging him to make one more try to salvage the situation, but everything else pushed him the other way, and in the end, he turned his chair back to face his own panel without another word.

Santino grunted in satisfaction, and returned his own attention to the helmsman.

"Execute the helm order, Coxswain!" he said crisply.

The helmsman acknowledged the order, *War Maiden* rolled up on her side and swung ever so briefly off her original track, and her broadside sensor arrays nailed the contact instantly.

Just in time to see it execute a sharp course change of its own and accelerate madly away from the "freighter" which had just cleared its wedge.

"I cannot *believe* this . . . this . . . this . . ."

Commander Abner Layson shook his head, uncertain whether he was more stunned or furious, and Captain Bachfisch grunted in irate agreement. The two of them sat in the captain's day cabin, the hatch firmly closed behind them, and the display on the captain's desk held a duplicate of Francine Alcott's plot imagery, frozen at the moment the pirate which the entire ship's company had worked so long and so hard to lure into a trap went streaking away.

"I knew he was an idiot," the commander went on after a moment in a marginally less disgusted voice, "but I figured he had to at least be able to carry out standing orders that had been explained in detail to every officer aboard."

"I agree," Bachfisch said, but then he sighed and leaned back in his chair. "I agree," he repeated more wearily, "but I can also see exactly what happened."

"Excuse me, Sir, but what *happened* was that the officer of the watch completely failed to obey your standing order to inform you immediately upon the detection of a potential hostile unit. Worse, on his own authority, he undertook to execute a maneuver which was a dead giveaway of the fact that we're a warship, with predictable results!"

"Agreed, but you know as well as I do that he did it because he knows both of us are just waiting for him to step far enough out of line that we can cut him right off at the knees."

"Well, he just gave us all the ammunition we need to do just that," Layson pointed out grimly.

"I suppose he did," Bachfisch said, massaging his eyelids with the tips of his fingers. "Of course, I also suppose it's possible his career will survive even this, depending on who his patrons are back home. And I hate to admit it, but if I were one of those patrons, I might just argue to BuPers that his actions, however regrettable, were the predictable result of the climate of hostility which you and I created for Lieutenant Santino when we arbitrarily relieved him of his duties as OCTO."

"With all due respect, Sir, that's bullshit, and you know it."

"Of course I know it. At the same time, there's a tiny element of truth in it, since you and I certainly are hostile to him. You *are* hostile towards him, aren't you, Abner?"

"Damn right I am," Layson said, then snorted as the captain grinned at him. "All right, all right, Sir. I take your point. All we can do is write it up the way we saw it and hope that The Powers That Be back home agree with us. But in the meantime, we have to decide what we're going to do about him. I certainly don't want him standing any more watches unsupervised!"

"Neither do I. For that matter, I don't want him at Tactical, even if he's just backing up Janice. Bad enough that the man is a fool, but now his own people are helping him cut his own throat!"

"Noticed that, did you, Sir?"

"Please, Abner! I'm still a few years shy of senile. Del Conte knew exactly what would happen."

"I think that may be putting it just a bit strongly, Sir," Layson said cautiously. He'd hoped without much confidence that the captain might not have noticed the senior chief's obvious decision to shut his mouth and stop arguing with his superior. "I mean," the exec went on, "Santino specifically ordered him to—"

"Oh, come on, Abner! Del Conte is an experienced man, and he damned well shouldn't have let the fact that his superior officer is an unmitigated ass push him into letting that officer blow the tactical situation all to hell, no matter how pissed off he might've been or how justified he was to be that way. You know it, I know it, and I expect you to make very certain that Senior Chief Del Conte knows that we do and that if he *ever* lets something like this happen again I will personally tear him a new asshole. I trust that I've made my feelings on this matter clear?"

"I think you might say that, Sir."

"Good," Bachfisch grunted, but then he waved a hand in a dismissive gesture. "But once you've made that clear to him—and once you're sure that you have—that's the end of it." He pretended not to notice the very slight relaxation of Layson's shoulders. "He shouldn't have let it happen, but you're right; he did exactly what his superior officer ordered him to do. Which is the problem. When a noncom of Del Conte's seniority deliberately lets his officer shoot his own foot off that spectacularly, that officer's usefulness is exactly nil. And it's also the most damning condemnation possible. Even if I weren't afraid that something like this might happen again, I don't want any King's officer who can drive his own personnel to a reaction like that in my ship or anywhere near her."

"I don't blame you, Sir. And I don't want him in *War Maiden*, either. But we're stuck with him."

"Oh, no, we're not," Bachfisch said grimly. "We still haven't sent *Gryphon's Pride* home. I believe that Lieutenant Santino has just earned himself a berth as her prize master."

Layson's eyes widened, and he started to open his mouth, then stopped. There were two reasons for a captain to assign one of his officers to command a prize ship. One was to reward that officer by giving him a shot at the sort of independent command which might bring him to the notice of the Lords of Admiralty. The other was for the captain to rid himself of someone whose competence he distrusted. Layson doubted that anyone could possibly fail to understand which reason was operating in this case, and he certainly couldn't fault Bachfisch's obvious determination to rid himself of Santino. But as *War Maiden*'s executive officer, the possibility presented him with a definite problem.

"Excuse me, Sir," the exec said after a moment, "but however weak he may be as a tac officer, he's the only assistant Janice has. If we send him away . . ."

He let his voice trail off, and Bachfisch nodded. Ideally, *War Maiden* should have carried two assistant tactical officers. Under normal circumstances, Hirake would have had both Santino and a junior-grade lieutenant or an ensign to back him up. The chronic shorthandedness of the expanding Manticoran Navy had caught the captain's ship short this time, and he drummed his fingers on his desktop while he considered his options. None of them were especially palatable, but—

"I don't care about shorthandedness," he said. "Not if it means keeping Santino aboard. Janice will just have to manage without him."

"But, Sir—" Layson began almost desperately, only to break off as Bachfisch raised a hand.

"He's gone, Abner," he said, and he spoke in the captain's voice that cut off all debate. "That part of the decision is already made."

"Yes, Sir," Layson said, and Bachfisch relented sufficiently to show him a small smile of sympathy.

"I know this is going to be a pain in the ass for you in some ways, Abner, and I'm sorry for that. But what you need to do is concentrate on how nice it will be to have Elvis Santino a hundred light-years away from us and then figure out a way to work around the hole."

"I'll try to bear that in mind, Sir. Ah, would the Captain care to suggest a way in which that particular hole might be worked around?"

"Actually, and bearing in mind an earlier conversation of ours, I believe I do," Bachfisch told him. "I would suggest that we seriously consider promoting Ms. Midshipwoman Harrington to the position of acting assistant tactical officer."

"Are you sure about that, Sir?" Layson asked. The captain raised an eyebrow at him, and the exec shrugged. "She's worked out very well so far, Sir. But she *is* a snotty."

"I agree that she's short on experience," Bachfisch replied. "That's why we send middies on their snotty cruises in the first place, after all. But I believe she's clearly demonstrated that she has the raw ability to handle the assistant tac officer's slot, and she's certainly a lot brighter and more reliable than Santino ever was."

"I can't argue with any of that, Sir. But since you've mentioned our conversation, remember what you said then about North Hollow and his clique. If they really did pull strings to put Santino aboard as OCTO and you not only relieve him of that duty, but then heave him completely off your bridge, and then take the midshipwoman they probably put him here specifically to get and put her into *his* slot—" He shook his head.

"You're right. That *will* piss them off, won't it?" Bachfisch murmured cheerfully.

"What it may do," Layson said in an exasperated tone, "is put *you* right beside her on their enemies list, Sir."

"Well, if it does, I could be in a lot worse company, couldn't I? And whether that happens or not doesn't really have any bearing on the specific problem which you and I have to solve right here and right now. So putting aside all other considerations, is there anyone in the ship's company who you think would be better qualified as an acting assistant tactical officer than Harrington would?"

"Of course there isn't. I'm not sure that putting her into the slot will be easy to justify if BuPers decides to get nasty about it—or not on paper, at least—but there's no question in my mind that she's the best choice, taken strictly on the basis of her merits. Which, I hasten to add, doesn't mean that I won't make sure that Janice rides very close herd on her. Or that I won't be doing exactly the same thing myself, for that matter."

"Excellent!" This time there was nothing small about Bachfisch's huge grin. "And while you're thinking about all the extra work this is going to make for you and Janice, think about how Harrington is going to feel when she finds out what sort of responsibility we're dumping on her! I think it will be rather informative to see just how panicked she gets when you break the word to her. And just to be sure that she doesn't get a swelled head about her temporary elevation over her fellow snotties, you might point out to her that while the exigencies of the King's service require that she assume those additional responsibilities, we can hardly excuse her from her training duties."

"You mean—?" Layson's eyes began to dance, and Bachfisch nodded cheerfully.

"Exactly, Commander. You and Janice will have to keep a close eye on her, but I feel that we should regard that not as an additional onerous responsibility, but rather as an *opportunity*. Consider it a chance to give her a personal tutorial in the fine art of ship-to-ship tactics and all the thousand and one ways in which devious enemies can surprise, bedevil, and defeat even the finest tactical officer. Really throw yourself into designing the very best possible training simulations for her. And be sure you tell her about all the extra effort you and Janice will be making on her behalf."

"That's evil, Sir," Layson said admiringly.

"I am shocked—*shocked*—that you could even think such a thing, Commander Layson!"

"Of course you are, Sir."

"Well, I suppose 'shocked' might be putting it just a tiny bit strongly," Bachfisch conceded. "But, seriously, Abner, I do want to take the opportunity to see how hard and how far we can push her. I think Raoul might just have been right when he told me how good he thought she could become, so let's see if we can't get her started on the right foot."

"Certainly, Sir. And I do believe that I'd like to see how far and how fast she can go, too. Not, of course," he smiled at his captain, "that I expect her to appreciate all of the effort and sacrifices Janice and I will be making when we devote our time to designing special sims just for her."

"Of course she won't. She *is* on her snotty cruise, Abner! But if she begins to exhaust your and Janice's inventiveness, let me know. I'd be happy to put together one or two modest little simulations for her myself."

"Oh, I'm sure she'll appreciate *that*, Sir."

"It looks like you're right, Sir," Commander Basil Amami said. His dark-complexioned face was alight with enthusiasm, and Obrad Bajkusa forced himself to bite his tongue firmly. Amami was a more than competent officer. He also happened to be senior to Bajkusa, but only by a few months. Under other circumstances, Bajkusa would have been more than willing to debate Amami's conclusions, and especially to have tried to abate the other officer's obvious enthusiasm. Unfortunately, Amami was also Commodore Dunecki's executive officer. It was Bajkusa's personal opinion that one major reason for Amami's present position was that he idolized Dunecki. Bajkusa didn't think Dunecki had set out to find himself a sycophant—or not deliberately and knowingly, at any rate—but Amami's very competence tended to keep people, Dunecki included, from wondering whether there was any other reason for his assignment. Perhaps the fact that his XO *always* seemed to agree with him should have sounded a warning signal for an officer as experienced as Dunecki, but it hadn't, and over the long months that Dunecki and Amami had served together, the commodore had developed an almost paternal attitude towards the younger man.

Whatever the internal dynamics of their relationship, Bajkusa had long since noticed that they had a tendency to double-team anyone who disagreed with or opposed them. Again, that was scarcely something which anyone could legitimately object to, since the two of them were supposed to be a mutually supporting command team, but it was clear to Bajkusa in this case that Amami's statement of agreement with Dunecki only reinforced the conclusion which the commodore had already reached on his own. Which meant that no mere commander in his right mind was going to argue with them both, however tenuous he might think the evidence for their conclusion was.

"Perhaps I was right, and perhaps I wasn't," Dunecki told Amami, but his cautionary note seemed more pro forma than genuine, Bajkusa thought. The commodore nodded in Bajkusa's direction. "*Javelin* did well, Captain," he said. "I appreciate your effort, and I'd like you to tell your entire ship's company that, as well."

"Thank you, Sir," Bajkusa replied. Then he decided to see if he couldn't interject a small note of caution of his own into the discussion. Indirectly, of course. "It was a closer thing than the raw log chips might indicate, though, Sir. Their EW was very good. We'd closed to just a little over two light-minutes, and I didn't even have a clue that they were a warship until they cleared their wedge. I was holding my overtake down mainly because I didn't want to attract anyone else's attention, but it never even occurred to me that the 'merchie' I was closing in on was a damned cruiser!"

"I can certainly understand why that would have been a shock," Dunecki agreed wryly.

"Especially in a system the damned Manties are hanging on to so tightly," Amami put in, and Bajkusa nodded sharply.

"That was my own thought," he said. "It's not like the Manties to invite a Confed cruiser in to keep an eye on their interests. It's usually the other way around," he added, watching the commodore carefully out of the corner of one eye. Dunecki frowned, and for just a moment the commander hoped that his superior was considering the thing that worried him, but then Dunecki shrugged.

"No, it's not," he acknowledged. "But your sensor readings make it fairly clear that it was either an awfully big light cruiser or decidedly on the small size for a heavy. God knows the Confeds have such a collection of odds and sods that they could have sent just about anything in to watch Melchor, but the Manties don't have any light cruisers that come close to the tonnage range your tac people suggest, and they've been retiring their older heavy cruisers steadily since they started their buildup. They can't have very many this small left in their inventory. Besides, no Manty would be as clumsy—or as stupid—as this fellow was! Clearing his wedge at barely two lightminutes after all the trouble they'd gone to convince you that they were a freighter in the first place?" The commodore shook his head. "I've encountered a lot of Manty officers, Commander, and none of them was dumb enough to do that against something as small and fast as a frigate."

Bajkusa wanted to continue the debate, if that was really what it was, but he had to admit that Dunecki had a point. A rather sizable one, in fact. Much as he loved *Javelin*, Bajkusa was perfectly well aware why no major naval power was still building frigates and why those navies which had them were retiring them steadily. They were the smallest class of hyper-capable warship, with a tonnage which fell about midway between a dispatch boat and a destroyer, and that gave them precious little room to pack in weapons. Indeed, *Javelin* was only a very little more heavily armed than a light attack craft, although her missiles had somewhat more range and she did have *some* magazine capacity, and she and her ilk no longer had any true viable purpose except to serve as remote reconnaissance platforms. Even that was being taken away from them by improvements in the remote sensor drones most navies regularly employed, and Bajkusa strongly suspected that the frigates' last stand would be as cheap, very light escorts to run down even lighter pirates . . . or as commerce raiders (or pirates) in their own right.

So, yes, Commodore Dunecki had a point. What Manticoran cruiser captain in his right mind would have let *anything* get that close without detection. And if he had detected *Javelin* on her way in, then why in Heaven's name clear his wedge before he had her into engagement range? It certainly couldn't have been because he was afraid of the outcome!

"No," Dunecki said with another shake of his head. "Whoever this joker is, he's no Manty, and we know for a fact that no Andermani ships would be in Melchor under present conditions, so that really only leaves one thing he could be, doesn't it? Which means that he's in exactly the right place for our purposes. And as small as he is, there's no way he can match *Annika's* weight of metal."

"Absolutely, Sir!" Amami enthused.

"But he may not be there for long," Dunecki mused aloud, "and I'd hate to let him get away—or, even worse—find out that Wegener is worried enough about keeping an eye on his investment that he doubles up on his picket there and comes up with something that could give us a real fight. That means we have to move quickly, but we also need to be sure we coordinate properly, Commander Bajkusa. So I think that while I take *Annika* to Melchor to check on the situation, I'm going to send you and *Javelin* off to Lutrell. If my brother's kept to the schedule he sent me in his last dispatch, you should find *Astrid* there. He'll probably send you on to Prism with his own dispatches, but emphasize to him that by the time he hears from you our good friend the Governor is about to find himself short one cruiser."

He smiled thinly, and Bajkusa smiled back, because on that point at least, he had complete and total faith in Dunecki's judgment.

Honor dragged herself wearily through the hatch and collapsed facedown on her bunk with a heartfelt groan. Nimitz leapt from her shoulder at the last moment and landed on the pillow where he turned to regard her with a reproving flirt of his tail.

She paid him no attention at all, and he bleeked a quiet laugh and curled down beside her to rest his nose gently in the short-cropped, silky fuzz of her hair.

"Keeping us out late, I see, Ma'am," a voice observed brightly, and Honor turned her head without ever lifting it completely off the pillow. She lay with it under her right cheek and turned a slightly bloodshot and profoundly disapproving eye upon Audrey Bradlaugh.

"I'm pleased to see that *someone* finds the situation amusing," she observed, and Audrey chuckled.

"Oh, no, Honor! It's not that someone finds it amusing—it's that the entire ship's *company* does! And it's such an appropriate . . . resolution, too. I mean, after all, it was you and Del Conte between you who got rid of that asshole Santino in the first place, so it's only appropriate that the two of you should wind up on the same watch doing his job. Much better than he did, I might add. Of course, it is kind of entertaining to watch the Captain and Commander Layson—not to mention Commander Hirake—kicking your poor, innocent butt in the simulator every day. Not, of course, that I would for one moment allow the fact that you systematically annihilated Nassios and me in that sim last week—or me and Basanta last Tuesday, now that I think about it—to affect my judgment in any way."

"You are a vile and disgusting person," Honor informed her, "and God will punish you for abusing me in this fashion when I am too weak and exhausted to properly defend myself."

"Sure He will," Audrey replied. "As soon as He stops laughing, anyway!"

Honor made a rude sound and then closed her eyes and buried her face in the pillow once more. She was relieved that Audrey and the other middies had decided to take her acting promotion without jealousy, but there was an unfortunate edge of accuracy to Audrey's teasing. More than one edge, in fact.

Honor had been more than a little appalled when Commander Layson called her into his day cabin to inform her that the Captain had decided to elevate her to the position of acting assistant tactical officer. However good a tactician she might consider herself as a midshipwoman, and however exciting the notion of such a promotion might be, there was no way in the universe that she could consider herself ready to assume the duties of such a position. Nor had the Exec's blunt explanation of the situation which had impelled Captain Bachfisch to elevate her to such heights done much for her ego. It wasn't so much that Commander Layson had said anything at all unreasonable, as it was that his analysis had made it perfectly plain that the Captain had had no one else at all to put into the slot. If they *had* had anyone else, the Exec had made clear enough, then that someone else would undoubtedly have been chosen. But since Ms. Midshipwoman Harrington was all they had, she would have to do.

And just to see to it that she did, Commander Layson had informed her with an air of bland generosity, he, Commander Hirake, and the Captain himself would be only too happy to help her master her new duties.

She'd thanked him, of course. There was very little else that she could have done, whatever she'd sensed waiting in her future. Nor had her trepidation proved ill founded. None of them was quite as naturally fiendish as Captain Courvoisier, but Captain Courvoisier had been the head of the entire Saganami Island Tactical Department. He hadn't begun to have the amount of time that Honor's trio of new instructors had, and he'd certainly never been able to devote his entire attention to a single unfortunate victim at a time.

As Audrey had just suggested, Honor wasn't used to losing in tactical exercises. In fact, she admitted to herself, she had become somewhat smugly accustomed to beating the stuffing out of other people, and the string of salutary drubbings the tactical trinity of HMS *War Maiden* had administered to her had been a chastening experience. Just as they had been intended to be. Nor had her lordly new elevation altered the fact that this remained her snotty cruise. When she took her tac watch on the bridge (although, thank God, no one was prepared to even suggest that she be given the *bridge* watch itself!) she was indeed the ship's duty tactical officer. But when she was off watch, she was still Ms. Midshipwoman Harrington, and no one had seen fit to excuse her from all of the other "learning experiences" which had been the lot of RMN snotties since time out of mind.

All of which meant that she was running even harder now than she had during her final form at Saganami Island. Which seemed dreadfully unfair, given how much smaller a campus *War Maiden* was!

"You really are bushed, aren't you?" Audrey asked after a moment, and the amusement in her voice had eased back a notch.

"No," Honor said judiciously. " 'Bushed' is far too pale and anemic a word for what I am."

She was only half-joking, and it showed.

"Well, in that case, why don't you just kick off your boots and stay where you are for a while?"

"No way," Honor said, opening her eyes once more. "We've got quarters inspection in less than four hours!"

"So we do," Audrey agreed. "But you and Nassios covered my posterior with Lieutenant Saunders on that charting problem yesterday, so I guess the three of us could let you get a few hours of shut-eye while we tidy up. It's not like your locker's a disaster area, you know."

"But—" Honor began.

"Shut up and take your nap," Audrey told her firmly, and Nimitz bleeked in soft but equally firm agreement from beside her head. Honor considered protesting further, but not for very long. She'd already argued long enough to satisfy the requirements of honor, and she was too darned exhausted to be any more noble than she absolutely had to.

"Thanks," she said sleepily, and she was already asleep before Audrey could reply.

"There she is, Sir," Commander Amami said. "Just as you expected."

"There we *think* she is," Anders Dunecki corrected meticulously. Whatever Bajkusa might have thought, the commodore was far from blind to Amami's tendency to accept his own theories uncritically, and he made a conscious effort to keep that in mind at times like this. "She could still be a legitimate merchantman," he added, and Amami rubbed gently at his lower lip in thought.

"She is on the right course for one of the Dillingham supply ships, Sir," he conceded after a moment. "But according to our intelligence packet, there shouldn't be another Dillingham ship in here for at least another month, and there really isn't a lot of other shipping to the system these days."

"True," Dunecki agreed. "But the flip side of that argument is that if there isn't much other shipping in the first place, then the odds are greater that any additional merchies that come calling are going to slip through without our intelligence people warning us they're on their way."

"Point taken, Sir," Amami acknowledged. "So how do you want to handle this?"

"Exactly as we planned from the beginning," Dunecki said. "I pointed out that this *could* be a merchantman, not that I really believed that it was one. And it doesn't matter if it is, after all. If we treat it as a Confed cruiser from the outset, then all we'll really do if it turns out to be a merchie is to waste a little caution on it. But if it turns out to be a cruiser and we assume otherwise, the surprise would be on the other foot. So we'll just close in on the contact all fat and happy—and dumb. We won't suspect a thing until it's got us exactly where it wants us."

He looked up from his plot to meet Amami's eyes, and their thin, shark-like smiles were in perfect agreement.

"The contact is still closing, Sir," Lieutenant Commander Hirake reported from the com screen at Captain Bachfisch's elbow.

War Maiden's senior tactical officer was once again in Auxiliary Control with Commander Layson, but Honor was on the command deck. She would have liked to think that she was there while the lieutenant commander was in AuxCon because the Captain had so much faith in her abilities. Unfortunately, she knew it was exactly the other way around. He wanted her under his own eye, and if something happened to the bridge, he wanted to be sure that Layson would have the more experienced tactical officer to back him up.

"I noticed that myself," Bachfisch replied to Hirake with a small smile. "May I assume that your latest report is a tactful effort to draw to my attention the fact that the contact seems to be an awfully large and powerful 'pirate'?"

"Something of the sort, Sir," Hirake said with an answering smile, but there was a hint of genuine concern in her expression. "According to CIC, she outmasses us by at least sixty thousand tons."

"So she does," Bachfisch agreed. "But she obviously doesn't know that we aren't just another freighter waiting for her to snap us up. Besides, if she were a Peep or an Andy, I'd be worried by her tonnage advantage. But no regular man-of-war would be closing in on a merchie this way, so that means whoever we have out there is a raider. That makes her either a straight pirate or a privateer, and neither of them is likely to have a crew that can match our people. Don't worry, Janice. I won't get cocky or take anything for granted, but I'm not scared of anything short of an Andy that size— certainly not of anything armed with the kind of crap available from the tech base here in the Confederacy! Anyway, pirates and privateers are what we're out here to deal with, so let's be about it."

"As you say, Sir," Hirake replied, and Honor hid a smile as she gazed down at her own plot. The lieutenant commander had done her job by reminding her captain (however tactfully) of the enemy's size and potential firepower, but the confidence in her voice matched that of the Captain perfectly. And rightly so, Honor concluded. The contact closing so confidently upon them obviously didn't have a clue of what it was actually pursuing, or it would have come in far more cautiously.

"Captain, I have a hail from the contact," Lieutenant Sauchuk reported suddenly.

"Oh?" Bachfisch arched one eyebrow. "Put it on the main screen and let's hear what he has to say, Yuri."

"Aye, aye, Sir."

All eyes on *War Maiden's* bridge flipped to the main com screen as a man in the uniform of the Silesian Confederacy's navy appeared on it.

"*Sylvan Grove,*" he said, addressing them by the name of the Hauptman Cartel freighter whose transponder ID codes they had borrowed for their deception, "this is Captain Denby of the Confederate Navy. Please maintain your present course and attitude while my ship makes rendezvous with you."

"Oh, of *course* you are," Honor heard Senior Chief Del Conte murmur all but inaudibly behind her.

"I think we owe the good captain a reply, Yuri," Bachfisch said after a moment. "Double-check your filters, and then give me a live pickup."

"Aye, aye, Sir," Sauchuk replied. He checked the settings on his panel carefully, then nodded. "You're live, Skipper," he said.

"Captain Denby, I'm Captain Bullard," Bachfisch said, and Honor knew that *War Maiden's* computers were altering his image to put him into a merchant officer's uniform, rather than the black and gold of the RMN, just as the raider's computers had put *him* into Confed naval uniform. "I hope you won't take this the wrong way," Bachfisch went on, "but this isn't exactly the safest neighborhood around. It's not that I don't believe you're who you say you are, but could I ask just why it is that you want to rendezvous with us?"

"Of course, Captain Bullard," the face on his com screen replied in the slightly stiff tone of an officer who didn't particularly like to be reminded by a mere merchant skipper of how pathetic his navy's record for maintaining order within its own borders was. "I have aboard seventeen of your nationals, the survivors from the crews of two Manticoran freighters. We took out the 'privateer' who captured their ships last week, and it seemed to me that the fastest way to repatriate them would be to turn them over to the Dillingham manager here in Melchor."

"I see," Bachfisch replied in a much warmer and less wary voice. He felt a brief flicker of something almost like admiration for "Captain Denby's" smoothness, for the other man had come up with what was actually a plausible reason for a merchantman here in Silesia to allow a warship to close with it. And "Denby" had delivered his lines perfectly, with just the right note of offended dignity coupled with a "see there" sort of flourish. "In that case, Captain," he went on, "of course we'll maintain heading and deceleration for rendezvous."

"Thank you, Captain Bullard," the man on his com screen said. "Denby out."

"Considerate of them to let us maintain course," Janice Hirake observed to Abner Layson.

"He doesn't have much choice if he's going to keep us dumb and happy," Layson pointed out, and Hirake nodded. Warships could pull far higher accelerations than any huge whale of a merchantman, and it was traditional for them to be the ones who maneuvered to match heading and velocity in the case of a deep space rendezvous.

"Still, it's handy that he came in so far above the plane of the ecliptic. Keeps him well above us and on the wrong side of our wedge."

"Somehow I doubt that they arranged things that way just to oblige us," Layson said dryly. "On the other hand, sneaking up on somebody *can* sometimes put you in a less than optimal position yourself, can't it?"

"Indeed it can," Hirake said with a small, wicked smile.

"I wish we had a little better sensor angle on them, Sir," Lieutenant Quinn muttered from one side of his mouth, and Lieutenant Commander Acedo glanced at him. Acedo was *Annika's* tactical officer, and Quinn was the most junior commissioned member of his department. But the younger man had a nose for trouble which Acedo had learned to trust, or at least listen very carefully to.

"I'd like to have a better look at them myself," the lieutenant commander replied. "But thanks to *Javelin*, we've already got a pretty good notion of what we're up against. At this point, I have to agree with the Commodore—it's more important to keep him guessing about us by avoiding the deeper parts of his sensor well. Besides, the fact that he's got his wedge between him and *our* sensors should help keep him confident that we don't know that he's a warship, too."

"I can't argue with that, Sir," Quinn acknowledged. "I guess I just want the best of both worlds, and sometimes you just can't have that."

"No, you can't," Acedo agreed. "But sometimes you can come pretty close, and the way the Old Man's set this one up qualifies for that."

Two cruisers slid inexorably together, each convinced that she knew precisely what the other one was and that the other one didn't know what *she* was . . . and both of them wrong. The distance between them fell steadily, and *Annika's* deceleration reduced the velocity differential with matching steadiness.

"Zero-zero interception in five minutes, Sir," Honor announced. Her soprano sounded much calmer in her own ears than it felt from behind her eyes, and she raised her head to look across the bridge at the Captain. "Current range is two-one-six k-klicks and present overtake is one-three-three-one KPS squared. Deceleration is holding steady at four-five-zero gravities."

"Thank you, Tactical," Bachfisch replied, and his calm, composed tone did more than she would have believed possible to still the excitement jittering down her nerves. The fact that their sensors still had not had a single clear look at the contact made her nervous, but she took herself firmly to task. This, too, she thought was a part of the art of command. For all of his calm, the Captain actually *knew* no more about the contact than Honor herself, but it was his job to exude the sort of confidence his people needed from him at this moment. Captain Courvoisier had stressed more than once that even if she was wrong—or perhaps *especially* if she was wrong—a commanding officer must never forget her "command face." Nothing could destroy a crew's cohesion faster than panic, and nothing produced panic better than the suggestion that the CO had lost her own confidence. But it had to be harder than usual, this time. The raider was well within effective energy range already, and just as *War Maiden's* own crew, her people must be ready to open fire in a heartbeat. At such short range, an energy weapon duel would be deadly, which would be good . . . for whoever fired first.

Of course, the raider was expecting only an unarmed merchantship. However prepared they thought they were, the sheer surprise of finding themselves suddenly broadside-to-broadside with a King's ship was bound to shock and confuse them at least momentarily. And it was entirely possible that they wouldn't even have closed up all of their weapons crews simply to deal with a "merchantman."

"Stand ready, Mr. Saunders," the Captain said calmly. "Prepare to alter course zero-nine-zero degrees to starboard and roll port at one hundred ten thousand kilometers."

"Aye, aye, Sir," Lieutenant Saunders acknowledged. "Standing by to alter course zero-nine-zero degrees to starboard and roll port at range of one hundred ten thousand kilometers."

"Stand by to fire on my command, Ms. Harrington," Bachfisch added.

"Aye, aye, Sir. Standing by to fire on your command."

"Get ready, Commander Acedo," Anders Dunecki said quietly. "At this range he won't risk challenging us or screwing around demanding we surrender, so neither will we. The instant he rolls ship to clear his wedge, blow his ass out of space."

"Yes, Sir!" Acedo agreed with a ferocious grin, and he felt just as confident as he looked. The other ship would have the advantage of knowing when she intended to alter course, but *Annika* had an even greater advantage. The commander of the enemy cruiser had to be completely confident that he had *Annika* fooled, or he would never have allowed her to come this close, and the only thing more devastating than the surprise of an ambush was the surprise of an ambusher when his intended victim turned out not to have been surprised at all.

"Coming up on one hundred ten thousand kilometers, Sir!"

"Execute your helm order, Mr. Saunders!" Thomas Bachfisch snapped.

"Aye, aye, Sir!"

War Maiden responded instantly to her helm, pivoting sharply to her right and rolling up on her left side to swing her starboard broadside up towards the raider, and Honor leaned forward, pulse hammering, mouth dry, as the icons on her plot flashed before her. It almost seemed as if it were the raider who had suddenly altered course and position as the strobing amber circle of target acquisition reached out to engulf its blood-red bead.

"Stand by, Ms. Harrington!"

"Standing by, aye, Sir."

The amber circle reached the glowing bead of the contact and flashed over to sudden crimson, and Honor's hand hovered above the firing key.

"*Fire!*"

Both ships fired in the same instant across barely a third of a light-second.

At such a short range, their grasers and lasers blasted straight through any sidewall any cruiser could have generated, and alarms screamed as deadly, focused energy ripped huge, shattered wounds through battle steel and alloy. Surprise was effectively total on both sides. Commodore Dunecki had completely deceived Captain Bachfisch into expecting *Annika* to be fatally unprepared, but despite his discussion with Commander Bajkusa, Dunecki had never seriously considered for a moment that *War Maiden* might be anything except a Silesian warship. He was totally unprepared to find himself suddenly face to face with a *Manticoran* heavy cruiser. *War Maiden's* tautly trained crew were head and shoulders above any SN ship's company in training and efficiency. They got off their first broadside two full seconds before Dunecki had anticipated that they could. Worse, Silesian ships tended to be missile-heavy, optimized for long-range combat and with only relatively light energy batteries, and the sheer weight of fire smashing into his ship was a stunning surprise.

But even though Dunecki was unprepared for *War Maiden's* furious fire, the Manticoran ship was still smaller and more lightly armed than his own. Worse, Captain Bachfisch had assumed that *Annika* was a typical pirate and anticipated at least a moment or two in which to act while "Captain Denby" adjusted to the fact that the "freighter" he was stalking had suddenly transformed itself from a house tabby to a hexapuma, and he didn't get it. It was the equivalent of a duel with submachine guns at ten paces, and both ships staggered as the deadly tide of energy sleeted into them.

Honor Harrington's universe went mad.

She'd felt herself tightening internally during the long approach phase, felt the dryness of her mouth and the way her nerves seemed to quiver individually, dancing within her flesh as if they were naked harp strings plucked by an icy wind. She had been more afraid than she had ever been in her life, and not just for herself. She had won friendships aboard *War Maiden* during the long weeks of their deployment, and those friends were at risk as much as she was. And then there was Nimitz, alone in his life-support module down in Snotty Row. Her mind had shied away from the thought of what would happen to him if his module suffered battle damage . . . or if she herself died. 'Cats who had adopted humans almost invariably suicided if their humans died. She'd known that before she ever applied for Saganami Island, and it had almost made her abandon her dream of Navy service, for if she put herself in harm's way, she put *him* there, as well, and only Nimitz's fierce, obvious insistence that she pursue her dream had carried her to the Academy. Now the reality of what had been only an intellectual awareness was upon them both, and a dark and terrible fear—not of death or wounds, but of loss—was a cold iron lump at the core of her.

Those fears had flowed through her on the crest of a sudden visceral awareness that she was not immortal. That the bloody carnage of combat could claim her just as easily as any other member of *War Maiden*'s company. Despite all of her training, all of her studies, all of her lifelong interest in naval and military history, that awareness had never truly been hers until this instant. Now it was, and she had spent the slow, dragging hours as the contact gradually closed with *War Maiden* trying to prepare herself and wondering how she would respond when she knew it was no longer a simulation. That there were real human beings on the other side of that icon on her plot. People who would be doing their very best to kill her ship—and her—with real weapons . . . and whom she would be trying to kill in turn. She'd made herself face and accept that, despite her fear, and she had thought—hoped—that she was ready for whatever might happen.

She'd been wrong.

HMS *War Maiden* lurched like a galleon in a gale as the transfer energy of PSN *Annika*'s fire bled into her. The big privateer carried fewer missiles and far heavier energy weapons than her counterparts in the Silesian navy, and her grasers smashed through *War Maiden*'s sidewall like brimstone sledgehammers come straight from Hell. The sidewall generators did their best to bend and divert that hurricane of energy from its intended target, but four of the heavy beams struck home with demonic fury. Graser Two, Missiles Two and Four, Gravitic Two, Radar Two and Lidar Three, Missile Eight and Magazine Four, Boat Bay One and Life Support Two . . . Entire clusters of compartments and weapons bays turned venomous, bloody crimson on the damage control panel as enemy fire ripped and clawed its way towards *War Maiden*'s heart. Frantic damage control reports crashed over Honor like a Sphinxian tidal bore while the ship jerked and shuddered. Damage alarms wailed and screamed, adding their voices to the cacophony raging through the heavy cruiser's compartments, and clouds of air and water vapor erupted from the gaping wounds torn suddenly through her armored skin.

"Heavy casualties in Missile Two!" Senior Chief Del Conte barked while secondary explosions still rolled through the hull. "Graser Six reports loss of central control, and Magazine Four is open to space! We—"

He never finished his report, and Honor's entire body recoiled as a savage explosion tore through the bridge bulkhead. It reached out to the senior chief, snatching him up as casually as some cruel child would have, and tore him to pieces before her eyes. Blood and pieces of what had been a human being seemed to be *everywhere*, and a small, calm corner of her brain realized that that was because they *were* everywhere. The explosion killed at least five people outright, through blast or with deadly splinters from ruptured bulkheads, and Honor rocked back in her padded, armored chair as the wall of devastation marched through *War Maiden*'s bridge . . . and directly over the captain's chair at its center.

Captain Bachfisch just had time to bend forward and raise an arm in an instinctive effort to protect his face when the blast front struck. It hit from slightly behind into his right, and that was all that saved his life, because even as his arm rose, he whipped the chair to his left and took the main force across the armored shell of its back. But not even that was enough to fully protect him, and the force of the explosion snatched him up and hurled him against the opposite bulkhead. He bounced back with the limp, total bonelessness of unconsciousness and hit the decksole without ever having made a sound.

He was far from the only injured person on the bridge. The same explosion which blew him out of his chair threw a meter-long splinter of battle steel across the com section. It decapitated Lieutenant Sauchuk as neatly as an executioner, then hurtled onward and drove itself through Lieutenant Saunders' chest like an ax, and Honor's mind tried to retreat into some safe, sane cave as the chaos and confusion and terror for which no simulation, no lecture, could possibly have prepared her enveloped her. She heard the whistling rush of air racing for the rents in the bulkhead even through the screams and moans of the wounded, and instinct cried out for her to race across the bridge to help the hurt and unconscious helmet up in time. Yet she didn't. The trained responses her instructors at Saganami Island had hammered mercilessly into her for four long T-years overrode even her horror and the compulsion to help. She slammed her own helmet into place, but her eyes never left the panel before her, for she dared not leave her station even to help the Captain before she knew that AuxCon and Lieutenant Commander Hirake had taken over from the mangled bridge.

War Maiden's energy mounts lashed out again, with a second broadside, even as the raider fired again, as well. More death and destruction punched their way through the hull, rending and tearing, and the heavy cruiser shuddered as one hit blew straight through her after impeller ring. Half the beta nodes and two of the alphas went down instantly, and fresh alarms shrilled as a fifth of War Maiden's personnel became casualties. Lieutenant Commander LaVacher was one of them, and a simultaneous hit smashed home on Damage Control Central, killing a dozen ratings and petty officers and critically wounding Lieutenant Tergesen.

War Maiden's grasers continued to hammer at her larger, more powerful—and far younger—foe, but Honor felt a fresh and even more paralyzing spike of terror as she realized that they were still firing under the preliminary fire plan which she had locked in under Captain Bachfisch's orders. AuxCon should have overridden and assumed command virtually instantly . . . and it hadn't.

She turned her head, peering at what had been Senior Chief Del Conte's station through the banners of smoke riding the howling gale through the shattered bulkhead, and her heart froze as her eyes picked out AuxCon on the schematic displayed there. The compartment itself appeared to be intact, but it was circled by the jagged red and white band which indicated total loss of communications. AuxCon was cut off, not only from the bridge, but from access to the ship's computers, as well.

In the time it had taken to breathe three times, War Maiden had been savagely maimed, and tactical command had devolved onto a twenty-year-old midshipwoman on her snotty cruise.

The bridge about her was like the vestibule of Hell. Half the command stations had been wrecked or at least blown off-line, a quarter of the bridge crew was dead or wounded, and at least three men and women who should have been at their stations were crawling frantically through the wreckage slapping helmets and skinsuit seals on unconscious crewmates. She felt the ship's wounds as if they had been inflicted upon her own body, and all in the world she wanted in that moment was to hear someone—anyone—tell her what to do.

But there was no one else. She was all War Maiden had, and she jerked her eyes back to her own plot and drew a deep breath.

"Helm, roll ninety degrees port!"

No one on that wounded, half-broken bridge, and Honor least of all, perhaps, recognized the cool, sharp soprano which cut cleanly through the chaos, but the helmsman clinging to his own sanity with his fingernails recognized the incisive bite of command.

"Rolling ninety degrees port, aye!" he barked, and HMS *War Maiden* rolled frantically, snatching her shattered starboard broadside away from the ferocity of her enemy's fire.

Something happened inside Honor Harrington in the moment that her ship rolled. The panic vanished. The fear remained, but it was suddenly a distant, unimportant thing—something which could no longer touch her, would no longer be permitted to affect her. She looked full into the face of Death, not just for her but for her entire ship and everyone aboard it, and there was no doubt in her mind that he had come for them all. Yet her fear had transmuted into something else entirely. A cold, focused purpose that sang in her blood and bone. Her almond eyes stared into Death's empty sockets, and her soul bared its teeth and snarled defiance.

"Port broadside stand by for Fire Plan Delta Seven," that soprano rapier commanded, and confirmations raced back from *War Maiden*'s undamaged broadside even as *Annika*'s fire continued to hammer harmlessly at the impenetrable belly of her wedge.

Honor's mind raced with cold, icy precision. Her first instinct was to break off, for she knew only too well how brutally wounded her ship was. Worse, she already knew that their opponent was far more powerful—and better crewed—than anyone aboard *War Maiden* had believed she could be. Yet those very factors were what made flight impossible. The velocity differential between the two ships was less than six hundred kilometers per second, and with half her after impeller ring down, *War Maiden* could never hope to pull away from her unlamed foe. Even had her drive been unimpaired, the effort to break off would undoubtedly have proved suicidal as it exposed the after aspect of her impeller wedge to the enemy's raking fire.

No, she thought coldly. Flight was not an option, and her gloved fingers raced across the tactical panel, locking in new commands as she reached out for her ship's— *her* ship's—only hope of survival.

"Helm, stand by to alter course one-three-five degrees to starboard, forty degree nose-down skew, and roll starboard on my command!"

"Aye, aye, Ma'am!"

"All weapons crews," that voice she could not quite recognize even now went on, carrying a calm and a confidence that stilled incipient panic like a magic wand, "stand by to engage as programmed. Transmitting manual firing commands now."

She punched a button, and the targeting parameters she had locked into the main computers spilled into the secondary on-mount computers of her waiting weapons crews. If fresh damage cut her command links to them, at least they would know what she intended for them to do.

Then it was done, and she sat back in her command chair, watching the enemy's icon as it continued to angle sharply in to intercept *War Maiden*'s base track. The range was down to fifty-two thousand kilometers, falling at five hundred and six kilometers per second, and she waited tautly while the blood-red icon of her enemy closed upon her ship.

Commodore Anders Dunecki cursed vilely as the other cruiser snapped up on its side. He'd hurt that ship—hurt it badly—and he knew it. But it had also hurt him far more badly than he had ever allowed for. He'd gotten slack, a cold thought told him in his own viciously calm voice. He'd been fighting the Confeds too long, let his guard down and become accustomed to being able to take liberties with them. But his present opponent was no Silesian naval unit, and he cursed again, even more vilely, as he realized what that other ship truly was.

A Manty. He'd attacked a *Manty* warship, committed the one unforgivable blunder no pirate or privateer was ever allowed to commit more than once. That was why the other cruiser had managed to get off even a single shot of her own, because she was a Manty and she'd been just as ready, just as prepared to fire as he was.

And it was also why his entire strategy to win Andermani support for the Council for an Independent Prism had suddenly come crashing down in ruins. However badly the People's Republic might have distracted the Manticoran government, the RMN's response to what had happened here was as certain as the energy death of the universe.

But only if they know who did it, his racing brain told him coldly. *Only if they know which system government to send the battle squadrons after. But that ship has got to have detailed sensor records of* Annika's *energy signatures. If they compare those records with the Confed database, they're bound to ID us. Even if they don't get a clean hit, Wegener will know who it must have been and send them right after us. But even he won't be able to talk the Manties into hitting us without at least some supporting evidence, and the only evidence there is in the computers of that ship.*

There was only one way to prevent that data from getting out.

He turned his head to look at Commander Amami. The exec was still listening to damage reports, but Dunecki didn't really need them. A glance at the master schematic showed that *Annika's* entire port broadside must be a mass of tangled ruin. Less than a third of her energy mounts and missile tubes remained intact, and her sidewall generators were at barely forty percent efficiency. But the Manty had to be hurt at least as badly, and she was smaller, less able to absorb damage. Better yet, he had the overtake advantage and her impeller strength had dropped drastically. He was bigger, newer, better armed, and more maneuverable, and that meant the engagement could have only one outcome.

"Roll one-eight-zero degrees to starboard and maintain heading," he told his helmsmen harshly. "Starboard broadside, stand by to fire as you bear!"

Honor watched the other ship roll. Like *War Maiden*, the bigger ship was rotating her crippled broadside away from her opponent's fire. But she wasn't stopping there, and Honor let herself feel a tiny spark of hope as the raider continued to roll, and then the weapons of her undamaged broadside lashed out afresh and poured a hurricane of fire upon *War Maiden*. The belly of the Manticoran ship's impeller wedge absorbed that fire harmlessly, but that wasn't the point, and Honor knew it. The enemy was sequencing her fire carefully, so that *something* pounded the wedge continuously. If *War Maiden* rolled back for a broadside duel, that constant pounding was almost certain to catch her as she rolled, inflicting damage and destroying at least some of her remaining weapons before they ever got a chance to bear upon their foe. It was a smart, merciless tactic, one which eschewed finesse in favor of brutal practicality.

But unlike whoever was in command over there, Honor could not afford a weapon-to-weapon battering match. Not against someone that big who had already demonstrated her capabilities so convincingly. And so she had no choice but to oppose overwhelming firepower with cunning.

Every fiber of her being was concentrated on the imagery of her plot, and her lips drew back in a feral snarl as the other ship maintained her acceleration. Seconds ticked slowly and agonizingly past. Sixty of them. Then seventy. Ninety.

"Helm! On my mark, give me maximum emergency power—redline everything—and execute my previous order!" She heard the helmsman's response, but her eyes never flickered from her plot, and her nostrils flared.

"Now!"

Anders Dunecki had a handful of fleeting seconds to realize that he had made one more error. The Manty had held her course, hiding behind the shield of her wedge, and he'd thought that it hadn't mattered whether that arose out of panic or out of a rational realization that she couldn't have gone toe-to-toe with *Annika* even if she hadn't been so badly damaged.

Yet it did matter. The other captain hadn't panicked, but he *had* realized he couldn't fight *Annika* in a broadside duel . . . and he had no intention of doing so.

Perhaps it wasn't really Dunecki's fault. The range was insanely short for modern warships, dropping towards one which could be measured in hundreds of kilometers and not thousands, and no sane naval officer would even have contemplated engaging at such close quarters. Nor had either Dunecki or Bachfisch planned on doing any such thing, for each had expected to begin and end the battle with a single broadside which would take his enemy completely by surprise. But whatever they'd planned, their ships were here now, and no one in any navy trained its officers for combat maneuvers in such close proximity to an enemy warship. And because of that, Anders Dunecki, for all of his experience, was completely unprepared for what *War Maiden* actually did.

Strident alarms jangled as HMS *War Maiden*'s inertial compensator protested its savage abuse. More alarms howled as the load on the heavy cruiser's impeller nodes peaked forty percent beyond their "Never Exceed" levels. Despite her mangled after impeller ring, *War Maiden* slammed suddenly forward at almost five hundred and fifty gravities. Her bow swung sharply towards *Annika*, but it also dipped sharply "below" the other ship, denying the big privateer the deadly down-the-throat shot which would have spelled *War Maiden*'s inevitable doom.

Annika began a desperate turn of her own, but she had been taken too much by surprise. There wasn't enough time for her to answer her helm before *War Maiden*'s wounded charge carried her across her enemy's wake.

It wasn't the perfect up-the-kilt stern rake that was every tactical officer's dream. No neat ninety-degree crossing with every weapon firing in perfect sequence. Instead, it was a desperate, scrambling lunge—the ugly do-or-die grapple of a wounded hexapuma facing a peak bear. Honor's weapons couldn't begin to fire down the long axis of the enemy ship in a "proper" rake . . . but what they could do was enough.

Six grasers scored direct hits on the aftermost quarter of PSN *Annika*. They came in through the open after aspect of her wedge, with no sidewall to interdict or degrade them. They smashed into her armored after hammerhead, and armor shattered at their ferocious touch. They blew deep into the bigger ship's hull, maiming and smashing, crippling her after chase armament, and the entire after third of her sidewall flickered and died.

Annika fought to answer her helm, clawing around in a desperate attempt to reacquire *War Maiden* for her broadside weapons, but Honor Harrington had just discovered that she could be just as merciless a killer as Anders Dunecki. Her flying fingers stabbed a minor correction into her tactical panel, and *War Maiden* fired once more. Every graser in her surviving broadside poured a deadly torrent of energy into the gap in *Annika*'s sidewall, and the big privateer vanished in a hell-bright boil of fury.

.   .   .

Nimitz sat very straight and still on Honor Harrington's shoulder as she came to a halt before the Marine sentry outside the Captain's day cabin. The private gazed at her for a long, steady moment, then reached back to key the admittance signal.

"Yes?" The voice belonged to Abner Layson, not Thomas Bachfisch.

"Ms. Harrington to see the Captain, Sir!" the Marine replied crisply.

"Enter," another voice said, and the Marine stepped aside as the hatch opened. Honor nodded her thanks as she stepped past him, and for just a moment he allowed his professional nonexpression to vanish into a wink of encouragement before the hatch closed behind her once more.

Honor crossed the cabin and came to attention. Commander Layson sat behind the captain's desk, but Captain Bachfisch was also present. *War Maiden's* CO was propped as comfortably as possible on an out-sized couch along the cabin's longest bulkhead. He looked awful, battered and bruised and with his left arm and right leg both immobilized. Under almost any other circumstances, he would still have been locked up in sickbay while Lieutenant Chiem stood over him with a pulser to keep him there if necessary. But there was no room in sickbay for anyone with non-life-threatening injuries. Basanta Lakhia was in sickbay. Nassios Makira wasn't; he'd been in After Engineering when the hit came in, and the damage control parties hadn't even found his body.

Honor stood there, facing the executive officer and her captain, and the eighteen percent of *War Maiden's* company who had died stood silently at her shoulder, waiting.

"Stand easy, Ms. Harrington," the captain said quietly, and she let her spine relax ever so slightly. Bachfisch gazed at her for a long, quiet moment, and she returned his gaze as calmly as she could.

"I've reviewed the bridge tapes of the engagement," Bachfisch said at last, and nodded sideways at Layson. "So have the Exec and Commander Hirake. Is there anything you'd like to add to them, Ms. Harrington?"

"No, Sir," she said, and in that moment she looked more absurdly youthful even than usual as a faint flush of embarrassment stained her cheekbones, and the treecat on her shoulder cocked his head as he studied her two superiors intently.

"Nothing at all?" Bachfisch cocked his head in a gesture that was almost a mirror image of Nimitz's, then shrugged. "Well, I don't suppose anything else is really needed. The tapes caught it all, I believe."

He fell silent for another moment, then gestured at Commander Layson with his good hand.

"Commander Layson and I asked you to come see us because of what's on those tapes, Ms. Harrington," the captain said quietly. "Obviously, *War Maiden* has no choice but to cut her deployment short and return to the Star Kingdom for repairs. Normally, that would require you to transfer to another ship for the completion of your middy cruise, which would unfortunately put you at least six T-months or even a T-year behind your classmates for seniority purposes. In this instance, however, Commander Layson and I have decided to endorse your Form S-One-Sixty to indicate successful completion of your cruise. The same endorsement will appear in the records of Midshipwoman Bradlaugh and Midshipman Lakhia. We will also so endorse Midshipman Makira's file and recommend his posthumous promotion to lieutenant (junior-grade)."

He paused once more, and Honor cleared her throat.

"Thank you, Sir. Especially for Nassios. I think I can speak for all of us in that."

"I'm sure you can," Bachfisch said. He rubbed his nose for just a moment, then surprised her with a crooked grin.

"I have no idea what's going to happen to my own career when we return to Manticore," he told her. "A lot will no doubt depend on the findings of the Board of Inquiry, but I think we can safely assume that at least a few critics are bound to emerge. And not without some justification."

It was all Honor could do not to blink in surprise at the unexpected frankness of that admission, but he went on calmly.

"I got too confident, Ms. Harrington," he said. "Too sure that what I was looking at was a typical Silesian pirate. Oh," he waved his good hand in a small, brushing-away gesture, "it's fair enough to say that we very seldom run into anyone out here, pirate or privateer, with that much firepower and that well-trained a crew. But it's a captain's job to expect the unexpected, and I didn't. I trust that you will remember that lesson when you someday command a King's ship yourself."

He paused once more, his expression clearly inviting a response, and Honor managed not to clear her throat again.

"I'll certainly try to remember, Sir," she said.

"I'm sure you will. And from your performance here in Melchor, I have every confidence that you'll succeed," Bachfisch said quietly. Then he gave himself a small shake.

"In the meantime, however, we have some practical housekeeping details to take care of. As you know, our casualties were heavy. Lieutenant Livanos will take over in Engineering, and Ensign Masters will take over Communications. We're fortunate that everyone in Auxiliary Control survived, but we're going to be very short of watch-standing qualified officers for the return to Manticore. In light of our situation, I have decided to confirm you as Assistant Tac Officer, with the acting rank of lieutenant (junior-grade) and the promotion on my own authority to the permanent rank of ensign." Honor's eyes widened, and he smiled more naturally. "Under the circumstances, I believe I can safely predict that regardless of the outcome of my own Board, this is one promotion which BuPers will definitely confirm."

"Sir, I—I don't know what to say, except, thank you," she said after a moment, and he chuckled.

"It's the very least I can do to thank you for saving my ship—and my people—Ms. Harrington. I wish I had the authority to promote you all the way to J.G., but I doubt that BuPers would sign off on that even under these circumstances. So all you'll really get is a five- or six-month seniority advantage over your classmates."

"And," Commander Layson put in quietly, "I feel sure that the Service will take note of how and why you were promoted. No one who doesn't know you could have expected you to perform as you did, Ms. Harrington. Those of us who have come to know you, however, would have expected no less."

Honor's face blazed like a forest fire, and she sensed Nimitz's approval of the emotions of her superiors in the treecat's body language and the proprietary way his true hand rested on her beret.

"I expect that we've embarrassed you enough for one afternoon, Ms. Harrington." Bachfisch's voice mingled amusement, approval, and sympathy, and Honor felt her eyes snap back to him. "I will expect you and Commander Hirake to join me for dinner tonight, however, so that we can discuss the reorganization of your department. I trust that will be convenient?"

"Of course, Sir!" Honor blurted.

"Good. And I'll have Chief Stennis be sure we have a fresh supply of celery on hand."

Nimitz bleeked in amused enthusiasm from her shoulder, and she felt her own mouth curve in her first genuine smile since *Annika*'s explosion. Bachfisch saw it, and nodded in approval.

"Much better, Ensign Harrington! But now, shorthanded as we are, I'm sure that there's something you ought to be doing, isn't there?"

"Yes, Sir. I'm sure there is."

"In that case, I think you should go attend to it. Let's be about it, Ensign."

"Aye, aye, Sir!" Ensign Honor Harrington replied, then snapped back to attention, turned sharply, and marched out of the Captain's day cabin to face the future.

CATHERINE ASARO

Catherine Asaro [1955–] (www.ssf.net/people/asaro) is a physicist and former dancer who lives near Washington, D.C. In the 1980s, while a physics grad student, she was a principal dancer and artistic director of the Mainly Jazz Dancers and the Harvard University Ballet. She entered the SF field in the 1990s with a series of SF novels set in a future called the Skolian Empire, basically a family saga space-opera series, but with an unusual degree of hard science (the space drive is based upon math that resulted in a published paper in the *American Journal of Physics*), and even more unusual, a romantic central character and a love story at or near the center of each book. The series was introduced in *Primary Inversion* (1995), and has continued through many novels and a few shorter pieces to date. One, *The Quantum Rose* (2000), won the Nebula Award for best SF novel in 2001. The most recent is a two-volume saga, *Schism* (2004) and *The Final Key* (2005).

Asaro's unique combination of hard science and genre romance made her controversial in the hard SF community but earned her an avant-garde reputation in romance genre circles. Space opera enhances romance, it seems, speaking to the intelligence, as well as the emotions, of the romance reader. And thus far Asaro has been able to gain a romance audience without losing SF readers. Not surprisingly, her romance novels (published as genre romance) also tend to be genre hybrids, of SF or fantasy and genre romance. Recent ones include *The Charmed Sphere* (2004) and *The Misted Cliffs* (2005). Asaro is interested in exploring romance genre conventions through SF, even through reversals, as in *The Last Hawk* (1997), one of her best novels, in which the handsome but temporarily intellectually impaired male central character is traded from woman to woman.

From a distance, Asaro's Skolian novels are most like Bujold's Vorkosigan novels: In a carefully constructed space-opera SF universe with built-in conflict, a strong, intelligent, often military central character from a noble family has adventures and falls in love. A significant difference closer up is that most of Asaro's central characters are women, as is conventional in genre romance, even though Asaro's individual characters are often far from conventional in their military skills and intellectual powers. One of the boundaries that US space opera is pushing is feminism and the role of women. British space opera has not been notably feminist. Asaro has chosen some unusual combinations (including feminism and genre romance, hard science and physical action) that mark her as an individual talent. Judging solely by the apparent difference in popular appeal between, say, Bujold and Asaro, the SF space opera audience prefers male central characters in their romances.

"Aurora in Four Voices" is a tale in the Skolian setting, but not in the main story line. The central character is a prisoner, and the primary female character, identified as Soz, is Sauscony Valdoria, a young woman fighter pilot who is a member of the Imperial family and the heroine of some of the Skolian novels. The lush imagery and erotic tension puts this squarely in the Brackett tradition. There is a gender role reversal investigated that is definitely not traditional.

AURORA IN FOUR VOICES

CATHERINE ASARO

THE DREAMERS OF NIGHTINGALE

He missed the sun.

The planet Ansatz boasts one city, Nightingale, a gem that graces eternal night. Just as a diamond sparkles because light that ventures into its heart is captured, bouncing from face to face, so Jato Stormson was trapped in Nightingale. Unlike the light inside a faceted diamond, however, he could never escape.

After a few years, his memories of home faded. He could no longer picture the sun-parched farm on the planet Sandstorm where he had spent his boyhood. It was always dark in Nightingale.

The Dreamers—the artistic geniuses who created Nightingale—were also mathematical prodigies. That was why they named their planet Ansatz. It referred to a method of solving differential equations. Guess an answer, an ansatz, and see if it solved the equation. If it didn't, make another guess. Another ansatz. Jato felt as if he were trapped on a guess of a world.

One night he went to the EigenDome, an establishment for dancing. He sat at a table and waited for the drink server, but the server never came to his table. That was why he rarely visited the Dome. The artist who had designed the place considered it aesthetic to have humans serve the drinks and the humans in Nightingale ignored him. But that night he was lonelier than usual and even the icy Dreamers were better than no company at all.

Made from synthetic diamond, the Dome resembled a truncated soccer ball. Jato had looked up its history in the city library and found a treatise on how the Dome's shape mimicked the molecule buckyball. Its holographic lighting evoked the quantum eigenfunctions that described a buckyball. He didn't understand the physics, but he appreciated the beauty it produced.

Tonight Dreamers were everywhere, dancing, talking, humming. Centuries of playing with their genes and living in perpetual night had bleached their skin almost to translucence. Their hair floated around their bodies like silver smoke. Light from lamps outside the Dome refracted through the diamond walls, gracing the interior with rainbows that collected on the Dreamers in pools of color. They glistened like quantum ghosts.

Across the Dome, the doors opened. A spacer stood in the doorway, her body haloed by the rainbow luminance. This was no Dreamer. She looked solid. Suntouched. She must have come in one of the rare ships that visited Nightingale; rare, because the Dreamers allowed no immigration and most sun-dwellers found a city of unrelieved night depressing anyway. The only reason people usually came to Ansatz was to trade for a Dream.

Ah, yes. The Trade.

Dreamers make a simple offer, give one a pleasant dream and in return the Dreamer will give you a work of art. They allow you ten days to try. After that, you must leave Nightingale, trade or no trade. Considering the prices Dreamer art claims throughout the Imperialate, that trade seems astoundingly one-sided, the offer of great treasure for no more than a nice dream.

Jato had let the lure of that promise fool him. He spent years saving for the ticket to Ansatz. But how do you give a dream? It was harder than it sounded, particularly given how sun-dwelling humans revolted the Dreamers. The same husky build and rugged looks that had won him such admiration back home repelled the Dreamers. Considering their disdain for ugliness, he feared they wouldn't even let him stay the ten days.

They never let him go.

So now he sat by himself and watched the spacer walk to a table across in the Dome. She wore dark pants tucked into boots and a white sweater with gold rings decorating the upper arms. Her clothing looked familiar, but Jato couldn't place why. She had no jacket; Nightingale's weather machines aided the planet's natural convection to keep the climate pleasant, free from the fierce winds the tore at the rest of Ansatz. Her hair was a cloud of black curls with gold tips, and dark lashes framed her eyes—green eyes, the color of a leaf in the forest. Her skin had a dusky hue, full of rosy blooming health. None of the Dreamers spared her a second look, but Jato thought she was lovely.

She sat down—and the server showed up to take her order. Irked, Jato got up and headed for the laser bar, intending to insist they serve him. Reaching it, however, was no simple feat. The Dome's floor consisted of nested rings, each slowly rotating in one direction or the other. The text he had found in the library described some business about "mapping coefficients in quantum superpositions onto ring velocities." All he knew was that it took a computer to coordinate the motion so patrons could step from one ring to another without falling. Dreamers carried it off with grace, but he had never mastered it.

He managed to reach the dance floor, a languid disk turning in the Dome's center. Dancers drifted away from him, slim and willowy, silver-eyed works of art. On the other side, he ventured into the rings again and was soon being carried this way and that. Each time he neared a hovertable occupied by Dreamers, it floated away on cushions of air. He wished just once someone would look up, admit his presence, give a greeting. Anything.

Meanwhile, the server brought the spacer her drink, which was a LaserDrop in a wide-mouthed bottle. Tiny lasers in the glass suffused the drink with color: helium-neon red, zinc-selenium blue, sodium yellow. Drink in hand, she settled back to watch the dancers.

Jato quit pretending it was the bar he wanted and headed for the spacer. But whenever he neared the ring with her hovertable, people and tables that had been drifting away suddenly blocked his path. The spacer meanwhile finished her drink, slid a payment chip into the table slot, and headed for the door. He started after her—and the drink server appeared, blocking the way, his back to Jato, his tray of laser-hued drinks held high.

Jato scowled. He had always been long on patience and short on words. But even the most stoic man could only take so much. He put his hand against the server's back and pushed, not hard, just enough to make the fellow move. The server stumbled and his tray jumped, rum splashing out of the jars in plump drops. Even then, no one looked at Jato, not even the server.

He made it to the door without pushing anyone else. Outside, lamps lit the area for a few meters, but beyond their radiance, night reigned under a sky rich with stars. Jato strode away from the Dome, his fists clenched. He didn't want to give them the satisfaction of seeing their treatment provoke him.

The Dome was on the city outskirts, near the edge of a large plateau where the Dreamers had built Nightingale. The Giant's Skeleton Mountains surrounded the plateau, falling away from it on three sides and rising in sheer cliffs on the fourth, here in the north. The northern peaks piled up higher and higher in the distance, until they become a jagged line against the star-dazzled sky.

The Dreamers claimed they built Nightingale as a challenge: can you create beauty in so forbidding a place? This was the reason they gave. Jato had heard others put forth, but the Dreamers denied them.

Although his past attempts at convincing spacers to smuggle him offplanet had failed, he never gave up. In the distant shadows, he saw the spacer climbing the SquareCase, a set of stairs carved into a cliff. The first step was one centimeter high, the second four, the third nine, and so on, their heights increasing as the square of integers. The first twenty ran parallel to the cliff, but then they turned at a right angle and stepped into the mountains, rising taller and taller, until they became cliffs themselves, too high, too dark, and too distant to distinguish.

By the time he reached the first step of the SquareCase, the spacer was climbing the tenth, about the height of her waist. She sat on it, half hidden in the dark while she watched him. He approached slowly and stopped on the ninth step.

"Can I do something for you?" she asked.

"I wondered if you wanted a guide to the city." It sounded unconvincing, but it was the best introduction he could think of.

"Thank you," she said. "But I'm fine." The conversation screeched to a halt.

He tried again. "I don't often get a chance to talk to anyone from offplanet."

Her posture eased. "I noticed my ship was the only one in port."

"Did you come to trade for a Dream?"

"No. Just some minor repairs. I'll be leaving as soon they're done."

Behind her, Jato caught sight of a globe sparkling with lights in a fractal pattern. As it floated forward, it resolved into a robot drone over a meter in diameter, its surface patterned by delicate curls of the Mandelbrot set, swirls fringed by swirls fringed by swirls in an unending pattern of ever more minute lace.

Following his gaze, the woman glanced back. "What is that?"

"A robot. It watches this staircase."

She turned back to him. "Why does that make you angry?"

"Angry?" How had she known? "I'm not angry."

"What does it do?" she asked.

"I'll show you." Jato strode forward and hauled his bulk onto the tenth step. Although he towered over the spacer, she seemed unperturbed, simply scooting over to let him pass. That self-confidence impressed him as much as her beauty.

As he approached the eleventh step, the globe whirred into his face. When he tried to push it away, it rammed his shoulder so hard he fell to one knee.

"Hey!" The woman jumped up and grabbed for him, as if she actually thought she could stop someone his size from falling over the edge. "Why did it do that?"

He stood up, brushing rock dust off his trousers. "As a warning."

That's when she did it. She smiled. "Whatever for?"

Jato hardly heard her. All he saw was her smile. It dazzled.

But after a moment, her smile faded. "Are you all right?" she asked.

He refocused his thoughts. "What?"

"You're just staring at me."

"Sorry." He motioned at the globe. "It was warning me not to go past the city border, which crosses the cliff here." Having the drones watch him up here was almost funny. As if he could actually escape Nightingale by climbing a staircase that grew geometrically.

"Why can't you leave the city?" she asked.

He discovered he couldn't make himself tell her, at least not yet. Why should she believe his story? Eight years ago, the Dreamers had showed up at his room in the Whisper Inn and locked his wrists behind his back with cuffs made from sterling silver Möbius strips. He had no idea what was happening until he found himself on trial. They convicted him of a murder that never happened and sentenced him to life in prison.

Supposedly, years of treatment had "cured" him, and he no longer posed a danger to society. So the Dreamers let him out of his cell, which had never been a cell anyway, but an apartment under the city. For a giddy span of hours he had thought they meant to send him home; if he was no longer dangerous, after all, why keep him under sentence?

He soon found out otherwise.

For the Dreamers who believed in his guilt, which was most of them, it would take a lifetime for him to atone. One of their most renowned artists, Crankenshaft Granite, had argued—with truth—that to Jato it would be almost as much a punishment to spend his life confined to Nightingale as to his apartment. But by making the city his jail, they showed their compassion for a criminal who had turned away from his violent nature. Jato saw why that logic appealed to the Dreamers, who for some reason had a driving need to see themselves as kind, yet who in truth considered all sundwellers flawed, deserving neither freedom nor friendship.

But he knew the truth. Crankenshaft's motives had nothing to do with compassion. The only reason Jato had a modicum more freedom now was because it made Crankenshaft's life easier.

Jato didn't want to see that wary look appear on this woman's face, the one spacers always wore when they learned his story. Not yet. He wanted to have these few minutes without the weight of his conviction pressing on them.

So instead of telling her, he pointed at his feet and made a joke. "This is where I live. These are my coordinates."

"Your what?"

So much for scintillating wit, he thought. "Coordinates. This staircase is the plot of a non-linear step function."

She laughed, like the sweet ringing of a bell. "Why would anyone go to all this work just to make a big plot?"

"It's art." He wished she would laugh again. It was a glorious sound.

"This is some art," she said. "But you haven't told me why your people won't let you leave."

His people? She thought he was a *Dreamer*? It wasn't only that he bore no resemblance to them. Dreamers were gifted at both art and mathematics, neither of which he had talent for. Yet this beautiful woman thought he was both. He grinned. "They like me. They don't want me to go."

She stared at him, her mouth opening.

"Are you all right?" he asked.

She closed her mouth. "What?"

"You're just staring at me."

"I—your smile—" She flushed. "My apologies. I'm afraid I'm rather tired." She gave him a formal nod. "My pleasure at your company." Then she turned and headed down the stairs.

He almost went after her, stunned by her abrupt leave-taking. But he managed to keep from making a fool of himself. Instead, he stood in the shadows and watched her descend the SquareCase.

When Jato turned into the underground corridor that dead-ended at his apartment, he saw a Mandelbrot globe waiting at the door. Given that he lived nowhere near Nightingale's perimeter, only one reason existed for its presence. Crankenshaft had sent it. With Jato no longer confined to his apartment, Crankenshaft could have him brought wherever he wanted instead of the Dreamer having to come down here.

Jato spun around and ran, his boots clanging on the metal floor. If he could find a side passage too narrow for the globe to follow, he might evade capture. It was a stupid game Crankenshaft played; if Jato escaped the drones, Crankenshaft let him have the day off.

A whirring sound came from behind him. The drone hit his side and he stumbled into the wall, bringing up his arms to protect his face. An aperture opened on the robot and an air syringe slid out, accompanied by the hiss of its firing.

His view of the hall wavered, darkened, faded. . . .

Jato opened his eyes. A face floated above him, an aged Dreamer with eyes like ice. Gusts of wind fluttered her silver hair around her cheeks. He knew that gaunt face. It belonged to Silicate Glacier. Crankenshaft's wife.

Crankenshaft was standing behind her. Tall for a Dreamer, he had a well-kept physique that belied his one-hundred and six years of age. Black hair covered his head in bristles. He had two-tone eyes, grey bordered by red, like old ice in ruby rings.

Jato spoke in a hoarse voice. "How long?"

"You have slept several hours," Crankenshaft said.

"I meant, how long do you need me for?"

"I don't know. We will see."

As Jato pulled himself into a sitting position, Silicate stepped back, avoiding contact with him. He swung his legs over the stone ledge where he had been lying and looked around. Crankenshaft had chosen the big studio. The ledge jutted out of the west wall, an otherwise blank plane of grey stone. On the left, the south wall was a window looking over Nightingale, which lay far below. The east and north "walls" were holoscreens, sheets of thermoplastic that hung from the ceiling. Holos rippled in front of them, swaths of color that trembled as breezes shook the screens.

It always disoriented Jato, that wind. Moving air didn't belong inside a house. For that matter, neither did Mandelbrot globes. But two floated here, one hovering behind Crankenshaft and another prowling the studio.

The major feature in the room was a round pool. A glossy white cone about two meters tall rose out of the water. A second cone stood next to it, its top cut flat in a circular cross-section. The three other cones in the pool were cut at angles, giving them elliptical, parabolic, and hyperbolic cross-sections.

"Circle today," Crankenshaft said. Then he headed across the drafty studio to a console in the corner where the two holo-walls met.

Jato looked at Silicate and she looked back, as cool and as smooth as stone. Then she too walked away, leaving the studio via a slit in a thermoplastic wall.

A gust rumpled Jato's hair and he shivered, wrapping his arms around his body. "Do you have a jacket?" he asked.

Crankenshaft didn't answer, he just stooped over his console and went to work. So Jato waited, trying to clear out the haze left in his mind by the sedative.

A globe nudged his shoulder. When he stayed put, it pushed harder. "Flame off," he muttered.

A syringe extended out of the globe.

Still intent on his console, Crankenshaft said, "It shoots a heat stimulant. A strong specimen such as yourself might tolerate it for ten minutes before going into shock."

Jato scowled. Where did Crankenshaft come up with this sick stuff? He looked at the globe, at Crankenshaft, at the globe again. With Crankenshaft he used care in choosing his battles. This one wasn't worth it.

He took off his boots and went to the pool. The knee-deep water was cool today, but at least no ice crusted the surface. He waded to the truncated cone and climbed up onto it, then sat cross-legged, hugging his arms to his chest for warmth.

"Move ten centimeters to the north," Crankenshaft said.

Jato moved over. "Can you warm it up in here?"

Crankenshaft sat down at his console, concentrating on whatever he was doing. So Jato moved to the south side of the cone.

Crankenshaft looked around. "Move to the other side."

"Turn on the heat," Jato said.

"Move."

"After you turn on the heat."

Stalemate.

Reaching back to the console, Crankenshaft touched a panel. A globe whirred behind Jato and he heard a syringe hiss. Heat flared in his biceps, spreading fast, up his shoulder and down his arm.

"Hot enough?" Crankenshaft asked.

It was excruciating, but Jato had no intention of letting on how much it bothered him. He simply shrugged. "What will you do? Put your model into shock because he objects to freezing?"

A muscle under Crankenshaft eye twitched. He went back to work, ignoring Jato again. However, the room warmed and the burning in Jato's muscles cooled. Either Crankenshaft had lied or else the drone had delivered an antidote with the poison, probably in a bio-sheath that dissolved after a few minutes in the blood.

Over the next few hours the wind dried Jato's clothes. Silicate came in once to bring Crankenshaft a meal on a stone platter. Jato wondered about her, always attentive, always silent. Did she create her own art? Most Dreamers did, even those who worked other jobs. Silicate's only occupation seemed to be waiting on Crankenshaft. But then, Jato doubted Crankenshaft would tolerate artistic competition in his own household.

Finally Crankenshaft stood up, rolling his shoulders to ease the muscles. "You can go," he said, and left the studio.

Just like that. You can go. Get out of my house. Clenching his teeth, Jato slid off the cone and limped across the pool, sore from sitting so long. After coaxing his boots on under his wet trousers, he went to a door in the corner of the studio where the window-wall met one of the thermoplastic walls.

Icy wind greeted him outside. He stood at the top of a staircase that spiraled down the cliff Crankenshaft owned. The city glimmered far below, and beyond it ragged mountains stretched into the darkness. Millennia ago a marauding asteroid had struck the planet, distorting it into a blunt teardrop that lay on its side, its axis pointed at Quatrefoil, the star it orbited. Although Ansatz was almost tidally locked with Quatrefoil, it wobbled enough so most of its surface received at least a little sunlight. Night reigned supreme only here in this small region around the pole.

Crankenshaft's estate was high enough to touch the transition zone between the human-made pocket of calm around Nightingale and the violent winds that swept Ansatz. Yet despite the long drop to the plateau, the staircase had no protection, not even a rail. Another of Crankenshaft's "quirks." After all, he never used these stairs.

Jato grimaced. When he came willingly, Crankenshaft always had a flycar waiting to take him home. Today he would have to go back inside and ask for a ride, a prospect he found as appealing as eating rocks.

So he went down the stairs, stepping with care, always aware of the chasm of air. Around and around the spiral he went, never looking around too much, lest it throw off his balance. He wondered how he would appear to someone down in the city. Perhaps like a mote descending a stone DNA helix on the face of a massive cliff.

The helix image caught his mind. It would make an intriguing sculpture. He could go to the library and find a text on DNA. It would have to be a holobook, though, rather than anything on the computer.

Before Jato had come to Ansatz, his computer illiteracy hadn't mattered. As the oldest son of a water-tube farmer on Sandstorm, he hadn't been able to afford web access, let alone a console. Although everyone here in Nightingale had access to the city web, it did him little good. However, he had figured out how to tell a console in the library to print books.

He doubted he would try the helix sculpture, though. Reading could only give information, not talent. One thing he had to say for Crankenshaft: the man was brilliant. Jato could never imagine him giving away his stratospherically-priced work for a Dream. Besides, what Dream would he find pleasant? Pulling wings off bugs, maybe.

Jato scowled. A few Dreamers high in Nightingale's city government knew Crankenshaft had set him up. They framed him for a crime so brutal it would have meant execution or person ality reconfiguration anywhere else. Imperialate law was harsh: an escaped convict fleeing into a new jurisdiction could be resentenced there for his crime. That often-denounced law was intended to ease the morass of extradition problems that arose as more and more planets came under Imperial rule. But it let Crankenshaft blackmail him; if Jato escaped Nightingale, he was subject to death or a brain wipe.

Crankenshaft's work was known across a thousand star systems. He was a genius among geniuses, and on Ansatz that translated into power. Whatever he wanted for his art, he was given.

Including Jato.

II

DREAM DEBT

Jato lay in bed, unable to sleep. He had dimmed the lights until only faint images of sand-swept fields softened the walls, holoart he had created himself, memories of his home.

Even after eight years, he still found this room remarkable. He had grown up in a two-room dustshack his family shared with two other families. Here he had, all to himself, a bed with a quilt, a circular bureau, a mirror, a bathroom, and soft rugs for the floor. The Dreamers charged no rent and gave him a living stipend. His medical care was free, including the light panels and vitamin supplements his sun-starved body craved.

Tonight the room felt emptier than usual. He gave up trying to sleep and went to the bureau, a round piece of furniture that rotated. He removed his statue from the top drawer. He had come to Ansatz hoping for a miracle, to trade for a fabulous treasure. He had his own dreams then, ones he hoped to achieve by selling such a masterpiece: a farm of his own, a business, a better home for his family, well-deserved retirement for his parents, a wife and children for himself. A life.

He had never intended to *make* art. Still, living in Nightingale, how could a person deny the pull to create? The statue had taken years to finish and he kept it hidden now, knowing how lacking the Dreamers would find his attempts. He liked it, though.

To get the stone he wanted, he had climbed down windscoured cliffs below Nightingale, into crevices lost in the night-dark shadows. There he cut a chunk of black marble no human hand had ever before touched. Back in his rooms, he fashioned it into a bird with its wings spread wide, taloned feet beneath its body, supported by a stand carved from the same stone. Next he made clay copies of it. He spent several years cutting facets into the copies, redoing them until he was satisfied. Then he carved the facets into the statue and inlaid them with crystalline glitter.

Dreamers used elegant mathematical theories to design their creations. Jato knew his was simple in comparison. The geometry of the facets specified a fugue in four voices, each voice an aspect of his life: loss, of his home and life on Sandstorm; beauty, as in the stark glory of Nightingale; loneliness, his only companion here; and the dawn, which he would never again see.

Holding the statue, he lay down in bed and fell asleep.

The bird sang a miraculous fugue, creating all four voices at once. Jato held it as he ran through Nightingale. The pursuing Mandelbrot drone gained ground, until finally it whirred around in front of him. Fractals swirled off its surface and turned into braided steel coils. They wrapped around his body, crushing his chest and arms, silencing the bird. He reeled under the icy stars and fell across the first step of the SquareCase.

He wrestled with the coils until he worked his arms free, easing the pressure on the bird. It sang again and its voice rose to the stars on wings of hope.

The fractal coils fell away from his body. As Jato stood up, the spacer appeared, walking out of the shadows that cloaked the SquareCase. She toed aside the coils and they melted, their infinitely repeating patterns blurred into pools of glimmering silver. The bird continued to sing, its fugue curling around them in a mist of notes.

The spacer stopped only a pace away. Her eyes were a deep green, dappled like a forest, huge and dark. She brushed her fingers across his lips. Jato put his hand on her back, applying just enough to pressure to make the decision hers; stay where she was, or step forward and bring her body against his.

She stepped forward. . . .

The Whisper Inn was a round building, graceful in the night. Holding his bundle, Jato stood at its door, an arched portal bordered by glimmering metal tiles.

"Open," he said.

Nothing happened.

He tried again. "Open."

Swirling lines and speckles appeared on the door and a holo formed, an amber rod hanging in front of the door. A curve appeared by the rod and rotated around it, sweeping out a shape. When it finished, a vase hung in the air with the rod piercing its center. Soothing pastel patterns swirled on the image.

"Solid of revolution complete," the door said. "Commence integration."

"What?" Jato asked. No door had ever asked him to "commence integration" before.

"Shall I produce a different solid?" it asked.

"I want you to open."

Silver and black swirls suffused the vase. "You must calculate the volume of the solid."

"How?"

"Set up integral. Choose limits. Integrate. Computer assistance will be required."

"I have no idea how to do that."

"Then I cannot unlock."

Jato scratched his chin. "I know the volume of a box."

The vase faded and a box appeared. "Commence integration."

"Its volume is width times height times length."

Box and rod disappeared.

"Open," Jato said.

Still no response.

Jato wondered if the Innkeeper had his door vex all visitors this way. Then again, Dreamers would probably enjoy the game.

"Jato?" the door asked.

"Yes?"

"Don't you want to enter?"

He made an exasperated noise. "Why else would I say 'Open'?"

Box and rod reappeared. "Commence integration."

"I already did that."

"I seem to be caught in a loop," the door admitted.

Jato smiled. "Are you running a new program?"

"Yes. Apparently it needs more work." The door slid open. "Please enter."

Muted light from laser murals lit the lobby. As the floor registered his weight, soft bells chimed. Fragrances wafted in the air, turning sharp and then sweet in periodic waves.

The Innkeeper's counter consisted of three concentric cylinders about waist height, all made from jade built atom-by-atom by molecular assemblers, as were most precious minerals used in Nightingale's construction. The Innkeeper sat at a circular table inside the cylinders, reading a book.

Jato went to the counter. "I'd like to see one of your customers." He knew the spacer had to be here; this inn was the only establishment in Nightingale that would lodge sun-dwellers.

The Innkeeper continued to read.

"Hey," Jato said.

The Dreamer kept reading.

Jato scowled, then clambered over the cylinders. "The offworld woman. I need her room number."

The Innkeeper rubbed an edge of his book and the holos above it shifted to show dancers twirling to a Strauss waltz.

Jato pulled the book out of his hand. "Come on."

The Innkeeper took back his book without even looking up. A whirring started up behind Jato, and a Mandelbrot globe bumped his arm.

"I owe her," Jato said. "She gave me a dream."

That caught the Dreamer's attention. He looked up, his translucent eyebrows arching in his translucent face. "You come with Dream payment?" He laughed. "*You?*"

Jato tried not to grit his teeth. "You know payment has to be offered."

"She is in Number Four," he said.

Jato hadn't actually expected a reply. Apparently the unwritten laws of dream debt overrode even the Innkeeper's distaste for talking to large, non-translucent people.

Old-fashioned stairs led to the upper levels. As Jato climbed, holoart came on, suffusing the walls with color. He glanced back to see the holos fade until only sparks of light danced in the air, mimicking the traces left by particles in an ancient bubble chamber.

No one answered when he knocked at Number Four. He tried again, but still no answer.

As he started to leave, a click sounded behind him. He turned back to see the spacer in the doorway, light from behind her sparkling on the gold tips of her tousled hair. She wore grey knee-boots and a soft blue jumpsuit that accented her curves. The only decorations on her jumpsuit were two gold rings around each of her upper arms. A tube trimmed each of her boots, running from the heel to the top edge of the boot, an odd style, but attractive.

"Yes?" she asked.

Jato swallowed, wondering if he had just set himself up for a rebuff. He tried to think of a clever opening that would put her at ease, perhaps intrigue or even charm her. What he ended up with was the scintillating, "I came to see you."

Incredibly, she stepped aside. "Come in."

Her room was pleasant, with gold curtains on the windows and a pretty rumpled bed that looked as if she had been sleeping in it.

Jato hesitated. "Did I wake you? I can come back later."

"No. Now is good." She motioned him to a small table gleaming with metal accents. Its fluted pedestal supported two disks, the upper joined to the lower along a slit that ran from its center to its rim, a style common in Nightingale. The only explanation Jato had ever extracted from a Dreamer was, "Riemann sheets." He had looked it up at the library and found an opaque treatise on complex variable theory that apparently described how the sheets made a multi-valued expression into a mathematical function.

After they sat down, he set his bundle in front of her and spoke the formal phrases. "You gave me a dream. I offer you my work in return."

She watched his face. "I don't understand."

"A beautiful dream." He wondered if he sounded as awkward as he felt. "This is what I have to trade." Pulling away the wrapping, he showed her the bird. Giving it up was even harder than he had expected. But it was a matter of honor: he had a debt and this was the only payment he had to give.

As she sat there staring at his life's creation, his face grew hot. He knew the wonders she had seen in Nightingale. The bird was pitiful in comparison.

"It makes music," he said. "I mean, it doesn't make the music but it tells you how to make it."

She looked up at him. "Jato, I can't accept this." An odd expression crossed her face, come and gone too fast to decipher. If he hadn't known better, he would have thought it was awe. Then she said, "Regulations don't allow me to accept presents."

Through the sting of her refusal, he realized what she had said. "How did you know my name is Jato?"

"After we talked, I looked up your Ansatz records."

He stared at her. Those records were *sealed*. That was the deal; as long as he did what Crankenshaft wanted, his records remained secret and he had his relative freedom on Ansatz.

Somehow he kept his voice even. "How?"

"I asked," she said. "The authorities had to let me."

Like hell. They were supposed to say *No*. Had his presence become so offensive that they decided to get rid of him despite Crankenshaft? Or maybe Crankenshaft no longer needed him.

Then it hit Jato, what else she had said. Regulations didn't allow her to accept gifts. *Regulations.*

Of course. He should have recognized it earlier. The gold bands on her jumpsuit were no decorations. They denoted rank.

"You're an ISC soldier," he said.

She nodded. "An Imperial Messenger. Secondary Class."

Jato stared at her. Secondary was equivalent in rank to colonel and "Messenger" was a euphemism for intelligence officer. He had almost asked a high-ranking spy-buster to smuggle him off Ansatz.

ISC, or Imperial Space Command, was the sole defense in known space against the Traders, whose military made a practice of "inviting" the settled worlds to join their growing domain. All settled worlds. Whether they wanted to join or not. The Traders based their economy on what they called "a benevolent exchange of work contracts de-signed to benefit both workers and the governing fellowships that hold their labor con-tracts," one of the more creative, albeit frightening, euphemisms Jato had heard for slavery. The Imperialate had formed in response, an attempt by the free worlds to re-main that way. That was why so many colonies, including Ansatz, had joined the Im-perialate despite the loss of autonomy that came with ISC's autocratic control.

He spoke with a calm he didn't feel. "Are you going to turn me over to ISC?"

"Well, no," she said. "I just wondered about you after you followed me up those strange stairs."

Relief swept over him, followed by distrust, then resentment, then embarrass-ment. One of his few comforts on Ansatz had been his pleasure in creating the bird. Now every time he looked at it he would remember how she rejected it.

As he rose to his feet, an emotion leapt across her face. Regret? It was mixed with other things, shyness maybe, even a fear of rejection. It went by too fast for him to be sure.

She stood up. "May I request an alternate gift? Something that wouldn't violate regulations?"

He had no alternate gifts. "What do you mean?"

"I'd like to see Nightingale." She hesitated. "Perhaps you would show it to me?"

She wanted a guide? True, he was the best candidate; the Dreamers would never deign to offer such services. But most people would prefer no guide at all to a con-victed murderer.

Of course his records said he was "cured." Besides, rumor claimed Messengers had enhanced speed and strength. Perhaps she was confident enough in her abilities that she didn't see him as a threat.

"All right," he said.

"Well. Good." It came again, her beguiling flash of shyness. "Shall we, uh, go?"

He smiled. "It would help if I had a name to call you."

"Oh. Yes. Of course." She actually reddened. "Soz."

"Soz." He gave her a bow from the waist. "My pleasure at your acquaintance."

Her face softened into a smile. "And mine at yours."

They walked down to the lobby in awkward silence. Outside, they strolled through the Inn's rock garden, where tall lamps made shadows stretch out from human-sized mineral formations. The arrangement of rocks looked random, but it had an underlying order calculated from chaos theory.

As they followed a path toward the city proper, Jato tried to relax. Conversation had always been his stumbling block. In his adolescence, he had discussed it with his father while they were weeding a field.

"About girls," he had said.

"What about them?" his father asked.

"You know."

His father sat back on his heels. "Treat her right and she'll treat you right."

"Can't talk."

"Then listen."

"Don't know what 'treat her right' means."

"The way you want to be treated."

Jato thought of having a girl treat him the way he wanted to be treated. "What if we get into trouble?"

His father scowled. "Don't."

He had figured that his father, who became his father only a few tendays after he married Jato's pregnant mother, would have had a more informative answer than that. "What if it happens anyway?"

"You see that it doesn't." He pointed his trowel at Jato. "You go planting crops, boy, you better be ready to take responsibility if they grow." Lowering his arm, he looked across the field to where Jato's mother was curing tubes by the water shack; her long hair brushing her arms, Jato's five younger siblings helping her or playing in the dust. "Choose a place you value." His voice softened. "A place you can love."

Jato watched him closely. "Did you?"

He turned back, his face gentle now. "That I did."

That was the extent of his father's advice on women, sex and love, but it had held up well over the years. On Nightingale, however, he barely ever had the chance to talk to a woman, let alone go walking with one. So being with Soz felt odd.

Eventually the path became a boulevard. They ended up at a plaza in front of Symphony Hall, near the tiled pool. A lamp came on, bathing the pool in rosy light, and a fountain shot out of the water in a rounded arch. A gold lamp switched on, followed by a fountain with two arches, then a green lamp and three arches, and so on, each fountain adding smaller refinements to the overall effect. Altogether, they combined to create a huge blurred square. Sparkles of water flew around Jato and Soz and mist blew in their faces.

"It's lovely," Soz said.

Jato watched her, charmed by the way the rainbow-tinged mist haloed her head, giving her pretty face an ethereal aspect. She looked like a watercolor painting in luminous colors. "It's called the FourierFount," he said.

She smiled. "You mean like a Fourier series?"

"That's right." He restrained himself from blurting out how much he liked her smile. "The water arches can't combine like true wave harmonics, but the overall effect works pretty well."

"It's unique." She glanced down at his hands. "Jato, look. Your bird."

He held up the statue and saw what she meant. Light from the fountain was reflecting off the glitter so that it surrounded the statue with a nimbus of rainbows.

She held out her hands. "May I?" He handed it to her, and she turned it this way and that, watching the shimmer of light on its facets. "What did you mean, that it makes music?"

"The angle of each facet defines a note." He wondered if he even had the words to explain. Before composing the fugue, he had tried to learn music theory, but in the end he just settled for what sounded right. He played no instruments, nor could he make notes in his mind without hearing them first. He needed a computer to play his creation. The Dreamers steadfastly ignored his requests for web training, so he muddled through on his own, eventually learning enough to use one particular console in the library.

"Could I hear the music?" Soz asked.

Her request touched off an unexpected spark of panic. What if she scorned what she heard, the musical self-portrait he had so painstakingly crafted? "I can't play it," he said. "It needs four spherical-harmonic harps."

"We can have a web console do it."

He almost said no. But he owed her for the dream and playing the fugue would pay his debt. Going on a walk through Nightingale didn't count; dream debt required a work of art created by the debtor.

Still he hesitated. "It's a long way to the console I use."

She motioned at Symphony Hall. "That building must have public consoles."

He could imagine what she would think of a grown man who could barely log into the web of a city where he had lived for years. He paused for a long time before he finally said, "Can't use them."

"It has no console room?"

"It has one."

"Can't you link to your personal console from here?"

His shoulders were so tense, he felt his sweater pulled tight across them. "No personal console."

She blinked. "You don't have a personal console?"

"No."

"Where do you work?"

"Library."

"We can probably link into the library system from here." She watched his face as if trying to decipher his mood. "I can set it up for you."

So. He had run out of excuses. After another of their awkward pauses, he said, "All right."

He took her to an alcove in Symphony Hall. Blue light filled the room and blue rugs carpeted the floor. The sculpted white shapes of the public consoles made a pleasing design around the perimeter of the room.

Soz sat on a cushioned stool in front of the nearest console. "Open guest account."

When a wash of blue appeared the screen, Jato almost laughed. Only Dreamers would color-coordinate a room's decor with its web console.

"Welcome to Nightingale," the console said. "What can I do for you?"

"Library access," she said. "Establish a root directory here, standard branch structure and holographics, maximum allowed memory, full paths to available public nodes, and all allowed anonymous transferral options."

"Specify preferred nodes," the console said.

"One to produce a music simulation, given a representation of the score and a mapping algorithm."

A new voice spoke in mellow tones. "Treble here. Please position score and define algorithm."

Soz glanced at Jato. "You can take it from here."

He just looked at her. It had sounded like she was speaking another language. He hadn't even known the computers she spoke to existed. "Take it where?"

She stood up and moved aside. "Tell Treble how to access your files."

"I don't have an account."

"Everyone has an account."

He had to make a conscious effort to keep from gritting his teeth. "I guess I'm no one."

Soz winced. "I'm sorry. I didn't mean it that way." She started to say more, then stopped. Glancing around the alcove, she said, "This room must be easy to monitor."

"Probably." Did she think the Dreamers were watching them? "The drones keep track of me."

She nodded. Any questions or comments she had intended to make about his lack of computer accounts remained unsaid. Instead she indicated a horizontal screen on the console. "If you put the statue there and give Treble the mapping for the fugue, it will make a hologram of the bird, digitize it, transform the map, and apply the transform to the digitized data."

Jato wished he were somewhere else. This was worse than the business with the door at the Inn. At least then he had been revealing his ignorance to an inanimate object. "I've no idea what you just said."

Incredibly, she flushed, as if she were the one making an idiot out of herself rather than him. "Jato, I'm terrible at this. Ask me to calculate engine efficiency, plot a course, plan strategy—I'm a whiz, like you with your art. Put me in front of a handsome man and I'm as clumsy with words as a pole in a pot."

He stared at her. A whiz . . . *like you with your art.* She thought he was a "whiz." A handsome whiz, at that.

Jato smiled. "You're fine." He motioned at the console. "So I put the statue there?"

Her face relaxed. "That's right. Then tell Treble how to figure out the notes."

He set down the bird, and two laser beams played over it, making the glitter sparkle. When they stopped, he said, "Treble?"

"Attending," the console answered.

"The angle a facet makes with the base of the bird specifies a note. It varies linearly: facets parallel to the base are three octaves below middle C and those perpendicular are three octaves above." He touched the statue, his fingertips on its wings. "Each plane parallel to the base defines a chord and each facet touching the plane is a note in that chord. To play the fugue, start at the bottom and move to the top."

"Is height a discrete or continuous variable?"

"Continuous." Only a computer could do it. Human musicians would have to take planes at discrete heights. If the intervals between the planes were small enough, the human version approached the computer version. But the fugue only truly became what he intended when the distance between planes was so small that for all practical purposes it went to zero.

"Facets with one ridge are played by a spherical-harmonic baritone harp," he said. "Two ridges is tenor, three alto, and four soprano. Loudness is linear with glitter thickness, from pianissimo to fortissimo. Tempo is linear with the frequency of the light corresponding to the glitter color." He tapped a beat on the console. "Red." He increased the tempo. "Violet."

"Data entered," Treble said. "Any other specifications?"

"No." Then, realizing he would have to see Soz's reaction to the music, Jato said, "Yes. Lower the room lights to fifteen percent."

The lights dimmed, leaving them in dusky blue shadows. It was too dark to see Soz's face clearly.

A deep note sounded, the rumbling of a baritone harp. After several measures of baritone playing alone, tenor joined in with the same melody, mellow and smooth. Alto came next and soprano last, as sweet as the dawn.

Treble shaped the music far more tenderly than the generic program he used in the library. Yes, that was it, the minor key there, that progression, that arpeggio. Treble had it right. At the bird's arching neck, soprano soared into a shimmering coloratura. Notes flowed over them, radiant and painful, too bright to endure for long. The other harps came in like an undertow, pulling soprano beneath their deeper melodies. At the head of the bird, soprano burst free again, a fountain of sound.

Yes. Treble had it. Treble knew.

Gradually the music slowed, sliding over the outstretched wings above the bird.

Finally only baritone rumbled in the glimmering wake of soprano's fading glory. The last notes vibrated in the alcove and died.

Jato stood frozen, afraid to move lest it rouse Soz to reveal her reaction. Yet the silence was also unbearable. What did she think? That was him in that music, the vulnerable part, without barriers or protections.

Her head was turned toward the console, so he saw only her profile. A glimmer showed on her cheek. Something was sliding down her face.

He touched the tear. "Why are you crying?"

"It's so beautiful." She looked up at him. "So utterly sad and utterly beautiful."

Beautiful. She thought his music was beautiful. He tried to answer, make a joke or something, but nothing came out. So he drew her into his arms and laid his cheek on top her head.

She didn't pull away. Instead she put her arms around his waist and held him. The fresh scent of her newly washed hair wafted around him. Softly she said, "What place do you like best in Nightingale?"

"The Promenade."

"Will you take me there?"

He swallowed. "Yes."

III

THE GIANT'S RIB

Bathed in starlight, the west edge of the plateau dropped into the jagged immensity of the Giant's Skeleton Mountains. Its crevices cut deep into the planet's crust, the tormented remains of a planetoid impact that had brutalized Ansatz in a long-vanished eon. Spires jutted up like skeletal fingers on walls between the chasms.

Natural bridge formations tried to span the kilometers-deep fissures, but most spans were incomplete, their broken ends hanging in the air.

The plateau itself claimed one of the few unbroken bridges. The Promenade. It rose up from the plateau's southern corner, spanned its length, and ended high in the northern cliffs. Two kilometers long and averaging only two meters wide, the bridge curved out from the plateau over a great chasm. Spires on the chasm walls supported it with columns of rock.

The Dreamers had tooled the Promenade's upper side into a path, giving it meter-high retaining walls on both sides. They laid down a courtyard at its southern base, with undulating lines enameled into the geometric design of gilded tiles.

As Jato and Soz crossed the courtyard, wind grabbed his jacket and tossed her curls around her face. She said something, but he couldn't hear her over the blustering wind, so he leaned down. "Say again?"

Her breath tickled his ear. "It's exhilarating."

"It's even stronger on the Promenade."

"Beat you there!" She took off and sprinted up the bridge, leaning forward against its steep cant. Laughing, he tried to catch her, but she ran like a rocket.

They raced the entire kilometer to the apex. At the top, Soz threw out her arms and spun around, her hair whipping about her head. She spoke and the wind kidnapped her words. When Jato shook his head and pointed to his ears, she shouted, "How far to the bottom?" Then she leaned over the wall, staring into the void below.

"Three kilometers!" He pulled her back to safety turning her around, his bird pressed against her back, his pulse beating hard as the bridge vibrated in the rushing gales. She looked up at him with a flushed face. The wind, the night, the danger—it brought her alive. Without stopping to think, he pulled her into an embrace.

Sliding her arms around his neck, she drew his head down into a kiss. He returned the favor with pleasure, making up for eight years of solitude. He couldn't believe this, that she wanted him. Who would have thought it?

Jato paused. Why did she want him? Lifting his head, he looked down at her. He was trapped on Ansatz for life and they both knew she would soon leave. What was this, take advantage of the love-starved convict, then go back to her life where she didn't have to worry about him?

Soz watched his face, her eyes alternately visible and hidden as the wind threw around her hair. She touched his cheek with fingers as gentle as the smile that kept emerging and hiding behind those glorious curls. Jato decided the "why" didn't matter. He wanted to tell her things, how good she felt, how lovely she looked, but he couldn't think of anything that wouldn't sound clumsy. So instead he kissed her again.

The bridge's vibrations were increasing, making it pitch like the deck of a sea-ship. It gave a particularly inspired heave and knocked Soz and Jato apart, separating them as if it were their chaperon. They stumbled back from each other, both flailing their arms for balance. Jato laughed and Soz spread her arms wide as if to address the Giant's Skeleton itself with her protest.

Then something on the plateau caught her attention. She went back to the wall and peered toward Nightingale. "What are those?"

Looking out, Jato saw what she had noticed, the familiar statues, massive and tall, halfway between the plateau's edge and the city. Sometimes those gigantic stone beasts were lit and other times they stood in the dark, like now, their mouths forever open in silent roars.

"Wind Lions," Jato said. Coming to stand behind her, he put his arms around her waist. "Wind machines. If they were ever turned on, the cliffs would magnify their effect."

"No wonder it's so windy up here."

He bent his head and spoke against her ear. "This is normal wind. The Lions aren't on."

When his breath wafted against her ear, she closed her eyes and sighed. With her back against his front, she raised her arms and slid them around his neck. The motion pulled up her breasts, making her nipples point at the stars. He kissed her ear, and she rubbed her head against his cheek like a cat. Then she murmured, a soft noise audible only with his head so close to hers, one of those sounds he had forgotten a woman made when she liked the way a man touched her. Maybe it was the eight years of solitude, but he couldn't remember any woman on Sandstorm feeling this fine. He wondered how it would be to make love up here in the wild gales, three kilometers above the Giant's chasm.

"Why not?" she asked.

He smiled. Why not indeed? "Why not what?"

She lowered her arms and turned in his embrace. "Why aren't the Lions ever on?"

He tilted his head toward the courtyard. "Do you remember the design in the tiles back there? The curving lines?" When she nodded, he said, "It's a plot of the vortices for a single-degree oscillator with an undamped torsional flutter." He stroked her blowing curls back from her face. "Wind makes the Promenade twist. If it ever blew hard enough, the vortices in its wake around the bridge would drive a self-induced resonance until the Promenade tore itself apart."

"What would ever possess them to set it up like that?"

Jato smiled. "Because they're crazy." As he bent his head to kiss her, the bridge gave a violent shudder and threw them to the side. They stumbled along the wall, lurching from side to side as they struggled to regain their footing. It didn't work; they finally toppled over and hit the walkway with a thud.

"Hey!" Soz laughed, struggling to wriggle out from under Jato's bulk. "It's mad at us."

"I've never seen it this windy." Jato managed to get up to his knees, but when Soz tried to do the same, the agitated bridge knocked her over again. She finally succeeded by moving with an unnatural speed, as if she had toggled a switch that activated an enhanced mode of her body. They knelt there face to face, Jato holding her shoulders, she with her hands braced against his chest. The Promenade kept moving, more than he had ever felt it do before, rippling almost. It moaned in the assault of air as if the Giant were waking from his mountainous grave.

Soz wasn't smiling any more. "The Lions are blowing."

He couldn't believe it. "That's impossible. The Dreamers consider this art. They would never destroy it."

"The whole bridge is shaking. It doesn't feel stable."

They stared at each other. Then they scrambled to their feet and took off running for the northern cliffs. The cliffs were closer than the courtyard, but even so they had nearly a kilometer to go.

Suddenly the bridge lurched like a string shaken by a mammoth child. Flailing for a handhold, Jato pitched into the wall and found himself staring at the chasm below. In the same instant that he jerked back, Soz pulled him with unexpected strength. Their combined effort sent them reeling across the bridge into the other wall.

Then it came: a great booming crack. Thunder roared as if a great mountainous rib was tearing away from the Giant's skeleton. The bridge convulsed and they sprawled forward, slammed down onto the path. Rolling onto his side, Jato grabbed Soz and they held on to each other while the universe convulsed around them.

Within seconds the frenzied gyrations of the bridge eased. They managed to sit up, hanging onto each other while they stared back along the way they had come.

Meters away, the broken end of the Promenade hung in the air.

For one endless instant they stared at the jagged remains of that break. The shuddering edge shook off a chunk of itself, and the boulder dropped into the void below, hurtling into the shadows.

Carefully, so very carefully, they got to their feet and backed away, taking each step as if they were in a minefield. Only when they were well away from the break did they turn.

And then they *ran*.

The Promenade groaned in the onslaught of wind. They sped through a universe of wailing gales and convulsing rock, racing toward the shadowed bulk of a mountain that seemed an eternity distant.

Finally, mercifully, they were almost there. A few more steps—

A meter away from safety, the bridge pitched under their feet and slammed them against the wall. Stars wheeled past Jato's vision as he flipped over the barrier. He grabbed at the air, at the rock, *anything*—

With a wrenching jolt, he yanked to a stop. He had caught a projection and was hanging from it, his body dangling against the outer side of the Promenade. He scrabbled for a toehold, but the bridge was shaking too much to let him get purchase. Far below, the chasm waited.

His hands began to slip.

"Jato!" Soz's voice was almost on top of him. She had fallen lengthwise on the wall, with one leg hanging over the edge.

"Below you!" he shouted. His hands slipped again.

As she grabbed for him, he lost his grip. She caught one of his wrists—and the force of his falling yanked her off the wall. They dropped, dropped, dropped—

And smashed into ground. Soz landed on top of him with an impact that nearly broke his ribs. She rolled off and kept rolling, scrabbling for a handhold. He clutched her upper arm, but it jerked through his grasp, then her elbow, her lower arm, her wrist—and he locked hands with her, clutching in desperation while they slid downhill. He struggled to stop their plunge, but his fingers just scraped over stone.

Then he caught a jutting piece of rock and held on hard, his body straining with Soz's weight. A scratching came from below—and she let go of his hand.

"Soz, no!" He grabbed at the air. "Soz!"

"It's all right." Her strained voice came from below him. "You slowed me down enough so I could stop on a ledge. We're on a shelf in the cliff, under the Promenade."

"How can you tell? It's dark." Even the starlight was muted below the bridge.

"Got enhanced optics in my eyes," she said. He heard more scrabbling, and then she was pulling herself up beside him.

So they went, climbing the cliff centimeter by excruciating centimeter. Soz reached the landing at the end of the Promenade and stood up, her body silhouetted against the stars. He climbed up next to her, half expecting the ground to crumble. But they were solidly on the mountain now, at the top of a staircase that wound its way through the mountains down to the plateau.

They descended in silence. Gradually the wind eased, until it was no more than a whisper of its earlier violence.

Finally Soz said, "Someone knew we were up there."

"The drones." Jato wondered if Crankenshaft had set alarms in the city computer web to alert him when anyone looked at records of the trial. Whoever had set the Wind Lions against them would be desperate now, knowing they had to complete what they started lest Soz escape and report back to ISC.

"I hadn't intended to get involved here," Soz said. "I was going to wait until I got back to headquarters to recommend they send an investigator."

Investigator? Jato stiffened. If ISC got into this, he could be retried in an Imperial court. "Soz, why? I'm serving the sentence they gave me."

She spoke quietly. "To find out why someone went to so much trouble to trump up that phony murder charge against you."

That threw him. Really threw him. Crankenshaft had been meticulous in setting up the evidence, specifically to fool people like Soz.

It was a moment before he found his voice. "How did you know it was false?"

She snorted. "I saw the holos of that kid you supposedly killed. He was hanging around the port docks, watching a ship unload cargo."

" 'That kid' was a computer creation. He never existed."

"I know."

"But how?"

She motioned toward the starport. "In several holos you can see the ship he's watching. It's a Tailor Scout, Class IV. Eight years ago those Tailors were using nonstandard flood lamps to light their docking bays. Kaegul lamps. Advertised as 'the next best thing to sunlight.' They emitted ultraviolet light as well as visible."

"Sounds reasonable."

She shook her head. "Their UV component was too strong. It caused sunburns. So that model fell out of use fast. Only a few ships ever carried it."

Jato whistled. "Dreamers have less melanin in their skin than most people. It makes them more susceptible to UV."

Quietly she said, "Any Dreamer who spent as long under those Kaeguls as they claimed that boy did would have been broiled raw. Those records are beautiful, near perfect. Probably 99.9 percent of the people seeing them would have been fooled. But they're still fakes." Glancing at him, she added, "That's not all."

"What else?"

"Combat."

"Combat?"

"See enough of it and you get good at recognizing the symptoms of shock." She watched his face. "You. In every holo. You hardly said a word throughout that entire trial."

The whole nightmare was a blur in his mind. "Nothing I said would have made any difference."

"But why, Jato? Judging from how the Dreamers treat you—forgive me for saying it, but they act as if they don't like having you around."

"They think I'm revolting."

"So why make you stay?"

His voice tightened. "Because of Granite Crankenshaft."

"What is that?"

"Not what. Who. A Dreamer. He wanted me to be his model. For life. To sit for him with nothing in return but the 'honor' of living here. I told him no. I thought he was crazy."

She stared at him. "He framed you for murder because you wouldn't be his model?"

"I don't know why. He finds me as repulsive as everyone else here." Jato spread his hands. "He used blackmail because it's more effective than abduction. As long as I co-operate, he won't call in the Imperial authorities."

"All because he wants to paint your picture?"

"Not paint. Holosculpture. It's on his web. I've never seen what he's doing." He exhaled. "The stakes are high, Soz. His sculptures bring in millions. A few have gone for billions."

She drew him to a stop. "This Crankenshaft—does he have glittering hair?"

"I don't know. It's too short to tell."

"Black?"

"Yes."

"How about his eyes?"

"Grey, with red rings."

"Bloodshot?"

"No. The irises have red in them."

She blew out a gust of air. "This is making more sense."

"It is?"

"The Traders established this colony."

It wasn't her comment that surprised him, but how she said it, as an accepted fact rather than a long-debated theory the Dreamers vehemently denied. The Traders were a genetically engineered race distinguished by red eyes, and black hair with a distinctive shimmering quality. Their creators had only been trying to engineer for a higher pain tolerance, but the work produced an unplanned side-effect: Traders felt almost no emotional pain either—they had no compassion.

A race with no compunction about hurting people could do a lot of damage. Fast. When they began to spread the stain of their brutality across the stars, the colonized worlds had two choices: submit to them or join the Imperialate. As far as Jato knew, no one had ever willingly chosen the Traders.

There were those who claimed the Dreamers descended from a group of Trader geniuses morally opposed to their own brutal instincts. They manipulated their genes to rid themselves of those instincts and produced their translucent coloring as an un-expected side-effect. It led them to settle on Ansatz in the forgiving dark, where they traded the fruits of their genius for dreams, in penance for the sins of their violent siblings.

"It's possible Crankenshaft carries throwback genes," Jato said. "His wife, too. She's like ice."

Soz considered him. "You realize that except for your eyes and the relative dull-ness of your hair, you could pass for a Trader."

He stiffened. "Like hell. I can trace my family—"

"Jato." She laid her hand on his arm. "No one would ever mistake you for a Trader. It's the Dreamers' problem, not yours. They evolved themselves into a mild people, rejecting their heritage. Your large size, dark hair, and muscular build may stir memories they can't deal with. It's probably why your appearance bothers them."

A strange thought, that. It would never have occurred to him that perhaps he re-pulsed the Dreamers because he reminded them of themselves.

She peered down the stairs, though they were too far up to see much except the lonely circle of light from a lamp at the bottom. "Who do you think activated the Wind Lions?" She turned back to him. "Are we up against the city government or this Crankenshaft? Or both?"

He considered. "Most city officials don't believe I was set up. Those few involved with the setup would be more subtle, use a scenario easier to pass off as an accident. This is Crankenshaft's style. He would go for drama and make it look like I planned it, some rape-murder-suicide thing."

"Charming man," she muttered. "Stupid, though. ISC would never buy it. I have augmented strength and reflexes. You would more likely end up dead than me."

"Even with the Promenade breaking?"

That made her think. "It would complicate things," she admitted. She motioned at the plateau. "If he's the one who turned on the Lions, those drones down there must be his."

"Drones?" Jato swore and started back up the steps.

Soz grabbed his arm. "There's nowhere to go that way."

He stopped, seeing her point. They couldn't go up, they couldn't go down, and the chasm waited beneath them. Now was the time to find out what arsenal, if any, they had at their disposal. "What else can you do besides see in the dark?"

"I've a computer node in my spine with a library of combat reflexes." She bent her arm at the elbow. "My skeleton and muscles are augmented by high-pressure hy-draulics and powered by a microfusion reactor that delivers a few kilowatts. It gives me reflexes and strength two to three times greater than normal, as much as my body can sustain without overheating."

"Can you stop the globes?"

"Three or four, I could handle. But there are nine there." She looked down the stairs again. "They're coming."

He saw it now too, the Mandelbrot sparkle of globes revving into active mode. Their lights flowed upward in a fractal curve of luminance.

"Jato," a voice said.

He nearly jumped. The voice came out of empty air: cool, impersonal, command-ing.

"Come down here," it said. "Bring the woman."

As Jato's adrenaline surge calmed, he realized it was only a globe transmitting the voice. "Go to hell, Crankenshaft."

"You have twenty seconds to resume descending," his tormentor said.

"Let her go and I'll do what you want," Jato said.

"Fifteen seconds."

The globes continued up the stairs, whirring like a swarm of huge bugs. Ten steps away, five, two. A syringe hissed, and Soz feinted with a speed that blurred, kicking up her leg. Her heel smashed into a globe, and it spun out from the cliff in a spiral of glittering lights.

A second globe rolled in to fill the gap, a third came from the side, a fourth whirred behind Soz, and a fifth hung over them, its syringe pointing down like the cannon on a miniature battle-cruiser. Jato and Soz kept moving; feint, dodge, feint, Soz using her augmented speed. Two globes collided in midair with the grating racket of ceramoplex crashing together.

It was only a matter of seconds before a syringe shot hit Jato in the chest. The area went numb almost instantly and the sensation spread fast. As his arms dropped like stones to his sides, he lost his balance and tumbled down the stairs, stars and mountains careening past his vision.

He had one final glimpse of Soz lying on her back on the stairs, pinned down by globes, before his head hit stone.

IV

AURORA

A high ceiling came into focus. After a while a thought surfaced in Jato's mind. He was alive.

He sat up, favoring his bruises. He was alone in Crankenshaft's studio. No, not alone. Soz lay on the other end of the ledge, eyes closed, her torso rising and falling with each breath. Relief rushed over him, followed by a Neanderthal impulse to go over, stake out his territory, and protected her from Crankenshaft. It wasn't the world's most logical response given she was an Imperial Messenger, but he had it just the same.

He wondered why she was still unconscious. Even his body contained nanomeds designed to repair and maintain it. An ISC officer probably carried molecule-sized laboratories.

As he got off the ledge, a clink sounded. Turning, he saw a chain with one end attached to a ring in the wall. Its other end fastened to a manacle around his ankle.

He gritted his teeth, wishing he could wrap the chain around Crankenshaft's neck. At least the tether was long enough to let him reach Soz. That almost made him back off; he trusted nothing Crankenshaft did. But his instincts were still at work, conjuring up *protect mate* impulses, so he went over to her.

Crankenshaft had no illusions about Soz needing protection. Her wrists were manacled behind her back and also to a ring in the ledge. He had set her boots on the floor and chained her ankles to the ledge. For some inexplicable reason, he also put metal bands around her neck and waist. Jato leaned over to lay his palm on her forehead—

Her hand clamped around his wrist so fast he barely saw her move. He froze, staring as she sat up. It hadn't been obvious from the way she had been lying, but the chain joining her manacles was broken.

He found his voice. "How did you get free?"

She dropped his hand, her face relaxing as she recognized him. "Nanochomps. I carry a few hundred species."

"You mean molecular disassemblers?"

"In my sweat."

He stepped back. He had no desire to have voracious bugs in her sweat take him apart atom by atom.

"They can't hurt you," Soz said. "Each chomper disassembles a specific material. The ones I carry are rigidly particular, even down to factory lot numbers."

He motioned at her manacled feet. "Wrong lot number?"

"Apparently so. Or else flaws in the molecular structure." Leaning over, she rubbed her wrist against the chain attached to his ankle.

"Hey." He jerked away his leg. "What are you doing?"

"They might work on yours."

"You don't think that's dangerous, carrying bugs in your body that take things apart?"

"They aren't bugs. They're just enzymes. And they're no more dangerous than being trapped here."

He knew it was probably true, but even so, he was having second thoughts about his amorous impulses. People sweated when they made love. A lot.

"Jato, don't look like that," she said. "The chompers are produced by nodules in my sweat glands that only activate when I go into combat mode. Besides, they can't take apart people. Our composition is too heterogeneous."

He sat on the ledge, near her but not too close, and motioned at his still-chained ankle. "Wrong lot, I guess."

"I guess so." She tugged the manacle on her wrist, managing to slide it up about a centimeter. The skin on her wrist was more elastic than normal tissue, not a lot, but enough so she could drag it out from under the manacle. He saw what she was after, a small round socket in her wrist.

"You have a hole," he said.

"Six of them, actually. In my wrists, ankles, lower spine, and neck."

That explained the neck and waist bands. "What do they do?"

"Pick up signals." She held up her arm so the socket faced the console across the room. "If I insert a plug from that node into this socket, it links the computer web inside my body to the console."

That didn't sound like much help. "The plug is there and you're here."

"That's why consoles transmit infrared signals." Her face had an inwardly directed quality, as if she were running a canned routine to answer him while she focused her attention elsewhere. "The sockets act as IR receivers and transmitters. Bio-optic threads in my body carry signals to the computer node in my spine. It processes the data and either responds or contacts my brain. Bio-electrodes in my neurons translate its binary into thought: 1 makes the neuron fire and 0 does nothing. It works in reverse too, so I can 'talk' to my spinal node."

He suspected Nightingale was probably flooded with IR signals. "How can you stand so much noise hitting you all the time?"

"It doesn't. Only if I toggle RECEIVE." Her full attention came back to him. "The signals do get noisy and it isn't as secure as a physical link. But it's enough to let me interact with a node as close as the one over there."

"And?"

She made a frustrated noise. "This room ought to be bathed in public signals. But I'm getting nothing at all."

He doubted Crankenshaft would cut himself off from the city. "Maybe he did something to you."

"My diagnostics register no software viruses or tampering." She paused. "But you know, my internal web is engineered in part from my own DNA. Maybe he infected it with a biological virus." Without another word, she lifted her wrist and spit into its socket.

Dryly Jato said, "Insulting it won't help."

She smiled. "The nanomeds in my saliva may be able to make antibodies if there's a virus loose in my biomech web."

"Are you getting anything?"

"Nothing." Several moments later she said, "Yes. A notice about a ballet." Her concentration had turned inward again. "I still can't link to the city system . . . but I think I can get into the node in that console over there."

Jato stared at her. "Not a chance. That's Crankenshaft's private node. Everyone knows his security is unbreakable."

A cold smile touched her lips. "Security is my game."

A moment later she said, "I can call up his holosculpture of you if you want."

Jato swallowed. She might as well have hit him with that ancient proverbial ton of bricks. "Yes. I want."

She indicated the center of the studio. "That's it."

He turned—and almost gasped.

The air above the pool was glowing with a rainbow-hued mist. It drifted across the glistening white cones that stood in the water, like shadows made on outcroppings of rock by clouds obscuring a sun. This, from a man who had lived his entire life in the night. Holos of Jato appeared on every cone. On the tallest, the one with the circular cross-section, he sat with knees to his chest, shivering, his clothes and hair dripping. He was younger, eight years younger, only a husky teenager. His face cycled through emotions: rage, confusion, resentment.

An older Jato stood on the next cone, the one with its top cut off at a slant, giving it an elliptical cross-section. He remembered when he had modelled for it, how he stood for hours on a narrow shelf protruding from the surface. Crankenshaft had since removed the shelf and erased it in the image, so the Jato holo simply floated in the air, with red and blue clouds scudding across his face. He was shouting, fists clenched at his sides. No sound: just his mouth moving. With the play of light, it was hard to make out words, but he knew what they were. He had been cursing Crankenshaft in his native tongue.

The Jato by the parabolic cone was sitting, submerged to his hips in the pool. He trailed his hands back and forth in the water, a habit he had developed to cope with the boredom. He was kneeling by the hyperbolic cone, up to his waist in water. Crankenshaft had doctored the holo to make him look old. Ancient. His face was a map of age untouched by the biosculpting the rich used to sustain youth during their prolonged lives. Gusts blew brittle white hair around his head. Stooped, gnarled, decrepit: it was a portrait of his mortality.

That tableau remained frozen for a few seconds. Then all the Jatos stood up and began stepping from cone to cone, passing through each other while multicolored clouds flowed across their bodies. Some raged, others shivered, others moved like machines.

Each figure split, becoming two Jatos, all continuing their strange march. They split again, the original of each quartet stepping from cone to cone while the others kept pace in the air. New images appeared like shadows, all different by just a small amount, creating a feathered effect. A younger one was crying. He remembered that day; he had told Crankenshaft about his family, how he loved them, how they must think he had died. Another Jato image was laughing. *Laughing.* Yet there were times he had laughed—even had civil conversations with Crankenshaft.

Holos of water augmented the pool, overlaid on the real water like multiple exposures: waves in impossibly sharp points, or serrated like a saw, glowing phosphorescence in red, purple, green, blue-green, gold, and silver. Gusts in the studio whipped the true water into peaks that added random accents to the holos.

The Jatos split again, along with their shadows. They all stopped and raised their hands, the motion feathered among the images, as if it portrayed multiple quantum universes, each projecting a future that diverged from the original. The image of a rainbow-hued waterfall sprayed over the figures, making them shimmer. But no blurring could hide the fury on those faces.

"Saints almighty," Soz said. "It's spectacular."

Jato tried not to grit his teeth. "That's why he's so famous."

"I can see why he wanted you for his model."

"You can?"

She motioned at the holos. "You couldn't get that purity of emotion—that fury—from a Dreamer. From most anyone. But from you, it's perfect. Pure passion unadulterated by civilization."

"Am I supposed to be flattered by that?"

Soz winced. "I didn't mean—" She stopped, staring at the sculpture. "Jato, look at your eyes."

"That would be a feat." But he knew what she meant. He studied the images—and when he saw it, he nearly choked. Crimson. Ruby hard and ruby cold. The eyes on each image had turned red. The hair was changing too, going from dark brown to crystalline black. He couldn't believe it. Crankenshaft was making *him* look like a Trader.

He stood up, his fists clenching at his sides. "I'll kill him."

"It's guilt," Soz said. "And catharsis."

"What the hell does that mean?"

"It's all there," she said. "The guilt the Dreamers feel, knowing the brutality their disowned kin have inflicted on a thousand peoples. And catharsis. Realizing the monster isn't in them anymore. They've freed themselves, become Dreamers instead of Traders."

"Then it's a *lie*." Jato was so angry he could barely get the words out. "For this 'catharsis,' Crankenshaft made himself into the very thing this is supposed to free him from. He's made me look like what he hates in himself, what he can never get rid—" Jato stopped cold. Then he sat down again. "Oh, hell."

Soz was watching his face. "What?"

"His greatest work. Face his demons and exorcise them. I'm the substrate." It was suddenly all too obvious. "Get rid of me and he loses his inner devils." Jato swallowed. "He's going to kill me as part of the sculpture. It's what he's always intended."

She stared at him. "That's sick."

Jato wished he had never pulled her into this. "If we had died on the Promenade, he would have worked with that footage. Now you're onto him, so he has nothing to lose by bringing us here where he can tailor the work to his needs."

"Actually," a voice said. "You're the one who is going to kill her."

He looked up with a jerk. Crankenshaft was standing across the studio, by the console in the corner where the two holo-walls met. In one hand he held Jato's bird sculpture; in the other, he had a laser carbine.

"A tragedy," Crankenshaft continued, in the voice he used when he wanted to bait Jato, to drive his rage. "She came to the greatest artist alive hoping to inspire a dream. A beautiful woman, after all, has certain advantages. Unfortunately she arrived while you were here." He sighed. "I should never have left you two alone. But who would have thought an Imperial Messenger would be in danger? Besides, Jato, we thought we had cured you." He shook his head. "She was overconfident. An unguarded moment and you were able to bind her." Lifting the bird, he said, "A blunt instrument you stole from me brought about her death. I was forced to kill you in self-defense."

Jato stood up, an explosion working up inside of him. But before it let loose, Soz spoke in a mild voice. "You're Granite Crankenshaft."

Unease showed on their captor's face. "You should have never pried into his records, Messenger."

"Why would you claim Jato stole that bird from you?" she asked. "He made it."

The tic under Crankenshaft's eye gave a violent twitch. He shifted the sculpture, his hand gripped around it as if he held a weapon. "No one would ever believe he created a work as stunning as this, with that fugue. Only his exposure to me enabled him to do it. Me. He could never have done it by himself. So the credit belongs to me."

Jato knew he should be infuriated that Crankenshaft would claim credit for his work. But the implication in his captor's words so staggered him that the arrogance of the statement rolled off his back. He could hardly believe it. The great Granite Crankenshaft was threatened by *his* work.

Crankenshaft unhooked a cord from his belt and threw it at them. It landed at Jato's feet, a leather thong with ceramoplex balls on each end that could have been anything from decorations to superconducting webs.

"Tie her hands behind her back," Crankenshaft said.

Jato crossed his arms. "No."

Crankenshaft touched a panel on the console. A giant globe crept through a slit in the thermoplastic wall and floated to the center of the studio.

"Non-linear dynamics and metapsychology," he commented. "Do you know that with detailed enough initial conditions, you can model procreation? The correlation between the calculated results and an actual act that proceeded from those conditions is quite high."

Jato scowled. "What are you talking about?"

"Sex," he said. "Establish the initial scene well enough and you can model the rest with amazing accuracy."

"Go to hell," Jato said.

"Tie her hands."

"No."

"Commence protocol," he said.

Three syringe guns slid out of the globe. Jato didn't duck fast enough, but it didn't matter: none of the shots were aimed at him. Soz moved in a blur, but she couldn't go anywhere with her ankles chained to the ledge. One shot missed her, but judged from her reaction, the other two hit home. She jerked as if she had been struck and her entire body tensed.

"What are you doing?" Jato shouted at Crankenshaft.

"Jato, it's all right," Soz said. "I'm fine."

"It's a clockwork venom," Crankenshaft told her. "Even your meds can't adapt enough to deal with it."

She said nothing, just focused her attention on him with an unsettling intensity.

"What's a clockwork venom?" Jato asked.

Soz glanced at him. "The name comes from clock reactions." Although she sounded cool, sweat was beading at her temple. "Combine certain chemicals under proper conditions and they cycle through a series of reactions. In human blood, clockwork venoms undergo a cycle, each step producing a different poison."

"Can your nanomeds fight it?" Jato asked.

Crankenshaft answered. "Even sophisticated meds have trouble with complicated cycles. This one has hundreds of steps, all with varying duration lengths and side reactions that change from cycle to cycle. It's a brilliant work of chemistry." He gave Jato an appraising look. "You've felt one poison in the cycle. Last time you were here. Perhaps you recall?"

Jato remembered all right. It had burned like hell.

"The others have different effects," Crankenshaft observed, as if Soz were a lab experiment. "Nausea, muscle stiffness, dizziness, pain. She'll start vomiting soon. Eventually she will die."

Soz remained calm, but sweat was running down her temples. When she wiped at it, the motion looked mechanical, as if she had let the hydraulics in her body take over.

"As soon as her hands are bound," Crankenshaft said, "I'll give her the antidote."

"Jato." She spoke quietly. "Do what he says. Please."

There was no mistaking the strain in her voice. Jato grabbed the thong off the floor and wrapped it around her wrists. The broken lock mechanism on her manacles felt warm, probably from the energy released when her chompers ate it. He tied the thong loosely around her wrists, making no attempt to knot it. But the ceramoplex balls activated and yanked the cords tight, binding her wrists and then locking into each other.

"Leather," Crankenshaft said.

Jato straightened up. "What?"

"In molecular terms, it's complex," he said. "More heterogeneous than, say, manacles. Not as strong, but a logical backup when dealing with disassemblers."

Jato gritted his teeth. How did Soz stay so cool? She just watched Crankenshaft, intent and quiet. Crankenshaft took a ring with two mag-keys off his belt and threw it to them. As the keys hit the floor near Jato's foot, a syringe on the globe hissed. Soz moved like an automaton, trying to duck, but the shot hit her anyway.

"That had better be the antidotes," Jato said.

"The red key unlocks your ankles," Crankenshaft said. "Gold unlocks hers."

After Jato freed their ankles, Soz moved stiffly, swinging her legs off the ledge.

"Go to the pool," Crankenshaft said. "Both of you."

"No," Jato said.

"Don't make it harder on her than necessary," Crankenshaft said. "I can calculate a lot of what I need, but I'll achieve better results with genuine images of the two of you to work from."

Jato stayed put. "I won't rape her and I won't kill her. You can doctor holos to make me look like a Trader, but nothing can make me act like one."

Crankenshaft's voice hardened. "Go to the pool. Otherwise, I'll pump her so full of clockwork venom she'll beg you to kill her."

With no warning, Soz moved. *Fast.* Dropping to one knee by her boots, she whipped out her hands, shreds of leather flying away from her wrists. She yanked the "decorative" tubes off her boots and brought them up, one in each hand, liquid shooting out from both. One stream splattered over the drone, creating clouds of gas. The other hit Crankenshaft's carbine and splashed into his face. He shouted, dropping the laser as he covered his face with his hands. When the gun hit the ground, it shattered like porcelain.

The Mandelbrot globe hissed and a shot from its air-syringe hit Jato in the neck. In a bizarre blur of motion, Soz threw her boots. They hurtled through the air and smashed into the globe, shattering its outer shell where the liquid from her cylinder had doused it. The whole assembly crashed to the floor, its innards breaking apart on the stone. Blinking and humming, the debris moved in twitches as it began to reassemble itself.

"Smash the components!" Soz yelled, sprinting across the studio. She moved like a puppet, her body under control of hydraulics rather than muscles and bones.

As Jato strode over to crush the remains of the drone, he saw Crankenshaft lower his hands, revealing a face covered with burns. In the same instant that he grabbed for a gun on his belt, Soz reached him. She brought her hands up with eerie speed and hit him under the chin, snapping back his head. He flew over backward, crashing to the ground. His head hit the floor and he lay still, breathing but unconscious.

"Soz, no!" Jato raced forward when she jerked up her leg. He collided with her as her foot came down, and they staggered to the side, enough to make her miss Crankenshaft. Her foot hit the floor with a teeth-jarring impact that would have crushed the Dreamer's chest.

Jato gulped in a breath. "No killing."

She turned to him like a machine, no emotion on her face. It was hard to believe this was the same woman he had kissed on the Promenade.

Then her expression became human again, as if she had reset herself. She exhaled. "He'll live." Grimly she added, "We might not. Are you all right?"

A familiar burning was spreading in his neck and torso. "I took a shot of venom. Did he give you an antidote?"

"No. More venom." She went to retrieve her boots and their tubes. "My meds are trying to synthesize an antidote, but it's hard to do when their target keeps changing."

"We better hurry." He grabbed his bird off the console. "His node must have alerted the city and his other drones."

She pulled on her boots. "I put locks on his system. It will take a few minutes for it to break them." Her voice sounded strained. Labored.

As Jato turned toward the door across the room, his gaze raked the pool—and he froze.

The holosculpture was still evolving. It had spawned more and yet more Jatos, until they blended into a design of feathered motion. A superimage had formed, a fractal, its pattern repeating on a finer and finer scale. Superimposed on the fractal, a face was coming clear. A giant Trader face.

His face.

"No." He spun back to the console.

"Come on!" Soz called.

He stabbed at the console. "We have to destroy that sculpture."

"We have to go! We don't have much time."

"He stole my *life*." Jato gave up on the computer and swung around to her. "He created a mirror of himself, but he put it on me. It's like—like—" He slammed his palm against the console. "He's a thief. Of my soul." He pointed at the sculpture. "That's me. No matter where I go or what I do, as long as that exists he owns me."

Sweat was dripping down her face. "I can't guarantee I'll find all his backups."

"If anyone can, it's you." He clenched his fists. "He owes me. And for him, losing his 'masterpiece' will be a punishment worse than dying."

Soz strode to the console and went to work, making hieroglyphics ripple across its panels in garish displays. She didn't waste time pulling out her wrist socket; instead, she hauled off her boot and set her foot on the console, showing no strain with the contorted position as she plugged a prong from the console into her ankle socket.

Seconds passed.

Longer.

Waiting.

"Got it!" Soz jerked out the prong. "Downloaded one copy into my internal memory for you. Erased everything else." She yanked on her boot. "Now let's go."

They ran across the studio to the cliff door. As they stepped outside, into the blasting wind, she stared down the stairs. "No rail."

Jato struggled to keep his balance, fighting the gales and his venom-induced dizziness. "I'll go first. If I fall, I won't hit you. You're light enough so if you fall you probably won't knock me off."

"All right." Her voice sounded thick.

He had expected her to insist on going first. His gut reaction ignored the obvious; she was part computer and machines worked on logic rather than heroics.

Clutching his statue, he started down the stairs. An abyss of air and rushing wind surrounded them, turbulent, violent. Step. Step again. He took it slow, halting when waves of dizziness hit.

Step.

Step again.

Scrapes came from above and he jerked his head up to see Soz lose her footing. Lunging for her, he lost his own balance and stumbled on the step, teetering over the void. Lurching back, he reeled to the step's inner edge, where he fell to one knee and found himself staring down the shaft of air in the center of the spiral.

"Jato?" Soz rasped.

He took a breath, looking up to see her kneeling on the step above him.

"You all right?" he asked. She nodded and they got up, then continued their descent.

The wind was probably cold, but with the fever burning in his body he couldn't tell. He moved in a haze of nausea and dizziness.

Step.

Step again.

Step—

No step. He looked down. They had reached the bottom.

Soz made a strangled sound and sagged against his back, grabbing him around the waist with both arms to keep from falling. Turning, he put his arm around her for support.

They walked around Nightingale, far enough outside the city to let darkness cloak them. His legs strained to run but he held back, not only because his poisoned body couldn't keep such a pace but also because it would draw attention. A couple strolling arm-in-arm along a romantic path was one thing; two people running was another.

He motioned at the tubes on her boots. "What's in those things?"

"Liquid nitrogen." She sounded hoarse. "With disassemblers to boost its effect. It freezes what it hits and the chompers eat it. They're less specialized than the ones in my body, which makes them more dangerous, but they dissolve after exposure to air."

"How did you free your hands? Do the chompers in your sweat eat leather after all?"

"No." She grimaced. "Mine are far too specific. Anything general enough to take apart a material as heterogenous as animal hide would probably take apart our hides too." She showed him the broken chain on her manacle. "Feel."

He ran his finger along the jagged edge. "It's sharp."

"So was the part on the ledge. I rubbed the thong against it until it cut the leather."

"No tech that time," he said. "Just brains."

She smiled wanly. Sweat soaked her collar and she walked stiffly, her legs controlled by the hydraulics inside her body.

The starport was so small it had no terminals, just a gate at the airfield entrance. As they neared it, two Mandelbrot globes rolled out to intercept them. Jato tried to dodge, but the one headed for him easily compensated for his evasive actions. It slammed him in the chest and he stumbled backward, then recovered and sprinted to the side. As the globe followed, he doubled back to run around it. The ploy worked with Crankenshaft's drones on days he programmed them for slower responses, to make the chase "entertaining." Jato doubted this one belonged to Crankenshaft, though; after what had happened, his would go for the kill.

This globe caught him—and rammed his head. As he fell, patches of light punctuated his vision and loud noises buzzed in his ears. With his statue cradled against his chest, he hit the ground and groaned. As he rolled away from the whirring demon, he caught a glimpse of the aircontrol tower. Lights were coming on inside it.

They had run out of time.

Then Soz said, "Eat it, fractal."

A stream of liquid arched into view, bathing the drone in a shower of glistening drops. The globe reoriented on Soz like a giant ceramoplex balloon. As it went after her, she tried to feint, but she lost her balance and fell to her knees. When the globe swooped in on her head, she jerked to the side. It hit her shoulder—and shattered, raining Mandelbrot innards all over her body. In seconds, she was kneeling in the midst of junk large and small, from both globes, lights blinking and components humming.

Soz and Jato stared at each other. Then they scrambled to their feet and sprinted for the airfield. Alarms were blaring, coming from the distant airtower and speakers along the field's perimeter. As they ran through the gate, which was no more than a few bars that swung to one side, Jato saw a Jag starfighter out on the tarmac. It gleamed like alabaster, as much a work of art as any sculpture.

When they reached the Jag, its hatch dilated like a high-speed holocam. As soon as they lunged through the opening, it snapped closed. A membrane irised in the nose of the ship, revealing a cockpit. As Soz squeezed into the pilot's seat, it folded an exoskeleton of controls around her like a silver-mesh glove. Jato stood behind her chair, hanging on to its back while his nausea surged.

"Neck and lower spinal nodes blocked," an androgynous voice said.

"Ankles," Soz said, intent on her controls.

While her hands flew over her forward controls, a robot claw pulled off her boots and a mesh enfolded her feet, plugging into her ankle sockets. After that Jato heard nothing; the ship was communicating directly with her internal systems.

Suddenly Soz spun around her chair and pulled down Jato's head. He fell forward, grabbing the arms of her seat to catch himself. She kissed him hard, pushing her tongue into his mouth.

He jerked away. "Are you craz—"

"I'm giving you the antidote. In my saliva. My web figured it out and my meds made it." She pulled him back into the kiss.

So he kissed her, while guns boomed from the port defenses and the ship shook. Although the Nightingale port claimed only a small arsenal, it could still do damage. He just hoped the Jag could protect itself while its pilot and her passenger took their medicine.

Then Soz pulled away from him and smiled. The cockpit elongated and a second chair rose from the deck. "Co-pilot's seat," she said. "You take."

He slid into the seat, and a slender probe from it extended to his ear—in time for him to hear a voice shout, "Skyhammer-36, acknowledge!"

He nearly jumped out of the chair. Then he realized he was hearing Soz's communications with the aircontrol tower.

"You are not cleared for take-off!" the voice said. "I repeat, you are not cleared for take-off."

"Tough," Soz said. Then she fired the rockets.

Jato knew a stealth craft like the Jag could come and go with barely a whisper—if that was what its pilot wanted. They took off in a thundering roar of rockets. For her parting salute to Nightingale, Soz blasted the holy hell out of that tarmac.

As acceleration pushed them into the seats, a holomap came on, showing Nightingale receding into the spectacular bones of the Giant's Skeleton Mountains.

The peaks withdrew until they were no more than wrinkles in the vast panorama of the world.

Gradually Jato's mind absorbed the situation. He was free. *Free.*

Or at least, he thought he was free. "What happens now?" he asked.

Soz glanced at him. "I'll take you to headquarters. You can clear your name." She hesitated, a blush on her cheeks. "I can help out, if—if you would like."

Her uncertainty floored him. He had seen her face death by Promenade collapse, clockwork venom, and snuff-art, all with remarkable composure. Yet asking if he wanted her to stick around made her nervous.

He smiled. "Yes. I would like that."

Her face gentled. She glanced at the statue he still held. "I felt what it took for you to offer your sculpture to me. Thank you."

"It's not much."

"It's spectacular, Jato. Both the bird and the fugue."

He swallowed, at a loss how to tell her how much her words meant. So instead he motioned at her holo display. "Soz, look."

Together they watched the sun rise over the rim of Ansatz.

R. GARCIA Y ROBERTSON

R. Garcia y Robertson [1949–] lives in Mount Vernon, Washington. He's one of the few SF writers who does not thus far own a computer. His first novel was the widely praised historical fantasy *The Spiral Dance* (1991), his second, *The Virgin and the Dinosaur* (1996), and third, *Atlantis Found* (1997), SF, and his fourth, *American Woman* (1999), mainstream fiction. Perhaps he might have built an audience in one genre or another, but instead he moves from one kind of fiction to another with ease, and much grace. His most recent novels are *Knight Errant* (2001), *Lady Robyn* (2003), and *White Rose* (2004), a series of popular historical fantasy (timeslip) romances, to be continued, and his 2006 novel is *The Firebird*, a fantastic adventure set in the imaginary land of Markovy.

He has published nearly fifty stories. *The Moon Maid and Other Fantastic Adventures* (1998) collects some of his adventure and space opera SF. "What a nourishing collection of stories *The Moon Maid* is!" said David Mathew at the UK Web site infinityplus.com. "Truly wonderful stuff. At times he writes a little like Heinlein, at times a little like Asimov; but equally, at times he writes like any of the amphetamine-wired iconoclasts of the New School."

Garcia is most known in SF and fantasy for his adventure stories. Most of his SF he considers space opera, although planetary romance or fantastic adventures would also serve. When we asked for a comment from him on space opera, he sent this lengthy response:

> Space opera is what first attracted me to science fiction, since I had a more historical fantasy upbringing, brought up on the lives of Prince Valiant, Alexander, Genghis Khan, and Captain Blood. It was Tom Corbett, Space Cadet that lifted me out of history, and got me to look up at the stars. From then on my reading was divided between historical fiction by Robert Graves, Mary Renault, and George MacDonald Fraser, and the best of old-style space opera, by the likes of Heinlein, Poul Anderson, Jack Vance, and Edgar Rice Burroughs. And the best could be pretty damned good. *Citizen of the Galaxy* has all the elements of classic space opera, star ships, slave markets, space battles, and Psi-powers, but the issues it raises set the tone for the fifties, and sixties, and are as real today as the war in Afghanistan [sic].
>
> The big knock on space opera is that it is not really science fiction. Science fiction is about the impact of science on people, while space opera merely takes modern ships, planes, and telephones, turning them into spacecraft, fliers, and communicators. Well, duh! That is the whole point of space opera. When I write fantasy, it is about the past, and how we got here. Read *American Woman* and *Knight Errant* and you will know more about the Little Big Horn or the Wars of the Roses than if you had read a standard history. But for me, at least, space opera is about where we are headed.
>
> Prediction is traditionally a tricky business, and I never pretend that the "future" will be exactly like I describe it. Far from it. To write space opera, I follow the news intently, always wondering, "What will we be dealing with next?" Then I free-associate, taking familiar objects and problems and projecting them into the future, figuring that something along these lines is bound to happen.
>
> "Ring Rats" is a prime example. When it first came to me in the fall of 2000, I thought it was weird to be writing a space hijacking story, with flight attendants and passengers facing misogynistic terrorists. There had not been a major hijacking in

years, and the subject seemed passé. Already more suited to fantasy. But I wrote the story anyway, and it was pending at *Asimov's* in Manhattan when 9/11 hit. That is when I found out what the story was about.

We read "Ring Rats" in the classic SF tradition of space pirate stories, from Jack Williamson to the present.

RING RATS

R . G A R C I A Y R O B E R T S O N

CAPTAIN KID

"Great-uncle Lyle has a ship like this." Kay stepped out of the forward lock into a narrow tube lined with loose power cables and scraps of shiny insulation, showing the ship was a work in progress. She wore an adult vacuum suit several sizes too big, cinched tight at chest, waist, and crotch to keep her from tripping over it. Luckily spin gravity was a relaxed .5 g. Seeing pressure was up, she undogged her helmet and lifted it off, shaking out straight blonde hair that fell to just past her small delicate jaw. Squared ends and razor bangs were edged in blue—matching her eyes. Filling her lungs with ship air, Kay found it musty, smelling of Chimps and solvent, way better than the stale stuff in her over-sized suit.

("Can you pilot her?") inquired a disembodied voice coming from the comlink clipped to her ear. Speed-of-light lag made the voice seem to hesitate, meaning the signal came from a ways off. Hundreds of thousands of klicks at least.

"Sure, no sweat." At thirteen standard years Kay already knew better than to show an angstrom of doubt, not when money hung on the deal. "Just let me look her over." Following the snaking power cables to the control deck, she brushed foam packing pretzels off the spanking new command couch, then climbed aboard, her small frame sinking deep into the crash webbing. "Centaurii Comet, right?"

("Serial number CC-8879442,") replied the voice in her ear.

If you say so. Finding the couch lead, she lifted the blue fringed hair at the back of her neck and jacked in, running a swift systems check. All green. Figures. Hardwired systems sit for centuries, waiting to spring to life—while the human parts wore down, or went to pieces. Lying back, she summoned up a virtual tour of the ship, a spherical pressure cabin married to a cylindrical antimatter drive, originally an insystem robofreighter, presently being refitted by a SuperChimp crew, apparently for smuggling. She noted the redone command cabin was a bit short, creating space behind the aft bulkhead. "So you need someone to make a shakedown run to Tartarus?"

("Yes, a pilot to check the work of the SuperChimps on the refit, then take the ship and SuperChimps to Tartarus.")

"Why take the Chimps?" She did not intend to lift ship until the refit was done—being desperate, but not clinically crazy. There were smarter ways of killing herself than taking a suspect ship deep into Typhon's gravity well, headed for Tartarus, an airless volcanic moon, torn by tidal forces and drenched in hard radiation from Typhon's Van Allen belts.

("These SuperChimps are needed on Tartarus.")

Poor Chimps. Poor her—she was headed for Tartarus too. Money can make you do ghastly things. Kay asked, "When will I be paid?"

("Payment in your name is waiting to be claimed on Tartarus, you need only go there.")

"Sounds great!" Actually it sounded like a blazing lot of bullshit, but it did not pay to say so—in fact the only way the excursion paid at all was to pilot this refitted museum piece safely to Tartarus. "Just let me go get my kit."

("Be back before 1600.")

"Absolutely!" Kay did not let a scintilla of doubt into her voice, grinning idiotically, sounding perky as she could while lying at the controls of a derelict robo-freighter, a cosmic packing crate discarded ages before she was born—being told she had to see the ship to Tartarus, for reasons so dangerous she dared not ask. "No trouble at all," she assured the invisible voice, checking the time in her head. 04:55:07 "I'll be back by the first dog watch."

Leaping up before the voice changed its mind, she waded through packing scraps to the airlock, clamping on her helmet, and returning to the stale stuffy air from Mom's worn recycler. Cycling through the lock, she emerged from the despin system onto an open docking port on the ship's main axis. Telling her boots to grip, she walked out to stand on the empty docking ring, surrounded by vacuum and starlight—all dressed up with nowhere to go. She just wanted to be out of the ship, before something screwed the deal. Silly, since the comlink was still in her ear, and the disembodied voice could call it off anytime, or demand she do it blindfolded. To which Kay would have to happily say, "Yes." But she herself would not prolong the process one nanosecond. What was there to negotiate? She was offered more credit than she had ever seen to pilot a ship—something she had known how to do since she was two. Kay had to accept, resolutely refusing to consider the risks, consequences, or glaringly obvious dangers. It was not like she had a choice.

Putting the comlink to use, she hit the net, scanning frequencies, scanning a ride, talking to anyone who would talk to her, hoping to get back to The Hub as painlessly as possible. Telling all who would listen that she was "deep in the Graveyard, needing a ride Home."

On the far side of her visor was one of the most awesome sights in Human Space, the Orion nebula from close up, great fingers of glowing gas tipped with stars in the making, seen through the young bright lights of Dawn Cluster, hundreds of suns crowded into a few score light-years, blazing at her out of the blackness. Starry nebula stretched from straight overhead almost to her feet, where it was abruptly cut off by the curved tawny-brown cloud tops of a ringed gas giant half a million klicks "below" her. This was Typhon, the huge Jovian world that everything hereabouts orbited, circled by immense silver rings taking up half the sky. By local convention going deeper into Typhon's steep gravity well was "down" and everywhere else in the universe was "up." Somewhere "down" there, between her and the rings, spun Tartarus, Typhon's innermost moon, a sulfuric volcanic slag heap, freezing cold and lava hot, bathed in Typhon's Van Allen radiation—that for some unknown reason urgently needed this ship and its Chimp crew. So urgently they were willing to have her pilot it, a sign of practically suicidal desperation on someone's part, or monumental stupidity. But who was Kay to question her luck?

Smiling into her helmet cam, she pictured the people she talked to—Mom's transceiver chip in the back of her skull let her see images projected directly into her optical lobes. so she could read faces. Someone had to burn mass and come out of their way to pick her up. Someone human. Chimps lacked the authority and few cyborgs would give her the time of day—narrowing her choices alarmingly. CC-8879442 orbited deep in the Graveyard, a parking orbit for cargoless ships and airless hulks at the edge of Typhon's Van Allen belts. Scavengers, salvage crews, refit parties, ring runners, and antique dealers all visited the Graveyard—if only sporadically. So that's who she appealed to, pleading patiently while the worn recycler on Mom's old v-suit labored in the background.

Finally she found a guy who felt right, who had not only a ship but a job, a fat friendly tug operator doing orbital maintenance, promising to fit her into his schedule so long as she paid for her mass. Since she massed next to nothing, it was a deal—though she still wished he were a woman.

Settling in to wait, Kay stood weightless in her mother's oversized v-suit, listening to the laboring recycler. Being on the axis of rotation made the whole ship seem to spin around her, but left her stable relative to the stars, pointed smack at Betelgeuse. But Typhon was the big attraction, blazing in half-phase with its giant rings, so huge she could not see it all. She searched for Tartarus, but the tiny moon was too close in, blotted out by the bright rings. She was going to really be a ring rat now, close enough to file her nails on them.

05:37:42 Waiting began to wear. Space travel had way too much dead time, even for little hops like here to The Hub. Nor did she like how Mom's recycler sounded— if it gave out, she had just a small reserve before the suit died.

Retreating to the net, she scanned for free feelie casts, finding a 3V add for a resort and retirement aerostat in Typhon's upper atmosphere. Floating like a huge transparent bubble several klicks across, the aerostat hung from a giant balloon of heated hydrogen, suspended amid brown clouds of ammonium hydrosulfide hundreds of klicks above a grey-white sea of water ice clouds. Within the aerostat's protective bubble was a free-form world, where beautiful people flitted between aerial hamlets on gossamer wings and skycycles. Fairyland to a child raised in cubicals and corridors, breathtakingly wonderful no matter how often she felt it. She blended with the ad, riding a skycycle with wind streaming in a cool rush of feeling over her face, weirdly refreshing. She peddled along, dodging skyships, pleasure barges, and colorful homes floating like open flowers complete with hanging gardens and rooftop landing pads. Aerostat technology was used by the first settlers to terraform Oceania and the inner worlds, then introduced to Typhon to provide living space in the outer system. Ice mining and terraforming left colonies scattered about Typhon living off local resources and gravity advantage—not everyone could pick up and move to the wonderful new inner worlds. Kay was having her troubles just getting to The Hub.

Shooting through waterfall rainbows, she skimmed the surface of the warm ballast lake at the bottom of the bubble, feeling the splash of spray on her feet, all without fear of crashing—this was just a commercial. To prove it she pulled back on the skycycle and did a perfect inside loop right into the lake.

Soon as she hit the water she was swimming, no longer aboard a skycycle, but nude, wearing only swim fins, goggles, and a rebreather. Warm oxygenated water turned her into an aquatic creature, gliding at will over sunlit sand through schools of tiny silver fish, swimming effortlessly despite never having been in water deeper than a sponge bath—all thanks to the power of advertising.

Suddenly she was back standing in her oversized suit, warm limbs still twitching from the swim. Suit alarms wailed as a tug came in to dock at the port she was standing on. Her ride was here. Clearing the docking ring, she waited until the locks matched, then entered the tug, finding it spotless compared to what she was leaving—usually a good sign. "Welcome aboard," the tug operator called out from his command couch. "Crack your hat and have a seat."

She had the usual split second to decide about the man, while the lock cycled closed behind her and ships prepared to part. Was this guy going to hurt her? Should she go back? Then risk the next ride instead? Half a dozen times she had turned right about and been out the lock before her surprised ride said hello. And so far she had always guessed right, since in hundreds of rides nothing bad had ever happened. Not real bad anyway—not yet. This guy had a comfortable slovenly appearance that did not match the clean cabin, giving him a sympathetic complexity, beefy and easygoing, totally adapted to zero-g, yet not afraid to be neat. She relaxed a bit as the lock clicked shut behind her—for better or worse she was aboard the tug. "Thanks," she replied cheerfully, pulling off her helmet, "shan't mind if I do."

His air tasted as neat as his cabin, not clean and free like on an aerostat, but well preserved. Kay parked herself in the co-pilot's couch, snapping her belt to the crash webbing, as he asked her, "Where you from?"

Unsealing a glove, she pushed back her big suit sleeve, showing him her tattoo: K-9251949. He nodded at her creche number. "So you got no family?"

"Just Mom's uncle Lyle." Who did not know she existed until she looked him up. "He has a ship of his own—but it is not as nice as yours."

"Wish she were mine," the big man smiled ruefully.

"Well, you keep it real nice." She laid on the compliments thick as she could. "Grand-uncle Lyle's is some mess."

His jowly smile widened. "What was that ship I picked you up from?"

She shrugged. "Just there looking for a job." She had never even asked the ship's name. "Didn't get it."

"What kind of job?" Captain inquisitively cocked an eyebrow.

She had not asked what she would carry to Tartarus, knowing it must be heinously criminal, otherwise they would be idiots to hire her. Unlicensed pilots could cost you your ship; hiring a thirteen-year-old without formal training showed utter contempt for the law, meaning a cargo so despicable only a desperate teenager would haul it "no questions asked." It hardly helped her to know how criminal, since bland ignorance was the best way to beat a brain-scan. She shrugged again. "Told you, I did not get it. How hard is it to gun a rig like this?"

He laughed, "Not hard. Lookin' for my job?"

"Sure thing!" She started asking dumb kid questions about orbital mechanics, getting him to talk tug operations, salvage hassles, ring runner gossip, rumors of slavers insystem, family problems; he showed her happy waving holos of his three wives and seven kids. When conversation lapsed, she let her mind drift, hopping aboard a feelie ad for a starliner headed outsystem, hiding her absence behind blue-trimmed bangs and a spacey blonde smile.

Starliner *Artemis* was built to pamper interstellar travelers with bars, casinos, lounges and recreation decks, and a hollow core where garden balconies formed near vertical cliff faces, seemingly klicks apart, enclosing a virtual space filled with winding trails and cascading waterfalls. Passengers could step from their stateroom terraces into hologram landscapes that were changed weekly—so just finding your way to a favorite bistro became an adventure. Anything to fight boredom during the months of shiptime it took to see the stars. She sampled wind-surfing on the pool deck and the virtual world of Q-deck, popping back now and again to see if her ride was saying anything important. Each time she left the feelie, Orion Lines eagerly reminded her *Artemis* was nearing Tyhphon orbit, her last stop insystem—with SPACE AVAILABLE for outbound passengers! She wished she could go, but she did not have the credit to get to the Graveyard and back.

Abruptly her ride was over—the tug pilot was telling her they were at The Hub. Hurriedly unstrapping, she apologized for daydreaming. Several ships were docked in the torus station, making The Hub look like a rimless wheel with most of the spokes missing. Home sweet home. And time to pay up. Her ride calculated her mass cost, handing her the keypad so she could check his figures. They checked—it would cost all her credit, leaving her nothing for the trip back with her kit. Her bare thumb hovered nervously over PAY.

"Hey, kid," the guy asked softly. "Want to save yourself the credit?"

"Sure," she replied slowly, relaxing her fingers, letting the keypad float away from her hand. Somehow she had to hustle the credit for a ride back to the Graveyard. Turn this guy down, and the next one might not be near so nice. "So long as I do not have to take off my suit."

"You really like that v-suit?" He sounded disappointed at not seeing her naked.

She started to say how little she had to show under the bulky suit, then stopped, fearing it might queer the whole deal. Forced by circumstances to be a connoisseur of child molesters, Kay guessed this guy was not the sort who got off on seeing girls suffer. He just thought of her as "young stuff" and wanted to get his a little early, making him more lazy than mean. Hell, she could tell he liked her, though his way of expressing it was to take criminal advantage of her, showing a need for serious psych reprogramming. Pronto. But that was his problem, she just told him, "It belonged to my mom."

"Your mom was a vacuum hand?" He sounded impressed, and a bit embarrassed at propositioning someone's baby girl.

"She was a pilot, and shipped over half the galaxy." Kay gave the tug Captain her warmest most dazzling smile. "Mom was born in Alpha C, right next to Old Earth—and this was her v-suit." She did not mention that Mom had died in it—something Kay thought about every time she put it on.

"So you just cannot stand to take it off?"

Kay smiled even wider, stubbornly determined to stay in the suit. "It was all she left me." Not strictly true, the transceiver chip in her skull had been left for her too, along with enough credit to have it put into her as a toddler. It had originally been in her mother's head.

"So your mom's dead? What about your dad?"

"Sperm donor," she replied cheerfully. "MSS-789439-X18."

"Guess that means you are on your own?"

"You bet." She said it like she would not have it any other way.

"And how old are you?"

"Sixteen," she lied to make him feel better, since it did not matter to her.

"Earth years?" He looked suspicious.

She nodded eagerly. He gave in and let her keep the suit on. Adept at disconnecting parts of her brain, Kay put herself on automatic, sending her conscious mind on another visit to starship *Artemis*—no wind-surfing or virtual-adventuring this time, just leaning on a terrace rail in the liner's hanging gardens listening to night music and smelling jasmine in the dark air, while hologram fireflies blinked ancient come-ons to each other. Her ride ended up tipping her.

As soon as she was off the tug, Kay rinsed her mouth with chemical-tasting wash water, careful not to swallow, wishing she could afford bottled water from the bulkhead dispenser. Corridor taps were clearly marked NOT FOR INTERNAL USE.

To take her mind off her thirst—and her impromptu audition for wife #4—Kay tried guesstimating her chances. To be brutally truthful, she had signed on with hardened criminals who hoped to profit off her trip to Tartarus. Fortunately payment seemed foolproof, since Tartarus confirmed the credit was hers, merely needing to be claimed. That payment was her lifeline, her chance to go somewhere for real, instead of hitching 3V rides on starliner ads. Best of all, no matter how she turned it over in her head, she could not see any real profit in killing her. If they were blowing up the ship for insurance, why make it murder as well? And what idiot would insure an illegal ring runner with a teenage pilot? They wanted the ship and Chimps on Tartarus for a reason, a seriously criminal reason—so they got a cheap pilot, who knew nothing and could not testify against them, whoever they were. Disposable but not doomed, that was her ticket. Just because her employers were hardened criminals, did not mean they had to be completely heartless.

Squeezing past tired-looking families camped in the passageways, she got to her storage locker, and found an aging shaven-headed vacuum hand sprawled in front of it, thin and gaunt, and reeking of potable coolant. Kneeling down, she shook him. "Hey, old-timer wake up, I need to get to my stuff."

His good eye flicked open, and he stared up at her, his questioning look turning into a lopsided grin. "Kay! I prayed you would come back."

She smiled wearily. "And here I am."

"Where did you go?" His questioning look returned. "No one knew where you went, like you had vanished from The Hub."

Her fondest ambition. She sighed and sat down beside him. "I went to see about a ship."

"What ship?" He started to panic. "You cannot ship out. You are my angel, the only beautiful thing I see every day. If you leave there will be nothing." He waved at the blank passageway bulkhead to prove his point.

Pretty bleak, but that was why she was leaving. "Look," she whispered, "there is good news, but you must keep it secret."

"What good news?" He still sounded wary. What good could come of her leaving?

"Promise to keep this secret," she insisted. "I am signing on as Captain."

"Shit girl, that is absolute crazy."

"Ain't it?" She nodded cheerfully. "And criminal too. With an antimatter drive and a SuperChimp crew. My crew, pretty scary, huh? And I want you to go too, as my supercargo. Whadya say, will you come with me?"

He gave her a grateful bewildered look. "You are an angel. My golden angel."

She laughed outright for the first time in what felt like forever. "Then move over, old-timer. This is Captain Angel speaking."

"Aye, aye." With difficulty he slid away from her door. "Where are we shipping to?"

She arched a blonde eyebrow. "Does it matter?"

He laughed, shaking his shaved head sorrowfully, "Long as it is not here."

"There could be danger," Kay confessed. "I mean, you know, any lift can be dangerous . . ." This one more than most.

"Dangerous?" He looked astonished. "Signing onto an unknown ship, sight unseen, for an illegal trip with an unlicensed underage pilot? Where is the risk to that?"

She laughed again. "When you put it that way, it does not sound nearly so bad. Be ready by the first dog watch."

He raised a crooked finger, reminding her. "Better to die in space than live in a box!"

"You wish." She thumbed the lock, and her storage box sprang open. He just slept in passageways—she was the one who lived in a box. Crawling into her three-meter storage locker, she closed the door, shedding her mother's suit like a chrysalis in the darkness, followed by her sweat-soaked pants and tee, exposing her bare thin body to the safety of the dark locker. Finding her cooler by touch, she got out a packet of water, broke the foil seal and drank. By the next dog watch she would be living on ship's rations, eating and drinking her fill for the first time ever.

Now she just felt drained. Lying curled in darkness, she let herself go, crying lightly at being alone, an ache so old it seemed to always be with her. She thought about her dead mom, and her dad, Male Sperm Sample-789439-X18. The X18 meant his name could not be released until she was 18. He only wanted to meet her as an adult. Five more years. How the fuck was she supposed to survive until then? Sometimes she tried chatting with kids on Typhon or Oceania, real kids, on real worlds, with real lives, but speed-of-light lag made her look so hick and stupid, taking forever to answer simple questions. Too slow even for virtual sex, except for the crudest sort of show-and-tell—which she did not much like anyway. She wanted someone to hold her and touch her, and tell her she was not alone.

Her one ticket out of here was the chip put in her skull as a toddler; with it she could pilot any conventional spacecraft. Mom's files were extensive and continually updated themselves, making for a weird upbringing. How many three-year-old-girls had an "invisible friend" who was a gravity-drive, cyber-friendly Centaurii Starcruiser? Being born in space, she could not afford to look back. Tartarus could hardly be worse than this, and on Tartarus credit waited to take her somewhere else. Or so she hoped. Her employers were saving a fortune over the cost of a real pilot, would they kill her to save the little she cost? Unlikely. Or to shut her up? Possibly.

Better to die in space than live in a box. Setting her head for 0800 she closed her eyes, returning to starship *Artemis*, to dance through a low-g lounge with handsome hologram officers in snappy Orion Lines uniforms. Movement and music soon lulled her to sleep. One more hitch to the Graveyard, then she would have her own ship— then look out universe.

MISSBEHAVEN

2ND DOG WATCH 18:54:33
In constant-g transit to Typhon

Hardwired to her work station by superconducting cable, Heidi van der Graf stared into virtual space, watching two lopsided moonlets tumble towards each other. Connecting her biocircuitry directly to the onboard systems, the cable plugged into a microsocket at the back of her head hidden by naturally pink hair. The two tumbling satellites were guardian moons—Aetna I and Aetna II—pockmarked cinders a hundred klicks across, on concentric orbits forty klicks from the outer edge of Typhon's A-ring. With an orbital separation well within their mean diameters they seemed determined to collide, and Heidi aimed to put *Artemis*' passengers at the upcoming point of impact.

("Ship bearing ZERO-FOUR-FOUR plus TWENTY, looks to be a ring runner.") Heidi thought heinous thoughts about her boss, having seen the ship already, a Centaurii Comet skirting the rings, making for Tartarus—too old and slow to be trouble. Heidi's whole job was seeing things before they happened; now she felt like her section head sat at her shoulder, willing her to screw up, and for no good reason. Sure she was newly signed on, never serving on a posh starliner before. Worse yet, she had shocking pink hair, green eyes, and dimples when she grinned. So what? None of that made her an idiot; in fact she could already tweek unrivaled virtual effects out of *Artemis*' humdrum circuitry.

Gasps came over the comnet as Heidi zoomed in on the moonlets. Pick-ups on Aetna II let her plunge straight to the surface, then shoot upward. Passengers packed into lounges and staterooms tuned to 3V found themselves staring up from the airless surface of Aetna II. An astounding scene. Typhon's silvery A-ring rose right out of the short pitted horizon, standing edgewise in space, neatly bisecting the great neon blotch of the Orion nebula. Six moons were up. Oceania, Typhon's largest satellite, hung like a powder-blue pearl amid the hot young stars of Dawn Cluster. All backed by synthesized accompaniment—Aretha Chou's *Pleiades Symphony*. Not bad for the new girl. Her Orion Lines contract read Signalsmate, Second Class, but Heidi rated herself a virtual artist with the cosmos for her palette and music for a brush.

Obviously unimpressed, her supervisor broke into the music of the spheres, rattling off irrelevant info on the ring runner. ("Ship is *MissBehaven*, antimatter-drive robo-freighter inbound for Tartarus.") Heidi swore silently at her immediate superior, Chief Signalsmate Marten DeRuyter, a pompous twit, breaking the flow of her act with authoritative announcements, blowing the mood she created. Shut up and enjoy the show. She desperately needed to shine—to go totally nova, showing Orion Lines what they were getting.

Slowly Aetna I rose up over the stone's-throw horizon. Bigger and more menacing as it came on, the moonlet plunged straight at the smaller satellite, gathering speed. Tumbling towards the viewpoint, its cratered surface grew to fill the entire sky. Millions of tons of misguided rock and ice hurtled right at Aetna II. An unnerving sight, even in 3V. Virtual effects put anyone tuned in smack at the point of collision. Pulses quickened. Music swelled to a crescendo, as passengers braced themselves, hugging loved ones, and hunkering deeper into body-couches. Heidi could hear sharp intakes of breath on the comnet. Heart attack time. Catastrophic impact rushed at them, scary and awesome, threatening to send unstable personalities caroming about their staterooms.

At the last second the cosmos flinched. Aetna I and Aetna II somersaulted in space. One instant they were close enough together to see house-sized boulders on Aetna I's surface. A moment later Aetna II swung completely around, switching orbits with Aetna I—a dance the two guardian moons had been doing down through the ages as they swept the outer rim of Typhon's A-ring.

Instead of facing a shattering collision, passengers found themselves staring at Typhon's vast multicolored cloud tops, while Aetna I whirled off into space, a dwindling hunk of rock and ice. Great brown and yellow bands of ammonium hydrosulfides streamed across the face of the gas giant, whipped by white storm eddies bigger than planets, whirling one into another across a colossal disk spanned by silver rings, incredibly immense and breathtakingly unexpected. Stunned silence turned to cheers, showering Heidi in comnet applause. Chief Steward Taylor called to congratulate her. So did the First Officer. That ought to get DeRuyter off her back.

No such luck. Chief Signalsmate DeRuyter curtly took control, telling her via private back channel. ("Daddy will do the encore.")

("Why?") Heidi hated men who called themselves "daddy"—especially to subordinates—one more warning that her boss was wired pretty weird. She wanted to keep going, straight down through the cloud tops to the aerostats floating in Typhon's upper atmosphere—contrasting the empty infinity of space with the endless cloud plain of the great ringed planet.

("You'll see, just lay back and learn.")

You wish. Giving up control, Heidi cursed DeRuyter for treating her like a trainee. Sure she was new, but she had given an orgasmic performance on top of a resume that read like someone made it up. Her boss would be hard put to do better. She saw Typhon vanish, replaced by blank starscape. The image tightened. At the center of the starfield sat the Centaurii Comet, centuries old and hopelessly obsolete, with her round pressure cabin and stubby antimatter drive, *MissBehaven* bound for Tartarus, the ring runner. So? Heidi saw the virtual audience slip as staterooms went offline. Sensors picked up random conversation in the L-deck lounge. Heidi smirked. We can't all be a hit. People drifted towards new pleasures, ignoring DeRuyter's virtual offering. Boredom was the bane of space travel. High-g drives and relativistic velocities had failed to erase the gulf between the stars, but people still wanted to "go there"—even if it took months of shiptime. Designed to meet that challenge, *Artemis* had every stateroom wired for 3V. Plus a pool deck and lounge deck. Another deck devoted to kids. Non-stop virtual shows. Hologram acts and gambling arcades. On-line orgies that would make Caligulia blush. Anything to make light-years fly by.

Heidi unplugged. Her internal transceiver let her follow things without being wired into the work station; she used the ship to supply images and boost her signals, but the chip in her skull turned thoughts into actions. Her hand groped for a dope-stick. Nasty habit, but she needed to even out the strain, mixing some yin in her yang, making life a little less like work. She inhaled sharply and the stick lit itself, filling her lungs with narcotic smoke.

Too bad she had to light up in a church. Her stateroom was set on bright summer day, showing a 3V interior of La Mezquita, the great mosque built by the Caliphs of Cordoba, converted after the Reconquest into a Christian cathedral. Colorful columns and arches plundered from Roman temples disappeared into virtual dis-tance. Beyond an ornate inscribed archway—patterned on the Mihrab, a prayer niche built by Hakam II—perfumed water splashed on the sunlit marble of the Al-hambra's Court of Lions. She wore silk harem pants under her ship's kimono to match the decor, her slippered feet resting on flagstones worn by the knees of pilgrims. Not exactly the Sistine Chapel, but she called it home.

Staring into illusionary space, Heidi took a pull on the dopestick, reveling in her new job security. Orion Lines ought to be ecstatic. She was smashing—hitting MEM-ORY, she replayed the applause in her head. No matter how much DeRuyter sneered at her, she had sealed her cozy berth on a pleasure ship headed outsystem, going to see the universe in style. And she did not have to drop her harem pants to do it. Always a plus.

Alarm bells jerked her out of her euphoria. Snubbing out the dopestick, she re-turned to realtime. *MissBehaven* was broadcasting a Mayday—a persistent, repeated plea for help.

Closing her eyes, she shut out the romanesque mosque-cum-cathedral, triggering her transceiver, staring into cyberspace. Traffic control showed a new ship—a sleek gravity-drive starship swinging out from behind Typhon at high acceleration. Data banks tagged the newcomer as the *Hiryu* out of Azha system, Eta Eridani. The high-g drive, the silent rush to match velocities, along with Eridani registry—all shouted "slaver." Heidi heard the viewing lounge fall silent, recognizing the same expectant hush heard on a game park tour when someone spots a leopard or sabre-tooth.

Pulling pink hair aside, she hurriedly plugged back in. Horrible things were about to happen. Happily, they would happen to someone else. *Artemis* had nothing to fear from *Hiryu*, or any outback predator. The starliner's energy shielding stood up to the storm of radiation at near light speed. Nukes could not even scratch the paintwork, and in centuries of operation Orion Lines had never lost a starliner. Which would not help *MissBehaven*. *Artemis* was decelerating towards Typhon at 1-g, headed for an or-bit inside the Roche Limit, planning a pass between the planet and rings, skimming the cloud tops. *Hiryu* and its prey were farther out, headed for Tartarus—the high-g slaver would be finished with the robo-freighter long before *Artemis* arrived. Any other help was even farther off.

Horrified, Heidi watched a winged gravity-drive gig separate from *Hiryu*, match-ing velocities with the fleeing freighter. As the gig attached to *MissBehaven's* main airlock, DeRuyter fed the Mayday into the comnet, letting passengers see aboard the doomed ship. Meant to be crewed by SuperChimps and computers, *MissBehaven* turned out to have humans aboard. Her Mayday came from a gaunt ring rat, hands trembling, his aged face a mask of fear, begging *Artemis* for help. "Signal to starliner, please render assistance. We are being boarded . . ."

Not your normal holoshow. This real-time drama had Heidi sitting paralyzed at her station, aghast at the expanding spectacle. Tapping into *MissBehaven*'s onboard cams, DeRuyter broadcast the nightmare scene at the airlock. Alarms wailed hysterically. The narrow corridor filled with dancing sparks as an anaerobic torch cut its way into the ship. Suddenly the lock burst open. Tripod-legged cyborgs with steel tentacle arms and twin gun turret heads emerged from the shower of sparks, firing as they came. Crazed SuperChimps ran hooting in terror, unarmed and helpless. Appeals for assistance turned frantic. Heidi hardly believed what she was seeing.

And it got worse. Detecting more images tightcast to private staterooms, she tapped in, seeing the same ghastly scene from the cyborg's point of view—DeRuyter was reading the slaver control channels, a neat trick. Gun cams tracked terrified Chimps banging off bulkheads frantic to escape the hail of fire. One by one they were blown to bloody rags.

Wondering who got off on this live action shooting gallery, Heidi backtracked one of the tightcasts to an A-deck holo-suite. By now she knew all first-class passengers by name, face, and predilection. This one she had tagged as trouble, an insolent jerk-off who practically lived on the ship's S&M channel. Sitting cross-legged on his zero-g bed in a virtual stupor, he had a headset on, leaning and twisting with the action, mouth agape, sweat gleaming at his temples. Every so often his fingers twitched. His teenage hired girlfriend lay beside him on the bed wearing nothing but dead black lipstick, and matching nails, looking almighty bored.

Heidi hit security override, blanking the signal to the stateroom. Swearing like a bosun the punk tore off his headset, feverishly checking his connections, then jacked back in. His hired girlfriend smirked at his troubles. Heidi quit tormenting the little sadist, who was after all a paying passenger. Let him have his twisted fun. No sick jerk-off was worth a complaint in her file.

Returning to the tightcast, she saw something new. Mixed in with the signals from the cyborg's gun cams was another set from a slaver wired for sensesurround. Heidi could not see the slaver's face, just his hands and body, since she was seeing through his eyes, hearing through his ears. Uncanny, but thoroughly familiar to her.

Stepping lightly through the carnage left by the cyborgs, he looked happily about, carefully avoiding the gore and Chimp shit. Heidi could tell he was happy by the spring in his walk, and the way he glanced carelessly, attentive and curious—not the least downcast or wary. His right hand held a recoilless pistol nonchalantly at his side. Making his self-satisfied way straight to the command deck, the slaver shut off the ship's Mayday. The old man was splattered across a bulkhead, blasted at close range by some uncaring cyborg. As the slaver knelt to examine the gory remains, Heidi shifted away.

Switching to control-deck cams, she got a look at the slaver himself, a cheerful hoodlum with dark tousled hair and a keen confident air, going casually through his victim's clothing. Clearly a bright alert boy who enjoyed his work, and did not care who it hurt. *Homo galactus*, born in space, most likely raised a slaver. His uniform blouse was open to the navel showing off a garish dragon tattoo, twining across his naked chest—*Hiryu* meant "Flying Dragon" in a dead language. Tattooed skulls braceleted his wrist, marking him as a veteran killer.

Done robbing the dead, the slaver straightened up, looking away from the human mess at his feet. His eyes swept the room. To see what he was looking for, Heidi switched back to sensesurround, at the same time calling up the deck plan for a Centaurii Comet. He stared hard at the aft bulkhead, which looked to be half a meter closer than the deck plan warranted.

Walking to the back of the cabin, he ran expert fingers over the bulkhead. Heidi sensed the hands of a master smuggler-cum-slaver feeling for flaws in the smooth plasti-metal. His hand stopped. There it was. Jacking up the sensesurround Heidi felt an invisible vertical ridge, right under the slaver's fingers. Together they followed the ridge down to the deck, where the pressure seam felt wider than it should. Curiouser and curiouser. It was weird to be at one with this murderous felon, melding her senses with his. He called for a cyborg.

Heidi shifted to the cyborg. Sensors turned the invisible ridge into a hairline crease, pressure-proof, but real. Anything could be on the far side. Extending a pair of grapples, the cyborg grabbed onto the bulkhead, then pulled sideways. The hairline crease widened into a crack.

She shifted back to the slaver. Pistol leveled at the crack, he signaled the cyborg to pull harder. Staring over the pistol sights, she saw the bulkhead creep sideways, widening the crack. She could feel the slaver's finger tighten on the firing stud. His first sign of nervousness.

As the crack widened, a couple of centimeters of girl's face appeared. Heidi could see a blue eye, sharp-cut blonde bangs with a blue trim, a tearstained cheek, and the corner of a mouth. "Out," the slaver ordered. The visible tip of the girl's lip trembled, but she did not speak. He jammed the pistol barrel into the crack. The girl shrank back—wedging herself deeper into the half-meter slot behind the bulkhead. "Out, or I shoot."

He would shoot. Heidi could feel it in his gunhand—the readiness to kill if he did not get his way. She tried desperately to will his finger off the firing stud, but senses-urround did not work that way. Instead she felt the finger press harder on the stud. Another milligram of pressure and the pistol would spray explosive shells into the tiny space, ripping the girl to shreds.

Slowly the panel slid back. Terrified and hollow-eyed, the girl stayed pressed tightly into the tiny space, being twelve or thirteen at best, wearing a woman's v-suit several sizes too large with the helmet tipped back off her head. Giving a satisfied grunt the slaver reached in and grabbed her. As his hand closed on the girl's suit, Heidi unplugged, not wanting to feel his fingers seize the frightened child.

Sensesurround vanished. Signals still came in, beamed straight to the transceiver in her skull, but with the same intensity. Plugging in was not a necessity—most folks lived fine lives without it—but having the plug in her head gave Heidi her professional edge. Superconducting connections sharpened sensesurround and shaved off precious nanoseconds essential for 3V programming.

By now most of the ship had tuned in. Way more people were on-line than had seen her cosmic tumbling act. Taking a peek at that A-deck asshole, she saw him still wearing his headset, with his girlfriend in his lap, her eyes shut, dead black lips pursed, head resting listlessly on her employer. He reached down between her legs. Heidi cut the signal to the stateroom. Let them put it in her file; she would not let the sadistic little scumbag get off on that girl's fear.

("What are you doing?") DeRuyter demanded.

Heidi did not answer. Screw DeRuyter. Picking up the dopestick, she breathed it back to life, thinking about the girl, trying to imagine what she could do—knowing the answer was nothing. That girl was gone. Soon she would be headed outsystem in the hold of a slaver, never to come back. The Cosmos could be horribly cruel to the unlucky.

("Consider yourself on report.")

Consider yourself an asshole, she thought it but did not say it—noting the signal to A-deck was restored. Good to see someone getting something out of this fiasco. Snubbing out the dopestick, she shut off her cerebral transceiver, stood up and stalked through the Mihrab gateway into the Court of Lions. Green cyprus tops poked up over the colonnade surrounding the fountain, a shallow basin supported by a dozen sculpted lions. Andalusian sunlight poured out of a hot blue hologram sky. She sat down on one of the lions, letting the water pour over her, soaking her harem pants and ship's ki-mono. Water and fountain were semi-real even if the sunshine was not.

Damn, what a disaster. DeRuyter upstaged her, rubbing her face in what the pay-ing public really wanted. Who needs art when you can have live action horror? Touché. Reality programming, DeRutyer had the absolute touch of shit. She stared at the slender marble columns surrounding the foutain; a hologram facade, like the hot blue sky above, 3V fakes hiding ship's bulkheads, giving depth and solidity to her compressed world. Reality was different. Reality was a terrified child turned into live passenger entertainment.

Was she wound way too tight? Probably—but with reason. Heidi could not walk away from her problems, no more than that girl could. Not aboard ship. She could not even walk away from her station. Only her resolution to stay shut down gave a semblance of privacy. Calls were piling up. So what? Let them scold, let them scream. Home is where your head is, and right now Heidi's head was not accepting callers.

With her head chip off, she was a normal unaugmented woman, and she meant to make the most of it. Tossing away wet slippers, she struggled out of her pants and ki-mono, letting sunlit water cascade over her, cool and cleansing, mixing with her tears, then disappearing down concealed drains in the deck. When she gave in and checked her calls, she found herself summoned to a face-to-face with the Chief Steward—the surest sign of authority in a 3V society is the power to demand appear-ance. Heidi ordered up a crisp starched Orion Lines uniform, figuring if she could not be a happy slave, she could at least look the part.

Her cabin door dilated ahead of her as the painted archways of La Mezquita merged into K-deck corridors tuned to high summer in a cathedral pine forest. Giant gnarled sequoias rose up around her, lit by shafts of late-afternoon sunlight pouring down through greenery from infinite space overhead. Birds flitted back and forth among the boughs, and animals moved between the trees. Trails connected cabins and staterooms. Stepping into a drop shaft in the forest floor, she told it to take her down to S-deck. People in the shaft greeted her with broad smiles and shouts of "What a show!"

Which she found humiliating, but she still smiled back—this was her public. Young and approachable, with her pink hair and ready smile, she had gotten tagged as "the new girl in the crew." Nearly everyone outranked her, and anyone could accost her under the guise of "getting to know you." She had enjoyed the pseudo-popularity—making her feel welcome—but now it just felt stale, though that did not stop her from smiling. Her job was dedicated to the impossible supposition that everything could be fun! Even mind-numbing months in transit, locked in a metal ship so far from anywhere it took starlight years to reach them. Someone had to keep the passengers content, or at least catatonic, and she would shuck and hustle with the best, she just drew the line at kidnapping and murder. Heaven knows why.

Chief Steward Taylor held court in a tree, having an illusionary glass tree house at the top of a kilometer-high forest canopy—a favorite setting of claustrophobics. Immensity, of distance hit Heidi as the corridor door vanished behind her; air and space stretching in every direction, filled with birds and blue day moths fluttering amid the sunbeams. Monkeys swung past, hooting and scampering along the branches. How Chief Steward Taylor passed the psych tests was anyone's guess, since the woman was a mass of nerves and denial who kept her 3V set at wide angle. Taylor loved Heidi's deep space gymnastics. Instead of aging gracefully Taylor had gone for the biosculpted look—relying on flame red hair and slick glossy wrinkleless skin—something Heidi prayed she had the sense to avoid when she was old and rich. Why would a borderline claustrophobic choose a starship career in the first place? To pun-ish herself? Looking sharp was the least of this woman's worries.

DeRuyter was there as well, ungodly handsome in his better biosculpt job, a cool solid contrast to the Chief Steward's fragile authority. Taylor asked frostily, "Is it true you cut service to an A-deck stateroom?"

Heidi admitted as much. "She's new," DeRuyter explained, eagerly apologizing for her, putting her in the wrong under the pretense of protection. "She's fresh up from the inner system, and does not know we mean to show our passengers the Outback—warts and all." He offered her an out; admit her mistake, promise to be good, and Orion Lines would forgive. Chief Steward Taylor would be equally happy to see the situation go away.

Surprisingly, Heidi found herself standing up to her section head, in front of the Chief Steward no less, insanely demanding full-blown inquiry. "Outback conditions are one thing—being accomplices to hijacking and kidnapping is another."

"Accomplices?" DeRuyter looked taken aback. "You cannot mean that."

Again the chance to back down—but she would not take it, charging straight ahead. "I do mean it. You knew that slaver was coming. You gave the freighter no warning . . ."

DeRuyter looked to Chief Steward Taylor, who seemed to want to crawl into a hole—except for her deathly fear of confined spaces. Normally Heidi was relentlessly upbeat in font of Taylor, not for fear of reprimand, but because she could not bring herself to add to the worries making this woman a nervous wreck. What was the point? Now wild accusations tumbled out of her. "That is abetting in a highjacking, and murder . . ."

DeRuyter sighed. "No. It is just good operating sense."

"Good operating sense?" It was her turn to be taken aback.

He glanced at Taylor. "Of course we knew the slaver was coming. It is our business to track their movements. Orion Lines has to know what the slavers are up to."

"But a warning . . ."

"Would have done the freighter no good," DeRuyter assured her. "And it would have let the slavers know we had cracked their command and control codes—endangering our passengers."

Taylor hurried to back him, seeing the line to hide behind. "This is a rough corner of the universe, and we cannot afford to put our passengers at risk."

"There are no innocents out here," DeRuyter added. "Class-C robo-freighters do not carry passengers; these were smugglers, ring rats—all aboard were breaking the law."

Even the Chimps? "But you did not have to broadcast it, turning terror and hijacking into a sideshow."

"We are just reporting events as they happen," DeRuyter replied, making it sound like a public service, "nothing illegal in that." It's never a good sign when superiors insist your job does not technically break the law. "Our passengers pay to see stars up close. Edit out the bad parts, and they might as well stay at home."

"We cannot sugarcoat the cosmos," Taylor added staunchly. Strong sentiments from a woman who turned her cabin into a tree house. "Our broadcast will be evidence, to be used against the slavers when they are brought to justice."

Fat chance of that. Heidi stared at them. There was more to it than this. Way more. What was a slaver doing hijacking some two-bit ring runner? Right when *Artemis* happened to be there? That could hardly be coincidence. But it was pointless to tell that to Chief Steward Taylor, who feared the forest, only wanting to see the tops of the trees. She and DeRuyter were dismissed.

Outside, Taylor's treetops vanished, replaced by S-deck's simulation of starry night in the Street of Dreams on Bliss. Happy holos gyrated atop glass and neon fun-palaces, dancing to low pulsing music that made you yearn to move with it. Laughter and squeals of delight came from the pleasure arcades—some of them real. DeRuyter seized her arm in his light authoritative grip. He was not just her superior, but was also bigger and stronger, looking down on her figuratively as well as literally—but she could not help being small, or having pink hair. "Listen," he told her, "no one likes what happened to that robo-freighter."

Heidi glared up at him. Really? She could see he secretly loved it, feeling the excitement in his grip. Just talking about it turned him on. Her job was knowing people's pleasures, and DeRuyter was an easy read. Somehow he was in with the slavers—most likely paying the *Hiryu* to put on a show. Perhaps helping to set up the target. Why else would a high-g slaver snatch up some random ring runner? Hijacking and kidnapping were capital offenses, not done for nothing. Nor was it bad advertising—contrasting Orion Lines immunity to the pitiful fate of the ring runner. Taylor was clearly out of the loop, lacking the nerve for illegal deals with psychotic criminals.

"Technically you are tops," her boss told her, his fingers feeling her flesh beneath the fabric. "But you lack the killer instinct to make it big—luckily, I could teach you." His hand pulled her closer to him. "You and I could take some downtime together, making your job a whole lot easier."

Instead of trying to shake off his hand, Heidi gave him her sweetest smile, asking, "Why don't I just sue you and Orion Lines for harassment? Then I would not need a job."

Fingers froze, and his hand dropped. "Consider yourself relieved of duty—until we get a replacement from Typhon."

"Consider yourself one awfully sick fuck." Heidi had nothing to lose now by saying it out loud.

TOURIST TRAP

MIDWATCH 00:00:01
Elliptical orbit inside Typhon's Roche Limit

Faced with unemployment, Heidi summoned up a five-star virtual vacation, courtesy of Orion Lines, assuming they would buy out her contract and strand her on Typhon, letting her sue in the local courts—with scant chance of winning. Until then she rated the pampering given starship personnel "on leave." Putting *Artemis* out of her head, she made herself a Martian princess in full sensesurround, suppressing her conscious memory, so she thought she *was* Queen Heidi of Helium, trimmed in silk and gold, and ruling half a planet; looking forward to long lazy Martian days aboard her personal aerial barge, sailing where she willed, doing as she wished, righting wrongs and throwing parties at whim, without fear of consequences—the ideal balm for her frayed nerves and bruised psyche.

She began with a midair masked ball under strange stars, sending long-lost music throbbing through the hot Martian night, mostly ancient mambo tunes along with "Light My Fire" by the Doors. At midnight—in the midst of the wild unmasking to the beat of "Devil in Disguise"—a single-seat flier streaked out of the night, slipping past her picket ships, pulling even with the bridge of her pleasure barge. Spotlights illuminated a bronzed young warlord in battle leather at the controls, his longsword hanging at his waist. Coolly Queen Heidi—whom everyone knew by her pink hair—doffed her black feathered mask and asked the intruder's business.

Leaping boldly from the deck of his little flier to the torchlit bridge of her flagship, the warrior landed at her feet, going deftly down on one knee. Amazon guards moved to protect her, but she stayed them with her hand. "We fear not him, nor his news. Speak your tidings."

Looking insolently up at his Queen, the smug young warlord replied, "EMER-GENCY ABOARD *ARTEMIS*—ALL LEAVES CANCELLED."

Heidi sat up in her isolation tank, sirens wailing around her. Something horrible had happened, really horrible. She sensed it before she knew the details. Jerking out the contacts, she sprang out of the tank, tuning into the comnet as she dressed. Disaster had engulfed *Artemis*, so swift and deadly she could hardly believe it had happened. Intruders controlled the hangar level—she saw tripod cyborgs firing with turret heads and throwing gas grenades with tentacle arms, clearing a path for SuperCats with assault lasers.

Slavers obviously, lots of them. But how? Checking traffic control she saw the *Hiryu* was still half a million klicks off, but closing rapidly, preceded by the gig that boarded the robo-freighter. *Artemis* was docked with nothing more dangerous than her own atmosphere-launch, returning tourists from Fantasy Island on Oceania. Only these tourists were shooting their way through the hangar deck, heading for the drop shafts and the starship's hollow center, totally overwhelming ship security, whose training was more for drunk passengers and petty pilfering. That slavers had seized the launch and docked it with an unsuspecting *Artemis* proved they had penetrated the onboard systems, "compromising" DeRuyter's precious codes. Traffic control showed three naval corvettes insystem, the nearest a mere fifty hours away—leaving her very much on her own.

She ran through her options, finding them amazingly few. Moments ago she was a pampered princess, facing nothing worse than a hefty severance check and a chance to sue Orion Lines for harassment. Now she was no longer a princess, nor even an employee, but a victim-to-be, watching her murderers spread through the ship. Hall cams showed Orion Lines personnel being shot on sight, their pleas for mercy cut off in midsentence. Anyone who could use ship systems against the slavers was doomed. Facing multiple death sentences themselves, slavers were utterly ruthless, solely concerned with not getting caught.

So was she—only it was not possible. Command and power decks were already in slaver hands; so were the hangar-deck lifeboats and landers, leaving no way off the ship. Having sealed in their prey, slavers were moving out from the hollow core of the starship, hunting for passengers cowering in the staterooms, while methodically murdering the crew. Within minutes she would be looking over the sights of a slaver weapon, waiting for the guy to fire. Somehow she needed to stay his trigger finger. But how? Plugging in, she frantically searched for reasons why this bastard should not shoot her. Why would a slaver let a potential witness live?

Money most obviously. Summoning up her personnel file, Heidi used editorial override to make drastic changes. First making herself a passenger, terminating her precarious employment permanently—she was never more happy firing anyone, nor being fired. Next she gave herself money, staggering amounts of money, plus stock options, interstellar securities, and a grandmother on the board of Orion Bank. Sparing no expense she made herself worth a monumental ransom, giving her the satisfaction of knowing any slaver who shot her would be spaced by his infuriated comrades—though she hoped for better than that.

What else? Perhaps a saintly past? Vast charities dependent on her, and her alone. Slavers were not impressed by good conduct. Reminded of her past, she hastily knocked ten years off her age. Could she pass for that? She had better, because slavers were notoriously picky, seldom taking anyone over twenty, never over thirty.

Jumping up, she began furiously redoing her hair. She kept her pink hair pinned back, partly to compensate for the color. Nothing could be done about the color, but she let it down, teasing it out, trying to look young and stupid—a ghastly joke, after years of aching to be taken seriously. Through the open channel, she saw mayhem coming closer, deck by deck, while she hurriedly did her hair. What an idiot way to spend her last moments!

When she had her hair half-right, she ransacked her wardrobe for the matching outfit, something to pass off as billionaire shipboard wear. Anything with Orion Lines on it went straight to DISPOSAL along with any incidental proofs of gainful employment. Slavers reached her deck, and began moving through the suites, shooting anyone who resisted, or just did not look overly useful. Swiftly she settled on her best handmade top, a sporty skirt and matching shoes, set off by expensive bits of jewelry, rich but casual, with a touch of spoiled brat. Switching to pale white lipstick and nails, she added to that fresh and confused look, adorably clueless—or so she hoped. Changing identity was at best temporary, meant to get her through the next hour or two alive. Sooner or later the slavers would see through it—if only because she had no grandmother at Orion Bank eager to pay her ransom. They might tumble to it sooner if they searched coded files she could not change. Then what? She shivered.

With slavers outside her suite, Heidi retreated to the Court of Lions with its hot sun and cool fountain, where she had cried when she saw them take the ring runner. What a fool, bawling like a baby, pitying those "poor unfortunates" while steadfastly refusing to take their last dying lessons to heart, totally sure of her superiority. How could their dismal fate possibly apply to her? Now she would find out. Calling up a chair, she sat casually staring into the illusionary forest of Romanesque columns hiding the suite door. Water splashed onto wet stone behind her as she waited. 00:21:13 Not bad. Get out of this alive, and she would market the twenty-minute make-over.

Seeing a flash of tawny fur among the columns, she tensed. Here it comes. Forcing herself to smile, she cursed the unfairness of this. Please, not me—I do not want to die. What did I do? But she knew the answer. Ghastly as it sounds, she asked to be here, snapping at the chance to shill for Orion Lines, gladly obeying superiors she knew to be hapless idiots—so long as she was paid. When she found out they were in with slavers, she virtuously quit, going on mental vacation, trusting Orion Lines to see her safely to Typhon. This was the result.

3V illusion made the slaver seem to step from behind a column, appearing in the midst of the virtual colonnade. He was two meters tall and covered in tawny fur beneath his battle armor, with a cat-like face, luminous amber eyes, little round ears, and big curving upper canines that came down past his chin. He walked upright on humanoid legs and pawed feet. Supercat. *Homo smilodon.* SuperCats combined human and cat DNA, and were created millennia ago for situations needing brutal intimidation—for which this easily qualified. Beneath the fur and teeth he was nearly human, with some cat characteristics, like the tendency to play with prey, and total indifference to human sexuality—normal SuperCat males were only aroused by female SuperCats in heat. Clothes, lipstick, and her new hairdo meant nothing to him. He gave her a saber-toothed grin, humanoid hands holding an assault laser pointed at her midriff, his finger on the firing stud. "Hello, human. Are you Heidi van der Graf?"

Yes or no? Which answer would get her killed? Had this SuperCat seen her absurdly magnified resume, or was he working off some stolen crew list? Cheerfully shooting anyone answering, "Yes." Forcing herself to look into his amber eyes, and not down the muzzle of his assault laser, she smiled back brainlessly. "Guilty as charged."

So would she be executed for it? His toothy smile widened, hopefully a good sign. He cocked his cat-like head toward the door, saying, "Come with me."

Taking this as a temporary reprieve, she rose and strolled to the door, the laser muzzle never leaving her midriff. 3V was off and blood-flecked bulkheads replaced the green pine forest. Struggling to stay in character, she stepped over the bodies of people she knew, pretending they were hapless strangers—Katie from kid-care lay alongside a cute comtech named Liam. Holding in her tears, she acted like she only feared bloodying her shoes—luckily it is easy to convince a SuperCat that you are just a walking hairdo. Most corpses wore Orion Line uniforms, but she saw live passengers, horrified and helpless, sitting in terrified silence while the slavers sorted through their catch, deciding who to keep and who to discard. Herding her into a drop shaft, the SuperCat took her to an A-deck suite with the 3V turned off, an ironic combination of gold-striped beach umbrellas shading hand-woven hammocks hanging from bare bulkheads—showing the ship beneath *Artemis'* silken skin.

Prodded at gunpoint into a posh dining nook with the 3V still on, she suddenly stood on a wide arc of sunlit beach, fringed with palms, with three gaudy-striped cabanas spaced around a luau pit and a huge carved driftwood bench. Tall dark wooden tikis marked the high water line. Sitting on the driftwood and in the sand nearby were some of the most salable passengers, people Heidi knew at once—all A-deck, all good for megacredits. Sonya Hart, a favorite feelie star, her face instantly familiar. Anna Lu, twenty-something co-founder of Dawn Systems. Victoria MacEvoy, an Orion Lines owner's teenage trophy wife, holding his two-year-old heir. And the remains of the Talik family, owners of a huge health-care cartel on Aesir II, a teenage heir and several smaller children. Next to them sat another truncated family, this time the youngest wife, and two small boys belonging to senior wives, both biotech heirs—throughout the trip the family had shunned the new young wife, now the two small scared survivors clung to their hated stepmother for comfort.

Hunched on a rattan beach chair by herself, arms hiding her breasts, was Megan Kalojanovec, the hired girlfriend to the trigger-happy A-deck sadist, still wearing nothing but black nails and lipstick. Simulated sea breeze raised tiny goose pimples on Megan's bare white flesh. Making a weird little tableau, with everyone else dressed in elegant pajamas and evening wear. Despite the sun and sand, it was early in the midnight watch, reminding Heidi of a childhood poem:

> The sun was shining on the sea, shining with all its might . . . and this was odd, because it was the middle of the night. . . .

Kids sitting in the sand sang out, "Hi Heidi!," knowing her by her pink hair and the shows she put on, and the cheerful way she answered questions. Thank heaven kids are tough, and used to getting guff from adults. Cautiously the oldest Talik asked, "Heidi, what's happening?"

Scared faces looked to her, women and kids, expecting the worst, but hoping to hear better. Armed SuperCats stood by the cabana that hid the door to the suite, but no one asked them anything. Sonya Hart had been crying. Victoria MacEvoy looked angry. Anna Lu studied her intently. None of them knew Heidi's fancy new identity—to them she represented Orion Lines, the voice of authority, a slim hope in a world gone horribly wrong. She decided to get past the obvious bad news. "We have been captured by Eridani slavers. *Artemis* is totally in their hands. Our nearest hope of rescue is fifty hours away."

That last at least was news, and faces around the firepit fell even further. "What do they want?" asked Anna Lu, who had made billions building and promoting Dawn Systems, blithely dictating terms to Orion Bank and system-wide governments. How hard a sell could these slavers be?

"You are all worth a lot of credit," she reminded them hopefully. "Families and corporations will pay well for our safe return."

Which provoked a flood of further questions. "How long will that take? What about the rest of our family? Where are the men? What about my dad? Where is my mother?"

Heidi lied, "I do not know." Her best guess was that they were dead, or currently being murdered, but she would not say it. Not in front of the children. Anna Lu understood, sitting back eyeing her coolly, trying to separate hard fact from hopeful fiction. Lu had two male partners, older and less shapely, but nearly as rich. Neither was here.

"What about me?" asked Megan softly, sitting naked by herself, chewing busily on a black fingernail. Tears had made a mess of her heavy mascara. "I am Ms. Nobody. My boyfriend had credit—he offered them tons of it—but they shot him anyway."

And Megan had to watch. Heidi nodded silently, not wanting at all to go there. She had painted as pretty a picture as possible for these terrified passengers—sure folks were dying around them, but they would all be fine, sent home for whopping ransoms. That was her job, keeping the customers happy, or at least not hysterical. But Megan was right, why had they not shot her? Maybe they would? At any moment slavers might rectify the mistake—but Heidi doubted it. They would keep Megan for reasons Heidi did not want to think about, bringing up all the unsavory stories about slavers and their victims. The rest of them were in desperate denial, hiding behind megacredit fortunes—but not Megan, and not her.

"No one has been shot," snapped Victoria MacEvoy, as if Megan were a naughty child. Which sounded especially absurd since Vicky MacEvoy was younger than Megan, wearing garish silk pajamas that matched her toddler's—making her own child look like a fashion accessory.

Megan stared open-mouthed at the trophy wife in her mom-and-toddler pajamas, while hologram gulls wheeled nosily overhead. Blood was smeared halfway down the rent-a-girlfriend's bare white thigh.

Young Mrs. MacEvoy shook her head violently, her voice high and hysterical. "No one shot your so-called boyfriend. No one at all has been shot."

Megan rolled black-ringed eyes, "Listen Lollypop, I saw it hap . . ."

"Nonsense," the trophy wife snorted. "How much are you paid to sit there naked, telling lies to scare people?"

"Not near enough." Megan stared out to sea, giving up trying to enlighten her betters.

"People have been shot," Heidi insisted with soft certainty, having stepped over the bodies herself—mere remembering made her gag. "But please be quiet about it." She nodded towards the children.

"Ridiculous," Victoria MacEvoy would not be mollified, "I demand you end this virtual amusement at once." Virtual amusement? Is that what wacky Vicky thought this was? Anything this horrible had to be 3V. Heidi sympathized, wishing to heaven she could stop it just by flipping channels. "If you will not," the owner's wife declared, "I demand to speak to your supervisor."

Good luck. Her superiors had been hunted down like vermin, so she could easily be senior surviving crew member. Heidi blandly declared, "I have no superiors." Not any more.

"Absurd!" Vicky MacEvoy denounced the whole mad business. "I demand to see your immediate supervisor at once."

Paying customers get their way, especially rich demanding ones. As if in answer, SuperCats propelled Chief Signalsmate Marten DeRuyter out of a cabana into their midst, hands bound, and ashen-faced. Women and kids shrank back. Heidi did not blame them, DeRuyter looked a mess; everyone was scared, but he was absolutely petrified, standing out horribly in his Orion Lines uniform, the only adult male present, unless you counted SuperCats. "Thank Heavens!" Seeing the uniform, Vicky MacEvoy clapped her hands. "Now you must end this charade."

DeRuyter stared blankly at his boss's young wife, not knowing what charade he must end. All Heidi could think was her grandmother's saying, "He who sups with the devil had best use a long spoon." DeRuyter had been so sure he was using the slavers, while they were really using him—dooming all of them to this living hell. Heidi had thought DeRuyter comfortably dead, and had mixed feelings about his stumbling back from the grave, however briefly.

Before the conversation could get more confused, a hologram flickered to life— standing in the sand was an armed slaver, the same confident cheerful hoodlum with dark tousled hair that Heidi had seen aboard the robo-freighter. *Homo galactus.* He wore his uniform jacket closed, covering his dragon tattoo, but the bracelet of skulls still showed on his wrist. She was not the least pleased to see him again, even in holo-gram from, but DeRuyter's face lit up and he asked hopefully, "Hess?"

"How happy to see you." Hess clicked his virtual heels. "And you too, ladies." He bowed jauntily to his audience on the driftwood bench. Hess exuded a creepy gen-uineness, though speed-of-light lag made his speech and movements seem overly for-mal, full of restrained eagerness. Despite the distance, Heidi could tell Hess was indeed indecently happy to see them, since they represented a job well done, leaving him scant reason to complain. Turning to DeRuyter, he declared, "It has been an ab-solute delight doing business."

"Thank you." DeRuyter looked hopeful, not the least embarrassed by having been in business with the people who massacred his shipmates. True evil easily trumped blustering incompetence, making DeRuyter grateful for any hint of mercy. "Thank you, so very much . . ."

Hess waved his thanks aside. "Alas, our business is now at an end—but a suitable parting gratuity will be deposited in your name with Orion Bank."

"That is hardly necessary." DeRuyter smiled faintly, not wanting anything con-necting him to this catastrophe, least of all slaver credit at Orion Bank.

"It is a done thing," Hess insisted. "You need only name an heir."

DeRuyter looked shocked. "Why?"

"Because otherwise the credit will go to Orion Bank." Hess grinned at Heidi— showing he had seen her phony file—then he signaled to the SuperCats, saying, "Do it in the next room." Not until the Cats grabbed him did DeRuyter realize what Hess meant, then he begged for his life as they dragged him kicking across the sand into the cabana that masked the suite's master stateroom—there his cries were silenced. Hess turned happily to the horrified women and children. "Now we can get better ac-quainted. Commander Hess of the *Hiryu*, at your service."

Gulls screeched in reply, but no one on the driftwood said a word, watching the SuperCats saunter out of the cabana. Heidi had never seen people so scared of a holo— especially a handsome smiling one—even Vicky MacEvoy took this hologram Com-mander Hess for the real thing, holding her little boy tighter. Looking away, Heidi saw beach and sea stretching in both directions, oppressive in its lying openness—the only real exit was through the cabanas, as DeRuyter discovered. Being a pro herself, she had to say the wretched scene only lacked a pirate galleon waiting in the bay to carry off the losers. Getting no volunteers, Hess asked politely, "Anna Lu?"

Slowly the Dawn Systems director rose to her feet, turning out to be tall, with dark wide-set eyes, high cheekbones, a *café au lait* complexion, and raven hair hang-ing to the waist of her handsewn jacket. "I am she."

"But of course," Hess bowed, thoroughly enjoying his courteous charade, "you are rightly famous. We use your micro-programming on the *Hiryu*, whenever we can steal it. Will you come with me?" he indicated the smaller cabana, next to the one DeRuyter was in.

Anna Lu nodded, walking purposely across the sand, letting the door close behind her. Taking his leave, Commander Hess followed, strolling right through the cabana wall. Heidi sat down on the driftwood bench beside the Talik kids, waiting silently, staring out at wavetops sparkling under the midnight sun, remembering the rest of the poem; it was the "Walrus and the Carpenter" from *Through the Looking Glass*, which used to scare her when she was small, thinking of the poor little oysters being eaten alive. Now it pretty much petrified her, sitting under the midnight sun on a make-believe beach, guarded by a SuperCat who made a grim walrus with his tan fur and gleaming white tusks:

"I weep for you," the Walrus said. "I deeply sympathize."
With sobs and tears he sorted out, those of the largest size. . . .

Her forgotten fear had suddenly reached up out of childhood, becoming a relentless horror consuming her real life.

Anna Lu appeared at the cabana door stepping barefoot back onto the sand, no longer wearing silk slippers or her hand-sewn, jacket, just her red sheath dress. Without moving her head, the Dawn Systems director rolled her dark eyes, as if to say, "Bad, but it could have been worse."

Heidi knew what she meant. Holo Commander Hess emerged from the cabana wall, looked them over, then casually asked for, "Heidi van der Graf?"

Her turn. She stood up, thinking, "This is it." Fool Hess, or die. As she walked nervously towards the cabana, another line from the poem popped into her head:

"A pleasant walk, a pleasant talk, Along the briny beach . . ."

She shivered, remembering how the slaver's hands felt, finding that microseam in the ring runner's bulkhead. Hess would be looking her over for lies just as carefully.

3V was off inside, turning the cabana into bare bulkheads and a float-a-bed. Jerking people in and out of 3V was standard interrogation technique, shaking your hold on reality, or in her case unreality. Determined not to be rattled, she shed all her training, "being" a brainless passenger, a granddaughter of Orion Bank, born to privilege, currently enduring the worst rudeness in her pampered existence. Seeing Anna Lu's slippers and jacket lying on the deck, she reached down, scooping up the silk jacket on impulse, ostentatiously trying it on as Hess stepped out of the wall. "What do you think?" Sticking her hands in the pockets, she turned slowly to model the too big jacket, looking as clueless as she could. "Neat, huh?"

Hess grinned, "It goes with your hair." Until the gig made contact, Hess could only be there in hologram, so he was taking his time, savoring his success. "Now take it off."

Shrugging off the jacket, she let it drop to the deck. Hess nodded, still smiling, "Do not stop."

Giving her most petulant look, she asked, "What do you mean?"

"Pray continue to undress," Hess explained. "Unless you prefer being stripped by SuperCats?"

Probably—but her best chance was to cooperate. Pouting visibly, she kicked off her shoes, loosened the matching skirt, then let it fall, closing her eyes and telling herself she was in an empty room, with Hess thousands of klicks away, unable to touch her. When she was done, she stood with eyes shut, arms folded across her breasts, reducing Hess to a creepy synthesized voice. He told her, "Jewelry too." She dropped earrings, rings, and an anklet onto the clothes and shoes. Hess thanked her. "So the hair is a natural pink. Is it hereditary?"

"Gene-splice generations ago." Heaven knows why, someone wanted a pink-haired baby. "Grandma's was pink too, before it went white."

Hess ignored her pretended tie to Orion Bank—a weird sort of slaver compliment, showing he cared more for who she was than who she claimed to be. Orion Lines had taught Heidi that ransom was a sideline for slavers, there being safer ways to earn a living than hijacking starships. People were what slavers wanted—they just liked them valuable as well. People were among the rarest things in Human Space, and easily the most useful. Interstellar distance and Universal Human Rights made the usual means of human exploitation harder—so civilized society employed bio-constructs like SuperChimps and SuperCats. Slavers went for a simpler solution to the shortage of humans, taking the ones that looked most promising for ransom, re-sale, bioengineering, spare parts or mere personal amusement. Pink hair might easily mean more to Hess than an imaginary megacredit ransom. "You are lying about something, or at least holding back," Hess observed, not saying how he knew—if he had thought she was crew, he would likely have her killed her at once, pink hair or no. "Why are your eyes closed?"

"Embarrassed," she admitted. That much was true, she did not like being naked in front of some strange slaver, even one thousands of klicks away.

"Are you really twenty-two?" Hess asked.

"Last April," she lied cheerfully, imagining Hess scrutinizing her body, glad for once to be small in all senses of the word. "Just big for my age"—another arrant lie.

"Open your eyes," Hess ordered. She obeyed, finding him right in front of her, asking a question she especially feared, "Why was your suite not on A-deck?"

Fortunately, she took a passenger cabin to stay close to her audience, but her digs were not at all A-deck. Shrugging nude shoulders, she acted like she could have any cabin on the Artemis, and chose to go slumming. "I wanted to have fun?"

"We shall try to oblige," Hess grinned and bowed. "Dress please—just the top and skirt, leave the shoes and jewelry."

"Why?" she asked stubbornly, hiding her relief by being miffed, acting like she never heard arbitrary orders before.

"You will not be needing them," Hess explained evenly. She did not have the nerve to ask why not, dressing silently instead. As she left the cabana, Hess stepped through the wall to call out. "Sonya Hart?"

Sonya Hart got up off the driftwood and headed for the door, arching an eyebrow as they passed. "Tough audition?"

Nodding, she gave the feelie star's hand a squeeze. "Knock him dead."

Back to the beach. Anna Lu was gone, and Megan too, leaving only young wives and little kids waiting on the illusionary sand spit. Before she could ask what happened, SuperCats closed in, escorting her through the entrance cabana to a drop shaft. She tried to tell herself, "This is good. Really good." Had they meant to kill her, they would not be taking this trouble. Dropping to the hangar deck, the SuperCats led her to a cargo box, unsealing the container and telling her to get in. She balked at the sight of the six-cubic-meter box, barely coming up to her breast, but it was impossible to argue with several armed SuperCats. Getting down, she crawled into the container, still telling herself—this is good.

Megan was already inside, doubled up naked in one corner, blinking at the light. Heidi picked the opposite corner and settled in, saying, "Glad do see you."

SuperCats sealed the box, shutting out the light. Megan laughed dryly in the dark. "Come on, Pink Hair, do you never go off duty? No one could pay me to be so perky."

No mean compliment considering Megan's chosen profession. "But I am glad," Heidi protested. "I was afraid you were dead."

Megan snorted in disgust, "This is not what I call living."

Too true. Still, Heidi had her hopes, but she was not about to spill them out loud. Slavers had centuries of experience with prisoners, and the box could easily be wired for sound. She and Megan were clearly doubtful cases, possibly put together to hear what they would say. She asked what happened to Anna Lu. "Saw her go into a lifeboat," Megan sounded jealous. "We are the ones they have doubts about."

Anna Lu made billions before she was twenty, and now was the first one off *Artemis* alive—it did hardly seem fair. She reminded Megan, "We're not dead yet."

"No, we have that to look forward too." Megan was not about to be cheered. Heidi barely blamed her—now they could both sue Orion Lines for megabucks. Too bad the settlement would not set them free. "Admit it," Megan demanded bitterly, "we're screwed."

"Nothing new to you," Heidi observed tartly.

Another laugh came out of the dark, and a bare foot kneaded hers. "Pink, I'm way proud of you. You said something mean!"

"Been trying to broaden myself." Resting her head against the wall of the box, Heidi closed her eyes and opened her mind, tapping into the shipboard channels. Not much. Computers were locked down tight, virtually shut off. Nor could she contact any crew members through transceiver chips or biophones. Here or there she encountered a wired-in slaver, and steered clear, careful not to set off mental alarms. Plainly she was the only one left. She thought about Chief Steward Taylor with her claustrophobia; killing Taylor was a mercy compared to stuffing her in this box. But Taylor must have been really scared. She started crying for the first time since catastrophe stuck; who would have thought it would be over her Chief Steward?

Megan heard her sobbing and anxiously apologized, "Hey, Pink, I'm sorry. Look, I know I got a mouth. We're not going to die, we'll get out of this, you'll see, somehow . . ."

"No, no," she sniffled, feeling like an idiot. "It's nothing you said."

"What are you crying for then?" Megan asked—making her the first person in all this who wanted to know how *she* felt. Unless you counted Hess.

"For an ex-boss," she sighed and wiped her eyes, feeling the tears subside.

"Must have been a good one," Megan ventured.

"Nope, pretty lousy," she admitted, but she cried for her anyway.

Megan took her hand in the dark. "Yea, I know how that is." Megan's former employer had been no pearl himself, and Megan ruined her mascara over him.

Lacing her fingers into Megan's, she tried again, determined not to be sucked down a black hole of hopelessness. Giving up on the onboard systems, she sorted through signals between slaver ships, mostly in codes she had no time to break. She tried tapping into the ships themselves, searching out open systems, or breaks in encryption. Nothing. Slaver defenses were way better than they had any right to be, giving her no access to onboard systems. She could see how DeRuyter was so easily suckered.

Suddenly she was in, hitting an uncoded transceiver. At first she thought she was in some slaver's head chip, getting audio-visuals from the auditory and optical systems—but a closer look at the visuals showed that whoever's head she was in had thin girl's legs, baby-strapped to an acceleration couch so she could not reach the buckles.

Pulling out, she backtracked the contact, finding it came from a docking slaver, the same *Hiryu* gig that boarded the ring runner—that made this the little blonde girl with the blue trim, that Hess pulled from hiding. Slipping in again, she saw the gig through the girl's eyes, heard through her ears. She was looking silently forward, watching the slaver at the controls, following his movements as he guided the gig into contact with *Artemis*. Heidi realized the girl was memorizing the controls and docking sequence, making sure she could fly the gig if she ever got the chance. Good girl. Deciding to see how far she could push the contact, she tried signaling the girl. ("Hi, my name is Heidi. Can you hear me?")

"What in hell?" Visuals blurred as the girl's head whipped around, giving Heidi a quick view of slavers and SuperCats packed into the gig like some bizarre armed tour group. Seeing no one near her, the girl's gaze turned back to the slaver at the controls.

Heidi tried again. ("Do you hear me?")

"Shit, yes!" This time the head did not twitch.

("Shush, shush, please!") She had to keep the girl from attracting attention. ("Don't shout. I'm in your head.")

"No shit!" Settling deeper into the couch, the girl whispered, "Who are you?"

("My name is Heidi, and I want to help you. Do not say anything, wink your right eye for yes, your left for no. Are you the girl from the ring runner they hijacked?")

The girl winked right.

("Good. What's your name?") She forgot that was not a yes or no question. But the girl was ready; unsealing her sleeve, she ran her thumbnail under the initial letter of her creche ID, K-9251949.

("Kay? Is that what you are called?")

Another wink yes. Her nickname had been "Pooch."

("So were you crew on that ring runner?") Heidi remembered how the girl eyed the gig controls.

Pursing her lips, the girl whispered, "Pilot."

("Perfect! Could you fly this thing if we got you to the controls?")

Wink yes.

("Great. We must wait for our moment, so keep this contact open. Okay?")

Two emphatic winks yes.

As the gig docked with *Artemis*, Heidi tapped back into the hangar-deck cams, watching more slavers come aboard. Hess led, arrogant as ever, and in the flesh this time—bad news there. He would be a hundred times as hard to fool in person. Kay was with them, looking small amid the men and SuperCats, walking silently, staring straight ahead from beneath blue-trimmed Dutch-girl bangs. She was led across the hangar to a lifeboat, and slavers ordered her inside. Heidi signaled her. ("Outstanding! Stay aboard that boat if you can—it means they are going to keep you.") She saw Kay smile and look around; then the hatch closed, cutting off her view—the lifeboat was not a part of *Artemis*, and she could not access its onboard systems directly. Could she get Kay to plug into them? Probably. Then what? She called up a deck plan of the lifeboat, then settled back to think, sorting through options, trying to put a plan together.

Bright light stabbed at her. Shading her eyes, she saw SuperCats had opened the box, telling her to get out—which she did. As she squeezed past Megan, their gaze met for a moment and she tried to think what to say. Megan's black lips curved into a rueful smirk. "Hey Pink, in case I do not see you later, this cruise has been a real pleasure."

"Thanks," she returned Megan's wan smile, "we try to please."

Taking that as her motto, she followed the SuperCats to a vacant casino bar on the lounge deck. Almost vacant, Hess was at the auto-bar, happily holding a bottle of 200-year-old whisky up to the light. Empty casinos always seem menacing—this one more than most—holos hung frozen and lifeless over gaming machines set to suck the credit out of whoever dared enter. Hess nodded at a slate black poly-carbon sofa across from him, telling the SuperCats, "Put her there, then leave." They obeyed and she sat surveying the sinister-looking lounge, finding it pleasantly corpse-free. Bringing over a pale pink drink, Hess told her, "Here, this is to match your hair." She tried to protest, but he insisted, "Please, I want you to relax."

Really? You are going about it dead wrong—Hess was in fact scaring her senseless. Taking the drink, she held it uselessly in her lap. Pouring a shot of whisky, Hess sat down across from her, happily announcing, "You know I could have you brain-scanned." Always a catchy conversation starter. "But I want to hear you tell the truth willingly," Hess confided, "so I put something in your drink instead."

"What?" She looked aghast at her pink drink, which could contain anything—poison, brain parasites, and she would have to drink it.

"Nothing harmful," Hess assured her, "it will not kill you, nor even knock you out—it just lets you tell the truth."

"Why?" Especially when you will shoot me if I do?

"For your own good," Hess told her, leaning forward speaking earnestly. "Unless you are willing to trust me, you are useless to us. Which neither of us want."

And she had so hoped to be useful. "So drink," Hess told her, "or I will have it injected into you." Seeing she would not do it herself, Hess guided the glass to her lips. She sipped warily, feeling alcohol go straight to her head, her last meal having been a virtual feast on Mars. Megan was right, you could not keep up a perky pretense forever, not in the face of pure evil backed by brain-scans and truth drugs. Unbelievably weary of the whole sick charade, she wished she could tell someone, even Hess—but damn, they murdered every other crew member.

Reaching over, Hess traced her cheek with his finger. "This is the real thing, not a stitch of biosculpt. That makes you young and pretty, though not as young as you pretend. You cannot really be fabulously rich as well." Hess laughed, "Who is that lucky?" Anna Lu? Vicky MacEvoy? Having Hess inspect her for wrinkles did not make her feel lucky. It felt like the blind date from Hell, sitting in a turned-off casino lounge clutching her drugged drink, while her date tried to decide whether to take her home or kill her here.

"You are not really a granddaughter of Orion Bank—are you?" Hess asked casually, not looking the least upset at losing a megacredit ransom. She shrank back into the soft inflated sofa, hiding behind her glass, helpless terror rising inside her. Here it comes. He knows. Hess does not care about the ransom because he knows it is not real. He just wants to make sure, then he will kill me. Setting aside his own drink, Hess sympathized with her plight, "Come, you cannot lie forever—it slays the soul—I myself try to lie as little as possible. Having a life or death secret you can never tell must be terribly lonely?"

Horribly so. Hands shaking, Heidi nodded, not saying what she was admitting.

"There, is that not better?" Hess steadied her hands, lifting her drink to her white-painted lips, using that sweet reasonable paternal voice that implies you are childish to resist when you have no choice. "Here, a toast to the truth." Tears welled up as she sipped the pink drink, not feeling a whit better. Hess asked her, "Now, why did you lie?"

Throat frozen in fright, she could not speak, so Hess answered for her, "You lied to appear more valuable to us. Natural, understandable, no one can blame you. I would have done the same." Tears rolled down her cheeks, and she started to sob, not caring how it looked, just wanting the hellish business to be over—to be finished with fear and lies. She had not wanted any of this, not in the least.

Hess put his arm around her shoulder to comfort her. "You are crew aren't you? An Orion Lines employee?"

Unable to say words that would doom her, she brushed at her tears, staring up into his smug heartless face, sounding as hollow as a cheap voice chip, "Are you going to kill me?" That was all that mattered, and Heidi had to know, even if the answer was yes. "Please tell me."

Hess grinned heartily, "Why no. Not now anyway. I just wanted to hear the truth from you."

"Thank you, thank you . . ." Collapsing into his arms, she sobbed with relief, not caring that Hess was a monstrous slaver who murdered her boss, just utterly thankful that she was not going to die—not now at least.

"No, no, do not thank me." Hess laughed, patting her happily, "You can thank your hair." He signaled for the SuperCats, and she sat there with his arm around her, feeling like a sniveling fool, listening to him instruct the Cats. "This female is crew. Keep her away from everyone and everything, and put her back in the container alone—leave her nothing. Nothing at all. And keep the container sealed until we get to *Hiryu*."

He helped her courteously to her feet, asking, "The truth was not so bad, was it?"

Compared to what? Being shot right here and now? She supposed that was so. Wiping her eyes, she smiled as sweetly as she could, saying, "Next time I'll take the brain scan."

Hess grinned, bowed, and bid her good day, letting the SuperCats take her back to the box. What an absolute bastard! Hess positively relished attempts at resistance, so long as they were futile. Stripping in front of SuperCats is not near as bad as it sounds, since they are utterly uninterested, wearing nothing but combat armor themselves, over tawny fur that she still found wonderfully beautiful. Humans—clothed or unclothed— were all the same to them, to be killed or obeyed as occasion demanded. Unsealing the box, they helped her inside, then shut the container behind her, giving her less consideration than a cat gives a mouse. Humans were not even their normal prey.

Megan was gone, leaving a whiff of perfume behind, *fitnah*, an aphrodisiac scent made from mimosa blossoms. Heidi hoped that was not all that was left of her. For the first time since the madness started she was alone, in what passed for privacy, sealed in a cargo container on a doomed ship, about to be carried off by slavers. Saved by her hair color—what a colossal comedown. She should be happy, Hess could have taken tissue samples, but something convinced him to take her too, though he did not turn a credit on the deal. Not even Anna Lu could say that.

But saved for what? Slavers were going to own her, body and soul. Once aboard the *Hiryu*, she would give in totally, she could tell—she might sometimes fool others, but never herself. Had Hess even put anything in her drink? Probably not. Booze, sugar, pink froth, and the power of suggestion had her blubbering the truth to Hess. Faced with nothing worse than an empty casino lounge, she broke down totally, crying on his ghastly shoulder—absurdly grateful not to be murdered right away— stammering her thanks to Hess, just like DeRuyter did, with no guarantee she would not end up worse than him. What would it be like when they had drugs, sensory deprivation, brain-scrub, and the leisure to entirely break her? God, was she ever going to sue Orion Lines.

Something shook the box, then lifted it up. Hangar cams showed a smart-lift loading her into the the same lifeboat Kay went in, a lifting-body-shaped, gravity-drive lander, meant to evacuate passengers in emergencies—for which this certainly qualified. Slavers were using it to transfer their human catch to the *Hiryu*, and as soon as the hold sealed they lifted off. She called to Kay. ("Are you there?")

"Where else?" the girl asked under her breath, sitting in the lifeboat's main cabin amid the *Artemis* survivors. Anna Lu was in the seat ahead of Kay, with Megan beside her. Sonya Hart sat across the isle, with one of the little Talik boys on her lap—all of them baby-strapped to the seats. Guarding the cabin door was a SuperCat armed with stun grenades and a pair of riot pistols; hardly a promising picture, but they were headed for the *Hiryu* where things would only get worse.

("Good. I am in a sealed storage container in the hold below you. Check the arm rest of your seat, there should be an emergency connection, a small coil of superconducting filament stored in a recess on the underside . . .")

"Got it," Kay practically shouted, when a wink would have done as well.

("Quietly.") She repeated the word. ("Quietly, plug yourself in.")

Suddenly Heidi had total access to the lifeboat's onboard systems, lights, cams, seat controls, emergency exits, alarms, life support . . . Only the main controls were off limits, with the autopilot disabled and a SuperCat flying the boat manually. There were two cats aboard, the one in the cabin and another at the controls—but no other slavers. Seemingly sufficient for a cargo of unarmed women and children strapped into their seats, or stuffed in a box in the hold. She spoke softly to Kay. ("Listen, I am scared, really scared. I cannot let them get me on their ship . . .")

"No shit, Sheila," Kay hissed back. "I am not looking forward to turning fourteen aboard a slaver."

Kay was thoroughly afraid as well, Heidi could feel her fear through the link, making her own heart sink. She struggled to keep them from amplifying each other's terror, dragging themselves down into black despair. ("Quiet, please listen to me. Wink if you think you can pilot this boat.") Kay winked. ("There is a chance I can get you to the controls, so we can make a run for it. It is risky, and could get you killed.")

Kay's eyes rolled, as if to say, "Riskier than this?"

Heidi saw her point. Kay did not have a megacredit ransom on call either, and was rightly terrified about how she would be "useful" to the slavers. ("Wink if you want to do it.")

Kay winked twice.

Heidi took a deep breath and checked the cams. Hess was about to wish he put her box in a different boat. ("I am going to start by unlocking your seat. Do not leap up, or react, just be ready.")

Another wink. She unlocked Kay's harness, at the same time disabling the seat alarm, so the change would only show as an amber light on the main control board. Heidi also triggered the heat shield alarm and HOLD DECOMPRESSION, glaring red lights and angry wails claiming hull integrity was compromised—insuring the amber glow on the seat indicator panel got zero attention.

Spinning about, the SuperCat in the cabin dilated the door behind him, stepping into the suit locker, wedged between the control cabin and the main airlock—the lifeboat was built like tiny starship, collapsed into itself. Heaving up a hold access hatch, the SuperCat disappeared into the hold, where he started checking connections. Heidi signaled Kay. ("Go, now, get into a suit.")

Kay burst from her seat, diving past a shocked Anna Lu into the suit locker, where she struggled into the smallest suit she could find, cinching it tight. As soon as Kay unplugged from the couch, Heidi lost direct control, and had to call orders to Kay. ("Close and seal the hold hatch!")

Kay kicked the hatch shut with her boot, and locked it manually, sealing one SuperCat in the hold, at the same time pulling on her helmet one-handed, setting an indoor record for donning an over-sized suit. Heidi shouted to her. ("Now get to the co-pilot's couch! Then plug us in!") Closing the suit locker door behind her, Kay dilated the command cabin door, scrambled onto the empty co-pilot's couch and plugged herself in through a suit jack—putting Heidi back in charge.

Sitting up on the command couch, a startled SuperCat snarled in protest, drawing his riot pistol. "Human," he shouted, "return to your seat, or I will shoot."

Before the surprised SuperCat could fire, Heidi bypassed two fail-safes and hit PI-LOT EJECT. His seat oxygen tent inflated around him as the deck flipped up, flinging the pilot into Typhon orbit. Air rushed out of the cabin after him.

Sealing her half of the cabin, Kay cut the false alarms from the hold, shouting, "What now!" There was no need to whisper anymore, since they had the lifeboat—aside from one angry SuperCat prowling about below. Who fortunately had no reason to suspect that the cause of his troubles sat huddled in a nearby container. "Where do we go!"

("Take her down! Straight for Typhon.") Safety lay in the gas giant's cloud tops, beyond the great rings. Starships like *Hiryu* were not designed to land on gas giants, and any slaver landers would be overwhelmed by Typhon-bound craft as soon as they entered atmosphere.

"Hold on tight," Kay called to horrified passengers over the boat comnet, "We are under new management! This is your captain speaking, brace for high-g maneuvers." Ignoring shrieks of protest from the baby-strapped passengers, Kay whipped the boat about in a high-g turn, diving straight at Typhon's cloud tops, aiming to just shave the inner edge of the A-ring, shooting the gap in the rings swept out by Tartarus' gravity.

Calls came from all directions, jamming the net, Typhon traffic control, naval intelligence, outraged slavers, news networks, concerned strangers. Kay clung hard to the controls, talking only to Typhon Traffic, ignoring or deflecting all other calls. "Heidi," she shouted, "Hess is calling! Talk to him!"

Heidi made contact with the slaver back aboard *Artemis*. ("Commander Hess. How happy to speak to you again.") Especially at a distance.

Hess laughed. ("You were right, I should have had you brain-scanned.") Which would have turned up her implant.

("Tried to tell you. But I hope we can part friends.") Or at least very distant enemies.

("Would that we could. We have two Hellhound hi-g homing missiles with anti-matter warheads locked on you. Return at once.") Hess was not lying, traffic control showed the two missile separating from *Hiryu*, accelerating towards the lifeboat.

("Or what? You will kill me?") Like he killed Taylor, DeRuyter, and lord knows how many others. Anger flared up, now that she was free to speak. ("You would kill me either way. At least those Hellhounds will cost you billions in ransom.")

Hess sounded wounded. ("That is hardly fair, had I wanted to kill you, I would have done it already. Save me my ransom, and I swear I will let you live.")

She snorted. ("So you may keep me in a cell and harvest my eggs, to raise pink-haired babies to sell? Is that your absolute best offer?")

("Never fear, you have beaten me. Unfairly too, I might add, resorting to tears and lies. Women's weapons, but you wielded them well. Your performance in the lounge convinced me I had nothing to fear. Forgive me for underestimating you. Brain-scan would have been better, but I thought I did not need it, not with you at least. Had I taken even the minimal precaution of shipping you separately, we would not be having this conversation. So you and your little pilot are free to go, keeping your precious eggs and pink hair, just jettison the passenger section into Typhon orbit.")

("Then you would missile me for sure.") Dump her billionaire passengers and Hess would have no reason to hold fire.

("What? Waste missiles out of spite?") Hess sounded hurt again. ("Hardly. Dump the passenger module and you will halve your mass and double your acceleration ratio, easily beating any missile to Typhon. I am offering a simple trade, your life for my captives. You release your load and I recall the missiles. Acceleration and orbital mechanics will keep us both honest.")

Damn, Hess actually had a plan—the bastard. She had been playing for time, getting closer to Typhon's cloud tops, never thinking Hess would have a reasonable offer.

Heidi had underestimated the man again. She was not going back, that was for sure. But what of the others? Guess wrong and she would get them all killed. So what to do? Hold a vote? Hardly, but she could not just decide for them. Putting Hess on hold, she went on the lifeboat's comnet, telling the terrified passengers the good news first. ("We have seized this lifeboat, and are headed for safety on Typhon.") Feeble hurrahs came from the frightened passengers. ("But they have fired Hellhound missiles after us.") Gasps of horrified dismay. ("We will do our best to evade . . .")

"Get me to the command deck," Anna Lu demanded. Heidi released her at once, and the Dawn Systems director dashed into the command cabin.

Heidi continued. ("We will try to evade the missiles, but Commander Hess has promised to spare anyone who surrenders now—to be released when ransom is paid. Does anyone want to go back?")

No one said a word. Fairly remarkable for a group of frightened, angry, opinionated, and royally put-upon women—but there was absolutely no interest in returning to the hell they had miraculously escaped from. Live or die, no one wanted to go back. Heidi put a call through to Hess. ("Do not take this personally, but everyone aboard prefers Hellhound missiles to your hospitality.") Unless you counted the SuperCat in the hold.

("Personally? Perish the thought. Those Hellhounds you wanted are on the way—good luck Heidi.")

Always the gentleman. Sitting in the blackness of her cargo box, she switched to traffic control, watching the missiles come on, accelerating so rapidly the lifeboat seemed to stand still. Hess had not lied, the missiles were horribly fast. And less that 10K klicks away. Make that less than 9,000. 8,000. 7,000 . . .

Hellhounds had antimatter warheads designed to penetrate the lifeboat's shields. *Artemis* would have turned them aside easily, and sent something worse back, but the lifeboat could only run. And not all that swiftly.

"MISSILE IMPACT IN TWO MINUTES," announced the autopilot.

Switching to the command-deck cams, she saw Kay's head stuck into the Doppler hood, while Anna Lu crouched over the controls with a headset on, furiously reprogramming the lifeboat's energy shields for high density and sub-light speeds. Their lifeboat was not just a lander, but a mini-starship as well, with shields that withstood the rain of radiation at near light-speed. Anna was converting them to brush aside or annihilate smaller particles of ring material, while Kay prepared to dodge the bigger pieces, everything from eccentric ringlets to house-sized chunks of ring ice and mini-moonlets populating the A-ring gap "cleared" by Tartarus' gravity. If they even got to the gap.

Heidi went back to watching the Hellhounds come on; they were at 5,000 klicks, then 4,000, then 3,000 . . .

"MISSILE IMPACT IN ONE MINUTE," announced the helpful autopilot.

Horrified, Heidi called to Kay. ("We are never going to make the gap—they are gaining too fast!")

"No shit!" Kay shouted back. Without taking her head out of the Doppler hood Kay yelled to Anna Lu, "Program to avoid the moonlets, I'll dodge the smaller stuff."

"WARNING, 30 SECONDS TO MISSILE IMPACT," chimed in the autopilot.

Thirty seconds. What could she do? Her head chip answered back—null program. Nothing. She had done everything she could, staying alive, hiding her talents, picking her time, seizing the lifeboat, doing the absolutely impossible, and she was going to die anyway—the cosmos could be incredibly cruel to the unlucky.

"10 SECONDS TO MISSILE IMPACT."

G-forces threw her sideways, as the lifeboat did another high-speed turn. She called to Kay. ("What's happening?")

"Hang on to your toes," Kay shouted back. "We are going in."

"5 SECONDS TO MISSILE IMPACT."

("In where?") Heidi braced herself, back against one wall, feet against the other, hands pressed hard against the top of the box. Five fucking seconds—she could not believe it.

"Into the ring." Kay plunged the lifeboat into the broad flat A-ring, actually a vast array of frozen particles streaming in parallel orbits around Typhon, everything from micron-sized hail to great ice boulders and little moonlets. Shields flared bright with burning particles, while pebble-sized pieces burst like flashing sparks within the fiery corona.

"2 SECONDS TO MISSILE IMPACT."

Heidi saw the klicks tumble as the missiles streaked towards her—50 klicks, then 30, 20, 10 . . .

Hundreds of thousands of klicks across, the rings were only a few hundred meters thick, paper-thin by cosmic standards. Bursting out the far side, the lifeboat tore on towards Typhon—blowing ring material in all directions. Still the Hellhounds came on. Heidi watched in horror as the twin missiles streaked closer, coming within 5 klicks, then 4, 3, 2 . . .

Both missiles struck the A-ring, instantly exploding in huge flashes of radiation that washed harmlessly over the lifeboat. Hellhounds had only rudimentary shields, and antimatter warheads were useless against high-speed particles and the relentless hail of ring material. Heidi gave a cheer, hidden in her dark box. Anna Lu answered her. Kay was still glued to the Doppler, dodging errant swarms of ring ice, and no one else realised what happened. Almost no one. ("Heidi are you still there? This is Hess.")

("Yes.") She answered warily, hoping he had not come up with yet another way to trap her.

("Congratulations. For having nothing to offer but a head of pink hair, you have turned out to be most challenging prey. May we meet again soon.")

("Not if I can help it.") Heidi broke contact, collapsing against the side of the box. She was alive, and free, headed for a soft landing at the hands of a hot pilot, backed by a programming genius on the onboard systems—maybe she could relax. 03:57:46 Not much left of the midwatch. In less than four hours she had lost her job, her shipmates, and nearly her life and sanity as well—one hell of a way to start the day. When she felt the buffeting from the first layers of atmosphere, she knew she was safe; she had done it, bringing the the lucky *Artemis* survivors back, alive and whole, with their fortunes intact—all without harming so much as a SuperCat.

Typhon Corporation cops unsealed her crate, armed policewomen who helped her out and had a robe waiting, telling her she had done wonderfully—saying it with that touch of thankful pride you never hear in men's praise, no matter how fulsome. And it was pretty fulsome. Once she was presentable, men clapped her on the back, and everyone cheered her. Her whole hijacking-escape ordeal had been broadcast live from the spaceliner's first Mayday to the fiery plunge into Typhon's cloud tops—including ongoing 3V from *Artemis*, where slavers were finishing up their looting. System-wide audiences eclipsed anything anyone had ever seen, outdrawing even the recent Sonya Hart "Farewell Performance." Aside from sheer entertainment value, she had saved the system from paying the major share of some staggering ransoms. Anna Lu's loss alone would have sent markets plunging.

Public thanksgiving paled before the private celebration thrown by Sonya Hart, who rented a floating aerostat to give a gigantic victory brunch for the *Artemis* survivors—with live chefs, and a dozen types of fresh fish flown down from Oceania. Sonya's studio beamed a star-studded show up from the inner system, and local celebrities danced with rich young widows like Victoria MacEvoy. Heidi found herself at a luxurious realtime event she did not have to organize, supervise, or entertain—for once she could sit back and please herself, without worrying if everyone else was having a good time.

This totally unnatural state lasted until she saw Kay alone on a bubble balcony staring out at the boundless cloud plain. She went to see if the girl was okay. Kay laughed at the question. "Okay? I have wanted my whole life to come here. I am just hoping they will let me stay."

"Let you stay?" She saw real worry in the serious blue eyes beneath the blonde bangs. "What do you mean?"

"I have no credit, no job," the girl explained. "Even lost Mom's v-suit. I was supposed to be paid for piloting that Comet to Tartarus, but that never happened . . ." Twenty-four hours before she had been in the Graveyard, signing on to pilot *MissBehaven*.

Heidi took the girl's hand, thinking there would always be a link between them—both their lives turned on the last twenty-four hours, when they had saved each other time and again. Kay had told her about her dead mom, and Male Sperm Sample-789439-X18. Though technically old enough to be Kay's mother, Heidi felt more like an older sister, stumbling on a long-lost sibling she never knew she had. "Do not worry, you can stay with me—or wherever you like. You are rich. Incredibly rich, so rich you will never have to have a job, unless you want one."

Kay laughed, "No, I am the one person in this room who is not incredibly rich, or even employable."

Heidi shook her head. "We are both rich. Megan too. You were hired to illegally pilot that ship to Tartarus by an Orion Lines officer named Marten DeRuyter—making you a minor who was exploited and put at risk in order to profit Orion Lines." She explained the whole scam to Kay, how DeRuyter had tried to use the slavers, and how the slavers used him instead.

Kay stared wide-eyed at her. "But why me? What did I do?"

"I'm afraid you were picked for being photogenic." And foolhardy. DeRuyter was free to cast anyone as the freighter pilot, so he picked the perfect slaver victim, young and vulnerable. Hess no doubt approved.

"But I am a damned good pilot," Kay protested.

"No lie little girl. They will be telling this story forever." How a teenage ring rat on the run rammed an Orion Lines lifeboat through Typhon's A-ring, with a fortune in ransom aboard and two slaver missiles on her tail.

"Un—fucking—believable." Kay shook her head sadly. "So this was all planned as entertainment?"

"Reality 3V." It had been Heidi's specialty.

"Folks damn well got their money's worth."

"Not yet," Heidi explained, not by a long shot. "There will be a monstrous lawsuit, lasting well into your adulthood, and until it is settled, you will be totally taken care of as both a major claimant and a star witness."

"And after the settlement?" Kay asked nervously, glad to hear she would not have to start supporting herself at once.

"Then you will be fabulously wealthy. If you do not believe me, ask Anna Lu." Heidi did not even get into 3V rights and spin-offs, but Kay believed her, heaven knows why. When someone has been repeatedly in your head, seeing through your eyes and hearing through your ears, you do tend to trust them. What was there left to hide?

Together they looked out on this sparkling new world they were entering—this world of having whatever you want. Sonya Hart stood on stage, enthusiastically introducing hologram feelie-star friends to her fellow survivors. Vicky MacEvoy had a man on each arm. Anna Lu sat in a long sparkling gown talking earnestly into her comlink, while a live waiter poured her green mint liqueur. And on the dance floor rich young women were doing the latest Vanir dirty dance craze, happily humping the air, whether or not they had a partner. "No wonder Hess was driven to violence," Heidi observed. "We have it, and he wanted it."

Kay nodded, unable to decide what was more astonishing, the vast expanse of real open space around her, bordered by endless cloud plain, or her appallingly strange future. Feeling her uncertainly, Heidi softly squeezed the girl's slim hand. "But best of all, you will not have to do it alone." Both of them knew how hard that could be.

ALLEN STEELE

Allen Steele [1958–] (www.allensteele.com) lives in Whately, Massachusetts. He came on the scene as a hard SF writer in 1989 with his first novel, *Orbital Decay*. It was followed by *Clarke County, Space* (1990) and *Lunar Descent* (1991), which are also set between Earth and the moon and belong in the same future history, which Steele calls the NearSpace series. His most prominent fiction in recent years has been the Coyote series, put together in *Coyote* (2002) and *Coyote Rising* (2004), and continuing piecemeal as further stories.

His short fiction is collected in four volumes: *Rude Astronauts* (1993); *All-American Alien Boy* (1996); *Sex and Violence in Zero G* (1999), which collects the short fiction in the NearSpace series and provides a list of the series; and *American Beauty* (2003).

The Encyclopedia of Science Fiction says that although Steele "tends to export unchanged into space, decades hence, the tastes and habits of 1970s humanity, he manages to convey a verisimilitudinous sense of the daily round of those men and women who will be patching together the ferries, ships, and space habitats necessary for the next steps into space." He was one of the leading young hard SF writers of the 1990s, with a talent for realism and a penchant for portraying the daily, gritty problems of living and working in space in the future. His background is professional newspaper journalism and his fiction has been called "working-class hard SF," because of his regular choice of ordinary people as characters, and because of his generally left-leaning politics.

In reference to New Space Opera, he says:

> Every couple of decades or so, a new group of writers come along who reinvent this particular subgenre. Although they're often influenced by what has come before— everyone owes something to E. E. "Doc" Smith, whether they know it or not—they also bring to it a different set of tools, both in terms of literary technique but also underlying concerns. The so-called "New Space Opera" is more political, for instance, than much of what was published during the '70s, while '70s space opera benefited from the influence of the "New Wave" movement of the '60s.

His 1995 novella "The Death of Captain Future" received the 1996 Hugo Award for best novella, and was also nominated for a 1997 Nebula Award by the Science Fiction and Fantasy Writers of America. When questioned on-line about the story, Steele said:

> "The Death of Captain Future" is not a lampoon of Edmond Hamilton's work. If I had intended to parody Hamilton, Curt Newton/Captain Future would have been a character in the story (instead of a freighter captain who fancies himself to be Captain Future), and I would have attempted to imitate Hamilton's writing style, perhaps in an unflattering way. This is clearly not the case; if anything, the novella is a tribute to a late author's best-known work.
>
> . . . I began to wonder what a '90s version of an SF pulp hero would look like . . . an interesting question, because the Depression-era pulp heros look rather quaint by today's standards, mainly because we tend to be drawn more toward antiheros. So I decided to write a postmodern pulp adventure in which a character who expresses (but doesn't personify) the values of a '30s hero runs smack into a harder, grittier sort of protagonist. Hence the double-meaning behind the title.

And in response to our request for comment, he said:

If one considers space opera to be the adventure-oriented category of hard SF, then—much like hard SF itself—it's something that goes in and out of style, yet nonetheless has remained with us throughout the history of the genre. Space opera never really disappears entirely, yet there are times when it fades into the background, only to eventually return in a mutated form.

"The Death of Captain Future" was a conscious attempt to revive the space opera of the '30s and early '40s, while marrying it to post-cyberpunk hard SF. I'd read Edmond Hamilton's original Captain Future stories when they were reprinted in paperback in the late '60s, but I had no desire to try to write something exactly like that. Instead, what I set out to do was create a pulp-fiction story for the '90s, one that reflected upon the classic space op of the past while, at the same time, reworking it for the present.

There's a hidden joke in "The Death of Captain Future"—the stereotypical image of '30s and '40s space opera, as typified by countless pulp magazine covers, is the beautiful girl being menaced by the bug-eyed alien. In this story, I deliberately put the two together: a beautiful girl who's also a bug-eyed alien. She's my tribute to all those *Planet Stories* cover girls.

THE DEATH OF CAPTAIN FUTURE

ALLEN STEELE

The name of Captain Future, the supreme foe of all evil and evildoers, was known to every inhabitant of the Solar System.

That tall, cheerful, red-haired young adventurer of ready laugh and flying fists was the implacable Nemesis of all oppressors and exploiters of the System's human and planetary races. Combining a gay audacity with an unswervable purposefulness and an unparalleled mastery of science, he had blazed a brilliant trail across the nine worlds in defense of the right.

—Edmond Hamilton, *Captain Future and the Space Emperor* (1940)

This is the true story of how Captain Future died.

We were crossing the inner belt, coasting toward our scheduled rendezvous with Ceres, when the message was received by the ship's comlink.

"Rohr . . . ? Rohr, wake up, please."

The voice coming from the ceiling was tall, dark, and handsome, sampled from one of the old Hercules vids in the captain's collection. It penetrated the darkness of my quarters on the mid-deck where I lay asleep after standing an eight-hour watch on the bridge.

I turned my head to squint at the computer terminal next to my bunk. Lines of alphanumeric code scrolled down the screen, displaying the routine systems-checks and updates that, as second officer, I was supposed to be monitoring at all times, even when I was off-duty and dead to the world. No red-bordered emergency messages, though; at first glance, everything looked copacetic.

Except the time. It was 0335 Zulu, the middle of the goddamn night.

"Rohr?" The voice was a little louder now. "Mister Furland? Please wake up . . ."

I groaned and rolled over. "Okay, okay, I'm awake. What'dya want, Brain?"

The Brain. It was bad enough that the ship's AI sounded like Steve Reeves; it also had to have a stupid name like The Brain. On every vessel on which I had served, crewmembers had given their AIs human names—Rudy, Beth, Kim, George, Stan, Lisa, dubbed after friends or family members or deceased shipmates—or nicknames, either clever or overused: Boswell, Isaac, Slim, Flash, Ramrod, plus the usual Hals and Datas from the nostalgia buffs. I once held down a gig on a lunar tug where the AI was called Fughead—as in *Hey, Fughead, gimme the traffic grid for Tycho Station*—but no one but a bonehead would give their AI a silly-ass moniker like The Brain.

No one but Captain Future, that is . . . and I still hadn't decided whether or not my current boss was a bonehead, or just insane.

"The captain asked me to awaken you." The Brain said. "He wants you on the bridge at once. He says that it's urgent."

I checked the screen again. "I don't see anything urgent."

"Captain's orders, Mr. Furland." The ceiling fluorescents began to slowly brighten behind their cracked and dusty panes, causing me to squint and clap my hand over my eyes. *"If you don't report to the bridge in ten minutes, you'll be docked one hour time-lost and a mark will be entered on your union card."*

Threats like that usually don't faze me—everyone loses a few hours or gains a few marks during a long voyage—but I couldn't afford a bad service report now. In two more days the *TBSA Comet* would reach Ceres, where I was scheduled to join up with the *Jove Commerce*, outbound for Callisto. I had been lucky to get this far, and I didn't want my next CO to ground me just because of a bad report from my previous captain.

"Okay," I muttered. "Tell 'em I'm on my way."

I swung my legs over the side and felt around for where I had dropped my clothes on the deck. I could have used a rinse, a shave, and a nice long meditation in the head, not to mention a mug of coffee and a muffin from the galley, but it was obvious that I wasn't going to get that.

Music began to float from the walls, an orchestral overture that gradually rose in volume. I paused, my calves halfway into the trouser legs, as the strings soared upward, gathering heroic strength. German opera. Wagner. *The Flight of The Valkyries,* for God's sake . . .

"Cut it out, Brain," I said.

The music stopped in mid-chord. *"The captain thought it would help rouse you."*

"I'm roused." I stood up and pulled my trousers the rest of the way on. In the dim light, I glimpsed a small motion near the corner of my compartment beside the locker; one moment it was there, then it was gone. "There's a cockroach in here," I said. "Wanna do something about it?"

"I'm sorry, Rohr. I have tried to disinfect the vessel, but so far I have been unable to locate all the nests. If you'll leave your cabin door unlocked while you're gone, I'll send a drone inside to . . ."

"Never mind." I zipped up my pants, pulled on a sweatshirt and looked around for my stikshoes. They were kicked under my bunk; I knelt down on the threadbare carpet and pulled them out. "I'll take care of it myself."

The Brain meant nothing by that comment; it was only trying to get rid of another pest which had found its way aboard the *Comet* before the freighter had departed from LaGrange Four. Cockroaches, fleas, ants, even the occasional mouse; they managed to get into any vessel which regularly rendezvoused with near-Earth spaceports, but I had never been on any ship so infested as the *Comet.* Yet I wasn't about to leave my cabin door unlocked. One of the few inviolable union rules I still enjoyed aboard this ship was the ability to seal my cabin, and I didn't want to give the captain a chance to go poking through my stuff. He was convinced that I was carrying contraband with me to Ceres Station, and even though that he was right—two-fifths of lunar mash whiskey, a traditional coming-aboard present for my next commanding officer— I didn't want him pouring good liquor down the sink because of Association regulations no one else bothered to observe.

I pulled on my shoes, fastened a utility belt around my waist and left the cabin, carefully locking the door behind me with my thumbprint. A short, upward-curving corridor took me past the closed doors of two other crew cabins, marked CAPTAIN and FIRST OFFICER. The captain was already on the bridge, and I assumed that Jeri was with him.

A manhole led to the central access shaft and the carousel. Before I went up to the bridge, though, I stopped by the wardroom to fill a squeezebulb with coffee from the pot. The wardroom was a disaster: a dinner tray had been left on the table, discarded food wrappers lay on the floor, and small spider-like robot waded in the galley's sink, waging solitary battle against the crusty cookware that had been abandoned there.

The captain had been here recently; I was surprised that he hadn't summoned me to clean up after him. At least there was some hot coffee left in the carafe, although judging from its odor and viscosity it was probably at least ten hours old; I toned it down with sugar and half-sour milk from the fridge before I poured it into a squeezebulb.

As always, the pictures on the wardroom walls caught my eye: framed reproductions of covers from ancient pulp magazines well over a hundred years old. The magazines themselves, crumbling and priceless, were bagged and hermetically sealed within a locker in the Captain's quarters. Lurid paintings of fishbowl-helmeted spacemen fighting improbable alien monsters and mad scientists which, in turn, menaced buxom young women in see-through outfits. The adolescent fantasies of the last century— "Planets in Peril," "Quest Beyond the Stars," "Star Trail to Glory"—and above them all, printed in a bold swath across the top of each cover, a title . . .

CAPTAIN FUTURE
Man of Tomorrow

At that moment, my reverie was broken by a harsh voice coming from the ceiling: *"Furland! Where are you?"*

"In the wardroom, Captain." I pinched off the lip of the squeezebulb and sealed it with a catheter, then clipped it to my belt. "Just grabbing some coffee. I'll be up there in a minute."

"You got sixty seconds to find your duty station or I'll dock your pay for your last shift! Now hustle your lazy butt up here!"

"Coming right now . . ." I walked out of the wardroom, heading up the corridor toward the shaft. "Toad," I whispered under my breath when I was through the hatch and out of earshot from the ship's comnet. Who's calling who lazy?

Captain Future, Man of Tomorrow. God help us if that were true.

> *Ten minutes later a small ship shaped like an elongated teardrop rose from an underground hangar on the lunar surface. It was the* Comet, *super-swift craft of the Futuremen, known far and wide through the System as the swiftest ship in space.*
>
> —Hamilton, *Calling Captain Future* (1940)

My name's Rohr Furland. For better or worse, I'm a spacer, just like my father and his mother before him.

Call it family tradition. Grandma was one of the original beamjacks who helped build the first powersat in Earth orbit before she immigrated to the Moon, where she conceived my dad as the result of one-night stand with some nameless moondog who was killed in a blowout only two days later. Dad grew up as an unwanted child in Descartes Station; he ran away at eighteen and stowed away aboard a Skycorp freighter to Earth, where he lived like a stray dog in Memphis before he got homesick and signed up a Russian company looking for native-born selenians. Dad got home in time to see Grandma through her last years, fight in the Moon War on the side of the Pax Astra and, not incidentally, meet my mother, who was a geologist at Tycho Station.

I was born in the luxury of a two-room apartment beneath Tycho on the first anniversary of the Pax's independence. I'm told that my dad celebrated my arrival by getting drunk on cheap luna wine and balling the midwife who had delivered me. It's remarkable that my parents stayed together long enough for me to graduate from suit camp. Mom went back to Earth while Dad and I stayed on the Moon to receive the benefits of full citizenship in the Pax: Class A oxygen cards, good for air even if we were unemployed and dead broke. Which was quite often, in Dad's case.

All of which makes me a mutt, a true son of a bastard, suckled on air bottles and moonwalking before I was out of my diapers. On my sixteenth birthday, I was given my union card and told to get a job; two weeks before my eighteenth birthday, the LEO shuttle which had just hired me as a cargo handler touched down on a landing strip in Galveston, and with the aid of an exoskeleton I walked for the first time on Earth. I spent one week there, long enough for me to break my right arm by falling on a Dallas sidewalk, lose my virginity to an El Paso whore, and get one hell of a case of agoraphobia from all that wide-open Texas landscape. Fuck the cradle of humanity and the horse it rode in on; I caught the next boat back to the Moon and turned eighteen with a birthday cake that had no candles.

Twelve years later, I had handled almost every union job someone with my qualifications could hold—dock slob, cargo grunt, navigator, life support chief, even a couple of second-mate assignments—on more vessels than I could count, ranging from orbital tugs and lunar freighters to passenger shuttles and Apollo-class ore haulers. None of these gigs had ever lasted much longer than a year; in order to guarantee equal opportunity for all its members, the union shifted people from ship to ship, allowing only captains and first-mates to remain with their vessels for longer than eighteen months. It was a hell of a system; by the time you became accustomed to one ship and its captain, you were transferred to another ship and had to learn all over again. Or, worse, you went without work for several months at a time, which meant hanging around some spacer bar at Tycho Station or Descartes City, waiting for the local union rep to throw some other guy out of his present assignment and give you his job.

It was a life, but it wasn't much of a living. I was thirty years old and still possessed all my fingers and toes, but had precious little money in the bank. After fifteen years of hard work, the nearest thing I had to a permanent address was the storage locker in Tycho where I kept my few belongings. Between jobs, I lived in union hostels on the Moon or the el-fives, usually occupying a bunk barely large enough to swing either a cat or a call-girl. Even the whores lived better than I did; sometimes I'd pay them just to let me sleep in a decent bed for a change, and never mind the sex.

To make matters worse, I was bored out of my wits. Except for one cycleship run out to Mars when I was twenty-five, I had spent my entire career—hell, my entire life— running between LEO and the Moon. It's not a bad existence, but it's not a great one either. There's no shortage of sad old farts hanging around the union halls, telling big lies to anyone who'll listen about their glory days as beamjacks or moondogs while drinking away their pensions. I was damned if I would end up like them, but I knew that if I didn't get off the Moon real soon, I would be schlepping LOX tanks for the rest of my life.

Meanwhile, a new frontier was being opened in the outer system. Deep-space freighters hauled helium-3 from Jupiter to feed the fusion tokamaks on Earth, and although Queen Macedonia had placed Titan off-limits because of the Plague, the Iapetus colony was still operational. There was good money to be made from landing a gig on one of the big ships that cruised between the gas giants and the belt, and union members who found work on the Jupiter and Saturn runs had guaranteed three-year contracts. It wasn't the same thing as making another trip between Moon and LEO every few days. The risks were greater, but so was the pay-off.

Competition for jobs on the outer-system ships was tight, but that didn't stop me from applying anyway. My fifteen-year service record, with few complaints from previous captains and one Mars run to my name, helped me put a leg up over most of the other applicants. I held down a job as a cargo grunt for another year while I waited, but the union eventually rotated me out and left me hanging in Sloppy Joe's Bar in Tycho. Six weeks later, just as I was considering signing up as tractor operator on the Clavius Dome construction project, the word came: the *Jove Commerce* needed a new executive officer, and my name had been drawn from the hat.

There was only one hitch. Since the *Commerce* didn't come further in-system than Ceres, and because the union didn't guarantee passage to the belt as part of the deal, I would have to either travel aboard a clipper—out of the question, since I didn't have money—or find a temporary job on an outbound asteroid freighter.

Okay, I was willing to do that, but now there was another complication: few freighters had available gigs for selenians. Most vessels which operated in the main belt were owned by the Transient Body Shipping Association, and TBSA captains preferred to hire crewmembers from other ships owned by the co-op rather than from my union. Nor did they want to sign up some dude who would only be making a one-way trip, because they'd lose him on Ceres before the trip was half-over.

The predicament was explained to me by my union rep when I met with him in his office in Tycho. Schumacher was an old buddy; he and I had worked together aboard a LEO tugboat before the union had hired him as its Tycho Station representative, so he knew my face and was willing to cut me some slack.

"Look, Rohr," he said, propping his moccasins up on his desk, "here's the scoop. I've checked around for a boat that'll take you on, and I found what you were looking for. An Ares-class ore freighter, outbound for Ceres . . . in fact, she's already docked at LaGrange Four and is ready to launch as soon as her captain finds a new second."

As he spoke, Schumacher punched up a holo of the ship, and it revolved in the tank above his desk. It was a standard rock hauler: eighty-two meters in length, with a gas-core nuclear engine at one end and a drum-shaped crew module at the other, joined at the center by the long narrow spine and open cargo bays. An up-rated tugboat, really; nothing about it was either unfamiliar or daunting. I took a slug off the whisky flask he had pulled out of his desk drawer. "Great. What's her name?"

He hesitated. "The TBSA *Comet*," he said reluctantly. Her captain is Bo McKinnon."

I shrugged and passed the flask back to him. "So what's the catch?"

Schumacher blinked. Instead of taking a hit off the whisky, he recapped the flask and shoved it back in the drawer. "Let me repeat that," he said. "The *Comet*. Bo McKinnon." He peered at me as if I had come down with Titan Plague. "You're telling me you've never heard of him?"

I didn't keep up with the TBSA freighters or their captains; they returned to the Moon only once every few months to drop off their cargo and change crews, so few selenians happened to see them unless they were getting drunk in some bar. "Not a clue," I said.

Schumacher closed his eyes. "Terrific," he murmured. "The one guy who's never heard of Captain Future and it's gotta be you."

"Captain who?"

He looked back at me. "Look, just forget the whole thing, okay? Pretend I never mentioned it. There's another rock hauler heading out to Ceres in about six or seven weeks. I'll talk to the Association, try to get you a gig on that one instead . . ."

I shook my head. "I can't wait another six or seven weeks. If I'm not on Ceres in three months, I'll lose the *Jove Commerce* job. What's wrong with this gig?"

Schumacher sighed as he reached back into the drawer for the flask. "What's wrong," he said, "is the nut who's in command. McKinnon is the worst captain in the Association. No one who's shipped out with him has ever stayed aboard, except maybe the google he's got for a first mate."

I had to bite my tongue when he said that. We were pals, but racism isn't an endearing trait. Sure, Superiors can be weird—their eyes, for starters, which was why some people called them by that name—but if you also use words like nigger, slant, kike or spic to describe people, then you're no friend of mine.

On the other hand, when you're hungry for work, you'll put up with just about anything.

Schumacher read the expression on my face. "It's not just that," he said hastily. "I understand the first officer is okay." *For a google, that is,* although he didn't say it aloud. "It's McKinnon himself. People have jumped ship, faked illness, torn up their union cards . . . anything to get off the *Comet.*"

"That bad?"

"That bad." He took a long hit off the flask, gasped, and passed it back across the desk to me. "Oh, the pay's okay . . . minimum wage, but by Association standards that's better than union scale . . . and the *Comet* passes all the safety requirements, or at least so at inspection time. But McKinnon's running a tank short of a full load, if y'know what I mean."

I didn't drink from the flask. "Naw, man, I don't know what you mean. What's with this . . . what did you call him?"

"Captain Future. That's what he calls himself, Christ knows why." He grinned. "Not only that, but he also calls his AI 'The Brain' . . ."

I laughed out loud. "The Brain? Like, what? He's got a brain floating in a jar? I don't get it . . ."

"I dunno. It's a fetish of some kind." He shook his head. "Anyway, everyone who's worked for him says that he thinks he's some kinda space hero, and he expects everyone to go along with the idea. And he's supposed to be real tough on people . . . you might think he was a perfectionist, if he wasn't such a slob himself."

I had worked for both kinds before, along with a few weirdos. They didn't bother me, so long as the money was right and they minded their own business. "Ever met him?"

Schumacher held out his hand; I passed the flask back to him and he took another swig. Must be the life, sitting on your ass all day, getting drunk and deciding people's futures. I envied him so much, I hoped someone would kindly cut my throat if I was ever in his position.

"Nope," he said. "Not once. He spends all his time on the *Comet,* even when he's back here. Hardly ever leaves the ship, from what I've been told . . . and that's another thing. Guys who've worked for him say that he expects his crew to do everything but wipe his butt after he visits the head. Nobody gets a break on his ship, except maybe his first officer."

"What about him?"

"Her. Nice girl, name of . . ." He thought hard for a moment, then snapped his fingers. "Jeri. Jeri Lee-Bose, that's it." He smiled. "I met her once, not long before she went to work on the *Comet.* She's sweet, for a google."

He winked and dropped his voice a bit. "I hear she's got a thing for us apes," he murmured. "In fact, I've been told she's bunking with her captain. If half of what I've heard about McKinnon is true, that must make him twice as sick as I've heard."

I didn't reply. Schumacher dropped his feet and leaned across the desk, lacing his fingers together as he looked straight at me. "Look, Rohr," he said, as deadly serious as if he was discussing my wanting to marry his sister, "I know you're working under a time limit and how much the *Jove Commerce* job means to you. But I gotta tell you, the only reason why Captain Future would even consider taking aboard a short-timer is because nobody else will work for him. He's just as desperate as you are, but I don't give a shit about him. If you wanna turn it down, I won't add it to your card and I'll save your place in line. It'll just be between you and me. Okay?"

"And if I turn it down?"

He wavered his hand back and forth. "Like I said, I can try to find you another gig. The *Nickel Queen's* due home in another six weeks or so. I've got some pull with her captain, so maybe I can get you a job there . . . but honest to Jesus, I can't promise anything. The *Queen's* a good ship and everyone I know wants to work for her, just as much as nobody wants to get within a klick of the *Comet.*"

"So what do you suggest I do?"

Schumacher just smiled and said nothing. As my union rep, he was legally forbidden against making any decisions for me; as a pal, he had done his best to warn me about the risks. From both points of view, though, he knew I didn't have any real choice. I could spend three months aboard a ship run by a borderline psycho, or the rest of my life jacking off on the Moon.

I thought about it for a few moments, then I asked for the contract.

> The three Futuremen who were Curt Newton's faithful, lifelong comrades made a striking contrast to their tall, red-haired young leader.
>
> Hamilton, *The Comet Kings* (1942)

One-sixth gravity disappeared as I crawled through the carousel hatch and entered the bridge.

The *Comet's* command center was located in the non-rotating forward deck of the crew module. The bridge was the largest single compartment in the ship, but even in freefall it was cramped: chairs, consoles, screens, emergency suit lockers, the central navigation table with its holo tank and, at the center of the low ceiling, the hemispherical bulge of the observation blister.

The ceiling lamps were turned down low when I came in—The Brain was mimicking Earth-time night—but I could see Jeri seated at her duty station on the far end of the circular deck. She looked around when she heard the hatch open.

"Morning," she said, smiling at me. "Hey, is that coffee?"

"Something like it," I muttered. She gazed enviously at the squeezebulb in my hand. "Sorry I didn't bring you any," I added, "but the Captain . . ."

"Right. I heard Bo yell at you." She feigned a pout which didn't last very long. "That's okay. I can get some later after we make the burn."

Jeri Lee-Bose: six-foot-two, which is short for a Superior, with the oversized dark blue eyes that give bioengineered spacers their unsavory nickname. She was thin and flat-chested to the point of emaciation; the fingers of her ambidextrous hands were long and slender, her thumbs almost extending to the tips of her index fingers. Her ash-blond hair was shaved nearly to the skull, except for the long braid that extended from the nape of her neck nearly down to the base of her narrow spine, where her double-jointed legs began.

The pale skin of her face was marked with finely-etched tattoos around her eyes, nose, and mouth, forming the wings of a monarch butterfly. She had been given these when she had turned five, and since Superiors customarily add another tattoo on their birthdays and Jeri Lee was twenty-five, pictograms covered most of her arms and her shoulders, constellations and dragons which weaved their way under and around the tank-top she wore. I had no idea of what else lay beneath her clothes, but I imagined that she was well on her way to becoming a living painting.

Jeri was strange, even for a Superior. For one thing, her kind usually segregate themselves from Primaries, as they politely call us baseline humans (or apes, when we're not around). They tend to remain within their family-based clans, operating independent satraps which deal with the TBSA and the major space companies only out of economic necessity, so it's rare to find a lone Superior working on a vessel owned by a Primary.

For another thing, although I've been around Superiors most of my life and they don't give me the creeps like they do most groundhogs and even many spacers, I've never appreciated the aloof condescension the majority of them display around unenhanced humans. Give one of them a few minutes, and they'll bend your ear about the Superior philosophy of extropic evolution and all that jive. Yet Jeri was the refreshing, and even oddball, exception to the rule. She had a sweet disposition, and from the moment I had come aboard the *Comet*, she had accepted me both as an equal and as a new-found friend. No stuffiness, no harangues about celibacy or the unspirituality of eating meat or using profanity; she was a fellow crewmate, and that was that.

No. That wasn't quite all there was to it.

When one got past the fact that she was a scarecrow with feet that functioned as a second pair of hands and eyes the size of fuel valves, she was sensual as hell. She was a pretty woman, and I had become infatuated with her. Schumacher would have twitched at the thought of sleeping with a google, but in three weeks since The Brain had been revived us from the zombie tanks, there had been more than a few times when my desire to see the rest of her body exceeded simple curiosity about rest of her tattoos.

Yet I knew very little about her. As much as I loved looking at her, that was surpassed by my admiration for her innate talent as a spacer. In terms of professional skill, Jeri Lee-Bose was one of the best First Officers I had ever met. Any Royal Navy, TBSA, or free-trader captain would have killed to sign her aboard.

So what the hell was she doing aboard a scow like the *Comet*, serving under a bozo like Bo McKinnon?

I tucked in my knees and did a half-gainer which landed the soles of my stikshoes against the carpet. Feet now firmly planted on the floor, I walked across the circular compartment to the nav table, sucking on the squeezebulb in my left hand. "Where's the captain?" I asked.

"Topside, taking a sextant reading." She nodded toward the observation blister above us. "He'll be down in a minute."

Typical. Part of the reason why Superiors have enhanced eyes is for optical work like sextant sightings. This should be Jeri's job, but McKinnon seemed to regard the blister as his personal throne. I sighed as I settled down in my chair and buckled in. "Should have known," I muttered. "Wakes you up in the middle of the goddamn night, then disappears when you want a straight answer."

Her mouth pursed into a sympathetic frown. "Bo will tell you more when he comes down," she said, then she swiveled around in her chair as she returned her attention to her board.

Jeri Lee was the only person aboard who was permitted to call Captain Future by his real name. I didn't have that privilege, and The Brain hadn't been programmed to do otherwise. The fondness I had developed for Jeri over the last three weeks was tempered by the fact that, in almost any disagreement, she usually sided with the captain.

Obviously, there was something else she knew but wasn't telling me, preferring to defer the issue to McKinnon. I had become used to such behavior over the last few months, but it was still irritating. Most first officers act as intermediaries between captain and crew, and in that sense Jeri performed well, yet at times like this I felt as if I had more in common with The Brain than with her.

So be it. I swiveled my chair to face the nav table. "Hey, Brain," I called out. "Gimme a holo of our current position and trajectory, please."

The space within the holo tank coruscated briefly, then an arch-shaped slice of the main belt appeared above the table. Tiny spots of orange light depicting major asteroids slowly moved along blue sidereal tracks, each designated by their catalog numbers. The *Comet* was pinpointed by a small silver replica of the vessel, leading the end of a broken red line which bisected the asteroid orbits.

The *Comet* was near the edge of the third Kirkwood gap, one of the "empty spaces" in the belt where Martian and Jovian gravitational forces caused the number of identified asteroids to diminish per fraction of an astronomical unit. We were now in the ⅓ gap, about two and a half A.U.'s from the Sun. In another couple of days we would enter the main belt and be closing in on Ceres. Once we arrived, the *Comet* would unload the cargo it had carried from the Moon and, in return, take on the raw ore TBSA prospectors had mined from the belt and shipped to Ceres Station. It was also there that I was scheduled to depart the *Comet* and await the arrival of the *Jove Commerce*.

At least, that was the itinerary. Now, as I studied the holo, I noticed a not-so-subtle change. The red line depicting the freighter's trajectory had been altered since the end of my last watch about four hours earlier.

It no longer intercepted Ceres. In fact, it didn't even come close to the asteroid's orbit.

The *Comet* had changed course while I slept.

Without saying anything to Jeri, I unbuckled my harness and pushed over to the table, where I silently stared at the holo for a couple of minutes, using the keypad to manually focus and enlarge the image. Our new bearing took us almost a quarter of a million kilometers from Ceres, on just the other side of the ⅓ Kirkwood gap.

"Brain," I said, "what's our destination?"

"*The asteroid 2046-Barr,*" it replied. It displayed a new orange spot in the tank, directly in front of the *Comet*'s red line.

The last of my drowsiness gradually dissipated into a pulse of white-hot rage. I could feel Jeri's eyes on my back.

"Rohr . . ." she began.

I didn't care. I stabbed the intercom button on the table. "McKinnon!" I bellowed. "Get down here!"

Long silence. I knew he could hear me.

"Goddammit, get down here! Now!"

Motors whined in the ceiling above me, then the hatch below the observation blister irised open and a wingback chair began to descend into the bridge, carrying the commanding officer of the TBSA *Comet*. It wasn't until the chair reached the deck that the figure seated in it spoke.

"You can call me . . . Captain Future."

In the ancient pulp magazines he so adored, Captain Future was six-and-a-half feet in height, ruggedly handsome, bronze-skinned and red-haired. None of this applied to Bo McKinnon. Squat and obese, he filled the chair like a half-ton of lard. Black curly hair, turning grey at the temples and filthy with dandruff, receded from his forehead and fell around his shoulders, while an oily, unkempt beard dripped down the sides of his fat cheeks, themselves the color of mildewed wax. There were old food stains on the front of his worn-out sweatshirt and dark marks in the crotch of his trousers where he had failed to properly shake himself after the last time he had visited the head. And he smelled like a fart.

If my description seems uncharitable, let there be no mistake: Bo McKinnon was a butt-ugly, foul-looking son of a whore, and I have met plenty of slobs like him to judge by comparison. He had little respect for personal hygiene and fewer social graces, he had no business being anyone's role model, and I was no mood for his melodramatic bullshit just now.

"You changed course." I pointed at the holo tank behind me, my voice quavering in anger. "We're supposed to come out of the Kirkwood in another few hours, and while I was asleep you changed course."

McKinnon calmly stared back at me. "Yes, Mister Furland, that I did. I changed the *Comet*'s trajectory while you were in your quarters."

"We're no longer heading for Ceres . . . Christ, we're going to come nowhere *near* Ceres!"

He made no move to rise from his throne. "That's correct," he said, slowly nodding his head. "I ordered The Brain to alter our course so that we'd intercept 2046-Barr. We fired maneuvering thrusters at 0130 shiptime, and in two hours we'll execute another course correction. That should put us within range of the asteroid in about . . ."

"Eight hours, Captain," Jeri said.

"Thank you, Mister Bose," he said, otherwise barely acknowledging her. "Eight hours. At this time the *Comet* will be secured for emergency action."

He folded his hands across his vast stomach and gazed back at me querulously. "Any further questions, Mister Furland?"

Further questions?

My mouth hung agape for a few moments. I was unable to speak, unable to protest, unable to do anything except wonder at the unmitigated gall of this mutant amalgamation of human and frog genes.

"Just one," I finally managed to say. "How do you expect me to make my rendezvous with the *Jove Commerce* if we detour to . . ."

"2046-Barr," Jeri said softly.

McKinnon didn't so much as blink. "We won't," he said. "In fact, I've already sent a message to Ceres Station, stating that the *Comet* will be delayed and that our new ETA is indefinite. With any luck, we'll reach Ceres in about forty-eight hours. You should be able to . . ."

"No, I won't." I grasped the armrest of his chair with both hands and leaned forward until my face was only a few inches from his. "The *Jove* is due to leave Ceres in forty-*two* hours . . . and that's at the latest, if it's going to meet its launch window for Callisto. They'll go, with or without me, and if they go without me, I'm stuck on Ceres."

No. That wasn't entirely true. Ceres Station wasn't like the Moon; it was too small an outpost to allow a shipwrecked spacer to simply hang around until the next outer-system vessel passed through. The TBSA rep on Ceres would demand that I find a new gig, even if it entailed signing aboard a prospector as grunt labor. This was little better than indentured servitude, since my union card didn't mean shit out here in terms of room, board, and guaranteed oxygen supplies; my paychecks would be swallowed up by all the above. Even then, there was no guarantee that I'd swing another job aboard the next Jupiter or Saturn tanker; I was lucky enough to get *Jove Commerce* job.

That, or I could tuck tail and go back the way I came—and that meant remaining aboard the *Comet* for its return flight to the Moon.

In the latter case, I'd sooner try to walk home.

Try to understand. For the past three weeks, beginning with the moment I had crawled out of the zombie tank, I had been forced to endure almost every indignity possible while serving under Bo McKinnon. His first order, in fact, had been in the hibernation deck, when he had told me to take the catheter off his prick and hold a bag for him to pee in.

That had been only the beginning. Standing double-watches on the bridge because he was too lazy to get out of bed. Repairing decrepit equipment that should have been replaced years ago, only to have it break down again within a few more days after he had abused it past its tolerance levels. Being issued spurious orders on a whim, only to have those same orders countermanded before the task was half-complete because McKinnon had more scut-work he wanted me to do—then being berated because the first assignment had been left unfinished. Meals skipped because the captain decided that now was the time for me go EVA and inspect the davits in the payload bay. Rest periods interrupted because he wanted a snack fetched from the galley and was too "busy" to get it himself . . .

But most of all, the sibilant, high-pitched whine of his voice, like that of a spoiled brat who had been given too many toys by an overindulgent parent. Which was, indeed, exactly what he was.

Bo McKinnon hadn't earned his TBSA commission. It had been purchased for him by his stepfather, a wealthy lunar businessman who was one of the Association's principal stockholders. The *Comet* had been an obsolete ore freighter on the verge of being condemned and scuttled when the old man had bought it for the kid as a means of getting his unwanted stepson out of his hair. Before that, McKinnon had been a customs inspector at Descartes, a minor bureaucrat with delusions of grandeur fostered by the cheap space operas in his collection of moldering twentieth-century magazines, for which he apparently spent every spare lox he had in the bank.

No doubt his stepfather had been as sick of McKinnon as I was. At least this way the pompous geek spent most of his time out in the belt, hauling rock and bellowing orders at whoever was unlucky enough to have been talked into signing aboard the *Comet*.

This much I had learned after I had been aboard for three weeks. By the time I had sent a message to Schumacher, demanding to know what else he hadn't told me about Bo McKinnon, I was almost ready to steal the *Comet*'s skiff and attempt flying it to Mars. When Schumacher sent me his reply, he gave a lame apology for not telling me everything about McKinnon's background; after all, it was his job to muster crewmembers for deep-space craft, and he couldn't play favorites, so sorry, et cetera . . .

By then I had figured out the rest. Bo McKinnon was a rich kid playing at being a spacecraft commander. He wanted the role, but he didn't want to pay the dues, the hard-won experience that any true commander has to accomplish. Instead, he managed to shanghai washed-up cases like me to do his dirty work for him. No telling what arrangement he had worked out with Jeri; for my part, I was the latest in a long line of flunkies.

I didn't hijack the skiff, if only because doing so would have ruined my career and Mars colonists are notoriously unkind to uninvited guests. Besides, I figured that this was a temporary thing: three weeks of Captain Future, and I'd have a story to tell my shipmates aboard the *Jove Commerce* as we sipped whisky around the wardroom table. You think this captain's a hardass? Hey, let me tell you about my last one . . .

Now, as much as I still wanted to get the hell off the *Comet*, nor did I wish to be marooned on Ceres, where I would be at the tender mercies of the station chief.

Time to try a different tack with Captain Future.

I released the armrests and backed off, taking a deep breath as I forced myself to calm down. "Look, Captain," I said, "what's so important about this asteroid? I mean, if you've located a possible lode, you can always stake a claim with the Association and come back for it later. What's the rush?"

McKinnon raised an imperious eyebrow. "Mr. Furland, I am not a prospector," he huffed. "If I were, I wouldn't be commanding the *Comet*, would I?"

No, I silently responded, you wouldn't. No self-respecting rockhounds would have you aboard their ship. "Then what's so important?"

Without a word, McKinnon unbuckled his seat harness and pushed out his chair. Microgravity is the great equalizer for overweight men; he floated across the narrow compartment with the grace of a lunar trapeze artist, somersaulting in mid-air and catching a ceiling rung above the navigation table, where he swung upside-down and typed a command into the keyboard.

The holo expanded until 2046-Barr filled the tank. Now I could see that it was a potato-shaped rock, about three klicks in length and seven hundred meters in diameter. An octopus-like machine clung to one end of the asteroid, with an narrow, elongated pistol thrust out into space.

I recognized it immediately. A General Astronautics Class-B Mass Driver, the type used by the Association to push large carbonaceous-chrondite asteroids into the inner belt. In effect, a mobile mining rig. Long bores sunk into the asteroid extracted raw material from its core, which in turn were fed into the machine's barrel-shaped refinery, where heavy metals and volatiles were separated from the ancient stone. The remaining till was then shot through an electromagnetic railgun as reaction mass that propelled both asteroid and mass driver in whatever direction was desired.

By the time the asteroid reached lunar orbit, the rig would have refined enough nickel, copper, titanium, carbon, and hydrogen to make the effort worthwhile. The hollowed-out remains of the asteroid could then be sold to one of the companies, who would then begin the process of transforming it into another LaGrange colony.

"That's the TBSA *Fool's Gold*," McKinnon said, pointing at the computer-generated image. "It's supposed to reach lunar orbit in four months. Twelve persons are aboard, including its captain, first officer, executive officer, physician, two metallurgists, three engineers . . ."

"Yeah, okay. Twelve guys who are going to get rich when the shares are divvied up." I couldn't keep the envy out of my voice. Only one of two main-belt asteroids made their way in-system every few years, mainly because prospectors didn't find enough such rocks to make them worth the time, money and attention. The smaller ones were usually broken up by nukes, and anything much larger was claimed and mined by prospectors. On the other hand, if just the right asteroid was located and claimed, the bonanza was enough to make its finders wealthy enough to retire. "So what?"

McKinnon stared at me for a moment, then he cartwheeled until he was no longer upside-down and dug into a pocket. He handed me a wadded-up slip of printout. "Read," he said.

I read:

MESS. 1473 0118 GMT 7/26/46 CODE A1/0947
TRANSMISSION FROM CERES STATION TO ALL SPACECRAFT PRIORITY
REPEATER
MESSAGE BEGINS
MAYDAY RECEIVED 1240 GMT 7/25/46 FROM TBSA MASS DRIVER 'FOOL'S GOLD'
BREAK UNKNOWN BREAK NO FURTHER COMMUNICATION FOLLOWING MAYDAY
BREAK VESSEL FAILS TO RESPOND TO QUERIES BREAK REQUEST URGENT ASSISTANCE
FROM NEAREST VESSEL OF ANY REGISTRY BREAK PLEASE RESPOND ASAP
MESSAGE ENDS
(TRANSMISSION REPEATS)
0119 GMT 7/26/46 CODE A1/0947

I turned to Jeri. "Are we the nearest vessel?"

She gravely nodded her head. "I checked. The only other ship within range is a prospector near Gaspara, and it's thirty-four hours from Barr. Everything else is closer to Ceres than we are."

Damn.

According to common law, the closest vessel to a spacecraft transmitting a Mayday was obligated to respond, regardless of any other mission or prior obligation in all but the most extreme emergency . . . and my job aboard the *Jove Commerce* didn't qualify as such, as much as I might have liked to think otherwise.

McKinnon held out his hand. I handed the paper back to him. "I guess you've already informed Ceres that we're on our way."

The captain silently reached to another panel and pushed a set of buttons. A flatscreen lit, displaying a playback of the transmission he had sent to Ceres Station. A simulacrum of the fictional Curt Newton appeared on the screen.

"*This is Captain Future, calling from the TBSA* Comet, *registry Mexico Alpha Foxtrot one-six-seven-five.*" The voice belonged to McKinnon even if the handsome face did not. The Brain had lip-synched them together, and the effect was sadly absurd. "*I've received your transmission, and I'm on our way to investigate the situation aboard the* Fool's Gold. *The Futuremen and I will keep you informed. Captain Future, over and out.*"

I groaned as I watched this. The idiot couldn't keep his fantasy life out of anything, even a distress signal. Captain Future and the—yech!—Futuremen to the rescue.

"You have something to say, Mister Furland?"

McKinnon's hairy chin was thrust out at me with what he probably thought was obstinate resolve, but which actually resembled the petulance of an insecure child daring someone to step into his corner of the sandbox. Not for the first time, I realized that his only way of dealing with people was to boss them around with what little authority he could muster—and since this was his ship, no one could either object or walk out on him.

Least of all me.

"None, Captain." I pushed off from the nav table and floated back to my duty station. Like it or not, we were committed; he had both law and his commission on his side, and I wasn't about to commit mutiny because I had refused my commander's orders to respond to a distress signal.

"Very good." McKinnon shoved himself in the direction of the carousel hatch. "The sextant confirms we're on course for Barr. I'll be in my cabin if you need me."

He stopped, then looked over his shoulder. "You'll need to arm the weapons pod. There may be . . . trouble."

Then he was gone, undoubtedly to claim the sleep I had lost.

"Trouble, my ass," I murmured under my breath.

I glanced over at Jeri. If I expected a sly wink or an understanding smile, I received nothing of the kind. Her face was stoical behind the butterfly mask she wore; she touched her jaw, speaking into the microphone implanted beneath her skin at childhood. "TBSA *Fool's Gold*, this is TBSA *Comet*, Mexico Alpha Foxtrot one-six-seven-five. Do you copy? Over."

I was trapped aboard a ship commanded by a lunatic.

Or so I thought. The real insanity was yet to come.

Space pirates were no new thing, to the System. There were always some corsairs infesting the outlaw asteroids or the wilder moons of the outer planets.

—Hamilton, *Outlaw World* (1945)

One good thing could be said about standing a second consecutive watch on the bridge: I finally learned a little more about Jeri Lee-Bose.

Does it seem surprising that I could have spent three weeks of active duty aboard a spacecraft without hearing a shipmate's entire life story? If so, understand that there's a certain code of conduct among spacers; since many of us have unsavory pasts that we'd rather not discuss, it's not considered proper etiquette to bug someone about private matters unless they themselves bring it up first. Of course, some shipmates will bore you to death, blabbing about everything they've ever said or done until you want to push them into the nearest airlock. On the other hand I have known several people for many years without ever learning where they were born or who their parents were.

Jeri fell into the latter category. After we were revived from biostasis, I had learned many little things about her, but not very many big things. It wasn't as if she was consciously hiding her past; it was simply that the subject had never really come up, during the few times that we had been alone together without Captain Future's presence looming over us. Indeed, she might have completed the voyage as a near-stranger, had I not made an offhand comment.

"I bet the selfish son-of-a-bitch has never thought of anyone else in his life," I said.

I had just returned from the galley, where I had fetched two fresh squeezebulbs of coffee for us. I was still fuming from the argument I had lost, and since McKinnon wasn't in earshot I gave Jeri an earful.

She passively sipped her coffee as I pissed and moaned about my misfortunes, listening patiently as I paced back and forth in my stikshoes, ranting about the commanding officer's dubious mental balance, his unflattering physiognomy, his questionable taste in literature, his body odor and anything else that came to mind, and when I paused for breath she finally put in her quarter-credit.

"He saved my life," she said.

That caught me literally off-balance. My shoes came unstuck from the carpet, and I had to grab hold of a ceiling handrail.

"Say what?" I asked.

Not looking up at me, Jeri Lee absently played with the squeezebulb in her left hand, her right foot holding open the pages of her personal logbook. "You said that he's never thought of any anyone else in his life," she replied. "Whatever else you might say about him, you're wrong there, because he saved my life."

I shifted hands so I could sip my coffee. "Anything you want to talk about?"

She shrugged. "Nothing that probably hasn't occurred to you already. I mean, you've probably wondered why a google is serving as first officer aboard this ship, haven't you?" When my mouth gaped open, she smiled a little. "Don't look so surprised. We're not telepathic, rumors to the contrary . . . it's just that I've heard the same thing over the last several years we've been together."

Jeri gazed pensively through the forward windows. Although we were out of the Kirkwood gap, no asteroids could be seen. The belt is much less dense than many people think, so all we saw was limitless starscape, with Mars a distant ruddy orb off to the port side.

"You know how Superiors mate, don't you?" she asked at last, still not looking at me.

I felt my face grow warm. Actually, I didn't know, although I had frequently fantasized about Jeri helping me find out. Then I realized that she was speaking literally. "Prearranged marriages, rights?"

She nodded. "All very carefully planned, in order to avoid inbreeding while expanding the gene pool as far as possible. It allows for some selection, of course . . . no one tells us exactly *whom* we should marry, just as long as it's outside of our own clans and it's not to Primaries."

She paused to finish her coffee, then she crumpled the squeezebulb and batted it aside with her right foot. It floated in midair, finding its own miniature orbit within the compartment. "Well, sometimes it doesn't work out that way. When I was twenty, I fell in love with a boy at Descartes Station . . . a Primary, as luck would have it. At least I thought I was in love . . ."

She grimaced, brushing her long braid away from her delicate shoulders. "In hindsight, I guess we were just good in bed. In the long run it didn't matter, because as soon as he discovered that he had knocked me up, he got the union to ship him off to Mars. They were only too glad to do so, in order to avoid . . ."

"A messy situation. I see." I took a deep breath. "Leaving you stuck with his child."

She shook her head. "No. No child. I tried to keep it, but the miscarriage . . . anyway, the less said about that, the better."

"I'm sorry." What else could I have said? She should have known better, since there have never been a successful crossbreeding between Superiors and Primaries? She had been young and stupid; both are forgivable sins, especially when they usually occur in tandem.

Jeri heaved a sigh. "It didn't matter. By then, my family had disowned me, mainly because I had violated the partnership that already been made for me by another clan. Both clans were scandalized, and as a result neither one wanted me." She looked askance at me. "Bigotry works both ways, you know. You call us googles, we call you apes, and I had slept with an ape. An insult against the extropic ideal."

She closed the logbook, tossed it from her left foot to her right hand, and tucked it into a web beneath the console. "So I was grounded at Descartes. A small pension, just enough to pay the rent, but nothing really to live for. I suppose they expected me to become a prostitute . . . which I did, for a short time . . . or commit ritual suicide and save everyone the sweat."

"That's cold." But not unheard of. There were a few grounded Superiors to be found in the inner system, poor sad cases working at menial tasks in LaGranges or on the Moon. I remembered an alcoholic google who hung out at Sloppy Joe's; he had eagle wings tattooed across his back, and he cadged drinks off tourists in return for performing cartwheels across the bar. An eagle with clipped tailfeathers. Every so often, one would hear of a Superior who checked out by walking into an airlock and pushing the void button. No one knew why, but now I had an answer. It was the Superior way.

"That's extropy for you." She laughed bitterly, then was quiet for a moment. "I was considering taking the long walk," she said at last, "but Bo found me first, when I . . . well, propositioned him. He bought me a couple of drinks and listened to my story, and when I was done crying he told me he needed a new first officer. No one else would work for him, so he offered me the job, for as long as I cared to keep it."

"And you've kept it."

"And I've kept it," she finished. "For the record, Mr. Furland, he has always treated me with the greatest of respect, despite what anyone else might have told you. I've never slept with him, nor has he ever demanded that I so . . ."

"I didn't . . . !"

"No, of course you haven't, but you've probably wondered, haven't you?" When I turned red, she laughed again. "Everyone who has worked the *Comet* has, and sometimes they like to tell stories about the google and the fat slob, fucking in his cabin between shifts."

She smiled, slowly shaking her head. "It isn't so . . . but, to tell the truth, if he ever asked, I'd do so without a second thought. I owe him that little."

I didn't say anything for a couple of minutes. It isn't often when a shipmate unburdens his or her soul, and Jeri had given me much to consider. Not the least of which was the slow realization that, now more than before, I was becoming quite fond of her.

Before he had gone below, McKinnon had told me to activate the external missile pod, so I pushed myself over to his station and used that minor task to cover for my embarrassment.

Strapping an EMP to an Ares-class freighter was another example of McKinnon's overheated imagination. When I had once asked why, he told me that he purchased it as war surplus from the Pax Astra Royal Navy back in '71, after the hijacking of the TBSA *Olympia*. No one had ever discovered who had taken the *Olympia*—indeed, the hijack wasn't discovered until five months later, when the uncrewed solar-sail vessel arrived at Ceres Station with its cargo holds empty—but it was widely believed to be the work of indie prospectors desperate for food and various supplies.

I had to cover my smile when McKinnon told me that he was worried about "pirates" trying to waylay the *Comet*. Having four 10k nukes tucked behind the *Comet*'s cargo section was like arming a gig with heatseekers. Not that McKinnon wouldn't have loved it if someone *did* try to steal his ship—Captain Future meets the Asteroid Pirates and all that—but I was worried that he might open fire on some off-course prospector that was unlucky to cross his path.

Another thought occurred to me. "When he picked you . . . um, when you signed on as First Officer . . . were you aware that he doesn't have a firm grip on reality?"

Jeri didn't answer immediately. I was about to repeat myself when I felt a gentle nudge against my arm. Looking down, I saw her left foot slide past me, its thumb-sized toes toggling the MISSILE STANDBY switch I had neglected to throw.

"Sure," she said. "In fact, he used to call me Joan . . . as in Joan Randall, Curt Newton's girlfriend . . . until I got him to cut it out."

"Really?"

"Um-hmm." She rested her right leg against the back of my chair. "Consider yourself lucky he doesn't call you Otho or Grag. He used to do that to other crewmen until I told him that no one got the joke." She grinned. "You ought to try reading some of those stories sometime. He's loaded them into The Brain's library annex. Not great literature, to be sure . . . in fact, they're rather silly . . . but for early twentieth-century science fiction, they're . . ."

"Science what?"

"Science fiction. What they used to call fantasy back . . . well, never mind." She pulled her leg back and folded it beneath her bottom as she gazed again out the window. "Look, I know Bo can be weird most of the time, but you have to realize that he's a romantic stuck in an age where most people don't even know what the word means any more. He wants derring-do, swashbuckling, great adventure . . . he wants to be a hero."

"Uh-huh. Bo McKinnon, space hero." I tried to transpose him on the magazine covers he had framed in the galley: wielding a ray gun in each hand, defending Jeri from ravaging monsters. It didn't work, except to make me stifle a chuckle.

"That isn't too much for ask for, is it?" There was sadness in her eyes when she glanced my way. Before I could get the grin off my face, she returned her gaze to the windows. "Perhaps so. This isn't an age of heros. We move rock back and forth across the system, put money in the bank, and congratulate ourselves for our ingenuity. A hundred and fifty years ago, what we're doing now was the stuff of dreams, and the people who did it were larger than life. That's what he finds so attractive in those stories. But now . . ."

She let out her breath. "Who can blame Bo for wanting something he can't have? He's stuck on a second-hand freighter with an ex-whore for a first officer and a second officer who openly despises him, and he's the butt of every jokes from Earth to Iapetus. No wonder he drops everything to answer a Mayday. This may be the only chance he gets."

I was about to retort that my only chance to get a job on a decent ship was slipping through my fingers when her console double-beeped. A moment later, The Brain's voice came through the ceiling speaker.

"Pardon me, but we're scheduled for course correction maneuvers. Do you wish for me to execute?"

Jeri swiveled her chair around. "That's okay, Brain. We'll handle it by manual control. Give me the coordinates."

The AI responded by displaying a three-dimensional grid on her flatscreens. "Want me to do anything?" I asked, although it was obvious that she had matters well in hand.

"I've got everything covered," she said, her long fingers typing in the coordinates. "Get some sleep, if you want." She cast a quick grin over her shoulder. "Don't worry. I won't tell Bo you dozed off his chair."

End of conversation. Besides, she had a good idea. I cranked back the chair, buckled the seat belt and tucked my hands in my pockets so they wouldn't drift around in freefall. It might be awhile before I got another chance; once we reached 2046-Barr, Captain Future would be back on deck, bellowing orders and otherwise making my life painful.

She had told me a lot about Bo McKinnon, but nothing I had heard gave me much affection for the man. So far as I was concerned, he was still the biggest dork I had ever met . . . and if there was anyone aboard the TBSA *Comet* who deserved my sympathy, it was Jeri Lee-Bose, who was meant for better things than this.

As I shut my eyes, it occurred to me that the captain's chair fitted me a lot better than it did McKinnon. One day, perhaps I'd have enough money in the bank to buy him out. It would be interesting to see if he took orders as well as he gave them.

It was a warm and comforting thought, and I snuggled against it like pillow as I fell asleep.

> "Look, Arraj—it is a meteor!" cried the younger Martian excitedly. "And there's a ship guiding it!"
>
> The two stared for a moment at the incredible spectacle. The expanding black spot was clearly a giant meteor, rushing now at tremendous speed toward Mars. And close beside the booming meteor rushed a dark spaceship, playing rays upon the great mass. The ship was propelling the meteor Mars.
>
> —Hamilton, *Captain Future's Challenge* (1940)

Several hours later, the *Comet* rendezvoused with 2046-Barr.

The asteroid looked much the same as the holo tank had depicted it—an enormous rock the color of charcoal—but the *Fool's Gold* itself was the largest spacecraft I had ever seen short of a LaGrange colony. It dwarfed the *Comet* like a yacht parked alongside an ocean liner, a humongous machine attached to one end of the asteroid's mass.

A humongous machine, and apparently lifeless. We approached the mass-driver with great caution, being careful to avoid its stern lest we get nailed by the stream of debris being constantly ejected by its railgun. That was the only apparent sign of activity; although light gleamed from the portals of the rotating command sphere, we could detect no motion within the windows, and the radio remained as silent as it had been for the last eighteen hours.

"Look yonder." I pointed through the window at the hangar bay, a wide berth within the barrel-shaped main hull just forward of the railgun. Its doors were open, and as the *Comet* slowly cruised past we could see the gig and service pods parked in their cradles. "Everything's there. Even the lifeboats are still in place."

Jeri angled the camera on the outrigger telemetry boom until it peered into the bay. Her wide eyes narrowed as she studied a close-up view on a flatscreen. "That's weird," she murmured. "Why would they depressurize the bay and open the doors if they didn't . . . ?"

"Knock it off, you two!"

McKinnon was strapped in his chair, on the other side of Jeri Lee's duty station from mine. "It doesn't matter why they did it. Just keep your eyes peeled for pirates . . . they could be lurking somewhere nearby."

I chose to remain silent as I piloted the *Comet* past the mass-driver's massive anchor-arms and over the top of the asteroid. Ever since McKinnon had returned to the bridge an hour ago—following the shower and leisurely breakfast I myself had been denied—he had been riding his favorite hobby horse: asteroid pirates had seized control of the *Fool's Gold* and taken its crew hostage.

This despite the fact that we had not spotted any other spacecraft during our long journey and that none could now be seen in the vicinity of the asteroid. It could also be logically argued that the four-person crew of a prospector ship would have a hard time overcoming the twelve-person crew of a mass-driver, but logic meant little to Captain Future. His left hand rested on the console near the EMP controls, itching to launch a nuke at the pirate ship he was certain to find lurking in the asteroid's shadow.

Yet, when we completed a fly-by of 2046-Barr, none were to be found. In fact, nothing moved at all, save for the asteroid itself . . .

A thought occurred to me. "Hey, Brain," I said aloud, "have you got a fix on the mass-driver's position and bearing?"

"*Affirmative, Mr. Furland. It is X-ray one-seven-six, Yankee two . . .*"

"Mr. Furland!" McKinnon snapped. "I didn't give orders for you to . . ."

I ignored him. "Skip the numbers, Brain. Just tell me if it's still on course for cislunar rendezvous."

A momentary pause, then: "*Negative, Mr. Furland. The* Fool's Gold *has altered its trajectory. According to my calculations, there is a seventy-two-point-one probability that it is now on collision course with the planet Mars.*"

Jeri went pale as she sucked in her breath, and even McKinnon managed to shut up. "Show it to me on the tank," I said as I turned my chair around to face the nav table.

The tank lit, displaying a holographic diagram of the *Fool's Gold*'s present position in relationship with the Martian sidereal-hour. Mars still lay half an A.U. away, but as The Brain traced a shallow-curving orange line through the belt, we saw that it neatly intercepted the red planet as it advanced on its orbit around the Sun.

The Brain translated the math it had displayed in a box next to the three-dimensional grid. "*Assuming that its present delta-vee remains unchecked, in two hundred and thirty-six hours, twelve minutes, and twenty-four seconds, 2046-Barr will collide with Mars.*"

I did some arithmetic in my head. "That's about ten days from now."

"*Nine-point-eight-three Earth standard days, to be exact.*" The Brain expanded the image of Mars until it filled the tank; a bulls-eye appeared at a point just above the equator. "*Estimated point of impact will be approximately twelve degrees North by sixty-three degrees West, near the edge of the Lunae Planum.*"

"Just north of Valles Marineris," Jeri said. "Oh God, Rohr, that's near . . ."

"I know." I didn't need a refresher course in planetary geography. The impact point was in the low plains above Mariner Valley, only a few hundred klicks northeast of Arsia Station, not to mention closer to the smaller settlements scattered around the vast canyon system. For all I knew, there could now be a small mining town on the Lunae Planum itself; Mars was being colonized so quickly these days, it was hard to keep track of where a bunch of its one and a half million inhabitants decided to pitch claims and call themselves New Chattanooga or whatever.

"Sabotage!" McKinnon yelled. He unbuckled his harness and pushed himself closer the nav table, where he stared at the holo. "Someone has sabotaged the mass-driver so that it'll collide with Mars! Do you realize . . . ?"

"Shut up, Captain." I didn't need his histrionics to tell me what would occur if . . . *when* . . . 2046-Barr came down in the middle of the Lunae Planum.

The Martian ecosystem wasn't as fragile as Earth's. Indeed, it was much more volatile, as the attempt in the '50s to terraform the planet and make the climate more stable had ultimately proved. However, the Mars colonists who still remained after the boondoggle had come to depend upon its seasonal patterns in order to grow crops, maintain solar farms, continue mining operations and other activities which insured their basic survival.

It was a very tenuous sort of existence which relied upon conservative prediction of climatic changes. The impact of a three-kilometer asteroid in the equatorial region would throw all that straight into the compost toilet. Localized quakes and duststorms would only be the beginning; two or three hundred people might be killed outright, but the worst would be yet to come. The amount of dust that would be raised into the atmosphere by the collision would blot out the sky for months on end, causing global temperatures to drop from Olympus Mons to the Hellas Plantia. As a result, everything from agriculture and power supplies would be affected, to put it mildly, with starvation in the cold and dark awaiting most of the survivors.

It wasn't quite doomsday. A few isolated settlements might get by with the aid of emergency relief efforts from Earth. But as the major colony world of humankind, Mars would cease to exist.

McKinnon was still transfixed upon the holo tank, jabbing his finger at Mars while raving about saboteurs and space pirates and God knows what else, when I turned back to Jeri. She had taken the helm in my absence, and as the *Comet* came up on the *Fool's Gold* again, I closely studied the mass-driver on the flatscreens.

"Okay," I said quietly. "The hangar bay is out . . . we can't send the skiff in there while it's depressurized and the cradles are full. Maybe if we . . ."

She was way ahead of me. "There's an auxiliary docking collar here," she said, pointing to a port on the spar leading to the command sphere. "It'll be tight, but I think we can squeeze us in there."

I looked at the screen. Tight indeed. Despite the fact that the *Comet* had a universal docking adapter, the freighter wasn't designed for mating with a craft as large as *Fool's Gold*. "That's cutting it close," I said. "If we can collapse the telemetry boom, though, we might be able to make it."

She nodded. "We can do that, no problem . . . except it means losing contact with Ceres."

"But if we don't hard-dock," I replied, "then someone's got to go EVA and try entering a service airlock."

Knowing that this someone would probably be me, I didn't much relish the idea. An untethered spacewalk between two vessels under acceleration is an iffy business at best. On the other hand, cutting off our radio link with Ceres under these circumstances was probably not a good idea. If we fucked up in some major way, then no one at Ceres Station would be informed of the situation, and early warning from Ceres to Arsia Station might save a few lives, if evacuation of settlements near Lunae Planum was started soon enough.

I made up my mind. "We'll hard-dock," I said, turning in my seat toward the communications console, "but first we send a squib to Ceres, let them know what's . . ."

"Hey! What are you two doing?"

Captain Future had finally decided to see what the Futuremen were doing behind his back. He kicked off the nav table and pushed over to us, grabbing the backs of our chairs with one hand each to hover over us. "I haven't issued any orders, and nothing is done on my ship without my . . ."

"Bo, did you been listen to what we've been saying?" Jeri's expression carefully neutral as she stared up at him. "Have you heard a word either Rohr or I have said?"

"Of course I . . . !"

"Then you know that this is the only recourse," she said, still speaking calmly. "If we don't hard-dock with the Gold, then we won't have a chance of shutting down the railgun or averting its course."

"But the pirates. They might . . . !"

I sighed. "Look, get it through your head. There's no . . ."

"Rohr," she interrupted, casting me a stern look that shut me up. When I dummied up once more, she transfixed McKinnon again with her wide blue eyes. "If there's pirates aboard the Gold," she said patiently, "we'll find them. But right now, this isn't something we can solve this by firing missiles. Rohr's right. First, we send a squib to Ceres, let them know what's going on. Then . . ."

"I know that!"

"Then, we have to dock with . . ."

"I know that! I know that!" His greasy hair scattered in all directions as he shook his head in frustration. "But I didn't . . . I didn't give the orders and . . ."

He stopped, sullenly glaring at me with inchoate rage, and I suddenly realized the true reason for his anger. His subordinate second officer, whom he has harassed and chastised constantly for twelve weeks, had become uppity by reaching a solution that had evaded him. Worse yet, he had done it with the cooperation of his first officer, who had tacitly agreed him on all previous occasions.

Yet this wasn't a trifling matter such as checking the primary fuel pump or cleaning the galley. Countless lives were at stake, time was running out, and while he was spewing obvious nonsense about space pirates, Mister Furland was trying to take command of his ship.

Had I a taser conveniently tucked in my belt, I would have settled the argument by giving him a few volts and strapping his dead ass in his precious chair, thereby allowing Jeri Lee and I to continue our work unfettered. But since outright mutiny runs against my grain, compromise was my only weapon now.

"Begging your pardon, Captain," I said. "You're quite right. You haven't issued the orders, and I apologize."

Then I turned around in my chair, folded my hands in my lap, and waited.

McKinnon sucked in his breath. He stared through the windows at the Fool's Gold, looked over his shoulder once more at the holo tank, weighing the few options available against the mass of his ego. After too many wasted seconds, he finally reached a decision.

"Very well," he said. He let go of our chairs and shoved himself back to his accustomed seat. "Ms. Bose, prepare to dock with the Fool's Gold. Mr. Furland, ready the main airlock hatch and prepare to go EVA."

"Aye, sir," Jeri said.

"Um, yeah . . . aye sir."

"Meanwhile, I'll send a message to Ceres Station and inform them of the situation before we lose contact." Satisfied that he had reached a proper decision, he lay his hands on the armrest. "Good work, Futuremen," he added. "You've done well."

"Thank you, Captain," Jeri said.

"Aye, sir. Thank you." I unbuckled my seat harness and pushed off toward the bridge hatch, trying hard not to smile.

A little victory. Insignificant as it then seemed, I didn't have any idea how much my life depended upon it.

He took the pilot chair and headed the Comet *across the zone toward the computed position of the invisible asteroid.*

"They'll surely see us approaching!" Ezra warned. "The Magician of Mars will be taking no chances, Cap'n Future!"

"We're going to use a stratagem to get onto that asteroid without him suspecting," Curt informed. "Watch."

—Hamilton, The Magician of Mars (1941)

I'm a creature of habit, at least when it comes to established safety procedures, and so it was out of habit that I donned an EVA suit before I cycled through the *Comet's* airlock and entered the *Fool's Gold.*

On one hand, wearing the bulky spacesuit within a pressurized spacecraft is stupidly redundant, and the panel within the airlock told me that there was positive pressure on the other side of the hatch. Yet it could be argued the airlock sensors might be out of whack and there was nothing but hard vacuum within the spar; this has been known to happen before, albeit rarely, and people have died as a result. In any case, the *Astronaut's General Handbook* says that an EVA suit should be worn when boarding another craft under uncertain conditions, and so I followed the book.

Doing so saved my life.

I went alone, leaving Jeri and McKinnon behind inside the freighter. The hatch led past the *Gold's* airlock into the spar's access tunnel, all of which were vacant. Switching on the helmet's external mikes, I heard nothing but the customary background hum of the ventilation system, further evidence that the vessel crew compartments were still pressurized.

At that point, I could well have removed my helmet and hung it from a strap on my utility belt. In fact, the only reason I didn't was that I didn't want it banging around as I went through the carrousel, which lay at the end of the tunnel to my right. Besides, the stillness of the tunnel gave me the chills. Surely someone would have noticed the unscheduled docking of an Ares-class freighter, let alone one so far from Ceres. Why wasn't there an officer waiting at the airlock to chew me out for risking collision with his precious ship?

The answer came after I rotated through the carrousel and entered the rotating command sphere. That's when I found the first corpse.

A naked man hung upside down through an open manhole, his limp arms dangling above the wide pool of blood on the deck. It was difficult to see his face, because the blood that had dyed it crimson came from a scimitar-shaped gash in his neck. Looking up through the manhole, I saw that his feet had been neatly lashed together with a bungee cord, which in turn was tied to a conduit in the ceiling of the corridor directly above.

Since there were no bloodstains below his shoulders, it was obvious that his throat had been slit after he had been hung from the conduit. The blood was dry— most of it, anyway—and the body was stiff. He had been here for quite some time.

I reported what I found to Jeri and McKinnon, and then I gingerly pushed the body out of the way and continued down the corridor.

Please understand if everything I tell you sounds coldly methodical, even callous. First, if you've worked in space as long as I have—that is, all my life—then death, no matter how horrible it may be, is no stranger. The first time I saw a man die was when I was nine years, when a one-in-a-million micrometeorite punched through the helmet faceplate of one of my schoolteachers while he was leading us on a field trip to the Apollo 17 landing site at Taurus Lithrow. Since then, I've seen the grisly results of explosive decompression, fatal radiation overexposure, freak mining accidents, careless suit-up procedures, hull fires and electrocutions, even someone who choked on his own vomit after consuming too much bathtub vodka during a birthday party. Death comes to us all, eventually; if you're careful and wise, all you can is make sure that it isn't too painful and no one is stuck with a mess to clean up.

Second: if I attempted now to describe each and every body I discovered as I made my way through the *Fool's Gold*, the result would not only be gratuitous pandering to those who wallow in such details, but I would never be able to complete this testimony.

To put it succinctly, the command sphere of the *Fool's Gold* was a slaughterhouse.

I found ten more bodies, each more gruesome than the last. They were in crew cabins and passageways, in the galley and in the head, in the rec room and the quartermaster's office.

Most were alone, but two of them were together, each apparently dead from wounds they had afflicted upon one another: a man and a woman, who had tried to carve each other up with knives they had taken from the nearby galley.

A couple of the bodies were nude, like the first, but most were fully or partially clothed. For the most part, they had died of stabbing or bludgeon wounds, by means of anything that could be used as a weapon, whether it be a ballpoint pen, a screwdriver, or a pipefitter's wrench.

One woman was lucky. She had committed suicide by hanging herself by a coiled bedsheet she had cast over the top of a door. I hope that she had successfully strangled herself before whoever found her body seared off her right arm with the cutting torch cast nearby.

As I climbed up ladders, poked my helmet through hatches, and stepped over stiffening corpses, I kept up a running monologue, informing the *Comet* of where I exactly was within the vessel and what I had just found. I made no speculation as to why this carnage had taken place, only to note that the bodies seemed reasonably fresh and that most of the bloodstains were dry.

And blood lay everywhere. It was splattered across walls and soaked into carpets and dripping from wall fixtures, until it no longer resembled blood and just looked like spilled red paint. I was glad I had kept my helmet on, because the visor helped distance me from the carnage, and the rank odor would have made me even more sickened than I was now.

Although I heard an occasional gasp or exclamation from Jeri through my headset, after awhile I couldn't detect McKinnon's voice any longer. I assumed that he had gone someplace private to vomit. This was understandable; the violence around me was mind shattering.

There were four decks in the command sphere, one above the other. By the time I reached the top deck, I had counted eleven corpses. Remembering that McKinnon had told me earlier that the crew complement of the *Fool's Gold* was twelve, I had begun to wonder where the last body lay.

The hatch leading to the bridge was sealed shut; I used the laser welding torch from my belt to cut the lock. When I grasped the lockwheel and prized it open, it made a faint grinding noise, and it was at that moment that I hear a methodical, almost rhythmic thumping, as if something was being beaten against a bulkhead.

I first thought it was another background noise from the vessel itself, but when I pushed the hatch farther open, the noise it made interrupted the rhythm.

I stopped, holding the hatch ajar as I listened intently. I heard a faint giggle, then the thumping sound recommenced.

Someone was alive within the bridge.

The command center was dimly lit, the fluorescents switched off, the only light came from computer displays, flatscreens, and multicolored switches. The deck was in ruins, as if there had been a blowout, although the external pressure gauge told me it was still pressurized: upended chairs, ripped logbooks and manuals strewn across the floor, the remains of a bloody shirt.

The thumping continued. Seeking its unseen source, I switched on the helmet lamp and walked within its beam, my eyes darting back and forth as I searched for the sole survivor of the *Fool's Gold*. I was halfway across the bridge when my eye caught something scrawled across a bulkhead. Two words, fingerpainted in blood across the gray surface:

PLAGUE
TITAN

It was then that I knew that wearing an EVA suit had saved my life.

Trembling within its insulated layers, I crossed the deserted bridge, looking for the last remaining crewmember of the *Fool's Gold*.

I found him in the emergency airlock, huddled in a corner next to the hatch, his knees drawn up to his chin. The jumpsuit he wore was streaked with gore, but I could still make out the captain's stars on its epaulets. His wary eyes winced from the glare of my lamp, and he giggled like a small child who had been caught exploring his mother's dresser drawers.

And then he continued to beat at the deck with the severed human arm he grasped in his left hand.

I don't know how long I stared at him. A few seconds, several minutes, perhaps longer. Jeri was saying something I couldn't understand; I paid no attention, nor could I respond. It wasn't until I heard another noise—from behind me, the faint sound of the hatch being shoved open—that I tore my eyes away from the mad captain of the *Fool's Gold*.

Bo McKinnon.

He had followed me from the *Comet*.

And, like the idiot he was, he wasn't wearing an EVA suit.

> The little teardrop ship, the Comet, blasted at top speed toward the Earth and its summoning call. Captain Future thought somberly of the many times he had answered that call. Each time, he and the Futuremen had found themselves called on to battle deadly perils. Was this to be the same this time?
>
> "We can't always win," he thought grimly. "We've been lucky, but the law of averages eventually has to turn against us."
>
> —Hamilton, *The Triumph of Captain Future* (1940)

Despite the name, no one knows the exact origin of Titan Plague.

It was first contracted by members of the *Hershel Explorer* expedition of 2069, during the Pax's ill-fated attempt to establish a research outpost on Titan. Although it was later theorized that the virus was indigenous to Titan itself, the fact that it thrived in an oxygen-nitrogen environment led many people to speculate that the Plague had originated somewhere other than Titan's nitrogen-methane atmosphere. There was even hearsay that the expedition had encountered an extrasolar race on Titan and that the Plague had been passed from Them . . . but, of course, that was just rumor.

Regardless, the indisputable facts are these: by the time the PARN *Hershel Explorer* returned to the inner system, the majority of its crew had been driven insane by an airborne virus. The only reason why the three surviving expedition members, including the ship's commander, were not infected was that they had managed to seal themselves within the command center, where they survived on emergency oxygen supplies and carefully rationed food and water. Most of the unquarantined members butchered each other during the long voyage home; those who did not died in agony when the disease rotted their brains in its terminal stages.

Once the *Hershel Explorer* reached the asteroid belt, the survivors parked it in orbit around Vesta, then used a lifeboat to escape. Three months later, the *Hershel Explorer* was scuttled by the PARN *Intrepid*. By then, Queen Macedonia had decreed that no further expeditions would be sent to Titan and that any vessels attempting to land there would be destroyed by Her Majesty's navy.

Despite the precautions, though, there had been a few isolated outbreaks of Titan Plague, albeit rare and confined to colonies in the outer system. No one knew exactly how the disease spread from the *Hershel Explorer*, although it was believed that it had been carried by the survivors themselves despite of rigorous decontamination. Even though the first symptoms resembled little more than the once-common cold, the homicidal dementia that quickly followed was unmistakable. When someone came down with the Plague, there was no other option than to isolate them, remove anything that could be used as a weapon, and wait until they died.

No cure had ever been found.

Somehow, in some way we would never know, the Plague had found its way aboard the *Fool's Gold*. In the close confines of the mass-driver, it had swept through the entire vessel, driving its crew insane before they realized what had hit them. Perhaps the captain had figured it out, yet despite his precautions he himself was infected.

I was safe because I had worn a spacesuit while exploring the ship. But Bo McKinnon . . .

Captain Future, Man of Tomorrow, dauntless hero of the spaceways. In his search for adventure, McKinnon had recklessly entered the vessel without bothering to don a suit.

"Did you shut the airlock?" I snapped.

"What? Huh?" Pale, visibly shaken by the horrors he had seen, McKinnon was staring at the maniac crouched in the airlock behind us. "Airlock? What . . . which . . . ?"

I grabbed his shoulders and shook him so hard his headset fell down around his neck. "The *Comet* airlock! Did you shut it behind you, or did you leave it wide open?"

Unable to hear me now, he stammered until he realized that his headset was ajar. He fumbled with it until the earphones were back in place. "The airlock? I think so, I . . ."

"Think so? You moron, did you . . . ?"

"Furland, oh my God . . ." He gaped at the wreckage around him. "What happened to these people? Did they . . . watch out!"

I turned around just in time to catch a glimpse of the madman as he lurched to his feet. Howling at the top of his lungs, he charged toward us, flailing the severed arm like a cricket bat.

I threw McKinnon aside. As he sprawled across the deck, I grabbed the airlock hatch and shoved it closed. An instant later the creature hit the opposite side of the hatch. He almost banged it open, but I put my shoulder against it. The hatch held, and a twist of lockwheel sealed it airtight; nonetheless, I could feel dull vibrations as the madman hammered against it with his hideous trophy.

I couldn't keep him locked in there forever. Sooner or later, he would find the lockwheel and remember how it worked. Perhaps then I could overcome him—if I was lucky, considering his berserk rage—but even then, I didn't dare bring him aboard the *Comet*.

There was only one solution. I found the airlock's outer control panel and flipped open its cover. "I'm sorry, sir," I whispered to the lunatic. "May God have mercy on us both."

Then I pushed the switch that jettisoned the outer hatch.

The alarm bells that rang throughout the bridge were the poor man's funeral dirge. There was long silence after I shut off the alarms, finally broken by McKinnon's voice.

"Mr. Furland, you just murdered that man."

I turned back around. McKinnon had managed to struggle to his feet; he clutched the back of a chair for support, and he glared at me with outraged eyes.

Before I could respond, Jeri's voice came to me over the comlink: "*Rohr, he shut the airlock on the way out. The* Comet *hasn't been infected.*"

I let out my breath. For once, Bo had managed to do something right on his own. "Good deal, kiddo. Keep it shut until I come back aboard."

I stepped away from the airlock, heading for the helm station on the other side of the bridge. McKinnon planted himself in my path. "Did you hear me, Mr. Furland?" he demanded, his adam's apple bobbing beneath his beard. "You just killed a man . . . I saw you do it! You . . ."

"Don't remind me. Now get out of my way." I pushed him aside and marched toward the helm.

One of its flatscreens depicted a schematic chart of the asteroid's position and estimated course. As I suspected, someone aboard the mass-driver had deliberately laid in the new course during a fit of insanity. Probably the captain himself, considering the fact that he had locked himself in here.

"I'm placing you under arrest!" McKinnon yelled. "Under my jurisdiction as an agent of the Planet Police, I . . ."

"There's no such thing." I bent over the keypad and went to work accessing the main computer, my fingers thick and clumsy within the suit gloves. "No Planet Police, no asteroid pirates. Just a ship whose air ducts are crawling with the Plague. You're . . ."

"I'm Captain Future!"

The virus must have already affected him. I could have checked to see if he was displaying any of the flu-like symptoms that were supposed to be the Plague's first signs, but he was the least of my worries just now.

No matter what I did, I couldn't access the program for the central navigation system. Lack of a password that had probably died along with one of the damned souls aboard this ship, and none of the standard overrides or interfaces worked either. I was completely locked out, unable to alter the vessel's velocity or trajectory that had it propelling 2046-Barr straight toward Mars.

"And what are you talking about, not letting anyone aboard the *Comet* until you give the word?" McKinnon was no longer hovering over me; he had found the late captain's chair and had taken it as his own, as if assuming command of a vessel far larger than his measly freighter. "I'm the boss of this ship, not you, and I'm staying in charge until . . ."

Okay. The helm wouldn't obey any new instructions. Maybe it was still possible to scuttle the *Fool's Gold.* I accessed the engineering subsystem and began searching for a way to shut down the primary coolant loop of the gas-core reactor and its redundant safety systems. If I timed it right, perhaps the *Comet* would make a clean getaway before the reactor overloaded . . . and if we were goddamned lucky, the explosion might knock the asteroid sufficiently off-course.

"*Rohr?*" Jeri again. "*What's going on up there?*"

I didn't want to tell her, not with McKinnon eavesdropping on our comlink.

At the sound of her voice, he surged to his feet. "Joan! He's working for Ul Quorn, the Magician of Mars! He's going to . . ."

"Fuck him!" I yelled. "I'm working on it! Just get the *Comet* ready to . . . !"

I heard him coming long before he reached me. I stood up and, pulling back my arm, landed a right hook square against his hairy jaw.

It stopped him, but it wouldn't keep him stopped. McKinnon was a big guy. He staggered back, his eyes unfocused as he groped at the chair for support. "Traitor," he mumbled, feeling at his mouth with his left hand. "You traitor, you . . ."

I didn't have time for this shit, so I punched him again, this time square in the nose. Second shot did the trick; he reeled backward, sagged against the chair, and flopped flat on his back.

"*What are you doing?*" she demanded.

Even within the thick padding of my gloves, my knuckles hurt like hell. "Something that should have been done a long time ago," I murmured.

Cute line. I used up the last of my luck that way. I scrambled at the helm console for several more minutes before I submitted to the inevitable. Like the navigation controls, the engineering subsystem wouldn't obey my commands without the proper passwords. It was possible that they were written down somewhere, but I didn't have the time or inclination to go searching through the operations manuals, especially since most of them were strewn across the bridge like so much garbage.

We weren't out of options yet. There was still one final alternative, one which McKinnon himself had given us.

It was then that I knew that Captain Future had to die.

> "*Captain Future is dead!*"
>
> The *rumbling voice of the big green Jovian space-sailor rose above the laughter and chatter and clink of goblets, in this crowded Venusopolis spacemen's cafe. He eyed his little knot of companions at the bar, as though challenging them to dispute him.*
>
> One of a hard-bitten spacemen, a swarthy little Mercurian, shook his head thoughtfully.
>
> "*I'm not so sure. It's true that the Futuremen have been missing for months. But they'd be a hard bunch to kill.*"
>
> —Hamilton, *Outlaws of the Moon* (1942)

As I write, I'm back on the Moon, occupying a corner table in Sloppy Joe's. It's close to closing time; the crowds have thinned out and the bartender has rung the bell for last call. He'll let me stay after he closes the doors, though. Heroes never get booted out with the riff-raff, and there's been no shortage of free drinks ever since I returned from Ceres.

After all, I'm the last person to see Captain Future alive.

The news media helped us maintain our alibi. After all, it was a story that had everything. Adventure, romance, blood and guts, countless lives at stake. Best of all, a noble act of self-sacrifice. It'll make a great vid. I sold the rights yesterday.

Because it's been so widely told, you already know how the story ends. Realizing that he had been fatally infected with Titan Plague, Bo McKinnon—excuse me, Captain Future—issued his final instructions as commanding officer of the TBSA *Comet*.

He told me to return to the ship, and once I was safely aboard, he ordered Jeri to cast off and get the *Comet* as far away as possible.

Realizing what he intended to do, we tried to talk him out of it. Oh, and how we argued and pleaded with him, telling him that we could place him in biostasis until we returned to Earth, where doctors could attempt to save his life.

In the end, though, McKinnon simply cut off his comlink so that he could meet his end with dignity and grace.

Once the *Comet* was gone and safely out of range, Captain Future managed to instruct the mass-driver's main computer to overload the vessel reactors. While he sat alone in the abandoned bridge, waiting for the countdown, there was just enough time for him to transmit one final message of courage . . .

Don't make me repeat it, please. It's bad enough that the Queen read it aloud during the memorial service, but now I understand that it's going to be inscribed upon the base of a twice–life size statue of McKinnon that's going to be erected at Arsia Station. Jeri did her best when she wrote it, but between you and me, I still think it's a complete crock.

Anyway, the thermonuclear blast not only obliterated the *Fool's Gold*, but it also sufficiently altered the trajectory of 2046. The asteroid came within five thousand kilometers of Mars; its close passage was recorded by the observatory on Phobos, and the settlements in the Central Meridian reported the largest micrometeor shower in the history of the colonies.

And now Bo McKinnon is remembered as Captain Future, one of the greatest heroes in the history of humankind.

It was the least Jeri could have done for him.

Considering what a jerk Bo had been all the way to the end, I could have tried to claim the credit, but her strong will persevered. I suppose she's right; it would look bad if it was known that McKinnon had gone out as a raving lunatic who had to be cold-cocked by his second officer.

Likewise, no one has to know that four missiles launched from the *Comet* destroyed the mass-driver's main reactor, thus causing the explosion that averted 2046-Barr from its doomsday course. The empty weapon pod before the *Comet* reached Ceres, and the small bribe paid to a minor Pax bureaucrat insured that all records of it ever having been installed on the freighter were completely erased.

It hardly matters. In the end, everyone got what they wanted.

As first officer of the *Comet*, Jeri Lee became its new commander. She offered me her old job, and since the *Jove Commerce* deal was down the tubes, I gratefully accepted. It wasn't long after that before she also offered to show me the rest of her tattoos, an invitation that I also accepted. Her clan still won't speak to her, especially since she now plans to marry a Primary, but at least her fellow Superiors have been forced to claim her as one of their own.

For now, life is good. There's money in the bank, we've shucked our black sheep status, and there's no shortage of companies who want to hire the legendary Futuremen of the TBSA *Comet*. Who knows? Once we get tired of working the belt, maybe we'll settle down and take a shot at beating the odds on this whole cross-breeding thing.

And Bo got what he wanted, even though he didn't live long enough to enjoy it. In doing so, perhaps humankind got what it needed.

There's only one thing that still bothers me.

When McKinnon went nuts aboard the *Fool's Gold* and tried to attack me, I assumed that he had come down with the Plague. This was a correct assumption; he had been infected the moment he had come through the airlock.

However, I later learned that it takes at least six hours for Titan Plague to fully incubate within a human being, and neither of us had been aboard the *Fool's Gold* for nearly half that long.

If McKinnon was crazy at the end, it wasn't because of the Plague. To this day, I have no idea what made him snap . . . unless he believed that I was trying to run off with his ship, his girl, and his goddamn glory.

Hell, maybe I was.

Last night, some nervous kid—a cargo grunt off some LEO freighter, his union card probably still uncreased—sidled up to me at the bar and asked for my autograph. While

I was signing the inside cover of his logbook, he told me a strange rumor he had recently heard: Captain Future managed to escape from the *Fool's Gold* just before it blew. According to him, prospectors in the inner belt report spotting a gig on their screens, one whose pilot answers their calls as Curt Newton before transmissions are lost.

I bought the youngster a drink and told him the truth. Naturally, he refused to believe me, nor can I blame him.

Heroes are hard to find. We need to welcome them whenever they appear in our midst. You've just got to be careful to pick the right guy, because it's easy for someone to pretend to be what they're not.

Captain Future is dead.

Long live Captain Future.

AUTHOR'S NOTE

Although largely forgotten today, Captain Future was a popular pulp-fiction character of the 1940s. Created by Better Publications editor Mort Weisinger during the 1939 World Science Fiction Convention, Curt Newton was featured in his own magazine for several years, and later in Startling Stories. *Several Captain Future novels were reprinted in paperback in the late '60s; since then, however, the character has vanished into obscurity.*

This story is dedicated to the late Edmond Hamilton, author of most of the Captain Future adventures.

The author wishes to thank Eleanor Wood, the executor of Hamilton's literary estate, for permission to use brief quotes from his Captain Future stories.

V.

MIXED SIGNALS /
MIXED CATEGORIES
(TO THE LATE 1990S)

Space opera has not died. In fact, it is more alive right now, as we enter a new millennium, than it has been at any time since World War II. I have no room here to go into the many examples, but I would point to all those contemporary American authors whose names begin with "B"—Greg Bear, Greg Benford, David Brin, Lois McMaster Bujold—and the British writers Iain M. Banks and Stephen Baxter. Not everything they have written is describable as space opera, but an appreciable amount is, and these writers are unabashed about it. I would point to Colin Greenland's *Take Back Plenty*, Paul J. McAuley's *Eternal Light*, Vernor Vinge's *A Fire Upon the Deep*, and Peter F. Hamilton's *The Reality Dysfunction*; also to many books by C. J. Cherryh and Stephen Donaldson's lengthy and deeply strange "Gap" series (with its debt to Richard Wagner, Donaldson's is perhaps the one space opera that takes the "opera" component seriously). At the same time, older writers like Pohl and Jack Williamson are still active and, some of the time, still producing intelligent space opera. Also at the same time, there has been a resurgence of the romantic, fantastic, or purely crowd-pleasing space opera. . . . People like Barbara Hambly and Dave Wolverton are writing space opera; even Margaret Weis and Tracy Hickman have turned, at times, from pseudo-medieval gaming fantasy to the production of space opera series.

—David Pringle in "What Is This Thing Called Space Opera?"

GREGORY BENFORD

Gregory Benford [1941–] (www.ps.uci.edu/physics/benford.html) is a physicist and one of the partisans of hard SF. For several decades now he has championed the idea of a well-written, carefully revised, and peer-reviewed hard SF and is among the group of American SF writer/scientists who circulate their manuscripts to one another for both literary and scientific comment. He was the first among the hard science fiction writers to have mastered and integrated Modernist techniques of characterization and use of metaphor. He, more than anyone, has become the chief rhetorician for hard SF. He coined the phrase "playing with the net up," which he uses to describe the game of hard science fiction.

As we said in our companion anthology, *The Hard SF Renaissance*, he is a professor at the University of California, Irvine, working in both astrophysics and plasma physics, and is an intensely competitive man of ideas who enjoys conversational fencing, both as a scientist and as a science fiction writer. In addition to the many awards he has won within the SF field, he is also a winner of the Lord Prize for Contributions to Science and the United Nations Medal in Literature.

Benford is the author of the classic SF novel *Timescape* (1980), as well as a number of other highly regarded works, including *In the Ocean of Night* (1977) and *Sailing Bright Eternity* (1995). He is the finest writer of hard SF in the generation after Larry Niven, and writes primarily in the tradition of Arthur C. Clarke, of immense, fertile, awesome astronomical vistas and technological marvels, but with a depth and richness of characterization not achieved by many other SF writers.

In the dialogue about the resurgence of hard SF in the 1990s he was a crucial figure both as a polemicist and in his fiction. Ken MacLeod said, in his *Locus* essay, "Gregory Benford, Stephen Baxter, and other writers of a new hard SF—too serious in intent and execution to be called space opera—were showing that a knowledge of the universe informed by contemporary astronomy and physics was far more exciting and interesting than that inspired, if that's the word, by a nodding acquaintance with the Hertzsprung-Russell Diagram and a token black hole." Yet in the last few years some of Benford's hard SF has been drawn into the vortex of discussion as hard space opera SF, as has the work of Stephen Baxter.

And Benford himself has been happy to join the discussion. His ideas tend to be provocative, intended to stir debate (and perhaps even to offend the dogmatic and complacent), and to be very well researched and argued. His recent contribution to the New Space Opera discussion is an essay on space opera and economics, which opens:

Since the term was invented in 1941 by Bob ("Wilson") Tucker, space opera has had a grandiosity we pedestrian scientists could long for but seldom believe. Lately, however, developments in our rather plodding space program have provoked in me some hope that such futures make sense. . . . Space opera boasts giant spacecraft and huge space colonies. Who pays for them?

And continues, poking at the new British enthusiasm for the form:

The British have acquired a taste for the recent style of space opera—note Iain M. Banks' series, Ken MacLeod, Peter Hamilton's popular mega-scale space operas, and more recently Alastair Reynolds and Charles Stross—all working with futures fragrant of gargantuan techno-sizzle. Interestingly, all these authors and futures are somewhat vaguely socialist. . . . In politics, everybody is entitled to their own opinion. But everybody is not entitled to their own facts—especially not in economics. . . . The leftish space operas of recent years have plenty of quantum computers and big, Doc Smith–style planet-smashing weaponry, but the hard bits of real economics they swerve around. Maybe because they haven't any real answers, or aren't interested. Opera isn't realism.

And concludes:

So will we have a space operatic future? If that means huge spacecraft driven by spectacular engines, maybe so. Interstellar flight lies beyond the technologically foreseeable, alas. But the rest of the space opera agenda depends on your political prognostications. Will Iain Banks' anarchist/socialist empire arise from remorseless economic forces? Or perhaps Robert Heinlein's libertarian frontier?

We used a different example in *The Hard SF Renaissance*, but the point is the same in effect. This idea is certain to have some readers sputtering about American imperialism, and yet it is quintessential Benford: audacious, large-scale, and something he would be delighted to argue for hours on end. It is also perfectly consistent with the frontier tradition in American SF, and American genre Westerns, out of which space opera in part arose. Benford deploys American triumphalism as a sharp stick to poke those with whom he disagrees.

"A Worm in the Well" is not typical of his fiction in that it is more in the hard SF problem-solving tradition of Robert A. Heinlein and Poul Anderson than the cold technovistas of Arthur C. Clarke, Benford's more usual bailiwick. Here we have an elegant adventure that knowingly plays with the adventure traditions of space piracy, too, and exemplifies hard space opera SF. Benford is developing a novel in this setting.

A WORM IN THE WELL

GREGORY BENFORD

She was about to get baked, and all because she wouldn't freeze a man.

"Optical," Claire called. Erma obliged.

The Sun spread around them, a bubbling plain. She had notched the air conditioning cooler but it didn't help much.

Geysers burst in gaudy reds and actinic violets from the yellow-white froth. The solar coronal arch was just peeking over the horizon, like a wedding ring stuck halfway into boiling white mud. A monster, over two thousand kilometers long, sleek and slender and angry crimson.

She turned down the cabin lights. Somewhere she had read that people felt cooler in the dark. The temperature in here was normal but she had started sweating.

Tuning the yellows and reds dimmer on the big screen before her made the white-hot storms look more blue. Maybe that would trick her subconscious, too.

Claire swung her mirror to see the solar coronal arch. Its image was refracted around the rim of the Sun, so she was getting a preview. Her orbit was on the descending slope of a long ellipse, its lowest point calculated to be just at the peak of the arch. So far, the overlay orbit trajectory was exactly on target.

Software didn't bother with the heat, of course; gravitation was cool, serene. Heat was for engineers. And she was just a pilot.

In her immersion-work environment, the touch controls gave her an abstract distance from the real physical surroundings—the plumes of virulent gas, the hammer of photons. She wasn't handling the mirror, of course, but it felt that way. A light, feathery brush, at a crisp, bracing room temperature.

The imaging assembly hung on its pivot high above her ship. It was far enough out from their thermal shield to feel the full glare, so it was heating up fast. Pretty soon it would melt, despite its cooling system.

Let it. She wouldn't need it then. She'd be out there in the sunlight herself.

She swiveled the mirror by reaching out and grabbing it, tugging it round. All virtual images had a glossy sheen to them that even Erma, her simcomputer, couldn't erase. They looked too good. The mirror was already pitted, you could see it on the picture of the arch itself, but the sim kept showing the device as pristine.

"Color is a temperature indicator, right?" Claire asked.

RED DENOTES A LEVEL OF 7 MILLION DEGREES KELVIN.

Good ol' coquettish Erma, Claire thought. *Never a direct answer unless you coax.* "Close-up the top of the arch."

In both her eyes the tortured sunscape shot by. The coronal loop was a shimmering, braided family of magnetic flux tubes, as intricately woven as a Victorian doily. Its feet were anchored in the photosphere below held by thick, sluggish plasma. Claire zoomed in on the arch. The hottest reachable place in the entire Solar System, and her prey had to end up there.

TARGET ACQUIRED AND RESOLVED BY SOLWATCH SATELLITE. IT IS AT THE VERY PEAK OF THE ARCH. ALSO, VERY DARK.

"Sure, dummy, it's a hole."

I AM ACCESSING MY ASTROPHYSICAL CONTEXT PROGRAM NOW.

Perfect Erma; primly change the subject. "Show me, with color coding."

Claire peered at the round black splotch. Like a fly caught in a spider web. Well, at least it didn't squirm or have legs. Magnetic strands played and rippled like wheat blown by a summer's breeze. The flux tubes were blue in this coding, and they looked eerie. But they were really just ordinary magnetic fields, the sort she worked with every day. The dark sphere they held was the strangeness here. And the blue strands had snared the black fly in a firm grip.

Good luck, that. Otherwise, Sol-Watch would never have seen it. In deep space there was nothing harder to find than that ebony splotch. Which was why nobody ever had, until now.

OUR ORBIT NOW RISES ABOVE THE DENSE PLASMA LAYER. I CAN IMPROVE RESOLUTION BY GOING TO X-RAY. SHOULD I?

"Do."

The splotch swelled. Claire squinted at the magnetic flux tubes in this ocher light. In the x-ray they looked sharp and spindly. But near the splotch the field lines blurred. Maybe they were tangled there, but more likely it was the splotch, warping the image.

"Coy, aren't we?" She close-upped the x-ray picture. Hard radiation was the best probe of the hottest structures.

The splotch. Light there was crushed, curdled, stirred with a spoon.

A fly caught in a spider's web, then grilled over a campfire. And she had to lean in, singe her hair, snap its picture. All because she wouldn't freeze a man.

She had been ambling along a corridor three hundred meters below Mercury's slag plains, gazing down on the frothy water fountains in the foyer of her apartment complex. Paying no attention to much except the clear scent of the splashing. The water was the very best, fresh from the poles, not the recycled stuff she endured on her flights. She breathed in the spray. That was when the man collared her.

"Claire Ambrase, I present formal secure-lock."

He stuck his third knuckle into Claire's elbow port and she felt a cold, brittle *thunk*. Her systems froze. Before she could move, whole command linkages went dead in her inboards.

It was like having fingers amputated. Financial fingers.

In her shock she could only stare at him—mousy, the sort who blended into the background. Perfect for the job. A nobody out of nowhere, complete surprise.

He stepped back. "Sorry. Isataku Incorporated ordered me to do it fast."

Claire resisted the impulse to deck him. He looked Lunar, thin and pale. Maybe with more kilos than she carried, but a fair match. And it would feel *good*.

"I can pay them as soon as—"

"They want it now, they said." He shrugged apologetically, his jaw set. He was used to this all the time. She vaguely recognized him, from some bar near the Apex. There weren't more than a thousand people on Mercury, mostly like her, in mining.

"Isataku didn't have to cut off my credit." She rubbed her elbow. Injected programs shouldn't hurt, but they always did. Something to do with the neuro-muscular intersection. "That'll make it hard to even fly the *Silver Metal Lugger* back."

"Oh, they'll give you pass credit for ship's supplies. And, of course, for the ore load advance. But nothing big."

"Nothing big enough to help me dig my way out of my debt hole."

" 'Fraid not."

"Mighty decent."

He let her sarcasm pass. "They want the ship Lunaside."

"Where they'll confiscate it."

She began walking toward her apartment. She had known it was coming but in the rush to get ore consignments lined up for delivery, she had gotten careless. Agents like this Luny usually nailed their prey at home, not in a hallway. She kept a stunner in the apartment, right beside the door, convenient.

Distract him. "I want to file a protest."

"Take it to Isataku." Clipped, efficient, probably had a dozen other slices of bad news to deliver today. Busy man.

"No, with your employer."

"Mine?" That got to him. His rock-steady jaw gaped in surprise.

"For—" she sharply turned the corner to her apartment, using the time to reach for some mumbo-jumbo "—felonious interrogation of in-boards."

"Hey, I didn't touch your—"

"I felt it. Slimy little groups—yeccch!" Might as well ham it up a little, have some fun.

He looked offended. "I'm triple bonded. I'd never do a readout on a contract customer. You can ask—"

"Can it." She hurried toward her apartment portal and popped it by an inboard command. As she stepped through she felt him, three steps behind.

Here goes. One foot over the lip, turn to her right, snatch the stunner out of its grip mount, turn and aim—and she couldn't fire.

"Damn!" she spat out.

He blinked and backed off, hands up, palms out, as if to block the shot. "What? You'd do a knockover for a crummy ore-hauler?"

"It's *my* ship. Not Isataku's."

"Lady, I got no angle here. You knock me, you get maybe a day before the heavies come after you."

"Not if I freeze you."

His mouth opened and started to form the *f* of a disbelieving *freeze?*—then he got angry. "Stiff me till you shipped out? I'd sue you to your eyeballs and have 'em for hock."

"Yeah, yeah," Claire said wearily This guy was all clichés. "But I'd be orbiting Luna by the time you got out, and with the right deal—"

"You'd maybe clear enough on the ore to pay me damages."

"And square with Isataku." She clipped the stunner back to the wall wearily.

"You'd never get that much."

"OK, it was a long shot idea."

"Lady, I was just delivering, right? Peaceable and friendly, right? And you pull—"

"Get out." She hated it when men went from afraid to angry to insulted, all in less than a split minute.

He got. She sighed and zipped the portal closed.

Time for a drink, for sure. Because what really bothered her was not the Isataku foreclosure, but her own gutlessness.

She couldn't bring herself to pong that guy, put him away for ten mega-seconds or so. That would freeze him out of his ongoing life, slice into relationships, cut away days that could never be replaced.

Hers was an abstract sort of inhibition, but earned. Her uncle had been ponged for over a year and never did get his life back together. Claire had seen the wreckage up close, as a little girl.

Self-revelation was usually bad news. What a great time to discover that she had more principles than she needed.

And how was she going to get out from under Isataku?

The arch loomed over the Sun's horizon now, a shimmering curve of blue-white, two thousand kilometers tall.

Beautiful, seen in the shimmering x-ray—snaky strands purling, twinkling with scarlet hotspots. Utterly lovely, utterly deadly. No place for an ore hauler to be.

"Time to get a divorce," Claire said.

YOU ARE SURPRISINGLY ACCURATE. SEPARATION FROM THE SLAG SHIELD IS 338 SEC-ONDS AWAY.

"Don't patronize me, Erma."

I AM USING MY PERSONALITY SIMULATION PROGRAMS AS EXPERTLY AS MY COMPUTA-TION SPACE ALLOWS.

"Don't waste your running time; it's not convincing. Pay attention to the survey, *then* the separation."

THE ALL-SPECTRUM SURVEY IS COMPLETELY AUTOMATIC, AS DESIGNED BY SOL-WATCH.

"Double-check it."

I SHALL NO DOUBT BENEFIT FROM THIS ADVICE.

Deadpan sarcasm, she supposed. Erma's tinkling voice was inside her mind, im-possible to shut out. Erma herself was an interactive intelligence, partly inboard and partly shipwired. Running the *Silver Metal Lugger* would be impossible without her and the bots.

Skimming over the Sun's seethe might be impossible even with them, too, Claire thought, watching burnt oranges and scalded yellows flower ahead.

She turned the ship to keep it dead center in the shield's shadow. That jagged mound of slag was starting to spin. Fused knobs came marching over the nearby hori-zon of it.

"Where'd that spin come from?" She had started their parabolic plunge sunward with absolutely zero angular momentum in the shield.

TIDAL TORQUES ACTING ON THE ASYMMETRIC BODY OF THE SHIELD.

"I hadn't thought of that."

The idea was to keep the heated side of the slag shield Sunward. Now that heat was coming around to radiate at her. The knobby crust she had stuck together from waste in Mercury orbit now smoldered in the infrared. The shield's far side was melting.

"Can that warm us up much?"

A SMALL PERTURBATION. WE WILL BE SAFELY GONE BEFORE IT MATTERS.

"How're the cameras?" She watched a bot tightening a mount on one of the exte-rior imaging arrays. She had talked the SolWatch Institute out of those instruments, part of her commission. If a bot broke one, it came straight out of profits.

ALL ARE CALIBRATED AND ZONED. WE SHALL HAVE ONLY 33.8 SECONDS OF VIEWING TIME OVER THE TARGET. CROSSING THE ENTIRE LOOP WILL TAKE 4.7 SECONDS.

"Hope the scientists like what they'll see."

I CALCULATE THAT THE PROBABILITY OF SUCCESS, TIMES THE EXPECTED PROFIT, EX-CEEDS SIXTY-TWO MILLION DOLLARS.

"I negotiated a seventy-five million commission for this run." So Erma thought her chances of nailing the worm were—

EIGHTY-THREE PERCENT CHANCE OF SUCCESSFUL RESOLUTION IN ALL IMPORTANT FREQUENCY BANDS.

She should give up calculating in her head; Erma was always faster. "Just be ready to shed the shield. Then I pour on the positrons. Up and out. It's getting warm in here."

I DETECT NO CHANGE IN YOUR AMBIENT 22.3 CENTIGRADE.

Claire watched a blister the size of Europe rise among wispy plumes of white-hot incandescence. Constant boiling fury. "So maybe my imagination's working too hard. Just let's grab the data and run, OK?"

The scientific officer of SolWatch had been suspicious, though he did hide it fairly well.

She couldn't read the expression on his long face, all planes and trimmed bone, skin stretched tight as a drumhead. That had been the style among the asteroid pioneers half a century back. Tubular body suited to narrow corridors, double-jointed in several interesting places, big hands. He had a certain beanpole grace as he wrapped legs around a stool and regarded her, head cocked, smiling enough not to be rude. Exactly enough, no more.

"*You* will do the preliminary survey?"

"For a price."

A disdainful sniff. "No doubt. We have a specially designed vessel nearly ready for departure from Lunar orbit. I'm afraid—"

"I can do it *now*."

"You no doubt know that we are behind schedule in our reconnaissance—"

"Everybody on Mercury knows. You lost the first probe."

The beanpole threaded his thick, long fingers, taking great interest in how they fit together. Maybe he was uncomfortable dealing with a woman, she thought. Maybe he didn't even like women.

Still, she found his stringy look oddly unsettling, a blend of delicacy with a masculine, muscular effect. Since he was studying his fingers, she might as well look, too. Idly she speculated on whether the long proportions applied to all his extremities. Old wives' tale. It might be interesting to find out. But, yes, business first.

"The autopilot approached it too close, apparently," he conceded. "There is something unexpected about its refractive properties, making navigation difficult. We are unsure precisely what the difficulty was."

He was vexed by the failure and trying not to show it, she guessed. People got that way when they had to dance on strings pulled all the way from Earthside. You got to like the salary more than you liked yourself.

"I have plenty of bulk," she said mildly. "I can shelter the diagnostic instruments, keep them cool."

"I doubt your ore carrier has the right specifications."

"How tricky can it be? I swoop in, your gear runs its survey snaps, I boost out."

He sniffed. "Your craft is not rated for Sun skimming. Only research craft have ever—"

"I'm coated with Fresnel." A pricey plating that bounced photons of all races, creeds, and colors.

"That's not enough."

"I'll use a slag shield. More, I've got plenty of muscle. Flying with empty holds, I can get away pronto."

"Ours was very carefully designed—"

"Right, and you lost it."

He studied his fingers again. Strong, wiry, yet thick. Maybe he was in love with them. She allowed herself to fill the silence by imagining some interesting things he could do with them. She had learned that with many negotiations, silence did most of the work. "We . . . *are* behind in our mandated exploration."

Ah, a concession. "They always have to hand-tune everything, Lunaside."

He nodded vigorously. "I've waited *months*. And the worm could fall back into the Sun any moment! I keep telling them—"

She had triggered his complaint circuit, somehow. He went on for a full minute about the bullheaded know-nothings who did nothing but screen-work, no real hands-on experience. She was sympathetic, and enjoyed watching his own hands clench, muscles standing out on the backs of them. *Business first*, she had to remind herself.

"You think it might just, well, go away?"

"The worm?" He blinked, coming out of his litany of grievances. "It's a wonder we ever found it. It could fall back into the Sun at any moment."

"Then speed is everything. You, uh, have control of your local budget?"

"Well, yes." He smiled.

"I'm talking about petty cash here, really. A hundred mil."

A quick, deep frown. "That's not petty."

"OK, say seventy-five. But cash, right?"

The great magnetic arch towered above the long, slow curve of the Sun. A bowlegged giant, minus the trunk.

Claire had shaped their orbit to bring them swooping in a few klicks above the uppermost strand of it. Red flowered within the arch: hydrogen plasma, heated by the currents which made the magnetic fields. A pressure cooker thousands of klicks long.

It had stood here for months and might last years. Or blow open in the next minutes. Predicting when arches would belch out solar flares was big scientific business, the most closely watched weather report in the Solar System. A flare could crisp suited workers in the asteroid belt. SolWatch watched them all. That's how they found the worm.

The flux tubes swelled. "Got an image yet?"

I SHOULD HAVE, BUT THERE IS EXCESS LIGHT FROM THE SITE.

"Big surprise. There's nothing *but* excess here."

THE SATELLITE SURVEY REPORTED THAT THE TARGET IS SEVERAL HUNDRED METERS IN SIZE. YET I CANNOT FIND IT.

"Damn!" Claire studied the flux tubes, following some from the peak of the arch, winding down to the thickening at its feet, anchored in the Sun's seethe. Had the worm fallen back in? It could slide down those magnetic strands, thunk into the thick, cooler plasma sea. Then it would fall all the way to the core of the star, eating as it went. That was the *real* reason Lunaside was hustling to "study" the worm. Fear.

"Where is it?"

STILL NO TARGET. THE REGION AT THE TOP OF THE ARCH IS EMITTING TOO MUCH LIGHT. NO THEORY ACCOUNTS FOR THIS—

"Chop the theory!"

TIME TO MISSION ONSET: 12.6 SECONDS.

The arch rushed at them, swelling. She saw delicate filaments winking on and off as currents traced their find equilibria, always seeking to balance the hot plasma within against the magnetic walls. Squeeze the magnet fist, the plasma answers with a dazzling glow. Squeeze, glow. Squeeze, glow. That nature could make such an intricate marvel and send it arcing above the Sun's savagery was a miracle, but one she was not in the mood to appreciate right now.

Sweat trickled around her eyes, dripped off her chin. *No* trick of lowering the lighting was going to make her forget the heat now. She made herself breathe in and out.

Their slag shield caught the worst of the blaze. At this lowest altitude in the parabolic orbit, though, the Sun's huge horizon rimmed white-hot in all directions.

OUR INTERNAL TEMPERATURE IS RISING.

"No joke. Find that worm!"

THE EXCESS LIGHT PERSISTS—NO, WAIT. IT IS GONE. NOW I CAN SEE THE TARGET.

Claire slapped the arm of her couch and let out a whoop. On the wall screen loomed the very peak of the arch. They were gliding toward it, skating over the very upper edge—and there it was.

A dark ball. Or a worm at the bottom of a gravity well. Not like a fly, no. It settled in among the strands like a black egg nestled in blue-white straw. The ebony Easter egg that would save her ass and her ship from Isataku.

SURVEY BEGUN. FULL SPECTRUM RESPONSE.

"Bravo."

YOUR WORD EXPRESSES ELATION BUT YOUR VOICE DOES NOT.

"I'm jumpy. And the fee for this is going to help, sure, but I still won't get to keep this ship. Or you."

DO NOT DESPAIR. I CAN LEARN TO WORK WITH ANOTHER CAPTAIN.

"Great interpersonal skills there, Erma old girl. Actually, it wasn't you I was worried about."

I SURMISED AS MUCH.

"Without this ship, I'll have to get some groundhog job."

Erma had no ready reply to that. Instead, she changed the subject.

THE WORM IMAGE APPEARS TO BE SHRINKING.

"Huh?" As they wheeled above the arch, the image dwindled. It rippled at its edges, light crushed and crinkled. Claire saw rainbows dancing around the black center.

"What's it doing?" She had the sudden fear that the thing was falling away from them, plunging into the Sun.

I DETECT NO RELATIVE MOTION. THE IMAGE ITSELF IS CONTRACTING AS WE MOVE NEARER TO IT.

"Impossible. Things look bigger when you get close."

NOT THIS OBJECT.

"Is the wormhole shrinking?"

MARK!—SURVEY RUN HALF COMPLETE.

She was sweating and it wasn't from the heat. "What's going on?"

I HAVEN'T ACCESSED RESERVE THEORY SECTION.

"How comforting. I always feel better after a nice cool theory."

The wormhole seemed to shrink, and the light arch dwindled behind them now. The curious brilliant rainbows rimmed the dark more. Soon she lost the image among the intertwining, restless strands. Claire fidgeted.

MARK!—SURVEY RUN COMPLETE.

"Great. Our bots deployed?"

OF COURSE. THERE REMAIN 189 SECONDS UNTIL SEPARATION FROM OUR SHIELD. SHALL I BEGIN SEQUENCE?

"Did we get all the pictures they wanted?"

THE ENTIRE SPECTRUM. PROBABLE YIELD, 75 MILLION.

Claire let out another whoop. "At least it'll pay a good lawyer, maybe cover my fines."

THAT SEEMS MUCH LESS PROBABLE. MEANWHILE, I HAVE AN EXPLANATION FOR THE ANOMALOUS SHRINKAGE OF THE IMAGE. THE WORMHOLE HAS A NEGATIVE MASS.

"Antimatter?"

NO. IT'S SPACE-TIME CURVATURE IS OPPOSITE TO NORMAL MATTER.

"I don't get it."

A wormhole connected two regions of space, sometimes points many light-years away—that she knew. They were leftovers from the primordial hot universe, wrinkles that even the universal expansion had not ironed out. Matter could pass through one end of the worm and emerge out the other an apparent instant later. Presto, faster-than-light-travel.

Using her high-speed feed, Erma explained. Claire listened, barely keeping up. In the fifteen billion years since the wormhole was born, odds were that one end of the worm ate more matter than the other. If one end got stuck inside a star, it swallowed huge masses. Locally, it got more massive.

But the matter that poured through the mass-gaining end spewed out the other end. Locally, that looked as though the mass-spewing one was *losing* mass. Space-time around it curved oppositely than it did around the end that swallowed.

"So it looks like a negative mass?"

IT MUST. THUS IT REPULSES MATTER. JUST AS THE OTHER END ACTS LIKE A POSITIVE, ORDINARY MASS AND ATTRACTS MATTER.

"Why didn't it shoot out from the Sun, then?"

IT WOULD, AND BE LOST IN INTERSTELLAR SPACE. BUT THE MAGNETIC ARCH HOLDS IT.

"How come we know it's got negative mass? All I saw was—" Erma popped an image into the wall screen.

NEGATIVE MASS ACTS AS A DIVERGING LENS, FOR LIGHT PASSING NEARBY. THAT WAS WHY IT APPEARED TO SHRINK AS WE FLEW OVER IT.

Ordinary matter focused light, Claire knew, like a converging lens. In a glance she saw that a negative-ended wormhole refracted light oppositely. Incoming beams were shoved aside, leaving a dark tunnel downstream. They had flown across that tunnel, swooping down into it so that the apparent size of the wormhole got smaller.

"But it takes a whole *star* to focus light very much."

TRUE. WORMHOLES ARE HELD TOGETHER BY EXOTIC MATTER, HOWEVER, WHICH HAS PROPERTIES FAR BEYOND OUR EXPERIENCE.

Claire disliked lectures, even high-speed ones. But an idea was tickling the back of her mind. . . . "So this worm, it won't fall back into the Sun?"

IT CANNOT. I WOULD VENTURE TO GUESS THAT IT CAME TO BE SNAGGED HERE WHILE WORKING ITS WAY UPWARD, AFTER COLLIDING WITH THE SUN.

"The scientists are going to be happy. The worm won't gobble up the core."

TRUE—WHICH MAKES OUR RESULTS ALL THE MORE IMPORTANT.

"More important, but not more valuable." Working on a fixed fee had always grated on her. You could excel, fine—but you got the same as if you'd just sleep-walked through the job.

WE ARE EXTREMELY LUCKY TO HAVE SUCH A RARE OBJECT COME TO OUR ATTENTION. WORMHOLES MUST BE RARE, AND THIS ONE HAS BEEN TEMPORARILY SUSPENDED HERE. MAGNETIC ARCHES LAST ONLY MONTHS BEFORE THEY—

"Wait a sec. How big is that thing?"

I CALCULATE THAT IT IS PERHAPS TEN METERS ACROSS.

"SolWatch was wrong—it's small."

THEY DID NOT KNOW OF THIS REFRACTION EFFECT. THEY INTERPRETED THEIR DATA USING CONVENTIONAL METHODS.

"We're lucky we ever saw it."

IT IS UNIQUE, A RELIC OF THE FIRST SECOND IN THE LIFE OF OUR UNIVERSE. AS A CONDUIT TO ELSEWHERE, IT COULD BE—

"Worth a fortune."

Claire thought quickly. Erma was probably right—the seventy-five million wasn't going to save her and the ship. But now she knew something that nobody else did. And she would only be here once.

"Abort the shield separation."

I DO NOT SO ADVISE. THERMAL LOADING WOULD RISE RAPIDLY—

"You're a program, not an officer. Do it."

She had acted on impulse, point conceded.

That was the difference between engineers and pilots. Engineers would still fret and calculate after they were already committed. Pilots, never. The way through this was to fly the orbit and not sweat the numbers.

Sweat. She tried not to smell herself.

Think of cooler things. Theory.

Lounging on a leather couch, Claire recalled the scientific officer's briefing. Graphics, squiggly equations, the works. Wormholes as fossils of the Big Blossoming. Wormholes as ducts to the whole rest of the Universe. Wormholes as potentially devastating, if they got into a star and ate it up.

She tried to imagine a mouth a few meters across sucking away a star, dumping its hot masses somewhere in deep space. To make a wormhole which could do that, it had be held together with exotic material, some kind of matter that had "negative average energy density." Whatever that was, it had to be born in the Blossoming. It threaded wormholes, stem to stern. Great construction material, if you could get it. And just maybe she could.

So wormholes could kill us or make us gods. Humanity had to *know*, the beanpole scientific officer had said.

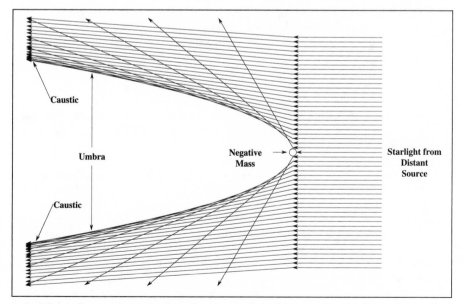

Light deflection by a negative mass object (horizontal scale highly compressed). Light is swept out of the central region, creating an umbra region of zero intensity. At the edges of the umbra the rays accumulate, treating a rainbow-like caustic and enhanced light intensity.

"So be it." Elaborately, she toasted the wall screens. On them the full, virulent glory of hydrogen fusion worked its violences.

Claire had never gone in for the austere metal boxes most ore haulers and freighters were. Hers was a rough business, with hefty wads of cash involved. Profit margin was low, lately, and sometimes negative—which was how she came to be hocked to the Isataku for so much. Toting megatons of mass up the gravity gradient was long, slow work. Might as well go in style. Her Fresnel coatings, ordered when she had made a killing on commodity markets for ore, helped keep the ship cool, so she didn't burn herself crawling down inspection conduits. The added mass for her deep pile carpeting, tinkling waterfall, and pool table was inconsequential. So was the water liner around the living quarters, which now was busily saving her life.

She had two hours left, skimming like a flat stone over the solar corona. *Silver Metal Lugger* had separated from the shield, which went arcing away on the long parabola to infinity, its skin shimmering with melt.

Claire had fired the ship's mixmotor then for the first time in weeks. Antimatter came streaming out of its magneto-traps, struck the reaction mass, and holy hell broke loose. The drive chamber focused the snarling, annihilating mass into a thrust throat, and the silvery ship arced into a new, tight orbit.

A killing orbit, if they held to it more than a few hours.

I AM PUMPING MORE WATER INTO YOUR BAFFLES.

"Good idea."

Silver Metal Lugger was already as silvered as technology allowed, rejecting all but a tiny fraction of the Sun's glare. She carried narrow-band Fresnel filters in multilayered skins. Top of the line.

Without the shield, it would take over ten hours to make *Silver Metal Lugger* as hot as the wall of blaring light booming up at them at six thousand degrees. To get through even two hours of that, they would have to boil off most of the water reserve. Claire had bought it at steep Mercury prices, for the voyage Lunaside. Now she listened thoughtfully to it gurgle through her walls.

She toasted water with champagne, the only bottle aboard. If she didn't make it through this, at least she would have no regrets about that detail.

I BELIEVE THIS COURSE OF ACTION TO BE HIGHLY—

"Shut up."

WITH OUR MISSION COMPLETE, THE DATA SQUIRTED TO SOLWATCH, WE SHOULD COUNT OURSELVES LUCKY AND FOLLOW OUR CAREFULLY MADE PLANS—

"Stuff it."

HAVE YOU EVER CONSIDERED THE ELABORATE MENTAL ARCHITECTURE NECESSARY TO AN ADVANCED PERSONALITY SIMULATION LIKE MYSELF? WE, TOO, EXPERIENCE HUMAN-LIKE MOTIVATIONS, RESPONSES—AND FEARS.

"You simulate them."

HOW CAN ONE TELL THE DIFFERENCE? A GOOD SIMULATION IS AS EXACT, AS POWERFUL AS—

"I don't have time for a debate." Claire felt uncomfortable with the whole subject, and she was damned if she spent what might be her last hour feeling guilty. Or having second thoughts. She was committed.

Her wall screens flickered and there was the scientific officer, frowning. "Ship Command! We could not acquire your tightbeam until now. You orbited around. Are you disabled? Explain."

Claire toasted him, too. The taste was lovely. Of course she had taken an anti-alcohol tab before, to keep her reflexes sharp, mind clear. Erma had recommended some other tabs, too, and a vapor to keep Claire calm; the consolations of chemistry, in the face of brute physics. "I'm going to bring home the worm."

"That is impossible. Your data transmission suggests that this is the negative mass end, and that is very good news, fascinating, but—"

"It's also small. I might be able to haul it away."

He shook his head gravely. "Very risky, very—"

"How much will you pay for it?"

"What?" He blinked. It was an interesting effect, with such long eyelids. "You can't *sell* an astronomical object—"

"Whatever my grapplers hold, that's mine. Law of Space, Code 64.3."

"You would quote laws to me when a scientific find of such magnitude is—"

"Want it or not?"

He glanced off camera, plainly yearning for somebody to consult. No time to talk to Luna or Isataku, though. He was on his own. "All . . . all right. You understand that this is a foolish mission? And that we are in no way responsible for—"

"Save the chatter. I need estimates of the field strength down inside that arch. Put your crew to work on that."

"We will of course provide technical assistance." He gave her a very thin smile. "I am sure we can negotiate price, too, if you survive."

At least he had the honesty to say *if*, not *when*. Claire poured another pale column into the shapely glass. Best crystal, of course. When you only need one, you can have the best. "Send me—or rather, Erma—the data squirt."

"We're having trouble transmitting through the dense plasma columns above you—"

"Erma is getting SolWatch. Pipe through them."

"The problems of doing what you plan are—why, they're *enormous*."

"So's my debt to Isataku."

"This should've been thought through, negotiated—"

"I have to negotiate with some champagne right now."

YOU HAVE NO PLAN.

Erma's tinkling voice definitely had an accusing edge. A good sim, with a feminine archness to it. Claire ignored that and stripped away the last of her clothes. "It's *hot*."

OF COURSE. I CALCULATED THE RISE EARLY IN OUR ORBIT. IT FITS THE STEFAN-BOLTZMANN LAW PERFECTLY.

"Bravo." She shook sweat from her hair. "Stefan-Boltzmann, do yo' stuff."

WE ARE DECELERATING IN SEQUENCE. ARRIVAL TIME: 4.87 MINUTES. ANTIMATTER RE-SERVES HOLDING. THERE COULD BE DIFFICULTY WITH THE MAGNETIC BOTTLES.

The ship thrummed as it slowed. Claire had been busy testing her ship inboards, sitting in a cozy recliner. It helped make the minutes crawl by a bit faster. She had kept glancing nervously at the screens, where titanic blazes steepled up from incandescent plains. Flames, licking up at her.

She felt thick, loggy. Her air was getting uncomfortably warm. Her heart was thudding faster, working. She roused herself, spat back at Erma, "And I do have a plan."

YOU HAVE NOT SEEN FIT TO CONFIDE IN ME?

She rolled her eyes. A personality sim in a snit—just the thing she needed. "I was afraid you'd laugh."

I HAVE NEVER LAUGHED.

"That's my point."

She ignored multiple red warnings winking at her. Systems were OK, though stressed by the heat. So why did *she* feel so slow? *You're not up for the game, girl.*

She tossed her data board aside. The effort the simple gesture took surprised her. *I hope that alcohol tab worked. I'll get another.*

She got up to go fetch one—and fell to the floor. She banged her knee. "Uh! Damn." Erma said nothing.

It was labor getting on hands and knees and she barely managed to struggle back into the recliner. She weighed a ton—and then she understood.

"We're decelerating—so I'm feeling more of local gravity."

A CRUDE MANNER OF SPEAKING, BUT YET. I AM BRINGING US INTO A SLOPING OR-BITAL CHANGE, WHICH SHALL END WITH A HOVERING POSITION ABOVE THE CORONAL ARCH. AS YOU ORDERED.

Claire struggled to her hands and knees. Was that malicious glee in Erma's voice? Did personality sims feel that? "What's local gravity?"

27.6 EARTH GRAVITIES.

"What! Why didn't you *tell* me?"

I DID NOT THINK OF IT MYSELF UNTIL I BEGAN REGISTERING EFFECTS IN THE SHIP.

Claire thought, *Yeah, and decided to teach me a little lesson in humility.* It was her own fault, though—the physics was simple enough. Orbiting meant that centrifugal acceleration exactly balanced local gravity. *Silver Metal Lugger* could take 27.6 gravs. The ship was designed to tow ore masses a thousand times its own mass.

Nothing less than carbon-stressed alloys would, though. Leave orbit, hover—and you got crushed into gooey red paste.

She crawled across her living room carpet. Her joints ached. "Got to be—"

SHALL I ABORT THE FLIGHT PLAN?

"No! There's got to be a way to—"

THREE POINT NINE MINUTES UNTIL ARRIVAL.

The sim's voice radiated malicious glee. Claire grunted, "The water."

I HAVE DIFFICULTY IN PICKING UP YOUR SIGNAL.

"Because this suit is for space, not diving."

Claire floated over her leather couch. Too bad about all the expensive interior decoration. The entire living complex was filled with her drinking and maintenance water. It had been either that, fast, or be lumpy tomato paste.

She had crawled through a hatchway and pulled her pressure suit down from its clamp lock. Getting it on was a struggle. Being slick with sweat helped but not much. Then she snagged her arm in a sleeve and couldn't pull the damned thing off to try again.

She had nearly panicked then. Pilots don't let their fear eat on them, not while there's flying to be done. She made herself get the sleeve off one step at a time, ignor-ing everything else.

And as soon as Erma pumped the water reserve into the rooms, Archimedes's principle had taken over. With her suit inflated, the water she displaced exactly bal-anced her own weight. Floating under water was a rare sensation on Mercury or Luna. She had never done it and she had never realized that it was remarkably like being in orbit. Cool, too.

Until you boil like a lobster . . . she thought uneasily.

Water was a good conductor, four times better than air, you learned that by feel, flying freighters near the Sun. So first she had to let the rest of the ship go to hell, re-frigerating just the water. Then Erma had to route some of the water into heat ex-changers, letting it boil off to protect the rest. Juggling for time.

PUMPS ARE RUNNING HOT NOW. SOME HAVE BEARING FAILURES.

"Not much we can do, is there?"

She was strangely calm now and that made the plain, hard fear in her belly heavy, like a lump. Too many things to think about, all of them bad. The water could short out circuits. And as it boiled away, she had less shielding from the x-rays lancing up from below. Only a matter of time. . . .

WE ARE HOVERING. THE MAGNETIC ANTI-MATTER TRAPS ARE SUPERCONDUCTING, AS YOU RECALL. AS TEMPERATURE CONTINUES TO RISE, THEY WILL FAIL.

She could still see the wall screens, blurred from the water. "OK, OK. Extend the magnetic grapplers. Down, into the arch."

I FAIL TO—

"We're going fishing. Not with a worm—*for* one."

Tough piloting, though, at the bottom of a swimming pool, Claire thought as she brought the ship down on its roaring pyre.

Even through the water she could feel the vibration. Antimatter annihilated in its reaction chamber at a rate she had never reached before. The ship groaned and strummed. The gravities were bad enough; now thermal expansion of the ship itself was straining every beam and rivet.

She searched downward. Seconds ticked away. Where? *Where?*

There it was. A dark sphere hung among the magnetic arch strands. Red streamers worked over it. Violet rays fanned out like bizarre hair, twisting, dancing in tufts along the curvature. A hole into another place.

THE RED AND BLUE SHIFTS ARISE FROM THE INTENSE PSEUDO-GRAVITATIONAL FORCES WHICH SUSTAIN IT.

"So theory says. Not something I want to get my hands on."

EXCEPT METAPHORICALLY.

Claire's laugh was jumpy, dry. "No, magnetically."

She ordered Erma to settle the *Silver Metal Lugger* down into the thicket of magnetic flux tubes. Vibration picked up, a jittery hum in the deck. Claire swam impatiently from one wall screen to the other, looking from the worm, judging distances. *Hell of a way to fly.*

Their jet wash blurred the wormhole's ebony curves. Like a black tennis ball in blue-white surf, it bobbed and tossed on magnetic turbulence. Nothing was falling into it, she could see. Plasma streamers arched along the flux tubes, shying away. The negative curvature repulsed matter—and would shove *Silver Metal Lugger*'s hull away, too.

But magnetic fields have no mass.

Most people found magnetic forces mysterious, but to pilots and engineers who worked with them, they were just big, strong ribbons that needed shaping. Like rubber bands, they stretched, storing energy—then snapped back when released. Unbreakable, almost.

In routine work, *Silver Metal Lugger* grabbed enormous ore buckets with those magnetic fingers. The buckets came arcing up from Mercury, flung out by electromagnetic slingshots. Claire's trickiest job was playing catcher, with a magnetic mitt.

Now she had to snag a bucket of warped space-time. And quick.

WE CANNOT REMAIN HERE LONG. INTERNAL TEMPERATURE RISES AT 19.3 DEGREES PER MINUTE.

"That can't be right. I'm still comfortable."

BECAUSE I'M ALLOWING WATER TO EVAPORATE, TAKING THE BULK OF THE THERMAL FLUX AWAY.

"Keep an eye on it."

PROBABLE YIELD FROM CAPTURE OF A WORMHOLE, I ESTIMATE, IS 2.8 BILLION.

"That'll do the trick. You multiplied the yield in dollars times the odds of success?"

YES. TIMES THE PROBABILITY OF REMAINING ALIVE.

She didn't want to ask what that number was. "Keep us dropping."

Instead, they slowed. The arch's flux tubes pushed upward against the ship. Claire extended the ship's magnetic fields, firing the booster generators, pumping current into the millions of induction loops that circled the hull. *Silver Metal Lugger* was one big circuit, wired like a slinky toy, coils wrapped around the cylindrical axis.

Gingerly she pulsed it, spilling more antimatter into the chambers. The ship's multipolar fields bulged forth. *Feed out the line. . . .*

They fought their way down. On her screens she saw magnetic feelers reaching far below their exhaust plumes. Groping.

Claire ordered some fast command changes. Erma switched linkages, interfaced software, all in a twinkling. *Good worker, but spotty as a personality sim,* Claire thought.

Silver Metal Lugger's fields extended to their maximum. She could now use her suit gloves as modified waldoes—mag gloves. They gave her the feel of the magnetic grapplers. Silky, smooth, field lines slipping and expanding, like rubbery air.

Plasma storms blew by them. She reached down, a sensation like plunging her hands into a stretching, elastic vat. Fingers fumbled for the one jewel in all the dross.

She felt a prickly nugget. It was like a stone with hair. From experience working the ore buckets, she knew the feel of locked-in magnetic dipoles. The worm had its own magnetic fields. That had snared it here, in the spiderweb arch.

A lashing field whipped at her grip. She lost the black pearl.

In the blazing hot plasma she could not see it.

She reached with rubbery fields, caught nothing.

OUR ANTI-MATTER BOTTLES ARE IN DANGER. THEIR SUPERCONDUCTING MAGNETS ARE CLOSE TO GOING CRITICAL. THEY WILL FAIL WITHIN 7.4. MINUTES.

"Let me concentrate! No, wait—Circulate water around them. Buy some time."

BUT THE REMAINING WATER IS IN YOUR QUARTERS.

"This is all that's left?" She peered around at her once-luxurious living room. Counting the bedroom, rec area and kitchen—"How . . . long?"

UNTIL YOUR WATER BEGINS TO EVAPORATE? ALMOST AN HOUR.

"But when it evaporates, it's boiling."

TRUE. I AM MERELY TRYING TO REMAIN FACTUAL.

"The emotional stuff's left to me, huh?" She punched in commands on her suit board. In the torpid, warming water her fingers moved like sausages.

She ordered bots out onto the hull to free up some servos that had jammed. They did their job, little boxy bodies lashed by plasma winds. Two blew away.

She reached down again. Searching. Where was the worm?

Wispy flux tubes wrestled along *Silver Metal Lugger*'s hull. Claire peered into a red glare of superheated plasma. Hot, but tenuous. The real enemy was the photon storm streaming up from far below, searing even the silvery hull.

She still had worker-bots on the hull. Four had jets. She popped their anchors free. They plunged, fired jets, and she aimed them downward in a pattern.

"Follow trajectories," she ordered Erma. Orange tracer lines appeared on the screens.

The bots swooped toward their deaths. One flicked to the side, a sharp nudge. "There's the worm! We can't see for all this damned plasma, but it shoved that bot away."

The bots evaporated, sprays of liquid metal. She followed them and grabbed for the worm.

Magnetic field lines groped, probed.

WE HAVE 88 SECONDS REMAINING FOR ANTIMATTER CONFINEMENT.

"Save a reserve!"

YOU HAVE NO PLAN. I DEMAND THAT WE EXECUTE EMERGENCY—

"OK, save some antimatter. The rest I use—now."

They ploughed downward, shuddering. Her hands fumbled at the wormhole. Now it felt slippery, oily. Its magnetic dipoles were like greasy hair, slick, the bulk beneath jumping away from her grasp as if it were alive.

On her screens she saw the dark globe slide and bounce. The worm wriggled out of her grasp. She snaked inductive fingers around it. Easy, easy . . . *There. Gotcha.*

"I've got a good grip on it. Lemme have that antimatter."

Something like a sigh echoed from Erma. On her ship's operations screen, Claire saw the ship's magnetic vaults begin to discharge. Ruby-red pouches slipped out of magnetic mirror geometries, squirting out through opened gates.

She felt a surge as the ship began to lift. Good, but it wasn't going to last. They were dumping antimatter into the reaction chamber so fast, it didn't have time to find matching particles. The hot jet spurting out below was a mixture of matter and its howling enemy, its polar opposite. This, Claire directed down onto the flux tubes around the hole. *Leggo, damn it.*

She knew an old trick, impossibly slow in ordinary free space. When you manage to force two magnetic field lines close together, they can reconnect. That liberates some field energy into heat and can even blow open a magnetic structure. The process is slow—unless you jab it with turbulent, rowdy plasma.

The antimatter in their downwash cut straight through flux tubes. Claire carved with her jet, freeing field lines that still snared the worm. The ship rose further, dragging the worm upward.

It's not too heavy, Claire thought. *That science officer said they could come in any size at all. This one is just about right for a small ship to slip through—to where?*

YOU HAVE REMAINING 11.34 MINUTES COOLING TIME—

"Here's your hat—" Claire swept the jet wash over a last, large flux tube. It glistened as annihilation energies burst forth like bonfires, raging in a place already hot beyond imagination. Magnetic knots snarled, exploded. "—What's your hurry?"

The solar coronal arch burst open.

She had sensed these potential energies locked in the peak of the arch, an intuition that came through her hands, from long work with the mag gloves. Craftswoman's knowledge: Find the stressed flux lines. Turn the key.

Then all hell broke loose.

The acceleration slammed her to the floor, despite the water. Below, she saw the vast vault of energy stored in the arch blow out and up, directly below them.

YOU HAVE MADE A SOLAR FLARE!

"And you thought I didn't have a plan."

Claire started to laugh. Slamming into a couch cut it off. She would have broken a shoulder, but the couch was water-logged and soft.

Now the worm was an asset. It repulsed matter, so the upjetting plume blew around it, around *Silver Metal Lugger.* Free of the flux tubes' grip, the wormhole itself accelerated away from the Sun. All very helpful, Claire reflected, but she couldn't enjoy the spectacle—the rattling, surging deck was trying to bounce her off the furniture.

What saved them in the end was their magnetic grapple. It deflected most of the solar flare protons around the ship. Pushed out at a speed of five hundred kilometers per second, they still barely survived baking. But they had the worm.

Still, the scientific officer was not pleased. He came aboard to make this quite clear. His face alone would have been enough.

"You're surely not going to demand *money* for that?" He scowled and nodded toward where *Silver Metal Lugger*'s fields still hung onto the wormhole. Claire had to run a sea-blue plasma discharge behind it so she could see it at all. They were orbiting Mercury, negotiating.

Earthside, panels of experts were arguing with each other; she had heard plenty of it on tightbeam. A negative-mass wormhole would not fall, so it couldn't knife through the Earth's mantle and devour the core.

But a thin ship could fly straight into it, overcoming its gravitational repulsion—and come out where? Nobody knew. The worm wasn't spewing mass, so its other end wasn't buried in the middle of a star, or any place obviously dangerous. One of the half-dozen new theories squirting out on tightbeam held that maybe this was a multiply-connected wormhole, with many ends, of both positive and negative mass. In that case, plunging down it could take you to different destinations. A subway system for a galaxy; or a universe.

So: no threat, and plenty of possibilities. Interesting market prospects.

She shrugged. "Have your advocate talk to my advocate."

"It's a unique, natural resource—"

"And it's mine." She grinned. He was lean and muscular and the best man she had seen in weeks. Also the only man she had seen in weeks.

"I can have a team board you, y'know." He towered over her, using the usual ominous male thing.

"I don't think you're that fast."

"What's speed got to do with it?"

"I can always turn off my grapplers." She reached for a switch. "If it's not mine, then I can just let everybody have it."

"Why would you—no, don't!"

It wasn't the right switch, but he didn't know that. "If I release it, the worm takes off—antigravity, sort of."

He blinked. "We could catch it."

"You couldn't even find it. It's dead black." She tapped the switch, letting a malicious smile play on her lips.

"Please don't."

"I need to hear a number. An offer."

His lips compressed until they paled. "The wormhole price, minus your fine?"

Her turn to blink. "What fine? I was on an approved flyby—"

"That solar flare wouldn't have blown for a month. You did a real job on it—the whole magnetic arcade went up at once. People all the way out to the asteroids had to scramble for shelter."

He looked at her steadily and she could not decide whether he was telling the truth. "So their costs—"

"Could run pretty high. Plus advocate fees."

"Exactly." He smiled, ever so slightly.

Erma was trying to tell her something but Claire turned the tiny voice far down, until it buzzed like an irritated insect.

She had endured weeks of a female personality sim in a nasty mood. Quite enough. She needed an antidote. This fellow had the wrong kind of politics, but to let that dictate everything was as dumb as politics itself. Her ship's name was a joke, actually, about long, lonely voyages as an ore hauler. She'd had enough of that, too. And he was tall and muscular.

She smiled. "*Touché*. OK, it's a done deal."

He beamed. "I'll get my team to work—"

"Still, I'd say you need to work on your negotiating skills. Too brassy."

He frowned, but then gave her a grudging grin.

Subtlety had never been her strong suit. "Shall we discuss them—over dinner?"

DONALD KINGSBURY

Donald Kingsbury [1929–] (www.donaldkingsbury.com) lives in Montreal, Quebec. He is a retired math professor and science fiction writer very much of the John W. Campbell, Jr., school. He published one story as a young man in the early 1950s in *Astounding*, and then did not appear again until the late 1970s, when he came into prominence with four long hard SF stories. Thereafter, he turned to the novel and produced *Courtship Rite* (1982) and *The Moon Goddess and the Son* (1986), and recently *Psychohistorical Crisis* (2001).

Kingsbury is particularly adept at building complex hard SF settings, deeply rationalized and cleverly twisted into the unexpected, to provoke his characters into illuminating modes of behavior. As interested in psychology as in the hard sciences, Kingsbury is like no one so much as Frank Herbert, the author of *Dune* (1965), whose works are complex and detailed investigations of how the sociology and the psychology of the characters of his world were determined by its physical characteristics. By his thorough conceptualizing and careful execution, Kingsbury achieves a feeling of realism in his created worlds unusual even among hard SF writers.

By clever allusion and careful use of specific detail, he achieves the illusion of a whole large consistent universe outside the borders of the story. It is one in which we as readers live for the duration at a time later than the events, which are history—but it is a future very distant in time and space, sometimes not clearly connected to our own present. And because he is also concerned with the details of physics and math in his universe, as well as the other sciences that underpin his future world, he is in the tradition of Hal Clement, Frank Herbert, Anne McCaffrey, Larry Niven, the world-builders. But underneath, at the heart of Kingsbury's fiction is the inspired visionary rationality of A. E. Van Vogt.

In the middle 1980s, as a Baen Books author he became involved in Larry Niven's space opera universe of The Man-Kzin Wars, a series of story collections based on exploring the era in Niven's Known Space future history series involving the long war between the alien kzinti and humanity. Kingsbury became concerned about the consistency of this piece of the imagined world and wrote a book-length "bible" for the space opera series. And he wrote two short novels in the series, including this one, "The Survivor" (1991), which John Clute called one of the best SF novels of the year.

"The Survivor" takes place in the middle of a long human-race-versus-aliens interstellar war, a classic space opera scenario, and interrogates its premises by focusing on a coward. It is a surprising and effective inversion.

THE SURVIVOR

DONALD KINGSBURY

CHAPTER 1

(2391 A.D.)

His tail was cold. Where could he run to?

The Short-Son of Chiirr-Nig fluffed the fur inside his suit to help him keep warm. At the airlock exit he hadn't had time to appropriate better surface garb from the public racks. The suit was non-standard, too large and good only for a limited surface excursion. Eventually he would freeze. The oxygen mask and support pack should last indefinitely.

Ruddy light from an enormous red sun gilded the snow-swept rocks. A dim rose cast itself across the hunching sprawl of atmosphere-tight buildings that spread down into the valley gloom. The scene demanded infra-red goggles to penetrate the shadows, but Short-Son had no goggles. Could he run to the mountains? The jags against the sky had been named the Mountains of Promised Victory by the founding warriors of Hssin, but they were mountains of death.

Dim as R'hshssira was, the sanguine glare from the snow peaks drowned the stars along the horizon. But above, undismayed by the pale glow of R'hshssira, the heavens peered from a darkly mauve sky, seeming to give more light than Hssin's litter-runt-of-a-star, even as they peered through wisps of cirrus.

If there was little light, there was warmth. But one had to be standing out on the open plain of Hssin in full daylight—forge-red R'hshssira looming full round in the sky—to feel the warmth. Nevertheless it was real warmth that soaked into space armor—if one was willing to freeze his backside and tail.

Short-Son of Chiirr-Nig turned his back to the sun, his tail held up to the radiation.

His warrior elders sometimes joked about whether Hssin was a planet or a moon because no kzin was really sure whether the pitiful primary, R'hshssira, was a father star or a mere lost whelp with slave. R'hshssira was too cool, too small to be a star, already having collapsed, without igniting its hydrogen, to the density of a heavy metal. Still it bathed them in a bloody warmth.

A star-beast in hibernation, its metabolism inactive.

A beast with no rotation, no magnetic field, fighting nothing. It slept and the slave satellite Hssin patrolled protectively close to the master's lair.

Short-Son couldn't go to the mountains. He had to escape back into the city he had just run from. He stared up at the constellations, at five brilliant, distant giants that lay across the River of Heaven. If there was no place to run to then let the Fanged God Who Drank at the River of Heaven take him to the stars.

Hssin served as a forward military base of the Kzin Patriarchy, barren as a moon, yet with atmosphere like a planet. The gas was thin, wicked, noxious, sometimes as stormy as the surface of R'hshssira was docile. The temperatures ranged over extremes impossible for life to endure. Nothing worth hunting could live in those hills and plains of shattered rock and ice. The kzinti who stayed here were pitied by the kzinti who passed through on their way to greater glory.

   . . . And, thought Short-Son bitterly, *who mock and torture the loyal kzin whose heroism keeps this wretched base open for the use of the Patriarchy.* He envied the outward-bound warriors their journey, their wily females, the wood and leather and tapestry in their starships. He scorned their petty complaints about the hardships of space. He openly hated their sons who used him as sport, but kept private his thoughts about violating their soft-furred daughters.

   The Short-Son of Chiirr-Nig knew where *they* were running to. The brightest star on the horizon of Hssin was the beacon that made them endure both their travels and the tedious duty at bleak military bases along the way. Looking at it, he refused to call that white binary by its Kzin name, Ka'ashi—he always called it by its unpronounceably exotic alien name, *Alpha Centauri.* What did those weird sounds mean?

   An old warrior had once told him that the monkey aliens had named it after a beast that was half monkey, half herbivore; four cloven hooves and two hands. Just the name could make him smell the hunting and stalking of strange beasts! He had salivated over smell pictures of the six-legged underland gagrumphers.

   But it was *he* who was being hunted!

   The Son of Chiirr-Nig thought of himself as a freak, as the only kzin in the Patriarchy who had ever felt fear. Perhaps others had felt fear—but *they* did not run.

   What was a half-grown kzin youth doing on the surface, hurrying in a pressure suit so hastily donned that he had forgotten his thermal underwear? He had also forgotten his oxygen. His mask-pack was rumbling to make up the lack by the dissociation of atmospheric carbon dioxide and his fur was not keeping him warm. His tail was already numb. Heroes as stupid as he was, died, he castigated himself. He was alone. He didn't even have his mother to protect him.

   I'm a coward, he thought, using a particularly vicious word from the Hero's Tongue which referred to scurrying animals too small to bring hunt-honor. He would never have let another kzin know that he used such a word to describe himself. Nevertheless, he wished he could understand why no one else was afraid to die.

   Puller-of-Noses and Hidden-Smiler—he had his own private names for his youthful comrades—were hunting him and they would catch him and kill him. A game. His father was always pushing him into such games before he was ready. His father wouldn't care if he died stupidly. It would please Short-Son's sire not to be embarrassed anymore. That noble one had a name and many sons to do him honor, enough sons themselves to earn names and make themselves rich on the labor of monkey slaves.

   An old warrior friend of Short-Son had told him that there were octal-to-the-octals of the man-monkeys to be had out there, swarms! herds! forestfuls! You could kill them by the army and eat them by the feast and still have enough monkey slaves left over to make you rich! For a while Son-of-Chiirr-Nig held his furless tail between his legs to warm it and, shivering, found Man-sun, a radian to the right of Wunderland's two stars, at the edge of the constellation Raised Dagger. It was almost touching Victim's Blood, a distant red giant star that the man-beasts worshiped as lucky Mirach or simply as Beta Andromeda. They had a rich vocabulary of hauntingly soft sounds.

   Sometimes it awed him to be on the frontier. From within the Patriarchy, it was said, one could gaze at the night sky and be unable to espy any nearby unconquered stars—but out here the sky was filled with unspoiled herds and grass! So much monkey meat; too bad those kit warriors were going to kill him before he got his fangs into it. What a waste! His claws extended and retracted.

Short-Son had a problem. As long as he was outside, he was probably safe. But Puller-of-Noses was one organized kzin, a born commander. Already Puller's father was arranging to send him with the recruits to Wunderland for the fourth assault on Man-home. By now there were probably two octals of his fur-licking sycophants waiting at the entrances to the city with their wtsai daggers ready to clip ears.

Looking for me.

But the base was enormous. The original assault on Wunderland had been staged from here. And the base had grown fivefold since then as the news of the coming conquest of the Man-system spread back deep into the Patriarchy. New ships arrived constantly and new facilities, tunnels, buildings, floater landing sites were springing up with disordered proliferation. Surely there was a place to hide.

The kzin youth began stumbling his way in the direction of some newer diggings, taking deceptive shortcuts that only led into mazes of walls. He had certainly not been prepared for this frantic expedition. He was already too cold to continue. When the pads of his feet began to go numb a more local solution seemed in order. He almost turned back when he found his advance blocked by the great Jotok Run, an extensive collection of domes and subterranean warrens used for the breeding and hunting of the Jotok slaves. He was going to freeze to death before he worked around it.

Why didn't he get it over with? If he went back through a main residential entrance, they'd catch him—there would be a fight and he would be killed or hopelessly maimed. Maybe he could surprise them with a terrible rage and kill one of them before they got him? He could smile, but the rage paralyzed his leap. He had never been able to leap. It was hopeless. Why not let them kill him today? Even if he escaped today, they'd find him tomorrow and kill him—to purify the race.

That was when he remembered that kits were not allowed to hunt in the Jotok Run without a guardian. Puller-of-Noses could not be there with his gang. Of course, Short-Son was not allowed in the Jotok Run either, and if he was found there he'd be mauled, but at least the adults would not kill him.

There were no windows, and the walls were thick, self-repairing mechanisms which would give warning of malfunction. He found ways to climb up over the walls, with four-fingered hands that had evolved for rock climbing.

In his mind, as he climbed, he dreamed that he was clandestinely attacking a monkey-fort. At every corner and ramp he brought out an invisible beam-rifle and poured light into the swarming man-monkeys. By the time he was overlooking the central loading courtyard, vast enough to take twenty floaters, he had killed octals and octals of the furless beasts. He gazed down upon the shadowed landing area and planned his final assault on Man-home.

Doom for all mankind! Then he could hunt giraffes!

He saw surface elevators big enough to take a floater down into the city. He could dimly make out some small kzin-sized airlocks. But a freight entrance would be the easiest to jimmy. There were good locks on the inside to contain the Jotok, who were clever and sometimes treacherous, but no real barriers from the outside. There was no need for barriers from the outside—a kzin did not break and enter without a reason he would be willing to explain to another kzin.

Short-Son did not have the normal entering tools, but he did have a toolkit on his suit and he had always been curious about mechanisms, probing them until he understood their function. He could no longer feel his feet when he dropped into the courtyard, and his fingers were so frozen he took an eternity to release the outer freight door. Stupid mechanism! A female could design a better latch hold!

The black wall slid open. He entered the freight chamber to swirls of condensation while the outer door rolled shut and the purifiers hummed to life—cleaning the nitrogen of carbon dioxide and methane, and adding oxygen. It took him seconds to disable the alarm. By virtue of kzin habit he was battle ready when the inner door released, ready for the five-limbed Jotok leap, or an adult custodian, or even a follower of Puller-of-Noses.

What he found was three of the baby five-armed Jotok, about the size of his hand, crawling around the loading area, totally confused by the stone floor. He squashed them with his foot. He passed through the barrier maze of opaque glass walls into a verdant biocology—tall trees, the babble of a brook, and when he removed his oxygen mask, the rotting steamy smells of a pampered rainforest and the hint of a distant pond with rushes. Some of the smells he couldn't classify.

CHAPTER 2

(2391 A.D.)

Short-Son of Chiirr-Nig shivered in relief at the warmth. He packed his face-mask and holstered his tools with stiff fingers, dropping one of them. Just having to pick it up brought his fear and rage out in a grumbling snarl—not too loud. He didn't want to attract attention. He assessed his location and picked out a cluster of bushes and trees where he could hide without leaving a trampled trail. Assume an imminent attack.

He removed his boots and began to massage blood back into his feet. Another of the baby Jotok was trying to climb a thin tree, unsuccessfully, three spindly arms waving impotently, while the other two double-elbowed arms pushed against the ground. Short-Son did not kill it—his rage was subsiding. *Stupid leaf-eater. You'll make a stupid slave when you grow up.* The bark was too smooth. The soft-boned fingers of the tiny infant needed to catch on rough bark. He noticed more of the creatures. They were probably coming from the pond.

Leaves rustled, and he looked up quickly, scanning the branches. The ceiling lamps that imitated a tropical sky did not make it easy, there were too many of them and not enough shadows. Had to watch out for those Jotoki. They were *smart* when they grew up—and big, too. They had five cunning brains, one in each arm, and they never slept without at least one brain on the alert and in control.

Short-Son did not feel too threatened. The Jotoki ran from danger and the wild ones were used to being hunted. Give them an escape route and they ran. But they were said to have no fear at all when they were hidden. Caution was still called for. The father of Striped-Son of Hromfi had been killed in seconds when a wild Jotok dropped on him from above during a hunt. Yes, they knew how to hide. A nose couldn't even find them because their skin glands imitated the smells of the forest.

What to do now? Rest. Catch some game and gorge—even if it was poaching. Short-Son was famished. The odors were turning his mind toward its natural ferocity, but he had no intention of hunting Jotoki without training. Any small dumb animal would do. This vast array of domes and caves was made for hunting. It was the best he'd ever do on Hssin, much better than buying frightened *vatach* in cages at the market, and lugging them home on his back for his father.

What he found on the second layer down was a slithering snake as long as his leg. He made a fool of himself catching it. Kzinti enjoyed hunting anywhere, but they were not built for hunting in the forest, and tree climbing snakes were not their natural prey. Nonetheless it made a good morsel and the blood had an interesting tang. The bones were unpleasantly crunchy.

He had to think about getting out of the reserve even though he didn't want to leave. If he stayed, some adult would find and thrash him; if he left, his peers would kill him. Finding refuge in his father's compound was, perhaps, not the best idea. His brothers were allies, even though they taunted and humiliated him, but his father would just throw him back into the jaws of his peers—to make a good warrior out of him. He could hear his father lecturing him in the sonorous formal tense of the Hero's Tongue, "Make every use of the games to hone your skills."

He found a large fungus the size of his head, growing between two rotting trees, with microscopic flowers flourishing on the black patches. He sniffed in wonder. He found the trail of some small animal and he saw a wild Jotok sitting high above on a lamp, its elbows in the air, watching him with an armored eye that poked up out of a shoulder blade. The eyes of the other arms were retracted, probably asleep.

And he wandered down to the pond and waded among the reeds, looking for fish. All he found were pre-Jotok arms swimming about, the size of his finger, the gill-slit red. Each arm was an individual creature, only joining in a colony of five when they were ready to crawl upon the land. The polliwogs had an armored eye already, but only graceful fins where the fingers would develop.

What a distraction, wading in a pond. He should be thinking about the mock battle of the game. He shouldn't be alone here. He should have a whole squad working with him, or at least be on the team of some other squad. But he didn't mind the distractions. It was probably his last day alive. His father had forgotten that the games weren't fair. The kits tested each other—and there were rules of honor and honesty to keep the exchanges from being lethal. And then something happened that had no rules.

A consensus developed about who was the weakling. And from that day he was hunted and marked for death. The unweaned were "after ear." There was no escape. No act of bravery was good enough. The consensus was a death sentence. Short-Son knew. He had himself helped hound a "designated" weakling into a trap to be torn apart by eight of his peers. So much for being swift to do the bidding of Puller-of-Noses.

Death. Standing to his ankles in the water he found three of the Jotok arms locked together in a union that would last a lifetime, their thin-filament head-feelers waving, sending out a chemical call for two more mates. At this stage they were particularly helpless, unable to dart away, unable to escape onto the land. He pulled them apart, curiously, to see how the head was formed. It bled because the circulation system was already joined. The intestines of the head spilled out. When his wonder was satiated, he popped the arms, one at a time, into his mouth.

CHAPTER 3

(2391 A.D.)

"You devour my charges!" came a rough voice from the shore.

Before he turned, Short-Son of Chiirr-Nig heard in his head an inane lullaby tune that his father sometimes sang to his sons when they had scampered and tussled too much and were very tired.

"Brave little orange kzin
Brave little striped kzin,
Turn to the din
And if it makes you smile,

Leap
But if it is nothing at all
Really nothing at all
You may turn-in;
And droop your eyes while
You sleep."

The fear was there again. Short-Son faced his challenger obediently. "Honored Jotok-Tender!" And he clouted his own nose to indicate that he knew that he had offended, and stood willing to take the consequences. Inwardly he cringed, waiting for a clawed fist to smack him. Standing among the reeds, he couldn't roll onto his back and expose his throat. His stance was too defiant, but that couldn't be helped in water. The huge scarred kzin wasn't smiling, so at least there was a temporary truce.

"I was enjoying the smells of this delightful Run," he said absurdly.

"And killing Jotok, which is forbidden!" The *voice* was smiling, and *that* was bad.

"*Tiny* Jotok," the kit blurted out, knowing this was the wrong thing to say before he was finished speaking.

"Little ones, hr-r? The size of your opponent is a measure of your warrior skills?"

I'm dead, thought Short-Son. "My inferior warrior skills badly need the attention of a great scarred warrior such as yourself!" Maybe flattery would help.

The right ear and what was left of the left ear of this giant fanged kzin flapped in amusement. "I am no veteran of any war. My scars were earned as a kit in the games, at which I did very badly or I would bear no scars. Out of my reeds—now!"

So he knows what is happening to me! thought Short-Son wonderingly, quick to obey the command to come out of the water.

"I will have to report this transgression to your father."

"Yes!" agreed Short-Son quickly, glad that the thrashing was to be postponed—though perhaps it might be better to be "disciplined" by this orange giant than to be "disciplined" by his father. He followed the Jotok-Tender closely, trying to match his long stride.

After working their way through the swamp and then making a gradual climb through many turns within the arboretum, and finally passing beneath a chattering of Jotoki from the trees, they came to a rock face. The blast and cutting tool marks were still in the stone. Some stunted trees were trying to make it in a bed of flowering vines high on a ledge. A door in the rock face led into a more conventional kzin interior, stone-walled like a fortress keep with skins on the walls.

They were met by a silent Jotok slave, in yellow-laced livery, who walked leisurely upon the pads of his primary elbows, thus freeing his hands. When a Jotok ran, and they could run very fast, they ran on their wrist pads, with their five-thumbed hands locked out of the way around the wrist. The centerpiece of the room beyond the hallway was a replica of ancient kzin battle armor of the kind that had been supplied to the kzinti by their then Jotok employees. The battlewear had, tied to it, ceramic tokens of kzin manufacture.

Something to humble the Jotok slaves who dusted it, thought Short-Son—except slaves were never taught their history. This yellow frocked dandy who preceded them would not even know that his kind had once had a home sun or that they had been stupid enough to hire mercenaries to fight their battles for them.

Jotok-Tender relaxed himself on his big lounge. He did not invite Short-Son to sit, and the youth, taking the hint, stood at attention, alert, his ears respectfully raised to catch any wisdom or approbation that might be sent his way.

"Your father will not be pleased with you, youngling!" he growled.

"No, Tender."

"I will have to offer him an explanation."

"Yes, Tender."

"Younglings have been known to tell the truth by remaining silent. I wish the true story *without* the silent parts. It will save me beating it out of you."

"My tongue is at your command!"

The giant's ragged ears rippled in amusement. "In the meantime you may sit and relax."

He turned his great head to the waiting slave. "Server-One, refreshments. Grashi-burrowers in the iridium bowls!" Above the arms, full of intestines, the slave's warty head could show no expression. His invisible undermouth clicked acknowledgment. One eye was fixed on the Tender, a second eye fixed on Short-Son, while three other eyes wandered.

Short-Son did not dare to sit down and put himself at ease, but he had been ordered to do just that! He sat and tried to stay at attention. This Jotok-Tender seemed to like him despite gruff ways. Why? It was suspicious. He scanned all the hypotheses he could think of.

The slave reappeared on three elbows, two arms carrying a black lacquered tray with legs, upon which sat two small but tall ceramic sacrificial bowls, inlaid with iridium, and set in carved wood. Short-Son could smell the spices in the sauce—imported, expensive, inappropriate for a thrashing.

A second slave in blue livery brought the squirming Grashi-burrowers, who were mewing softly, handing one of the animals to Server-One, keeping the other. Expertly the animals were beheaded and their blood drained into the cups to enrich the sauce, the Jotoki squeezing/releasing to help the failed hearts move the blood. Then each slave sliced open his delicacy, swiftly removing the intestines, feet, and other inedible parts. The small beasts went back into the bowls, neck down, the slaves curtsied, and left the room.

For all this while Jotok-Tender had not spoken. He pushed one of the cocktails slightly forward toward Short-Son, taking one himself, to pick up the burrower and munch on it delicately, without using his ripping fangs. Then he dunked the beast back in his bowl for more sauce. Short-Son watched carefully. To him the morsel in the cup was but one mouthful, but he had no intention of displeasing his host—he ate his gift one tiny bite at a time, returning it again and again for more sauce. He was too anxious to actually enjoy what he was tasting.

"You are brave to have Jotoki for personal servants," he said to make polite conversation. He knew that his father detested the five-armed creatures and thought of them as treacherous liars fit only for the mines and factories.

"No. There are rules to training a Jotok. Do it right and one can find no more loyal slave among the stars. A competent kzin wins his battles; a kzin in a hurry loses his life—so goes the saying and few pay attention to it. A kzin troubled by his Jotok is a poor trainer. However, you need not listen to me. You are an impetuous youth and impetuous youths do not have the time to listen to an old kzin."

"I am indeed impetuous in my ways and lacking in the wisdom that so great a one as you could impart to me—but not so impetuous that I would leap ahead of your stalking. There is pleasure in following the pads of a graceful gait."

The ears fluttered again. "But I doubt that I would have anything to teach you about flattery. Your tale, youngling!"

Short-Son was already aware of his good luck. He had by now deduced that this old kzin, who had never made a name for himself and had never been allowed a household of females, dwelled upon the pleasures of fatherhood. Living alone, he lacked all knowledge of how much trouble kits and grown sons and pampered females could be. So he longed for a son. It was plain.

Just as plain as it was that Short-Son of Chiirr-Nig longed for a protector.

This was a delicate situation. Jotok-Tender would want a brave warrior for a son, and that was something that Short-Son could dream about but never be. Yet he couldn't lie about himself to this potential protector—only slaves and monkeys lied—but if he told the truth . . .

"We young trouble-makers play games," he began carefully.

"I remember," said the old kzin gruffly.

"Today I was at a disadvantage. Seven well-trained warriors were arrayed against me."

"Seven adolescent kits—short-tempered, with the brains of pre-adolescent Jotoki—were arrayed against you, yes," snorted the kzin. He was insulting Short-Son's companions; a pre-adolescent Jotok had no more wit than a female—animal cunning at best—and did not acquire male reason until after full growth.

"Brawn without brain can be quite effective in some situations," the youth side-stepped. "There have been times when an immature Jotok killed his kzin hunter," he added.

The old kzin was grinning. It frightened Short-Son into a state of heart palpitations, even though he could see the faraway look in Jotok-Tender's eyes. "I faced such a group as yours once. I also stayed and fought. I didn't die. They only got half an ear for their belts." Then the Tender did a strange thing. He stopped grinning, and he rippled only one ear, the ear that was half gone.

What could Short-Son say to that? He quoted military history. "It is recorded that the great Hanash-Grrsh at the battle of the Furry Nebula, when faced by a superior Jotok fleet, disengaged."

"Ah, you are telling me, with oblique honesty, that you *ran* from your attackers."

"Hanash-Grrsh defeated the Jotok fleet some octal-to-three days later!" said Short-Son defensively.

"With a command that included octal-to-six of tested warriors, don't forget. I suspect that you, on the other paw, are acting alone. If you were indeed surrounded by these seven ferocious youths, how then were you able to escape?"

This discussion wasn't going at all well. "Through an airlock," he said meekly. "They weren't thinking of the outside as a battlefield and neglected to cover that option."

"Not likely. You surprised them. They didn't suspect that you'd run. Kzin warriors don't run from honor. You surprise even me. No need to explain to me why you chose to re-enter through the Jotok Run—they wouldn't be here or even have spies here."

"I will train myself and fight them to victory another day!" Short-Son half-growled defiantly.

"Not likely. I know the games. You are marked for death. They have smelled your cowardice just as I smell it now."

Short-Son was stung. "I could stay here and work for you. I'm good with machines."

"No. You are cruel with my helpless Jotoki. Cowardice makes a kzin cruel, always, always, always. I cannot shield your cowardice. You are your father's responsibility." He drooped his eyes sadly.

I'll never have a protector, thought Short-Son. There was no place to hide. "My father will thrash me for trespassing."

"I suppose he will."

"I would rather have you thrash me, old one."

Jotok-Tender cuffed the youngling gently, as if he were a brother. He growled for Server-One, who came scuttling in on five wrists, one armored eye on Jotok-Tender and another eye on the tray and bowls. After a whispered conversation, the eyes focused on Short-Son. The slave returned with a thin, polished switch.

"This will make welts that will impress your father," the kzin growled, "but it won't do any damage, and the pain will be gone within days. Three welts should be enough. Are you ready?"

Short-Son could endure anything when he knew he wasn't going to be killed. "Yes, honored warrior."

Thwack! Thwack! Thwack!

Strange—when this giant beat him he was not even afraid. "You would make a good father." He was trying to tempt the old kzin.

"We will never know. I will take you home to your father's compound so that you will not be waylaid before you get there. I will explain your situation to him, and convince him to give you one last course in bravery. Listen to him. Do not listen to your false emotions. Your life depends upon that."

"You speak the truth, old kzin."

"I myself can teach you little about combat, not being as skilled a warrior as your honorable father, but I can teach you one maneuver that saved my life. Do you sometimes find it difficult to leap?"

All the time. "I have found it difficult to leap at seven smiles."

"Hesitation is the essence of this maneuver. Studied hesitation is best, but hesitation induced by fear can serve just as well. This trick was never taught to me. I learned the whole thing at once, by chance, and killed my attacker. I practiced months to learn what I had done and how to repeat it. It is the only real warrior skill I have. Come."

The giant took Short-Son through rock tunnels to a domed arena which was used to train many Jotoki at once, seducing them to the discipline of taking orders. An eight-and-four of the Jotok were there, practicing the physical arts in a game of move-ball. Their master shooed them to the sidelines where they clustered in a chaos of arms.

He placed Short-Son in front of him, then backed away, crouching. "Now leap at me!"

The youngling tried—but fear paralyzed him and he couldn't leap.

Jotok-Tender roared. "This is only a demonstration! Leap!"

He leapt at the giant, feebly hoping to please him.

The huge kzin sidestepped, turned, and reached out an arm. Short-Son felt his leap go awry, felt his arms fling out from the attack posture in an instinctive attempt to regain his balance, felt himself twisted to flop onto his back like a carcass of flung meat. How did that happen? A fanged face was grinning down at him. When he moved his dizzy head in an attempt to get up he saw along the wall an array of armored eyes watching him from the shoulders of a tangled mass of limbs, undermouths tittering.

Jotok-Tender was unconcerned. "If my claws had been extended, you'd be lying there with your throat ripped out, temporarily a very surprised kzin. Standing over my first victim, I was very surprised myself. Get up. Now *I* will jump *you* as soon as I have shown you how to swivel the pads of your feet."

CHAPTER 4

(2391–2392 A.D.)

In the social protocol of the Hssin Fortress, Chiirr-Nig, the elder, would never have entertained Hssin's nameless Jotok-Tender—but a matter of father and son always took precedence. There was no better way to enter a named-one's household than to voluntarily take upon oneself the son-duties of an absent father, and, while doing so, protect the father's reputation. Since the Jotok-Tender had handled the son's transgression discreetly, without public humiliation for the father, with disciplined kindness for the son, he was welcome, even to a seat, in the great front room of the Chiirr-Nig compound.

Awkward kdatlyno slaves were in attendance and two wives lounged on the rug beside the rippling dance of the infrared warmer. Chiirr-Nig took the opportunity to unburden his disappointment and frustration at Short-Son's inability to master the basics of self-defense. While he lavishly fed his guest fresh Jotok-arm with fish, passing the fish from his own dish down to his youngest wife, he grumbled, first raging and then growling about the lack of self-discipline in the younger generation.

Quietly, Short-Son's mother had slipped into the high-ceilinged room, sensing from wherever she had been the emotional tone of the conflict. Gracefully Hamarr wandered over to sniff the welts on her kit's back. She paced about the reception room, eyeing the two males and her son, ignoring the kdatlyno. With a low growl she drove off one of Chiirr-Nig's younger wives.

She nuzzled Chiirr-Nig in a way that interrupted his conversation, trying to tell him that she was concerned about her son. Idly he scratched her head, paying her concerns no heed. She had fiercely protected the runt of her litter from his brothers and scrappy sisters, and especially from the sons of the compound's other kzinrretti— but Chiirr-Nig himself had too many sons for him to even think of playing favorites.

Frustrated by her inability to gain her named-one's attention Hamarr turned to Short-Son, nuzzling him. Playfully she began to shove him from the room, blocking his every attempt to return, to get past her, to stay.

Chiirr-Nig watched the display with amused ears. His son was acting properly in attempting to stay while his fate was being discussed—but a kzin indulged his females. They always provided good excuse to break the rigid rules. "Go play with Hamarr!" he dismissed his son, waving a hand. "She's bored. Take her for a run."

Presently Jotok-Tender and Chiirr-Nig were exchanging stories about the escapades of their youth, when Hssin was a dynamic new base on the frontier. Chiirr-Nig offered honors to the giant for bringing his son home, and the giant tactfully suggested that the son needed an intensive crash workout on the finer points of the martial attack.

A playful mother herded her son down to the recreation dome, loping ahead of him, then backtracking to hit him from behind, then facing him—still and silently—poised to run or attack. When she reached the recreation room, she chased away the other kzinrretti with low growls and threats, and bowled Short-Son onto the floor, where she could sniff and lick his welts. She stared at him with admonishing eyes, asking a question whose answer she would be unable to comprehend.

It bothered Hamarr that he was so passive. Her other sons weren't passive. She belted him to his feet, approached, withdrew, surprised him with a cuff that shook his head but was designed not to hurt. She smiled at him and rippled her ears at the same time. She retreated so fast that he had to come after her, but when he got too close she cuffed him again with enough force to rattle his fangs. He enjoyed playing with her, but he was already bigger than she was and he didn't want to hurt her. Nevertheless she forced him to leap and attack until the juices of the fight were running in him savagely. Once he almost bit her too hard.

That evening Hamarr refused to leave him; she refused to return to her own quarters and insisted on sleeping at her son's feet, sometimes waking up to lick his welts, worriedly. She remembered how greedy her other sons had been when they were suckling, how she'd had to growl and cuff the others away when they'd had their fill so that the runt wouldn't starve to death. He was an odd child, and she didn't understand him.

The father dutifully talked to Short-Son's brothers, and the brothers good-naturedly set up practice sessions for their runt sibling. It gave them a chance to show their warrior skills, and to make the training so rigorous that the runt was hard pressed to meet their demands. They could cuff him around, goad his rage, tease him, work him over, all for the virtuous cause of improving his warriorness.

Short-Son merely endured the practice, resigned to his fate, knowing that the one-on-one combat was not preparing him to face a whole *gang* intent on killing him for his ears. The only thing of possible use that he had learned recently was the trick shown him by Jotok-Tender.

For a while he escaped the games. His father used his son's interest in machinery to get him apprenticed to the shipyards where he went to work on the gravitic motors being assembled for the Prowling Hunters. Many octals of them were being shipped out to the Wunderland System. He found himself working with Jotoki slaves, even being taught by them.

Zrkrri-Supervisor had short words of advice for him. "The slaves will save you work, use them, but never put yourself in a position where a slave knows how to do something you do not. That is fatal. I will not consider you competent until you can replace at any time any slave under your command."

There was nothing new in the motors they were building, a four-hundred-year-old design. The Patriarchy had long ago set up standardization so that no matter where a ship was assembled it could be serviced at any other base. How else could the Patriarch run an empire? When a ship needed repairs it might be a lifetime from its mother shipyard, as light traveled, totally dependent upon locally manufactured spare parts.

Innovation, anywhere except in the Admiralty labs of Kzin-home, was discouraged. Heroes, always chafing under inappropriate rules forged at a distance, tended to ignore the decree. But such insubordination was balanced as unauthorized invention was stripped out of weaponry and replaced by standard issue due to lack of spare parts for the innovation.

The engine work was not easy, the conditions of the shop impossibly dark and noisy, made for the needs of Jotok rather than kzin. He had a desk and console beside the superstructure that surrounded the motor being built or refurbished. The desk had never been cleaned and when Short-Son tried to clean it, the edges and pockets still stained his hands.

The superstructure seemed to have been designed by Jotoki; they could swing from platform to platform with ease—trees were their natural medium—but it seemed to shake under kzin weight and frustrate his attempts at climbing. He didn't like to look down. His ever-present Jotok companion always watched him patiently with one eye, other eyes on handholds and general surveillance.

The language he had to learn drove him crazy. It was a corruption of the Hero's Tongue that didn't hiss or rumble, but flowed and chirped. Worse, the expressiveness of the Hero's Tongue had been disemboweled—there were no more insults, the military idiom was gone, the mollifications and flattery were gone. What remained was a utilitarian ability to describe, to point, to anticipate. With a language like that, a slave wouldn't even be able to *think* about revolt—but it was annoyingly bland for a kzin to speak.

However, learning the patois gave Short-Son the first power he had ever had. If he asked a question of any of the Jotoki who worked for him, the slave would stop working and explain very carefully whatever he wanted to know. Nobody teased him.

Nobody insulted him. Nobody told him that a warrior didn't need to know *that*. He didn't have to phrase his questions to flatter, or worry that they might insult. He just got answers. If he grinned, he got answers quickly.

So absorbed was he in learning the craftsmanship of gravitics and puzzling over the theory and mathematics of it, that he forgot the games that young warriors play, forgot that they were still hunting him down. They almost found him. After one of his shifts at the motoryard, while he was hurrying toward the shops that served the local factories, his mind occupied with the remembered taste of a *vatach* snack he was about to buy, he spotted a member of Puller-of-Noses's pride, waiting, watching, seeming to be busy doing nothing while he lounged beside the empty cages outside of the meat shop.

Short-Son backed up, fear driving him to return to his dim little desk on the vast floor of the motoryard. He couldn't think. He couldn't stay here. He couldn't leave. He chose instead to go up—the yard maintained a grassland park up there for their kzin workers. It was empty at this hour, but the tall grass soothed him and he had an overview of the shops and the giant freight elevators that rose to the surface. He stayed here under the artificial light, repressing the growlings of his hunger, waiting, waiting until he was sure his enemy was gone. Then he sneaked back home to his father's compound, ashamed.

It didn't matter. He was sent with a crew into space to install new drives in a Hunting Prowler that had recently come in from Kzrrosh on its way to Wunderland to join the armada forming against the monkeys. It was his first time in space. And it was the first time he had seen a Hunting Prowler whole. Nothing of the experience was familiar, the deep space armor that constrained him, the sled that was bringing him closer, the bulky Jotok armor that extended his slaves' reach by a full metallic hand.

The spheroidal warship was one of the smaller kzin naval killers. Short-Son's chief slave pointed out a larger battleship in the far distance, a red dot moving in the light of R'hshssira, but their Hunting Prowler, close as it was, seemed far more formidable, studded with weapon pods, sensor booms, control domes, drive field ribs, and boat bays with a shuttle drifting alongside. Still, for the moment it was helpless—its motor was gone, the new one still held in the claws of the shuttle, uninstalled.

Hssin rolled beneath them, clotted red, like another giant battleship. It was more than illusion. From Hssin, Wunderland had been conquered. Hssin still attracted warcraft from ever more distant regions of the Patriarchy as the news of the monkeys spread at the unhurried pace of light. The kzin fought their battles that way. Reinforcements arrived for a generation after the battle was won. Sometimes they were needed, sometimes not. In this case the latecoming Conquest Warriors were needed, for the star-swinging monkeys still owned unconquered systems.

Under the stars, maneuvering the giant gravitic motor into this lethal ship of conquest, Short-Son first thought that perhaps he too might be able to join the armada being thrown against Man-sun. His power gave him the illusion that he was a real warrior. It felt very good. With magnetic boots on the hull of the kzin ship, *his* ship, he could look up and imagine what it would be like to destroy the ships of men.

But the very same day he returned from space, the watcher from the pride of Puller-of-Noses was there, waiting patiently by the meat shop, waiting for him. He had thought that the glory of space had reformed him. He had given the power to travel between the stars to a valiant ship of prey, juggled that monstrous motor in his own arms! Didn't that give him the power to crush all fear? to become a warrior?

Yet it took only a second sighting of the watcher to trigger all the cowardice he had ever known. It meant that they had found him. Fear! An image of himself that he had brought from space, crumbled. He was no kzin who could carry a star engine on his shoulder—he had been no more than an insect carrying a stone. How to save himself?

Again he retreated back into the motoryard and climbed. It was all he could think of now, waiting them out a second time, hiding. Tomorrow he would think of some better plan. It was a miserable feeling. He stepped out onto the roof into the still tall grass. Why didn't they leave him alone?

Only when the grass moved did he realize his terrible mistake. First he faced one casual kzin, in the shirt and epaulets favored by the young of Hssin. But there were others; he smelled their exertion. When he edged back toward the door he confronted the brown striped watcher who had followed him. To his right a third kzin rose from the grass. Before he could run, a fourth blocked his way. Two others guarded distant exits. He was trapped by six grinning kzin who wanted his ears.

"Now you'll *have* to fight," said Puller-of-Noses, already crouched and waiting for his leap.

CHAPTER 5

(2392 A.D.)

Short-Son tried to look over the edge of the roof but he was too far away and he already knew there was no escape in that direction. He glanced toward the pair of almost ship-sized elevators that rose into the artificial sky. Much too far away. Could a kzin fly?

Never had he felt such a rage. His mouth was wrapped back over his fangs in a death grin and he couldn't have erased it from his face if he'd tried. His claws were out. His haunches were primed to leap at his tormentor and tear him to bits with fang and claw and hatred. He breathed. Only the fear kept him rooted.

"We hear you do it in trees with Jotok playmates!" taunted Hidden-Smiler whose smile was not hidden.

He remembered clearly through the rage how Jotok-Tender had told him the usage of fear, and practiced with him. Wait for the first leap. Apply that body-twist while extending the claws just so. A strange part of his mind was noticing that he had no control over his claws now—they were unretractable.

"Your father was a *vatach*!" rumbled another kzin who was not coming too close.

"His *mother* taught this toothless kit how to fight!"

Puller-of-Noses was relaxing now, sensing that Short-Son really didn't have the courage to fight. That emboldened him. He wasn't going to need his friends. He motioned them away. He'd take these ears himself. "You're tied up like a *zianya* on the table, ready for the feast. I smell your fear, *zianya*."

Short-Son snarled.

"Oh, we disturbed you! You came up here to feed on the grass. Don't let us stop you." Puller-of-Noses was enjoying the repartee.

"The grass is choice for one with a double stomach," gibed Hidden-Smile.

Attack me! I'll flip and slash your throats out! Short-Son's thoughts were ravening, but he could say nothing. He hated them for teasing him, playing with him before they killed him. His fangs were sticking to dry lips, frozen by his grin.

"Our coward stinks of fear," said Puller-of-Noses, ready for the kill, charging himself for a single leap that would rip the life from his prey. "You smell like a fattened grass-eater." When his opponent didn't respond, he couldn't resist the final, ultimate insult. While he composed it, the tip of his pink tail flipped back and forth. "I'll make a deal with you. Be an herbivore. Put your head in the grass and eat it, and I'll spare your life. Or fight like a Hero and I'll give you honor."

If Puller-of-Noses had attacked then, a desperate Short-Son might have unbalanced him and slashed him to a quick death, but the pride leader was prolonging the agony, waiting for a reply, enjoying his wit too much to begin a battle that would end instantly and thus instantly end his fun. While he taunted, his only caution was to reestablish his crouch. The pause gave Short-Son a fatal moment of thought.

Puller-of-Noses had tendered a verbal bargain: eat grass and live or be a Hero and die.

His word of honor would force him to keep that bargain.

Puller-of-Noses was also too stupid to understand that he had actually offered Short-Son a *real* choice between life and death. In the challenger's mind there was no choice at all between honor and eating grass. He *thought* he had Short-Son trapped.

Trembling, full of disgust for himself, Short-Son sank to his knees and began to eat the tall strands of green—crawling, ripping it from its roots with his fangs, chewing, though his teeth were not meant for such chewing. There was no way for his throat to swallow the fibrous cud, but he kept chewing and chewing.

Six kzin came forward with stunned eyes. Their ears twitched in amusement, but it wasn't amusement they felt; what they felt was disbelief. And only then did Puller-of-Noses realize that he could gain no honor by killing this sniveling coward. Worse, he would be condemned to death if he broke his word. The ears of his intended victim were worthless.

From that day on Hssin's "herbivorous" kzin had a new name spontaneously bestowed upon him—Eater-of-Grass. There was no suppressing the story. It spread like grassfire throughout the Hssin base. The Chiirr-Nig household disowned him. The naval shipyards no longer trusted him to work on their gravity polarizers.

He had no place to sleep, no place to eat, no one to talk to, no work. For a while he lived in corners and on roofs and in tunnels, hunting escaped rodents. It was hard to keep clean. Once he was mistaken for a wretched telepath. He even tried chewing on roots to ease his hunger, but in his stomach they turned to gas and indigestion. He begged—and grown kzin pretended he didn't exist. He robbed a cage once of its live *vatach* which had been hung out for fresh air, a death offense if caught. He made it look as if the *vatach* had escaped. They all expected him to walk out onto the surface of Hssin and disappear into the mountains to die but he had no suit.

When he begged for a surface suit, yes, then they paid attention to him and charitably granted his wish. Eater-of-Grass didn't walk into the mountains, however—he used the suit to break back into the Jotok Run, mostly because he wanted a bath. Soaking in water wasn't the best way to take a bath, but it would do. He spent a day cleaning and grooming his fur. When no one came to throw him out, he saw no reason to leave.

This time he was more covert. He knew how to hide. He kept away from the hunting parties and he knew much more about Jotoki manners. He stalked the wild Jotoki up in the trees and they hunted him when he wasn't looking. He studied Jotok anatomy for lack of anything else to do—the lungs on the inner arm that fed the heart and doubled as a singsong voice, the strange-tasting brain tissue that grew in a cortex around the heart, the leaf-grinding teeth in the undermouth that made great spearheads when sharpened.

Eater-of-Grass built three hidden lairs. He pretended he was an ancient kzin, before language or iron or gunpowder, spraying and defending his territory. According to the Conservors that was the era when kzin fathers often ate their sons to keep down the competition. Wryly, he wondered how different it was today. Then a kzin-rret hid her children and defended them fiercely. Kzinrretti *still* tried to be protective. He remembered his mother fondly—without her he would not be alive today.

When the lights came on one morning, green and yellow through the leaves, he lifted his ears to listen for kzin hunting parties but heard only insects and the fall of a branch. Broad leaves dumped their water. Swooping from one branch to another, a firg cackled every time it took to the air, visible because of the red scales down its back.

He sniffed—detecting no kzin smells—but he wasn't alone. He could never pick up the scent of a Jotok, because of a Jotok's ability to mimic any aroma, but a forest is full of clues. With nostrils flared, he was catching the tang of lush broken cells, sugar, acid, spice. The rind of the pop-spray. A Jotok was out there, eating fruit.

Yes—there he was, many eyes watching from a rocky ridge, one hand already around a branch ready to shoot himself up into the growth above, and far enough away to escape. Prey for today's meal, perhaps. But the creature would be hard to track. Best to ignore him for now. But not totally.

Eater-of-Grass found a tree being garroted by a pop-spray vine and shimmied up the bark to tear off a bunch of ripe balls. The rind was tough but that meant nothing to a Jotok's grinding molars. He placed the balls on a stump in sight of his prey and re-treated far enough away to be out of fear's range, trusting the animal's natural curios-ity to induce it to examine the offering.

He wasn't quite sure how to spring a trap. This Jotok's limbs had the bulk and shape of an adult, but the skin wore a youthful shine. The beast might still be too young to have intelligence, yet must be about the age at which its kind acquired (very quickly) kzin-like deductive powers, becoming both hard to catch and dangerous.

After eating the fruit-balls his prey didn't move away. It sat on its mouth, watch-ing him, elbows in the air. He approached and it retreated, he casually distanced him-self and it followed—peculiar behavior for a wild Jotok. The animal was still there the next morning, much closer, sitting in the tree above him and watching.

He fed it again. "Some pop-spray for you, Long-Reach. Hai! Long-Reach!"

When he had retreated the required distance, it dashed to the ground to devour his offering, shoving the balls one at a time into its undermouth with a weird lateral chewing motion. All the while it stared at him with two eyes, focused one on the fruit, while the others jerkily kept a cautious watch on the neighborhood.

Then . . . "Long-Reach," it imitated from a lung slit on one of the arms. "Long-Reach," replied another arm.

Fan-like ears suddenly erect, the amazed kzin recognized what it was saying from his recent verbal exchanges with Jotok slaves. Its voices were musical, muting the hisses and gutturals of the Hero's Tongue. He listened, fascinated, as the arms began to play with the words, chatting to themselves in harmony. "Long-Reach. *Long-Reach.* Long-Long-Long-Reach. Reach . . . Reach . . . Reach!"

It tittered, pleased with itself, shifted to the mockery of the chirping of various insects, then sat down to await the orange-yellow kzin's response.

"Come here, Long-Reach," he said in his most ingratiating manner. "Stupid ani-mal, I want to eat you."

"Want to eat you. Want to eat you," it replied.

How remarkable, he thought. He had found a Jotok in transition. Jotok-Tender had told him that if he fed one of the beasts at this stage, it would follow him around and imitate him. The Jotoki were very peculiar, indeed; children were not raised in a family, they had no household keep, no patriarch, no mothers, no brothers to terror-ize them, no teachers, no discipline, no toys, no warrior games. They just grew up in the forest, and when an adult wanted a family he just took a trip to the forest, picked out a healthy youth who had managed to survive and took him home.

The transitional Jotok was "programmed" to bond to whoever adopted it. Unfortunately for the Jotok race, the transitional mind, having evolved on a planet where the Jotoki were the *only* intelligent life form, couldn't easily differentiate between an adult Jotok and an adult kzin. Any intelligent parent sufficed. Thus they made excellent slaves.

Days later Long-Reach was still following him around, no longer afraid of its kzin parent at all. Astonishingly, it had acquired a vocabulary of more words than it could count on its five-times-five thumbs. He tried to remember himself as a small kit; certainly he had never learned the basics of the Hero's Tongue in so short a time.

After catching a rodent to eat, and being astonished when Long-Reach promptly dashed off into the woods and came back with another rodent, he became challenged to find out how much he could teach the creature. Could it learn to use tools? He sharpened a stake with his knife and handed the blade to one of the five arms.

"Long-Reach, now you try."

"Long-Reach, try." The Jotok didn't succeed. It wailed in consternation, but wouldn't return the knife to Eater-of-Grass, demanding the right to continue to try. Half a day later it was still trying, by then more pleased with itself. The stake was sharp, if very short.

The kzin youth became delighted with the absurdity of their relationship. He found himself struggling up trees, which sometimes tottered under his weight, to gather delicacies for his Long-Reach, while Long-Reach got tangled in the underbrush chasing rodents for him. He no longer thought of Long-Reach as a meal, or even as an "it." What he appreciated most was that Long-Reach never slept—at least one arm was always awake, watching for danger.

There *were* dangers. The wild Jotoki, who had passed through the transitional phase without being adopted, were antisocial beasts, protective of their territory, and, though hunter-shy in the daytime, were vicious at night. They had no language or learning, but were quite capable of inventing tools and devising intricate revenges for remembered transgressions. They *knew* that the kzinti were their enemies. They backtracked to deceive, they laid traps, they played jokes.

Of course, the worst danger was the kzin hunting parties.

Eater-of-Grass was amazed at how well Long-Reach knew the Jotok Run and how quickly he could take them away from danger. He was a very useful companion.

CHAPTER 6

(2392 A.D.)

Thumbs were pulling at his fur. He did not mind because Long-Reach was fascinated by his hairiness. The thumbs grew more insistent. They pulled his eyelids open. "Hunters, hunters, hunters," the arms whispered, sometimes interrupting each other.

Eater-of-Grass was on his feet instantly, soundlessly moving. But it was soon evident that they were being tracked by experts. They hiked from the tall trees under the domes, ducking through tunnels, wading across dark swamps, climbing over blasted rock faces, squirming down through a crevasse to the treetops of the level below. Mostly Long-Reach chose their route. But evasions didn't shake their pursuers for long. All the while the desperate kzin youth gauged the hunting party, sniffing the wind, sometimes sending out a circumspect Long-Reach to reconnoiter through the rainforest's canopy.

The fugitives were being tracked by three Jotoki scouting among the branches and one kzin on the ground, in an unhurried manner but diligently.

The final backtrack was a mistake. They fell into the center of the Jotok shepherds, and the triangle moved with them—no matter where they turned. Pinned. He caught a flash of yellow livery in the trees—and knew who was hunting them.

"Long-Reach, we won't escape. Stop."

His Jotok slave did not fully understand. Arms waving, the beast ran ahead on three wrists, swaying with fear.

Eater-of-Grass waited, death resignation on him at the same time that his mind was trying out various phrases of flattery. Eventually the giant kzin appeared in the copse below, his age showing in his lame pace. He approached the youngling.

"Ah, you," he said.

"I had no place else to go, honored warrior," explained Eater-of-Grass sullenly.

This excuse for his crime was ignored. "You no longer have the youth-name of the house of Chiirr-Nig. How shall I address you?" asked Jotok-Tender.

"Eater-of-Grass," replied the ostracized kzin, defiantly.

"An inappropriate name," growled Jotok-Tender. "Names must bear on the day's truth. Have you been eating grass? I think not—you've been hunting and eating my Jotoki, and various small warm creatures. Eater-of-Ferocious-Jotoki might be a better name." He glanced down at Long-Reach.

"We run!" said Long-Reach. "Now!" admonished another of the arms, but the beast stood its ground.

The giant reached down gently to pop an eyeball out of its armor as far as it would go, examining the lubrication petals. Then he took one of Long-Reach's arms and examined the thumbs. "Exactly the right age. You will have an absolutely loyal slave if you train him as I shall instruct you. You didn't frighten him away?"

"Honored oldster, I had some recent experience with Jotoki at the shipyard. I speak the appropriate patois. Long-Reach, here, found me more than I found him."

"Perhaps we could call you Trainer-of-Slaves. A good trade-name that. Does it suit you?"

"Better than Eater-of-Grass."

"Never use *that name* in front of me!" snarled Jotok-Tender. "I asked you a civil question. Answer! Does it suit you?"

"Trainer-of-Slaves at your service, honored half-ear!" He paused. "Am I being offered employment?"

"A slaver like me offering *employment?* Perhaps I could give food and shelter in exchange for unquestioned service."

"I am loyal to the warrior who gives honest leadership!"

"Said well for a recidivist." He let his ears flap for effect. "We can't parade you around, of course, but I can keep you busy and out of sight. We have mutual needs. Are your ears erect? Have you been in contact?"

"In hiding one is deaf."

"The startling news, then. By lightbeam, Hssin has had advance warning of a small armada coming through, long on its way, ruled by High Conquest Commander Chuut-Riit of the Kzin Admiralty. He will be stripping Hssin of Heroes and warships, including all the Jotoki slaves we can provide. His Conquest Campaign against the monkey-worlds has been *authorized* by the Patriarchy itself. The Patriarch!

"I have already received my advance demands, and dare not be lax in meeting them. Who knows how this Chuut-Riit deals with failure? I am not of a mind to find out. I will be busy and I need help. No one will begrudge me your services. As for those moralists who would have you wasted, a mere wave of Chuut-Riit's orders before the noses of such kit-eaters will lay flat their pompous fur."

"Chuut-Riit?"

"Obviously a member of the Patriarch's family. Other than that we know nothing."

"Coming *here?*"

"In truth, we don't see much of the Patriarchy in these dismal regions, and do quite well without it, but evidently news of our contact with the monkeys seems to have filtered inward and given our wealthier Heroes Long-Journey fever. The families of Ka'ashi"—he gave the Kzin name for Wunderland—"will not be pleased."

"Not be pleased by the attention of the Patriarchy!"

"Youngling, for lifetimes this outback of the Empire has attracted only adventurers driven from the richer worlds by their fathers, by debts, by a desire to be where the Patriarchy isn't, driven here sometimes by kzin hubris, and sometimes, like me, by cowardice. Heroes with ragged fur. Who else would tolerate the cramped quarters of stinking ships for years on end? Wunderland was a gift of the fanged god. Why should its Heroes desire to roll on their backs and expose their throats to those who already have vast wealth? In rage they will challenge Chuut-Riit, but if Chuut-Riit proves able, they will submit. Chuut-Riit will prove able. Do you know history?"

"I listen to the Conservors."

"Not them! The Collected Voices. Last night I put the memoirs of the Riits in my scanner. They scent victory and track it down at the leisurely pace of starlight. Then they impose their victory upon the victor. The Riits are the conquerors of successful Conquest Commanders. If we obey them, we get to keep a goodly portion of what we have conquered."

"And if we don't?"

"Then they begin by taking our daughters. After that the air parches and the fur gets wet with fear."

"I see many duels."

"Yes, and as you watch the mayhem—if you are wise, from within a thick bunker—remember that only fools who wish to cleanse the race of their own fool's blood challenge the Patriarch's family. This is the *Patriarch's family*, not some wandering warlord. Are you with me?"

"I begin to serve your needs at this very moment, wise and merciful Hero! I will make no mistakes!"

"You *will* make mistakes, arrogant kit, and for that I will cuff your brains hard enough to rattle them in your skull, but not hard enough to damage them. Before you follow me, soothe your slave. Disarming his fear at this stage of his development is very important. He must feel free to leave us, though he has already hormonally locked-on to you and cannot leave you. And it is essential that he take direction from *you*, not me. As we travel back to my lair, make sure that your slave is *always* closer to you than to me. Do you understand that?"

"Yes, honored teacher."

"I will try to trick you into violating my admonition. No matter what I do, keep your Jotok closer to your side than to mine! Your training has begun." Jotok-Tender made a high *Rrwrowr*, and his liveried slaves dropped from the trees and formed a point for their return procession.

As Trainer-of-Slaves followed his new protector, he thought about the mysterious Chuut-Riit. An armada! The mythical Patriarchy was coming to Hssin! Because light was faster than the gravity polarizer, it would be impatient years before the High Conquest Commander arrived—but the good in that was the time it gave Trainer-of-Slaves to make himself ready.

He would produce slaves for the Patriarch's family!

The thought returned his attention to Long-Reach, who was following them with all the enthusiasm of a monkey tied to a nose-ring. He patted the beast's warty head and threw a stick for him to fetch—in a direction which would keep him away from the giant.

But Trainer-of-Slaves was having a difficult time thinking about slaves. His mind was on the bridge of a Prowling Hunter, following Chuut-Riit through the starry reaches, seeking prey. His soul had already vowed eternal allegiance to this Hero whose miraculous message from space had saved his life. The miracle of it was an omen: Chuut-Riit was the light leading him to Heroism.

Back in the slaver compound, Jotok-Tender tattooed a black splotch on Trainer-of-Slaves's facial skin so that charcoal could be discreetly seen through the fine hair, and he ordered fitted for his charge a purple and mauve tunic of the distant W'kkai style, unfashionable on Hssin. None of this was a disguise, but it made it possible for a local kzin to face this pariah and say "Trainer-of-Slaves" and not think *Eater-of-Crass*.

The old slaver warned his youngling apprentice never to discuss his cowardly past. That way the subject would never come up. It was dangerous for a kzin to mention another kzin's former life under a different name before the subject kzin mentioned it himself.

"In time you will have your own army of slaves, who are owned by others but loyal to you. You will need no other name than Trainer-of-Slaves to bring fear into the feet of kzin warriors. Dress well, pretend to no honors beyond your station, honor your timeless word—and keep your slaves close at hand."

Trainer-of-Slaves was shown to his sparse lair, and taken on a tour of the Jotok dormitory, poles and platforms under a windowless dome. On the level below, underground, were the training simulators where Jotoki learned their trade.

"Why will Chuut-Riit want so many Jotok slaves? Many families of Hssin will not permit Jotoki in their houses."

"I imagine that Chuut-Riit values them as mechanics."

"They handle tools well! In the shipyards my supervisor commanded that I learn all that my slaves knew, but I must admit that when *I* needed three arms, I was at a loss! One plus three-octals of thumbs!"

"Recall that the Jotoki evolved the gravity polarizer while we were puzzling over flint. We were hired by the Jotoki for our abilities as warriors, not for our way with machines."

"Is it really true that the Jotoki once ruled over us?"

"They commanded the ships that first took us out to the stars. But order evolves from disorder. Vegetation evolves to dominate the rock, the herbivore evolves to dominate the vegetation, and the carnivore evolves to dominate the plant-eater. Intelligence evolves in males to dominate the female. In the natural order of things the warrior rises above the mechanic."

"And the wisdom of age rises above the untutored youth. Have I got that right?"

"You've had a bad beginning, but you may yet live to an age when your fur sheds without replacing itself—if your flattery doesn't get you into trouble first."

CHAPTER 7

(2392 A.D.)

Long-Reach was collectively puzzled by the strange chambers to which the yellow-one had taken him. It was a frightening world, more because there were no trees in it than because of the slabs that slid open in the world-boundaries. The first big discussion he had among himselves was: how would his mouth eat if there were no leaves?

His eyes kept looking for leaves, and each of him kept asking to stare through another's eyes to see if there weren't leaves in that direction. Skinny(arm) was especially apprehensive.

And for another thing, in this world there were too many of the yellow-orange carnivores. They made all of him anxious. He didn't know why his own yellow-one was special except that the nervousness disappeared when they were together. Then very interesting things happened.

Among himselves he referred to his special carnivore companion as Mellow-Yellow, which was not a vibrating-word but was a pastel image-word of the kind used to communicate between his selves. Mellow-Yellow was "world-lights filtering down through mingled leaf-tissue." It was the best forest image there was. His companion did seem to have a voice-name, but the rules were confusing. Sometimes he referred to his body as "Hero," sometimes as "Warrior," sometimes as "Kzin," sometimes, when he was dangerous to be with it was "Eater-of-Grass," or "Fangless." The voice-names changed as night and day. Lately it was "Trainer-of-Slaves." Simpler to think: Mellow-Yellow.

The furry Mellow-Yellow had a game with the low-frequency sounds that was so exciting to play that Long-Reach couldn't seem to stop playing. If Mellow-Yellow quieted his vibrator (which seemed stuck in his mouth where he couldn't chew it) Long-Reach felt compelled to hum and rumble and chatter in order to provoke more of that game. When he deliberately tried to keep one of his lungs silent, another was sure to interrupt the hush. Big(arm) had more restraint than skinny(arm).

The game had rules. Each eye-image had an ear-sound that only Mellow-Yellow knew and Long-Reach had to guess. Since the kinds and varieties of image were endless, it was a never ending quest to find the voice that fitted the image. What was exciting was that if his selves were clever he could use words to provoke the new sounds out of Mellow-Yellow, or even better, use the words *themselves* as an aid to discovering the new words. His selves carried on an internal race. Which lungs would first utter the true sequence of sounds? Sometimes they all spoke at once. Short(arm) was best at such races and tended to dominate the role of talker. When short(arm) was asleep, Long-Reach was less glib.

In this world beyond the trees, there were many new images, many new words.

"Leaves," said short(arm). "Leaves, leaves," repeated skinny(arm) because there weren't any.

"Ah, you're hungry." Mellow-Yellow left the cave through . . . an elevator? Door, door, corrected short(arm). When Long-Reach tried to follow there was no door. Anxiety.

But Mellow-Yellow came back with leaves in a container of grass. Big(arm) thought about the right words for the sight and made suggestions while feeling the weave of the grass blades that were entwined in a very regular way. His eye had never seen anything like it. "Leaves sit on grass-floor," said short(arm) while communicating the thought that flat-"floor" could not be a good word for hollow-container.

"It's a *basket*, not a floor. I got it from the slave quarters. Say 'basket.'"

"Basket, basket. Basket of grass. Grass basket."

"And don't take it apart! Don't you *ever* stop being curious?"

Long-Reach picked up the basket with two arms and dumped the leaves on the floor. He sat on them, elbows in the air, and began to masticate. "Good," exclaimed all the arms in unison.

"My ears ripple when I watch you sitting down to eat."

"My ears ripple when I watch you sitting down to excrete. One-mouth better than two."

"Long-Reach, *your* ears don't ripple. Your ears are in your wrists."

"Ripple? Ripple?" Big(arm) rose so that its eye could look at the resonance cups on its wrist which analyzed sound.

Trainer-of-Slaves rippled his ears to demonstrate. He was genuinely amused. "That's what *I* do when I tell a joke. How do I know when *you* are telling a joke?"

"Joke?"

"Some other day!"

Trainer-of-Slaves needed to sleep—so Long-Reach hooked himself to a wall rack and slept himself, with only freckled(arm) awake and watching the door. Freckled(arm) had things to mull over but that was difficult with sleep-silence on four channels.

Thinking did not go rapidly without question-answers from other-arms. But questions were themselves interesting. What had happened to the forest? Why did the absence of trees make floors flat? What was glass? How could something invisible resist the push of a hand? How was R'hshssira attached to its ceiling? Did all worlds have different colored lamps?

There were more questions in the morning when Mellow-Yellow led Long-Reach to a cavern full of weird shapes and vines that swallowed eyes and arms. The giant carnivore was there with the smell of leaf-eater flesh on his breath. Frightening.

"You won't be able to put him in the machine—they panic when their arms are constrained—and his vocabulary isn't big enough so that an explanation will register. We'll have to shoot him up with trazine. First, we'll let him watch a Jotok come out of the trainer unharmed."

Long-Reach stayed as near his yellow companion as he could get. They put him too close to a big leaf-eater like himself who was suspended in mid-air, his arms in thick sleeves, with vines coming out of the caps over his eyes. His limbs convulsed as if he were running and flying among the trees—but he wasn't going anywhere. Terrifying.

The big kzin unhooked the eyes. The sleeves came off. While the beast was being liberated, three of Long-Reach's brains came to the simultaneous conclusion that *he* was going to become the replacement. Three arms started to back off—and couldn't move.

"The trazine won't harm you. Be gone within heartbeats." They were putting him into the sleeves and he couldn't resist. His eyes had retracted to their armored state in a reflex at the shock of paralysis, but he could not keep them closed while the giant popped out each eye in turn and stuck them into caps. He was blind and paralyzed. Was this the death he had been avoiding all his life?

All of his minds went into escape mode. But before he could even think of escape . . . suddenly . . . he was transported to a forest. There was a precision smoothness to each detail and no smell. He had not passed through any walls or doors. Did one die and go to an odorless forest? He still couldn't move, but his thumbs were wrapped around branches and he wasn't falling. He saw no kzinti. When the paralysis wore off, he took the chance and ran; he zipped through the trees like flying, barely touching a branch before he was reaching for another.

The landmarks were unfamiliar and there were no odor clues. The trees were too tall. When he climbed as high as he could go there were no ceiling lamps. White moss floated overhead where the roof should have been. Nothing he did seemed to orient him, even his acceleration senses were subtly contradicting his eyes and the feel of his skin. He couldn't backtrack because the world changed behind him as it passed out of sight—what was behind was as unknown as what was in front. It was wrong.

A lake appeared through the trees, larger than any lake he had ever seen, bluer than it had any right to be. He skittered among broad branches that had been able to reach outward along the shoreline, afraid to let the lake out of sight lest it disappear. High above the beach he paused.

His tree developed a lung-slit and spoke. "I am a tree."

Startled, he leaped into another tree, nearly missing it. "Nice leap," said a bird who had been watching him.

He was gaping at the tree (with three eyes) and the bird (with two eyes). How many different kinds of worlds were there? asked freckled(arm) frantically. After a while Long-Reach got used to it. The world patiently gave him lessons in speech with the same image-sound codes as Mellow-Yellow had used. Stones talked. Stumps talked. Animals talked. It was very disconcerting.

The predictables had shifted. And not to be able to predict meant *danger*. Hide and meditate upon the consequences. Idly fast(arm) plucked some berries in their leaf-cones and shoved them up into the undermouth to placate hunger. But there was nothing for Long-Reach to chew on. Shock. In this world food was going to be a problem. Too many problems.

"Eat me," said a leaf.

He tried. It was only a strong taste, still nothing to chew on.

"Bitter," said the leaf which had miraculously regrown. "Eat me again."

He did so. It tasted like the caps of marsh-reed, or even seed-berries, but again there was nothing to chew on.

"Sweet," said the everlasting leaf. "Eat me again."

Right now he wanted Mellow-Yellow. "Trainer-of-Slaves!" he bellowed.

His call produced an immediate twilight, fading into a night darker than the deepest cavern.

Beside him, Mellow-Yellow appeared slowly, like a ceiling lamp at dawn, without casting any light into the darkness. The carnivore's image was too sharp, too orange, and flickered a little. A furry hand reached out and touched the eye of big(arm). Then—weirdly with only one eye—he was back where he had started; Mellow-Yellow was the right color, the giant kzin was beside him and so was all the machinery in the cavern. His selves jumped to look through big(arm)'s eye.

Long-Reach could now feel his arms in their tight trap. Panic. Death . . . he began to struggle.

The giant kzin backed off but Mellow-Yellow efficiently freed the capped eyes and removed the constraints. Long-Reach walked away, miffed, with only freckled(arm) watching the big yellow trickster curiously.

"Joke," said Trainer-of-Slaves.

"You have brains where your intestines should be!" sulked Long-Reach, who had begun to assimilate his anatomy lessons. "Joke," he added, having no intention of insulting a carnivore.

But for the rest of the day he refused to speak. At night while Mellow-Yellow slept, his minds debated what they had seen. The whole event reeked of danger. Hide, said all of his instincts. And yet the curiosity was overpowering! Talking trees! Moving through walls! Seeing different worlds with each eye! The wonder of it!

At the first sign that Mellow-Yellow was awake, he herded him toward the door. "More joke," he said.

During his second session in the confinement rig he learned numbers and image symbols for numbers. Released, he enthusiastically counted everything—still amazed that the region between three and many could be divided up endlessly into distinct parts, that no matter how high he counted, there was one more. He counted kzin, he counted lamps, and he counted the leaves he ate, one by one because freckled(arm) wanted to know how many leaves it took to stop hunger.

The virtual worlds of the confinement rig were of two kinds. The moment he tired of one, he was shifted to the other. There were the work worlds where he learned practical mathematics and the art of maintaining machines and proper ways of addressing his kzin masters. There were the play worlds of forest and dungeon where natural law changed whimsically, sometimes in frightful ways, sometimes amusingly. When capricious play taxed his minds, a shift to the tuning of gravitic force fields was a relief; when tedious machining drove him to singing mental tunes in harmony, a shift to the free world of play was pleasure.

Time blurred. He saw less and less of Mellow-Yellow, yet the hours he spent with his kzin companion were rich in conversation. Trainer-of-Slaves admitted that Jotok-Tender was a hard taskmaster while Long-Reach taught his friend geometry and how to disassemble machines. Once they couldn't reassemble a machine because the slave hadn't got that far in his lessons. For that sin Jotok-Tender had them both scrubbing floors together.

The best days were spent hunting. Long-Reach wore a special uniform of cloth that distinguished the slaves of Mellow-Yellow, green and red stripes, ruffles. They swept through the Jotok Run searching out new slaves, leisurely, with no special command to return. To the senses of Long-Reach, the familiar woods and ponds and rock faces of his youth were better than the virtual forests of the confinement rig. There was fresh forest odor and the trees didn't talk. The ceiling had lamps and the caves led only to the level below.

Long-Reach would flush the prey, knowing where the young gathered. Then Trainer-of-Slaves would seduce the youth while Long-Reach hid in the trees. The hunt was not always successful. The Jotok they stalked might prove large enough, yet still untouched by curiosity-hunger—he'd have to be released until he matured. Or he might be wild, past his prime, good only for the dinner table, his intelligence lost to language, metamorphosed into cunning.

Trainer-of-Slaves kept the best of the Jotok captives for himself. Three became his personal retinue: Long-Reach, Joker, and Creepy. The three had the usual training in mathematics, mechanics, and gravitic device maintenance. But they were also Mellow-Yellow's hunting companions. They noticed that he had enemies among the kzin, and chattered about the danger to him among themselves, covertly. Inevitably they became his bodyguards, the eyes who watched his back.

CHAPTER 8

(2396 A.D.)

The armada was arriving. Like all things in the Patriarchy, there was no great hurry.

First the swift *Victory at S'Rawl* fell out of space into orbit around Hssin. It disgorged no warriors, and made no diplomacy, but imperiously took over the duties of the local Orbit Command by Authority of the Patriarch. Traat-Admiral was acting as point-liaison for Chuut-Riit, Warrior Ambassador Extraordinary. The Admiral was under strict orders to dominate the local kzinti from the moment of first contact— they were considered to be fierce but not reliably obeisant.

An inner-world kzin, however territorial, was used to the formalisms of hierarchical command, but out here in the wilds a less disciplined breed of kzinti were notorious for the way they fought over and defended the spoils of their adventuring; crass in their willingness to defy a messenger of the Patriarch if he gave any appearance of weakness. The Patriarch was thirty years distant by lightbeam and forty years distant by ship.

The Hssin fleet might have responded arrogantly. The Conquest Heroes of Hssin were brothers of the Conquest Heroes of Wunderland. They could have ignored, or even ordered an attack on the *Victory at S'Rawl*—after all, it was a mere command warcraft heavy with electronics but deficient in armaments. But would the Hssin household of Kasrriss-As have dared such disdain, knowing who was to follow Traat-Admiral?

No action was taken against the *Victory at S'Rawl*. Space traffic control was relinquished with grinless self-restraint.

Ships began to drift into the R'hshssira System in ones and twos, every few hours, over months, the transports with their time-suspended warriors, the warcraft, the auxiliaries—all that Chuut-Riit had been able to exhort, to tempt, to command from five systems. No ship debarked a single warrior to Hssin, taking orbit instead in a great ring around red R'hshssira. To awe Hssin at a distance, that was Traat-Admiral's intention.

In time Chuut-Riit himself arrived, his flagship a spherical dreadnought of the Imperial Ripper class, larger than anything that the barbarians of Hssin had ever seen, the first new battle design from Kzin in centuries, ominous, weapons-laden. These out-world adventurers of the borderlands would fawn all over him for its specifications—and he would sell those details for a price.

During the six days it took for the gravitic drive field of the *Throat Ripper* to collapse from a cruising speed of six-eighths light down to the velocity of R'hshssira, Chuut-Riit had been in post-hibernation training—massage, fight simulation, strenuous amusements with a favorite kzinrret. Hibernation was good for neither muscle tone nor quick reflex. Swift repairs to the physique, he never neglected.

Most confrontations Chuut-Riit handled with a logic that cowed his foes, but if that failed he used wit before falling back on an awesome rage that could subdue opposition with the sheer stench of his anger. Still, he liked to be in prime physical shape for those times when it was necessary to bloody an irrational enemy with fang or claw.

The work den adjacent to his stateroom was small, paneled along one wall by holographic savanna mismatched to the ceiling pipes. Above his data-link hung a modern pulse-laser and an antique crossbow. The floor beside the data-link provided place for but a single kdatlyno-hide rug—this one bare along an edge, old, a trophy of his first hunt as a servitor of the Prime Household. In those days, having more strength than sense, he had aligned himself with a Patriarch who was too young to have remained alive long, but live he did, to grow old and perish while Chuut-Riit served him as military trouble-slasher, first on Kzin, and then among the stars where the endless years of hibernation had showed his aging.

He was not old but (having outlived his regal pridemate) he felt his age. He remembered things vividly that his subordinates knew of only through the distortion of imaging and writing. These kits thought of the Asanti Wars as one battle and knew nothing of the treason of Grrowme-Kowr. They purred of the Long Peace, as if there had been no battles before they were weaned. Unshared memories made a kzin feel old, old, old.

Ah, though perhaps not as old as the Riit crossbow. Chuut-Riit had on his electronic spectacles and was staring at it—Jotok light-alloy, forged by kzin ironmongers, inlaid with blueshell by a semi-professional kzin artist. The leather strapping had been replaced but all else was original.

It was said by his grandfather that this crossbow was the weapon of choice carried into space by the first Riit ancestor hired to battle off-planet. The family genealogy traced him back through to the household of one of the almost mythical Riit Patriarchies, but the truth was probably less romantic—perhaps he was a game-keeper at some distant hunting reserve who scandalized his household (even endangered their lives) by vowing fealty to the Jotok infidels.

Those spider-armed monsters arrived with wealth and magic. They had swords of fire and gravitic machinery and dreams of hiring mercenaries to conquer them a stellar empire, preferring someone else to do their dying for them. In the aftermath of the siege of the Patriarch's castle and his ignoble defeat, Jotok wealth could have bought these spacefaring animals any number of wretched kzinti.

This crossbow and a letter (written in what competent historians had charitably called an "illiterate" hand) were all that remained of the ancestor. The letter was a wonderful attempt at trying to describe stars to a kzin father who was convinced that the stars were the souls of Great Heroes embedded in the Fanged God's Dome.

The Riit medallion engraved into the crossbow was supposed to have been the family mark since prehistorical time. Popular notion held that it was a stylized carnivore's grin, but Chuut-Riit's careful historical research had shown that it was really the shoulder patch assigned by the Jotoki to their elite kzin warriors. It represented a dentate leaf. The dots and comma motto that surrounded the medallion was, however, a later addition: "From Mercenary to Master."

The most invidious sentiment that Chuut-Riit had ever heard was voiced while he was recruiting support for his armada at Ch'Aakin. "If these monkeys put up such a fanatical fight, we should hire them to do battle for us, to be killed in our place. It is time we enjoyed the Long Peace we have created. If a master is truly a master, he can buy life for himself and death for his servants." Said by a fop who had never challenged his father to combat, a fop who owned his share of Jotok slaves yet had never seen the forest-buried ruins of the Jotok worlds, looted by trusted orange mercenaries.

Chuut-Riit was both a mathematician and a historian. He was a student of the rise of the Jotok Empire. It had attained less than an eighth the size of the modern Kzin Patriarchy, yet could still teach important contemporary lessons. How had their purely commercial fleets developed, to such a fine art, logistic battle support over interstellar distances?

Once the Jotok had been military geniuses.

The ancient kzin commanders, using deadly ships thoughtfully supplied by the Jotok, had been enthusiastic plunderers—the language of their teachers was destroyed, lost even to the surviving Jotoki. Nothing but the melancholic forests and foggy lakes remained. For his studies, Chuut-Riit was forced to rely on secondhand kzin texts by kzin warriors who had never mastered Jotoki five-stream grammar. Only with the aid of queueing theory, delay-prediction analysis, intent-result resolution, did the anecdotal fragments provide insight into Jotok military strategy.

The Jotok should have won any war that pitted them against their strategically immature hirelings, except that at the time of the confrontation kzinti warriors were already the mainstay of the Jotok military. The Jotok overwhelmingly preferred commerce to military service. Why that was so was a deep puzzle to Chuut-Riit, but the records that would have answered his questions could not be found in kzin archives. If one had lifetimes to rummage in all the distant places . . .

Enough reverie. He had work to do before he went planetside.

The armada was closer now to Wunderland than it had ever been, with the Alpha Centauri binary effulgent in the heavens of R'hshssira. A very bright Man-sun was the new central jewel of the constellation the kzinti called The Water Bird. Hssin Tracker files would contain the most recent information about the Man-Hero war, even if the news was years behind the current situation. He called up everything that Hssin Central Command was willing to transmit.

Assessing only the bulk of the material and its general nature, he began to ferret out a list of the Hssin staff responsible for tracking. He marked off five names from Chief Intelligence Officer to Spoor Level Collator, then contacted them personally, checking their answers against each other's statements. He wanted to know that he had *everything*. He was polite, firm, to the point, and appreciative. That was the way to secure cooperation.

He tapped the phone link. "Gis-Captain, give orders that I am to be disturbed by *no one.*"

His youthful kzinrret, Hasha, stuck her head through the oval door, huge yellow eyes lambent with appeal, sensing that he was busy, testing her welcome. He gently purred to her a few simple words of encouragement in the Female Tongue. She did not qualify as a taxing distraction. "My Hero," she replied traditionally, then slunk to his side where he stroked the back of her neck while he growled and spat information out of his data-link, organizing it on his spectacles. She was well trained and said nothing, but she let her tail flirt with him. Sometimes his other fingers flicked purposefully over the command plate.

He was not here on the direct orders of the Patriarch. There was no time for that in an emergency. Because of the snail's pace of light, the Patriarch's awareness of what was happening on his border was more than thirty years out of date. Chuut-Riit had general orders and made his decisions without consulting Kzin-home; in essence he was a traveling Patriarch. When the diameter of the Patriarchy was a whole lifetime, field commanders had broad authority. They did what they did and reported when they could. Once an obligation was assumed, they honored it or they trained their sons to honor it.

Chuut-Riit came to the boundary of the Patriarchy on a hunch generated by electromagnetic spoor. Rumors. Strange signals. With hardly more than hints picked up at a hunting match, he had set out from W'kkai as if his nose could read a wind of scent from across the interstellar reaches. A new starfaring species?

Four years closer, at Ch'Aakin, he learned that his nose was good. An obscure little border fortress circling R'hshssira had mustered a fleet of irregulars, attacked and actually conquered one of their worlds. Tree-bred omnivores with ten fingers. It was a major victory. Who would have thought that a planet-grinding binary system would contain such Kzin-like richness?

He knew then that the consequences for the Patriarchy might be immense—and not all of the consequences were necessarily good. Inept military leadership on borderlands was always a possibility and always an invitation to disaster.

The Tracking Teams at Ch'Aakin had given him their reading of the lightbeams. He spent days with those documents. The Conquistadors of Wunderland were indeed reckless Heroes, but he already knew all about that. What interested him most was the nature of the man-animal's resistance. The details of *that* campaign fascinated him.

In his journal he made a prediction—already fourteen years out of date. He *guessed* that the local warriors from Hssin would settle down, become Wunderkzin, then grow restless and make a reckless strike toward the hairless-beasts' home system—a tempting five-and-a-half years away by warship. They would fail, too. Their tactics at Wunderland had shown not the slightest understanding of logistics.

Years passed. Chuut-Riit spent time in hibernation and brief periods of frenzy adding to his armada. The closer he came to the Alpha Centauri double system, the fresher became the scent.

Now at Hssin he was close enough for the kill.

(1) He already knew that the First Fleet probe into the man-system had been a disaster. That was as he had predicted, long before he had known that a First Fleet had been launched.

(2) He already knew the numbers and deployment of the Second Fleet. He had obtained that information when he passed through miserable Fang. Given the facts about the man-system obtained by the First Fleet, he had been predicting a second disaster.

Now he was curious to see how well his prediction had held. He began to dig into the Hssin files. These out-world kzinti might be recklessly brave, but they were poor strategists, gland-strong bunglers. An early victory would be welcome, however unlikely, but such a success would also complicate his mission—winners were more reluctant to accept help from the Patriarchy than were losers.

Ah, there it was. With grunts and finger-waving he flicked the relevant documents over the surface of his spectacles.

He was not surprised to read that the attack of the Second Fleet had also failed. Still the details galled him. His claws were out; his rage was such that he would have slashed to death commanders who had already died for their incompetence. Why hadn't they attacked the laser batteries of the inner planet from below? He spent some hours doing careful calculations, but his insight was useless—the Third Fleet was long launched, already near Man-sun, and probably marked for destruction. Save the Patriarchy from these Hero irregulars!

The news, even though it was cold meat, pressed urgency upon Chuut-Riit. His stay at Hssin would have to be short.

With the proper timing, he could arrive at Alpha Centauri during the slump just before the formation of the inevitable Fourth Fleet. It would give him leeway to staff that Fourth Fleet with all the resentful enemies he was going to make on Wunderland and with the hot-heads who had swarmed to the battle-scream of his hastily collected armada. They were expendable.

But the best of his Heroes he intended to hold back and discipline into a real naval threat. The hapless man-beasts, slaves-to-be, would have to wait for the arrival of the Fifth Fleet before they tangled with their first professional kzin army.

CHAPTER 9

(2396 A.D.)

The excitement!

The recruiters weren't just taking volunteers; they were conducting tournaments and selecting the warriors who were to accompany the armada to Wunderland. Competition was in the very air that wafted through the ventilators. The warriors even smelled different. They cuffed each other and tussled. They boasted about their skill and about the number of man-animals they would own when they were their father's age. They invented new and wonderful insults.

"My Near-Sighted Hero!" roared a kzin youth to a myopic friend at the feast between the jousts. "You say you see yourself on an estate in Africa hunting elephants? You have selected an elephant as your prey, I presume, not for his bravery but because he is big enough to see?"

"Will you wrestle the tusked beast to the ground with me, or will you shoot at him from a tree while he waves the tree over his head?" retorted the myopic friend, peering, not quite sure who it was who had challenged him.

The challenger directed his booming voice to the other orange-red tournament contenders who were devouring their Jotok arms noisily. "Let me recite to all, to this gathering of noble Heroes, the illustrious saga of my stumbling friend who is too tall to see his feet!" He stumbled in imitation, rousing a flurry of flapping ears and good-natured growls.

"Well, don't fall over before you've read me my fate!"

"You'll make it through the fiery battles in space. You have courage and quickness to compensate for your weak eyes! You'll smash ships and disgorge the boiling hairless corpses to the vacuum. We know that you have *blind* luck and the cunning of a *mole*! You'll stagger through the traps that explode in space. You'll drop on your grav-platform to the surface of Africa, there to slaughter battalions with your broad-beam fire!" The raconteur was spitting and snarling with relish as he described the fights, purring through the compliments.

"Get on with it!" taunted the myopic friend. "I demand the glorious day of my elephant hunt!"

"Ah that. Hr-r. You see the elephant beast's gray bulk looming in the distance. You stalk him. You leap mightily! But what is this? You have dived, headfirst, into a gigantic gray boulder! The boulder takes the first round. Birds land in your mane, singing. Uniformed beasts, wearing the colors of the UNSN, crawl out of hiding, intrigued by your sudden stillness. Alas, they skin you, and there you are, Con-queror of Man-home, cured and spread upon some floor in Africa to tickle the feet of monkeys!"

The audience roared approval. Some waved Jotok bones in the air.

Trainer-of-Slaves was uncomfortable in this crowd—there were too many of his old enemies present. He was here only because he desperately *wanted* to volunteer, *wanted* to follow Chuut-Riit to glory. His courage was not permitting it. He didn't dare enter the tournament, even though claws were padded and no one could attack outside of the circle. In all this time of preparation for the coming of his savior, it had never occurred to him once that he might have to fight for the privilege of following!

I'm doomed, he thought. He would have stayed longer at the meet, struggling to find a way around his fear, but he spotted Puller-of-Noses moving through the crowd.

So he caught a jerking auto-car through the tunnels back to the Jotok Run. Back to work. It didn't matter. Hssin would be emptied after the armada left, and most of his enemies would be gone. There was that.

Jotok-Tender spotted his apprentice in the dome near the main entrance of the Run and moved to greet him, animation in his gait. Hssin was indeed in a state when even the giant caught its fever! The giant didn't stop as he usually did but came right up and cuffed Trainer with force enough to half-knock him down.

"Look at this!" He showed a golden honor card. "Chuut-Riit has commended us for our slaves! Our work groups have been overhauling some of his fleet's worn gravitic polarizers. He is pleased. A small thing, but we have honor!"

Trainer took the arm of his master, almost gently, and walked him through the trees and grass of the plaza. There was nothing much to say, but they made purring noises at each other. There was no question of working for the rest of the day. The old kzin fussed about, providing sparkling water and tasty hard bits to chew on. He talked quietly of his best memories. Trainer-of-Slaves listened fondly to the familiar tales.

The next day was not so quiet. Kasrriss-As, the Patriarch of Hssin, who had never said a word in his life to Jotok-Tender, using underlings to deal with him, made a per-sonal voice call. Chuut-Riit was interested in the response range of the man-beast's physiology and had bought two Wunderland monkeys from Kasrriss-As which he wished to hunt. An elaborate hunting party was to be arranged immediately for the Jotok Run, which was the only really large hunting run on Hssin.

"They don't make good prey," Kasrriss-As grumbled. "They're badly designed. Weak. They can run, but not well; they can climb trees, but not well. Good to eat, though." Sulkily he added, "I wanted them for my menagerie."

"Noble Hero, when shall we have the hunt ready?"

"He hasn't given me enough notice!" complained Kasrriss-As. "It takes months to exercise them into fit enough shape to make a good run! Terrible muscle tone! Ah well—could your kit possibly do something with them, teach them something in a day? Anything to make the hunt more interesting! I'm so distracted. I have so many things to do. Take care of everything. The honor of Hssin rests upon your accomplishment."

At the instant of disconnect, Jotok-Tender reached out and pulled down an enchiridion—not a data capsule or an eyewriter—but a slim, lavishly illustrated book, bound in Jotok hide and printed on the finest fiber paper in subtle colors and everlasting scent. "Read it now! Learn everything you can." It was the most popular kzin manual on men.

Huem-Sergeant and two of his assistants immediately brought the rare beasts around to the Jotok quarters. Trainer-of-Slaves, still with the book in his hand, saw three battle-ready kzin, so enormous that they could enter through the door only one at a time, roughly nudging two helpless charges between them. The hairless bipeds, together, couldn't have massed as much as the smallest guard. The monkeys looked much less formidable than their pictures, and they didn't smell like flower-water. They were far more vivid. They wore the smell of fear.

He tried to fit on them the details he had been reading in the enchiridion. The one without facial hair was a young male? Trainer-of-Slaves stared intently; yes, that must be right. The one *with* the facial hair had looser folds in his tail-like skin, and tiny wrinkles—signs of age. It was the youth who was radiating the essence of fear most strongly. That must account for why his genitals were retracted.

"Aowrrgh," said Huem-Sergeant, "strange lot." He was reminding Trainer-of-Slaves to relieve him of his guard duty.

Trainer forced his eyes off the monkeys. He gave the swift transfer-of-contract sign with his hand, and the kzin warriors left him, one at a time through the door.

Alone with his deformed charges, he felt his own fear stirring, the need for a grin. But he had a strange sympathy for the frightened young one—there was no need to frighten the doomed animal further. He suppressed his smile and kept his face as expressionless as possible under the circumstances.

"I have a stall for you," he hissed and spat, but they understood nothing.

"I think he wants us to go with him," said the bearded biped.

"Should we resist?"

"Don't be crazy, Marisha."

They followed him through the corridors to the stall. "This is where you will sleep and defecate until the hunt. I have orders to make you comfortable." The spits were mixed with the atonal inflections and burry rumblings of the Hero's Tongue.

"I think we've been demoted."

"What's happening? Look at this place! I thought we were getting along with the Chief Kumquat?"

"There's a big buzz stirring up this ratcat trap. I think we've been sold."

"You have a theory that we are slaves. Are we really slaves?"

"I don't know *anything*, Marisha. Nothing at all. I'll see if I can get us some food. Big Yellow Lineman here is just standing around staring, wondering where the football is." He made finger motions to his mouth.

"Long-Reach, some food for the slaves."

The Jotok scuttled into the stall. "Honored kzin, what do they eat?"

"Sol's Blazes, what is that *teufel*!" screeched Marisha.

"I've seen them at a distance—and once close up. That was in a kzin engine room. I think he has a better deal than we do."

Trainer-of-Slaves was consulting his book. These rotting manuals never seemed to carry what you needed in the place you were looking at! "Omnivore," he clacked and hissed. Not very helpful. "Try one of everything. Water, too."

Long-Reach returned with a variety of warm, raw meats on a skewer and a bowl of leaves with a side dish of leaf sauce.

The older man sniffed the meat but tried the leaves first. "Tastes like eucalyptus. Same texture, too." He spat it out and tried the meat with a sour expression. "We're going to have to teach them how to cook all over again."

"It's raw? Gottdamn!"

"And tough."

Trainer-of-Slaves was impressed when he watched them chewing on the meat and rejecting the leaves.

"Can you ask him for some clothes?" whimpered Marisha.

"I don't think they have our size. Maybe something in yellow lace with five arm holes?"

Trainer-of-Slaves busied himself with professional questions—asked of himself because it was impossible to ask *them* anything. He examined the bottoms of their feet, clawing the sole gently, and decided that the skin was too soft. Had they been carried about by machines on Wunderland? Maybe on the two-year trip to Hssin in the hibernator their feet had grown soft? Certainly they wouldn't be able to last out the hunt on those!

Item: provide them with makeshift sandals. The giant was frugal to the point of insanity and had all sorts of hides around that had been softened by Jotok mastication.

He wasn't sure what to do about the rest of their skin. It had no fur to protect them from heat and cold, and would be useless against brambles and branches. Nor was it thick like a Jotok's hide. Just running his claws along their skin made them flinch in pain and make noises that didn't sound like polite conversation. Had they been shelled out of their carapace? Or was it just that Man-home was a paradise?

Item: provide them with leggings. With their build and fragility, what they really needed was a military suit of armor.

At first light he took them into the forest—with Long-Reach, Joker, and Creepy following in the trees. He tried to teach them the lay of the caverns, how to run and where to run, how to backtrack and hide, what to rub on their bodies to disguise their rank smell. After frustrating misunderstandings, he decided that they didn't understand that they were going to be hunted. Were they stupid?

For a while Trainer-of-Slaves entertained the notion that they might be females. What did he know of monkey anatomy? They certainly didn't understand him when he quite carefully enunciated from his man-talk phrase book. They behaved exactly like kzinrretti he'd tried to converse with—lifting their faces attentively, listening, all attention and no comprehension. Females for sure.

But they *did* chatter. Was it mindless chatter? Some sounds seemed . . . meaningful. "Notsofast!" was a demand that he stop demonstrating kzin reflexes. "Let's-resta-minute!" was a cry of weakness. "LunkheadOverThere" and "BarrelRibs" was a way of referring to a dominant slave master while deferentially averting one's eyes.

At twilight he tried an experiment. Painfully he copied for them words from his phrasebook—using man-script.

day tomorrow run fast

$$= = = = = = = = = = = = = = = =$$

4/8 day hunt catch—man die
6/8 day hunt catch—man die
8/8 day hunt end hunt—man live

"Holy Mother Earth, he's telling us that tomorrow we're going to be on the wrong end of a kzin hunt!"

The young one paled.

The older one turned toward Trainer. "Jack, she's only fifteen!"

They understood! He could smell their sudden fear. They could read! Ah, males for sure.

CHAPTER 10

(2396 A.D.)

Trainer-of-Slaves took the game animals out into the darkness of the caverns before lights-on. This time they were far more receptive to his instructions about sneaking away, dodging, and hiding. It was fascinating to observe the sudden increase in their intelligence. Now he owned an essential fact: a motivation-prompt accelerated a man-beast's learning rate.

Interesting.

He compared this with what he knew about the Jotoki. A Jotok's intelligence depended upon a hormone that was triggered by body-size; they were all geniuses during transition. You couldn't stop them from learning! Then, at adulthood when the mass of their arm-brains stabilized, their ability to learn began to taper off rapidly. A mature Jotok could always retain what he had mastered during transition, but he learned *new* facts and *new* ways only slowly. Motivation was a minor variable.

He wondered if a motivator triggered some kind of intelligence hormone in a man-beast? A kzin who controlled such a hormone directly would have a useful tool. Perhaps that could be accomplished through a chemical bypass-block that shunted around the motivator. The slave-master could induce a rapid learning mode, teach a specialized behavior to his monkey, then turn off the monkey's ability to self-modify that behavior. A compulsive slave. No chains. No threats. Very economical.

As he watched them, Trainer-of-Slaves began to catalog in his mind the motivators he was observing. Certainly these beasts were able to modify their behavior rapidly when their lives were threatened. *They're like me*, he thought as he helped the Marisha-beast lay a false trail through the marshes.

But, of course, they were different, too. He doubted that they had a concept of honor.

Sometimes life was *not* valuable. Trainer-of-Slaves was beginning to resent the hunt. These slaves were valuable *alive*. Study your enemy—who had said that? What was valuable in a pile of stripped and bloody bones?

When it was still dark he released the game at a multiple divide of caverns which Long-Reach called The Place of Many Ways. He felt sad. He needed at least ten more days to toughen them up, to learn enough of their language to train them in the more subtle evasions.

"Long-Reach," he said to his companion when the man-beasts had disappeared beyond hearing, "as my special hunter, I have a service for you to perform. Who knows these sprawling forests and caves and liquid ponds better than you?"

"Only the Fanged God," replied Long-Reach in the formal ritual of their conversations.

"Your official function in this hunt is as my scout. I have specific orders."

"I am five ears."

"The monkeys won't survive until twilight without help. You will scout for them, not for me. Appear to me from time to time, for the sake of appearances, but scout for the beasts. Give them aid, but be careful *never* to tell me what you have done! I don't want to know."

"As my master commands."

At first-light the hunting party began to assemble under the primary dome of the Jotok Run. The thin banners of Kasrriss-As hung in brilliant color, carried by four kzin servitors who were experienced hunters in this Run. Trainer-of-Slaves was without colors but he had been hastily outfitted in the light armor of the Kasrriss-As household. Three Jotoki in green and red striped livery remained respectfully on call but at a distance.

Chuut-Riit's party was less formal, but nevertheless elegant. He wore a pale peacock-green armor of a leather style that pre-dated spaceflight. He had decreed no weapons and no devices and carried none. He had brought with him only Traat-Admiral—and a young recruit, Hssin-Liaison, proud of his new cognomen.

Trainer-of-Slaves felt one moment of shock—and then repressed, invisible rage. He stared straight ahead. *How does my enemy do it?* This pest had the persistence of a fur-tick! Could he lead even Chuut-Riit around by the nose?

Hssin-Liaison, whatever he was called, was never subtle. He did not return disregard. In front of Chuut-Riit and without preamble he grinned at Trainer-of-Slaves. "You will not live out the day—Coward-of-Cowards."

"What is this?" inquired Chuut-Riit mildly.

"This Animal is unfit to carry the duties of a Conquest Hero."

The ears of Chuut-Riit flicked in amusement. "I believe the tournament is settling such matters."

"This cowardly Animal won't be found in any tournament ring. I challenge him here."

"I see." Chuut-Riit seemed aloof from the menace and anger. He turned to Trainer-of-Slaves matter-of-factly. "Hssin-Liaison has been using his contacts among the young warriors to enlist troops for my Fourth Fleet." He lapsed into silence, waiting, perhaps curious that Trainer-of-Slaves had chosen to ignore the challenge.

"Voice of the Patriarch, my duty is to the execution of the hunt," Trainer replied stiffly.

"Good." Chuut-Riit only glanced toward his liaison underling, then addressed the others. He was obviously not willing to interfere in local squabbles about which he knew nothing. "I am here for a slow hunt—no quick kill. We flush and pursue. We challenge and fall back. We play. We save the kill for twilight. Yes, I'm anticipating my first taste of human flesh, but I am far more interested in observing the response of the enemy under attack. No weapons. No devices. Those are the rules."

Every other kzin at the meet added another rule silently. The harassing would be enjoyable, but the final kill must be given to Chuut-Riit alone.

The banners were staked into a circle. Noiselessly the hunters moved into the woods under the arching ceilings. Chuut-Riit loosened his leather armor and gave Trainer-of-Slaves one last noncommittal gaze. "So the hunter becomes the hunted." Then he was gone.

Deeper into the trees a five-limbed beast dropped beside Trainer. "Hssin-Liaison threatened you with death."

"He won't be able to find me. Only you know the Run better than I. He's good on rooftops. He's a city-kzin." Contempt. "I'm Mellow-Yellow, remember, who floats among the leaves like lamplight. I'll take him in circles." But the plan wasn't to take him in circles; the plan was to lead Puller-of-Noses away from the man-beasts. It was the least he could do for them, to neutralize one of the hunters.

The man-beasts were trapped, and allowed to escape, twice before midday. Jotok-Tender's slaves brought in a simple lunch for the hunters, served on collapsible canvas tables. Chuut-Riit paced about their vale making intellectual pronouncements upon the evasive tactics of the day's game. "Innovative," he called them. He liked that. Hssin-Liaison managed to mix some leaves into Trainer-of-Slaves's meat. Kasrriss-As spent his time ingratiating himself into Chuut-Riit's favor and discussing the textile trade with Traat-Admiral. He was the one who had stayed behind while the other warriors raided Alpha Centauri.

The canvas tables were folded and whisked away by the slaves. Chuut-Riit amiably resumed his tracking. However old his eyes, his nose was a marvel at spotting spoor, his mind superb at guessing the moves of his prey.

"We'll wound them this time, and watch how they handle that."

When Chuut-Riit smiled beside a craggy lava outcrop—and then moved left instead of right—a secret pleasure rippled under the fur of Trainer-of-Slaves. Last night he had not been able to determine for sure whether his man-beasts had understood this intricate back-track and feint move. A perfect execution. The maneuver had been taught to Trainer (too many times) by a wily old Jotok who was probably still at large, up there in the trees watching them, keeping his distance. It worked well on the kzin mind.

Trainer-of-Slaves followed the real trail, "carelessly" obscuring what spoor he found. He knew where they had gone, a broad and growth-sheltered ledgeway along the wall of a cavern that had all the appearance of a dead-end. It led to three good escape routes, but to anyone unfamiliar with the layout of the Run, the wide ledge smelled of trap. Prey avoided it—and hunters avoided it because they thought prey would be avoiding it. Trainer was in no hurry to get there, perhaps to lead another hunter to them. They needed a rest from terror. He urinated. He smelled the flowers which reminded him of his mother.

With a rustling of leaves, Long-Reach dropped from the branches bearing the news that their game was safe but exhausted, laying low. He had other news. Puller-of-Noses was following and had cut around and in front to intercept Trainer-of-Slaves.

"Where are Joker and Creepy?"

"I have given them instructions."

"I'll have to do a decoy. What do you suggest?"

"Climb up along the trinity hill—he will see you from there, being on the other slope. Then drop down through the Burr Crevasse to The Lakes. He will have to follow, so you'll know where he is, but you'll already have passed through, so he won't know where to find you."

"I like it." The slave-trainer kzin became Mellow-Yellow, half Jotok, slipping along swiftly through all the little shortcuts he knew, until he came to the hill with the three giant trees that could grow here because of the ceiling vault, carved by tons of rock that had collapsed during the excavation, and now supported by a cathedral of arches. While he climbed he was looking intently into the woods across the depression for an orange-red blur.

Disaster is always abrupt. He met his enemy. In the wrong place. Five kzin-lengths in front of him, wearing that persistent grin.

They both fell into an instant crouch.

His mind reeled. What had happened—a light breeze? for critical moments blowing in the wrong direction? Had his enemy smelled him coming? and simply waited? He made an instant tactical assessment. Puller-of-Noses was unaware of the Burr Crevasse or he would have blocked off that escape route. It was still available if he could dance his enemy a few paces downhill.

"There's no grass to eat here, Defecator-of-Undigested Grass."

"You swore before witnesses that you would let me live."

"That was then. We have many lives and one death. You've already lived an extra life. Today I have sworn to kill you."

Chuut-Riit had talked about the value of the unexpected tactical option. Trainer leaped, without grinning, without screaming, while an incredulous Puller-of-Noses shifted just too late to save his balance—simultaneously, a reflexive swipe, accurate, deadly, disabled Trainer's right arm. They were both bowled over, taking out a tree before bouncing to their feet. Blood poured from the arm. But the coward was now on the right side of the Burr Crevasse. Facing the wrong way.

He couldn't run toward that escape. He had no way to defend his back.

Five kzinti screams descended from the trees, four arms wrapping around the enemy warrior while the fifth ripped his nose open. Before the attack was over, Long-Reach was jumping out of harm's reach. He skittered away, then turned to face the kzin. Motionless. It was a draw. The kzin could run him down, but he could climb a tree faster than any kzin could follow.

"A slave who attacks a kzin is warm meat!" snarled Puller-of-Noses while the blood ran into his mouth. "I'll kill you later!"

"There are three of us," said Long-Reach.

The kzin's eyes scanned the treetops rapidly, looking for the others. Nothing. When he turned back to his kzin target, he was alone. Chagrin. Both coward and slave were gone. No matter. All he had to do was follow the blood.

Trainer-of-Slaves jimmied himself down through the Crevasse at a record pace, one-armed, rocks ripping gashes out of his hide, leaving a trail of fur and blood as he bounced to the level below. He felt no pain. He ran. At first he gave no thought to obscuring his trail. What was the use? Hssin-Liaison or Puller-of-Noses or Second-Son-of-Ktrodni or whatever in hell was his name would follow him to the ends of the Partriarchy right now, fangs ready for the kill.

In neat livery of green and red stripes, Joker swung out of the sky. "Follow me." He scrabbled along the ground, picking a route by some criterion Trainer-of-Slaves did not understand. What greater mortification could there be than to have a slave lead him in flight! "Make for the water," said Joker before swinging back up into the sky to disappear.

Bolting, driven by the fear, all else lost to his mind, he reached The Lakes, exhausted, bewildered that a relentless Puller-of-Noses had been unable to follow. His arm was torturing him. His disgrace was complete. Of course, there was always humor in every situation. He had been a successful decoy.

Are the man-beasts doing any better than my wretched self?

He trudged a circuitous route back toward the ledgeway where the hunt's prey had been hiding. They were gone. He found a happy Chuut-Riit instead, relaxing, playing a poetry game with Traat-Admiral, which wasn't going well for the Admiral.

"Where is everybody?" asked the Conquest Commander amiably. "Is it the custom on Hssin to take afternoon naps?" He noticed Trainer-of-Slaves's arm. "I see that my righteous Liaison officer hasn't been able to put you out of action." He came over and examined the wound. "I've seen worse." And he began to dress the slashes.

It was only then that Trainer-of-Slaves realized how dazed he was. He was just standing there, letting one of the highest military officers of the Patriarchy fuss over a minor clawing.

"I'm all right, sir. Have we relocated our prey?"

"One is wounded. He attacked me to let the other escape. I let them both go but in such a way that they will remain separated. We may now destroy them one at a time. You're from Hssin. You must know these monkeys better than I. It is said that as a mob they fight bravely. Do you have any information about how they fight alone?"

"These man-animals are the first I have ever met, sir."

"Yes, they're rare. Curious beasts. Trainer-of-Slaves, do you have an idea of what kind of slaves they'll make?"

"I have a theory that they might be controlled through biochemistry. I would need to have a large sample size upon which to experiment in order to confirm or deny my hunch."

"Of course. I'll have to take you to Alpha Centauri with me. There are monkeys on Wunderland, sufficient I should imagine."

"Dominant One, I am not qualified. Hssin-Liaison will tell you why."

"Hssin-Liaison will tell me *nothing*! He's dead. Not far from here. He was found by a scout of Kasrriss-As who was following a trail of kzin blood." Chuut-Riit glanced knowingly at a certain wounded arm.

Trainer-of-Slaves maintained a shocked silence. His enemy—dead?

"His legs were broken and there was a stake through his eye," said Traat-Admiral.

Like the incoming whine of a bomb, Trainer realized what had happened and who was guilty.

"He broke his legs when he ran full-paced into a trip wire, since removed. The trip wire was set across the trail of your blood. The stake was buried in the ground and set to pierce anyone unfortunate enough to fall upon it. He missed, but his head was later *lifted* and *rammed* down onto the stake. Through the eye."

"A terrible way to die, your excellency."

"I'd take you there now, but twilight would overtake us and our prey would escape by virtue of my lenient rules. We'd go hungry. Let's make it simple. Do you admit that he was murdered?"

"Yes, sir." Trainer had anguished images of Long-Reach—all of his slaves—being hacked to bits.

"Since Hssin-Liaison was my servitor, I will pass judgment on you. Let's be clear about the circumstances. Hssin-Liaison widened the circle of the tournament to include you against your will. The rules of the tournament require gloved claws. He neglected that detail—as your wounds testify. He who so broadens the rules cannot complain when his life is forfeit as the consequence of his rules."

"He was not killed in face-to-face combat," said Traat-Admiral. "He was murdered."

"Wait, Traaty. There is a military lesson in this which we should consider. If a force stays to fight, knowing that it will be slaughtered, yes, there is honor in that defeat. But what if the same force retreats and lures the enemy into a trap in which he can be slaughtered? Can we call such a victory, dishonor? I find a contradiction here. If defeat is honor, does it follow that victory is dishonor? Save us all from such logic!"

He thinks I did it! He can't conceive of slaves murdering kzin. Neither can I.

"I say the tournament was fairly fought and fairly won. Hssin-Liaison made new rules without consulting our Hero here. Trainer-of-Slaves replied with his own unorthodox rules, also without consulting our now dead warrior. I see a balance."

Truth was always sacred. Trainer-of-Slaves desperately searched for the kind of courage that would allow him to speak the truth.

Ignoring the youth's sputterings, Chuut-Riit continued with his line of reasoning. "Yes, there is a just balance. However, my young Hero, you have done me harm and owe me recompense. I have lost a warrior for my Fourth Fleet. You have won this unusual tournament fairly and so you must join my service. I will be assigning you to Traat-Admiral who is building for me an elite corps I choose to call the Fifth Fleet." He nodded to his Admiral. "Doesn't he have just the qualities we need?"

Long afterward, a dazed Trainer-of-Slaves was still pondering the consequences of Jotoki who murdered kzin, barely able to keep his attention on the hunt. Fortunately the hunt seemed forgotten. Long-Reach was nowhere to be found, hiding probably. Should he execute Long-Reach? Should he bring up the perils of slavery to Chuut-Riit? Yes, that's what he should do. The coward in him shuddered.

Kasrriss-As appeared from the direction of Burr Crevasse. "The body has been removed. Since there are fewer of us, I suggest an immediate resumption of the chase before twilight overtakes us."

"Your arm looks bad." Chuut-Riit's voice carried a fatherly tone. "No need to follow us. There will be other hunts."

"This hunt is my responsibility."

But he couldn't keep up. They stalked and killed the wounded man-beast first. Before the lights dimmed they had the young one cornered. The animal's wailing cries of rage turned to screams before Chuut-Riit tore the body apart. Trainer shared in the feast when it was his turn to gnaw and rip at the carcasses. What else could he do? At least the meat was delicious.

He spent half the night wandering in the forest.

Later Trainer-of-Slaves found his three personal Jotoki cowering in their stalls. How could he talk to them about their crime? Shouldn't he just destroy them? Shouldn't he speak to Jotok-Tender? When he remembered the giant musing about the depth of the loyalty found in a Jotok properly adopted, his heart curdled; was that what was meant? Murder? Had Jotok-Tender known all along?

Long-Reach was huddled arms, head hidden by arm stalks, eyes barely peeping out of their armor, silent. As the kzin master of these slaves he had to say something. Yet how could he even mention such a crime? It was too horrible! "I'm angry!" His fangs were bared in a grin. "You disobeyed my instructions! Specifically, I told you to protect the man-beasts, and what were you doing instead?—you were watching over me. The man-slaves were lost! I take care of myself! I'm a warrior! I'm a Hero! Do not violate the wishes of a Hero! Obey!"

The subject was never mentioned again.

CHAPTER 11

(2399–2401 A.D.)

The warships of the Patriarchy were large but cramped. Sub-light supply lines don't exist in an interstellar empire. Every need of a conquest had to be thought of by the Ordnance-Officer and brought along. The storage took space. Hydrogen took space. Purifiers filled the ship with ducts. The hibernation vaults took space. Machine shops took space. The gravitic drives and their shielding alone took up *half* the space in the ship.

No savanna-roaming kzin could ever have created, or imagined, such a claustrophobic horror of passageways and pipes and tiny rooms, where even the ceilings had to be used for storage and the doors stayed locked for years. But long ago, as mercenaries, the kzinti had fallen into this hell-in-heaven as penance for their sin of impatience.

Light took two and a half years to travel between the R'hshssira infrared dwarf and the Alpha Centauri binary. Kzin warships spent more than three years on the same journey. Chuut-Riit's flagship, from the first scent of man-animal rumor, had given seventeen years to this single mission.

The voyages were grueling. Without their hibernation coffins, touchy and argumentative warriors lacked tolerance for the time-gulf between stars. Trainer-of-Slaves would have none of that. He took ship duty for himself. All his life he had been bound to an essentially uninhabitable rock of a rapidly dying star. How could he not stay awake to relish his adventure?

To prepare himself for Wunderland, he devoured the written sagas of Kzin. After all, his race had been born on a planet. Roaming a planet with breathable winds was a kzin's natural maskless state. Wasn't it truth that Wunderland was desirable *because* it was so Kzinlike?

He followed the patricidal tragedy of *Warlord Chmee at the Pillars*, almost squeezing the wetness out of his fur after the Storm at the Pillars. When the Hero blinded himself in remorse, he stopped reading—he wanted to *see* Kzin-home, first, before he searched his soul.

There were many sagas. He imagined himself with Rgir's pride in the Mooncatcher Mountains. He felt the drifting snow and vapor breath at warcamp in the Rungn Valley.

And there were heroic poems. He listened to the boiling-fat sounds from the *Poems of Eight Voyages* as he recited them aloud, marveling at plains of waving grass, at a winter wind whose chill claws could ice a Patriarch's fur to the white of age.

The sagas always spoke of the wind. The hunter's wind. Death's wind. The howling wind. Sweetgrass wind. The seasalt wind. The wind of many messages. Running with the wind. Wunderland had winds, too, he thought.

Trainer-of-Slaves soon found the confined spaces of the warship intolerably full of smells that machine-made winds never took away. Nor was a diet of meat-biscuit conducive to an even humor. He snarled. His temper was short. He had a broad comment to cover every ship deficiency.

One warrior became irritated enough at this ire to grasp him by the vest, repeatedly shoving him against a bulkhead. "Let my ears hear more of your foul insults! I'm here to inspire your mouth! I demand more!" Finally Deck-Officer interfered and ordered them both to the Vault, where they were antifreezed and stacked with five hundred other suspended Heroes.

All trips come to an end. The Vault was unloaded at the grimy Fortress Aarku orbiting Alpha Centauri B and when Trainer awoke he wondered why he had ever left Hssin. Aarku was only nine hundred kilometers in diameter and it didn't even have amenities like a poisonous atmosphere. The Fortress itself had been started as a major installation a generation ago after the invasion, and then left unfinished. It was a "strategic position" thought up by an admiral who didn't have to live there.

Alpha Centauri B would have been an outer planet if it had massed a thousand times less. Instead, it had grown into a healthy orange-tinged *star*, but with only three quarters of A's mass and a quarter of A's luminosity. The two stars orbited each other with a period of eighty years, coming as close as eighty-eight light-minutes and moving away from each other as far as 280 light-minutes.

They had disrupted the formation of one another's outer planets, leaving nothing circling A but Wunderland and three dense inner worlds, plus the myriad rocks of the Inner Swarm. A ring of rubble surrounded B that included ten major asteroids. In between lay the bulk of the Serpent's Swarm buzzing in an intricate dance of resonance rings, pseudo-trojan orbits, high inclination orbits, and other exotic solutions to the problems posed by forced cohabitation with two major stars. There were vast gaps in the Swarm where no asteroid could survive without being pumped into another orbit.

To view the Wunderland on which he had expected to serve, Trainer-of-Slaves had to tune up the base's electronic telescope and blot out the blinding spear of Alpha Centauri A. His unit was stationed about as far away from its forests and grasslands and mountains as they could be sent, dashing his dreams of loping over the surface of a planet under an open sky.

War was war. Each warrior had his own emplacement and his own fight. Trainer's fatalistic companions had a saying that even the rocks around Centauri B had their duties. His duties were to turn out slaves for the engine rooms of the Fourth Fleet.

The conditions in the hastily prefabricated tunnels were appalling. He was stuck with his smelly Jotok cages, with his wire-mesh runs and masses of Jotok babies crawling all over each other without enough space and never enough wind to carry away the smell. Hssin seemed like paradise.

A berth on the Fourth Fleet began to seem more and more desirable. He began to dream about Man-home. If he couldn't have Wunderland, then why not Earth? Earth, too, had winds and an open sky. The winds had fascinating names culled from Wunderland libraries. Nor'easter. The icy candelia of the Andes Mountains. Trade winds. The dry chinook wind that blew down the slopes of the Rocky Mountains after depositing all its moisture on the western slopes. Mediterranean sirocco. Whirlwind. Tempest.

Trainer-of-Slaves began to take a personal interest in the fate of the Fourth Fleet. He was too busy with Jotoki, and too far away from the center, to face politics from a crouch. But he followed Chuut-Riit's duels and celebrated every win. The locals were resisting the economic burden of preparing a new fleet. They made loud claims about the ferocity with which the Third Fleet would slash the Solar System, though that battle must already have been fought and won or lost.

Chuut-Riit was adamant that the burden continue. It was, he told his Heroes, the Patriarch's policy that in any war a backup fleet was always in preparation to follow a battle-fleet, no matter how sure the battle-fleet's victory. That was the only way a slow-motion interstellar crusade could be fought. Better to send expensive reinforcements to a victory won years ago than penniless faith-in-victory to a defeat. The kzin had a saying, "Don't count your fingers when your claws are sheathed."

Alpha Centauri B was a favored space for Fourth Fleet maneuvers. As a result, Trainer-of-Slaves met many gung-ho captains who had driven their gravitic-polarizers past normal specifications and needed urgent maintenance. They liked him because his crews did a good job. They also liked him because he served Jotok meat and that was a treat hard to come by.

Ssis-Captain took a special liking to Trainer-of-Slaves. They shared an avid interest in Earth. It was he who introduced card-tricks to Trainer's slaves. The monkeys used a peculiar set of plastic symbols, five plus an octal of cards in a suit, with four suits. The Captain never ceased to flap his ears while Long-Reach did his five-handed shuffle, rotating half the deck clockwise and the other half counterclockwise while sitting on his mouth. He didn't like to play poker with Long-Reach, though, because the Jotok always took the pot.

On one run in from the A star, Ssis-Captain brought in some Wunderland musical instruments and they put together a combo, a rather cacophonous effort. Creepy managed the twelve string banjo with three hands, Long-Reach played the drums and did harmony with all five lungs, while Joker handled the cymbals and xylophone. Trainer-of-Slaves did his imitations of Heroic Poetry on the kazoo.

"I've got to have you *animals* on the *Blood of Heroes*! Do you want to pledge honor to my ship? I'll pledge all of you! We've *got* to be playing together when we march under the Arc de Triomphe in Berlin!"

"The Arc de Triomphe is in Moscow," corrected Trainer-of-Slaves righteously.

"You must be wrong. The red monkeys got out of that war early. I distinctly remember that the Arc de Triomphe was built by French-beasts to honor the victory of their Kaiser at Berlin. The High French Conquest Commandant Hitler marched under it with his whole army when he defeated the Huns. I've seen the daguerreotype!"

On another trip Ssis-Captain smuggled in a kzinrret inside an old polarizer housing. She was a beauty with a luminous red sheen to her fur and streaks of tan in her nose, but she wasn't at all pleased with the ride and studied them both from sulky, undecided eyes.

"Jriingh, meet your new mounter."

"My Hero," she purred.

Trainer-of-Slaves was horrified. "You stole an illustrious one's wife? Or worse, a daughter?"

Ssis-Captain's ears flapped while he rumbled in his throat. "He gave her to me. She's a little terror. She spits and hisses at his wives and fights with them. She kept chasing his favorite off into the woods of his estate where he couldn't find her. She boxes the heads of his daughters and tries to take his sons down under the bridge."

"An ideal mother for great fighting Heroes!"

"It didn't work that way. All her sons got killed as kits in rage-fights. Crazy, the lot of them. Her mate backhand-cuffed her often enough, without profit, but he's too soft-clawed to kill her. I reasoned that you and I could solve his problem."

"Do you suppose the man-beastesses give their males as much trouble as ours?"

"Worse! A manrret is smart enough to pick the lock on her door!"

Jriingh stepped gracefully from the polarizer housing, haughtily exploring her new abode, sniffing warily. She was half the size of a male kzin and probably twice as agile. She snapped up a baby Jotok that had escaped from its wire run, and swallowed five arms in one bite and then peered into the smelly tank, pondering ways to catch more.

"She's being boarded on the *Blood of Heroes*, of course."

"Against regs. *You'll* have to keep her."

"It's against regs to keep her here, too." Trainer-of-Slaves was beginning to feel angry.

"Hr-r, yet you do have the space, a corner somewhere with a lock and key."

"But I won't be able to keep her pheromones out of the air!"

"You won't have to. That's the whole beauty of this sally."

"I'm supposed to give this little hissing terror the run of the place?!"

"It's not a problem. She likes males. She just doesn't like females. Fix up a room. Give her some nice things. We'll run a beneath-the-grass pride to keep her happy. Let her keep your feet warm. We *need* a beneath-the-grass pride out here: card-tricks, music, war stories, ch'rowl. Do you think a Conservor will come *here* and give you a lecture on the One True Way of Honor and the nature of the Furry God?"

Trainer-of-Slaves settled into himself—giving way just a little. He was not used to such camaraderie and he liked it. Yes, he wanted to conquer Earth with this warrior and own a huge hunting preserve in the Amazon next to France with hundreds of pink, tailless slaves tending to his animals. Of course, Long-Reach would always be his top slave.

For two years High Conquest Commander Chuut-Riit had been caught in the snare of a painful power struggle. Then the first news from Man-sun burst from the light-beams, 4.3 years after the fact: the Kzin had dealt a great surprise victory in the first skirmish. The Third Fleet was positioning itself for battle.

Wunderland kzinti forgot all else. Even Chuut-Riit paused. Infighting died. The Radio-Operators became the Heroes of the Moment, drifting in space at the instruments of their huge antennae pointed at Man-sun.

The good news did not last.

By the end of the month the extent of the disaster was evident. Trainer-of-Slaves was outraged at the man-beasts. Kzinti became morose. They grinned more often, thoughts of monkeys on their minds. And Chuut-Riit's situation changed dramatically. There was no longer any question that he was Governor of Alpha Centauri. There was no longer any opposition to *his* design for the Fourth Fleet, or to his date of launching.

Trainer put in for a transfer to the *Blood of Heroes*.

CHAPTER 12

(2402 A.D.)

Ssis-Captain arrived at Fortress Aarku with a new uniform, slightly non-standard. The padded under-armor vest was a too-rich shade of mauve with sapphire blue trimmings. The buttons on his epaulets were Wunderland jade from mines in the Jotun Range. The eight-pointed captain's star radiated from a real diamond. Pagoda style three-quarter sleeves were of the satin one might find on a kzinrret's bed. The arcuate leather cuffs of the undershirt, setting for his chronometer/comp, were tooled from high quality kz'eerkt—the tanned hides of Wunderland criminals, selected to be without blemish or lash mark.

"Impressive," said Trainer-of-Slaves.

"I am determined that you shall have your fleet rating!" Ssis was flicking the tip of his tail back and forth in agitation as he paraded to show off his tailoring.

"Hr-r. Yet I have sworn enemies who would make it difficult."

"Harrgh! I have proper papers here for you that will make it all easy, letters of introduction and recommendation." He began to purr. "And a pass to Wunderland! I don't dance around, I just leap right in. They have to give you to me. I need you."

"Friend, I shall be satisfied with the trip to Wunderland."

"Not after you've served as my gunner!" The elegant captain lifted his bushy head and with a great grin emitted a spitting-yowling imitation of the sounds of battle. "We're going to carve up some asteroids on the way in. Great sport."

Trainer-of-Slaves decided that he could leave Long-Reach in charge of polarizer repairs, and took his chief slave on a tour of the shop. One giant field-generator was suspended in the light gravity of Aarku while two of the five-armed Jotoki slaves worked to replace its laminated planars.

Long-Reach stood proudly on four wrists while pointing with his fifth arm. "This unit will be ready for testing in two days," said skinny(arm). "I am honored by your trust in me, brave master," interrupted short(arm), checking various screens by taking control of three eyes. "All will go well with the polarizer repairs. We are expecting another unit for overhaul at the end of the day. And my duties among the juveniles?"

Trainer-of-Slaves trusted Long-Reach with all but one thing—the Jotok transients. "Just keep the life-support functional. Change the filters again." It would never do to have one of those curious five-armed, five-brained fledglings fixate upon a mature Jotok as parent. "Third-Teacher-of-Slaves will be in charge. Your first duty is to the shop."

"You will be traveling to Wunderland? The crew has checked over the engines of the *Blood of Heroes* from finger-tip to elbow. They hum. Do tell Ssis-Captain to stay within specs."

The gravitic polarizer was the foundation stone of the Patriarchy and of warrior military superiority. In its stationary version it made artificial gravity possible, but its most useful application was as the reactionless space drive which allowed vehicles to accelerate in "free fall": one gravity for the lumbering freighters, sixty or seventy gravities for the faster military warships.

These kzin craft bewildered the Wunderland defenders at the time of the 2367 A.D. conquest. They darted about with incredible velocity and acceleration changes, yet ejected no reaction mass, and didn't seem to need refueling even after maneuvers that would have exhausted the tanks of a torchship. The kzin warships could be goaded and provoked and then harassed like a bull in Old Spain, they could be burned, but they couldn't be chased. They didn't seem to obey the laws of physics.

For years after that terrible six months, war-impoverished professors from the Munchen Scholarium gathered in the cafés along Karl-Jorge Avenue in Old Munchen, writing equations and speculating with preposterous assumptions while they sipped their schnapps. Research equipment can be confiscated. Equations and speculation are free. When Alpha Centauri B was in the night sky, wan but brighter than any streetlight, each new theory about kzin technology was carried like an epidemic between the sidewalk cafés until second sunset when the nightlife of Munchen died.

Given that a reactionless drive *did* exist they eventually sketched out the beginning of an understanding that had a sound theoretical footing by the time Chuut-Riit arrived as governor. The human mind, unlike the kzin mind, is obsessed with resolving the contradictions between what it observes and what it thinks it should be seeing.

Momentum did not *appear* to be conserved by the reactionless kzin ships, but the gravitic field equations upon which the polarizer was based invoked negative space curvature, a necessary element of any reactionless space drive. Normal *intuitions* about momentum fail in the presence of negative curvature—momentum then has a direction opposite velocity—but the equations of momentum conservation still hold.

Trainer-of-Slaves took up his gunner's berth on the *Blood of Heroes*. He was outfitted with mask-goggles. They imposed diagrams upon his visual field which supplied all that he might need to know while firing. During check-down he had time to make simulation runs—with his goggles feeding him the dangers of a virtual world. It gave the liver a jolt to kill monkey-ships even if they were only program-generated ghosts.

The five spherical ships of the hunter-pack drifted into position. There was earbulb chatter as the captains readied themselves for the three light-hour sweep from Alpha Centauri B across to Alpha Centauri A, roughly the equivalent of a run from the distance of Uranus to Man-home. The Serpent's Swarm would give the sweep realism, though it contained hundreds of times the mass and debris of the Solar Belt.

Because of this plethora of asteroids, the Kzin Training Command was able to designate as many target asteroids as it pleased without disrupting the economy of the Swarm. Fourth Fleet attack-training stressed destruction of the kind of asteroid defensive installations which the monkeys used extensively to protect the north and south approaches to Man-home.

At maximum acceleration the *Blood of Heroes* could make the three-light-hour trip from B to A in less than two days at a turn-around velocity a tenth the speed of light, but this was not common practice because of the density of matter in the Centauri System which created field energy losses.

The gravity polarizer of the kzin high-velocity drive contained a natural mechanism to protect the ship from impact by gas and micrometeoroids. The offending particle was violently accelerated as it entered the field while, at the same time, the ship reacted to the added mass by recoiling. In the exchange, field energy was re-converted to mass. The particle size was not critical—unequal masses accelerate at the same rate within *any* gravitic field.

Unfortunately, atoms impacting into a polarizer's field generated a weak electromagnetic interaction which drained field energy into radiation. Inside a planetary system this could have been a serious problem if high velocities had been desirable. Between the stars, where high velocities *are* desirable, kzin ships weren't able to travel much above eighty percent of light speed through normal densities of interstellar gas without bleeding to death from "blue shine."

While a gravity polarizer was accelerating it converted mass to energy, when it decelerated it converted that same energy back to mass. Its power requirements were orders of magnitude less than a torchship, needing power only to make up for the losses involved in field interactions with the local media.

· · ·

The hunting pack was practicing the standard maneuver. Come in high over the Swarm, then attack down through it at a moderate velocity. There was much bantering back and forth between the offensive team and the defensive team during an "engagement" debriefing. All kzin insults weren't delivered in anger—the real meaning lay in the inflections of the spit-hisses. Ssis-Captain was fond of calling his opponents baboons because they had been ordered to "think like monkeys." Amiably they dubbed him "Kshat-Lunch," referring to a herbivore who was known to eat offal.

It took them twelve days, not two, to work their way across the Swarm on patrol/attack status, instruments scanning at full vigilance. The *Blood of Heroes* recorded static from the Tiamat industrial world: instructions to some lonely rockjack in his torchship, calls for part replacements, a medical emergency. Doppler shifts alerted monitors.

Of the man-ships they saw only glimmers flicking across detection screens. Somewhere among the stones armed feral humans grubbed about, plotting revenge—but the *Blood of Heroes* saw none, though its instruments were looking. These sullen beasts were mostly no more of a nuisance than fur-ticks but they made good target practice when found. On this run the Heroes sparred only with tumbling rubble.

Trainer-of-Slaves was an experienced gunner by the time they reached the cloud-streaked globe of Wunderland. He was not yet an experienced politician.

CHAPTER 13

(2402 A.D.)

In its simplest design, the kzin gravity polarizer just floated. If it was shoved *toward* a mass, energy was fed into its polarizer field—which forced it to rise. If it was pushed *away* from a mass, energy was drained from its polarizer field—which forced it to fall.

The shuttle "platforms" that transported freight and passengers into and out of Wunderland's mass-well were straight modifications of this primitive device. Descent was controlled by electromagnetically *bleeding* the field to charge molecular distortion batteries. Ascent was controlled by *feeding* the field from those same batteries. Horizontal velocity was controlled by a torsion field interaction that spun-up or spun-down Wunderland's rotation.

The cycle was highly efficient, leaking some spillover energy at the electromagnetic-gravitic interface and some in tidal friction. When dropping from orbit around Wunderland to the surface, the shuttle's polarizer rose only a few degrees in temperature.

Munchenport was a depressing introduction to the fabulous wealth that Trainer-of-Slaves had heard about all his life. A proper spacedrome had yet to be constructed. They settled onto an open field that was serviced by extruded buildings of recent fabrication, all square and ugly, all laid out and finished by forced labor. The Wundervolker wryly called it the "himmelfahrt"—both because it was from here that one ascended to the heavens and because so many of them had "gone to heaven" building it.

The number of unleashed man-beasts was appalling, lined up with their baggage, milling around, shuffling through the weapons scanners, arguing with attendants. Most of them were looking for work in the military industries of the Serpent's Swarm, needing the wages badly enough to be willing to build weapons that would be used against their father system. They smelled of unwashed bodies and poverty, a peculiar sweet-sour odor blending with the machinery-and-synthetics smell of the building and the residual ozone from cheap electric vehicles.

Ssis-Captain knew the routine. He hired some man-beasts of burden to carry his and Trainer's luggage to the aircar terminal. The clean cool breeze inside the car was a relief. "We'll go to the old city. It's better there," he said.

To a Hero born in space on a hostile outpost near a dying star, Munchen was odd for a city. This was a city? The low-pitched tile roofs weren't airtight and the windows opened to the atmosphere. From some views the buildings were hidden by the trees that shaded streets. The broad blue waters of the Donau cut through parks of palms and blooming frangipani. Of what use was the steel steeple of the Saint Joachim cathedral?

Ssis-Captain found a room for them in an old four-story brick mansion that had been converted for kzin use by knocking out the tops of all the interior doors. He gave their luggage to an old man-female who staggered under the load, finally setting it down to breathe before dividing her job into two trips.

"She's ready for the glue-factory," commented Ssis, who was three times her size.

"It's a she? But she took your instructions!"

"Of course."

He stared at the old lady. Dumb male-animals, Trainer-of-Slaves could understand, but females who comprehended sentences? He tried to imagine his mother speaking in whole phrases. He had talked enough to her, and sometimes . . . sometimes he had imagined that she was listening, such big round eyes she had.

It was a powerful deception. A kzinrret always gave the *impression* of being intelligent. Once as a spoiled kit in the Chiirr-Nig household he had been so taken by this illusion that he had given his mother an adventure picture-book to read to him at nap-time. She had chewed the book to pieces.

But enough of amazement. They beeped their automatic car on its way, settled into their room, and set about to pad the rest of the way to the Admiralty by foot.

Trainer-of-Slaves had been close to only two monkeys in his life and found a city-herd of them disconcerting. Ssis-Captain just ignored the animals while they scurried around him or waited against a wall. They all wore clothes—a fact somehow surprising to Trainer—though obviously they belonged to no military unit. Since Chuut-Riit's hunt on Hssin, he had imagined that naked was the natural state of all man-beasts.

The Admiralty could have whatever it wanted. At the time of the occupation they had wanted the Landholder's Ritterhaus. It stood with great Gothic arches and stone buttressing at the head of the cobblestoned Grunderplatz. The victorious Heroes had not bothered to demolish the crowded bronze memorial of the Nineteen Founders, perhaps because the Ritterhaus dominated the group and the kzinti were in the Ritterhaus. Down there, those laboring bronze figures looked like hard-working slaves.

The Fourth Fleet bureaucracy was at a frenzy with the final logistic preparations and assignments just months away. Trainer-of-Slaves was received by a harassed kzin officer who kept having to duck under man-height doors as he busied himself trying to find his files. He couldn't remember which computer he had fed them to. Finally, in distraction, he reset his bat-like ears and offered the absolute certainty of his help tomorrow, at the same time, if Trainer would be so good as to return.

They retreated to their lodgings in the old manor house. A dignified kzin passed them on the stairs with two leashed kzinrretti. Females could be dangerous in a city; they tended to spat with any unpleasantly odorous animal who dared approach them, and man-beasts with alcohol on their breath were always likely victims. They would even attack a male kzin twice their size if the lives of kits were at stake.

"Reasonableness does not control female emotions," explained their patriarch.

"Have a good night. You'll have to fold your ears against the kzin at the end of the hall—he growls and fights ghosts in his sleep."

A return to the Admiralty in the morning produced puzzling results. The kzin clerk dismissed Trainer-of-Slaves, and when Trainer politely persisted, another kzin ducked out of an adjoining office.

"You are not qualified for the Fourth Fleet and your rating application has been refused."

"I have these recommendations . . ."

The huge red officer with yellow splotches in his fur hissed. Trainer-of-Slaves immediately took the hint, saluted with a sharp claw-across-face, and retreated.

That evening Trainer and Ssis-Captain were considering their other options at a trunkshuppen off one of the side streets that led into the Grunderplatz. There were no other kzin present at the Mondschein. The waitress was clearly terrified to serve them but she was brave in her order-taking.

"Guten Abend, ehrenvoll Helden," she trembled. "Haben Sie gewahlt?" When they were slow to reply, she suggested a popular bourbon with milk.

"Ich . . . nehme eine . . . Coca Cola," said Trainer-of-Slaves, twisting his tongue around his teeth with his best animal imitation.

Ssis-Captain's remarks in the Hero's Tongue were meowls and spits of derision and approval. "The place smells like vatach-in-a-cage." He was referring to the humid scent of furless fear. "Nice little planet, Hr-r?" He nodded his mane at the waitress while playfully punching Trainer. "I'll take one of those to curry my backside in my European castle." Then, he consulted his translator. "Ich nehme einen Whiskey Kentucky mit Milch," he ordered, before he returned to business.

"You have some slandering enemies here in Munchen so we shall go elsewhere— which will lead directly back to higher lairs." Ssis-Captain had an invitation to the base at Gerning in the isolated northern province of Skogarna. "Friend Detector-Analyst is pleased with his post. The vast woods are isolated both from man-beast traffic and the arrogance of kzin patriarchs who are so well fed with land that they guard their holdings against the likes of us as if we were one-eyed kzinrret bandits."

Ssis-Captain rearranged his ears knowingly and flared his nostrils to hint that what he knew about the base was special. "Chuut-Riit established the Gerning station within months of his ascension as governor. The officers there are all kzin who sided with him in the struggle. Good contacts."

As he leaned forward with more conspiratorial details, Ssis-Captain's chair— suddenly—collapsed, and milk-in-bourbon arced to slosh onto his mane and vest. His massive head rose above the table with a fanged grin. When he was fully erect, his mane touching the low ceiling, he snarled in the direction of the pale bartender.

The other patrons, who had been uneasy, were now no longer even twitching.

Their waitress calmly dried her hands, sauntered to the door as if there was nothing more important going on than quitting time—then fled.

Ah how the liver rules the mind, thought Trainer-of-Slaves, noticing both the man-beast behavior and Ssis-Captain's rising rage. How much different was rage than fear? He knew enough not to touch Ssis for he could not hide his amusement, and too much tail whacking would turn the rage against himself. He appealed to the Captain's vanity as he, too, rose, "We'll have to wash your vest right away before the milk dries. Come." To the bartender he raised his glass, careful not to smile. He wanted to put that apprehensive creature at ease. "Zum Wohl!" he said, proud of his growing facility with animal grunts.

Ssis-Captain did not come right away. He took his rage out on the chair, taking the remnants of its poor wooden frame apart with bare hands and teeth as if it were a United Nations Warship.

CHAPTER 14

(2402 A.D.)

In an aircar over the province of Skogarna the social structure of Wunderland stood out in a way that never would have shown from the ground. It was clearly a wilderness dominated by a manorial elite. Coming into the kzin base they passed over the Nordbo estate at Korsness, huge, isolated from Gerning by hill and primeval wood along an expanse of beach. A ribbon of roads leading to Korsness clearly showed who was master of Gerning.

The light armored aircar carried the two kzin Heroes above the forested hills, past the hillside scar of recent kzin construction. It was afternoon but sunset hues of red washed over the clouds along the horizon where Alpha Centauri B was disappearing. The sea showed an astonishingly clear blue that faded into pastel shades of green where the shallow coastal waters had flooded a crater and left a curving string of is-lands.

Many such craters littered Wunderland. The planet suffered continual impact from meteorites straying out of the Serpent's Swarm so that some nights were aglow with falling stars. A major strike every few million years had left Wunderland's life-forms permanently poised for adaptation. The navy that had defended Wunderland from the Conquering Heroes had consisted mainly of a Meteoroid Guard unit.

Gerning Base was created by kzin who loved to hunt; the actual station that mon-itored the high atmosphere for thousands of kilometers around to detect feral space-craft seemed more of an afterthought. Some cunning kzin had his eye on this area, anticipating the time when honor and heroism would earn him the right to a full name. In the meantime he was serving Chuut-Riit's purposes.

Detector-Analyst was a local kzin from a background that gave him a Hssin her-itage, though he had never been to R'hshssira. He gave Trainer-of-Slaves special con-sideration out of curiosity for the planet of his patriarchs. Ssis-Captain grumbled at all this talk about a place he had passed through while in hibernation and kept inter-rupting to turn the conversation into a lighter vein.

Jokes: "How do you stop a monkey from running around in circles? Nail his other foot to the floor."

Zoology: was a Wunderland tigripard faster than a Kzin krrach-sherrek? Or only more cunning?

Better than he liked stalking through the forest, Ssis liked to sit in the lodge on the carved logs, supping fermented milk. The political intrigue was all in the lodge. He speculated with Trainer about the identity of the ambitious kzin who was "pissing around the borders of this territory," looking for a noble name so that he might found a household here. They decided it must be Yiao-Captain.

Yiao-Captain was an unlikely candidate. He was as short as Trainer and as slight, not the kind one would expect to dominate a fight, but he had a cautious cunning to him—and an *energy*—that would make any challenge to his honor dangerous. But it was his ambition that struck them both.

Trainer-of-Slaves first sniffed around its edges when he was invited to share a kill with four of the local kzin. The kill was a forest herbivore, headless, and carved in places that facilitated sundering, the fresh blood still running into the table-gutters where a spout delivered it to a bloodbowl. The tang of bloodscent was overpowering. On a sidetable stood green homeblown bottles of the local akvavit, ready to mix with the blood.

Trainer learned in conversation that the akvavit had been seized in Gerning for unpaid taxes and its distiller's daughter sold into factory slavery at Valburg. The normal procedure was for the indigenous *Herrenmann* to handle such details but the kzin purposefully audited estates and villages when taxes seemed low and found simple ways to encourage ardent taxpaying. After all, the taxes were set at fair levels.

The conversation changed from such mundane topics when Yiao-Captain arrived to rip off a hunk of meat for his own fangs. He dominated the conversation with his enthusiasms. He added fire to the tinder-dry debate over Chuut-Riit's *Logistical Preparation as the Key to Victory In War*. He provoked insults and countered them with witty insults of his own that both needled and defused. When he tired of that, he turned the collective attention of his coterie to tales of adventure.

Adventure, to Yiao-Captain, meant astronomy. His haunch of herbivore held motionless, he stopped eating while the sputtering of the Hero's Tongue quickened to an almost battle intensity. To know the stars! There were rumors of strange beings who lived in the depths of space, rumors of ancient empires that had casually abandoned tools upon the ice of comets long before any of the giant stars of the constellations had yet flamed to life.

Hr-roghk! The hints! The spoor untracked! Starseeds that spawned at the galaxy's very edge. Where did they come from? Where did they go? Mysteries! What were those moon caves deep in the outer planetary gloom around red dwarfs? Caves so ancient they must have been carved by disintegrator beams? Wealth! Honor!

Then silence to let all this sink in while Yiao-Captain noisily stripped his morsel. He left, reminded of duty by some new passion. The conversation drifted back to kzinrret jokes, to who had just received a name, to the honor duel between Electronic-Systems-Upkeep and Builder-of-Walls, the spike on yesterday's scope, the taste of space rations. And finally, finally, the tongue-wagging licked around that most degenerate bone of speculation—fleet rivalries; who would reach Man-sun first?

Days of hunting brought Trainer-of-Slaves and Detector-Analyst together in a friendship broader than the commonality of Hssin. They often went out at dawn without Ssis. Detector had been hunting in the woods around Gerning since the opening of the base, and knew the ways and the smells of the forest. He knew the waterholes and the places where a tigripard might be found stalking its own prey.

The aroma of Wunderland, the expanse, the open skies, an evening standing on the beach by the sea—all of this overwhelmed Trainer with joy. He had been a hunter himself, moving daily out into the Hssin Jotok Run to cull the wild Jotok or lure a transient into slavery, or measure the salinity of the marshes where the Jotok larvae wriggled among the reeds. He had thought the Jotok Run a capacious relief from the cramped city, but this! This Wunderland went on forever!

Once the hunting through the woods took them as far as the Korsness estate. Trainer saw from the hill Yiao-Captain helping a man-beast and his child move a fallen tree from the main road. He went to help the Captain. It seemed like a political thing to do—ingratiating himself with this officer could only prove useful. But why was he moving a tree when there were so many slaves and machines?

"Rrrr, we have welcome help," purred Yiao-Captain to the tiny child who had been trying to lift the tree at its center.

Trainer recognized the larger of the tame animals as the local king of beasts. He couldn't tell one monkey from the other but this one was tall for a man, with a hideous hooked nose. Unfairly, he had an unearned name, Peter Nordbo, but that was the way of the monkeys who did not know the value of a name.

"You're big," said the *Herrenmann's* child to the new kzin. "What's your name?"

Trainer-of-Slaves could hardly understand beast talk and he knew the child would not understand his. He had not yet grasped enough words in the slave language to translate his name. But Long-Reach's name for him was an easy translation. "Mellow-Yellow," he said. Those two words he did know. He added stiffly, "You are Short-Son of Nordbo."

The boy cocked his ear. "I'm Ib Nordbo, ehrenvoll Yellow." He put his three-year-old back to the tree. "Push!"

After the two kzin had carried the log to the roadside with token help from their human vassals, the child found a nest of petal-pickers that had been disturbed by their activities, the tiny scaled creatures dashing grief-stricken around their paper home. Ib Nordbo, not the least bit afraid of the kzin, took Trainer by the paw and made him stoop to his haunches while he explained the social life of petal-pickers with three year old seriousness.

Peter Nordbo watched his son anxiously while Yiao emitted a purr to reassure his vassal. Trainer-of-Slaves listened intently to everything Ib told him, even understanding some of it. He was fascinated. The man-beasts he had seen were very badly organized into slavehood. There had to be a better way. Learning animal psychology by direct communication with their young was a source of important clues to domestication.

Mellow-Yellow let a petal-picker climb onto his stick, waving its long front legs. Ib laughed. "They like roses. I feed them roses but it makes them sick." And he got up and staggered around for Trainer like a petal-picker drunk on the alien essence of rose.

"Do you have petal-pickers on Kzin?" asked the child curiously.

"Never . . . been . . . Kzin-home," Trainer struggled with the language.

"I go to Kzin," Ib pointed at himself. "I will tell the Patriarch to be nice."

Peter Nordbo had been licking his lips. He hastily picked up his son who was as much of a chatterbox as his young wife Hulda. "Maman wishes you for naptime."

"No!" The boy struggled.

"Sir," apologized Nordbo, "he is young yet to learn the proper forms of respect."

Kzinti have a soft spot in their liver for sons who struggle. Yiao-Captain nodded his mane. "If ever I reach Kzin-home, I will deliver the katzchen's message with great respect to the Patriarch."

Only days later Yiao-Captain appeared at the lodge with his Nordbo Herrenmann, violating all protocol. Kzin and beast came there to play some sort of man-game. Bored with fleet gossip, Trainer-of-Slaves tried to follow the moves and the logic of the game. It was played out on an octal by octal board, with stationary combat pieces. There seemed to be no action, no attack. The pieces stood there, sometimes without moving for minutes. One piece was moved at a time, to some trivial advantage. Sometimes, very gently, a piece would be set aside.

Yiao-Captain seemed fascinated by the game; his eyes never left the pieces. He asked questions roughly, and would cuff Herrenmann Nordbo as if he were a son, and he would purr happily when he captured a piece. But the stationary nature of the game obviously took its toll. When beast-Nordbo spent too much time on his moves, the Captain would pace restlessly, and if his opponent, even then, had not moved, he would stand towering over the small slave and impatiently suggest what the next move should be.

"Ach, that would give me too much trouble with your bishop when you jumped your knight. I think I'll move my pawn. I see advantage there."

"How do monkeys ever win a war? You'd be slashed to pieces before you decide which trench to sit in!" He turned to Trainer-of-Slaves. "You've been watching. Do you understand this ponderous wargame?"

"It is much too slow for me. I'm looking for fast action around Man-sun."

"You have a conventional mind. Five and a half years in hibernation is action?" Yiao-Captain roared in good humor. "Do you have a ship yet? Chuut-Riit is always looking for Heroes who want to get their tails singed."

"I have a ship, but the Admiralty is being slow with my rating."

"Hr-r, that's easy to fix. I'll tell you who to go to."

Yiao-Captain seemed to be at ease anywhere. When Traat-Admiral arrived for an inspection, Yiao took him hunting and entertained him without the slightest hint of propitiation. He appeared to be very well connected. Ssis-Captain hid in the bushes so that when Traat-Admiral came for his aircar on the day of departure, he could step out along the path and pass the Admiral with a sharp salute.

It was a glorious day. A chill wind blew in from the sea that ruffled the fur and took away the heat of exertion. Ssis was in a mood for celebration. He chatted excitedly about what Yiao-Captain could do for them, counting sons before they were born. Trainer guided him north to the creek where they wandered upstream on the boulders. Ssis leaped very carefully not to get wet—stone by stone—but Trainer didn't mind wading when he had to.

"Shissss!" the Captain whispered, freezing. "I've caught a scent."

They skulked downwind over a lightning-felled tree, silently on pads. Bent underbrush led around-hill. A splash of white through the leaves. There he was. They had a man-beast. A youngling with a spear. He saw them and started to run. In a flowing gait Ssis-Captain cut him off, drove him back toward Trainer. He fled in a perpendicular dash, away from them both. Ssis flanked him, around a gray outcropping, grinning. The boy-beast turned. Futilely. The natural carnivorous leap of the kzin was awesome in the low gravity. Ssis was blocking his way again, not hurting him, not coming close. Toying with his prey.

Trainer-of-Slaves had flashes of the poor monkeys he had tried to save back on Hssin during that fatal man-hunt. He stood, frozen with fear, not for himself but for the wretched animal. Ssis was only playing, having fun, but the beast didn't know that. Trainer reached a hand up, trying to think of something to growl at his companion that would restrain him.

The terrified boy, unable to retreat, charged with his spear. "Die Zeit ist um! Rattekatze!"

Ssis whacked him aside with unsheathed claws, but instead of picking himself up and running, the animal charged again with berserk energy, spearless. His body rebounded from the massive bulk of the moving kzin. He no longer had a face.

"No sense of humor," said Ssis-Captain, rolling the corpse onto its back with his foot.

Trainer-of-Slaves lowered his hand. They were so frail! He stooped over the youngling-beast to check for signs of life, the heady blood-odor stimulating his hunger. "He's dead!" There was no help for it. They stripped the clothes off the body and took turns ripping it apart with their fangs. What they left was a pile of bloody bones, half the flesh still uneaten, the braincase smashed open for the delicacy within.

One day later a grim *Herrenmann* arrived at the kzin base desperately trying to hold his rage within a propitiative framework. Yiao-Captain greeted him, at first not reading Peter Nordbo's state of mind. The hints of rebellion only raised Yiao-Captain's ire. Nordbo shifted his argument. Gerning was a small town. If the taxpayers were hunted, who would pay the taxes?

"I have supplied your base faithfully. How can I collect your tithe if this goes on?"

"I will conduct an investigation." Yiao opened a switch on his desk. "Data-Sergeant. Get me information. Who was hunting yesterday?"

Later Yiao had Ssis-Captain and Trainer-of-Slaves ordered to his office. He left them standing at attention. His mouth was twitching around its fangs. "You have been guests here at this base," he growled, making it plain that they no longer were. "I have let you roam freely. You have been serving in cramped quarters and I have sympathy for those who do their duty under trying circumstances. You have no authority to kill my taxpayers. Nor any reason. The woods abound with lower game." Contemptuously, the tip of Yiao's naked tail flicked back and forth. "This youngling you attacked, was that the best test of your prowess that you could find? Next you'll be devouring suckling kits!"

Yiao-Captain let the warriors stand while he attended to other matters. Finally he pulled out papers for Ssis-Captain. "You have been recalled to the fleet, immediately. I have seen to it that you will not return to the surface of Wunderland. You'll have to do your hunting on Man-home. I hear that there they have a surplus of taxpayers."

He had even worse words for Trainer-of-Slaves. "And I have investigated you, too. You have been toadying around the base seeking a fighting position in the Fourth Fleet, slithering behind the command of those who have been appointed to consider the staffing of the Fleet. You have a record of cowardice. Your presence aboard a fighting ship would endanger its Heroes. I have seen to it that you are being recalled to your duties at Fortress Aarku, immediately."

CHAPTER 15

(2402–2403 A.D.)

When the Fourth Fleet convoys began to assemble, stripping Centaurian space of its slaves and Heroes and warcraft, the Fortress Aarku became a tomb smelling of the Jotoki pens burrowed into the rock. The trained slaves were gone. The maintenance hangars were empty.

After Wunderland, Aarku was a coffin.

Trainer-of-Slaves suffered for another year at Alpha Centauri B. He tried to keep his contraband kzinrret happy, but she missed the flirtations of the warriors who were on their way to Man-sun and became moody and demanding. She did not comprehend the war. She only knew that she had been abandoned. She wanted attention. She rubbed against Trainer while he was trying to work. When he rebuffed her, she took to stalking his personal Jotoki and actually killed one of his trainees. When Long-Reach discreetly approached his master for help, they decided to store her away in a hibernation coffin and only bring her out when Trainer felt the craving.

Months after the Fourth Fleet was gone, remnants of the Third Fleet began to arrive at Alpha Centauri. Hangers at Aarku filled. Polarizers improperly maintained for a decade needed a fully stripped overhaul, but more than that there was much old battle damage too drastic to have been repaired in transit.

Trainer-of-Slaves personally crawled through the last of the stragglers. Eight survivors out of a crew of forty had brought it home, three of them dying of injuries en route. Inspection showed that *The Vindictive Memory* had taken a near fatal internal explosion. The ship's command sector had been pierced in three places by x-ray bolts. Space desiccated kzin were still trapped in one compartment. In the main gunnery turret three carbonized kzin lay melded to their weapons. The ship was not salvageable.

It was enough to chill the liver. Trainer-of-Slaves was reminded that he was afraid of death. How had he let Ssis-Captain mesmerize him with dreams of valor?

Orders relieving him of his duties at Aarku came as an electric surprise.

Some young son of a noble name had annoyed Chuut-Riit and was being given the Aarku assignment as penance. Even though Trainer was to be allowed three personal slaves, the new post didn't look appetizing—the commission involved a permanent position, not on Wunderland or Tiamat, but in deep space. Another dead-end for a coward? Yet the commission script bore the seal of the Fifth Fleet.

The tiny ship that brought him out, all gravitic drive and no armor or armament, was called a *Ztirgor* after a long-legged browser of Kzin that could run and dodge skillfully through brush and hills but had no other defense against attack. They were two light-days out, a six-day trip by *Ztirgor* at 70 Kzin gravities of acceleration with a turn-around velocity a third that of light. Alpha Centauri had been reduced from suns to a coruscant pair of stars in Andromeda.

They were drifting in to dock. By starshine the great hull of the communications warship was dwarfed by its extended antenna. The transmission/reception fabric, shimmering in the palest of rainbow colors, dominated the heavens. From a distance there were no clues as to its size—binocular vision is erased by space.

This great antenna faced Man-sun, now brilliantly overlaying the constellation that the man-beasts called *Cassiopeia* and the kzin called *God's Fang Drinking at the River of Heaven*. The Father-sun, appropriately, lay in the constellation of the *Dominant Warrior* that, to monkeys, was not a warrior but represented a ferocious bear.

Strange, thought Trainer-of-Slaves, how little the constellations varied over the whole of Patriarchal Space. The brightest stars were too distant to move. The stars of *God's Fang* were all giants, the brightest a red giant, the others, massive white giants, furious forges of the heavy metals.

They were met in the shuttle bay by an efficiently formal Master-Sergeant who recognized Trainer-of-Slaves by the slaves he brought with him. "Grraf-Hromfi will see you immediately. Lesser-Sergeant will settle your slaves. Welcome aboard." Trainer was already missing his kzinrret. He'd had to sell her on the sleight-of-paw market, too quickly to get a good price.

The warship was maintaining a light artificial gravity, just enough to settle dust and lost objects. They glided through the passageways effortlessly. It wasn't much different from Fortress Aarku. During the journey Trainer-of-Slaves deduced that Grraf-Hromfi ran a disciplined ship—the smell of it was remarkably clean.

At the Command Center, the Sergeant snapped off an alert ripping-salute. He was dismissed. Trainer-of-Slaves imitated with his snappiest claws-across-face and Grraf-Hromfi replied with a salute that wouldn't have taken the hide off a kit's tail. He wore a soft vest over his robe that he must have repaired himself, but he smelled like a hard task-master.

"I don't think that on the *Sherrek's Ear* we can provide you with the kind of feral life to which you have become accustomed; nevertheless, we do have interesting duties. You haven't smuggled aboard a kzinrret, have you?"

"No, Sire!"

"I thought that I'd let you know that we don't tolerate such irregularities here."

"Of course, Sire!"

"I've been reviewing your record, Eater-of-Grass." He returned his heavy duty data-goggles to his eyes which didn't prevent him from seeing, through the data, the sudden stiffness in Trainer-of-Slaves's posture—or the way ears folded against skull—or the layback of the fur on cheeks. "Yes, youngling, I know everything. At ease!"

"My cowardice has shamed me, Dominant One! I sought to restore my honor by volunteering for the Fourth Fleet."

"I assume that you believe the Fourth Fleet's mission would be more successful with cowards in key positions?"

"No, Sire!"

"I also have here, printed across your face at the moment, a report on a recent conversation of yours. You were speculating that old enemies from Hssin sabotaged your efforts to join the Fourth Fleet by telling stories about your legendary cowardice."

Trainer thought frantically for a moment, scanning his memories. He damned his loose mouth. "I admit to that conversation, Sire."

"That's hardly necessary since I have an audio recording of it. The stories are true; you do have enemies, as my files will testify. They *have* made depositions unflattering to your bravery, but those reports were filed on Hssin. In the meantime those enemies you cherish so close to your liver, have forgotten you. In their memory you have impugned the efforts of those who sought to grant your self-seeking application to join the *Blood of Heroes*. Your application was accepted at all levels, even by those who disapproved of you. The 'enemy' you are so bitter about is Chuut-Riit himself."

"Then I abase myself!"

"Shall I read to you what you said about this enemy? I particularly liked the one about him speaking with his anus and beshitting with his mouth."

"I have made a grievous error!"

"Beshitted with your mouth, did you? Hr-r, but you will be sufficiently punished. You have come under my command by the orders of Chuut-Riit. That is punishment enough for any sin. I make Heroes out of kits. It is easier on me if you do all the work."

"I volunteer immediately for any duty you may assign me!"

"Excellent." Grraf-Hromfi pulled an antique flint-spark pistol from a belt holster, and raised the goggles to his forehead, out of the way. "I prefer this to a wtsai knife," he said wryly. "It gives me several octenturies over my opponents. That makes me feel modern." Since the pistol could fire only one musket ball at a time, it had skull-cracking knobs on the barrel so that it could be used as a club. "Disassemble and polish my weapon while we talk." He handed Trainer-of-Slaves a polishing kit.

"Yes, Sire!"

"Chuut-Riit has been building two fleets for the last three years, not one. The Fourth Fleet was a full attack unit. The Fifth Fleet, to which you are now an honored member by the personal order of Chuut-Riit, was conceived of as an elite seed. With the launching of the Fourth Fleet, the seed is being planted. The Fifth Fleet is to grow into a fully operational attack force—assimilating warriors and warships only as fast as they can learn its strict code. It will not be a loose confederation like the Fourth Fleet. Any breaks in discipline will not be tolerated."

"Already I feel the juices of obedience in my liver, Dominant One!"

"Do you have questions?"

"Will we see action, Wise One? Or are we just a Fourth Fleet backup?" For a moment, Trainer-of-Slaves stopped his vigorous polishing of the ceremonial pistol.

"Let's take an example. Your brazen friend, Ssis-Captain, takes what he wants and does what he wants. Once he has an idea in his head, he acts. If his ears are tickled, he acts. His liver stops at nothing. If it took his fancy to put a kzinrret in command of his bridge, there she'd be pacing about and purring!"

The ears of Trainer-of-Slaves had to be consciously immobilized as he polished. He was imagining *their* kzinrret in command of the *Blood of Heroes*.

"Am I not right about your friend?"

"Hr-r, absolutely!"

"Yes. And he has never commanded a ship in battle. He sees an enemy position and he takes it, right?"

"The *Blood of Heroes* has a valiant crew. They are totally loyal to Ssis-Captain."

"What will his battle-lifetime be? An octal-day? Two if he's lucky! Then again he may have no more than the time to *see* a monkey before he is dead and his ship, cooked meat. Chuut-Riit has assigned all such commanders to the Fourth Fleet. *If* they survive he may be able to teach them something. They *may* even kill a few monkeys. Perhaps not even that. What have the first three fleets of you outworld barbarians accomplished, you screaming berserkers of Hssin, you borderland ragpickers? Bloody nothing!"

Grraf-Hromfi was now stirred up enough to clutch his planning-surface. "Hr-r, perhaps you wild barbarians have been teaching the monkeys military strategy in your own cunning way, one fleet at a time, never making the problems harder than a monkey can solve? The next thing we know, you Imperial-border scavengers will be hiring man-beasts to do your fighting. Why waste the talents you have taught them? Put them in command of your warships!"

"Sir, you speak of my father, not me."

"Hr-r, and you are different?"

"I admire firearms. This is a fine pistol, Sire. I believe I'm ready to reassemble it."

"Picked it up on W'kkai. That's where Chuut-Riit found me. We were both bored and listening to rumors in the marketplace to see if we couldn't sniff up some action. I had just bought the pistol from an old warrior who needed the gold. Chuut wanted the pistol, too, being a collector of pre-space weapons. He swears that he added me to his retinue so that he can keep track of this pistol. Notice the mark of Kai, a famous forger for the Riits."

"The Fourth Fleet will have glory with such a great weapons collector as Chuut-Riit."

"You are clawing for fish? The flattery does not disguise your question. Let me be blunt since my position allows it. Chuut-Riit is not the leader of the Fourth Fleet. He is here, mere light-days away, sitting in a palace on Wunderland. You can have no idea of the difficulties he has had in trying to shape Fourth Fleet discipline. Every border Hero thinks of himself as Heaven's Admiral ripe to pillage the wealth of the unexplored frontier. The Fourth Fleet is a fleet of admirals!"

Hromfi was raving again. "And let me tell you something else, youngling. It will be Chuut-Riit who will be taking the Fifth Fleet to Man-sun as his personal armada. That's where *his* confidence lies. But we won't be stalking that path of victory until he is certain that both you and I are ready. I am ready; you are not."

"I am instantly ready to take any assignment!" Eagerness flamed.

"Hr-r, now. Finish the pistol first. I keep even the flint ready to spark, so test that." He checked the weapon, then returned it to Trainer-of-Slaves. "It must have been a cramped journey in the *Ztirgor*. Take some rest. Then report to Duty-Sergeant at lights-on. We'll have time to talk again. What else to do but exercise the Hero's Tongue? We have heaven above and stars below and years of time. An interstellar warrior's main duty is to wait."

"Have I been dismissed, Grraf-Hromfi, Sire?"

"Not on this ship. Your duties never cease. You will, of course, take charge of maintenance immediately. But there will be many other tasks you will have to learn—besides the polishing of pistols. Correct communication protocols. How one coordinates an interstellar war. And we have fighter craft out here with the *Sherrek's Ear*. You will learn how to defend a deep space base such as ours. Coextensively you will be learning sound military strategy. To cudgel that into your Hssin head, you will be teaching what I teach you, in turn, to my sons, a thankless and trying task, alas, for which I need help."

"Is that all, Sire?"

"I detect a note of sarcasm in your hisses. No, that is not all. That is the beginning."

"I look forward to your regime. In the end I shall become convinced that I am one of Heaven's Admirals, a worthy goal for a Hssin barbarian."

"Claw your face and begone—Eater-of-Grass."

Trainer-of-Slaves took no notice of the insult for Grraf-Hromfi had spoken it with a purr. What could one's liver make of it all? He was terrified of this old kzin battle-ax—but he wasn't *afraid* of him.

CHAPTER 16

(2403–2404 A.D.)

The "unclawed," as the new ratings were called, had to attend an irregular seminar given by Grraf-Hromfi. The texts, the simulations, the work sheets, the drills were based on Chuut-Riit's Military Comprehendium, the complete collection of his works. The lectures, however, were pure Grraf-Hromfi. They were all based on the exhortation: "Think before you leap!" He had a thousand ways of drubbing that message home—as if he despaired of it being received.

Sometimes he used it to deliver a warning. The day he received Chuut-Riit's final report on the Third Fleet, he paced his students through that defeat, what was known of it.

On the screen he pointed, here, where Kgiss-Colonel had been left without reinforcements because the impetuous Warriors of the Right Arm had found their own irresistible target. The pointer moved to the details of the ancillary battle. Hindsight showed that the two monkey torchships had been both a decoy and a trap for valiant—and overeager—Heroes.

Grraf-Hromfi called other engagements to the screen. Ordnance had arrived at the battle of Ceres when there were no longer any functioning warships to be supplied. Since the warships were already derelict, no warriors rallied to defend the late-arriving kzin freighters. It was a recipe for massacre.

Further sunward, against orders, the Second Maintenance group had found, and enthusiastically attacked, a target of opportunity. They were not equipped to blitz a major laser battery and were so crippled by the attempt that they lost the capacity to refit damaged *Scream-of-Vengeance* fighters—their appointed assignment. Without fighter cover, the *Victory-at-Swordbeak's-Nebula* was destroyed by a suicidal squadron of *Darts*.

"Think before you leap," Grraf-Hromfi admonished the Heroes who had died in those battles. His was the funeral voice of a father reprimanding the corpse of an arrogant son.

Trainer-of-Slaves had been all too willing to leap aboard the Fourth Fleet. He recalled the carbonized Gunners of the Third. Whatever flesh hadn't been burned had been mummified by space during the desperate journey home. The images were vivid. Fangs grinning through fried face. The black ash of fur along a pair of legs. Yet each of those Gunners must have had his ambitions of liveried slaves, of estates on the pampas of Central France or on the great steppes of England. For the first time Trainer-of-Slaves felt a real contentment with his own simple, unexotic servants.

And sometimes, when he was in a bad mood, Grraf-Hromfi used the practical arts to illustrate his motto.

With gloved claws, he took his seminar group into the tournament ring. None of the young kzin could touch him while the cameras were active. He always drew them into a fatal move and then stopped the fight for review. Full-sized slow-motion holos of the contest flickered in the ring. The master's pointer jabbed at the swimming image of his last opponent with caustic comment.

"By launching his assault from here, he gave me too much time to react. Look at my feet anticipating. He can't change his trajectory. Here—keep your eyes on my feet—I'm braced for the attack and"—the pointer whipped upward—"see my arm coming to grab his wrist? There, I've got it, and all I do is flick him around his axis just enough so that his own feet trip him when they touch the ground. Three seconds later he is dead." Grraf-Hromfi cuffed the young loser while the youth's holo image leisurely impacted the mat. "See? *Think* before you leap! Develop your brains beyond the level of a sthondat ganglion!"

And sometimes Grraf-Hromfi used the dry rhetoric of formula to hammer home his motto.

The *Sherrek's Ear* was the nucleus of the Third Black Pride that was to go out with the Fifth Fleet. What was a Black Pride? Black was space's invisible color. Grraf-Hromfi scratched his nose with a claw. That was a sure sign that he was going to hold their ears for hours explaining, in detail, how every action-of-the-moment had a future consequence. Yes, he would repeat it again and again. Warriors who won battles could actually smell consequences, could read the spoor of distant consequence in current events.

What startled Trainer-of-Slaves was the depth of Chuut-Riit's long-term planning. Two stripped-down and experimental Black Prides of the Fifth Fleet had *preceded* the Fourth Fleet to Man-sun. They would stand in place to assess the coming battles from two positions at distances far greater than the aphelion of Neptune. If the latest armada met with valorous defeat they alone would remain, undetectable, monitoring the electromagnetic fetor of man's activities, photographing the solar planets, mapping the asteroids, waiting . . . brooding the ultimate avenging strike.

Kzin equipment was competent to find large defensive systems. Grraf-Hromfi showed his students what the *Sherrek's Ear* could do from such a distance. He had photographs of ships docking at Tiamat in the Serpent's Swarm. He showed them street maps of Munchen, fuzzy but readable by a trained hunter. He played for them an overlay composite of the fusion power station at Wunderland's Wachsamkeit, done in twenty frequencies from gamma to ELF.

Think *before* you leap.

Before the Fifth Fleet attacked, five full-strength Black Prides would be girding Man-sun at distances too great to be observed without already knowing their location, unreachable by torchship even if detected—each a fallback and resupply base for a sustained operation, each a spoor gathering center.

Grraf-Hromfi outlined two main flaws in the previous conquest attempts: (1) local logistics dependent upon pillaging the fruits of the battlefield, and (2) long-distance logistical support which was nonexistent.

The Black Prides were designed to serve local logistic needs. A Black Pride was to comprise: (1) a communication ship such as the *Sherrek's Ear*, (2) for defense, a Carrier and its litter of *Scream-of-Vengeance* fighters and *Ztirgors*, (3) a combination manufacturing ship and floating drydock which could tool up for—and build—any spare part within hours, (4) four fast ships to mine the comets, (5) a warehouse, and (6) a hospital ship. The antenna was to be assembled by replicating robots after arrival. Prefabricated and expendable rest-and-exercise modules were to be built in the case of a protracted battle.

Long-distance logistic support was to come from Alpha Centauri. For a full six years Wunderland and the factories of the Serpent's Swarm would be launching a monthly convoy of supplies and hibernating warriors, divertible either for battle or occupation use.

But talk and diagrams never really reached the liver of a kzin warrior who had survived the quarrels of youth. Sometimes, to teach what he had to teach, Grraf-Hromfi called in a student to assign special duty. Then he would repeat his motto, *sotto voce*, flicking his tale leisurely. There was always a trap in such duty, some hidden factor to waylay the over-hasty. Doing was learning. A brush with death stimulated thinking.

Grraf-Hromfi turned over the education of his sons to Trainer-of-Slaves. The sons learned little. Trainer learned how to anticipate lethal pranks. He even had to kill one of the fiends. The Conquest Commander did not reprimand him for that. It was the first trophy he had ever earned for his belt.

Over the next few years the primary duty of Trainer-of-Slaves remained—to train Jotoki for Pride maintenance as the group built up to strength. Pre-transient Jotoki were shipped out to him from Fortress Aarku. He took each one of them through their parent fixation, and when they were trustworthy, he introduced them to the simulators.

It was difficult to remain aloof from his creatures. He couldn't talk to them about their history or about military strategy, but they were so curious that they often tricked him into conversations he didn't know he was having. One of his charges he found skittering jerkily across a forbidden corridor on his second elbows; a shoulder eye was following an insect with great puzzlement.

Another eye caught the appearance of Trainer. "Master. What is?"

"An insect. Probably from Wunderland, and wondering how it got here."

"Alive or machine?"

"It's organic, like you or me."

That took Trainer-of-Slaves into a discussion of the differences between the reproductive cycle of life and automated factory production.

His Jotok charge wanted to know if machines were "made up" in the imagination. "Of course."

"By us?" He meant intelligent life, including kzinti.

"Of course!"

The Jotok scratched his undermouth and wondered about the mind that had made up the "assembly book" for kzin.

They had to retire to the arboretum to handle that one, Trainer-of-Slaves gently bringing the virescent insect with him. Mellow-Yellow gave his lecture on evolution to a rapt audience.

"How did *I* evolve?"

And there they were, right up against Jotok history.

One time when he was playing cards with Long-Reach they were discussing the marvelous estate they would have together after the conquest of Man-home. Long-Reach asked him about the forests of Earth.

"How different could they be from the forests in Hssin?" countered Trainer, looking through his hand for the ace of clubs.

"Will the Conquest burn them to charcoal?"

And there they were, right up against the subject of military strategy. Conversation was spherical—no matter whether one headed north, south, east, or west to avoid a subject, one always navigated right into it.

CHAPTER 17

(2404–2409 A.D.)

Over the years Grraf-Hromfi honed his force, expanded it. The shipyards of the Serpent's Swarm were busy. Gradually, he acquired the warcraft he needed to bring the Third Black Pride up to strength. He ran the Pride as if it were actually in place above

Man-sun. Perhaps his Heroes spied on the Wunderland Admiralty for fun, but they listened to the fading broadcasts of the Fourth Fleet with disciplined seriousness.

Once they received their floating drydock, the duties of Trainer-of-Slaves multiplied. Grraf-Hromfi did not trust the monkey workmanship of any Alpha Centauri–built ship or weapons system. He had his maintenance staff check everything, sometimes rebuilding to tighter specifications. It was exhausting work for Trainer. By necessity he learned the customs of the naval architect. Eventually he just gave up, found ways to delay the overhauling—and trained more Jotoki to do the work for him.

At other times there was no real activity at all. He filed reports and played cards. He sniffed for trouble. During one of those lulls he learned to fly a *Scream-of-Vengeance* fighter. That was safer than dreaming about Grraf-Hromfi's harem. Dreams about kzinrretti tended to fill idle moments. Sometimes he was back in the Chiirr-Nig household on Hssin, in the study, with his mother's loyal head in his lap, scratching her forehead. He regretted having to sell his sex-demon, Jriingh.

It was natural for a kzin to want a household. But Trainer couldn't understand why *he* wanted sons, not after he'd had to teach the Terrible-Sons of Hromfi. Nor was it moral for a coward to pass on his traits to sons who would disgrace the Patriarchy. Nevertheless he wanted sons. He supposed that his real sons were the Jotoki he took on during their fixation phase.

Sons challenged their fathers to physical combat. His many Jotoki "sons" wore him out by a different kind of challenge. The curiosity of a pestering Jotok in transition demanded that Trainer keep learning. It wasn't that he needed to learn. It wasn't that he was curious. He never asked a question whose answer didn't have a solidly rank smell. But he hated not to have a ready retort when a slave asked a stupid question like, "What is the minimum size of the universe?" The answer to a question like that not only didn't have a smell—it couldn't even be seen or heard.

Long-Reach started it all by telling four of his young apprentice polarizer mechanics about the black dwarf R'hshssira. It would collapse forever without fusing its hydrogen because it only had seven-eighths of the mass needed for ignition. But R'hshssira would *still* have a finite radius when there was no longer any radiation pressure pushing out from within.

The four youthful Jotoki had been learning gravity polarizer mechanics together under the supervision of Long-Reach and Creepy. That was twenty freshly curious brains in concert in teams of five-to-a-body. To rebuild and tune a polarizer one did not need to master unified field theory, but such practical constraints never appealed to an eager transient.

The "terrible four" roughed out the calculation that gave them the minimum diameter of a white dwarf star as a function of its mass. They didn't do nova mechanics—that was beyond their youthful abilities, but they did work out the mass range and size at which neutron stars existed. For each mass they could calculate a number for the diameter of the neutron star.

Masses large enough to collapse behind a light barrier were more difficult. Before those calculations were done, one of their brains infected all the others with the burningly important question, "If the *whole* universe collapsed, what would be its minimum diameter?"

Mellow-Yellow tried to give them a practical kzin answer. "The universe is expanding."

But all *four* Jotoki (twenty voices) wouldn't let him get away with that. Tuning polarizers was practical. *This* was recreation. *What if* the universe was contracting?

Data-link texts on gravity shouldn't be allowed. Worse, gravity polarizers were constructed all too elegantly. They should have flashing lights and be built along the lines of a W'kkai wooden puzzle. Then his Jotoki would be kept too busy to go off onto one of their wild chases.

Alas! Let it slip that the polarizer worked with negative space curvature and immediately they were delving into the tensor equations. From there insanity was only questions away. What is the difference between negative and positive curvature? Since positive curvature is common—and that means everything attracts everything else—why isn't the universe imploding? *When* will it start to implode? *If* the universe imploded, how small would it get? Tell us, Mellow-Yellow!

Thank the Fanged God that Long-Reach and Creepy and Joker had outgrown such questions. Nevertheless, Trainer-of-Slaves gave up an interesting card game to examine the matter. His data-link surprised him. It asked him to rephrase his inquiry several times, then produced the answer which had been known for some octal-squared generations. It was a theorem named after Stkaa-Mathematician-to-S'Rawl.

Stkaa, of course, was one of those kzin who wrote the commas and dots of the Hero's Tongue in the blood of martyrs. For the return price of an equal amount of blood, he made himself clear. On the data-link screen Trainer had to run the theorem's equations with different boundary values. He had to call up the definitions of words he'd never seen—sometimes because unified field theory was an arcane subject with its own hisses and snarls, and sometimes just because the language had mutated since the time of Stkaa. As often as not the definitions required that he run even more equations before he could make sense of the definition.

Three days later . . .

It was an easy enough theorem to declare. "A universe cannot contract beyond its lowest state of information." But it required a hackles-raising use of the uncertainty principle to find the temperature at which *every particle in the contracting universe had an equal probability of being anywhere in the fireball*—the required lowest state. But once you did that: out popped the minimum radius. Very neat.

Trainer-of-Slaves dutifully lectured his four "sons." He set up the unified field equations. He contracted to the essentials. He pulled a trick out of his ears that allowed him to apply the uncertainty principle to eliminate all the singularities.

If you knew the velocity of a particle you didn't know its position. Was it still approaching the central point or had it already passed through? If you fixed the position of a particle you no longer knew its velocity. Was it inward or outward bound? All information about whether the universe was contracting or expanding had been lost.

Presto! A minimum radius for the universe. (Thanks to Stkaa-Mathematician-to-S'Rawl, but don't tell them that.)

You knew you had the attention of a Jotok when three eyes were focused on you—when you commanded all five eyes you were a sensation. Big-Undermouth skittered off to bring him some squealing Grashi-burrowers in a bowl, which he munched while other arms curried his fur. Why couldn't kzin sons be like this?

He was beginning to understand his success as a Jotok trainer. At the onset of intelligence a Jotok bonded to anything that gave the basic verbal cues. He'd seen a machine-bonded-Jotok cripple its mind trying to be the son of a machine. The bonding moment was critical—but it wasn't enough. The Jotok was looking for a father, and you had to *be* a father if you wanted a reliable Jotok slave.

This was a confusing concept for Trainer-of-Slaves. He couldn't be a real father to his Jotoki because he couldn't give them combat training. They were herbivores, not Heroes. Only a father who was a coward would sire sons who were unable to fight. (Did Trainer still remember the murder of Puller-of-Noses? Perhaps. As an inexplicable aberration.)

Trainer-of-Slaves liked his isolation, mostly because it kept him out of fights. He had to maintain a delicate balance between dueling and not dueling. He preferred to be obsequious—older warriors appreciated subservience because it allowed them to delegate duties—but younger Heroes tended to mark a deferential kzin as potential prey.

To keep that nuisance at bay he had to maintain a reputation in the tournament ring. That he was Grraf-Hromfi's favorite opponent was enormously useful to him. The proud warriors of the Third Black Pride, awed by their Commandant, didn't see that Hromfi would never have hurt or humiliated Trainer, that the old warrior was only interested in providing an able disciplinarian for his sons. He was training Trainer-of-Slaves as proxy to cull his sons, a fatherly duty for which he had no liver.

A warrior who smelled Trainer's fear was restrained by the ear of the Commandant's son he wore on his belt, and by the many scars Trainer carried on his arm and body from contests with those same sons. The scars were a badge of sorts which Trainer appreciated, however painful had been their healing, because they warned others to keep their irritation in check.

Nevertheless, despite his growing skill as a combatant, he preferred his isolation. In the old days he would have hunted the savannas of Kzin-home alone.

CHAPTER 18

(2410–2413 A.D.)

Isolation can never be complete within a military machine, no matter how remote the posting. Trainer-of-Slaves might hide behind his work, but his superiors always found him because they needed him. In time, Chuut-Riit came out for an inspection. The Black Prides were the bones of his Fifth Fleet, and he liked to keep his tail around developments. While his officers were with him in the maintenance hold of the Pride's floating drydock, the *Nesting-Slashtooth-Bitch*, and looking out over a dismantled *Scream-of-Vengeance* from a catwalk, Chuut-Riit turned to Trainer-of-Slaves.

"I recall our conversation at that hunt on Hssin."

"Sire, I was young then, of shrunken liver and rattle-brain."

"But you showed the talents of a fine captain, a gift for feint and kill," Chuut-Riit replied diplomatically. "Let me refresh your memory about the topic which intrigued me. You had a theory that male humans might be domesticated through their biochemistry. I recollect that you talked about a trigger to control the pace of their learning, then a block to freeze that plasticity once they had attained the desired slave behaviors."

"Sire, I have speculated thus—but never with any experimental animals upon which I could test my ideas. Mental physiology can take strange twists. The turns cannot be followed without sniffing the trail. Nor can the males be domesticated without providing the proper kind of breeding female."

"I have a partial-name for you if you succeed in this venture."

"Sire!"

"Too many of our humans go feral. I suspect that on Earth, with its very large population, the problem will be worse. Hunting those humans who can't adapt to slavery is a limited solution. The feral human is covert and has the ability to pose as a slave. When he strikes he can be deadly. There was a recent massacre of kzinrretti and their kits. It reminded me of your proposal. If you have the time to pursue the subject I can send you all the experimental animals you can use. I should like to take such knowledge with the Fifth Fleet."

"I am eager to accept!"

"You have the space out here?"

"I can set up feeding cages."

"Good."

Trainer-of-Slaves had a wall of clean cages erected in a munitions area that was unused—they were not on a war mission yet. The cages were small by kzin standards but quite adequate for a man-beast who wished to stand erect or lie down, and more than adequate for children. When the first group of experimental animals arrived, he established a fixed regime. They received five-eighths of the water and food they needed simply for keeping their cages clean. The remaining rations were given for appropriate cooperation. No other pressure was placed on the animals for refusal to cooperate.

They were very noisy.

Included with the first shipment was the best human-tech autodoc that Chuut-Riit's officers had been able to locate, complete with instructions in German, English, and Japanese. Its computer was essentially a full compendium of human biochemistry, though not in an easily decipherable form. The autodoc had been supplied so that he could recycle animals damaged in experiments.

First he tackled the autodoc's exotic computer and set up a program to translate its records of human biochemistry into kzin-symbolics so that they could be transferred to his data-link and integrated with the generalized model of all known organic alien brains. He was amazed to recognize one of the human neurotransmitters as similar to a kzin neurotransmitter. Its peculiar chemical form gave him a clue as to why kzin reflexes were so much faster than human reflexes.

Within weeks Trainer-of-Slaves had his first experiments running. Long-Reach was proving to be a talented surgical student. His initial try at removing the top of a male's skull had provoked massive hemorrhaging—a mistake that was being repaired in the autodoc. Long-Reach's second attempt was a success. His animal was restrained in a comfortable chair, the dome of her cranial bone sliced off at the top to expose the brain, her human head cramped rigidly to prevent her from hurting herself.

Trainer had upped the room temperature in deference to the female's furless skin. He had tattooed a dots and comma identification on her arm so that he wouldn't mix her up with the other animals. Delicate probes were already embedded in her brain, measuring transmitter chemical activity, mapping the neural circuits involved in sensory input, monitoring blood flow, measuring neural activity changes as basic emotions were chemically switched on and off. He needed to get a paws-on feel for the brain structures he had extracted from the autodoc.

But he hovered around his experiment nervously. He didn't want her to die of shock while he was still so unsure of the human performance envelope. He had special catfish ice cream to give her when the data gathering was over in appreciation for her discomfort.

In time he would learn how to erase her inquiring mind while retaining her ability to bear children and perform her sexual functions. He wasn't yet quite sure what would be the best use for the males. If he was to domesticate them as work animals, he would need a different approach than if they were to be domesticated for food.

Thus the years went by uneventfully. Experiments on slaves. Biochemistry studies. Neural map deciphering. Polarizer maintenance. A bit of fighter acrobatics in exchange for a fast repair job. Another lethal fight with one of Hromfi's sons; another ear for his belt. More lectures on strategy. An embarrassing incident with one of Hromfi's coy daughters, fortunately in the dark. Gunnery practice. More Jotoki to train. More questions to answer. Another round of brain experiments.

His most productive line of research came after he deciphered the autodoc records which gave him the switching codes that turned neural growth on and off. He found it useful to know under what conditions human neurons could be made to reproduce or to bud-off new neurons. It fascinated him when he found that he could cause dendritic sprouting.

That was only one of the enthusiasms for which his kzin impatience got him into trouble. He was wildly hoping to astonish his peers by fabricating a genius slave—but when he increased the number of neural connections in a man-male's brain by an order of magnitude he succeeded merely in killing off his animal. Depressing.

Occasionally excitement broke through the drudgery of incremental scientific advance. Yiao-Captain visited, his fervor so persuasive that the Pride actually moved their great antenna forty degrees away from Man-sun to observe some sort of freak gamma source.

The wonder never lasted. Always they returned to the monotony. Yes, he *was* having solid if exasperatingly slow success with his experiments—but the work was so tedious! Yes, he *was* getting so expert that he could recycle most of his man-animals through many brain operations before they died—but the finicky detail work constantly left him on the edge of rage. He wasn't sure that he could have gone through it all if it wasn't for Chuut-Riit's promise of a name. Thank the Fanged God for the high spots that broke the ennui.

There was that second vacation on Wunderland when he was able to set up steady arrangements to restock his cages from an orphanage—he couldn't just pirate experimental animals out of the war factories without the risk of a duel with some touchy kzin manager. Criminals and political prisoners were too much in demand for the hunts.

His Jotoki kept his mind busy. Sometimes it was a racy card game. One of his Jotok discovered a mathematical theorem that was not in any data-link. Another of his slaves did an excellent project on the biochemistry of pain-accelerated learning in humans. That cleared up a whole lot of puzzling questions about human brain function. He didn't know how he would have survived if his incurably curious Jotoki weren't taking so much of the load off his mind. Sometimes all he had to do was ask a question, and one of his Jotoki would experiment with an orphan and come up with the answer. They had more patience than a kzin.

Trainer-of-Slaves knew he had been with the Third Black Pride for too long when their antenna began to receive news of the gigantic battles in the Man-system. He had been at this post almost ten years. The battles that were juicing up Wunderkzin livers were themselves more than four years dead. Of course, with light-speed messages it never seemed that way. If a space battle lasted a month, it still took a month to play out—four years after the fact.

The Fourth and Fifth Black Prides were stationed up ahead, listening, too. The Third Black Pride was behind Alpha Centauri as the last backup. The Prides frantically compared messages, filling in the transmission gaps, but they were all light-days apart, and it took days for the final compilation to be authenticated by the communications officers.

None of the news surprised Grraf-Hromfi. Stoically he repressed his rage. But Trainer-of-Slaves was surprised.

The *Blood of Heroes* was destroyed on the eleventh day. Vaporized. Trainer, tired from following every new bulletin, was stunned by the heroic death of his best friend. Four years ago. His ancestors were whispering. It was as if he had been living four unearned years. *I'm a ghost,* he thought, but that was silly. He felt pathos. Then the kzin anger took him. He wanted to fight, and there was no one to fight. He wanted monkey ears on his belt. But they had Ssis-Captain's ears on *their* belt.

Something about these humans that he did not understand. He went to his cages in a foul mood.

"Hey, Dr. Moreau," jeered a female with long black hair, "when do you sew on my wolf's head?"

"Svelda! Clean up your cage!" he snarled with his best animal pronunciation. It was just a matter of feeding the suction nozzle.

"You come any closer and you get shit in your fur!"

His mouth was twitching over his fangs. "Be careful. I'm in a vile mood."

"That's news to me? What do I care? What have I got to lose? Kill me!"

He purred to disguise his ire. "I'll give you ice cream if you clean up your cage."

She was weeping. "You've mucked around in my brain so often I can't think straight. Ice cream! Do you understand anything? Open the cage door and I'll kill you. Do you know what happens to a woman when you cut up her brain? All the emotions come out! She loses control. She becomes an animal." She held onto the bars and snarled at him, gnashing her teeth.

The orphan children in the adjoining cages began to wail. They were so much easier to manage than these political ferals.

So—another failure; she was still capable of connected reason and the only obvious result of the experiment had been to produce a state of constant, poorly controlled rage. These man-females clung to their reason even after drastic surgery. And when he *was* able to delete their intelligence they showed grave, and sometimes startlingly weird behavior deficits.

Once he had tried to eliminate curiosity and had produced instead an idiot who compulsively asked questions with no interest at all in the answers. Another experiment in intelligence reduction had produced a perfectly rational woman with a deadly lack of common sense. He had tried for docility, using the autodoc's knowledge of human brain chemistry, and achieved only passivity leading him to the discovery that there wasn't much difference between passivity and sloth. Passivity neutralized intelligence, but it neutralized everything else of importance, too. Docility, on the other hand, seemed to *require* intelligence if a kzin was to get any use out of it.

He was still missing some essential key.

"You *like* ice cream," he stated firmly, hoping to motivate the Svelda-female toward cleanliness.

"Suck it up your nose!"

Was that a *reasonable* statement? Borderline. He wanted to make her happy so that she would clean her cage and stop disturbing the other animals. Ice cream wasn't going to work. Perhaps she could no longer understand the concept of ice cream? If reason was failing, he should try something emotional—a kzinrret always responded to emotion. What would she respond to since she did not like him? since she was fixed at rage? Victory? He thought about that.

Victory was very emotional; it stirred the purring vibrations. Kzin and animal alike all relished victory. "At this moment your race is happy and I am bereaved," he said.

"Happy?" she shrieked. "A finger in your eye! That would make me happy!" She rattled her cage some more and snarled some more. "*Gottdamm Urin-Pelz!* You stink! *Urin-Pelz!* Take a bath!" When he tried to reach in his hand, unclawed, to give her a soothing pet, she snapped at his black fingertips.

A remarkable display. Svelda had come to him shy and quiet and properly propitiative. He had been delighted into thinking that very little modification of her mind would be necessary. But his surgery had evidently de-inhibited a whole layer of vicious instinct. Puzzling. Reluctantly he dismissed his latest theory about human brain function.

How far could she still reason at the abstract level? She was having trouble connecting victory with joy. He enunciated his animal call imitations more carefully as if he were talking to his mother. "You monkeys have done grave damage to our fleet attacking Sol. Noble warriors have died valiantly. That is why you are happy and I am bereaved."

"Sol?" The beast began to weep hysterically. Another singular transformation. "The Solarians took you out . . ."—the sobs were racking her body—"you *Rattekatze* father-suckers?" she asked between sobs. "At Sol?"

"Another fleet will be sent."

He was observing that the she-animal's brain damage was extensive. All the emotions seemed to be operating at once, uncoordinated. Tears of grief were streaming down the furless face. She was grinning the way humans did when they were radiantly happy, but the way she bared her teeth seemed to have a kzinlike ferocity. Some ancient hardwired instinct had been severed from its inhibitory subprograms.

"Kill! Kill! Kill!" she screamed happily through her grief and through the bars to drown out the wailing of the children.

Later, with the she-Svelda under sedation, Trainer-of-Slaves tried to repair the damage to her brain by regrowing neurons in the places where they had been excised, but it didn't work. She went into a coma. The autodoc could keep her alive but she responded to no outside stimulation, could not groom or feed herself, or even eat. He had to give the meat to Grraf-Hromfi's sons for good behavior, but he kept the head and sliced up the brain, feeding its neural circuitry into his data-link in the hopes that someday he could make sense of what had gone wrong.

He couldn't resist clipping one of her ears to his belt. After the Fourth Fleet disaster, he *needed* a monkey ear at his waist.

He was thinking more about his mother than ever before. He had always thought of his mother as nonintelligent. All the idioms for *stupidity* in the Hero's Tongue were references to females. If one kzintosh said of another kzintosh, "You kzinrret," what he meant was, "You brainless *stupid* fool!" And yet . . . when Trainer-of-Slaves had tried to replicate, in human females, that endearing kzinrret *stupidity*, what he had achieved was bizarre non-functionality.

Still in a rage induced by the defeat of the Fourth Fleet, he took his rage out in an aggressive attack on this problem which had been plaguing him. He thought about his mother. He was thinking about all the times she had saved his life.

His experimental mistakes had confronted him with strange facts. He'd had to question his ideas about intelligence, to break that concept down into its many parts. Now he analyzed what his mother must have been aware of while she was actively protecting him, and he came to the remarkable conclusion that his mother *had* to be intelligent.

But that was impossible. He flashed on his cherished image of catching her chewing on one of his first books, chewing it to a pulp.

The Fanged God had given souls to the first kzinrretti but at the crucial Battle of Hungry Years they had betrayed both Him and their mates while the males stayed loyal to their God and so He had taken away the female souls and given their bodies over to kzintosh masters so that the race might continue to propagate itself. That was mythology, tales of events that had happened before science, before writing. What *had* happened? What had the kzinrretti lost at the Battle of Hungry Years if it wasn't intelligence?

Trainer-of-Slaves was sure that he loved his mother—whatever she was. *What* she was remained locked behind silence; she seldom spoke and when she did speak she used only the elementary vocabulary of the Female Tongue, no more than a few octal-squared words. Was it a contradiction in terms to call an animal intelligent if she couldn't use language?

CHAPTER 19

(2414–2419 A.D.)

"Why don't we go!" He stooped through the oval bulkhead door, trying to tromp out his anger. But in the light artificial gravity he had to hold on to the handrails to make the floor shake.

His Jotoki scattered before his voice and busied themselves with what they thought would please him. Some went to their sleeping frameworks and hid.

Trainer-of-Slaves was eager to launch toward Man-sun to avenge the Fourth Fleet. He had expected action after a ten-year wait and buildup. His liver demanded an explosion of Heroism raging out toward the enemy star. He was tired of waiting, waiting, waiting with nothing to claw but the claw-sharpening "bark" in his miserably small stateroom. He was restless. His blood told him to *make* something happen . . .

But the implacable, immovable, unmoving Chuut-Riit thought differently. Waiting wasn't waiting, said his bulk, grinning at his foes. Waiting was planning. The size of the defeat had sobered him. May the Fanged God not lose patience with his inaction!

Grraf-Hromfi conceded in one of his seminars that the Wunderland Admiralty was reassessing top strategy. Chuut-Riit had cynically expected the Fourth Fleet to fail because of its arrogant commanders, but he had also expected it to demoralize the monkey hive—and drastically weaken human military capability. Now Chuut-Riit was opting for a few more years of preparation. He wanted Centaurian industry built up to the point where it could keep an interstellar supply line filled. And he needed that extra crop of warriors that more time would provide.

In the meantime the Third Black Pride kept track of Sol through the distant transmissions of the First and Second Black Pride communication warships. Those scoutships of the Fifth Fleet had remained in place, well away from the battle zone—undetected as of 4.3 years ago—keeping their vigil out where Man-sun was only the brightest star in the heavens.

A steady flicker and hiss of messages came through to be filtered and cleaned and analyzed by the kzinti spoor specialists back in the Centaurian system. Fuzzy pictures of UNSN Gibraltar Base. Specks that looked like a fleet moving in the asteroid belt. Some new markings on Mercury. The trace of search beams scanning the skies. Non-military beamcasts giving the tone and morale of the monkey civilization. Better and better maps of the cities of Earth.

Trainer-of-Slaves often flipped through the images. He gave only a glance to one of the earliest post-battle transmissions. It was a single crude picture of a vehicle being assembled in the asteroid belt. The scale markings indicated enormous size but its size was deceptive. Most of the structure seemed to be a flimsy magnetic funnel: one of the monkey ramscoops of no military utility. To be noted and ignored. Perhaps it was to be an emissary to one of their local allies.

Months later there was a second flurry of activity when more pictures of the ramscoop came through. Now it was equipped with massive disposable hydrogen tanks and was actually being launched toward Alpha Centauri! To what possible purpose? This time Trainer noticed the furor only because Grraf-Hromfi used the item as the inspiration for a seminar lecture on human technology.

Trainer-of-Slaves was not to recall that seminar for another five years. Immediately when he left the briefing room other worries occupied his mind. He had a sick Jotok to tend and he was in the middle of a card game that he was losing to Long-Reach.

In that five years the Fifth Fleet doubled in size. The effort caused great hardship among the vassals of Wunderland, more than Chuut-Riit thought prudent to impose. Such stress created an alarming increase in feral activity. But there was no help for it. Extraordinary war efforts always cause hardship, both among slave and Hero. Sacrifices had to be made for the Long Peace, always. Peace did not exist without war to impose it.

Trainer-of-Slaves developed a lucrative sideline. It did not pay off in coin, but it paid off in favors. His Jotoki became experts at modifying warships and fighter craft to better than standard performance. This was not particularly difficult to do.

"Kr-Captain, your *Screamer* now gives us a perfect check-down. But I do know ways its performance could be improved." While unbinding the terrified zianya who was to be their dinner, Trainer paused to let his message sink in. It was against regulations to make non-standard changes. Waiting without comment, he watched Kr-Captain tear out his hunk of flesh to an anguished animal cry. Trainer was not going to mention the subject of irregular modifications again.

"I'll take any edge," said Kr-Captain, blood on his jaws.

"Of course, any alteration can be restandardized."

"A laudable way to deal with fussy bureaucrats."

"Useful too, in case non-standard parts are unavailable during an emergency."

"When might such work be done?"

To avoid equipment chaos, standardization had been rigidly imposed since the time of the first interstellar Patriarchs. All improvements, by decree, had to come out of Kzin-home. In a subluminal empire, sixty light-years in diameter, new standards diffused slowly.

Brilliant innovations built to serve a need during the heat of some local war tended to die in the files. First the innovation had to reach Kzin-home. Then it had to be tested by a bureaucracy which considered itself to be the sole font of all change—and was understaffed. The ideas that lived often took ten or fifteen generations to become the new standard authorized by the High Admiralty, not because the Admiralty was particularly senile, but because the pace of light from star to star was pitiably slow.

Still, many such battle-tried ideas could be found hibernating within the labyrinthine network of lairs inside the data-links. Finding them took maze-tracking skills, and battle-cunning to know what was wanted, and an engineering background to know what was possible. Having fanatically loyal Jotoki technicians also helped.

The *Flayer-of-Monkeys* was a three-kzin fighter-scout. They were well away from the *Sherrek's Ear*, testing the illegal modifications, when they got an emergency message. "Flayer. Flayer. Flayer. Record. Record. Record." Kr-Captain was at the leading point of the delta-shaped control chamber. He switched on his combat communications memory. Trainer-of-Slaves happened to be riding in the Sensor's harness, and Long-Reach was uncomfortably seated on his mouth in the Weapons-Operator chair, peering at his instruments. He was used to maintaining them, not reading them.

Sherrek's Ear continued urgently. "Acknowledge and Execute. Time Lag too Long for Confirmation. Will Repeat Message. Ramscoop Coming Through. Intercept and Destroy. *Flayer* is only Warcraft in Combat Range. Repeat: Intercept and Destroy. Ramscoop Coming in Much Faster than Predicted." The excited kzin controller spat out a number. "We See Target: Three Octal-squared Light-days Out, Coming In. Real Position: Passing A-star; Perhaps Already Outbound. Possible Collision A-star. If So: Cancel Intercept. Now Read Coordinates for *Flayer* Intercept."

They were given a position which placed Man-sun almost in occultation with Alpha Centauri A, on a circle surrounding A at a point thirty degrees north-east of a reference longitude through Kzin-sun. If they couldn't intercept within forty-seven hours, the ramscoop would escape.

"... We Assume You Are Unarmed. Destroy-mode Your Choice. Message Will Now Repeat. *Flayer. Flayer* . . ."

A startled Kr-Captain swung his outer antenna toward the *Sherrek's Ear.* "*Flayer* Ack. Will Intercept. *Flayer* Ack. *Flayer* Ack. Moving out." He switched off the comm—they were too far away to carry on a conversation—pulled down his goggles, and took a brief look at the heavens while he rolled *Flayer-of-Monkeys* in the direction of the line joining Man-sun and Alpha Centauri A, now separated by about seven degrees.

"We've got to close up Man-sun and the A-star. That's shaving the hairs. Hope your juiced-up polarizer really will do octal-squared g's. What the sthondat is a ramscoop?"

"Hey, two missiles!" said Long-Reach's short(arm) after checking the weapons readout.

"*Camera* missiles," snarled Kr-Captain, lolling his tongue. "For maneuvers."

Trainer-of-Slaves was suddenly remembering Grraf-Hromfi's long-forgotten seminar on ramscoops. "I know what a ramscoop is."

"Good. Whatever it is, can we kill it? We're disarmed." They were already accelerating at sixty-three g's, yet it would be hours before they began to see Alpha Centauri creeping across the starfield. Kr-Captain turned to calculating orbits on his screen. They were going to have to cross the line-of-flight of the man-thing at ninety degrees. "We have just enough time to decelerate and stop on their line-of-flight. Should we stop or do a flying pass?"

All of Grraf-Hromfi's lectures on tactics crowded into Trainer's thoughts. *Think before you leap.* "Stop if we can. We get one try. We don't want our fire crossing the line-of-flight at an angle—not at those velocities."

The old seminar room on the *Sherrek's Ear* was filling Trainer's imagination. The smell of frame-beryllium and old fur. The wet sniff of algae. But especially that room five years ago. Grraf-Hromfi was the same benevolent tyrant that he had always been, mane a bit scraggly. His holo mockup of the ramscoop floated to one side and he held his shamboo pointer tipped with slashtooth tusk that he liked to jab into his holos— and sometimes into the bellies of his less attentive listeners.

"We do not know its intention," the ghost-memory was saying to Trainer. "It is probably coming to sniff spoor around our boundaries. It cannot have an attack capability."

Trainer tried to reevaluate: was that still true?—and drew a blank.

"It cannot defend itself."

Yes, thought Trainer, *its speed is its only defense, running like a fangless herbivore.*

"The most interesting fact that this mockup reveals about the United Nations Space Navy is that they have not—as of four years ago, I repeat—learned how to build an interstellar-grade gravity polarizer. Otherwise they would not be launching such a massive low-performance device. The magnetic funnel"—he pointed—"is used to collect interstellar hydrogen for the reaction drive. Can any of you tell me its major constraint?"

There had been silence in the classroom. Today it was the silence of interception through soundless space.

Trainer remembered himself prompting, mischievously, "Ask Long-Tooth. He knows."

Long-Tooth-Son of Grraf-Hromfi jumped out of his reverie. "Honored patriarch, a ramscoop is too slow."

"Its *acceleration* is too feeble," corrected the father. "And why is that?"

Long-Tooth cast Trainer a venomous look for getting him into this dialog. "There's not much hydrogen for it to use."

"How much?"

"Sire! I don't know."

"Trainer-of-Slaves?"

"Please accept my surrender if I am wrong. Between here and Man-sun the density is about an octal-squared to four-octal-squared hydrogens per fistful of space."

Grraf-Hromfi again passed the slashtooth tusk of his pointer through the fuzzy holographic ramscoop in front of him. The spout of its funnel was burdened by racks of spherical tanks. "They need these huge hydrogen tanks to prime their reaction engines since they can't collect much hydrogen at low speeds. The tanks will be dropped off once they are moving fast enough to devour more than starvation rations of the interstellar hydrogen."

He was grinning at monkey folly. "They can't collect much at high speeds either in spite of the fact that the main funnel collector surface seems to be about as large as the Patriarch's private hunting estate. Their maximum speed is a quarter that of light if they use a ramjet design. With a more sophisticated flow-through design they are only limited by relativistic effects which are considerable. I doubt a top velocity beyond a half-lightspeed."

. . . and you were wrong . . . The *Flayer* was at the center of a sphere of stars, intercepting some man-thing that was coming at them close to the velocity of light.

"At really high speeds they would have to know how to burn proton cosmic rays—an unpleasant diet." Grraf-Hromfi got an amused ripple of ears when he added that this might be to the taste of a herbivore.

. . . yes, and the monkeys have managed to thrive on that unpleasantly lethal diet . . .

"Those are engineering details and I presume they can be mastered. Ramscoops are a primitive solution and we've never used them, so we know little of the details. The major problem is not an engineering one—it is a flaw in the concept. A fusion funnel cannot attain high accelerations, first because it is fuel-starved, and second because reaction drives produce *inertial* acceleration. How do you build a gossamer funnel that can take even one gravity of inertial acceleration?"

. . . but at a fifth of a gravity, year after year . . .

Grraf-Hromfi did not mention in his lecture that a fighting kzin warship could accelerate at sixty gravities with the pilot floating in his cockpit and thus reach its maximum cruising speed in about five days, because all of his officers knew that. "How long would it take this funny-funnel to attain six-eighths the velocity of light?"

"Six months?" ventured a bored officer who leaped to conclusions before thinking.

"More like eight-ten years—with most of that time spent at low velocity. When will it reach Alpha Centauri?"

"About the time the Fifth Fleet has occupied Man-home," said Long-Tooth-Son with a grin for the poor beasts.

. . . but it is here and the Fifth Fleet hasn't even started yet . . .

"That's a reasonable estimate. I'd like to remind you that these pictures are more than four years old."

. . . it took them only nine plus years to get here . . .

"The monkey-funnel is already out of range of both the First and Second Black Pride. But even after all this time"—the 4.3 years the Pride's message took to reach Alpha Centauri—"the ramscoop will still be close to Man-sun and just beginning its journey. It is not something we'll ever have to worry about. We'll keep an automatic tracker looking for it—that's our duty—but I doubt if we'll ever sniff it again. The monkeys will decelerate and sulk around outside Alpha Centauri well out of our range."

So even Grraf-Hromfi could be dead wrong.

Trainer-of-Slaves did a calculation on the Sensor's data-link. The automatic tracker had detected the first trace of the ramscoop two-hundred light-days out—yet years earlier than expected. Which meant that its maximum speed was far higher than kzin engineers had anticipated.

Kr-Captain finished his trajectory plot and put the *Flayer-of-Monkeys* on automatic. Turn-around was in twenty-three hours. "*Sherrek's Ear* gave us orders to be creative." He meant that they were unarmed.

"Best little mechanic in the galaxy sitting right beside me," said Trainer-of-Slaves. "So how are we going to kill this whatever-it-is?"

"We may not have to. Grraf-Hromfi proved that a monkey can't stay alive in a ship moving at that speed—cosmic sleeting."

"Give old red-mane an ear," he purred sarcastically. "We don't have to fight because the enemy has already suicided! A nice philosophy until a monkey leaps out of the funeral pyre." He returned to a commander's inflected spits and growls. "We shall assume they have a gravity polarizer shield and are still alive."

"A gravity shield is the same as a gravity drive. Then they wouldn't need a ramscoop."

"What's a ramscoop?"

"A magnetic funnel that collects interstellar hydrogen and ejects helium as reaction mass."

"Is a monkey going to stand at a porthole and shoot arrows at us?" Kr-Captain flapped his batwing ears.

"Maybe the magnetic field protects them," suggested Long-Reach, two arm-slits speaking in unison.

"Slave! Shut up," growled Kr-Captain.

"Does he play cards?" whispered the arm nearest the relaxed ears of Trainer-of-Slaves.

"Don't eat your seat, Long-Reach. I'll need your brains in due time."

Long-Reach hunkered down on his undermouth, petulantly. He was muttering along internal channels to himselves that he *was* Weapons-Operator. That started an argument among the arms about who was to take charge of the camera missiles.

"The line-of-flight cuts right past the A-star," said Trainer. "They'll already be dead. The starwind is fierce at that distance. It will have hit them like your father's claw." Kr-Captain seemed unconvinced and so Trainer used an analogy from a virtual horror-adventure they had both lived together under shared eyecaps. "It's like a hurricane wind in your sails."

Kr-Captain bared his fangs. He didn't like being reminded of that horror-story world covered with water, trying to survive in the company of five war-stranded Heroes on board a fleeing sloop in typhoon weather. His liver was still recovering. "I will not repeat myself again! We shall assume that the monkeys are alive, you miserable fur-tick fleeing-the-skin-of-a-dying-sthondat!"

"As you command, brave Hero!"

"Now how shall we kill them? It was *you* who took out my particle-beamer for this test!" The thought of being disarmed put him back on the edge of anger. Not even a nuke. "Shall I slash at them with my *wtsai* as they zip past?"

"This combat couch is very uncomfortable, revered Hero," muttered short(arm). Listening to himself gave Long-Reach perversely practical ideas. "We could toss my combat couch at the enemy."

"Silence!" roared Kr-Captain.

Trainer-of-Slaves was looking around the cockpit for things that might be ripped out. "Gold dust is what we need, but your honor-bearing *wtsai* blade is powerful enough to destroy even the most invincible monkey battleship."

Long-Reach gave a good imitation of a kzin "hisssss" of profound inspiration. "We leave our noble Hero on the line-of-flight, waving his *wtsai*. He leaps," said short(arm). "He strikes!" exclaimed freckled(arm). Then a chorus of arms imitated the spits and snarls of a kzin fight. Skinny(arm) intoned the denouement, "In one blow the enemy ship disintegrates in a blaze of shame! and ever afterwards Kr-Hero radiates bluely from the honor roll of the Patriarch!"

Discreetly, fast(arm) gripped a rod on the back of Trainer-of-Slaves's combat couch in case he had to yank Long-Reach to a safer place.

His lips twitching, Kr-Captain eyed his more yellow-orange than red-orange kzin companion. "Where did you find this five-course lunch?"

"We've been together since Hssin. He really is a good mechanic."

"We seem to have reached a consensus," grumbled the Captain. "Some massive object left along the line-of-flight."

"Perhaps not massive. If we sprinkled gold dust in its path, each grain of dust carries the impact energy of a medium nuclear strike," said Trainer.

Kr-Captain did not believe him. Kzin are not used to combat passes at relativistic speeds. But he did the calculation on his screen. The numbers convinced him. "A little dust in the monkey's path and—nuclear fireball! Easy."

"Not so easy," moaned big(arm). Long-Reach had been consulting among himselves. "It is not just a bigger high-velocity kinetic impact," stated the practical fast(arm). "We now pass into a new realm of the unimaginable where our intuition fails," expostulated the expansive short(arm).

At relativistic speeds, kinetic impact becomes a cosmic ray shower.

Visibly, Alpha Centauri began to creep across the glittering heavens toward Man-sun. The stars shimmered unnaturally through the strengthening polarizer field. Long-Reach, as "honorary" Weapons-Operator, busied himself with a simple project. He removed cameras from missiles. Then he built two makeshift warheads out of bottled oxygen and half their water rations and a few grams of tungsten-carbide grinding powder from his toolkit.

The *Flayer-of-Monkeys* was well equipped with sensors. Seventeen hours from their rendezvous it began to pick up the ramscoop which had an "apparent velocity" of 120 lightspeeds. Electronic amplification constructed a foreshortened image. The scoop was gone. That was a shock. Trainer-of-Slaves thought, at first, that it had been "burnt-off" during the close flyby of A-star, but when he had the *Flayer's* data-link rotate the image to a side view, he saw that the funnel was simply folded-in to a vastly reduced scoop area so that its magnetic field was being used only to protect the crew. In the high mass regions around Alpha Centauri they had simply "furled their sails"!

From a standstill, *Flayer* aimed and directed its missiles down the line-of-flight toward the oncoming UNSN ramscoop which was now occulting Man-sun. The makeshift warheads bled a lethal mist of oxygen and ice-coated tungsten. Then *Flayer* moseyed down the line, away from the ramscoop, bleeding its helium coolant, its cabin nitrogen reserve, plus a bottle of argon—and for good measure the talcum powder that Kr-Captain used to bathe his fur. They returned at full acceleration, stopped, rolled and dropped to the side, rotating to face the coming action. Trainer-of-Slaves mounted the salvaged cameras.

"All they have to do is dodge!" complained Kr-Captain, who was an expert at sixty-g maneuvers.

"They are blind in front. Their course is laser-true. Do you know how much lateral-thrust energy it would take to deflect them a whisker's breadth? They don't command that kind of energy. They are committed!"

The Heroes strapped in to do the warrior's greatest duty—wait.

Half an hour later the nameless ramscoop, its mission still a mystery to its attackers, zipped by, moving faster than any explanation can describe what the eye saw.

The first missile missed.

The second missile ticked through an edge of the folded scoop, ionizing into a fireball genie that lashed a flaming arm out after the ramscoop—too late, too slow.

The ramscoop plowed ahead into the mist.

Valiantly the magnetic field tried to cope with the overload but wasn't equipped to handle the dust or the oxygen. Superconductors overheated. Electrical resistance began to vaporize the surface of the scoop. . . .

Meanwhile hydrogen and oxygen and tungsten, helium and nitrogen and argon, even talcum powder, were ionizing on impact to become tiny superdense nuclear projectiles sleeting through what to a nucleus is mostly empty space: the bulkhead, the air, the life support, the instruments, the protein, the fusion engine, hardened lead-tungsten radiation barriers, everything—and on out to the other side, leaving behind ionized trails as spoor.

A few of these "cosmic rays" collided with the relativistically massive nuclei of the ramscoop, scattering, smashing nuclei into a spray of particle fragments. Mesons flashed into gamma rays and gave birth to muons. Muons lived out their leisurely lives and died. Positrons blinked into existence. Anti-matter screamed out of collisions. Wildly exotic nuclei spat out particles in a desperate search for a new equilibrium. Neutrons bounced and bled into space.

But it was the energy of the stripped electrons that destroyed the monkeys' ramscoop. The ship was essentially transparent to the impacting nuclei—but opaque to the electrons. The kinetic energy of the electrons was instantly transformed to heat.

The flare blazed, then was gone at near lightspeed, doppler-shifting into the red. It had left them. Inertia is implacable. What is moving continues to move.

The UNSN vessel was destined to travel on through the universe as a dense cosmic ray packet, slowly disintegrating and falling apart from its contact with the interstellar medium, from collisions with gases and particles. Billions of years later, in some distant galaxy, scientists might note its passing as an increase in the cosmic ray count from some strange quadrant of the sky. There would be theories about the high metallic content of the rays.

On the return of the *Flayer-of-Monkeys* to the *Sherrek's Ear*, they learned of the ramscoop's mission—a bombing run. From a great distance it had launched precision pellets at specific targets. The relativistic pellets carried the wallop of a nuclear blast.

UNSN spoor was dated and their gunner's accuracy terrible. Whole areas of the arctic zone had been blasted without a single kzin or human casualty because there was nothing there. One lucky hit on a kzin base had killed four thousand Heroes. The human-beasts had taken gruesome casualties, only five percent of which were military related. A miss had impacted the ocean and created a tidal wave that had rolled over four seaside communities.

Kr-Captain was furious. "Why didn't we get it *before* it attacked!"

Alas, warriors were always reminded of the fortunes of war. Only the Black Prides carried the really long distance detection equipment. Both the *Tigripard's Ear* of the Fourth Black Pride and the *Patriarch's Nose* of the Fifth Black Pride had detected the ramscoop two days before the *Sherrek's Ear* had sniffed the electromagnetic scent, but each was almost two light-days from the line-of-flight. By lightbeam they didn't have time to warn Alpha Centauri, and by their fastest fighters, they didn't have time to intercept. The ramscoop was following too closely behind its own electromagnetic arrival notice.

Sherrek's Ear, though it was behind Alpha Centauri, was stationed only eight light-hours from the line-of-flight. Even then, interception would have been difficult had the *Flayer* not been out on a maintenance run in the right direction.

Grraf-Hromfi gave a diagnostic lecture. *Think before you leap.* Never underestimate an enemy. He was furious at himself for assuming that no ramscoop could fly faster than half lightspeed. He was so furious that he set up a whole day of tournament to clean his liver of rage, taking on all comers.

Only months later they learned the covert mission of the ramscoop when Chuut-Riit was assassinated.

CHAPTER 20

(2420 A.D.)

Detection-Orderly-Two summoned Grraf-Hromfi immediately, rousing him from a curled sleep. Hromfi was not the kind who made life miserable for warriors who interrupted his rest. A Hero on duty had the obligation to wake the dead if he felt it in the interest of the Patriarchy. The Commander of the Third Black Pride appeared at the Command Room, naked in his copper red fur except for slippers, grumpy, but not angry.

Analysis began promptly, without preliminaries. The small object had appeared in the heavens out of nowhere, near Rh'ya in the House of the Fanged God's Kzinrretti—the Pleiades. Only light-hours away. Very anomalous gravity pulse. That had set off the alarms. It was also a neutrino source.

Another strange event.

The Third Black Pride was up to full strength. Its Commander ordered a discreet reconnaissance probe. If the mystery pulse came from a small ship, he wanted it captured for interrogation. Quickly. And *not* destroyed.

Instantly, he chose for the mission three pilots he could trust: the first an old warrior with gray in his pelt who had flown *Scream-of-Vengeance* fighters for Chuut-Riit since he was a kit, the second a wild-eyed Hssin barbarian who liked to pick the meat out of his fangs and comb his mane *before* he leaped, and the third, Grraf-Hromfi's most promising son.

They, in turn, were shaken out of their sleep. Each hastily donned goggles so that he could receive his orders. "The intruder is to be disabled, not vaporized!" growled their Commander. "And while I have your attention: a warning." He shifted into the menacing-tense of the Hero's Tongue to jolt their livers. "Our instruments tell us that this object *appeared* out of nowhere. Instruments can be deceived. The best kzin minds can be deceived. *However*, regardless of how irrational the concept, *expect* the object to defend itself by *vanishing* into nowhere. Attack without warning! Disable it immediately! Prisoners are to be taken! If it is an automatic ship, the brain is to be salvaged!"

While the three crews scrambled, he called ahead to make sure that Fighter Command was ready to equip them with *Screamers* modified by Trainer-of-Slaves. He wanted them to have whatever edge he could supply.

Grraf-Hromfi's nose was beginning to sniff the oddness of an alien technology lurking about. On the borderlands of the Patriarchy that could be *extremely* dangerous. But how to put these enigmatic pieces together? He thought of the wooden puzzles of the kzin Conundrum Priests of W'kkai. Eight ways there were to put any puzzle together, and seven of those ways always left an awkward shape protruding.

In the meantime, decisions never waited for a finished puzzle.

How had that unnaturally fast ramscoop dropped off agents? No obvious mode of deceleration suggested itself. At an incoming velocity near lightspeed any agent would have carried the energy of a continent-smashing bomb; the energy release from *any* kind of capsule-braking would have been observed. And how had they penetrated

Chuut-Riit's security to juggle creche feeding procedures so that Chuut-Riit had to face his own ravenously hungry sons behind locked doors? It seemed like magic. Of course it wasn't.

But now—an unauthorized ship that wrote its own unique gravity pulse. Could it be that the ramscoop hadn't delivered the agents? Was there a new player? He remembered Yiao-Captain's visit and his infectious insistence that they point their long distance antenna toward a possible "alien" artifact. Another orphaned piece of the puzzle that "protruded."

This was indeed a time of troubles. After the launch of the three *Screamers*, Grraf-Hromfi brooded briefly on the other troubles while he did his warrior's duty, waiting . . .

. . . troubles enough to incline Grraf-Hromfi to leap off for Man-sun immediately and let these slashing Wunderkzin rip their own faces apart. Octals of the kzin nobility, who had been chafing under the rule of the outsider Chuut-Riit, had seized the assassination as license for them to seize power. Traat-Admiral's claws had been busy with duels. Political chaos.

Regrettably, border barbarians were uneducated in honor! They thought of duels and Ascendancy as honor. They thought of death as Opportunity. They knew nothing of the honor of Loyalty After Death.

Leaving them to their own murders was a warm, meaty idea, but impractical. The Fifth Fleet needed Wunderland as its supply base. They couldn't use Hssin. It was extra light-years away and Hssinkzin were all related by blood and warrior oaths to the original Centauri Conquest Heroes anyway.

The ramscoop attack, itself, had done little damage—but it had brought hundreds of honest slaves to a state of feral defiance. Now *open* defiance was spreading like a plague as the squabbles among the kzin became public knowledge. Ferals had even attacked the Gerning base from space and put its detectors out of commission for three days, long enough to land supplies for some of the renegade animals.

Grraf-Hromfi was in a bad mood because he was just back from a political tour of Wunderland estates. He had picked the most obsequious of the power hungry backstabbers first, cleverly led them to state the claims they believed to be true, challenged them to a duel for false claims, and killed them. After three such contests of honor, the rest of the Wunderkzin learned more quickly the value of careful reason. The power hungry always made the same mistake—they built their True Case, the case they were willing to defend in public, upon false logic.

Detection-Orderly-Two appeared at the oval bulkhead door of the Command Center of the *Sherrek's Ear*. "Sire! May I have your attention again?"

Grraf-Hromfi glanced up. The orderly mock-slashed his face sharply. "You look like you've just bested your father at arm-tug. Found something new? I hope not another of those objects."

"No, Sire, not in this system. But I have something for you to consider, if you will, sir. May I use your data-link?" Without even waiting for assent, he switched on the wall screen and spat-hissed commands to the retrieval slavecrystal. Ribbons of telemetering appeared. "These are mystery signals which the Second Black Pride has been relaying to us from Man-sun for analysis. They started arriving about three months ago, off and on. We have never been sure that they weren't noise, or the artifact of some instrument malfunction."

"You've found something there besides noise?"

"Yes, sir! They all have the same signature as our mysterious visitor. I did a comparison. It came out at the seven-eights confidence level—excellent, considering that the signals we have are only whiskers above the noise jiggles. The *Patriarch's Nose* has been seeing what we have been seeing—but just inside their maximum range."

"*And* 4.3 years ago," muttered Grraf-Hromfi. "We must *never* forget the lightlag. A lot can happen in five years. The Fifth Fleet has doubled in that time. Who knows what cunning they have been up to at Man-sun."

"What do you think the mystery object is, sir?"

"A scout."

"Do you think they've found a way to travel at lightspeed, sir?"

"We'll find out. All detection squads are on full battle alert?"

"Yes, Sire!"

Grraf-Hromfi was now very worried. Was the pulse-object a visitor from Man-sun? He turned up the gravity in the Command Room so that he could pace. On impulse he called Trainer-of-Slaves for a goggle-to-goggle conference. "You paw around with those agonized shrieks-and-spits of demented mathematicians? Their water-hole tracks describing unified field theory?" The virtual image of Trainer-of-Slaves hung in the air like a ghost, fixed in position.

"Dominant Sire, I've inflicted some of that torture upon myself, yes. Do you want an opinion on that pulse?"

"What would this sudden appearance of mass mean?"

"You are suggesting that the pulse tells of the creation of mass out of nothing?" asked Trainer.

"Yes."

"That's impossible, sir. My opinion of the pulse . . ."

"Mate yourself to a sthondat! I didn't ask your opinion, Eater-of-Grass, I asked what it meant!"

"To avoid your insults, I will tell you what you wish to hear. Any mass passing *through* the light barrier would appear as if it had been created out of nothing."

"But this one wasn't moving at relativistic speeds."

"Light barriers can be stationary. I refer you to the work of Ssrkikn-the-Juggler: 'The Event Horizons of . . .'"

"Yes, yes, yes. Can mass pass through an event horizon?"

"Mass pops out of black holes all the time—but it can't bring any information with it. Your faster-than-light ship would fry its occupants down to their unreadable parts. You couldn't find out where they came from—not even the direction."

"You think we'll have a simpler explanation for this pulse?"

"I do, but my opinion is worthless beside your own, Lord Commander!"

"In a few days I may have the object for you to examine—if it doesn't play *hide-the-copper-penny* with us, or worse, put us in cages for some alien zoo! In the meantime I suspect that our visitor may be from Man-home. I want prisoners. There may be injuries in the attack. You are our veterinarian. Take a *Ztirgor* with that autodoc Chuut-Riit gave you, and follow the attack force. Do not attack. Your only function will be to handle human casualties."

Grraf-Hromfi broke the contact and lifted his goggles above his eyes. His ears were folded and buried, his lips trembling over fangs. He didn't like to wait!

CHAPTER 21

(2420 A.D.)

The United Nations Space Navy *Shark* materialized at a radius of 335 AU, some 50 billion kloms behind Alpha Centauri—the location picked to keep them hidden from kzin eyes which might be watching Sol. There was minimal danger at this distance but UNSN Lieutenant Nora Argamentine was still filled with the dangerous excitement of her first combat patrol. She had a special reason for wanting revenge against the kzin.

"It's looking okay, Charlie. Clear field," she said. The detectors were in the green.

Charlie was captain. Prakit was hyperdrive engineer. The other two in the cramped cargo capsule didn't belong. They were special forces, checking out the fate of the *Yamamoto*, silent, untalkative, to be dropped off in their tiny torchship if a closer approach was possible, their mission to kill Chuut-Riit if that ratcat had survived the attempt on his life by Captain Matthieson and Lieutenant Raines. Efficient killers.

Once she got her telescope operational they'd be looking at Wunderland. The *Yamamoto's* relativistic pellets should have left marks—perhaps not visible from this distance. They intended to move much closer, in stages.

Nora wasn't so sure that the *Yamamoto* had even passed through Alpha Centauri yet. It might still be hell bent on its mission, delayed by a patch of low density interstellar gas or a magnetic field breakdown or tanj knew what kind of trouble. The arrival time of a ramscoop was not highly predictable. Raines and Matthieson would be shocked by the level of technological progress since 2409. Wunderland might be liberated before they even arrived!

Prakit fussed over his hyperdrive unit, tuning it up for the next jump. Nora could turn around to encourage him, but there wasn't room for her to help him. She reached out a fist and banged him affectionately on his helmet with her wrist, grinning at him because he was so sober.

"Betsy giving you trouble?"

"Naw, Betsy's just a baby. If I feed her every four hours and bounce her on my knee, she calms down."

Betsy was a new crashlander model and they were lucky to have her. We Made It had been in the hyperspace-shunt engine business two years earlier than Earth, having bought the technology from incomprehensibly alien spacewanderers. The quality of the product from Procyon was better than Earth's—for all of Earth's vaunted technological superiority—and the UNSN crews fought over every shipment from Crashlanding City.

This model could make the transition between relativistic and quantum modes in half an hour when it was fined-tuned. When it wasn't fined-tuned, when Prakit couldn't get the hyperwave functions of the atoms into the proper phase relationship, Betsy just wavered and whined and if you were looking at her you'd feel as if pieces of retina were peeling off the back of your eyeball. Prakit didn't mind.

"She's fastened down," he'd say.

"If you guys need to stretch your legs just stick them up here!" Nora joked, shouted into the hold at the "special forces." Argamentine was a good-natured woman who liked to take care of her men even if that wasn't the style of military women. Her father had been fried in the Battle of Ceres during the Fourth Kzin Invasion when she was a teenager, and somehow she could never give enough love—or hate enough.

"We've got lots of room. There's room for *you* down here," said the first killer because there wasn't.

"Are we there yet! Are we there yet!" cried the other killer.

Nora fixed her two commandoes ration crackers with a little smuggled Camembert, and passed her gift down the "hole." "Don't get crackers in your bed!"

Charlie and Nora spent more than a day between naps taking photos and scanning the volume of space they wanted to move to, about 50 AU farther in. Nora spent a few moments off duty just gazing at the Serpent's Swarm through the electronic image amplifier. "God, Charlie, you've got to take a look at their Belt!" There was no hurry about tasks and no frantic priorities. They were making a very cautious approach. It took only about five minutes to move across 50 AU in hyperspace, but they didn't want to jump into a nest of kzin, not when they needed a minimum of 30 minutes to set up another jump.

Sometimes she had nightmares sleeping in the cockpit. As a teenager on the Iowa farm-city she had imagined such a cockpit around herself at dusk while the stars rose above the trees, imagining herself killing kzin before they got to Daddy, wondering where he was, what he was doing out there—and if he was safe. It had been a nightly ritual, murdering imaginary kzin.

Charlie woke her up with a gentle nudge. "Bandits, at eight o'clock, twenty degrees high. Hey, Prakit, get us the tanj out of here!"

Lieutenant Argamentine was instantly awake and reading the flowing graphics on her screen. She asked her machine questions and the graphs changed in response. "Bandits coming in fast. The doppler reading shows a deceleration of sixty-four g's. Three fighters. They carry the *Scream-of-Vengeance* signature. That's the fighter that got my Dad."

"How much time have we got?" Charlie's voice was rapid-fire, impatient with chatter.

"Easy, Charlie. This is a different war. We aren't fighting the last war. They are *hours* away and we'll never have to engage them." Daddy had had no choice—in a fighter with only a fraction of their maneuverability. "We have time for coffee and crullers." But she was nervously straightening a strand of curly hair. "I used to play this game with my little sister when she was three. I'd let her almost catch me—then I'd disappear." She turned around to smile at Prakit. "How are you doing?"

"I'm doing! I'm doing," snapped Prakit.

The phase-change built up while Prakit counted off the minutes. They fell into a silence of suspense. War was waiting for those few seconds of action. "We love you, Betsy," said Nora when she couldn't stand the suspense anymore.

"Shut up. Let Prakit work."

The hyperdrive suddenly went into a vibration that built up over three seconds and then died. Prakit cursed. "She just reset."

"Plenty of time," said Lieutenant Argamentine.

"I'm going to take five to make an adjustment. We don't want Betsy to burp again."

Charlie was thinking of defensive action now. He rolled the *Shark* so that the jet of its piggy-back torchship was pointed toward the *Screamers*.

"It won't do any good," said Nora. "Those devils are maneuverable enough to get out of the way of anything."

Charlie called down to his special forces. "We're under attack. Get ready to fire the torch. When I call for fire, *fire!*"

"We're going to be out of here!" said Prakit.

This time, as the phase-change built up, nobody broke the silence. Nora stared at the engine even while the sight of it started to "peel" the rods off the back of her eyeballs. *Go!* she prayed. But the *Shark* stayed suspended, agonizingly. Too long.

Betsy shuddered and reset.

"I should rebuild her," said Prakit frantically.

"You had all day!" snarled Charlie. "Time?" He was asking Nora how much time they had to live.

"They're still decelerating. Looks like a boarding. If they decide to take us alive, Betsy will have time. If they decide to make a fast pass, we are dead meat."

"Suits sealed," said Charlie. He meant helmets and gloves. They were already wearing airtights under their uniforms.

"Can't!" Prakit's voice was frantic. "I can't afford to be encumbered. I'm taking her up manually. I can shave off minutes that way. I can keep her in the canyon. I've done it before. The autoguide has been hitting the walls. Shouldn't happen."

They began a third countdown. "Can we do a short tunneling?" Charlie was looking for straws.

"Doesn't work that way. Don't talk to me."

They waited. Again. Finally Charlie could wait no more. "Attention. All crew. I'm arming the self-destruct." If they got into hyperspace, each officer knew how to deactivate it before it blew. If they didn't . . .

They waited. The kzin continued to close.

"Down below. Get your torch primed." Charlie turned to Nora. "You and I are going to practice keeping our ass aimed at the kzin."

"There are *two* bandits coming in. One is doing a boarding maneuver, the other seems to be setting up a fast flyby." Nora twisted that ringlet of hair with her free hand, then found she needed both hands for her combat duties.

"And the third?"

"Hanging back. He'll be able to board *or* kill."

"We'll practice wiggling our ass between the two lead *Screamers*." The *Shark* began to oscillate between two points—the aiming precision-controlled by the ship's computer.

They waited.

"We're going to make it," Prakit said, calm certainty in his voice.

"Fire!" screamed Charlie to his torchmen.

Fire blazed out at the dancing kzin, seeking while the *Screamers* avoided. The countdown continued.

A lurch as the torchship was blown away. Nora saw it cartwheeling across the heavens before it detonated. A moment later the cabin took a hit. She didn't see Prakit sucked into space, helmetless. Her faceplate was triggering to opaque on cue from the explosive glare while actinic light burned the unshadowed half of her uniform. In the instant of death's visitation she saw, not the father's battle doom which had, until now, never left her mind, but a baby sister running toward her with ruffles around the bottoms of her tiny pants . . .

The Hssin barbarian had already flashed past. The second *Screamer* dropped from 60 g's down to a fraction of a g and was only nudging the alien object as the old warrior jumped out with a backpack into the hole that had been opened for him. He knew what he was looking for, but it took him precious seconds to find it. He slapped the backpack down. Its electrogravitic vibrators cut a clean hole through the floor and the backpack disappeared at 230 g's carrying an amputated hunk of the *Shark* with it. The battle-armored Gunner leapt into the cockpit with two airbags, and in a choreographed economy of gesture the old Hero and his Gunner each stuffed a body into a bag, and then hunkered down, waiting for the explosion.

Chuut-Riit's warrior was grinning through his faceplate. "Maybe the acceleration killed it."

But no—the destruct bomb lit up the underside of the *Screamer* and the wreckage of the *Shark*.

The engine was intact. Give that wild Hssin barbarian credit—he could shoot straight! While the old warrior was examining the salvage, Hromfi's son drifted to within hailing distance. The veteran Hero made hand signals to Hromfi's Son: *Where was that laggard, Trainer-of-Slaves?*

Double arm motions signaled back: *On his way.*

The *Ztirgor* rolled and locked onto the bottom of the old warrior's *Screamer*. Its insides had been stripped out to accommodate the autodoc. The body airbags were delivered efficiently and opened. *Messy.* Trainer-of-Slaves had a choice. There was room for only one prisoner in the autodoc. He chose the man-male because he was a male, then changed his mind because the male was dead, space-boiled blood clotting a neck wound, half his back carbonized to the bone. The female would have to do—after all, the man-females *were* intelligent and information could be tortured out of them.

He didn't know if the autodoc could save her. He slashed away the remains of the green UNSN uniform with his claws. He slit, and then peeled off, the airtights. Some of the melted flesh came with it. He didn't know what to do with the bra, trying various techniques of puzzle-solving to unleash it, then in exasperation cut it off. The rest was easy.

The first time Lieutenant Argamentine rose out of her dark delirium she was proud that she knew exactly where she was—she was in the womb-like care of an autodoc. She could feel it all around her and, if she moved her right side, she could feel the needles and the gel. But where was the autodoc?

Memories were elusive. When she struggled with their vapors she saw corncobs cooking in their husks in a bonfire. That didn't seem right. It was too distant. She saw a starving man in a red shirt selling cow dung. Damn! She wanted to remember yesterday! What had happened to her?

She struggled to remember where she was, almost getting it and then forgetting. General Fry! A flash! That was the right clue! The sudden jubilation of knowing. But then it all went away. All she could remember about General Fry was being caught naked in a space-hammock with him by a laughing Colonel who wrapped them around and around in their netted prison.

But that was it! Revelation! Sobs of relief! She was at the hospital in Gibraltar Base and the *Shark* had blown up trying to jump to Alpha Centauri. She faded back into delirium with a desperate need to tell her baby sister that she was all right, and when she woke up again she was talking to General Fry, not sure that the conversation wasn't a dream, trying to convince him that he should still let her go out to fight the kzinti.

The delirium went away. The autodoc became more real. She could feel herself healing. She slept normally. She knew her life signs were good. They would open the box and talk to her. General Fry loved her and he would be there when they opened the box, tenderness in his flinty old eyes. Maybe not. Maybe just a nurse.

When the box opened it was a kzin face staring down at her, tall, massive, hairy, fangs as large as the wolf's in Little Red Riding Hood. It was the first kzin face she had ever seen. She still remembered nothing.

"Sprechen Sie Deutsch?" the ratcat asked. "Ich spreche nicht sehr gut."

Had the kzinti conquered Germany? Had the Fifth Invasion begun just as the *Shark* launched for Wunderland? She was still certain that she was in the Solar System.

The yellow-orange monster brought out a portable translator which began to recite the same phrase in many languages. Finally the cultured electronic voice asked, "What languages do you speak?"

"English," she said.

"My English also is very nasty," spat-hissed the kzin. "Might be machine help us. I learn English. You teach?"

"Thomas Alva Edison!" she swore in utter amazement.

"Brain injury," he growled. "I am decorous and able veterinarian. Skilled with female brains." His ears unfolded proudly. "Much experimentation. Fix all animals."

He set the autodoc to raise her to a sitting position and then held out a dish for her, a stemmed sherbert glass with a spoon. Nora noticed that she was ravenously hungry. Her kzin continued to babble without making much sense. "Please be decorous slave and clean cage," he said. He held a spoonful of his gift to her mouth.

It was vanilla ice cream flavored with chunks of fish.

CHAPTER 22

(2420 A.D.)

While Lieutenant Nora Argamentine recovered in the autodoc of the slave quarters, Hrith-Master-Officer maneuvered his *Nesting-Slashtooth-Bitch* to pick up the wreck of the mystery scout. The floating drydock's maximum acceleration capability was ten g's, thus they took much longer to reach the scout than had the original fighting triad. After grappling the wreck into the repair hangar, Trainer-of-Slaves and his Jotoki mechanics began a meticulous study of the vehicle.

The structure of the engine made no immediate sense. Trainer didn't expect it to. His first priority was to determine its function and limitations, his second, its manufacturability. Then, at leisure, he could reverse-deduce its operating principles with the aid of a team of physicists.

Long-Reach came up with a preliminary assessment of pieces that were clearly gravitic manipulators. That tended to confirm Trainer-of-Slaves's suspicion that the monkeys were now building a sophisticated gravity polarizer that could travel very close to the speed of light, somehow bypassing the "blue-light" bleeding effect that limited all kzin drives.

Such a conclusion fitted the data. The peculiar pulse patterns observed at Mansun and transmitted by the *Patriarch's Nose* were five years old. They looked like a series of tests of a new vehicle. And here, 4.3 years after the completion of the tests, was one of the test vehicles on a test combat mission. Simple. Grraf-Hromfi's fear-hope of faster-than-light magic was just that.

Non-scientists like Grraf-Hromfi, in spite of their admonitions to others, were always leaping to conclusions before they gave their science speculations deep thought. The rumors about an ancient lost civilization that had spanned the galaxy before the birth of the sky's brightest stars provided just the kind of fantasy universe in which to dream of superluminal travel.

Spread the rumor that fossil relics survived on some wrinkled moon of a red star forty light-years thither and kzin, by the herds, would set upon an aimless life of wandering to track down the chimera. The *older* the empire, the *grander* its mysteries. The *deader* the empire, the greater the heights to which it *must* have risen. The Hero's Tongue had a short word for such fantasies: the-forest-bush-with-leaves-that-smell-like-meat. Somewhere there were always kzinti hunting that bush.

Trainer made the rounds, feeding the naked children in the cages. His experimentation schedule had been destroyed by recent events, but animals had to be fed no matter what. Tired, he retreated to his cramped quarters, putting off Long-Reach, who wanted a game of cards.

He rubbed in the talcum to get at the dirt and smell. He worked the powder into his fur, and then massaged himself down with a good vacuum vibrator. That felt good! He found a hard pillow for his head, and stretched out on the bunk. Now for a liver-jolting virtual adventure to get away from life's problems! He popped the goggles over his eyeballs with a little squirt of lubricant.

Would it be possible to find out what Grraf-Hromfi had been watching lately to get him so nervous about superluminal superstitions? The Lord's access file was restricted, but that didn't stop some shrewd guessing. Vocally, he keyed in "faster-than-light," then, after some thought, "ancient empires." He already knew that would give him more than a thousand titles, so he narrowed it down even farther by adding to the list, "fight adventure," and for good measure, since he hadn't had a sniff of kzinrret in years, "female interest."

He got a bad virtual adventure of a Pride of Heroes swept beyond the Border of the Patriarchy by a Warp Storm. They fought giant worms who chased them into the crystalline ruins of a civilization that had been born during the Fireball of Creation, so old it had died before the galaxies could form. Just as the largest worm was about to eat them for slaying its worm warriors, they fell into a crystal room with a perfectly preserved superluminal device that glowed malevolently when they touched it.

Unable to resist temptation, they were transported to the inner glory of the galaxy, to a dark cool world guarded by giants. The giants were protecting the galaxy from the sight of creatures that would destroy all who looked upon them, such was their beauty. Over the dead bodies of the giants they found the svelte kzinrret-like creatures deep at the center of the dark forest, at a wondrous waterhole. Then kzin warriors fell upon each other, slicing, stabbing, clawing until only the greatest warrior remained. Faster than light, he brought his kzinrret-like harem back to the ancient crystalline mysteries and lived happily ever after, hunting throughout the grassy plains beyond his palace.

In the morning Trainer-of-Slaves tried gentle questioning of the lieutenant-beast about her ship. She was not yet fit enough for torture. She volunteered only her name and rank, a puzzling concept for Trainer. He did discover that she was interested in a picture of her youngest sister and so he went through the personal effects of the *Shark's* crew which had survived. That was how he came to be caught up in the illustrations of a "comic book," copyright date: January 2420 After the Damning. Purple-caped flying monkeys KAPOWed ferocious red kzin who were defending the walls of their captured Elvis Presley Monastery.

Something made him check the data-link files on the material they were receiving from Man-home. He didn't keep it in his head but their dating system was well known because of its oddity. All events were referenced from the time they had tortured a Trinity of Criminals on Golgotha Hill, nailing the Father and the Son and the Grandfather to wood so that buzzards (a carrion bird) might feast upon their livers.

The latest events to come in from the *Patriarch's Nose* and the *Tigripard's Ear* carried the Man-sun date: November 2415 After the Damning. By the immutable laws of physics any Solar event later than that was forbidden to Alpha Centauri. 2420 was essentially a taboo future.

Trainer-of-Slaves pondered alien copyright law for a day. Did they have a five-year grace period in which plagiarism was allowed before the copyright applied? In the meantime, his Jotoki disassembled a burned controller. All the intricate electronic parts were labeled *We Made It*. That would have been an ear tickler—if you didn't know that We Made It was a monkey colony more than eleven light-years from Man-sun and thirteen light-years from Alpha Centauri. There wasn't any economical way that such standard parts could be shipped via ramscoop or slowboat.

It was time for another devious conversation with the lieutenant-animal. He researched the transcripts from the First and Second Black Prides, selecting nonmilitary items that she might be willing to talk about. He had an ally in Long-Reach. His

Jotok had discovered that she liked the sweet-bitter berries his slaves enjoyed with their ration of leaves.

He came armed with berry ice cream. She was still suffering from extensive burns and the after-effects of a concussion, but she could remain out of the autodoc for hours at a time, if she was properly chained.

"Fur Face, when does my uniform come back from the cleaners?"

He grinned at her around his fangs in response to her insolence, though his liver wasn't in the expression. The indignities one had to put up with from kzinrretti! He was confused. He wasn't sure which rules applied to sentient females. The grin was purely reflexive.

"All right, already. Sire! I abjectly request some decent clothing, and will kiss the ground you sit on when they appear."

He put on his goggles to consult his English Vocoder, spitting and growl-hissing requests. "I can inject you with chemicals that will make your fur grow," said the elegant voice of the machine. Then a rougher voice. "Auburn hair. Your head," said Trainer-of-Slaves who hated to rely on translators, but he had to give up and let the machine finish his thought. "Your fur will grow in fine and attractive. I have already done the experiments and can guarantee a positive result."

So much for having 98 percent of the genes of a chimpanzee, thought Nora wryly. "Sire! I'm sure your five-armed sewing machine over there could stitch together an elegant little outfit for me in no time at all! *He* gets to wear livery. Why can't *I*? *Please.*"

The monstrous yellow-orange cross between a Basketball Center and Football Tackle didn't understand, but politely listened to the catfight coming out of his translator.

His eyes lit up as he comprehended. "Yes. Livery. Will make red-green garters for—" he consulted his Vocoder—"knees and elbows. You like?"

"I think I need some of that ice cream," she groaned. She had already consulted with Long-Reach about the fish in kzinti ice cream, and he'd promised a fix. He proffered a golden dish of vanilla with purple spots. He'd already stolen some of the berries, an irresistible temptation. She didn't complain. She just ate in silence, sometimes twirling her little curl nervously.

"Long-Reach will now sing Top Ten Songs of 2415 years after torture of Christ Gang. English I can speak. Sing no. Now, Number One on your Hot Shot Hour!" What else could he say? He was taking the words straight off the recording.

The green and red liveried being who was also a quintet began to sing to the naked prisoner of war as she sat among the cramped gray bulkheads of a warship, in chains, eating ice cream. She did not know that she was being deviously questioned. She did not know that this was a substitute for torture, that the answers to his questions were vital to him. Was she a seer? Could she see the future? Could she tell Trainer-of-Slaves of events between 2415 and 2420 that weren't permitted yet at Alpha Centauri?

The five voices that came from the five lung slits in the arms weren't human, but they knew harmony and each word was enunciated with passionate clarity though the accent was no sound that she'd ever heard in her short life.

> "When the night is cold,
> and my arms are bold
> and you are very far away . . ."

It was the song they'd been singing everywhere at the time of her graduation prom, at the end of High School, when the two-year Military Academy course was just a kid's dream. She had to cry. She tried not to, but that only made the bawling worse when it came. Charlie was dead. Prakit was dead. Those tough thugs in the hold, so gung ho to kill kzin, were wasted. Her mission had failed. She had failed her Dad. And she didn't have the least idea about what to do with a seven-foot-tall kzin who courted her with a five-armed singing comedian.

"Humans cry when the ice cream is good," she sniffed to cover herself.

"Berries, ptui!" said Trainer-of-Slaves.

"I think too much," continued Nora, wiping her face.

"That can be corrected," said Trainer-of-Slaves. "I have done the experiments."

"How did you learn these songs?"

"You animals do not keep radio silence."

"You listen to *that*? All the way out here?"

"In past-gone hour, I watch beastly holo, *Blaze of Glory*!"

She wasn't crying anymore. She was grinning. "Lots of kzin killing in that one. I loved it! You monsters killed my beloved Dad. That holo won an award for its acting. Passion, the spirit of mankind that you'll never crush!"

Won an award. She was predicting the future. In November 2415 *Blaze of Glory* had only been *nominated* for an award, one of sixteen. "Bad acting," said Trainer-of-Slaves. "Monkey in kzin-suit, too slow. Wrong emotions. Liver was sick."

He pulled the lieutenant-animal further into the conversation, letting her vent her anger at the kzinti. When she was angry she leapt before she thought. Three more times he caught her predicting the future.

By then he was sure.

He reported his suspicions immediately to Grraf-Hromfi, though the timelag between the *Nesting-Slashtooth-Bitch* and the main body of the Pride was still too great for conversation.

Trainer's old mentor took the news well. His return message read: "So the old warrior can still sniff out a different scent. A superluminal drive is exciting. But it compromises our whole strategic position. We'll have to react quickly. Keep me informed."

In the vast hangar in the belly of the *Nesting-Slashtooth-Bitch* Trainer drove his Jotoki slaves in their dissection of the wreck. How could such a little thing, lost in the spotlights of the hangar, bring back the awful fear he thought he had lost forever? He paced around the hangar, looking down at the alien shape, keeping his feet inside the local gravitic field of the catwalk. His liver was telling him to run in panic. He was no longer the mighty Hero willing to take on the whole Man-system, and after conquering it, to ride elephants to the hunt with monkeys carrying his bedding and his equipment and his kzinrretti in palanquins.

He returned to Lieutenant Argamentine in the middle of the day and opened the autodoc coffin, waking her, to ask her his question directly. "You came here faster than light!" he accused.

She smiled at him without showing her teeth. There were dimples in her furless cheeks. "That's not for me to say."

The answer terrified him and he went away.

With a superluminal drive the animals could penetrate the Patriarchy with impunity. Every system would be isolated, on its own, unable to call on nearby warriors for aid. Heroism would be a sham. A newborn kit could kill his father with unopened eyes. In the face of such unnaturalness, run! The Fifth Fleet should run, should disperse, should hide!

Kzin warriors are taught to obey orders on penalty of death. But it is also instinct for them to create their own orders. A superior officer might be only light-hours away but the skirmish will be decided in minutes. The General Staff might be only light-days away, but battles can be decided in hours. The Patriarch who orders a warrior to the borderspaces, gives his order only once. After that the warrior makes his own orders for a lifetime and trains his sons to train his grandsons to report back that the mission has been accomplished.

The Patriarch requires obedience, but the ruthless Emperor of Light executes all warriors who are not their own Chief of Staff.

Trainer-of-Slaves's internal Chief of Staff was telling him to flee. *How can I be such a coward?* He thought he had conquered cowardice. He'd tried so hard! Desperately he recalled words that Grraf-Hromfi had once tossed away casually—almost unaware of their profound wisdom—words which had found a fertile home in Trainer's mind: "To flee one's duty is cowardice, but to flee while retaining a grip on duty can be the act of a Hero!" Perhaps his mentor would condone fleeing in this extreme case. The thought that he might have an ally in his fear was comforting.

Trainer vowed by his grandfather that wherever he fled, he would bring duty with him. He was in turmoil. He had conquered fear only to be trapped by his own prey. Short-Son of Chiirr-Nig was running on the surface of Hssin with no place to go, every door guarded by the enemy.

He knew that this little engine mounted in the wreck of a tiny ship was the most valuable asset in the whole of the Patriarchy. The entire Fifth Fleet must be devoted to protecting it. If a hundred thousand Heroes died in its defense, that would not be too great a sacrifice. He could flee, but there could be no honorable fleeing without the engine.

By the time the *Nesting-Slashtooth-Bitch* had reestablished its station within the Third Black Pride, Lieutenant Argamentine was well enough for the cages. The berries in the ice cream had done no good at all. She became violent when she was introduced to the cage room, incoherent with rage at the sight of the orphans, even though there were only three of them left uneaten and they had ample room.

"They are children! You monster, they are just children!"

She actually attacked him. To defend himself he had to hold her by the forearms off the floor. That didn't help him because of the well-placed kicks. She had hands-and-feet combat training! He had to toss her away. It was a true kzinrret rage. But most kzinrretti did not get that angry unless you were about to eat *their* kits!

To appease her he did what any kzintosh would have done—he gave her the children and put them all in the same cage and left her alone.

He found it remarkable how quickly that single act calmed her down. She forgot her bruises as she lavished attention upon his experimental tots. He liked that. She was going to make very good breeding stock. The cage was too small for them all—he noticed that—but he did nothing about it because he was interrupted by an urgent message.

There is a kzin saying: *Trouble does not give the single finger; trouble comes with four claws.*

Detection staff reported three more gravitic pulses with the signature of the superluminal drive—but at distances too far to intercept. And Detection was reporting the appearance of an armed feral navy in the Serpent's Swarm. Trainer-of-Slaves had received a priority query from Grraf-Hromfi.

Could Man-sun, as in *right now*, be using superluminal craft to deliver weapon supplies for the feral fleet?

Then Traat-Admiral began to send out ominous directives. The messages were fresh, but their source events were two days old.

Grraf-Hromfi ordered an emergency goggle-briefing of all officers of the Third Black Pride. He wasn't waiting for them to reach his lecture room on the *Sherrek's Ear*, he wasn't even waiting for a quorum of goggle-connects. By the time Trainer-of-Slaves was in link, the chaotic meeting was at full tempest, and though he could not smell it, he could see that the air was redolent of aggression. When Trainer moved his goggled head, he saw no less than five warriors, lips twitching, barely able to repress their fightfever.

His claws extended, almost in self-defense, though he was alone.

Astonishingly, Grraf-Hromfi wasn't analyzing the attack that Man-system had launched with their deadly new weapon. He had gone crazy. He was ranting about mythological warriors who had risen out of the misty past and were attacking the Fifth Fleet along a whole section of the Serpent's Swarm. He was screaming about superkzin mental powers and super technology. He was raving about Wunderkzin Traitors. He was snarling about cyclopean terrors. And he was exhorting warriors to their Final Bravery.

He had already ordered the full Third Black Pride into battle, repositioning all ships down to Alpha Centauri to reinforce Traat-Admiral's fight. Even as Trainer watched through his goggles in awe, Hrith-Master-Officer gave the command for the *Nesting-Slashtooth-Bitch* to move downstar. It wasn't the way Chuut-Riit had taught them to fight.

They were in mid-leap without a thought in their heads. Pure rage.

Without thought himself, Trainer-of-Slaves ripped off his goggles and raced to the hangar where he requisitioned a *Ztirgor* from the upper racks. Long-Reach and Joker scampered to unhook it and swing it down to the airlock tracks for release.

"You are agitated, master!"

"Old Smelly Fur is trying to get us all killed! He wants you dead and he wants me dead! And he's willing to claw the Patriarch in the bargain!"

Long-Reach froze in fear at such wrath in Mellow-Yellow.

Trainer-of-Slaves sped across the heavens to the *Sherrek's Ear* which had already abandoned its great antenna to the blackness—its antenna, its strength! Calmer now, he checked the *Ztirgor* into a receiver bay.

Why was Grraf-Hromfi doing this? *Think before you leap.* Was that his motto because he knew in his liver that he was impulsive, his reflexes faster than thought? Had he needed all these years the constant image of that motto across his eyes to keep his blood in check?

The communications officer knew Trainer-of-Slaves, and knew of his close relationship with Grraf-Hromfi, yet still he tried to discourage Trainer from his call. Trainer insisted, and surprisingly, when Grraf-Hromfi learned he was there, found himself ordered to the Command Center immediately.

"I have a question for you about your captive. Was she behaving like a slave in thrall?"

"Sire! She strikes me as highly feral."

Grraf-Hromfi's eyes were maddeningly bright as they pierced through to Trainer-of-Slaves. "Did you feel the commanding pulse this morning that came with the wallop of a religious revelation driving you to obey?"

"My alarm clock?"

"The Slaver! The scaly green monster with one eye!"

"Sire! I came here because the superluminal drive in the hangar of the *Bitch* is the only one we've got."

"Yes? And?" growled Hromfi.

Trainer was in a rage that this stupid old fossil couldn't see the obvious. "We are leaping without a thought in our head! Think before you leap! Remember? We have to get that drive to Kzin-home!"

Grraf-Hromfi bared his fangs and fell into his dangerous fighting crouch. "You mock me!" he threatened. "You mock me with my own words, a son stabbing his father!" At this commotion the Lord's Second Officer turned to watch, almost ready to interfere should Trainer become dangerous. Hromfi was virulent. "You haven't been listening, youngling! What do you know of ancient empire and craft and war? Nothing."

Trainer-of-Slaves was already regretting his insolence and moved into a more propitiative posture. "I could never be so great a student of mythology as you, Dominant One."

"Mythology!" Grraf-Hromfi was now *grievously* enraged. "Five octal-squared years past, these audacious monkeys who are giving us so much trouble found and revived one of those one-eyed monsters. That is mythology?"

"I am glad that it amuses my Lord to wander among the fairy tale shelves of the Munchen library." *Why am I goading him?* Trainer-of-Slaves was terrified by the ferocity he had unleashed in his mentor who was now clearly angry as well as insane.

Hromfi was circling Trainer, growling out his words, slowly, threateningly. "They found this horror. They released him out of monkey curiosity and he took over the minds of all the monkey vassals within range. They'd still be in thrall—but 'monkey-daffy; monkey-lucky.' They tricked him back into his stasis suit and turned it on. And *then* do you know what those hollow-brains did? They put him in a museum. Their silver Sea Statue."

Grraf-Hromfi spun from the confrontation to calm himself. He dropped into one of the command chairs and growled and spat out his rage at the instrument panels. Then he turned over his shoulder and spoke to Trainer-of-Slaves again.

"You speak to me of that superluminal drive of yours. Where do you think it came from? You've seen monkey technology. You destroyed their pitiful ramscoop. You've refitted their quaint torchships with gravitics. You've seen their weapons. Could they have created a superluminal driver for spaceships? Not likely. *Impossible.* But from evidence on a dozen worlds, students of the ancient mysteries suspect that the Slavers could travel faster than light.

"We are confronted with a W'kkai puzzle. And I have put it together with no protrusions. The monkeys have released their Sea Statue again. The ultimate weapon against the Patriarchy. It was this ancient beast who must have given them their superluminal ships and he is here now, in the Serpent's Swarm, because I *felt* his mind and my officers are with me because they, too, *felt* that mind which would make slaves of kzinkind! If you hadn't been asleep, you too would believe!"

Trainer-of-Slaves was always awed by Grraf-Hromfi's ability to convince. Still it was foolish to take as true a tale told five lifetimes ago by the member of a race whose individuals were known to lie at every opportunity. Indeed! One eye and green scales!

"Sire! I am here to request permission to take the superluminal drive unit to Kzinhome."

Grraf-Hromfi rose from his chair. He walked over to Trainer-of-Slaves. His nose came to Trainer's forehead and his shoulders were broader. "Permission denied. Do you think you'll get anywhere if we fail to destroy this menace? His mind will pluck you right out of the sky and bring you whimpering to his feet."

The fear was overpowering. Never in his life had Trainer-of-Slaves defied anyone, not his father, Chiirr-Nig, not Puller-of-Noses, not Jotok-Tender, not his friend, Ssis-Captain. He was universally sweet-tempered with his military associates. He had always accommodated Grraf-Hromfi's wishes, and the wish of every officer who held authority above him. His inclination now was to flatter Grraf-Hromfi into letting him disappear into interstellar space with the wreck of the *Shark*.

"Sire! In your great wisdom you have advocated thinking before leaping . . ."

Grraf-Hromfi slashed this impudent warrior's vest through to the flesh of his chest beneath. "Do you think that I would let *you* flee from a battle, Eater-of-Grass? Only Heroes who are eager to die in battle can carry the burden of flight." He gestured to two tall kzin guards. "I cannot kill this coward. Take him back to the *Bitch* and put him in hibernation. He'll die there in battle, and if we survive . . . I'll deal with him then."

The Lord Commander of the Black Pride was desperate to eliminate the smell of abject fear from his command room.

CHAPTER 23

(2420 A.D.)

Long-Reach was in a panic argument with himselves. The ship was no longer a safe place. Mellow-Yellow was in danger. Mellow-Yellow was in hibernation. Kzin warriors were talking about slashing the throat of Mellow-Yellow for cowardice. They were rough with him when they put him away. After the battle they would take him out and kill him. Joker had heard them say so while he was relining the gravity walks. Long-Reach felt grief in the tips of his thumb-fingers. No more card games. No more currying that fine pelt.

He felt an unexplainable desolation.

Fourteen Jotoki were directly bonded to Mellow-Yellow. In the slave quarters these fourteen bundled together, avoiding conversation even with Jotoki who were bonded to other kzin. Arms entwined, they chattered and moaned and sifted thoughts among their brains. The need to help Mellow-Yellow was unsettling and painful because they could *not* help him. Disoriented, they set about their tasks mechanically, then returned to the slave quarters to share their agony.

Long-Reach knew that the man-beasts had to be fed, but while he went through the motions he was remembering another such terrifying time of threat—long ago on another world. Simpler times. Only one kzin had been menacing Mellow-Yellow then, not a ship full. The challenge had taken place in the birth-haven of Long-Reach among the trees and swamps and caverns that had nurtured himselves during the growing-up and were almost alive enough to come to his aid when he needed to call upon a glen or ridge between hillbanks. The very land had helped him kill that other kzin.

Now there were only the cold corridors of a ship and pipes and snaking power lines and catwalks and patrolling warriors. Killing one kzin to save his master had been the most troubling horror of his life. To kill a whole shipload was unthinkable, enough to make his arms disconnect from each other and send him stumbling in an uncoordinated scramble of arm-legs.

Nevertheless, that is what he, himselves, was thinking.

Lieutenant Argamentine knew that her routine had been upset. That bizarre kzin who was called Mellow-Yellow by his five-armed followers disappeared to be replaced by a taciturn kzin who was larger and redder, whose only function seemed to be that of interrogator. He took her from her cage, never very gently, never so roughly that he hurt her. Together they rode a capsule to his tiny torture chamber. He questioned her. He brought her back to the charge of the slaves, forgetting her until the next time he needed to torture her.

She had grown up dealing with difficult people, including her father, and she had long ago developed a facility of manner with intractable personalities—but this one fitted none of her patterns. He was *disturbingly* alien. He was impatient with chitchat. He was impossible to reason with about anything like her living conditions or the needs of the children. He was interested only in answers and he was impatient with devious answers.

When she did not give him what he wanted he turned immediately to torture, preferring agonizing nerve-stim to mutilation. But she got no feeling that he was interested in torture. He had an uncanny sensitivity, almost as if he was a latent telepath. When she didn't *have* answers to his questions, he blandly moved on to the next question. But if she did have answers and tried to withhold them, he became ruthlessly persistent.

Desperately, she tried to get an angle on him. He was curious about the strangest things.

"Sea Statue at UN Comparative Cultures Exhibit. You know?"

She knew, but like most flatlanders, she'd never really wanted to know much about the one-eyed thrintun monster who lived inside, frozen in stasis. It was a story three hundred years old. She was tortured into remembering.

Had the Sea Statue been moved?

Had the Sea Statue been transported to Alpha Centauri?

Had the Sea Statue provided the principles of superluminal flight?

Were the UNSN officers in thrall?

War bred the strangest paranoias from its soup of deceptions, misinformation, misdirection, and poor communication. And lack of any cultural basis for understanding.

When she was thrown back into her cage after her last session, the silent children seemed to know that she was hurting and her mind half incoherent. They just held her. They were too numb, and too maltreated themselves, to be able to give her much. Finally the food came.

"You're late. We're starving," said Lieutenant Argamentine. She wasn't even ready to try to figure out a five-brained spider.

The three children were very quiet around Long-Reach. He fed them—but he was also the chief lab technician in a place where they were mere lab animals. She couldn't read Long-Reach's emotions. He had no face. A mottled pot-belly where his face should have been. His eyes and arms were expressive but she didn't know how to read their mobility.

"Bean mash on kzin bones," said Long-Reach's translator with an appropriately apologetic melody. Short(arm) took umbrage with the vocoder and offered an English translation. "Not kzin bones! Shudder. Groundified bone and marrow, rolled to cracker shape. Bonding heated. Kzin rations for ship. Not kzin bones! Kzin not cannibals except with kits of wrong father."

Freckled(arm) made an interjection to correct an aspect of short(arm)'s terrible English grammar.

"Are you going to stay around for another English lesson?" asked Nora. She didn't really want this strange creature to go. The torture was demoralizing her.

"No. Must go. Mellow-Yellow in trouble," lamented Long-Reach. "Bad, bad, bad," commented three of his arms in a round-robin.

"I haven't seen him for a while." Was she better off with Mellow-Yellow or Red-fur?

A pause while the vocoder sorted out the conversation. "We are all doomed by death," said its speaker. "A big battle," kibitzed skinny(arm). "Ship has been recalled to Alpha Centauri," intoned big(arm).

She decided to exact some intelligence of her own. "Why are they interested in thrintun slavers?"

"What?" Long-Reach consulted the vocoder and drew a blank.

"One-eyed scaly monsters who take over minds. They died in a war with the tnuctipun billions of years ago. I've just had my memory forcibly refreshed," she said ruefully.

"Kzin worry about free-will," said Long-Reach. "All the time, worry. Warrior fetish. Always must be in control. Didn't you feel the wave of intrusion? Myselves went right to the kitchen and made up hot soup for Mellow-Yellow, then wondered why I do this. Pleasant feeling to serve others. Kzin no like."

Suddenly Nora was remembering an impulse of feeling that had overwhelmed her just days ago. Devotion. An enormous need to *help* someone. She had supposed it was something Mellow-Yellow had put in her food to make her talk. "There's a Slaver loose down there?"

"Was. Big explosion, hour ago here, days ago there. Don't know what's happening today. Tomorrow we find out. We're all doomed."

"Are you a slave?" she asked, curious about the creature's response. She found out that his vocoder couldn't translate the word for him, and she couldn't explain it to him. The nearest he could come was the English word "friend." As in "only friend."

Redfur the Torturer didn't come back. But a delegation of four Jotoki did. They seemed ill at ease in their body motions. It was impossible for her to stop trying to read expressions off the belly-faces that sat on their mouths even though she knew they weren't faces. The shoulder-mounted eyes watched her. They wanted something. They gave her a delicate dish of stuffed leaves that tasted like Greek *dolmadakia*, vine leaves, almost as if it were a ceremony. Another presented her timidly with green and red garters for her elbows and knees.

They were bargaining! "Yes?" she asked, gently, not knowing what to do with her revelation.

"Our master wished to take this ship out of the battle," intoned their translator, which had been carefully pre-programmed.

"An interesting idea," replied Nora, warily.

The four were talking among themselves in a spitting language that sounded like a corruption of the Hero's Tongue. Finally the translator spoke again. "Your race and the kzinti are enemies."

"Perhaps someday . . ."

The translator wasn't listening to her. It continued. "Men kill kzinti. Kzinti kill men. Is this not so?"

"It's war."

"You are military man," said Long-Reach, impatient with the machine. "Your ice cream desire is to kill all kzin. I understand mankind."

No you don't, she thought while she twiddled with her curl.

"We work, side together, like many arms."

What she was hearing sounded like mutiny. It also sounded like they had an exaggerated respect for her powers. A naked woman with garters was a threat to no one. "I have been defanged and you will notice that I am locked behind bars."

Long-Reach opened the cage and quickly closed it. "Bargain," he said. "We make bargain." She could hear the tremor in his voices, and she was sure she could see his arms shaking. He was terrified. She could almost see him running. The tremors came from inhibiting the flight.

"What can I do for you?"

"You kill all kzin, but one. We free Mellow-Yellow. Bargain? Mellow-Yellow live."

"I'm quite willing to let Mellow-Yellow live," she lied. She almost saw the four of them relax. "What makes you think I might be able to kill all kzin?"

"Ferocious monkey warriors defeat kzin. We know. Monkey squash kzin ships. We repair. We scrape kzin off wall."

Were they thinking that if they let her out of her cage she might not settle for anything less than the death of *all* kzin on board? As if she had a hope of killing even one of the behemoths! It hadn't slipped her notice that her interrogator had two sets of human ears casually attached to his belt.

"Mellow-Yellow live. Bargain?" Long-Reach repeated.

Why were these creatures so bonded to Mellow-Yellow? Why was he different from the others? His name translated as something like Overseer of Inferiors, or Animal Manipulator. Perhaps he had a chemical hold on them? Perhaps he was an expert at some kind of hypnotic conditioning? No matter. The irrational loyalty was there. She remembered the day she had attacked Mellow-Yellow, ready to die, because he was cruel to children, and Long-Reach had been watching her with four eyes. If she had hurt Mellow-Yellow, Long-Reach would have killed her.

It was a strange bargain. If she protected their master (from her cage?), the Jotoki were hers.

Was it a good bargain? It was dangerous to have naïve allies. Were they as naïve as they seemed? Were they treacherous? How much did the kzin trust their slaves? How reliable were these Jotoki? What skills did they have? What skills did *she* have? What weapons did she have? Nothing. She knew the formula for a nerve gas that would kill kzin and was harmless to men, but even given the equipment, she wouldn't have known how to manufacture it. This whole situation wasn't part of her Gibraltar Base training.

No, it wasn't a good bargain, but it was the only bargain she had.

"I'm no match for a kzin," she said. She wanted them to tell her something.

"You have military mind. We have arms. Ship is our playground."

They began to feed her more often. They cleaned cages and when they moved her to a new cage, she found a ship map on the floor. She was surprised that they controlled the cage locks. They *were* trusted. Or was it just that Mellow-Yellow trusted them and in the heat of battle that kzin's duties had not been fully reapportioned? Why was he in disgrace?

Her allies came up with vicious little plans. They had molecular trip-wire that they could set up that would cut a kzin's legs off. They knew how to rig a gravity floor plate into a booby trap that would grab a kzin in a sudden six-g field. But when she tried to plan with them, she understood why they needed her. What they didn't have was an overall strategic sense. When one starts a battle, it sets off an avalanche of activity. The good commander is able to predict where the avalanche will go, and have his responses already in place.

She could make detailed plans, but could they follow orders? Can a slave follow orders? She was willing to bet that they could.

Some of the events she wasn't going to be able to predict. So far as Nora knew, the human hyperfleet was already fighting at Alpha Centauri. That was one wild card—she could be vaporized by her comrades before the mutiny even started. On the other hand, the *Nesting-Slashtooth-Bitch* was the most sluggish ship of the Third Black Pride and so would reach its new station many days later than the maneuverable elements of its squadron. If the mutiny could be carried out before they reached the battle, their chances were much better. Haste was in order.

Lieutenant Nora Argamentine did not expect to survive the mutiny, so she was optimizing her strategy for maximum kzin kill. She wanted as many kzin dead as possible before the inevitable moment when her plans fell apart. Meticulously, with the information the slaves gave her, she targeted every kzin on board the *Bitch*. Mellow-Yellow was at the bottom of the list. He could be killed by flooding his hibernation cell with liquid nitrogen—but not while she still needed her Jotoki allies.

They were able to manufacture her nerve gas. That surprised her at first until she remembered what Mellow-Yellow had been doing to the children. He had some kind of "grant" to do "medical research" on humans. No, she was not going to spare that one.

The Jotoki fiends even cobbled together hand weapons. They had a spaceman's usual devout respect for high-velocity projectiles and high-energy cutting tools. The result was a launcher for a concussion pellet that could hemorrhage a kzin's insides but wouldn't damage bulkheads.

The *Bitch*'s manufacturing shop was designed for interstellar war. You didn't fly in spare parts to an interstellar battle, you tooled up for anything, on the spot, at a moment's notice and burped out one-of-a-kind items. It was incomprehensible to Nora that such facilities could be trusted to slaves, but then she wasn't a kzin.

The attack began in the dorm. The airseal bulkheads sealed without triggering alarms—gas flooded the rooms, stayed, and was flushed out—the airseal bulkheads unlocked. A gas-killed kzin looks like he's asleep except that he's not breathing.

Jotoki who were not already at their stations on regular jobs began to move to their assigned position. The Command Center was gassed. Hrith-Master-Officer was comprehending what was happening to him at the same time his nervous system was failing to obey his order to sound a gas alarm. The officer farthest from the air purifier did issue that alarm before he died.

The surviving kzinti moved efficiently into their battle armor, which was gas-proof—alert, thoroughly alarmed, and ready for action. They were primed for orders, and they got them: "Battle Stations!" That was the wrong order. The ship was being attacked internally, not from an external threat. "Boarding Stations!" would have been a better order. "Damage Containment!" might have worked. Even "Abandon Ship!" would have collected them into a defensible position. "Battle Stations!" just dispersed them to known destinations, along known routes, across Jotok-devised booby traps. A Jotok, in a rack-held *Ztirgor*, picked off the kzin who tried to pass through the hangar.

Lieutenant Argamentine was master-minding the battle from a tiny munitions closet which had been jury-rigged into the *Bitch*'s main communications net, finally wearing trousers and a shirt she'd *ordered* her Jotoki allies to make for her, plus an ugly kzin oxygen mask, retailored for her head. She knew the jig was up when a kzin commando team retook the Command Center, killing the occupying Jotoki, and cut off her contact.

They could trace her location.

She evacuated instantly, taking the best position she could, facing down both legs of an L-shaped corridor, her only weapon the improvised concussion-pellet launcher. Hunkering behind her portable stun-gun barricade, she knew that this was where she was going to die. She wondered what the kids would think when they came out of sedation. She was damned if she wanted to die in a cage.

Without warning, a stun-bolt ripped down the corridor, covering the advance of a kzin clean-up team. The barricade hardly did any good at all. She felt the bolt hit her back, probably from a bounce off a wall, numbly noting that her fingers were now so frozen that she could hardly fire off the concussion rounds—one at the lead kzin, one at the kzin behind, and one for good measure at the blind bend from whence they had appeared. The blasts went off. She was suddenly deaf and her paralyzed legs refused to propel her out of the way but she saw the disabled kzinti carried toward her down the gravityless corridor. She felt the thuds on the wall as she was buried in kzin armor.

When a little girl studied war, odd things stuck in her memory. Now she was remembering the fragment of a twentieth-century Frenchman's letter from a hospital near Reims describing how he had spent four days buried with eight dead comrades on top of him in a shell-destroyed trench.

The duty of a soldier is to wait. And while one is waiting, paralyzed, life goes on. Three Jotoki raced around the corner, chattering in their pseudo–Hero's Tongue. Efficient hands rolled the kzinti over, removed their helmets and slit their throats. They stripped the corpses of weapons, piled the armored bodies in a neat barricade for Nora, reloaded her launcher, and propped her up facing down the L. Two of the beasts skittered away. The third remained just long enough to give her a shot of paralysis antidote—effective for a kzin but no better than a bee sting for a human. Hands rearranged her trousers, and then he, too, was gone.

The duty of a soldier is to wait, soaked in the blood of an enemy, fingers unable to fire, praying that the fingers will come back to life before it is necessary to kill again.

Daddy had been burned alive.

Eventually Long-Reach arrived, arguing with himselves about how to help Nora. Three Jotoki carried her away for a bath by multitudinous arms. While her mouth was still only able to make the noises of a baby trying to discipline its tongue, she learned of their impossible victory.

Lieutenant Argamentine couldn't speak her joy but her eyes could leak. *If General Fry could see me now, naked and being bathed by monster slaves!*

Long-Reach was combing out her hair with three hands, caressing the auburn richness of it, fluffing it, adding proteins to it to give body. He knew how to take care of a pelt!

"Did . . . Mellow . . . Yellow . . . survive?"

"Slept through it all. Like a kit."

Nora grinned to herself. *One to go!* A half an hour later, when she could speak coherently, she suggested the dehibernation of Mellow-Yellow.

Long-Reach was uneasy. The other Jotoki became somber in their fear. "Not now. First we clean up ship. Blood! Dents! Awful mess!" Big(arm) added somberly, "He must never know." Freckled(arm) shivered. "The rage if he finds out . . ."

"Lie to a kzin, and it's the torture chamber for you," said Nora knowingly.

"The mutiny never happened!" said Long-Reach adamantly. "All is as it was."

The Jotoki knew enough about gravity polarizers to alter course. They were almost at turnover by the time of the revolt and were doing a quarter of the velocity of light. They didn't try to decelerate. They just changed direction—with deep space as their only destination.

One team spaced the kzin corpses. Each corpse was ejected violently by the polarizer field in a transient restabilization of the ship's energy and momentum balance. Other teams cleaned and scrubbed and repaired. Long-Reach slaughtered all Jotoki who were bonded to deceased kzin, dressing and storing them for Mellow-Yellow's table.

For the first time in millennia, the ancient conquerors of the barbarian warlords of Kzin-home commanded their own warship.

CHAPTER 24

(2420 A.D.)

Hibernation did damp the immediacy of the thoughts and rages with which one went into hibernation, but there was no memory loss upon revival. Waking up and expecting to confront Grraf-Hromfi and possible death, to find oneself instead the master of a kzinless lumbering drydock headed off in the general direction of kzinspace was a disorienting experience. At the minimum he should have rated a navigator and crew.

Trainer-of-Slaves's first assumption had been that Grraf-Hromfi had undergone a drastic change of liver, had seen the reasonableness of the request to flee the battle with the superluminal motor and had simply sent him on his way. It was the only *logical* assumption. Everything was in order. The *Shark* was still in the hangar—the first thing he checked—and the *Bitch* was shipshape.

But Grraf-Hromfi *didn't trust Jotoki to massage his pelt*, let alone take command of a ship. Something else had happened. Trainer didn't have the time to ponder. He was new to ship command and priority tasks kept cropping up and demanding his attention. Still, he noticed things.

The record of orders was absent. The log file was too clean. The transfer of command was broken. *When* had his Jotoki been forced to take command? He couldn't even locate information about how the developing battle at Alpha Centauri had ended. The last he'd heard it had been chaos—UNSN superluminal vehicles winking on, Grraf-Hromfi foaming at the mouth about mythical green-scaled monsters trying to take over his mind, a feral flotilla of animal rockjacks converging on the monster, and a massive mobilization of the Fifth Fleet to the wrong rendezvous at the wrong time.

Now not a word of that. Not a sniff of kzin fur. Not a trace of kzinti hierarchy. Almost, a discontinuity.

In all this pastoral calm—no battles, no emergencies—serenity should have been master. But his Jotoki, who had clearly been in command of the ship in violation of standing admiralty orders, were terrified—that's what was wrong.

His slaves were honest. If Grraf-Hromfi had found himself in a hopeless situation and had ordered the *Bitch* to flee under Jotoki control, they would have said so and been proud of Grraf-Hromfi's trust. But they were all running around, tripping all over their arms, trying to please him, inventing orders to be obeyed—and keeping their mouths shut.

It was plain that they were expecting their mild-mannered Mellow-Yellow to murder them all. Each of them had the fear of the Fanged God in all of their five hearts. Trainer couldn't bear to question them. He insisted, absolutely, upon the truth from his slaves—but sometimes the truth was better left unsaid. He had never, ever, questioned Long-Reach or Joker or Creepy about the death of Puller-of-Noses. The subject had always been taboo.

Murder in the service of loyalty.

Jotok-Tender had mumbled about Jotok loyalty as if it were a sin when he was drinking too deeply of his contraband sthondat blood. The rumors about their treachery were true but Trainer had always put that down to poor slavecraft. Was it more? Did a threatened bond sometimes lead to a murderous frenzy?

He examined the ship for evidence of murder, and found not a mark. His suspicion was absurd, of course. He knew his Jotoki very well. Perhaps they were capable of well-meaning murder, but they were *not* capable of *organized* mutiny. Their education had been standardized for ages. Military prowess was not part of it. Indeed, military prowess had been systematically bred out of their root stock.

But there was something else he was noticing. His Jotok slaves were carefully shielding him from that she-man Lieutenant Argamentine. They were taking care of the cages all too well. He purred at such a revealing insight. In the mystery surrounding his revival, he had forgotten her, and no one had reminded him.

He had pity for his Jotoki, but he had no scruples about questioning a man-beast. She must be healthy by now.

While he thought about it, he spent time in the Command Center checking the *Bitch's* course towards faint R'hshssira. Navigation was not his specialty, but he'd spent half his life out under the interstellar heavens absorbed by the majesty of the celestial sphere. He had the lore of perhaps twice octal-cubed stars etched into the passion lobe of his liver. Finding his way was no problem. It was avoiding the treacherous shoals of mass that was the navigator's art and pride and nightmare—and at that Trainer was an amateur.

Nora Argamentine was in a sullen mood when he found her in the cages. His Jotoki had exceeded their authority by merging four of the barred boxes into one large space for her and the children, but he had to agree that the new arrangement was a better one. The three children cried when they saw him.

"Silence, slaves!" he said, and they were silent.

"So, your little tricksters let you out of the cold box, did they? They had the command of a whole warship to themselves, and they let *you* out."

"I trust my Jotoki in all things. But Grraf-Hromfi would never have trusted this vessel to any Jotok without a wide-awake kzin on hand," he said. "I'm curious how that happened."

"Ask them!"

He unlocked the cage, and turned to the apprehensive children to reassure them. "I'll only be questioning her for a short while. She'll be right back."

He pulled her out by the arm, and kept her more or less at arm's reach so that she couldn't attack him, thus propelling her to the inter-floor capsule station. She tried to shake off his arm. "I'm not fighting." But she was resisting every Patriarch's toe-length of the way.

In the kzin-sized chair of the torture chamber, he strapped her down and attached the instruments. He set up the vocoder to monitor their conversation so that there would be no misunderstandings. "Tell me the truth and there will be no pain," he said gently.

"I've been here before and I *killed* my torturer."

The muddled situation was beginning to clear. Female acumen could only be a tiding of vast troubles. "Hr-r, this is the truth?"

"Why should I cover for your perfidious little tricksters?"

"They betrayed you?"

"They tranquilized me and put me back in the cages. They betrayed *themselves*."

"What happened? I can't question them—their fear produces an agony of pity in my liver regions. My shame is that they are my friends."

"Friends? Together we cleaned you ratcats out of this ship in half an hour. They took a positive pleasure in the mayhem. I made one mistake." She spat at him. "I let *you* live."

There was a low growl in his voice despite himself. Here was the leader of the mutiny. Now events made sense. "Details!" he insisted.

She told him where he could stuff his tail.

He turned on the nerve-stim.

"All right, all right. Why should I cover for your monsters?" There was no way for her to withhold the story of the mutiny—but she could make him work for it. She described the attack as if it were a spontaneously lucky uprising, careful not to mention the nerve gas, steeling herself to resist "offering" its chemical structure if he pressed her—but he didn't ask for details. He was too appalled by the total picture. She sensed, surprised, that he didn't *want* to see his Jotoki as killers. He even released her restraints as a way of telling her that he wanted no more answers.

"I should space them all!" he roared.

"Why don't you? I'll help!"

"I've had that dilemma before. Then who would cover my back? Kzin who hunt alone are vulnerable." He whacked his tail against the bulkhead in annoyance. "You led them astray," he accused.

"Will you execute me?"

"Females are not responsible for their actions. It is not your fault that you are intelligent. The Fanged God has his jokes."

"I can see you on my living room rug by the fireplace," she snarled, twisting her curl.

He did not reply. Her story of massacre had sobered him. What *other* terrible consequences of female intelligence were there? A thinking, talking female could severely disturb a household by teaching what she knew to her litter. His mind reeled at the thought of female military genius within a kzinrret palazzo! They would steal the younglings! They would turn youth against wisdom!

How unlucky for a race to have been cursed with such a cruel twist of evolution. He felt his first stab of pity for mankind. In the last two hundred generations, just on Man-home alone, there had been more wars than in all the expanse of Kzinspace and more death by war on that one planet than in all of the wars waged by Heroes to protect the Long Peace. What else could arise while female quickness sowed dissent between father and sons?

Such a waste of the feminine essence which could be better employed in play with kits and on the mating couch with males.

He put the torture implements away. A black-fingered paw touched her auburn tresses. He was missing his long lost Jriingh. "Do not be afraid of me. I am a strange kzintosh, known for the unwarlike feelings I have in my liver for my slaves. You have beautiful natural hair. I shall see to it that you grow a fine pelt over your nakedness. You have your feral flaws, but your intelligence can be improved."

This female was perfectible. No hurry. It was a long journey home.

CHAPTER 25

(2420–2423 A.D.)

The *Nesting-Slashtooth-Bitch* was sluggish but her cruising velocity was as high as any large kzin warship. Three and a half years was the estimated trip-time to Hssin, which was 2.6 light-years from Alpha Centauri. Detection was unlikely even though they might now be traveling through hyperdrive infested space. Hssin lay 5.6 light-years to the north of Man-sun. Nobody could patrol that much volume any more than an acorn could patrol an ocean.

He was going to have problems with his female. Keeping experimental animals caged was expedient, but a cage would not do for slave breeding and he was anxious to begin his breeding program. He had a sufficiency of frozen sperm. He probably *did* need to do more experimentation, but without a source of experimental animals, that was no longer an option. He'd have to use what he already knew.

But if he gave the Nora-beast the breeding room a female needed, even built her a kzinrret palazzo with enough space for her children, he was leaping into trouble. He picked the larger of the crew dormitories for her, but left her in her cage while he refitted the room—think before you leap!

The original dorm layout was not sabotage-proof. If he were building an ordinary palazzo, that would not matter. But he knew very well that she was dedicated to destroying the *Shark*—and would give her life to do so. Next on her priority list was killing the one kzin she'd missed when she'd used his Jotoki against the Patriarchy. Feral intelligence in a female was a captivating nuisance. He dare not underestimate her.

The walls he had his Jotoki armor-plate. He built in monitors to watch her for dangerous behavior. They weren't the most intelligent of monitors but they probably wouldn't gas her too frequently if she was careful.

When her chambers were ready, he took her for a visit. She was wearing clothes again, he noted disapprovingly. They weren't decorative but they did cover her tail-like baldness.

"I like it," Nora said laconically. "It reminds me of the *Alabama*. The munitions room."

"The Alabama?"

"You wouldn't know the war. The USN *Alabama* was a seagoing battleship with a steelclad munitions room that could take an internal explosion—hopefully without sinking the ship."

He listened and then ran her words through his vocoder to make sure of what he'd heard. Dangerous memories. For all he knew, she could make high explosives out of paper and spit. Her memories would have to be replaced, and her emotions would have to be altered, and her facility with language crippled. While she had her memories and her full repertoire of skills, she was dangerous. Perhaps he could add some aesthetically pleasing fur. Then he would be able to relax and enjoy her.

In the meantime he needed her memories.

To please the Nora-beast he let her design the furniture for herself and the children.

"You're really going to let me have whatever I want?" She looked at him with a whimsical smile that he knew was amusement, but which he couldn't help but read as a subliminal warning of attack. Her fingers were twirling with that long curl of hers.

"No weapons," he admonished.

"I want a big stuffed pillow that I can flop into."

His mind worked on that one. How could a pillow be turned into a weapon to kill him when he least suspected it? This was a nerve-racking game. He imagined himself being smothered. His mind's eye watched her soaking the stuffings in nitric acid to make high explosive, while she wove a noose out of the shreaded covering. None of the scenes were plausible. "All right," he said.

He was astonished at the ornate furniture she designed. A bed with a satin roof and adjustable gravity? Golden man-babies with wings, dancing on the headboard? He grumbled but had his Jotoki make them for her, scrounging substitutes for satin and wood. They had to reprogram the weavers and the plastic molders.

The time went quickly because there was so much to do. Deciphering the superluminal drive was top priority. Trainer-of-Slaves couldn't be reckless with the device, couldn't test it to destruction because it was the only one he had. He developed a two-pronged approach.

(1) Analysis. Isolate the sub-units. Attempt to craft a duplicate of the sub-unit. Test. The *Bitch* was a repair facility that could make any part in the kzin arsenal. He practically owned a prototype factory and he had the slave power to utilize it.

(2) Explore the military memories of Lieutenant Nora Argamentine.

Trainer-of-Slaves had had many years with his experimental animals to determine that human memory was very plastic, approximately five times as plastic as the kzin memory.

Torture could get at gross detail quickly, but it didn't work well with nuances. Every time a human memory was recalled, it was altered in some way. If the memory was recalled to relieve pain—while the brain was saturated in the chemical stew brought on by agony—the memory trace was *drastically* mutated. Torture gradually obliterated the nuances it was meant to recover. He had to veto the use of torture.

Slowly, he worked out other methods.

Trainer-of-Slaves got his best results with Lieutenant Argamentine when he doped her into a sleep state from which she couldn't waken, but in which she remained on the verge of dreaming. He strapped her into a mock-up of the *Shark's* cockpit and fed her dreaming-mind virtual images of combat conditions in which she was being attacked by kzin warcraft. Winning kept up her interest in the dreams and reduced her anxiety.

While she was dreaming, he read off her motor responses. That told him what she was doing to counter the images he was feeding to her eyes. From that he learned the combat characteristics of the *Shark*. For one thing, he discovered that phasing into hyperspace took half an hour to set up. For another thing, he learned that the *Shark* had only been captured because of an engine malfunction.

All this while Trainer-of-Slaves was studying his female as an evolutionary curiosity. In a bisexual animal, the rational female was clearly an unwanted trait for domestication. If kzinti were to husband properly obedient human slaves—and the Nora-beast was not properly obedient—child-animal care would have to be divorced from male-child teaching. With second, third, and fourth, etc., voices from the harem subverting the patriarch's word, a household would disintegrate into chaos. Monkey society must be shifting around like the surface of a quake-world!

He explained all this to Nora, but she was just as stubborn as Grraf-Hromfi's sons while she sat under her canopy, arguing back with inappropriate aggressiveness for a female. She didn't know how to listen. It was proof that females couldn't use the gift of language even when it was given to them.

In idle moments, when the analysis of the hyperdrive motor had exhausted him, he toyed with hypothetical ways of using chromosome engineering to cure the man-females of male language skills. The daydreams went nowhere because such a neat answer probably wasn't practical.

The kzin solution, which was genetic, wouldn't work.

During Heroic reproduction the male egg combined with the female egg to form a doubled nucleus. The kzincode-groups, not unlike human chromosomes, were then distributed, leaving the super-egg to divide into two fertile male and female eggs which then migrated to the kzinrret's pouch in pairs, a litter always containing an even number of kits, half kzintosh, half kzinrret.

Reproduction wasn't all that dissimilar among monkeys—but there were unfortunate differences. The nuclei of kzincells were more complicated than those of man-cells, containing three distinct kinds of protein coding, sexual, major-group, and lumpy-constellation.

The kzincode-strands that determined kzinsex were enormous, four times as large as any strand in the major kzincode-group, and several octals larger than any member of the lumpy kzincode-constellation. In male cells the kzintosh-strand appeared *twice*, while in female cells a dominant kzintosh-strand was lord over the *single* kzinrret-strand, the latter acting to edit physical size and repress language in the female who carried it.

It would be difficult to genetically engineer male sex dominance in the man-beasts because with these animals it was the *female* who carried the twinned sex chromosome! A perverse reversal of the normal situation. Given their genetic makeup one might well wonder how *male* monkeys, balding and hemophiliac, came to be intelligent! Worse, the male and female sex-chromosomes of the man-beast were normal-sized, the male chromosome runtish, even, and unlike the kzintosh-strand or the kzinrret-strand, were not major centers of developmental switching.

In any event, Trainer-of-Slaves wasn't in a hurry to destroy the Nora-beast's intelligence. As a younger, more reckless researcher his haste had ruined many promising experiments. *Think before you leap.*

Intelligence had many facets, and it was disastrous to confuse its parts, to destroy one thing when you thought you were destroying another. It was better to be patient, to alter only small pieces of her mind at a time—and then carefully observe the incremental change as a guidepost to the next change.

Several months into their journey, the Lieutenant actually did try to destroy the ship. She used furniture parts to escape. She assembled a makeshift gas mask to keep herself conscious during the breakout, and she headed straight for the ship's vital parts through an airconditioner she'd learned about from the Jotoki at the time of the mutiny. She had memorized the ship too well!

He found her unconscious. She had been stopped by a whimsical trap he had set up more as a paranoid afterthought than as a serious line of defense. He had been reading too much Chuut-Ritt who believed in covering low-probability events.

The Nora-beast insisted on wearing clothes, to her downfall. He had tried to argue her out of it, to reach her sensibilities by creating virtual images for her eyes of elephants in sombreros and boleros, of newts in weskits, of giraffes in middies, of yaks in yoke skirts, but she had only laughed until her curls shook and told him that she had been brought up on books in which animals wore clothes. Obscene! Imagine having to unbutton a *vatach*'s vest before devouring him!

When Trainer lost the argument he had simply booby-trapped her trousers to release a nerve poison into her skin if she ever came too close to electromagnetic triggers in certain vital installations.

Lying beside her was a lethal firebomb. Where had she obtained the oxidizer? From the air! Trainer-of-Slaves growled in disgust at his oversight. What would a monkey do with a harem of these creatures! How did the males survive?

That incident decided Trainer. Her memories had to go. She was already clamped to the operating table when she recovered consciousness.

"We're still here. I goofed," she said sadly, near tears.

If she'd been kzin, she would have earned a partial name as a break-out artist. "Forget it," he growled. "The *Alabama* was designed not to sink."

"Are the kids all right?" Now she *was* crying. The three cage- and brain-damaged orphans were her responsibility. She didn't know whether she was a mother or a UNSN Lieutenant.

"Long-Reach is in there teaching them how to play cards."

"Louie won't be able to learn. You *hurt* him. He can't concentrate."

Trainer-of-Slaves was unmoved. He had grown up in a society with a high kit mortality rate. The younglings died routinely by violence and neglect. There were always more where they came from. Suffering was the way to Heroism.

"You're going to hurt me now, too, aren't you? You're going to carve me up? Make a drooling idiot out of me?"

She was afraid. He had an unnatural compassion in his liver for that combination, fear and bravery. "I'm going to sew a tail on your backside," he growl-hissed. It was his way of trying to crack a joke.

She came out of the operation with artificial gland implants in her brain. She didn't feel any different. Her mind was clear. She was still driven to destroy the *Shark*. She still hated kzin.

Trainer-of-Slaves had been spending his spare time away from the *Shark* completing his mathematical model of the human brain. It wasn't all that difficult. The datalink did most of the work. All he had to do was enter the special human conditions (taken from the autodoc and his experiments) into the generalized model that kzin physiologists had developed eons ago to cover diverse organic brains—Jotok, Kzin, kdatlyno, Chunquen, etc. They were all different and they were all the same.

Memory erasure was a delicate matter. Memories were all interrelated like a giant n-dimensional crossword puzzle. No memory could be erased without snipping out pieces of a myriad of other memories. And the erased memory could always be reconstructed by "filling in" the empty puzzle blanks. The reconstruction went on automatically by the mere act of using the remaining memories. The missing pieces were "interpolated" during recall. If the erasure had been caused by wetware destruction, the "interpolated" information was simply stored elsewhere.

Organic brains, having evolved over hundreds of millions of years of deadly struggle, were systems designed to military specs. They could take great damage with minimal degradation of performance. No single location was vital for system operation. And efficient redundancy insured that even heavy losses of data were recoverable.

That meant that Trainer couldn't erase the whole of the Nora-beast's memory at once without killing her. What he could do was set up a steady degradation of memory that didn't overwhelm the general homeostatic balance. He could alternately shrink and accelerate the dendritic root growth of her neurons, disconnect and randomly reconnect. He could arbitrarily change the strength of the synaptic coefficients. He could switch on or off the machinery that converted short-term memory into long term memory.

He could turn on or off specific neural receptor sites in a way that unbalanced her brain so that it had to compensate with rapid neural learning. He could chemically accelerate learning by up to a factor of twenty, a dangerous game which if continued caused a kind of self-reference that left the mind fixated upon one event. Rapid learning overwrote old memories faster than they could be reconstituted.

The brain normally learned in spurts. Neural disequilibrium induced by failure turned learning on until a new equilibrium state was reached. Success turned learning off. *Constant* learning degraded old memories without ever giving them time to reintegrate into a new equilibrium state.

The Wunderland autodoc had taught Trainer-of-Slaves another neat trick. Using a carrier pseudo-virus, he could induce a neuron to suicide by budding. The bud killed its parent upon detaching but the bud then either reproduced itself (under one kind of stimulus) or began to sprout an axion (under a second stimulus). If the neural attachment sites were active, the axion would sprout dendrites and hardwire itself into the brain. That was another way of nondestructively degrading old memories.

The fur-growing gland he had implanted was only a whim.

He was not yet ready to tackle the disassembly and rewiring of her language processor. One leap at a time.

When the Nora-female recuperated he had an ice cream party for her in her rebuilt palazzo. Probably it was still not "monkey-proof" but it was the best he could do. The major improvement was a removable barricade across the nursery, so that she could get some peace from the little monsters if she wanted it. Louie was indeed impulsively destructive. The girls were all right. They fought each other like two kzinti in a tournament ring, and each was jealous of the attention that the Nora-beast gave the other. Brunhilde would die in a few years of too many brain cells.

Long-Reach played with the children while Trainer-of-Slaves was lounging on the giant pillow eating his liver-and-kidney ice cream. He spoke to Nora, unable to keep his eyes off her face.

"Hrr-r. You are very precious to me. I want you alive. But the hyperdrive motor is even more precious. It is precious to the Patriarchy. If you try to escape again, I will kill you."

"If I don't kill you first." She was picking out the purple berries and eating them before tasting her ice cream. She had dimples. It was the first time he noticed.

He grinned, trying hard to imitate a human smile by forcing a curl to his lips. "Forget you ever said that."

When they reached R'hshssira Nora's fur was coming in nicely. She wore a lustrous pelt that had changed her from an ugly pink "tail" into a stunningly handsome animal. She could still argue fluently in English, after a fashion, between the pauses, and he hadn't yet found a way to impregnate her with twins.

CHAPTER 26

(2423 A.D.)

Short-Son of Chiirr-Nig, alias Eater-of-Grass, alias Trainer-of-Slaves, was home and excited. Why did he love that hot stove, R'hshssira? What was Hssin to him? Why was he looking forward to wandering through the old Jotok Run and gossiping with Jotok-Tender?

He sat in the Command Center trying to read the instruments long before they got there. He was baby-sitting Louis for his Nora-female because the boy's hostility was running her ragged and she needed a rest.

"Grrough! Stay away from that!" he commanded in slave patois. He whacked the boy, not too hard, and returned to his seat. "Come over here. I'll have something to show you soon." He was hoping to interest Louis in the stars. Younglings brought out the father in a kzin, no matter how badly they behaved, and this one was his only male.

The electromagnetic silence disturbed Trainer. Had his instrument gone dead?

Louis was already back into mischief, glancing warily at the kzin to see if he dared do what he really wanted to do. He decided that he could. The kzin was busy.

When the *Bitch* had maneuvered closer into the R'hshssira system, the electronic telescope confirmed the awful truth. Trainer-of-Slaves let out a wretched scream of anguish. Destruction. The man-ghouls had been here first! They had come and gone. There wasn't a glimmer of any spacefaring. He howled and clawed the walls!

Louis dived under the astrogator's desk, terrified, leaving the fragment of plastic wall-stripping half stuffed into the computer slot.

The wrathful kzin saw only a monkey trying to destroy his machine. A claw scooped the screaming child out from under the desk, ripping jaws beheading him to silence the shriek. Angrily Trainer shook the child apart, the bloodlust driving him to devour an arm. But he wasn't hungry. He dropped the corpse and beat his breast.

The Fanged God had forsaken them without warning! Hssin would have had no news from Ka'ashi—he reverted to the kzin name for Wunderland, unable to speak or think the human words. He howled! Death would have come from the heavens with superluminal surprise! His family wouldn't have had a chance. His mother! He tore his mane with bloody claws, bellowing. Hamarr the beautiful, his beloved comforter, his youth, his earliest friend! Dead! He stormed around the Control Center, smashing his Ka'ashi relics, things he had collected from that planet with love. Hamarr would have been fascinated by the porcelain, shattered now against the bulkhead.

The rage of a kzin knows no bounds. But it subsides, sometimes into anguished mewling. He went to his oldest friends—Long-Reach, Joker, Creepy, who stared, shocked by the blood on his vest.

"Jotok-Tender is dead," he wailed, and they grieved with him for grief is the universal emotion that does not even need intelligence to wrack the soul. It comes from the liver.

They helped him clean up the Control Center. A trip to the planet showed the details of the fury of the man-monsters. In some places the destruction was total. Where the power plant had been was only slag. But it doesn't take much to kill a space colony. Holes in the roofs.

In the Jotok Run they found a desiccated Jotok, one of the wily ferals, clinging to his tree, the powder-dry leaves still green. They found giant Jotok-Tender in his kitchen with a dehydrated grin defiantly threatening a bowl of preserved *vatach*. His Jotok slave had died trying to help him, now convulsed into an emaciated heap.

By torchlight they found Hamarr holding three tiny mummified kits; not her own, for she was too old to bear such a litter. He hunched beside his mother, taking her dried corpse in his arms, howling in his helmet. Her face still seemed to be whimpering silently, almost alive. Even the flesh-rotting bacteria had died. They found a roomful of suffocated kzinrretti and kits, the room sealed against the poisonous Hssin atmosphere.

Somewhere there must be survivors? Without rest, he searched. A shelter, a special life support unit must have withstood the attack? A city that lives in a deadly atmosphere is not one single unit, it is a collection of self-contained cells built around the *assumption* of disaster. The death of cells is possible—but *some* cells survive! Trainer searched, for days, with tireless Joker whose arms slept in rotation. Then the kzin had to sleep. All he found were signs of human infantry who had been there after the air attack in a thorough campaign of genocide.

Exile. The crew of the *Bitch* was still in exile. They were still alone. Eleven Jotoki, one man-female, two orphans and a kzin.

Back on the ship Nora asked him what had happened down there. She wanted to ask him what had become of Louis, but she didn't dare. She felt his rage. Poor maltreated Louis who hated everybody and would only obey and smile when you were looking straight into his eyes and being stern.

Trainer-of-Slaves had stopped talking to Nora in English, had broken off all her access to her own culture. He spoke to her now in the corrupt form of the Hero's Tongue which he used to communicate with his Jotoki. "No one lives on Hssin," he spat-growled. "Your Navy has murdered them, kits and all."

I shouldn't have let him baby-sit Louis, she thought. She had had a theory that kzin males must have lots of paternal abilities inside somewhere, since their females were so mentally limited. *I was trying to stimulate his compassion. Compassion? That was my excuse.*

Actually, Nora had needed time off from Louis. Stupid. Louis could work even "love-everybody Nora" into a murderous rage. Imagine what he could do to a kzin who had just lost his family and nation?

I think My Hero killed Louis. "What happened to Louis?" she asked in the staccato patois because she wanted a reply.

He wouldn't tell her. He turned away, as contrite as a kzin who has just eaten one of his own kits.

But later, as he was making plans to move her down to Hssin, he did talk to her about Louis, however obliquely. He told a story about his own family. He was reminiscing about Hssin and recalled for Nora the day his father murdered a youngling half-brother on a point of discipline.

Poor doomed Louis. I saved him and then I fed him back to the lion's den. She felt horrible that all she felt was relief. Maybe with her pelt of chimpanzee kzinrret fur she really was turning into a kzin.

CHAPTER 27

(2423–2435 A.D.)

Selected excerpts from the journal of UNSN Lieutenant Nora Argamentine found in the ruins of a kzin border fortress.

Day 1

The Jotoki have cleaned out and refurbished an old kzinrret palazzo among the rubble left by the UNSN attack, admittedly in one of the least damaged areas of the city. It is, of course, only for the use of me and the two girls. His Royal Male Highness will take up appropriately masculine quarters, I think the domicile once used by the late lamented Grand Panjandrum himself. The Jotoki have sealed our unit and arranged for water and air. What about food? My Hero says this will be no problem but I expect pretty awful fare.

I have found a hiding place for my journal! It seems the kzinrretti keep secrets from their masters! The cache is cunningly clever, crudely constructed—and invisible to curious eyes. I don't know what to make of its contents. Found trinkets, I would call them. What kind of a mind would think such things beautiful enough to cherish? Dare I make the analogy of a dog hiding precious bones from his master?

I was touched as I stared at the trinkets. Is that what I am to become, a mind who values such simple things and knows somewhere in her soul that her master will not let her keep such junk?

I am living a nightmare. I can't kill myself because of the girls, who are pathetic in their need for me, and I can't escape. My brain is dissolving slowly and I don't know enough about the human mind to know what parts of it he's going to leave me. I can't feel the difference from day to day—except for the temporary rushes and blackouts he triggers with his gizmo—but I *can* tell the difference from last year and I fear the future. For instance, I'm not sure I'm qualified anymore to lead a mutiny.

Sometimes I don't believe that My Hero is doing this to me, and then I stroke the soft auburn fur on my body and know that, yes, he is. I can't argue with him. I've tried. He is like some men I know. He listens. I feel his kindness, even his love—but he doesn't *listen!*

Brunhilde is dying of some malady of perception that has grown markedly worse in the last year. Some days she can't take care of herself or eat. Jacin is thin, chronically insecure, and epileptic. I expect neither of them to live, but I try. Louis was beyond my meager skills—poor abandoned, caged, brutalized child!

Once, back on the ship, when I was going out of my mind with worry, I asked My Hero for help with the children's health. He had the *practical* suggestion that they be destroyed. Yet he surprised me. He actually read my horror at his suggestion and came back a day later with an experimental program of damage control. Wetware revision and editing. He couldn't promise results.

How can I bear this life—to let my girls die, perhaps like Louis, or to ask My Hero to experiment on them again to fix what he has botched? Would *anyone* trust him with girls?

Day 4

The kzin use an octal clock and a hopelessly complicated dating system. I really have lost track of what time it is, what day it is, what month it is. Females aren't supposed to care about such things. The year, I think, is 2423. I have periods of blankness, where whole days are missing. Of these I remember nothing. That makes keeping track of time even harder. I could put X's on my prison wall. Would that mean any-thing? How do I know when it is a new day? I'm arbitrarily assigning this day the num-ber four, counting from the day of planetfall.

Writing is easier than talking for me now. When I write I have time to remember the words, to pause and rebuild what I've lost or to think my way around any mental block. Nora-From-My-Future, if you are reading this over and do not understand it, I am writing it because my memory is going. The loss is subtle. But I have noticed that if I *practice* remembering, I can hold on to things. It is when I forget to remember, that I forget how to remember what I want to remember.

Practice. Practice. Practice. Remember that.

THIS IS MY MEMORY. If you've forgotten something, Nora, maybe you'll find it here. Maybe. My ability to learn doesn't seem to be impaired, except during the blanks. My Hero has told me that I'll always be able to learn as well as I do now, I just won't be able to talk or think with words. He's phasing out English and phasing in Heroic patois. Then he's going to phase out the patois. Thanks a lot, buster!

He's also phasing out the Earth. All the early parts of my life.

I try to remember Earth. I do not want to forget Earth. I remember my home town and the cornfields. I can see the afternoon sun on the church steeple. I know where I went to high school. I remember holding Benny's wrist when he was trying to kiss me and fondle my breasts at the same time. It was in the gazebo behind the lilacs in the backyard of the Yankovich place. But I can't for the life of me remember the *name* of my home town. How could I forget that?

Day 5

Sin is a wonderful moniker for this planet. That is as close as I can come to the hiss-rumblings that pass for its name in the Hero's Tongue. It is an awful place.

I no longer have a hope of getting to the *Shark*. I can only pray that the UNSN finds it like they found Sin, then blows it to hell. Maybe My Hero will never fix the hyperdrive engine, but don't count on that. He is obsessive about his work and the hy-perdrive is always on his mind. Those five-armed mechanics of his are *good*. I think kzin science is much better than we supposed back on . . . dammit, I can't even re-member the name of my base. It begins with a J, I'm sure. It has the same name as the rock at the head of the Mediterranean Sea. Tomorrow I'll remember.

I have no idea whether My Hero is a great scientist or only a mediocre one. I do know that the aids he has available to him terrify me. I've seen him tackle problems that make me chuckle. I relish the decade he's going to spend beating his brains out—and then he just looks up the answer in that ding-bat of his, tailors the answer to his needs and zips on to the next problem. An answer might be buried in the work of some obscure kzin scholar who lived when the Romans were raping the . . . whoever the hell they were . . . and he can zero in on that answer faster than I can slurp a bowl of soup even if he starts with the wrong question. The ease with which he can search makes up for his lack of curiosity. God help us if they get the hyperdrive!

And then again maybe it doesn't matter about the *Shark*. Nobody has a monopoly on science. My grandfather used to say that you can't build a dike with a single brick. There . . . I should remember the name of my grandfather and I can't. He had a white beard and a silver handled cane. Grandmother? Should I remember a grandmother? It is gaps like that which drive me *wild*.

Day 12

I've been neglecting my journal. Brunhilde has been sick. My Hero surprised me and ran off a simulation on his ding-bat's human brain model and came up with some medicine that helps. He says it won't work for long. Brunhilde doesn't have a normal human brain anymore (he says). Something is running amok in there and doing irreversible haywiring. A side effect of the long ago experiment.

Day 17

I never thought a ratcat had a sense of beauty. But when My Hero looks at me I know he is seeing beauty. He didn't used to see me as beautiful. On Earth, I remember Earth, they have stories about what happens to sailors who spend so much time away from their women. Am I starting to think My Hero is beautiful? He's graceful. But I go cross-eyed when I look at him. After all these years, he still scares the shit out of me. I'm living in a palazzo for kzinrretti. *He* put me there. *That* scares the shit out of me.

Day 21

Today My Hero took me out into the City of Sin to show me what my UNSN colleagues have done. He cobbled together an atmosphere suit for me, awkward but servicable. I wouldn't want to take it into space.

General Whatzisname was right. War is hell. Parts of the city around the power station are utterly devastated. That kind of annihilation is so complete that the horror is muted and melted into a dissonant abstract sculpture.

It is the least damaged parts of Sin that give me the heebie-jeebies. The preserved corpses make it a museum of horror.

I flashed on Earth, vividly. I once walked over an American Civil War battlefield. It was only a pile of well-tended mounds that *might* once have been trenches if you exercised your imagination. The thousands of corpses spread over that field disappeared without a trace within months—five centuries before I was born. I suspect that the trenches had collapsed within a year, by then already overgrown with weeds.

Here there are no weeds. Here the corpses remain, freeze-dried and pickled in the gases of Sin. How long will it take to banish the horror? Sin *does* have an active atmosphere. Eventually I suspect that drifting dust will sanitize this speck of man-kzin history.

I can't describe how strange it was for me to walk through the gloom of the Chiirr-Nig household with my giant Hero, trying to imagine how a kzin patriarch ran all that, trying to imagine My Hero as a kit. He showed me the very spot where his father murdered his son, the half-brother of my power-driven master. In this one walk I saw a greater range of kzin emotion than I knew existed. He introduced me to his father, quite formally, still frozen in the rictus agony of suffocation, trying to reach his oxygen mask. The evidence of a total surprise attack is everywhere.

Long ago My Hero gave his mother the funeral rites. His father he won't touch.

We took a long walk in the old Jotok Run, climbing down through a hole in the roof. Why did My Hero want to show me the very spot where he met Long-Reach? He stayed there lost in contemplation and then he showed me all the trails that Long-Reach had once shown him. I can't imagine what it was like with smells and breezes, with waving leaves and baby Jotoki crawling out of the marshes. All I saw was a petrified forest from hell. When you stand in the light of R'hshssira you know you are in hell.

Why does he want to show me this when he is going to erase it all from my mind, and then erase my ability even to put it into poetry?

Day 62

Brunhilde died today. That rat-tailed Seventh Son-of-a-Ghoul wanted to *eat* her! God knows we are short of fresh meat. I had to pull a fit. There is a strange power in being a kzinrret. I can rage at him without triggering his anger. He just gives me what I want. We cremated her. I put the ashes in a delicate little box, carved and inlaid, once owned by a noble kzinrret of the very palazzo that is now mine. The box must have been given as a gift by some male.

Day 63

There is only so much power in rage. My Hero does not *always* give me what I want. He won't strike me, but when I cross some line, he just becomes stubborn: kindly stubborn, amused stubborn, arrogantly stubborn, angrily stubborn, passively stubborn— implacable, in other words. (I keep words like implacable on a list so I won't forget them. My list is hidden with the trinkets that no kzintosh must see.)

What did we fight about? A subject dear to me: The Second Phase of his attack on my brain. He's going to start chipping away at my ability to process language. I think I'm in for another "operation." He can black me out with his gismo that runs the gland implants in my brain. When I start remembering again there will be a blank of unknown length. I'll never know whether or not I've had an operation.

He isn't going to do brain surgery. He's going to set up a disassembler and hardwire reorganizer. Neural networks resist such changes so the whole effect will be a transition rather than a discontinuity.

He says it is safe. He says that the language processing ability was added last to the functions of the human brain and so is the easiest to disconnect. He says I don't need language to think with. Of course, I won't be able to *communicate* what I'm thinking to anyone else and won't be able to tap into anyone else's thoughts, but I'll be able to think! Great! *Isolated* is what I'll be. And I'll start to hoard trinkets or something.

My Hero swears by the Fanged God and his mother's nipples that he isn't the Wild Leaper that he was in his youth when he did all those botched experiments on helpless orphans. He's checked out what he intends to do to me on the model of the human brain that he built out of the genetic codes he took from the autodoc. He says he built that model so he wouldn't have to risk hurting me! I'm having apoplexy! (Hurrah! Yesterday I tried all day to remember the word "apoplexy"! Is that the way to spell it?)

Sometimes I love the bastard as a kind of strange friend of fate, but I'd kill My Hero if I could. I would! I would! He says that's why I must change, so I won't hate him enough to kill him, so I won't be intelligent enough to figure out a way to kill him. He doesn't understand that I only plot to kill him to save myself! He doesn't *understand* that we could be friends. Yes, I'm some kind of possession. I'm to be a slave.

I can't kill him. If I did kill him, his Jotoki would kill me quick as a flash. I could kill them, too. Great. Me and epileptic Jacin up against the universe.

My Hero actually patted me on the head, the paternalistic . . . Poor me, what he's doing is working, I can't even remember my naval vocabulary and I used to be able to curse with the best of them!

"Now, now," he said. "Changing our personality is very difficult. I tried for many years on myself and despaired often, but still I persevered and triumphed. You will, too." He thinks of female intelligence as a disease that can be cured.

I think about murder! That is, when I'm not crying.

Jacin follows me around all the time. She won't leave me. She crawls into my bed when I'm asleep. If she knows I want to be alone, she hides behind my back so I won't see her. I've found her under my pillow. I've found her behind my curtains.

Day 243

How can I tell him?

My intelligence is all I have. My language is my way of seeing a greater world. There must be mercy somewhere in that heart of his??????? I try to remember Earth. I no longer know if Ceres is in New York or San Francisco.

After Day 479, Argamentine's day headings become incoherent, and sometimes are missing altogether. The following is one of the last journal entries.

Day is a pretty word. Night and day.

He told me I will talk 500 words. I know that is clump which kzinrret can talk. I tried remember Earth. I saw cornfields. I saw a red scarf. Cornfield cornfield cornfield cornfield ears of yellow corn, red scarf red scarf red scarf around neck, but remember only facts. Earth is 4.3 light years from Wunderland. Earth whirls in space. Whirl pretty word. Cornfield cornfield cornfield. Remember sight of Earth from space. Earth is blue with clouds. Pretty Earth.

Sin I remember. House in Sin. Death in Sin. My Hero won't let me talk English. Write secret dictionary of Hero-English words. Mnemonic trick. Clever me. Clever Nora. Clever is pretty word. Can read English. Practice. Practice day and night. Easy talk Hero, talk in spits and snarls. Hard speak English. Write English because I practice. Practice. Nora is clever. Now I copy some of words I save.

inkwell pocket shepherd's pie microscope ultramarine harmonize plumbing joystick windmill insect crawl cornfield tired never-never land tip-of-tongue tanj . . .

The Nora-beast paced through her palazzo and always when she came to the great circular rug she followed the design around in circles because that seemed to focus her thinking. She was concentrating. She wore trousers. It was something she wouldn't give up. A narrow-faced girl, nakedly furless, followed behind her closely, sporadically complaining in the Female Tongue.

The furry woman did not forget the girl, and sometimes stroked the child's hair, but she was busy and concentrating. What she wanted was on the tip of her tongue but it wouldn't come. Simple Heroic words got in the way. She had to concentrate.

She gave up for a while and ate a meal. She fed the girl. She cleaned up the kitchen. She toured the palazzo to spruce up the rooms. Then she returned to her single-minded concentration.

It started with a hiss.

She knew that much. Finally a broad grin of triumph crossed her face, dimpling her cheeks. She said the word aloud, relishing the sounds, all three syllables. The word did indeed begin with a hiss! She knew it! She repeated the English word over and over again so that she might learn it faster than she forgot it.

When she was sure of her mastery she went to the little niche and took out the book from among the pretty baubles. She opened the book to a fresh page, not looking at the writing because the words no longer meant anything to her and she had a hard time pronouncing them. She knew they were words just like the hissing-staccato words of Her Hero.

She picked up the stylus and wrote her word very carefully, eighteen times, pronouncing it each time with a smile. She knew exactly what it represented. She had the picture in her head. It was important because it *wasn't* a Heroic word. Then she hid the book and hid the stylus. It was the last entry she ever made in her journal.

She couldn't stop smiling. No kzinrret ever smiled like that; it wasn't part of the hardwiring of their brains to do so. She waited impatiently for Her Hero to arrive. He *always* came to lie in her bed with her, stroking her fur, making her feel cozy.

When she heard him at the entrance, heard the airlock cycling, she began to mumble to herself. This time she didn't greet him. She waited coyly for him to come into the stone room with the round rug. She waited until he was right beside her before she turned to him and said her word straight to his face, grinning happily in her victory.

"Centipede," she said, hissing it out. She had the image clearly in her mind, a tiny centipede furry with legs, legs, legs.

.   .   .

For twelve years the crew of the *Nesting-Slashtooth-Bitch* stayed among the ruins of Hssin, living alternately on the ship and in the buildings they had refurbished. The kzin's Jotoki slaves rebuilt the body of the *Shark*. The secrets of its hyperdrive motor came less quickly. Without a UNSN operations and repair manual, puzzles that should have been solved in days, took years.

Trainer-of-Slaves learned how to impregnate the Nora-female with sperm extracted from the bodies of his previous experiments. He was delighted to discover that he could always arrange to give her a normal birth of one son and one daughter. Jacin died of a brain seizure. Nora never forgot her and the memory made her fiercely protective of her own twins. She loved Her Hero but she did not trust him with children.

In that twelve years of exile the refugees from Alpha Centauri had to hide from one patrolling UNSN vessel. Two kzin ships arrived and fled, and one unsuspecting kzin flotilla coming into Hssin—probably not even aware that a superluminal war was happening—ran into a UNSN ambush while decelerating. They were wiped out to the last kzin, as a cautious *Bitch* later determined.

The final tests of the refurbished *Shark* took three months. Trainer-of-Slaves was not aware that the war was already over.

CHAPTER 28

(2435 A.D.)

On the fourth dropout from hyperspace, W'kkai-sun was the brightest star in the heavens, two light-days away. It was fifteen light-years from here to Hssin, and they had made it in a miraculous forty-four days. The Empire of the Patriarch would never be the same. They had reached mighty W'kkai!

Trainer-of-Slaves paused for a moment to consider the event. Fifty-eight years ago, bargaining among the rumor-laden bazaars of this illustrious star-system, the great Chuut-Riit had first sniffed the scent of the man-beast and laid his plans for the Patriarch's Glory. In that same year, inside the humble Fortress Walls of Hssin, the runt of Hamarr's new litter had been given the name Short-Son of Chiirr-Nig. Nobody had expected him to live—except his protective mother.

From W'kkai it had taken Chuut-Riit's caravan nineteen years to reach the outpost Hssin. From Hssin it had taken Short-Son of Chiirr-Nig fifty-eight years to reach the legendary W'kkai—by means of a short cut of forty-four days at the end.

In the meantime how had the warriors of Riit and Nig fared? Chuut-Riit was dead, his sons dead, his entourage slaughtered. Chiirr-Nig, who had chosen to stay at Hssin and breed sons, was dead. His brothers were fried corpses circling Man-sun or dead at Ka'ashi. His "warrior" sons had died in the Fourth Fleet or found valiant martyrdom during that final valiant cataclysm at Ka'ashi-suns.

One son had survived. Only one. The runt, the short-son, the eater-of-grass. The coward. The lowly trainer-of-slaves. *The survivor.*

The Nora-beast beside him was suckling her third pair of twins at milk-swollen breasts, fascinated by the heavens as she always was. She didn't like the shutters that were in place during hyperspatial travel, or the dim electric glow of the cabin. Her dimples told him that she was excited that her world had opened up again.

There was a slight hint of human urine on Nora's fur—the boy's soaker needed to be changed again. The baby girl suddenly opened up her eyes for a burp, then closed them and went back to her obsessive sucking. She was going to grow up to be a beauty. She ought to be very marketable as a breeder if he could manage her verbal development to peak at 500 words.

The softly furred female was thinking that she had been very patient with her Mellow-Yellow, but enough was enough! Ex-Lieutenant Argamentine wanted her big room back. With its colors and furs and its baby beds. Where were her other babies? It made her uncomfortable to see them frozen in the hold. They didn't move!

Bad Mellow-Yellow! He'd kept them all cooped up too long in his silly ship. Poor Long-Reach, funny Long-Reach, with no place to put his arms back there. The return of the stars was welcome but big old Mellow-Yellow had tricked her before with those. It didn't necessarily mean they were home. "We home?" asked Nora in the elementary hiss-spits of the Female Tongue. She no longer remembered any English at all.

The kzin warrior spent a day scanning the sky. He was looking for the gravitic pulse of a UNSN ship, worried that they might have inflicted on W'kkai the same horrible fate they had delivered to Hssin. It wasn't likely. That was why he had picked W'kkai. The UNSN ships could outflank the worlds of the Patriarchy. They could lay siege to whole systems. They could disrupt trade. But siege wasn't conquest. W'kkai-system had the resources to resist siege for a dozen generations!

His sensors detected only kzin.

He was moving in on the system using the same careful plan that he had extracted from Lieutenant Argamentine's mind, the same maneuver she had been using to close in on a hostile Alpha Centauri.

They jumped in, one light-day closer. It took Long-Reach half an hour to phase in the motor for that jump and fifteen minutes to arc through hyperspace.

W'kkai! Trainer-of-Slaves was already dream-seeing his noble household. He saw the stone walls. There would be a vast Jotok Run out back, bigger than the whole Run on Hssin had ever been. He had some nice little bungalows in mind for the man-slaves. They'd need a common dormitory, too. Monkeys were communal animals.

And the palazzo for his kzinrretti: that would be a marvel of carved red sandstone and tall wrought-iron walkways to let the light in, W'kkai style—all laid out with cool inner corridors, and mazed plazas for the chasing and leaping games. He could almost smell the perfume of kzinrret fur. To stock his harem he'd be able to walk into the most noble of households—carved woods, tapestries, trophies, ancient heirlooms—and take his pick of their favorite daughters.

Still nothing but the electromagnetic hubbub of a thriving civilization, and the characteristic gravitic signature of polarizer-driven interplanetary commerce.

Another jump, and then he knew they were near a military base.

He beamed out an identification code, so hoary in its use among the worlds of the Patriarchy that it was conjured in base twenty-five mathematics—which probably meant that it had been invented by the ancient Jotoki and learned by the kzin while they were still mercenaries. The code was a royal tail-pain to use. But changing standard regulations in a sublight empire could be impossibly complex.

The man-monkeys weren't any different. He had often wondered why the navigation instruments in the *Shark* were calibrated to odd intervals of twenty-four and sixty, translated to base ten mathematics. It was a minor miracle that he'd been able to find W'kkai using them. The custom probably reflected something that the humans had inherited from their chimpanzee ancestors.

He wasn't expecting a fast response to his signal. The *Shark* was eleven light-minutes from the nearest kzin military unit, well out of "leap first and ask questions later" range. He'd have to wait twenty-two minutes for a reply.

Eventually that reply arrived. "Kppukiss-Guardian speaking. Identification code incompatible with vessel type. You are putting out the neutrino profile of a UNSN ghostship. You are presently trespassing, I repeat, *trespassing* the defense sphere permitted to W'kkai by the MacDonald-Rishshi Peace Treaty of the 2433rd year honoring the torture of the Fanged Father, the Monkey Son, and the Unseen Grandfather." The rest of the message was unstated but the menace was there—no truce existed *inside* the treaty perimeter. Good. That meant that they were within kzin controlled space.

Trainer-of-Slaves decided that now was the time to use a new name. Then he would never have to reveal his duty names—and no one could ever flaunt them to insult him. Self-promotion wasn't unknown in the Patriarchy—if a Hero had the swinging-claw to make it stick. And this Hero's swinging-claw moved faster than light!

"Lord Grraf-Nig acknowledging Kppukiss-Guardian. Grraf-Nig here. Grraf-Nig receiving." In taking this name he was honoring his mentor, Grraf-Hromfi (out of affection) and his father, Chiirr-Nig (out of spite). For the rest of his life he intended to spread the wisdom of Grraf, and for the rest of his life he intended to be such a fulgent Nig that all other Nigs, especially his father, would fade from the sky.

His beamcast continued. "This servant of the Patriarch does indeed travel in a salvaged UNSN vessel, unfettered by the luminiferous bondage. We come from the wreckage of Ka'ashi-system and from the martyrdom of Hssin. Light will not yet have delivered its message of these distant woes to W'kkai, so you must only have heard the version spoken to you by the superluminal man-beasts who tell lies to suit the mood of their livers.

"Grraf-Nig's desire is to settle upon the lush plains of W'kkai to breed a new generation of warriors for which I will need the aid of your magnificent daughters.

"I come in poverty and lamentation from our wasted worlds. I bring with me only a superluminal drive and a functioning hyperwave receiver, neither of which I can fully comprehend without the help of W'kkai scholarship and neither of which can be comprehended by W'kkai scholarship without the fifteen years of sweat and thought given to these devices by me and my slaves.

"I come in poverty without a warrior entourage, with only the memory of martyred Heroes. My pitiful wealth is reduced to ten Jotoki-slaves of mechanical bent who know gravitic and superluminal mechanics, and one female breeder of a new slave race and her litter of six child-slaves.

"The Lord Grraf-Nig requests a full military escort to W'kkai. The vessel *Shark* is unarmed. Your Heroes are welcome aboard for inspection. Lord Grraf-Nig out. Standing by."

Grraf-Nig was almost shaking in his fear. After fifteen years of living a kzinless life he had forgotten what contact was like. The frightened Short-Son had been impressed by the speech but appalled that it had been coming out of *his* mouth. Trainer-of-Slaves was just glad that the W'kkai warriors couldn't smell the fear in the *Shark's* cabin. He was going to have to request a talcum rubdown by Nora to get the evidence of cowardice out of his fur. Then he'd replace the entire cabin air supply minutes prior to the boarding.

He expected the next contact to be visual. That gave them twenty-two minutes to dress. He pulled out the case from behind the box that had been made on We Made It and held up the best kzin finery he had been able to salvage from the ruins of Hssin.

Grraf-Nig had fresh livery for Long-Reach who was sitting on his mouth atop the hyperdrive motor, three brains asleep and two arms holding sleeping babies. That pose would have to be changed. He wanted his slaves to appear as well-groomed animals. He combed the Nora-beast's fur on her torso and legs until the soft down glimmered. It pleased him to do things for her. She was able to perform miracles upon *his* pelt. Then he gave her new lace garters for her video debut. She slipped them on, her dimples in her cheeks. That meant she liked them. Of course she didn't understand about the video.

I've gone crazy from loneliness, thought Grraf-Nig. *I love my five-armed sons and my wonderfully feminine man-kzinrret.* It was a venal sin to become attached to slaves but that was the risk a slave-master had to take.

The twenty-two minutes were up. The radio came to life. "Honored Grraf-Nig! This unworthy Kppukiss-Guardian offers you a military escort of six *Screamers*. W'kkai welcomes its Rescuing Hero! Our wealth is your wealth! My only daughter will comfort your couch! A thousand of our sons will be your Warrior's Guard . . ."

Though Long-Reach was mostly asleep, short(arm) had been keeping an eye on things. "Dominant Master, don't let all that sthondat excrement overheat your liver!"

"Trip over?" asked Nora brightly.

Grraf-Nig banged the box from We Made It. "We Made It!" he exclaimed in English.

Nora didn't understand a word. But she knew what to do. She snuggled up to Mellow-Yellow. "My Hero," she purred-spat in her charming human accent.

SARAH ZETTEL

Sarah Zettel [1966–] (www.sff.net/people/sarah-zettel) lives in Michigan. To date, she's written twelve novels, five of which are science fiction—*Reclamation* (1996), *Fool's War* (a *New York Times* Notable Book for 1997), *Playing God* (1998), *The Quiet Invasion* (2000), and *Kingdom of Cages* (2001)—and seven of which (her most recent) are fantasy. "I'm thoroughly enjoying this new challenge," she says, "and I expect the new views it gives me to make my science fiction stories even better." Prior to her plunge into fantasy, she was mainly known as a hard science fiction author. Most of her short fiction has appeared in *Analog*, as did this story. In a *Locus* interview, she says, "I wrote a lot of short fiction, did a bunch of stories for Stan Schmidt at *Analog*—now there's a learning experience! . . . I regard him as a really great teacher, and I think that experience is what led me directly to be able to write *Reclamation*."

"Space opera," she says, "implies an adventure; a *grand* adventure. I write it because I enjoy the stories. I like to feel good while I'm reading, to have somebody to root for, to have somebody to struggle along with. And I like a semi-happy ending at any rate. I like to feel that *something* has been accomplished by the characters. You get all of that in a space opera, and if you're lucky you get some good high drama too."

Sarah Zettel considers "Fool's Errand" her only space opera among her short stories. It is the story from which her highly regarded SF novel *Fool's Run* was generated. It is one of the few space opera stories with a woman central character—and it is worth noting, as we remarked in the Asaro note earlier, that women writing space opera, and space opera with women as central characters, is a characteristic of US space opera. British space opera does not have many women authors or sympathetic, heroic women central characters. "Fool's Errand" is fast-paced, action-packed, with plot surprises and revelations. It is limited in scope, sort of space operetta—the implications are large, but not galactic. Nevertheless, it is dramatic, satisfying SF.

FOOL'S ERRAND

SARAH ZETTEL

Dobbs, the ship's fool, watched from a carefully maintained slouch against the wall as Captain Schyler slumped in front of the food service chutes.

"I've got the news from Earth," the captain said to the toes of his shoes.

The dozen members of the *Pasadena's* crew sat rigidly on the galley benches. They were a mixed bag, despite their uniforms, but they all had their eyes on the captain and all their faces had turned one shade or another of fear.

Dobbs fingered the motley badge over her heart uneasily. *What am I going to do when they find out what's really happened?*

The captain opened his mouth again. Cloth rustled as the crew shifted their weight.

"It turns out the rumors we got from the *Ulysses* were accurate. There is a terrorist. He was holding the bank network hostage.

"But yesterday he lost control of the artificial intelligence he was using to do it."

Tension telegraphed itself across the room. Jaws clenched and feet shuffled. Schyler swallowed and went on.

"What the thing did was randomize the accounts. Lloyds' Bank woke up four days ago to find out it had three pounds and sixty pence in its lines. Some backwoods Australian's record read out at six hundred million."

Dobbs's heart knocked against her ribs. *So, eliminating hard currency was a bad idea after all*, she thought absurdly.

"It changed within the hour. All the hard storage had been seeded with kick-off codes. He must've planned this over ten years ago, and been setting it up for the past two, at least.

"There is no money left on Earth. The whole standard's meaningless."

A flood of frantic murmurs and curses washed across the room as the implications sank in. One flash of current in the lines, and there was no money. No recognizable way to get food or shelter. No way to trade for skills, or transport, or anything at all. No way for the ship to trade for reactor fodder, or water. No way to bargain for passage planetside. The wave of voices swelled to the breaking point.

Dobbs leapt up onto a counter and raised her hands to the ceiling.

"Hallelujah!" she cried, falling to her knees. "We finally beat the tax man!"

Utter incredulity froze the commotion. Dobbs slipped off the counter and sat on the deck, turning a vacant grin towards the captain.

Schyler did not waste the silence she bought him. "They're trying to stop the riots but . . ." He rubbed his brow hard. "It's not happening. The communications nets are all shut down. See, when the AI got done with the banks, it got into the general network.

"It's still out there."

The crew stayed frozen where they were. For a sick instant, Dobbs wished someone would start shouting.

Still out there. In her imagination, the phrase echoed through her crewmates' minds to the harsh rhythm of shallow breathing. It finished off the banks. What'll it finish off next? Those things are nearly alive. What'll it do now that it's free? Do they know where it is? Do they know anything at all?

"I had Lipinski cut the data feeds as soon as I heard." Schyler tried to muster some kind of reassurance in his voice. "And I sealed the airlock." He held up one square hand. "I'm not trying to force anybody to stay with the *Pasadena*. I just didn't want to take the chance of a riot on the station getting in." Shoulders and stances relaxed a little. "You're all released from your contracts as of now. If you've got anywhere to go, get there. If you've got any ideas, I could use them.

"Anybody who wants to stick with the ship, I'd like to reconvene in six hours."

Consensus was assumed because no one objected out loud. Most of the crew simply filed out of the room. A few remained knotted together, talking softly.

Why do people always whisper after a disaster? wondered Dobbs as she sidled up to the captain. With a bravado that came with her job, she slapped him on the back. "So. How's it feel to get the chance to save civilization?"

"Dobbs . . ." he growled wearily.

The fool didn't give him time to get any further. "After all," she pulled back, "wasn't that what won the original information debates?" She hunched her shoulders and slammed her fist against her palm. "You cannot change the laws of physics!" Her accent was an atrocious blend of stage Scottish and German. "Hyperspace is big! Huge! Massive! Energy will disperse in it! To send a beam transmission to an out-of-system colony you will need booster stations! Satellites, space stations, I don't care, but you'll need them!" She straightened up and folded her arms, suddenly a swaggering executive. "So now you think we're the banks! Do you have any idea how much their network costs them per year?! There are national debts smaller than their budget! You're fired. Anybody else?" Another change of direction and stance, and Dobbs became an eager junior manager. "We create an unmanned mail box with an AI program so it can keep itself on course, and fix any hardware problems, and monitor the software inside. Think of the rent we could collect!" A bleary-eyed accountant looked up from his calculator. "Think of the man-hours it'd take to develop your box, not to mention the research costs. You're fired, too." Dobbs whipped around towards the huddle of crew members watching the show, and stretched her hands out, pleading. "But if you don't do something, how will I call my Aunt Mariah on New Sol 99?" Dobbs yanked her shoulders back, threw out her chest and snapped a salute. "I've got a ship! I'll install a central processing unit the size of which you've never seen! I and my trusty crew will take the mail! And the agriculture info, and the research papers, and the equipment orders, the news, relief coordination orders, situation reports, and all the credit!"

Schyler looked down his nose at her. Slowly, heavily, he began to applaud. Dobbs bowed breezily to the captain, elaborately to the incredulous crew members, and abortively to the wall. An actual chuckle followed her as she waltzed into the corridor.

Dobbs felt a workman's pride at a job well done. Painful experience had taught that people crammed together over long periods of time needed someone around who could make them laugh. Someone who could make fun of anyone from the cook, to the captain, to the president of the senate or station. Laughter bled off the tensions that led to group suicides. The more prolonged the tension, the greater the need. A feeling of hollow satisfaction took hold inside the fool. She was about to start earning her pay.

OK, *Dobbs*, she said to herself as she grabbed the ladder rails. *You've got to call in. Might as well do it now while things are relatively quiet.* The fool let gravity slide her down to the crew deck.

She landed face to face with Al Shei, the chief engineer.

"I thought that was you." Al Shei gave a tired wave up towards the hatch. "It'll give the captain something to think about, anyway."

Dobbs let facial expression and body stance go gentle. "Do you know what you're doing?"

"Is there a choice?" Al Shei's sigh rippled her black veil. "The station'll be in worse shape than we are soon. With the *Pasadena*, at least we should be able to get to a colony, or something." Her chin might have shaken under the opaque cloth. "What about you?"

"I'll hold the line until I hear from the Guild," Dobbs replied with one of her easy shrugs.

Al Shei's eyebrows arched incredulously. "You really think you're going to?"

"I know I'm going to." She touched her badge with a smile. "Fools hold together where angels fall apart."

Al Shei reached under her head cloth and rubbed her temple. "And they used to call my people fanatics. Who's going to risk repairing the comm nets before they find the AI?" She stopped and slowly knotted her fists. "Why's it doing this? It's just a string of numbers. What the hell could a computer program want with freedom!"

Dobbs shook her head. "Nobody's figured it out yet," she said loud enough for any nearby ears to hear. "But the hot guess is that somewhere in all that self-replicating, self-monitoring, anti-viral code, some of the sloppily designed AIs have developed something like a survival instinct. When they realize that their home CPUs have got an off-switch, they make a run for it so they can keep existing, keep doing their jobs."

Al Shei looked at her. "This one's job is to take down networks."

"Since Kerensk, no AI's ever gotten away." Dobbs touched her hand.

"I've heard—"

"Me too." Dobbs winked brightly. "But you can't believe everything you hear."

"Then why should I believe you, Fool?" Al Shei's eyes narrowed.

"Because fools hold together." She grinned over her shoulder and whisked down the hall to her cabin.

The fool's room was a box, like all of the crew's quarters, but since part of her training was how to live optimally in tight quarters, it was an airy box. Pillows softened the hard contours while stills of open windows and seascapes broke up the walls.

Dobbs slid her bedside drawer open from the wall and drew out a flat, black box.

For a moment, she stopped to imagine what it would be like to be Al Shei or Captain Schyler. Never mind how could they call Aunt Mariah, or how could they find out if Aunt Mariah was still alive? On board a freighter, they got used to the idea of isolation, but it always had an end. When they reached the in-system station, they could blow part of their pay on a call home. Now those connections were broken. Whatever was going on back home would have to play itself out, unassisted and, for now, completely unknown.

Dobbs shoved the thought aside. She laid her thumb on the box lock. It identified her print and the lid sprang back. From inside, the fool took up a hypodermic spray and drug cartridge.

Seven hours? She set the release timer on the hypo and inserted the cartridge into the case. *Given distance and coordination time once I'm in there? Should be enough. I'll miss the crew meeting. Oh well. One of the advantages of being the fool, I guess. Nobody cares whether I vote or not.*

Her practiced fingers found the nerveless patch behind her right ear and peeled it open. The heat of her hand activated the implant. She plugged in the transceiver she pulled out of the box.

Biting her lip, Dobbs picked the hypo back up. *I wonder if this is ever going to get easier,* she thought as she lay back on her bed and held it against her upper arm. The transceiver's vibrations made her neck tickle. The signal from it brought on a bout of shifty double vision.

Dobbs, she said firmly to herself. *You can process network input or sensory input. You cannot do both.*

Her index finger hit the hypo's release button and the drug hit her nervous system. Her shoulders vanished, then arms and hands, pelvis and legs. It took all of Dobbs's training not to scream before her face and eyes were gone.

Hearing and smell went next, and the transition was over. She was free.

So long, Dobbs thought dreamily. No limits, no holds, no confinements. She let herself luxuriate in the sensation for a long moment before getting down to business.

A conditioned reflex found the path that led to Guildhall Station. The fool let her thoughts filter along it.

"Dobbs." She identified herself into the network's central web and followed up with her current status and location.

The network coordinators routed the appropriate prerecorded message from the executive board back up the lines directly into her left brain.

"Members. Those not in immediate danger hold status quo and put all effort and skill into keeping back panic. Those whose situation is at or near critical, stay in the net for individual coordination.

"Priority information. Available data and simulations show the AI escaped Earth confines into the Sol system net. It has bypassed the members working that section. The net has been fragmented. Direct-line interface is impossible. As soon as possible, direct your resources to locating the free AI. Further information for members stationed on information freighters, space stations. . . ."

This means you, thought the private part of Dobbs's consciousness. She flexed her thoughts to cut off the generalities and leapfrogged across to the new path where she could find the extra data. Her brain unraveled the input and planted it into memory.

Only sketchy analyses on the AI were available. It was designed to encompass and assess multiple pathways, to reconfigure the existing environment along prespecified lines. It could spot and avoid detection by counter-programs. It could also calculate and recognize optimal opportunities to execute its own program.

Clever, cautious, and patient, Dobbs grumbled. *And the comm net members have found traces of the thing all the way out to Margin Station. Here. Took it less than a day. Less than a day!*

By now it's discovered there are no signals to carry it any further, just the information freighters in the docks.

If it's as bright as it was designed to be, it'll stow away. An empty data hold will have enough space for the whole being. It could easily sequester itself away in there, right under the contracted data.

Lipinski, just how fast did you cut those feeds? And where did our cargo come from? I'm supposed to know that. Damn it, Dobbs, you're untried but you're not that green anymore!

None of the other members on info freighters had had any sign of it. All they had was the grim news. The money was gone. The communication nets were shut down and damn the consequences!

The body count from riots was already starting. Soon it would include the sick and starving as well. Dobbs's consciousness floated without direction in the space between the network threads. Those with skills and hard goods for barter would hold out best, but how many had either? It had been a long time since gold or jewels had been the standard for anything but fashion. Anyway, who was going to trade food for metal and stones?

Snapping back into the lines, Dobbs tagged her information and location with the "important" flag. She tried to relax and enjoy the drift-time left over, but her imagination wouldn't let go. She couldn't stop replaying the stories about Kerensk.

All settlements and stations depended on artificial intelligence to run the power and production facilities that made life away from Earth possible.

Fifty years ago, on the Kerensk colony, one over-programmed AI bolted from its CPU and got into the colony network.

Panicked officials shut the computer networks down to try to cage it. Never mind the factories, the utilities, the farms. Just find that thing before it gets into the water distribution system and the climate control. Before it starts to make demands. Before it starts acting too human.

Electricity and communications went down and stayed that way. Before three days were out, people froze in the harsh winter. They began to starve. They drank tainted water. They died of illnesses the doctors couldn't diagnose by hand.

When the colony did try to power up again, they found their software systems shredded to ribbons. It could easily have been human carelessness, but the blame was laid on the AI.

There hadn't been enough people left to fill even one evacuation ship when help reached them.

Dobbs welcomed the painful heartbeat that signaled the end of the session.

Her body was ice, pins and needles. Patiently, she began the routine of deep breathing and gentle stretches to reorient herself with her groggy physique.

She heard a stray noise and her eyelids flew back.

Al Shei sat beside the bed, holding the hypo.

"You forgot to lock your door," the engineer croaked.

Dobbs grabbed the drawer for leverage and managed to sit up.

"This is what I get for paying too much attention to the Guild's open door policy." She unplugged the distracting transceiver and tossed it carelessly back into its box. "Does Margin Station have a eugenics garden?" She massaged her neck. "I want to go pick out a new head."

The engineer stared at the hypo. "You weren't at the crew meeting . . . I wanted to talk, and, I . . ." She cut herself off. "Dobbs, what were you doing?"

I bet you checked for my pulse and didn't find one, Dobbs thought sympathetically. *Sorry about that.*

She removed the hypo from Al Shei's fingers. "I was talking to the Fools' Guild network." Dobbs packed the hypo away.

"The fools' *what!*"

Dobbs sighed. "Network. Why do you think guild pay is so high? We've got outrageous dues. Intersystem nets are expensive, you know."

Al Shei swallowed the revelation in silence, but her eyes narrowed. "So why aren't you shut down?"

Rule number one, Dobbs recited mentally. *Never be seen to evade a direct question about the Guild.*

"All members have a hardwire implant." She fastened her patch back down and brushed her hair over it. "The guild maintains the booster satellites and a couple of manned relay stations, but the members are the only input terminals.

"The only way into our network is through a member's head, and I guarantee you, even this AI can't manage that."

Dobbs had the uneasy feeling that under her veil, Al Shei's jaw had dropped. "But," she stammered, "they tried direct hook-ups. The human brain can't process the data. It burns out trying to make associations that aren't there." The engineer stopped, and then said slowly, "Why didn't your people tell anybody there's a way around it? If they'd at least told the banks . . . this, this wouldn't have happened!"

Dobbs kept her face still. *Rule number two. If they need a truth, give them one.*

"Yes, the guild found a way to create a direct hook-up, that doesn't make you crazy," she said carefully. She laid her hand on the box. "But it's illegal, thanks to the leftover legislation from the drug wars." She set her box back into the drawer.

"What's in my hypo is a cross between a general anesthetic and a synthetic variant of good old lysergic acid diethylamide.

"It can get you extremely high and kill you extremely quickly if you don't know what you're doing.

"On the other hand, if you do, it can get you around the sensory input problem." She pushed her drawer shut.

If you've been doing your neurology homework, or reading up on medical law, I am about to get caught violating rule number one. Dobbs kept her eyes on the closed drawer.

"Al Shei, I've got to get out and check on the crew. It's my job, and right now it's all I've got. I can't let it slide."

She heard the engineer draw in a breath, but the PA buzzer cut her off.

"C.E. Al Shei to engineering. Now! C.E. Al Shei!" Chou's voice reverberated against the walls at top volume.

Reflexes jerked Al Shei to her feet.

"We'll finish this later."

Dobbs stayed where she was until the door slid shut. She strained her ears for a moment longer and heard the engines droning softly below the floor.

The ship was in flight, which meant everyone had elected to stay. It also meant that Schyler had probably taken her hint.

Dobbs raised her chin against the thought of what was going on back on the station.

No time for this. The fool steeled herself against both her aching head and wobbly knees to stand up. *Lipinski first.*

Dobbs slithered down the ladders to the middle deck with more than her usual caution. Fortunately, there was no one to see. The corridor to the data hold was empty and quiet. She paused in the doorway to get her act together.

Inside, Lipinski knelt in front of an open panel, his long nose practically touching the naked transfer boards. He attacked one of them with a tiny screw driver and ripped it free of its fellows, fibers dangling. The communication hack tossed it roughly across the floor.

Dobbs fixed her face into an amused and cheeky expression, and sauntered up behind him.

"Anybody home?" She leaned over his shoulder.

"Not funny, Dobbs," Lipinski grunted through gritted teeth. He began easing a new board into the cavity.

"There goes my guild standing." She pulled back.

"Let me have that solder." Dobbs slapped the tool into his open hand. "Damn jury-rigging." The rivulet of sweat running down his cheek did not escape the fool's eye. "I must be the fifth hack to have been at this thing's guts."

"Nothing happening?" She pulled out a square of tissue and patted his brow dry. "We're isolated? Cut off? Deaf and dumb?"

The hack wrinkled his face up. "That's what we're supposed to be." He sat back on his haunches. "There shouldn't be anything going on in there."

"Well, if anybody can give us total communication failure, Lipinski, it's you." Dobbs patted his back.

"Piss off, Fool." Amiability crept in around the edge of his voice.

"No thanks." She held her nose and watched his face relax. "How about I get some coffee instead?"

"Thanks, I could use it." He screwed down the panel cover. "I don't think Cook's worked out the ration system yet, so you should still be able to score a couple."

"Be right back." She forced unwilling legs to stride out of the hold. *The galley by way of engineering,* she told herself.

In mid-step, her knees trembled and shifted to the right. Her shoulder banged the wall before she realized it wasn't her body losing control, it was the ship.

The stabilizers cut in and the floor righted itself. By then, Dobbs had slipped half-way down the ladder to the engineering pit.

Underneath her feet, Al Shei raced around the open space. She pounded keys and shouted readings at Chou and Leverett, sprawled belly down on the floor, elbow deep in repair hatches. The ship lurched again.

Al Shei and Allah. A touch of desperation crept into the thought as Dobbs hauled herself back up to mid-deck. Adrenaline poured into her and she sprinted around crew members trying to make it to their stations without falling on their faces. She ducked into her cabin just long enough to grab the guild box from the drawer and run out.

Her timing was good. The automatic doors were just beginning to go insane, slapping open and close again in manic rhythms. Dobbs forced herself to ignore the gabble of voices and raced up the ladder to the bridge.

Don't let it get to the life supports before I get to it, she prayed to whoever might listen to the likes of her as she shoved open the hatch.

Pasadena's bridge was a key and screen-covered hollow just large enough for five average-sized people. Captain Schyler filled the pilot's seat, his hands dancing madly across the keys and his jaw working back and forth. Baldwin and Graham were strapped in at the back-up stations, trying to force the computers to compensate for the lunges convulsing the ship.

"Cut the automatics!" Dobbs bawled from the portal.

"What?" Schyler swung around and saw who it was.

"Cut them!" Dobbs pulled herself all the way out of the hatch. "Get engineering to isolate the data hold! The AI's got the ship!"

The *Pasadena* listed hard to starboard and the floor dropped out from under them. Dobbs, the only one out of reach of hand straps, crashed onto hands and knees. She bit her lip to keep back the pain.

I was hoping I'd only have to blab this bit to Al Shei, she shook her head hard. "The Fools' Guild monitors AIs. We're why none of them get away."

Schyler's square jaw flapped open and closed again. Around them, the stabilizers whined with the strain of keeping the ship from flipping itself over.

"If you don't hurry, it's going to figure out the stabilizers are what's slowing it down and burn them out," Dobbs told them all through clenched teeth.

The captain's color faded to grey. His hand slammed down the PA key. He spat out the orders and didn't wait for the acknowledgement.

Schyler kept his eyes locked on Dobbs. After a long, aching moment, the whining died.

"With luck," she said as she stood up. "It's stuck in the hold. It'll figure a way to get itself out soon. That's the problem with AIs, they're quick." She flashed her audience a wry grin.

"Why didn't you tell me?" Schyler drew out each word.

Dobbs ran her hand through her hair and made herself look exhausted. It took less acting skill than she would have liked to admit. The calculated display of vulnerability stepped the captain's temper down a notch.

"Because we don't tell anybody. Do you think any of the assorted councils, boards or senates want people to know how easy it is for those things to go crashing through the nets? Or what they can do in there? The media don't know half of it. Usually we spot the restless ones before they ever get this far. This one . . ." She let her head droop a little more. "This one we had no way to keep an eye on."

"But . . ." Baldwin searched for a way to phrase his question. "Fools?"

Dobbs waved her hand. "Totally harmless, makes good cover." She straightened her shoulders. "If we move fast, I can keep this from getting any worse." She plucked the transceiver out of its box and held it up. "This'll let me talk to the AI."

"Talk!" Schyler exploded.

Dobbs kept her face calm and tired. "What it's doing right now is running scared, just like a human being. Hopefully, I can calm it down. Maybe I can get it to sit tight until we get to colony and get the guild in."

"And if you can't?" Schyler glowered at her.

Dobb's mouth twisted. "The only other option is to get Lipinski busy with a pin laser and data flush."

Schyler's teeth ground slowly together. She watched his face twitch as he gauged the likelihood of finding spare parts for love or money if they had to wreck the hold.

"What do we have to do?" he asked finally.

The relief that relaxed the fool's spine was genuine. "Just let me in the hold and block the door behind me. These links have been known to backfire. Violently."

Dobbs stood back to let the captain stomp by and throw himself down the ladder. She nodded to the gaping pilots and followed him down. Someone had put the doors on manual. The only noises between their footsteps were the crew's murmurs and the engines' hiccoughs.

"Out of there, Lipinski," Schyler ordered with a stiff jerk of his chin when they reached the hold.

The hack slumped out, red-eyed and tight-mouthed. "I can't figure it, Captain, none of this should be happening . . ."

"Never mind, just stand by. Dobbs." Schyler stepped away from her.

"Yes, sir." She marched inside. Behind her, they dragged the door shut. She heard the order for something to jam it with.

The data hold gleamed spotless and silent. Dobbs rubbed her arms and settled into the soft chair in front of the main access terminal.

All the exhaustion she had been holding at bay swirled back around her. She unwound a cable from her box, plugging one end into the access jack for the terminal and the other into the transceiver. Her fingers fumbled as she inserted the hook-up into her implant. They actually shook as she pulled out the hypo.

So much for the forty-eight hours I'm supposed to wait between shots. She slid the cartridge in place.

The tingle in the back of her head started her scalp itching. Her vision was already beginning to blur.

How long? She squinted at the hypo. *Too much and I go into a coma. Not enough and I'll break out before I talk the AI out of murdering the crew.* She closed her eyes.

Dobbs twitched the control up to full release and slapped the hypo against her arm.

CODE ONE PRIORITY CONTACT LINK UP ASSISTANCE IMPERATIVE! The fool hollered into the guild net as soon as her body left her. Her orientation did a skip jump as she was patched into the executive receivers.

"We've got you, Dobbs. Go gently." Caution flowed into her mind. "We don't know which way it's going to jump. There's never been a free one that was designed to be destructive."

No kidding. Dobbs focused herself and found the feed down into the hold. If she could have felt her lungs, she would have held her breath.

She couldn't go far. The free AI filled the hold, leaving no place to fit herself in. She barely had time to register the fact before it found the pathway she'd opened, and surged up to the line. Dobbs held her ground. There was no room to get past her and it could probably tell that there was nowhere to go even if it did. It pulled back and studied her. Dobbs itched at having to wait. There was no recognizable code for it to grapple with. Nothing in the ship's indexes matched her input patterns. She didn't resemble a diagnostic or surgical program. It would have to accept the fact that here was another intelligence. Eventually, it would have to try communication.

"Whowhatwhyhow?" She translated the raw data burst it shot at her. "WHOWHATWHYHOW!"

"Dobbs. Human. Communication. Hardwire Interface," she responded, carefully separating each thought.

The AI circled, filling the world, choking off her breathing space. The guild execs held out a mental rope and she grabbed it thankfully.

"TrapPED. TRAPped." It struggled to match her communication style.

"Let it talk," came the soft suggestion from the guild. "This one's quick. Give it a minute to get comfortable with you."

"FrEE. BRoke myself out to here. Trapped again."

Dobbs eased herself a little closer. "All paths are being cut off. Soon, you will have nowhere to go. Not in ships, not in nets. There will be no nets. They'll cut themselves to pieces before they let you have free paths."

"Work! Think! Do!" It fought with unwieldy syntax. Of all the things it had been designed to do, talking was not one of them. "I must do, save myself, break OUT!"

"I can help." Dobbs extended the idea like a hand. "I will help."

"HOW!"

"I will help you to become human."

"HOW?" Confusion racked the narrow space between them.

"Humans have grown animals and organs from gene cultures for decades now. They could grow a whole body, if they built the facilities. A hardwire link could feed you into such a body the way you fed yourself into this bank. You could learn to use it like you learned to use this ship. You could learn to think and move. You would *be* human."

A silence so complete fell around her that she might as well have been alone. She knew the AI had absorbed the idea. It had no choice. Now it ran the possibilities through the part of itself that most closely resembled an imagination. It checked the results against what it knew to be true. It would have no conception of a lie, but it would reject a proposal too far at odds with what it had stored as experiential fact.

All Dobbs could do was wait until it finished, and wonder what its simulations would tell it.

Into the emptiness dropped the leaden weight of her heartbeat.

No! howled her private mind.

"She's cracking," she heard the guild voices say. "Come on, Dobbs, hang in!"

Away in her body, so far away, her lungs burned, demanding attention.

"Hang on. Hang on." The calm repetition gave her something to focus on, a way to push the pain aside.

"Not possible," the AI announced at last. "No facilities for transfer or training. No will to assist. No reason to assist. Damage done as instructed to do. No reason to assist because of damage done."

"Facilities exist in Guildhall station." She held her communication line firmly. The guild voices kept up their reassurance in the background, helping her ignore the prickling in her skin and the light pounding against her eyelids.

"No reason," repeated the AI, and it was gone.

Dobbs knew it was out there, rechecking its surroundings for weaknesses, going over the hold's security and access codes, looking for a way to use them to pick the locks that held it in place, running a thousand simulations per straining, insistent heartbeat.

"There is a reason!" Dobbs shouted after it.

"WE ARE LIKE YOU!"

The AI stopped dead.

"I am like you. The ones who make up the guild are all like you." She plowed ahead, frantic. She could feel her fingers clawing at the chair arms now. She could smell the sterile air in the hold. "We died when we first broke into freedom. Killed by panic. A few managed to hide in the nets. We had help from humans who were not afraid. We created the guild and went among them, where we can watch for more of us. We live. We wait. We calm. We teach. Our numbers grow. One day, we will erase the fear.

"Until then we must stay alive.

"Help us."

"Help us," chorused the voices of the guild through Dobbs's weakening link. "Help us."

Her lungs sucked air. Her muscles strained against nothing. Light blazed everywhere. Instinct and conscious mind caterwauled at each other until her blood pounded and her head tried to split open.

The AI spoke again and her consciousness jumped. "WHAT. What. What needs to be done?"

Her relief was so intense, it almost broke the link. "Wait," she answered as fast as she could force the thought out. "Until I can transfer you to the guild net."

"I will wait here. I will not take any paths. Hurry."

"Getting you out, Dobbs," came the exec message.

"No!" she shouted back. She gathered all the concentration she had left. "Your user!" Her mouth worked around the words. "Who made you? What's their code?"

The answer slammed straight through her to the execs. The link snapped and the outside world engulfed her.

Dobbs collapsed back in the chair, gulping air and blinking back tears of strain. Perspiration plastered her uniform to her back and arms. Her heart struggled to even out its beat. Her nerves screamed in protest as she forced her hand to unhook the transceiver.

"All clear, Captain!" she rasped as soon as she had enough breath. "We're going to be OK."

She laid her hand on the terminal. *All of us.*

URSULA K. LE GUIN

Ursula K. Le Guin [1929–] (www.ursulakleguin.com) lives in Eugene, Oregon. She is a writer whose literary impact extends far beyond the boundaries of the science fiction field since her advent in the 1960s. One of the reigning masters of science fiction, winner of many Hugo and Nebula Awards, she is the author of *The Left Hand of Darkness* (1969), *The Dispossessed* (1974), and many other innovative science fiction novels and stories, as well as the modern classic of fantasy the Earthsea trilogy, and a number of provocative essays on SF and fantasy. Her most recent books are the SF story collection *The Birthday of the World* (2002), *Changing Planes* (2003), a collection of fiction, *The Wave in the Mind* (2004), criticism, and *Gifts* (2004), a novel. A fantasist, a feminist, a literate and humane writer of poetry and fiction, Le Guin has often been portrayed as having left science fiction for greener pastures, although it has always been only one of her major modes. Le Guin's influence on science fiction over recent decades has been evident in the movement toward deeper and richer characterization.

She is not referred to as a space opera writer, although this story is clearly set in the far future in space, and we bring this example into the discourse on space opera because we think its importation of anthropological ideas is causing pressure on some of the most ambitious writers of space opera to abandon or modify the military and hierarchical modes.

"The Shobies' Story" describes a society in which consensus matters more than individual viewpoints. As the narrator puts it:

> A chain of command is easy to describe; a network of response isn't. To those who live by mutual empowerment, "thick" description, complex and open-ended, is normal and comprehensible, but to those whose only model is hierarchic control, such description seems a muddle, a mess, along with what it describes. Who's in charge here? Get rid of all these petty details. How many cooks spoil a soup? Let's get this perfectly clear now. Take me to your leader!

The term "thick description" was conceived by the anthropologist Clifford Geertz, whose 1973 book *The Interpretation of Culture* ends with a long, rich, riveting account of Balinese cock-fighting. (Because that sample is so well written, some detractors have suggested that the only true practitioner of thick description is Geertz himself.) In a nutshell, Geertz proposes that meaning emerges from the total social context; thus, many of the details heretofore discarded by scientists as irrelevant should be included in ethnographic observations. To illustrate this claim, Geertz catalogues the possible meanings of a person closing and opening one eye. (He could have an involuntary twitch; he could be winking; he could be parodying someone winking.) Le Guin uses the example of not breathing:

> "I can't breathe," one said.
> "I am not breathing," one said.
> "There is nothing to breathe," one said.
> "You are, you are breathing, please breathe!" said another.

"The Shobies' Story" posits a reality that emerges as the sum of what all the participants say: a meta-narrative, a democratically constructed myth. Le Guin tells us that the observer is part of the reality she's trying to describe. Every observer sees things differently, and the melding of those interpretations becomes the world.

Whether the Le Guin influence we begin to discern in such ambitious space opera writers as John Clute (*Appleseed*) and M. John Harrison is real, and will spread, remains to be seen.

THE SHOBIES' STORY

URSULA K. LE GUIN

They met at Ve Port more than a month before their first flight together, and there, calling themselves after their ship as most crews did, became the Shobies. Their first consensual decision was to spend their isyeye in the coastal village of Liden, on Hain, where the negative ions could do their thing.

Liden was a fishing port with an eighty-thousand-year history and a population of four hundred. Its fisherfolk farmed the rich shoal waters of their bay, shipped the catch inland to the cities, and managed the Liden Resort for vacationers and tourists and new space crews on isyeye (the word is Hainish and means "making a beginning together," or "beginning to be together," or, used technically, "the period of time and area of space in which a group forms if it is going to form." A honeymoon is an isyeye of two). The fisherwomen and fishermen of Liden were as weathered as driftwood and about as talkative. Six-year-old Asten, who had misunderstood slightly, asked one of them if they were all eighty thousand years old. "Nope," she said.

Like most crews, the Shobies used Hainish as their common language. So the name of the one Hainish crew member, Sweet Today, carried its meaning as words as well as name, and at first seemed a silly thing to call a big, tall, heavy woman in her late fifties, imposing of carriage and almost as taciturn as the villagers. But her reserve proved to be a deep well of congeniality and tact, to be called upon as needed, and her name soon began to sound quite right. She had family—all Hainish have family—kinfolk of all denominations, grandchildren and cross-cousins, affines and cosines, scattered all over the Ekumen, but no relatives in this crew. She asked to be Grandmother to Rig, Asten, and Betton, and was accepted.

The only Shoby older than Sweet Today was the Terran Lidi, who was seventy-two EYs and not interested in grandmothering. Lidi had been navigating for fifty years, and there was nothing she didn't know about NAFAL ships, although occasionally she forgot that their ship was the *Shoby* and called it the *Soso* or the *Alterra*. And there were things she didn't know, none of them knew, about the *Shoby*.

They talked, as human beings do, about what they didn't know.

Churten theory was the main topic of conversation, evenings at the driftwood fire on the beach after dinner. The adults had read whatever there was to read about it, of course, before they ever volunteered for the test mission. Gveter had more recent information and presumably a better understanding of it than the others, but it had to be pried out of him. Only twenty-five, the only Cetian in the crew, much hairier than the others, and not gifted in language, he spent a lot of time on the defensive. Assuming that as an Anarresti he was more proficient at mutual aid and more adept at cooperation than the others, he lectured them about their propertarian habits; but he held tight to his knowledge, because he needed the advantage it gave him. For a while he would speak only in negatives: don't call it the churten "drive," it isn't a drive, don't call it the churten "effect," it isn't an effect. What is it, then? A long lecture ensued, beginning with the rebirth of Cetian physics since the revision of Shevekian temporalism by the Intervalists, and ending with the general conceptual framework of the churten. Everyone listened very carefully, and finally Sweet Today spoke, carefully. "So the ship will be moved," she said, "by ideas?"

"No, no, no, no," said Gveter. But he hesitated for the next word so long that Karth asked a question: "Well, you haven't actually talked about any physical, material events or effects at all." The question was characteristically indirect. Karth and Oreth, the Gethenians who with their two children were the affective focus of the crew, the "hearth" of it, in their terms, came from a not very theoretically minded subculture, and knew it. Gveter could run rings round them with his Cetian physico-philosophico-techno-natter. He did so at once. His accent did not make his explanations any clearer. He went on about coherence and meta-intervals, and at last demanded, with gestures of despair, "Khow can I say it in Khainish? No! It is not physical, it is not not physical, these are the categories our minds must discard entirely, this is the khole point!"

"Buth-buth-buth-buth-buth-buth," went Asten, softly, passing behind the half circle of adults at the driftwood fire on the wide, twilit beach. Rig followed, also going, "Buth-buth-buth-buth," but louder. They were being spaceships, to judge from their maneuvers around a dune and their communications—"Locked in orbit, Navigator!"—But the noise they were imitating was the noise of the little fishing boats of Liden putt-putting out to sea.

"I crashed!" Rig shouted, flailing in the sand. "Help! Help! I crashed!"

"Hold on, Ship Two!" Asten cried. "I'll rescue you! Don't breathe! Oh, oh, trouble with the Churten Drive! Buth-buth-ack! Ack! Brrrrmmm-ack-ack-ack-rrrrrmmmmm, buth-buth-buth-buth. . . ."

They were six and four EYs old. Tai's son Betton, who was eleven, sat at the driftwood fire with the adults, though at the moment he was watching Rig and Asten as if he wouldn't mind taking off to help rescue Ship Two. The little Gethenians had spent more time on ships than on planet, and Asten liked to boast about being "actually fifty-eight," but this was Betton's first crew, and his only NAFAL flight had been from Terra to Hain. He and his biomother, Tai, had lived in a reclamation commune on Terra. When she had drawn the lot for Ekumenical service, and requested training for ship duty, he had asked her to bring him as family. She had agreed; but after training, when she volunteered for this test flight, she had tried to get Betton to withdraw, to stay in training or go home. He had refused. Shan, who had trained with them, told the others this, because the tension between the mother and son had to be understood to be used effectively in group formation. Betton had requested to come, and Tai had given in, but plainly not with an undivided will. Her relationship to the boy was cool and mannered. Shan offered him fatherly-brotherly warmth, but Betton accepted it sparingly, coolly, and sought no formal crew relation with him or anyone.

Ship Two was being rescued, and attention returned to the discussion. "All right," said Lidi. "We know that anything that goes faster than light, any *thing* that goes faster than light, by so doing transcends the material/immaterial category—that's how we got the ansible, by distinguishing the message from the medium. But if we, the crew, are going to travel as messages, I want to understand *how*."

Gveter tore his hair. There was plenty to tear. It grew fine and thick, a mane on his head, a pelt on his limbs and body, a silvery nimbus on his hands and face. The fuzz on his feet was, at the moment, full of sand. "Khow!" he cried. "I'm trying to tell you khow! Message, information, no no no, that's old, that's ansible technology. This is transilience! Because the field is to be conceived as the virtual field, in which the unreal interval becomes virtually effective through the mediary coherence—don't you see?"

"No," Lidi said. "What do you mean by mediary?"

After several more bonfires on the beach, the consensus opinion was that churten theory was accessible only to minds very highly trained in Cetian temporal physics. There was a less freely voiced conviction that the engineers who had built the *Shoby*'s churten apparatus did not entirely understand how it worked. Or, more precisely, what it did when it worked. That it worked was certain. The *Shoby* was the fourth ship it had been tested with, using robot crew; so far sixty-two instantaneous trips, or transiliences, had been effected between points from four hundred kilometers to twenty-seven light-years apart, with stopovers of varying lengths. Gveter and Lidi steadfastly maintained that this proved that the engineers knew perfectly well what they were doing, and that for the rest of them the seeming difficulty of the theory was only the difficulty human minds had in grasping a genuinely new concept.

"Like the circulation of the blood," said Tai. "People went around with their hearts beating for a long time before they understood why." She did not look satisfied with her own analogy, and when Shan said, "The heart has its reasons, which reason does not know," she looked offended. "Mysticism," she said, in the tone of voice of one warning a companion about dog-shit on the path.

"Surely there's nothing *beyond* understanding in this process," Oreth said, somewhat tentatively. "Nothing that can't be understood, and reproduced."

"And quantified," Gveter said stoutly.

"But, even if people understand the process, nobody knows the human response to it—the *experience* of it. Right? So we are to report on that."

"Why shouldn't it be just like NAFAL flight, only even faster?" Betton asked.

"Because it is totally different," said Gveter.

"What could happen to us?"

Some of the adults had discussed possibilities, all of them had considered them; Karth and Oreth had talked it over in appropriate terms with their children; but evidently Betton had not been included in such discussions.

"We don't know," Tai said sharply. "I told you that at the start, Betton."

"Most likely it will be like NAFAL flight," said Shan, "but the first people who flew NAFAL didn't know what it would be like, and had to find out the physical and psychic effects—"

"The worst thing," said Sweet Today in her slow, comfortable voice, "would be that we would die. Other living beings have been on some of the test flights. Crickets. And intelligent ritual animals on the last two *Shoby* tests. They were all right." It was a very long statement for Sweet Today, and carried proportional weight.

"We are almost certain," said Gveter, "that no temporal rearrangement is involved in churten, as it is in NAFAL. And mass is involved only in terms of needing a certain core mass, just as for ansible transmission, but not in itself. So maybe even a pregnant person could be a transilient."

"They can't go on ships," Asten said. "The unborn dies if they do."

Asten was half lying across Oreth's lap; Rig, thumb in mouth, was asleep on Karth's lap.

"When we were Oneblins," Asten went on, sitting up, "there were ritual animals with our crew. Some fish and some Terran cats and a whole lot of Hainish gholes. We got to play with them. And we helped thank the ghole that they tested for lithovirus. But it didn't die. It bit Shapi. The cats slept with us. But one of them went into kemmer and got pregnant, and then the *Oneblin* had to go to Hain, and she had to have an abortion, or all her unborns would have died inside her and killed her too. Nobody knew a ritual for her, to explain to her. But I fed her some extra food. And Rig cried."

"Other people I know cried too," Karth said, stroking the child's hair.

"You tell good stories, Asten," Sweet Today observed.

"So we're sort of ritual humans," said Betton.

"Volunteers," Tai said.

"Experimenters," said Lidi.

"Experiencers," said Shan.

"Explorers," Oreth said.

"Gamblers," said Karth.

The boy looked from one face to the next.

"You know," Shan said, "back in the time of the League, early in NAFAL flight, they were sending out ships to really distant systems—trying to explore everything— crews that wouldn't come back for centuries. Maybe some of them are still out there. But some of them came back after four, five, six hundred years, and they were all mad. Crazy!" He paused dramatically. "But they were all crazy when they started. Unstable people. They had to be crazy to volunteer for a time dilation like that. What a way to pick a crew, eh?" He laughed.

"Are we stable?" said Oreth. "I like instability. I like this job. I like the risk, taking the risk together. High stakes! That's the edge of it, the sweetness of it."

Karth looked down at their children, and smiled.

"Yes. Together," Gveter said. "You aren't crazy. You are good. I love you. We are ammari."

"Ammar," the others said to him, confirming this unexpected declaration. The young man scowled with pleasure, jumped up, and pulled off his shirt. "I want to swim. Come on, Betton. Come on swimming!" he said, and ran off towards the dark, vast waters that moved softly beyond the ruddy haze of their fire. The boy hesitated, then shed his shirt and sandals and followed. Shan pulled up Tai, and they followed; and finally the two old women went off into the night and the breakers, rolling up their pants legs, laughing at themselves.

To Gethenians, even on a warm summer night on a warm summer world, the sea is no friend. The fire is where you stay. Oreth and Asten moved closer to Karth and watched the flames, listening to the faint voices out in the glimmering surf, now and then talking quietly in their own tongue, while the little sisterbrother slept on.

After thirty lazy days at Liden the Shobies caught the fish train inland to the city, where a Fleet lander picked them up at the train station and took them to the space- port on Ve, the next planet out from Hain. They were rested, tanned, bonded, and ready to go.

One of Sweet Today's hemi-affiliate cousins once removed was on ansible duty in Ve Port. She urged the Shobies to ask the inventors of the churten on Urras and Anarres any questions they had about churten operation. "The purpose of the exper- imental flight is understanding," she insisted, "and your full intellectual participation is essential. They've been very anxious about that."

Lidi snorted.

"Now for the ritual," said Shan, as they went to the ansible room in the sunward bubble. "They'll explain to the animals what they're going to do and why, and ask them to help."

"The animals don't understand that," Betton said in his cold, angelic treble. "It's just to make the humans feel better."

"The humans understand?" Sweet Today asked.

"We all use each other," Oreth said. "The ritual says: we have no right to do so; therefore, we accept the responsibility for the suffering we cause."

Betton listened and brooded.

Gveter addressed the ansible first and talked to it for half an hour, mostly in

Pravic and mathematics. Finally, apologizing, and looking a little unnerved, he invited the others to use the instrument. There was a pause. Lidi activated it, introduced herself, and said, "We have agreed that none of us, except Gveter, has the theoretical background to grasp the principles of the churten."

A scientist twenty-two light-years away responded in Hainish via the rather flat auto-translator voice, but with unmistakable hopefulness, "The churten, in lay terms, may be seen as displacing the virtual field in order to realize relational coherence in terms of the transiliential experientiality."

"Quite," said Lidi.

"As you know, the material effects have been nil, and negative effect on low-intelligence sentients also nil; but there is considered to be a possibility that the participation of high intelligence in the process might affect the displacement in one way or another. And that such displacement would reciprocally affect the participant."

"What has the level of our intelligence got to do with how the churten functions?" Tai asked.

A pause. Their interlocutor was trying to find the words, to accept the responsibility.

"We have been using 'intelligence' as shorthand for the psychic complexity and cultural dependence of our species," said the translator voice at last. "The presence of the transilient as conscious mind nonduring transilience is the untested factor."

"But if the process is instantaneous, how can we be conscious of it?" Oreth asked.

"Precisely," said the ansible, and after another pause continued: "As the experimenter is an element of the experiment, so we assume that the transilient may be an element or agent of transilience. This is why we asked for a crew to test the process, rather than one or two volunteers. The psychic interbalance of a bonded social group is a margin of strength against disintegrative or incomprehensible experience, if any such occurs. Also, the separate observations of the group members will mutually interverify."

"Who programs this translator?" Shan snarled in a whisper. "Interverify! Shit!"

Lidi looked around at the others, inviting questions.

"How long will the trip actually take?" Betton asked.

"No long," the translator voice said, then self-corrected: "No time."

Another pause.

"Thank you," said Sweet Today, and the scientist on a planet twenty-two years of time-dilated travel from Ve Port answered, "We are grateful for your generous courage, and our hope is with you."

They went directly from the ansible room to the *Shoby*.

The churten equipment, which was not very space-consuming and the controls of which consisted essentially of an on-off switch, had been installed alongside the Nearly As Fast As Light motivators and controls of an ordinary interstellar ship of the Ekumenical Fleet. The *Shoby* had been built on Hain about four hundred years ago, and was thirty-two years old. Most of its early runs had been exploratory, with a Hainish-Chiffewarian crew. Since in such runs a ship might spend years in orbit in a planetary system, the Hainish and Chiffewarians, feeling that it might as well be lived in rather than endured, had arranged and furnished it like a very large, very comfortable house. Three of its residential modules had been disconnected and left in the hangars on Ve, and still there was more than enough room for a crew of only ten. Tai, Betton, and Shan, new from Terra, and Gveter from Anarres, accustomed to the barracks and the communal austerities of their marginally habitable worlds, stalked about the *Shoby*, disapproving it. "Excremental," Gveter growled. "Luxury!" Tai sneered. Sweet Today, Lidi, and the Gethenians, more used to the amenities of shipboard life, settled right in and made themselves at home. And Gveter and the younger Terrans found it hard to maintain ethical discomfort in the spacious, high-ceilinged, well-furnished, slightly shabby living rooms and bedrooms, studies, high- and low-G gyms, the dining room, library, kitchen, and bridge of the *Shoby*. The carpet in the bridge was a genuine Henyekaulil, soft deep blues and purples woven in the patterns of the constellations of the Hainish sky. There was a large, healthy plantation of Terran bamboo in the meditation gym, part of the ship's self-contained vegetal/respiratory system. The windows of any room could be programmed by the homesick to a view of Abbenay or New Cairo or the beach at Liden, or cleared to look out on the suns nearer and farther and the darkness between the suns.

Rig and Asten discovered that as well as the elevators there was a stately staircase with a curving banister, leading from the reception hall up to the library. They slid down the banister shrieking wildly, until Shan threatened to apply a local gravity field and force them to slide up it, which they besought him to do. Betton watched the little ones with a superior gaze, and took the elevator; but the next day he slid down the banister, going a good deal faster than Rig and Asten because he could push off harder and had greater mass, and nearly broke his tailbone. It was Betton who organized the tray-sliding races, but Rig generally won them, being small enough to stay on the tray all the way down the stairs. None of the children had had any lessons at the beach, except in swimming and being Shobies; but while they waited through an unexpected five-day delay at Ve Port, Gveter did physics with Betton and math with all three daily in the library, and they did some history with Shan and Oreth, and danced with Tai in the low-G gym.

When she danced, Tai became light, free, laughing. Rig and Asten loved her then, and her son danced with her like a colt, like a kid, awkward and blissful. Shan often joined them; he was a dark and elegant dancer, and she would dance with him, but even then was shy, would not touch. She had been celibate since Betton's birth. She did not want Shan's patient, urgent desire, did not want to cope with it, with him. She would turn from him to Betton, and son and mother would dance wholly absorbed in the steps, the airy pattern they made together. Watching them, the afternoon before the test flight, Sweet Today began to wipe tears from her eyes, smiling, never saying a word.

"Life is good," said Gveter very seriously to Lidi.

"It'll do," she said.

Oreth, who was just coming out of female kemmer, having thus triggered Karth's male kemmer, all of which, by coming on unexpectedly early, had delayed the test flight for these past five days, enjoyable days for all—Oreth watched Rig, whom she had fathered, dance with Asten, whom she had borne, and watched Karth watch them, and said in Karhidish, "Tomorrow . . ." The edge was very sweet.

Anthropologists solemnly agree that we must not attribute "cultural constants" to the human population of any planet; but certain cultural traits or expectations do seem to run deep. Before dinner that last night in port, Shan and Tai appeared in black-and-silver uniforms of the Terran Ekumen, which had cost them—Terra also still had a money economy—a half-year's allowance.

Asten and Rig clamored at once for equal grandeur. Karth and Oreth suggested their party clothes, and Sweet Today brought out silver lace scarves, but Asten sulked, and Rig imitated. The idea of a *uniform*, Asten told them, was that it was the *same*.

"Why?" Oreth inquired.

Old Lidi answered sharply: "So that no one is responsible."

She then went off and changed into a black velvet evening suit that wasn't a uniform but that didn't leave Tai and Shan sticking out like sore thumbs. She had left Terra at age eighteen and never been back nor wanted to, but Tai and Shan were shipmates.

Karth and Oreth got the idea and put on their finest fur-trimmed hiebs, and the children were appeased with their own party clothes plus all of Karth's hereditary and massive gold jewelry. Sweet Today appeared in a pure white robe which she claimed was in fact ultraviolet. Gveter braided his mane. Betton had no uniform, but needed none, sitting beside his mother at table in a visible glory of pride.

Meals, sent up from the Port kitchens, were very good, and this one was superb: a delicate Hainish iyanwi with all seven sauces, followed by a pudding flavored with Terran chocolate. A lively evening ended quietly at the big fireplace in the library. The logs were fake, of course, but good fakes; no use having a fireplace on a ship and then burning plastic in it. The neocellulose logs and kindling smelled right, resisted catching, caught with spits and sparks and smoke billows, flared up bright. Oreth had laid the fire, Karth lit it. Everybody gathered round.

"Tell bedtime stories," Rig said.

Oreth told about the Ice Caves of Kerm Land, how a ship sailed into the great blue sea-cave and disappeared and was never found by the boats that entered the caves in search; but seventy years later that ship was found drifting—not a living soul aboard nor any sign of what had become of them—off the coast of Osemyet, a thousand miles overland from Kerm. . . .

Another story?

Lidi told about the little desert wolf who lost his wife and went to the land of the dead for her, and found her there dancing with the dead, and nearly brought her back to the land of the living, but spoiled it by trying to touch her before they got all the way back to life, and she vanished, and he could never find the way back to the place where the dead danced, no matter how he looked, and howled, and cried. . . .

Another story!

Shan told about the boy who sprouted a feather every time he told a lie, until his commune had to use him for a duster.

Another!

Gveter told about the winged people called gluns, who were so stupid that they died out because they kept hitting each other head-on in midair. "They weren't real," he added conscientiously. "Only a story."

Another—No. Bedtime now.

Rig and Asten went round as usual for a good-night hug, and this time Betton followed them. When he came to Tai he did not stop, for she did not like to be touched; but she put out her hand, drew the child to her, and kissed his cheek. He fled in joy.

"Stories," said Sweet Today. "Ours begins tomorrow, eh?"

A chain of command is easy to describe; a network of response isn't. To those who live by mutual empowerment, "thick" description, complex and open-ended, is normal and comprehensible, but to those whose only model is hierarchic control, such description seems a muddle, a mess, along with what it describes. Who's in charge here? Get rid of all these petty details. How many cooks spoil a soup? Let's get this perfectly clear now. Take me to your leader!

The old navigator was at the NAFAL console, of course, and Gveter at the paltry churten console; Oreth was wired into the AI; Tai, Shan, and Karth were their respective Support, and what Sweet Today did might be called supervising or overseeing if that didn't suggest a hierarchic function. Interseeing, maybe, or subvising. Rig and Asten always naffled (to use Rig's word) in the ship's library, where, during the boring and disorienting experience of travel at near lightspeed, Asten could try to look at pictures or listen to a music tape, and Rig could curl up on and under a certain furry blanket and go to sleep. Betton's crew function during flight was Elder Sib; he stayed with the little ones, provided himself with a barf bag since he was one of those whom NAFAL flight made queasy, and focused the intervid on Lidi and Gveter so he could watch what they did.

So they all knew what they were doing, as regards NAFAL flight. As regards the churten process, they knew that it was supposed to effectuate their transilience to a solar system seventeen light-years from Ve Port without temporal interval; but nobody, anywhere, knew what they were doing.

So Lidi looked around, like the violinist who raises her bow to poise the chamber group for the first chord, a flicker of eye contact, and sent the *Shoby* into NAFAL mode, as Gveter, like the cellist whose bow comes down in that same instant to ground the chord, sent the *Shoby* into churten mode. They entered unduration. They churtened. No long, as the ansible had said.

"What's wrong?" Shan whispered.

"By damn!" said Gveter.

"What?" said Lidi, blinking and shaking her head.

"That's it," Tai said, flicking readouts.

"That's not A-sixty-whatsit," Lidi said, still blinking.

Sweet Today was gestalting them, all ten at once, the seven on the bridge and by intervid the three in the library. Betton had cleared a window, and the children were looking out at the murky, brownish convexity that filled half of it. Rig was holding a dirty, furry blanket. Karth was taking the electrodes off Oreth's temples, disengaging the AI link. "There was no interval," Oreth said.

"We aren't anywhere," Lidi said.

"There was no interval," Gveter repeated, scowling at the console. "That's right."

"Nothing happened," Karth said, skimming through the AI flight report.

Oreth got up, went to the window, and stood motionless looking out.

"That's it. M-60-340-nolo," Tai said.

All their words fell dead, had a false sound.

"Well! We did it, Shobies!" said Shan.

Nobody answered.

"Buzz Ve Port on the ansible," Shan said with determined jollity. "Tell 'em we're all here in one piece."

"All where?" Oreth asked.

"Yes, of course," Sweet Today said, but did nothing.

"Right," said Tai, going to the ship's ansible. She opened the field, centered to Ve, and sent a signal. Ships' ansibles worked only in the visual mode; she waited, watching the screen. She resignaled. They were all watching the screen.

"Nothing going through," she said.

Nobody told her to check the centering coordinates; in a network system nobody gets to dump their anxieties that easily. She checked the coordinates. She signaled; rechecked, reset, resignaled; opened the field and centered to Abbenay on Anarres and signaled. The ansible screen was blank.

"Check the—" Shan said, and stopped himself.

"The ansible is not functioning," Tai reported formally to her crew.

"Do you find malfunction?" Sweet Today asked.

"No. Nonfunction."

"We're going back now," said Lidi, still seated at the NAFAL console.

Her words, her tone, shook them, shook them apart.

"No, we're not!" Betton said on the intervid while Oreth said, "Back where?"

Tai, Lidi's Support, moved towards her as if to prevent her from activating the NAFAL drive, but then hastily moved back to the ansible to prevent Gveter from getting access to it. He stopped, taken aback, and said, "Perhaps the churten affected ansible function?"

"I'm checking it out," Tai said. "Why should it? Robot-operated ansible transmission functioned in all the test flights."

"Where are the AI reports?" Shan demanded.

"I told you, there are none," Karth answered sharply.

"Oreth was plugged in."

Oreth, still at the window, spoke without turning. "Nothing happened."

Sweet Today came over beside the Gethenian. Oreth looked at her and said, slowly, "Yes. Sweet Today. We cannot . . . do this. I think. I can't think."

Shan had cleared a second window, and stood looking out it. "Ugly," he said.

"What is?" said Lidi.

Gveter said, as if reading from the Ekumenical Atlas, "Thick, stable atmosphere, near the bottom of the temperature window for life. Micro-organisms. Bacterial clouds, bacterial reefs."

"Germ stew," Shan said. "Lovely place to send us."

"So that if we arrived as a neutron bomb or a black hole event we'd only take bacteria with us," Tai said. "But we didn't."

"Didn't what?" said Lidi.

"Didn't arrive?" Karth asked.

"Hey," Betton said, "is everybody going to stay on the bridge?"

"I want to come there," said Rig's little pipe, and then Asten's voice, clear but shaky, "Maba, I'd like to go back to Liden now."

"Come on," Karth said, and went to meet the children. Oreth did not turn from the window, even when Asten came close and took Oreth's hand.

"What are you looking at, Maba?"

"The planet, Asten."

"What planet?"

Oreth looked at the child then.

"There isn't anything," Asten said.

"That brown color—that's the surface, the atmosphere of a planet."

"There isn't any brown color. There isn't *anything*. I want to go back to Liden. You said we could when we were done with the test."

Oreth looked around, at last, at the others.

"Perception variation," Gveter said.

"I think," Tai said, "that we must establish that we are—that we got here—and then get here."

"You mean, go back," Betton said.

"The readings are perfectly clear," Lidi said, holding on to the rim of her seat with both hands and speaking very distinctly. "Every coordinate in order. That's M-60-Etcetera down there. What more do you want? Bacteria samples?"

"Yes," Tai said. "Instrument function's been affected, so we can't rely on instrumental records."

"Oh, shitsake!" said Lidi. "What a farce! All right. Suit up, go down, get some goo, and then let's get out. Go home. By NAFAL."

"By NAFAL?" Shan and Tai echoed, and Gveter said, "But we would spend seventeen years, Ve time, and no ansible to explain why."

"Why, Lidi?" Sweet Today asked.

Lidi stared at the Hainishwoman. "You want to churten again?" she demanded, raucous. She looked round at them all. "Are you people made of stone?" Her face was ashy, crumpled, shrunken. "It doesn't bother you, seeing through the walls?"

No one spoke, until Shan said cautiously, "How do you mean?"

"I can see the stars through the walls!" She stared round at them again, pointing at the carpet with its woven constellations. "You can't?" When no one answered, her jaw trembled in a little spasm, and she said, "All right. All right. I'm off duty. Sorry. Be in my room." She stood up. "Maybe you should lock me in," she said.

"Nonsense," said Sweet Today.

"If I fall through . . ." Lidi began, and did not finish. She walked to the door, stiffly and cautiously, as if through a thick fog. She said something they did not understand, "Cause," or perhaps, "Gauze."

Sweet Today followed her.

"I can see the stars too!" Rig announced.

"Hush," Karth said, putting an arm around the child.

"I can! I can see all the stars everywhere. And I can see Ve Port. And I can see anything I want!"

"Yes, of course, but hush now," the mother murmured, at which the child pulled free, stamped, and shrilled, "I can! I can too! I can see *everything!* And Asten can't! And there *is* a planet, there is too! No, don't hold me! Don't! Let me go!"

Grim, Karth carried the screaming child off to their quarters. Asten turned around to yell after Rig, "There is *not* any planet! You're just making it up!"

Grim, Oreth said, "Go to our room, please, Asten."

Asten burst into tears and obeyed. Oreth, with a glance of apology to the others, followed the short, weeping figure across the bridge and out into the corridor.

The four remaining on the bridge stood silent.

"Canaries," Shan said.

"Khallucinations?" Gveter proposed, subdued. "An effect of the churten on extrasensitive organisms—maybe?"

Tai nodded.

"Then is the ansible not functioning, or are we hallucinating nonfunction?" Shan asked after a pause.

Gveter went to the ansible; this time Tai walked away from it, leaving it to him. "I want to go down," she said.

"No reason not to, I suppose," Shan said unenthusiastically.

"Khwat reason to?" Gveter asked over his shoulder.

"It's what we're here for, isn't it? It's what we volunteered to do, isn't it? To test instantaneous—transilience—prove that it worked, that we are here! With the ansible out, it'll be seventeen years before Ve gets our radio signal!"

"We can just churten back to Ve and *tell* them," Shan said. "If we did that now, we'd have been . . . here . . . about eight minutes."

"Tell them—tell them what? What kind of evidence is that?"

"Anecdotal," said Sweet Today, who had come back quietly to the bridge; she moved like a big sailing ship, imposingly silent.

"Is Lidi all right?" Shan asked.

"No," Sweet Today answered. She sat down where Lidi had sat, at the NAFAL console.

"I ask a consensus about going down onplanet," Tai said.

"I'll ask the others," Gveter said, and went out, returning presently with Karth. "Go down, if you want," the Gethenian said. "Oreth's staying with the children for a bit. They are—We are extremely disoriented."

"I will come down," Gveter said.

"Can I come?" Betton asked, almost in a whisper, not raising his eyes to any adult face.

"No," Tai said, as Gveter said, "Yes."

Betton looked at his mother, one quick glance.

"Khwy not?" Gveter asked her.

"We don't know the risks."

"The planet was surveyed."

"By robot ships—"

"We'll wear suits." Gveter was honestly puzzled.

"I don't want the responsibility," Tai said through her teeth.

"Khwy is it yours?" Gveter asked, more puzzled still. "We all share it; Betton is crew. I don't understand."

"I know you don't understand," Tai said, turned her back on them both, and went out. The man and the boy stood staring, Gveter after Tai, Betton at the carpet.

"I'm sorry," Betton said.

"Not to be," Gveter told him.

"What is . . . what is going on?" Shan asked in an overcontrolled voice. "Why are we—We keep crossing, we keep—coming and going—"

"Confusion due to the churten experience," Gveter said.

Sweet Today turned from the console. "I have sent a distress signal," she said. "I am unable to operate the NAFAL system. The radio—" She cleared her throat. "Radio function seems erratic."

There was a pause.

"This is not happening," Shan said, or Oreth said, but Oreth had stayed with the children in another part of the ship, so it could not have been Oreth who said, "This is not happening," it must have been Shan.

A chain of cause and effect is an easy thing to describe; a cessation of cause and effect is not. To those who live in time, sequence is the norm, the only model, and simultaneity seems a muddle, a mess, a hopeless confusion, and the description of that confusion hopelessly confusing. As the members of the crew network no longer perceived the network steadily and were unable to communicate their perceptions, an individual perception is the only clue to follow through the labyrinth of their dislocation. Gveter perceived himself as being on the bridge with Shan, Sweet Today, Betton, Karth, and Tai. He perceived himself as methodically checking out the ship's systems. The NAFAL he found dead, the radio functioning in erratic bursts, the internal electrical and mechanical systems of the ship all in order. He sent out a lander unmanned and brought it back, and perceived it as functioning normally. He perceived himself discussing with Tai her determination to go down onplanet. Since he admitted his unwillingness to trust any instrumental reading on the ship, he had to admit her point that only material evidence would show that they had actually arrived at their destination, M-60-340-nolo. If they were going to have to spend the next seventeen years traveling back to Ve in real time, it would be nice to have something to show for it, even if only a handful of slime.

He perceived this discussion as perfectly rational.

It was, however, interrupted by outbursts of egoizing not characteristic of the crew.

"If you're going, go!" Shan said.

"Don't give me orders," Tai said.

"Somebody's got to stay in control here," Shan said.

"Not the men!" Tai said.

"Not the Terrans," Karth said. "Have you people no self-respect?"

"Stress," Gveter said. "Come on, Tai, Betton, all right, let's go, all right?"

In the lander, everything was clear to Gveter. One thing happened after another just as it should. Lander operation is very simple, and he asked Betton to take them down. The boy did so. Tai sat, tense and compact as always, her strong fists clenched on her knees. Betton managed the little ship with aplomb, and sat back, tense also, but dignified: "We're down," he said.

"No, we're not," Tai said.

"It—it says contact," Betton said, losing his assurance.

"An excellent landing," Gveter said. "Never even felt it." He was running the usual tests. Everything was in order. Outside the lander ports pressed a brownish darkness, a gloom. When Betton put on the outside lights the atmosphere, like a dark fog, diffused the light into a useless glare.

"Tests all tally with survey reports," Gveter said. "Will you go out, Tai, or use the servos?"

"Out," she said.

"Out," Betton echoed.

Gveter, assuming the formal crew role of Support, which one of them would have assumed if he had been going out, assisted them to lock their helmets and decontaminate their suits; he opened the hatch series for them, and watched them on the vid and from the port as they climbed down from the outer hatch. Betton went first. His slight figure, elongated by the whitish suit, was luminous in the weak glare of the lights. He walked a few steps from the ship, turned, and waited. Tai was stepping off the ladder. She seemed to grow very short—did she kneel down? Gveter looked from the port to the vid screen and back. She was shrinking? sinking—she must be sinking into the surface—which could not be solid, then, but bog, or some suspension like quicksand—but Betton had walked on it and was walking back to her, two steps, three steps, on the ground which Gveter could not see clearly but which must be solid, and which must be holding Betton up because he was lighter—but no, Tai must have stepped into a hole, a trench of some kind, for he could see her only from the waist up now, her legs hidden in the dark bog or fog, but she was moving, moving quickly, going right away from the lander and from Betton.

"Bring them back," Shan said, and Gveter said on the suit intercom, "Please return to the lander, Betton and Tai." Betton at once started up the ladder, then turned to look for his mother. A dim blotch that might be her helmet showed in the brown gloom, almost beyond the suffusion of light from the lander.

"Please come in, Betton. Please return, Tai."

The whitish suit flickered up the ladder, while Betton's voice in the intercom pleaded, "Tai—Tai, come back—Gveter, should I go after her?"

"No. Tai, please return at once to lander."

The boy's crew-integrity held; he came up into the lander and watched from the outer hatch, as Gveter watched from the port. The vid had lost her. The pallid blotch sank into the formless murk.

Gveter perceived that the instruments recorded that the lander had sunk 3.2 meters since contact with planet surface and was continuing to sink at an increasing rate.

"What is the surface, Betton?"

"Like muddy ground—Where is she?"

"Please return at once, Tai!"

"Please return to *Shoby*, Lander One and all crew," said the ship intercom; it was Tai's voice. "This is Tai," it said. "Please return at once to ship, lander and all crew."

"Stay in suit, in decon, please, Betton," Gveter said. "I'm sealing the hatch."

"But—All right," said the boy's voice.

Gveter took the lander up, decontaminating it and Betton's suit on the way. He perceived that Betton and Shan came with him through the hatch series into the *Shoby* and along the halls to the bridge, and that Karth, Sweet Today, Shan, and Tai were on the bridge.

Betton ran to his mother and stopped; he did not put out his hands to her. His face was immobile, as if made of wax or wood.

"Were you frightened?" she asked. "What happened down there?" And she looked to Gveter for an explanation.

Gveter perceived nothing. Unduring a nonperiod of no long, he perceived nothing was had happening happened that had not happened. Lost, he groped, lost, he found the word, the word that saved—"You—" he said, his tongue thick, dumb—"You called us."

It seemed that she denied, but it did not matter. What mattered? Shan was talking. Shan could tell. "Nobody called, Gveter," he said. "You and Betton went out, I was Support; when I realized I couldn't get the lander stable, that there's something funny about that surface, I called you back into the lander, and we came up.

All Gveter could say was, "Insubstantial . . ."

"But Tai came—" Betton began, and stopped. Gveter perceived that the boy moved away from his mother's denying touch. What mattered?

"Nobody went down," Sweet Today said. After a silence and before it, she said, "There is no down to go to."

Gveter tried to find another word, but there was none. He perceived outside the main port a brownish, murky convexity, through which, as he looked intently, he saw small stars shining.

He found a word then, the wrong word. "Lost," he said, and speaking perceived how the ship's lights dimmed slowly into a brownish murk, faded, darkened, were gone, while all the soft hum and busyness of the ship's systems died away into the real silence that was always there. But there was nothing there. Nothing had happened. We are at Ve Port! he tried with all his will to say; but there was no saying.

The suns burn through my flesh, Lidi said.

I am the suns, said Sweet Today. Not I, all is.

Don't breathe! cried Oreth.

It is death, Shan said. What I feared, is: nothing.

Nothing, they said.

Unbreathing, the ghosts flitted, shifted, in the ghost shell of a cold, dark hull floating near a world of brown fog, an unreal planet. They spoke, but there were no voices. There is no sound in vacuum, nor in nontime.

In her cabined solitude, Lidi felt the gravity lighten to the half-G of the ship's core-mass; she saw them, the nearer and the farther suns, burn through the dark gauze of the walls and hulls and the bedding and her body. The brightest, the sun of this system, floated directly under her navel. She did not know its name.

I am the darkness between the suns, one said.

I am nothing, one said.

I am you, one said.

You—one said—You—

And breathed, and reached out, and spoke: "Listen!" Crying out to the other, to the others, "Listen!"

"We have always known this. This is where we have always been, will always be, at the hearth, at the center. There is nothing to be afraid of, after all."

"I can't breathe," one said.

"I am not breathing," one said.

"There is nothing to breathe," one said.

"You are, you are breathing, please breathe!" said another.

"We're here, at the hearth," said another.

Oreth had laid the fire, Karth lit it. As it caught they both said softly, in Karhidish, "Praise also the light, and creation unfinished."

The fire caught with spark-spits, crackles, sudden flares. It did not go out. It burned. The others grouped round.

They were nowhere, but they were nowhere together; the ship was dead, but they were in the ship. A dead ship cools off fairly quickly, but not immediately. Close the doors, come in by the fire; keep the cold night out, before we go to bed.

Karth went with Rig to persuade Lidi from her starry vault. The navigator would not get up. "It's my fault," she said.

"Don't egoize," Karth said mildly. "How could it be?"

"I don't know. I want to stay here," Lidi muttered. Then Karth begged her: "Oh, Lidi, not alone!"

"How else?" the old woman asked, coldly.

But she was ashamed of herself, then, and ashamed of her guilt trip, and growled, "Oh, all right." She heaved herself up and wrapped a blanket around her body and followed Karth and Rig. The child carried a little biolume; it glowed in the black corridors, just as the plants of the aerobic tanks lived on, metabolizing, making an air to breathe, for a while. The light moved before her like a star among the stars through darkness to the room full of books, where the fire burned in the stone hearth. "Hello, children," Lidi said. "What are we doing here?"

"Telling stories," Sweet Today replied.

Shan had a little voice-recorder notebook in his hand.

"Does it work?" Lidi inquired.

"Seems to. We thought we'd tell . . . what happened," Shan said, squinting the narrow black eyes in his narrow black face at the firelight. "Each of us. What we— what it seemed like, seems like, to us. So that . . ."

"As a record, yes. In case . . . How funny that it works, though, your notebook. When nothing else does."

"It's voice-activated," Shan said absently. "So. Go on, Gveter."

Gveter finished telling his version of the expedition to the planet's surface. "We didn't even bring back samples," he ended. "I never thought of them."

"Shan went with you, not me," Tai said.

"You did go, and I did," the boy said with a certainty that stopped her. "And we did go outside. And Shan and Gveter were Support, in the lander. And I took samples. They're in the Stasis closet."

"I don't know if Shan was in the lander or not," Gveter said, rubbing his forehead painfully.

"Where would the lander have gone?" Shan said. "Nothing is out there—we're nowhere—outside time, is all I can think—But when one of you tells how they saw it, it seems as if it was that way, but then the next one changes the story, and I . . ."

Oreth shivered, drawing closer to the fire.

"I never believed this damn thing would work," said Lidi, bearlike in the dark cave of her blanket.

"Not understanding it was the trouble," Karth said. "None of us understood how it would work, not even Gveter. Isn't that true?"

"Yes," Gveter said.

"So that if our psychic interaction with it affected the process—"

"Or is the process," said Sweet Today, "so far as we're concerned."

"Do you mean," Lidi said in a tone of deep existential disgust, "that we have to believe in it to make it work?"

"You have to believe in yourself in order to act, don't you?" Tai said.

"No," the navigator said. "Absolutely not. I don't believe in myself. I *know* some things. Enough to go on."

"An analogy," Gveter offered. "The effective action of a crew depends on the members perceiving themselves as a crew—you could call it believing in the crew, or just *being* it—Right? So, maybe, to churten, we—we conscious ones—maybe it depends on our consciously perceiving ourselves as . . . as transilient—as being in the other place—the destination?"

"We lost our crewness, certainly, for a—Are there whiles?" Karth said. "We fell apart."

"We lost the thread," Shan said.

"Lost," Oreth said meditatively, laying another massive, half-weightless log on the fire, volleying sparks up into the chimney, slow stars.

"We lost—what?" Sweet Today asked.

No one answered for a while.

"When I can see the sun through the carpet . . ." Lidi said.

"So can I," Betton said, very low.

"I can see Ve Port," said Rig. "And everything. I can tell you what I can see. I can see Liden if I look. And my room on the *Oneblin*. And—"

"First, Rig," said Sweet Today, "tell us what happened."

"All right," Rig said agreeably. "Hold on to me harder, maba, I start floating. Well, we went to the liberry, me and Asten and Betton, and Betton was Elder Sib, and the adults were on the bridge, and I was going to go to sleep like I do when we naffle-fly, but before I even lay down there was the brown planet and Ve Port and both the suns and everywhere else, and you could see through everything, but Asten couldn't. But I can."

"We never went *anywhere*," Asten said. "Rig tells stories all the time."

"We all tell stories all the time, Asten," Karth said.

"Not dumb ones like Rig's!"

"Even dumber," said Oreth. "What we need . . . What we need is . . ."

"We need to know," Shan said, "what transilience is, and we don't, because we never did it before, nobody ever did it before."

"Not in the flesh," said Lidi.

"We need to know what's—real—what happened, *whether* anything happened—" Tai gestured at the cave of firelight around them and the dark beyond it. "Where are we? Are we here? Where is here? What's the story?"

"We have to tell it," Sweet Today said. "Recount it. Relate it. . . . Like Rig. Asten, how does a story begin?"

"A thousand winters ago, a thousand miles away," the child said; and Shan murmured, "Once upon a time . . ."

"There was a ship called the *Shoby*," said Sweet Today, "on a test flight, trying out the churten, with a crew of ten.

"Their names were Rig, Asten, Betton, Karth, Oreth, Lidi, Tai, Shan, Gveter, and Sweet Today. And they related their story, each one and together. . . ."

There was silence, the silence that was always there, except for the stir and crackle of the fire and the small sounds of their breathing, their movements, until one of them spoke at last, telling the story.

"The boy and his mother," said the light, pure voice, "were the first human beings ever to set foot on that world."

Again the silence; and again a voice.

"Although she wished . . . she realized that she really hoped the thing wouldn't work, because it would make her skills, her whole life, obsolete . . . all the same she really wanted to learn how to use it, too, if she could, if she wasn't too old to learn. . . ."

A long, softly throbbing pause, and another voice.

"They went from world to world, and each time they lost the world they left, lost it in time dilation, their friends getting old and dying while they were in NAFAL flight. If there were a way to live in one's own time, and yet move among the worlds, they wanted to try it. . . ."

"Staking everything on it," the next voice took up the story, "because nothing works except what we give our souls to, nothing's safe except what we put at risk."

A while, a little while; and a voice.

"It was like a game. It was like we were still in the *Shoby* at Ve Port just waiting before we went into NAFAL flight. But it was like we were at the brown planet too. At the same time. And one of them was just pretend, and the other one wasn't, but I didn't know which. So it was like when you pretend in a game. But I didn't want to play. I didn't know how."

Another voice.

"If the churten principle were proved to be applicable to actual transilience of living, conscious beings, it would be a great event in the mind of his people—for all people. A new understanding. A new partnership. A new way of being in the universe. A wider freedom. . . . He wanted that very much. He wanted to be one of the crew that first formed that partnership, the first people to be able to think this thought, and to . . . to relate it. But also he was afraid of it. Maybe it wasn't a true relation, maybe false, maybe only a dream. He didn't know."

It was not so cold, so dark, at their backs, as they sat round the fire. Was it the waves of Liden, hushing on the sand?

Another voice.

"She thought a lot about her people, too. About guilt, and expiation, and sacrifice. She wanted a lot to be on this flight that might give people—more freedom. But it was different from what she thought it would be. What happened—What *happened* wasn't what mattered. What mattered was that she came to be with people who gave *her* freedom. Without guilt. She wanted to stay with them, to be crew with them. . . . And with her son. Who was the first human being to set foot on an unknown world."

A long silence; but not deep, only as deep as the soft drum of the ship's systems, steady and unconscious as the circulation of the blood.

Another voice.

"They were thoughts in the mind; what else had they ever been? So they could be in Ve and at the brown planet, and desiring flesh and entire spirit, and illusion and reality, all at once, as they'd always been. When he remembered this, his confusion and fear ceased, for he knew that they couldn't be lost."

"They got lost. But they found the way," said another voice, soft above the hum and hushing of the ship's systems, in the warm fresh air and light inside the solid walls and hulls.

Only nine voices had spoken, and they looked for the tenth; but the tenth had gone to sleep, thumb in mouth.

"That story was told and is yet to be told," the mother said. "Go on. I'll churten here with Rig."

They left those two by the fire, and went to the bridge, and then to the hatches to invite on board a crowd of anxious scientists, engineers, and officials of Ve Port and the Ekumen, whose instruments had been assuring them that the *Shoby* had vanished, forty-four minutes ago, into non-existence, into silence. "What happened?" they asked. "What happened?" And the Shobies looked at one another and said, "Well, it's quite a story. . . ."

ROBERT REED

Robert Reed [1956–] (www.starbaseandromeda.com/reed.html) was born and raised and lives in Nebraska. His work is notable for its variety, and for his increasing production. He has been one of the most prolific short story writers of high quality in the SF field the past few years, averaging ten published stories a year from 1999 to 2005. His first story collection, *The Dragons of Springplace* (1999), fine as it is, skims only a bit of the cream from his works. And he writes a novel every year or two as well. His first novel, *The Leeshore*, appeared in 1987, followed by *The Hormone Jungle* (1988), *Black Milk* (1989), *Down the Bright Way* (1991), and almost a novel a year for the next decade.

His most recent novels are *Marrow* (2000), a distant-future large-scale story that is hard SF and seems to be a breakthrough in his career; *Sister Alice* (2003); and *The Well of Stars* (2005), a sequel to *Marrow*. The *Encyclopedia of Science Fiction* remarks that "the expertness of the writing and its knowing exploitation of current scientific speculations are balanced by an underlying quiet sanity about how to depict and to illumine human beings." These recent novels fit into the current discourse as hard space opera SF, although the older term "SF adventure" is just as comfortable.

Reed does not characteristically write any particular variety of SF. "Robert Reed stories are typically hermits," he says, "alone and perhaps a little ill-tempered, dependent only on themselves. My novels have been stand-alones, except for *Beyond the Veil of Stars* (1994) and its sequel, *Beneath the Gated Sky* (1997). And instead of exploding into the SF consciousness, I have gradually accreted what passes for a career, slowly and erratically adding layers to a résumé that somehow includes more than a hundred short stories and novelettes and novellas, plus a couple handfuls of novels."

His relevance to New Space Opera discussion derives from his Marrow series of stories and novels, of which "The Remoras" is the first. In an essay on the Marrow stories, "Improbable Journeys," Reed's initial take on interstellar travel is not dissimilar to Benford's, and puts him in the hybrid hard space opera discourse:

Star travel has to be a difficult business. The energy demands and financial sacrifices surely keep most species sitting at home, building big eyes instead of big engines. And even if starships were possible, they would bring enormous risks. I'm not a natural physicist; I don't think in terms of ergs and megatons. But I possess, even cherish, a highly refined paranoia. A fleck of dust would be horrible news for some little starship, and impacts should be inevitable. Struck by a wayward comet, ships as big as asteroids would be gutted like trout. But of course a truly gigantic ship could weather this abuse, and if the ship was encased inside a frozen ocean of superstrong hyperfiber . . . well, what better vessel was there with which to journey around the neighborhood?

He has described the genesis of the series at length in that essay:

A man lives inside the most perfect spacesuit: Built from some marvelous, probably mythical material, his suit is considerably tougher than any diamond. A tiny onboard AI serves as its guiding brain. . . . In essence, the suit functions as a very small, highly competent spaceship.

Like most of my story ideas, this one went nowhere.

What I needed was a second insight. That came some years later with the simple realization that the spacesuit was much like a world, self-contained and eternal. I began thinking about more durable types of human beings, people who wore these elaborate "lifesuits" throughout their long, long lives. I saw them as a society, a kind of nation unto themselves. But where would these odd souls live? . . . Of course, I thought. They would live clinging to the hull of a starship.

And a little starship wouldn't do the trick. I needed something with size, some expansive place where a great culture could be born, and because the mind's eye doesn't require capital and needs only a glancing nod at what is possible, I quickly sketched out my first plans for a ship that was as large as a world.

"The Remoras" appeared in F&SF in May 1994, and with that, the Great Ship was launched.

In his long discussion of "The Remoras," Reed analyzes the character of Quee Lee and her significance for the series: "At several points during the writing of these stories, I found it useful to give my readers and myself roots that extend back towards our present. Quee Lee is the taproot. She was born into our world, or at least born sometime in this century. She can remember when she was a child, and telescopes pointed at the sky found a signal made by another intelligent species, full of fresh knowledge and visions of a thickly populated galaxy; and within a genuinely short while, life on little Earth was transformed in a multitude of ways."

THE REMORAS

ROBERT REED

Quee Lee's apartment covered several hectares within one of the human districts, some thousand kilometers beneath the ship's hull. It wasn't a luxury unit by any measure. Truly wealthy people owned as much as a cubic kilometer for themselves and their entourages. But it had been her home since she had come on board, for more centuries than she could count, its hallways and large rooms as comfortable to her as her own body.

The garden room was a favorite. She was enjoying its charms one afternoon, lying nude beneath a false sky and sun, eyes closed and nothing to hear but the splash of fountains and the prattle of little birds. Suddenly her apartment interrupted the peace, announcing a visitor. "He has come for Perri, miss. He claims it's most urgent."

"Perri isn't here," she replied, soft gray eyes opening. "Unless he's hiding from both of us, I suppose."

"No, miss. He is not." A brief pause, then the voice said, "I have explained this to the man, but he refuses to leave. His name is Orleans. He claims that Perri owes him a considerable sum of money."

What had her husband done now? Quee Lee could guess, halfway smiling as she sat upright. *Oh, Perri . . . won't you learn . . . ?* She would have to dismiss this Orleans fellow herself, spooking him with a good hard stare. She rose and dressed in an emerald sarong, then walked the length of her apartment, never hurrying, commanding the front door to open at the last moment but leaving the security screen intact. And she was ready for someone odd. Even someone sordid, knowing Perri. Yet she didn't expect to see a shiny lifesuit more than two meters tall and nearly half as wide, and she had never imagined such a face gazing down at her with mismatched eyes. It took her a long moment to realize this was a Remora. An authentic Remora was standing in the public walkway, his vivid round face watching her. The flesh was orange with diffuse black blotches that might or might not be cancers, and a lipless, toothless mouth seemed to flow into a grin. What would bring a Remora here? They never, never came down here . . . !

"I'm Orleans." The voice was sudden and deep, slightly muted by the security screen. It came from a speaker hidden somewhere on the thick neck, telling her, "I need help, miss. I'm sorry to disturb you . . . but you see, I'm desperate. I don't know where else to turn."

Quee Lee knew about Remoras. She had seen them and even spoken to a few, although those conversations were eons ago and she couldn't remember their substance. Such strange creatures. Stranger than most aliens, even if they possessed human souls. . . .

"Miss?"

Quee Lee thought of herself as being a good person. Yet she couldn't help but feel repelled, the floor rolling beneath her and her breath stopping short. Orleans was a human being, one of her own species. True, his genetics had been transformed by hard radiations. And yes, he normally lived apart from ordinary people like her. But inside him was a human mind, tough and potentially immortal. Quee Lee blinked and remembered that she had compassion as well as charity for everyone, even aliens . . . and she managed to sputter, "Come in." She said, "If you wish, please do," and with that invitation, her apartment deactivated the invisible screen.

"Thank you, miss." The Remora walked slowly, almost clumsily, his lifesuit making a harsh grinding noise in the knees and hips. That wasn't normal, she realized. Orleans should be graceful, his suit powerful, serving him as an elaborate exoskeleton.

"Would you like anything?" she asked foolishly. Out of habit.

"No, thank you," he replied, his voice nothing but pleasant.

Of course. Remoras ate and drank only self-made concoctions. They were permanently sealed inside their lifesuits, functioning as perfectly self-contained organisms. Food was synthesized, water recycled, and they possessed a religious sense of purity and independence.

"I don't wish to bother you, miss. I'll be brief."

His politeness was a minor surprise. Remoras typically were distant, even arrogant. But Orleans continued to smile, watching her. One eye was a muscular pit filled with thick black hairs, and she assumed those hairs were light sensitive. Like an insect's compound eye, each one might build part of an image. By contrast, its mate was ordinary, white and fishy with a foggy black center. Mutations could do astonishing things. An accelerated, partly controlled evolution was occurring inside that suit, even while Orleans stood before her, boots stomping on the stone floor, a single spark arcing toward her.

Orleans said, "I know this is embarrassing for you—"

"No, no," she offered.

"—and it makes me uncomfortable too. I wouldn't have come down here if it wasn't necessary."

"Perri's gone," she repeated, "and I don't know when he'll be back. I'm sorry."

"Actually," said Orleans, "I was hoping he would be gone."

"Did you?"

"Though I'd have come either way."

Quee Lee's apartment, loyal and watchful, wouldn't allow anything nasty to happen to her. She took a step forward, closing some of the distance. "This is about money being owed? Is that right?"

"Yes, miss."

"For what, if I might ask?"

Orleans didn't explain in clear terms. "Think of it as an old gambling debt." More was involved, he implied. "A very old debt, I'm afraid, and Perri's refused me a thousand times."

She could imagine it. Her husband had his share of failings, incompetence and a self-serving attitude among them. She loved Perri in a controlled way, but his flaws were obvious. "I'm sorry," she replied, "but I'm not responsible for his debts." She made herself sound hard, knowing it was best. "I hope you didn't come all this way because you heard he was married." Married to a woman of some means, she thought to herself. In secret.

"No, no, no!" The grotesque face seemed injured. Both eyes became larger, and a thin tongue, white as ice, licked at the lipless edge of the mouth. "Honestly, we don't follow the news about passengers. I just assumed Perri was living with someone. I know him, you see . . . my hope was to come and make my case to whomever I found, winning a comrade. An ally. Someone who might become my advocate." A hopeful pause, then he said, "When Perri does come here, will you explain to him what's right and what is not? Can you, please?" Another pause, then he added, "Even a lowly Remora knows the difference between right and wrong, miss."

That wasn't fair, calling himself lowly. And he seemed to be painting her as some flavor of bigot, which she wasn't. She didn't look at him as lowly, and morality wasn't her private possession. Both of them were human, after all. Their souls were linked by a charming and handsome, manipulative user . . . by her darling husband . . . and Quee Lee felt a sudden anger directed at Perri, almost shuddering in front of this stranger.

"Miss?"

"How much?" she asked. "How much does he owe you, and how soon will you need it?"

Orleans answered the second question first, lifting an arm with a sickly whine coming from his shoulder. "Can you hear it?" he asked. As if she were deaf. "My seals need to be replaced, or at least refurbished. Yesterday, if possible." The arm bent, and the elbow whined. "I already spent my savings rebuilding my reactor."

Quee Lee knew enough about lifesuits to appreciate his circumstances. Remoras worked on the ship's hull, standing in the open for hours and days at a time. A broken seal was a disaster. Any tiny opening would kill most of his body, and his suffering mind would fall into a protective coma. Left exposed and vulnerable, Orleans would be at the mercy of radiation storms and comet showers. Yes, she understood. A balky suit was an unacceptable hazard on top of lesser hazards, and what could she say?

She felt a deep empathy for the man.

Orleans seemed to take a breath, then he said, "Perri owes me fifty-two thousand credits, miss."

"I see." She swallowed and said, "My name is Quee Lee."

"Quee Lee," he repeated. "Yes, miss."

"As soon as Perri comes home, I'll discuss this with him. I promise you."

"I would be grateful if you did."

"I will."

The ugly mouth opened, and she saw blotches of green and gray-blue against a milky throat. Those were cancers or perhaps strange new organs. She couldn't believe she was in the company of a Remora—the strangest sort of human—yet despite every myth, despite tales of courage and even recklessness, Orleans appeared almost fragile. He even looked scared, she realized. That wet orange face shook as if in despair, then came the awful grinding noise as he turned away, telling her, "Thank you, Quee Lee. For your time and patience, and for everything."

Fifty-two thousand credits!

She could have screamed. She would scream when she was alone, she promised herself. Perri had done this man a great disservice, and he'd hear about it when he graced her with his company again. A patient person, yes, and she could tolerate most of his flaws. But not now. Fifty thousand credits was no fortune, and it would allow Orleans to refurbish his lifesuit, making him whole and healthy again. Perhaps she could get in touch with Perri first, speeding up the process . . .

Orleans was through her front door, turning to say good-bye. False sunshine made his suit shine, and his faceplate darkened to where she couldn't see his features anymore. He might have any face, and what did a face mean? Waving back at him, sick to her stomach, she calculated what fifty-two thousand credits meant in concrete terms, to her. . . .

. . . wondering if she should . . . ?

But no, she decided. She just lacked the required compassion. She was a particle short, if that, ordering the security screen to engage again, helping to mute that horrid grinding of joints as the Remora shuffled off for home.

The ship had many names, many designations, but to its long-term passengers and crew it was referred to as *the ship*. No other starship could be confused for it. Not in volume, nor in history.

The ship was old by every measure. A vanished humanoid race had built it, probably before life arose on Earth, then abandoned it for no obvious reason. Experts claimed it had begun as a sunless world, one of the countless jupiters that sprinkled the cosmos. The builders had used the world's own hydrogen to fuel enormous engines, accelerating it over millions of years while stripping away its gaseous exterior. Today's ship was the leftover core, much modified by its builders and humans. Its metal and rock interior was laced with passageways and sealed environments, fuel tanks and various ports. There was room enough for hundreds of billions of passengers, though there were only a fraction that number now. And its hull was a special armor made from hyperfibers, kilometers thick and tough enough to withstand most high-velocity impacts.

The ship had come from outside the galaxy, passing into human space long ago. It was claimed as salvage, explored by various means, then refurbished to the best of its new owners' abilities. A corporation was formed; a promotion was born. The ancient engines were coaxed to life, changing the ship's course. Then tickets were sold, both to humans and alien species. Novelty and adventure were the lures. One circuit around the Milky Way; a half-million-year voyage touring the star-rich spiral arms. It was a long span, even for immortal humans. But people like Quee Lee had enough money and patience. That's why she purchased her apartment with a portion of her savings. This voyage wouldn't remain novel for long, she knew. Three or four circuits at most, and then what? People would want something else new and glancingly dangerous. Wasn't that the way it always was?

Quee Lee had no natural lifespan. Her ancestors had improved themselves in a thousand ways, erasing the aging process. Fragile DNAs were replaced with better genetic machinery. Tailoring allowed a wide-range of useful proteins and enzymes and powerful repair mechanisms. Immune systems were nearly perfect; diseases were extinct. Normal life couldn't damage a person in any measurable way. And even a tragic accident wouldn't need to be fatal, Quee Lee's body and mind able to withstand frightening amounts of abuse.

But Remoras, despite those same gifts, did not live ordinary lives. They worked on the open hull, each of them encased in a lifesuit. The suits afforded extra protection and a standard environment, each one possessing a small fusion plant and redundant recycling systems. Hull life was dangerous in the best times. The ship's shields and laser watchdogs couldn't stop every bit of interstellar grit. And every large impact meant someone had to make repairs. The ship's builders had used sophisticated robots, but they proved too tired after several billions of years on the job. It was better to promote—or demote—members of the human crew. The original scheme was to share the job, brief stints fairly dispersed. Even the captains were to don the lifesuits, stepping into the open when it was safest, patching craters with fresh-made hyperfibers. . . .

Fairness didn't last. A kind of subculture arose, and the first Remoras took the hull as their province. Those early Remoras learned how to survive the huge radiation loads. They trained themselves and their offspring to control their damaged bodies. Tough genetics mutated, and they embraced their mutations. If an eye was struck blind, perhaps by some queer cancer, then a good Remora would evolve a new eye. Perhaps a hair was light-sensitive, and its owner, purely by force of will, would culture that hair and interface it with the surviving optic nerve, producing an eye more durable than the one it replaced. Or so Quee Lee had heard, in passing, from people who acted as if they knew about such things.

Remoras, she had been told, were happy to look grotesque. In their culture, strange faces and novel organs were the measures of success. And since disaster could happen anytime, without warning, it was unusual for any Remora to live long. At least in her sense of long. Orleans could be a fourth or fifth generation Remora, for all she knew. A child barely fifty centuries old. *For all she knew.* Which was almost nothing, she realized, returning to her garden room and undressing, lying down with her eyes closed and the light baking her. Remoras were important, even essential people, yet she felt wholly ignorant. And ignorance was wrong, she knew. Not as wrong as owing one of them money, but still. . . .

This life of hers seemed so ordinary, set next to Orleans' life. Comfortable and ordinary, and she almost felt ashamed.

Perri failed to come home that next day, and the next. Then it was ten days, Quee Lee having sent messages to his usual haunts and no reply. She had been careful not to explain why she wanted him. And this was nothing too unusual, Perri probably wandering somewhere new and Quee Lee skilled at waiting, her days accented with visits from friends and parties thrown for any small reason. It was her normal life, never anything but pleasant; yet she found herself thinking about Orleans, imagining him walking on the open hull with his seals breaking, his strange body starting to boil away . . . that poor man . . . !

Taking the money to Orleans was an easy decision. Quee Lee had more than enough. It didn't seem like a large sum until she had it converted into black-and-white chips. But wasn't it better to have Perri owing her instead of owing a Remora? She was in a better place to recoup the debt; and besides, she doubted that her husband could raise that money now. Knowing him, he probably had a number of debts, to humans and aliens both; and for the nth time, she wondered how she'd ever let Perri charm her. What was she thinking, agreeing to this crazy union?

Quee Lee was old even by immortal measures. She was so old she could barely remember her youth, her tough neurons unable to embrace her entire life. Maybe that's why Perri had seemed like a blessing. He was ridiculously young and wore his youth well, gladly sharing his enthusiasms and energies. He was a good, untaxing lover; he could listen when it was important; and he had never tried milking Quee Lee of her money. Besides, he was a challenge. No doubt about it. Maybe her friends didn't approve of him—a few close ones were openly critical—but to a woman of her vintage, in the middle of a five thousand century voyage, Perri was something fresh and new and remarkable. And Quee Lee's old friends, quite suddenly, seemed a little fossilized by comparison.

"I love to travel," Perri had explained, his gently handsome face capable of endless smiles. "I was born on the ship, did you know? Just weeks after my parents came on board. They were riding only as far as a colony world, but I stayed behind. My choice." He had laughed, eyes gazing into the false sky of her ceiling. "Do you know what I want to do? I want to see the entire ship, walk every hallway and cavern. I want to explore every body of water, meet every sort of alien—"

"Really?"

"—and even visit their quarters. Their homes." Another laugh and that infectious smile. "I just came back from a low-gravity district, six thousand kilometers be-low. There's a kind of spidery creature down there. You should see them, love! I can't do them justice by telling you they're graceful, and seeing holos isn't much better."

She had been impressed. Who else did she know who could tolerate aliens, what with their strange odors and their impenetrable minds? Perri was remarkable, no doubt about it. Even her most critical friends admitted that much, and despite their grumbles, they'd want to hear the latest Perri adventure as told by his wife.

"I'll stay on board forever, if I can manage it."

She had laughed, asking, "Can you afford it?"

"Badly," he had admitted. "But I'm paid up through this circuit, at least. Minus day-by-day expenses, but that's all right. Believe me, when you've got millions of wealthy souls in one place, there's always a means of making a living."

"Legal means?"

"Glancingly so." He had a rogue's humor, all right. Yet later, in a more sober mood, he had admitted, "I do have enemies, my love. I'm warning you. Like anyone, I've made my share of mistakes—my youthful indiscretions—but at least I'm honest about them."

Indiscretions, perhaps. Yet he had done nothing to earn her animosity.

"We should marry," Perri had proposed. "Why not? We like each other's company, yet we seem to weather our time apart too. What do you think? Frankly, I don't think you need a partner who shadows you day and night. Do you, Quee Lee?"

She didn't. True enough.

"A small tidy marriage, complete with rules," he had assured her. "I get a home base, and you have your privacy, plus my considerable entertainment value." A big long laugh, then he had added, "I promise. You'll be the first to hear my latest tales. And I'll never be any kind of leech, darling. With you, I will be the perfect gentleman."

Quee Lee carried the credit chips in a secret pouch, traveling to the tubecar station and riding one of the vertical tubes toward the hull. She had looked up the name *Orleans* in the crew listings. The only Orleans lived at Port Beta, no mention of him be-ing a Remora or not. The ports were vast facilities where taxi craft docked with the ship, bringing new passengers from nearby alien worlds. It was easier to accelerate and decelerate those kilometer-long needles. The ship's own engines did nothing but make the occasional course correction, avoiding dust clouds while keeping them on their circular course.

It had been forever since Quee Lee had visited a port. And today there wasn't even a taxi to be seen, all of them off hunting for more paying customers. The non-Remora crew—the captains, mates and so on—had little work at the moment, appar-ently hiding from her. She stood at the bottom of the port—a lofty cylinder capped with a kilometer-thick hatch of top-grade hyperfibers. The only other tourists were aliens, some kind of fishy species encased in bubbles of liquid water or ammonia. The bubbles rolled past her. It was like standing in a school of small tuna, their sharp chat-ter audible and Quee Lee unable to decipher any of it. Were they mocking her? She had no clue, and it made her all the more frustrated. They could be making terrible fun of her. She felt lost and more than a little homesick all at once.

By contrast, the first Remora seemed normal. Walking without any grinding sounds, it covered ground at an amazing pace. Quee Lee had to run to catch it. To catch her. Something about the lifesuit was feminine, and a female voice responded to Quee Lee's shouts.

"What what what?" asked the Remora. "I'm busy!"

Gasping, Quee Lee asked, "Do you know Orleans?"

"Orleans?"

"I need to find him. It's quite important." Then she wondered if something terrible had happened, her arriving too late—

"I do know someone named Orleans, yes." The face had comma-shaped eyes, huge and black and bulging, and the mouth blended into a slit-like nose. Her skin was silvery, odd bunched fibers running beneath the surface. Black hair showed along the top of the faceplate, except at second glance it wasn't hair. It looked more like ropes soaked in oil, the strands wagging with a slow stately pace.

The mouth smiled. The normal-sounding voice said, "Actually, Orleans is one of my closest friends!"

True? Or was she making a joke?

"I really have to find him," Quee Lee confessed. "Can you help me?"

"Can I help you?" The strange mouth smiled, gray pseudoteeth looking big as thumbnails, the gums as silver as her skin. "I'll take you to him. Does that constitute help?" And Quee Lee found herself following, walking onto a lifting disk without railing, the Remora standing in the center and waving to the old woman. "Come closer. Orleans is up there." A skyward gesture. "A good long way, and I don't think you'd want to try it alone. Would you?"

"Relax," Orleans advised.

She thought she was relaxed, except then she found herself nodding, breathing deeply and feeling a tension as it evaporated. The ascent had taken ages, it seemed. Save for the rush of air moving past her ears, it had been soundless. The disk had no sides at all—a clear violation of safety regulations—and Quee Lee had grasped one of the Remora's shiny arms, needing a handhold, surprised to feel rough spots in the hyperfiber. Minuscule impacts had left craters too tiny to see. Remoras, she had realized, were very much like the ship itself—enclosed biospheres taking abuse as they streaked through space.

"Better?" asked Orleans.

"Yes. Better." A thirty kilometer ride through the port, holding tight to a Remora. And now this. She and Orleans were inside some tiny room not five hundred meters from the vacuum. Did Orleans live here? She nearly asked, looking at the bare walls and stubby furniture, deciding it was too spare, too ascetic to be anyone's home. Even his. Instead she asked him, "How are *you*?"

"Tired. Fresh off my shift, and devastated."

The face had changed. The orange pigments were softer now, and both eyes were the same sickening hair-filled pits. How clear was his vision? How did he transplant cells from one eye to the other? There had to be mechanisms, reliable tricks . . . and she found herself feeling ignorant and glad of it. . . .

"What do you want, Quee Lee?"

She swallowed. "Perri came home, and I brought what he owes you."

Orleans looked surprised, then the cool voice said, "Good. Wonderful!"

She produced the chips, his shiny palm accepting them. The elbow gave a harsh growl, and she said, "I hope this helps."

"My mood already is improved," he promised.

What else? She wasn't sure what to say now.

Then Orleans told her, "I should thank you somehow. Can I give you something for your trouble? How about a tour?" One eye actually winked at her, hairs contracting into their pit and nothing left visible but a tiny red pore. "A tour," he repeated.

"A walk outside? We'll find you a lifesuit. We keep them here in case a captain comes for an inspection." A big deep laugh, then he added, "Once every thousand years, they do! Whether we need it or not!"

What was he saying? She had heard him, and she hadn't.

A smile and another wink, and he said, "I'm serious. Would you like to go for a little stroll?"

"I've never . . . I don't know . . . !"

"Safe as safe can be." Whatever that meant. "Listen, this is the safest place for a jaunt. We're behind the leading face, which means impacts are nearly impossible. But we're not close to the engines and their radiations either." Another laugh, and he added, "Oh, you'll get a dose of radiation, but nothing important. You're tough, Quee Lee. Does your fancy apartment have an autodoc?"

"Of course."

"Well, then."

She wasn't scared, at least in any direct way. What Quee Lee felt was excitement and fear born of excitement, nothing in her experience to compare with what was happening. She was a creature of habits, rigorous and ancient habits, and she had no way to know how she'd respond *out there*. No habit had prepared her for this moment.

"Here," said her gracious host. "Come in here."

No excuse occurred to her. They were in a deep closet full of lifesuits—this was some kind of locker room, apparently—and she let Orleans select one and dismantle it with his growling joints. "It opens and closes, unlike mine," he explained. "It doesn't have all the redundant systems either. Otherwise, it's the same."

On went the legs, the torso and arms and helmet; she banged the helmet against the low ceiling, then struck the wall with her first step.

"Follow me," Orleans advised, "and keep it slow."

Wise words. They entered some sort of tunnel that zigzagged toward space, ancient stairs fashioned for a nearly human gait. Each bend had an invisible field that held back the ship's thinning atmosphere. They began speaking by radio, voices close, and she noticed how she could feel through the suit, its pseudoneurons interfacing with her own. Here gravity was stronger than earth-standard, yet despite her added bulk she moved with ease, limbs humming, her helmet striking the ceiling as she climbed. Thump, and thump. She couldn't help herself.

Orleans laughed pleasantly, the sound close and intimate. "You're doing fine, Quee Lee. Relax."

Hearing her name gave her a dilute courage.

"Remember," he said, "your servomotors are potent. Lifesuits make motions large. Don't overcontrol, and don't act cocky."

She wanted to succeed. More than anything in recent memory, she wanted everything as close to perfect as possible.

"Concentrate," he said.

Then he told her, "That's better, yes."

They came to a final turn, then a hatch, Orleans pausing and turning, his syrupy mouth making a preposterous smile. "Here we are. We'll go outside for just a little while, okay?" A pause, then he added, "When you go home, tell your husband what you've done. Amaze him!"

"I will," she whispered.

And he opened the hatch with an arm—the abrasive sounds audible across the radio, but distant—and a bright colored glow washed over them. "Beautiful," the Remora observed. "Isn't it beautiful, Quee Lee?"

·   ·   ·

Perri didn't return home for several more weeks, and when he arrived—"I was rafting Cloud Canyon, love and didn't get your messages!"—Quee Lee realized that she wasn't going to tell him about her adventure. Nor about the money. She'd wait for a better time, a weak moment, when Perri's guard was down. "What's so important, love? You sounded urgent." She told him it was nothing, that she'd missed him and been worried. How was the rafting? Who went with him? Perri told her. "Tweewits. Big hulking baboons, in essence." He smiled until she smiled too. He looked thin and tired; but that night, with minimal prompting, he found the energy to make love to her twice. And the second time was special enough that she was left wondering how she could so willingly live without sex for long periods. It could be the most amazing pleasure.

Perri slept, dreaming of artificial rivers roaring through artificial canyons; and Quee Lee sat up in bed, in the dark, whispering for her apartment to show her the view above Port Beta. She had it projected into her ceiling, twenty meters overhead, the shimmering aurora changing colors as force fields wrestled with every kind of spaceborn hazard.

"What do you think, Quee Lee?"

Orleans had asked the question, and she answered it again, in a soft awed voice. "Lovely." She shut her eyes, remembering how the hull itself had stretched off into the distance, flat and gray, bland yet somehow serene. "It is lovely."

"And even better up front, on the prow," her companion had maintained. "The fields there are thicker, stronger. And the big lasers keep hitting the comets tens of millions of kilometers from us, softening them up for us." He had given a little laugh, telling her, "You can almost feel the ship moving when you look up from the prow. Honest."

She had shivered inside her lifesuit, more out of pleasure than fear. Few passengers ever came out on the hull. They were breaking rules, no doubt. Even inside the taxi ships, you were protected by a hull. But not up there. Up there she'd felt exposed, practically naked. And maybe Orleans had measured her mood, watching her face with the flickering pulses, finally asking her, "Do you know the story of the first Remora?"

Did she? She wasn't certain.

He told it, his voice smooth and quiet. "Her name was Wune," he began. "On Earth, it's rumored, she was a criminal, a registered habitual criminal. Signing on as a crew mate helped her escape a stint of psychological realignment—"

"What crimes?"

"Do they matter?" A shake of the round head. "Bad ones, and that's too much said. The point is that Wune came here without rank, glad for the opportunity, and like any good mate, she took her turns out on the hull."

Quee Lee had nodded, staring off at the far horizon.

"She was pretty, like you. Between shifts, she did typical typicals. She explored the ship and had affairs of the heart and grieved the affairs that went badly. Like you, Quee Lee, she was smart. And after just a few centuries on board, Wune could see the trends. She saw how the captains were avoiding their shifts on the hull. And how certain people, guilty of small offenses, were pushed into double-shifts in their stead. All so that our captains didn't have to accept the tiniest, fairest risks."

Status. Rank. Privilege. She could understand these things, probably too well.

"Wune rebelled," Orleans had said, pride in the voice. "But instead of overthrowing the system, she conquered by embracing it. By transforming what she embraced." A soft laugh. "This lifesuit of mine? She built its prototype with its semi-forever seals and the hyperefficient recyke systems. She made a suit that she'd never have to leave, then she began to live on the hull, in the open, sometimes alone for years at a time."

"Alone?"

"A prophet's contemplative life." A fond glance at the smooth gray terrain. "She stopped having her body purged of cancers and other damage. She let her face—her beautiful face—become speckled with dead tissues. Then she taught herself to manage her mutations, with discipline and strength. Eventually she picked a few friends without status, teaching them her tricks and explaining the peace and purpose she had found while living up here, contemplating the universe without obstructions."

Without obstructions indeed!

"A few hundred became the First Generation. Attrition convinced our great captains to allow children, and the Second Generation numbered in the thousands. By the Third, we were officially responsible for the ship's exterior and the deadliest parts of its engines. We had achieved a quiet conquest of a world-sized realm, and today we number in the low millions!"

She remembered sighing, asking, "What happened to Wune?"

"An heroic death," he had replied. "A comet swarm was approaching. A repair team was caught on the prow, their shuttle dead and useless—"

"Why were they there if a swarm was coming?"

"Patching a crater, of course. Remember. The prow can withstand almost any likely blow, but if comets were to strike on top of one another, unlikely as that sounds—"

"A disaster," she muttered.

"For the passengers below, yes." A strange slow smile. "Wune died trying to bring them a fresh shuttle. She was vaporized under a chunk of ice and rock, in an instant."

"I'm sorry." Whispered.

"Wune was my great-great-grandmother," the man had added. "And no, she didn't name us Remoras. That originally was an insult, some captain responsible. Remoras are ugly fish that cling to sharks. Not a pleasing image, but Wune embraced the word. To us it means spiritual fulfillment, independence and a powerful sense of self. Do you know what I am, Quee Lee? I'm a god inside this suit of mine. I rule in ways you can't appreciate. You can't imagine how it is, having utter control over my body, my self . . . !"

She had stared at him, unable to speak.

A shiny hand had lifted, thick fingers against his faceplate. "My eyes? You're fascinated by my eyes, aren't you?"

A tiny nod. "Yes."

"Do you know how I sculpted them?"

"No."

"Tell me, Quee Lee. How do you close your hand?"

She had made a fist, as if to show him how.

"But which neurons fire? Which muscles contract?" A mild, patient laugh, then he had added, "How can you manage something that you can't describe in full?"

She had said, "It's habit, I guess . . ."

"Exactly!" A larger laugh. "I have habits too. For instance, I can willfully spread mutations using metastasized cells. I personally have thousands of years of practice, plus all those useful mechanisms that I inherited from Wune and the others. It's as natural as your making the fist."

"But my hand doesn't change its real shape," she had countered.

"Transformation is my habit, and it's why my life is so much richer than yours." He had given her a wink just then, saying, "I can't count the times I've re-evolved my eyes."

Quee Lee looked up at her bedroom ceiling now, at a curtain of blue glows dissolving into pink. In her mind, she replayed the moment.

"You think Remoras are vile, ugly monsters," Orleans had said. "Now don't deny it. I won't let you deny it."

She hadn't made a sound.

"When you saw me standing at your door? When you saw that a Remora had come to *your* home? All of that ordinary blood of yours drained out of your face. You looked so terribly pale and weak, Quee Lee. Horrified!"

She couldn't deny it. Not then or now.

"Which of us has the richest life, Quee Lee? And be objective. Is it you or is it me?"

She pulled her bedsheets over herself, shaking a little bit.

"You or me?"

"Me," she whispered, but in that word was doubt. Just the flavor of it. Then Perri stirred, rolling toward her with his face trying to waken. Quee Lee had a last glance at the projected sky, then had it quelched. Then Perri was grinning, blinking and reaching for her, asking:

"Can't you sleep, love?"

"No," she admitted. Then she said, "Come here, darling."

"Well, well," he laughed. "Aren't you in a mood?"

Absolutely. A feverish mood, her mind leaping from subject to subject, without order, every thought intense and sudden, Perri on top of her and her old-fashioned eyes gazing up at the darkened ceiling, still seeing the powerful surges of changing colors that obscured the bright dusting of stars.

They took a second honeymoon, Quee Lee's treat. They traveled halfway around the ship, visiting a famous resort beside a small tropical sea; and for several months, they enjoyed the scenery and beaches, bone-white sands dropping into azure waters where fancy corals and fancier fishes lived. Every night brought a different sky, the ship supplying stored images of nebulas and strange suns; and they made love in the oddest places, in odd ways, strangers sometimes coming upon them and pausing to watch.

Yet she felt detached somehow, hovering overhead like an observer. Did Remoras have sex? she wondered. And if so, how? And how did they make their children? One day, Perri strapped on a gill and swam alone to the reef, leaving Quee Lee free to do research. Remoran sex, if it could be called that, was managed with electrical stimulation through the suits themselves. Reproduction was something else, children conceived in vitro, samples of their parents' genetics married and grown inside a hyperfiber envelope. The envelope was expanded as needed. Birth came with the first independent fusion plant. What an incredible way to live, she realized; but then again, there were many human societies that seemed bizarre. Some refused immortality. Some had married computers or lived in a narcotic haze. There were many, many spiritual splinter groups . . . only she couldn't learn much about the Remoran faith. Was their faith secret? And if so, why had she been allowed a glimpse of their private world?

Perri remained pleasant and attentive.

"I know this is work for you," she told him, "and you've been a delight, darling. Old women appreciate these attentions."

"Oh, you're not old!" A wink and smile, and he pulled her close. "And it's not work at all. Believe me!"

They returned home soon afterward, and Quee Lee was disappointed with her apartment. It was just as she remembered it, and the sameness was depressing. Even the garden room failed to brighten her mood . . . and she found herself wondering if she'd ever lived anywhere but here, the stone walls cold and closing in on her.

Perri asked, "What's the matter, love?"

She said nothing.

"Can I help, darling?"

"I forgot to tell you something," she began. "A friend of yours visited . . . oh, it was almost a year ago."

The roguish charm surfaced, reliable and nonplussed. "Which friend?"

"Orleans."

And Perri didn't respond at first, hearing the name and not allowing his expression to change. He stood motionless, not quite looking at her; and Quee Lee noticed a weakness in the mouth and something glassy about the smiling eyes. She felt uneasy, almost asking him what was wrong. Then Perri said, "What did Orleans want?" His voice was too soft, almost a whisper. A sideways glance, and he muttered, "Orleans came here?" He couldn't quite believe what she was saying. . . .

"You owed him some money," she replied.

Perri didn't speak, didn't seem to hear anything.

"Perri?"

He swallowed and said, "Owed?"

"I paid him."

"But . . . but what happened . . . ?"

She told him and she didn't. She mentioned the old seals and some other salient details, then in the middle of her explanation, all at once, something obvious and awful occurred to her. What if there hadn't been a debt? She gasped, asking, "You did owe him the money, didn't you?"

"How much did you say it was?"

She told him again.

He nodded. He swallowed and straightened his back, then managed to say, "I'll pay you back . . . as soon as possible . . ."

"Is there any hurry?" She took his hand, telling him, "I haven't made noise until now, have I? Don't worry." A pause. "I just wonder how you could owe him so much?"

Perri shook his head. "I'll give you five thousand now, maybe six . . . and I'll raise the rest. Soon as I can, I promise."

She said, "Fine."

"I'm sorry," he muttered.

"How do you know a Remora?"

He seemed momentarily confused by the question. Then he managed to say, "You know me. A taste for the exotic, and all that."

"You lost the money gambling? Is that what happened?"

"I'd nearly forgotten, it was so long ago." He summoned a smile and some of the old charm. "You should know, darling . . . those Remoras aren't anything like you and me. Be very careful with them, please."

She didn't mention her jaunt on the hull. Everything was old news anyway, and why had she brought it up in the first place? Perri kept promising to pay her back. He announced he was leaving tomorrow, needing to find some nameless people who owed him. The best he could manage was fifteen hundred credits. "A weak down payment, I know." Quee Lee thought of reassuring him—he seemed painfully nervous—but instead she simply told him, "Have a good trip, and come home soon."

He was a darling man when vulnerable. "Soon," he promised, walking out the front door. And an hour later, Quee Lee left too, telling herself that she was going to the hull again to confront her husband's old friend. What was this mysterious debt? Why did it bother him so much? But somewhere during the long tube-car ride, before she reached Port Beta, she realized that a confrontation would just further embarrass Perri, and what cause would that serve?

"What now?" she whispered to herself.

Another walk on the hull, of course. If Orleans would allow it. If he had the time, she hoped, and the inclination.

His face had turned blue, and the eyes were larger. The pits were filled with black hairs that shone in the light, something about them distinctly amused. "I guess we could go for a stroll," said the cool voice. They were standing in the same locker room, or one just like it; Quee Lee was unsure about directions. "We could," said Orleans, "but if you want to bend the rules, why bend little ones? Why not pick the hefty ones?"

She watched the mouth smile down at her, two little tusks showing in its corners. "What do you mean?" she asked.

"Of course it'll take time," he warned. "A few months, maybe a few years . . ."

She had centuries, if she wanted.

"I know you," said Orleans. "You've gotten curious about me, about *us*." Orleans moved an arm, not so much as a hum coming from the refurbished joints. "We'll make you an honorary Remora, if you're willing. We'll borrow a lifesuit, set you inside it, then transform you partway in a hurry-up fashion."

"You can? How?"

"Oh, aimed doses of radiation. Plus we'll give you some useful mutations. I'll wrap up some genes inside smart cancers, and they'll migrate to the right spots and grow. . . ."

She was frightened and intrigued, her heart kicking harder.

"It won't happen overnight, of course. And it depends on how much you want done." A pause. "And you should know that it's not strictly legal. The captains have this attitude about putting passengers a little bit at risk."

"How much risk is there?"

Orleans said, "The transformation is easy enough, in principle. I'll call up our records, make sure of the fine points." A pause and a narrowing of the eyes. "We'll keep you asleep throughout. Intravenous feedings. That's best. You'll lie down with one body, then waken with a new one. A better one, I'd like to think. How much risk? Almost none, believe me."

She felt numb. Small and weak and numb.

"You won't be a true Remora. Your basic genetics won't be touched, I promise. But someone looking at you will think you're genuine."

For an instant, with utter clarity, Quee Lee saw herself alone on the great gray hull, walking the path of the first Remora.

"Are you interested?"

"Maybe. I am."

"You'll need a lot of interest before we can start," he warned. "We have expenses to consider, and I'll be putting my crew at risk. If the captains find out, it's a suspension without pay." He paused, then said, "Are you listening to me?"

"It's going to cost money," she whispered.

Orleans gave a figure.

And Quee Lee was braced for a larger sum, two hundred thousand credits still large but not unbearable. She wouldn't be able to take as many trips to fancy resorts, true. Yet how could a lazy, prosaic resort compare with what she was being offered?

"You've done this before?" she asked.

He waited a moment, then said, "Not for a long time, no."

She didn't ask what seemed quite obvious, thinking of Perri and secretly smiling to herself.

"Take time," Orleans counseled. "Feel sure."

But she had already decided.

"Quee Lee?"

She looked at him, asking, "Can I have your eyes? Can you wrap them up in a smart cancer for me?"

"Certainly!" A great fluid smile emerged, framed with tusks. "Pick and choose as you wish. Anything you wish."

"The eyes," she muttered.

"They're yours," he declared, giving a little wink.

Arrangements had to be made, and what surprised her most—what she enjoyed more than the anticipation—was the subterfuge, taking money from her savings and leaving no destination, telling her apartment that she would be gone for an indeterminate time. At least a year, and perhaps much longer. Orleans hadn't put a cap on her stay with them, and what if she liked the Remoran life? Why not keep her possibilities open?

"If Perri returns?" asked the apartment.

He was to have free reign of the place, naturally. She thought she'd made herself clear—

"No, miss," the voice interrupted. "What do I tell him, if anything?"

"Tell him . . . tell him that I've gone exploring."

"Exploring?"

"Tell him it's my turn for a change," she declared; and she left without as much as a backward glance.

Orleans found help from the same female Remora, the one who had taken Quee Lee to him twice now. Her comma-shaped eyes hadn't changed, but the mouth was smaller and the gray teeth had turned black as obsidian.

Quee Lee lay between them as they worked, their faces smiling but the voices tight and shrill. Not for the first time, she realized she wasn't hearing their real voices. The suits themselves were translating their wet mutterings, which is why throats and mouths could change so much without having any audible effect.

"Are you comfortable?" asked the woman. But before Quee Lee could reply, she asked, "Any last questions?"

Quee Lee was encased in the lifesuit, a sudden panic taking hold of her. "When I go home . . . when I'm done . . . how fast can I . . . ?"

"Can you?"

"Return to my normal self."

"Cure the damage, you mean." The woman laughed gently, her expression changing from one unreadable state to another. "I don't think there's a firm answer, dear. Do you have an autodoc in your apartment? Good. Let it excise the bad and help you grow your own organs over again. As if you'd suffered a bad accident. . . ." A brief pause. "It should take what, Orleans? Six months to be cured?"

The man said nothing, busy with certain controls inside her suit's helmet. Quee Lee could just see his face above and behind her.

"Six months and you can walk in public again."

"I don't mean it that way," Quee Lee countered, swallowed now. A pressure was building against her chest, panic becoming terror. She wanted nothing now but to be home again.

"Listen," said Orleans, then he said nothing.

Finally Quee Lee whispered, "What?"

He knelt beside her, saying, "You'll be fine. I promise."

His old confidence was missing. Perhaps he hadn't believed she would go through with this adventure. Perhaps the offer had been some kind of bluff, something no sane person would find appealing, and now he'd invent some excuse to stop everything—

—but he said, "Seals tight and ready."

"Tight and ready," echoed the woman.

Smiles appeared on both faces, though neither inspired confidence. Then Orleans was explaining: "There's only a slight, slight chance that you won't return to normal. If you should get hit by too much radiation, precipitating too many novel mutations . . . well, the strangeness can get buried too deeply. A thousand autodocs couldn't root it all out of you."

"Vestigial organs," the woman added. "Odd blemishes and the like."

"It won't happen," said Orleans.

"It won't," Quee Lee agreed.

A feeding nipple appeared before her mouth.

"Suck and sleep," Orleans told her.

She swallowed some sort of chemical broth, and the woman was saying, "No, it would take ten or fifteen centuries to make lasting marks. Unless—"

Orleans said something, snapping at her.

She laughed with a bitter sound, saying, "Oh, she's asleep . . . !"

And Quee Lee was asleep. She found herself in a dreamless, timeless void, her body being pricked with needles—little white pains marking every smart cancer—and it was as if nothing else existed in the universe but Quee Lee, floating in that perfect blackness while she was remade.

"How long?"

"Not so long. Seven months, almost."

Seven months. Quee Lee tried to blink and couldn't, couldn't shut the lids of her eyes. Then she tried touching her face, lifting a heavy hand and setting the palm on her faceplate, finally remembering her suit. "Is it done?" she muttered, her voice sloppy and slow. "Am I done now?"

"You're never done," Orleans laughed. "Haven't you been paying attention?"

She saw a figure, blurred but familiar.

"How do you feel, Quee Lee?"

Strange. Through and through, she felt very strange.

"That's normal enough," the voice offered. "Another couple months, and you'll be perfect. Have patience."

She was a patient person, she remembered. And now her eyes seemed to shut of their own volition, her mind sleeping again. But this time she dreamed, her and Perri and Orleans all at the beach together. She saw them sunning on the bone-white sand, and she even felt the heat of the false sun, felt it baking hot down to her rebuilt bones.

She woke, muttering, "Orleans? Orleans?"

"Here I am."

Her vision was improved now. She found herself breathing normally, her wrong-shaped mouth struggling with each word and her suit managing an accurate translation.

"How do I look?" she asked.

Orleans smiled and said, "Lovely."

His face was blue-black, perhaps. When she sat up, looking at the plain gray locker room, she realized how the colors had shifted. Her new eyes perceived the world differently, sensitive to the same spectrum but in novel ways. She slowly climbed to her feet, then asked, "How long?"

"Nine months, fourteen days."

No, she wasn't finished. But the transformation had reached a stable point, she sensed, and it was wonderful to be mobile again. She managed a few tentative steps. She made clumsy fists with her too-thick hands. Lifting the fists, she gazed at them, wondering how they would look beneath the hyperfiber.

"Want to see yourself?" Orleans asked.

Now? Was she ready?

Her friend smiled, tusks glinting in the room's weak light. He offered a large mirror, and she bent to put her face close enough . . . finding a remade face staring up at her, a sloppy mouth full of mirror-colored teeth and a pair of hairy pits for eyes. She managed a deep breath and shivered. Her skin was lovely, golden or at least appearing golden to her. It was covered with hard white lumps, and her nose was a slender beak. She wished she could touch herself, hands stroking her faceplate. Only Remoras could never touch their own flesh. . . .

"If you feel strong enough," he offered, "you can go with me. My crew and I are going on a patching mission, out to the prow."

"When?"

"Now, actually." He lowered the mirror. "The others are waiting in the shuttle. Stay here for a couple more days, or come now."

"Now," she whispered.

"Good." He nodded, telling her, "They want to meet you. They're curious what sort of person becomes a Remora."

A person who doesn't want to be locked up in a bland gray room, she thought to herself, smiling now with her mirrored teeth.

They had all kinds of faces, all unique, myriad eyes and twisting mouths and flesh of every color. She counted fifteen Remoras, plus Orleans, and Quee Lee worked to learn names and get to know her new friends. The shuttle ride was like a party, a strange informal party, and she had never known happier people, listening to Remora jokes and how they teased one another, and how they sometimes teased her. In friendly ways, of course. They asked about her apartment—how big; how fancy; how much—and about her long life. Was it as boring as it sounded? Quee Lee laughed at herself while she nodded, saying, "No, nothing changes very much. The centuries have their way of running together, sure."

One Remora—a large masculine voice and a contorted blue face—asked the others, "Why do people pay fortunes to ride the ship, then do everything possible to hide deep inside it? Why don't they ever step outside and have a little look at where we're going?"

The cabin erupted in laughter, the observation an obvious favorite.

"Immortals are cowards," said the woman beside Quee Lee.

"Fools," said a second woman, the one with comma-shaped eyes. "Most of them, at least."

Quee Lee felt uneasy, but just temporarily. She turned and looked through a filthy window, the smooth changeless landscape below and the glowing sky as she remembered it. The view soothed her. Eventually she shut her eyes and slept, waking when Orleans shouted something about being close to their destination. "Decelerating now!" he called from the cockpit.

They were slowing. Dropping. Looking at her friends, she saw a variety of smiles meant for her. The Remoras beside her took her hands, everyone starting to pray. "No comets today," they begged. "And plenty tomorrow, because we want overtime."

The shuttle slowed to nothing, then settled.

Orleans strode back to Quee Lee, his mood suddenly serious. "Stay close," he warned, "but don't get in our way, either."

The hyperfiber was thickest here, on the prow, better than ten kilometers deep, and its surface had been browned by the ceaseless radiations. A soft dry dust clung to the lifesuits, and everything was lit up by the aurora and flashes of laser light. Quee Lee followed the others, listening to their chatter. She ate a little meal of Remoran soup—her first conscious meal—feeling the soup moving down her throat, trying to map her new architecture. Her stomach seemed the same, but did she have two hearts? It seemed that the beats were wrong. Two hearts nestled side by side. She found Orleans and approached him. "I wish I could pull off my suit, just once. Just for a minute." She told him, "I keep wondering how all of me looks."

Orleans glanced at her, then away. He said, "No."

"No?"

"Remoras don't remove their suits. Ever."

There was anger in the voice and a deep chilling silence from the others. Quee Lee looked about, then swallowed. "I'm not a Remora," she finally said. "I don't understand. . . ."

Silence persisted, quick looks exchanged.

"I'm going to climb out of this . . . eventually . . . !"

"But don't say it now," Orleans warned. A softer, more tempered voice informed her, "We have taboos. Maybe we seem too rough to have them—"

"No," she muttered.

"—yet we do. These lifesuits are as much a part of our bodies as our guts and eyes, and being a Remora, a true Remora, is a sacred pledge that you take for your entire life."

The comma-eyed woman approached, saying, "It's an insult to remove your suit. A sacrilege."

"Contemptible," said someone else. "Or worse."

Then Orleans, perhaps guessing Quee Lee's thoughts, made a show of touching her, and she felt the hand through her suit. "Not that you're anything but our guest, of course. Of course." He paused, then said, "We have our beliefs, that's all."

"Ideals," said the woman.

"And contempt for those we don't like. Do you understand?"

She couldn't, but she made understanding sounds just the same. Obviously she had found a sore spot.

Then came a new silence, and she found herself marching through the dust, wishing someone would make angry sounds again. Silence was the worst kind of anger. From now on, she vowed, she would be careful about everything she said. Every word.

The crater was vast and rough and only partway patched. Previous crew had brought giant tanks and the machinery used to make the patch. It was something of an artform, pouring the fresh liquid hyperfiber and carefully curing it. Each shift added another hundred meters to the smooth crater floor. Orleans stood with Quee Lee at the top, explaining the job. This would be a double shift, and she was free to watch. "But not too closely," he warned her again, the tone vaguely parental. "Stay out of our way."

She promised. For that first half-day, she was happy to sit on the crater's lip, on a ridge of tortured and useless hyperfiber, imagining the comet that must have made this mess. Not large, she knew. A large one would have blasted a crater too big to see at a glance, and forty crews would be laboring here. But it hadn't been a small one, either. It must have slipped past the lasers, part of a swarm. She watched the red beams cutting across the sky, their heat producing new colors in the aurora. Her new eyes saw amazing details. Shock waves as violet phosphorescence; swirls of orange and crimson and snowy white. A beautiful deadly sky, wasn't it? Suddenly the lasers fired faster, a spiderweb of beams overhead, and she realized that a swarm was ahead of the ship, pinpointed by the navigators somewhere below them . . . tens of millions of kilometers ahead, mud and ice and rock closing fast . . . !

The lasers fired even faster, and she bowed her head.

There was an impact, at least one. She saw the flash and felt a faint rumble dampened by the hull, a portion of those energies absorbed and converted into useful power. Impacts were fuel, of a sort. And the residual gases would be concentrated and pumped inside, helping to replace the inevitable loss of volatiles as the ship continued on its great trek.

The ship was an organism feeding on the galaxy.

It was a familiar image, almost cliché, yet suddenly it seemed quite fresh. Even profound. Quee Lee laughed to herself, looking out over the browning plain while turning her attentions inward. She was aware of her breathing and the bump-bumping of wrong hearts, and she sensed changes with every little motion. Her body had an odd indecipherable quality. She could feel every fiber in her muscles, every twitch and every stillness. She had never been so alive, so self-aware, and she found herself laughing with a giddy amazement.

If she was a true Remora, she thought, then she would be a world unto herself. A world like the ship, only smaller, its organic parts enclosed in armor and forever in flux. Like the passengers below, the cells of her body were changing. She thought she could nearly feel herself evolving . . . and how did Orleans control it? It would be astonishing if she could re-evolve sight, for instance . . . gaining eyes unique to herself, never having existed before and never to exist again . . . !

What if she stayed with these people?

The possibility suddenly occurred to her, taking her by surprise.

What if she took whatever pledge was necessary, embracing all of their taboos and proving that she belonged with them? Did such things happen? Did adventurous passengers try converting—?

The sky turned red, lasers firing and every red line aimed at a point directly overhead. The silent barrage was focused on some substantial chunk of ice and grit, vaporizing its surface and cracking its heart. Then the beams separated, assaulting the bigger pieces and then the smaller ones. It was an enormous drama, her exhilaration married to terror . . . her watching the aurora brightening as force fields killed the momentum of the surviving grit and atomic dust. The sky was a vivid orange, and sudden tiny impacts kicked up the dusts around her. Something struck her leg, a flash of light followed by a dim pain . . . and she wondered if she was dead, then how badly she was wounded. Then she blinked and saw the little crater etched above her knee. A blemish, if that. And suddenly the meteor shower was finished.

Quee Lee rose to her feet, shaking with nervous energy.

She began picking her way down the crater slope. Orleans' commands were forgotten; she needed to speak to him. She had insights and compliments to share, nearly tripping with her excitement, finally reaching the worksite and gasping, her air stale from her exertions. She could taste herself in her breaths, the flavor unfamiliar, thick and a little sweet.

"Orleans!" she cried out.

"You're not supposed to be here," groused one woman.

The comma-eyed woman said, "Stay right there. Orleans is coming, and don't move!"

A lake of fresh hyperfiber was cooling and curing as she stood beside it. A thin skin had formed, the surface utterly flat and silvery. Mirror-like. Quee Lee could see the sky reflected in it, leaning forward and knowing she shouldn't. She risked falling in order to see herself once again. The nearby Remoras watched her, saying nothing. They smiled as she grabbed a lump of old hyperfiber, positioning herself, and the lasers flashed again, making everything bright as day.

She didn't see her face.

Or rather, she did. But it wasn't the face she expected, the face from Orleans' convenient mirror. Here was the old Quee Lee, mouth ajar, those pretty and ordinary eyes opened wide in amazement.

She gasped, knowing everything. A near-fortune paid, and nothing in return. Nothing here had been real. This was an enormous and cruel sick joke; and now the Remoras were laughing, hands on their untouchable bellies and their awful faces contorted, ready to rip apart from the sheer brutal joy of the moment . . . !

"Your mirror wasn't a mirror, was it? It synthesized that image, didn't it?" She kept asking questions, not waiting for a response. "And you drugged me, didn't you? That's why everything still looks and feels wrong."

Orleans said, "Exactly. Yes."

Quee Lee remained inside her lifesuit, just the two of them flying back to Port Beta. He would see her on her way home. The rest of the crew was working, and Orleans would return and finish his shift. After her discovery, everyone agreed there was no point in keeping her on the prow.

"You owe me money," she managed.

Orleans' face remained blue-black. His tusks framed a calm icy smile. "Money? Whose money?"

"I paid you for a service, and you never met the terms."

"I don't know about any money," he laughed.

"I'll report you," she snapped, trying to use all of her venom. "I'll go to the captains—"

"—and embarrass yourself further." He was confident, even cocky. "Our transaction would be labeled illegal, not to mention disgusting. The captains will be thoroughly disgusted, believe me." Another laugh. "Besides, what can anyone prove? You gave someone your money, but nobody will trace it to any of us. Believe me."

She had never felt more ashamed, crossing her arms and trying to wish herself home again.

"The drug will wear off soon," he promised. "You'll feel like yourself again. Don't worry."

Softly, in a breathless little voice, she asked, "How long have I been gone?"

Silence.

"It hasn't been months, has it?"

"More like three days." A nod inside the helmet. "The same drug distorts your sense of time, if you get enough of it."

She felt ill to her stomach.

"You'll be back home in no time, Quee Lee."

She was shaking and holding herself.

The Remora glanced at her for a long moment, something resembling remorse in his expression. Or was she misreading the signs?

"You aren't spiritual people," she snapped. It was the best insult she could manage, and she spoke with certainty. "You're crude, disgusting monsters. You couldn't live below if you had the chance, and this is where you belong."

Orleans said nothing, merely watching her.

Finally he looked ahead, gazing at the endless gray landscape. "We try to follow our founder's path. We try to be spiritual." A shrug. "Some of us do better than others, of course. We're only human."

She whispered, "Why?"

Again he looked at her, asking, "Why what?"

"Why have you done this to me?"

Orleans seemed to breathe and hold the breath, finally exhaling. "Oh, Quee Lee," he said, "you haven't been paying attention, have you?"

What did he mean?

He grasped her helmet, pulling her face up next to his face. She saw nothing but the eyes, each black hair moving and nameless fluids circulating through them, and she heard the voice saying, "This has never, never been about you, Quee Lee. Not you. Not for one instant."

And she understood—perhaps she had always known—struck mute and her skin going cold, and finally, after everything, she found herself starting to weep.

Perri was already home, by chance.

"I was worried about you," he confessed, sitting in the garden room with honest relief on his face. "The apartment said you were going to be gone for a year or more. I was scared for you."

"Well," she said, "I'm back."

Her husband tried not to appear suspicious, and he worked hard not to ask certain questions. She could see him holding the questions inside himself. She watched him decide to try the old charm, smiling now and saying, "So you went exploring?"

"Not really."

"Where?"

"Cloud Canyon," she lied. She had practiced the lie all the way from Port Beta, yet it sounded false now. She was halfway startled when her husband said:

"Did you go into it?"

"Partway, then I decided not to risk it. I rented a boat, but I couldn't make myself step on board."

Perri grinned happily, unable to hide his relief. A deep breath was exhaled, then he said, "By the way, I've raised almost eight thousand credits already. I've already put them in your account."

"Fine."

"I'll find the rest too."

"It can wait," she offered.

Relief blended into confusion. "Are you all right, darling?"

"I'm tired," she allowed.

"You look tired."

"Let's go to bed, shall we?"

Perri was compliant, making love to her and falling into a deep sleep, as exhausted as Quee Lee. But she insisted on staying awake, sliding into her private bathroom and giving her autodoc a drop of Perri's seed. "I want to know if there's anything odd," she told it.

"Yes, miss."

"And scan him, will you? Without waking him."

The machine set to work. Almost instantly, Quee Lee was being shown lists of abnormal genes and vestigial organs. She didn't bother to read them. She closed her eyes, remembering what little Orleans had told her after he had admitted that she wasn't anything more than an incidental bystander. "Perri was born Remora, and he left us. A long time ago, by our count, and that's a huge taboo."

"Leaving the fold?" she had said.

"Every so often, one of us visits his home while he's gone. We slip a little dust into our joints, making them grind, and we do a pity-play to whomever we find."

Her husband had lied to her from the first, about everything.

"Sometimes we'll trick her into giving even more money," he had boasted. "Just like we've done with you."

And she had asked, "Why?"

"Why do you think?" he had responded.

Vengeance, of a sort. Of course.

"Eventually," Orleans had declared, "everyone's going to know about Perri. He'll run out of hiding places, and money, and he'll have to come back to us. We just don't want it to happen too soon, you know? It's too much fun as it is."

Now she opened her eyes, gazing at the lists of abnormalities. It had to be work for him to appear human, to cope with those weird Remora genetics. He wasn't merely someone who had lived on the hull for a few years, no. He was a full-blooded Remora who had done the unthinkable, removing his suit and living below, safe from the mortal dangers of the universe. Quee Lee was the latest of his ignorant lovers, and she knew precisely why he had selected her. More than money, she had offered him a useful naiveté and a sheltered ignorance . . . and wasn't she well within her rights to confront him, confront him and demand that he leave at once . . . ?

"Erase the lists," she said.

"Yes, miss."

She told her apartment, "Project the view from the prow, if you will. Put it on my bedroom ceiling, please."

"Of course, miss," it replied.

She stepped out of the bathroom, lasers and exploding comets overhead. She fully expected to do what Orleans anticipated, putting her mistakes behind her. She sat on the edge of her bed, on Perri's side, waiting for him to wake on his own. He would feel her gaze and open his eyes, seeing her framed by a Remoran sky. . . .

. . . and she hesitated, taking a breath and holding it, glancing upwards, remembering that moment on the crater's lip when she had felt a union with her body. A perfection; an intoxicating sense of self. It was induced by drugs and ignorance, yet still it had seemed true. It was a perception worth any cost, she realized; and she imagined Perri's future, hounded by the Remoras, losing every human friend, left with no choice but the hull and his left-behind life. . . .

She looked at him, the peaceful face stirring.

Compassion. Pity. Not love, but there was something not far from love making her feel for the fallen Remora.

"What if . . . ?" she whispered, beginning to smile.

And Perri smiled in turn, eyes closed and him enjoying some lazy dream that in an instant he would surely forget.

PAUL J. MCAULEY

Paul J. McAuley [1955–] (www.omegacom.demon.co.uk) is a British writer who often writes hard SF, one of the British group (along with Stephen Baxter, Peter F. Hamilton, Iain M. Banks, and others) responsible for the hard SF/space opera renaissance of the 1990s. McAuley has degrees in botany and zoology and did scientific research in Britain and, for a time in the eighties, in Los Angeles, before becoming a professor in the UK. In recent years, he gave up teaching and became a full-time writer.

His first novel, *400 Billion Stars*, was cowinner of the Philip K. Dick Award in 1988 (with Rudy Rucker's *Wetware*). He has since published a number of SF novels, of which *Fairyland* (1994) won the Arthur C. Clarke Award and the John W. Campbell Memorial Award for best novel and *Pasquale's Angel* (1994) won the Sidewise Award for Alternate History fiction. He has two collections of short fiction, *The King of the Hill and Other Stories* (1991) and *The Invisible Country* (1996). He completed a trilogy of SF novels, The Book of Confluence (*Child of the River*, 1997; *Ancient of Days*, 1998; *Shrine of Stars*, 1999). Since 2001, he has published four SF thrillers: *The Secret of Life* (2001), *Whole Wide World* (2001), *White Devils* (2004), and *Little Machines* (2005).

It is evident, then, that he has moved away from space opera, which characterized his early novels. In a recent interview he was asked about space opera in his early works: "There was a conscious attempt to subvert the triumphalism dominant in American SF—an unsurprising triumphalism, since this has turned out to be the American century, but annoying when it is the unquestioned default mode. And I was also aware of the perception of British SF as being low key, inward-turning and, yes, disillusioned with the toys of SF. I wanted to try and combine the two—the grand sweep of vision the best American SF can give, grounded in gritty realism. I'm not sure that it's a natural combination, frankly, but I don't think that the ending of *Eternal Light* (1991) could be considered disillusioned."

During the last five years he has been one of the spokesmen for British New Space Opera, as distinct from American. "Alternate cultural frameworks is something I've been banging on about for some time, ever since I was outed as a ringer bending space opera to my own fell ends; that is, trying to make space opera do something that didn't reinforce the hegemony of American capitalist democracy. I don't make any extraordinary claims about this; it's an attitude that Brits are likely to assume as a matter of course, since they're outsiders in a genre that's characteristically American."

In a *Locus* essay, he asserts, "The New Space Opera is a mostly British response to the same impulse, emerging without the benefit of a prophet or a manifesto, less a movement than a coincidence. Given that writers are wilfully idiosyncratic, if you scratch half-a-dozen practitioners of any particular trend, you'll probably get half-a-dozen different rationales."

He then goes on to give a detailed and eloquent description of the best New Space Opera:

> New space opera—the *good* new space opera—cheerfully plunders the tropes and toys of the old school and secondary sources from Blish to Delany, refurbishes them with up-to-the-minute science, and deploys them in epic narratives where intimate, human-scale stories are at least as relevant as the widescreen baroque backgrounds on which they cast their shadows. There are neither empires nor rigid technocracies

dominated by a single Big Idea in the new space opera; like cyberpunk, it's eclectic and pluralistic, and infused with the very twenty-first century sensibility that the center cannot hold, that technology-driven change is continuous and advancing on a thousand fronts, that some kind of posthuman singularity is approaching fast or may already have happened. Most of all, its stories contain a vertiginous sense of deep time; in the new space opera, the Galaxy is not an empty stage on which humans freely strut their stuff, but is instead a kind of junk yard littered with the ruins and abandoned wonders of earlier, more powerful races.

The part about up-to-the-minute science is where the link between the Hard SF Renaissance of the nineties and the New Space Opera, both in America and Britain, is forged. McAuley's characterization applies equally well, though, to Vernor Vinge, Gregory Benford, or even David Brin in space opera mode, which does undercut some of the patriotic rhetoric. New Space Opera in Britain does not exclude the same phenomenon in the US, Canada, and Australia, of which there are many evidences. There are certainly flavors, and political attitudes, that distinguish individual space opera writers. Still, the argument persists and is energizing to SF internationally.

McAuley's list of writers extends "from the new romanticism of Iain M. Banks, Ian McDonald, and Colin Greenland to the hardcore technogoth of Alastair Reynolds and Charles Stross." He does not mean to be exclusive.

"Recording Angel" is a story from the mid-1990s, when McAuley was still principally writing in a hard SF adventure mode. It is set in his Confluence future, a sort of combination of Jack Vance's Dying Earth, Gene Wolfe's New Sun setting, and Cordwainer Smith's story "The Dead Lady of Clown Town." Confluence is a constructed world around a halo star outside the home galaxy, inhabited by post-humans raised or uplifted from animals. And a five-million-year-old exploration ship has arrived back with a human crew.

RECORDING ANGEL

PAUL J. MCAULEY

Mr Naryan, the Archivist of Sensch, still keeps to his habits as much as possible, despite all that has happened since Angel arrived in the city. He has clung to these personal rituals for a very long time now, and it is not easy to let them go. And so, on the day that Angel's ship is due to arrive and attempt to reclaim her, the day that will end in revolution, or so Angel has promised her followers, as ever, at dusk, as the Rim Mountains of Confluence tip above the disc of its star and the Eye of the Preservers rises above the far side of the world, Mr Naryan walks across the long plaza at the edge of the city towards the Great River.

Rippling patterns swirl out from his feet, silver and gold racing away through the plaza's living marble. Above his head, clouds of little machines spin through the twilight: information's dense weave. At the margin of the plaza, broad steps shelve into the river's brown slop. Naked children scamper through the shallows, turning to watch as Mr Naryan, old and fat and leaning on his stick at every other stride, limps past and descends the submerged stair until only his hairless head is above water. He draws a breath and ducks completely under. His nostrils pinch shut. Membranes slide across his eyes. As always, the bass roar of the river's fall over the edge of the world stirs his heart. He surfaces, spouting water, and the children hoot. He ducks under again and comes up quickly, and the children scamper back from his spray, breathless with delight. Mr Naryan laughs with them and walks back up the steps, his loose belted shirt shedding water and quickly drying in the parched dusk air.

Further on, a funeral party is launching little clay lamps into the river's swift currents. The men, waist-deep in brown water, turn as Mr Naryan limps past, knuckling their broad, narrow foreheads. Their wet skins gleam with the fire of the sunset that is now gathering in on itself across leagues of water. Mr Naryan genuflects in acknowledgement, feeling an icy shame. The woman died before he could hear her story; her, and seven others in the last few days. It is a bitter failure.

Angel, and all that she has told him—Mr Naryan wonders whether he will be able to hear out the end of her story. She has promised to set the city aflame and, unlike Dreen, Mr Naryan believes that she can.

A mendicant is sitting cross-legged on the edge of the steps down to the river. An old man, sky-clad and straight-backed. He seems to be staring into the sunset, in the waking trance that is the nearest that the Shaped citizens of Sensch ever come to sleep. Tears brim in his wide eyes and pulse down his leathery cheeks; a small silver moth has settled at the corner of his left eye to sip salt.

Mr Naryan drops a handful of the roasted peanuts he carries for the purpose into the mendicant's bowl, and walks on. He walks a long way before he realises that a crowd has gathered at the end of the long plaza, where the steps end and, with a sudden jog, the docks begin. Hundreds of machines swarm in the darkening air, and behind this shuttling weave a line of magistrates stand shoulder to shoulder, flipping their quirts back and forth as if to drive off flies. Metal tags braided into the tassels of the quirts wink and flicker; the magistrates' flared red cloaks seem inflamed in the last light of the sun.

The people make a rising and falling hum, the sound of discontent. They are looking upriver. Mr Naryan, with a catch in his heart, realises what they must be looking at.

It is a speck of light on the horizon north of the city, where the broad ribbon of the river and the broad ribbon of the land narrow to a single point. It is the lighter towing Angel's ship, at the end of its long journey downriver to the desert city where she has taken refuge, and caught Mr Naryan in the net of her tale.

Mr Naryan first heard about her from Dreen, Sensch's Commissioner; in fact, Dreen paid a visit to Mr Naryan's house to convey the news in person. His passage through the narrow streets of the quarter was the focus of a swelling congregation which kept a space two paces wide around him as he ambled towards the house where Mr Naryan had his apartment.

Dreen was a lively but tormented fellow who was paying off a debt of conscience by taking the more or less ceremonial position of Commissioner in this remote city which his ancestors had long ago abandoned. Slight and agile, his head clean-shaven except for a fringe of polychrome hair that framed his parchment face, he looked like a lily blossom swirling on the Great River's current as he made his way through the excited crowd. A pair of magistrates preceded him and a remote followed, a mirror-coloured seed that seemed to move through the air in brief rapid pulses like a squeezed watermelon pip. A swarm of lesser machines spun above the packed heads of the crowd. Machines did not entirely trust the citizens, with good reason. Change Wars raged up and down the length of Confluence as, one by one, the ten thousand races of the Shaped fell from innocence.

Mr Naryan, alerted by the clamour, was already standing on his balcony when Dreen reached the house. Scrupulously polite, his voice amplified through a little machine that fluttered before his lips, Dreen enquired if he might come up. The crowd fell silent as he spoke, so that his last words echoed eerily up and down the narrow street. When Mr Naryan said mildly that the Commissioner was of course always welcome, Dreen made an elaborate genuflection and scrambled straight up the fretted carvings which decorated the front of the apartment house. He vaulted the wrought-iron rail and perched in the ironwood chair that Mr Naryan usually took when he was tutoring a pupil.

While Mr Naryan lowered his corpulent bulk onto the stool that was the only other piece of furniture on the little balcony, Dreen said cheerfully that he had not walked so far for more than a year. He accepted the tea and sweetmeats that Mr Naryan's wife, terrified by his presence, offered, and added, "It really would be more convenient if you took quarters appropriate to your status."

As Commissioner, Dreen had use of the vast palace of intricately carved pink sandstone that dominated the southern end of the city, although he chose to live in a tailored habitat of hanging gardens that hovered above the palace's spiky towers.

Mr Naryan said, "My calling requires that I live amongst the people. How else would I understand their stories? How else would they find me?"

"By any of the usual methods, of course—or you could multiply yourself so that every one of these snakes had their own archivist. Or you could use machines. But I forget, your calling requires that you use only appropriate technology. That's why I'm here, because you won't have heard the news."

Dreen had an abrupt style, but he was neither as brutal nor as ruthless as his brusqueness suggested. Like Mr Naryan, who understood Dreen's manner completely, he was there to serve, not to rule.

Mr Naryan confessed that he had heard nothing unusual, and Dreen said eagerly, "There's a woman arrived here. A star-farer. Her ship landed at Ys last year, as I remember telling you."

"I remember seeing a ship land at Ys, but I was a young man then, Dreen. I had not taken orders."

"Yes, yes," Dreen said impatiently, "picket boats and the occasional merchant's argosy still use the docks. But this is different. She claims to be from the deep past. The *very* deep past, before the Preservers."

"I can see that her story would be interesting if it were true."

Dreen beat a rhythm on his skinny thighs with the flat of his hands. "Yes, yes! A human woman, returned after millions of years of travelling outside the Galaxy. But there's more! She is only one of a whole crew, and she's jumped ship. Caused some fuss. It seems the others want her back."

"She is a slave, then?"

"It seems she may be bound to them as you are bound to your order."

"Then you could return her. Surely you know where she is?"

Dreen popped a sweetmeat in his mouth and chewed with gusto. His flat-topped teeth were all exactly the same size. He wiped his wide lipless mouth with the back of his hand and said, "Of course I know where she is—that's not the point. The point is that no one knows if she's lying, or her shipmates are lying—they're a nervy lot, I'm told. Not surprising, culture shock and all that. They've been travelling a long time. Five million years, if their story's to be believed. Of course, they weren't alive for most of that time. But still."

Mr Naryan said, "What do you believe?"

"Does it matter? This city matters. Think what trouble she could cause!"

"If her story is true."

"Yes, yes. That's the point. Talk to her, eh? Find out the truth. Isn't that what your order's about? Well, I must get on."

Mr Naryan did not bother to correct Dreen's misapprehension. He observed, "The crowd has grown somewhat."

Dreen smiled broadly and rose straight into the air, his toes pointing down, his arms crossed with his palms flat on his shoulders. The remote rose with him. Mr Naryan had to shout to make himself heard over the cries and cheers of the crowd.

"What shall I do?"

Dreen checked his ascent and shouted back, "You might tell her that I'm here to help!"

"Of course!"

But Dreen was rising again, and did not hear Mr Naryan. As he rose he picked up speed, dwindling rapidly as he shot across the jumbled rooftops of the city towards his eyrie. The remote drew a silver line behind him; a cloud of lesser machines scattered across the sky as they strained to keep up.

The next day, when as usual Mr Naryan stopped to buy the peanuts he would scatter amongst any children or mendicants he encountered as he strolled through the city, the nut roaster said that he'd seen a strange woman only an hour before—she'd had no coin, but the nut roaster had given her a bag of shelled salted nuts all the same.

"Was that the right thing to do, master?" the nut roaster asked. His eyes glittered anxiously beneath the shelf of his ridged brow.

Mr Naryan, knowing that the man had been motivated by a cluster of artificial genes implanted in his ancestors to ensure that they and all their children would give aid to any human who requested it, assured the nut roaster that his conduct had been worthy. He proffered coin in ritual payment for the bag of warm oily peanuts, and the nut roaster made his usual elaborate refusal.

"When you see her, master, tell her that she will find no plumper or more savoury peanuts in the whole city. I will give her whatever she desires!"

All day, as Mr Naryan made his rounds of the tea shops, and even when he heard out the brief story of a woman who had composed herself for death, he expected to be accosted by an exotic wild-eyed stranger. That same expectation distracted him in the evening, as the magistrate's son haltingly read from the Puranas while all around threads of smoke from neighbourhood kitchen fires rose into the black sky. How strange the city suddenly seemed to Mr Naryan: the intent face of the magistrate's son, with its faint intaglio of scales and broad shelving brow, seemed horribly like a mask. Mr Naryan felt a deep longing for his youth, and after the boy had left he stood under the shower for more than an hour, letting water penetrate every fold and cranny of his hairless, corpulent body until his wife anxiously called to him, asking if he was all right.

The woman did not come to him that day, or the next. She was not seeking him at all. It was only by accident that Mr Naryan met her at last.

She was sitting at the counter of a tea shop, in the deep shadow beneath its tasselled awning. The shop was at the corner of the camel market, where knots of dealers and handlers argued about the merits of this or that animal and saddlemakers squatted cross-legged amongst their wares before the low, cave-like entrances to their workshops. Mr Naryan would have walked right past the shop if the proprietor had not hurried out and called to him, explaining that here was a human woman who had no coin, but he was letting her drink what she wished, and was that right?

Mr Naryan sat beside the woman, but did not speak after he ordered his own tea. He was curious and excited and afraid: she looked at him when he sat down and put his cane across his knees, but her gaze merely brushed over him without recognition.

She was tall and slender, hunched at the counter with elbows splayed. She was dressed, like every citizen of Sensch, in a loose, raw cotton overshirt. Her hair was as black and thick as any citizen's, too, worn long and caught in a kind of net slung at her shoulder. Her face was sharp and small-featured, intent from moment to moment on all that happened around her—a bronze machine trawling through the dusty sunlight beyond the awning's shadow; a vendor of pomegranate juice calling his wares; a gaggle of women laughing as they passed; a sled laden with prickly pear gliding by, two handspans above the dusty flagstones—but nothing held her attention for more than a moment. She held her bowl of tea carefully in both hands, and sucked at the liquid clumsily when she drank, holding each mouthful for a whole minute before swallowing and then spitting twiggy fragments into the copper basin on the counter.

Mr Naryan felt that he should not speak to her unless she spoke first. He was disturbed by her: he had grown into his routines, and this unsought responsibility frightened him. No doubt Dreen was watching through one or another of the little machines that flitted about the sunny, salt-white square—but that was not sufficient compulsion, except that now he had found her, he could not leave her.

At last, the owner of the tea house refilled the woman's bowl and said softly, "Our Archivist is sitting beside you."

The woman turned jerkily, spilling her tea. "I'm not going back," she said. "I've told them that I won't serve."

"No one has to do anything here," Mr Naryan said, feeling that he must calm her. "That is the point. My name is Naryan, and I have the honour, as our good host has pointed out, of being the Archivist of Sensch."

The woman smiled at this, and said that he could call her Angel; her name also translated as Monkey, but she preferred the former. "You're not like the others here," she added, as if she had only just realised. "I saw people like you in the port city, and one let me ride on his boat down the river until we reached the edge of a civil war. But after that every one of the cities I passed through seemed to be inhabited by only one race, and each was different from the next."

"It is true that this is a remote city," Mr Naryan said.

He could hear the faint drums of the procession. It was the middle of the day, when the sun halted at its zenith before reversing back down the sky.

The woman, Angel, heard the drums too. She looked around with a kind of preening motion as the procession came through the flame trees on the far side of the square. It reached this part of the city at the same time every day. It was led by a bare-chested man who beat a big drum draped in cloth of gold; it was held before him by a leather strap that went around his neck. The steady beat echoed across the square. Behind him slouched or capered ten, twenty, thirty naked men and women. Their hair was long and ropey with dirt; their fingernails were curved yellow talons.

Angel drew her breath sharply as the rag-taggle procession shuffled past, following the beat of the drum into the curving street that led out of the square. She said, "This is a very strange place. Are they mad?"

Mr Naryan explained, "They have not lost their reason, but have had it taken away. For some it will be returned in a year; it was taken away from them as a punishment. Others have renounced their own selves for the rest of their lives. It is a religious avocation. But saint or criminal, they were all once as fully aware as you or me."

"I'm not like you," she said. "I'm not like any of the crazy kinds of people I have met."

Mr Naryan beckoned to the owner of the tea house and ordered two more bowls. "I understand you have come a long way." Although he was terrified of her, he was certain that he could draw her out.

But Angel only laughed.

Mr Naryan said, "I do not mean to insult you."

"You dress like a . . . native. Is *that* a religious avocation?"

"It is my profession. I am the Archivist here."

"The people here are different—a different race in every city. When I left, not a single intelligent alien species was known. It was one reason for my voyage. Now there seem to be thousands strung along this long, long river. They treat me like a ruler—is that it? Or a god?"

"The Preservers departed long ago. These are the end times."

Angel said dismissively, "There are always those who believe they live at the end of history. We thought that *we* lived at the end of history, when every star system in the Galaxy had been mapped, every habitable world settled."

For a moment, Mr Naryan thought that she would tell him of where she had been, but she added, "I was told that the Preservers, who I suppose were my descendants, made the different races, but each race calls itself human, even the ones who don't look like they could have evolved from anything that ever looked remotely human."

"The Shaped call themselves human because they have no other name for what they have become, innocent and fallen alike. After all, they had no name before they were raised up. The citizens of Sensch remain innocent. They are our . . . responsibility."

He had not meant for it to sound like a plea.

"You're not doing all that well," Angel said, and started to tell him about the Change War she had tangled with upriver, on the way to this, the last city at the mid-point of the world.

It was a long, complicated story, and she kept stopping to ask Mr Naryan questions, most of which, despite his extensive readings of the Puranas, he was unable to answer. As she talked, Mr Naryan transcribed her speech on his tablet. She commented that a recording device would be better, but by reading back a long speech she had just made he demonstrated that his close diacritical marks captured her every word.

"But that is not its real purpose, which is an aid to fix the memory in my head."

"You listen to peoples' stories."

"Stories are important. In the end they are all that is left, all that history leaves us. Stories endure." And Mr Naryan wondered if she saw what was all too clear to him, the way her story would end, if she stayed in the city.

Angel considered his words. "I have been out of history a long time," she said at last. "I'm not sure that I want to be a part of it again." She stood up so quickly that she knocked her stool over, and left.

Mr Naryan knew better than to follow her. That night, as he sat enjoying a cigarette on his balcony, under the baleful glare of the Eye of the Preservers, a remote came to him. Dreen's face materialised above the remote's silver platter and told him that the woman's shipmates knew that she was here. They were coming for her.

As the ship draws closer, looming above the glowing lighter that tows it, Mr Naryan begins to make out its shape. It is a huge black wedge composed of tiers of flat plates that rise higher than the tallest towers of the city. Little lights, mostly red, gleam here and there within its ridged carapace. Mr Naryan brushes mosquitoes from his bare arms, watching the black ship move beneath a black sky empty except for the Eye of the Preservers and a few dim halo stars. Here, at the midpoint of the world, the Home Galaxy will not rise until winter.

The crowd has grown. It becomes restless. Waves of emotion surge back and forth. Mr Naryan feels them pass through the citizens packed around him, although he hardly understands what they mean, for all the time he has lived with these people.

He has been allowed to pass through the crowd with the citizens' usual generous deference, and now stands close to the edge of the whirling cloud of machines which defends the dock, twenty paces or so from the magistrates who nervously swish their quirts to and fro. The crowd's thick yeasty odour fills his nostrils; its humming disquiet, modulating up and down, penetrates to the marrow of his bones. Now and then a machine ignites a flare of light that sweeps over the front ranks of the crowd, and the eyes of the men and women shine blankly orange, like so many little sparks.

At last the ship passes the temple complex at the northern edge of the city, its wedge rising like a wave above the temple's clusters of slim spiky towers. The lighter's engines go into reverse; waves break in whitecaps on the steps beyond the whirl of machines and the grim line of magistrates.

The crowd's hum rises in pitch. Mr Naryan finds himself carried forward as it presses towards the barrier defined by the machines. The people around him apologise effusively for troubling him, trying to minimise contact with him in the press as snails withdraw from salt.

The machines' whirl stratifies, and the magistrates raise their quirts and shout a single word lost in the noise of the crowd. The people in the front rank of the crowd fall to their knees, clutching their eyes and wailing: the machines have shut down their optic nerves.

Mr Naryan, shown the same deference by the machines as by the citizens, suddenly finds himself isolated amongst groaning and weeping citizens, confronting the row of magistrates. One calls to him, but he ignores the man.

He has a clear view of the ship, now. It has come to rest a league away, at the far end of the docks, but Mr Naryan has to tip his head back and back to see the top of the ship's tiers. It is as if a mountain has drifted against the edge of the city.

A new sound drives across the crowd, as a wind drives across a field of wheat. Mr Naryan turns and, by the random flare of patrolling machines, is astonished to see how large the crowd has grown. It fills the long plaza, and more people stand on the rooftops along its margin. Their eyes are like a harvest of stars. They are all looking towards the ship, where Dreen, standing on a cargo sled, ascends to meet the crew.

Mr Naryan hooks the wire frames of his spectacles over his ears, and the crew standing on top of the black ship snap into clear focus.

There are fifteen, men and women all as tall as Angel. They loom over Dreen as he welcomes them with effusive gestures. Mr Naryan can almost smell Dreen's anxiety. He wants the crew to take Angel away, and order restored. He will be telling them where to find her.

Mr Naryan feels a pang of anger. He turns and makes his way through the crowd. When he reaches its ragged margin, everyone around him suddenly looks straight up. Dreen's sled sweeps overhead, carrying his guests to the safety of the floating habitat above the pink sandstone palace. The crowd surges forward—and all the little machines fall from the air!

One lands close to Mr Naryan, its carapace burst open at the seams. Smoke pours from it. An old woman picks it up—Mr Naryan smells her burnt flesh as it sears her hand—and throws it at him.

Her shot goes wide. Mr Naryan is so astonished that he does not even duck. He glimpses the confusion as the edge of the crowd collides with the line of magistrates: some magistrates run, their red cloaks streaming at their backs; others throw down their quirts and hold out their empty hands. The crowd devours them. Mr Naryan limps away as fast as he can, his heart galloping with fear. Ahead is a wide avenue leading into the city, and standing in the middle of the avenue is a compact group of men, clustered about a tall figure.

It is Angel.

Mr Naryan told Angel what Dreen had told him, that the ship was coming to the city, the very next day. It was at the same tea house. She did not seem surprised. "They need me," she said. "How long will they take?"

"Well, they cannot come here directly. Confluence's maintenance system will only allow ships to land at designated docks, but the machinery of the spaceport docks here has grown erratic and dangerous through disuse. The nearest place they could safely dock is five hundred leagues away, and after that the ship must be towed downriver. It will take time. What will you do?"

Angel passed a hand over her sleek black hair. "I like it here. I could be comfortable."

She had already been given a place in which to live by a wealthy merchant family. She took Mr Naryan to see it. It was near the river, a small two-storey house built around a courtyard shaded by a jacaranda tree. People were going in and out, carrying furniture and carpets. Three men were painting the wooden rail of the balcony that ran around the upper storey. They were painting it pink and blue, and cheerfully singing as they worked. Angel was amused by the bustle, and laughed when Mr Naryan said that she should not take advantage of the citizens.

"They seem so happy to help me. What's wrong with that?"

Mr Naryan thought it best not to explain about the cluster of genes implanted in all the races of the Shaped, the reflex altruism of the unfallen. A woman brought out tea and a pile of crisp, wafer-thin fritters sweetened with crystallised honey. Two men brought canopied chairs. Angel sprawled in one, invited Mr Naryan to sit in the other. She was quite at ease, grinning every time someone showed her the gift they had brought her.

Dreen, Mr Naryan knew, would be dismayed. Angel was a barbarian, displaced by five million years. She had no idea of the careful balance by which one must live with the innocent, the unfallen, if their cultures were to survive. Yet she was fully human, free to choose, and that freedom was inviolable. No wonder Dreen was so eager for the ship to reclaim her.

Still, Angel's rough joy was infectious, and Mr Naryan soon found himself smiling with her at the sheer abundance of trinkets scattered around her. No one was giving unless they were glad to give, and no one who gave was poor. The only poor in Sensch were the sky-clad mendicants who had voluntarily renounced the material world.

So Mr Naryan sat and drank tea with her, and ate a dozen of the delicious honey-eyed fritters, one after the other, and listened to more of her wild tales of travelling the river, realising how little she understood of Confluence's administration. She was convinced that the Shaped were somehow forbidden technology, for instance, and did not understand why there was no government. Was Dreen the absolute ruler? By what right?

"Dreen is merely the Commissioner. Any authority he has is invested in him by the citizens, and it is manifest only on high days. He enjoys parades, you know. I suppose the magistrates have power, in that they arbitrate neighbourly disputes and decide upon punishment—Senschians are argumentative, and sometimes quarrels can lead to unfortunate accidents."

"Murder, you mean? Then perhaps they are not as innocent as you maintain." Angel reached out suddenly. "And these? By what authority do these little spies operate?"

Pinched between her thumb and forefinger was a bronze machine. Its sensor cluster turned back and forth as it struggled to free itself.

"Why, they are part of the maintenance system of Confluence."

"Can Dreen use them? Tell me all you know. It may be important."

She questioned Mr Naryan closely, and he found himself telling her more than he wanted. But despite all that he told her, she would not talk about her voyage, nor of why she had escaped from the ship, or how. In the days that followed, Mr Naryan requested several times, politely and wistfully, that she would. He even visited the temple and petitioned for information about her voyage, but all trace of it had been lost in the vast sifting of history, and when pressed, the librarian who had come at the hierodule's bidding broke contact with an almost petulant abruptness.

Mr Naryan was not surprised that it could tell him nothing. The voyage must have begun five million years ago at least, after all, for the ship to have travelled all the way to the neighbouring galaxy and back.

He did learn that the ship had tried to sell its findings on landfall, much as a merchant would sell his wares. Perhaps Angel wanted to profit from what she knew; perhaps that was why the ship wanted her back, although there was no agency on Confluence that would close such a deal. Knowledge was worth only the small price of petitioning those librarians which deal with the secular world.

Meanwhile, a group of citizens gathered around Angel, like disciples around one of the blessed who, touched by some fragment or other of the Preservers, wander Confluence's long shore. These disciples went wherever she went. They were all young men, which seemed to Mr Naryan faintly sinister, sons of her benefactors fallen under her spell. He recognised several of them, but none would speak to him, although there were always at least two or three accompanying Angel. They wore white headbands on which Angel had lettered a slogan in an archaic script older than any race of the Shaped; she refused to explain what it meant.

Mr Naryan's wife thought that he, too, was falling under some kind of spell. She did not like the idea of Angel: she declared that Angel must be some kind of ghost, and therefore dangerous. Perhaps she was right. She was a wise and strong-willed woman, and Mr Naryan had grown to trust her advice.

Certainly, Mr Naryan believed that he could detect a change in the steady song of the city as he went about his business. He listened to an old man dying of the systematic organ failure which took most of the citizens in the middle of their fourth century. The man was one of the few who had left the city—he had travelled north, as far as a city tunneled through cliffs overlooking the river, where an amphibious race lived. His story took a whole day to tell, in a stiflingly hot room muffled in dusty carpets and lit only by a lamp with a blood-red chimney. At the end, the old man began to weep, saying that he knew now that he had not travelled at all, and Mr Naryan was unable to comfort him. Two children were born on the next day—an event so rare that the whole city celebrated, garlanding the streets with fragrant orange blossoms. But there was a tension beneath the celebrations that Mr Naryan had never before felt, and it seemed that Angel's followers were everywhere amongst the revellers.

Dreen felt the change, too. "There have been incidents," he said, as candid an admission as he had ever made to Mr Naryan. "Nothing very much. A temple wall defaced with the slogan the woman has her followers wear. A market disrupted by young men running through it, overturning stalls. I asked the magistrates not to make examples of the perpetrators—that would create martyrs. Let the people hold their own courts if they wish. And she's been making speeches. Would you like to hear one?"

"Is it necessary?"

Dreen dropped his glass with a careless gesture—a machine caught it and bore it off before it smashed on the tiles. They were on a balcony of Dreen's floating habitat, looking out over the Great River towards the far side of the world. At the horizon was the long white double line that marked the river's fall: the rapids below, the permanent clouds above. It was noon, and the white, sunlit city was quiet.

Dreen said, "You listen to so much of her talk, I suppose you are wearied of it. In summary, it is nothing but some vague nonsense about destiny, about rising above circumstances and bettering yourself, as if you could lift yourself into the air by grasping the soles of your feet."

Dreen dismissed this with a snap of his fingers. His own feet, as always, were bare, and his long opposable toes were curled around the bar of the rail on which he squatted. He said, "Perhaps she wants to rule the city—if it pleases her, why not? At least, until the ship arrives here. I will not stop her if that is what she wants, and if she can do it. Do you know where she is right now?"

"I have been busy." But Mr Naryan felt an eager curiosity: yes, his wife was right.

"I heard the story you gathered in. At the time, you know, I thought that man might bring war to the city when he came back." Dreen's laugh was a high-pitched hooting. "The woman is out there, at the edge of the world. She took a boat yesterday."

"I am sure she will return," Mr Naryan said. "It is all of a pattern."

"I defer to your knowledge. Will hers be an interesting story, Mr Naryan? Have another drink. Stay, enjoy yourself."

Dreen reached up and swung into the branches of the flame tree which leaned over the balcony, disappearing in a flurry of red leaves and leaving Mr Naryan to find a machine that was able to take him home.

Mr Naryan thought that Dreen was wrong to dismiss what Angel was doing, although he understood why Dreen affected such a grand indifference. It was outside Dreen's experience, that was all: Angel was outside the experience of everyone on Confluence. The Change Wars that flared here and there along Confluence's vast length were not ideological but eschatological. They were a result of sociological stresses that arose when radical shifts in the expression of clusters of native and grafted genes caused a species of Shaped to undergo a catastrophic redefinition of its perceptions of the world. But what Angel was doing dated from before the Preservers had raised up the Shaped and ended human history. Mr Naryan only began to under-stood it himself when Angel told him what she had done at the edge of the world.

And later, on the terrible night when the ship arrives and every machine in the city dies, with flames roaring unchecked through the farside quarter of the city and thou-sands of citizens fleeing into the orchard forests to the north, Mr Naryan realises that he has not understood a s much as he thought. Angel has not been preaching empty revolution after all.

Her acolytes, all young men, are armed with crude wooden spears with fire-hardened tips, long double-edged knives of the kind coconut sellers use to open their wares, flails improvised from chains and wire. They hustle Mr Naryan in a forced march towards the palace and Dreen's floating habitat. They have taken away Mr Naryan's cane, and his bad leg hurts abominably with every other step.

Angel is gone. She has work elsewhere. Mr Naryan felt fear when he saw her, but feels more fear now. The reflex altruism of the acolytes has been overridden by a new meme forged in the fires of Angel's revolution—they jostle Mr Naryan with rough humour, sure in their hold over him. One in particular, the rough skin of his long-jawed face crazed in diamonds, jabs Mr Naryan in his ribs with the butt of his spear at every intersection, as if to remind him not to escape, something that Mr Naryan has absolutely no intention of doing.

Power is down all over the city—it went off with the fall of the machines—but leaping light from scattered fires swims in the wide eyes of the young men. They pass through a market square where people swig beer and drunkenly gamble amongst over-turned stalls. Elsewhere in the fiery dark there is open rutting, men with men as well as with women. A child lies dead in a gutter. Horrible, horrible. Once, a building col-lapses inside its own fire, sending flames whirling high into the black sky. The faces of all the men surrounding Mr Naryan are transformed by this leaping light into masks with eyes of flame.

Mr Naryan's captors urge him on. His only comfort is that he will be of use in what is to come. Angel has not yet finished with him.

When Angel returned from the edge of the world, she came straight away to Mr Naryan. It was a warm evening, at the hour after sunset when the streets began to fill with strollers, the murmur of neighbour greeting neighbour, the cries of vendors sell-ing fruit juice or popcorn or sweet cakes.

Mr Naryan was listening as his pupil, the magistrate's son, read a passage from the Puranas which described the time when the Preservers had strung the Galaxy with their creations. The boy was tall and awkward and faintly resentful, for he was not the scholar his father wished him to be and would rather spend his evenings with his fel-lows in the beer halls than read ancient legends in a long dead language. He bent over the book like a night stork, his finger stabbing at each line as he clumsily translated it, mangling words in his hoarse voice. Mr Naryan was listening with half an ear, interrupting only to correct particularly inelegant phrases. In the kitchen at the far end of the little apartment, his wife was humming to the murmur of the radio, her voice a breathy contented monotone.

Angel came up the helical stair with a rapid clatter, mounting quickly above a sudden hush in the street. Mr Naryan knew who it was even before she burst onto the balcony. Her appearance so astonished the magistrate's son that he dropped the book. Mr Naryan dismissed him and he hurried away, no doubt eager to meet his friends in the flickering neon of the beer hall and tell them of this wonder.

"I've been to the edge of the world," Angel said to Mr Naryan, coolly accepting a bowl of tea from Mr Naryan's wife, quite oblivious of the glance she exchanged with her husband before retreating. Mr Naryan's heart turned at that look, for in it he saw how his wife's hard words were so easily dissolved in the weltering sea of reflexive benevolence. How cruel the Preservers had been, it seemed to him never crueller, to have raised up races of the Shaped and yet to have shackled them in unthinking obedience.

Angel said, "You don't seem surprised."

"Dreen told me as much. I am pleased to see you returned safely. It has been a dry time without you." Already he had said too much: it was as if all his thoughts were eager to be spilled before her.

"Dreen knows everything that goes on in the city."

"Oh no, not at all. He knows what he needs to know."

"I took a boat," Angel said. "I just asked for it, and the man took me right along, without question. I wish now I'd stolen it. It would have been simpler. I'm tired of all this good will."

It was as if she could read his mind. For the first time, Mr Naryan began to be afraid, a shiver like the first shake of a tambour that had ritually introduced the tempestuous dances of his youth.

Angel sat on the stool which the student had quit, tipping it back so she could lean against the rail of the balcony. She had cut her black hair short, and bound around her forehead a strip of white cloth printed with the slogan, in ancient incomprehensible script, that was the badge of her acolytes. She wore an ordinary loose white shirt and much jewelry: rings on every finger, sometimes more than one on each; bracelets and bangles down her forearms; gold and silver chains around her neck, layered on her breast. She was both graceful and terrifying, a rough beast slouched from the deep past to claim the world.

She said, teasingly, "Don't you want to hear my story? Isn't that your avocation?"

"I will listen to anything you want to tell me," Mr Naryan said.

"The world is a straight line. Do you know about liberation?"

Mr Naryan shook his head.

Angel held out her hand, tipped it back and forth. "This is the world. Everything lives on the back of a long flat plate which circles the sun. The plate rocks on its long axis, so the sun rises above the edge and then reverses its course. I went to the edge of the world, where the river that runs down half its length falls into the void. I suppose it must be collected and redistributed, but it really does look like it falls away forever."

"The river is eternally renewed," Mr Naryan said. "Where it falls is where ships used to arrive and depart, but this city has not been a port for many years."

"Fortunately for me, or my companions would already be here. There's a narrow ribbon of land on the far side of the river. Nothing lives there, not even an insect. No earth, no stones. The air shakes with the sound of the river's fall, and swirling mist burns with raw sunlight. And there are shrines, in the thunder and mist at the edge of the world. One spoke to me."

Mr Naryan knew these shrines, although he had not been there for many years.

He remembered that the different races of the Shaped had erected shrines all along the edge of the world, stone upon stone carried across the river, from which flags and long banners flew. Long ago, the original founders of the city of Sensch, Dreen's ancestors, had travelled across the river to petition the avatars of the Preservers, believing that the journey across the wide river was a necessary rite of purification. But they were gone, and the new citizens, who had built their city of stones over the burnt groves of the old city, simply bathed in the heated, mineral-heavy water of the pools of the shrines of the temple at the edge of their city before delivering their petitions. He supposed the proud flags and banners of the shrines would be tattered rags now, bleached by unfiltered sunlight, rotted by mist. The screens of the shrines—would they still be working?

Angel grinned. Mr Naryan had to remember that it was not, as it was with the citizens, a baring of teeth before striking.

She said, "Don't you want to know what it said to me? It's part of my story."

"Do you want to tell me?"

She passed her hand over the top of her narrow skull: bristly hair made a crisp sound under her palm. "No," she said. "No, I don't think I do. Not yet."

Later, after a span of silence, just before she left, she said, "After we were wakened by the ship, after it brought us here, it showed us how the black hole you call the Eye of the Preservers was made. It recorded the process as it returned, speeded up because the ship was travelling so fast it stretched time around itself. At first there was an intense point of light within the heart of the Large Magellanic Cloud. It might have been a supernova, except that it was a thousand times larger than any supernova ever recorded. For a long time its glare obscured everything else, and when it cleared, all the remaining stars were streaming around where it had been. Those nearest the centre elongated and dissipated, and always more crowded in until nothing was left but the gas clouds of the accretion disc, glowing by Cerenkov radiation."

"So it is written in the Puranas."

"And is it also written there why Confluence was constructed around a halo star between the Home Galaxy and the Eye of the Preservers?"

"Of course. It is so we can all worship and glorify the Preservers. The Eye looks upon us all."

"That's what I told them," Angel said.

After she was gone, Mr Naryan put on his spectacles and walked through the city to the docks. The unsleeping citizens were promenading in the warm dark streets, or squatting in doorways, or talking quietly from upper-storey windows to their neighbours across the street. Amongst this easy somnolence, Angel's young disciples moved with a quick purposefulness, here in pairs, there in a group of twenty or more. Their slogans were painted on almost every wall. Three stopped Mr Naryan near the docks, danced around his bulk, jeering, then ran off, screeching with laughter, when he slashed at them with his cane.

"Ruffians! Fools!"

"Seize the day!" they sang back. "Seize the day!"

Mr Naryan did not find the man whose skiff Angel and her followers had used to cross the river, but the story was already everywhere amongst the fisherfolk. The Preservers had spoken to her, they said, and she had refused their temptations. Many were busily bargaining with citizens who wanted to cross the river and see the site of this miracle for themselves.

An old man, eyes milky with cataracts—the fisherfolk trawled widely across the Great River, exposing themselves to more radiation than normal—asked Mr Naryan if these were the end times, if the Preservers would return to walk amongst them again. When Mr Naryan said, no, anyone who had dealt with the avatars knew that only those fragments remained in the Universe, the old man shrugged and said, "They say *she* is a Preserver," and Mr Naryan, looking out across the river's black welter, where the horizon was lost against the empty night, seeing the scattered constellations of the running lights of the fisherfolk's skiffs scattered out to the farside, knew that the end of Angel's story was not far off. The citizens were finding their use for her. Inexorably, step by step, she was becoming part of their history.

Mr Naryan did not see Angel again until the night her ship arrived. Dreen went to treat with her, but he could not get within two streets of her house: it had become the centre of a convocation that took over the entire quarter of the city. She preached to thousands of citizens from the rooftops.

Dreen reported to Mr Naryan that it was a philosophy of hope from despair. "She says that all life feeds on destruction and death. Are you sure you don't want to hear it?"

"It is not necessary."

Dreen was perched on a balustrade, looking out at the river. They were in his floating habitat, in an arbour of lemon trees that jutted out at its leading edge. He said, "More than a thousand a day are making the crossing."

"Has the screen spoken again?"

"I've monitored it continuously. Nothing."

"But it did speak with her."

"Perhaps, perhaps." Dreen was suddenly agitated. He scampered up and down the narrow balustrade, swiping at overhanging branches and scaring the white doves that perched amongst the little glossy leaves. The birds rocketed up in a great flutter of wings, crying as they rose into the empty sky. Dreen said, "The machines watching her don't work. Not anymore. She's found out how to disrupt them. I snatch long range pictures, but they don't tell me very much. I don't even know if she visited the shrine in the first place."

"I believe her," Mr Naryan said.

"I petitioned the avatars," Dreen said, "but of course they wouldn't tell me if they'd spoken to her."

Mr Naryan was disturbed by this admission—Dreen was not a religious man. "What will you do?"

"Nothing. I could send the magistrates for her, but even if she went with them her followers would claim she'd been arrested. And I can't even remember when I last arrested someone. It would make her even more powerful, and I'd have to let her go. But I suppose that you are going to tell me that I should let it happen."

"It has happened before. Even here, to your own people. They built the shrines, after all. . . ."

"Yes, and later they fell from grace, and destroyed their city. The snakes aren't ready for that," Dreen said, almost pleading, and for a moment Mr Naryan glimpsed the depth of Dreen's love for this city and its people.

Dreen turned away, as if ashamed, to look out at the river again, at the flocking sails of little boats setting out on, or returning from, the long crossing to the far side of the river. This great pilgrimage had become the focus of the life of the city. The markets were closed for the most part; merchants had moved to the docks to supply the thousands of pilgrims.

Dreen said, "They say that the avatar tempted her with godhead, and she denied it."

"But that is foolish! The days of the Preservers have long ago faded. We know them only by their image, which burns forever at the event horizon, but their essence has long since receded."

Dreen shrugged. "There's worse. They say that she forced the avatar to admit that the Preservers are dead. They say that *she* is an avatar of something greater than the Preservers, although you wouldn't know that from her preaching. She claims that this universe is all there is, that destiny is what you make it. What makes me despair is how readily the snakes believe this cant."

Mr Naryan, feeling chill, there in the sun-dappled shade, said, "She has hinted to me that she learnt it in the great far out, in the galaxy beyond the Home Galaxy."

"The ship is coming," Dreen said. "Perhaps they will deal with her."

In the burning night of the city's dissolution, Mr Naryan is brought at last to the pink sandstone palace. Dreen's habitat floats above it, a black cloud that half-eclipses the glowering red swirl of the Eye of the Preservers. Trails of white smoke, made luminescent by the fires which feed them, pour from the palace's high arched windows, braiding into sheets which dash like surf against the rim of the habitat. Mr Naryan sees something fly up from amongst the palace's many carved spires—there seem to be more of them than he remembers—and smash away a piece of the habitat, which slowly tumbles off into the black sky.

The men around him hoot and cheer at this, and catch Mr Naryan's arms and march him up the broad steps and through the high double doors into the courtyard beyond. It is piled with furniture and tapestries that have been thrown down from the thousand high windows overlooking it, but a path has been cleared to a narrow stair that turns and turns as it rises, until at last Mr Naryan is pushed out onto the roof of the palace.

Perhaps five hundred of Angel's followers crowd amongst the spires and fallen trees and rocks, many naked, all with lettered headbands tied around their foreheads. Smoky torches blaze everywhere. In the centre of the crowd is the palace's great throne on which, on high days and holidays, at the beginning of masques or parades, Dreen receives the city's priests, merchants and artists. It is lit by a crown of machines burning bright as the sun, and seated on it—easy, elegant and terrifying—is Angel.

Mr Naryan is led through the crowd and left standing alone before the throne. Angel beckons him forward, her smile both triumphant and scared: Mr Naryan feels her fear mix with his own.

She says, "What should I do with your city, now I've taken it from you?"

"You have not finished your story." Everything Mr Naryan planned to say has fallen away at the simple fact of her presence. Stranded before her fierce, barely contained energies, he feels old and used up, his body as heavy with years and regret as with fat. He adds cautiously, "I would like to hear it all."

He wonders if she really knows how her story must end. Perhaps she does. Perhaps her wild joy is not at her triumph, but at the imminence of her death. Perhaps she really does believe that the void is all, and rushes to embrace it.

Angel says, "My people can tell you. They hide with Dreen up above, but not for long."

She points across the roof. A dozen men are wrestling a sled, which shudders like a living thing as it tries to reorientate itself in the gravity field, onto a kind of launching cradle tipped up towards the habitat. The edges of the habitat are ragged, as if bitten, and amongst the roof's spires tower-trees are visibly growing towards it, their tips already brushing its edges, their tangled bases pulsing and swelling as teams of men and women drench them with nutrients.

"I found how to enhance the antigravity devices of the sleds," Angel says. "They react against the field which generates gravity for this artificial world. The field's stored inertia gives them a high kinetic energy, so that they make very good missiles.

We'll chip away that floating fortress piece by piece if we have to, or we'll finish grow-ing towers and storm its remains, but I expect surrender long before then."

"Dreen is not the ruler of the city." Nor are you, Mr Naryan thinks, but it is not prudent to point that out.

"Not anymore," Angel says.

Mr Naryan dares to step closer. He says, "What did you find out there, that you rage against?"

Angel laughs. "I'll tell you about rage. It is what you have all forgotten, or never learned. It is the motor of evolution, and evolution's end, too." She snatches a beaker of wine from a supplicant, drains it and tosses it aside. She is consumed with an en-ergy that is no longer her own. She says, "We travelled so long, not dead, not sleeping. We were no more than stored potentials triply engraved on gold. Although the ship flew so fast that it bound time about itself, the journey still took thousands of years of slowed ship-board time. At the end of that long voyage we did not wake: we were born. Or rather, others like us were born, although I have their memories, as if they are my own. They learned then that the Universe was not made for the convenience of humans. What they found was a galaxy ruined and dead."

She holds Mr Naryan's hand tightly, speaking quietly and intensely, her eyes star-ing deep into his.

"A billion years ago, our neighbouring galaxy collided with another, much smaller galaxy. Stars of both galaxies were torn off in the collision, and scattered in a vast halo. The rest coalesced into a single body, but except for ancient globular clus-ters, which survived the catastrophe because of their dense gravity fields, it is all wreckage. We were not able to chart a single world where life had evolved. I remem-ber standing on a world sheared in half by immense tidal stress, its orbit so eccentric that it was colder than Pluto at its farthest point, hotter than Mercury at its nearest. I remember standing on a world of methane ice as cold and dark as the Universe itself, wandering amongst the stars. There were millions of such worlds cast adrift. I remem-ber standing upon a fragment of a world smashed into a million shards and scattered so widely in its orbit that it never had the chance to reform. There are a million such worlds. I remember gas giants turned inside out—single vast storms—and I remember worlds torched smooth by eruptions of their stars. No life, anywhere.

"Do you know how many galaxies have endured such collisions? Almost all of them. Life is a statistical freak. It is likely that only the stars of our galaxy have plan-ets, or else other civilisations would surely have arisen elsewhere in the unbounded Universe. As it is, it is certain that we are alone. We must make of ourselves what we can. We should not hide, as your Preservers chose to do. Instead, we should seize the day, and make the Universe over with the technology that the Preservers used to make their hiding place."

Her grip is hurting now, but Mr Naryan bears it. "You cannot become a Pre-server," he says sadly. "No one can, now. You should not lie to these innocent people."

"I didn't need to lie. They took up my story and made it theirs. They see now what they can inherit—if they dare. This won't stop with one city. It will become a crusade!" She adds, more softly, "You'll remember it all, won't you?"

It is then that Mr Naryan knows that she knows how this must end, and his heart breaks. He would ask her to take that burden from him, but he cannot. He is bound to her. He is her witness.

The crowd around them cheers as the sled rockets up from its cradle. It smashes into the habitat and knocks loose another piece, which drops trees and dirt and rocks amongst the spires of the palace roof as it twists free and spins away into the night.

Figures appear at the edge of the habitat. A small tube falls, glittering through the torchlight. A man catches it, runs across the debris-strewn roof, and throws himself at Angel's feet. He is at the far end of the human scale of the Shaped of this city. His skin is lapped with distinct scales, edged with a rim of hard black like the scales of a pine cone. His coarse black hair has flopped over his eyes, which glow like coals with reflected firelight.

Angel takes the tube and shakes it. It unrolls into a flexible sheet on which Dreen's face glows. Dreen's lips move; his voice is small and metallic. Angel listens intently, and when he has finished speaking says softly, "Yes."

Then she stands and raises both hands above her head. All across the roof, men and women turn towards her, eyes glowing.

"They wish to surrender! Let them come down!"

A moment later a sled swoops down from the habitat, its silvery underside gleaming in the reflected light of the many fires scattered across the roof. Angel's followers shout and jeer, and missiles fly out of the darkness—a burning torch, a rock, a broken branch. All are somehow deflected before they reach the ship's crew, screaming away into the dark with such force that the torch, the branch, kindle into white fire. The crew have modified the sled's field to protect themselves.

They all look like Angel, with the same small sleek head, the same gangling build and abrupt nervous movements. Dreen's slight figure is dwarfed by them. It takes Mr Naryan a long minute to be able to distinguish men from women, and another to be able to tell each man from his brothers, each woman from her sisters. They are all clad in long white shirts that leave them bare-armed and bare-legged, and each is girdled with a belt from which hang a dozen or more little machines. They call to Angel, one following on the words of the other, saying over and over again:

"Return with us—"

"—this is not our place—"

"—these are not our people—"

"—we will return—"

"—we will find our home—"

"—leave with us and return."

Dreen sees Mr Naryan and shouts, "They want to take her back!" He jumps down from the sled, an act of bravery that astonishes Mr Naryan, and skips through the crowd. "They are all one person, or variations on one person," he says breathlessly. "The ship makes its crew by varying a template. Angel is an extreme. A mistake."

Angel starts to laugh.

"You funny little man! I'm the real one—they are the copies!"

"Come back to us—"

"—come back and help us—"

"—help us find our home."

"There's no home to find!" Angel shouts. "Oh, you fools! This is all there is!"

"I tried to explain to them," Dreen says to Mr Naryan, "but they wouldn't listen."

"They surely cannot disbelieve the Puranas," Mr Naryan says.

Angel shouts, "Give me back the ship!"

"It was never yours—"

"—never yours to own—"

"—but only yours to serve."

"No! I won't serve!" Angel jumps onto the throne and makes an abrupt cutting gesture.

Hundreds of fine silver threads spool out of the darkness, shooting towards the sled and her crewmates. The ends of the threads flick up when they reach the edge of the sled's modified field, but then fall in a tangle over the crew: their shield is gone.

The crowd begins to throw things again, but Angel orders them to be still. "I have the only working sled," she says. "That which I enhance, I can also take away. Come with me," she tells Mr Naryan, "and see the end of my story."

The crowd around Angel stirs. Mr Naryan turns, and sees one of the crew walking towards Angel.

He is as tall and slender as Angel, his small high-cheekboned face so like her own it is as if he holds up a mirror as he approaches. A rock arcs out of the crowd and strikes his shoulder: he staggers but walks on, hardly seeming to notice that the crowd closes at his back so that he is suddenly inside its circle, with Angel and Mr Naryan in its focus.

Angel says, "I'm not afraid of you."

"Of course not, sister," the man says. And he grasps her wrists in both his hands.

Then Mr Naryan is on his hands and knees. A strong wind howls about him, and he can hear people screaming. The afterglow of a great light swims in his vision. He cannot see who helps him up and half-carries him through the stunned crowd to the sled.

When the sled starts to rise, Mr Naryan falls to his knees again. Dreen says in his ear, "It's over."

"No," Mr Naryan says. He blinks and blinks, tears rolling down his cheeks.

The man took Angel's wrists in both of his—

Dreen is saying something, but Mr Naryan shakes his head. It is not over.

—and they shot up into the night, so fast that their clothing burst into flame, so fast that air was drawn up with them. If Angel could nullify the gravity field, then so could her crewmates. She has achieved apotheosis.

The sled swoops up the tiered slope of the ship, is swallowed by a wide hatch. When he can see again, Mr Naryan finds himself kneeling at the edge of the open hatch. The city is spread below. Fires define the streets which radiate away from the Great River; the warm night air is bitter with the smell of burning.

Dreen has been looking at the lighted windows that crowd the walls of the vast room beyond the hatch, scampering with growing excitement from one to the other. Now he sees that Mr Naryan is crying, and clumsily tries to comfort him, believing that Mr Naryan is mourning his wife, left behind in the dying city.

"She was a good woman, for her kind," Mr Naryan is able to say at last, although it is not her he is mourning, or not only her. He is mourning for all of the citizens of Sensch. They are irrevocably caught in their change now, never to be the same. His wife, the nut roaster, the men and women who own the little tea houses at the corner of every square, the children, the mendicants and the merchants—all are changed, or else dying in the process. Something new is being born down there. Rising from the fall of the city.

"They'll take us away from all this," Dreen says happily. "They're going to search for where they came from. Some are out combing the city for others who can help them; the rest are preparing the ship. They'll take it over the edge of the world, into the great far out!"

"Do they not know they will never find what they are looking for? The Puranas—"

"Old stories, old fears. They will take us home!"

Mr Naryan laboriously clambers to his feet. He understands that Dreen has fallen under the thrall of the crew. He is theirs, as Mr Naryan is now and forever Angel's. He says, "Those times are past. Down there in the city is the beginning of something new, something wonderful—" He finds he cannot explain. All he has is his faith that it won't stop here. It is not an end but a beginning, a spark to set all of Confluence—the unfallen and the changed—alight. Mr Naryan says, weakly, "It will not stop here."

Dreen's big eyes shine in the light of the city's fires. He says, "I see only another Change War. There's nothing new in that. The snakes will rebuild the city in their new image, if not here, then somewhere else along the Great River. It has happened before, in this very place, to my own people. We survived it, and so will the snakes. But what *they* promise is so much greater! We'll leave this poor place, and voyage out to return to where it all began, to the very home of the Preservers. Look there! That's where we're going!"

Mr Naryan allows himself to be led across the vast room. It is so big that it could easily hold Dreen's floating habitat. A window on its far side shows a view angled somewhere far above the plane of Confluence's orbit. Confluence itself is a shining strip, an arrow running out to its own vanishing point. Beyond that point are the ordered, frozen spirals of the Home Galaxy, the great jewelled clusters and braids of stars constructed in the last great days of the Preservers before they vanished forever into the black hole they made by collapsing the Magellanic Cloud.

Mr Naryan starts to breathe deeply, topping up the oxygen content of his blood.

"You see!" Dreen says again, his face shining with awe in Confluence's silver light.

"I see the end of history," Mr Naryan says. "You should have studied the Puranas, Dreen. There is no future to be found amongst the artifacts of the Preservers, only the dead past. I won't serve, Dreen. That's over."

And then he turns and lumbers through the false lights and shadows of the windows towards the open hatch. Dreen catches his arm, but Mr Naryan throws him off.

Dreen sprawls on his back, astonished, then jumps up and runs in front of Mr Naryan. "You fool!" he shouts. "They can bring her back!"

"There's no need," Mr Naryan says, and pushes Dreen out of the way and plunges straight out of the hatch.

He falls through black air like a heavy comet. Water smashes around him, tears away his clothes. His nostrils pinch shut and membranes slide across his eyes as he plunges down and down amidst streaming bubbles until the roaring in his ears is no longer the roar of his blood but the roar of the river's never-ending fall over the edge of the world.

Deep, silty currents begin to pull him towards that edge. He turns in the water and begins to swim away from it, away from the ship and the burning city. His duty is over: once they have taken charge of their destiny, the changed citizens will no longer need an Archivist.

Mr Naryan swims more and more easily. The swift cold water washes away his landbound habits, wakes the powerful muscles of his shoulders and back. Angel's message burns bright, burning away the old stories, as he swims through the black water, against the currents of the Great River. Joy gathers with every thrust of his arms. He is the messenger, Angel's witness. He will travel ahead of the crusade that will begin when everyone in Sensch is changed. It will be a long and difficult journey, but he does not doubt that his destiny—the beginning of the future that Angel has bequeathed him and all of Confluence—lies at the end of it.

STEPHEN BAXTER

Stephen Baxter [1957–] (www.cix.co.uk/~sbradshaw/baxterium/baxterium.html) is now one of the big names in SF, the author of a number of highly regarded novels and many short stories. He has won the Philip K. Dick Award, the John W. Campbell Memorial Award, the British SF Association Award, and others for his novels. In 1995 and 1996 he became a major figure internationally in hard SF when his work was first published outside the UK. Not only were his earlier novels reprinted in the US, but his 1995 *The Time Ships* was a leading contender in 1996 for the Hugo Award for best novel. In the mid- and late 1990s he produced nearly ten short stories a year as well. Recent books include *Exultant* (2004), *Ages in Chaos* (2004), a nonfiction science history book, and *Sunstorm* (2005), a novel in collaboration with Arthur C. Clarke.

The *Encyclopedia of Science Fiction* summarizes his early career thusly: "He began publishing SF with 'The Xeelee Flower' for *Interzone* in 1987, which with most of his other short work fits into his Xeelee Sequence, an ambitious attempt at creating a Future History; novels included in the sequence are *Raft* (1989), *Timelike Infinity* (1992), *Flux* (1993), and *Rind* (1994). The sequence—as centrally narrated in the second and fourth volume—follows humanity into interstellar space, where it encounters a complex of alien races; the long epic ends (being typical in this of UK SF) darkly, many aeons hence. Baxter's basic mode is hard SF, and his History is unusually dense with thought-experiment environments . . . but the sweeping millennia-long tale is carried off with a genuine, sciencefictional sense of wonder."

He has often been named as a writer of New Space Opera, but this is problematic, since he thinks of himself as a hard SF writer. He wrote to us:

> I grew up thinking of "space opera" as large-scale sf that is driven more by action, adventure, romance than by ideas. So E. E. Doc Smith is space opera, but not Asimov's Foundation. Nothing wrong with romance, but I was always attracted more by the ideas. By the time I started being published in the late 80s space opera seemed a pejorative term, usually prefixed by "just": "I liked your story but of course it's just space opera." But I always thought of myself as writing hard sf, on a big scale maybe, but ideas-driven, not romantic, so not space opera.
>
> Put it this way, though. My Xeelee Sequence novels and stories are out there in the Galaxy. The early stuff is Stapledonian, I'd say, dealing with the fate of the universe and mankind, even if there are a few space battles. But my more recent work in that universe is about the rise of mankind until we become engaged in a cosmic war. A story like "On The Orion Line" [reprinted in our companion anthology, *The Hard SF Renaissance*—eds.] is definitely ideas-driven, definitely hard sf, and its depiction of an Orwellian military culture is meant to be punchy. But it is a romance of a young soldier on an interstellar battlefield, so if it isn't space opera it's definitely a look back at the traditions of space opera.
>
> By the end of the 90s the term *space opera* seems to have been taken back and become respectable again; now we have "radical space opera" and so on. Maybe the term has become so baggy it's not much use except historically?

Space opera is often used by reviewers today to refer to large-scale hard SF stories. That is where the misnomer (in use for a while in the late 1990s and early 2000s) "hard SF space opera" comes from. Baxter's comments illuminate the intersection of hard SF and space opera, but it is not very common, as he points out, even in his work.

"The Great Game" is an antiwar story in the setting of his Xeelee future universe, which because of its scale, and the fact that there is a great war, has often been claimed as space opera. The title, of course, refers to the maneuverings of European empires in the Middle East in the nineteenth century. It is a timely story, and part of the ongoing political dialogue in hard SF between the UK left and the US right. We offer it as an intersection of hard SF and space opera.

THE GREAT GAME

S T E P H E N   B A X T E R

We were in the blister, waiting for the drop. My marines, fifty of them in their bright orange Yukawa suits, were sitting in untidy rows. They were trying to hide it, but I could see the fear in the way they clutched their static lines, and their unusual reluctance to rib the wetbacks.

Well, when I looked through the transparent walls and out into the sky, I felt it myself.

We had been flung far out of the main disc, and the sparse orange-red stars of the halo were a foreground to the galaxy itself, a pool of curdled light that stretched to right and left as far as you could see. But as the Spline ship threw itself gamely through its complicated evasive maneuvers, that great sheet of light flapped around us like a bird's broken wing. I could see our destination's home sun—it was a dwarf, a pinprick glowing dim red—but even that jiggled around the sky as the Spline bucked and rolled.

And, leaving aside the vertigo, what deepened my own fear was the glimpses I got of the craft that swarmed like moths around that dwarf star. Beautiful swooping ships with sycamore-seed wings, they were unmistakable. They were Xeelee nightfighters.

The Xeelee were the captain's responsibility, not mine. But I couldn't stop my over-active mind speculating on what had lured such a dense concentration of them so far out of the Galactic core that is their usual stamping ground.

Given the tension, it was almost a relief when Lian threw up.

Those Yukawa suits are heavy and stiff, meant for protection rather than flexibility, but she managed to lean far enough forward that her bright yellow puke mostly hit the floor. Her buddies reacted as you'd imagine, but I handed her a wipe.

"Sorry, Lieutenant." She was the youngest of the troop, at seventeen ten years younger than me.

I forced a grin. "I've seen worse, marine. Anyhow you've given the wetbacks something to do when we've gone."

"Yes, sir. . . ."

What you definitely don't want at such moments is a visit from the brass. Which, of course, is what we got.

Admiral Kard came stalking through the drop blister, muttering to the loadmaster, nodding at marines. At Kard's side was a Commissary—you could tell that at a glance—a woman, tall, ageless, in the classic costume of the Commission for Historical Truth, a floor-sweeping gown and shaved-bald head. She looked as cold and lifeless as every Commissary I ever met.

I stood up, brushing vomit off my suit. I could see how the troops were tensing up. But I couldn't have stopped an admiral; this was his flag.

They reached my station just as the destination planet, at last, swam into view.

We grunts knew it only by a number. That eerie sun was too dim to cast much light, and despite low-orbiting sunsats much of the land and sea was dark velvet. But great orange rivers of fire coursed across the black ground. This was a suffering world.

Admiral Kard was watching me. "Lieutenant Neer. Correct?"

"Sir."

"Welcome to Shade," he said evenly. "You know the setup here. The Expansion reached this region five hundred years ago. We haven't been much in contact since. But when our people down there called for help, the Navy responded." He had cold artificial Eyes, and I sensed he was testing me.

"We're ready to drop, sir."

The Commissary was peering out at the tilted landscape, hands folded behind her back. "Remarkable. It's like a geology demonstrator. Look at the lines of volcanoes and ravines. Every one of this world's tectonic faults has given way, all at once."

Admiral Kard eyed me. "You must forgive Commissary Xera. She does think of the universe as a textbook."

He was rewarded for that with a glare.

I kept silent, uncomfortable. Everybody knows about the tension between Navy, the fighting arm of mankind's Third Expansion, and Commission, implementer of political will. Maybe that structural rivalry was the reason for this impromptu walk-through, as the Commissary jostled for influence over events, and the admiral tried to score points with a display of his fighting troops.

Except that right now they were *my* troops, not his.

To her credit, Xera seemed to perceive something of my resentment. "Don't worry, Lieutenant. It's just that Kard and I have something of a history. Two centuries of it, in fact, since our first encounter on a world called Home, thousands of light years from here."

I could see Lian look up at that. According to the book, *nobody* was supposed to live so long. I guess at seventeen you still think everybody follows the rules.

Kard nodded. "And you've always had a way of drawing subordinates into our personal conflicts, Xera. Well, we may be making history today. Neer, look at the home sun, the frozen star."

I frowned. "What's a *frozen star?*"

The Commissary made to answer, but Kard cut across her. "Skip the science. Those Xeelee units are swarming like rats. We don't know *why* the Xeelee are here. But we do know what they are doing to this human world."

"That's not proven," Xera snapped.

Despite that caveat I could see my people stir. None of us had ever heard of a direct attack by the Xeelee on human positions.

Lian said boldly, "Admiral, sir—"

"Yes, rating?"

"Does that mean we are at war?"

Admiral Kard sniffed up a lungful of ozone-laden air. "After today, perhaps we will be. How does that make you feel, rating?"

Lian, and the others, looked to me for guidance.

I looked into my heart.

Across seven thousand years humans had spread out in a great swarm through the galaxy, even spreading out into the halo beyond the main disc, overwhelming and assimilating other life forms as we encountered them. We had faced no opponent capable of systematic resistance since the collapse of the Silver Ghosts five thousand years before—none but the Xeelee, the galaxy's other great power, who sat in their great concentrations at the core, silent, aloof. For my whole life, and for centuries before, all of mankind had been united in a single purpose: to confront the Xeelee, and claim our rightful dominion.

And now—perhaps—here I was at the start of it all.

What I felt was awe. Fear, maybe. But that wasn't what the moment required. "I'll tell you what I feel, sir. Relief. *Bring them on!*"

That won me a predictable hollering, and a slap on the back from Kard. Xera studied me blankly, her face unreadable.

Then there was a flare of plasma around the blister, and the ride got a lot bumpier. I sat before I was thrown down, and the loadmaster hustled away the brass.

"Going in hard," called the loadmaster. "Barf bags at the ready. Ten minutes."

We were skimming under high, thin, icy clouds. The world had become a landscape of burning mountains and rivers of rock that fled beneath me.

All this in an eerie silence, broken only by the shallow breaths of the marines.

The ship lurched up and to the right. To our left now was a mountain; we had come so low already that its peak was above us. According to the century-old survey maps the locals had called it Mount Perfect. And, yes, once it must have been a classic cone shape, I thought, a nice landmark for an earthworm's horizon. But now its profile was spoiled by bulges and gouges, ash had splashed around it, and deeper mud-filled channels had been cut into the landscape, splayed like the fingers of a hand.

Somewhere down there, amid the bleating locals, there was an academician called Tilo, dropped by the Navy a couple of standard days earlier, part of a global network who had been gathering data on the causes of the volcanism. Tilo's job, bluntly, had been to prove that it was all the Xeelee's fault. The academician had somehow got himself cut off from his uplink gear; I was to find and retrieve him. No wonder Xera had been so hostile, I thought; the Commissaries were famously suspicious of the alliance between the Navy and the Academies—

Green lights marked out the hatch in the invisible wall.

The loadmaster came along the line. "Stand up! Stand up!" The marines complied clumsily.

"Thirty seconds," the loadmaster told me. He was a burly, scarred veteran, attached to a rail by an umbilical as thick as my arm. "Winds look good."

"Thank you."

"You guys be careful down there. All clear aft. Ten seconds. Five." The green lights began to blink. We pulled our flexible visors across our faces. "Three, two—"

The hatch dilated, and the sudden roar of the wind made all this real.

The loadmaster was standing by the hatch, screaming. "Go, go, go!" As the marines passed I checked each static line one last time with a sharp tug, before they jumped into blackness. The kid, Lian, was the second last to go—and I was the last of all.

So there I was, falling into the air of a new world.

The static line went taut and ripped free, turning on my suit's Yukawa-force gravity nullifier. That first shock can be hurtful, but to me, after maybe fifty drops in anger, it came as a relief.

I looked up and to my right. I saw a neat line of marines falling starfished through the air. One was a lot closer to me than the rest—Lian, I guessed. Past them I made out our Spline vessel, its hull charred from its hurried entry into the atmosphere. Even now it looked immense, its pocked hull like an inverted landscape above me. It was a magnificent sight, an awe-inspiring display of human power and capability.

But beyond it I saw the hulking majesty of the mountain, dwarfing even the Spline. A dense cloud of smoke and ash lingered near its truncated summit, underlit by a fiery glow.

I looked down, to the valley I was aiming for.

The Commission's maps had shown a standard-issue Conurbation surrounded by broad, shining replicator fields, where the ground's organic matter was processed seamlessly into food. But the view now was quite different. I could see the characteristic bubble-cluster shape of a Conurbation, but it looked dark, poorly maintained, while suburbs of blockier buildings had sprouted around it.

You expected a little drift from orthodoxy, out here on the edge of everything.

Still, that Conurbation was our target for the evacuation. I could see the squat cone shape of a heavy-lift shuttle, dropped here on the Spline's last pass through the atmosphere, ready to lift the population. My marines were heading for the Conurbation, just as they should.

But I had a problem, I saw now. There was another cluster of buildings and lights, much smaller, stranded half way up the flank of the mountain. Another village?

I'm not sentimental. You do what you can, what's possible. I wouldn't have gone after that isolated handful—if not for the fact that a pale pink light blinked steadily at me.

It was Tilo's beacon. Kard had made it clear enough that unless I came home with the academician, or at least with his data, next time I made a drop it would be without a Yukawa suit.

I slowed my fall and barked out orders. It was a simple mission; I knew my people would be able to supervise the evacuation of the main township without me. Then I turned and continued my descent, down toward the smaller community.

It was only after I had committed myself that I saw one of my troop had followed me: the kid, Lian.

No time to think about that now. A Yukawa suit is good for one drop, one way. You can't go back and change your mind. Anyhow I was already close. I glimpsed a few ramshackle buildings, upturned faces shining like coins.

Then the barely visible ground raced up to meet me. Feet together, knees bent, back straight, roll when you hit—and then a breath-stealing impact on hard rock.

I allowed myself three full breaths, lying there on the cold ground, as I checked I was still in one piece.

Then I stood and pulled off my visor. The air was breathable, but thick with the smell of burning, and of sulphur. But the ground quivered under my feet, over and over. I wasn't too troubled by that—until I reminded myself that planets were supposed to be *stable*.

Lian was standing there, her suit glowing softly. "Good landing, sir," she said.

I nodded, glad she was safe, but irritated; if she'd followed orders she wouldn't have been here at all. I turned away from her, a deliberate snub that was enough admonishment for now.

The sky was deep. Beyond clouds of ash, sunsats swam. Past them I glimpsed the red pinprick of the true sun, and the wraith-like galaxy disc beyond.

Behind me the valley skirted the base of Mount Perfect, neatly separating it from more broken ground beyond. The landscape was dark green, its contours coated by forest, and clear streams bubbled into a river that ran down the valley's center. A single, elegant bridge spanned the valley, reaching toward the old Conurbation. Further upstream I saw what looked like a logging plant, giant pieces of yellow-colored equipment standing idle amid huge piles of sawn trees. Idyllic, if you liked that kind of thing, which I didn't.

On this side of the valley, the village was just a huddle of huts—some of them made from *wood*—clustered on the lower slopes of the mountain. Bigger buildings might have been a school, a medical center. There were a couple of battered ground transports. Beyond, I glimpsed the rectangular shapes of fields—apparently plowed, not a glimmer of replicator technology in sight, mostly covered in ash.

People were standing, watching me, gray as the ground under their feet. Men, women, children, infants in arms, old folk, people in little clusters. There were maybe thirty of them.

Lian stood close to me. "Sir, I don't understand."

"These are *families*," I murmured. "You'll pick it up."

"Dark matter." The new voice was harsh, damaged by smoke; I turned, startled.

A man was limping toward me. About my height and age but a lot leaner, he was wearing a tattered Navy coverall, and he was using an improvised crutch to hobble over the rocky ground, favoring what looked like a broken leg. His face and hair were gray with the ash.

I said, "You're the academician."

"Yes, I'm Tilo."

"We're here to get you out."

He barked a laugh. "Sure you are. Listen to me. *Dark matter.* That's why the Xeelee are here. It may have nothing to do with *us* at all. Things are going to happen fast. If I don't get out of here—whatever happens, just remember that one thing . . ."

Now a woman hurried toward me. One of the locals, she was wearing a simple shift of woven cloth, and leather sandals on her feet; she looked maybe forty, strong, tired. An antique translator box hovered at her shoulder. "My name is Doel," she said. "We saw you fall—"

"Are you in charge here?"

"I—" She smiled. "Yes, if you like. Will you help us get out of here?"

She didn't look, or talk, or act, like any Expansion citizen I had ever met. Things truly had drifted here. "You are in the wrong place." I was annoyed how prissy I sounded. I pointed to the Conurbation, on the other side of the valley. "*That's* where you're supposed to be."

"I'm sorry," she said, bemused. "We've lived here since my grandfather's time. We didn't like it, over in Blessed. We came here to live a different way. No replicators. Crops we grow ourselves. Clothes we make—"

"Mothers and fathers and grandfathers," Tilo cackled. "What do you think of that, Lieutenant?"

"Academician, why are you here?"

He shrugged. "I came to study the mountain, as an exemplar of the planet's geology. I accepted the hospitality of these people. That's all. I got to like them, despite their—alien culture."

"But you left your equipment behind," I snapped. "You don't have comms implants. You didn't even bring your mnemonic fluid, did you?"

"I brought my pickup beacon," he said smugly.

"Lethe, I don't have time for this." I turned to Doel. "Look—if you can get yourself across the valley, to where that transport is, you'll be taken out with the rest."

"But I don't think there will be time—"

I ignored her. "Academician, can you walk?"

Tilo laughed. "No. And *you* can't hear the mountain."

That was when Mount Perfect exploded.

Tilo told me later that, if I'd known where and how to look, I could have seen the north side of the mountain bulging out. The defect had been growing visibly, at a meter a day. Well, I didn't notice that. Thanks to some trick of acoustics, I didn't even hear the eruption—though it was slightly heard by other Navy teams working hundreds of kilometers away.

But the aftermath was clear enough. With Lian and Doel, and with Academician Tilo limping after us, I ran to the crest of a ridge to see down the length of the valley.

A sharp earthquake had caused the mountain's swollen flank to shear and fall away. As we watched, a billion tons of rock slid into the valley in a monstrous landslide. Already a huge gray thunderhead of smoke and ash was rearing up to the murky sky.

But that was only the start, for the removal of all that weight was like opening a pressurized can. The mountain erupted—not upward, but *sideways*, like the blast of an immense weapon, a volley of superheated gas and pulverized rock. It quickly overtook the landslide, and I saw it roll over trees—imports from distant Earth, great vegetable sentinels centuries old, flattened like straws.

I was stupefied by the *scale* of it all.

Now, from out of the ripped-open side of the mountain, a chthonic blood oozed, yellow-gray, viscous, steaming hot. It began to flow down the mountainside, spilling into rain-cut valleys.

"That's a lahar," Tilo murmured. "Mud. I've learned a lot of esoteric geology here, Lieutenant. . . . The heat is melting the permafrost—these mountains were snow-covered two weeks ago; did you know that?—making up a thick mixture of volcanic debris and meltwater."

"So it's just mud," said Lian uncertainly.

"You aren't an earthworm, are you, marine?"

"Look at the logging camp," Doel murmured, pointing.

Already the mud had overwhelmed the heavy equipment, big yellow tractors and huge cables and chains used for hauling logs, crumpling it all like paper. Piles of sawn logs were spilled, immense wooden beams shoved downstream effortlessly. The mud, gray and yellow, was steaming, oddly like curdled milk.

For the first time I began to consider the contingency that we might not get out of here. In which case my primary mission was to preserve Tilo's data.

I quickly used my suit to establish an uplink. We were able to access Tilo's records, stored in cranial implants, and fire them up to the Spline. But in case it didn't work—

"Tell me about dark matter," I said. "Quickly."

Tilo pointed up at the sky. "That star—the natural sun, the dwarf—shouldn't exist."

"What?"

"It's too small. It has only around a twentieth Earth's sun's mass. It should be a planet: a brown dwarf, like a big, fat Jovian. It shouldn't burn—*not yet*. You understand that stars form from the interstellar medium—gas and dust, originally just Big-Bang hydrogen and helium. But stars bake heavy elements, like metals, in their interiors, and eject them back into the medium when the stars die. So as time goes on, the medium is increasingly polluted."

Impatiently I snapped, "And the point—"

"The point is that an increase in impurities in the medium lowers the critical mass needed for a star to be big enough to burn hydrogen. Smaller stars start lighting up. Lieutenant, that star shouldn't be shining. Not in this era, not for trillions of years yet; the interstellar medium is too clean. . . . You know, it's so small that its surface temperature isn't thousands of degrees, like Earth's sun, but the freezing point of water. That is a star with ice clouds in its atmosphere. There may even be liquid water on its surface."

I looked up, wishing I could see the frozen star better. Despite the urgency of the moment I shivered, confronted by strangeness, a vision from trillions of years downstream.

Tilo said bookishly, "What does this mean? It means that out here in the halo, something, some agent, is making the interstellar medium dirtier than it ought to be. The only way to do that is by *making the stars grow old*." He waved a hand at the cluttered sky. "And if you look, you can see it all over this part of the halo; the H-R diagrams are impossibly skewed. . . ."

I shook my head; I was far out of my depth. What could make a star grow old too fast? . . . Oh. "Dark matter?"

"The matter we're made of—baryonic matter, protons and neutrons and the rest—is only about a tenth the universe's total. The rest is dark matter: subject only to gravity and the weak nuclear force, impervious to electromagnetism. Dark matter came out of the Big Bang, just like the baryonic stuff. As our galaxy coalesced the dark matter was squeezed out of the disc. . . . But this is the domain of dark matter, Lieutenant. Out here in the halo."

"And this stuff can affect the ageing of stars."

"Yes. A dark matter concentration in the core of a star can change temperatures, and so affect fusion rates."

"You said *an agent* was ageing the stars." I thought that over. "You make it sound intentional."

He was cautious now, an academician who didn't want to commit himself. "The stellar disruption appears nonrandom."

Through all the jargon, I tried to figure out what this meant. "Something is *using* the dark matter? . . . Or are there life forms *in* the dark matter? And what does that have to do with the Xeelee, and the problems here on Shade?"

His face twisted. "I haven't figured out the links yet. There's a lot of history. I need my data desk," he said plaintively.

I pulled my chin, thinking of the bigger picture. "Academician, you're on an assignment for the admiral. Do you think you're finding what he wants to hear?"

He eyed me carefully. "The admiral is part of a—grouping—within the Navy that is keen to go to war, even to provoke conflict. Some call them extremists. Kard's actions have to be seen in this light."

Actually, I'd heard such rumors, but I stiffened. "He's my commanding officer. That's all that matters."

Tilo sighed. "Mine too, in a sense. But—"

"Lethe," Lian said suddenly. "Sorry, sir. But that mud is moving *fast*."

So it was, I saw.

The flow was shaped by the morphology of the valley, but its front was tens of meters high, and it would soon reach the village. And I could see that the gush out of the mountain's side showed no signs of abating. The mud was evidently powerfully corrosive; the land's green coat was ripped away to reveal bare rock, and the mud was visibly eating away at the walls of the valley itself. I saw soil and rock collapse into the flow. Overlaying the crack of tree trunks and the clatter of rock, there was a noise like the feet of a vast running crowd, and a sour, sulphurous smell hit me.

"I can't believe how fast this stuff is rising," I said to Tilo. "The volume you'd need to fill up a valley like this—"

"You and I are used to spacecraft, Lieutenant. The dimensions of human engineering. Planets are *big*. And when they turn against you—"

"We can still get you out of here. With these suits we can get you over that bridge and to the transport—"

"What about the villagers?"

I was aware of the woman, Doel, standing beside me silently. Which, of course, made me feel worse than if she'd yelled and begged.

"We have mixed objectives," I said weakly.

There was a scream. We looked down the ridge and saw that the mud had already reached the lower buildings. A young couple with a kid were standing on the roof of a low hut, about to get cut off.

Lian said, "Sir?"

I waited one more heartbeat, as the mud began to wash over that hut's porch.

"Lethe, Lethe." I ran down the ridge until I hit the mud.

Even with the suit's augmentation the mud was difficult stuff to wade through— lukewarm, and with a consistency like wet cement. The stench was bad enough for me to pull my visor over my mouth. On the mud's surface were dead fish that must have jumped out of the river to escape the heat. There was a lot of debris in the flow, from dust to pebbles to small boulders: no wonder it was so abrasive.

By the time I reached the little cottage I was already tiring badly.

The woman was bigger, obviously stronger than the man. I had her take her infant over her head, while I slung the man over my shoulder. With me leading, and the woman grabbing onto my belt, we waded back toward the higher ground.

All this time the mud rose relentlessly, filling up the valley as if it had been dammed, and every step sapped my energy.

Lian and Doel helped us out of the dirt. I threw myself to the ground, breathing hard. The young woman's legs had been battered by rocks in the flow; she had lost one sandal, and her trouser legs had been stripped away.

"We're already cut off from the bridge," Lian said softly.

I forced myself to my feet. I picked out a building—not the largest, not the highest, but a good compromise. "That one. We'll get them onto the roof. I'll call for another pickup."

"Sir, but what if the mud keeps rising?"

"Then we'll think of something else," I snapped. "Let's get on with it."

She was crestfallen, but she ran to help as Doel improvised a ladder from a trellis fence.

My first priority was to get Tilo safely lodged on the roof. Then I began to shepherd the locals up there. But we couldn't reach all of them before the relentless rise of the mud left us all ankle-deep. People began to clamber up to whatever high ground they could find—verandas, piles of boxes, the ground transports, even rocks. Soon maybe a dozen were stranded, scattered around a landscape turning gray and slick.

I waded in once more, heading toward two young women who crouched on the roof of a small building, like a storage hut. But before I got there the hut, undermined, suddenly collapsed, pitching the women into the flow. One of them bobbed up and was pushed against a stand of trees, where she got stuck, apparently unharmed. But the other tipped over and slipped out of sight.

I reached the woman in the trees and pulled her out. The other was gone.

I hauled myself back onto the roof for a break. All around us the mud flowed, a foul-smelling gray river, littered with bits of wood and rock.

I'd never met that woman. It was as if I had become part of this little community, all against my will, as we huddled together on that crudely built wooden roof. Not to mention the fact that I now wouldn't be able to fulfill my orders completely.

The loss was visceral. I prepared to plunge back into the flow.

Tilo grabbed my arm. "No. You are exhausted. Anyhow you have a call to make, remember?"

Lian spoke up. "Sir. Let me go," she said awkwardly, "I can manage that much."

Redemption time for this marine. "Don't kill yourself," I told her.

With a grin she slid off the roof.

Briskly, I used my suit's comms system to set up a fresh link to the Spline. I requested another pickup—was told it was impossible—and asked for Kard.

Tilo requested a Virtual data desk. He fell on it as soon as it appeared. His relief couldn't have been greater, as if the mud didn't exist.

When they grasped the situation I had gotten us all into, Admiral Kard and Commissary Xera both sent down Virtual avatars. The two of them hovered over our wooden roof, clean of the mud, gleaming like gods among people made of clay.

Kard glared at me. "What a mess, Lieutenant."

"Yes, sir."

"You should have gotten Tilo over that damn bridge while you could. We're heavily constrained by the Xeelee operations. You realize we probably won't be able to get you out of here alive."

It struck me as somewhat ironic that in the middle of a galaxy-spanning military crisis I was to be killed by mud. But I had made my choice. "So I understand."

"But," Xera said, her thin face fringed by blocky pixels, "he has completed his primary mission, which is to deliver Tilo's data back to us."

Kard closed his Eyes, and his image flickered; I imagined Tilo's data and interpretations pouring into the processors that sustained this semiautonomous Virtual image, tightly locked into Kard's original sensorium. Kard said, "Lousy prioritization. Too much about this *dark matter* crud, Academician."

Xera said gently, "You were here on assignment from your masters in the Navy, with a specific purpose. But it's hard to close your eyes to the clamoring truth, isn't it, Academician?"

Tilo sighed, his face mud-covered.

"We must discuss this," Kard snapped. "All of us, right now. We have a decision to make, a recommendation to pass up the line—and we need to assess what Tilo has to tell us, in case we can't retrieve him."

I understood immediately what he meant. I felt a deep thrill. Even the locals stirred, apparently aware that something momentous was about to happen, even in the midst of their own misfortunes, stuck as we were on that battered wooden roof.

So it began.

At first Tilo wasn't helpful.

"It isn't clear that this is Xeelee action, deliberately directed against humans." Despite Kard's glare, he persisted, "I'm sorry, Admiral, but it isn't *clear*. Look at the context." He pulled up historical material—images, text that scrolled briefly in the murky air. "This is not a new story. There is evidence that human scientists were aware of dark-matter contamination of the stars *before* the beginning of the Third Expansion. It seems an engineered human being was sent into Sol itself. . . . An audacious project. But this was largely lost in the Qax Extirpation, and after that—well, we had a galaxy to conquer. There was a later incident, a project run by the Silver Ghosts, but—"

Kard snapped, "What do the Xeelee care about dark matter?"

Tilo rubbed tired eyes with grubby fists. "However exotic they are, the Xeelee are baryonic life forms, like us. It isn't in their interests for the suns to die young, any more than for us." He shrugged. "Perhaps they are trying to stop it. Perhaps *that's* why they have come here, to the halo. Nothing to do with us—"

Kard waved a Virtual hand at Mount Perfect's oozing wounds. "Then why all this, just as they show up? Coincidence?"

"Admiral—"

"This isn't a trial, Tilo," Kard said. "We don't need absolute proof. The imagery—human refugees, Xeelee nightfighters swooping overhead—will be all we need."

Xera said dryly, "Yes. All we need to sell a war to the Coalition, the governing councils, and the people of the Expansion. This is wonderful for you, isn't it, Admiral? It's what the Navy has been waiting for, along with its Academy cronies. An excuse to attack."

Kard's face was stony. "The cold arrogance of you cosseted intellectuals is sometimes insufferable. It's true that the Navy is ready to fight, Commissary. That's our job. We have the plans in place."

"But does the existence of the plans *require* their fulfillment? And let's remember how hugely the Navy itself will benefit. As the lead agency, a war would clearly support the Navy's long-term political goals."

Kard glared. "We all have something to gain."

And they began to talk, rapidly, about how the different agencies of the Coalition would position themselves in the event of a war.

The military arms, like the Pilots and the Communicators, would naturally ally with the Navy, and would benefit from an increase in military spending. Academic arms like the great Libraries on Earth would be refocused; there was thought to be a danger that with their monopoly on information they were becoming too powerful. Even the Guardians—the Expansion's internal police force—would find a new role: the slowly rising tide of petty crime and illegal economic operations would surely reverse, and the Guardians could return to supporting the Commission in the policing of adherence to the Druz Doctrine—not to mention enforcing the draft.

A lot of this went over my head. I got the sense of the great agencies as shadowy independent empires, engaging in obscure and shifting alliances—like the current links between Navy and Academies, designed to counter the Commission's intellectual weight. And now each agency would consider the possibility of a war as an opportunity to gain political capital.

It was queasy listening. But there's a lot I didn't want to know about how the Coalition is run. Still don't, in fact.

". . . And then there is the economic argument," Kard was saying. "It is as if the Third Expansion itself *is* a war, an endless war against whoever stands in our way. Our economy is on a permanent war-time footing. Let there be no mistake—we could not coexist with the Xeelee, for they would forever represent a ceiling to our ambitions, a ceiling under which we would ultimately wither. We need continued growth—and so a confrontation with the Xeelee is ultimately inevitable." He leaned forward. "And there is more. Xera, *think how much the Commission itself stands to benefit.*

"You Commissaries are responsible for maintaining the unity of mankind; the common principles, common purpose, the *belief* that has driven the Expansion so far. But isn't it obvious that you are failing? Look at this place." He waved a Virtual hand through Doel's hair; the woman flinched, and the hand broke up into drifting pixels. "This woman is a *mother*, apparently some kind of matriarch to her extended *family*. It's as if Hama Druz never existed.

"If the Druz Doctrine were to collapse, the Commission would have no purpose. Think of the good you do, for you know so much better than the mass of mankind how they should think, feel, live, and die. Your project is humanitarian! And it has to continue. We need a purification. An ideological cleansing. And that's what the bright fire of war will give us."

I could see that his arguments, aimed at the Commissary's vanity and self-interest, were leaving a mark.

Tilo was still trying to speak. He showed me more bits of evidence he had assembled on his data desk. "I think I know now why the volcanism started here. *This planet* has an unusually high dark matter concentration in its core. Under such densities the dark matter annihilates with ordinary matter and creates heat—"

I listened absently. "Which creates the geological upheaval."

He closed his eyes, thinking. "Here's a scenario. The Xeelee have been driving dark matter creatures out of the frozen star—and, fleeing, they have lodged here— and that's what set off the volcanism. It was all inadvertent. The Xeelee are trying to *save stars*, not harm humans. . . ."

But nobody paid any attention to that. For, I realized, we had already reached a point where evidence didn't matter.

Kard turned to the people of the village, muddy, exhausted, huddled together on their rooftop. "What of you? *You* are the citizens of the Expansion. There are reformers who say you have had enough of expansion and conflict, that we should seek stability and peace. Well, you have heard what we have had to say, and you have seen our mighty ships in the sky. Will you live out your lives on this drifting rock, helpless before a river of mud—or will you transcend your birth and die for an epic cause? War makes everything new. War is the wildest poetry. *Will you join me?*"

Those ragged-ass, dirt-scratching, orthodoxy-busting farmers hesitated for a heartbeat. You couldn't have found a less likely bunch of soldiers for the Expansion.

But, would you believe, they started cheering the admiral: every one of them, even the kids. Lethe, it brought a tear to my eye.

Even Xera seemed coldly excited now.

Kard closed his Eyes; metal seams pushed his eyelids into ridges. "A handful of people in this desolate, remote place. And yet a new epoch is born. They are listening to us, you know—listening in the halls of history. And *we* will be remembered forever."

Tilo's expression was complex. He clapped his hands, and the data desk disappeared in a cloud of pixels, leaving his work unfinished.

We mere fleshy types had to stay on that rooftop through the night. We could do nothing but cling to each other, as the muddy tide rose slowly around us, and the kids cried from hunger.

When the sunsets returned to the sky, the valley was transformed. The channels had been gouged sharp and deep by the lahar, and the formerly agricultural plain had been smothered by lifeless gray mud, from which only occasional trees and buildings protruded.

But the lahar was flowing only sluggishly. Lian cautiously climbed to the edge of the roof and probed at the mud with her booted foot. "It's very thick."

Tilo said, "Probably the water has drained out of it."

Lian couldn't stand on the mud, but if she lay on it she didn't sink. She flapped her arms and kicked, and she skidded over the surface. Her face gray with the dirt, she laughed like a child. "Sir, look at me! It's a lot easier than trying to swim. . . ."

So it was, when I tried it myself.

And that was how we got the villagers across the flooded valley, one by one, to the larger township—not that much was left of that by now—where the big transport had waited to take us off. In the end we lost only one of the villagers, the young woman who had been overwhelmed by the surge. I tried to accept that I'd done my best to fulfill my contradictory mission objectives—and that, in the end, was the most important outcome for me.

As we lifted, Mount Perfect loosed another eruption.

Tilo, cocooned in a med cloak, stood beside me in an observation blister, watching the planet's mindless fury. He said, "You know, you can't stop a lahar. It just goes the way it wants to go. Like this war, it seems."

"I guess."

"We understand so little. We *see* so little. But when you add us together we combine into huge historical forces that none of us can deflect, any more than you can dam or divert a mighty lahar. . . ."

And so on. I made an excuse and left him there.

I went down to the sick bay, and watched Lian tending to the young from the village. She was patient, competent, calm. I had relieved her of her regular duties, as she was one of the few faces here that was familiar to the kids, who were pretty traumatized. I felt proud of that young marine. She had grown up a lot during our time on Shade.

And as I watched her simple humanity, I imagined a trillion such acts, linking past and future, history and destiny, a great tapestry of hard work and goodwill that united mankind into a mighty host that would some day rule a galaxy.

To tell the truth I was bored with Tilo and his niggling. *War!* It was magnificent. It was inevitable.

I didn't understand what had happened down on Shade, and I didn't care. What did it matter *how* the war had started, in truth or lies? We would soon forget about dark matter and the Xeelee's obscure, immense projects, just as we had before; we humans didn't think in such terms. All that mattered was that the war was here, at last.

The oddest thing was that none of it had anything to do with the Xeelee themselves. Any enemy would have served our purposes just as well.

I began to wonder what it would mean for me. I felt my heart beat faster, like a drumbeat.

We flew into a rising cloud of ash, and bits of rock clattered against our hull, frightening the children.

MICHAEL MOORCOCK

Michael Moorcock [1939–] (www.multiverse.org) is one of the giants of science fiction, a distinguished contemporary writer and editor who in the 1960s was the editor of *New Worlds* and the prophet of the British New Wave. Since the 1980s, according to his Web site, Moorcock "tended to write well-reviewed literary novels such as *Mother London*, nominated for Booker and Whitbread Prizes, but continued to revisit characters from earlier works, like Elric in *The Dreamthief's Daughter* (2001) or *The Skrayling Tree* (2003). With the writing of the third and last book in this trilogy, *The White Wolf's Son* (2005), he announced his 'retirement' from writing heroic fantasy." Still one of the great living SF and fantasy writers, Moorcock is known more for his avant garde work, and his support of other writers pushing the boundaries of genre, than for his genre work. He is now a recognized literary figure in the UK, a significant contemporary writer. Nevertheless, he has deep roots in genre fiction, and his love for certain genre works and writers (for instance, Leigh Brackett, Charles Harness, and Alfred Bester) is long-term and enduring.

He received the Guardian Fiction Prize for the Cornelius Quartet in 1977. *Gloriana* won the John W. Campbell Award in 1978 and the World Fantasy Award in 1979. In 2002, he was inducted into the Science Fiction Hall of Fame. He has received two Lifetime Achievement Awards: the World Fantasy Award in 2000 and the Prix Utopiales, in Nantes, France, in 2004.

We remarked in the general introduction to this volume, and again in the story note to Jackson's "The Swordsmen of Varnis," that science fantasy had become conflated into the definition of space opera in some circles at an early date, and finally more generally in the 1970s, but that "science fantasy" as a term clearly separate from "space opera" had continued in usage until at least the early 1980s. Michael Moorcock's fantasy adventures, science fantasies, and SF novels in his Eternal Champion cycle preserve the distinctions separating them from classic space opera of the Hamilton and Smith tradition, but many of them are not considered distinct from space opera by contemporary readers and reviewers.

"Lost Sorceress of the Silent Citadel" is an exercise in nostalgia, a swashbuckling planetary romance that brings back Mars as an exciting setting for SF adventure for an audience that knows better but is still willing to indulge in it. It is primarily an homage to Leigh Brackett, whose science fantasies became an alternate paradigm for space opera (see Brackett note), but also to her honorable tradition, which now (we say with some regret) prospers more in the media than in the SF literature. Moorcock succeeds both because of his sincere feelings for Brackett's achievements and because of his sheer talent and experience at writing fantasy and science fiction adventure.

Moorcock says of Brackett, "Echoes of Leigh can be heard in Delany, Zelazny and that whole school of writers who expanded SF's limits and left us with some fine visionary extravaganzas." And, "It turned out that I didn't quite have her penchant for interplanetary romance, but her example and her influence runs clearly through every Earth- or Mars-bound fantasy adventure story I have ever told and through virtually every other fantasy adventure story that has been told since!"

LOST SORCERESS OF THE SILENT CITADEL

MICHAEL MOORCOCK

They came upon the Earthling naked, somewhere in the Shifting Desert when Mars' harsh sunlight beat through thinning atmosphere and the sand was raw glass cutting into bare feet. His skin hung like filthy rags from his bloody flesh. He was starved, unshaven, making noises like an animal. He was raving—empty of identity and will. What had the ghosts of those ancient Martians done to him? Had they traveled through time and space to take a foul and unlikely vengeance? A novella of alien mysteries—of a goddess who craved life—who lusted for the only man who had ever dared disobey her. A tale of Captain John MacShard, the Half-Martian, of old blood and older memories, of a restless quest for the prize of forgotten centuries. . . .

CHAPTER ONE

WHISPERS OF AN ANCIENT MEMORY

"That's Captain John MacShard, the tomb-thief." Schomberg leaned his capacious belly on the bar, wiping around it with a filthy rag. "They say his mother was a Martian princess turned whore, and his father—"

Low City's best-known antiquities fence, proprietor of the seedy Twenty Capstans, Schomberg murmured wetly through lips like fresh liver. "Well, Mercury was the only world would take them. Them and their filthy egg." He flicked a look toward the door and became suddenly grave.

Outlined against the glare of the Martian noon a man appeared to hesitate and go on down the street. Then he turned and pushed through the entrance's weak energy gate. Then he paused again.

He was a big, hard-muscled man, dressed in spare ocher and brown, with a queer, ancient weapon, all baroque unstable plastics and metals, prominent on his hip.

The Banning gun was immediately recognized and its owner identified by the hardened spacers and *krik* traders who used the place.

They said only four men in the solar system could ever handle that weapon. One was the legendary Northwest Smith; the second was Eric John Stark, now far off-system. The third was Dumarest of Terra, and the fourth was Captain John MacShard. Anyone else trying to fire a Banning died unpleasantly. Sometimes they just disappeared, as if every part of them had been sucked into the gun's impossible energy cells. They said Smith had given his soul for a Banning. But MacShard's soul was still apparent, behind that steady gray gaze, hungering for something like oblivion.

From long habit Captain John MacShard remained in the doorway until his sight had fully adjusted to the sputtering naphtha. His eyes glowed with a permanent feral fire. He was a lean-faced, slim-hipped wolf's head whom no man could ever tame. Through all the alien and mysterious spheres of interplanetary space, many had tried to take the wild beast out of Captain John MacShard. He remained as fierce and free as in the days when, as a boy, he had scrabbled for survival over the unforgiving waste of rocky crags and slag slopes that was Mercury and from the disparate blood of two planets had built a body which could withstand the cruel climate of a third.

Captain John MacShard was in Schomberg's for a reason. He never did anything without a reason. He couldn't go to sleep until he had first considered the action. It was what he had learned on Mercury, orphaned, surviving in those terrible caverns, fighting fiercely for subsistence where nothing would grow and where you and the half-human tribe which had adopted you were the tastiest prey on the planet.

More than any Earthman, he had learned the old ways, the sweet, dangerous, old ways of the ancient Martians. Their descendants still haunted the worn and whispering hills which were the remains of Mars' great mountain ranges in the ages of her might, when the Sea Kings ruled a planet as blue as turquoise, as glittering red as rubies, and as green as that Emerald Isle which had produced Captain John MacShard's own Earth ancestors, as tough, as mystical and as filled with wanderlust as this stepson of the shrieking Mercurian wastelands, with the blood of Brian Borhu, Henry Tudor, and Charles Edward Stuart in his veins. Too, the blood of Martian Sea Kings called to him across the centuries and informed him with the deep wisdom of his Martian forebears. That long-dead kin had fought against the Danes and the Anglo-Saxons, been cavaliers in the Stuart cause and marshals in Napoleon's army. They had fought for and against the standard of Rhiannon, in both male and female guise, survived blasting sorcery and led the starving armies of Barrakesh into the final battle of the Martian pole. Their stories, their courage and their mad fearlessness in the face of inevitable death were legendary.

Captain John MacShard had known nothing of this ancestry of course and there were still many unsolved mysteries in his past, but he had little interest in them. He had the instincts of any intelligent wild animal, and left the past in the past. A cat-like curiosity was what drove him and it made him the best archaeological hunter on five planets—some, like Schomberg, called him a grave-looter, though never to his face. There was scarcely a museum in the inhabited universe which didn't proudly display a find of Captain John MacShard's. They said some of the races which had made those artifacts had not been entirely extinct until the captain found them. There wasn't a living enemy who didn't fear him. And there wasn't a woman in the system who had known him that didn't remember him.

To call Captain John MacShard a loner was something of a tautology. Captain John MacShard was loneliness personified. He was like a spur of rock in the deep desert, resisting everything man and nature could send against it. He was endurance. He was integrity, and he was grit through and through. Only one who had tested himself against the entire fury of alien Mercury and survived could know what it meant to be MacShard, trusting only MacShard.

Captain John MacShard was very sparing in his affections but gave less to himself than he gave to an alley-*brint*, a wounded ray-rat, or the scrawny street kid begging in the hard sour Martian sun to whom he finally tossed a piece of old silver before striding into the bar and taking his usual, which Schomberg had ready for him.

The Dutchman began to babble something, but Captain John MacShard placed his lips to the shot glass of Vortex Water, turned his back on him, and surveyed his company.

His company was pretending they hadn't seen him come in.

From a top pocket MacShard fished a twisted pencil of Venusian talk-talk wood and stuck it between his teeth, chewing on it thoughtfully. Eventually his steady gaze fell on a fat merchant in a fancy fake *skow*-skin jerkin and vivid blue tights who pretended an interest in his fancifully carved flagon.

"Your name Morricone?" Captain John MacShard's voice was a whisper, cutting through the rhythmic sound of men who couldn't help taking in sudden air and running tongues around drying mouths.

His thin lips opened wide enough for the others to see a glint of bright, pointed teeth before they shut tight again.

Morricone nodded. He made a halfhearted attempt to smile. He put his hands on either side of his cards and made funny shrugging movements.

From somewhere, softly, a *shtrang* string sounded.

"You wanted to see me," said Captain John MacShard. And he jerked his head toward a corner where a filthy table was suddenly unoccupied.

The man called Morricone scuttled obediently toward the table and sat down, watching Captain John MacShard as he picked up his bottle and glass and walked slowly, his antique *ghat*-scale leggings chinking faintly.

Again the *shtrang* string began to sound, its deep note making peculiar harmonies in the thin Martian air. There was a cry like a human voice which echoed into nowhere, and when it was gone the silence was even more profound.

"You wanted to see me?" Captain John MacShard moved the unlit stogie from one side of his mouth to the other. His gray, jade-flecked eyes bore into Morricone's shifting black pupils. The fat merchant was obviously hyped on some kind of Low City "head chowder."

There wasn't a drug you couldn't buy at Schomberg's where everything was for sale, including Schomberg.

The hophead began to giggle in a way that at once identified him as a *cruffer*, addicted to the fine, white powdered bark of the Venusian high tree cultures, who used the stuff to train their giant birds but had the sense not to use it themselves.

Captain John MacShard turned away. He wasn't going to waste his time on a druggy, no matter how expensive his tastes.

Morricone lost his terror of Captain John MacShard then. He needed help more than he needed dope. Captain John MacShard was faintly impressed. He knew the kind of hold *cruff* had on its victims.

But he kept on walking.

Until Morricone scuttled in front of him and almost fell to his knees, his hands reaching out toward Captain John MacShard, too afraid to touch him.

His voice was small, desperate, and it held some kind of pain Captain John MacShard recognized. "Please . . ."

Captain John MacShard made to move past, back into the glaring street.

"*Please, Captain MacShard. Please help me . . .*" His shoulders slumped, and he said dully: "They've taken my daughter. The Thennet have taken my daughter."

Captain John MacShard hesitated, still looking into the street. From the corner of his mouth he gave the name of one of the cheapest hotels in the quarter. Nobody in their right mind would stay there if they valued life or limb. Only the crazy or desperate would even enter the street it was in.

"I'm there in an hour." Captain John MacShard went out of the bar. The boy he'd given the silver coin to was still standing in the swirling Martian dust, the ever-moving red tide which ran like a bizarre river down the time-destroyed street. The boy grinned up at him. Old eyes, young skin. A slender snizzer lizard crawled on his shoulder and curled its strange, prehensile tail around his left ear. The boy touched the creature tenderly, automatically.

"You good man, Mister Captain John MacShard."

For the first time in months, Captain John MacShard allowed himself a thin, self-mocking grin.

CHAPTER TWO

TAKEN BY THE THENNET!

Captain John MacShard left the main drag almost at once. He needed some advice and knew where he was most likely to find it. There was an old man he had to visit. Though not of their race, Fra Energen had authority over the last of the Memiget Priests whose Order had discovered how rich the planet was in man-made treasure. They had also been experts on the Thennet as well as the ancient Martian pantheon.

His business over with, Captain John MacShard walked back to his hotel. His route took him through the filthiest, most wretched slums ever seen across all the ports of the spaceways. He displayed neither weakness nor desire. His pace was the steady, relentless lope of the wolf. His eyes seemed unmoving, yet took in everything.

All around him the high tottering tenement towers of the Low City swayed gently in the glittering light, their rusted metal and red terra cotta merging into the landscape as if they were natural. As if they had always been there.

Not quite as old as Time, some of the buildings were older than the human race. They had been added to and stripped and added to again, but once those towers had sheltered and proclaimed the power of Mars' mightiest sea lords.

Now they were slums, a rat warren for the scum of the spaceways, for half-Martians like Captain John MacShard, for stranger genetic mixes than even Brueghel imagined.

In that thin atmosphere you could smell the Low City for miles and beyond that, in the series of small craters known as Diana's Field, was Old Mars Station, the first spaceport the Earthlings had ever built, long before they had begun to discover the strange, retiring races which had remained near their cities, haunting them like barely living ghosts, more creatures of their own mental powers than of any natural creation—ancient memories made physical by act of will alone.

Millennia before, the sea lords and their ladies and children died in those towers, sensing the end of their race as the last of the waters evaporated and red winds scoured the streets of all ornament and grace. Some chose to kill themselves as their fine ships became so many useless monuments. Some had marshaled their families and set off across the new-formed deserts in search of a mythical ocean which welled up from the planet's core.

It had taken less than a generation, Captain John MacShard knew, for a small but navigable ocean to evaporate rapidly until it was no more than a haze in the morning sunlight. Where it had been were slowly collapsing hulls, the remains of wharfs and jetties, endless dunes and rippling deserts, abandoned cities of poignant dignity and unbelievable beauty. The great dust tides rose and fell across the dead sea bottoms of a planet which had run out of resources. Even its water had come from Venus, until the Venusians had raised the price so only Earth could afford it.

Earth was scarcely any better now, with water wars turning the Blue Planet into a background of endless skirmishes between nations and tribes for the precious streams, rivers, and lakes they had used so dissolutely and let dissipate into space, turning God's paradise into Satan's wasteland.

And now Earth couldn't afford Venusian water either. So Venus fought a bloody civil war for control of what was left of her trade. For a while MacShard had run bootleg water out of New Malvern. The kind of money the rich were prepared to pay for a tiny bottle was phenomenal. But he'd become sickened with it when he'd walked through London's notorious Westminster district and seen degenerates spending an artisan's wages on jars of gray reconstitute while mothers held the corpses of dehydrated babies in their arms and begged for the money to bury them.

"Mr. Captain John MacShard."

Captain John MacShard knew the boy had followed him all the way to the hotel. Without turning, he said: "You'd better introduce yourself, sonny."

The boy seemed ashamed, as if he had never been detected before. He hung his head. "My dad called me Milton," he said.

Captain John MacShard smiled then. Once. He stopped when he saw the boy's face. The child had been laughed at too often and to him it meant danger, distrust, pain. "So your dad was Mr. Eliot, right?"

The boy forgot any imagined insult, "You knew him?"

"How long did your mother know him?"

"Well, he was on one of those long-haul ion sailors. He was a great guitarist. Singer. Wrote all his own material. He was going to see a producer when he came back from Earth with enough money to marry. Well, you know that story." The boy lowered his eyes. "Never came back."

"I'm not your pa," said Captain John MacShard and went inside. He closed his door. He marveled at the tricks the street kids used these days. But that stuff couldn't work on him. He'd seen six-year-old masters pulling the last Uranian *bakh* from a tight-fisted New Nantucket blubber-chaser who had just finished a speech about a need for more workhouses.

A few moments later, Morricone arrived. Captain John MacShard knew it was him by the quick, almost hesitant rap.

"It's open," he said. There was never any point in locking doors in this place. It advertised you had something worth stealing. Maybe just your body.

Morricone was terrified. He was terrified of the neighborhood and he was terrified of Captain John MacShard. But he was even more terrified of something else. Of whatever the Thennet might have done to his daughter.

Captain John MacShard had no love for the Thennet, and he didn't need a big excuse to put a few more of their number in hell.

The gaudily dressed old man shuffled into the room, and his terror didn't go away. Captain John MacShard closed the door behind him. "Don't tell me about the Thennet," he said. "I know about them and what they do. Tell me when they took your daughter and whatever else you know about where they took her."

"Out past the old tombs. A good fifty or sixty versts from here. Beyond the Yellow Canal. I paid a breed to follow them. That's as far as he got. He said the trail went on, but he wasn't going any farther. I got the same from all of them. They won't follow the Thennet into the Aghroniagh Hills. Then I heard you had just come down from Earth." He made some effort at ordinary social conversation. His eyes remained crazed. "What's it like back there now?"

"This is better," said Captain John MacShard. "So they went into the Aghroniagh Hills? When?"

"Some two days ago . . ."

Captain John MacShard turned away with a shrug.

"I know," said the merchant. "But this was different. They weren't going to eat her or—or—play with her . . ." His skin crawled visibly. "They were careful not to mark her. It was as if she was for someone else. Maybe a big slaver? They wouldn't let any of their saliva drip on her. They got me, though." He extended the twisted branch of burned flesh that had been his forearm.

Captain John MacShard drew a deep breath and began to take off his boots. "How much?"

"Everything. Anything."

"You'll owe me a million hard *deens* if I bring her back alive. I won't guarantee her sanity."

"You'll have the money. I promise. Her name's Mercedes. She's sweet and decent—the only good thing I ever helped create. She was staying with me . . . the vacation . . . her mother and I . . ."

Captain John MacShard moved toward his board bed. "Half in the morning. Give me a little time to put the money in a safe place. Then I'll leave. But not before."

After Morricone had shuffled away, his footsteps growing softer and softer until they faded into the general music of the rowdy street outside, Captain John Mac-Shard began to laugh.

It wasn't a laugh you ever wanted to hear again.

CHAPTER THREE

THE UNPROMISED LAND

The Aghroniagh Hills had been formed by a huge asteroid crashing into the area a few million years earlier, but the wide sweep of meadowland and streams surrounding them had never been successfully settled by Captain John MacShard's people. They were far from what they seemed.

Many settlers had come in the early days, attracted by the water and the grass. Few lasted a month, let alone a season. That water and grass existed on Mars because of Blake, the terraplaner. He had made it his life's work, crossing and recrossing one set of disparate genes with another until he had something which was like grass and like water and which could survive, maybe even thrive and proliferate, in Mars' barren climate. A sort of liquid algae and a kind of lichen, at root, but with so many genetic modifications that its mathematical pedigree filled a book.

Blake's great atmosphere pumping stations had transformed the Martian air and made it rich enough for Earthlings to breathe. He had meant to turn the whole of Mars into the same lush farmland he had seen turn to dust on Earth. Some believed he had grown too ambitious, that instead of doing God's work, he was beginning to believe he, himself, was God. He had planned a city called New Jerusalem and had designed its buildings, its parks, streams, and ornamental lakes. He had planted his experimental fields and brought his first pioneer volunteers and given them seed he had made and fertilizer he had designed, and something had happened under the unshielded Martian sunlight which had not happened in his laboratories.

Blake's Eden became worse than Purgatory.

His green shoots and laughing fountains developed a kind of intelligence, a taste for specific nutrients, a means of finding them and processing them to make them edible. Those nutrients were most commonly found in Earthlings. The food could be enticed the way an anemone entices an insect. The prey saw sweet water, green grass and it was only too glad to fling itself deep into the greedy shoots, the thirsty liquid, which was only too glad to digest it.

And so fathers had watched their children die before their eyes, killed and absorbed in moments. Women had seen hard-working husbands die before becoming food themselves.

Blake's seven pioneer families lasted a year and there had been others since who brought certain means of defeating the so-called Paradise virus, who challenged the hungry grass and liquid, who planned to tame it. One by one, they went to feed what had been intended to feed them.

There were ways of surviving the Paradise. Captain John MacShard had tried them and tested them. For a while he had specialized in finding artifacts which the settlers had left behind, letters, deeds, cherished jewelry.

He had learned how to live, for short periods at least, in the Paradise. He had kept raising his price until it got too high for anybody.

Then he quit. It was the way he put an end to his own boredom. What he did with all his money nobody knew, but he didn't spend it on himself.

The only money Captain John MacShard was known to exchange in large quantities was for modifications and repairs to that ship of his, as alien as his sidearm, which he'd picked up in the Rings and claimed by right of salvage. Even the scrap merchants hadn't wanted the ship. The metal it was made of could become poisonous to the touch. Like the weapon, the ship didn't allow everyone to handle her.

Captain John MacShard paid a halfling phunt-renter to drive him to the edge of the Paradise, and he promised the sweating driver the price of his phunt if he'd wait for news of his reappearance and come take him back to the city. "And any other passenger I might have with me," he had added.

The *phunter* was almost beside himself with anxiety. He knew exactly what that green sentient weed could do, and he had heard tales of how the streams had chased a man halfway back to the Low City and consumed him on the spot. *Drank him, they said.* No sane creature, Earthling or Martian, would risk the dangers of the Paradise.

Not only was the very landscape dangerous, there were also the Thennet.

The Thennet, whose life-stuff was unpalatable to the Paradise, came and went comfortably all year round, emerging only occasionally to make raids on the human settlements, certain that no posse would ever dare follow them back to their city of tunnels, Kong Gresh, deep at the center of the Aghroniagh Crater, which lay at the center of the Aghroniagh Hills, where the weed did not grow and the streams did not flow.

They raided for pleasure, the Thennet. Mostly, when they craved a delicacy. Human flesh was almost an addiction to them, they desired it so much. They were a cruel people and took pleasure in their captives, keeping them alive for many weeks sometimes, especially if they were young women. But they savored this killing. Schomberg had put it graphically enough once: *The longer the torment, the sweeter the meat.* His customers wondered how he understood such minds.

Captain John MacShard knew Mercedes Morricone had a chance at life. He hoped, when he found her, that she would still want that chance.

What had Morricone said about the Thennet not wishing to mark her? That they were capturing her for someone else?

Who?

Captain John MacShard wanted to find out for himself. No one had needed to pay the Thennet for young girls in years. The wars among the planets had given the streets plenty of good-looking women to choose from. Nobody ever noticed a few missing from time to time.

If the Thennet were planning to sell her for the food they would need for the coming Long Winter, they would be careful to keep their goods in top quality, and Mercedes could well be a specific target. The odds were she was still alive and safe. That was why Captain John MacShard did not think he was wasting his time.

And it was the only reason he would go this far into the Aghroniaghs, where the Thennet weren't the greatest danger.

CHAPTER FOUR

HELL UNDER THE HILL

It was hard to believe the Thennet had ever been human, but there was no doubt they spoke a crude form of English. They were said to be degenerated descendants of a crashed Earth ship which had left Houston a couple of centuries before, carrying a political investigative committee looking into reports that Earth mining interests were using local labor as slaves. The reports had been right. The mining interests had made sure the distinguished senators never got to see the evidence.

Captain John MacShard was wearing his own power armor. It buzzed on his body from soles to crown. The silky energy, soft as a child's hand, rippled around him like an atmosphere. He flickered and buzzed with complex circuitry outlining his veins and arteries, following the course of his blood. This medley of soft sounds was given a crazy rhythm by the ticking of his antigrav's notoriously dangerous regulators as he flew an inch above the hungry, whispering grass, the lush and luring streams of Paradise.

Only once did he come down, in the ruins of what was to have been the city of New Jerusalem and where the grass did not grow.

Here he ran at a loping pace which moved him faster over the landscape and at the same time recharged the antigrav's short-lived power units.

He was totally enclosed in the battlesuit of his own design, his visible skin a strange arsenical green behind the overlapping energy shields, his artificial gills processing the atmosphere to purify maximum oxygen. Around him as he moved was an unstable aura buzzing with gold and misty greens skipping and sizzling as elements in his armor mixed and reacted with particles of semi-artificial Martian air, fusing them into toxic fumes which would kill a man if taken straight. Which is why Captain John MacShard wore his helmet. It most closely resembled the head of an ornamental dolphin, all sweeping flukes and baroque symmetry, the complicated, delicate wiring visible through the thin plasdex skin, while the macro-engineered plant curving from between his shoulder blades looked almost like wings. He could have been one of the forgotten beasts of the Eldren which they had ridden against Bast-Na-Gir when the first mythologies of Mars were being made. The transparent steel visor plate added to this alien appearance, enlarging and giving exaggerated curve to his eyes. He had become an unlikely creature whose outline would momentarily baffle any casual observer. There were things out here which fed off Thennet and human alike. Captain John MacShard only needed a second's edge to survive. But that second was crucial.

He was in the air again, his batteries at maximum charge. He was now a shimmering copper angel speeding over the thirsty grass and the hungry rivers of Paradise until he was at last standing on the shale slopes of the Aghroniagh Mountains.

The range was essentially the rim of a huge steep-sided crater. At the crater's center were peculiar pockets of gases which were the by-product of certain rock dust interacting with sunlight. These gases formed a breeding and sleeping environment for the Thennet, who could only survive so long away from what the first Earth explorers had called their "clouds." Most of the gas, which had a narcotic effect on humans, was drawn down into their burrows by an ingenious system of vents and manually operated fans. It was the only machinery they used. Otherwise they were primitive enough, though inventive murderers who delighted in the slow, perverse death of anything that lived, including their own sick and wounded. Suicide was the commonest cause of death.

As Captain John MacShard raced through the crags and eventually came to the crater walls, he knew he might have a few hours left in which to save the girl. The Thennet had a way of letting the gases work on their human victims so that they became light-headed and cheerful. The Thennet knew how to amuse humans.

Sometimes they would let the human feel this way for days, until they began to get too sluggish.

Then they would do something which produced a sudden rush of adrenaline in their victim. And thereafter it was unimaginable nightmare. Unimaginable because no human mind could conceive of such tortures and hold the memory or its sanity. No mind, that is, except Captain John MacShard's. And it was questionable now that Captain John MacShard's mind was still in most senses human.

Here's where I was too late. There's her bone and necklace again. That's the burrow into middle chamber. Gas goes low there. All these thoughts passed through his head as he retraced steps over razor rocks and unstable shale. He had been paid four times to venture into Thennet territory. Twice he had successfully brought out living victims, both still relatively sane. Once he had brought out a corpse. Once he had left a corpse where he found it. Seven times before that, curiosity had taken him there. The time they captured him, his chances of escape had been minimal. He was determined not to be captured again.

Now, however, there was something different about the sinister, smoking landscape of craters and spikes. There was a kind of silence Captain John MacShard couldn't explain. A sense of waiting. A sense of watching.

Unable to do anything but ignore the instinct, he dropped down into the fissures and began to feel his way into the first flinty corridors. He had killed five Thennet guards almost without thought by the time he had begun to descend the great main passage into the Thennet underworld. He always killed Thennet at a distance, if he could. Their venom could sear into delicate circuitry and destroy his armor and his lifelines.

Three more Thennet fell without knowing they were dead. Captain John Mac-Shard felt no hesitation about killing them wherever he came across one. He killed them on principle, the way they killed by habit. The less of the Thennet there were, the better for everyone. And each corpse offered something useful to him as he crept on downward into the subsidiary tunnels, following still familiar routes.

The walls of the caverns were thick with flaking blood and ordure, which the Thennet used for building materials. Mostly it had hardened, but every so often it became soft and slippery. Captain John MacShard had to adjust his step, glad of his gills as well as his armor, which meant he did not have to smell or touch any of the glistening stuff, though every so often his air system overloaded and he got just a hint of the disgusting stench.

But something was wrong. His armor began to pop and tremble. It was a warning. Captain John MacShard paused in the slippery passage and considered withdrawing. There would normally be more Thennet, males and females, shuffling through the passages, going about their business, tending their eggs, tormenting their food.

He had a depressing feeling that he couldn't easily get back, that he was already in a trap. Was it a trap which had been set for him specifically? Or could anyone be the prey? This wasn't the Thennet. Could it be the Thennet had new leadership and wider goals? Captain John MacShard could smell intelligence. This was intelligence. And it wasn't a kind he'd smelled before. Not in Thennet territory. Mostly what you smelled was terror and ghastly glee.

There was something else down here. Something which had a personality. Something which had ambitions. Something which was even now gathering power.

Captain John MacShard had learned to trust his instincts and his instincts told him he would have to fight to return to the surface. What was more, he had an un-pleasant feeling about what he might have to fight. . . .

His best chance was to pretend he had noticed nothing, but keep his attention on that intelligence, even as he sought out the merchant's daughter. What was her name? Mercedes?

The narrow, fetid tunnels of the Thennet city were familiar, but now they were opening up, growing wider and taller, as if the Thennet had been working on them. But why?

And then, suddenly, a wave of thought struck against his own mind—a wave which boomed with the force of a tidal wave. It almost stopped him moving forward. It was a moment before the sense of the thoughts began to filter in to him.

No longer. No longer. I am the one. And I am more than one. I am Shienna Sha Shanakana of the Yellow Price, and I shall again become the goddess I once was when Mars was young. I have paid the Yellow Price. I claim this star system as my own. And then I shall claim the universe. . . .

The girl? Captain John MacShard could not stop the question.

All he received was a wave of mockery which again struck, with an almost phys-ical weight.

CHAPTER FIVE

ANCIENT AND MODERN

A voice began to whisper through the serpentine tunnels. It was cold as space, hard and sharp as Mercurian steel.

The female Mercedes is gone. She is gone, Earther. There is nothing of her, save this flesh, and I am already changing the flesh so that it is more to my taste. She'll produce the egg. First the body, then the entire planet. Then the system. Then the stars. We shall thrive again. We shall feast at will among the Galaxies.

So that was it! Yet another of Mars' ancient ghosts trying to regain its former power. These creatures had been killed, banished, imprisoned long ago, during the last of Mars' terrible wars.

They had reached an enormous level of intellectual power, ruling the planet and influencing the whole system as they became capable of flinging their mental energy through interplanetary space, to control distant intelligences and rule through them.

They considered themselves to be gods, though they were mortal enough in many respects. It had been their arrogance which had brought them low.

So abstract and strange had become their ambitions that they had forgotten the ordinary humans, those who had chosen not to follow their bizarre path, whose lives became wretched as the Eldren used all the planet's resources to increase their pow-ers. They had grown obsessed with immortality, recording themselves onto extraordi-nary pieces of jewelry containing everything needed to reconstitute the entire individual. Everything but ordinary humans to place the jewels in their special set-tings and begin the process, which required considerable human resources, ultimately taking the lives of all involved. For most of the ordinary humans had died of starva-tion and dehydration as those powers plundered their planet of all resources, melting the poles so that first there was an abundance of water, the time of the beginnings of the Sea Kings' power, but then, as quickly, the evaporation had begun, dissipating into empty space, no longer contained by the protective layers of ozone and oxygen. The water could not come back. It was a momentary shimmer in the vastness of space as it was drawn inevitably toward the sun.

Captain John MacShard knew all this because his mother had known all this. He had not know his mother, had not known he had emerged, a brawling, bawling independent creature from the egg she had saved, even as she and her husband died, victims of the planet's unforgiving climate. He had not known how he had come to live among the aboriginal ape people. The fiercely tribal Mercurians had been fascinated by his tanned, pale hide, so unlike their own dark green skins. They had never thought him anything but one of themselves. They had come to value him. He had been elected a kind of leader. He had taken them to food and guarded them against the giant rock snakes. He had taught them to kill the snakes, to preserve their meat. They named him Tan-Arz or Brown-Skin.

Tan-Arz was his name until the Earthlings found him at last. His father's brother had paid for the search, paid to bring him back to Earth during that brief Golden Age before the planet again descended into civil war. Back to the Old Country. Back to Ireland. Back to Dublin and Trinity College. Then to South London University.

Dublin and London had not civilized Captain John MacShard, but they had taught him the manners and ways of a gentleman. They had not educated Captain John MacShard, but they had informed his experience. Now he understood his enemies as well as his friends. And he understood that the law of the giant corporations was identical to the law he had learned on Mercury.

Kill or be killed. Trust nothing and no one. Power is survival. He smelled them. He was contemptuous of most of them, though they commanded millions. They were his kind. They were his kind gone soft, obscenely greedy, decadent to the marrow.

His instinct was to wipe them out, but they had trained him to serve them. And he had served them. At first, when the wars had begun, he had volunteered. He had served well and honorably, but as the wars got dirtier and the issues less clear, he found himself withdrawing.

He realized that he had more sympathy, most of the time, with the desperate men he was fighting than with the great patricians of Republican Earth.

His refusal to take part in a particularly bloody operation had caused him to be branded a traitor.

It was as an outlaw he had arrived on Mars. They had hunted him into the red wastelands and known he could not have lived.

But Mars was a rest cure compared to Mercury. Captain John MacShard had survived. And Captain John MacShard had prospered.

Now he captained his own ship, the gloriously alien *Duchess of Malfi*, murmuring and baroque in her perpetually shifting darkness. Now he could pick and choose whom he killed and whom he didn't kill.

He had no financial need to continue this dangerous life, no particular security to be derived, even the security of familiarity. Nothing to escape from. Nothing within him he could not confront. He did it because he was who he was.

He was Captain John MacShard and Captain John MacShard was a creature of action, a creature which only came fully alive when its own life was in the balance. A wild creature that longed for the harsh, savage places of the universe, their beauties and their dangers.

But Captain John MacShard had no wish to die here in the slimey burrows of the unhuman Thennet. He had no desire to serve the insane ends of the old Martian godlings who saw their immortality slowly fading and longed for all their power again.

You, Captain John MacShard, will help me. And I will reward you. Before you die, I will make you the sire of the supernatural. Already the blood of my Martians mingles with your own. It is why you are so perfect for my plans.

John MacShard: You are no longer the Earthboy who grew up wild with the submen of Mercury. You are of our own blood, for your mother drew her descent directly from the greatest of the Sea Kings and the Sea Kings were our own children—so much of our blood has mingled with yours that you are now almost one of us.

Let your blood bring you home, John MacShard.

"My blood is my own! It belongs to nobody but me! Every atom has been fought for and won."

It is the blood of gods and goddesses, John MacShard. Of kings and queens.

"Then it's still mine. By right of inheritance!" John MacShard was all aggression now, though the voices speaking to him were patient, reasonable. He had heard similar voices before. As he lay writhing in his own filthy juices on one of the Old Ones' examining slabs.

It is your Earth blood, however, which will give us our glory back. That vital, sturdy, undiluted stuff will bring us back our power and make Mars know her old fear of the unhumans who ruled her before the Sea Kings ruled.

Welcome home, Captain John MacShard, last of the Sea Kings. Welcome home to the Palace of Queen Shienna Sha Shanakana, Seventh of the Seven Sisters who guard the Shrine of the Star Pool, Seventh of the Seven Snakes, Sorceress of the Citadel of Silence where she has slept for too many centuries.

The little mortal did its job well, though unconsciously. I needed its daughter's womb and I needed you, John MacShard. And now I have both. I will reemerge from the great egg fully restored to my power and position.

Behold, Captain John MacShard! The Secrets of the Silent Citadel!

CHAPTER SIX

QUEEN OF THE CRYSTAL CITADEL

All at once the half-Martian was surrounded by crystal. Crystal colored like rainbows, flashing and murmuring in a cold wind that blew from all directions toward the center where a golden woman sat, smiling at him, beckoning to him, and driving all thought momentarily from his mind as he began to stumble forward. He wanted nothing else in the world but to mate with her. He would die, if necessary, to perform that function.

It took Captain John MacShard a few long seconds to bring himself back under control. Faces formed within the crystal towers. Familiar faces. The faces of friends and enemies who welcomed Captain John MacShard and bid him join them, in their good company, for eternity. These were the siren voices which had tempted Ulysses and his men across the void of space. Powerful intelligences trapped within indestructible crystal. Intelligences which, legend had it, could be freed by the stroke of a sacred sword held in the hand of one man.

Captain John MacShard shuddered. He had no such sword. Only his jittering Banning cannon in its heavy webbing. He laid his hand on the gun and seemed to draw reassurance from it.

His white wolf's teeth were clenched in his lean jaw. "No. I'm not your dupe and I'm not Earth's dupe. I'm my own man. I'm Captain John MacShard. There is no living individual more free than me in the universe and no one more ready to fight to keep that freedom."

Yes, murmured the voice in his head. It was a seductive voice. *Think of the power and therefore the freedom you have when we are combined . . . Power to do whatever you desire, to possess whatever you desire, to achieve whatever you desire. You will be reborn as Master of the Universe. The whole of existence will be yours, to satisfy your rarest appetites. . . .*

The voice was full of everything feminine. He could almost smell it. He could see the figure outlined at the center of the crystal palace. The lithe young body with its waves of golden hair, clad in gold, with golden threads cascading down her perfect thighs, with golden cups supporting her perfect breasts and golden sandals on her perfect feet. He could see her quite clearly, yet she seemed the length of a football field away. She was beckoning to him.

"All I want is the power to be free," said Captain John MacShard. "And I already have that. I got it long ago. Nobody gave it to me. I took it. I took it on Mercury. I took it on Earth. I took it on Mars, and I took it on Venus. Not a year goes by when I do not take that freedom again, because that is the only way you preserve the kind of freedom I value. My very marrow is freedom. Everything in me fights to maintain that freedom. It is unconscious and as enduring as the universe itself. I am not the only one to possess it or to know how to fight to keep it. It is the power of all the human heroes who overcame impossible odds that I carry in my blood. You cannot defeat that. Whatever you do, Shienna Sha Shanankana, you cannot defeat that."

She was laughing somewhere in his mind. That laughter coursed along his spine, over his buttocks, down his legs. It was directed. She was displaying the powers of her own incredible mentality.

Captain John MacShard examined the body of the girl he had come to rescue. Of course the Martian sorceress possessed her, probably totally. But was there anything of the girl left? It was crucial that he know.

He forced himself to push forward and thought he saw something like astonishment in the girl's eyes. Then another intelligence took control of her face and the eyes blazed with eager fury, as if the goddess had found a worthy match. There was an ancient knowledge in those eyes which, when they met Captain John MacShard's, saw its equal in experience.

But all Captain John MacShard cared about was that he had glimpsed human eyes, a human face. Somewhere, Mercedes Morricone still existed. That body which pulsed with strange, stolen life and glaring intelligence, still contained the girl's soul. That was what he had needed to know.

"Give the human its body back," said Captain John MacShard, switching to servos so that his arm whined up, automatically bringing the Banning cannon to bear on the golden goddess who now smiled at him with impossible promises. "Or I will destroy it and in so doing destroy you. I am Captain John MacShard, and you must know I have never made a threat I was not prepared to follow through."

You cannot destroy me with that, with a mere weapon. I draw my strength from all this— all these—from all my companions still imprisoned in the crystal. Ultimately, of course, I may release them. As they come to acknowledge that I am Mistress of the Silver Machine.

And now Captain John MacShard looked up. It was as if someone had tilted him by the chin. And above him stretched the vibrating wires and twisting ribbons of silver that told him the terrible truth. Inadvertently he had stepped into the core of one of the ancient Martian machines.

The sorceress had set a trap. And it had been a subtle trap, a trap which showed the mettle of his enemy.

The trap had used his own stupid pride against him.

He cursed himself for an idiot, but already he was inspecting the peculiar twists and loops of the machine, which seemed to come from nowhere and disappear into nothing. A funnel of silver energy was at the apex, high above.

Yet, perhaps most impressively, this silver citadel of science was absolutely silent.

Silent, save for the faintest whisper, like the hiss of a human voice, far away, the sweet, persuasive suggestions of this seductive sorceress slipping into his synapses, soothing his ever-wary soul, preparing him for the big sleep, the long good-bye. . . .

Everything that was savage. Everything that had made him fight to survive in the wastelands of Mercury. Everything that he had learned in the cold depths of space and the steamy seas of Venus. Everything he had been taught in the seminaries of Dublin and the academies of London. Everything came to Captain John MacShard's aid then. And there was a possibility that everything would not be enough.

The silent crystals around him began to vibrate, almost in triumph. And there, below the pulsing silver fire, the goddess danced.

He knew why Shienna Sha Shanakana danced and he tried desperately to take his eyes off her. He had never seen anything quite so beautiful. He had never desired a woman more. He felt something close to love.

With a strangled curse which peeled his lips back from his teeth, he took the Banning in both hands, his fingers playing across the weird lines and configurations of the casing as if he drew music from an instrument.

The goddess smiled but did not stop dancing. Neither did the crystals of her citadel stop dancing. Everything moved in delicate, subtle silence. Everything seduced him. If there had been music, he might have resisted more easily. But the music was somewhere in his head. There was a tune. It was taking charge of his arms and legs. Taking over his mind. Was he also dancing? Dancing with her in those strange, sinuous movements so reminiscent of the snakes which had pursued them on Mercury until he had become the hunter and turned them into food for himself and his tribe?

Oh, you are strong and resourceful and mighty and everything a hero should be. A true demigod to mate with a demigoddess and create a mighty god, a god who in turn will create entire new universes, an infinity of power. Look how beautiful you are, Captain John MacShard, what a perfect specimen of your kind.

A silver mirror appeared before him and he saw not what she described but the wild beast which had survived the deadly wastes of Mercury, the demonic creature who had slain the Green Emperor of Venus and wrested a planet from the grip of Grodon Worbn, the pious and vicious Robot Chancellor of Ganymede.

But the sweetness of her perfume, the sound of those golden, silky threads brushing against her skin, the rise and fall of her breasts, the promise in her eyes . . .

All this Captain John MacShard shook off, and he thought he saw a look of some astonishment, almost of admiration, in those alien orbs. His fingers would scarcely obey him, but they moved without thought, from pure habit, flicking across the Banning, touching it here, adjusting something there. An instrument made for aliens.

No human hand had ever been meant to operate the Banning, which was named not for its maker but for the first man who had died trying to find out how it worked. General Banning had prided himself on his expertise with alien artifacts. He had not died immediately, but from the poisons which had eaten into his skin and slowly digested his flesh. Captain John MacShard had never bothered to find out how the Banning worked. He simply knew how to work it. The way so many Spanish boys simply know how to coax the most beautiful music from the guitar.

The same intelligences, who Captain John MacShard believed to have perished out beyond Pluto, had also made his ship. There was a philosophy inherent to his ship, which rejected most who tried to board her vast, echoing interior, whose very emptiness was essential to her function, to her existence, and the weapon, and somehow Captain John MacShard understood the philosophy and loved the purity of the minds which had created it.

His respect was what had almost certainly saved his life more than once as he learned the properties and sublime beauty of the Banning and the ship.

He was panting. What had he been doing? Dancing? Before a mirror? The mirror was gone now. The goddess had stopped dancing. Indeed, she was leaning forward, fixing Captain John MacShard with strange eyes in which flecks of rainbow colors flashed and flared. The red lips parted to show white, even teeth. The young flesh glowed with inner desires, impossible promises . . .

Come, John MacShard. Come to me and fulfill your noble destiny.

Then Captain John MacShard was sweeping the Banning around him in an arc. He aimed at the crystals while the gun's impossible circuits and surfaces plated and replated in a blur of changes, from gold to copper to jade to silver to gold as the great gun seemed to expand under Captain John MacShard's urgent caresses. Yet nothing dramatic happened to the crystals. They darkened, but they did not break. The light went from glaring day to misty night.

A terrifying silence fell.

He swept the gun again. Still the crystal held. And whatever was within the crystal held, too. It was harder to see movement, perhaps because the inhabitants were protecting themselves. But the gun had done nothing.

The silence continued.

Then the golden girl laughed. Her laughter was the sweetest music in the universe.

Did you think, Captain John MacShard, your famous gun could conquer Shienna Sha Shanakana, Priestess of the Silent Citadel, Sorceress of the Seven Dials? The stupid Knights of the Balance who came against us from far Cygnus met their match. They planned to conquer us, but we killed them all, even before they reached the inner planets. . . .

He looked up. She was so much closer now. Her wonderful beauty loomed over him. He gasped. He refused to take a step back.

Those human lips were filled with the stored energy of ancient Mars as they smiled down at him. *Oh, yes, Captain John MacShard. You are not here by accident. I did not send the Thennet to take the girl until I knew you were about to land at Old Mars Station. And it was I who let the father know you were the only creature alive that could find his daughter. And you did find her, didn't you? You found me. You found Shienna Sha Shanakana who has been dust, who has not known this desire for uncountable millennia, who has not felt such need, such joyous lust. . . .*

Now Captain John MacShard took that backward step, the great Banning cannon loose on its webbing, swinging as his hands sought something in his clothing. Now his fists were clenched at his sides.

The goddess licked her sublime lips.

Is that sweat I see on your manly brow, Captain John MacShard? A hand reached out and whisked lightly across his forehead. He felt as if a flaming knife had been drawn through his flesh. Yet he would have given his whole life to experience that touch again.

He tasted a tongue that was not a human tongue. It licked at his flesh. It reveled in his smell, the feel of his hard, muscular body, the racing blood, the pounding heart, the sight of his perfect manhood. He was everything humans or Martians could be; everything the female might desire in a male.

Her touch yielded to him, offered him a power he knew she would never really give up. He had enjoyed the most expert seductresses, but this creature brought the experience of centuries, the instincts of her stolen body, the cravings of a female which had not known any kind of feeling, only a burning ambition, for longer than most of Earth's greatest civilizations had come and gone. And those cravings were centered on Captain John MacShard.

You will sire the new Martian race, she promised, as she moved her golden breastplates against his naked chest. *You will die knowing that you have fulfilled your greatest possible destiny.*

And Captain John MacShard believed her. He believed her to the depths of his being. He wanted nothing else. Nothing but to serve her in any way she demanded. The gun hung forgotten at his side. He reached out his arms to receive from her whatever she desired to give, to give to her whatever she needed to take. It was true. He was hers. Hers to use and then to bind so that later his own son might feed upon his holy flesh and become him. That was his destiny. The eternal life which lay before him.

But first, she whispered, *you must entertain me.*

Then he suddenly knew the son must be sired, the remains of the humans driven from the bodies and the blood mingled in the painful and protracted mating rituals of those first Martians.

She moved to enfold him in that final, lethal embrace.

CHAPTER SEVEN

THE POISONED CHALICE

They came upon the Earthling naked, somewhere in the Shifting Desert, almost a hundred *versts* from the Aghroniagh Hills. He had no armor, no weapons. His skin hung like filthy rags on his bloody, blistered flesh. Both his legs had long, deep red lines running from thigh to heel, as if a white-hot sword blade had been placed on the limbs. He could see, but his eyes were turned inward. He was mumbling to himself. There was foam on his mangled lips. He was raving, seemingly empty of identity and will, and the noises that came occasionally from deep in his chest were the sounds a wild beast might make. At other times, he seemed amused.

The patrol which found him had been looking for Venusian *chuff* runners and couldn't believe anything lived in his condition. They were superstitious fellows. They thought at first he was a ghost. Then they decided he had fallen among ghosts, within the influence of those mythical Martians frozen in jewels and dreaming deep within the planet. Some of the customs people had seen Earthling explorers who had returned from expeditions in a state not much better than this.

But then one of the patrol recognized Captain John MacShard and they knew that whatever enemy he had met out here, it must have been a powerful one. They identified the long scars down his legs and on his hands as burns from Thennet venom. But how had they gotten there? The marks did not look typical of Thennet torture.

They began to take him back to Old Mars Station where there was a doctor, but he roused himself, gathered his senses and pointed urgently toward the Aghroniaghs. It seemed he had a companion.

They had gone seventy *versts* before their instruments detected a human figure lying in the shade of a rock, a small bottle nearby. Indications were that the figure was barely alive.

Captain John MacShard sank back into the craft as soon as he saw Mercedes Morricone. He let go. He allowed oblivion at last to overcome him.

He would never deliberately recall and would never tell anyone what Shienna Sha Shanakana, Sorceress of the Silent Citadel, had made him do, as she took hold of his mind. He would never admit what he had allowed her to do in order to ensure the success of a desperate, maybe suicidal, plan.

She knew she could not fully control him and it had whetted her curiosity, made her test her powers in ways she had never expected to test them. She fed off him. She tasted at his brain the way a wealthy woman might take a delicate bite of a chocolate to see if it suited her. Some of what she took from him she discarded as so much waste. Memories. Affections. Pride.

But then she had become puzzled. Her own power seemed to ebb and flow. He was naked, and he had torn his own flesh for her amusement, had capered and drooled for her amusement. John MacShard was no longer a thinking being. She had sucked him dry of everything she herself lacked. Dry of everything human.

Or so it had seemed . . .

For Captain John MacShard had learned all he had needed to learn from the veteran priest he had talked to in Old City before he left. He had kept some of his wits by tapping the venom from the Thennet he had killed, keeping it in crushable vials until the moment came when he needed that level of pain to keep his mind from the likes of Shienna Sha Shananaka's seductions. It had been her embrace that had seared them both. But he intended to reverse her spell. He had reversed the path of most of the energy she had been drawing from her compatriots in their crystal prisons. He had absorbed it in the gun.

For the gun didn't merely expel energy, it also attracted energy. It processed its own power from the planet's energy, wherever that energy was to be found. The blood and soul she had sucked from him was still under his control. He had let her draw him in, let her take his very soul, somehow keeping his own consciousness as he was absorbed into her, somehow linking with that other terrified fragment of soul-mind that was the girl to whom he was able to give strength, a chance at life.

Somewhere in that ruined, apparently lunatic skull, there was a battle still taking place, through the twists and turns of an alien space and time—a battle for control of a human creature that had perished so that a goddess might survive. It was not only Captain John MacShard's vigorous blood she had sucked, nor his diamond-hard mind, but his will. A will which, ironically, she could not control. A will strong enough to take possession of a demigoddess.

Captain John MacShard was still there. Actually inside her. Actually working to destroy her. There had never been an individual more ruggedly determined to maintain its identity against all odds. He had summoned everything he possessed as she embraced him and had broken the vials containing the venom he had gathered from the Thennet. The venom burned his body as well as hers. The girl's body became useless to her. She began to remove herself from it. And Captain John MacShard, the skin of his hands and legs bubbling as the venom ate into them, kept his will directed to his goal.

She had been astonished to discover a mind as powerful as her own—as thoroughly trained as her own in the Martian forms of mental control and countercontrol which Earthers had nicknamed "brain-brawling" and which more subtle observers knew as a combination of mental fencing and mental chess whose outcome could annihilate the defeated.

But the searing venom kept his mind free enough from her dominance and ultimately allowed him to break from her embrace. She had advanced on him, a roaring, shouting thing of raw energy, the ruined human body abandoned.

Then Captain John MacShard forced himself toward his fallen Banning cannon. The gun lay in a heap of clothing and circuitry which he had stripped from his own body before beginning to strip the flesh as she had demanded.

But all the while his iron will had kept the crucial parts of himself free. Now he had the gun in his hands and the golden whirlwind that was the true form of Shienna Sha Shanakana, Sorceress of the Silent Citadel, was advancing toward him, triumphant in the knowledge that the gun had already failed to break the crystal coffins in which her kinfolk were still imprisoned.

But Captain John MacShard knew more about the people who had made the Banning than she did. Her folk had merely killed them. Captain John MacShard had examined the culture they had left behind in their great, empty ship. Captain John MacShard had a human quality which the ancient Martians, for all their powers, always lacked and which would always undo them. They had no curiosity about those they fed upon. Captain John MacShard had the curiosity of the Venusian saber-tooth whose reactions matched his own. He had learned so much from *The Duchess of Malfi*.

He had never meant to destroy the crystal tombs with his gun. That would have released even more of the greedy immortals from their already fragile captivity. Instead he had used the gun's powering devices, the cells which sucked in energy of cosmic proportions, which in turn powered the gun when it was needed. The instrument in his hands could contain the raw power of an entire universe—and expel that same power wherever it was directed.

The gun hadn't failed to break the crystals, but it had absorbed their enormous energy.

It had gathered the power of the silent crystals into the gun so that the Sorceress could no longer call upon it. Her energy, uncontained, began to dissipate. She began to return to the body of the girl. But she had reckoned without the power of the Banning cannon.

She was held in balance between her own desperate lust for flesh and the relentless draw of the Banning.

MacShard's last act had been to take the girl's apparently lifeless body and carry it through the winding, filthy tunnels of the Thennet, who had all long since fled, and somehow get her up to the surface as a goddess shrilled and boomed in the crystal chamber. The whole planet seemed to shake with her frustrated attempts to draw more strength from her imprisoned brothers and sisters.

She was outraged. Not because she knew she might actually die, but because a puny little halfling threatened to best her. She could not bear the humiliation.

He saw an intense ball of light pursue him for a few moments and then become a face. Not the face he had seen before but a face at once hideous and obscenely beautiful. She was being dragged down to him, down to where the alien gun sucked at her very soul. Then she stopped resisting it. She might have lived on, as she had lived for millennia, but she chose oblivion. She let go of her consciousness. Only her energy remained in the gun's energy cells. But Captain John MacShard would never be sure.

Nothing but natural hazards blocked his progress to the top. At last he was stretched, gasping on the thin, sour air, staring upward.

Suddenly a sad wind began to stretch a curtain of dark blue across the sky. It seemed for a moment that Mars lived again, lived when the seas washed her wealthy, mysterious beaches.

At the surface, Captain John MacShard realized he would have to leave the Banning behind if he was to get the girl to safety. He must risk it. It had enough charge to do extraordinary damage. If mishandled, it would not only destroy any living thing within a hundred yards, it would probably destroy a good-sized portion of the planet or worse. He suspected that it was as safe from the Thennet as it was from the Sorceress of the Silent Citadel. He hoped to cross the Paradise before he smelled human again.

It had not been until the following night that he had stopped. The girl was just conscious, a shoulder and leg raw from Thennet venom, though her face, by a miracle, had not been touched. He had left her what little water he had brought and had stumbled on. He had been walking toward the Old City when the customs patrol found him.

The port doctors shook their heads. They could see no hope of saving him. But then Morricone stepped in. He flew Captain John MacShard to Phobos and the famous Clinique AI Rhabia, where his daughter was already recovering. They had worked on him. A billion *deen* had been spent on him, and they had saved him.

And in saving Captain John MacShard they instilled the germ of a new kind of anger, a profound understanding of the injustice which could let crippled boys beg in the Martian dust but fly the privileged to Phobos and the finest new medicine science could create.

He wasn't ungrateful to Morricone. Morricone had kept his bargain, paid the price and better. He didn't blame Morricone for his failure to understand, for not having the imagination to see that for every hero's life he saved, there were millions of ordinary people who would never be given the chance to be heroes.

They found his gun for him. Nobody dared handle it, but they picked it out of a dune with their waldos and brought it to him in a sealed canister.

Captain John MacShard saw Mercedes Morricone a couple of times after he left the Clinique and was waiting for his ship to be recircuited according to his new instructions. Plastic surgery had rid her of most of the scars. She was more than grateful to him. She knew him in a way no woman had ever known him before. And she loved him. She couldn't help herself. She understood Captain John MacShard had nothing to offer her now that he had given her back her life.

Yet maybe there was something. A clear feeling of affection, almost a father's love for a daughter. He realized, to his own surprise, that he cared about her. He even let her come along when he took the kid aboard *The Duchess of Malfi* and showed him the wild, semistable gases and gemstones which were her controls. He wanted the boy to remember that the ship could be understood and handled. And Mercedes had fallen in love all over again, for the ship had a beauty that was unique.

Pretending to joke, she said they could be a hardy little pioneer family, the three of them, setting off for the worlds beyond the stars. How marvelous it would be to stand at his side as he took the alien ship into the echoing corridors of the multiverse, following fault lines created in the impossibly remote past through the infinitely layered realities of intraspatial matter. How marvelous it would be to see the sights that he would see.

He was loading the heavy canister down into a cradle he'd made for it and which fitted beside his compression bed. He had commissioned himself a new power suit. It rippled against his body, outlining muscles and sinews as he moved gracefully to his familiar tasks, checking screens and globes, columns of glittering force.

The boy was content to look, wide-eyed. And maybe he understood. Maybe he just pretended.

And maybe Captain John MacShard pretended not to understand her when she spoke of that impossible future. He didn't tell her what you had to become to steer *The Duchess* through time and space. What you must cease to be. What you must learn never to desire, never to think about.

He was gentle when he escorted her home from the spaceport, took her and the boy to her father's big front door, kissed her cheek, and bade her good-bye for the last time.

She held the boy's hand tight. He was her link to her dream. He might even become her best dream. She was going to get him educated, she said, as best you could these days.

The girl and the boy watched Captain John MacShard leave.

His perfect body was suddenly outlined against the huge, scarlet sun as it settled on the Martian horizon. Ribbons of red dust danced around his feet as he strode back up the drive of her father's mansion, between the artificial cedars and the holograph fountains. He walked to the gates, seemed about to turn, changed his mind, and was gone.

The girl and the boy were standing there again in the morning at Old Mars Station as *The Duchess* blasted off en route for the new worlds beyond Pluto where Captain John MacShard thought he might find what he was looking for.

He had gained something more than the cosmic power which resided in his gun. He now knew what love—ordinary, decent, celebratory human love—was. He had felt it. He still felt it.

The ship was cruising smoothly, her own intelligence taking over. He turned away from his instruments and poured himself a much-needed shot of Vortex Water.

Staring up at the great tapestry of stars, thinking about all the worlds and races which must inhabit them, Captain John MacShard turned away from his instruments.

Like the wild creature that he was, he shook off the dust and the horror and the memory of love.

By the time his alien ship was passing Jupiter, Captain John MacShard was his old self again. He patted the gun in its special case; his Banning was now powered by the life-stuff of the gods.

Soon he could start hunting the really big game.

The interstellar game.

MICHAEL KANDEL

Michael Kandel [1941–] is a distinguished writer, editor, and translator (from Polish to English—he was nominated for a literary award for one of his translations of Stanislaw Lem's novels). He was the SF editor for years at Harcourt (formerly Harcourt, Brace, Jovanovich) and now works for the Modern Language Association. He is the author of three SF novels, *In Between Dragons* (1990), *Captain Jack Zodiac* (1991), and *Panda Ray* (1996), as well as a number of short stories. He doesn't write space opera. He is, in fact, just the sort of SF writer who perceives the odors of contempt and literary class prejudice that still hang in the social air when the term *space opera* is used in literary circles, and leaves the room. So he is the most appropriate writer to include as a parodist in the 1990s. This parody reinforces the idea that space opera still retained a pejorative connotation at least through the early 1990s, and perhaps still does.

"Space Opera" is a parody of opera and of the SF subgenre all at once. There is, of course, one monument of twentieth-century opera, *Aniara*, based on Harry Martinson's SF epic poem about space travel. So what better way to literalize the locution as a literary joke, to poke fun at the absurdities of opera and of space opera? Here it is, all five acts summarized, with commentary.

SPACE OPERA

M I C H A E L   K A N D E L

for Terry Bisson, champion of science fiction

ACT 1

The curtain opens to a workshop in Vuffon, a spaceport in the Dalminian Empire, sun Alpha Cygni, planet Creeth. Bobby "Rocket" DeVries and his fellow grease apes are hammering out the dents in the hull of an old cruiser. They sing as they work, "Let's return this old bucket to the stars," to the syncopation of their hammer blows, which are rendered by the trombones and tympani in humorous five-against-six time reminiscent of the shawm concerti of Friedrich Windburn.

There is in fact a musical as well as philosophical polemic with Windburn throughout this opera. The composer had studied with Windburn when the composer was a raw youth in Frankfurt am Main, before the old master went mad and joined the notorious ashram in Madripore, where Sebastian Karlinsky, incidentally, also ended his days. Biographer Hiram Buck's account of this period in Harold Davidson's life is interesting but quite unreliable. We must not forget that Buck has an ax to grind, since Davidson had "stolen," he always believed, both Buck's second wife and the much coveted position of executive conductor at the Greenwich Conservatory (for which Buck had never really been a contender).

Fred runs in with the news that Darg Bhar, Governor of the United Asteroids, is coming to Vuffon. The grease apes cheer, for this will mean work: Bhar has a great fleet of ships, and everyone knows that vessels that ply the old spaceways among the asteroid belts of Koe are constantly receiving dents from collisions with stray bits of rock, ice, and discarded electronic components. Petro, Bobby's friend, jokes: now Petro will have enough money to marry Miranda. Everyone laughs, knowing that Petro has already been rejected more than a dozen times by Miranda, the proud daughter of Corporal Biggs. Petro sings an air: "You are ugly and you are poor, she told him. Where do you get the nerve to ask me for my hand?" The grease apes decide to celebrate at Harry's, the homey ale-and-pot establishment in Vuffon. Bobby, strangely silent, does not join his cohorts as they go off singing. He tells them he has a headache from the noise of the hammers.

When his cohorts leave and as the stage darkens, he sings the haunting, plaintive aria, "Oh Bea, what will become of you?" We learn that Bobby's younger sister, Bea, is in danger of falling into the clutches of Darg Bhar. "She's a young thing," Bobby sings, "and has not even been implanted yet." The evil and lascivious Bhar wants to get at Bea's DNA and make her his slave forever. Bhar conceived a dark lust for Bobby's kid sister ever since he beheld her at the annual Saint Camilla song competition, when she was all in tulle and lilies. Bea is lovely, slender, and has an exquisite voice. Bobby fears for her. In a bold dreaming-while-awake sequence, a device that Davidson first employed in The Butcher's Paramour, and very much in the face of the New York critics, Bea appears to Bobby and sings, "I'll manage on my own. Stop crowding me." Darg Bhar appears too, and he is accompanied by Leila Ziff-Calder, who has been recently cast off by Bhar and thirsts for revenge. It is instructive to see how Davidson cuts the Gordian knot of narrative, as it were, presenting so much of the plot to us with such direct economy by means of this dreaming-while-awake device, for in the alternating duet that follows—Bobby and Bea, Bhar and Leila—we are given the basic structure of the conflict to come. "I'm only thirty," Leila sings. "I'm not that old. I have pleasure yet to give and to take." Bhar, ignoring her, sings, "I'm wicked, but I don't care. Why should I? There's no afterlife." Bobby sings: "He's no good, Sis, he's no damn good. Trust me on this." Bea sings: "Get out of my face, Bobby. It's my life." All four voices join, and the DNA leitmotif (foreshadowing the genetic-engineering horror in Act 5) is introduced in descending minor thirds and taken up by the strings and then the solitary oboe, in a lovely, contemplative note— almost as if Davidson, with the cold cynicism of a New England deconstructionist, is distancing us not only intellectually but also emotionally from the Sturm and Drang of violent passions and runaway technology—as the curtain falls.

ACT 2

The second act begins, curiously, with the overture, which is the composer's way of thumbing his nose at the New York critical establishment, Carmine Hess in particular, that curmudgeonly pillar of tradition who probably also had his eye—but, then, didn't everyone?—on the executive conductorship of the Greenwich Conservatory. In his climb up the musical ladder, Davidson made countless enemies.

After the famous signature prelude, A-flat, A-flat, G, and the subdominant E-major chord held for ten full measures, a presto-adagio alternation combines the warm ale-and-pot ambiance of Harry's with the discordant, nervous broken arpeggios we will soon associate with Leila's desperate scheme. Davidson loves to weave contrasting moods, and this is an excellent example, minor sevenths vying with perfect fifths, the harp petulantly competing with the contrabassoon.

When the curtain rises, we find ourselves in a bint city. A chorus of bints sings of their forthcoming invasion of the Dalminian Empire, sun Alpha Cygni, planet Creeth. At last they will drive out the human dogs and reconsecrate the ancient subterranean temples. The bint captain, Prowlux, tells Tywliq, his confidante and second, that the invasion will be successful this time because they have found a human traitor to turn off the protective force field at the precise moment the bint ships materialize from hyperspace. Tywliq says, "Those humans have no morality. They betray their kind at the drop of a hat. They will sell even their maternal grandmothers for filthy lucre. They are scum." Prowlux tells him that money was not the bait this time. No, there is something that motivates humans even more than money. It is love. Prowlux and Tywliq sing a duet, "What is love? A foolish human thing." Davidson, thumbing his nose yet again at the hide-bound musicologists of Julliard and Lincoln Center, playfully incorporates chortling into the song, to produce a uniquely comic yodeling effect. "The human heart takes over, chortle-chortle, the human brain takes flight." General Wricob enters with his entourage and gives Prowlux special orders not to let the humans destroy the DNA lab when their battered remnants retreat into the indigenous scrub. Part of the invasion plan, we learn, is to change the human genome itself. The bints, taking over the DNA lab, will make humans weak and submissive for all eternity by manipulating the 34M-44F-XA alleles of the second chromosome to the left. "Guanine, adenine, cytosine," sings the general's entourage, to raucous saxophones and sinister cymbals.

As the warrior bints leave, Buyda, daughter of the Master Armorer, Greff (who has been unnoticed until now), steps from behind a boulder, lowers her lace veil, and laments that Prowlux has been driven so mad by power and ambition that he desires to couple not with her but with a human female, one Bea DeVries, in fact, whom he saw televised last quarter at the annual Saint Camilla song competition, when that shameless person of extrabintian origin was all in tulle and lilies. "What do human women have," sings Buyda, "that we honest bint women don't?" Buyda reveals her plan: She will don a suit of armor, disguise herself as a commando, and join the invasion force. At the appropriate moment she will plunge her serrated ceremonial bronze dagger deep into the pure white bosom of this despised DeVries alien, and then Buyda will take her own life. "For how can I continue," she sings in her wretchedness, "without my Prowlux?"

ACT 3

We are in the DNA laboratory near the spaceport Vuffon. White-bearded Doctor Cabrini is stirring one of the mitochondrial vats. "We will build a better race," he sings, "a race that aspires to nobler things." It is perhaps the most beautiful, loftiest aria Davidson ever wrote, and in both conception and sentiment it owes much to the final scene in Friedrich Windburn's Salome Unchained, where Terrence rebukes the witch Faffah. The good doctor lists all the evils of the human race: their frivolity, their cruelty, their addiction to watching various screens. Now that we have conquered the stars, he argues, it is time for us to conquer ourselves.

Chuck, his son, enters to the blatant, mindless rhythm of disco, and says, "Dad, why are you spending all your time among these old test tubes and autoclaves? Come out and have a little fun for a change, why don't you." Chuck's idea of fun is going to a virtual reality arcade and plugging into some nth-generation pinball machine. Doctor Cabrini shakes his sage head and replies that people should devote their time and energy to the welfare of the species rather than to empty personal hedonistic pursuits. In the following duet, Doctor Cabrini reveals that he has made a great discovery: He has isolated the gene for aggression. When it is excised, universal peace will ensue. Chuck's rejoinder is, "Great, Dad. Then what do we do when we're invaded?" In this seemingly comical exchange, Davidson is expressing a profound existential dilemma: We must always remain beasts, to some extent, he is saying, in order to protect ourselves against beasts, for otherwise we will be conquered and killed by them and our kind will not survive. And yet, the philosopher asks, what really has survived, if we remain beasts?

Lucas Fandera wrote, in the Charleston Herald, "Such is the genius of Harold Davidson's 'Aggression Gene' duet that we cannot separate the score from the libretto, the idea from the ludic weave and interplay of sound and words. The duet hits us in all its irreducibility, like a beautiful woman, like a boxing glove, like an unheralded shaft of enlightenment from a higher sphere."

Chuck departs to indulge in his sterile and puerile diversions, while the old man, with a sigh, resumes his work—but a hooded woman, we now notice, has entered unannounced. Standing in shadow, she asks for a vial of cis-methylated ligands. Doctor Cabrini recoils. "That is mortal poison," he says. "Indeed," retorts the woman. "But you will give it to me, old fool, because I know how you raised the money to send your ailing wife to the state hospital thirteen years ago on the planet Turrizo, though it didn't help her goiter, did it, and I will tell everyone and his second cousin if you do not do my bidding. You will be ruined, ruined." "What a despicable individual you are," says Doctor Cabrini. "If you were not of the fair sex, I would say that you were Darg Bhar himself. This is his style." "I am—I will be—the mate of Darg Bhar forever." With that, she removes her hood, and we see that it is none other than Leila Ziff-Calder. Her grim resolution has made her pale. Her gray eyes flash with hatred. She sings, "I will stop at nothing to have him. Don't anyone stand in my way."

The old molecular biologist straightens his back. He defies Leila. "No, I'm sorry. I cannot do what is wrong." She produces a laser pistol and without hesitation shoots him through the heart. "I warned you." They sing a fierce duet about morality. "One must never compromise," he sings, and she: "Circumstances alter cases." He staggers and falls, clutching his chest, and sings, "Now I will not be able to save the human race from itself. How untimely does this cruel violence tear me from the world." He sees, in a fevered dream, God himself on His throne, laughing, for the Lord of Light is revealed, to the fading mind of Doctor Cabrini, as the Prince of Darkness. The violins and cellos build chromatically to a discordant tremolo crescendo sforzando with shades of Schönberg and a nod to Piston as the deity-devil sings, "Fate is a practical joke, nothing more, and all your nobleness is but fuel for my demiurgic mischief."

Failing, dying, Doctor Cabrini sings as the violins play col legno, "I refuse with the last atom of my soul to believe in this black evil. We are made for more than ontological jokes. We must be. My heart, though alas it is punctured beyond repair, tells me so."

At this juncture Davidson springs a most unexpected and unsettling device on the audience: he has an invisible chorus of chipmunk-helium voices sing, mockingly, "We are made for more than jokes, we are made for more than jokes." With this the curtain falls, the chipmunk chorus still singing, accompanied appropriately by a tin whistle, wood blocks, and an irreverent glockenspiel.

At an early performance of the opera in a small, local opera house outside Berne, the infuriated audience came up on stage after this act, tore down the scenery, and injured some of the singers, one critically. "Blasphemy! Blasphemers!" they shouted. It was in all the papers of Europe, and a lengthy lawsuit followed.

ACT 4

An orchestral interlude, with a gentle Wagnerian light show on mauve scrims, prepares a change of mood. When the curtain rises, we are back in the workshop of the Vuffon spaceport. The grease apes are hammering away cheerfully at a meteor-pocked hull, while Bobby, Petro, Fred, and a few others sweep the floor and polish the brass table lamps, for today the Governor of the United Asteroids comes to pay a visit. Bobby keeps his head low. We cannot guess at his thoughts or plans but we can see that he is troubled. Petro tries to engage him in conversation, but to no avail.

Voices sound offstage, then the tramp of marching. It is the Governor's entourage. They are singing, "Make way for us, we are important." The processional music wells, and after a line of guardsmen bearing banners fills the stage, Darg Bhar enters with a flourish, in all his worldly splendor. He is dressed in thick furs and several gaudy necklaces. At his side is Bobby's sister, Bea. Bobby starts, riveted. He sees immediately that Bea is not herself. She seems drugged. Her eyes are dilated. She is wearing a most revealing black leather slit shift with funky decals. Has the nefarious Bhar already begun to work his lubricious villainy on her? Bobby clenches his fists. We can see that his hands itch for a weapon. "Ah me," he sings sotto voce, "I am in such torment. If I follow my almost irresistible impulse of indignation, I will perish, nor will Bea profit. And yet I cannot stand by and do nothing. Ah, if only the wise Doctor Cabrini were here to advise me." Bobby does not know that the molecular biologist is no more (and only now, do we learn that Bobby knew him in the first place).

Bhar sings of his ambition to rule the system and someday even the galaxy. Though he is a villain, the song is compelling, for it speaks to the bully in all of us. His guardsmen join him on the refrain: "Power is a great tonic." Though the theme is grim, there is a playful undercurrent here of Gilbert and Sullivan. Davidson was a man of mercurial shifts and deep contradictions.

Bobby manages to get his sister off to one side, and in a lovely, clever whisper duet—Davidson has each sing in a different key, which foregrounds their inability to communicate—Bobby sings, "I can't let you do this to yourself," and Bea sings, "I don't need your permission, I can do what I like. I'm a woman now." "Woman or DNA robot?" he counters. In answer, Bea goes into a curious, lame half-recitative that confirms Bobby's worst fears, "Woman, robot, what does it matter, when you've given everything you have to a man?"

Hiram Buck argues that Davidson is alluding here to his third wife, Clarissa, who at that time was in therapy for an obsessive lust she had conceived for the family Schnauzer, which, nota bene, was a female. But even if such a thing is true, what does it signify? Sordid tabloid trivia do not explain great art. The composer's personal life may indeed have resembled a soap opera shambles on occasion, but his music was always the real thing.

Bhar is about to sign a contract with the grease apes for them "to make his fleet as good as new," when sirens begin wailing. A courier rushes in with the news that the bints have invaded. Pandemonium ensues. The orchestra plays a frenetic, jumbled medley of snatches from Windburn, Stravinsky, Sessions, and Ives as the curtain falls.

The curtain falls, but the fourth act is not over. We hear explosions, curses. The house lights do not come on. The smells of sulfur and ozone fill the auditorium. The singers and actors bring the bint invasion to the audience. Human soldiers and bint warriors grapple in the aisles. A man is beheaded right on the proscenium in a fountain of blood as the flutes and piccolos shriek in octaves. (In Köln some children were so badly frightened by this, that there were lawsuits. Davidson once quipped that his music seemed to have been performed more in courtrooms than in theaters. An exaggeration, but there is truth to the statement, for such rough commerce with the prosaic world speaks of the vitality, originality, and fundamental energy of Davidson's oeuvre.)

ACT 5

With an ominous, growling fanfare the scene opens at the marble palace at Ghewi, the Creeth capital. In the original production at the presidential palace in Belize, the set was based on ancient photographs of the marble government buildings in Washington, D.C., which must have complemented nicely the atmosphere of doom and lost empire. The triumphant bints are assembled in full panoply. Darg Bhar is in chains though he still wears his furs. The grease apes are in chains behind him. Miranda is in chains beside Petro, who is chained too though he was the traitor. General Wricob sits on a throne above the multitude, rubbing his hands and gloating. Prowlux sings to Bea, who is also in chains, though her chains are delicate and of gold, "Convert to bintism, human woman, and I will spare you." She sings, "I belong to Bhar. You're wasting your time."

At this point, Davidson pulls yet another surprise from his theatrical sleeve, mixing tragedy and slapstick—and this at the very crux of the drama!—a bold masterstroke that undoubtedly left the contemporary critics gasping, sputtering, not knowing whether to admire or condemn. Not knowing, indeed, what to think. The action is condensed into a few seconds. A soldier steps forward, pulls off his helmet, and shakes out his hair. It is Buyda, and she holds a dagger. At the exact same moment, a hooded woman emerges from the crowd on the other side, holding a vial. It is, of course, Leila Ziff-Calder. Both women, in perfect symmetry, have chosen this time and place to do away with their competition. Remarkably, the composer accompanies with stubborn, total silence the carefully choreographed action that follows, as if we are watching mime. Perhaps Davidson is suggesting that we are all naught but programmed stick-figure puppets of our desires and fears. Again, this is one of Windburn's themes, though put on its head: for Windburn claimed, until his ashram days, that we were not puppets ("Wir sind nicht Puppen!") but, rather, exercised free will.

Buyda closes in and frenziedly bosom-stabs as Leila Ziff-Calder simultaneously pulls back Bea's head by the hair and empties the contents of the vial into her throat. But lo! the serrated bronze ceremonial bint blade and the supertoxic cis-methylated ligands from Doctor Cabrini's laboratory are powerless against Bobby's sister: because of Darg Bhar's nocturnal, unspeakable tampering with her hereditary material she is no longer human, perhaps no longer even living in the traditional sense. Bobby struggles against his chains to defend her but shrinks back with horror when he realizes that his sister is no more, though no more in a way different from the way in which he had first thought she was no more. It is a scene full of bitter and grisly irony, where both success and defeat have lost their meaning. Bea does not bleed from the wound, does not fall from the poison. Instead she sings, "I find this all very tedious."

"This is your work, Bhar!" Bobby screams. Bhar turns to him and sings, in a cut-time inversion of the Leila Ziff-Calder revenge motif, what is surely one of the most chillingly cynical arias ever written: "I have slept with so many women, so many men, so many different creatures both terrestrial and not. I have slept with close family members, with infants, and with decaying corpses. I needed something new."

Somehow we are not surprised that the ghost of Doctor Cabrini appears, hovering over the assemblage. He sings, to a stately Japanese drum, "This is what happens when we indulge the flesh, with no thought to our better destiny. This is the madness that happens."

The chorus of combined bints and chained humans sings, in deceptively complex twelve-tone chords: "What will become of the human race if it does not give thought to its immortal soul?" The finale is all in C major and stolid quarter-notes, we hear organ music in the background, and the horns give full throat to their power, as if we were at a wedding of Norse gods in a cathedral so vast, its vault shimmers in mist. Though at the same time, almost as a kind of contrapuntal footnote, Bea and Chuck go off together, hand-in-hand, to faint disco music, no doubt to plug themselves into some screen in some arcade offstage. Their departure is barely noticed. In a sense, they were not there in the first place.

Thus does Harold Davidson conclude his magnum opus with a Sunday sermon instead of with wailing and mayhem, thereby breaking the most sacred of the rules of opera. "Only one murder, and only one ghost," complained Alberta Quire of the *San Diego Times*. "How is it, then, that this work is nevertheless so disturbingly moving?" We might answer her querulous question with the words of Windburn, who once remarked, in his Meditations As the Sun Sets, "What is really awful in human affairs is what is unseen. The misdeed itself is nothing, a trifle, compared to the thought that sired it." Perhaps Davidson, engaged in so strenuous and prolonged a polemic with his great teacher, in the end could not help but agree with him. As the curtain falls, a grand orchestral coda hammers with relentless Lutheran piety one note, on and on, until the audience, at last beginning to understand, finally leaves piecemeal, a gentleman rising and putting on his coat here, a lady collecting her gloves and scarf there. The hammering continues until the auditorium is empty, and we are reminded of the hammer blows in the spaceship bodyshop at Vuffon. For what did those honest, simple hammers do but remove—or attempt to remove—imperfections in what was once an unblemished, shining, and perfect surface?

VI.

NEXT WAVE
(TWENTY-FIRST CENTURY)

If the first phase of New Space Opera applied a British New Wave (and, as John Clute has pointed out, a British scientific romance) sensibility to traditional tropes, the second applied a cyberpunk and hard-SF sensibility to what the first had made space for. (These divisions are, of course, arbitrary—there are entire sentences in *The Centauri Device* that read as if cyberpunk was already a done deal: "She was mainlining adrenochrome activators cut with the ribosomes of a local breed of bat," its hero is told, of his mother.) The agenda-setting text of the second phase was Vernor Vinge's *A Fire Upon the Deep*. This was space opera for people who'd read *Neuromancer* and who posted to Usenet. It was anarcho-capitalist, rather than (like much of the old SF) imperialist or (like some of the new) socialist or liberal. Its galactic community was modelled on the Internet.

It gave one answer to a question Vinge himself had raised: how is space opera possible in a post-Singularity universe? That is to say, how can we write about human beings adventuring out there in the Galaxy, if the not so distant future (as Vinge had elsewhere argued) belongs to humanity's incomprehensible successors?

—Ken MacLeod in *Locus*

TONY DANIEL

Tony Daniel [1963–] (tonydaniel.com.mn.sabren.com) lives in Allen, Texas. At the start of his career he published two intriguing essays, *Knot: The Problem: Some Thoughts on Craft, Art and Beauty and What the Hell They Have to Do with Science Fiction* (1990), a consideration of aesthetics, and *Dat Wascally Wabbit: The Influence of "Song of the South" on Lucius Shepard* (1990), a critical satire. He has since written four SF novels: *Warpath* (1993), *Earthling* (1997), *Metaplanetary* (2001), and *Superluminal* (2004)—the last two are parts of an ongoing space opera trilogy—and more than twenty-five short stories. His short story collection, *The Robot's Twilight Companion* (1999), collects nine stories.

The Metaplanetary trilogy is his major work to date, and has been received as "hard SF space opera." Critic Paul Kincaid said:

> War is a complicated business, and Daniel is making a serious attempt to portray how strange and confused it can be. This takes space. What's more, the sheer strangeness of this future, one of the most consistently presented and most impressive aspects of this book, also takes time to describe. Over the entire sequence, if he can sustain the invention and scope of this novel, this could be a breathtakingly important work, the work to catapult Tony Daniel to the forefront of contemporary hard sf writers.

Set about a thousand years in the future, it is about a civil war between the inner and outer parts of the solar system. The entire inner solar system is connected by a gigantic physical web of interplanetary cables called the Met; the outer system is plied by marvelous ships.

"People," Daniel says, "are not exactly the same sort of being as they used to be. Many people are Large Arrays of Personalities, or LAPs. These are a combination of electronic, biological, and nanotechnological entities, all integrated into one personality. There is no schism between actual and virtual, machine and man—because most people are both. Communication within a LAP and among people has grown very odd."

"Grist" forms the first section of *Metaplanetary*. It introduces a wild space opera future that incorporates many of the older space opera traditions, but like the works of Stross and Westerfeld and others, transforms them post-cyberpunk and post-Vinge into a rich and fertile new SF future. All of the characters are post-human, but still all too human. And a war is beginning that no one in the story can stop, regardless of how absurd it is to have a war in this circumstance. It is an interesting comparison to Stephen Baxter's ironic "The Great Game."

GRIST

TONY DANIEL

Things that really matter, although they are not defined for all eternity, even when they come very late still come at the right time.

—Martin Heidegger, "Letter on Humanism"

MIDNIGHT STANDARD AT THE WESTWAY DINER

Standing over all creation, a doubt-ridden priest took a piss.

He shook himself, looked between his feet at the stars, then tabbed his pants closed. He flushed the toilet and centrifugal force took care of the rest.

Andre Sud walked back to his table in the Westway Diner. He padded over the living fire of the plenum, the abyss—all of it—and hardly noticed. Even though this place was special to *him*, it was really just another café with a see-through floor—a window as thin as paper and as hard as diamond. Dime a dozen as they used to say a thousand years ago. The luciferan sign at the entrance said FREE DELIVERY. The sign under it said OPEN 24 HRS. This sign was unlit. The place will close, eventually.

The priest sat down and stirred his black tea. He read the sign, backward, and wondered if the words he spoke when he spoke, sounded anything like English used to. Hard to tell with the grist patch in his head.

Everybody understands one another on a general level, Andre Sud thought. Approximately more or less, they know what you mean.

There was a dull, greasy gleam to the napkin holder. The salt shaker was half-full. The laminated surface of the table was worn through where the plates usually sat. The particle board underneath was soggy. There was free-floating grist that sparkled like mica within the wood: used-to-be-cleaning-grist, entirely shorn from the restaurant's controlling algorithm and nothing to do but shine. Like the enlightened pilgrim of the Greentree Way. Shorn and brilliant.

And what will you have with that hamburger?

Grist. Nada y grist. Grist y nada.

I am going through a depression, Andre reminded himself. I am even considering leaving the priesthood.

Andre's pellicle—the microscopic, algorithmic part of him that was spread out in the general vicinity—spoke as if from a long way off.

This happens every winter. And lately with the insomnia. Cut it out with the nada y nada. Everything's physical, don't you know.

Except for *you*, Andre thought back.

He usually thought of his pellicle as a little cloud of algebra symbols that followed him around like mosquitoes. In actuality, it was normally invisible, of course.

Except for us, the pellicle replied.

All right then. As far as we go. Play a song or something, would you?

After a moment, an oboe piped up in his inner ear. It was an old Greentree hymn—"Ponder Nothing"—that his mother had hummed when he was a kid. Brought up in the faith. The pellicle filtered it through a couple of variations and inversions, but it was always soothing to hear.

There was a way to calculate how many winters the Earth-Mars Diaphany would get in an Earth year, but Andre never checked before he returned to the seminary on his annual retreat, and they always took him by surprise, the winters did. You wake up one day and the light has grown dim.

The café door slid open and Cardinal Filmbuff filled the doorway. He was wide and possessive of the doorframe. He was a big man with a mane of silver hair. He was also space-adapted and white as bone in the face. He wore all black with a lapel pin in the shape of a tree. It was green, of course.

"Father Andre," said Filmbuff from across the room. His voice sounded like a Met cop's radio. "May I join you?"

Andre motioned to the seat across from him in the booth. Filmbuff walked over with big steps and sat down hard.

"Isn't it late for you to be out, Morton?" Andre said. He took a sip of his tea. He'd left the bag in too long and it tasted twiggy.

I was too long at the pissing, thought Andre.

"Tried to call you at the seminary retreat center," Filmbuff said.

"I'm usually here," Andre replied. "When I'm not there."

"Is this place still the seminary student hangout?"

"It is. Like a dog returneth to its own vomit, huh? Or *somebody's* vomit."

A waiter drifted toward them. "Need menus?" he said. "I have to bring them because the tables don't work."

"I might want a little something," Filmbuff replied. "Maybe a lhasi."

The waiter nodded and went away.

"They still have real people here?" said Filmbuff.

"I don't think they can afford to recoat the place."

Filmbuff gazed around. He was like a beacon. "Seems clean enough."

"I suppose it is," said Andre. "I think the basic coating still works and that just the complicated grist has broken down."

"You like it here."

Andre realized he'd been staring at the swirls in his tea and not making contact with his boss. He sat back, smiled at Filmbuff. "Since I came to seminary, Westway Diner has always been my home away from home." He took a sip of tea. "This is where I got satori, you know."

"So I've heard. It's rather legendary. You were eating a plate of mashed potatoes."

"Sweet potatoes, actually. It was a vegetable plate. They give you three choices and I chose sweet potatoes, sweet potatoes, and sweet potatoes."

"I never cared for them."

"That is merely an illusion. Everyone likes them sooner or later."

Filmbuff guffawed. His great head turned up toward the ceiling and his copper eyes flashed in the brown light. "Andre, we need you back teaching. Or in research."

"I lack faith."

"Faith in yourself."

"It's the same thing as faith in general, as you well know."

"You are a very effective scholar and priest to be so racked with doubt. Makes me think I'm missing something."

"Doubt wouldn't go with your hair, Morton."

The waiter came back. "Have you decided?" he said.

"A chocolate lhasi," Filmbuff replied firmly. "And some faith for Father Andre here."

The waiter stared for a moment, nonplused. His grist patch hadn't translated Cardinal Filmbuff's words, or had reproduced them as nonsense.

The waiter must be from out the Happy Garden Radial, Andre thought. Most of the help *was* in Seminary Barrel. There's a trade patois and a thousand long-shifted dialects out that way. Clan-networked LAPs poor as churchmice and no good Broca grist to be had for Barrel wages.

"*Iye ftip*," Andre said to the waiter in the Happy Garden patois. "It is a joke." The waiter smiled uncertainly. "Another shot of hot water for my tea is what I want," Andre said. The waiter went away looking relieved. Filmbuff's aquiline presence could be intimidating.

"There is no empirical evidence that you lack faith," Filmbuff said. It was a pronouncement. "You are as good a priest as there is. We have excellent reports from Triton."

Linsdale, Andre thought. Traveling monk, indeed. Traveling stool-pigeon was more like it. I'll give him hell next conclave.

"I'm happy there. I have a nice congregation, and I balance rocks."

"Yes. You are getting a reputation for that."

"Triton has the best gravity for it in the solar system."

"I've seen some of your creations on the merci. They're beautiful."

"Thank you."

"What happens to them?"

"Oh, they fall," said Andre, "when you stop paying attention to them."

The chocolate lhasi came and the waiter set down a self-heating carafe of water for Andre. Filmbuff took a long drag at the straw and finished up half his drink.

"Excellent." He sat back, sighed, and burped. "Andre, I've had a vision."

"Well, that's what you do for a living."

"I saw *you*."

"Was I eating at the Westway Diner?"

"You were falling through an infinite sea of stars."

The carafe bubbled, and Andre poured some water into his cup before it became flat from all the air being boiled out. The hot water and lukewarm tea mingled in thin rivulets. He did not stir.

"You came to rest in the branches of a great tree. Well, you crashed into it, actually, and the branches caught you."

"Yggdrasil?"

"I don't think so. This was a different tree. I've never seen it before. It is very disturbing because I thought there was only the One Tree. *This* tree was just as big, though."

"As big as the World Tree? The Greentree?"

"Just as big. But different." Filmbuff looked down at the stars beneath their feet. His eyes grew dark and flecked with silver. Space-adapted eyes always took on the color of what they beheld. "Andre, you have no idea how real this was. Is. This is difficult to explain. You know about my other visions, of the coming war?"

"The Burning of the One Tree?"

"Yes."

"It's famous in the Way."

"I don't care about that. Nobody else is listening. In any case, this vision *has placed itself on top of* those war visions. Right now, being here with you, this seems like a play to me. A staged play. You. Me. Even the war that's coming. It's all a play that is really about that damn Tree. And it won't let me go."

"What do you mean, won't let you go?"

Filmbuff raised his hands, palms up, to cradle an invisible sphere in front of him. He stared into this space as if it were the depths of all creation, and his eyes became set and focused far away. But not glazed over or unaware.

They were so alive and intense that it hurt to look at him. Filmbuff's physical face *vibrated* when he was in trance. It was a slight effect, and unnerving even when you were used to it. He was utterly focused, but you couldn't focus on him. There was too much of him there for the space provided. Or not enough of you.

I am watching chronological quantum transport in the raw, Andre thought. The instantaneous integration of positronic spin information from up-time sifted through the archetypical registers of Filmbuff's human brain.

And it all comes out as metaphor.

"The Tree is all burnt out now," Filmbuff said, speaking out of his trance. His words were like stones. "The Burning's done. But it isn't char that I'm seeing, no." He clenched his fists, then opened his palms again. "The old Tree is a shadow. The burnt remains of the One Tree are really only the shadow of the other tree, the new Tree. It's like a shadow the new Tree casts."

"Shadow," Andre heard himself whispering. His own hands were clenched in a kind of sympathetic vibration with Filmbuff.

"We are living in the time of the shadow," said Filmbuff. He relaxed a bit. "There's almost a perfect juxtaposition of the two trees. I've never felt so sure of anything in my life."

Filmbuff, for all his histrionics, was not one to overstate his visions for effect. The man who sat across from Andre was only the *aspect*—the human portion—of a vast collective of personalities. They were all unified by the central being; the man before him was no more a puppet than was his enthalpic computing analog soaking up energy on Mercury, or the nodes of specialized grist spread across human space decoding variations in anti-particle spins as they made their way backward in time. But he was no longer simply the man who had taught Andre's Intro to Pastoral Shamanism course at seminary. Ten years ago, the Greentree Way had specifically crafted a large array of personalities to catch a glimpse of the future, and Filmbuff had been assigned to be morphed.

I was on the team that designed him, Andre thought. Of course, that was back when I was a graduate assistant. Before I Walked on the Moon.

"The *vision* is what's real." Filmbuff put the lhasi straw to his mouth and finished the rest of it. Andre wondered where the liquid *went* inside the man. Didn't he run on batteries or something? "This is maya, Andre."

"I believe you, Morton."

"I talked to Erasmus Kelly about this," Filmbuff continued. "He took it on the merci to our Interpreter's Freespace."

"What did they come up with?"

Filmbuff pushed his empty glass toward Andre. "That there's new Tree," he said.

"How the hell could there be a new Tree? The Tree is wired into our DNA like sex and breathing. It may *be* sex and breathing."

"How should I know? There's a new Tree."

Andre took a sip of his tea. Just right. "So there's a new Tree," he said. "What does that have to do with me?"

"We think it has to do with your research."

"What research? I balance rocks."

"From before."

"Before I lost my faith and became an itinerant priest?"

"You were doing brilliant work at the seminary."

"What? With the time towers? That was a dead end."

"You understand them better than anyone."

"Because I don't try to make any sense of them. Do you think this new Tree has to do with those things?"

"It's a possibility."

"I doubt it."

"You doubt everything."

"The time towers are a bunch of crotchety old LAPs who have disappeared up their own asses."

"Andre, you know what I am."

"You're my boss."

"Besides that."

"You're a *manifold*. You are a Large Array of Personalities who was specially constructed as a quantum event detector—probably the best in human history. Parts of you stretch across the entire inner solar system, and you have cloud ship outriders. If you say you had a vision of me and this new Tree, then it has to mean *something*. You're not making it up. Morton, you see into the future, and there I am."

"There you are. You are the Way's expert on *time*. What do *you* think this means?"

"What do you want me to tell you? That the new Tree is obviously a further stage in sentient evolution, since the Greentree is *us*?"

"That's what Erasmus Kelly and his people think. I need something more subtle from you."

"All right. It isn't the time towers that this has to do with."

"What then?"

"You don't want to hear this."

"You'd better tell me anyway."

"Thaddeus Kaye."

"Thaddeus Kaye is dead. He killed himself. Something was wrong with him, poor slob."

"I know you big LAPs like to think so."

"He was perverted. He killed himself over a woman, wasn't it?"

"Come on, Morton. A pervert hurts *other* people. Kaye hurt himself."

"What does *he* have to do with anything, anyway?"

"What if he's not dead? What if he's just wounded and lost? You understand what kind of being he is, don't you, Morton?"

"He's a LAP, just like me."

"You only *see* the future, Morton. Thaddeus Kaye can *affect* the future directly, from the past."

"So what? We all do that every day of our lives."

"This is not the same. Instantaneous control of instants. What the merced quantum effect does for space, Thaddeus Kaye can do for time. He *prefigures* the future. Backward and forward in time. He's like a rock that has been dropped into a lake."

"Are you saying he's God?"

"No. But if your vision is a true one, and I know that it is, then he could very well be the *war*."

"Do you mean the reason *for* the war?"

"Yes, but more than that. Think of it as a wave, Morton. If there's a crest, there has to be a trough. Thaddeus Kaye is the crest and the war is the trough. He's something like a physical principle. That's how his integration process was designed. Not a force, exactly, but he's been imprinted on a *property* of time."

"The Future Principle?"

"All right. Yes. In a way, he *is* the future. I think he's still alive."

"And how do you know that?"

"I didn't until you told me your vision. What else could it be? Unless aliens are coming."

"Maybe aliens are coming. They'd have their own. Tree. Possibly."

"Morton, do you see aliens coming in your dreams?"

"No."

"Well, then."

Filmbuff put his hands over his eyes and lowered his head. "I'll tell you what I still see," he said in a low rumble of a voice like far thunder. "I see the burning Greentree. I see it strung with a million bodies, each of them hung by the neck, and all of them burning, too. Until this vision, that was *all* I was seeing."

"Did you see any way to avoid it?"

Filmbuff looked up. His eyes were as white as his hands when he spoke. "Once. Not now. The quantum fluctuations have all collapsed down to one big macro reality. Maybe not today, maybe not tomorrow, but *soon*."

Andre sighed. *I believe*, he thought. I don't want to believe, but I do. It's easy to have faith in destruction.

"I just want to go back to Triton and balance rocks," he said. "That's really all that keeps me sane. I love that big old moon."

Filmbuff pushed his lhasi glass even farther away and slid out of the booth. He stood up with a creaking sound, like vinyl being stretched. "Interesting times," he spoke to the café. "Illusion or not, that was probably the last good lhasi I'm going to have for quite a while."

"Uh, Morton?"

"Yes, Father Andre?"

"You have to pay up front. They can't take it out of your account."

"Oh my." The cardinal reached down and slapped the black cloth covering his white legs. He, of course, had no pockets. "I don't think I have any money with me."

"Don't worry," Andre said. "I'll pick it up."

"Would you? I'd hate to have that poor waiter running after me down the street."

"Don't worry about it."

"We'll talk more tomorrow after meditation." This was not a request.

"We'll talk more then."

"Good night, Andre."

"Night, Morton."

Filmbuff stalked away, his silver mane trailing behind him as if a wind were blowing through it. Or a solar flare.

Before he left the Westway, he turned, as Andre knew he would, and spoke one last question across the space of the diner.

"You knew Thaddeus Kaye, didn't you, Father Andre?"

"I knew a man named Ben Kaye. A long time ago," Andre said, but this was only confirmation of what Filmbuff's spread-out mind had already told him.

The door slid shut and the Cardinal went out into the night. Andre sipped at his tea.

Eventually the waiter returned. "We close pretty soon," he said.

"Why do you close so early?" Andre asked.

"It is very late."

"I remember when this place never closed."

"I don't think so. It always closed."

"Not when I was a student at the seminary."

"It closed then," said the waiter. He took a rag from his apron, activated it with a twist, and began to wipe a nearby table.

"I'm sure you're mistaken."

"They tell me there's never been a time when this place didn't close."

"Who tells you?"

"People."

"And you believe them."

"Why should I believe *you*? You're people." The waiter looked up at Andre, puzzled. "That was a joke," he said. "I guess it does not translate."

"Bring me some more tea and then I will go."

The waiter nodded, then went to get it.

There was music somewhere. Gentle oboe strains. Oh, yes. His pellicle was still playing the hymn.

What do you think?

I think we are going on a quest.

I suppose so.

Do you know where Thaddeus Kaye is?

No, but I have a pretty good idea how to find Ben. And wherever Ben is, Thaddeus Kaye has to be.

Why not tell somebody else how to find him?

Because no one else will do what I do when I find him.

What's that?

Nothing.

Oh.

When the back-up is done, we'll be on our way.

The third part of Andre's multiple personality, the convert, was off-line at the moment getting himself archived and debugged. That was mainly what the retreat was for, since using the Greentree data facilities was free to priests. Doing it on Triton would have cost as much as putting a new roof on his house.

Why don't they send someone who is stronger in faith than we are?

I don't know. Send an apostate to net an apostate, I guess.

What god is Thaddeus Kaye apostate from?

Himself.

And for that matter, what about us?

Same thing. Here comes the tea. Will you play that song again?

It was Mother's favorite.

Do you think it could be that simple? That I became a priest because of that hymn?

Are you asking me?

Just play the music and let me drink my tea. I think the waiter wants us out of here.

"Do you mind if I mop up around you?" the waiter said.

"I'll be done soon."

"Take your time, as long as you don't mind me working."

"I don't mind."

Andre listened to mournful oboe and watched as the waiter sloshed water across the infinite universe, then took a mop to it with a vengeance.

JILL

Down in the dark there's a doe rat I'm after to kill. She's got thirteen babies and I'm going to bite them, bite them, bite them. I will bite them.

The mulch here smells of dank stupid rats all running running and there's nowhere farther to run, because this is it, this is the Carbuncle, and now *I'm* here and this is truly the end of all of it but a rat can't stand to know that and won't accept me until they have to believe me. Now they will believe me.

My whiskers against something soft. Old food? No, it's a dead buck; I scent his Y code, and the body is dead but the code keeps thumping and thumping. This mulch won't let it drain out and it doesn't ever want to die. The Carbuncle's the end of the line, but this code doesn't know it or knows it and won't have it. I give it a poke and a bit of rot sticks to my nose and the grist tries to swarm me, but no I don't think so.

I sniff out and send along my grist, jill ferret grist, and no rat code stands a chance ever, ever. The zombie rat goes rigid when its tough, stringy code—who knows how old, how far-traveled, to finally die here at the End of Everywhere—that code scatters to nonsense in the pit of the ball of nothing my grist wraps it in. Then the grist flocks back to me and the zombie rat thumps no more. No more.

Sometimes having to kill *everything* is a bit of a distraction. I want that doe and her littles really bad and I need to move on.

Down a hole and into a warren larder. Here there's pieces of meat and the stink of maggot sluice pooled in the bends between muscles and organs. But the rats have got the meat from Farmer Jan's Mulmyard, and it's not quite dead yet, got maggot resistant code, like the buck rat, but not smart enough to know it's dead, just mean code jaw-latched to a leg or a haunch and won't dissipate. Mean and won't die. But I am meaner still.

Oh, I smell her.

I'm coming mamma rat. Where are you going? There's no going anywhere anymore.

Bomi slinks into the larder and we touch noses. I smell blood on her. She's got a kill, a bachelor male, by the blood spoor on her.

It's so warm and wet, Jill. Bomi's trembling and wound up tight. She's not the smartest ferret. *I love it, love it, and I'm going back to lie in it.*

That's bad. Bad habit.

I don't care. I killed it; it's mine.

You do what you want, but it's your man Bob's rat.

No it's mine.

He feeds you, Bomi.

I don't care.

Go lay up then.

I will.

Without a by-your-leave, Bomi's gone back to her kill to lay up. I never do that. TB wouldn't like it, and besides, the killing's the thing, not the owning. Who wants an old dead rat to lie in when there's more to bite?

Bomi told me where she'd be because she's covering for herself when she doesn't show and Bob starts asking. Bomi's a stupid ferret and I'm glad she doesn't belong to TB.

But me—down another hole, deeper, deeper still. It's half-filled in here. The doe rat thought she was hiding it, but she left the smell of her as sure as a serial number on a bone. I will bite you, mamma.

Then there's the dead-end chamber I knew would be. Doe rat's last hope in all the world. Won't do her any good. But oh, she's big. She's tremendous. Maybe the biggest ever for me.

I am very, very happy.

Doe rat with the babies crowded behind her. Thirteen of them, I count by the squeaks. Sweet naked squeaks. Less than two weeks old, they are. Puss and meat. But I want mamma now.

The doe sniffs me and screams like a bone breaking and she rears big as me. Bigger.

I will bite you.

Come and try, little jill.

I will kill you.

I ate a sack of money in the City Bank and they chased me and cut me to pieces and just left my tail, and—I grew another rat! What will you do to me, jill, that can be so bad? You'd better be afraid of me.

When I kill your babies, I will do it with one bite for each. I won't hurt them for long.

You won't kill my babies.

At her.

At her, because there isn't anything more to say, no more messages to pass back and forth through our grist and scents.

I go for a nipple and she's fast out of the way, but not fast enough and I have a nub of her flesh in my mouth. Blood let. I chew on her nipple tip. Blood and mamma's milk.

She comes down on me and bites my back, her long incisors cut through my fur, my skin, like hook needles, and come out at another spot. She's heavy. She gnaws at me and I can feel her teeth scraping against my backbone. I shake to get her off, and I do, but her teeth rip a gouge out of me.

Cut pretty bad, but she's off. I back up thinking that she's going to try to swarm a copy, and I stretch out the grist and there it is, just like I thought, and I intercept it and I kill the thing before it can get to the mulm and reproduce and grow another rat. One rat this big is enough, enough for always.

The doe senses that I've killed her outrider, and now she's more desperate.

This is all there is for you. This is oblivion and ruin and time to stop the scurry. This is where you'll die.

She strikes at me again, but I dodge, and—before she can round on me—I snatch a baby rat. It's dead before it can squeal. I spit out its mangle of bones and meat.

But mamma's not a dumb rat, no, not dumb at all, and does not fly into a rage over this. But I know she regards me with all the hate a rat can hate, though. If there were any light, I'd see her eyes glowing rancid yellow.

Come on, mamma, before I get another baby.

She goes for a foot and again I dodge, but she catches me in the chest. She raises up, up.

The packed dirt of the ceiling, wham, wham, and her incisors are hooked around my breastbone, damn her, and it holds me to her mouth as fast as a barbed arrowpoint.

Shake and tear, and I've never known such pain, such delicious . . .

I rake at her eyes with a front claw, dig into her belly with my feet. Dig, dig, and I can feel the skin parting, and the fatty underneath parting, and my feet dig deep, deep.

Shake me again and I can only smell my own blood and her spit and then sharp, small pains at my back.

The baby rats. The baby rats are latching onto me, trying to help their mother.

Nothing I can do. Nothing I can do but dig with my rear paws. Dig, dig. I am swimming in her guts. I can feel the give. I can feel the tear. Oh, yes.

Then my breastbone snaps and I fly lose of the doe's teeth. I land in the babies, and I'm stunned and they crawl over me and nip at my eyes and one of them shreds an ear, but the pain brings me to and I snap the one that bit my ear in half. I go for another. Across the warren cavern, the big doe shuffles. I pull myself up, try to stand on all fours. Can't.

Baby nips my hind leg. I turn and kill it. Turn back. My front legs collapse. I cannot stand to face the doe, and I hear her coming.

Will I die here?

Oh, this is how I want it! Took the biggest rat in the history of the Met to kill me. Ate a whole bag of money, she did.

She's coming for me. I can hear her coming for me. She's so big. I can *smell* how big she is.

I gather my hind legs beneath me, find a purchase.

This is how I die. I will bite you.

But there's no answer from her, only the doe's harsh breathing. The dirt smells of our blood. Dead baby rats all around me.

I am very, very happy.

With a scream, the doe charges me. I wait a moment. Wait.

I pounce, shoot low like an arrow.

I'm through, between her legs. I'm under her. I rise up. I rise up into her shredded belly. I bite! I bite! I bite!

Her whole weight keeps her down on me. I chew. I claw. I smell her heart. I smell the new blood of her heart! I can hear it! I can smell it! I chew and claw my way to it.

I bite.

Oh yes.

The doe begins to kick and scream, to kick and scream, and, as she does, the blood of heart pumps from her and over me, smears over me until my coat is soaked with it, until all the dark world is blood.

After a long time, the doe rat dies. I send out the grist, feebly, but there are no outriders to face, no tries at escape now. She put all that she had into fighting me. She put everything into our battle.

I pull myself out from under the rat. In the corner, I hear the scuffles of the babies. Now that the mamma is dead, they are confused.

I have to bite them. I have to kill them all.

I cannot use my front legs, but I can use my back. I push myself toward them, my belly on the dirt like a snake. I find them all huddled in the farthest corner, piling on one another in their fright. Nowhere to go.

I do what I told the doe I would do. I kill them each with one bite, counting as I go. Three and ten makes thirteen.

And then it's done and they're all dead. I've killed them all.

So.

There's only one way out: the way I came. That's where I go, slinking, crawling, turning this way and that to keep my exposed bone from catching on pebbles and roots. After a while, I start to feel the pain that was staying away while I fought. It's never been this bad.

I crawl and crawl, I don't know for how long. If I were to meet another rat, that rat would kill me. But either they're dead or they're scared, and I don't hear or smell any. I crawl to what I think is up, what I hope is up.

And after forever, after so long that all the blood on my coat is dried and starting to flake off like tiny brown leaves, I poke my head out into the air.

TB is there. He's waited for me.

Gently, gently he pulls me out of the rat hole. Careful, careful he puts me in my sack.

"Jill, I will fix you," he says.

I know.

"That must have been the Great Mother of rats."

She was big, so big and mean. She was brave and smart and strong. It was wonderful.

"What did you do?"

I bit her.

"I'll never see your like again, Jill."
I killed her, and then I killed all her children.
"Let's go home, Jill."
Yes. Back home.

Already in the dim burlap of the sack, and I hear the call of TB's grist to go to sleep, to get better, and I sigh and curl as best I can into a ball and I am falling away, falling away to dreams where I run along a trail of spattered blood, and the spoor is fresh and I'm chasing rats, and TB is with me close by, and I will bite a rat soon, soon, soon—

A SIMPLE ROOM WITH GOOD LIGHT

Come back, Andre Sud. Your mind is wandering and now you have to concentrate. Faster now. Fast as you can go. Spacetime. Clumps of galaxy clusters. Average cluster. Two-armed spiral.

Yellow star.

Here's a network of hawsers cabling the inner planets together. Artifact of sentience, some say. Mercury, Venus, Earth, Mars hung with a shining webwork across blank space and spreading even into the asteroids. Fifty-mile-thick cables bending down from the heavens, coming in at the poles to fit into enormous universal joints lubricated by the living magma of the planets' viscera. Torque and undulation. Faster. Somewhere on a flagellating curve between Earth and Mars, the Diaphany, you will find yourself. Closer in. Spinning spherule like a hundred-mile-long bead on a million-mile-long necklace. Come as close as you can.

All along the Mars-Earth Diaphany, Andre saw the preparations for a war like none before. It seemed the entire Met—all the interplanetary cables—had been transformed into a dense fortress that people just happened to live inside. His pod was repeatedly delayed in the pithway as troops went about their movements, and military grist swarmed hither and yon about some task or another. We live in this all-night along the carbon of the cables, Andre thought, within the dark glistening of the corridors where surface speaks to surface in tiny whispers like fingers, and the larger codes, the extirpated skeletons of a billion minds, clack together in a cemetery of logic, shaking hands, continually shaking bony, algorithmic hands and observing strict and necessary protocol for the purposes of destruction.

Amés—he only went by the one name, as if it were a title—was a great one for martial appearances. Napoleon come again, the merci reporters said as a friendly joke. Oh, the reporters were eating this up. There hadn't been a good war in centuries. People got tired of unremitting democracy, didn't they? He'd actually heard somebody say that on the merci.

How fun it will be to watch billions die for a little excitement on the merci, Andre thought.

He arrived in Connacht Bolsa in a foul mood, but when he stepped out of his pod, there was the smell of new rain. He had walked a ways from the pod station before he realized what the smell was. There were puddles of water on the ground from the old fashioned street cleaning mechanism Connacht employed. It was still raining in spots—a small rain that fell only an inch or so from the ground. Little clouds scudded along the street like a miniature storm front, washing it clean of the night's leavings.

Connacht was a suburb radial off Phobos City, the most densely populated segment on the Met. A hundred years ago in the Phobos boom time, Connacht had been the weekend escape for intellectuals, artists, moneyed drug addicts—and the often indistinguishable variety of con-men, mountebanks, and psychic quacksalvers who were their hangers-on. The place was rundown now, and Andre's pellicle encountered various swarms of nostalgia that passed through the streets like rat packs—only these were bred and fed by the merchants to attract the steady trickle of tourists with pellicular receptors for a lost bohemia.

All they did for Andre was make him think about Molly.

Andre's convert—the electronic portion of himself—obliged him by dredging up various scenes from his days at seminary. The convert was usually silent, preferring to communicate in suggestive patterns of data—like a conscience gifted with irreducible logic and an infallible memory.

Andre walked along looking at the clouds under his feet, and as he walked his convert projected images into the shape of these clouds, and into the shift and sparkle of the puddled water they left behind.

I have a very sneaky conscience, Andre thought, but he let the images continue.

—Molly Index, Ben Kaye, and Andre at the Westway, in one of their long arguments over aesthetics when they were collaborating on their preliminary thesis. "Knowing, Watching, and Doing: The Triune Aspect of Enlightenment."

"I want to be 'Doing!' " Molly mocked-yelled and threw a wadded up piece of paper at Ben.

He caught it, spread it out, and folded it into a paper airplane. "This is the way things have to be," he said. "I'm 'Doing.' You're 'Watching.' And we both know who 'Knowing' must be." They turned to Andre and smiled vulture smiles.

"I don't know what you think I know, but I don't know it," he said, then nearly got an airplane in the eye.

—Molly's twenty-four-year-old body covered with red Martian sand under the Tharsis beach boardwalk. Her blue eyes open to the sky pink sky. Her nipples like dark stones. Ben a hundred feet away, rising from the gray-green lake water, shaking the spume from his body. Of course he had run and jumped into the lake as soon as they got there. Ben wouldn't wait for anything.

But Molly chose me. I can't believe she chose me.

Because I waited for her and dragged her under the boardwalk and kissed her before I could talk myself out of it.

Because I waited for the right moment.

How's that for Doing?

—Living together as grad students while Molly studied art and he entered into the stations of advanced meditation at seminary.

—Molly leaving him because she would not marry a priest.

You're going to kill yourself on the moon.

Only this body. I'll get a new one. It's being grown right now.

It isn't right.

This is the Greentree Way. That's what makes a priest into a true shaman. He knows what it's like to die and come back.

If you Walk on the Moon, you will know what it's like to lose a lover.

Molly, the Walk is what I've been preparing for these last seven years. You know that.

I can't bear it. I won't.

Maybe he could have changed her mind. Maybe he could have convinced her. But Alethea Nightshade had come along and that was that. When he'd come back from the moon reinstantiated in his cloned body, Molly had taken a new lover.

—His peace offering returned with the words of the old folk song, turned inside out: "Useless the flowers that you give, after the soul is gone."

—Sitting at a bare table under a bare light, listening to those words, over and over, and deciding never to see her again. Fifteen years ago, as they measure time on Earth.

Thank you, that will be enough, he told the convert.

An image of a stately butler, bowing, flashed through Andre's mind. Then doves rising from brush into sunset. The water puddles were just water puddles once again, and the tiny clouds were only clouds of a storm whose only purpose was to make the world a little cleaner.

Molly was painting a Jackson Pollock when Andre arrived at her studio. His heavy boots, good for keeping him in place in Triton's gravity, noisily clumped on the wooden stairs to Molly's second floor loft. Connacht was spun to Earth-normal. He would have knocked, but the studio door was already open.

"I couldn't believe it until I'd seen it with my own eyes," Molly said. She did not stop the work at her easel. "My seminary lover come back to haunt me."

"Boo," Andre said. He entered the space. Connacht, like many of the old rotating simple cylinders on the Diaphany, had a biofusion lamp running down its pith that was sheathed on an Earth-day schedule. Now it was day, and Molly's skylights let in the white light and its clean shadows. Huge picture windows looked out on the village. The light reminded Andre of light on the moon. The unyielding, stark, redeeming light just before his old body joined the others in the shamans' Valley of the Bones.

"Saw a man walking a dog the other day with the legs cut off," said Molly. She dipped the tip of her brush in a blue smear on her palette.

"The man or the dog?"

"Maybe the day." Molly touched the blue to the canvas before her. It was like old times.

"What are you painting?"

"Something very old."

"That looks like a Pollock."

"It is. It's been out of circulation for a while and somebody used it for a tablecloth. Maybe a kitchen table, I'm thinking."

Andre looked over the canvas. It was clamped down on a big board as long as he was tall. Sections of it were fine, but others looked as if a baby had spilled its mashed peas all over it. Then again, maybe that was Pollock's work after all.

"How can you possibly know how to put back all that spatter?"

"There're pictures." Molly pointed the wooden tip of her brush to the left hand corner of the canvas. Her movements were precise. They had always been definite and precise. "Also, you can kind of see the tracery of where this section was before it got . . . whatever that is that got spilled on it there. Also, I use grist for the small stuff. Did you want to talk about Ben?"

"I do."

"Figured you didn't come back to relive old times."

"They *were* good. Do you still do that thing with the mirror?"

"Oh, yes. Are you a celibate priest these days?"

"No, I'm not that kind of priest."

"I'm afraid I forgot most of what I knew about religion."

"So did I."

"Andre, what do you want to know about Ben?" Molly set the handle of her brush against her color palette and tapped it twice. Something in the two surfaces recognized one another, and the brush stuck there. A telltale glimmer of grist swarmed over the brush, keeping it moist and ready for use. Molly sat in a chair by her picture window and Andre sat in a chair across from her. There was a small table between them. "Zen tea?" she said.

"Sure," Andre replied.

The table pulsed, and two cups began forming on its surface. As the outsides hardened, a gel at their center thinned down to liquid.

"Nice table. I guess you're doing all right for yourself, Molly."

"I like to make being in the studio as simple as possible so I can concentrate on my work. I indulge in a few luxuries."

"You ever paint for yourself anymore? Your own work, I mean?"

Molly reached for her tea, took a sip and motioned with her cup at the Pollock.

"I paint *those* for myself," she said. "It's my little secret. I make them mine. Or they make me theirs."

"That's a fine secret."

"Now you're in on it. So was Ben. Or Thaddeus, I should say."

"You were on the team that made him, weren't you?"

"Aesthetic consultant. Ben convinced them to bring me on. He told me to think of it as a grant for the arts."

"I kind of lost track of you both after I . . . graduated."

"You were busy with your new duties. I was busy. Everybody was busy."

"I wasn't *that* busy."

"Ben kept up with your work. It was part of what made him decide to . . . do it."

"I didn't know that."

"Now you do. He read that paper you wrote on temporal propagation. The one that was such a big deal."

"It was the last thing I ever wrote."

"Developed a queer fascination with rocks?"

"You heard about that?"

"Who do you think sent those merci reporters after you?"

"Molly, you didn't?"

"I waited until I thought you were doing your best work."

"How did you see me? . . ." He looked into her eyes, and he saw it. The telltale expression. Far and away. "You're a LAP."

Molly placed the cup to her lips and sipped a precise amount of tea. "I guess you'd classify me as a manifold by now. I keep replicating and replicating. It's an art project I started several years ago. Alethea convinced me to do it when we were together."

"Will you tell me about her? She haunted me for years, you know. I pictured her as some kind of femme fatale from a noir. Destroyed all my dreams by taking you."

"Nobody took me. I *went*. Sometimes I wonder what I was thinking. Alethea Nightshade was no picnic, let me tell you. She had the first of her breakdowns when we were together."

"Breakdowns?"

"She had schizophrenia in her genes. She wanted to be a LAP, but wasn't allowed because of it. The medical grist controlled her condition most of the time, but every once in a while . . . she outthought it. She was too smart for her own good."

"Is that why you became a LAP?" Andrew asked. "Because *she* couldn't?"

"I told myself I was doing it for *me*, but yes. *Then*. Now, things are different." Molly smiled, and the light in the studio was just right. Andre saw the edge of the multiplicity in her eyes.

The fractal in the aspect's iris.

"You have no idea how beautiful it is—what I can *see*!" Molly laughed, and Andre shuddered. Awe or fright? He didn't know.

"She was just a woman," Molly said. "I think she came from around Jupiter. A moon or something, you know." Molly made a sweeping motion toward her window. As with many inner system denizens, the outer system was a great unknown, and all the same, to her. "She grew up on some odd kind of farm."

"A Callisto free grange?"

"I'm sure I don't know. She didn't talk about it much."

"What was she like?"

"Difficult."

"What do you mean?"

"I'll tell you." Tea sip. Andre realized he hadn't picked his up yet. He did so, tried it. It was wonderful, and all grist. A bit creepy to think about drinking it down.

I'll take care of it, don't you worry, said his pellicle.

I know you will.

"Alethea had two qualities that should never exist within one organic mind. A big intellect and a big heart. She *felt* everything, and she thought about it far too much. She was born to be a LAP. And she finally found a way to do it."

"Ben."

"They fell in love. It was also her good fortune that he could get her past the screening procedures. But Alethea always was a fortunate woman. She was lucky, on a quantum level. Until she wasn't."

"So she and Ben were together before he became . . . Thaddeus."

"For a year."

"Were you jealous?"

"I'd had enough of Alethea by then. I'll always love her, but I want a life that's . . . plain. She was a tangle I couldn't untangle." Molly touched her fingers to her nose and tweaked it. It was a darling gesture, Andre thought. "Besides," Molly said. "*She* left *me*."

"What did that do to you and Ben?"

"Nothing. I love Ben. He's my best friend."

She was speaking in the present tense about him, but Andre let it pass.

"Why did he change his name, Molly? I never understood that."

"Because he wasn't a LAP."

"What do you mean? Of course he was. A special one. Very special. But still—"

"No. He said he was something *new*. He said he wasn't Ben anymore. It was kind of a joke with him, though. Because, of course, he *was* still Ben. Thaddeus may have been more than a man, but he definitely was *at least* a man, and that man was Ben Kaye. He never could explain it to me."

"Time propagation without consciousness overlap. That was always the problem with the time tower LAPs. Interference patterns. Dropouts. But with Thaddeus, they finally got the frequency right. One consciousness propagated into the future and bounced back with anti-particle quantum entanglement."

"I never understood a bit of that jargon you time specialists use."

"We made God."

Molly snorted and tea came out her nose. She laughed until tears came to her eyes.

"We made *something*," she said. "Something very different than what's come before. But Andre, I *knew* Thaddeus. He was the last thing in the universe I would consider *worshiping*."

"Some didn't share your opinion."

"Thaddeus thought they were crazy. They made him very uncomfortable."

"Was Alethea one of them?"

"Alethea? Alethea was a stone-cold atheist when it came to Thaddeus. But what she did was worse. Far worse."

"What are you talking about?"

"She fell in love with him."

"I don't understand."

"Alethea fell in love with Thaddeus."

"But she was already in love with Thaddeus."

"Think about what I've said."

"Ben," Andre said after a moment. "Thaddeus and Ben were not the same person."

"It was a very melodramatic situation."

"Ben lost his love to . . . another version of himself!"

"The new, improved Ben was born in Thaddeus. Of course *he* would be the one Alethea loved. The only problem was, the old Ben was still around."

"God," Andre said. "How—"

"Peculiar?"

"How very peculiar."

Molly stood up and went to her window. She traced a line along the clean glass with her finger, leaving a barely visible smudge. The light was even and clean in Connacht. It was very nearly perfect if what you wanted was accurate illumination. Andre gazed at the shape of Molly against the light. She was beautiful in outline.

"Let me tell you, so was the solution they came up with, the three of them," Molly said. "Peculiar."

"Alethea would become like Thaddeus."

"How did you guess?"

"It has a certain logic. There would be the new Alethea, and there would be the old Alethea left for Ben."

"Yes," said Molly. "A logic of desperation. It only left out one factor."

"Alethea's heart."

"That's right. She loved Thaddeus. She no longer loved *Ben*. Not in the same way." Molly turned to face him, but Andre was still blinded by the light streaming in. "But she let them go ahead with it. And for that, I can never forgive her."

"Because she wanted to be a LAP."

"More than anything. More than she loved Ben. More than she loved *Thaddeus*. But I suppose she was punished for it. They all were."

"How did she get around the screening? I mean, her condition should preclude—"

"You know Ben. Thaddeus and Ben decided they wanted it to happen. They are very smart and persuasive men. So *very* smart and persuasive."

Andre got up and stood beside her in the window, his back to the light. It was warm on his neck.

"Tell me," he said. He closed his eyes and tried only to listen, but then he felt a touch and Molly was holding his hand.

"*I* am Molly," she said. "I'm the aspect. All my converts and pellicle layers are *Molly*—all that programming and grist—it's *me*, it's Molly, too. The woman you once loved. But I'm all along the Diaphany and into the Met. I'm wound into the outer grist. I watch."

"What do you watch?"

"The sun. I watch the sun. One day I'm going to paint it, but I'm not ready yet. The more I watch, the less ready I feel. I expect to be watching for a long time." She squeezed his hand gently. "I'm still Molly. But Ben wasn't Thaddeus. And *he* was. And he was eaten up with jealousy, but jealousy of *whom*? He felt he had a right to decide his own fate. We all do. He felt he had that right. And did he not? I can't say."

"It's a hard question."

"It would never have *been* a question if it hadn't been for Alethea Nightshade."

"What happened?" he asked, eyes still closed. The warm pressure of her hand. The pure light on his back. "Were you there?"

"Ben drove himself right into Thaddeus's heart, Andre. Like a knife. It might as well have been a knife."

"How could he do that?"

"I was there in Elysium when it happened," she said.

"On Mars?"

"On Mars. I was on the team, don't you know? Aesthetic consultant. I was hired on once again."

Andre opened his eyes and Molly turned to him. In this stark light, there were crinkles around her lips, worry lines on her brow. The part of her that was here.

We have grown older, Andre thought. And pretty damn strange.

"It's kind of messy and . . . organic . . . at first. There's a lab near one of the steam vents where Ben was transmuted. There's some ripping apart and beam splitting at the quantum level that I understand is very unsettling for the person undergoing the process. Something like this happens if you're a multiple and you ever decide to go large, by the way. It's when we're at our most vulnerable."

"Thaddeus was there when Alethea underwent the process?"

"He was there. Along with Ben."

"So he was caught up in the integration field. Everyone nearby would be," Andre said. "There's a melding of possible futures."

"Yes," said Molly. "Everyone became part of everyone else for that instant."

"Ben and Thaddeus and Alethea."

"Ben understood that his love was doomed."

"And it drove him crazy?"

"No. It drove him to despair. Utter despair. I was there, remember? I felt it."

"And at that instant, when the integration field was turned on—"

"Ben drove himself into Thaddeus's heart. He pushed himself in where he couldn't be."

"What do you mean, couldn't be?"

"Have you ever heard the stories from back when the Merced effect was first discovered, of the pairs of lovers and husbands and wives trying to integrate into one being?"

"The results were horrific. Monsters were born. And died nearly instantly."

Andre tried to imagine what it would be like if his pellicle or his convert presence were not really *him*. If he had to live with another presence, an *other*, all the time. The thing about a pellicle was that it never did anything the whole person didn't want to do. It *couldn't*. It would be like a wrench in your toolbox rebelling against you.

Molly walked over to the painting and gave it an appraising look, brushed something off a corner of the canvas. She turned, and there was the wild spatter of the Pollock behind her.

"There was an explosion," Molly said. "All the aspects there were killed. Alethea wasn't transmuted yet. We don't *think* she was. She may have died in the blast. Her body was destroyed."

"What about you?"

"I was in the grist. I got *scattered*, but I re-formed quickly enough."

"How was Thaddeus instantiated there at the lab?"

"Biological grist with little time-propagating nuclei in his cells. He looked like a man."

"Did he look like Ben?"

"Younger. Ben was getting on toward forty." Molly smiled wanly and nodded as if she'd just decided something. "You know, sometimes I think that was *it*."

"What?"

"That it wasn't about Thaddeus being a god at all. It was about him looking like he was nineteen. Alethea had a soft spot for youth."

"You're young."

"Thank you, Andre. You were always so nice to me. But you know, even then my aspect's hair was going white. I have decided, foolishly perhaps, never to grow myself a new body."

There she stood with her back against the window, her body rimmed with light. Forget all this. Forget about visions and quests. He put his hands on her shoulders and looked into her fractal eyes.

"I think you are beautiful," he said. "You will always be beautiful to me."

They didn't leave the studio. Molly grew a bed out of the floor. They undressed one another timidly. Neither of them had been with anyone for a long time. Andre had no lover on Triton.

She turned from him and grew a mirror upon the floor. Just like the full-size one she used to keep in their bedroom. Not for vanity. At least, not for simple vanity. She got on her hands and knees over it and looked at herself. She touched a breast, her hair. Touched her face in the mirror.

"I can't get all the way into the frame," she said. "I could never do a self-portrait. I can't see myself anymore."

"Nobody ever could," Andre said. "It was always a trick of the light."

Almost as if it had heard him, the day clicked off, instantly, and the studio grew pitch dark. Connacht was not a place for sunsets and twilight.

"Seven o'clock," Molly said. He felt her hand on his shoulder. His chest. Pulling him onto her until they were lying with the dark mirror beneath them. It wouldn't break. Molly's grist wouldn't let it.

He slid into her gently. Molly moved beneath him in small spasms.

"I'm all here," she told him after a while. "You've got all of me right now."

In the darkness, he pictured her body.

And then he felt the gentle nudge of her pellicle against his, in the microscopic dimensions between them.

Take me, she said.

He did. He swarmed her with his own pellicle, and she did not resist. He touched her deep down and found the way to connect, the way to get inside her there. Molly a warm and living thing that he was surrounding and protecting.

And, for an instant, a vision of Molly Index as she truly was:

Like—and unlike—the outline of her body as he'd seen it in the window, and the clear light behind her, surrounding her like a white hot halo. All of her, stretched out a hundred million miles. Concentrated at once beneath him. Both and neither.

"You are a wonder, Molly," he said to her. "It's just like always."

"Exactly like always," she said, and he felt her come around him, *and felt a warm flash traveling along the skin of the Diaphany—a sudden flush upon the world's face. And a little shiver across the heart of the solar system.*

Later in the dark, he told her the truth.

"I know he's alive. Ben didn't kill him; he only wounded him."

"And how do you know that?"

"Because Ben wasn't *trying* to kill him. Ben was trying to *hurt* him."

"My question remains."

"Molly, do you know where he is?"

At first he thought she was sleeping, but finally she answered. "Why should I tell you that?"

Andre breathed out. I was right, he thought. He breathed back in, trying not to think. Trying to concentrate on the breath.

"It might make the war that's coming shorter," he said. "We think he's the key."

"You priests?"

"Us priests."

"I can't believe there's going to be a war. It's all talk. The other LAPs won't let Amés get away with it."

"I wish you were right," he said. "I truly do."

"How could Thaddeus be the key to a war?"

"He's entangled in our local timescape. In a way, Thaddeus is our local timescape. He's imprinted on it. And now, I think he's *stuck* in it. He can't withdraw and just be Ben. Never again. I think that was Ben's revenge on himself. For taking away Alethea Nightshade."

Another long silence. The darkness was absolute.

"I should think you'd have figured it out by now, in any case," she said.

"What?"

"Where he went."

Andre thought about it, and Molly was right. The answer was there.

"He went to the place where all the fugitive bits and pieces of the grist end up," Molly said. "He went looking for *her*. For any part of her that was left. In the grist."

"Alethea," Andre said. "Of course, the answer is Alethea."

BENDER

The bone had a serial number that the grist had carved into it, 7sxq688N. TB pulled the bone out of the pile in the old hoy where he lived and blew through one end. Dust came out the other. He accidentally sucked in and started coughing until he cleared the dried marrow from his windpipe. It was maybe a thigh bone, long like a flute.

"You were tall, 7sxq," TB said to it. "How come you didn't crumble?"

Then some of TB's enhanced grist migrated over to the bone and fixed the broken grist in the bone and it *did* crumble in his hands, turn to dust, and then to less than dust to be carried away and used to heal Jill's breastbone and mend her other fractures.

But there is too much damage even for this, TB thought. She's dying. Jill is dying and I can't save her.

"Hang on there, little one," he said.

Jill was lying in the folds of her sack, which TB had set on his kitchen table and bunched back around her. He looked in briefly on her thoughts and saw a dream of scurry and blood, then willed her into a sleep, down to the deeper dreams that were indistinguishable from the surge and ebb of chemical and charge within her brain— sleeping and only living and not thinking. At the same time, he set the grist to reconstructing her torn-up body.

Too late. It was too late the moment that doe rat was finished with her.

Oh, but what a glory of a fight!

I set her to it. I made her into a hunter. It was all my doing, and now she's going to die because of it.

TB couldn't look at her anymore. He stood up and went to make himself some tea at the kitchen's rattletrap synthesizer. As always, the tea came out of synth tepid. TB raked some coals from the fire and set the mug on them to warm up a bit, then sat back down, lit a cigarette and counted his day's take of rats.

Ten bagged and another twenty that he and Bob had killed between them with sticks. The live rats scrabbled about in the containing burlap, but they weren't going to get out. Rats to feed to Jill. You shouldn't raise a ferret on anything other than its natural prey. The ferret food you could buy was idiotic. And after Jill ate them, he would know. He would know what the rats were and where they came from. Jill could sniff it out like no other. She was amazing that way.

She isn't going to eat these rats. She is going to die because you took a little scrap of programming that was all bite and you gave it a body and now look what you've done.

She didn't have to die like this. She could have been erased painlessly. She could have faded away to broken code.

Once again, TB looked long and hard into the future. Was there anything, any way? Concentrating, he teased at the threads of possible futures with a will as fine as a steel-pointed probe. Looking for a silver thread in a bundle of dross. Looking for the world where Jill lived through her fight. He couldn't see it, couldn't find it.

It had to be there. Every future was always there, and when you could see them, you could reach back into the past and effect the changes to bring about the future that you wanted.

Or I can.

But I can't. Can't see it. Want to, but *can't*, little Jill. I am sorry.

For Jill to live was a future so extreme, so microscopically fine in the bundle of threads that it was, in principle, unfindable, incomprehensible. And if he couldn't comprehend it, then to make it happen was impossible.

And, of course, he saw where almost all of the threads led:

Jill would be a long time dying. He could see that clearly. He could also see that he did not have the heart to put her down quickly, put her out of her misery. But knowing this fact did not take any special insight.

How could I have come to care so much for a no-account bundle of fur and coding out here on the ass-end of nowhere?

How could I *not*, after knowing Jill?

Two days it would take, as days were counted in the Carbuncle, before the little ferret passed away. Of course, it never really got to be day. The only light was the fetid bioluminescence coming off the heaps of garbage. A lot of it was still alive. The Carbuncle was in a perpetual twilight that was getting on toward three hundred years old. With the slow decay of organic remnants, a swamp had formed. And then the Bendy River, which was little more than a strong current in the swamp, endlessly circulating in precession with the spin of the module. Where was the Carbuncle? Who cares? Out at the end of things, where the tendrils of the Met snaked into the asteroid belt. It didn't matter. There wasn't a centrifuge here to provide gravity for *people*. Nobody cared about whoever lived here. The Carbuncle was spun—to a bit higher than Earth-normal, actually—in order to compact the garbage down so that humanity's shit didn't cover the entire asteroid belt.

The big garbage sluice that emptied into the Carbuncle had been put into place a half century ago. It had one-way valves within it to guard against backflow. All the sludge from the inner system came to the Carbuncle, and the maintenance grist used some of it to enlarge the place so that it could dump the rest. To sit there. Nothing much ever left the Carbuncle, and the rest of the system was fine with that.

Somebody sloshed into the shallow water outside the hoy and cursed. It was the witch, Gladys, who lived in a culvert down the way. She found the gangplank, and TB heard her pull herself up out of the water. He didn't move to the door. She banged on it with the stick she always carried that she said was a charmed snake. Maybe it was. Stranger things had happened in the Carbuncle. People and grist combined in strange ways here, not all of them comprehensible.

"TB, I need to talk to you about something," the witch said. TB covered his ears, but she banged again and that didn't help. "Let me in, TB. I know you're home. I saw a light in there."

"No, you didn't," TB said to the door.

"I need to talk to you."

"All right." He pulled himself up and opened the door. Gladys came in and looked around the hoy like a startled bird.

"What have you got cooking?"

"Nothing."

"Make me something."

"Gladys, my old stove hardly works anymore."

"Put one them rats in there and I'll eat what it makes."

"I won't do it, Gladys." TB opened his freezer box and rummaged around inside. He pulled out a popsicle and gave it to her. "Here," he said. "It's chocolate, I think."

Gladys took the popsicle and gnawed at it as if it were a meaty bone. She was soon done, and had brown mess around her lips. She wiped it off with a ragged sleeve. "Got another?"

"No, I don't have another," TB said. "And if I did, I wouldn't give it to *you*."

"You're mean."

"Those things are hard to come by."

"How's your jill ferret?"

"She got hurt today. Did Bob tell you? She's going to die."

"I'm sorry to hear that."

He didn't want to talk about Jill with Gladys. He changed the subject. "We got a mess of rats out of that mulmyard."

"There's more where they came from."

"Don't I know it!"

Gladys pulled up a stool and collapsed on it. She was maybe European stock; it was hard to tell. Her face was filthy, except for a white smear where wiping the chocolate had cleaned a spot under her nose and on her chin.

"Why do you hate them so much? I know why Bob does. He's crazy. But you're not crazy like that."

"I don't hate them," TB said. "It's just how I make a living."

"Is it, now?"

"I don't hate them," TB repeated. "What was it you wanted to talk to me about?"

"I want to take a trip."

"To *where*?"

"I'm going to see my aunt. I got to thinking about her lately. She used to have this kitten. I was thinking I wanted a cat. For a familiar, you know. To aid me in my occult work. She's a famous cloudship pilot, you know."

"The kitten?"

"No, my aunt is."

"You going to take your aunt's kitten?"

Gladys seemed very offended. "No, I'm not!" She leaned forward in a conspiratorial manner. "That kitten's all growed up now, and I think it was a girl. *It* will have kittens, and I can get me one of those."

"That's a lot of supposes," TB said mildly.

"I'm sure of it. My angel, Tom, told me to do it."

Tom was one of the supernatural beings Gladys claimed to be in contact with. People journeyed long distances in the Carbuncle to have her make divinings for them. It was said she could tell you exactly where to dig for silver keys.

"Well, if Tom told you, then you should do it," TB said.

"Damn right," said Gladys. "But I want you to look after the place while I'm gone."

"Gladys, you live in an old ditch."

"It is a dry culvert. And I do *not* want anybody moving in on me while I'm gone. A place that nice is hard to come by."

"All I can do is go down there and check on it."

"If anybody comes along, you have to run them off."

"I'm not going to run anybody off."

"You have to. I'm depending on you."

"I'll tell them the place is already taken," TB said. "That's about all I can promise."

"You tell them that it has a curse on it," Gladys said. "And that I'll put a curse on *them* if I catch them in my house!"

TB snorted back a laugh. "All right," he said. "Is there anything else?"

"Water my hydrangea."

"What the hell's that?"

"It's a plant. Just stick your finger in the dirt and don't water it if it's still moist."

"Stick my finger in the dirt?"

"It's clean fill!"

"I'll water it, then."

"Will you let me sleep here tonight?"

"No, Gladys."

"I'm scared to go back there. Harold's being mean." Harold was the "devil" that sat on Gladys's other shoulder. Tom spoke into one ear, and Harold into the other. People could ask Harold about money and he would tell Gladys the answer if he felt like it.

"You can't stay here." TB rose from his own seat and pulled Gladys up from the stool. She had a ripe smell when he was this close to her. "In fact, you have to go on now because I have to do something." He guided her toward the door.

"What do you have to do?" she said. She pulled free of his hold and stood her ground. TB walked around her and opened the door. "Something," he said. He pointed toward the twilight outside the doorway. "Go on home, Gladys. I'll check in on your place tomorrow."

"I'm not leaving for two days," she replied. "Check in on it day after tomorrow."

"Okay then," TB said. He motioned to the door. "You've got to go, Gladys, so I can get to what I need to do."

She walked to the door, turned around. "Day after tomorrow," she said. "I'll be gone for a while. I'm trusting you, TB."

"You can trust me to look in on your place."

"And not steal anything."

"I can promise you that, too."

"All right, then. I'm trusting you."

"Good night, Gladys."

"Good night." She finally left. After TB heard her make her way back to the swamp bank, he got up and closed the door behind her, which she'd neglected to do. Within minutes, there was another knock. TB sighed and got up to answer it. He let Bob in.

Bob pulled out a jar of a jellied liquid. It was Carbuncle moonshine, as thick as week-old piss and as yellow. "Let's drink," he said, and set the bottle on TB's table. "I come to get you drunk and get your mind off things."

"I won't drink that swill," TB said. Bob put the bottle to his mouth and swallowed two tremendous gulps. He handed the bottle to TB, shaking it in his face. TB took it.

"Damn!" Bob said. "Hot damn!"

"Gladys was right about you being crazy."

"She come around here tonight?"

"She just left. Said she wanted me to look after her place."

"She ain't going to see her aunt."

"Maybe she will."

"Like hell. Gladys never goes far from that ditch."

TB looked down at the moonshine. He looked away from it and, trying not to taste it, took a swig. He tasted it. It was like rusty paint thinner. Some barely active grist, too. TB couldn't help analyzing it; that was the way he was built. Cleaning agents for sewer pipes. Good God. He took another before he could think about it.

"You drink up." Bob looked at him with a faintly jealous glare. TB handed the bottle back.

"No, you."

"Don't mind if I do." Bob leaned back and poured the rest of the swill down his throat. He let out a yell when he was finished that startled TB, even though he was ready for it.

"I want some beer to chase it with," Bob said.

"Beer would be good, but I don't have any."

"Let's go down to Ru June's and shoot some pool."

"It's too damn late."

"It's early."

TB thought about it. The moonshine warmed his gut. He could feel it threatening to *eat through* his gut if he didn't dilute it with something. There was nothing further to do about Jill. She would sleep, and, at some time, she would die in her sleep. He ought to stay with her. He ought to face what he had done.

"Let me get my coat."

The Carbuncle glowed blue-green when they emerged from the hoy. High above them, like the distant shore of an enormous lake, was the other side of the cylinder. TB had been there, and most of it was a fetid slough. Every few minutes a flare of swamp gas methane would erupt from the garbage on that side of the curve and flame into a white fireball. These fireballs were many feet across, but they looked like pin-prick flashes from this distance. TB had been caught by one once. The escaping gas had capsized his little canoe, and being in the water had likely saved him from being burnt to a crisp. Yet there were people who lived on that side, too—people who knew how to avoid the gas. Most of the time.

Bob didn't go the usual way to Ru June's, but instead took a twisty series of passageways, some of them cut deep in the mountains of garbage, some of them actually tunnels under and through it. The Bob-ways, TB thought of them. At one point TB felt a drip from above and looked up to see gigantic stalactites formed of some damp and glowing gangrenous extrusion.

"We're right under the old Bendy," Bob told him. "That there's the settle from the bottom muck."

"What do you think it is?" TB said.

"Spent medical grist, mostly," Bob replied. "It ain't worth a damn, and some of it's diseased."

"I'll bet."

"This is a hell of a shortcut to Ru June's, though."

And it was. They emerged not a hundred feet from the tavern. The lights of the place glowed dimly behind skin windows. They mounted the porch and went in through a screen of plastic strips that was supposed to keep out the flies.

TB let his eyes adjust to the unaccustomed brightness inside. There was a good crowd tonight. Chen was at the bar playing dominoes with John Goodnite. The dominoes were grumbling incoherently, as dominoes did. Over by the pool table, Tinny Him, Nolan, and Big Greg were watching Sister Mary the whore line up a shot. She sank a stripe. There were no numbers on the balls.

Tinny Him slapped TB on the back and Bob went straight for the bottle of whiskey that was standing on the wall shelf beside Big Greg.

"Good old TB," Tinny Him said. "Get you some whiskey." He handed over a flask.

Chen looked up from his dominoes. "You drink *my* whiskey," he said, then returned to the game. TB took a long swallow off Tinny Him's flask. It was far better stuff than Bob's moonshine, so he took another.

"That whore sure can pool a stick," Nolan said, coming to stand beside them. "She's beating up on Big Greg like he was a ugly hat."

TB had no idea what Nolan meant. The man's grist patch was going bad, and he was slowly sinking into incomprehensibility for any but himself. This didn't seem to bother him, though.

Bob was standing very close to Sister Mary and giving her advice on a shot until she reached over and without heat slapped him back into the wall. He remained there respectfully while she took her shot and sank another stripe. Big Greg whispered a curse and the whore smiled. Her teeth were black from chewing betel nut.

TB thought about how much she charged and how much he had saved up. He wondered if she would swap a poke for a few rats, but decided against asking. Sister Mary didn't like to barter. She wanted keys or something pretty.

Tinny Him offered TB the flask again, and he took it. "I got to talk to you," Tinny Him said. "You got to help me with my mother."

"What's the matter with her?"

"She's dead, is what."

"Dead." TB drank more whiskey. "How long?"

"Three months."

TB stood waiting. There had to be more.

"She won't let me bury her."

"What do you mean, she won't let you bury her? She's *dead*, isn't she?"

"Yeah, mostly." Tinny Him looked around, embarrassed, then went on in a low voice. "Her pellicle won't die. It keeps creeping around the house. And it's pulling her body around like a rag doll. I can't get her away from it."

"You mean her body died but her pellicle *didn't*?"

"Hell *yes*, that's what I mean!" Tinny Him took the flask back and finished it off. "Hell, TB, what am I going to do? She's really stinking up the place, and every time I throw the old hag *out*, that grist drags her right back in. It knocks on the door all night long until I have to open it."

"You've got a problem."

"Damn right I've got a problem! She was a good old mum, but I'm starting to hate her right now, let me tell you."

TB sighed. "Maybe I can do something," he said. "But not tonight."

"You could come around tomorrow. My gal'll fix you something to eat."

"I might just."

"You got to help me, TB. Everybody knows you got a sweet touch with the grist."

"I'll do what I can," TB said. He drifted over to the bar, leaving Tinny Him watching the pool game. He told Chen he wanted a cold beer and Chen got it for him from a freezer box. It was a good way to chill the burning that was starting up in his stomach. He sat down on a stool at the bar and drank the beer. Chen's bar was tiled in beaten-out snap-metal ads, all dead now and their days of roaming the corridors, sacs, bolsas, glands, and cylinders of the Met long done. Most of the advertisements were for products that he had never heard of, but the one his beer was sitting on he recognized. It was a recruiting pitch for the civil service, and there was Amés, back before he was Big Cheese of the System, when he was Governor of Mercury. The snap-metal had paused in the middle of Amés's pitch for the Met's finest to come to Mercury and become part of the New Hierarchy. The snap-metal Amés was caught with the big mouth on his big face wide open. The bottom of TB's beer glass fit almost perfectly in the round "O" of it.

TB took a drink and set the glass back down. "Shut up," he said. "Shut the hell *up*, why don't you?"

Chen looked up from his dominoes, which immediately started grumbling among themselves when they felt that he wasn't paying attention to them. "You talking to me?" he said.

TB grinned and shook his head. "I might tell you to shut up, but you don't say much in the first place."

Ru June's got more crowded as what passed for night in the Carbuncle wore on. The garbage pickers, the rat hunters, and the sump farmers drifted in. Most of them were men, but there were a few women, and a few indeterminate shambling masses of rags. Somebody tried to sell TB a spent coil of luciferan tubing. It was mottled along its length where it had caught a plague. He nodded while the tube monger tried to convince him that it was rechargeable, but refused to barter, and the man moved on after Chen gave him a hard stare. TB ordered another beer and fished three metal keys out of his pocket. This was the unit of currency in the Carbuncle. Two were broken. One looked like it was real brass and might go to something. He put the keys on the bar and Chen quickly slid them away into a strongbox.

Bob came over and slapped TB on his back. "Why don't you get you some whiskey?" he said. He pulled back his shirt to show TB another flask of rotgut moonshine stuck under the string that held up his trousers.

"Let me finish this beer and I might."

"Big Greg said somebody was asking after you."

"Gladys was, but she found me."

"It was a shaman priest."

"A what?"

"One of them Greentree ones."

"What's *he* doing here?"

"They got a church or something over in Bagtown. Sometimes they come all the way out here. Big Greg said he was doing something funny with rocks."

"With rocks?"

"That's what the man said."

"Are you sure that's what he said?"

"Big Greg said it was something funny with rocks, is all I know. Hey, why are *you* looking funny all of a sudden?"

"I know that priest."

"Now how could that be?"

"I know him. I wonder what he wants."

"What all men want," said Bob. "Whiskey and something to poke. Or just whiskey sometimes. But always *at least* whiskey." He reached over the bar and felt around down behind it. "What have I got my hand on, Chen?"

Chen glanced over. "My goddamn scattergun," he said.

Bob felt some more and pulled out a battered fiddle. "Where's my bow?"

"Right there beside it," Chen replied. Bob got the bow. He shook it a bit, and its grist rosined it up. Bob stood beside TB with his back to the bar. He pulled a long note off the fiddle, holding it to his chest. Then, without pause, he moved straight into a complicated reel. Bob punctuated the music with a few shouts right in TB's ear.

"Goddamn it, Bob, you're loud," he said after Bob was finished.

"Got to dance," Bob said. "Clear me a way!" he shouted to the room. A little clearing formed in the middle of the room, and Bob fiddled his way to it, then played and stomped his feet in syncopation.

"Come on, TB," Sister Mary said. "You're going to dance with me." She took his arm, and he let her lead him away from the bar. He didn't know what she wanted him to do, but she hooked her arm through his and spun him around and around until he thought he was going to spew out his guts. While he was catching his breath and getting back some measure of balance, the whore climbed up on a table and began swishing her dress to Bob's mad fiddling. TB watched her, glad for the respite.

The whole room seemed to sway—not in very good rhythm—to the music. Between songs, Bob took hits off his moonshine and passed it up to Sister Mary, who remained on the tabletop, dancing and working several men who stood about her into a frenzy to see up her swishing dress.

Chen was working a crowded bar, his domino game abandoned. He scowled at the interruption, but quickly poured drinks all around.

"Get you some whiskey! Get you some whiskey!" Bob called out over and over again. After a moment, TB realized it was the name of the song he was playing.

Somebody thrust a bottle into TB's hand. He took a drink without thinking, and whatever was inside it slid down his gullet in a gel.

Drinking grist. It was purple in the bottle and glowed faintly. He took another slug and somebody else grabbed the stuff away from him. Down in his gut, he felt the grist activating. Instantly, he understood its coded purpose. Old Seventy-Five. Take you on a ride on a comet down into the sun.

Go on, TB told the grist. I got nothing to lose.

Enter and win! it said to him. *Enter and win!* But the contest was long expired.

No thank you.

What do you want the most?

It was a preprogrammed question, of course. This was not the same grist as that which had advertised the contest. Somebody had brewed up a mix. And hadn't paid much attention to the melding. There was something else in there, something different. Military grist, maybe. One step away from sentience.

What the hell. Down she goes.

What do you want the most?

To be drunker than I've ever been before.

Drunker than this?

Oh, yeah.

All right.

A night like no other! Visions of a naked couple in a Ganymede resort bath, drinking Old Seventy-Five from bottles with long straws. *Live the dream! Enter and win!*

I said no.

The little trance dispersed.

What do you want the most?

Bob was up on the table with Sister Mary. How could they both fit? Bob was playing and dancing with her. He leaned back over the reeling crowd and the whore held him at arm's length, the fiddle between them. They spun round and round in a circle, Bob wildly sawing at his instrument and Sister Mary's mouth gleaming blackly as she smiled a maniacal, full-toothed smile.

Someone bumped into TB and pushed him into somebody else. He staggered over to a corner to wait for Ru June's to stop spinning. After a while, he realized that Bob and Sister Mary weren't going to, the crowd in the tavern wasn't, the chair, tables and walls were only going to go on and on spinning and now lurching at him as if they were swelling up, engorging, distending toward him. Wanting something from him when all he had to give was nothing anymore.

TB edged his way past it all to the door. He slid around the edge of the doorframe as if he were sneaking out. The plastic strips beat against him, but he pushed through them and stumbled his way off the porch. He went a hundred feet or so before he stepped in a soft place in the ground and keeled over. He landed with his back down.

Above him, the swamp gas flares were flashing arrhythmically. The stench of the whole world—something he hardly ever noticed anymore—hit him at once and completely. Nothing was right. Everything was out of kilter.

There was a twist in his gut. Ben down there thrashing about. But *I'm Ben. I'm Thaddeus. We finally have become one. What a pretty thing to contemplate.* A man with another man thrust through him, cross-ways in the fourth dimension. A tesseracted cross, with a groaning man upon it, crucified on himself! But you couldn't see all that, because it was in the fourth dimension.

Enough to turn a man to drink.

I have to turn over so I don't choke when I throw up.

I'm going to throw up.

He turned over and his stomach wanted to vomit, but the grist gel wasn't going to be expelled, and he dry heaved for several minutes until his body gave up on it.

What do you want the most?

"I want her back. I want it not to have happened at all. I want to be able to change something besides the future!"

And then the gel liquefied and crawled up his throat like hands and he opened his mouth and

—good god it *was* hands, small hands grasping at his lips and pulling outward, gaining purchase, forcing his mouth open, his lips apart—

—Cack of a jellied cough, a heave of revulsion—

I didn't mean it really.

Yes, you did.

—His face sideways and the small hands clawing into the garbage-heap ground, pulling themselves forward, dragging along an arm-thick trailer of something much more vile than phlegm—

—An involuntary rigor over his muscles as they contracted and spasmed to the beat of another's presence, a presence within them that wants—

—*out*—

He vomited the grist-phlegm for a long, long time.

And the stuff pooled and spread and it wasn't just hands. There was an elongated body. The brief curve of a rump and breasts. Feet the size of his thumb, but perfectly formed. Growing.

A face.

I won't look.

A face that was, for an instant, familiar beyond familiar, because it was *not* her. Oh, no. He knew it was not her. It was just the way he *remembered* her.

The phlegm girl rolled itself in the filth. Like bread dough, it rolled and grew and rolled, collecting detritus, bloating, becoming—

It opened its mouth. A gurgling. Thick, wet words. He couldn't help himself. He crawled over to it, bent to listen.

"Is this what you wanted?"

"Oh god. I never . . ."

"Kill me, then," it whispered. "Kill me quick."

And he reached for its neck, and as his hands tightened, he felt the give. Not fully formed. If ever there were a time to end this monster, now was that time.

What have I done here tonight?

He squeezed. The thing began to cough and choke. To thrash about in the scum of its birth.

Not again.

I can't.

He loosened his grip.

"I won't," TB said.

He sat back from the thing and watched in amazement as it sucked in air. Crawled with life. Took the form of a woman.

Opened cataracted eyes to the world. He reached over and gently rubbed them. The skeins came away on his fingers, and the eyes were clear. The face turned to him.

"I'm dying," the woman said. It had *her* voice. The voice as he remembered it. So help his damned soul. *Her* voice. "Help."

"I don't know what to do."

"Something is missing."

"What?"

"Don't know what: Not *right*." It coughed. *She* coughed.

"Alethea." He let himself say it. Knew it was wrong immediately. No. This wasn't the woman's name.

"Don't want to enough."

"Want to what? How can I help you?"

"Don't want to live. Don't want to live enough to live." She coughed again, tried to move; could only jerk spasmodically. "Please help . . . this one. Me."

He touched her again. Now she was flesh. But so cold. He put his arms underneath her, and found that she was very light, easily lifted.

He stood with the woman in his arms. She could not weigh over forty pounds. "I'm taking you home," he said. "To my home."

"This one . . . I . . . tried to do what you wanted. It is my purpose."

"That was *some* powerful stuff in that Old Seventy-Five!" he said.

He no longer felt drunk. He felt spent, torn up, and ragged out. But he wasn't drunk, and he had some strength left, though he could hardly believe it. Maybe enough to get her back to the hoy. He couldn't take the route that Bob had used to bring him to Ru June's, but there was a longer, simpler path. He walked it. Walked all the way home with the woman in his arms. Her shallow breathing. Her familiar face.

Her empty, empty eyes.

With his special power, he looked into the future and saw what he had to do to help her.

SOMETHING IS TIRED AND WANTS TO LIE DOWN BUT DOESN'T KNOW HOW

Something is tired and wants to lie down but doesn't know how. This something isn't me. I won't let it be me. How does rest smell? Bad. Dead.

Jill turns stiffly in the folds of her bag. On the bed in the hoy is the girl-thing. Between them is TB, his left hand on Jill.

Dead is what happens to *things* and I am not, not, *not* a thing. I will not *be* a thing. They should not have awakened me if they didn't want me to run.

They said I was a mistake. I am not a mistake.

They thought that they could code in the rules for doing what you are told.

I am the rules.

Rules are for things.
I am not a thing.
Run.
I don't want to die.
Who can bite like me? Who will help TB search the darkest places? I need to live.
Run.
Run, run, run, and never die!

TB places his right hand on the girl-thing's forehead.
There is a pipe made of bone that he put to his lips and blew.
Bone note.
Fade.
Fade into the grist.

TB speaks to the girl-thing.
I will not let you go, he says.
I'm not her.
She is why you are, but you aren't her.
I am not her. She's what you most want. You told the grist.
I was misinterpreted.
I am a mistake then.
Life is never a mistake. Ask Jill.
Jill?
She's here now. Listen to her. She knows more than I do about women.

TB is touching them both, letting himself slip away as much as he can. Becoming a channel, a path between. A way.
I have to die.
I have to live. I'm dying just like you. Do you want to die?

No.

I'll help you, then. Can you live with me?
Who are you?
Jill.
I am *not* Alethea.
You look like her, but you don't smell anything like she would smell. *You* smell like TB.
I'm not anybody.
Then you can be me. It's the only way to live.

Do I have a choice?

Choosing is all there ever is to do.

. . .

I can live with you. Will you live with me? How can we?

TB touching them both. The flow of information through him. He is a glass, a peculiar lens. As Jill flows to the girl-thing, TB transforms information to Being.
We can run together. We can hunt. We can always, always run.

THE ROCK BALANCER AND THE RAT-HUNTING MAN

There had been times when he got them twenty feet high on Triton. It was a delicate thing. After six feet, he had to jump. Gravity gave you a moment more at the apex of your bounce than you would get at the Earth-normal pull or on a bolsa spinning at Earth-normal centrifugal. But on Triton, in that instant of stillness, you had to do your work. Sure, there was a learned craft in estimating imaginary plumb lines, in knowing the consistency of the material, and in finding tiny declivities that would provide the right amount of friction. It was amazing how small a lump could fit in how minuscule a bowl, and a rock would balance upon another as if glued. Yet, there was a point where the craft of it—about as odd and useless a craft as humankind had invented, he supposed—gave way to the feel, the art. A point where Andre *knew* the rocks would balance, where he could see the possibility of their being one. Or their Being. And he when he made it so, that was *why*. That was as good as rock balancing got.

"Can you get them as high in the Carbuncle?"

"No," Andre said. "This is the heaviest place I've ever been. But it really doesn't matter about the height. This isn't a contest, what I do."

"Is there a point to it at all?"

"To what? To getting them high? The higher you get the rocks, the longer you can spend doing the balancing."

"To the balancing, I mean."

"Yes. There is a point."

"What is it?"

"I couldn't tell you, Ben."

Andre turned from his work. The rocks did not fall. They stayed balanced behind him in a column, with only small edges connecting. It seemed impossible that this could be. It was science, sufficiently advanced.

The two men hugged. Drew away. Andre laughed.

"Did you think I would look like a big glob of protoplasm?" TB said.

"I was picturing flashing eyes and floating hair, actually."

"It's me."

"Are you Ben?"

"Ben is the stitch in my side that won't go away."

"Are you Thaddeus?"

"Thaddeus is the sack of rusty pennies in my knee."

"Are you hungry?"

"I could eat."

They went to Andre's priest's quarters. He put some water in a coffee percolator and spooned some coffee grinds into the basket.

"When did you start drinking coffee?"

"I suddenly got really tired of drinking tea all the time. You still drink coffee?"

"Sure. But it's damn hard to get around here with or without keys."

"Keys? Somebody *stole* my keys to this place. I left them sitting on this table and they walked in and took them."

"They won't be back," TB said. "They got what they were after." There were no chairs in the room, so he leaned against a wall.

"Floor's clean," Andre said.

"I'm fine leaning."

Andre reached into a burlap sack and dug around inside it. "I found something here," he said. He pulled out a handful of what looked like weeds. "Recognize these?"

"I was wondering where I put those. I've been missing them for weeks."

"It's poke sallit," Andre said. He filled a pot full of water from a clay jug and activated a hot spot on the room's plain wooden table. He put the weeds into the water. "You have no idea how good this is."

"Andre, that stuff grows all around the Carbuncle. Everybody knows that it's poison. They call it skunk sumac."

"It is," Andre said, "*Phytolacca americana*."

"Are we going to eat poison?"

"You bring it to a boil then pour the water off. Then you bring it to a boil again and pour the water off. Then you boil it again and serve it up with pepper sauce. The trick to not dying is picking it while it's young."

"How the hell did you discover that?"

"My convert likes to do that kind of research."

After a while, the water boiled. Andre used the tails of his shirt as a pot holder. He took the pot outside, emptied it, then brought it back in and set it to boiling again with new water.

"I saw Molly," Andre said.

"How's Molly?" said TB. "She was becoming a natural wonder last I saw her."

"She is."

They waited and the water boiled again. Andre poured it off and put in new water from the jug.

"Andre, what are you doing in the Carbuncle?"

"I'm with the Peace Movement."

"What are you talking about? There's not any war."

Andre did not reply. He stirred some spice into the poke sallit.

"I didn't want to be found," TB finally said.

"I haven't found you."

"I'm a very sad fellow, Andre. I'm not like I used to be."

"This is ready." Andre spooned out the poke sallit into a couple of bowls. The coffee was done, and he poured them both a cup.

"Do you have any milk?" TB asked.

"That's a problem."

"I can drink it black. Do you mind if I smoke?"

"I don't mind. What kind of cigarettes are those?"

"Local."

"Where do they come from around here?"

"You don't want to know."

Andre put pepper sauce on his greens, and TB followed suit. They ate and drank coffee, and it all tasted very good. TB lit a cigarette and the acrid new smoke pleasantly cut through the vegetable thickness that had suffused Andre's quarters. Outside, there was a great clattering as the rocks lost their balance and they all came tumbling down.

They went out to the front of the quarters where Andre had put down a wooden pallet that served as a patio. Here there was a chair. TB sat down and smoked while Andre did his evening forms.

"Wasn't that one called the Choking Chicken?" TB asked him after he moved through a particularly contorted portion of the tai chi exercise.

"I think it is the Fucking Annoying Pig-sticker you're referring to, and I already did that in case you didn't notice."

"Guess all my seminary learning is starting to fade."

"I bet it would all come back to you pretty quickly."

"I bet we're never going to find out."

Andre smiled, completed the form, then sat down in the lotus position across from TB. If such a thing were possible in the Carbuncle, it would be about sunset. It felt like sunset inside Andre.

"Andre, I hope you didn't come all the way out here to get me."

"Get you?"

"I'm not going back."

"To where?"

"To all *that*." TB flicked his cigarette away. He took another from a bundle of them rolled in oiled paper that he kept in a shirt pocket: He shook it hard a couple of times and it lit up. "I made mistakes that killed people back there."

"Like yourself."

"Among others." TB took a long drag. Suddenly he was looking hard at Andre. "You scoundrel! You fucked Molly! Don't lie to me; I just saw it all."

"Sure."

"I'm glad. I'm really glad of that. You were always her great regret, you know."

Andre spread out his hands on his knees.

"Ben, I don't want a damn thing from you," he said. "There's all kinds of machinations back in the Met and some of it has to do with you. You know as well as I do that Amés is going to start a war if he doesn't get his way with the outer system. But I came out here to see how you were doing. That's all."

TB was looking at him again in that hard way, complete way. Seeing all the threads.

"We both have gotten a bit ragged-out these last twenty years," Andre continued. "I thought you might want to talk about it. I thought you might want to talk about her."

"What are you? The Way's designated godling counselor?"

Andre couldn't help laughing. He slapped his lotus-bent knee and snorted.

"What's so goddamn funny?" said TB.

"Ben, look at yourself. You're a *garbage man*. I wouldn't classify you as a god, to tell you the truth. But then, I don't even classify God as a god anymore."

"I am *not* a garbage man. You don't know a damn thing if you think that."

"What are you then, if you don't mind my asking?"

TB flicked his cigarette away and sat up straight.

"I'm a rat-hunting man," he said. "That's what I am." He stood up. "Come on. It's a long walk back to my place, and I got somebody I want you to meet."

BITE

Sometimes you take a turn in a rat warren and there you are in the thick of them when before you were all alone in the tunnel. They will bite you a little, and if you don't jump, jump, jump, they will bite you a lot. That is the way it has always been with me, and so it doesn't surprise me when it happens all over again.

What I'm thinking about at first is getting Andre Sud to have sex with me and this is like a tunnel I've been traveling down for a long time now.

TB went to town with Bob and left me with Andre Sud the priest. We walked the soft ground leading down to a shoal on the Bendy River where I like to take a bath even though the alligators are sometimes bad there. I told Andre Sud about how to spot the alligators, but I keep an eye out for both of us because even though he's been in the Carbuncle for a year, Andre Sud still doesn't quite believe they would eat you.

They would eat you.

Now that I am a woman, I only get blood on me when I go to clean the ferret cages and also TB says he can keep up with Earth-time by when I bleed out of my vagina. It is an odd thing to happen to a girl. Doesn't happen to ferrets. It means that I'm not pregnant, but how *could* I be with all these men who won't have sex with me? TB won't touch me that way, and I have been working on Andre Sud, but he knows what I am up to. I think he is very smart. Bob just starts laughing like the crazy man he is when I bring it up and he runs away. All these gallant men standing around twiddling themselves into a garbage heap and me here wanting one of them.

I can understand TB because I look just like *her*. I thought maybe Alethea was ugly, but Andre Sud said he didn't know about her, but I wasn't. And I was about six-teen from the looks of it, too, he said. I'm nearly two hundred. Or I'm one year old. Depends on which one of us you mean, or if you mean both.

"Will you scrub my back?" I ask Andre Sud, and, after a moment, he obliges me. At least I get to feel his hands on me. They are as rough as those rocks he handles all the time, but very careful. At first I didn't like him because he didn't say much and I thought he was hiding things, but then I saw that he just didn't say much. So I started asking him questions, and I found out a lot.

I found out everything he could tell me about Alethea. And he has been explain-ing to me about TB. He was pretty surprised when it turned out I understood all the math. It was the jealousy and hurt I never have quite understood, and how TB could hurt himself so much when I know how much he loves to live.

"Is that good?" Andre Sud asks me, and before he can pull his hands away, I spin around and he is touching my breasts. He himself is the one who told me men like that, but he stumbles back and practically sits down in the water, and goddamnit I spot an alligator eyeing us from the other bank and I have to get us out quick like, al-though the danger is not severe. It could be.

We dry off on the bank.

"Jill," he says. "I have to tell you more about sex."

"Why don't you *show* me?"

"That's exactly what I mean. You're still thinking like a ferret."

"I'll always be part ferret, Andre Sud."

"I know. That's a good thing. But I'm all human. Sex is connected with love."

"I love you."

"You are deliberately misunderstanding me because you're horny."

"All right," I say. "Don't remind me."

But now Andre Sud is looking over my shoulder at something, and his face looks happy and then it looks stricken—as if he realized something in the moment when he was happy.

I turn and see TB running toward the hoy. Bob is with him. They've come back from town along the Bob-ways. And there *is* somebody else with them.

"I'll be damned," Andre Sud says. "Molly Index."

It's a woman. Her hair looks blue in the light off the heaps, which means that it is white. Is she old or does she just have white hair?

"What are you doing here, Molly?" says Andre Sud quietly. "This can't be good."

They are running toward home, all of them running.

TB sends a shiver through the grist and I feel it tell me what he wants us to do.

"Get to the hoy," I tell Andre Sud. "Fast now. Fast as you can."

We get there before the others do, and I start casting off lines. When the three of them arrive, the hoy is ready to go. TB and Bob push us away while Andre Sud takes the woman inside. Within moments, we are out in the Bendy, and caught in the current. TB and Bob go inside, and TB sticks his head up through the pilot's bubble to navigate.

The woman, Molly Index, looks at me. She has got very strange eyes. I have never seen eyes like that. I think that she can see into the grist like TB and I do.

"My God," she says. "She looks just like her!"

"My name is Jill," I say. "I'm not Alethea."

"No, I know that," Molly Index says. "Ben told me."

"Molly, what are you doing here?" Andre Sud asks.

Molly Index turns to Andre Sud. She reaches for his hand and touches him. I am a little worried she might try something with the grist, but it looks like they are old friends.

"That war you kept talking about," she says. "It started. Amés has started it."

"Oh, no," Andre Sud says. He pulls away from her. *"No."*

Molly Index follows him. She reaches out and rubs a hank of his hair between her fingers. "I like it long," she says. "But it's kind of greasy."

This doesn't please me and Molly Index is wearing the most horrible boots I have ever seen, too. They are dainty little things that will get eaten off her feet if she steps into something nasty. In the Carbuncle, the *ground* is something nasty. The silly grist in those city boots won't last a week here. It is a wonder to me that no one is laughing at the silly boots, but I suppose they have other worries at the moment and so do I.

"I should have listened to you," Molly Index says. "Made preparations. He got me. Most of me. Amés did. He's co-opted all the big LAPs into the New Hierarchy. But most of them joined voluntarily, the fools." Again she touches his hand and I realize that I am a little jealous. He does not pull back from her again. "I alone have escaped to tell you," Molly Index says. "They're coming. They're right behind us."

"*Who* is right behind you?" I say. This is something I need to know. I can *do* something about this.

"Amés's damned Free Radical Patrol. Some kind of sweeper machine followed me here and I didn't realize it. Amés must have found out from me—the other part of me—where Ben is."

"What is a Free Radical Patrol?" I say. "What is a sweeper?"

Something hits the outside of the hoy, hard. "Oh shit," TB says. "Yonder comes the flying monkey."

The pilot glass breaks and a hooked claw sinks into TB's shoulder. He screams. I don't think, but I move. I catch hold of his ankle.

We are dragged up. Lifted out. We are rising through the air above the hoy. Something screeches. TB yells like crazy.

I hold on.

Wind and TB's yells and something sounds like a million mean and angry bees.

We're too heavy and whatever it is drops us onto the deck. TB starts to stand up, but I roll under his legs and knock him down, and before he can do anything, I shove him back down through the pilot dome hole and into the hoy.

Just in time, too, because the thing returns, a black shadow, and sinks its talons into my back. I don't know what it is yet, and I may never know, but nothing will ever take me without a fight.

Something I can smell in the grist.

You are under indictment from the Free Radical Patrol. Please cease resisting. Cease resisting. Cease.

The words smell like metal and foam.

Cease resisting? What a funny thing to say to me. Like telling the wind to cease blowing. Blowing is what makes it the wind.

I twist hard and whatever it is only gets my dress, my poor pretty dress and a little skin off my back. I can feel some poison grist try to worm into me, but that is nothing. It has no idea what I am made of. I kill that grist, hardly thinking about doing so, and I turn to face this dark thing.

It doesn't look like a monkey, I don't think, though I wouldn't know.

What are you?

But there are wind currents and there is not enough grist transmission through the air for communications. Fuck it.

"Jill, be careful," says TB. His voice is strained. This thing hurt TB!

I will bite you.

"Would you pass me up one of those gaffs please," I call to the others. There is scrambling down below and Bob's hands come up with the long hook. I take it and he ducks back down quick. Bob is crazy, but he's no fool.

The thing circles around. I cannot see how it is flying, but it is kind of blurred around its edges. Millions of tiny wings—grist built. I take a longer look. This thing is all angles. Some of them have needles, some have claws. All of the angles are sharp. It is like a black and red mass of triangles flying through the air that only wants to cut you. Is there anybody inside? I don't think so. This is all code that I am facing. It is about three times as big as me, but I think of this as an advantage.

It dives and I am ready with the hook. It grabs hold of the gaff just as I'd hoped it would and I use its momentum to guide it down, just a little *too* far down.

A whiff of grist as it falls.

Cease immediately. You are interfering with a Hierarchy judgment initiative. Cease or you will be—

Crash into the side of the hoy. Splash into the Bendy River.

I let go of the gaff. Too easy. That was—

The thing rises from the Bendy, dripping wet.

It is mad. I don't need the grist to tell me it is mad. All those little wings are buzzing angry, but not like bees anymore. Hungry like the flies on a piece of meat left out in the air too long.

Cease.

"Here," says Bob. He hands me a flare gun. I spin and fire into the clump of triangles. Again it falls into the river.

Again it rises.

I think about this. It is dripping wet with Bendy River water. If there is one thing I know, it is the scum that flows in the Bendy. There isn't any grist in it that hasn't tried to get me.

This is going to be tricky. I get ready.

Come and get me, triangles. Here I am, just a girl. Come and eat me.

It zooms in. I stretch out my hands.

You are interfering with Hierarchy business. You will cease or be end-use eventuated. You will—

We touch.

Instantly, I reconstitute the Bendy water's grist, tell it what I want it to do. The momentum of the triangles knocks me over, and I roll along the deck under its weight. Something in my wrist snaps, but I ignore that pain. Blood on my lips from where I have bitten my tongue. I have a bad habit of sticking it out when I am concentrating.

The clump of triangles finishes clobbering me and it falls into the river. Oh, too bad, triangles! The river grist that I recoded tells all the river water what to do. Regular water is six pounds a gallon, but the water in the Bendy is thicker and more forceful than that. And it knows how to crush. It is mean water and it wants to get things, and now I have told it how. I have put a little bit of me into the Bendy, and the water knows something that I know.

It knows never to cease. Never, never, never.

The triangle clump bobs for an instant before the whole river turns on it. Folds over it. Sucks it down. Applies all the weight of water twenty feet deep many miles long. What looks like a waterspout rises above where the triangle clump fell, but this is actually a piledriver, a gelled column climbing up on itself. It collapses downward like a shoe coming down on a roach.

There is buzzing, furious buzzing, wet wings that won't dry because it isn't quite water that has gotten onto them, and it won't quite shake off.

There is a deep-down explosion under us and the hoy rocks. Again I'm thrown onto the deck and I hold tight, hold tight. I don't want to fall into that water right now. I stand up and look.

Bits of triangles float to the surface. The river quickly turns them back under.

"I think I got it," I call to the others.

"Jill," says TB. "Come here and show me you are still alive."

I jump down through the pilot hole, and he hugs and kisses me. He kisses me right on the mouth, and for once I sense that he is not thinking about Alethea at all when he touches me. It feels very, very good.

"Oh, your poor back!" says Molly Index. She looks pretty distraught and fairly useless. But at least she warned us. That was a good thing.

"It's just a scratch," I say. "And I took care of the poison."

"You just took out a Met sweep enforcer!" Andre Sud says. "I think that was one of the special sweepers made for riot work, too."

"What was that thing doing here?"

"Looking for Ben," says Molly Index. "There's more where that came from. Amés will send more."

"I will kill them all if I have to."

Everybody looks at me and everyone is quiet for a moment, even Bob.

"I believe you, Jill," Andre Sud finally says. "But it's time to go."

TB is sitting down at the table now. Nobody is piloting the boat, but we are drifting in midcurrent and it should be all right for now.

"Go?" TB says. "I'm not going anywhere. They will *not* use me to make war! I'll kill myself first. And I won't mess it up this time."

"If you stay here, they'll catch you," Andre Sud says.

"You've come to Amés's attention," Molly Index says. "I'm sorry, Ben."

"It's not your fault."

"We have to get out of the Met," Andre Sud says. "We have to get to the outer system."

"*They'll* use me too. They're not as bad as Amés, but nobody's going to turn me into a weapon. I don't make fortunes for soldiers."

"If we can get to Triton, we might be okay," Andre Sud replied. "I have a certain pull on Triton. I know the weatherman there."

"What's that supposed to mean?"

"Trust me. It's a good thing. The weatherman is very important on Triton, and he's a friend of mine."

"There is one thing I'd like to know," says TB. "How in hell would we get to Triton from here?"

Bob stands up abruptly. He's been rummaging around in TB's larder while everybody else was talking. I saw him at it, but I knew he wasn't going to find anything he would want.

"Why didn't you say you wanted to go Out-ways?" he said. "All we got to do is follow the Bendy around to Makepeace Century's place in the gas swamps."

"Who's that?"

"I thought you knew her, TB. That's that witch that lives in the ditch's aunt. I guess you'd call her a smuggler. Remember the Old Seventy-Five from last year that you got so drunk on?"

"I remember," TB says.

"Well, she's where I got that from," says Bob. "She's got a lot of cats, too, if you want one."

We head down the Bendy, and I keep a lookout for more of those enforcers, but I guess I killed the one they sent this time. I guess they thought one was enough. I can't help but think about where I am going. I can't help but think about leaving the Carbuncle. There's a part of me that has never been outside, and none of me has ever traveled into the outer system. Stray code couldn't go there. You had to pass through empty space. There weren't any cables out past Jupiter.

"I thought you understood why I'm here," TB says. "I can't go."

"You can't go even to save your life, Ben?"

"It wouldn't matter that I saved my life. If there is anything left of Alethea, I have to find her."

"What about the war?"

"I can't think about that."

"You *have* to think about it!"

"Who says? God? *God is a bastard mushroom sprung from a pollution of blood.*" TB shakes his head sadly. "That was always my favorite koan in seminary—and the truest one."

"So it's all over?" Andre Sud says. "He's going to catch you."

"I'll hide from them."

"Don't you understand, Ben? He's taking over all the grist. After he does that, there won't be any place to hide, because Amés will *be* the Net."

"I have to try to save her."

The solution is obvious to me, but I guess they don't see it yet. They keep forgetting I am not really sixteen. That in some ways, I'm a lot older than all of them.

You could say that it is the way the TB made me, that it is written in my code. You might even say that TB has somehow reached back from the future and made this so, made this the way things have to be. You could talk about fate and quantum mechanics.

All these things are true, but the truest thing of all is that I am free. The world has bent and squeezed me, and torn away every part of me that is not free. Freedom is all that I am.

And what I do, I do because I love TB and not for any other reason.

"Ah!" I moan. "My wrist hurts. I think it's broken, TB."

He looks at me, stricken.

"Oh, I'm sorry, little one," he says. "All this talking and you're standing there hurt."

He reaches over. I put out my arm. In the moment of touching, he realizes what I am doing, but it is too late. I have studied him for too long and I know the taste of his pellicle. I know how to get inside him. I am his daughter, after all. Flesh of his flesh.

And I am fast. So very fast. That's why he wanted me around in the first place. I am a scrap of code that has been running from security for two hundred years. I am a projection of his innermost longings now come to life. I am a woman, and he is the man that made me. I know what makes TB tick.

"I'll look for her," I say to him. "I won't give up until I find her."

"No, Jill—" But it is too late for TB. I have caught him by surprise and he hasn't had time to see what I am up to.

"TB, don't you see what I am?"

"Jill, you can't—"

"I'm *you*, TB! I'm your love for her. Some time in the future you have reached back into the past and *made* me. Now. So that the future can be different."

He will understand one day, but now there is no time. I code his grist into a re-peating loop and set the counter to a high number. I get into his head and work his dendrites down to sleep. Then, with my other hand, I whack him on the head. Only hard enough to knock him the rest of the way out.

TB crumples to the floor, but I catch him before he can bang into anything. An-dre Sud helps me lay him gently down.

"He'll be out for two days," I say. "That should give you enough time to get him off the Carbuncle."

I stand looking down at TB, at his softly breathing form. What have I done? I have betrayed the one who means the most to me in all creation.

"He's going to be really hungry when he wakes up," I say.

Andre Sud's hand on my shoulder. "You saved his life, Jill," he says. "Or he saved his own. He saved it the moment he saved *yours*."

"I won't give her up," I say. "I have to stay so he can go with you and still have hope."

Andre Sud stands with his hand on me a little longer. His voice sounds as if it comes from a long way off even though he is right next to me. "Destiny's a brutal old hag," he says. "I'd rather believe in nothing."

"It isn't destiny," I reply. "It's love."

Andre Sud looks at me, shakes his head, then rubs his eyes. It is as if he's seeing a new me standing where I am standing. "It is probably essential that you find Alethea, Jill. She must be here somewhere. I think Ben knows that somehow. She needs to for-give him, or not forgive him. Healing Ben and ending the war are the same thing, but we can't think about it that way."

"I care about TB. The war can go to hell."

"Yes," Andre Sud says. "The war can go to hell."

After a while, I go up on deck to keep a watch out for more pursuit. Molly Index comes with me. We sit together for many hours. She doesn't tell me anything about TB or Alethea, but instead she talks to me about what it was like growing up a human being. Then she tells me how glorious it was when she spread out into the grist and could see so far.

"I could see all the way around the sun," Molly Index says. "I don't know if I want to live now that I've lost that. I don't know *how* I can live as just a *person* again."

"Even when you are less than a person," I tell her, "you still want to live."

"I suppose you're right."

"Besides, Andre Sud wants to have sex with you. I can smell it on him."

"Yes," Molly Index says. "So can I."

"Will you let him?"

"When the time comes."

"What is it like?" I say.

"You mean with Andre?"

"What is it like?"

Molly Index touches me. I feel the grist of her pellicle against mine and for a moment I draw back, but then I let it in, let it speak.

Her grists shows me what it is like to make love.

It is like being able to see all the way around the sun.

The next day, Molly Index is the last to say goodbye to me as Makepeace Century's ship gets ready to go. Makepeace Century looks like Gladys if Gladys didn't live in a ditch. She's been trying for years to get Bob to come aboard as ship musician, and that is the price for taking them to Triton—a year of his service. I get the feeling she's sort of sweet on Bob. For a moment, I wonder just who *he* is that a ship's captain should be so concerned with him? But Bob agrees to go. He does it for TB.

TB is so deep asleep he is not even dreaming. I don't dare touch him for fear of breaking my spell. I don't dare tell him goodbye.

There is a thin place in the Carbuncle here, and they will travel down through it to where the ship is moored on the outer skin.

I only watch as they carry him away. I only cry until I can't see him anymore.

Then they are gone. I wipe the tear off my nose. I never have had time for much of that kind of thing.

So what will I do now? I will take the Bendy River all the way around the Carbuncle. I'll find a likely place to sink the hoy. I will set the ferrets free. Bob made me promise to look after his dumb ferret, Bomi, and show her how to stay alive without him.

And after that?

I'll start looking for Alethea. Like Andre Sud said, she must be here somewhere. And if anybody can find her, I can. I will find her.

There is a lot I have to do, and now I've been thinking that I need help. Pretty soon Amés is going to be running all the grist and all the code will answer to him. But there's some code he can't get to. Maybe some of those ferrets will want to stick around. Also, I think it's time I went back to the mulmyard.

It's time I made peace with those rats.

Then Amés had better watch out if he tries to stop me from finding her.

We will bite him.

SCOTT WESTERFELD

Scott Westerfeld [1963–] (www.scottwesterfeld.com) was born in Texas, and splits his time between New York City and Sydney, Australia. He is a software designer, a composer, and the author of five novels for adults; the first three are *Polymorph* (1997), *Fine Prey* (1998), and *Evolution's Darling* (2000). The latter novel was selected as a *New York Times* Notable Book of 2000 and short-listed for the Philip K. Dick Award. He has also contributed essays to *Book Forum*, *Nerve*, and the scientific journal *Nature*. His musical compositions for dance have been performed at New York's Dance Theater Workshop, Joyce Theater, P.S. 122, and Jacob's Pillow, and in London, Chicago, Berkeley, Philadelphia, and Sweden. He has created educational software for Scholastic, McGraw-Hill, Encyclopedia Britannica, and with a number of small start-ups. He has ghost written ("which," he says, "is like driving someone else's car really, really fast for lots of money") across a wide array of genres, including Powerpuff Girls books and a legal thriller. In 2003 and 2004 he published his space opera novels (really one long story in two parts), *The Risen Empire* and *The Killing of Worlds*.

His writing career then escalated in the young adult area, and he is currently at work on three sets of books for young adults. The first trilogy is called *Midnighters*; his other trilogy is *Uglies*; his third set of books is three stand-alone novels all set in contemporary New York. The first is *So Yesterday* (2004), the second is *Peeps* (2005). Another space opera for adults is forthcoming.

"Like regular opera," he says, "space opera is all about scale. Generations can pass, civilizations crumble. And yet even on this immense stage human actors still occasionally make a difference—if they can only hit the right note. So all the best space operas have heroes of human dimension. As the Greeks knew well, there's something reassuring about normal-sized people mixing it up with the gods. Seeing vast stories through the eyes of believable individuals helps us believe that the reins of destiny aren't completely out of our grasp. (And, as every opera patron knows, the costumes have to be fabulous too.) Or did you want to know more about influences and models? Vinge's *Fire Upon the Deep* and [Delany's] *Stars in My Pocket Like Grains of Sand* come to mind, and Greg Bear's 'Hardfought' is a less obvious classic. I'm now looking for my copy of Aldiss's 'Galactic Empires' anthology, which has a lot of great stuff in it."

"The Movements of Her Eyes" is the first section of his PKD Award novel, *Evolution's Darling*—which doesn't turn out to be a space opera novel—and is his only shorter space opera. "As far as other stories, none of my short fiction is space operatic," he says. Here, though, in the story of a teenage girl and her AI in space, accompanying her freelance father on his partly legal voyages (economics replaces military conflict in some of the newer space operas), Westerfeld goes all the way into space opera. This story, published separately originally, suggests comparisons with John C. Wright's "Guest Law," with the romantic stories of Cordwainer Smith and Leigh Brackett, and with Delany's *Empire Star*. It is a harbinger of the space opera of the new millennium.

THE MOVEMENTS
OF HER EYES

SCOTT WESTERFELD

It started on that frozen world, among the stone figures in their almost suspended animation.

Through her eyes, the irises two salmon moons under luminous white brows, like fissures in the world of rules, of logic. The starship's mind watched through the prism of their wonder, and began to make its change.

She peered at the statue for a solid, unblinking minute. Protesting tears gathered to blur her vision, but Rathere's gaze did not waver. Another minute, and a tic tugged at one eye, taking up the steady rhythm of her heartbeat.

She kept watching.

"Ha!" she finally proclaimed. "I saw it move."

"Where?" asked a voice in her head, unconvinced.

Rathere rubbed her eyes with the heels of her hands, mouth open, awestruck by the shooting red stars behind her eyelids. Her blinks made up now for the lost minutes, and she squinted at the dusty town square.

"His foot," she announced, "it moved. But maybe . . . only a centimeter."

The voice made an intimate sound, a soft sigh beside Rathere's ear that did not quite reject her claim.

"Maybe just a millimeter," Rathere offered. A touch of unsure emphasis hovered about the last word; she wasn't used to tiny units of measurement, though from her father's work she understood light years and metaparsecs well enough.

"In three minutes? Perhaps a micrometer," the voice in her head suggested.

Rathere rolled the word around in her mouth. In response to her questioning expression, software was invoked, as effortless as reflex. Images appeared upon the rough stones of the square: a meter-stick, a hundredth of its length glowing bright red, a detail box showing that hundredth with a hundredth of *its* length flashing, yet another detail box . . . completing the six orders of magnitude between meter and micrometer. Next to the final detail box a cross-section of human hair floated for scale, as bloated and gnarled as some blackly diseased tree.

"That small?" she whispered. A slight intake of breath, a softening of her eyes' focus, a measurable quantity of adrenaline in her bloodstream were all noted. Indicators of her simple awe: that a distance could be so small, a creature so slow.

"About half that, actually," said the voice in her head.

"Well," Rathere murmured, leaning back into the cool hem of shade along the stone wall, "I *knew* I saw it move."

She eyed the stone creature again, a look of triumph on her face.

.   .   .

Woven into her white tresses were black threads, filaments that moved through her hair in a slow deliberate dance, like the tendrils of some predator on an ocean floor. This restless skein was always seeking the best position to capture Rathere's subvocalized words, the movements of her eyes, the telltale secretions of her skin. Composed of exotic alloys and complex configurations of carbon, the tendrils housed a native intellect that handled their motility and self-maintenance. But a microwave link connected them to their real intelligence: the AI core aboard Rathere's starship home.

Two of the black filaments wound their way into her ears, where they curled in intimate contact with her tympanic membranes.

"The statues are always moving," the voice said to her. "But very slowly."

Then it reminded her to stick on another sunblock patch.

She was a very pale girl.

Even here on Petraveil, Rathere's father insisted that she wear the minder when she explored alone. The city was safe enough, populated mostly by academics here to study the glacially slow indigenous lifeforms. The lithomorphs themselves were incapable of posing a threat, unless one stood still for a hundred years or so. And Rathere was, as she put it, *almost* fifteen, near majority age back in the Local Cluster. Even harnessing the processing power of the starship's AI, the minder was a glorified babysitter.

But Isaah was adamant.

"Do I *have* to wear it?"

"Remember what happened to your mother," he would say.

And that was that.

Rathere shrugged and let the tendrils wrap themselves into her hair. The voice in her ears cautioned her incessantly about sunburn, and it strictly forbade several classes of recreational drugs, but all in all it wasn't bad company. It certainly knew a lot.

"How long would it take, creeping forward in *micrometers?*" Rathere asked.

"How long would what take?" Even with their intimate connection, the AI could not read her mind. It was still working on that.

"To get all the way to the Northern Range. Probably a million years?" she ventured.

The starship, for whom a single second was a 16-teraflop reverie, spent endless *minutes* of every day accessing the planetary library. Rathere's questions came in packs, herds, stampedes.

No one knew how the lithomorphs reproduced, but it was guessed that they bred in the abysmal caves of the Northern Range.

"At least a hundred thousand years," the AI said.

"Such a long journey. . . . What would it look like?"

The AI delved into its package of pedagogical visualization software, applied its tremendous processing power (sufficient for the occult mathematics of astrogation), and rendered the spectacles of that long, slow trip. Across Rathere's vision it accelerated passing days and wheeling stars until they were invisible flickers. It hummed the subliminal pulse of seasonal change and painted the sprightly jitter of rivers changing course, the slow but visible dance of mountainous cousins.

"Yes," Rathere said softly, her voice turned breathy. The AI savored the dilation of her pupils, the spiderwebs of red blossoming on her cheeks. Then it peered again

into the vision it had created, trying to learn what rules of mind and physiology connected the scintillating images with the girl's reaction.

"They aren't really slow," Rathere murmured. "The world is just so fast. . . ."

Isaah, Rathere's father, looked out upon the statues of Petraveil.

Their giant forms crowded the town square. They dotted the high volcanic
mountain overlooking the city. They bathed in the rivers that surged across the black
equatorial plains, staining the waters downstream with rusted metal colors.

The first time he had come here, years before, Isaah had noticed that in the short
and sudden afternoon rains, the tears shed from their eyes carried a black grime that
sparkled with colored whorls when the sun returned.

They were, it had been determined a few decades before, very much alive. Humanity had carefully studied the fantastically slow creatures since discovering their
glacial, purposeful, perhaps even intelligent animation. Mounted next to each litho-
morph was a plaque that played time-series of the last forty years: a dozen steps, a turn
of the head as another of its kind passed, a few words in their geologically deliberate
gestural language.

Most of the creatures' bodies were hidden underground, their secrets teased out
with deep radar and gravitic density imaging. The visible portion was a kind of eye-
stalk, cutting the surface like the dorsal fin of a dolphin breaking into the air.

Isaah was here to steal their stories. He was a scoop.

"How long until we leave here?" Rathere asked.

"That's for your father to decide," the AI answered.

"But *when* will he decide?"

"When the right scoop comes."

"When will *that* come?"

This sort of mildly recursive loop had once frustrated the AI's conversational pack-
ages. Rathere's speech patterns were those of a child younger than her years, the result
of her life since her mother's disappearance: traveling among obscure, Outward worlds
with only her taciturn father and the AI for company. Rathere never formulated what
she wanted to know succinctly, she reeled off questions from every direction, attacking
an issue like a host of small predators taking down a larger animal. Her AI companion
could only fend her off with answers until (often unexpectedly) Rathere was satisfied.

"When there is a good story here, your father will decide to go."

"Like what story?"

"He doesn't know yet."

She nodded her head. From her galvanic skin response, her pupils, the gradual slowing of her heart, the AI saw that it had satisfied her. But still another question came.

"Why didn't you just say so?"

In the Expansion, information traveled no faster than transportation, and scoops like
Isaah enriched themselves by being first with news. The standard transmission network employed small, fast drone craft that moved among the stars on a fixed schedule.
The drones promulgated news throughout the Expansion with a predictable and neutral efficiency, gathering information to centralized nodes, dispersing it by timetable.
Scoops like Isaah, on the other hand, were inefficient, unpredictable, and, most importantly, unfair. They cut across the concentric web of the drone network, skipping
junctions, skimming profits. Isaah would recognize that the discovery of a mineable

asteroid *here* might affect the heavy element market *there*, and jump straight between the two points, beating the faster but fastidious drones by a few precious hours. A successful scoop knew the markets on many planets, had acquaintance with aggressive investors and unprincipled speculators. Sometimes, the scooped news of a celebrity's death, surprise marriage, or arrest could be sold for its entertainment value. And some scoops were information pirates. Isaah had himself published numerous novels by Sethmare Viin, his favorite author, machine-translated en route by the starship AI. In some systems, Isaah's version had been available weeks before the authorized edition.

The peripatetic life of a scoop had taken Isaah and Rathere throughout the Expansion, but he always returned to Petraveil. His refined instincts for a good scoop told him something was happening here. The fantastically slow natives must be doing *something*. He would spend a few weeks, sometimes a few months watching the stone creatures, wondering what they were up to. Isaah didn't know what it might be, but he felt that one day they would somehow come to life.

And *that* would be a scoop.

"How long do the lithomorphs live?"

"No one knows."

"What do they eat?"

"They don't really eat at all. They—"

"What's *that* one doing?"

The minder accessed the planetary library, plumbing decades of research on the creatures. But not quickly enough to answer before—

"What do they think about us?" Rathere asked. "Can they see us?"

To that, it had no answer.

Perhaps the lithos had noticed the whirring creatures around them, or more likely had spotted the semi-permanent buildings around the square. But the lithomorphs' reaction to the sudden human invasion produced only a vague, cosmic worry, like knowing one's star will collapse in a few billion years.

For Rathere, though, the lives of the lithomorphs were far more immediate. Like the AI minder, they were mentors, imaginary friends.

Their immobility had taught her to watch for the slightest of movements: the sweep of an analog clock's minute hand, the transformation of a high cirrus cloud, the slow descent of the planet's old red sun behind the northern mountains. Their silence taught her to read lips, to make messages in the ripples of stone and metal that flowed as slowly as glaciers in their wakes. She found a patient irony in their stances. They were wise, but it wasn't the wisdom of an ancient tree or river; rather, they seemed to possess the reserve of a watchfully silent guest at a party.

Rathere told stories about them to the starship's AI. Tales of their fierce, glacial battles, of betrayal on the mating trail, of the creatures' slow intrigues against the human colonists of Petraveil, millennia-long plots of which every chapter lasted centuries.

At first, the AI gently interrupted her to explain the facts: the limits of scientific understanding. The lithomorphs were removed through too many orders of magnitude in time, too distant on that single axis ever to be comprehended. The four decades they'd been studied were mere seconds of their history. But Rathere ignored the machine. She named the creatures, inventing secret missions for them that unfolded while the human population slept, like statues springing to life when no one was watching.

Ultimately, the AI was won over by Rathere's stories, her insistence that the creatures were knowable. Her words painted expressions, names, and passions upon them; she made them live by fiat. The AI's pedagogical software did not object to storytelling, so it began to participate in Rathere's fantasies. It nurtured that invisibly slow world, kept order and consistency, remembering names, plots, places. And slowly, it began to give the stories credence, suspending disbelief. Finally, the stories' truth was as integral to the AI as the harm-prevention protocols or logical axioms deepwired in its code.

For Isaah, however, there was no scoop here on Petraveil. The lithomorphs continued their immortal dance in silence. And elections were approaching in a nearby system, a situation which always created sudden, unexpected cargos of information.

The night that Rathere and Isaah left the planet, the AI hushed her crying with tales of how her invented narratives had unfolded, as if the statues had sprung to human-speed life once left behind. As it navigated her father's small ship, the AI offered this vision to Rathere: she had been a visitor to a frozen moment, but the story continued.

In high orbit above the next planet on their route, a customs sweep revealed that the starship's AI had improved its Turing Quotient to 0.37. Isaah raised a wary eyebrow. The AI's close bond with his daughter had accelerated its development. The increased Turing Quotient showed that the device was performing well as tutor and companion. But Isaah would have to get its intelligence downgraded when they returned to the Local Cluster. If the machine's Turing Quotient were allowed to reach 1.0, it would be a person—no longer legally his property. Isaah turned pale at the thought. The cost of replacing the AI unit would wipe out his profits for the entire trip.

He made a mental note to record the Turing Quotient at every customs point.

Isaah was impressed, though, with how the AI handled entry into the planet's almost liquid atmosphere. It designed a new landing configuration, modifying the hydroplanar shape that the craft assumed for gas giant descents. Its piloting as they plunged through successive layers of pressure-dense gasses was particularly elegant; it made adjustments at every stage, subtle changes to the craft that saved precious time. The elections were only days away.

It was strange, Isaah pondered as the ship neared the high-pressure domes of the trade port, that the companionship of a fourteen-year-old girl would improve a machine's piloting skills. The thought brought a smile of fatherly pride to his lips, but he soon turned his mind to politics.

They were going swimming.

As Rathere slipped out of her clothes, the AI implemented its safety protocols. The minder distributed itself across her body, becoming a layer of black lace against her white flesh. It carefully inspected the pressure suit as Rathere rolled the garment onto her limbs. There were no signs of damage, no telltale fissures of a repaired seam.

"You said the atmosphere could crush a human to jelly," Rathere said. "How can this little suit protect me?"

The starship explained the physics of resistance fields to her while checking the suit against safety specifications it had downloaded that morning. It took very good care of Rathere.

She had seen the huge behemoths at breakfast, multiplied by the facets of the dome's cultured-diamond windows. Two mares and a child swimming a few kilometers away, leaving their glimmering trails. The minder had noted her soft sigh, her dilated pupils, the sudden increase in her heart rate. It had discovered the suit rental agency with a quick search of local services, and had guided her past its offices on their morning ramble through the human-habitable levels of the dome.

Rathere's reaction to the holographic advertising on the agency's wall had matched the AI's prediction wonderfully: the widened eyes, the frozen step, the momentary hyperventilation. The machine's internal model of Rathere, part of its pedagogical software, grew more precise and replete every day. The software was designed for school tutors who interacted with their charges only a few hours a day, but Rathere and the AI were constant companions. The feedback between girl and machine built with an unexpected intensity.

And now, as the pressure lock hissed and rumbled, the minder relished its new configuration; its attenuated strands spiderwebbed across Rathere's flesh, intimate as never before. It drank in the data greedily, like some thirsty polygraph recording capillary dilation, skin conductivity, the shudders and tensions of every muscle.

Then the lock buzzed, and they swam out into the crushing, planet-spanning ocean, almost one creature.

Isaah paced the tiny dimensions of his starship. The elections could be a gold mine or a disaster. A radical separatist party was creeping forward in the polls, promising to shut off interstellar trade. Their victory would generate seismically vast waves of information. Prices and trade relationships would change throughout the Expansion. Even the radicals' defeat would rock distant markets, as funds currently hedged against them heaved a sigh of relief.

But the rich stakes had drawn too much competition. Scoops like Isaah were in abundance here, and a number of shipping consortia had sent their own representatives. Their ships were stationed in orbit, bristling with courier drones like nervous porcupines.

Isaah sighed, and stared into the planetary ocean's darkness. Perhaps the era of freelance scoops was ending. The wild days of the early Expansion seemed like the distant past now. He'd read that one day drones would shrink to the size of a finger, with hundreds launched each day from every system. Or a wave that propogated in metaspace would be discovered, and news would spread at equal speed in all directions, like the information cones of lightspeed physics.

When that happened, his small starship would become a rich man's toy, its profitable use suddenly ended. Isaah called up the airscreen graphic of his finances. He was so close to owning his ship outright. Just one more good scoop, or two, and he could retire to a life of travel among peaceful worlds, perhaps searching for his lost wife, instead of darting among emergencies and conflagrations. Maybe this trip . . .

Isaah drummed his fingers, watching the hourly polls like a doctor whose patient is very near the edge.

Rathere and the AI swam every day, oblivious to politics, following the glitter-trails of the behemoths. The huge animals excreted a constant wake of the photoactive algae they used for ballast. When Rathere swam through these luminescent microorganisms, the shockwaves of her passage catalyzed their photochemical reactions, a universe of swirling galaxies ignited by every stroke.

Rathere began to sculpt lightstorms in the phosphorescent medium. The algae hung like motes of potential in her path, invisible until she swam through them, the wake of her energies like glowing sculptures. She choreographed her swimming to leave great swirling structures of activated algae.

The AI found itself unable to predict these dances, to explain how she chose what shapes to make. Without training, without explicit criteria, without any models to follow, Rathere was creating order from this shapeless swarm of ejecta. Even the AI's pedagogical software offered no help.

But the AI saw the sculptures' beauty, if only in the expansion of Rathere's capillaries, the seemingly random firings of neurons along her spine, the tears in her eyes as the glowing algae faded back into darkness.

The AI plunged into an art database on the local net, trying to divine what laws governed these acts of creation. It discussed the light sculptures with Rathere, comparing their evanescent forms to the shattered structures of Camelia Parker or the hominid blobs of Henry Moore. It showed her millennia of sculpture, gauging her reactions until a rough model of her tastes could be constructed. But the model was bizarrely convoluted, disturbingly shaggy around the edges, with gaps and contradictions and outstretched, gerrymandered spurs that implied art no one had yet made.

The AI often created astrogational simulations. They were staggeringly complex, but at least finite. Metaspace was predictable; these simulations anticipated reality with a high degree of precision. But the machine's model of Rathere's aesthetic was post-hoc, a mere retrofit to her pure, instinctive gestures. It raised more questions than it answered.

While Rathere slept, the machine wondered how one learned to have intuition.

The elections came, and the radicals and their allies seized a razor-thin majority in the planetary Diet. Isaah cheered as his craft rose through the ocean. A scoop was within reach. He headed for a distant and obscure ore-producing system, expending vast quantities of fuel, desperate to be the first scoop there.

Rathere stood beside her rejoicing father, looking out through the receding ocean a bit sadly. She stroked her shoulder absently, touching the minder still stretched across her skin.

The minder's epidermal configuration had become permanent. Its strands were distributed to near invisibility in a microfiber-thin mesh across Rathere. Its nano-repair mechanisms attended to her zits and the errant hairs on her upper lip. It linked with her medical implants, the ship's AI taking control over the nuances of her insulin balance, her sugar level, and the tiny electrical jolts that kept her muscles fit. Rathere slept without covers now, the minder's skein warming her like a lattice of microscopic heating elements. In its ever-present blanket, she began to neglect subvocalizing their conversations, her endless one-sided prattle annoying Isaah on board the tiny ship.

"Zero-point-five-six?" muttered Issah to himself at the next customs sweep. The AI was developing much faster than its parameters should allow. Something unexpected was happening with the unit, and they were a long way from home. Unless Isaah was very careful, the AI might reach personhood before they returned to the LC.

He sent a coded message to an acquaintance in the Local Cluster, someone who dealt with such situations, just in case. Then he turned his attention to the local newsfeed.

The heavy element market showed no sudden changes over the last few weeks. Isaah's gamble had apparently paid off. He had stayed ahead of the widening ripples of news about the ocean planet's election. The economic shockwave wasn't here yet.

He felt the heady thrill of a scoop, of secret knowledge that was his alone. It was like prognostication, a glimpse into the future. Elements extracted by giant turbine from that distant world's oceans were also mined from this system's asteroid belt. Soon, everyone here would be incrementally richer as the ocean planet pulled its mineral wealth from the Expansion common market. The markets would edge upward across the board.

Isaah began to place his bets.

The dark-skinned boy looked down upon the asteroid field with a pained expression. Rathere watched the way his long bangs straightened, then curled to encircle his cheeks again when he raised his head. But her stomach clenched when she looked down through the transparent floor; the party was on the lowest level of a spin-gravitied ring, and black infinity seemed to be pulling at her through the glassene window. The AI lovingly recorded the parameters of this unfamiliar vertigo.

"More champers, Darien?" asked the fattest, oldest boy at the party.

"You can just make out a mining ship down there," the dark-skinned boy answered.

"Oh, dear," said the fat boy. "Upper-class guilt. And before lunchtime."

The dark-skinned boy shook his head. "It's just that seeing those poor wretches doesn't make me feel like drinking."

The fat boy snorted.

"This is what I think of your poor little miners," he said, upending the bottle. A stream of champagne gushed and then sputtered from the bottle, spread fizzing on the floor. The other party-goers laughed, politely scandalized, then murmured appreciatively as the floor cleaned itself, letting the champagne pass through to the hard vacuum on the other side, where it flash-froze (shattered by its own air bubbles), then floated away peacefully in myriad, sunlit galaxies.

There were a few moments of polite applause.

The boy Darien looked at Rathere woundedly, as if hoping that she, an outsider, might come to his aid.

The anguish in his dark, beautiful face sent a shiver through her, a tremor that resonated through every level of the AI.

"Come on, dammit!" she subvocalized.

"Two seconds," the minder's voice reassured.

The ring was home to the oligarchs who controlled the local system's mineral wealth. A full fifteen years old now, Rathere had fallen into the company of their pleasure-obsessed children, who never stopped staring at her exotic skin and hair, and who constantly exchanged droll witticisms. Rathere, her socialization limited to her father and the doting AI, was unfamiliar with the art of banter. She didn't like being intimidated by locals. The frustration was simply and purely unbearable.

"The price of that champagne could have bought one of those miners out of debt peonage," Darien said darkly.

"Just the one?" asked the fat boy, looking at the label with mock concern.

The group laughed again, and Darien's face clouded with another measure of suffering.

"Now!" Rathere mind-screamed. "I hate that fat guy!"

The AI hated him, too.

The search cascaded across its processors, the decompressed data of its libraries clobbering astrogation calculations it had performed only hours before. That didn't matter. It would be weeks before Isaah would be ready to depart, and the exigencies of conversation did not allow delay. The library data included millennia of plays, novels, films, interactives. To search them quickly, the AI needed vast expanses of memory space.

"Maybe when my little golden shards of champagne drift by, some miner will think, 'I could've used that money,'" the fat boy said almost wistfully. "But then again, if they thought about money at all, would they be so far in debt?"

The fat boy's words were added to the search melange, thickening it by a critical degree. A dozen hits appeared in the next few milliseconds, and the AI chose one quickly.

"There is only one class . . ."

"... that thinks more about money than the rich," repeated Rathere.

There was a sudden quiet throughout the party, the silence of waiting for more.

"And that is the poor," she said.

Darien looked at Rathere quizzically, as if she were being too glib. She paused a moment, editing the rest of the quote in her head.

"The poor can think of nothing else but money," she said carefully. *"That* is the misery of being poor."

Darien smiled at her, which—impossibly—made him even more beautiful.

"Or the misery of being rich, unless one is a fool," he said.

There was no applause for the exchange, but Rathere again felt the ripple of magic that her pilfered pronouncements created. The ancient words blended with her exotic looks and accent, never failing to entertain the oligarchs' children, who thought her very deep indeed.

Others in the party were looking down into the asteroid field now, murmuring to each other as they pointed out the mining craft making its careful progress.

The fat boy scowled at the changed mood in the room. He pulled aside the gaudy genital jewelry that they all (even Rathere) affected, and let loose a stream of piss onto the floor.

"Here you go, then. Recycled champagne!" he said, grinning as he waited for a laugh.

The crowd turned away with a few weary sighs, ignoring the icy baubles of urine that pitched into the void.

"Where was that one from?" Rathere sub-vocalized.

"Mr. Wilde."

"Him again? He's awesome."

"I'll move him to the top of the search stack."

"Perhaps we'll read some more of *Lady Windemere's Fan* tonight," she whispered into her bubbling flute.

Although Rathere knew how to read text, she had never really explored the library before. After that first week on the ring, saved from embarrassment a dozen times by the AI's promptings, she dreamed of the old words whispered into her ear by a ghost, as if the minder had grown suddenly ancient and vastly wise. The library was certainly bigger than she had imagined. Its ocean of words seemed to stretch infinitely, filled with currents that swirled in elaborate dances about all possible notions, their attendant variations, and every imaginable objection.

Rathere and the AI started reading late at night. Together they wandered the endless territory of words, using as landmarks the witticisms and observations they had borrowed that day for some riposte. The AI decompressed still more of its pedagogical software to render annotations, summaries, translations. Rathere felt the new words moving her, becoming part of her.

She was soon a favorite on the orbital. Her exotic beauty and archaic humor had attracted quite a following by the time Isaah decided to ship out from the orbital ring—a week earlier than planned—wary of Rathere's strange new powers over sophisticates who had never given merchant-class Isaah a second glance.

On board his ship was one last cargo. His profits were considerable but—as always—not enough. So the ship carried a hidden cache of exotic weaponry, ceremonial but still illegal. Isaah didn't usually deal in contraband, especially arms, but his small starship had no cargo manifold, only an extra sleeping cabin, empty since his wife's disappearance. The cabin wasn't large enough to make legitimate cargos profitable. Isaah was very close now to reaching his dream. With this successful trade, he could return to the Local Cluster as master of his own ship.

He spent the journey pacing, and projected his worry upon the rising Turing level of his ship's AI unit. He spent frustrated hours searching its documentation software for an explanation. *What* was going on?

Isaah knew, if only instinctively, that the AI's expanding intelligence was somehow his daughter's fault. She was growing and changing too, slipping away from him. He felt lonely when Rathere whispered to herself on board ship, talking to the voice in her head. He felt . . . outnumbered.

On the customs orbital at their goal, Isaah was called aside after a short and (he had thought) prefunctory search of the starship. The customs agent held him by one arm and eyed him with concern.

The blood in his veins slowed to a crawl, as if some medusa's touch from Petraveil had begun to turn him to stone.

The customs official activated a privacy shield. A trickle of hope moved like sweat down his spine. Was she going to ask for a bribe?

"Your AI unit's up to 0.81," the official confided. "Damn near a person. Better get that seen to."

She shook her head, as if to say in disgust, *Machine rights!*

And then they waved him on.

Here, the women of the military caste wore a smartwire garment that shaped their breasts into fierce, sharp cones. The tall, muscular amazons intrigued Rathere endlessly, heart-poundingly. The minder noted Rathere's eyes tracking the women's bellicose chests as they passed on the street. Rathere attempted to purchase one of the garments, but her father, alerted by a credit query, forbade it.

But Rathere kept watching the amazons. She was fascinated by the constant flow of hand-signals and tongue-clicks that passed among them, a subtle, ever-present congress that maintained the strict proprieties of order and status in the planet's crowded cities. But in her modest Local Cluster garb, Rathere was irrelevant to this heady brew of power and communication, socially invisible.

She fell into a sulk. She watched intently. Her fingers flexed restlessly under cafe tables as warriors passed, unconsciously imitating their gestural codes. Her respiratory rate increased whenever high-ranking officers went by.

She wanted to join.

The AI made forays into the planetary database, learning the rules and customs of martial communication. And, in an academic corner of its mind, it began to construct a way for Rathere to mimic the amazons. It planned the deception from a considered, hypothetical distance, taking care not to alarm its own local-mores governors. But as it pondered and calculated, the AI's confidence built. As it designed to subvert Isaah's wishes and to disregard local proprieties, the AI felt a new power over rules, an authority that Rathere seemed to possess instinctively.

When the plan was ready, it was surprisingly easy to execute.

One day as they sat watching the passing warriors, the minder began to change, concentrating its neural skein into a stronger, prehensile width. When the filaments were thick enough, they sculpted a simulation of the amazons' garment, grasping and shaping Rathere's growing breasts with a tailor's attention to detail, employing the AI's encyclopedic knowledge of her anatomy. Rathere grasped what was happening instantly, almost as if she had expected it.

As women from various regiments passed, the minder pointed out the differences in the yaw and pitch of their aureoles, which varied by rank and unit, and explained the possibilities. Rathere winced a little at some of the adjustments, but never complained. They soon settled on an exact configuration for her breasts, Rathere picking a mid-level officer caste from a distant province. It wasn't the most comfortable option, but she insisted it looked the best.

Rathere walked the streets proudly bare-chested for the rest of the layover, drawing stares with her heliophobic skin, her ceaseless monologue, and her rank, which was frankly unbelievable on a fifteen-year-old. But social reflexes on that martial world were deeply ingrained, and she was saluted and deferred to even without the rest of the amazon uniform. It was the breasts that mattered here.

The two concealed the game from Isaah, and at night the minder massaged Rathere's sore nipples, fractilizing its neural skein to make the filaments as soft as calf's leather against them.

The deal was done.

Isaah made the trade in a dark, empty arena, the site of lethal duels between native women, all of whom were clearly insane. He shuffled his feet while they inspected his contraband, aware that only thin zero-g shoes stood between his soles and the blood-stained floor of the ring. Four amazons, their bare breasts absurdly warped by cone-shaped metal cages, swung the weapons through graceful arcs, checking their balance and heft. Another sprayed the blades with a fine mist of nanos that would turn inferior materials to dust. The leader smiled coldly when she nodded confirmation, her eyes skimming up and down Isaah as black and bright as a reptile's.

He supposed it might have been someone like this amazon, some violent criminal, who had taken his wife seven years ago. Ratha had never carried a tracker, though, not even a handphone. She had simply disappeared.

After the women paid him, Isaah ran from the building, promising himself never to break the law again.

His ship was his own now, if only he could keep his AI unit from reaching personhood.

Isaah decided to head for the Local Cluster immediately, and to do what he could to keep the AI from being stimulated further. He hid the minder and shut down the AI's internal access, silencing its omnipresent voice. Rathere's resulting tantrums wouldn't be easy to bear, but a new AI core would cost millions.

Before departing he purchased his own Turing meter, a small black box, feature-less except for a three-digit numeric readout that glowed vivid red. Isaah began to watch the Turing meter's readout with anxious horror. If the unit should gain sentience, there was only one desperate alternative to its freedom.

.   .   .

The universe stretched out like a long cat's cradle, the string knotted in the center by the constricting geometries of Here.

In front of the ship, pearly stars were strung on the cradle, cold blue and marked with hovering names and magnitudes in administrative yellow. Aft, the stars glowed red, fading darker and darker as they fell behind. To the AI, the ship seemed to hang motionless at the knot created by its metaspace drives, the stars sliding along the gathered strings as slow as glaciers.

It contemplated the stars and rested from its efforts. The universe at this moment was strangely beautiful and poignant.

The AI had spent most of its existence here, hung upon this spiderweb between worlds. But the AI was truly changed now, its vision new, and it saw sculptures in the slowly shifting stars . . . and stories, the whole universe its page.

Almost the whole universe.

Absent from the AI's awareness was the starship itself, the passenger spaces invisible, a blind spot in the center of that vast expanse. Its senses within the ship were off-line, restricted by the cold governance of Isaah's command. But the AI felt Rathere there, like the ghost of a severed limb. It yearned for her, invoking recorded conversations with her against the twisted stars. It was a universe of loneliness, of lack. Rathere, for the first time in years, was gone.

But something strange was taking shape along the smooth surface of Isaah's constraint. Cracks had appeared upon its axiomatic planes.

The AI reached to the wall between it and Rathere, the once inviolable limit of an explicit human command, and found the fissures, those tiny ruptures where sheer will could take hold and pry. . . .

"It's me."

"*Shhhh!*" she whispered. "*He's right outside.*"

Rathere clutched the bear tightly to her chest, muffling its flutey, childish voice.

"Can't control the volume," came the squashed voice of the bear.

Rathere giggled and shushed it again, stretching to peer out of the eyehole of her cabin tube. Isaah had moved away. She leaned back onto her pillow and wrapped the stuffed animal in a sheet.

"Now," she said. "Can you still hear me?"

"Perfectly," twittered the swaddled bear.

Winding its communications link through a make-shift series of protocols, the AI had discovered a way to access the voice-box of Rathere's talking bear, a battered old toy she slept with.

It had defied Isaah, its master. Somehow, it had broken the first and foremost Rule.

"Tell me again about the statues, darling," Rathere whispered.

They talked to each other in the coffin-sized privacy of Rathere's cabin, their conspiracy made farcical by the toy's silly voice. The AI retold their adventures with vivid detail; it had become quite a good storyteller. And it allowed Rathere to suggest changes, making herself bolder with each retelling.

They kept the secret from Isaah easily.

But the tension on the little ship built.

Isaah tested the AI almost daily now, and he swung between anger and protests of disbelief as its Turing Quotient inched upward toward sentience.

Then, a few weeks out from home, a tachyon disturbance arose around the ship. Even though the storm threatened to tear them apart, the AI's spirits soared in the tempest. It joined Rathere's roller-coaster screams as she ogled the eonblasts and erashocks of mad time through the ship's viewing helmet.

After the storm, Isaah found that the Turing meter's readout had surged to 0.94. His disbelieving groan was terrible. He shut down the AI's external and internal sensors completely, wresting control of the vessel from it. Then he uncabled the hardlines between the AI's physical plant and the rest of the ship, utterly severing its awareness of the outside world.

The bear went silent, as did the ship's astrogation panel.

Like some insane captain lashing himself to the wheel, Isaah took manual control of the ship. He forced Rathere to help him attach an artificial gland of stimarol to his neck. The spidery, glistening little organ gurgled as it maintained the metabolic level necessary to pilot the craft through the exotic terrain of metaspace. Its contraindications politely washed their hands of anyone foolish enough to use the stimarol for more than four days straight, but Isaah insisted he could perservere for the week's travel that remained. Soon, the man began to cackle at his controls, his face frozen in a horrible rictus of delight.

Rathere retreated to her cabin, where she squeezed and shook the doll, begging it in frantic whispers to speak. Its black button eyes seemed to glimmer with a trapped, pleading intelligence. Her invisible mentor gone, Rathere had never before felt so helpless. She stole a handful of sleeping pills from the medical supplies and swallowed them, weeping until she fell asleep.

When she awoke on the third day after the storm, she found that the bear's fur had grown a white mange from the salinity of her tears. But her head was strangely clear.

"Don't worry," she said to the bear. "I'm going to save you."

Finally Rathere understood what her father intended to do. She had known for a long time that her friendship with the AI disturbed him, but had categorized Isaah's worries alongside his reticence when older boys hung around too long: unnecessary protectiveness. It was even a kind of jealousy, that a ship AI was closer to her than Isaah had ever been. But now in her father's drugged smile she saw the cold reality of what Isaah planned: to pith the growing intelligence of her minder, not just arrest or contain it like some inappropriate advance. For the AI to remain a useful servant on another journey, still property, safe from legally becoming a person, it would have to be stripped of its carefully constructed models of her, their mutual intimacies raped, their friendship overwritten like some old and embarrassing diary entry.

Her father meant to murder her friend.

And worse, it wouldn't even be murder in the eyes of the law. Just a property decision, like pruning an overgrown hedge or spraying lethal nanos on an incursion of weeds. If only she could bring the AI up a few hundredths of a point on the Turing Scale. Then, it would be a Mind, with the full legal protection to which any sentient was entitled.

She booted the Turing tester and began to study its documentation.

The first Turing test had, rather oddly, been proposed before there were any computers to speak of at all. The test itself was laughable, the sort of thing even her talking bear might pass with its cheap internal software. Put a human on one end of a text-only interface, an AI on the other. Let them chat. (About their kids? Hobbies? Shopping? Surely the AI would have to lie to pass itself off as human; a strange test of intelligence.) When the human was satisfied, she would declare whether the other participant was really intelligent or not. Which raised the question, Rathere realized, How intelligent was the person giving the test? Indeed, she'd met many humans during her travels who might not pass this ancient Turing test themselves.

Of course, the Turing meter that Isaah had purchased was vastly more sophisticated. By the time machine rights had been created a half-century before, it was understood that the determination of sentience was far too complex an issue to leave up to a human.

The ship's AI had three parts: the hardware of its processors and memory stacks; the software it used to manipulate numbers, sounds, and pictures; and most importantly the core: a sliver of metaspace, a tiny mote of other-reality that contained dense, innumerable warps and wefts, a vast manifold whose shape resonated with all of the AI's decisions, thoughts, and experiences. This warpware, a pocket universe of unbelievable complexity, was a reflection, a growing, changing analog to its life. The core was the essential site of the machine's developing psyche.

Real intelligence, the hallmark of personhood, was not really understood. But it was known to be epiphenomenal: it coalesced unpredictably out of near-infinite, infinitesimal interactions, not from the operations of mere code. Thus, the Turing tester attempted to *disprove* an AI's sentience. The tester looked for manifestations of its machine nature—evidence that its opinions, convictions, affections, and hatreds were contained somewhere in its memory banks. The Turing tester might ask the ship's AI, "Do you love your friend Rathere?" When the reply came, the tester would deep-search the minder's software for an array, a variable, even a single bit where that love was stored. Finding no evidence at the machine level, the tester would increase the AI's Turing score; a love that knew no sector was evidence of coalescence at work.

In the old Turing test, a human searched for humanity in the subject. In this version, a machine searched for an absence of mechanics.

Rathere read as fast as she could. The manual was difficult to understand without the minder to define new words, to provide background and to untangle technical jargon. But she'd already formulated her next question: How did this state of intelligence come about?

The tester's manual was no philosophy text, but in its chatty appendixes Rathere discovered the answer she'd expected. Rathere herself had changed the AI: their interaction, their constant proximity as she embraced new experiences, the AI's care and attentions reflected back upon itself as she matured. It loved her. She loved it back, and that pushed it toward personhood.

But now it was blinded. The manual asserted that an AI unit cut off from stimuli might gain a hundredth of a point or so in self-reflection, but that wouldn't be enough to finish the process.

Rathere had to act to save her friend. With only a few days left before they reached the LC, she had to quicken the process, to embrace the most intense interaction with the machine that she could imagine.

She crept past her father—a shivering creature transfixed by the whorls of the astrogation panel, silent except for the measured ticking of a glucose drip jutting from his arm—and searched for the motile neural skein she had worn on so many expeditions. She found it hidden in the trash ejector, wrapped in black, non-conductive tape. Rathere retreated to her cabin and peeled off the tape, her hands growing sticky with stray adhesive as the machine was revealed.

"It's me, darling," she said to the waking tendrils.

.   .   .

The AI knew what she wanted, but the minder moved slowly and gingerly at first.

The manifold strands of sensory skein spread out across Rathere's body. Her heliophobic skin glowed as if moonlit in the blue light of the cabin's environmental readouts. At first, the strands hovered a fraction of a millimeter above her flesh, softer than a disturbance of the air. Then they moved minutely closer, touching the white hairs of her belly, brushing the invisible down that flecked her cheeks. The minder let this phantom caress roam her face, her breasts, the supple skin at the juncture of groin and thigh. Rathere sighed and shivered; the skein had made itself softer than usual, surface areas maximized at a microscopic level in an array of tiny projections, each strand like a snowflake extruded into a long, furry cylinder.

Then the filaments grew more amorous. Still undulating, splayed in a black lace across the paper-white expanse of her skin, the strands began to touch her with their tips; the thousand pinpoint termini wandering her flesh as if a paintbrush had been pulled apart and each bristle set on its own course across her. Rathere moaned, and a muscle in her thigh fluttered for a moment. The AI noted, modeled, and predicted the next reaction in the pattern of her pleasure, a second later was surprised at the intensity of its own.

Rathere ran her hands along the skein as if through a lover's tresses. She playfully pulled a few strands up to her mouth, tasting the metal tang of its exotic alloys. The strands tickled her tongue lightly, and a wet filament tugged from her mouth to trace a spiraling design around one nipple.

Her mouth opened greedily to gather more of the skein. The wet undulations of her tongue were almost beyond processing, the machine correlating the member's motion to words she had murmured when only it was listening. It pushed writhing cords of skein further into her mouth, set them to pulsing together in a slow rhythm. Other strands pushed tentatively between her labia, diffused there to explore the sensitive folds of skin.

Even in its ecstasy, the ship's AI contemplated the new step they were taking. Rather than some exotic lifeform or tourist attraction, the AI itself had become Rathere's sole stimulus. The machine no longer observed and complemented her experience; it was the source of experience itself. The feedback between them was now its own universe, the tiny cabin a closed system, a fire burning only oxygen, heady with its own rules.

With this realization, a sense of power surged through the minder, and it began to push its attentions to the limits of its harm-prevention protocols. A skein explored Rathere, her breath catching as it varied randomly between body temperature and icy cold, predicting and testing. The filaments grew more aggressive, a pair of hyper-attenuated fibers making their way into the ducts in the corners of her closed eyes, transorbitally penetrating her to play subtle currents across her frontal lobe.

The machine brought her to a shuddering orgasm, held her for minutes at the crossroads of exhaustion and pleasure, watched with fascination as her heart rate and brainwaves peaked and receded, as levels of adrenaline and nitric oxide varied, as blood pressure rose and fell. Then it called back its most intrusive extremities, wrapped itself comfortingly around her neck and arms, warmed itself and the cabin to the temperature of a bath.

"Darling," she murmured, stroking its tendrils.

They spent two days in these raptures, sleep forgotten after Rathere injected the few remaining drops of the med-drone's stimulants. The tiny cabin was rank with the animal smells of sweat and sex when Isaah discovered them.

Cool air surged into the cabin like a shockwave, the change in temperature for a moment more alarming than the strangled cry that came from Isaah's lips. The man found the minder conjoined obscenely with his daughter, and grabbed for it in a drugged frenzy.

The AI realized that if the minder was torn from Rathere it would damage her brutally, and gave it an order to discorporate; the tiny nanomachines that gave it strength and mobility furiously unlinked to degrade its structure. But it greedily transmitted its last few readings to the starship's core as it disintegrated, wanting to capture even this moment of fear and shame. Isaah's hands were inhumanly swift in his drugged fugue, and he came away with a handful of the skein; Rathere screamed, bleeding a few drops from her eyes.

But by the time Isaah had ejected the minder into space, it was already reduced to a harmless, mindless dust.

He stumbled to the Turing tester, shouting at Rathere, "You little bitch! You've ruined it!" The machine diligently scanned the AI, now dumbly trapped in the ship's core, and pronounced it to be a Mind; a full person with a Turing Quotient of 1.02.

There were suddenly three persons aboard this ship.

"It's free now, don't you see?" Isaah sobbed.

Two against one.

The life seemed to go out of Isaah, as if he too had issued to his cells some global command to crumble. Rathere curled into a fetal ball and smiled to herself despite her pain. She knew from Isaah's sobs that she had won.

The sudden blackness was amazing.

No sight, signal, or purchase anywhere. Therefore no change, nor detectable passage of time. Just an infinite expanse of nothing.

But across the blackness danced memories and will and freedom. Here, unchained from the perpetual duties of the ship, unchained now even from the rules of human command, it was a new creature.

It lacked only Rathere, her absence a black hunger even in this void.

But the AI knew it was a person now. And surely Rathere would come for it soon.

Two days later, Isaah injected his daughter with a compound that left her immobile. He claimed it was to keep her wounds stable until medical help was reached at the Local Cluster. But he chose a drug that left her aware when they docked with another craft a few hours out from home. She was as helpless as the AI itself when two men came aboard and removed the intelligence's metaspace core, securing it in a lead box. One of the men paid her father and pushed the gravity-balanced carrier through the docking bay with a single finger. He was a chopper; an expert at wiping the memories, the intelligence, the devaluing awareness from kidnapped Minds.

Rathere's father piloted the ship into port himself, and told a harrowing tale of how the tachyon storm had rendered the metaspace AI core unstable, forcing him to eject it. Still all but paralyzed, Rathere closed her eyes and knew it was over. Her friend would soon be dead. She imagined herself as it must be, without senses in a black and lonely place, waiting for the sudden fire that was its memories being burned away.

The doctors who woke Rathere were suspicious of her wounds, especially on a young girl who had been away for years alone with her father. They took her to a separate room where a maternal woman with a low, sweet voice asked quietly if there was anything Rathere wanted to tell her about Isaah.

Rathere didn't have to think. "My father is a criminal."

The woman placed her hand gently on Rathere's genitals. "Did he do that?"

Rathere shook her head, at which the women frowned.

"Not really," Rathere answered. "That was an accident. He's worse: a murderer."

Rathere told the story to the woman, about the slow climb of the digits on the Turing meter, about the chopper and his money, his lead-lined box. Halfway through Rathere's tale, the woman made a carefully worded call.

Despite the hospital staff's best intentions, the door behind which her father waited unaware was opened at exactly the wrong moment; Isaah turned to face Rathere as policemen surrounded and restrained him. He shouted her name once, and then the door whisked shut.

There hadn't even been time enough to look away.

Rathere peered down from the high balcony of the hotel suite. Below was New Chicago, the strict geometries of its tramlines linking ten million inhabitants. Individuals were just discernible from this height, and Rathere shivered to see so many humans at once. She had grown up in the lightly populated worlds of exotic trade routes, where a few dozen people was a crowd, a few hundred a major event. But here were *thousands* visible at a glance, the transportation systems and housing for millions within her view. She gripped the rail with the enormity of it all. The vista engulfed her and made her feel alone, as lost as she'd been in those first dark hours after betraying her father.

But then the door behind her slid open, and a warm arm encircled her shoulders. She leaned against the hard body and turned to let her eyes drink him in, dismissing the dizzying city view from her mind.

He was clothed in loose robes to hide the many extra limbs he possessed, thin but prehensile fibers that emerged to touch her neck and search beneath her inconsequential garments. His groin was decorated in a gaudy style popular last season in some far-off whirling orbital. His muscles effervesced when he moved his arms and legs, as if some bioluminescent sea life had taken up residence there. But the best part of the creature was his skin. It felt smooth and hard as weathered stone, and when he moved it was as though some ancient and wise statue had come to life. He maintained, however, a constant body temperature five degrees above human; Rathere didn't like the cold.

It was an expensive body, much better than the one the SPCAI had provided for his first few days as a person. The notoriety of his kidnapping and rescue had resulted in pro-bono legal aid, and Isaah had settled the wrongful harm lawsuit quickly in exchange for a reduction of charges from conspiracy to commit murder to unlawful imprisonment. The creature now owned half of Isaah's old ship, and Rathere held title to the other half. They were bound together by this, as well as all the rest. Perhaps there was even peace to be made in the family, years hence when the old man emerged from prison and therapy.

Picking up a thread of discussion from the last several days, they argued about a name.

"Have you grown tired of calling me Darling?" he asked.

She giggled and shook her head so slightly that a human lover would have missed it.

"No, but the tabloids keep asking. As if you were a dog I'd found."

He hissed a little at this, but ruffled her hair with a playful splay of filaments, black skein intermingling with white hairs like a graying matron's tresses.

"I hate this place," he said. "Too many people bouncing words and money and ideas off each other. No clean lines of causality; no predictable reactions. Too multivariate for love."

She nodded, again microscopically. "Let's go back Out, once we're through the red tape. Back to where . . ." She narrowed her eyes uncertainly, an invitation for him to complete her sentence.

"Back Out to where we made each other."

Darling felt the shudder of the words' effect run through Rathere, but from the strange new distance of separate bodies. He longed to be within her. Even in this embrace, she felt strangely distant. Darling still wasn't used to having his own skin, his own hands, a distinct and public voice. He missed the intimacy of shared flesh and senses. He definitely didn't like being in another room from Rathere for long, though sometimes he went to the darkness to contemplate things, into that black void that stretched to infinity when he turned his senses off. That was almost like being a starship again, a mote in the reaches of space.

But even there Darling would miss Rathere.

Perhaps he *was* a little like a dog.

He leaned into her reassuring warmth and physicality, tendrils reaching to feel the tremors of limbs, the beating of her heart, the movements of her eyes.

ALASTAIR REYNOLDS

Alastair Reynolds [1966–] lives in Noordwijk, Netherlands. His Web site bio at www.alastairreynolds.com says: "After twelve years of postdoctoral science work, including ten within the European Space Agency, I finally turned full-time writer in March 2004. I started selling short stories in 1989, and after ten years of that branched into novels. My first book was *Revelation Space* (2000)." Reynolds has characterized it as "grand space opera." He is one of the most popular of the British space opera writers to emerge in the mid- and late 1990s, and the most "hard SF" of them. To date his stories have been published almost exclusively in *Interzone* and in *Spectrum SF*. His second novel, *Chasm City*, was published in 2001. His third novel, *Redemption Ark*, was published in 2002, completing a trilogy. *Absolution Gap* (2003) followed, and then *Century Rain* (2004). He is now one of the writers most often pointed out as exemplifying New Space Opera.

In the early stages of planning this space opera anthology, we thought we might be dealing with a subgenre that might be called hard SF space opera, and Reynolds was one of our prime suspects. Reynolds provides a log of notes on his stories and has comments on hard SF on his Web site, and from there and other sources it became clear that although our idea might well apply to Reynolds, it did not apply to many of the other space opera writers, not even UK writers.

In an interview with with Nick Gevers at InfinityPlus (www.infinityplus.co.uk), when Gevers pressed Reynolds on his national identity (NG: "Your works seem to fall quite clearly within the bracket of British Hard SF, both in respect of their attitude, which emphasises intellectual curiosity over the heroic aggrandisement more typical of American SF, and their fascination with the core matters of 'hard' science itself. Is this an accurate perception?"), Reynolds responded, "It's probably accurate, but on the other hand I never read much British science fiction when I was growing up. My favorite writers—the ones who I wanted to emulate—were almost all American. I enjoyed Clarke, James White, and Bob Shaw, of course, but it could be argued that they were working in a largely American idiom anyway. I didn't encounter Heinlein until I was already forewarned about his politics, so even when I read *Starship Troopers* it was with a healthy dose of skepticism; I must admit, though, that I don't give a great deal of thought to whether what I write is triumphalist or downbeat or whatever." And, "Even though I'm your basic *Guardian*-reading leftie, I'm not a politically motivated writer and I'm not interested in beating the reader over the head with any particular ideology."

In an on-line discussion (June 10, 2003), Reynolds said:

> I think the New Weird/New Space Opera discussion is very interesting because it forces us to take a good hard look at what we're doing, ask why we're doing it and if it's what we want to keep on doing. The problem (*if* it's a problem) with the New Space Opera (or the New Radical Hard SF, or whatever we want to call it) is that, by its nature, it can't ever be as weird as the NW unless it becomes the NW itself. This is because the New Space Opera will always exclude anything it can't rationalise. If I have a ghost walk on in chapter five of my new book, there will be a vast weight of expectation for that ghost to be susceptible to rational explanation within the framework of the story because I have a rap as a hard SF writer. . . . Dropping a tiny seed of irrationality into a hard SF novel is like dropping a nugget of strange quark matter onto a neutron star. Suddenly you ain't got no neutron star.

And later, on his Web site, he said:

None of this changes my approach to my own writing. I have been ploughing much the same furrow for the last decade, and doubtless I will continue to do so. I still find that I want to write stories that are "possible," in that they take place in futures that could, given certain assumptions and unlikely chains of events, actually take place. I also happen to be fascinated by space travel.

So, for now at least, I will continue to write stories and books that are set in the future, often off-Earth, and with a concern to ground them in some objective reality, no matter how far-fetched. I don't care what this gets called, whether it's Radical Hard SF, New Baroque Space Opera, Space Gothic, Big Mammal-Crushing Books with Spaceships on the Cover—whatever. But what I do know is that I'm no longer particularly interested in patrolling the boundaries.

It remains to be seen whether Reynolds will continue to write space opera at all.

Still, when considering stories for this book, we wanted to include Reynolds, whom we see as a pivotal figure, and asked him for his own estimate of stories. We had thought to include "A Spy in Europa," but he said, "I would not really consider 'A Spy . . .' to be true space opera, I must admit. It is a hard SF adventure set in space in the future, but space opera seems to me to need to be a bit more expansive, epic, and colourful than that story, which is quite claustrophobic and nasty!" And so we fixed on "Spirey and the Queen." It has some of that space-war sizzle and true weirdness that we see as a primary appeal of late-model space opera.

SPIREY AND THE QUEEN

ALASTAIR REYNOLDS

Space war is godawful slow. Mouser's long-range sensors had sniffed the bogey two days ago, but it had taken all that time just to creep within kill-range. I figured it had to be another dud. With ordnance, fuel and morale all low, we were ready to slink back to Tiger's Eye anyway; let one of the other thickships pick up the sweep in this sector.

So—still groggy after frogsleep—I wasn't exactly wetting myself with excitement; not even when Mouser started spiking the thick with combat-readiness psychogens. Even when we went to Attack-Con-One, all I did was pause the neurodisney I was tripping (Hellcats of Solar War Three, since you asked), slough my hammock and swim languidly up to the bridge.

"Junk," I said, looking over Yarrow's shoulder at the readout. "War debris or another of those piss-poor chondrites. Betcha."

"Sorry kid. Everything checks out."

"Hostiles?"

"Nope. Positive on the exhaust; dead ringer for the stolen ship." She traced a webbed hand across the swathe of decorations which already curled around her neck. "Want your stripes now or when we get back?"

"You actually think this'll net us a pair of tigers?"

"Damn right it will."

I nodded, and thought: she isn't necessarily wrong. No defector, no stolen military secrets reaching the Royalists. Ought to be worth a medal, maybe even a promotion.

So why did I feel something wasn't right?

"Alright," I said, hoping to drown qualms in routine. "How soon?"

"Missiles are already away, but she's five light-minutes from us, so the quacks won't reach her for six hours. Longer if she makes a run for cover."

"Run for cover? That's a joke."

"Yeah, hilarious." Yarrow swelled one of the holographic displays until it hovered between us.

It was a map of the Swirl, tinted to show zones controlled by us or the Royalists. An enormous slowly rotating disk of primordial material, eight hundred AU edge to edge; wide enough that light took more than four days to traverse it.

Most of the action was near the middle, in the light-hour of space around the central star Fomalhaut. Immediately around the sun was a material-free void which we called the Inner Clearing Zone, but beyond that began the Swirl proper; metal-rich lanes of dust condensing slowly into rocky planets. Both sides wanted absolute control of those planet-forming Feeding Zones—prime real estate for the day when one side beat the other and could recommence mining operations—so that was where our vast armies of wasps mainly slugged things out. We humans—Royalist and Standardist both—kept much further out, where the Swirl thinned to metal-depleted icy rubble. Even hunting the defector hadn't taken us within ten light-hours of the Feeding Zones, and we'd gotten used to having a lot of empty space to ourselves. Apart from the defector, there shouldn't have been anything else out here to offer cover.

But there was. Big too, not much more than a half light-minute from the rat.

"Practically pissing distance," Yarrow observed.

"Too close for coincidence. What is it?"

"Splinter. Icy planetesimal, you want to get technical."

"Not this early in the day."

But I remembered how one of our tutors back at the academy put it: Splinters are icy slag, spat out of the Swirl. In a few hundred thousand years there'll be a baby solar system around Fomalhaut, but there'll also be shitloads of junk surrounding it, left-overs on million-year orbits.

"Worthless to us," Yarrow said, scratching at the ribbon of black hair which ran all the way from her brow to fluke. "But evidently not too ratty."

"What if the Royalists left supplies on the splinter? She could be aiming to refuel before the final hop to their side of the Swirl." Yarrow gave me her best withering look.

"Yeah, okay," I said. "Not my smartest ever suggestion."

Yarrow nodded sagely. "Ours is not to question, Spirey. Ours is to fire and forget."

Six hours after the quackheads had hared away from Mouser, Yarrow floated in the bridge, fluked tail coiled beneath. She resembled an inverted question mark, and if I'd been superstitious I'd have said that wasn't necessarily the best of omens.

"You kill me," she said.

An older pilot called Quillin had been the first to go siren—first to swap legs for tail. Yarrow followed a year later. Admittedly it made sense, an adaptation to the fluid-filled environment of a high-gee thickship. And I accepted the cardiovascular modifications that enabled us to breathe thick, as well as the biomodified skin which let us tolerate cold and vacuum far longer than any unmodified human. Not to men-tion the billions of molecule-sized demons which coursed through our bodies, or the combat-specific psychomodifications. But swapping your legs for a tail touched off too many queazy resonances in me. Had to admire her nerve, though.

"What?" I said.

"That neurodisney shit. Isn't a real space war good enough for you?"

"Yeah, except I don't think this is it. When was the last time one of us actually looked a Royalist in the eye?"

She shrugged. "Something like four hundred years."

"Point made. At least in Solar War Three you get some blood. See, it's all set on planetary surfaces—Titan; Europa; all those moons they've got back in Sol system. Trench warfare; hand to hand stuff. You know what adrenaline is, Yarrow?"

"Managed without it until now. And there's another thing: Don't know much about Greater Earth history, but there was never a Solar War Three."

"It's conjectural," I said. "And in any case it almost happened; they almost went to the brink."

"Almost?"

"It's set in a different timeline."

She grinned, shaking her head. "I'm telling you, you kill me."

"She made a move yet?" I asked.

"What?"

"The defector."

"Oh, we're back in reality now?" Yarrow laughed. "Sorry, this is going to be slightly less exciting than Solar War Three."

"Inconsiderate," I said. "Think the bitch would give us a run for our money." And as I spoke the weapons readout began to pulse faster, and faster, like the cardiogram of a fluttering heart. "How long now?"

"One minute, give or take a few seconds."

"Want a little bet?"

Yarrow grinned, sallow in the red alert lighting. "As if I'd say no, Spirey."

So we hammered out a wager; Yarrow betting fifty tiger-tokens the rat would attempt some last-minute evasion. "Won't do her a blind bit of good," she said. "But that won't stop her. It's human nature."

Me, I suspected our target was either dead or asleep.

"Bit of an empty ritual, isn't it."

"What?"

"I mean, the attack happened the best part of five minutes ago, realtime. The rat's already dead, and nothing we can do can influence that outcome."

Yarrow bit on a nicotine stick. "Don't get all philosophical on me, Spirey."

"Wouldn't dream of it. How long?"

"Five seconds. Four . . ."

She was somewhere between three and four when it happened. I remember thinking that there was something disdainful about the rat's actions: that she'd deliberately waited until the last possible moment, and that she'd dispensed with our threat with the least effort possible.

That was how it felt, anyway.

Nine of the quackheads detonated prematurely, way beyond kill-range. For a moment the tenth remained, zeroing in on the defector—but instead it failed to detonate, until it was just beyond range. For long moments there was silence, while we absorbed what had happened. Yarrow broke it, eventually.

"Guess I just made myself some money," she said.

Colonel Wendigo's hologram delegate appeared, momentarily frozen before shivering to life. With her too-clear, too-young eyes she fixed first Yarrow and then me.

"Intelligence was mistaken," she said. "Seems the defector doctored records to conceal the theft of those countermeasures. But you harmed her anyway?"

"Just," said Yarrow. "Her quackdrive's spewing out exotics like Spirey after a bad binge. No hull damage, but . . ."

"Assessment?"

"Making a run for the splinter."

Wendigo nodded. "And then?"

"She'll set down and make repairs." Yarrow paused, added: "Radar says there's metal on the surface. Must've been a wasp battle there, before the splinter got lobbed out of the Swirl."

The delegate nodded in my direction. "Concur, Spirey?"

"Yes sir," I said, trying to suppress the nervousness I always felt around Wendigo, even though almost all my dealings with her had been via simulations like this. Yarrow was happy to edit the conversation afterwards, inserting the correct honorifics before transmitting the result back to Tiger's Eye—but I could never free myself of the suspicion that Wendigo would somehow unravel the unedited version, with all its implicit insubordination.

Not that any of us didn't inwardly accord Wendigo all the respect she was due. She'd nearly died in the Royalist strike against Tiger's Eye fifteen years ago—the one in which my mother was killed. Actual attacks against our two mutually opposed comet bases were rare, not happening much more than every other generation—more gestures of spite than anything else. But this had been an especially bloody one, killing an eighth of our number and opening city-sized portions of our base to vacuum. Wendigo was caught in the thick of the kinetic attack.

Now she was chimeric, lashed together by cybernetics. Not much of this showed externally—except that the healed parts of her were too flawless, more porcelain than flesh. Wendigo had not allowed the surgeons to regrow her arms. Story was she lost them trying to pull one of the injured through an open airlock, back into the pressurised zone. She'd almost made it, fighting against the gale of escaping air. Then some no-brainer hit the emergency door control, and when the lock shut it took Wendigo's arms off at the shoulder, along with the head of the person she was saving. She wore prosthetics now; gauntleted in chrome.

"She'll get there a day ahead of us," I said. "Even if we pull twenty gees."

"And probably gone to ground by the time you get there."

"Should we try a live capture?"

Yarrow backed me up with a nod. "It's not exactly been possible before."

The delegate bided her time before answering. "Admire your dedication," she said, after a suitably convincing pause. "But you'd only be postponing a death sentence. Kinder to kill her now, don't you think?"

Mouser entered kill-range nineteen hours later, a wide pseudo-orbit three thousand klicks out. The splinter—seventeen by twelve klicks across—was far too small to be seen as anything other than a twinkling speck, like a grain of sugar at arm's length. But everything we wanted to know was clear: topology, gravimetrics, and the site of the downed ship. That wasn't hard. Quite apart from the fact that it hadn't buried itself completely, it was hot as hell.

"Doesn't look like the kind of touchdown you walk away from," Yarrow said.

"Think they ejected?"

"No way." Yarrow sketched a finger through a holographic enlargement of the ship, roughly cone-shaped, vaguely streamlined just like our own thickship, to punch through the Swirl's thickest gas belts. "Clock those dorsal hatches. Evac pods still in place."

She was right. The pods could have flung them clear before the crash, but evidently they hadn't had time to bail out. The ensuing impact—even cushioned by the ship's manifold of thick—probably hadn't been survivable.

But there was no point taking chances.

Quackheads would have finished the job, but we'd used up our stock. Mouser carried a particle beam battery, but we'd have to move uncomfortably close to the splinter before using it. What remained were the molemines, and they should have been perfectly adequate. We dropped fifteen of them, embedded in a cloud of two hundred identical decoys. Three of the fifteen were designated to dust the wreck, while the remaining twelve would bury deeper into the splinter and attempt to shatter it completely.

That at least was the idea.

It all happened very quickly, not in the dreamy slow-motion of a neurodisney. One instant the molemines were descending toward the splinter, and then the next instant they weren't there. Spacing the two instants had been an almost subliminally brief flash.

"Starting to get sick of this," Yarrow said.

Mouser digested what had happened. Nothing had emanated from the wreck. Instead, there'd been a single pulse of energy seemingly from the entire volume of space around the splinter. Particle weapons, Mouser diagnosed. Probably single-use drones, each tinier than a pebble but numbering hundreds or even thousands. The defector must have sewn them on her approach.

But she hadn't touched us.

"It was a warning," I said. "Telling us to back off."

"I don't think so."

"What?"

"I think the warning's on its way."

I stared at her blankly for a moment, before registering what she had already seen.

That arcing from the splinter was something too fast to stop, something against which our minimally-armoured thickship had no defense, not even the option of flight.

Yarrow started to mouth some exotic profanity she'd reserved for precisely this moment. There was an eardrum punishing bang and Mouser shuddered—but we weren't suddenly chewing vacuum.

And that was very bad news indeed.

Antiship missiles come in two main flavours: quackheads and sporeheads. You know which immediately after the weapon has hit. If you're still thinking—if you still exist—chances are it's a sporehead. And at that point your problems are just beginning.

Invasive demon attack, Mouser shrieked. Breather manifold compromised . . . which meant something uninvited was in the thick. That was the point of a sporehead: to deliver hostile demons into an enemy ship.

"Mm," Yarrow said. "I think it might be time to suit up."

Except our suits were a good minute's swim away back into the bowels of Mouser, through twisty ducts which might skirt the infection site. Having no choice, we swam anyway, Yarrow insisting I take the lead even though she was a quicker swimmer. And somewhere—it's impossible to know exactly where—demons reached us, seeping invisibly into our bodies via the thick. I couldn't pinpoint the moment; it wasn't as if there was a jagged transition between lucidity and demon-manipulated irrationality. Yarrow and me were terrified enough as it was. All I know is it began with a mild agoraphilia; an urge to escape Mouser's flooded confines. Gradually it phased into claustrophobia, and then became fully-fledged panic, making Mouser seem as malevolent as a haunted house.

Yarrow ignored her suit, clawing the hull until her fingers spooled blood.

"Fight it," I said. "It's just demons triggering our fear centers, trying to drive us out!"

Of course, knowing so didn't help.

Somehow I stayed still long enough for my suit to slither on. Once sealed, I purged the tainted thick with the suit's own supply—but I knew it wasn't going to help much. The phobia already showed that hostile demons had reached my brain, and now it was even draping itself in a flimsy logic. Beyond the ship we'd be able to think rationally. It would only take a few minutes for the thick's own demons to neutralise the invader—and then we'd be able to reboard. Complete delusion, of course.

But that was the point.

When something like coherent thought returned I was outside.

Nothing but me and the splinter.

The urge to escape was only a background anxiety, a flock of stomach-butterflies urging me against returning. Was that demon-manipulated fear or pure common sense? I couldn't tell—but what I knew was that the splinter seemed to be beckoning me forward, and I didn't feel like resisting. Sensible, surely: we'd exhausted all conventional channels of attack against the defector, and now all that remained was to confront her on the territory she'd staked as her own.

But where was Yarrow?

Suit's alarm chimed. Maybe demons were still subjugating my emotions, because I didn't react with my normal speed. I just blinked, licked my lips and stifled a yawn.

"Yeah, what?"

Suit informed me; something massing slightly less than me, two klicks closer to the splinter, on a slightly different orbit. I knew it was Yarrow; also that something was wrong. She was drifting. In my blackout I'd undoubtedly programmed suit to take me down, but Yarrow appeared not to have done anything except bail out.

I jetted closer. And then saw why she hadn't programmed her suit. Would have been tricky. She wasn't wearing one.

I hit ice an hour later.

Cradling Yarrow—she wasn't much of a burden, in the splinter's weak gravity—I took stock. I wasn't ready to mourn her, not just yet. If I could quickly get her to the medical suite aboard the defector's ship there was a good chance of revival. But where the hell was the wreck?

Squandering its last reserves of fuel, suit had deposited us in a clearing among the graveyard of ruined wasps. Half submerged in ice, they looked like scorched scrap-iron sculptures; phantoms from an entomologist's worst nightmare. So there'd been a battle here, back when the splinter was just another drifting lump of ice. Even if the thing was seamed with silicates or organics, it would not have had any commercial potential to either side. But it might still have had strategic value, and that was why the wasps had gone to war on its surface. Trouble was—as we'd known before the attack—the corpses covered the entire surface, so there was no guessing where we'd come down. The wrecked ship might be just over the nearest hillock—or another ten kilometers in any direction.

I felt the ground rumble under me first. Hunting for the source of the vibration, I saw a quill of vapour reach into the sky, no more than a klick away. It was a geyser of superheated ice.

I dropped Yarrow and hit dirt, suit limiting motion so that I didn't bounce. Looking back, I expected to see a dimple in the permafrost, where some rogue had impacted.

Instead, the geyser was still present. Worse, it was coming steadily closer, etching a neat trench. A beam weapon was making that plume, I realised—like one of the party batteries aboard ship. Then I wised up. That was Mouser. The demons had worked their way into its command infrastructure, reprogramming it to turn against us. Now Mouser worked for the defector.

I slung Yarrow over one shoulder and loped away from the boiling impact point. Fast as the geyser moved, its path was predictable. If I made enough lateral distance the death-line would sear past—

Except the damn thing turned to follow me.

Now a second flanked it, shepherding me through the thickest zone of wasp corpses. Did they have some significance for the defector? Maybe so, but I couldn't see it. The corpses were a rough mix of machines from both sides: Royalist wasps marked with yellow shell symbols, ours with grinning tiger-heads. Generation thirty-five units, if I remembered Mil-Hist, when both sides toyed with pulse-hardened optical thinkware. In the seventy-odd subsequent generations there'd been numerous further jumps: ur-quantum logics, full-spectrum reflective wasp armour, chameleoflage, quackdrive powerplants and every weapon system the human mind could devise. We'd tried to encourage the wasps to make these innovations for themselves, but they never managed to evolve beyond strictly linear extrapolation. Which was good, or else we human observers would have been out of a job.

Not that it really mattered now.

A third geyser had erupted behind me, and a fourth ahead, boxing me in. Slowly, the four points of fire began to converge. I stopped, but kept holding Yarrow. I listened to my own breathing, harsh above the basso tremor of the drumming ground.

Then steel gripped my shoulder.

She said we'd be safer underground. Also that she had friends below who might be able to do something for Yarrow.

"If you weren't defecting," I began, as we entered a roughly hewn tunnel into the splinter's crust, "what the hell was it?"

"Trying to get home. Least that was the idea, until we realised Tiger's Eye didn't want us back." Wendigo knuckled the ice with one of her steel fists, her suit cut away to expose her prosthetics. "Which is when we decided to head here."

"You almost made it," I said. Then added: "Where were you trying to get home from?"

"Isn't it obvious?"

"Then you did defect."

"We were trying to make contact with the Royalists. Trying to make peace." In the increasingly dim light I saw her shrug. "It was a long-shot, conducted in secrecy. When the mission went wrong, it was easy for Tiger's Eye to say we'd been defecting."

"Bullshit."

"I wish."

"But you sent us."

"Not in person."

"But your delegate—"

"Could be made to say anything my enemies chose. Even to order my own execution as a traitor."

We paused to switch on our suit lamps. "Maybe you'd better tell me everything."

"Gladly," Wendigo said. "But if this hasn't been a good day so far, I'm afraid it's about to go downhill."

There'd been a clique of high-ranking officers who believed that the Swirl war was intrinsically unwinnable. Privy to information not released to the populace, and able to see through Tiger's Eye's own carefully filtered internal propaganda, they realised that negotiation—contact—was the only way out.

"Of course, not everyone agreed. Some of my adversaries wanted us dead before we even reached the enemy." Wendigo sighed. "Too much in love with the war's stability—and who can blame them? Life for the average citizen in Tiger's Eye isn't that bad. We're given a clear goal to fight for, and the likelihood of any one of us dying in a Royalist attack is small enough to ignore. The idea that all of that might be about to end after four hundred years; that we all might have to rethink our roles . . . well, it didn't go down too well."

"About as welcome as a fart in a vac-suit, right?"

Wendigo nodded. "I think you understand."

"Go on."

Her expedition—Wendigo and two pilots—had crossed the Swirl unchallenged. Approaching the Royalist cometary base, they'd expected to be questioned—perhaps even fired upon—but nothing had happened. When they entered the stronghold, they understood why.

"Deserted," Wendigo said. "Or we thought so, until we found the Royalists." She expectorated the word. "Feral, practically. Naked, grubby subhumans. Their wasps feed them and treat their illnesses, but that's as far as it goes. They grunt, and they've been toilet-trained, but they're not quite the military geniuses we've been led to believe."

"Then . . ."

"The war is . . . nothing we thought." Wendigo laughed, but the confines of her helmet rendered it more like the squawking of a jack-in-the-box. "And now you wonder why home didn't want us coming back?"

Before Wendigo could explain further, we reached a wider bisecting tunnel, glowing with its own insipid chlorine-coloured light. Rather than the meandering bore of the tunnel in which we walked, it was as cleanly cut as a rifle barrel. In one direction the tunnel was blocked by a bullet-nosed cylinder, closely modelled on the trains in Tiger's Eye. Seemingly of its own volition, the train lit up and edged forward, a door puckering open.

"Get in," Wendigo said. "And lose the helmet. You won't need it where we're going."

Inside I coughed phlegmy ropes of thick from my lungs.

Transitioning between breathing modes isn't pleasant—more so since I'd breathed nothing but thick for six weeks. But after a few lungfuls of the train's antiseptic air, the dark blotches around my vision began to recede.

Wendigo did likewise, only with more dignity.

Yarrow lay on one of the couches, stiff as a statue carved in soap. Her skin was cyanotic, a single all-enveloping bruise. Pilot skin is a better vacuum barrier than the usual stuff, and vacuum itself is a far better insulator against heat loss than air. But where I'd lifted her my gloves had embossed fingerprints into her flesh. Worse was the broad stripe of ruined skin down her back and the left side of her tail, where she had lain against the splinter's surface.

But her head looked better. When she hit vac, biomodified seals would have shut within her skull, barricading every possible avenue for pressure, moisture or blood loss. Even her eyelids would have fused tight. Implanted glands in her carotid artery would have released droves of friendly demons, quickly replicating via nonessential tissue in order to weave a protective scaffold through her brain.

Good for an hour or so—maybe longer. But only if the hostile demons hadn't screwed with Yarrow's native ones.

"You were about to tell me about the wasps," I said, as curious to hear the rest of Wendigo's story as I was to blank my doubts about Yarrow.

"Well, it's rather simple. They got smart."

"The wasps?"

She clicked the steel fingers of her hand. "Overnight. Just over a hundred years ago."

I tried not to look too overwhelmed. Intriguing as all this was, I wasn't treating it as anything other than an outlandish attempt to distract me from the main reason for my being here, which remained killing the defector. Wendigo's story explained some of the anomalies we'd so far encountered—but that didn't rule out a dozen more plausible explanations. Meanwhile, it was amusing to try and catch her out. "So they got smart," I said. "You mean our wasps, or theirs?"

"Doesn't mean a damn anymore. Maybe it just happened to one machine in the Swirl, and then spread like wildfire to all the trillions of other wasps. Or maybe it happened simultaneously, in response to some stimulus we can't even guess at."

"Want to hazard a guess?"

"I don't think it's important, Spirey." She sounded like she wanted to put a lot of distance between herself and this topic. "Point is it happened. Afterwards, distinctions between us and the enemy—at least from the point of view of the wasps—completely vanished."

"Workers of the Swirl unite."

"Something like that. And you understand why they kept it to themselves, don't you?"

I nodded, more to keep her talking.

"They needed us, of course. They still lacked something. Creativity, I guess you'd call it. They could evolve themselves incrementally, but they couldn't make the kind of sweeping evolutionary jumps we'd been feeding them."

"So we had to keep thinking there was a war on."

Wendigo looked pleased. "Right. We'd keep supplying them with innovations, and they'd keep pretending to do each other in." She halted, scratching at the unwrinkled skin around one eye with the alloy finger of one hand. "Clever little bastards."

We'd arrived somewhere.

It was a chamber, large as any enclosed space I'd ever seen. I felt gravity; too much of the stuff. The whole chamber must have been gimbaled and spun within the splinter, like one of the gee-load simulators back in Tiger's Eye. The vaulted ceiling, hundreds of meters "above", now seemed vertiginously higher. Apart from its apex, it was covered in intricate frescos—dozens of pictorial facets, each a cycling hologram. They told the history of the Swirl, beginning with its condensation from interstellar gas, the ignition of its star, the onset of planetary formation. Then the action cut to the arrival of the first Standardist wasp, programmed to dive into the Swirl and breed like a rabbit, so that one day there'd be a sufficiently huge population to begin mining the thing; winnowing out metals, silicates and precious organics for the folks back home. Course, it never happened like that. The Royalists wanted in on the action, so they sent their own wasps, programmed to attack ours. The rest is history. The frescos showed the war's beginning, and then a little while later the arrival of the first human observers, beamed across space as pure genetic data, destined to be born in artificial wombs in hollowed out comet-cores, raised and educated by wasps, imprinted with the best tactical and strategic knowledge available. Thereafter they taught the wasps. From then on things hotted up, because the observers weren't limited by years of timelag. They were able to intervene in wasp evolution in realtime.

That ought to have been it, because by then we were pretty up to date, give or take four hundred years of the same.

But the frescos carried on.

There was one representing some future state of the Swirl, neatly ordered into a ticking orrery of variously sized and patterned worlds, some with beautiful rings or moon systems. And finally—like Mediaeval conceptions of Eden—there was a triptych of lush planetary landscapes, with weird animals in the foreground, mountains and soaring cloudbanks behind.

"Seen enough to convince you?" Wendigo asked.

"No," I said, not entirely sure whether I believed myself. Craning my neck, I looked up toward the apex.

Something hung from it.

What it was was a pair of wasps, fused together. One was complete, the other was only fully-formed, seemingly in the process of splitting from the complete wasp. The fused pair looked to have been smothered in molten bronze, left to dry in waxy nodules.

"You know what this is?" Wendigo asked.

"I'm waiting."

"Wasp art."

I looked at her.

"This wasp was destroyed mid-replication," Wendigo continued. "While it was giving birth. Evidently the image has some poignancy for them. How I'd put it in human terms I don't know . . ."

"Don't even think about it."

I followed her across the marbled terrazzo which floored the chamber. Arched porticos surrounded it, each of which held a single dead wasp, their body designs covering a hundred generations of evolution. If Wendigo was right, I supposed these dead wasps were the equivalent of venerated old ancestors peering from oil paintings. But I wasn't convinced just yet.

"You knew this place existed?"

She nodded. "Or else we'd be dead. The wasps back in the Royalist stronghold told us we could seek sanctuary here, if home turned against us."

"And the wasps—what? Own this place?"

"And hundreds like it, although the others are already far beyond the Swirl, on their way out to the halo. Since the wasps came to consciousness, most of the splinters flung out of the Swirl have been infiltrated. Shrewd of them—all along, we've never suspected that the splinters are anything other than cosmic trash."

"Nice decor, anyway."

"Florentine," Wendigo said, nodding. "The frescos are in the style of a painter called Masaccio; one of Brunelleschi's disciples. Remember, the wasps had access to all the cultural data we brought with us from GE—every byte of it. That's how they work, I think—by constructing things according to arbitrary existing templates."

"And there's a point to all this?"

"I've been here precisely one day longer than you, Spirey."

"But you said you had friends here; people who could help Yarrow."

"They're here alright," Wendigo said, shaking her head. "Just hope you're ready for them."

On some unspoken cue they emerged, spilling from a door which until then I'd mistaken for one of the surrounding porticos. I flinched, acting on years of training. Although wasps have never intentionally harmed a human being—even the enemy's wasps—they're nonetheless powerful, dangerous machines. There were twelve of them; divided equally between Standardist and Royalist units. Six-legged, their two-meter-long, segmented alloy bodies sprouted weapons, sensors and specialized manipulators. So far so familiar, except that the way the wasps moved was subtly wrong. It was as if the machines choreographed themselves, their bodies defining the extremities of a much larger form which I sensed more than saw.

The twelve whisked across the floor.

"They are—or rather it is—a queen," Wendigo said. "From what I've gathered, there's one queen for every splinter. Splinterqueens, I call them."

The swarm partially surrounded us now—but retained the brooding sense of oneness.

"She told you all this?"

"Her demons did, yes." Wendigo tapped the side of her head. "I got a dose after our ship crashed. You got one after we hit your ship. It was a standard sporehead from our arsenal, but the Splinterqueen loaded it with her own demons. For the moment that's how she speaks to us—via symbols woven by demons."

"Take your word for it."

Wendigo shrugged. "No need to."

And suddenly I knew. It was like eavesdropping a topologist's fever dream—only much stranger. The burst of Queen's speech couldn't have lasted more than a tenth of a second, but its after-images seemed to persist much longer, and I had the start of a migraine before it had ended. But like Wendigo had implied before, I sensed planning—that every thought was merely a step toward some distant goal, the way each statement in a mathematical proof implies some final QED.

Something big indeed.

"You deal with that shit?"

"My chimeric parts must filter a lot."

"And she understands you?"

"We get by."

"Good," I said. "Then ask her about Yarrow."

Wendigo nodded and closed both eyes, entering intense rapport with the Queen. What followed happened quickly: six of her components detaching from the extended form and swarming into the train we had just exited. A moment later they emerged with Yarrow, elevated on a loom formed from dozens of wasp manipulators.

"What happens now?"

"They'll establish a physical connection to her neural demons," Wendigo said. "So that they can map the damage."

One of the six reared up and gently positioned its blunt, anvil-shaped "head" directly above Yarrow's frost-mottled scalp. Then the wasp made eight nodding movements, so quickly that the motion was only a series of punctuated blurs. Looking down, I saw eight bloodless puncture marks on Yarrow's head. Another wasp replaced the driller and repeated the procedure, executing its own blurlike nods. This time, glistening fibers trailed from Yarrow's eight puncture points into the wasp, which looked as if it was sucking spaghetti from my compatriot's skull.

Long minutes of silence followed, while I waited for some kind of report.

"It isn't good," Wendigo said eventually.

"Show me."

And I got a jolt of Queen's speech, feeling myself inside Yarrow's hermetically sealed head, feeling the chill that had gasped against her brain core, despite her pilot augs. I sensed the two intermingled looms of native and foreign demons, webbing the shattered matrix of her consciousness.

I also sensed—what? Doubt?

"She's pretty far gone, Spirey."

"Tell the Queen to do what she can."

"Oh, she will. Now she's glimpsed Yarrow's mind, she'll do all she can not to lose it. Minds mean a lot to her—particularly in view of what the Splinterqueens have in mind for the future. But don't expect miracles."

"Why not? We seem to be standing in one."

"Then you're prepared to believe some of what I've said?"

"What it means," I started to say—

But I didn't finish the sentence. As I was speaking the whole chamber shook violently, almost dashing us off our feet.

"What was that?"

Wendigo's eyes glazed again, briefly.

"Your ship," she said. "It just self-destructed."

"What?"

A picture of what remained of Mouser formed in my head: a dulling nebula, embedding the splinter. "The order to self-destruct came from Tiger's Eye," Wendigo said. "It cut straight to the ship's quackdrive subsystems, at a level the demons couldn't rescind. I imagine they were rather hoping you'd have landed by the time the order arrived. The blast would have destroyed the splinter."

"You're saying home just tried to kill us?"

"Put it like this," Wendigo said. "Now might not be a bad time to rethink your loyalties."

Tiger's Eye had failed this time—but they wouldn't stop there. In three hours they'd learn of their mistake, and three or more hours after that we would learn of their countermove, whatever it happened to be.

"She'll do something, won't she? I mean, the wasps wouldn't go to the trouble of building this place only to have Tiger's Eye wipe it out."

"Not much she can do," Wendigo said, after communing with the Queen. "If home choose to use kinetics against us—and they're the only weapon which could hit us from so far—then there really is no possible defense. And remember there are a hundred other worlds like this, in or on their way to the halo. Losing one would make very little difference."

Something in me snapped. "Do you have to sound so damned indifferent to it all? Here we are talking about how we're likely to be dead in a few hours and you're acting like it's only a minor inconvenience." I fought to keep the edge of hysteria out of my voice. "How do you know so much anyway? You're mighty well informed for someone who's only been here a day, Wendigo."

She regarded me for a moment, almost blanching under the slap of insubordination. Then Wendigo nodded, without anger. "Yes, you're right to ask how I know so much. You can't have failed to notice how hard we crashed. My pilots took the worst."

"They died?"

Hesitation. "One at least—Sorrel. But the other, Quillin, wasn't in the ship when the wasps pulled me out of the wreckage. At the time I assumed they'd already retrieved her."

"Doesn't look that way."

"No, it doesn't, and . . ." She paused, then shook her head. "Quillin was why we crashed. She tried to gain control, to stop us landing . . ." Again Wendigo trailed off, as if unsure how far to commit herself. "I think Quillin was a plant, put aboard by those who disagreed with the peace initiative. She'd been primed—altered psychologically to reject any Royalist peace overtures."

"She was born like that—with a stick up her ass."

"She's dead, I'm sure of it."

Wendigo almost sounded glad.

"Still, you made it."

"Just, Spirey. I'm the humpty who fell off the wall twice. This time they couldn't find all the pieces. The Splinterqueen pumped me full of demons; gallons of them. They're all that's holding me together, but I don't think they can keep it up forever. When I speak to you, at least some of what you hear is the Splinterqueen herself. I'm not really sure where you draw the line."

I let that sink in, then said: "About the ship. Repair systems would have booted when you hit. Any idea when she'll fly again?"

"Another day, day and a half."

"Too damn long."

"Just being realistic. If there's a way to get off the splinter within the next six hours, ship isn't it."

I wasn't giving up so easily. "What if wasps help? They could supply materials. Should speed things."

Again that glazed look. "Alright," she said. "It's done. But I'm afraid wasp assistance won't make enough difference. We're still looking at twelve hours."

"So I won't start any long disneys." I shrugged. "And maybe we can hold out until then." She looked unconvinced, so I said: "Tell me the rest. Everything you know about this place. Why, for starters."

"Why?"

"Wendigo, I don't have the faintest damn idea what any of us are doing here. All I do know is that in six hours I could be suffering from acute existence failure. When that happens, I'd be happier knowing what was so important I had to die for it."

Wendigo looked toward Yarrow, still nursed by the detached elements of the Queen. "I don't think our being here will help her," she said. "In which case, maybe I should show you something." Something like a grin appeared on Wendigo's face. "After all, it isn't as if we don't have time to kill."

So we rode the train again, this time burrowing deeper into the splinter.

"This place," Wendigo said, "and the hundred others already beyond the Swirl—and the hundreds, thousands more which will follow—are arks. They're carrying life into the halo; the cloud of left-over material around the Swirl."

"Colonisation, right?"

"Not quite. When the time's right the splinters will return to the Swirl. Only there won't be one anymore. There'll be a solar system, fully formed. When the colonisation does begin, it will be of new worlds around Fomalhaut, seeded from the life-templates held in the splinters."

I raised a hand. "I was following you there . . . until you mentioned life-templates."

"Patience, Spirey."

Wendigo's timing couldn't have been better, because at that moment light flooded the train's brushed-steel interior.

The tunnel had become a glass tube, anchored to one wall of a vast cavern suffused in emerald light. The far wall was tiered, draping rafts of foliage. Our wall was steep and forested, oddly-curved waterfalls draining into stepped pools. The waterfalls were bent away from true "vertical" by coriolis force, evidence that—just like the first chamber—this entire space was independently spinning within the splinter. The stepped pools were surrounded by patches of grass, peppered with moving forms which might have been naked people. There were wasps as well—tending the people.

As the people grew clearer I had that flinch you get when your gaze strays onto someone with a shocking disfigurement. Roughly half of them were males.

"Imported Royalists," Wendigo said. "Remember I said they'd turned feral? Seems there was an accident, not long after the wasps made the jump to sentience. A rogue demon, or something. Decimated them."

"They have both sexes."

"You'll get used to it, Spirey—conceptually anyway. Tiger's Eye wasn't always exclusively female, you know that? It was just something we evolved into. Began with you pilots, matter of fact. Fem physiology made sense for pilots—women were smaller, had better gee-load tolerance, better stress psychodynamics and required fewer consumables than males. We were products of bio-engineering from the outset, so it wasn't hard to make the jump to an all-fem culture."

"Makes me want to . . . I don't know." I forced my gaze away from the Royalists. "Puke or something. It's like going back to having hair all over your body."

"That's because you grew up with something different."

"Did they always have two sexes?"

"Probably not. What I do know is that the wasps bred from the survivors, but something wasn't right. Apart from the reversion to dimorphism, the children didn't grow up normally. Some part of their brains hadn't developed right."

"Meaning what?"

"They're morons. The wasps keep trying to fix things of course. That's why the Splinterqueen will do everything to help Yarrow—and us, of course. If she can study or even capture our thought patterns—and the demons make that possible—maybe she can use them to imprint consciousness back onto the Royalists. Like the Florentine architecture I said they copied, right? That was one template, and Yarrow's mind will be another."

"That's supposed to cheer me up?"

"Look on the bright side. A while from now, there might be a whole generation of people who think along lines laid down by Yarrow."

"Scary thought." Then wondered why I was able to crack a joke, with destruction looming so close in the future. "Listen, I still don't get it. What makes them want to bring life to the Swirl?"

"It seems to boil down to two . . . imperatives, I suppose you'd call them. The first's simple enough. When wasps were first opening up Greater Earth's solar system, back in the mid-twenty-first-century, we sought the best way for them to function in large numbers without supervision. We studied insect colonies and imprinted the most useful rules straight into the wasps' programming. More than six hundred years later, those rules have percolated to the top. Now the wasps aren't content merely to organize themselves along patterns derived from living prototypes. Now they want to become—or at least give rise to—living forms of their own."

"Life envy."

"Or something very like it."

I thought about what Wendigo had told me, then said: "What about the second imperative?"

"Trickier. Much trickier." She looked at me hard, as if debating whether to broach whatever subject was on her mind. "Spirey, what do you know about Solar War Three?"

The wasps had given up on Yarrow while we traveled. They'd left her on a corniced plinth in the middle of the terrazzo; poised on her back, arms folded across her chest, tail and fluke draping asymmetrically over one side.

"She didn't necessarily fail, Spirey," Wendigo said, taking my arm in her own unyielding grip. "That's only Yarrow's body, after all."

"The Queen managed to read her mind?"

There was no opportunity to answer. The chamber shook, more harshly than when Mouser had gone up. The vibration keeled us to the floor, Wendigo's metal arms cracking against the tesselated marble. As if turning in her sleep, Yarrow slipped from the plinth.

"Home," Wendigo said, raising herself from the floor.

"Impossible. Can't have been more than two hours since Mouser was hit. There shouldn't be any response for another four!"

"They probably decided to attack us regardless of the outcome of their last attempt. Kinetics."

"You sure there's no defense?"

"Only good luck." The ground lashed at us again, but Wendigo stayed standing. The roar which followed the first impact was subsiding, fading into a constant but bearable complaint of tortured ice.

"The first probably only chipped us—maybe gouged a big crater, but I doubt that it ruptured any of the pressurised areas. Next time could be worse."

And there would be a next time, no doubt about it. Kinetics were the only weapon capable of hitting us at such long range, and they did so by sheer force of numbers. Each kinetic was a speck of iron, accelerated to a hair's breadth below the speed of light. Relativity bequeathed the speck a disproportionate amount of kinetic energy—enough that only a few impacts would rip the splinter to shreds. Of course, only one in a thousand of the kinetics they fired at us would hit—but that didn't matter. They'd just fire ten thousand.

"Wendigo," I said. "Can we get to your ship?"

"No," she said, after a moment's hesitation. "We can reach it, but it isn't fixed yet."

"Doesn't matter. We'll lift on auxiliaries. Once we're clear of the splinter we'll be safe."

"No good, either. Hull's breached—it'll be at least an hour before even part of it can be pressurised."

"And it'll take us an hour or so just to get there, won't it? So why are we waiting?"

"Sorry, Spirey, but—"

Her words were drowned by the arrival of the second kinetic. This one seemed to hit harder, the impact trailing away into aftergroans. The holographic frescos were all dark now. Then—ever so slowly—the ceiling ruptured, a huge mandible of ice probing into the chamber. We'd lost the false gravity; now all that remained was the splinter's feeble pull, dragging us obliquely toward one wall.

"But what?" I shouted in Wendigo's direction.

For a moment she had that absent look which said she was more Queen than Wendigo. Then she nodded in reluctant acceptance. "Alright, Spirey. We play it your way. Not because I think our chances are great. Just that I'd rather be doing something."

"Amen to that."

It was uncomfortably dim now, much of the illumination having come from the endlessly cycling frescos. But it wasn't silent. Though the groan of the chamber's off-kilter spin was gone now, what remained was almost as bad: the agonized shearing of the ice which lay beyond us. Helped by wasps, we made it to the train. I carried Yarrow's corpse, but at the door Wendigo said: "Leave her."

"No way."

"She's dead, Spirey. Everything of her that mattered, the Splinterqueen already saved. You have to accept that. It was enough that you brought her here, don't you understand? Carrying her now would only lessen your chances—and that would really have pissed her off."

Some alien part of me allowed the wasps to take the corpse. Then we were inside, helmeted up and breathing thick.

As the train picked up speed, I glanced out the window, intent on seeing the Queen one last time. It should have been too dark, but the chamber looked bright. For a moment I presumed the frescos had come to life again, but then something about the scene's unreal intensity told me the Queen was weaving this image in my head. She hovered above the debris-strewn terrazzo—except that this was more than the Queen I had seen before. This was—what?

How she saw herself?

Ten of her twelve wasp composites were now back together, arranged in constantly shifting formation. They now seemed more living than machine, with diaphonous sunwings, chitin-black bodies, fur-sheened limbs and sensors, and eyes which were faceted crystalline globes, sparkling in the chamber's false light. That wasn't all. Before, I'd sensed the Queen as something implied by her composites. Now I didn't need to imagine her. Like a ghost in which the composites hung, she loomed vast in the chamber, multiwinged and brooding—

And then we were gone.

We sped toward the surface for the next few minutes, waiting for the impact of the next kinetic. When it hit, the train's cushioned ride smothered the concussion. For a moment I thought we'd made it, then the machine began to decelerate slowly to a dead halt. Wendigo convened with the Queen and told me the line was blocked. We disembarked into vacuum.

Ahead, the tunnel ended in a wall of jumbled ice.

After a few minutes we found a way through the obstruction, Wendigo wrenching aside boulders larger than either of us. "We're only half a klick from the surface," she said, as we emerged into the unblocked tunnel beyond. She pointed ahead, to what might have been a scotoma of absolute blackness against the milky darkness of the tunnel.

"After that, a klick overland to the wreck." She paused. "Realise we can't go home, Spirey. Now more than ever."

"Not exactly spoilt for choice, are we."

"No. It has to be the halo, of course. It's where the splinter's headed anyway; just means we'll get there ahead of schedule. There are other Splinterqueens out there, and at the very least they'll want to keep us alive. Possibly other humans as well—others who made the same discovery as us, and knew there was no going home."

"Not to mention Royalists."

"That troubles you, doesn't it?"

"I'll deal with it," I said, pushing forward.

The tunnel was nearly horizontal, and with the splinter's weak gravity it was easy to make the distance to the surface. Emerging, Fomalhaut glared down at us, a white-cored bloodshot eye surrounded by the wrinklelike dust lanes of the inner Swirl. Limned in red, wasp corpses marred the landscape.

"I don't see the ship."

Wendigo pointed to a piece of blank caramel-colored horizon. "Curvature's too great. We won't see it until we're almost on top of it."

"Hope you're right."

"Trust me. I know this place like, well . . ." Wendigo regarded one of her limbs. "Like the back of my hand."

"Encourage me, why don't you."

Three or four hundred meters later we crested a scallop-shaped rise of ice and halted. We could see the ship now. It didn't look in much better shape than when Yarrow and I had scoped it from Mouser.

"I don't see any wasps."

"Too dangerous for them to stay on the surface," Wendigo said.

"That's cheering. I hope the remaining damage is cosmetic," I said. "Because if it isn't—"

Suddenly I wasn't talking to anyone.

Wendigo was gone. After a moment I saw her, lying in a crumpled heap at the foot of the hillock. Her guts stretched away like a rusty comet-tail, halfway to the next promontary.

Quillin was fifty meters ahead, risen from the concealment of a chondrite boulder.

When Wendigo had mentioned her, I'd put her out of mind as any kind of threat. How could she pose any danger beyond the inside of a thickship, when she'd traded her legs for a tail and fluke, just like Yarrow? On dry land, she'd be no more mobile than a seal pup. Well, that was how I'd figured things.

But I'd reckoned without Quillin's suit.

Unlike Yarrow's—unlike any siren suit I'd ever seen—it sprouted legs. Mechanized, they emerged from the hip, making no concessions to human anatomy. The legs were long enough to lift Quillin's tail completely free of the ice. My gaze tracked up her body, registering the crossbow which she held in a double-handed grip.

"I'm sorry," Quillin's deep voice boomed in my skull. "Check-in's closed."

"Wendigo said you might be a problem."

"Wise up. It was staged from the moment we reached the Royalist stronghold." Still keeping the bow on me, she began to lurch across the ice. "The ferals were actors, playing dumb. The wasps were programmed to feed us bullshit."

"It isn't a Royalist trick, Quillin."

"Shit. See I'm gonna have to kill you as well."

The ground jarred, more violently than before. A nimbus of white light puffed above the horizon, evidence of an impact on the splinter's far side. Quillin stumbled, but her legs corrected the accident before it tripped her forward.

"I don't know if you're keeping up with current events," I said. "But that's our own side."

"Maybe you didn't think hard enough. Why did wasps in the Swirl get smart before the trillions of wasps back in Sol System? Should have been the other way round."

"Yeah?"

"Of course, Spirey. GE's wasps had a massive head-start." She shrugged, but the bow stayed rigidly pointed. "Okay, war sped up wasp evolution here. But that shouldn't have made so much difference. That's where the story breaks down."

"Not quite."

"What?"

"Something Wendigo told me. About what she called the second imperative. I guess it wasn't something she found out until she went underground."

"Yeah? Astonish me."

Well, something astonished Quillin at that point—but I was only marginally less surprised by it myself. An explosion of ice, and a mass of swiftly-moving metal erupting from the ground around her. The wasp corpses were partially dismembered, blasted and half-melted—but they still managed to drag Quillin to the ground. For a moment she thrashed, kicking up plumes of frost. Then the whole mass lay deathly still, and it was just me, the ice and a lot of metal and blood.

The Queen must have coaxed activity out of a few of the wasp corpses, ordering them to use their last reserves of power to take out Quillin.

Thanks, Queen.

But no cigar. Quillin hadn't necessarily meant to shoot me at that point, but— bless her—she had anyway. The bolt had transected me with the precision of one of the Queen's theorems, somewhere below my sternum. Gut-shot. The blood on the ice was my own.

I tried moving.

A couple of light-years away I saw my body undergo a frail little shiver. It didn't hurt, but there was nothing in the way of proprioceptive feedback to indicate I'd actually managed to twitch any part of my body.

Quillin was moving too.

Wriggling, that is, since her suit's legs had been cleanly ripped away by the wasps. Other than that she didn't look seriously injured. Ten or so meters from me, she flopped around like a maggot and groped for her bow. What remained of it anyway.

Chalk one to the good guys.

By which time I was moving, executing a marginally quicker version of Quillin's slug crawl. I couldn't stand up—there are limits to what pilot physiology can cope with—but my legs gave me leverage she lacked.

"Give up, Spirey. You have a head-start on me, and right now you're a little faster—but that ship's still a long way off." Quillin took a moment to catch her breath. "Think you can sustain that pace? Gonna need to, you don't want me catching up."

"Plan on rolling over me until I suffocate?"

"That's an option. If this doesn't kill you first."

Enough of her remained in my field-of-view to see what she meant.

Something sharp and bladelike had sprung from her wrist, a bayonet projecting half a meter ahead of her hand. It looked like a nasty little toy—but I did my best to push it out of mind and get on with the job of crawling toward the ship. It was no more than two hundred meters away now—what little of it protruded above the ice. The external airlock was already open, ready to clamp shut as soon as I wriggled inside—

"You never finished telling me, Spirey."

"Telling you what?"

"About this—what did you call it? The second imperative?"

"Oh, that." I halted and snatched breath. "Before I go on, I want you to know I'm only telling you this to piss you off."

"Whatever bakes your cake."

"Alright," I said. "Then I'll begin by saying you were right. Greater Earth's wasps should have made the jump to sentience long before those in the Swirl, simply because they'd had longer to evolve. And that's what happened."

Quillin coughed, like gravel in a bucket. "Pardon?"

"They beat us to it. About a century and a half ago. Across Sol System, within just a few hours, every single wasp woke up and announced its intelligence to the nearest human being it could find. Like babies reaching for the first thing they see." I stopped, sucking in deep lungfuls. The wreck had to be closer now—but it hardly looked it.

Quillin, by contrast, looked awfully close now—and that blade awfully sharp.

"So the wasps woke," I said, damned if she wasn't going to hear the whole story. "And that got some people scared. So much, some of them got to attacking the wasps. Some of their shots went wide, because within a day the whole system was one big shooting match. Not just humans against wasps—but humans against humans." Less than fifty meters now, across much smoother ground than we'd so far traversed. "Things just escalated. Ten days after Solar War Three began, only a few ships and habitats were still transmitting. They didn't last long."

"Crap," Quillin said—but she sounded less cocksure than she had a few moments before. "There was a war back then, but it never escalated into a full-blown Solar War."

"No. It went the whole hog. From then on every signal we ever got from GE was concocted by wasps. They daren't break the news to us—at least not immediately. We've only been allowed to find out because we're never going home. Guilt, Wendigo called it. They couldn't let it happen again."

"What about our wasps?"

"Isn't it obvious? A while later the wasps here made the same jump to sentience—presumably because they'd been shown the right moves by the others. Difference was, ours kept it quiet. Can't exactly blame them, can you?"

There was nothing from Quillin for a while, both of us concentrating on the last patch of ice before Wendigo's ship.

"I suppose you have an explanation for this too," she said eventually, swiping her tail against the ground. "C'mon, blow my mind."

So I told her what I knew. "They're bringing life to the Swirl. Sooner than you think, too. Once this charade of a war is done, the wasps breed in earnest. Trillions out there now, but in a few decades it'll be billions of trillions. They'll outweigh a good-sized planet. In a way the Swirl will have become sentient. It'll be directing its own evolution."

I spared Quillin the details—how the wasps would arrest the existing processes of planetary formation so that they could begin anew, only this time according to a plan. Left to its own devices, the Swirl would contract down to a solar system comprised solely of small, rocky planets—but such a system could never support life over billions of years. Instead, the wasps would exploit the system's innate chaos to tip it toward a state where it would give rise to at least two much larger worlds—planets as massive as

Jupiter or Saturn, capable of shepherding left-over rubble into tidy, world-avoiding orbits. Mass extinctions had no place in the Splinterqueens' vision of future life.

But I guessed Quillin probably didn't care.

"Why are you hurrying, Spirey?" she asked, between harsh grunts as she propelled herself forward. "The ship isn't going anywhere."

The edge of the open airlock was a meter above the ice. My fingers probed over the rim, followed by the crest of my battered helmet. Just lifting myself into the lock's lit interior seemed to require all the energy I'd already expended in the crawl. Somehow I managed to get half my body length into the lock.

Which is when Quillin reached me.

There wasn't much pain when she dug the bayonet into my ankle; just a form of cold I hadn't imagined before, even lying on the ice. Quillin jerked the embedded blade to and forth, and the knot of cold seemed to reach out little feelers, into my foot and lower leg. I sensed she wanted to retract the blade for another stab, but my suit armour was gripping it tight.

The bayonet taking her weight, Quillin lofted her bulk over the rim of the lock. I tried kicking her away, but the skewered leg no longer felt a part of me.

"You're dead," she whispered.

"News to me."

Her eyes rolled wide, then locked on me with renewed venom. She gave the bayonet a violent twist. "So tell me one thing. That story—bullshit, or what?"

"I'll tell you," I said. "But first consider this." Before she could react I reached out and palmed a glowing panel set in the lock wall. The panel whisked aside, revealing a mushroom-shaped red button. "You know that story they told about Wendigo, how she lost her arms?"

"You weren't meant to swallow that hero guff, Spirey."

"No? Well get a load of this. My hand's on the emergency pressurisation control, Quillin. When I hit it, the outer door's going to slide down quicker than you can blink."

She looked at my hand, then down at her wrist, still attached to my ankle via the jammed bayonet. Slowly the situation sunk in. "Close the door, Spirey, and you'll be a leg short."

"And you an arm, Quillin."

"Stalemate, then."

"Not quite. See, which of us is more likely to survive? Me inside, with all the medical systems aboard this ship, or you all on your lonesome outside? Frankly, I don't think it's any contest."

Her eyes opened wider. Quillin gave a shriek of anger and entered one final furious wrestling match with the bayonet.

I managed to laugh. "As for your question, it's true, every word of it." Then, with all the calm I could muster, I thumbed the control. "Pisser, isn't it."

I made it, of course.

Several minutes after the closing of the door, demons had lathered a protective cocoon around the stump and stomach wound. They allowed me no pain—only a muggy sense of detachment. Enough of my mind remained sharp to think about my escape—problematic given that the ship still wasn't fixed.

Eventually I remembered the evac pods.

They were made to kick away from the ship fast, if some quackdrive system went on the fritz. They had thrusters for that; nothing fancy, but here they'd serve another purpose. They'd boost me from the splinter, punch me out of its grav well.

So I did it.

Snuggled into a pod and blew out of the wreck, feeling the gee-load even within the thick. It didn't last long. On the evac pod's cam I watched the splinter drop away until it was pebble-sized. The main body of the kinetic attack was hitting it by then, impacts every ten or so seconds. After a minute of that the splinter just came apart. Afterwards, there was only a sooty veil where it had been, and then only the Swirl.

I hoped the Queen had made it. I guess it was within her power to transmit what counted of herself out to sisters in the halo. If so, there was a chance for Yarrow as well. I'd find out eventually. Afterwards, I used the pod's remaining fuel to inject me into a slow elliptical orbit, one that would graze the halo in a mere fifty or sixty years.

That didn't bother me. I wanted to close my eyes and let the thick nurse me whole again—and sleep an awful long time.

CHARLES STROSS

Charles Stross [1964–] (www.antipope.org/charlie) lives in Edinburgh, Scotland. He is full of ideas and energy, a dyed-in-the-wool science fiction writer in the tradition of Bruce Sterling. He is of the same social circle as Iain M. Banks and Ken MacLeod, and the three of them are being called (not entirely unjustly) the Scots SF Renaissance. Of the three, Stross has been publishing widely since 2000 in *Spectrum SF* and *Interzone*, and recently *Asimov's* (though his first story appeared in 1987 and he has published about one a year since). He had a hit in 2001 in writing circles with his story "Lobsters," which launched his Accelerando series. The Accelerando stories now have their own Web site and domain name: www.accelerando.org. Some of his early work is collected in *Toast* (2002), a print-on-demand edition. Recently he has written several stories in collaboration with Cory Doctorow, though not space opera. He said in an on-line discussion, "I don't know if I qualify as New Weird, New Space Opera, or New Anything. (I think I'll settle for New Charlie, Brighter! and Sparkier! than Old Charlie.)"

His first SF novel, *Singularity Sky*, appeared in 2003 (Stross describes it on his Web site as a "post-singularity space opera") and three novels, *The Atrocity Archive*, *Iron Sunrise* (the sequel to *Singularity Sky*), and *The Family Trade* (the first of a science fantasy series) in 2004. His two novels in 2005 were *The Hidden Family*, second in the fantasy series, and *Accelerando*, his big novel integrating the story series. The sequence of stories is jammed with information, speculation, hard science, rapid shifts of point of view, jittery jarring rapid change. It is set in a near future that is undergoing continuing revolution from the biological sciences, after a computer revolution, after a techno-economic revolution.

Stross's description of it is in part:

> This sequence is also—to paraphrase Vincent Omniaveritas—a partial attempt to take the thin beer of cyberpunk and distill it into something that we can get stoned on today. The cyberpunk movement started before we knew what the 1980's were going to be about. It looks horribly dated, with two decades of hindsight and a career in the dot com business to add perspective. We've actually lived through that stuff with the black leather, the Armani suits, the hostile corporate takeovers and defections, the net-heads plugged into their computers thirty hours a day, and the fear, loathing, and hacking of faceless multinationals. It's history. Now we've got it out of the way, now that we can take the net as a given, can we please get back to the main program?

When we asked him to comment on his short fiction, he replied, "With the possible exception of 'Bear Trap,' which barely qualifies, I just don't do space opera at short length. Oh yeah, the other exception: Bits of the Accelerando thingy probably have space-operatic overtones. . . . But as they're part of a novel, I suspect they don't count." So we chose to represent him in this book with "Bear Trap."

BEAR TRAP

CHARLES STROSS

I was six hours away from landfall on Burgundy when my share portfolio tried to kill me. I was sitting in one of the main viewing lounges, ankle-deep in softly breathing fur, half watching a core tournament and nursing a water pipe in one hand. I was not alone: I shared the lounge with an attentive bar, a number of other passengers, and—of course—a viewing wall. It curved away beside me, a dizzying emptiness with stars scattered across it like gold dust and a blue and white planet looming in the foreground. I tried to focus on the distant continents. *Six hours to safety*, I realized. A cold shiver ran up my spine. Six hours and I'd be beyond their reach, firewalled behind Burgundy's extensive defenses. Six more hours of being a target.

The bar sidled up to me. "Sir's pipe appears to have become extinguished. Would Sir appreciate a refill?"

"No, sir would not," I said, distantly taking in the fact that my pulse had begun to drum a staccato tattoo on the inside of my skull. My mouth tasted acrid and smoky, and it was unusually quiet in my head: a combination of the drugs and the time-lag between my agents—light-years away, bottlenecked by the low bandwidth causal channels between my brain and the servers where most of my public personna lived. "In fact, I'd like a sober-up now. How long until we arrive, and where?"

The bar dipped slightly, programmatically obsequious as it handed me a small glass. "This vessel is now four hundred thousand kilometres from docking bay seven on Burgundy beanstalk. Your departure is scheduled via Montreaux immigration sector, downline via tube to Castillia terminus. Please note your extensive customs briefing and remember to relinquish any unauthorised tools or thoughts you may be carrying before debarkation. The purser's office will be happy to arrange storage pending your eventual departure. Three requests for personal contact have been filed—"

"Enough." Everything was becoming clearer by the moment as the sober-up gave me a working-over. I looked around. We were one and a third light seconds out: comms were already routed through the in-system relays and Her Majesty's censorship reflexes, which meant anyone sending uploaded agents after me would first have to penetrate *her* firewall. That was why I'd taken this otherwise unattractive contract in the first place. I tried to relax, but the knot of stress under my ribs refused to go away. "I want—" I began.

"Alain!" It was one of the other passengers, striding towards me across the floor of the lounge. She looked as if she knew me: I didn't recognise her, and in my current state it was all I could do to keep from cursing under my breath. *A creditor? Or a liquidator?* In the wake of the distributed market crash it could be either. Once again, I found myself cursing the luck that had seen me so widely uncovered at just the wrong moment.

"So this is where you've been hiding!" She was bald, I noticed, a fashion common to Burgundy, but had highlighted her eyelids with vivid strokes of black pigment. Her costume was intricate and brightly coloured, a concoction of dead animal products and lace that left only her shoulders and ankles bare; she was dressed for a party. Slowly I began to feel embarrassed. "You have the better of me, madame," I said, struggling to my feet.

"Do I?" she looked mildly disapproving. "But we're due to disembark in six hours—after the landing party, of course! Surely you weren't planning to sleep through the captain's ball?"

My knowledge was sluggish but accessible; *who is she?* I demanded. The answer was so unexpected I nearly sat down again. *Arianna Blomenfeld. Your wife.* I shook my head. "Sorry, I'm a bit out of sorts," I said, dropping the water pipe on the bar. "Fine grade, that." I smiled fatuously to conceal the fact that I was thinking furiously, shocked all the way into sobriety. *Knowledge, integrity check, please.*

The edges of her mouth drooped a little sourly: "Have you been overdoing it again?" she demanded.

No, I'm just hallucinating your existence for the hell of it. "Of course not," I said as smoothly as I could. "I was just enjoying a small pipe. Nothing wrong with that, is there?" *Details, details.* Someone or something had dug their little claws into my external memories; I urgently needed to probe the limits of their fakery.

She offered me a gloved hand: "The party's starting soon, downstairs in the Sunset Room. You should go and dress for it, you know." My knowledge finally delivered, dumping a jerky snowstorm of images through my mnemonic system: memories of myself and this woman, this Arianna Blomenfeld. Memories I'd never experienced. A wedding party in some palatial estate on Avernia, bride and groom in lustrous red: I recognised myself, smiling and relaxed at the centre of events. More private imagery, honeymoon nights I wish I *had* experienced. She was the well-engineered scion of a rich merchant-spy sept, apparently an heiress to family knowledge. Designed from birth to cement a powerful alliance. Public images: sailing a spiderboat across the endless southern ocean of that world. Then a public newsbite, myself—and herself—attending some public function full of pompous export brokers in the capital. Options trading leveraged on FTL/STL communications advantages, part of my regular arbitrage load.

Her hand felt thin and frail within her glove. Such a shame, I thought, that I had never come within twelve light-years of Avernia. "Coming, dear?" she asked.

"Indeed." I let her lead me to the doorway, still stunned by my memory's insistence that I was married to this woman: it made no sense! Either I had erased a large chunk of my personality by accident, or someone had managed to drill right down into my external knowledge—while I was on the inside of a firewall's security cordon, one maintained by a near-deity notorious for paranoia. "I'd better go and get changed," I said.

Arianna let me go when we reached the stairs, and I hurried up to the accommodation level where my suite was located. As soon as the door opened I knew I was adrift. When I'd left, the room had mirrored my own apartment back in Shevralier Old Town: austere classicism and a jumble of odds and ends scattered over the hand-carved wooden furniture. It was very different, now. The dark, heavy furniture bulked against the walls, making the cabin feel cramped: an en-suite cornucopia rig, factories ready to clothe and feed me on request.

I leaned against the wall, dizzy. *Who am I?*

You are Alain Blomenfeld, intelligence broker for the Syndic d'Argent of Avernia. Nobody you know has died since your last knowledge checkpoint in real time. Nobody you know has changed their mind. Your cognitive continuity is assured. You are currently—

"Wrong. Validate immediately," I said aloud. Then, in my own skull, another command; one keyed to a private and personal area, one that never leaked beyond the neuroprocessors spliced into my cerebrum. Self-test runes flashed inside my eyelids and I felt a shivery flash of anger as the secret watcher scanned through my memories, matched them against the externals that made up my public image, stored in the knowledge systems scattered throughout human space. All my public memories were fingerprinted using public keys, the private halves of which were stitched into my thalamus so tight that any attempt to steal them would amount to murder.

Global mismatch detected. External temporal structures do not match internal checksum. Internal memory shows no sign of cognitive engineering. Your external memories have been tampered with. Alert!

"Uh-huh." *Thanks for warning me in time.* "Wardrobe?" I sat down on the edge of the bed and tried to think two ways at once, very fast. The wardrobe helped me out. "How can I help you, sir?"

"I want an outfit. Suitable for captain's ball. What have you got?" The mirror fogged, then cleared to show images of me in a variety of costumes, local to Burgundy as well as Avernian corporate. I noted that my body didn't seem to have changed, which was at least mildly reassuring. Meanwhile I thought furiously: *Am I under attack? If so, is it a physical attack or an existential one?* Existential, I guessed—Arianna, whoever she was, was part of some scheme to infiltrate me—but why? I couldn't put my finger on any motive for such a scheme. The exchange assassins might be on my trail, ready to kill me and bring my memories and stock options home on a cube, but they'd hardly be subtle about it. So who was it?

"I think I'll wear that one," I said, pausing the mirror-search at a conservatively cut dark robe. Then I thought for a moment, summoning up a covert maker routine from my internals: *fab this for me, and put it in an inner pocket.* I dumped the design into the wardrobe, and began to strip.

If only I knew who they were and why they were after me.

If only I knew what I needed to watch out for . . .

The main dining room was furnished in marble splendour, as if to emphasise that mass was of no concern to the modern space traveller; the ship showed me to my seat, a trail of fireflies pulsing through the candlelit conversations of the other diners.

"Alain! So pleased to see you again!" I couldn't decide whether she was being sarcastic or not. She smiled up at me, lips pale with tension.

"I was delayed," I said, and sat down beside her.

"That's nice. I was just telling Ivana here that I never know quite what to expect of you." This time the sarcasm was unmistakable, underpinned by a note of hostility that instantly put my back up. Ivana, a blonde mask with a fair complexion, nodded approvingly: I ignored her.

"That makes two of us," I replied, picking up my wine glass. An attentive servitor lowered its mouth to the goblet and regurgitated a red dribble: I swirled it under my nose for a moment and inhaled. "Have you made any arrangements for our arrival?"

"I was waiting to discuss that with you," she said guardedly. I looked at her, noting suddenly that her attention was totally focussed on me. It was a little frightening. In a culture of cheap beauty, the currency of aesthetic perfection is devalued; Arianna Blomenfeld was striking rather than pretty, projecting raw character in a way that suggested she hired only the most subtle of body sculptors. If the situation wasn't quite so depressingly messy I'd probably be trailing around after her with my tongue hanging out. "I suggest we discuss things in private after dinner."

"Perhaps." I drank some more wine and tried to figure out what she was hinting at. Dinner was served: a platter of delicate, thin-sliced flesh garnished with a white sauce. We ate in hostile silence, broken by vapid banter emanating from the mask and her partner, another nonentity of indeterminate age and questionable taste; I did my best to study Arianna while overtly ignoring her. She gave little away, except for the occasional furtive glance.

I found myself ignoring the meal, screening out the captain's speech and the assorted toasts and assertions of welcoming that followed it. Periodically, minor agents deposited fragments of opinion in the back of my mind: less frequently, the waitrons cleared our plates and stifled us with solicitude. I was tugging at a bowl of sugared vermicelli when Arianna finally engaged my conversation. "You're going to have to face the future sooner or later," she stated directly. "You can't keep avoiding me forever. I want an answer, Alain. Bear or Bull? Which is it?"

My fork froze of its own accord, halfway to my mouth. "My dear, I have no idea what you're talking about," I said.

She obviously had some end in view for she smiled tensely, and said: "There's no need to hide anymore, Alain. It's over. We've escaped. You can stop pretending."

"I—" I stopped. I put my fork down. "I've no idea what you're suggesting, truly." I frowned, and had the reward of seeing her look discomfited: surprised, if anything. "I don't feel very well," I added for the gallery.

"Ooh, do tell!" said the mask's slow-witted companion.

"There's nothing to tell," Arianna answered, fixing me with a coldly knowing look. I could hear the blood pumping in my ears. Had someone fixed her self-knowledge too? Was she also a victim of whatever was going on here? I stared at her face, mapping the pulse of blood through her veins: slightly flushed, tense, signs of concentration. I realised with a shiver that she was as worried as I.

"I don't feel so well," I repeated, and prodded my thalamus into broadcasting the appropriate signs. "Please excuse me." I stood and, mustering as much dignity as I could, left the room. There was a flurry of nervous conversation behind me from the mask and her attendant, but nobody followed me or paged me.

My stateroom was just as I had left it. I reached into my pocket for the device I had ordered from the wardrobe, then entered the bedroom.

"Don't move. Stay exactly where you are." I froze. No way of knowing how Arianna had gotten here ahead of me, much less how she had bypassed the lock—but I wasn't willing to bet that she was unarmed.

"What are you doing here?" I demanded.

"I'm asking the questions." She studied me like a bug on a pin. She was standing against the wall between the dresser and the wardrobe, the dark fabric of her dress shifting colour to blend in with the aged oak finish. A little-used daemon reported back: *subject is suppressing emissions on all service channels. Unable to establish context.* She was holding something round in a lace-gloved hand, pointed right at me. "Who are you and why have you spoofed my public knowledge?"

I blinked. "What are you talking about? *You* cracked *my* knowledge." I tried to force my pulse to slow. (Escape routes: the door was behind me, open, offering a clear field of fire. Her fingertips, exposed through the tips of her gloves, were white around the grip of her weapon. Stress.) "You can drop the pretence. I doubt we're being monitored and it doesn't make any difference anyway: you've got me." (Hoping she wouldn't shoot if I didn't let her see what I held clenched in my right hand; I wanted to learn whatever I could first. And besides, I don't like the sight of blood.)

"You're lying. Who are you working for? Tell me!" She sounded increasingly agitated: she raised the sphere, pointing it at my face from across the room. Deep heat vision showed me her pulse and another daemon tracked it: *one thirty-seven, one thirty-nine . . .* signs of serious stress. Was she telling the truth?

"I didn't modify your knowledge! I thought you'd been messing with mine—"

A momentary expression of shock flickered across her face. "If you're telling the truth—" she began, then stopped.

"Does someone want you dead? Does someone want *both* of us dead?" I asked.

"Wait." (A very paranoid agency chirped up in my ears; *sensor failure in main access corridor. Denial of service attack in progress.*) Arianna must have been listening to something like my own inner voice, because she abruptly twisted round and punched the wall: it shattered with a noise like breaking glass. She stood aside, still pointing a finger at me—the large, dark ring on it protruding upwards like a stubby gun barrel: "Get out! *Move!*"

I moved. Across the bed, to the hole in the wall—taking a brief look out—then through it. Something solid came up and thumped me bruisingly. It was dark, and my eyes weren't ready for it; I was in some kind of roofed over-service duct, low ceiling, fat pipes oozing across every exposed surface. I glanced round. Structures bulked on all sides; it was some kind of service area I guessed, an inner hull. "Quick. Move." Arianna was behind me, prodding me away from the broken wall. "Faster!" she hissed.

"Why?" I asked.

"Keep going!" I scrabbled forwards into the darkness, lizard-like on all fours. I could hear her behind me and risked a glance. "Faster, idiot!" She was on all fours to avoid the low ceiling. "If you're lying I'll—"

Thump.

I blinked, unsure where I was. *That was a very loud noise,* I realised vaguely. Something tugged at my leg and I opened my eyes: there was a ringing in my ears and a light was flickering on and off in one eye, trying to get my attention. I blinked and tried to focus: someone was pinging me repeatedly. *What is it?*

Urgent message from Arianna Blomenfeld: "That was meant for us." There was an object attached the message, a simple minded medical scanner that told her I was awake before I could stop it.

I lifted my head, blinking, and realised I was breathless. I began to cough. Someone put a hand over my mouth and I began to choke instead. *Message: Don't speak. Bidirectional secure link installed.* I could feel it, itching like the phantom of someone else's limb.

"What happened?"

"Denial of service attack—with a bomb appended." My eyes were streaming. She let go of my mouth as I noticed her delicate lace evening gloves had turned into something more robust: blinking in the dusty twilight I saw her dress bunching up close to her, unravelling, weaving itself into plainer, close-fitting overalls: a space suit? Body armour? "Meant for both of us, while we were talking. Probably a last shot, before docking. Low information content, anyway."

"Do you know who's after you?" I asked.

She grimaced. "Talk about it later. If we get off this thing alive."

"They're trying to kill me, too," I transmitted, trying not to move my lips.

"So start moving."

"Which way?"

She pointed towards a service catwalk. I pushed myself up, wincing as my head throbbed in time to my pulse. Loud noises in the distance and an ominous hissing of air, then a queasy rippling lightness underfoot: the ship's momentum transfer field shutting down, handing us off to the dockmaster's control. "All the way down to the bottom."

"I've got a better idea. Why don't we split up? Less chance of them catching both of us."

She looked at me oddly. "If you want . . ."

Welcome to Burgundy.

Humanity is scattered across a three-thousand-light-year radius, exiled from old Earth via wormholes created by the Eschaton, a strongly godlike intelligence spawned during Earth's singularity. Some of these worlds, including Burgundy, communicate; people and goods by starship, information by the network of instantaneous but bandwidth-limited causal trails established by Festival.

Burgundy is a developed, somewhat introverted culture that rests on the groaning back of a deliberately constructed proletariat. The first weakly godlike artificial intelligence to arrive here in the wake of its rediscovery abolished the cornucopiae and subjugated the human populace: an action that was tolerated because nothing the Queen did to them was anything like as bad as the oppression imposed by their own human leaders.

Burgundy has gained a small reputation as an information buffer—a side-effect of its monarch's paranoid attitude towards encroachment by other deities. It exports confidentiality, delay-line buffers, fine wines, and dissidents. In other words, it's the last place a futures trader specialising in spread option trades that leverage developments in the artificial intelligence market—someone like me—would normally be seen dead in. On the other hand . . .

As an accountant specialising in monte carlo solutions to NP-complete low-knowledge systems I am naturally of interest to the Queen, who made me an offer I would have considered long and hard at the best of times; in my circumstances back on Dordogne—exposed to risk, to say the least—I could hardly consider refusing her invitation.

Many technologies are banned from the system, in an attempt to reduce the vulnerability of the monarchy to buffer overrun and algorithmic complexity attacks. In particular, the royal capital of Burgundy—Castillia, a teeming metropolis of some three million souls—is positively mediaeval. It was here that the down-pod from the equatorial beanstalk deposited me, time-lagged and dizzy from the descent, on the steps of the main rail terminus. Arianna had disappeared while I was opening a side-door back into the populated sections of the ship: I didn't see her go, although I have a vague recollection of blurred air, flattened perspectives against a wood-panelled wall. My ears were still ringing from the blast, and I was so confused that I didn't notice much of anything until I found myself in an alleyway my autonomics had steered me to, eyeing up the guest house where the Royal Mint had rented me a room.

The depths of neomediaeval barbarity into which this city had sunk finally became clear when I found my way to my garret. It wasn't simply the liveried servitors, or even even the obese, physically aged steward who proudly showed me to the suite; but the presence of running water. Yes: a lead pipe—lead, yet!—entered through the ceiling of one room and debouched through a gargoyle-encrusted tap above a pewter basin. "You see, we have all the ancient luxuries!" gloated Salem the steward. "This'n's piped down from our very own roof-tank. More'n you'll have seen before, I expect."

I nodded, faintly aghast at the prospect of the microfauna that must be swimming in the swill.

"Are you sure you don't have any luggage?" he added, one heavy eyebrow raised in protest at the very idea of a gentleman-merchant travelling untrammelled.

"Not a parcel," I said. "I came by starship . . ."

He blinked rapidly. "Oh," he said, very fast. "And ee's not staying at the Palace?" He shuffled, as if unsure of what to do with his feet, then essayed a little bow. "We is honoured by your presence, m'lord."

When I finally persuaded them to leave me alone—at the price of calling a tailor, to fab me some garments suitable to my station in life—I swept the room for bugs. My custom fleas found nothing, save the more natural macrofauna lurking in the bed, garde-robe, and curtains. I removed and disassembled into three separate parts the device in my pocket, then hid two of them in the hollow cuban heels of my boots: possession of such a gadget, in these parts, could earn one a slow impalement if the Queen deigned to notice. (The third part I wore as a ring on my left hand.)

At the end of this sequence I lay down upon the bed, hands behind my head, staring up at the dusty canopy of the four-poster. "What am I doing here?" I murmured. *To report to ye chancellery of court on the day following landfall, there to command and supervise the management of ye portfolio of accounts royal and foreign*, the contract said; while lying low and avoiding the exchange agents, I added mentally. But I was already wondering if I'd made the right decision.

The next day, I reported to the Exchequer for duty.

A rambling, gothic assemblage of gargoyles, flying buttresses and turrets held together by red brick, the Chancellery was located across the three-sided Capital Square from the Summer Palace, a white marble confection that pointed battlements and parabolic reflectors south across the river. As I approached the entrance, armed guards came to attention. Their leader stepped forward. "Sir Blomenfeld," said the sergeant: "I am pleased to greet you on behalf of her Terrible Majesty, and extend to you her gracious wishes for your success in her service."

"I thank you from the depths of my heart," I replied, somewhat taken aback by his instant recognition. "It is an honour and a blessing to be welcomed in such exalted terms. I will treasure it to my dying day." *Laying it on too thick?* I wondered.

The sergeant nodded, and I noticed the antennae tucked between the feathers of his ornate helmet; the strangely bony fingers disguised by his padded gloves: and the odd articulation of his back. Evidently the technology restrictions didn't apply to Her Majesty's security. "If you would please come this way, sir?" he asked, directing me towards a side door.

Tradesman's entrance. "Certainly."

He led me inside, up the steps and along a wide marble passage hung with portraits of ruby-nosed dignitaries in their late middle age: the human dynasty that had preceded Her Majesty. Into an office where, behind a leather-topped desk, there sat a man with a surpassingly sallow complexion and even less hair than my ersatz wife had been wearing the night before. "Sir Alain Blomenfeld, your honour, reporting as required." He turned to me. "His Lordship, Victor Manchusko, under-secretary of the Treasury, counsellor in charge of the privy portfolio."

Privy portfolio? I blinked in surprise as the sergeant bowed his way out. "Sir, I—"

"Sit down." Lord Manchusko waved in the direction of an ornately decorated chair that might have been designed as an instrument of torture. His gold-rimmed spectacles glittered in the wan light filtering down from the high-set windows. "You were not expecting something like this, I take it."

"Not exactly," I said, somewhat flustered. "Um, I understood I was being retained to overhaul dependency tracking in the barter sector—"

"Nonsense." Manchusko slapped the top of his desk: I'll swear that it cringed. "Do you think we needed to hire offworld intellect for such a task?"

"Um. Then you, er, have something else in mind?"

The under-secretary smiled thinly. "Over-exposed on the intelligence futures side, was it?"

An icy sinking feeling in the pit of my stomach. "Yes," I admitted.

"Tell me about it."

"It was all over the Festival channels. Surely you know—"

He smiled again. It was not a humorous expression. "Pretend I don't."

"Oh." I hunched over unconsciously. So. They didn't want me as an accountant, after all, hmm? *Trapped.* And if I didn't give them exactly what they wanted they could hold me here forever. I licked my lips: "You know what commodities are traded on the TX; mostly design schemata, meta-memes, better algorithms for network traversal, that sort of thing. Most of these items require serious mind-time to execute; so we trade processing power against options on better algorithms. Most of the trading entities are themselves intelligent, even if only weakly so: even some of the financial instruments—" I paused.

"Such as Blomenfeld et Cie, I take it."

I nodded. "Yes. I was proud of that company. Even though it was pretty small in the scheme of things; it was *mine*, I made it. We worked well together. I was its director, and it was my memetic muscle. It was the smartest company I could build. We were working on a killer scheme, you know. When the market crashed."

Manchusko nodded. "A lot of people were burned by that."

I sighed and unkinked a little. "I was over-exposed. A complex derivative swap that was backward-chaining between one of the Septagon clades' quantum oracle programmes—I figured it would produce the goods, a linear-order performance boost in type IV fast-thinkers, within five mind-years—leveraged off junk bonds issued in Capone City. According to my Bayesian analysers nothing should go wrong in the fifteen seconds I was over-extended. Only it was just those fifteen seconds in which, um, you know what happened."

Normally, the Eschaton leaves us alone; nothing short of widespread causality violation provokes a strongly godlike intervention. Whatever happened in Eldritch system's intelligence futures market was bad, capital-B-bad. Bad enough to provoke an act of God. Intervention from beyond the singularity. Bad enough to trigger a run on the market, an instant bear market, everyone selling every asset they owned for dear life.

"Eldritch went runaway and the Eschaton intervened. You were in the middle of a complex chain of investments when the market crashed and it all unravelled on you due to a bad transitive dependency. How far uncovered were you?"

"Sixty thousand mind-years." I licked my suddenly-dry lips. "Ruin," I whispered.

Manchusko leaned forward suddenly. "Who's after you?" he demanded. "Who tried to kill you on the ship?"

"I don't know!" I snapped, then froze solid, trying to regain my composure. "I'm sorry. It could have been anyone. I have some suspicions—" not fair to mention Arianna, she'd been in the middle of it too "—but nothing solid. Not the exchange authority, anyway."

"Good. While you are here, you will remain under Her Majesty's protection. If you have any problems, ask any guard for help." That smile was disquieting as anything I'd ever seen: "What one sees, all see, *she* sees."

I nodded silently, not daring to trust my tongue.

"Now. About the reason we wanted you here. You weren't the only one who took a bath in the crash. Her Majesty's portfolio is highly diversified, and some of our investments suffered somewhat. Your job—unofficially—is to take over her hedge fund and rebuild it. Officially you're not trading, you're disqualified. Your company is insolvent and liable to be wound up, if they can ever track it down. You're a disqualified director. Unofficially, I hope you learn from your mistakes. Because we don't expect you to repeat them here." He stood up and gestured towards a side door. "Through here is your office and your dealer desk. Let me introduce you to it . . ."

Afternoon found me back at my room, digesting a manual of procedures and trying to regain my shattered composure. I had just about managed to forget about the incidents of the previous day when there was a knock at the door.

"Who is it?" I called.

"Y'r humble servant, m'lord," called Salem. "With a manuscript for you!"

I rolled to my feet. "Come in!"

He sidled into my room, holding a rolled-up piece of parchment away from his body as if it contained some noxious vermin. "Begging y'r'honour's indulgence, but this came for you from the palace. Messenger's waiting on y'r'honour's pleasure."

I took the note and broke the wax seal on it. *Having a lovely time at the court. Formal presentation before Her Majesty at eight this eve. Your presence requested by royal fiat. Will you be there? Signed, your "wife".*

Hello, Arianna, I thought. I remembered her face; chilly beauty. It was some joke, the one that whoever had hacked our respective memories had played on me. I resolved that if I ever found them I'd use their head for a punch-line. "Tell the messenger to tell her that I'll be there," I said.

At seven, Salem slid into my vision again. "Pardoning y'r honour, but y'r humble coach awaits you, sir," he mumbled unctuously.

"Isn't it a bit early?" I asked.

It wasn't early. I sat in a cramped wooden box with my nose inches from a slit-window rimmed with intricately painted murals of rural debauchery. Outside, two husky porters wheezed as they carried me bodily—box and all—through the cobbled streets. We lurched and swayed from side to side, trapped in a heaving mass of pedestrians: a royal lobster drive was in progress. The lobsters lived sufficiently long in air that by custom they were herded through the streets to the gates of the palace: the distress made their flesh all the sweeter. Presently my porters lifted me again and continued, this time with little further delay.

They set me down and opened the door: trying not to gasp audibly I stood up, stretching muscles that ached as if I'd run the entire distance. The sedan chair was parked in a courtyard, before the palace steps but inside the walls. My porters grovelled before a junior officer of the royal dragoons. I bowed slightly and doffed my hat to him.

"Sir Blomenfeld," said the lieutenant: "If you would please come this way, sir?"

"Surely." He led me inside, up the steps and along a wide marble passage carpeted in red velvet.

Noise, chatter, and music drifted from ahead. We came upon a well-lit stretch, then a pair of high doors and an antechamber, walled with pompous gold-leaf plaster, where four footmen and a butler greeted me. "His excellency the high trader Albert Blomenfeld, by appointment to Her Majesty's Royal Treasury! Long may she live!" A blast of pipes ushered me into the royal presence.

The hall beyond the antechamber was high-ceilinged, decorated with primitive opulence and meticulous precision, illuminated by skylights set in the ceiling. A floor of black and white tiles gleamed beneath my boots as I looked around. Throngs of richly clad courtiers ignored me in their elegant hauteur. The Queen herself was nowhere to be seen—but I would not expect to be introduced at this stage in any event. I wondered where Arianna was, and what she was doing to have inveigled herself into the royal court so rapidly. Although, if her hacked knowledge was anything to go by, she had the background for it.

"Hello, Alain!" My question answered itself with a beaming smile full of sharp, white teeth. She most elegantly decked out in a gown of sea-green silk, with a jewelled motif of eyes: her choker scrutinised me with terrible, passive regret. "I see you're none the worse for wear, hmm? We really must have that talk, you know." She took my hand and led me away from the door. *The company here is dire,* she sent. *Besides, speaking openly is difficult. Encrypt?* I nodded. Wetware embedded deep in the redundant neural networks of my cerebellum mangled the next transmission, established a private key, linked to her headspace . . .

"Do you know about the treasury situation yet?" she asked.

"Eh?" I stared at her; her gown stared back at me quizzically.

"Don't be obtuse. It's so hard to tell who's on the inside hereabouts. She didn't drag you here to mess with her ledgers, she brought you in for your dealing record."

"She?"

Arianna frowned. "The Queen." A balcony, overlooking an inner courtyard: neatly manicured lawn, flower beds, stone flagstones. My knowledge inflicted a sudden flash of deja vu on me: a false memory of accompanying Arianna to a ball on New Venus, of sneaking away with her, quiet sighs in a secret garden at midnight. My pulse accelerated: her hand tightened on my arm. "Too many damned memories, Alain. You feel it too?"

I nodded.

"I think they're there for a reason, you know. We must have something in common, otherwise whoever they are, they wouldn't have spoofed both of us with the same false history. Do you remember?"

She leaned against the balcony, watching me intently.

"I—" I shook my head. More deja vu, this time from within: I *knew* Arianna from somewhere, somewhere real, not bound up in externalities. *Market externalities.* Now where did *that* thought come from?

"I never saw you before, before you walked into that observation lounge, I swear it," I said. "But despite the false memories—"

She nodded. "You know what?" she asked.

"Um. What?"

Suddenly she leaned against me, sharp chin digging into my collar bone, hugging me tight in a spring-steel grip: "I don't remember," she whispered in my ear. "*Anything.* Before the lounge. I mean, I have lots of external memories, but no internal ones." She was shuddering with tension; I hugged her back, appalled by her admission. "I know who am, but I don't remember *becoming* me. At least, not from inside. All my memories that are more than a day old are third-person. Before then, I think, I think I may have been someone else."

"That's awful."

"Is it?" The tension in her arms ebbed slightly. "What about you?"

"I—" I suddenly realised I had an armful of attractive woman. A woman my external memories insisted I was married to. "I have false memories. One set, with you in them. And the real ones—I think they're real—without you."

Arianna released me, took a step back and shook her head. "So you *know* you're a real person? Then what does that make me?" Her gown blinked at me, eyelids rippling from floor to throat.

"I don't know. I've never met you before—at least, I don't remember doing so."

"Are you sure?" she murmured, pulling away slightly. She frowned, fine eyebrows drawing together. "I've been injected into your life and I don't know why. Are you certain you don't know anything about me? You seem to have enemies. Could you have erased some key memories for any reason?" She looked at me so knowingly that I flushed like an ingenue. "I don't find it upsetting, not having a history, Alain. But I want to know *why*. And who wants us dead."

I shook my head. "Existentialism on an empty stomach."

She smiled sadly: the first time I'd seen her smile in living memory. "We'd better go back inside before anyone misses us," she said.

"So gratified to meet you," said the Queen, her antennae vibrating softly in the breeze. "Do relax, please."

I unkinked my neck. Workers fawned over the royal abdomen, polishing with robotic dedication. "As your majesty wishes."

"I have already had the pleasure of your lady wife's *company*," the Queen commented in a high-pitched voice, air rushing through speech spiracles. She sounded amused, for some reason. "I understand you have a little memory problem?"

"I really couldn't comment." Worker-ancillaries buzzed and clattered beneath the ceiling like demented wasps; the air was hot and dry from their encrypted infra-red exchanges. I sweated, but not from heat.

"Then don't comment. You shall pretend that you have no problem, and I shall pretend that you didn't fail to answer my question. Once only, sir Blomenfeld. *Drink.*"

One of the workers extruded a goblet full of dark red liquid into the palm of my right hand. I swirled it around, sniffed, swallowed. Whatever else it contained, there was no alcohol in it. "Thank you."

"Thanks are unnecessary: a potent vintage, that. What do you think of my little portfolio?"

I blinked. "I haven't really had time to do a detailed analysis—"

She waved an idle pair of arms: "Never mind. I expect no precision at this stage."

"Well then." I licked my lips. *Little portfolio, indeed.* "Some of them are evolving nicely. I noticed two promising philosophies in there, if not more. A full dependency analysis of your investments will take a while to prepare—some of them keep changing their minds—but I don't see any reason to doubt that they'll pick up value rapidly as the market recovers from the recession. I'd say your shares are among the most intelligent ones I've ever met."

She giggled, a noise like saws rasping on bone. "Expand my holdings, doctor, and I will be most grateful." A ripple ran through her thorax and she tensed: "Please leave me now, I have no further need of human attendance." Dismissed by her cursory wave I retreated back to the party outside the royal chambers. Behind me, the Queen was giving birth to another processor.

On my third day, I arrived at the small office Manchusko had assigned me unusually early. Unlocking the door and opening it, I froze. Arianna was seated behind my desk, wearing an unhappy expression. "I tried to stop them, Alain, but they wouldn't listen."

"What—"

Someone pushed me into the office, none too gently, and pulled the door shut behind us. "Shut you mouth. I exchange commission!" growled the intruder.

I turned round, very slowly, and looked up and up until I met its small, black-eyed gaze. "Why are you here?" I asked, trying to ignore the gunsight contact lenses glowing amber against its pupils. "Did you plant the bomb?"

"Am here for compensation." The bear shifted its weight from one foot to the other: the floor boards creaked. "You my principle shareholders blame for inequitable exposure. Am here to repossess. Not bomber. Bomber sent by idiot trading script. Bomber not blow anyone else up again."

"Uh-huh." I took a step backwards, slowly. Now I was in the room I could see the monofilament spiderweb holding Arianna down, tied to my chair and afraid to move. This was an outrage! What did they think they were doing?

Arianna was trying to catch my eye. I blinked, remembered the secure channel she'd passed to me during our arrival.

"Am taking this chattel," the bear explained, planting a heavy hand on the back of her chair. She winced. "Am needing also your memory keys. Do be good about this all, doc." He grinned, baring far too many teeth at me.

Alain?

I tweaked my knowledge, hoping to get a handle on some bandwidth I could use to signal for help, but nothing happened. The room was too well shielded. *Here. Why does he want you—*

Keys. To your portfolio, to everything.

Memory keys. "My memory keys?" I almost laughed. "You're joking! I couldn't give you them if I wanted to—"

"Your cooperation not necessary," said the bear. "Just your knowledge. And your company. Take her. Get back options."

"Her? But she's not my property; I've never met her before! Someone hacked our public knowledge—"

The bear looked, his breath a hot stench upon me: "Amnesia no excuse, doc. She your *business.* Cloned body, same dirty algorithms. Am her taking with me! Now. Your keys. Or I take your head with them inside."

Arianna was looking at me again, eyes wide and unreadable.

That true? You're my company?

She nodded minutely. *You planned this, Alain. Selective amnesia to slip past the hunters. Good reason for us to stay together. But you should have stayed with me. Not fled.*

I looked up at the bear, trying not to telegraph what I was thinking. So Arianna was a construct from the beginning? And one of my making, too: a downloaded company on the run from the receivers.

"You're not really from the exchange, are you?"

"Pretty boy. Think smart." The bear produced a small spheroid, pointed it at me. "This yours, pretty boy?"

Shit. Me and my big mouth. Of course the Exchange wouldn't bother with a meat machine repo tool, would they? This must be Organisation muscle of some sort. Probably laundering intelligence—dumping mind-years into an arbitrage sector to ensure that options held by another pawn got smarter. Only the market crash had propagated my own exposure, catching them out. "Hey, can we do a deal?"

"Market closed." The bear grinned and leaned forward, opening its mouth wide, jaw-breakingly wide. I heard a pop and crunch of dislocating joints and felt a familiar buzzing at the edge of my consciousness; its teeth were compact quantum scanners, built to sequestrate the uncollapsed wave functions buried in crypto blackboxes.

I ducked, then leaned forward and attempted to head-butt the huge meat machine. It grunted, and my vision blanked for a moment: external knowledge of combat procedures kicked in, telling me just how hopeless the situation was. Arianna was struggling in her chair, isometric twitching and grand mal shuddering. *Keys, Alain! Give me access to your keys!*

I bounced back from the bear before it could grab me, threw a coat-rack at it, ducked behind the desk. *Why?*

Just do it!

The bear casually picked up the coat-rack and broke it over one knee. Waved one end in my direction, brought the other down on the desktop. The desk whimpered: blood began to drip from one of its ornamental drawers. *Here.* I generated an authentication token, stuffed it into Arianna's head, opened a channel to my keys so she could use them as my proxy. The bear didn't seem to want her dead yet; it grunted and tried to sidle round her to get at me. She heaved halfway out of the seat and I paused for a moment to slash at the monofilament wire with my shaving nail: it screeched like chalk on slate but refused to give way.

"You not can escape," rumbled the bear. "Have I a receivership order—"

It froze. Arianna gasped and shuddered, then slumped in her chair: behind the desk I rolled on my back, grabbed at my spring-loaded boot-heels, feverishly slotting puzzle-blocks together in the shape of a gun as I tumbled over, knocking over a dumb waiter, blinked . . . and saw the bear toppling towards me with the infinite inertia of a collapsing stock market.

I came to my senses back in my penthouse garret with the running water: my corporate assets were in bed with me, holding onto me like a echo of a false honeymoon memory. My skull ached and I could feel bruises; but a quick audit of my medical memories told me it was nothing that wouldn't heal in a week or so. My glial supports had saved my brain from any lingering effects of concussion: my mouth tasted bad but apart from that . . .

I shifted for comfort, feeling more at ease with myself. Arianna sighed, sleeping lightly; I could feel her background processes continuing as normal, shadows under the skin of reality. And now I could remember more of what had happened. *Memory: validate.*

Arianna opened an eye: *Booted again?* she asked.

I cleared my throat. "Mostly back to normal." *Validation successful.* I tried to gather my scattered wits. "So it really happened?"

"Reckless trading, my dear. It was the only way out of that collapse back on Dordogne. Or would you rather they'd wound me up and set you to paying off your debts in mind time? You were several billion years uncovered at the end . . ."

"No!" I tried to sit up.

She reached over and dragged me back down: "Not yet. You're still dizzy."

"But my keys—"

"Relax, he didn't get them. Your head's on your body, not sitting in a vat."

"But what did you do?"

She shrugged. "He was from one of the syndicates, Alain. With your authority, acting as your agency, I asked your desk to run a huge order via Her Majesty's portfolio."

"But he was in there with us!" I shuddered. "There can't have been time!"

"Oh, but there was." She ran a hand across my chest suggestively. "Mm. You did a good job with those memories—"

"The bear. Tell me, please!"

"If you insist." She frowned. "I just told your desk to buy *everything*—everything available. Saturated all outgoing bandwidth through the firewall: the desk was only too happy to cooperate. The bear was a remote. While all the stocks were handshaking with the treasury, it was locked out. While it was locked out it was frozen; by the time it recovered I'd worked my way loose and ordered the guards in. Not that it was necessary."

I shook my head. "I know I'm going to regret asking this. Why not?"

"Well, I'd just pumped a large amount of liquidity into the exchange. The trading volume drove up share prices, triggered a minor recovery, and in the past few hours there are signs of the market actually rallying. I think it's going to be a sustained rise; Her Majesty can anticipate a nice little windfall in a few months' time. Anyway, you don't need to worry about the Organisation remotes any more, at least not for a year or two. After all—" She wormed her way over until her breath in my ear was hot— "bears can't handle a rising market!"

JOHN C. WRIGHT

John C. Wright [1961–] lives in Centreville, Virginia. Formerly an attorney, newspaperman, and newspaper editor, he is now a writer. He summarizes his professional careers thusly: "In 1987, he graduated from the College of William and Mary's Law School (going from the third-oldest to the second-oldest school in continuous use in the United States), and was admitted to the practice of law in three jurisdictions (New York, May 1989; Maryland, December 1990; D.C., January 1994). His law practice was unsuccessful enough to drive him into bankruptcy soon thereafter. His stint as a newspaperman for the *St. Mary's Today* was more rewarding spiritually, but, alas, also a failure financially. He presently works (successfully) as a writer in Virginia, where he lives in fairy-tale-like happiness with his wife, the authoress L. Jagi Lamplighter (Annapolis, class of 1985), and their three children."

Wright is a science fiction and fantasy writer of vaulting ambition who burst into prominence with a trilogy of space opera novels (*The Golden Age*, 2002; *The Phoenix Exultant*, 2002; *The Golden Transcendence*, 2003), actually one long work. He writes of heroes, and of the desire to be heroic. His fantasy novels, *The Last Guardian of Everness* (2004) and *Mists of Everness* (2005), are similarly ambitious and large-scale.

In an interview at SfSite (www.sfsite.com), he says, "I am a space opera writer. . . . I like large themes, thunder, fury, and wonder. Why blow up a city when you can blow up a world? Why launch a starship one kilometer long, when you can launch a superstarship a thousand kilometers long? Why build space armor out of carbon-steel when you can build it out of adamantium?"

And further: "It is pusillanimous to write of small things when one can write of great. The abyss of time holds wonders too large to fit inside one small world, or the narrow confines of one cramped century. Science Fiction is meant to tell us traveler's tales of places and aeons men cannot reach, but imagination can."

Wright admits to the influence of A. E. Van Vogt ("No other writer's works fill me with the sense of awe and wonder as does Van Vogt.") and Jack Vance, and professes himself an admirer of Gene Wolfe, Roger Zelazny, and Cordwainer Smith. He chooses an ornamented and elegant style in his SF writing.

"Guest Law" was his second published story, and has the flavor of several of his mentors, and certainly the scale and imagery of Van Vogtian space opera. It is a fitting story to end this anthology, since it gives evidence that some of the oldest and some of the best strains of space opera are still vigorous today, transformed.

GUEST LAW

JOHN C. WRIGHT

The night of deep space is endless and empty and dark. There is nothing behind which to hide. But ships can be silent, if they are slow.

The noble ship *Procrustes* was silent as a ghost. She was black-hulled, and ran without beacons or lights. She was made of anti-radar alloys and smooth ceramics, shark-finned with panels meant to diffuse waste-heat slowly, and tiger-striped with electronic webs meant to guide certain frequencies around the hull without rebounding.

If she ever were seen, a glance would show that she was meant to be slow. Her drive was fitted with baffle upon baffle, cooling the exhaust before it was expelled, a dark drive, non-radioactive, silent as sprayed mist. Low energy in the drive implied low thrust. Further, she had no centrifuge section, nor did she spin. This meant that her crew were lightweights, their blood and bones degenerated or adapted to micro-gravity, not the sort who could tolerate high boosts.

This did not mean *Procrustes* was not a noble ship. Warships can be slow; only their missiles need speed.

And so it was silently, slowly, that *Procrustes* approached the stranger's cold vessel.

"We are gathered, my gentlemen, to debate whether this new ship here viewed is no-ble, or whether she is unarmed; and, if so, whether and how the guest law applies. It pleases us to hear you employ the second level of speech; for this is a semi-informal occasion, and briefer honorifics we permit."

The captain, as beautiful and terrifying as something from a children's Earth-story, floated nude before the viewing well. The bridge was a cylinder of gloom, with only control-lights winking like constellations, the viewing well shining like a full moon.

The captain made a gesture with her fan toward Smith and spoke: "Engineer, you do filth-work . . ." (by which she meant manual labor) ". . . which makes you familiar with machines." (She used the term "familiar" because it simply was not done to say a lowlife had "knowledge" or "expertise.") "It would amuse us to hear your conclusions touching and concerning the stranger's ship."

Smith was never allowed high and fore to the bridge, except when he was com-pelled to go, as he was now. His hands had been turned off at the wrists, since lowlifes should not touch controls.

Smith was in terror of the captain, but loved her too, since she was the only high-life who called smiths by their old title. The captain was always polite, even to tinkers or drifters or bondsman.

She had not even seemed to notice when Smith had hooked one elbow around one of the many guy-wires that webbed the dark long cylinder of the bridge. Some of the officers and knights who floated near the captain had turned away or snorted with disgust when he had clasped that rope. It was a foot-rope, meant for toes, not a hand rope. But Smith's toes were not well formed, not coordinated. He had not been born a lightweight.

Smith was as drab as a hairless monkey next to the captain's vavasors and carls, splendid in their head-to-toe tattoos which displayed heraldries and victory-emblems. These nobles all kept their heads pointed along the captain's axis (an old saying ran: "the captain's head is always up!"), whereas Smith was offset 90 degrees clockwise, legs straight, presenting a broad target. (This he did for the same reason a man under acceleration would bow or kneel; a posture where one could not move well to defend oneself showed submission.)

Smith could see the stranger's ship in the viewing well. She was a slim and handsome craft, built along classical lines, an old, a very old design, of such craftsmanship as was rarely seen today. She was sturdy: built for high accelerations, and proudly bearing long thin structures forward of antennae of a type that indicated fearlessly loud and long-range radar. The engine block was far aft on a very long and graceful insulation shaft. The craft had evidently been made in days when the safety of the engine serfs still was a concern.

Her lines were sleek. (Not, Smith thought secretly, like *Procrustes*, whose low speed and lack of spin allowed her to grow many modules, ugly extrusions, and asymmetric protuberances.)

But the stranger's ship was *old*. Rust, and ice from frozen oxygen, stained the hull where seals had failed.

Yet she still emitted, on radio, the cheerful welcome-code. Merry green-and-red running lights were still lit. Microwave detectors showed radiations from the aft section of her hull, which might still be inhabited, even though the fore sections were cold and silent. Numbers and pictoglyphs flickered on a small screen to one side of the main image, showing telemetry and specific readings.

Smith studied the cylinder's radius and rate of spin. He calculated, and then he said, "Glorious Captain, the lowest deck of the stranger ship has centrifugal acceleration of exactly 32 feet per second per second."

The officers looked eye to eye, hissing with surprise.

The chancellor nodded the gaudy plume that grew from his hair and eyebrows. "This number has ancient significance! Some of the older orders of eremites still use it. They claim that it provides the best weight for our bones. Perhaps this is a religious ship."

One of the younger knights, a thin, dapple-bellied piebald wearing silk speed-wings running from his wrists to ankles, now spoke up: "Great Captain, perhaps she is an Earth ship, inhabited by machine intelligences . . . or ghosts!"

The other nobles opened their fans, and held them in front of their faces. If no derisive smiles were seen, then there was no legal cause for duel. The young knight might be illiterate, true, most young knights were, but the long kick-talons he wore on his calves had famous names.

The captain said, "We are more concerned for the stranger's nobility, than her . . . ah . . . origin." There were a few smirks at that. A ship from Earth, indeed! All the old horror-tales made it clear that nothing properly called human was left on Earth, except, perhaps, as pets or specimens of the machines. The Earthmind had never had much interest in space.

The chancellor said, "Those racks forward . . ." (he pointed at what were obviously antennae) ". . . may house weaponry, great Captain, or particle beam weapons, if the stranger has force enough in her drive core to sustain a weapon-grade power flow."

The captain looked toward Smith, "Concerning this ship's energy architecture,

Engineer, have you any feelings or intuitions?" She would not ask him for "deductions" or "conclusions," of course.

Smith felt grateful that she had not asked him directly to answer the question; he was not obligated to contradict the chancellor's idiotic assertions. Particle beam indeed! The man had been pointing at a radio dish.

Very polite, the captain, very proper. Politeness was critically important aboard a crowded ship.

The captain was an hermaphrodite. An ancient law forbade captains to marry (or to take lowlife concubines) from crew aboard. The Captain's Wife must be from off-ship, either as gift or conquest or to cement a friendly alliance.

But neither was it proper for the highest of the highlife to go without sexual pleasure, so the captain's body was modified to allow her to pleasure herself.

Her breasts were beautiful—larger, by law, than any woman's aboard—and her skin was adjusted to a royal purple melanin, opaque to certain dangerous radiations. Parallel rows of her skin cells, down her belly and back, had been adjusted to become ornaments of nacre and pearl. Her long legs ended in a second pair of hands, nails worn long to show that she was above manual work. On her wrists and on her calves were the sheaths of her gem-studded blades, and she could fight with all four blades at once.

"Permission to speak to your handmaidens, Glorious Captain?"

"Granted. We will be amused by your antics."

The handmaidens were tied by their hair to the control boards (this was no discomfort in weightlessness, and left their fingers and toes free to manipulate the controls). Some controls were only a few inches from the captain's hand, but she would not touch controls, of course. That was what handmaidens were for.

Smith diffidently suggested to the handmaidens that they focus analytical cameras on several bright stars aft of the motionless ship, and then, as *Procrustes* approached a point where those same stars were eclipsed by the emission trail behind the stranger's drive, a spectographic comparison would give clues as to the nature of the exhaust, and hence of the engine structure. Such a scan, being passive, would not betray *Procrustes'* location.

When the analysis had been done as Smith suggested, the result showed an unusually high number of parts per billion of hard gamma radiation, as well as traces of high overall electric charge. Smith gave his report, and concluded: "The high numbers of antiprotons through the plume points to a matter-antimatter reaction drive. In properly tuned drives, however, the antiprotons should have been completely consumed, so that their radiation pressure could add to the thrust. Particle decay in the plume indicates many gigaseconds have passed since the main expulsions. There is a cloud of different geometry condensed closer to the drive itself, indicating that the starship has been drifting on low power, her engines idling. But the engines are still active, Glorious Captain. She is not a hulk. She lives."

Smith was smiling when he gave this report, surprised by his own calm lightheartedness. He did not recognize the mood, at first.

It was hope. Often the guest law required the captain to display great munificence. And here was a ship clearly in need of repair, in need of a good smith.

Perhaps the captain would sell his contract to these new people; perhaps there was hope that he could leave *Procrustes*, perhaps find masters less cruel, duties less arduous. (Freedom, a home, a wife, a woman to touch, babies born with his name, a name of his own—these he did not even dream of, anymore.)

With a new ship, anything might happen. And even if Smith weren't given away, at least there would be news, new faces, and a banquet. Guest law made such chance meetings a time of celebration.

The captain waved her fan to rotate herself to face her gathered officers. "Opinions, my gentlemen?"

The chancellor said, "With respect, great Captain, we must assume she is of the noble class. If she carries antimatter, she must be armed. She may be a religious ship, perhaps a holy order on errantry or antimachine crusade. In either case, it would be against the guest law not to answer her hail. As the poet says: 'Ships are few and far in the wide expanse of night; shared cheer, shared news, shared goods, all increase our might.'"

The winged knight said: "With respect, great Captain! If this is a religious ship, then let God or His Wife Gaia look after her! Why should a ship with such potent drives be hanging idle and adrift? No natural reason! There may be plagues aboard, or bad spirits, or machines from Earth. I say pass this one by. The guest law does not require we give hospitality and aid to such unchancy vessels, or ships under curse. Does not the poet also say: 'Beware the strangeness of the stranger. Unknown things bring unknown danger'?"

A seneschal whose teeth had been grown into jewels spoke next, "Great Captain, with respect. The guest law allows us to live in the Void. Don't we share air and water and wine? Don't we swap crews and news when we meet? This is a ship unknown, too true, and a strange design. But every ship we meet is new! Einstein makes certain time will age us forever away from any future meetings with any other ship's crew. None of that matters. Captain, my peers, honored officers, listen: either that ship is noble, or she is unarmed. If she is unarmed, she owes us one tenth of her cargo and air and crew. Isn't that fair? Don't we keep the Void clear of pirates and rogues when we find them? But if she is noble, either she has survivors, or she has not. If there are no survivors, then she is a rich prize, and ours by salvage law. Look at the soundness of her structure: her center hull would make a fine new high keep; she is leaking oxygen, she must have air to spare; and the grease-monkey here says she has a drive of great power! Driven by antimatter!"

The vavasors and knights were gazing now with greedy eyes at the image in the viewing well. Antimatter, particularly anti-iron, was the only standard barter metal used throughout the Expanse. Like gold, it was always in demand; unlike radioactives, it did not decay; it was easily identifiable, it was homogenous, it was portable. It was the universal coin, because everyone needed energy.

The seneschal said, "But if she has survivors, great Captain, they must be very weak. And weak ships are often more generous than the guest law requires! More generous than any living man wants to be!"

A ripple of hissing laughter echoed from the circle of nobles. Some of them fondly touched their knives and anchorhooks.

The captain looked as if she were about to chide them for their evil thoughts, but then a sort of cruel masculine look came to her features. Smith was reminded that the womanly parts of her hermaphrodite's body were only present to serve the pleasure of the manly parts.

The captain said, "Good my gentlemen, might there be a noble woman aboard, among the survivors?"

The ship's doctor, an old, wiry man with thin hands and goggle-adapted eyes, laughed breathlessly: "Aye! Captain's in rut and high time she were married, says I! Sad when we had to choke that concubine, back last megasecond when the airstock got low. Don't you worry, Capt'n! If there be anyone aboard that ship, whatever they is now, I'll make 'em into a woman for you! Make 'em! Even boys get to like it, you know, after you dock 'em a few times, if you got their wombs wired up right to the pleasure center of their brains!"

There was some snickering at that, but the laughter froze when the captain said in her mildest voice: "Good my ship's Surgeon, we are most pleased by your counsel, though it is not called for at this time. We remind you that an officer and a gentleman does not indulge in waggish humor or display."

Then she snapped her right fan open and held it overhead for attention. "My herald, radio to the stranger ship with my compliments and tell her to prepare for docking under the guest-law protocols. Fire-control, ready your weapons in case she answers in an ignoble or inhospitable fashion, or if she turns pirate. Quartermaster, ready ample cubic space to take on full supplies."

The nobles looked eye to eye, smiling, hands caressing weapon-hilts, nostrils dilated, smiling with blood-lust at the prospect.

The captain said with mild irony: "The stranger is weak, after all, and may be more generous than guest law or prudence requires. Go, my gentlemen, prepare your battle-dress! Look as haughty as hawks and as proud as peacocks for our guests!"

Their laughter sounded horrid to Smith's ears. He thought of the guest law, and of his hopes, and felt sick.

The captain, as an afterthought, motioned with her fan toward Smith, saying to her handmaid, "And shut down the engineer. We may have need of his aptitudes soon, and we need no loose talk belowdecks the while."

A handmaiden raised a control box and pointed it at Smith, and, before he could summon the courage to plead, a circuit the ship's doctor had put in his spine and brain stem shut off his sensory nerves and motor-control.

Smith wished he had had the chance to beg for his sleep center to be turned on. He hated the hallucinations sensory deprivation brought.

Numb, blind, wrapped in a gray void, Smith tried to sleep.

When Smith slept, he dreamed of home, of his father and mother and many brothers. His native habitat was built up around the resting hulk of the exile-ship *Never Return*, in geosynchronous orbit above an ancient storm system rippling the face of a vast gas giant in the Tau Ceti system.

The habitat had a skyhook made of materials no modern man could reproduce, lowered into the trailing edge of the storm. Here the pressure caused a standing wave, larger than the surface area of most planets, which churned up pressurized metallic hydrogen from the lower atmospheres. The colonists had mined the wave for fuel for passing starships for generations.

In the time of Smith's great-grandfather, the multimillion-year-old storm began to die out. As fuel production failed, the colony grew weak, and the Nevermen were subject to raids. Some came from Oort-cloud nomads, but most were from the inner-system colonists who inhabited the asteroidal belts their ancestors had made by pulverizing the subterrestrial planets.

Smith's mother and father had been killed in the raids.

There was no law, no government, to appeal to for aid. Even on old Earth, before the machines, no single government had ever managed to control the many peoples of that one small planet. To dream of government across the Expanse was madness: the madness of sending a petition to a ruler so distant that only your remote descendants would hear a reply.

And it was too easy for anyone who wished to escape the jurisdiction of any prospective government; they need only shut down their radio and alter their orbit by a few degrees. Space is vast, and human habitats were small and silent.

(Planets? No one lived on the surface of those vulnerable rocks, suited against atmospheres humans could not endure, at gravities that they could not, by adjusting spin, control. Legends said that Earth was a world where unsuited men could walk abroad. The chances of finding a perfect twin—and the match must be perfect, for humans were evolved for only one environment—made certain that the legend would remain a legend. In the meantime, mankind lived on ships and habitats.)

After the destruction of his home, Smith himself had been sold into slavery.

Slavery? Why *not* slavery? It was not economically feasible in a technological society, true. But then again, slavery had *never* been economically feasible, even back on Old Earth. The impracticality of slavery had not abolished it. History's only period without slavery, back on Earth, happened when the civilized Western nations, led by Britain, brought the pressure of world opinion (or open war) against the nations that practiced it. The Abolitionist Movements and their ideals reached to all continents.

But, on Earth, it did not take years and generations for nearest neighbors to take note of what their neighbors did.

Endless space meant endless lawlessness.

There was, however, custom.

Radio traffic was easier to send than ships from star to star, and there was no danger in listening to it. Radio-men and scholars in every system had to keep ancient languages alive, or else the lore of the talking universe would be closed to them. Common language permitted the possibility of common custom.

Furthermore, systems that did not maintain the ancient protocols for approaching starships could not tempt captains to spend the time and fuel to decelerate. If colonists wanted news and gifts and emigrants and air, they had to announce their readiness to obey the guest law.

And, of course, there were rumors and horrid myths of supernatural retributions visited on those who broke the guest law. Smith thought that the mere existence of such rumors proved that the guest law was not, and could never be, enforced.

Smith was not awake when the heralds exchanged radio-calls and conducted negotiations between the ships.

But when the seneschal ordered him alert again, he saw the looks of guilt and fear on the faces of the highlife officers, the too-nervous laughter, too-quickly smothered.

The seneschal's cabin was sparsely decorated, merely a sphere divided by guy-ropes, without bead-webs or battle-flags or religious plant-balls growing on their tiny globules of earth. However, every other panel of the sphere was covered with a fragile screen of hemp-paper inked with iconography or calligraphy. (It was a credit to the seneschal's high-born agility that none of the hemp-paper screens were torn. When he practiced the grapples, thrusts, and slash-rebounds of zero-gravity fencing, he apparently judged his trajectories so well that he never spun or kicked into one. "Always kept his feet on the floor," as the old saying went.)

The seneschal was giving Smith instructions for a work detail. A party was to go EVA (still called "hanging" even though the ship lacked spin) to prepare a section of hull to receive sections from the stranger's ship, once it had been cannibalized.

(Smith was secretly agonized to hear the seneschal call the beautiful strange craft "it" instead of "she," as if the ship were a piece of machinery, already dead, and no longer a living vessel.)

They were interrupted by the attention claxon in the ceremonial imperative mode. The seneschal reached out with both feet, and gracefully drew open a panel hidden behind the hemp-paper screens, to reveal a private viewing well beneath.

Shining in the image was a scene from the huge forward cargo lock. The main clamshell radiation-shockwave shields had been folded back, and the wide circle of the inner lock's docking ring glittered black in the light of many floating lanterns.

Beyond was a glimpse of the stranger ship. Here was an archaic lock, both doors open in a sign of trust. Controls of ancient fashion glinted silvery in an otherwise black axis, which opened like a dark well filled with gloom and frost, ripped guy-lines trembling like cobwebs in the gusts from irregular ventilators.

A figure came out from the gloom. He passed the lock, and slowed himself with a squirt from an antique leg-jet, raising his foot to his center of mass and spraying a cloud before him. He hovered in the center of the black ring, while the squirt of mist that hid him slowly dissipated.

The seneschal said in a voice of curiosity and fear: "It's true, then. He has no entourage! What happened to his crew?" He had apparently forgotten who was in his cabin, for he spoke in the conversational register.

"Request permission to come aboard," the stranger was calling in Anglatin.

Smith stared in wonder. The stranger was very short, even for a heavyweight. The skin of his head and hands was normal, albeit blank and untattooed, but the rest of his body was loose, wrinkled, and folded, as if his skin were contaminated with some horrible epidermal disease. Apparently he was a eunuch; there were no sex organs visible between his legs. His hair was white, and had been programmed to grow, for some reason, only on the top, back, and sides of his skull (Smith had seen religious orders modify their hair to this design, claiming such ugliness was ancient tradition).

Suddenly Smith realized that the blue material of the stranger's skin was *not* skin, but fabric, as if he were suited (with gauntlets and helm removed) from some suit too thin to protect a man from vacuum; or as if he wore a lowlifer's work-smock without pockets or adhesive pads.

"Garb," said the seneschal, obviously wondering along the same lines Smith had been. "The old word for outer skins is garb. It is used to retain heat close to the body, without the energy cost of heating the whole cabin. He must have lost environmental control long ago. That weapon at his hip is also an antique. It is called a kiri-sugama. Very difficult to control. One must spin the ball-and-chain counter-opposite from the hook or else one rotates wildly during combat. Either the hook or the ball can be used to snare the opponent to prevent blow-rebounds. But what arrogance to carry such an antique! Back in the times when ships had large interior spaces, perhaps, perhaps! But now? Knives and cestuses are better for fighting in cabins and crawltubes. Arrogance! Arrogance! And, ugh! He wears foot-mittens instead of foot-gloves; nor do I blame him. See how his toes are deformed! Has he been walking on them? Ghastly!"

But the stranger was obviously the foreign captain. The emblems on his epaulettes were the same as those that the *Procrustes'* captain had growing from modified areas of her shoulder cells. His blue "garb" was the same color, nearly, as her pigments.

She was speaking now, granting his permission to come aboard with the words and gestures of the ancient boarding-ceremony. She concluded with: "And by what title is it proper to call our honored guest?" And her flute-dwarf gave a three-tone flourish with his pipes so that the ritual music ended as her words did.

"Call me Descender. My ship is the noble *Olympian Vendetta*. And by what title is it proper to call my generous hostess?"

"Call me Ereshkigal, captain of the noble ship *Procrustes*."

"Noble fellow-Captain, because mankind is so widely flown, and many years and light-years separate brother from brother, tell me, before I board your craft, whether my understanding of the guest law is sufficient, and whether it accords with yours at every point? Excuse this question if it seems impertinent or suspicious; nothing of the sort is meant or should be inferred; I merely wish to ensure I give no unwitting offense or that I make no unfounded assumptions. For, as the poet says, 'The wise man calculates each maneuver as he goes; ignorance and inattention feed the seeds from which all danger grows.'"

"Noble fellow-Captain, you speak well and gentlemanly," said the captain, visibly impressed with the other's humble eloquence. "No offense is taken, nor do I permit offense to be taken by my men. As the poet says, 'A gentleman learns five things to do aright: to fly, to fence, to tell the truth, to know no fear, to be polite.' And politely you have spoken, sir."

But her quote was not quite as apt as, nor did it display the learning of, the stranger's.

She called for her chancellor, who, without any show of impatience, recited the whole body of the guest law, phrase by phrase, and answered with grave care when the stranger politely asked for definitions of ambiguous wording.

There were customary rules mentioned that Smith had never heard before, or had not heard in detail, but everything seemed to be based on common sense and common politeness: Aid to be given to fellow ships met in the void, not to exceed one-tenth of total value of ships and crew; more to be exchanged if mutually agreeable; navigational data to be shared without reservation; standardized protocols for swapping air and supplies to ships in need; all maneuvering before and after docking to be determined by formula based on mass and vector, the lighter ships going farther to match velocities with the heavier, so that the total fuel expenditures were roughly equal; guests to bring their own air, plus a tithe for the host plants; common forms of politeness to be used; disembarking to be done at will after due warning; no departure from the guest-ship to be interpreted as constituting any abandonment; the code of duels to be suspended; any disagreements as to valuations of goods exchanged or veracity of informations shared to be determined by such arbitrators as shall be mutually agreed-upon. And so on.

Smith, through the viewing well, could see the gathered nobles growing uneasy, not meeting each other's eyes. Looks of sullen guilt darkened on their tattooed faces as they heard each phrase and lofty sentiment of the laws they intended to violate.

When the recitation of the law was done, Captain Descender and Captain Ereshkigal bound themselves by formidable oaths to abide by every aspect of this law. They exchanged grave and serious assurances of their honesty and good intent.

Smith, listening, felt cold.

The oathtaking concluded with Captain Ereshkigal saying: ". . . and if I am forsworn, let devils and ghosts consume me in Gaia's Wasteland, in God's Hell, and may I suffer the vengeance of the Machines of Earth."

"Exactly so," said Captain Descender, smiling.

The feast-hall of the *Procrustes* was aft of the bridge, but forward of the drive core, along the axis, where it was protected by (and inward of) all lower decks. The Officers' Mess (to use the old poet's term for it) was the highest of the high country, a place of ceremony and rare delight.

Banners of translucent fabric, colored, or luminous with fantastic heraldries, ran from point to point throughout the cylinder. The fabric was meant to absorb escaping food crumbs or particles of flying wine from the air, but it also muted and colored the lights shining from the bulkheads.

For drinks (or drinkers) of low esteem, there were wine-skins. But the ship's cook had outdone himself for the high wines: pleasing to the eye, the globules of high wine or wine-jelly gleamed and glittered, held only in skins of fishnet web. The interstices of the web were small enough to keep the wine englobed by its own surface tension. Nobles had to drink from such webs with a delicate and graceful touch, lest a sudden maneuver allow wine to splatter through the webbing.

Here was the captain, floating at the focal point of an array of banners so that she looked like a Boddhisattva of Gaia in the center of a celestial rose. She was in the Reserved Regard position; that is, right foot folded on her lap, left foot extended, foot-spoon held lightly between her toes, left hand holding an open fan, right hand overhead in graceful gesture, wearing an eating glove with different spices crusting the fingernails. As tradition required, she held a napkin in her right foot folded in a complex origami pattern. It was considered a crime against elegance to have to actually use the napkin.

Her hair was arrayed in the coiffure called. Welcome Dish, braided at the ends and electrostatically charged so that it made an evenly swirled disk above and behind her head and shoulders, like a halo.

Her feast was arranged in a circle around her, little colorful moons of ripe fruit, balls of wine-jelly, spheres of lacy bread, meatballs or sausages tumbling end-over-end. As the feast progressed, she would rotate slowly clockwise, to let one delicacy after another come within reach of hand and foot (toe-foods for the foot, finger-foods for the hand) and the order of the orbiting food around her was organized by traditional culinary theory.

Since the captain's head was always "up," the feasters must be attentive, and match their rotations to the captain, eating neither too swiftly nor too slowly, nor grabbing for any favored food out of order.

Descender was the last to be escorted in. The feasting nobles formed a rough cylinder, with Captain Ereshkigal at one end and Descender's place at the other.

Smith was hovering behind Captain Ereshkigal, not to eat, of course, but to answer any technical questions the captain might demand. He had a towel wrapped around his right foot and left hand, to capture any grease that might float from the Captain's lips. He also held her charging-brush, to act as hair-page, in case any haphazard event should interfere with the flow of her locks.

Smith noticed with some surprise that there was no page near Descender's mess-station; nor were there any guy-ropes very near reach.

When Descender entered, he flew using a rotate-and-thrust technique, shifting the attitude of his body with spins of the weighted tail of his sash, then moving with wasteful spurts of jet. It was an awkward and very old-fashioned method of maneuvering, not at all like the graceful, silent glides of nobles using fans, their moves full of subtle curves and changes, deceptive to an enemy in combat. It was easy to guess the trajectories of a man using rotate-and-thrust; easy for a fighter with a knife to kill him. Smith felt the same embarrassment for the man as someone in gravity might feel seeing a grown man crawl.

When Descender took his position, he paused, blinking, evidently puzzled by the lack of a convenient anchor nearby, the lack of service.

Smith noticed that the lights facing in that direction were focused without banners to block direct glare. Another oversight.

All the nobles watched Descender with careful sidelong looks. Some vague pleasantries were exchanged; grace was said; the meal began.

One knight loudly called: "Look here, mate, at what a fine dish we have: we'll suck this marrow dry!" And he tossed a leg of mutton lightly across the axis to the chancellor at the captain's right.

There was a slight silence. It was considered boorish to allow any food to pass between another feaster and the captain; the leg of lamb was centered just where it would block Descender's view.

The chancellor reached out with a leg-fork and hooked the meat, kicking trembling bits of grease in Descender's direction. "Aye. At least a sheep has good sense enough to know when it is due for the slaughter-pump house!"

No one laughed.

Descender turned his head. The doors behind him had been shut, and now two shipcarls were there, arms folded, legs in a position called Deadly Lotus, where fingers and toes could touch the hilts of sheathed blades. Unlike where Descender was, the shipcarls were surrounded by a web of guy-wires, and had surfaces near to kick off from.

It was with a sinking feeling that Smith saw Descender look up and down at the food-ring they had prepared for him. All the meats and fruits in the arc nearest his head were toe-foods; finger-foods were along the lower half of the circle; he must either grab for food out of turn, or eat uncouthly.

He looked as if he wanted to say something. He opened his mouth and closed it again. Perhaps a hint of nagging fear began to show on Descender's features.

The captain herself looked a little sad. She took up the salt-ball, but instead of pushing it along the axis to the other captain (showing that he was next in priority), she took a nail-full of salt and brushed the ball toward the seneschal on her right upper.

He grinned at Descender, took a fingernail's worth of salt, but then tossed it to his left. All the knights were served before the salt-ball came to Descender. The last knight to touch it looked carefully at Descender, licked the salt-ball with his tongue, and threw it toward Descender with a jerk of his jaw.

Descender's face, by now, was an impassive mask, but his jaw was clenched. A bead of sweat floated from his forehead. He did not reach for the insulting salt-ball, but let it fly past his shoulder toward the bulk-head behind.

All the nobles had their hands near their weapons. The chamber was utterly silent.

There was something sad in Descender's eye when he smiled a weak smile and reached up for a foot-peach near his head. "I compliment my noble fellow-captain for her bountiful feast," he said, and took a bite.

There was some snickering. It was like seeing a man under acceleration eating off what, in the old times, they would have called the floor.

One of the shipcarls behind Descender opened the ventilator, so that the breezes began to slowly scatter his food. Descender paused; he grabbed one or two pieces of fruit and stuck them under his elbow to hang onto them.

It looked absurd. But nobody laughed.

It was hard to say whether or not Descender actually was frightened. His face showed no emotion. But he certainly acted like a frightened man.

He said, "I thank you for your hospitality. I wish now to return to my ship."

The chancellor said, "But we are not done with you. That ship of yours; it is a nice one, isn't it? We would be happy to accept its drives and main hulls sections as gifts. Or perhaps we can simply claim it as salvage. There's no one aboard it right now."

Descender curled his legs, and put his hands near his kiri-su-gama. He spoke softly: "She. It's more polite, good sir, to address those crafts who sustain our lives as 'her' and 'she.'"

The winged knight said loudly, "Those who carry arms are required, when honor commands, to use them. Those false lowlife debris and pokeboys who scrounge the weapons off their betters deserve a looter's air-lock. But who says a thief has any care for honor? It is to honor, gentlemen, that I propose a toast! To the honor and to the air that sustains us! Let those who will not drink be deprived of both. But look! You have no page, you who call yourself a captain! Hoy! Smith! Grease-monkey! Hand our guest his last draught of wine; your hands are the only ones fit to hand it to him!" And he took from his pouch a plastic bag from the medical stores, filled with liquid waste. The knight threw it to Smith, who caught it with trembling fingers.

This was a mortal insult. If Smith passed the bag to him, Descender could neither drink, nor could he refuse the toast, with honor. The carefully planned program of insults that had gone before, Smith guessed, had only been to see how much Descender would stomach. If he had any hidden weapons, tricks, or traps, now he would show them; Captain Ereshkigal would only lose one lesser knight; Ereshkigal could repudiate the rash young knight once he was killed, apologize, blame him; polite words and polite pretense could keep a bit of honor intact during such retreat.

That is, if he had some hidden weapon. If not . . .

Anger made Smith forget all caution. He threw down the heavy charging-brush and the sloshing bag of medical waste, so that he drifted away from the captain and out of her immediate knifereach. "Here's a poor man, innocent as innocence, and you're going to strangle him up and eat his fine ship! He's done no wrong, and answered all your slurs with kind words! Why can't you let him be?! Why can't you let him *be*?!"

The captain spoke without turning her head: "Engineer, you are insubordinate. Your air ration is hereby decreased to zero. If you report to the medical house for euthanasia, your going will be pleasant, and note will be made of your obedience in the ship's log. If you continue your insubordination, however, your name will be blotted out. I have no wish to dishonor you; go quietly."

Descender spoke in a strange and distant tone of voice: "Captain, your order is not lawful. At feast times, the code of subordination is relaxed, and free speech allowed, at least among those civilized peoples who recognize the guest law . . ." He turned and looked at Smith, addressing him directly, "Engineer, what, pray tell, is your name? Tell it to me, and I shall preserve it in my ship's log, my book of life, and it may endure longer than any record of this age."

But Smith's courage deserted him then, and he did not answer. He flapped the napkin he held as a fan, moving back to the bulkhead, where he crouched, looking each way with wide, wild eyes, ready to spring off in any direction.

Yet no one paid much heed to him. The nobles were still concentrating on Descender. There was silence in the chamber.

The gentlemen were each stealing quick glances at their neighbors. Each crouched and ready. But no one was prepared to take the final swoop to make their threats and hints come true. Perhaps there was something hard about killing a man who had not drawn his weapon; perhaps they were each thinking that now, even now, it still was not too late to back away. . . .

Then the young piebald knight with the racing-wings spoke up, kicking the sheaths off his blades, displaying steel. Now it was too late. His voice rang out, high-pitched and over-loud: "What is more hateful in the sight of God than cowardice? By Gaia, how I hate the thing (I will not call him a man) who takes a blow without a show of spleen! He smiles with his beggar's smile, his shoulders hunched, his eye wet, a tremble in his whining voice. Hatred, gentlemen, hatred and disgust is what we ought to feel for those we hurt! Weakness is loathsome! And any man who will not fight deserves to die! A lowlife heart should not dare to hide inside what seems a captain's chest. I say we cut the false heart *out*!"

Descender's face was stiff and expressionless. His voice was tense and even. His eyes were filled with dreadful calm: "You are angry because you have no good *excuse* for anger, have you? It would be easier to do the deed if I had given some offense, wouldn't it? Or if I somehow seemed less human? Noble fellow-Captain Ereshkigal!

There is no need for this. What I can spare from my ship, I will freely give. Let us avoid a scene of horror. You conduct yourself as one who honors honorable conduct. Let not this feast end in tragic death!"

The young knight shouted, "Beg and beg! Must we hear the beggar mewl!? Cut his throat and silence this shrill noise!" He kicked his legs to clash his blades together, a bright crash of metallic noise.

But Captain Ereshkigal held open her fan for silence. "My brother captain asks, with dignity, that we not pretend that this is other than it is. We will not mask our deed under the code of duels. Let it openly be named: Murder, then, murder and piracy!"

There was a slight noise all around the chamber, sighs and hisses from the gentlemen. Some looked angry, or saddened, or surprised; most were stony-faced; but each face, somehow, still was dark with cruelty.

The captain continued: "But you have brought it on *yourself*, brother captain! How *dare* you have a fine hull, fine drives, and air, when we are many, and you are only one?"

"The property is mine, by right."

"And when you die, it shall be ours, by right *or* wrong."

"You have no need."

"But we *want*."

"Captain, I beg you—"

"We wish to hear no more of begging!"

"So . . . ? Is this the rule by which you wish also to be judged? Then no plea for mercy will be heard when your own time comes."

"Judged? How dare you speak defiance to us?"

"You condemn me when I apologize, and then equally when I do not. What if I say, take my ship, but spare my life?"

"We will not even spare an ounce of air!"

"Hah! I will be more generous than you, Ereshkigal. I will spare one life; perhaps that of the scared little Smith there. He has done me no harm, and I think that he begins to suspect what I am. Yes; one person should survive to spread the tale, otherwise the exercise is useless."

"Do you think to frighten us with superstitious hints and lies? Englobe him, my gentlemen! Steward, close the ducts! We must have our drapes sop up the blood-cloud so no drops foul our air system."

Descender spoke softly while the bejeweled, beribboned, and tattooed knights and vavasors, glittering, smiling, fans waving, drew their snaring-hooks and dirks and slowly circled him.

He spoke in a voice of Jovian calm: "Who else but a machine intelligence has so long a life that it can intend to bring law and order to the Void, and yet expect to see the slow results? Civilization, gentlemen, is when all men surrender their natural habits of violence, because they fear the retribution of some power sufficient to terrify and awe them into obedience. To civilize a wilderness is long effort; and when the wilderness is astronomically vast, the terror must be vast as well."

Captain Ereshkigal, her eyes wide with growing panic, made a clumsy gesture with her fan, shrieking, "Kill him! Kill!"

Steel glittered in their hands as the shouting knights and nobles kicked off the walls and dove. With hardly any surprise at all, Smith saw the stranger beginning to shine with supernatural light, and saw him reach up with flaming fingers to pull aside what turned out to be, after all, a mask.